THE NORTON
INTRODUCTION TO
THE SHORT NOVEL

Second Edition

Jerome Beaty
Emory University

THE NORTON
INTRODUCTION TO
THE SHORT NOVEL

Second Edition

W · W · NORTON & COMPANY · NEW YORK · LONDON

Library of Congress Cataloging-in-Publication Data
The Norton introduction to the short novel.
1. Fiction—19th century.   2. Fiction—20th century.
I. Beaty, Jerome, 1924–
PN6120.2.N63   1987   808.83   86-12541
ISBN 0-393-95564-8

W. W. Norton & Company, Inc., 500 Fifth Avenue, New York, N.Y. 10110
W. W. Norton & Company, Ltd., 37 Great Russell Street, London WC1B 3NU

4 5 6 7 8 9 0

CONTENTS

FOREWORD

Of the thirteen short novels in this collection, seven are American (that is, North American), three English, two European (one written in Russian, the other in German), and one South American. They are spread fairly evenly—though with a little bunching at the two ends—over the past century. While there is geographical and historical range, however, the selection is not meant to be representative of the short novel as a whole in space or time, but primarily to offer interesting and challenging reading experiences of various kinds.

Though the novels may be read in any order and may profitably be grouped in a variety of ways, a bound book necessitates some fixed order, so they are arranged here chronologically, by date of publication. This arrangement has the virtue of not imposing an interpretive or editorial order on the novels, while not being entirely arbitrary or meaningless: we can say with some certainty, for example, that Toni Morrison or Philip Roth might have read *Daisy Miller* or *The Death of Iván Ilyich*, but that neither Henry James nor Tolstoy read either *Sula* or *Goodbye, Columbus.*

The "Introduction" defines the short novel in terms of its length, the formal and thematic consequences or corollaries of its length, and the effect of these on the experience of reading such a work. Preceding each novel is a brief headnote with enough biographical and other detail (about the author's other works, his or her theory of fiction—whatever seems fitting and useful) to prepare the reader to experience, appreciate, and understand the novel as fully as possible during a first reading. There are, as is usual in Norton books, informational footnotes designed to help the reader understand the text without either forcing upon the reader the editor's interpretation or unnecessarily burdening the text with what can be found in a standard desk dictionary. Following each novel is an "Afterword" discussing one or more aspects of the work that seem to the editor necessary to experience or understand the novel more fully. These are not meant to be definitive—they are very brief—but to generate thought, discussion, and even, I hope, controversy and excitement.

Just as in choosing the novels I have sought to provide the reader with stimulating and enjoyable material, so in writing the accompanying matter I have aimed at making the full power and pleasure of the novels readily accessible for the college and university student for whom this book is designed. Ready access, however, does not imply effortlessness or passive consumption, but rather an invitation to engage the imagined worlds of the novels actively and deeply, seeking new perspectives on new worlds and new experiences, and consequently new perspectives on our own world, our own experience.

If all my friends, family, colleagues, teachers, students, and acquaintances were to get their due, which of them could escape an acknowledgment of direct or indirect assistance in editing this anthology? I shall here name a few and beg the others to forgive me my debts.

I would like to thank all my colleagues at Emory University, but in particular Michaelyn Burnette, William B. Dillingham, Peter W. Dowell, Ricardo Gutierrez, viii FOREWORD

Leon Mandell, Gayla McGlamery, Sondra O'Neale, Lisa Rosenstein, Carlos Rojas, Ronald Schuchard, John Sitter, and Floyd Watkins. I wish to thank as well T. E. and Margaret Blom (University of British Columbia), Norman Feltes (York University), John Foley (University of Missouri), Kristin Hunter (University of Pennsylvania), George L. Levine (Rutgers University), William Morgan (Illinois State University), Douglas Peterson (Michigan State University), and Melissa Walker (Mercer University).

Andrew Beaty lent many hours of assistance; Mrs. Trudy Kretchman was unfailingly cooperative. For their relief, much thanks.

I wish to express my gratitude also to Toni Morrison for granting us permission to reprint her splendid short novel *Sula* and for supplying some information for the notes which would otherwise have eluded me.

At W. W. Norton & Company, I would particularly like to thank my friend and the editor's editor Barry Wade; for advice and encouragement, John Benedict; for assistance and patience, Roberta Flechner, Diane O'Connor, Nancy Palmquist, Heather Warren and Victoria Thys.

Meaghan and Caelin Beaty gave up many hours of story and play time while their father was reading and editing short novels, and my wife, V. Elaine Beaty, took up the slack cheerfully, and rendered continuous assistance, encouragement, and constructive critical comment. I promise to thank them when I get home.

J.B.

INTRODUCTION

For some readers and some instructional purposes, short stories are too short. And for some, most novels are too long. But short novels are just right. That's one of the reasons I prefer the term *short novel* to *novella* and *novelette:* the adjective echoes *short* story, and the noun tells you it's a *novel,* thus emphasizing its happy position between the two.

The length that normally qualifies a work to be considered a short *novel* rather than short *story* is about 15,000 words (twenty-five or so pages in this volume); when short novels get beyond 50,000 words they sometimes lose the adjective and are novels plain and simple. Length usually allows short novels to have more of everything than a short story. They can accommodate a larger cast of characters and develop them more fully; they can have more incidents or a more complicated plot; they can have more scenes (dramatized incidents in which characters think, talk, or do something over a brief, continuous period of time), or more—and more widely spaced—settings, and they can take place over longer stretches and in more discriminated moments of time. They can thus expand in various ways the scope, breadth, and depth of short stories. The compact form of the short story is particularly suited to stories of initiation, of sudden insight and illumination; the more leisurely novel is better suited to narratives of growth and change, of quest and development. The short novel is happily suited to either, or a blending of both.

The shortest of the short novels in this collection, *The Beggar Maid,* has many of the qualities of the full-length novel. It is made up of a goodly number of separate scenes, spread out over a number of years and over much of Canada; it has a fairly large cast of particularized characters (though it concentrates on two) and a rather large number of incidents. It is, however, a story of development. On the other hand, *Daisy Miller* has relatively few dramatized scenes, characters, and incidents, and is primarily a story of discovery or sudden illumination. It is, however, seldom thought of as anything other than a short novel. In its case, primarily length—more than 25,000 words—is no doubt the determining factor. The short novel can be as simple as a short story (but not when it's as short) and as complex as a novel (but not too, too long); it is a happy hybrid.

Sheer length is important not only as one characteristic of the work, but also in our experience of reading the work, something that happens to—but is also created by—the reader. Though one can put down a short story and later pick it up again, it seems designed to be read in a sitting; to absorb the reader for one period of time, come to a point of illumination or reversal and then let the reader go back to a reality that is spatially unchanged from that which was there when the story was begun (you've been sitting in the same spot), temporally changed only slightly (it hasn't taken you long to read it), and psychologically unchanged *except for the effect, vision, insight of the story itself* (not much has happened to you outside the reading).

Though there are novels (novels unmodified by "short") that can be read by non-speedreading readers in a sitting (a famous critic in the mid-nineteenth century picked up *Jane Eyre* one evening and, as he put it, "married Mr. Rochester at three o'clock the next morning"), the novel as such does not seem to be designed to be read so. Some novels have been published serially, in weekly or monthly installments, so that contemporary readers could not gobble them down; and most are divided into parts or chapters that seem to offer convenient stopping points. This elapsed reading time (and time between sittings) seems to me not insignificant. The reader may or may not resume the same position in chair or bed, may or may not have had illuminating or harrowing or meaningful experiences between readings, but he or she has done something (eaten dinner? answered the phone? gone skiing for a weekend?), and has both left the world of the fiction and, somewhere in the back or front of the mind, thought or felt something about the novel being read. The reader picking up the novel again must make a new entry into the fictional world as a more or less changed and different reader. It is the depth of the experience of reading a novel—more than the depth or breadth of its theme or its analysis of character or its vision—that may be the most significant difference between short story and novel.

Here again, mere length leaves the short novel in between. Short novels such as *Daisy Miller* (though it was serialized and so, on first appearance, could not have been read at once), *Dr. Jekyll and Mr. Hyde, The Metamorphosis,* can be read in a single (though fairly long) sitting. However, *Daisy Miller* is divided into two, *Metamorphosis* three, and *Iván Ilyich* twelve numbered chapters, and *Jekyll and Hyde* is divided into ten titled segments. These divisions are invitations to put the book down for a moment or longer, or at least to pause; to prepare for a shift of scene or time or to think back over what has happened so far, and to project some sort of pattern of expectation of what may come next. Even if we do not put a short novel down and let its development—and our expectations—ferment between reading sessions, its relative length requires punctuated pauses to process and store the information, perceptions, emotions, and relationships we are confronting.

Though our capacities differ, and individual works differ markedly, it is often possible to hold not only the details but even the memory of our responses to a *short story* in our minds when we finish it (especially after repeated readings). It is extremely difficult, at least for me, to remember a *short novel* in detail and to recall my point-by-point responses to it fully no matter how many times I have read it; it's like trying to carry an overstuffed bag of groceries or too high a pile of books—something inevitably falls. (And while you're retrieving it, two or three other things fall.) I can remember the witty, worldly tone at the beginning of *Daisy Miller* right now (though I usually don't), but I am not sure I can reconstruct my responses and expectations during the reading of that first page or so of the story.

As you see, when I talk about reading a story or novel, I'm not only talking about understanding it, interpreting it, or abstracting a meaning, but about *experiencing* it. It is difficult to pin down just what one means by the "experience" of reading a work of fiction—everything relevant that is going on in your head and nervous system as you read, perhaps. Reducing this complex activity to its simplest terms, we can talk about your taking in the information or data of the story (although language differs from data in that it bears the history of its culture and usage and its active rather than inert), going on to gather new "data," and making a pattern of what you are taking in, and so anticipating what will happen or be revealed next. When you read on, your expectations are disappointed, altered or fulfilled, new pieces are picked up and new patterns projected. Reading fiction is, then, in part a guessing game.

This reading process is unconscious; we usually do not watch our own minds as we read. But before we begin the thirteen short novels in this volume, let's look at the kinds of things that might be happening in our minds as we read them. The beginning is always a good place to begin, but let's begin before the beginning, with the title. There's no fictional "past" here; we have—or so we ought to assume for the sake of the guessing—no prior information as we read *The Strange Case of Dr. Jekyll and Mr. Hyde:* "case" suggests a detective story or crime, "strange" that it will not be like ordinary "cases." Even with only these two counters to go on, a pool of vague possibilities begins to form, waiting for more detail to shape it into a concrete expectation or set of expectations of what is to happen next. Even apparently neutral titles like *Daisy Miller* arouse some anticipation: we know that a person of that name is likely to appear and to be central or significant in the narrative to follow.

Though we can learn something from a title, exploration does not carry us very far in understanding the complex network of activities involved in reading and understanding a long work like a novel, even what we call a short novel. It probably would be not only impractical but misleading to stop to examine our mental activities and pattern-making after reading each word, phrase, or sentence of a prose narrative. To pause to analyze response, recapitulation, and expectation at the end of each paragraph would make some sense—we do, after all, have to shift our eyes back to the beginning of the next line, as we do in reading lines of poetry—but to pause and analyze so often would be cumbersome. Moreover, there is a larger and more appropriate unit of punctuation in a novel, one that is governed—usually consciously so—by the author to control our reading pace, making us pause, and inviting us to recapitulate and to anticipate what is to come. That unit is the chapter. *Eréndira* and *The Beggar Maid* are divided into units only by spacing—skipped lines—but the other short novels in this volume are all more formally divided into chapters headed by titles, dates, the names of characters, or numbers, and many of them are also divided into smaller units by spacing and other typographical devices. *Daisy Miller* is divided into only two chapters, *Ethan Frome* into ten. *Sula* is divided into two parts, eleven chapters headed by dates, and more than three dozen smaller units, mostly by spacing but several times by one or another set of printer's marks; *As I Lay Dying* is divided into almost sixty sections headed by fifteen different characters' names.

Let us look briefly at how that form of "punctuation" called the chapter can work in pacing our reading and therefore in generating or controlling our expectations. In Tolstoy's *The Death of Iván Ilyich*, the first chapter ends with Iván Ilyich's best friend, Peter Ivánovich, having just left Iván Ilyich's newly widowed wife, joining his and Iván Ilyich's other friends at cards, finding "them just finishing the first rubber, so that it was quite convenient for him to cut in." The pause forces us to think back over the brief chapter in which Iván Ilyich's death has been greeted by friends and family with only a show of sorrow but with self-interested questions of how that death will affect their own convenience and material conditions. What developments do we expect? What would surprise us? The punctuation of the chapter-ending has made us, consciously or unconsciously, frame some possibilities if we are reading attentively and following the author's pacing of our reading. Not every one of us will anticipate the same future for the story. Some of us will be drawing a blank, not able to frame an expectation; others will have one plot we are pretty sure will be followed; still others may have three, five, eight possibilities more or less vaguely floating through our minds.

Let us settle on just two fairly obvious possibilities. At this point we feel sorry for Iván Ilyich: neither his friends nor his wife seems truly to mourn him. Poor Iván: perhaps the rest of the novel will flash back over his life and show us how the poor man—maybe from the time he was a baby—was mistreated, misunderstood. We may anticipate, in other words, a sentimental journey into Iván Ilyich's past. (And perhaps some or all of us are prepared for such a narrative because we have all felt misunderstood, undervalued, ignored, or unrecognized for the splendid person we are, at one time or another.) The second obvious possibility is that all the selfish nonmourners, friends and widow alike, will be followed to their unmourned deaths, where each will get his or her just deserts. We may anticipate, in other words, a tale of moral retaliation. Since the story has scarcely begun and we can see we have nearly forty pages to go, either of these expectations—each requiring considerable space and development—would be possible.

But what if we hold both these anticipated plots consciously or unconsciously in mind? One of them is bound to be wrong. Would it not be better just to have the right one in mind? Or none at all, and just wait and see? Or suppose both of them are wrong? If we carefully put two and two together and come up with five, what is the advantage of informed anticipation?

A well-structured novel will play fair with you, offering at appropriate points all the necessary signals or clues to what will happen next, not just springing new and essential information on you at the last minute ("Meanwhile, unknown to our hero, the Marines were just on the other side of the hill . . ."). It is this playing fair that makes an ending satisfying or, when you look back on it, inevitable. Novels also offer a number of reasonable but false signals, red herrings, to get you off the scent, so that in a well-structured novel the ending, though inevitable, is also surprising. When we find that leads are false, that our expectations or guesses are wrong, we discard them, and with the new evidence we have gathered from the narrative we project a new pattern of events to come.

Old expectations and patterns seem about as useful as used tubes of toothpaste, we may feel: next time through the story we'll know better than to expect Sula to leave Ajax, or to suspect Hyde of forging Jekyll's signature or blackmailing him. Not so. The "wrong guesses" signalled by the text (not the free-floating guesses that may from time to time without reason pop into our heads or be made up) remain part of the text as a reading experience. The false expectations may be irrelevant to the outcome of the novel, but they are not irrelevant to the novel: they represent one of the choices made in defining the world of this particular novel; they represent one of the ways our expectation of reality is being redefined; they say, "This is a fictional world or view of reality in which two plus two might equal five, but doesn't," and they say, "This is a fictional world which does not even entertain the possibility that two plus two might equal three."

Novels differ as much in the questions they raise, in what *might* have happened in them but did not, as they do in what does happen. In a novel there are a great many more expectations, a great many more things that might have been than there are in a short story. Even if a short novel and a short story were to "say" the same thing, embody the same theme or abstraction, the short novel would usually be the richer. Just as an argument is the more convincing the more objections it raises and rebuts, so a fictional theme or vision may be the more fully realized (made real) the more alternative outcomes, explanations, visions it raises but dismisses. This can be done more readily in a long than in a short work.

So long as you are alert to your own mind's activity as you read, you will notice how breaks, marks, and formal chapter endings will pace your reading, push you to recapitulate and project; the "Afterwords" that follow each of the short novels will occasionally try to describe what happens to the reader at such a pause, as does the "Afterword" to The Death of Iván Ilyich, for example. You will notice too that not all the signals come from "inside" the text. We begin a novel usually with the expectation that the world of the fiction resembles our world as we see it, not necessarily in detail—we do not demand the ordinary—but in its "laws" or "physics," as it were. We expect this even of a novel whose title contains such words as "incredible" and "tale," and which begins with a most bizarre setting and set of circumstances, as does Innocent Eréndira. We are led by stages in that novel, however, to the extraordinary, the preposterous, and ultimately to the "incredible" or surreal. The *Metamorphosis* rapes rather than seduces our expectations of a more or less normative reality, but then, once we have granted the premise that a young man can wake one morning to find himself an insect, it follows that premise with remorseless "natural" consequences and logic. Reality as we know it outside a work furnishes us with expectations which the work can disappoint, alter, or fulfill like any other expectations.

Our expectations or guesses are also conditioned by the language of the novel, by literary tradition or our own experience of narratives and narrative patterns. *Heart of Darkness*, using nautical language, makes us feel like the ignorant landlubbers most of us are and opens us to the lessons of the sea and therefore of "life" Marlow has in store for us; in *Ethan Frome* we hear the voice of the narrator or author trying to put in words the pent-up, almost voiceless language of feeling of Ethan, as at the end of chapter IV: "Completely reassured, she shone on him through tear-hung lashes, and his soul swelled with pride as he saw how his tone subdued her."

Goodbye, Columbus begins when the young male narrator meets a girl named Brenda. Ah, ha! Boy-meets-girl. We know that story, and its various patterns and variations on "loses" and "gets." (We may be a little curious about how the title will figure, however.) *Daisy Miller* is another boy-meets-girl story, but the meeting does not take place quite so quickly: we first meet the "boy," Winterbourne, then Daisy's little brother, then Daisy herself. We are only a few paragraphs into the story, but just as the title of *Goodbye, Columbus* puts in our mind just a little curiosity not clearly related to the love story, so the opening description of Vevey and Lake Geneva in the James novel alerts us to the fashionable, social, cultural scene and its role in the love story and in the novel. So convention alerts us to a love story and detail alerts us to other, related or modifying expectations.

Expectations are not quite so simple, then, as we sometimes think them to be. Our minds can hold at once not only multiple possibilities for the outcome of a story but also have room for other related and unrelated stories or areas of experience. Whether the Bundrens will be able to get Addie buried in time and in Jefferson is a question that runs from first to last in *As I Lay Dying*, yet we have room in our heads to follow the various physical and psychological crises of Darl, Cash, Dewey Dell, and the others. We do not forget Addie's corpse, however; it comes to the foreground period-ically, and is the hub from which the other "stories" diverge.

Just as we began speaking about expectations in terms of the beginning, so, per-haps, we should conclude by talking about endings. In the beginning there is no "past" in our experience of the story: we seek to understand what we are reading in the present and to project the future. It would follow that at the end of the story we take in the last words, remembering all the past of the story, but not projecting a pattern of what will come in the future. The shape of the story is now complete, the final configuration is made (including not only the fulfilled expectations, but also all the things that might have been). At the end of *Daisy Miller* we not only know what she was really like, but we get a view of Winterbourne and of his learning something about her and about himself. The mystery of *Jekyll and Hyde* has been solved long before the ending, but at the conclusion we have the explanation and at least one final version of the meaning of it all.

Not all stories end so definitively, however. Sometimes, especially in a fairly com-plex novel, while the story has ended, our response to it and understanding of it have not taken final shape; but in other novels, the story itself has not really ended and we are left both with unresolved questions about meaning or vision and unresolved expectations about the future course of the lives with which we have been engaged. It's awkward to talk about endings in an introduction, because I don't want to give too much away and short-circuit any of your first responses or expectations. Let's just say that at the end of *The Fox* one character says to the other that he or she will feel better "over there."

> "Yes, I may. I can't tell. I can't tell what it will be like over there."
> "If only we could go soon!" —— said, with pain in —— voice.

We do not know how it will be "over there," whether the ending will be "happy" or not. We therefore do not know for sure how to interpret or evaluate what has happened to the characters in the story we have just finished reading and we are virtually being invited to complete the story ourselves, to write the ending, or an ending, or a stopping place. We are invited to continue recollecting what we have read, forming it into a present shape, to project a future pattern.

At the very end of *Old Mortality* one of the characters says,

> Let them tell their stories to each other. Let them go on explaining how things happened. I don't care. At least I can know the truth about what happens to me, she assured herself silently, making a promise to herself, in her hopefulness, her ignorance.

We have a double inconclusiveness. The first is a fairly conventional "open" or indefinite ending: we have heard a number of explanations of how things happened and none seems totally satisfactory and none seems totally wrong. We see how people interpret external reality in terms of their own perceptions, prejudices, and needs, so that no subjective explanation is adequate as an objective explanation, if there is such a thing. This is a conclusion, if an inconclusive one: we are invited to review in our minds all the versions of the past to which we have been subjected, perhaps to choose, perhaps to put together like a puzzle, perhaps simply to sigh at the difficulty of it all. But we are not asked to project a pattern of action or incident into the future beyond the moment at which the story ends—until the last five words or so. "Her ignorance"—she will not know the truth even about what will happen to her. We know a little of her life and a good deal about a long-deceased character named Amy and everyone's version of her life, and so we are virtually invited to put these together somehow and project a more or less definite future for the hopeful, ignorant woman who is thinking the final thoughts of the story.

I have some expectations, too. I am looking forward eagerly to your reading these thirteen short novels. I do not know (in my ignorance) how intensely you will enjoy them, but I expect (in my hopefulness) that you will enjoy them as much as I have in reading and thinking about them and readying them for you.

THE NORTON
INTRODUCTION TO
THE SHORT NOVEL

Second Edition

HENRY JAMES

Daisy Miller

Henry James (1843–1916) never married, had fairly little formal education, never held down a job, and, though not rich, never had to worry about money. He did little but travel, read and write, go to museums and theaters, dine out, and (with something of a stammer) talk.

The two most interesting things about his life—outside work—are, perhaps, his famous family and his obscure accident. His father was a philosophic and unorthodox religious writer; his older brother William was one of the first significant American psychologists and a famous philosopher; his sister Alice and two younger brothers rounded out a brilliant, intellectually active family. The accident occurred a few months after the beginning of the Civil War when he was pushed into a fence while trying to put out a small fire in Newport, Rhode Island. The result was what he called a "horrid even if an obscure hurt," and, characteristically, his reticence and ambiguity caused post-Freudian scholars to infer that the accident had something to do with his not marrying. His most authoritative biographer, Leon Edel, believes it was a slipped disc or similar back injury involving recurrent pain.

His travel began early—at six months he was in Paris—and in the late 1850s he spent five of his most formative years in Europe. He returned to Europe a few years after the end of the Civil War and by 1876 had decided to settle in England. Although his writing and reviewing had begun a dozen years before, his first novel, *Roderick Hudson*, did not appear until 1875. The flood was released and he published more than fifty books before his death in 1916.

James had a life-long addiction to the theater and in the early 1890s wrote more than half a dozen plays, two of which were produced and performed—both flopped. His best drama is in his fiction, which is dramatic in that the action takes place in rather lengthy scenes and primarily through dialogue; there is careful, significant, often symbolic use made of setting; and the intermediary or narrator which differentiates fiction from drama is, more and more as James's career progresses, replaced by a center of consciousness, a character spoken of in the third person through whose eye and mind we perceive the action, and, most often, in whose voice we are told of it. We can speak of "the drama of the mind" as characteristic of his novels, for the center *is* in the consciousness, the mind of the beholder; his works are about perception—the perception of the self and others—and if the dramatic nature of his theory and practice in writing fiction assures him a place in the history of literary craft and criticism, so his novels of the mind place him high in the history and development of the psychological novel.

Daisy Miller is an early work of Henry James but one in which several of his themes or preoccupations are already visible: "the international theme" (the American in Europe) and the search by the protagonist for the reality behind the appearance and actions of others. James and his protagonists ask fairly simple questions but the investigation is complex, the answers often tentative, and so the form of the short novel is very congenial to his genius and interests. Though we must name the full-length (even lengthy) novels such as *The Portrait of a Lady* (1881), *The Ambassadors* (1903), and *The Golden Bowl* (1904) among his greatest works, such short novels as *Daisy Miller, The Aspern Papers* (1888), *The Turn of the Screw* (1898), and *The Beast in the Jungle* (1901) are not only excellent examples of the form but are central to James's fiction.

Daisy Miller
A Study

I

A T THE LITTLE TOWN of Vevey, in Switzerland, there is a particularly comfortable hotel. There are, indeed, many hotels; for the entertainment of tourists is the business of the place, which, as many travellers will remember, is seated upon the edge of a remarkably blue lake[1]—a lake that it behoves every tourist to visit. The shore of the lake presents an unbroken array of establishments of this order, of every category, from the "grand hotel" of the newest fashion, with a chalk-white front, a hundred balconies, and a dozen flags flying from its roof, to the little Swiss *pension* of an elder day, with its name inscribed in German-looking lettering upon a pink or yellow wall, and an awkward summer-house in the angle of the garden. One of the hotels at Vevey, however, is famous, even classical, being distinguished from many of its upstart neighbours by an air both of luxury and of maturity. In this region, in the month of June, American travellers are extremely numerous; it may be said, indeed, that Vevey assumes at this period some of the characteristics of an American watering-place. There are sights and sounds which evoke a vision, an echo, of Newport and Saratoga.[2] There is a flitting hither and thither of "stylish" young girls, a rustling of muslin flounces, a rattle of dance music in the morning hours, a sound of high-pitched voices at all times. You receive an impression of these things at the excellent inn of the "Trois Couronnes,"[3] and are transported in fancy to the Ocean House or to Congress Hall. But at the "Trois Couronnes," it must be added, there are other features that are much at variance with these suggestions: neat German waiters, who look like secretaries of legation; Russian princesses sitting in the garden; little Polish boys walking about, held by the hand, with their governors; a view of the snowy crest of the Dent du Midi and the picturesque towers of the Castle of Chillon.[4]

I hardly know whether it was the analogies or the differences that were uppermost in the mind of a young American, who, two or three years ago, sat in the garden of the "Trois Couronnes," looking about him, rather idly, at some of the graceful objects I have mentioned. It was a beautiful summer morning, and in whatever fashion the young American looked at things, they must have seemed to him charming. He had come from Geneva the day before, by the little steamer, to see his aunt, who was staying at the hotel—Geneva having been for a long time his place of residence. But his aunt had a headache—his aunt had almost always a headache—and now she was shut up in her room, smelling camphor, so

---

1. Lake Geneva; Vevey is about ten miles east of Lausanne.
2. Newport, R.I., was a fashionable resort for the very rich, studded with palatial mansions; Saratoga Springs, N.Y., about thirty miles from Albany, a summer resort noted for its mineral springs, and from 1850 horse-racing, was considered the social center of America in the middle of the nineteenth century.
3. Three Crowns. Below: Ocean House was a

major hotel on Bellevue Avenue in Newport, Congress Hall on Broadway in Saratoga.
4. The ninth- to thirteenth-century castle at the eastern end of Lake Geneva was the residence of the counts of Savoy and the scene of the incarceration of "the prisoner of Chillon" made famous by Byron (see note on Bonivard, below); the Dent or Dents du Midi is a mountain group in Switzerland near the French border.

3

that he was at liberty to wander about. He was some seven-and-twenty years of age; when his friends spoke of him, they usually said that he was at Geneva, "studying." When his enemies spoke of him they said—but, after all, he had no enemies; he was an extremely amiable fellow, and universally liked. What I should say is, simply, that when certain persons spoke of him they affirmed that the reason of his spending so much time at Geneva was that he was extremely devoted to a lady who lived there— a foreign lady—a person older than himself. Very few Americans—indeed I think none—had ever seen this lady, about whom there were some singular stories. But Winterbourne had an old attachment for the little metropolis of Calvinism;[5] he had been put to school there as a boy, and he had afterwards gone to college there—circumstances which had led to his forming a great many youthful friendships. Many of these he had kept, and they were a source of great satisfaction to him.

After knocking at his aunt's door and learning that she was indisposed, he had taken a walk about the town, and then he had come in to his breakfast. He had now finished his breakfast, but he was drinking a small cup of coffee, which had been served to him on a little table in the garden by one of the waiters, who looked like an *attaché*. At last he finished his coffee and lit a cigarette. Presently a small boy came walking along the path—an urchin of nine or ten. The child, who was diminutive for his years, had an aged expression of countenance, a pale complexion, and sharp little features. He was dressed in knickerbockers, with red stockings, which displayed his poor little spindleshanks; he also wore a brilliant red cravat. He carried in his hand a long alpenstock, the sharp point of which he thrust into everything that he approached—the flower-beds, the garden benches, the trains of the ladies' dresses. In front of Winterbourne he paused, looking at him with a pair of bright penetrating little eyes.

"Will you give me a lump of sugar?" he asked, in a sharp hard little voice—a voice immature, and yet, somehow, not young.

Winterbourne glanced at the small table near him, on which his coffee-service rested, and saw that several morsels of sugar remained. "Yes, you may take one," he answered; "but I don't think sugar is good for little boys."

This little boy stepped forward and carefully selected three of the coveted fragments, two of which he buried in the pocket of his knickerbockers, depositing the other as promptly in another place. He poked his alpenstock, lance-fashion, into Winterbourne's bench, and tried to crack the lump of sugar with his teeth.

"Oh, blazes; it's har-r-d!" he exclaimed, pronouncing the adjective in a peculiar manner.

Winterbourne had immediately perceived that he might have the honour of claiming him as a fellow-countryman. "Take care you don't hurt your teeth," he said, paternally.

"I haven't got any teeth to hurt. They have all come out. I have only got seven teeth. My mother counted them last night, and one came out right afterwards. She said she'd slap me if any more came out. I can't help it. It's this old Europe. It's the climate that makes them come out. In America they didn't come out. It's these hotels."

5. Geneva, after John Calvin (1509–1564), leader of the Protestant Reformation there.

Winterbourne was much amused. "If you eat three lumps of sugar your mother will certainly slap you," he said.

"She's got to give me some candy, then," rejoined his young interlocutor. "I can't get any candy here—any American candy. American candy's the best candy."

"And are American little boys the best little boys?" asked Winterbourne.

"I don't know. I'm an American boy," said the child.

"I see you are one of the best!" laughed Winterbourne.

"Are you an American man?" pursued this vivacious infant. And then, on Winterbourne's affirmative reply—"American men are the best," he declared.

His companion thanked him for the compliment; and the child, who had now got astride of his alpenstock, stood looking about him, while he attacked a second lump of sugar. Winterbourne wondered if he himself had been like this in his infancy, for he had been brought to Europe at about this age.

"Here comes my sister!" cried the child, in a moment. "She's an American girl."

Winterbourne looked along the path and saw a beautiful young lady advancing. "American girls are the best girls," he said, cheerfully, to his young companion.

"My sister ain't the best!" the child declared. "She's always blowing[6] at me."

"I imagine that is your fault, not hers," said Winterbourne. The young lady meanwhile had drawn near. She was dressed in white muslin, with a hundred frills and flounces, and knots of pale-coloured ribbon. She was bare-headed; but she balanced in her hand a large parasol, with a deep border of embroidery; and she was strikingly, admirably pretty. "How pretty they are!" thought Winterbourne, straightening himself in his seat, as if he were prepared to rise.

The young lady paused in front of his bench, near the parapet of the garden, which overlooked the lake. The little boy had now converted his alpenstock into a vaulting-pole, by the aid of which he was springing about in the gravel, and kicking it up not a little.

"Randolph," said the young lady, "What *are* you doing?"

"I'm going up the Alps," replied Randolph. "This is the way!" And he gave another little jump, scattering the pebbles about Winterbourne's ears.

"That's the way they come down," said Winterbourne.

"He's an American man!" cried Randolph, in his little hard voice.

The young lady gave no heed to this announcement, but looked straight at her brother. "Well, I guess you had better be quiet," she simply observed.

It seemed to Winterbourne that he had been in a manner presented. He got up and stepped slowly towards the young girl, throwing away his cigarette. "This little boy and I have made acquaintance," he said, with great civility. In Geneva, as he had been perfectly aware, a young man was not at liberty to speak to a young unmarried lady except under certain rarely-occurring conditions; but here at Vevey, what conditions could

6. Speaking angrily, yelling.

be better than these?—a pretty American girl coming and standing in front of you in a garden. This pretty American girl, however, on hearing Winterbourne's observation, simply glanced at him; she then turned her head and looked over the parapet, at the lake and the opposite mountains. He wondered whether he had gone too far; but he decided that he must advance farther, rather than retreat. While he was thinking of something else to say, the young lady turned to the little boy again.

"I should like to know where you got that pole," she said.

"I bought it!" responded Randolph.

"You don't mean to say you're going to take it to Italy!"

"Yes, I am going to take it to Italy!" the child declared.

The young girl glanced over the front of her dress, and smoothed out a knot or two of ribbon. Then she rested her eyes upon the prospect again. "Well, I guess you had better leave it somewhere," she said, after a moment.

"Are you going to Italy?" Winterbourne inquired, in a tone of great respect.

The young lady glanced at him again. "Yes, sir," she replied. And she said nothing more.

"Are you—a—going over the Simplon?" Winterbourne pursued, a little embarrassed.

"I don't know," she said. "I suppose it's some mountain. Randolph, what mountain are we going over?"

"Going where?" the child demanded.

"To Italy," Winterbourne explained.

"I don't know," said Randolph. "I don't want to go to Italy. I want to go to America."

"Oh, Italy is a beautiful place!" rejoined the young man.

"Can you get candy there?" Randolph loudly inquired.

"I hope not," said his sister. "I guess you have had enough candy, and mother thinks so too."

"I haven't had any for ever so long—for a hundred weeks!" cried the boy, still jumping about.

The young lady inspected her flounces and smoothed her ribbons again; and Winterbourne presently risked an observation upon the beauty of the view. He was ceasing to be embarrassed, for he had begun to perceive that she was not in the least embarrassed herself. There had not been the slightest alteration in her charming complexion; she was evidently neither offended nor fluttered. If she looked another way when he spoke to her, and seemed not particularly to hear him, this was simply her habit, her manner. Yet, as he talked a little more, and pointed out some of the objects of interest in the view, with which she appeared quite unacquainted, she gradually gave him more of the benefit of her glance; and then he saw that this glance was perfectly direct and unshrinking. It was not, however, what would have been called an immodest glance, for the young girl's eyes were singularly honest and fresh. They were wonderfully pretty eyes; and, indeed, Winterbourne had not seen for a long time anything prettier than his fair countrywoman's various features—her complexion, her nose, her ears, her teeth. He had a great relish for feminine beauty; he was addicted to observing and analysing it; and as regards this young lady's face he made several observations. It was not at all insipid, but it was not exactly expressive; and though it was eminently delicate, Winterbourne mentally accused it—very forgivingly—of a want of finish. He thought it very possible that Master Randolph's sister was a coquette; he was sure she had a spirit of her own; but in her bright, sweet, superficial little visage, there was no mockery, no irony. Before long it became obvious that she was much disposed towards conversation. She told him that they were going to Rome for the winter—she and her mother and Randolph. She asked him if he was a "real American"; she wouldn't have taken him for one; he seemed more like a German—this was said after a little hesitation—especially when he spoke. Winterbourne, laughing, answered that he had met Germans who spoke like Americans; but that he had not, so far as he remembered, met an American who spoke like a German. Then he asked her if she would not be more comfortable in sitting upon the bench which he had just quitted. She answered that she liked standing up and walking about; but she presently sat down. She told him she was from New York State—"if you know where that is." Winterbourne learned more about her by catching hold of her small slippery brother and making him stand a few minutes by his side.

"Tell me your name, my boy," he said.

"Randolph C. Miller," said the boy, sharply. "And I'll tell you her name"; and he levelled his alpenstock at his sister.

"You had better wait till you are asked!" said this young lady, calmly.

"I should like very much to know your name," said Winterbourne.

"Her name is Daisy Miller!" cried the child. "But that isn't her real name; that isn't her name on her cards."

"It's a pity you haven't got one of my cards!" said Miss Miller.

"Her real name is Annie P. Miller," the boy went on.

"Ask him *his* name," said his sister, indicating Winterbourne.

But on this point Randolph seemed perfectly indifferent; he continued to supply information with regard to his own family. "My father's name is Ezra B. Miller," he announced. "My father ain't in Europe; my father's in a better place than Europe."

Winterbourne imagined for a moment that this was the manner in which the child had been taught to intimate that Mr. Miller had been removed to the sphere of celestial rewards. But Randolph immediately added, "My father's in Schenectady. He's got a big business. My father's rich, you bet."

"Well!" ejaculated Miss Miller, lowering her parasol and looking at the embroidered border. Winterbourne presently released the child, who departed, dragging his alpenstock along the path. "He doesn't like Europe," said the young girl. "He wants to go back."

"To Schenectady, you mean?"

"Yes; he wants to go right home. He hasn't got any boys here. There is one boy here, but he always goes round with a teacher; they won't let him play."

"And your brother hasn't any teacher?" Winterbourne inquired.

"Mother thought of getting him one, to travel round with us. There was a lady told her of a very good teacher; an American lady—perhaps you know her—Mrs. Sanders. I think she came from Boston. She told her of this teacher, and we thought of getting him to travel round with us. But Randolph said he didn't want a teacher travelling round with us. He said he wouldn't have lessons when he was in the cars.[7] And we *are* in the cars about half the time. There was an English lady we met in the cars—I think her name was Miss Featherstone; perhaps you know her. She wanted to know why I didn't give Randolph lessons—give him 'instruction,' she called it. I guess he could give me more instruction than I could give him. He's very smart."

"Yes," said Winterbourne; "he seems very smart."

"Mother's going to get a teacher for him as soon as we get to Italy. Can you get good teachers in Italy?"

"Very good, I should think," said Winterbourne.

"Or else she's going to find some school. He ought to learn some more. He's only nine. He's going to college." And in this way Miss Miller continued to converse upon the affairs of her family, and upon other topics. She sat there with her extremely pretty hands, ornamented with very brilliant rings, folded in her lap, and with her pretty eyes now resting upon those of Winterbourne, now wandering over the garden, the people who passed by, and the beautiful view. She talked to Winterbourne as if she had known him a long time. He found it very pleasant. It was many years since he had heard a young girl talk so much. It might have been said of this unknown young lady, who had come and sat down beside him upon a bench, that she chattered. She was very quiet, she sat in a charming tranquil attitude; but her lips and her eyes were constantly moving. She had a soft, slender, agreeable voice, and her tone was decidedly sociable. She gave Winterbourne a history of her movements and intentions, and those of her mother and brother, in Europe, and enumerated, in particular, the various hotels at which they had stopped. "That English lady in the cars," she said—"Miss Featherstone—asked me if we didn't all live in hotels in America. I told her I had never been in so many hotels in my life as since I came to Europe. I have never seen so many—it's nothing but hotels." But Miss Miller did not make this remark with a querulous accent; she appeared to be in the best humour with everything. She declared that the hotels were very good, when once you got used to their ways, and that Europe was perfectly sweet. She was not disappointed—not a bit. Perhaps it was because she had heard so much about it before. She had ever so many intimate friends that had been there ever so many times. And then she had had ever so many dresses and things from Paris. Whenever she put on a Paris dress she felt as if she were in Europe.

"It was a kind of a wishing-cap," said Winterbourne.

"Yes," said Miss Miller, without examining this analogy; "it always made me wish I was here. But I needn't have done that for dresses. I am sure they send all the pretty ones to America; you see the most frightful things here. The only thing I don't like," she proceeded, "is the society. There isn't any society; or, if there is, I don't know where it keeps itself. Do you? I suppose there is some society somewhere, but I haven't seen anything of it. I'm very fond of society, and I have always had a great deal of it. I don't mean only in Schenectady, but in New York. I used to go to New York every winter. In New York I had lots of society. Last winter I had seventeen dinners given me; and three of them were by gentlemen," added Daisy Miller. "I have more friends in New York than in Schenectady—more gentlemen friends; and more young lady friends

---

7. Railroad cars.

too," she resumed in a moment. She paused again for an instant; she was looking at Winterbourne with all her prettiness in her lively eyes and in her light, slightly monotonous smile. "I have always had," she said, "a great deal of gentlemen's society." Poor Winterbourne was amused, perplexed, and decidedly charmed. He had never yet heard a young girl express herself in just this fashion; never, at least, save in cases where to say such things seemed a kind of demonstrative evidence of a certain laxity of deportment. And yet was he to accuse Miss Daisy Miller of actual or potential *inconduite*,[8] as they said at Geneva? He felt that he had lived at Geneva so long that he had lost a good deal; he had become dishabituated to the American tone. Never, indeed, since he had grown old enough to appreciate things, had he encountered a young American girl of so pronounced a type as this. Certainly she was very charming; but how deucedly sociable! Was she simply a pretty girl from New York State—were they all like that, the pretty girls who had a good deal of gentlemen's society? Or was she also a designing, an audacious, an unscrupulous young person? Winterbourne had lost his instinct in this matter, and his reason could not help him. Miss Daisy Miller looked extremely innocent. Some people had told him that, after all, American girls were exceedingly innocent; and others had told him that, after all, they were not. He was inclined to think Miss Daisy Miller was a flirt—a pretty American flirt. He had never, as yet, had any relations with young ladies of this category. He had known, here in Europe, two or three women—persons older than Miss Daisy Miller, and provided, for respectability's sake, with husbands—who were great coquettes—dangerous, terrible women, with whom one's relations were liable to take a serious turn. But this young girl was not a coquette in that sense; she was very unsophisticated; she was only a pretty American flirt. Winterbourne was almost grateful for having found the formula that applied to Miss Daisy Miller. He leaned back in his seat; he remarked to himself that she had the most charming nose he had ever seen; he wondered what were the regular conditions and limitations of one's intercourse with a pretty American flirt. It presently became apparent that he was on the way to learn.

"Have you been to that old castle?" asked the young girl, pointing with her parasol to the far-gleaming walls of the Château de Chillon.

"Yes, formerly, more than once," said Winterbourne. "You too, I suppose, have seen it?"

"No; we haven't been there. I want to go there dreadfully. Of course I mean to go there. I wouldn't go away from here without having seen that old castle."

"It's a very pretty excursion," said Winterbourne, "and very easy to make. You can drive, you know, or you can go by the little steamer."

"You can go in the cars," said Miss Miller.

"Yes; you can go in the cars," Winterbourne assented.

"Our courier says they take you right up to the castle," the young girl continued. "We were going last week; but my mother gave out. She suffers dreadfully from dyspepsia. She said she couldn't go. Randolph wouldn't go either; he says he doesn't think much of old castles. But I guess we'll go this week, if we can get Randolph."

8. Improper behavior.

"Your brother is not interested in ancient monuments?" Winterbourne inquired, smiling.

"He says he don't care much about old castles. He's only nine. He wants to stay at the hotel. Mother's afraid to leave him alone, and the courier won't stay with him; so we haven't been to many places. But it will be too bad if we don't go up there." And Miss Miller pointed again at the Château de Chillon.

"I should think it might be arranged," said Winterbourne. "Couldn't you get some one to stay—for the afternoon—with Randolph?"

Miss Miller looked at him a moment; and then, very placidly—"I wish *you* would stay with him!" she said.

Winterbourne hesitated a moment. "I would much rather go to Chillon with you."

"With me?" asked the young girl, with the same placidity.

She didn't rise, blushing, as a young girl at Geneva would have done; and yet Winterbourne, conscious that he had been very bold, thought it possible she was offended. "With your mother," he answered very respectfully.

But it seemed that both his audacity and his respect were lost upon Miss Daisy Miller. "I guess my mother won't go, after all," she said. "She don't like to ride round in the afternoon. But did you really mean what you said just now; that you would like to go up there?"

"Most earnestly," Winterbourne declared.

"Then we may arrange it. If mother will stay with Randolph, I guess Eugenio will."

"Eugenio?" the young man inquired.

"Eugenio's our courier. He doesn't like to stay with Randolph; he's the most fastidious man I ever saw. But he's a splendid courier. I guess he'll stay at home with Randolph if mother does, and then we can go to the castle."

Winterbourne reflected for an instant as lucidly as possible—"we" could only mean Miss Daisy Miller and himself. This programme seemed almost too agreeable for credence; he felt as if he ought to kiss the young lady's hand. Possibly he would have done so—and quite spoiled the project; but at this moment another person—presumably Eugenio—appeared. A tall, handsome man, with superb whiskers, wearing a velvet morning coat and a brilliant watch-chain, approached Miss Miller, looking sharply at her companion. "Oh, Eugenio!" said Miss Miller, with the friendliest accent.

Eugenio had looked at Winterbourne from head to foot; he now bowed gravely to the young lady. "I have the honour to inform Mademoiselle that luncheon is upon the table."

Miss Miller slowly rose. "See here, Eugenio," she said. "I'm going to that old castle, any way."

"To the Château de Chillon, Mademoiselle?" the courier inquired. "Mademoiselle has made arrangements?" he added, in a tone which struck Winterbourne as very impertinent.

Eugenio's tone apparently threw, even to Miss Miller's own apprehension, a slightly ironical light upon the young girl's situation. She turned to Winterbourne, blushing a little—a very little. "You won't back out?" she said.

"I shall not be happy till we go!" he protested.

"And you are staying in this hotel?" she went on. "And you are really an American?"

The courier stood looking at Winterbourne, offensively. The young man, at least, thought his manner of looking an offence to Miss Miller; it conveyed an imputation that she "picked up" acquaintances. "I shall have the honour of presenting to you a person who will tell you all about me," he said, smiling, and referring to his aunt.

"Oh, well, we'll go some day," said Miss Miller. And she gave him a smile and turned away. She put up her parasol and walked back to the inn beside Eugenio. Winterbourne stood looking after her; and as she moved away, drawing her muslin furbelows over the gravel, said to himself that she had the *tournure*[9] of a princess.

He had, however, engaged to do more than proved feasible in promising to present his aunt, Mrs. Costello, to Miss Daisy Miller. As soon as the former lady had got better of her headache he waited upon her in her apartment; and, after the proper inquiries in regard to her health, he asked her if she had observed, in the hotel, an American family—a mamma, a daughter, and a little boy.

"And a courier?" said Mrs. Costello. "Oh yes, I have observed them. Seen them—heard them—and kept out of their way." Mrs. Costello was a widow with a fortune; a person of much distinction, who frequently intimated that, if she were not so dreadfully liable to sick-headaches, she would probably have left a deeper impress upon her time. She had a long pale face, a high nose, and a great deal of very striking white hair, which she wore in large puffs and *rouleaux*[1] over the top of her head. She had two sons married in New York, and another who was now in Europe. This young man was amusing himself at Homburg,[2] and, though he was on his travels, was rarely perceived to visit any particular city at the moment selected by his mother for her own appearance there. Her nephew, who had come up to Vevey expressly to see her, was therefore more attentive than those who, as she said, were nearer to her. He had imbibed at Geneva the idea that one must always be attentive to one's aunt. Mrs. Costello had not seen him for many years, and she was greatly pleased with him, manifesting her approbation by initiating him into many of the secrets of that social sway which, as she gave him to understand, she exerted in the American capital.[3] She admitted that she was very exclusive; but, if he were acquainted with New York, he would see that one had to be. And her picture of the minutely hierarchical constitution of the society of that city, which she presented to him in many different lights, was, to Winterbourne's imagination, almost oppressively striking.

He immediately perceived, from her tone, that Miss Daisy Miller's place in the social scale was low. "I am afraid you don't approve of them," he said.

"They are very common," Mrs. Costello declared. "They are the sort of Americans that one does one's duty by not—not accepting."

"Ah, you don't accept them?" said the young man.

"I can't, my dear Frederick. I would if I could, but I can't."

"The young girl is very pretty," said Winterbourne, in a moment.

"Of course she's pretty. But she is very common."

9. Figure, bearing.
1. Rolls.
2. Bad Homburg, famous spa and resort near

Frankfurt, Germany.
3. American social "capital," New York.

"I see what you mean, of course," said Winterbourne, after another pause.

"She has that charming look they all have," his aunt resumed. "I can't think where they pick it up; and she dresses in perfection—no, you don't know how well she dresses. I can't think where they get their taste."

"But, my dear aunt, she is not, after all, a Comanche savage."

"She is a young lady," said Mrs. Costello, "who has an intimacy with her mamma's courier!"

"An intimacy with the courier?" the young man demanded.

"Oh, the mother is just as bad! They treat the courier like a familiar friend—like a gentleman. I shouldn't wonder if he dines with them. Very likely they have never seen a man with such good manners, such fine clothes, so like a gentleman. He probably corresponds to the young lady's idea of a count. He sits with them in the garden, in the evening. I think he smokes."

Winterbourne listened with interest to these disclosures; they helped him to make up his mind about Miss Daisy. Evidently she was rather wild. "Well," he said, "I am not a courier, and yet she was very charming to me."

"You had better have said at first," said Mrs. Costello with dignity, "that you had made her acquaintance."

"We simply met in the garden, and we talked a bit."

"*Tout bonnement!*⁴ And pray what did you say?"

"I said I should take the liberty of introducing her to my admirable aunt."

"I am much obliged to you."

"It was to guarantee my respectability," said Winterbourne.

"And pray who is to guarantee hers?"

"Ah, you are cruel!" said the young man. "She's a very nice girl."

"You don't say that as if you believed it," Mrs. Costello observed.

"She is completely uncultivated," Winterbourne went on. "But she is wonderfully pretty, and, in short, she is very nice. To prove that I believe it, I am going to take her to the Château de Chillon."

"You two are going off there together? I should say it proved just the contrary. How long had you known her, may I ask, when this interesting project was formed? You haven't been twenty-four hours in the house."

"I had known her half an hour!" said Winterbourne, smiling.

"Dear me!" cried Mrs. Costello. "What a dreadful girl!"

Her nephew was silent for some moments. "You really think, then," he began earnestly, and with a desire for trustworthy information—"you really think that—" But he paused again.

"Think what, sir?" said his aunt.

"That she is the sort of young lady who expects a man—sooner or later—to carry her off?"

"I haven't the least idea what such young ladies expect a man to do. But I really think that you had better not meddle with little American girls that are uncultivated, as you call them. You have lived too long out of the country. You will be sure to make some great mistake. You are too innocent."

4. Very simply!

"My dear aunt, I am not so innocent," said Winterbourne, smiling and curling his moustache.

"You are too guilty, then!"

Winterbourne continued to curl his moustache, meditatively. "You won't let the poor girl know you, then?" he asked at last.

"Is it literally true that she is going to the Château de Chillon with you?"

"I think that she fully intends it."

"Then, my dear Frederick," said Mrs. Costello, "I must decline the honour of her acquaintance. I am an old woman, but I am not too old—thank Heaven—to be shocked!"

"But don't they all do these things—the young girls in America?" Winterbourne inquired.

Mrs. Costello stared a moment. "I should like to see my granddaughters do them!" she declared, grimly.

This seemed to throw some light upon the matter, for Winterbourne remembered to have heard that his pretty cousins in New York were "tremendous flirts." If, therefore, Miss Daisy Miller exceeded the liberal license allowed to these young ladies, it was probable that anything might be expected of her. Winterbourne was impatient to see her again, and he was vexed with himself that, by instinct, he should not appreciate her justly.

Though he was impatient to see her, he hardly knew what he should say to her about his aunt's refusal to become acquainted with her; but he discovered, promptly enough, that with Miss Daisy Miller there was no great need of walking on tiptoe. He found her that evening in the garden, wandering about in the warm starlight, like an indolent sylph, and swinging to and fro the largest fan he had ever beheld. It was ten o'clock. He had dined with his aunt, had been sitting with her since dinner, and had just taken leave of her till the morrow. Miss Daisy Miller seemed very glad to see him; she declared it was the longest evening she had ever passed.

"Have you been all alone?" he asked.

"I have been walking round with mother. But mother gets tired walking round," she answered.

"Has she gone to bed?"

"No; she doesn't like to go to bed," said the young girl. "She doesn't sleep—not three hours. She says she doesn't know how she lives. She's dreadfully nervous. I guess she sleeps more than she thinks. She's gone somewhere after Randolph; she wants to try to get him to go to bed. He doesn't like to go to bed."

"Let us hope she will persuade him," observed Winterbourne.

"She will talk to him all she can; but he doesn't like her to talk to him," said Miss Daisy, opening her fan. "She's going to try to get Eugenio to talk to him. But he isn't afraid of Eugenio. Eugenio's a splendid courier, but he can't make much impression on Randolph! I don't believe he'll go to bed before eleven." It appeared that Randolph's vigil was in fact triumphantly prolonged, for Winterbourne strolled about with the young girl for some time without meeting her mother. "I have been looking round for that lady you want to introduce me to," his companion resumed. "She's your aunt." Then, on Winterbourne's admitting the fact,

and expressing some curiosity as to how she had learned it, she said she
had heard all about Mrs. Costello from the chambermaid. She was very
quiet and very *comme il faut;* she wore white puffs; she spoke to no one,
and she never dined at the *table d'hôte.* Every two days she had a headache. "I think that's a lovely description, headache and all!" said Miss
Daisy, chattering along in her thin, gay voice. "I want to know her ever
so much. I know just what *your* aunt would be; I know I should like her.
She would be very exclusive. I like a lady to be exclusive; I'm dying to be
exclusive myself. Well, we *are* exclusive, mother and I. We don't speak to
every one—or they don't speak to us. I suppose it's about the same thing.
Any way, I shall be ever so glad to know your aunt."

Winterbourne was embarrassed. "She would be most happy," he said;
"but I am afraid those headaches will interfere "

The young girl looked at him through the dusk. "But I suppose she
doesn't have a headache every day," she said, sympathetically.

Winterbourne was silent a moment. "She tells me she does," he answered at last—not knowing what to say.

Miss Daisy Miller stopped and stood looking at him. Her prettiness was
still visible in the darkness; she was opening and closing her enormous
fan. "She doesn't want to know me!" she said, suddenly. "Why don't you
say so? You needn't be afraid. I'm not afraid!" And she gave a little laugh.

Winterbourne fancied there was a tremor in her voice; he was touched,
shocked, mortified by it. "My dear young lady," he protested, "she knows
no one. It's her wretched health."

The young girl walked on a few steps, laughing still. "You needn't be
afraid," she repeated. "Why should she want to know me?" Then she
paused again; she was close to the parapet of the garden, and in front of
her was the starlit lake. There was a vague sheen upon its surface, and in
the distance were dimly-seen mountain forms. Daisy Miller looked out
upon the mysterious prospect, and then she gave another little laugh.
"Gracious! she *is* exclusive!" she said. Winterbourne wondered whether
she was seriously wounded, and for a moment almost wished that her
sense of injury might be such as to make it becoming in him to attempt to
reassure and comfort her. He had a pleasant sense that she would be very
approachable for consolatory purposes. He felt then, for the instant, quite
ready to sacrifice his aunt, conversationally; to admit that she was a
proud, rude woman, and to declare that they needn't mind her. But before he had time to commit himself to this perilous mixture of gallantry
and impiety, the young lady, resuming her walk, gave an exclamation in
quite another tone. "Well; here's mother! I guess she hasn't got Randolph
to go to bed." The figure of a lady appeared, at a distance, very indistinct
in the darkness, and advancing with a slow and wavering movement. Suddenly it seemed to pause.

"Are you sure it is your mother? Can you distinguish her in this thick
dusk?" Winterbourne asked.

"Well!" cried Miss Daisy Miller, with a laugh, "I guess I know my own
mother. And when she has got on my shawl, too! She is always wearing
my things."

The lady in question, ceasing to advance, hovered vaguely about the
spot at which she had checked her steps.

"I am afraid your mother doesn't see you," said Winterbourne. "Or
perhaps," he added—thinking, with Miss Miller, the joke permissible—

"perhaps she feels guilty about your shawl."

"Oh, it's a fearful old thing!" the young girl replied, serenely. "I told her she could wear it. She won't come here, because she sees you."

"Ah, then," said Winterbourne, "I had better leave you."

"Oh, no; come on!" urged Miss Daisy Miller.

"I'm afraid your mother doesn't approve of my walking with you." Miss Miller gave him a serious glance. "It isn't for me; it's for you—that is, it's for *her*. Well; I don't know who it's for! But mother doesn't like any of my gentlemen friends. She's right down timid. She always makes a fuss if I introduce a gentleman. But I *do* introduce them—almost always. If I didn't introduce my gentlemen friends to mother," the young girl added, in her little soft, flat monotone, "I shouldn't think I was natural."

"To introduce me," said Winterbourne, "you must know my name." And he proceeded to pronounce it.

"Oh dear; I can't say all that!" said his companion, with a laugh. But by this time they had come up to Mrs. Miller, who, as they drew near, walked to the parapet of the garden and leaned upon it, looking intently at the lake and turning her back upon them. "Mother!" said the young girl in a tone of decision. Upon this the elder lady turned round. "Mr. Winterbourne," said Miss Daisy Miller, introducing the young man very frankly and prettily. "Common" she was, as Mrs. Costello had pronounced her; yet it was a wonder to Winterbourne that, with her commonness, she had a singularly delicate grace.

Her mother was a small, spare, light person, with a wandering eye, a very exiguous nose, and a large forehead, decorated with a certain amount of thin, much-frizzled hair. Like her daughter, Mrs. Miller was dressed with extreme elegance: she had enormous diamonds in her ears. So far as Winterbourne could observe, she gave him no greeting—she certainly was not looking at him. Daisy was near her, pulling her shawl straight. "What are you doing, poking round here?" this young lady inquired; but by no means with that harshness of accent which her choice of words may imply.

"I don't know," said her mother, turning towards the lake again.

"I shouldn't think you'd want that shawl!" Daisy exclaimed.

"Well—I do!" her mother answered, with a little laugh.

"Did you get Randolph to go to bed?" asked the young girl.

"No; I couldn't induce him," said Mrs. Miller, very gently. "He wants to talk to the waiter. He likes to talk to that waiter."

"I was telling Mr. Winterbourne," the young girl went on; and to the young man's ear her tone might have indicated that she had been uttering his name all her life.

"Oh yes!" said Winterbourne; "I have the pleasure of knowing your son."

Randolph's mamma was silent; she turned her attention to the lake. But at last she spoke. "Well, I don't see how he lives!"

"Anyhow, it isn't so bad as it was at Dover," said Daisy Miller.

"And what occurred at Dover?" Winterbourne asked.

"He wouldn't go to bed at all. I guess he sat up all night—in the public parlour. He wasn't in bed at twelve o'clock: I know that."

"It was half-past twelve," declared Mrs. Miller, with mild emphasis.

"Does he sleep much during the day?" Winterbourne demanded.

"I guess he doesn't sleep much," Daisy rejoined.

"I wish he would!" said her mother. "It seems as if he couldn't."

"I think he's real tiresome," Daisy pursued.

Then, for some moments, there was silence. "Well, Daisy Miller," said the elder lady, presently, "I shouldn't think you'd want to talk against your own brother!"

"Well, he *is* tiresome, mother," said Daisy, quite without the asperity of a retort.

"He's only nine," urged Mrs. Miller.

"Well, he wouldn't go to that castle," said the young girl. "I'm going there with Mr. Winterbourne."

To this announcement, very placidly made, Daisy's mamma offered no response. Winterbourne took for granted that she deeply disapproved of the projected excursion; but he said to himself that she was a simple, easily-managed person, and that a few deferential protestations would take the edge from her displeasure. "Yes," he began; "your daughter has kindly allowed me the honour of being her guide."

Mrs. Miller's wandering eyes atached themselves, with a sort of appealing air, to Daisy, who, however, strolled a few steps farther, gently humming to herself. "I presume you will go in the cars," said her mother.

"Yes; or in the boat," said Winterbourne.

"Well, of course, I don't know," Mrs. Miller rejoined. "I have never been to that castle."

"It is a pity you shouldn't go," said Winterbourne, beginning to feel reassured as to her opposition. And yet he was quite prepared to find that, as a matter of course, she meant to accompany her daughter.

"We've been thinking ever so much about going," she pursued; "but it seems as if we couldn't. Of course Daisy—she wants to go round. But there's a lady here—I don't know her name—she says she shouldn't think we'd want to go to see castles *here;* she should think we'd want to wait till we got to Italy. It seems as if there would be so many there," continued Mrs. Miller, with an air of increasing confidence. "Of course, we only want to see the principal ones. We visited several in England," she presently added.

"Ah yes! in England there are beautiful castles," said Winterbourne. "But Chillon, here, is very well worth seeing."

"Well, if Daisy feels up to it—" said Mrs. Miller, in a tone impregnated with a sense of the magnitude of the enterprise. "It seems as if there was nothing she wouldn't undertake."

"Oh, I think she'll enjoy it!" Winterbourne declared. And he desired more and more to make it a certainty that he was to have the privilege of a *tête-à-tête* with the young lady, who was still strolling along in front of them, softly vocalising. "You are not disposed, madam," he inquired, "to undertake it yourself?"

Daisy's mother looked at him an instant, askance, and then walked forward in silence. Then—"I guess she had better go alone," she said, simply.

Winterbourne observed to himself that this was a very different type of maternity from that of the vigilant matrons who massed themselves in the forefront of social intercourse in the dark old city at the other end of the lake. But his meditations were interrupted by hearing his name very distinctly pronounced by Mrs. Miller's unprotected daughter.

"Mr. Winterbourne!" murmured Daisy.

"Mademoiselle!" said the young man.

"Don't you want to take me out in a boat?"

"At present?" he asked.

"Of course!" said Daisy.

"Well, Annie Miller!" exclaimed her mother.

"I beg you, madam, to let her go," said Winterbourne, ardently; for he had never yet enjoyed the sensation of guiding through the summer starlight a skiff freighted with a fresh and beautiful young girl.

"I shouldn't think she'd want to," said her mother. "I should think she'd rather go indoors."

"I'm sure Mr. Winterbourne wants to take me," Daisy declared. "He's so awfully devoted!"

"I will row you over to Chillon in the starlight."

"I don't believe it!" said Daisy.

"Well!" ejaculated the elder lady again.

"You haven't spoken to me for half an hour," her daughter went on.

"I have been having some very pleasant conversation with your mother," said Winterbourne.

"Well; I want you to take me out in a boat!" Daisy repeated. They had all stopped, and she had turned round and was looking at Winterbourne. Her face wore a charming smile, her pretty eyes were gleaming, she was swinging her great fan about. No; it's impossible to be prettier than that, thought Winterbourne.

"There are half-a-dozen boats moored at that landing-place," he said, pointing to certain steps which descended from the garden to the lake. "If you will do me the honour to accept my arm, we will go and select one of them."

Daisy stood there smiling; she threw back her head and gave a little light laugh. "I like a gentleman to be formal!" she declared.

"I assure you it's a formal offer."

"I was bound I would make you say something," Daisy went on.

"You see it's not very difficult," said Winterbourne. "But I am afraid you are chaffing me."

"I think not, sir," remarked Mrs. Miller, very gently.

"Do, then, let me give you a row," he said to the young girl.

"It's quite lovely, the way you say that!" cried Daisy.

"It will be still more lovely to do it."

"Yes, it would be lovely!" said Daisy. But she made no movement to accompany him; she only stood there laughing.

"I should think you had better find out what time it is," interposed her mother.

"It is eleven o'clock, madam," said a voice, with a foreign accent, out of the neighboring darkness; and Winterbourne, turning, perceived the florid personage who was in attendance upon the two ladies. He had apparently just approached.

"Oh, Eugenio," said Daisy, "I am going out in a boat!"

Eugenio bowed. "At eleven o'clock, Mademoiselle?"

"I am going with Mr. Winterbourne. This very minute."

"Do tell her she can't," said Mrs. Miller to the courier.

"I think you had better not go out in a boat, Mademoiselle," Eugenio declared.

Winterbourne wished to Heaven this pretty girl were not so familiar with her courier; but he said nothing.

"I suppose you don't think it's proper!" Daisy exclaimed. "Eugenio doesn't think anything's proper."

"I am at your service," said Winterbourne.

"Does Mademoiselle propose to go alone?" asked Eugenio of Mrs. Miller.

"Oh no; with this gentleman!" answered Daisy's mamma.

The courier looked for a moment at Winterbourne—the latter thought he was smiling—and then, solemnly, with a bow, "As Mademoiselle pleases!" he said.

"Oh, I hoped you would make a fuss!" said Daisy. "I don't care to go now."

"I myself shall make a fuss if you don't go," said Winterbourne.

"That's all I want—a little fuss!" And the young girl began to laugh again.

"Mr. Randolph has gone to bed!" the courier announced, frigidly.

"Oh, Daisy; now we can go!" said Mrs. Miller.

Daisy turned away from Winterbourne, looking at him, smiling and fanning herself. "Good-night," she said; "I hope you are disappointed, or disgusted, or something!"

He looked at her, taking the hand she offered him. "I am puzzled," he answered.

"Well; I hope it won't keep you awake!" she said, very smartly; and, under the escort of the privileged Eugenio, the two ladies passed towards the house.

Winterbourne stood looking after them; he was indeed puzzled. He lingered beside the lake for a quarter of an hour, turning over the mystery of the young girl's sudden familiarities and caprices. But the only very definite conclusion he came to was that he should enjoy deucedly "going off" with her somewhere.

Two days afterwards he went off with her to the Castle of Chillon. He waited for her in the large hall of the hotel, where the couriers, the servants, the foreign tourists, were lounging about and staring. It was not the place he would have chosen, but she had appointed it. She came tripping downstairs, buttoning her long gloves, squeezing her folded parasol against her pretty figure, dressed in the perfection of a soberly elegant travelling costume. Winterbourne was a man of imagination and, as our ancestors used to say, of sensibility; as he looked at her dress and, on the great staircase, her little rapid, confiding step, he felt as if there were something romantic going forward. He could have believed he was going to elope with her. He passed out with her among all the idle people that were assembled there; they were all looking at her very hard; she had begun to chatter as soon as she joined him. Winterbourne's preference had been that they should be conveyed to Chillon in a carriage; but she expressed a lively wish to go in the little steamer; she declared that she had a passion for steamboats. There was always such a lovely breeze upon the water, and you saw such lots of people. The sail was not long, but Winterbourne's companion found time to say a great many things. To the young man himself their little excursion was so much of an escapade—an adventure—that, even allowing for her habitual sense of freedom, he had some expectation of seeing her regard it in the same way. But it must be confessed that, in this particular, he was disappointed. Daisy Miller was extremely animated, she was in charming spirits; but she was apparently

not at all excited; she was not fluttered; she avoided neither his eyes nor
those of any one else; she blushed neither when she looked at him nor
when she saw that people were looking at her. People continued to look
at her a great deal, and Winterbourne took much satisfaction in his pretty
companion's distinguished air. He had been a little afraid that she would
talk loud, laugh overmuch, and even, perhaps, desire to move about the
boat a good deal. But he quite forgot his fears; he sat smiling, with his
eyes upon her face, while, without moving from her place, she delivered
herself of a great number of original reflections. It was the most charming
garrulity he had ever heard. He had assented to the idea that she was
"common"; but was she so, after all, or was he simply getting used to her
commonness? Her conversation was chiefly of what metaphysicians term
the objective cast; but every now and then it took a subjective turn.

"What on *earth* are you so grave about?" she suddenly demanded, fixing her agreeable eyes upon Winterbourne's.

"Am I grave?" he asked. "I had an idea I was grinning from ear to ear."

"You look as if you were taking me to a funeral. If that's a grin, your
ears are very near together."

"Should you like me to dance a hornpipe on the deck?"

"Pray do, and I'll carry round your hat. It will pay the expenses of our
journey."

"I never was better pleased in my life," murmured Winterbourne.

She looked at him a moment, and then burst into a little laugh. "I like
to make you say those things! You're a queer mixture!"

In the castle, after they had landed, the subjective element decidedly
prevailed. Daisy tripped about the vaulted chambers, rustled her skirts in
the corkscrew staircases, flirted back with a pretty little cry and a shudder from the edge of the *oubliettes*, and turned a singularly well-shaped
ear to everything that Winterbourne told her about the place. But he saw
that she cared very little for feudal antiquities, and that the dusky traditions of Chillon made but a slight impression upon her. They had the
good fortune to have been able to walk about without other companion-
ship than that of the custodian; and Winterbourne arranged with this
functionary that they should not be hurried—that they should linger and
pause wherever they chose. The custodian interpreted the bargain gen-
erously—Winterbourne, on his side, had been generous—and ended by
leaving them quite to themselves. Miss Miller's observations were not remarkable for logical consistency; for anything she wanted to say she was
sure to find a pretext. She found a great many pretexts in the rugged
embrasures of Chillon for asking Winterbourne sudden questions about
himself—his family, his previous history, his tastes, his habits, his intentions—and for supplying information upon corresponding points in her
own personality. Of her own tastes, habits, and intentions Miss Miller was
prepared to give the most definite, and indeed the most favourable, account.

"Well; I hope you know enough!" she said to her companion, after he
had told her the history of the unhappy Bonivard.[5] "I never saw a man
that knew so much!" The history of Bonivard had evidently, as they say,
gone into one ear and out of the other. But Daisy went on to say that she

5. François de Bonivard—or Bonnivard—(c. 1493–
1570), a priest who supported the revolt of Geneva
against Charles III of Savoy, and who late in life became a Protestant, was imprisoned 1530–1536 in the
Castle of Chillon; he is the subject of Byron's poem
The Prisoner of Chillon.

wished Winterbourne would travel with them and "go round" with them; they might know something, in that case. "Don't you want to come and teach Randolph?" she asked. Winterbourne said that nothing could possibly please him so much; but that he had unfortunately other occupations. "Other occupations? I don't believe it!" said Miss Daisy. "What do you mean? You are not in business." The young man admitted that he was not in business; but he had engagements which, even within a day or two, would force him to go back to Geneva. "Oh, bother!" she said, "I don't believe it!" and she began to talk about something else. But a few moments later, when he was pointing out to her the pretty design of an antique fireplace, she broke out irrelevantly, "You don't mean to say you are going back to Geneva?"

"It is a melancholy fact that I shall have to return to Geneva tomorrow."

"Well, Mr. Winterbourne," said Daisy; "I think you're horrid!"

"Oh, don't say such dreadful things!" said Winterbourne—"just at the last."

"The last!" cried the young girl; "I call it the first. I have half a mind to leave you here and go straight back to the hotel alone." And for the next ten minutes she did nothing but call him horrid. Poor Winterbourne was fairly bewildered; no young lady had as yet done him the honour to be so agitated by the announcement of his movements. His companion, after this, ceased to pay any attention to the curiosities of Chillon or the beauties of the lake; she opened fire upon the mysterious charmer in Geneva, whom she appeared to have instantly taken it for granted that he was hurrying back to see. How did Miss Daisy Miller know that there was a charmer in Geneva? Winterbourne, who denied the existence of such a person, was quite unable to discover; and he was divided between amazement at the rapidity of her induction and amusement at the frankness of her *persiflage*. She seemed to him, in all this, an extraordinary mixture of innocence and crudity. "Does she never allow you more than three days at a time?" asked Daisy, ironically. "Doesn't she give you a vacation in summer? There's no one so hard worked, but they can get leave to go off somewhere at this season. I suppose, if you stay another day, she'll come after you in the boat. Do wait over till Friday, and I will go down to the landing to see her arrive!" Winterbourne began to think he had been wrong to feel disappointed in the temper in which the young lady had embarked. If he had missed the personal accent, the personal accent was now making its appearance. It sounded very distinctly, at last, in her telling him she would stop "teasing" him if he would promise her solemnly to come down to Rome in the winter.

"That's not a difficult promise to make," said Winterbourne. "My aunt has taken an apartment in Rome for the winter, and has already asked me to come and see her."

"I don't want you to come for your aunt," said Daisy; "I want you to come for me." And this was the only allusion that the young man was ever to hear her make to his invidious kinswoman. He declared that, at any rate, he would certainly come. After this Daisy stopped teasing. Winterbourne took a carriage, and they drove back to Vevey in the dusk; the young girl was very quiet.

In the evening Winterbourne mentioned to Mrs. Costello that he had spent the afternoon at Chillon with Miss Daisy Miller.

"The Americans—of the courier?" asked this lady.

"Ah, happily," said Winterbourne, "the courier stayed at home."

"She went with you all alone?"

"All alone."

Mrs. Costello sniffed a little at her smelling-bottle. "And that," she exclaimed, "is the young person you wanted me to know!"

II

Winterbourne, who had returned to Geneva the day after his excursion to Chillon, went to Rome towards the end of January. His aunt had been established there for several weeks, and he had received a couple of letters from her. "Those people you were so devoted to last summer at Vevey have turned up here, courier and all," she wrote. "They seem to have made several acquaintances, but the courier continues to be the most *intime*. The young lady, however, is also very intimate with some third-rate Italians, with whom she rackets about in a way that makes much talk. Bring me that pretty novel of Cherbuliez's—'Paule Méré'[6]—and don't come later than the 23rd."

In the natural course of events Winterbourne, on arriving in Rome, would presently have ascertained Mrs. Miller's address at the American banker's, and have gone to pay his compliments to Miss Daisy. "After what happened at Vevey I certainly think I may call upon them," he said to Mrs. Costello.

"If, after what happens—at Vevey and everywhere—you desire to keep up the acquaintance, you are very welcome. Of course a man may know every one. Men are welcome to the privilege!"

"Pray, what is it that happens—here, for instance?" Winterbourne demanded.

"The girl goes about alone with her foreigners. As to what happens farther, you must apply elsewhere for information. She has picked up half-a-dozen of the regular Roman fortune-hunters, and she takes them about to people's houses. When she comes to a party she brings with her a gentleman with a good deal of manner and a wonderful moustache."

"And where is the mother?"

"I haven't the least idea. They are very dreadful people."

Winterbourne meditated a moment. "They are very ignorant—very innocent only. Depend upon it they are not bad."

"They are hopelessly vulgar," said Mrs. Costello. "Whether or no being hopelessly vulgar is being 'bad' is a question for the metaphysicians. They are bad enough to dislike, at any rate; and for this short life that is quite enough."

The news that Daisy Miller was surrounded by a half-a-dozen wonderful moustaches checked Winterbourne's impulse to go straightway to see her. He had perhaps not definitely flattered himself that he had made an ineffaceable impression upon her heart, but he was annoyed at hearing of a state of affairs so little in harmony with an image that had lately flitted in and out of his own meditations; the image of a very pretty girl looking out of an old Roman window and asking herself urgently when Mr. Winterbourne would arrive. If, however, he determined to wait a little before

6. The second (1864) in a long series of novels by Victor Cherbuliez (1829–1899), novelist, art critic, and political writer.

reminding Miss Miller of his claims to her consideration, he went very soon to call upon two or three other friends. One of these friends was an American lady who had spent several winters at Geneva, where she had placed her children at school. She was a very accomplished woman, and she lived in the Via Gregoriana. Winterbourne found her in a little crimson drawing-room, on a third floor; the room was filled with southern sunshine. He had not been there ten minutes when the servant came in, announcing "Madame Mila!" This announcement was presently followed by the entrance of little Randolph Miller, who stopped in the middle of the room and stood staring at Winterbourne. An instant later his pretty sister crossed the threshold; and then, after a considerable interval, Mrs. Miller slowly advanced.

"I know you!" said Randolph.

"I'm sure you know a great many things," exclaimed Winterbourne, taking him by the hand. "How is your education coming on?"

Daisy was exchanging greetings very prettily with her hostess; but when she heard Winterbourne's voice she quickly turned her head. "Well, I declare!" she said.

"I told you I should come, you know," Winterbourne rejoined, smiling.

"Well—I didn't believe it," said Miss Daisy.

"I am much obliged to you," laughed the young man.

"You might have come to see me!" said Daisy.

"I arrived only yesterday."

"I don't believe that!" the young girl declared.

Winterbourne turned with a protesting smile to her mother; but this lady evaded his glance, and seating herself, fixed her eyes upon her son. "We've got a bigger place than this," said Randolph. "It's all gold on the walls."

Mrs. Miller turned uneasily in her chair. "I told you if I were to bring you you would say something!" she murmured.

"I told *you!*" Randolph exclaimed. "I tell *you*, sir!" he added jocosely, giving Winterbourne a thump on the knee. "It *is* bigger, too!"

Daisy had entered upon a lively conversation with her hostess; Winterbourne judged it becoming to address a few words to her mother. "I hope you have been well since we parted at Vevey," he said.

Mrs. Miller now certainly looked at him—at his chin. "Not very well, sir," she answered.

"She's got the dyspepsia," said Randolph. "I've got it too. Father's got it. I've got it worst!"

This announcement, instead of embarrassing Mrs. Miller, seemed to relieve her. "I suffer from the liver," she said. "I think it's this climate; it's less bracing than Schenectady, especially in the winter season. I don't know whether you know we reside at Schenectady. I was saying to Daisy that I certainly hadn't found any one like Dr. Davis, and I didn't believe I should. Oh, at Schenectady, he stands first; they think everything of him. He has so much to do, and yet there was nothing he wouldn't do for me. He said he never saw anything like my dyspepsia, but he was bound to cure it. I'm sure there was nothing he wouldn't try. He was just going to try something new when we came off. Mr. Miller wanted Daisy to see Europe for herself. But I wrote to Mr. Miller that it seems as if I couldn't get on without Dr. Davis. At Schenectady he stands at the very top; and there's a great deal of sickness there, too. It affects my sleep."

Winterbourne had a good deal of pathological gossip with Dr. Davis's patient, during which Daisy chattered unremittingly to her own companion. The young man asked Mrs. Miller how she was pleased with Rome. "Well, I must say I am disappointed," she answered. "We had heard so much about it; I suppose we had heard too much. But we couldn't help that. We had been led to expect something different."

"Ah, wait a little, and you will become very fond of it," said Winterbourne.

"I hate it worse and worse every day!" cried Randolph.

"You are like the infant Hannibal,"[7] said Winterbourne.

"No, I ain't!" Randolph declared, at a venture.

"You are not much like an infant," said his mother. "But we have seen places," she resumed, "that I should put a long way before Rome." And in reply to Winterbourne's interrogation, "There's Zurich," she observed; "I think Zurich is lovely; and we hadn't heard half so much about it."

"The best place we've seen is the City of Richmond!" said Randolph.

"He means the ship," his mother explained. "We crossed in that ship. Randolph had a good time on the City of Richmond."

"It's the best place I've seen," the child repeated. "Only it was turned the wrong way."

"Well, we've got to turn the right way some time," said Mrs. Miller, with a little laugh. Winterbourne expressed the hope that her daughter at least found some gratification in Rome, and she declared that Daisy was quite carried away. "It's on account of the society—the society's splendid. She goes round everywhere; she has made a great number of acquaintances. Of course she goes round more than I do. I must say they have been very sociable; they have taken her right in. And then she knows a great many gentlemen. Oh, she thinks there's nothing like Rome. Of course, it's a great deal pleasanter for a young lady if she knows plenty of gentlemen."

By this time Daisy had turned her attention again to Winterbourne. "I've been telling Mrs. Walker how mean you were!" the young girl announced.

"And what is the evidence you have offered?" asked Winterbourne, rather annoyed at Miss Miller's want of appreciation of the zeal of an admirer who on his way down to Rome had stopped neither at Bologna nor at Florence, simply because of a certain sentimental impatience. He remembered that a cynical compatriot had once told him that American women—the pretty ones, and this gave a largeness to the axiom—were at once the most exacting in the world and the least endowed with a sense of indebtedness.

"Why, you were awfully mean at Vevey," said Daisy. "You wouldn't do anything. You wouldn't stay there when I asked you."

"My dearest young lady," cried Winterbourne, with eloquence, "have I come all the way to Rome to encounter your reproaches?"

"Just hear him say that!" said Daisy to her hostess, giving a twist to a bow on this lady's dress. "Did you ever hear anything so quaint?"

"So quaint, my dear?" murmured Mrs. Walker, in the tone of a partisan of Winterbourne.

---

7. At the age of nine Hannibal was made by his father to swear enmity to Rome, victor over Carthage in the First Punic War (264–241 B.C.); in the Second Punic War (218–201 B.C.), Hannibal successfully led the Carthaginian army over the Alps to attack Rome.

"Well, I don't know," said Daisy, fingering Mrs. Walker's ribbons. "Mrs. Walker, I want to tell you something."

"Motherr," interposed Randolph, with his rough ends to his words, "I tell you you've got to go. Eugenio'll raise something!"

"I'm not afraid of Eugenio," said Daisy, with a toss of her head. "Look here, Mrs. Walker," she went on, "you know I'm coming to your party."

"I am delighted to hear it."

"I've got a lovely dress."

"I am very sure of that."

"But I want to ask a favour—permission to bring a friend."

"I shall be happy to see any of your friends," said Mrs. Walker, turning with a smile to Mrs. Miller.

"Oh, they are not my friends," answered Daisy's mamma, smiling shyly, in her own fashion. "I never spoke to them!"

"It's an intimate friend of mine—Mr. Giovanelli," said Daisy, without a tremor in her clear little voice, or a shadow on her brilliant little face.

Mrs. Walker was silent a moment, she gave a rapid glance at Winterbourne. "I shall be glad to see Mr. Giovanelli," she then said.

"He's an Italian," Daisy pursued, with the prettiest serenity. "He's a great friend of mine—he's the handsomest man in the world—except Mr. Winterbourne! He knows plenty of Italians, but he wants to know some Americans. He thinks ever so much of Americans. He's tremendously clever. He's perfectly lovely!"

It was settled that this brilliant personage should be brought to Mrs. Walker's party, and then Mrs. Miller prepared to take her leave. "I guess we'll go back to the hotel," she said.

"You may go back to the hotel, mother, but I'm going to take a walk," said Daisy.

"She's going to walk with Mr. Giovanelli," Randolph proclaimed.

"I am going to the Pincio,"[8] said Daisy, smiling.

"Alone, my dear—at this hour?" Mrs. Walker asked. The afternoon was drawing to a close—it was the hour for the throng of carriages and of contemplative pedestrians. "I don't think it's safe, my dear," said Mrs. Walker.

"Neither do I," subjoined Mrs. Miller. "You'll get the fever as sure as you live. Remember what Dr. Davis told you!"

"Give her some medicine before she goes," said Randolph.

The company had risen to its feet; Daisy, still showing her pretty teeth, bent over and kissed her hostess. "Mrs. Walker, you are too perfect," she said. "I'm not going alone; I am going to meet a friend."

"Your friend won't keep you from getting the fever," Mrs. Miller observed.

"Is it Mr. Giovanelli?" asked the hostess.

Winterbourne was watching the young girl; at this question his attention quickened. She stood there smiling and smoothing her bonnet-ribbons; she glanced at Winterbourne. Then, while she glanced and smiled, she answered without a shade of hesitation, "Mr. Giovanelli—the beautiful Giovanelli."

"My dear young friend," said Mrs. Walker, taking her hand, pleadingly, "don't walk off to the Pincio at this hour to meet a beautiful Italian."

8. A park in Rome.

"Well, he speaks English," said Mrs. Miller.

"Gracious me!" Daisy exclaimed, "I don't want to do anything improper. There's an easy way to settle it." She continued to glance at Winterbourne. "The Pincio is only a hundred yards distant, and if Mr. Winterbourne were as polite as he pretends he would offer to walk with me!"

Winterbourne's politeness hastened to affirm itself, and the young girl gave him gracious leave to accompany her. They passed downstairs before her mother, and at the door Winterbourne perceived Mrs. Miller's carriage drawn up, with the ornamental courier whose acquaintance he had made at Vevey seated within. "Good-bye, Eugenio!" cried Daisy, "I'm going to take a walk." The distance from the Via Gregoriana to the beautiful garden at the other end of the Pincian Hill is, in fact, rapidly traversed. As the day was splendid, however, and the concourse of vehicles, walkers, and loungers numerous, the young Americans found their progress much delayed. This fact was highly agreeable to Winterbourne, in spite of his consciousness of his singular situation. The slow-moving, idly-gazing Roman crowd, bestowed much attention upon the extremely pretty young foreign lady who was passing through it upon his arm; and he wondered what on earth had been in Daisy's mind when she proposed to expose herself, unattended, to its appreciation. His own mission, to her sense apparently, was to consign her to the hands of Mr. Giovanelli; but Winterbourne, at once annoyed and gratified, resolved that he would do no such thing.

"Why haven't you been to see me?" asked Daisy. "You can't get out of that."

"I have had the honour of telling you that I have only just stepped out of the train."

"You must have stayed in the train a good while after it stopped!" cried the young girl, with her little laugh. "I suppose you were asleep. You have had time to go to see Mrs. Walker."

"I knew Mrs. Walker——" Winterbourne began to explain.

"I knew where you knew her. You knew her at Geneva. She told me so. Well, you knew me at Vevey. That's just as good. So you ought to have come." She asked him no other question than this; she began to prattle about her own affairs. "We've got splendid rooms at the hotel; Eugenio says they're the best rooms in Rome. We are going to stay all winter—if we don't die of the fever; and I guess we'll stay then. It's a great deal nicer than I thought; I thought it would be fearfully quiet; I was sure it would be awfully poky. I was sure we should be going round all the time with one of those dreadful old men that explain about the pictures and things. But we only had about a week of that, and now I'm enjoying myself. I know ever so many people, and they are all so charming. The society's extremely select. There are all kinds—English, and Germans, and Italians. I think I like the English best. I like their style of conversation. But there are some lovely Americans. I never saw anything so hospitable. There's something or other every day. There's not much dancing; but I must say I never thought dancing was everything. I was always fond of conversation. I guess I shall have plenty at Mrs. Walker's—her rooms are so small." When they had passed the gate of the Pincian Gardens, Miss Miller began to wonder where Mr. Giovanelli might be. "We had better go straight to that place in front," she said, "where you look at the view."

"I certainly shall not help you to find him," Winterbourne declared.

"Then I shall find him without you," said Miss Daisy.

"You certainly won't leave me!" cried Winterbourne.

She burst into her little laugh. "Are you afraid you'll get lost—or run over? But there's Giovanelli, leaning against that tree. He's staring at the women in the carriages: did you ever see anything so cool?"

Winterbourne perceived at some distance a little man standing with folded arms, nursing his cane. He had a handsome face, an artfully-poised hat, a glass in one eye and a nosegay in his button-hole. Winterbourne looked at him a moment and then said, "Do you mean to speak to that man?"

"Do I mean to speak to him? Why, you don't suppose I mean to communicate by signs?"

"Pray understand, then," said Winterbourne, "that I intend to remain with you."

Daisy stopped and looked at him, without a sign of troubled consciousness in her face; with nothing but the presence of her charming eyes and her happy dimples. "Well, she's a cool one!" thought the young man.

"I don't like the way you say that," said Daisy, "It's too imperious."

"I beg your pardon if I say it wrong. The main point is to give you an idea of my meaning."

The young girl looked at him more gravely, but with eyes that were prettier than ever. "I have never allowed a gentleman to dictate to me, or to interfere with anything I do."

"I think you have made a mistake," said Winterbourne. "You should sometimes listen to a gentleman—the right one!"

Daisy began to laugh again. "I do nothing but listen to gentlemen!" she exclaimed. "Tell me if Mr. Giovanelli is the right one?"

The gentleman with the nosegay in his bosom had now perceived our two friends, and was approaching the young girl with obsequious rapidity. He bowed to Winterbourne as well as to the latter's companion; he had a brilliant smile, an intelligent eye; Winterbourne thought him not a bad-looking fellow. But he nevertheless said to Daisy—"No, he's not the right one."

Daisy evidently had a natural talent for performing introductions; she mentioned the name of each of her companions to the other. She strolled along with one of them on each side of her; Mr. Giovanelli, who spoke English very cleverly—Winterbourne afterwards learned that he had practiced the idiom upon a great many American heiresses—addressed her a great deal of very polite nonsense; he was extremely urbane, and the young American, who said nothing, reflected upon that profundity of Italian cleverness which enables people to appear more gracious in proportion as they are more acutely disappointed. Giovanelli, of course, had counted upon something more intimate; he had not bargained for a party of three. But he kept his temper in a manner which suggested far-stretching intentions. Winterbourne flattered himself that he had taken his measure. "He is not a gentleman," said the young American; "he is only a clever imitation of one. He is a music-master or a penny-a-liner,[9] or a third-rate artist. Damn his good looks!" Mr. Giovanelli had certainly a very pretty face; but Winterbourne felt a superior indignation at his own lovely fellow-

9. Hack writer.

countrywoman's not knowing the difference between a spurious gentle-man and a real one. Giovanelli chattered and jested and made himself wonderfully agreeable. It was true that if he was an imitation the imitation was very skillful. "Nevertheless," Winterbourne said to himself, "a nice girl ought to know!" And then he came back to the question whether this was in fact a nice girl. Would a nice girl—even allowing for her being a little American flirt—make a rendezvous with a presumably low-lived foreigner? The rendezvous in this case, indeed, had been in broad daylight, and in the most crowded corner of Rome; but was it not impossible to regard the choice of these circumstances as a proof of extreme cynicism? Singular though it may seem, Winterbourne was vexed that the young girl, in joining her *amoroso*,[1] should not appear more impatient of his own company, and he was vexed because of his inclination. It was impossible to regard her as a perfectly well-conducted young lady; she was wanting in a certain indispensable delicacy. It would therefore simplify matters greatly to be able to treat her as the object of one of those sentiments which are called by romancers "lawless passions." That she should seem to wish to get rid of him would help him to think more lightly of her, and to be able to think more lightly of her would make her much less perplexing. But Daisy, on this occasion, continued to present herself as an inscrutable combination of audacity and innocence.

She had been walking some quarter of an hour, attended by her two cavaliers, and responding in a tone of very childish gaiety, as it seemed to Winterbourne, to the pretty speeches of Mr. Giovanelli, when a carriage that had detached itself from the revolving train drew up beside the path. At the same moment Winterbourne perceived that his friend Mrs. Walker—the lady whose house he had lately left—was seated in the vehicle and was beckoning to him. Leaving Miss Miller's side, he hastened to obey her summons. Mrs. Walker was flushed; she wore an excited air. "It is really too dreadful," she said. "That girl must not do this sort of thing. She must not walk here with you two men. Fifty people have noticed her."

Winterbourne raised his eyebrows. "I think it's a pity to make too much fuss about it."

"It's a pity to let the girl ruin herself!"

"She is very innocent," said Winterbourne.

"She's very crazy!" cried Mrs. Walker. "Did you ever see anything so imbecile as her mother? After you had all left me, just now, I could not sit still for thinking of it. It seemed too pitiful, not even to attempt to save her. I ordered the carriage and put on my bonnet, and came here as quickly as possible. Thank heaven I have found you!"

"What do you propose to do with us?" asked Winterbourne, smiling.

"To ask her to get in, to drive her about here for half an hour, so that the world may see she is not running absolutely wild, and then to take her safely home."

"I don't think it's a very happy thought," said Winterbourne; "but you can try."

Mrs. Walker tried. The young man went in pursuit of Miss Miller, who had simply nodded and smiled at his interlocutrix in the carriage and had gone her way with her own companion. Daisy, on learning that Mrs.

1. Lover.

Walker wished to speak to her, retraced her steps with a perfect good grace, and with Mr. Giovanelli at her side. She declared that she was delighted to have a chance to present this gentleman to Mrs. Walker. She immediately achieved the introduction, and declared that she had never in her life seen anything so lovely as Mrs. Walker's carriage-rug.

"I am glad you admire it," said this lady, smiling sweetly. "Will you get in and let me put it over you?"

"Oh no, thank you," said Daisy. "I shall admire it much more as I see you driving round with it."

"Do get in and drive with me," said Mrs. Walker.

"That would be charming, but it's so enchanting just as I am!" and Daisy gave a brilliant glance at the gentlemen on either side of her.

"It may be enchanting, dear child, but it is not the custom here," urged Mrs. Walker, leaning forward in her victoria with her hands devoutly clasped.

"Well, it ought to be, then!" said Daisy. "If I didn't walk I should expire."

"You should walk with your mother, dear," cried the lady from Geneva losing patience.

"With my mother dear!" exclaimed the young girl. Winterbourne saw that she scented interference. "My mother never walked ten steps in her life. And then, you know," she added with a laugh, "I am more than five years old."

"You are old enough to be more reasonable. You are old enough, dear Miss Miller, to be talked about."

Daisy looked at Mrs. Walker, smiling intensely. "Talked about? What do you mean?"

"Come into my carriage and I will tell you."

Daisy turned her quickened glance again from one of the gentlemen beside her to the other. Mr. Giovanelli was bowing to and fro, rubbing down his gloves and laughing very agreeably; Winterbourne thought it a most unpleasant scene. "I don't think I want to know what you mean," said Daisy presently. "I don't think I should like it."

Winterbourne wished that Mrs. Walker would tuck in her carriage-rug and drive away; but this lady did not enjoy being defied, as she afterwards told him. "Should you prefer being thought a very reckless girl?" she demanded.

"Gracious me!" exclaimed Daisy. She looked again at Mr. Giovanelli, then she turned to Winterbourne. There was a little pink flush in her cheek; she was tremendously pretty. "Does Mr. Winterbourne think," she asked slowly, smiling, throwing back her head and glancing at him from head to foot, "that—to save my reputation—I ought to get into the carriage?"

Winterbourne coloured; for an instant he hesitated greatly. It seemed so strange to hear her speak that way of her "reputation." But he himself, in fact, must speak in accordance with gallantry. The finest gallantry, here, was simply to tell her the truth; and the truth, for Winterbourne, as the few indications I have been able to give have made him known to the reader, was that Daisy Miller should take Mrs. Walker's advice. He looked at her exquisite prettiness; and then he said very gently, "I think you should get into the carriage."

Daisy gave a violent laugh. "I never heard anything so stiff! If this is improper, Mrs. Walker," she pursued, "then I am all improper, and you must give me up. Good-bye; I hope you'll have a lovely ride!" and, with Mr. Giovanelli, who made a triumphantly obsequious salute, she turned away.

Mrs. Walker sat looking after her, and there were tears in Mrs. Walker's eyes. "Get in here, sir," she said to Winterbourne, indicating the place beside her. The young man answered that he felt bound to accompany Miss Miller; whereupon Mrs. Walker declared that if he refused her this favour she would never speak to him again. She was evidently in earnest. Winterbourne overtook Daisy and her companion, and offering the young girl his hand, told her that Mrs. Walker had made an imperious claim upon his society. He expected that in answer she would say something rather free, something to commit herself still farther to that "recklessness" from which Mrs. Walker had so charitably endeavoured to dissuade her. But she only shook his hand, hardly looking at him, while Mr. Giovanelli bade him farewell with a too emphatic flourish of the hat.

Winterbourne was not in the best possible humour as he took his seat in Mrs. Walker's victoria. "That was not clever of you," he said candidly, while the vehicle mingled again with the throng of carriages.

"In such a case," his companion answered, "I don't wish to be clever, I wish to be *earnest!*"

"Well, your earnestness has only offended her and put her off."

"It has happened very well," said Mrs. Walker. "If she is so perfectly determined to compromise herself, the sooner one knows it the better; one can act accordingly."

"I suspect she meant no harm," Winterbourne rejoined.

"So I thought a month ago. But she has been going too far."

"What has she been doing?"

"Everything that is not done here. Flirting with any man she could pick up; sitting in corners with mysterious Italians; dancing all the evening with the same partners; receiving visits at eleven o'clock at night. Her mother goes away when visitors come."

"But her brother," said Winterbourne, laughing, "sits up till midnight."

"He must be edified by what he sees. I'm told that at their hotel every one is talking about her, and that a smile goes round among the servants when a gentleman comes and asks for Miss Miller."

"The servants be hanged!" said Winterbourne angrily. "The poor girl's only fault," he presently added, "is that she is very uncultivated."

"She is naturally indelicate," Mrs. Walker declared. "Take that example this morning. How long had you known her at Vevey?"

"A couple of days."

"Fancy, then, her making it a personal matter that you should have left the place!"

Winterbourne was silent for some moments; then he said, "I suspect, Mrs. Walker, that you and I have lived too long at Geneva!" And he added a request that she should inform him with what particular design she had made him enter her carriage.

"I wished to beg you to cease your relations with Miss Miller—not to flirt with her—to give her no farther opportunity to expose herself—to let her alone, in short."

"I'm afraid I can't do that," said Winterbourne. "I like her extremely."

"All the more reason that you shouldn't help her to make a scandal."

"There shall be nothing scandalous in my attentions to her."

"There certainly will be in the way she takes them. But I have said what I had on my conscience," Mrs. Walker pursued. "If you wish to rejoin the young lady I will put you down. Here, by the way, you have a chance."

The carriage was traversing that part of the Pincian Garden which overhangs the wall of Rome and overlooks the beautiful Villa Borghese.[2] It is bordered by a large parapet, near which there are several seats. One of the seats, at a distance, was occupied by a gentleman and a lady, towards whom Mrs. Walker gave a toss of her head. At the same moment these persons rose and walked towards the parapet. Winterbourne had asked the coachman to stop; he now descended from the carriage. His companion looked at him a moment in silence; then, while he raised his hat, she drove majestically away. Winterbourne stood there; he had turned his eyes towards Daisy and her cavalier. They evidently saw no one; they were too deeply occupied with each other. When they reached the low garden wall they stood a moment looking off at the great flat-topped pine clusters of the Villa Borghese; then Giovanelli seated himself familiarly upon the broad ledge of the wall. The western sun in the opposite sky sent out a brilliant shaft through a couple of cloud-bars; whereupon Daisy's companion took her parasol out of her hands and opened it. She came a little nearer, and he held the parasol over her; then, still holding it, he let it rest upon her shoulder, so that both of their heads were hidden from Winterbourne. This young man lingered a moment, then he began to walk. But he walked—not towards the couple with the parasol; towards the residence of his aunt, Mrs. Costello.

He flattered himself on the following day that there was no smiling among the servants when he, at least, asked for Mrs. Miller at her hotel. This lady and her daughter, however, were not at home; and on the next day after, repeating his visit, Winterbourne again had the misfortune not to find them. Mrs. Walker's party took place on the evening of the third day, and in spite of the frigidity of his last interview with the hostess Winterbourne was among the guests. Mrs. Walker was one of those American ladies who, while residing abroad, make a point, in their own phrase, of studying European society; and she had on this occasion collected several specimens of her diversely-born fellow-mortals to serve, as it were, as text-books. When Winterbourne arrived Daisy Miller was not there; but in a few moments he saw her mother come in alone, very shyly and ruefully. Mrs. Miller's hair, above her exposed-looking temples, was more frizzled than ever. As she approached Mrs. Walker Winterbourne also drew near.

"You see I've come all alone," said poor Mrs. Miller. "I'm so frightened; I don't know what to do; it's the first time I've ever been to a party alone—especially in this country. I wanted to bring Randolph or Eugenio, or some one, but Daisy just pushed me off by myself. I ain't used to going round alone."

"And does not your daughter intend to favour us with her society?" demanded Mrs. Walker, impressively.

"Well, Daisy's all dressed," said Mrs. Miller, with that accent of the dispassionate, if not of the philosophic, historian, with which she always recorded the current incidents of her daughter's career. "She got dressed on purpose before dinner. But she's got a friend of hers there; that gentleman—the Italian—that she wanted to bring. They've got going at the piano; it seems as if they couldn't leave off. Mr. Giovanelli sings splendidly. But I guess they'll come before very long," concluded Mrs. Miller hopefully.

"I'm sorry she should come—in that way," said Mrs. Walker.

"Well, I told her that there was no use in her getting dressed before dinner if she was going to wait three hours," responded Daisy's mamma. "I didn't see the use of her putting on such a dress as that to sit round with Mr. Giovanelli."

"This is most horrible!" said Mrs. Walker, turning away and addressing herself to Winterbourne. "*Elle s'affiche.*³ It's her revenge for my having ventured to remonstrate with her. When she comes I shall not speak to her."

Daisy came after eleven o'clock, but she was not, on such an occasion, a young lady to wait to be spoken to. She rustled forward in radiant loveliness, smiling and chattering, carrying a large bouquet, and attended by Mr. Giovanelli. Every one stopped talking, and turned and looked at her. She came straight to Mrs. Walker. "I'm afraid you thought I never was coming, so I sent mother off to tell you. I wanted to make Mr. Giovanelli practise some things before he came; you know he sings beautifully, and I want you to ask him to sing. This is Mr. Giovanelli; you know I introduced him to you; he's got the most lovely voice, and he knows the most charming set of songs. I made him go over them this evening, on purpose; we had the greatest time at the hotel." Of all this Daisy delivered herself with the sweetest, brightest audibleness, looking now at her hostess and now round the room, while she gave a series of little pats, round her shoulders, to the edges of her dress. "Is there any one I know?" she asked.

"I think every one knows you!" said Mrs. Walker, pregnantly, and she gave a very cursory greeting to Mr. Giovanelli. This gentleman bore himself gallantly. He smiled and bowed, and showed his white teeth, he curled his moustaches and rolled his eyes, and performed all the proper functions of a handsome Italian at an evening party. He sang, very prettily, half a dozen songs, though Mrs. Walker afterwards declared that she had been quite unable to find out who asked him. It was apparently not Daisy who had given him his orders. Daisy sat at a distance from the piano, and though she had publicly, as it were, professed a high admiration for his singing, talked, not inaudibly, while it was going on.

"It's a pity these rooms are so small; we can't dance," she said to Winterbourne, as if she had seen him five minutes before.

"I am not sorry we can't dance," Winterbourne answered; "I don't dance."

"Of course you don't dance; you're too stiff," said Miss Daisy. "I hope you enjoyed your drive with Mrs. Walker."

"No, I didn't enjoy it; I prefered walking with you."

"We paired off, that was much better," said Daisy. "But did you ever hear anything so cool as Mrs. Walker's wanting me to get into her carriage and drop poor Mr. Giovanelli; and under the pretext that it was

3. She's trying to get herself talked about.

proper? People have different ideas! It would have been most unkind; he had been talking about that walk for ten days."

"He should not have talked about it at all," said Winterbourne; "he would never have proposed to a young lady of this country to walk about the streets with him."

"About the streets?" cried Daisy, with her pretty stare. "Where, then, would he have proposed to her to walk? The Pincio is not the streets either; and I, thank goodness, am not a young lady of this country. The young ladies of this country have a dreadfully poky time of it, so far as I can learn; I don't see why I should change my habits for *them*."

"I am afraid your habits are those of a flirt," said Winterbourne, gravely.

"Of course they are," she cried, giving him her little smiling stare again. "I'm a fearful, frightful flirt! Did you ever hear of a nice girl that was not? But I suppose you will tell me now that I am not a nice girl."

"You're a very nice girl, but I wish you would flirt with me, and me only," said Winterbourne.

"Ah! thank you, thank you very much; you are the last man I should think of flirting with. As I have had the pleasure of informing you, you are too stiff."

"You say that too often," said Winterbourne.

Daisy gave a delighted laugh. "If I could have the sweet hope of making you angry, I would say it again."

"Don't do that; when I am angry I'm stiffer than ever. But if you won't flirt with me, do cease at least to flirt with your friend at the piano; they don't understand that sort of thing here."

"I thought they understood nothing else!" exclaimed Daisy.

"Not in young unmarried women."

"It seems to me much more proper in young unmarried women than in old married ones," Daisy declared.

"Well," said Winterbourne, "when you deal with natives you must go by the custom of the place. Flirting is a purely American custom; it doesn't exist here. So when you show yourself in public with Mr. Giovanelli, and without your mother——"

"Gracious! poor mother!" interposed Daisy.

"Though you may be flirting, Mr. Giovanelli is not; he means something else."

"He isn't preaching, at any rate," said Daisy, with vivacity. "And if you want very much to know, we are neither of us flirting; we are too good friends for that; we are very intimate friends."

"Ah!" rejoined Winterbourne, "if you are in love with each other it is another affair."

She had allowed him up to this point to talk so frankly that he had no expectation of shocking her by this ejaculation; but she immediately got up, blushing visibly, and leaving him to exclaim mentally that little American flirts were the queerest creatures in the world. "Mr. Giovanelli, at least," she said, giving her interlocutor a single glance, "never says such very disagreeable things to me."

Winterbourne was bewildered; he stood staring. Mr. Giovanelli had finished singing; he left the piano and came over to Daisy. "Won't you come into the other room and have some tea?" he asked, bending before her, with his decorative smile.

Daisy turned to Winterbourne, beginning to smile again. He was still more preplexed, for this inconsequent smile made nothing clear, though it seemed to prove, indeed, that she had a sweetness and softness that reverted instinctively to the pardon of offences. "It has never occurred to Mr. Winterbourne to offer me any tea," she said, with her little tormenting manner.

"I have offered you advice," Winterbourne rejoined.

"I prefer weak tea!" cried Daisy, and she went off with the brilliant Giovanelli. She sat with him in the adjoining room, in the embrasure of the window, for the rest of the evening. There was an interesting performance at the piano, but neither of these young people gave heed to it. When Daisy came to take leave of Mrs. Walker, this lady conscientiously repaired the weakness of which she had been guilty at the moment of the young girl's arrival. She turned her back straight upon Miss Miller, and left her to depart with what grace she might. Winterbourne was standing near the door; he saw it all. Daisy turned very pale and looked at her mother, but Mrs. Miller was humbly unconscious of any violation of the usual social forms. She appeared, indeed, to have felt an incongruous impulse to draw attention to her own striking observance of them. "Goodnight, Mrs. Walker," she said; "we've had a beautiful evening. You see if I let Daisy come to parties without me, I don't want her to go away without me." Daisy turned away, looking with a pale grave face at the circle near the door; Winterbourne saw that, for the first moment, she was too much shocked and puzzled even for indignation. He on his side was greatly touched.

"That was very cruel," he said to Mrs. Walker.

"She never enters my drawing-room again," replied his hostess.

Since Winterbourne was not to meet her in Mrs. Walker's drawing-room, he went as often as possible to Mrs. Miller's hotel. The ladies were rarely at home, but when he found them the devoted Giovanelli was always present. Very often the polished little Roman was in the drawing-room with Daisy alone, Mrs. Miller being apparently constantly of the opinion that discretion is the better part of surveillance. Winterbourne noted, at first with surprise, that Daisy on these occasions was never embarrassed or annoyed by his own entrance; but he very presently began to feel that she had no more surprises for him; the unexpected in her behaviour was the only thing to expect. She showed no displeasure at her tête-à-tête with Giovanelli being interrupted; she could chatter as freshly and freely with two gentlemen as with one; there was always in her conversation the same odd mixture of audacity and puerility. Winterbourne remarked to himself that, if she was seriously interested in Giovanelli, it was very singular that she should not take more trouble to preserve the sanctity of their interviews, and he liked her the more for her innocent-looking indifference and her apparently inexhaustible good-humour. He could hardly have said why, but she seemed to him a girl who would never be jealous. At the risk of exciting a somewhat derisive smile on the reader's part, I may affirm that, with regard to the women who had hitherto interested him, it very often seemed to Winterbourne among the possibilities that, given certain contingencies, he should be afraid—literally afraid—of these ladies. He had a pleasant sense that he should never be afraid of Daisy Miller. It must be added that this sentiment was not altogether flattering to Daisy; it was part of his conviction, or rather of his apprehension, that she would prove a very light young person.

But she was evidently very much interested in Giovanelli. She looked at him whenever he spoke; she was perpetually telling him to do this and to do that; she was constantly "chaffing" and abusing him. She appeared completely to have forgotten that Winterbourne had said anything to displease her at Mrs. Walker's little party. One Sunday afternoon, having gone to St. Peter's with his aunt, Winterbourne perceived Daisy strolling about the great church in company with the inevitable Giovanelli. Presently he pointed out the young girl and her cavalier to Mrs. Costello. This lady looked at them a moment through her eye-glass, and then she said:

"That's what makes you so pensive in these days, eh?"

"I had not the least idea I was pensive," said the young man.

"You are very much preoccupied, you are thinking of something."

"And what is it," he asked, "that you accuse me of thinking of?"

"Of that young lady's—Miss Baker's, Miss Chandler's—what's her name?—Miss Miller's intrigue with that little barber's block."[4]

"Do you call it an intrigue," Winterbourne asked—"an affair that goes on with such peculiar publicity?"

"That's their folly," said Mrs. Costello, "it's not their merit."

"No," rejoined Winterbourne, with something of that pensiveness to which his aunt had alluded. "I don't believe that there is anything to be called an intrigue."

"I have heard a dozen people speak of it; they say she is quite carried away by him."

"They are certainly very intimate," said Winterbourne.

Mrs. Costello inspected the young couple again with her optical instrument. "He is very handsome. One easily sees how it is. She thinks him the most elegant man in the world, the finest gentleman. She has never seen anything like him; he is better even than the courier. It was the courier, probably, who introduced him, and if he succeeds in marrying the young lady, the courier will come in for a magnificent commission."

"I don't believe she thinks of marrying him," said Winterbourne, "and I don't believe he hopes to marry her."

"You may be very sure she thinks of nothing. She goes on from day to day, from hour to hour, as they did in the Golden Age. I can imagine nothing more vulgar. And at the same time," added Mrs. Costello, "depend upon it that she may tell you any moment that she is 'engaged.'"

"I think that is more than Giovanelli expects," said Winterbourne.

"Who is Giovanelli?"

"The little Italian. I have asked questions about him and learned something. He is apparently a perfectly respectable little man. I believe he is in a small way a *cavaliere avvocato*.[5] But he doesn't move in what are called the first circles. I think it is really not absolutely impossible that the courier introduced him. He is evidently immensely charmed with Miss Miller. If she thinks him the finest gentleman in the world, he, on his side, has never found himself in personal contact with such splendour, such opulence, such expensiveness, as this young lady's. And then she must seem to him wonderfully pretty and interesting. I rather doubt whether he dreams of marrying her. That must appear to him too impos-

---

4. Overdressed man.   5. Gentleman-lawyer.

sible a piece of luck. He has nothing but his handsome face to offer, and there is a substantial Mr. Miller in that mysterious land of dollars. Giovanelli knows that he hasn't a title to offer. If he were only a count or a *marchese!* He must wonder at his luck at the way they have taken him up."

"He accounts for it by his handsome face, and thinks Miss Miller a young lady *qui se passe ses fantaisies!*"[6] said Mrs. Costello.

"It is very true," Winterbourne pursued, "that Daisy and her mamma have not yet risen to that stage of—what shall I call it?—of culture, at which the idea of catching a count or a *marchese* begins. I believe that they are intellectually incapable of that conception."

"Ah! but the *cavaliere* can't believe it," said Mrs. Costello.

Of the observation excited by Daisy's "intrigue," Winterbourne gathered that day at St. Peter's sufficient evidence. A dozen of the American colonists in Rome came to talk with Mrs. Costello, who sat on a little portable stool at the base of one of the great pilasters. The vesper-service was going forward in splendid chants and organ-tones in the adjacent choir, and meanwhile, between Mrs. Costello and her friends, there was a great deal said about poor little Miss Miller's going really "too far." Winterbourne was not pleased with what he heard; but when, coming out upon the great steps of the church, he saw Daisy, who had emerged before him, get into an open cab with her accomplice and roll away through the cynical streets of Rome, he could not deny to himself that she was going very far indeed. He felt very sorry for her—not exactly that he believed that she had completely lost her head, but because it was painful to hear so much that was pretty and undefended and natural assigned to a vulgar place among the categories of disorder. He made an attempt after this to give a hint to Mrs. Miller. He met one day in the Corso a friend—a tourist like himself—who had just come out of the Doria Palace,[7] where he had been walking through the beautiful gallery. His friend talked for a moment about the superb portrait of Innocent X. by Velasquez, which hangs in one of the cabinets of the palace, and then said, "And in the same cabinet, by the way, I had the pleasure of contemplating a picture of a different kind—that pretty American girl whom you pointed out to me last week." In answer to Winterbourne's inquiries, his friend narrated that the pretty American girl—prettier than ever—was seated with a companion in the secluded nook in which the great papal portrait is enshrined.

"Who was her companion?" asked Winterbourne.

"A little Italian with a bouquet in his button-hole. The girl is delightfully pretty, but I thought I understood from you the other day that she was a young lady *du meilleur monde.*"[8]

"So she is!" answered Winterbourne; and having assured himself that his informant had seen Daisy and her companion but five minutes before, he jumped into a cab and went to call on Mrs. Miller. She was at home; but she apologised to him for receiving him in Daisy's absence.

"She's gone out somewhere with Mr. Giovanelli," said Mrs. Miller. "She's always going round with Mr. Giovanelli."

6. Who is indulging her whims.
7. The gallery contains many art treasures, including the 1649 portrait of Pope Innocent X by the Spanish painter Diego Rodríguez de Silva y Velás-quez (1599–1669). The Corso is one of the major streets of Rome.
8. Of the better class of society.

"I have noticed that they are very intimate," Winterbourne observed. "Oh! it seems as if they couldn't live without each other!" said Mrs. Miller. "Well, he's a real gentleman, anyhow. I keep telling Daisy she's engaged!"

"And what does Daisy say?"

"Oh, she says she isn't engaged. But she might as well be!" this impartial parent resumed. "She goes on as if she was. But I've made Mr. Giovanelli promise to tell me, if *she* doesn't. I should want to write to Mr. Miller about it—shouldn't you?"

Winterbourne replied that he certainly should; and the state of mind of Daisy's mamma struck him as so unprecedented in the annals of parental vigilance that he gave up as utterly irrelevant the attempt to place her upon her guard.

After this Daisy was never at home, and Winterbourne ceased to meet her at the houses of their common acquaintance, because, as he perceived, these shrewd people had quite made up their minds that she was going too far. They ceased to invite her, and they intimated that they desired to express to observant Europeans the great truth that, though Miss Daisy Miller was a young American lady, her behaviour was not representative—was regarded by her compatriots as abnormal. Winterbourne wondered how she felt about all the cold shoulders that were turned towards her, and sometimes it annoyed him to suspect that she did not feel at all. He said to himself that she was too light and childish, too uncultivated and unreasoning, too provincial, to have reflected upon her ostracism, or even to have perceived it. Then at other moments he believed that she carried about in her elegant and irresponsible little organism a defiant, passionate, perfectly observant consciousness of the impression she produced. He asked himself whether Daisy's defiance came from the consciousness of innocence or from her being, essentially, a young person of the reckless class. It must be admitted that holding oneself to a belief in Daisy's "innocence" came to seem to Winterbourne more and more a matter of fine-spun gallantry. As I have already had occasion to relate, he was angry at finding himself reduced to chopping logic about this young lady; he was vexed at his want of instinctive certitude as to how far her eccentricities were generic, national, and how far they were personal. From either view of them he had somehow missed her, and now it was too late. She was "carried away" by Mr. Giovanelli.

A few days after his brief interview with her mother, he encountered her in that beautiful abode of flowering desolation known as the Palace of the Cæsars. The early Roman spring had filled the air with bloom and perfume, and the rugged surface of the Palatine[9] was muffled with tender verdure. Daisy was strolling along the top of one of those great mounds of ruin that are embanked with mossy marble and paved with monumental inscriptions. It seemed to him that Rome had never been so lovely as just then. He stood looking off at the enchanting harmony of line and colour that remotely encircles the city, inhaling the softly humid odours, and feeling the freshness of the year and the antiquity of the place reaffirm themselves in mysterious interfusion. It seemed to him also that Daisy had never looked so pretty; but this had been an observation of his when-

---

9. One of the seven hills forming the center of ancient Rome.

ever he met her. Giovanelli was at her side, and Giovanelli too wore an aspect of even unwonted brilliancy.

"Well," said Daisy, "I should think you would be lonesome!"

"Lonesome?" asked Winterbourne.

"You are always going round by yourself. Can't you get any one to walk with you?"

"I am not so fortunate," said Winterbourne, "as your companion."

Giovanelli, from the first, had treated Winterbourne with distinguished politeness; he listened with a deferential air to his remarks; he laughed, punctiliously, at his pleasantries; he seemed disposed to testify to his belief that Winterbourne was a superior young man. He carried himself in no degree like a jealous wooer; he had obviously a great deal of tact; he had no objection to your expecting a little humility of him. It even seemed to Winterbourne at times that Giovanelli would find a certain mental relief in being able to have a private understanding with him—to say to him, as an intelligent man, that, bless you, *he* knew how extraordinary was this young lady, and didn't flatter himself with delusive—or at least *too* delusive—hopes of matrimony and dollars. On this occasion he strolled away from his companion to pluck a sprig of almond-blossom, which he carefully arranged in his button-hole.

"I know why you say that," said Daisy, watching Giovanelli. "Because you think I go round too much with *him!*" And she nodded at her attendant.

"Every one thinks so—if you care to know," said Winterbourne.

"Of course I care to know!" Daisy exclaimed seriously. "But I don't believe it. They are only pretending to be shocked. They don't really care a straw what I do. Besides, I don't go round so much."

"I think you will find they do care. They will show it—disagreeably."

Daisy looked at him a moment. "How disagreeably?"

"Haven't you noticed anything?" Winterbourne asked.

"I have noticed you. But I noticed you were as stiff as an umbrella the first time I saw you."

"You will find I am not so stiff as several others," said Winterborne, smiling.

"How shall I find it?"

"By going to see the others."

"What will they do to me?"

"They will give you the cold shoulder. Do you know what that means?"

Daisy was looking at him intently; she began to colour. "Do you mean as Mrs. Walker did the other night?"

"Exactly!" said Winterbourne.

She looked away at Giovanelli, who was decorating himself with his almond-blossom. Then looking back at Winterbourne—"I shouldn't think you would let people be so unkind!" she said.

"How can I help it?" he asked.

"I should think you would say something."

"I do say something;" and he paused a moment. "I say that your mother tells me that she believes you are engaged."

"Well, she does," said Daisy, very simply.

Winterbourne began to laugh. "And does Randolph believe it?" he asked.

"I guess Randolph doesn't believe anything," said Daisy. Randolph's scepticism excited Winterbourne to further hilarity, and he observed that Giovanelli was coming back to them. Daisy, observing it too, addressed herself again to her countryman. "Since you have mentioned it," she said, "I *am* engaged." . . . Winterbourne looked at her; he had stopped laughing. "You don't believe it!" she added.

He was silent a moment; and then, "Yes, I believe it!" he said.

"Oh no, you don't," she answered. "Well, then—I am not!"

The young girl and her cicerone were on their way to the gate of the enclosure, so that Winterbourne, who had but lately entered, presently took leave of them. A week afterwards he went to dine at a beautiful villa on the Cælian Hill, and, on arriving, dismissed his hired vehicle. The evening was charming, and he promised himself the satisfaction of walking home beneath the Arch of Constantine[1] and past the vaguely-lighted monuments of the Forum. There was a waning moon in the sky, and her radiance was not brilliant, but she was veiled in a thin cloud-curtain which seemed to diffuse and equalise it. When, on his return from the villa (it was eleven o'clock), Winterbourne approached the dusky circle of the Colosseum, it occurred to him, as a lover of the picturesque, that the interior, in the pale moonshine, would be well worth a glance. He turned aside and walked to one of the empty arches, near which, as he observed, an open carriage—one of the little Roman street cabs—was stationed. Then he passed in among the cavernous shadows of the great structure, and emerged upon the clear and silent arena. The place had never seemed to him more impressive. One-half of the gigantic circus[2] was in deep shade; the other was sleeping in the luminous dusk. As he stood there he began to murmur Byron's famous lines, out of "Manfred";[3] but before he had finished his quotation he remembered that if nocturnal meditations in the Colosseum are recommended by the poets, they are deprecated by the doctors. The historic atmosphere was there, certainly; but the historic atmosphere, scientifically considered, was no better than a villainous miasma. Winterbourne walked to the middle of the arena, to take a more general glance, intending thereafter to make a hasty retreat. The great cross in the centre was covered with shadow; it was only as he drew near it that he made it out distinctly. Then he saw that two persons were stationed upon the low steps which formed its base. One of these was a woman, seated; her companion was standing in front of her.

Presently the sound of the woman's voice came to him distinctly in the warm night air. "Well, he looks at us as one of the old lions or tigers may have looked at the Christian martyrs!" These were the words he heard, in the familiar accent of Miss Daisy Miller.

"Let us hope he is not very hungry," responded the ingenious Giovanelli. "He will have to take me first; you will serve for dessert!"

Winterbourne stopped, with a sort of horror; and, it must be added, with a sort of relief. It was as if a sudden illumination had been flashed upon the ambiguity of Daisy's behavior and the riddle had become easy to read. She was a young lady whom a gentleman need no longer be at

1. Triumphal arch erected about A.D. 315 honoring Constantine I's victory in 312 over Maxentius in the struggle for control of Rome. The Cælian is one of the seven hills. The Forum, now in ruins, was the marketplace and public area of ancient Rome.

2. Arena.
3. *Manfred* III, iv, 10–41, "I stood within the Coliseum's wall;/ 'Midst the chief relics of almighty Rome;/ The trees which grew along the broken arches/ Waved dark in the blue midnight . . . " etc.

pains to respect. He stood there looking at her—looking at her companion, and not reflecting that though he saw them vaguely, he himself must have been more brightly visible. He felt angry with himself that he had bothered so much about the right way of regarding Miss Daisy Miller. Then, as he was going to advance again, he checked himself; not from the fear that he was doing her injustice, but from a sense of the danger of appearing unbecomingly exhilarated by this sudden revulsion from cautious criticism. He turned away towards the entrance of the place; but as he did so he heard Daisy speak again.

"Why, it was Mr. Winterbourne! He saw me—and he cuts me!"

What a clever little reprobate she was, and how smartly she played an injured innocence! But he wouldn't cut her. Winterbourne came forward again, and went towards the great cross. Daisy had got up; Giovanelli lifted his hat. Winterbourne had now begun to think simply of the craziness, from a sanitary point of view, of a delicate young girl lounging away the evening in this nest of malaria. What if she *were* a clever little reprobate? that was no reason for her dying of the *perniciosa*.[4] "How long have you been here?" he asked, almost brutally.

Daisy, lovely in the flattering moonlight, looked at him a moment. Then—"All the evening," she answered gently. . . . "I never saw anything so pretty."

"I am afraid," said Winterbourne, "that you will not think Roman fever very pretty. This is the way people catch it. I wonder," he added, turning to Giovanelli, "that you, a native Roman, should countenance such a terrible indiscretion."

"Ah," said the handsome native, "for myself, I am not afraid."

"Neither am I—for you! I am speaking for this young lady."

Giovanelli lifted his well-shaped eyebrows and showed his brilliant teeth. But he took Winterbourne's rebuke with docility. "I told the Signorina it was a grave indiscretion; but when was the Signorina ever prudent?"

"I never was sick, and I don't mean to be!" the Signorina declared. "I don't look like much, but I'm healthy! I was bound to see the Colosseum by moonlight; I shouldn't have wanted to go home without that; and we have had the most beautiful time, haven't we, Mr. Giovanelli? If there has been any danger, Eugenio can give me some pills. He has got some splendid pills."

"I should advise you," said Winterbourne, "to drive home as fast as possible and take one!"

"What you say is very wise," Giovanelli rejoined. "I will go and make sure the carriage is at hand." And he went forward rapidly.

Daisy followed with Winterbourne. He kept looking at her; she seemed not in the least embarrassed. Winterbourne said nothing; Daisy chattered about the beauty of the place. "Well, I *have* seen the Colosseum by moonlight!" she exclaimed. "That's one good thing." Then, noticing Winterbourne's silence, she asked him why he didn't speak. He made no answer; he only began to laugh. They passed under one of the dark archways; Giovanelli was in front with the carriage. Here Daisy stopped a moment, looking at the young American. "*Did* you believe I was engaged the other day?" she asked.

4. Pernicious fever, malaria.

"It doesn't matter what I believed the other day," said Winterbourne, still laughing.

"Well, what do you believe now?"

"I believe that it makes very little difference whether you are engaged or not!"

He felt the young girl's pretty eyes fixed upon him through the thick gloom of the archway; she was apparently going to answer. But Giovanelli hurried her forward. "Quick, quick," he said; "if we get in by midnight we are quite safe."

Daisy took her seat in the carriage, and the fortunate Italian placed himself beside her. "Don't forget Eugenio's pills!" said Winterbourne, as he lifted his hat.

"I don't care," said Daisy, in a little strange tone, "whether I have Roman fever or not!" Upon this the cab-driver cracked his whip, and they rolled away over the desultory patches of the antique pavement.

Winterbourne—to do him justice, as it were—mentioned to no one that he had encountered Miss Miller, at midnight, in the Colosseum with a gentleman; but nevertheless, a couple of days later, the fact of her having been there under these circumstances was known to every member of the little American circle, and commented accordingly. Winterbourne reflected that they had of course known it at the hotel, and that, after Daisy's return, there had been an exchange of jokes between the porter and the cab-driver. But the young man was conscious, at the same moment, that it had ceased to be a matter of serious regret to him that the little American flirt should be "talked about" by low-minded menials. These people, a day or two later, had serious information to give: the little American flirt was alarmingly ill. Winterbourne, when the rumour came to him, immediately went to the hotel for more news. He found that two or three charitable friends had preceded him, and that they were being entertained in Mrs. Miller's salon by Randolph.

"It's going round at night," said Randolph—"that's what made her sick. She's always going round at night. I shouldn't think she'd want to—it's so plaguey dark. You can't see anything here at night, except when there's a moon. In America there's always a moon!" Mrs. Miller was invisible: she was now, at least, giving her daughter the advantage of her society. It was evident that Daisy was dangerously ill.

Winterbourne went often to ask for news of her, and once he saw Mrs. Miller, who, though deeply alarmed, was—rather to his surprise—perfectly composed, and, as it appeared, a most efficient and judicious nurse. She talked a good deal about Dr. Davis, but Winterbourne paid her the compliment of saying to himself that she was not, after all, such a monstrous goose. "Daisy spoke of you the other day," she said to him. "Half the time she doesn't know what she's saying, but that time I think she did. She gave me a message; she told me to tell you. She told me to tell you that she never was engaged to that handsome Italian. I am sure I am very glad; Mr. Giovanelli hasn't been near us since she was taken ill. I thought he was so much of a gentleman; but I don't call that very polite! A lady told me that he was afraid I was angry with him for taking Daisy round at night. Well, so I am; but I suppose he knows I'm a lady. I would scorn to scold him. Any way, she says she's not engaged. I don't know why she wanted you to know; but she said to me three times—'Mind you tell Mr. Winterbourne.' And then she told me to ask if you remembered the time you went to that castle, in Switzerland. But I said I wouldn't give any such messages as that. Only, if she is not engaged, I'm sure I'm glad to know it."

But, as Winterbourne had said, it mattered very little. A week after this the poor girl died; it had been a terrible case of the fever. Daisy's grave was in the little Protestant cemetery, in an angle of the wall of imperial Rome, beneath the cypresses and the thick spring flowers. Winterbourne stood there beside it, with a number of other mourners; a number larger than the scandal excited by the young lady's career would have led you to expect. Near him stood Giovanelli, who came nearer still before Winterbourne turned away. Giovanelli was very pale; on this occasion he had no flower in his button-hole; he seemed to wish to say something. At last he said, "She was the most beautiful young lady I ever saw, and the most amiable." And then he added in a moment, "And she was the most innocent."

Winterbourne looked at him, and presently repeated his words, "And the most innocent?"

"The most innocent!"

Winterbourne felt sore and angry. "Why the devil," he asked, "did you take her to that fatal place?"

Mr. Giovanelli's urbanity was apparently imperturbable. He looked on the ground a moment and then he said, "For myself, I had no fear; and she wanted to go."

"That was no reason!" Winterbourne declared.

The subtle Roman again dropped his eyes. "If she had lived, I should have got nothing. She would never have married me, I am sure."

"She would never have married you?"

"For a moment I hoped so. But no. I am sure."

Winterbourne listened to him; he stood staring at the raw protuberance among the April daisies. When he turned away again Mr. Giovanelli, with his light slow step, had retired.

Winterbourne almost immediately left Rome; but the following summer he again met his aunt, Mrs. Costello, at Vevey. Mrs. Costello was fond of Vevey. In the interval Winterbourne had often thought of Daisy Miller and her mystifying manners. One day he spoke of her to his aunt—said it was on his conscience that he had done her injustice.

"I am sure I don't know," said Mrs. Costello. "How did your injustice affect her?"

"She sent me a message before her death which I didn't understand at the time. But I have understood it since. She would have appreciated one's esteem."

"Is that a modest way," asked Mrs. Costello, "of saying that she would have reciprocated one's affection?"

Winterbourne offered no answer to this question; but he presently said, "You were right in that remark that you made last summer. I was booked to make a mistake. I have lived too long in foreign parts."

Nevertheless, he went back to live at Geneva, whence there continue to come the most contradictory accounts of his motives of sojourn: a report that he is "studying" hard—an intimation that he is much interested in a very clever foreign lady.

1878

AFTERWORD

For a short while *Daisy Miller* promises to be a sophisticated social novel, perhaps a comedy of manners, about Americans in Europe in the mid-1870s. There is a reasonably witty, somewhat cynical first-person narrator on-stage in the second paragraph who seems to know a great deal about the scene and about a certain young American—what his friends say about him, what others say; that he lives in Geneva, has some sort of attachment there and is satisfied, and that at the moment his aunt has (as she often does) a headache. But the narrator does not know quite everything: he is not entirely sure of ("I hardly know") the young man's thoughts. The first-person narrator soon withdraws, leaving us with Winterbourne, the young American, as the center of consciousness in the story, the one through whose eyes and mind we will see and interpret what is to happen. A boy appears, engaging Winterbourne in conversation. Soon his older sister appears, a beautiful American girl. Boy-meets-girl: the "real story" now seems underway.

There are those who say that in novels such as *Daisy Miller* Henry James invented the American Girl, especially the American-Girl-in-Europe. She is (or was) fresher and freer than her European counterpart, or, indeed, than her more "European-like" mother and grandmothers who took their manners and mores from the old country. She thus raises for both Europeans and more conventional Americans certain questions: What are these young girls really like? Independent in words and actions, unchaperoned, are they careless of conventions because of their innocence? Or is their freedom license: are they immoral as well as unconventional? If innocent, are they not in danger of being misunderstood, looked down upon, laughed at, victimized by the more worldly Europeans? These are the questions Winterbourne must ask himself, and since he is the center of consciousness for the rest of the novel, these are also the questions we ask. This is how our curiosity and suspense are aroused and maintained until the very end of the story.

This concern over sexual behavior, especially a woman's sexual behavior, is not necessarily evidence of a kind of prurience on Henry James's part, but rather was part of the contemporary social and moral code, a way of measuring the moral nature of the culture. The "world"—that is, the English-speaking world, which was then the most powerful portion—was then literally and figuratively "Victorian": Victoria had been queen for more than a third of a century. There have been several moral and sexual revolutions in the century that has passed since then, and the kinds of questions Winterbourne and his society upset themselves over may seem rather quaint nowadays, but there are underlying questions that still remain relevant. Where is the line between freedom and license, salutary restraint and tyranny? What can we really learn about others from appearance?

Because this questioning, this curiosity, this lust to know the truth about others is so prevalent in his work, Henry James is sometimes described as an eavesdropper—or even a voyeur—trying, for whatever reason, to live through other people, trying to learn about their lives because he has none of his own. But isn't this interest in others, in knowing what other people are like and how the world looks to them, central to our understanding of ourselves and to the world around us? And isn't it in large measure what literature is almost always about, and one of the chief reasons we read fiction—or look at pictures or films or listen to music or talk at cocktail parties, for that matter? So while "What is Daisy Miller really like?" is the question that drives—or nudges—our interest forward in the "detective" love story, it also pushes us into more profound cultural, moral, and psychological, not to mention literary, questions.

We are never allowed to forget in this "boy-meets-girl" story that the girl is an *American* girl (though we are, interestingly enough, sometimes likely to think that the "boy" is more European than American). The superiority of all things American is a major subject in the first scene, the first bit of dialogue between Winterbourne and Daisy's precocious and patriotic little brother. The Miller family, we soon learn, is typical, almost stereotypical, one kind of late nineteenth-century American tourist: those with "new," post-Civil War money, for the most part industrially earned, from what might then be considered the American West (that is, any section not on the narrow strand of the Eastern seaboard). Just as Daisy is a "new breed" of American girl, so this family is a new breed of American traveler in Europe—people like these did not tour Europe before the Civil War. Typically enough, too, the father of the family is not touring. He is home in Schenectady making still more of the money that permits his family to travel like their betters, and making it in the rather vulgar way of manufacturing useful objects. The mother is uneducated, obtuse, rather silly, and useless as a chaperone (if it ever dawned on her to act as chaperone). The girl is, as all American girls are, lovely, more gentle and genteel than her mother, more intelligent apparently, but, also apparently, very naïve. She is also spoiled, used to her own way—or is this just to say "free"? Her little brother is spoiled and forward and precocious, a little rude and bratty, but bright and in his way charming.

Winterbourne, our interpreter, is also an American, but a European resident. Daisy at first thinks he might even be a German. She finds him, for better and worse, stiff, formal, most un-American. Having lost touch with American—particularly new American—ways, Winterbourne has as much difficulty "reading" or understanding Daisy as would a true European. Moreover, Winterbourne is from New York—coastal, genteel America. His money, such as it is, no matter how it may have been originally made, we can be sure is "old." Eastern, Anglo-Saxon Americans in those days (and to some extent still?) looked to Europe and England in particular for their social and cultural models. Southern Europe—Latin, Catholic, old, old Europe, honored for its rich history and art, envied for its sensuous weather and flora—was considered as morally decadent as its ancient ruins. Northern Europe—Anglo-Saxon, Protestant, rich, cultured, established, civilized, and honorable—was the genteel American's heaven.

These views are, of course, merely stereotypes, and stereotypes have a bad reputation—deservedly so if all we know or want to know about people ends with pigeonholing them: man/woman, American/European, black/white, old/young, Catholic/Protestant. But, paradoxically, knowing people as individuals often involves first putting them in such a category *and then distinguishing them from other members of the category.* Stereotypes are, after all, only the biggest and coarsest of signs, and if we are going to have to read through appearances—words, gestures, actions, parentage, nationality, milieu—it makes sense to begin with the biggest sign or category, the stereotype, and begin discriminating more and more finely from there. This is what James will do.

Because this story is to a considerable degree about reading signs, we must be alert to those within the story. One such set of signs is that of the settings, the geography of the action. The novel opens in Vevey, described as having become virtually an American social resort, like the fashionable Newport in Rhode Island and Saratoga in New York State. It is into this rather elite society that the Millers "intrude." Visible from Vevey is the Castle of Chillon where centuries before an heroic antiauthoritarian cleric was imprisoned. That hero later became a Protestant, and so for some serves as a symbol of freedom from the tyranny of both church and state. He was commemorated in the early nineteenth century by Lord Byron, noted libertarian, libertine, and Romantic poet. The signs or signals of Vevey here at the very beginning of the novel thus are somewhat mixed, on the borderland between Catholicism and Protestantism, heroism and immorality, rigor and Romanticism.

Offstage is Geneva, where Winterbourne lives: the site of the Calvinist Reformation, it is associated with the most Protestant of Protestantism—the most rigorous intellectually and morally. Northeastern America was largely founded by such Protestants, from within and without the Anglican (or Episcopalian) church. The "Eastern Establishment," genteel America in the late nineteenth century, more or less identified with what was seen as the stricter morality and more ethical conduct of that religious orientation when compared to what was seen as the more lax and worldly Catholicism. Winterbourne, whatever his relationship to the older foreign lady, is—in his social standing and demeanor, his stiffness, formality, social and moral values—both a fitting representative of Establishment America and a resident of Calvinist Geneva.

But Geneva remains offstage. The novel's second long chapter (these two chapters are in some editions subdivided) is set in Rome, seat not only of the Roman Catholic church (stereotypically more experienced, worldly, jaded, decadent than the Protestant), but also the site of a great pre-Christian civilization with its long-past days of great power and glory and its long decline and fall into decadence and self-indulgence. The reader of signs, of stereotypes, finds that the settings heighten suspense. Vevey, ambivalently Protestant, moral and Romantic, is only vaguely threatening, just as Eugenio, the Italian guide, does not seem a terribly dangerous threat to Daisy's innocence. Daisy, at worst, is just being blindly indiscreet to let an underling even appear to be on an equal footing; it's enough to cause talk and shaking of heads in the conventional society of Winterbourne's aunt, nothing more. But Winterbourne and we never really take seriously the possibility that Daisy is having an affair with him, do we? In the second half of the story, however, a still (to our eyes) more unworthy and unsuitable suitor, Mr. Giovanelli—so Roman as to be almost sinister—appears. Daisy is equally indiscreet and incomparably more compromised. Even she recognizes that there might be a question of marriage—or something—involved. What is she up to?

Daisy Miller is both an early James novel and a rather short one—just over 25,000 words—and the changes rung on the central question of Daisy's guilt or innocence, vulgarity or freshness (is Annie P. or Daisy the more appropriate name for her?) are not inordinately complex. Later in his career James will leave us more uncertain than he does in *Daisy Miller* (is there any reason to doubt here Mr. Giovanelli's affirmation of Daisy's purity and her love for Winterbourne?). There will be times, too, later in his career, when the national stereotypes will not be so evident or flattering to us. It will be we Americans who, for all our naïveté, are shrewder, less bound by convention than our counterparts in Europe, more able to exploit them. We don't always play by the rules of cricket; poker is our game. Later, too, James will learn to twist and twist again the central interpretive question of character, sometimes to the extent of a very long novel like *The Golden Bowl*, which nonetheless has at its heart not much more of a sophisticated question than does *Daisy Miller* but requires a very much more complex and sophisticated journey in reading, unreading, rereading, and revising our reading of signs.

So on the one hand, James's questions are as simple as those of short stories: they are, one would think, capable of a yes or no answer, and that rather quickly, and so would not take up very much narrative space; but on the other, getting to that answer means seeing more and more and interpreting what we see at each stage, rigging and unrigging hypotheses—yes, no, maybe—with all the complexity of a full-length novel. Perhaps for that reason—simple questions, complex and tentative answers—James's concerns are very well suited to the intermediate form of the short novel. Though this collection begins with *Daisy Miller* because the novels are arranged chronologically, it is also a good novel to begin with because of its short-story-like simple center and its novel-like complications, moral, psychological, and social. We can follow it through, watching twist after twist; we can read it both for its narrative interest and its exploration of morality and conventions and ask of it such questions as "Why in its narrative and thematic logic does Daisy die?" We can also read it as a study of how the observing mind interprets—suggesting not only the role of stereotypes but of self-interest: To what degree does Winterbourne love Daisy? To what extent is his distrust of her merely his way of avoiding commitment, of refusing to acknowledge either that she cares for him or that she is capable of or worthy of being taken seriously as a beloved, a subject for a deep and permanent relationship? Is Daisy, finally, the subject or the object of the story?

LEO TOLSTOY

The Death of Iván Ilyich

If there is a "Shakespeare of the Novel," Tolstoy (1828–1910) would be a leading candidate for the title (which would have its own irony, since Tolstoy denied Shakespeare the supreme place in letters most people award him). One might argue whether his vast epic of a novel *War and Peace* (1863–1869) or the more compact (if still lengthy) *Anna Karénina* (1873–1876) is the pinnacle of his career, whether *The Death of Iván Ilyich* (1886) or *The Kreutzer Sonata* (1890) or even *Hadji Murad* (1896–1904) is the greatest of his short novels, but few would want to deny that such works, along with his other novels, short novels, and short stories, constitute a body of fiction of the first magnitude.

No life can "explain" such an accomplishment, but the life of Lyev Nikolayevich Tolstoy does itself read like a novel. Born into a noble family, orphaned before he was ten, studying first Oriental languages and then law at the University of Kazan but taking degrees in neither, Tolstoy settled on the family estate at Yásnaya Polyána, where he tried to improve the lot of his family's serfs—only to be rebuffed, in part by their suspicions. He served in the army in the Caucasian campaign and then around Sevastapol in the early 1850s, returning to Yásnaya Polyána to organize a school and to marry. After writing his two major long novels, the spoiled aristocrat, soldier, famous writer, found, as he tells us in *A Confession* (1884), that his life was "absurd . . . a stupid and spiteful joke," that he saw before him only death. He was "converted," first to the Russian Orthodox church, then along a winding path of theological study, toward a "primitive" Christianity like that which he imagined to be the faith of the Russian peasant. He opposed the military, capital punishment, pogroms (massacres, especially of Jews); he gave up alcohol, meat, and as much of his property, including copyrights of his later works, as his family would permit (his wife tried to have him declared incompetent). In 1910 he fled from home intending to enter a monastery but died in the railway station at Astápovo.

Much earlier, in 1859, four years before he himself was married, Tolstoy wrote a story called *Family Happiness* that foreshadows many of the great later scenes of happy marriage in *War and Peace* and *Anna Karénina* which we would otherwise attribute wholly to his own experience of marriage. There are scenes too in *War and Peace* which seem to "predict" what later happened to Tolstoy. Though he wrote about Iván Ilyich's crisis after having gone through his own, Iván's death "predicts" Tolstoy's. As he lay dying at Astápovo, he repeated in his delirium, "I do not understand what it is I have to do."

The Death of Iván Ilyich *

I

DURING AN INTERVAL in the Melvínski trial in the large building of the Law Courts the members and public prosecutor met in Iván Egórovich Shébek's private room, where the conversation turned on the celebrated Krasóvski case. Fëdor Vasílievich warmly maintained that it was not subject to their jurisdiction, Iván Egórovich maintained the contrary, while Peter Ivánovich, not having entered into the discussion at the start, took no part in it but looked through the *Gazette* which had just been handed in.

"Gentlemen," he said, "Iván Ilyich has died!"

"You don't say!"

"Here, read it yourself," replied Peter Ivánovich, handing Fëdor Vasílievich the paper still damp from the press. Surrounded by a black border were the words: "Praskóvya Fëdorovna Goloviná,[1] with profound sorrow, informs relatives and friends of the demise of her beloved husband Iván Ilyich Golovín, Member of the Court of Justice, which occurred on February the 4th of this year 1882. The funeral will take place on Friday at one o'clock in the afternoon."

Iván Ilyich had been a colleague of the gentlemen present and was liked by them all. He had been ill for some weeks with an illness said to be incurable. His post had been kept open for him, but there had been conjectures that in case of his death Alexéev might receive his appointment, and that either Vínnikov or Shtábel would succeed Alexéev. So on receiving the news of Iván Ilyich's death the first thought of each of the gentlemen in that private room was of the changes and promotions it might occasion among themselves or their acquaintances.

"I shall be sure to get Shtábel's place or Vínnikov's," thought Fëdor Vasílievich. "I was promised that long ago, and the promotion means an extra eight hundred rubles[2] a year for me besides the allowance."

"Now I must apply for my brother-in-law's transfer from Kalúga,"[3] thought Peter Ivánovich. "My wife will be very glad, and then she won't be able to say that I never do anything for her relations."

"I thought he would never leave his bed again," said Peter Ivánovich aloud. "It's very sad."

"But what really was the matter with him?"

"The doctors couldn't say—at least they could, but each of them said something different. When last I saw him I thought he was getting better."

"And I haven't been to see him since the holidays. I always meant to go."

"Had he any property?"

* Translated by Louise and Aylmer Maude.

1. Many Russian family names have masculine and feminine endings, so that Iván's name is *Golovín*, his wife's *Goloviná*. Russian "middle" names are patronymics—the father's name plus an ending that means "son of" or "daughter of": *Fëdorovna* = daughter of *Fëdor*; *Ilyich* = son of *Ilya*.

2. A ruble was then roughly equivalent to a dollar, though its modern purchasing power is difficult to calculate: perhaps four or five dollars per ruble is close enough.

3. City about one hundred miles southwest of Moscow.

"I think his wife had a little—but something quite trifling."

"We shall have to go to see her, but they live so terribly far away."

"Far away from you, you mean. Everything's far away from your place."

"You see, he never can forgive my living on the other side of the river," said Peter Ivánovich, smiling at Shébek. Then, still talking of the distances between different parts of the city, they returned to the Court.

Besides considerations as to the possible transfers and promotions likely to result from Iván Ilyich's death, the mere fact of the death of a near acquaintance aroused, as usual, in all who heard of it the complacent feeling that "it is he who is dead and not I."

Each one thought or felt, "Well, he's dead but I'm alive!" But the more intimate of Iván Ilyich's acquaintances, his so-called friends, could not help thinking also that they would now have to fulfil the very tiresome demands of propriety by attending the funeral service and paying a visit of condolence to the widow.

Fëdor Vasílievich and Peter Ivánovich had been his nearest acquaintances. Peter Ivánovich had studied law with Iván Ilyich and had considered himself to be under obligations to him.

Having told his wife at dinner-time of Iván Ilyich's death, and of his conjecture that it might be possible to get her brother transferred to their circuit, Peter Ivánovich sacrificed his usual nap, put on his evening clothes, and drove to Iván Ilyich's house.

At the entrance stood a carriage and two cabs. Leaning against the wall in the hall downstairs near the cloak-stand was a coffin-lid covered with cloth of gold, ornamented with gold cord and tassels, that had been polished up with metal powder. Two ladies in black were taking off their fur cloaks. Peter Ivánovich recognized one of them as Iván Ilyich's sister, but the other was a stranger to him. His colleague Schwartz was just coming downstairs, but on seeing Peter Ivánovich enter he stopped and winked at him, as if to say: "Iván Ilyich has made a mess of things—not like you and me."

Schwartz's face with his Piccadilly whiskers,[4] and his slim figure in evening dress, had as usual an air of elegant solemnity which contrasted with the playfulness of his character and had a special piquancy here, or so it seemed to Peter Ivánovich.

Peter Ivánovich allowed the ladies to precede him and slowly followed them upstairs. Schwartz did not come down but remained where he was, and Peter Ivánovich understood that he wanted to arrange where they should play bridge that evening. The ladies went upstairs to the widow's room, and Schwartz with seriously compressed lips but a playful look in his eyes, indicated by a twist of his eyebrows the room to the right where the body lay.

Peter Ivánovich, like everyone else on such occasions, entered feeling uncertain what he would have to do. All he knew was that at such times it is always safe to cross oneself. But he was not quite sure whether one should make obeisances while doing so. He therefore adopted a middle course. On entering the room he began crossing himself and made a slight movement resembling a bow. At the same time, as far as the motion of his

---

4. Sideburns carefully combed out and worn as long as possible, a fashion that died out in the 1880s.

head and arm allowed, he surveyed the room. Two young men—apparently nephews, one of whom was a high-school pupil—were leaving the room, crossing themselves as they did so. An old woman was standing motionless, and a lady with strangely arched eyebrows was saying something to her in a whisper. A vigorous, resolute Church Reader, in a frock-coat, was reading something in a loud voice with an expression that precluded any contradiction. The butler's assistant, Gerásim, stepping lightly in front of Peter Ivánovich, was strewing something on the floor. Noticing this, Peter Ivánovich was immediately aware of a faint odour of a decomposing body.

The last time he had called on Iván Ilyich, Peter Ivánovich had seen Gerásim in the study. Iván Ilyich had been particularly fond of him and he was performing the duty of a sick nurse.

Peter Ivánovich continued to make the sign of the cross slightly inclining his head in an intermediate direction between the coffin, the Reader, and the icons on the table in a corner of the room. Afterwards, when it seemed to him that his movement of his arm in crossing himself had gone on too long, he stopped and began to look at the corpse.

The dead man lay, as dead men always lie, in a specially heavy way, his rigid limbs sunk in the soft cushions of the coffin, with the head forever bowed on the pillow. His yellow waxen brow with bald patches over his sunken temples was thrust up in the way peculiar to the dead, the protruding nose seeming to press on the upper lip. He was much changed and had grown even thinner since Peter Ivánovich had last seen him, but, as is always the case with the dead, his face was handsomer and above all more dignified than when he was alive. The expression on the face said that what was necessary had been accomplished, and accomplished rightly. Besides this there was in that expression a reproach and a warning to the living. This warning seemed to Peter Ivánovich out of place, or at least not applicable to him. He felt a certain discomfort and so he hurriedly crossed himself once more and turned and went out of the door—too hurriedly and too regardless of propriety, as he himself was aware.

Schwartz was waiting for him in the adjoining room with legs spread wide apart and both hands toying with his top-hat behind his back. The mere sight of that playful, well-groomed, and elegant figure refreshed Peter Ivánovich. He felt that Schwartz was above all these happenings and would not surrender to any depressing influences. His very look said that this incident of a church service for Iván Ilyich could not be a sufficient reason for infringing the order of the session—in other words, that it would certainly not prevent his unwrapping a new pack of cards and shuffling them that evening while a footman placed four fresh candles on the table: in fact, that there was no reason for supposing that this incident would hinder their spending the evening agreeably. Indeed he said this in a whisper as Peter Ivánovich passed him, proposing that they should meet for a game at Fëdor Vasílievich's. But apparently Peter Ivánovich was not destined to play bridge that evening. Praskóvya Fëdorovna (a short, fat woman who despite all efforts to the contrary had continued to broaden steadily from her shoulders downwards and who had the same extraordinary arched eyebrows as the lady who had been standing by the coffin), dressed all in black, her head covered with lace, came out of her own room with some other ladies, conducted them to the room where the dead body lay, and said: "The service will begin immediately. Please go in."

Schwartz, making an indefinite bow, stood still, evidently neither accepting nor declining this invitation. Praskóvya Fëdorovna recognizing Peter Ivánovich, sighed, went close up to him, took his hand, and said: "I know you were a true friend to Iván Ilyich ..." and looked at him awaiting some suitable response. And Peter Ivánovich knew that, just as it had been the right thing to cross himself in that room, so what he had to do here was to press her hand, sigh, and say, "Believe me ..." So he did all this and as he did it felt that the desired result had been achieved: that both he and she were touched.

"Come with me. I want to speak to you before it begins," said the widow. "Give me your arm."

Peter Ivánovich gave her his arm and they went to the inner rooms, passing Schwartz who winked at Peter Ivánovich compassionately.

"That does for our bridge! Don't object if we find another player. Perhaps you can cut in when you do escape," said his playful look.

"Peter Ivánovich sighed still more deeply and despondently, and Praskóvya Fëdorovna pressed his arm gratefully. When they reached the drawing-room, upholstered in pink cretonne and lighted by a dim lamp, they sat down at the table—she on a sofa and Peter Ivánovich on a low hassock, the springs of which yielded spasmodically under his weight. Praskóvya Fëdorovna had been on the point of warning him to take another seat, but felt that such a warning was out of keeping with her present condition and so changed her mind. As he sat down on the hassock Peter Ivánovich recalled how Iván Ilyich had arranged this room and had consulted him regarding this pink cretonne with green leaves. The whole room was full of furniture and knick-knacks, and on her way to the sofa the lace of the widow's black shawl caught on the carved edge of the table. Peter Ivánovich rose to detach it, and the springs of the hassock, relieved of his weight, rose also and gave him a push. The widow began detaching her shawl herself, and Peter Ivánovich again sat down, suppressing the rebellious springs of the hassock under him. But the widow had not quite freed herself and Peter Ivánovich got up again, and again the hassock rebelled and even creaked. When this was all over she took out a clean cambric handkerchief and began to weep. The episode with the shawl and the struggle with the hassock had cooled Peter Ivánovich's emotions and he sat there with a sullen look on his face. This awkward situation was interrupted by Sokolóv, Iván Ilyich's butler, who came to report that the plot in the cemetery that Praskóvya Fëdorovna had chosen would cost two hundred rubles. She stopped weeping and, looking at Peter Ivánovich with the air of a victim, remarked in French[5] that it was very hard for her. Peter Ivánovich made a silent gesture signifying his full conviction that it must indeed be so.

"Please smoke," she said in a magnanimous yet crushed voice, and turned to discuss with Sokolóv the price of the plot for the grave.

Peter Ivánovich while lighting his cigarette heard her inquiring very circumstantially into the prices of different plots in the cemetery and finally decide which she would take. When that was done she gave instruc-

---

5. The Russian upper classes commonly spoke French.

tions about engaging the choir. Sokolóv then left the room.

"I look after everything myself," she told Peter Ivánovich, shifting the albums that lay on the table; and noticing that the table was endangered by his cigarette-ash, she immediately passed him an ash-tray, saying as she did so: "I consider it an affectation to say that my grief prevents my attending to practical affairs. On the contrary, if anything can—I won't say console me, but—distract me, it is seeing to everything concerning him." She again took out her handkerchief as if preparing to cry, but suddenly, as if mastering her feeling, she shook herself and began to speak calmly. "But there is something I want to talk to you about."

Peter Ivánovich bowed, keeping control of the springs of the hassock, which immediately began quivering under him.

"He suffered terribly the last few days."

"Did he?" said Peter Ivánovich.

"Oh, terribly! He screamed unceasingly, not for minutes but for hours. For the last three days he screamed incessantly. It was unendurable. I cannot understand how I bore it; you could hear him three rooms off. Oh, what I have suffered!"

"Is it possible that he was conscious all that time?" asked Peter Ivánovich.

"Yes," she whispered. "To the last moment. He took leave of us a quarter of an hour before he died, and asked us to take Vásya[6] away."

The thought of the sufferings of this man he had known so intimately, first as a merry little boy, then as a school-mate, and later as a grown-up colleague, suddenly struck Peter Ivánovich with horror, despite an unpleasant consciousness of his own and this woman's dissimulation. He again saw that brow, and that nose pressing down on the lip, and felt afraid for himself.

"Three days of frightful suffering and then death! Why, that might suddenly, at any time, happen to me," he thought, and for a moment felt terrified. But—he did not himself know how—the customary reflection at once occurred to him that this had happened to Iván Ilyich and not to him, and that it should not and could not happen to him, and that to think that it could would be yielding to depression which he ought not to do, as Schwartz's expression plainly showed. After which reflection Peter Ivánovich felt reassured, and began to ask with interest about the details of Iván Ilyich's death, as though death was an accident natural to Iván Ilyich but certainly not to himself.

After many details of the really dreadful physical sufferings Iván Ilyich had endured (which details he learnt only from the effect those sufferings had produced on Praskóvya Fëdorovna's nerves) the widow apparently found it necessary to get to business.

"Oh, Peter Ivánovich, how hard it is! How terribly, terribly hard!" and she again began to weep.

Peter Ivánovich sighed and waited for her to finish blowing her nose. When she had done so he said, "Believe me ..." and she again began talking and brought out what was evidently her chief concern with him— namely, to question him as to how she could obtain a grant of money from the government on the occasion of her husband's death. She made it appear that she was asking Peter Ivánovich's advice about her pension,

---

6. Nickname for Vasílii, Iván Ilyich's son.

but he soon saw that she already knew about that to the minutest detail, more even than he did himself. She knew how much could be got out of the government in consequence of her husband's death, but wanted to find out whether she could not possibly extract something more. Peter Ivánovich tried to think of some means of doing so, but after reflecting for a while and, out of propriety, condemning the government for its niggardliness, he said he thought that nothing more could be got. Then she sighed and evidently began to devise means of getting rid of her visitor. Noticing this, he put out his cigarette, rose, pressed her hand, and went out into the anteroom.

In the dining-room where the clock stood that Iván Ilyich had liked so much and had bought at an antique shop, Peter Ivánovich met a priest and a few acquaintances who had come to attend the service, and he recognized Iván Ilyich's daughter, a handsome young woman. She was in black and her slim figure appeared slimmer than ever. She had a gloomy, determined, almost angry expression, and bowed to Peter Ivánovich as though he were in some way to blame. Behind her, with the same offended look, stood a wealthy young man, an examining magistrate, whom Peter Ivánovich also knew and who was her fiancé, as he had heard. He bowed mournfully to them and was about to pass into the death-chamber, when from under the stairs appeared the figure of Iván Ilyich's schoolboy son, who was extremely like his father. He seemed a little Iván Ilyich, such as Peter Ivánovich remembered when they studied law together. His tear-stained eyes had in them the look that is seen in the eyes of boys of thirteen or fourteen who are not pure-minded. When he saw Peter Ivánovich he scowled morosely and shamefacedly. Peter Ivánovich nodded to him and entered the death-chamber. The service began: candles, groans, incense, tears, and sobs. Peter Ivánovich stood looking gloomily down at his feet. He did not look once at the dead man, did not yield to any depressing influence, and was one of the first to leave the room. There was no one in the anteroom, but Gerásim darted out of the dead man's room, rummaged with his strong hands among the fur coats to find Peter Ivánovich's and helped him on with it.

"Well, friend Gerásim," said Peter Ivánovich, so as to say something. "It's a sad affair, isn't it?"

"It's God's will. We shall all come to it some day," said Gerásim, displaying his teeth—the even, white teeth of a healthy peasant—and, like a man in the thick of urgent work, he briskly opened the front door, called the coachman, helped Peter Ivánovich into the sledge, and sprang back to the porch as if in readiness for what he had to do next.

Peter Ivánovich found the fresh air particularly pleasant after the smell of incense, the dead body, and carbolic acid.

"Where to, sir?" asked the coachman.

"It's not too late even now. . . . I'll call on Fëdor Vasílievich."

He accordingly drove there and found them just finishing the first rubber, so that it was quite convenient for him to cut in.

II

Iván Ilyich's life had been most simple and most ordinary and therefore most terrible.

He had been a member of the Court of Justice, and died at the age of forty-five. His father had been an official who after serving in various ministries and departments in Petersburg[7] had made the sort of career which brings men to positions from which by reason of their long service they cannot be dismissed, though they are obviously unfit to hold any responsible position, and for whom therefore posts are specially created, which though fictitious, carry salaries of from six to ten thousand rubles that are not fictitious, and in receipt of which they live on to a great age.

Such was the Privy Councillor and superfluous member of various superfluous institutions, Ilya Epímovich Golovín.

He had three sons, of whom Iván Ilyich was the second. The eldest son was following in his father's footsteps only in another department, and was already approaching that stage in the service at which a similar sinecure would be reached. The third son was a failure. He had ruined his prospects in a number of positions and was now serving in the railway department. His father and brothers, and still more their wives, not merely disliked meeting him, but avoided remembering his existence unless compelled to do so. His sister had married Baron Greff, a Petersburg official of her father's type. Iván Ilyich was le phénix de la famille[8] as people said. He was neither as cold and formal as his elder brother nor as wild as the younger, but was a happy mean between them—an intelligent, polished, lively and agreeable man. He had studied with his younger brother at the School of Law, but the latter had failed to complete the course and was expelled when he was in the fifth class. Iván Ilyich finished the course well. Even when he was at the School of Law he was just what he remained for the rest of his life: a capable, cheerful, good-natured, and sociable man, though strict in the fulfilment of what he considered to be his duty: and he considered his duty to be what was so considered by those in authority. Neither as a boy nor as a man was he a toady, but from early youth was by nature attracted to people of high station as a fly is drawn to the light, assimilating their ways and views of life and establishing friendly relations with them. All the enthusiasms of childhood and youth passed without leaving much trace on him; he succumbed to sensuality, to vanity, and latterly among the highest classes to liberalism, but always within limits which his instinct unfailingly indicated to him as correct.

At school he had done things which had formerly seemed to him very horrid and made him feel disgusted with himself when he did them; but when later on he saw that such actions were done by people of good position and that they did not regard them as wrong, he was able not exactly to regard them as right, but to forget about them entirely or not be at all troubled at remembering them.

Having graduated from the School of Law and qualified for the tenth rank of the civil service, and having received money from his father for his equipment, Iván Ilyich ordered himself clothes at Scharmer's, the fashionable tailor, hung a medallion inscribed respice finem[9] on his watchchain, took leave of his professor and the prince who was patron of the school, had a farewell dinner with his comrades at Donon's first-class restaurant, and with his new and fashionable portmanteau, linen, clothes, shaving and other toilet appliances, and a travelling rug, all purchased at the best shops, he set off for one of the provinces where, through his

7. St. Petersburg (now Leningrad), the capital of Russia (1712–1918) and its cultural and social center.

8. Prodigy of the family.
9. Look to (or consider) the end.

father's influence, he had been attached to the governor as an official for special service.

In the province Iván Ilyich soon arranged as easy and agreeable a position for himself as he had had at the School of Law. He performed his official tasks, made his career, and at the same time amused himself pleasantly and decorously. Occasionally he paid official visits to country districts, where he behaved with dignity both to his superiors and inferiors, and performed the duties entrusted to him, which related chiefly to the sectarians,[1] with an exactness and incorruptible honesty of which he could not but feel proud.

In official matters, despite his youth and taste for frivolous gaiety, he was exceedingly reserved, punctilious, and even severe; but in society he was often amusing and witty, and always good-natured, correct in his manner, and *bon enfant*[2] as the governor and his wife—with whom he was like one of the family—used to say of him.

In the province he had an affair with a lady who made advances to the elegant young lawyer, and there was also a milliner; and there were carousals with aides-de-camp who visited the district, and after-supper visits to a certain outlying street of doubtful reputation; and there was too some obsequiousness to his chief and even to his chief's wife, but all this was done with such a tone of good breeding that no hard names could be applied to it. It all came under the heading of the French saying: *Il faut que jeunesse se passe.*"[3] It was all done with clean hands, in clean linen, with French phrases, and above all among people of the best society and consequently with the approval of people of rank.

So Iván Ilyich served for five years and then came a change in his official life. The new and reformed judicial institutions were introduced, and new men were needed. Iván Ilyich became such a new man. He was offered the post of Examining Magistrate, and he accepted it though the post was in another province and obliged him to give up the connexions he had formed and to make new ones. His friends met to give him a send-off; they had a group-photograph taken and presented him with a silver cigarette-case, and he set off to his new post.

As examining magistrate Iván Ilyich was just as *comme il faut* and decorous a man, inspiring general respect and capable of separating his official duties from his private life, as he had been when acting as an official on special service. His duties now as examining magistrate were far more interesting and attractive than before. In his former position it had been pleasant to wear an undress uniform made by Scharmer, and to pass through the crowd of petitioners and officials who were timorously awaiting an audience with the governor, and who envied him as with free and easy gait he went straight into his chief's private room to have a cup of tea and a cigarette with him. But not many people had then been directly dependent on him—only police officials and the sectarians when he went on special missions—and he liked to treat them politely, almost as comrades, as if he were letting them feel that he who had the power to crush them was treating them in this simple, friendly way. There were then but few such people. But now, as an examining magistrate, Iván Ilyich felt that everyone without exception, even the most important and

---

1. A large sect (the "Old Believers") which had broken with the Orthodox church.
2. A good fellow.
3. Youth must have its fling. (Translators' note.)

self-satisfied, was in his power, and that he need only write a few words on a sheet of paper with a certain heading, and this or that important, self-satisfied person would be brought before him in the role of an accused person or a witness, and if he did not choose to allow him to sit down, would have to stand before him and answer his questions. Iván Ilyich never abused his power; he tried on the contrary to soften its expression, but the consciousness of it and of the possibility of softening its effect, supplied the chief interest and attraction of his office. In his work itself, especially in his examinations, he very soon acquired a method of eliminating all considerations irrelevant to the legal aspect of the case, and reducing even the most complicated case to a form in which it would be presented on paper only in its externals, completely excluding his personal opinion of the matter, while above all observing every prescribed formality. The work was new and Iván Ilyich was one of the first men to apply the new Code of 1864.[4]

On taking up the post of examining magistrate in a new town, he made new acquaintances and connexions, placed himself on a new footing, and assumed a somewhat different tone. He took up an attitude of rather dignified aloofness towards the provincial authorities, but picked out the best circle of legal gentlemen and wealthy gentry living in the town and assumed a tone of slight dissatisfaction with the government, of moderate liberalism, and of enlightened citizenship. At the same time, without at all altering the elegance of his toilet, he ceased shaving his chin and allowed his beard to grow as it pleased.

Iván Ilyich settled down very pleasantly in this new town. The society there, which inclined towards opposition to the governor, was friendly, his salary was larger, and he began to play *vint* [a form of bridge], which he found added not a little to the pleasure of life, for he had a capacity for cards, played good-humouredly, and calculated rapidly and astutely, so that he usually won.

After living there for two years he met his future wife, Praskóvya Fëdorovna Míkhel, who was the most attractive, clever, and brilliant girl of the set in which he moved, and among other amusements and relaxations from his labours as examining magistrate, Iván Ilyich established light and playful relations with her.

While he had been an official on special service he had been accustomed to dance, but now as an examining magistrate it was exceptional for him to do so. If he danced now, he did it as if to show that though he served under the reformed order of things, and had reached the fifth official rank, yet when it came to dancing he could do it better than most people. So at the end of an evening he sometimes danced with Praskóvya Fëdorovna, and it was chiefly during these dances that he captivated her. She fell in love with him. Iván Ilyich had at first no definite intention of marrying, but when the girl fell in love with him he said to himself: "Really, why shouldn't I marry?"

Praskóvya Fëdorovna came of a good family, was not bad looking, and had some little property. Iván Ilyich might have aspired to a more brilliant match, but even this was good. He had his salary, and she, he hoped, would have an equal income. She was well connected, and was a sweet,

---

4. The emancipation of the serfs in 1861 was fol-   ceedings. (Translators' note.)
lowed by a thorough all-round reform of judicial pro-

pretty, and thoroughly correct young woman. To say that Iván Ilyich married because he fell in love with Praskóvya Fëdorovna and found that she sympathized with his views of life would be as incorrect as to say that he married because his social circle approved of the match. He was swayed by both these considerations: the marriage gave him personal satisfaction, and at the same time it was considered the right thing by the most highly placed of his associates.

So Iván Ilyich got married.

The preparations for marriage and the beginning of married life, with its conjugal caresses, the new furniture, new crockery, and new linen, were very pleasant until his wife became pregnant—so that Iván Ilyich had begun to think that marriage would not impair the easy, agreeable, gay, and always decorous character of his life, approved of by society and regarded by himself as natural, but would even improve it. But from the first months of his wife's pregnancy, something new, unpleasant, depressing, and unseemly, and from which there was no way of escape, unexpectedly showed itself.

His wife, without any reason—*de gaieté de coeur*[5] as Iván Ilyich expressed it to himself—began to disturb the pleasure and propriety of their life. She began to be jealous without any cause, expected him to devote his whole attention to her, found fault with everything, and made coarse and ill-mannered scenes.

At first Iván Ilyich hoped to escape from the unpleasantness of this state of affairs by the same easy and decorous relation to life that had served him heretofore: he tried to ignore his wife's disagreeable moods, continued to live in his usual easy and pleasant way, invited friends to his house for a game of cards, and also tried going out to his club or spending his evenings with friends. But one day his wife began upbraiding him so vigorously, using such coarse words, and continued to abuse him every time he did not fulfil her demands, so resolutely and with such evident determination not to give way till he submitted—that is, till he stayed at home and was bored just as she was—that he became alarmed. He now realized that matrimony—at any rate with Praskóvya Fëdorovna—was not always conducive to the pleasures and amenities of life, but on the contrary often infringed both comfort and propriety, and that he must therefore entrench himself against such infringement. And Iván Ilyich began to seek for means of doing so. His official duties were the one thing that imposed upon Praskóvya Fëdorovna, and by means of his official work and the duties attached to it he began struggling with his wife to secure his own independence.

With the birth of their child, the attempts to feed it and the various failures in doing so, and with the real and imaginary illnesses of mother and child, in which Iván Ilyich's sympathy was demanded but about which he understood nothing, the need of securing for himself an existence outside his family life became still more imperative.

As his wife grew more irritable and exacting and Iván Ilyich transferred the centre of gravity of his life more and more to his official work, so did he grow to like his work better and became more ambitious than before.

Very soon, within a year of his wedding, Iván Ilyich had realized that marriage, though it may add some comforts to life, is in fact a very intricate and difficult affair towards which in order to perform one's duty, that

---

5. Wantonly.

is, to lead a decorous life approved of by society, one must adopt a definite attitude just as towards one's official duties.

And Iván Ilyich evolved such an attitude towards married life. He only required of it those conveniences—dinner at home, housewife, and bed—which it could give him, and above all that propriety of external forms required by public opinion. For the rest he looked for light-hearted pleasure and propriety, and was very thankful when he found them, but if he met with antagonism and querulousness he at once retired into his separate fenced-off world of official duties, where he found satisfaction.

Iván Ilyich was esteemed a good official, and after three years was made Assistant Public Prosecutor. His new duties, their importance, the possibility of indicting and imprisoning anyone he chose, the publicity his speeches received, and the success he had in all these things, made his work still more attractive.

More children came. His wife became more and more querulous and ill-tempered, but the attitude Iván Ilyich had adopted towards his home life rendered him almost impervious to her grumbling.

After seven years' service in that town he was transferred to another province as Public Prosecutor. They moved, but were short of money and his wife did not like the place they moved to. Though the salary was higher the cost of living was greater, besides which two of their children died and family life became still more unpleasant for him.

Praskóvya Fëdorovna blamed her husband for every inconvenience they encountered in their new home. Most of the conversations between husband and wife, especially as to the children's education, led to topics which recalled former disputes, and those disputes were apt to flare up again at any moment. There remained only those rare periods of amorousness which still came to them at times but did not last long. These were islets at which they anchored for a while and then again set out upon that ocean of veiled hostility which showed itself in their aloofness from one another. This aloofness might have grieved Iván Ilyich had he considered that it ought not to exist, but he now regarded the position as normal, and even made it the goal at which he aimed in family life. His aim was to free himself more and more from those unpleasantnesses and to give them a semblance of harmlessness and propriety. He attained this by spending less and less time with his family, and when obliged to be at home he tried to safeguard his position by the presence of outsiders. The chief thing however was that he had his official duties. The whole interest of his life now centered in the official world and that interest absorbed him. The consciousness of his power, being able to ruin anybody he wished to ruin, the importance, even the external dignity of his entry into court, or meetings with his subordinates, his success with superiors and inferiors, and above all his masterly handling of cases, of which he was conscious—all this gave him pleasure and filled his life, together with chats with his colleagues, dinners, and bridge. So that on the whole Iván Ilyich's life continued to flow as he considered it should do—pleasantly and properly.

So things continued for another seven years. His eldest daughter was already sixteen, another child had died, and only one son was left, a schoolboy and a subject of dissensions. Iván Ilyich wanted to put him in the School of Law, but to spite him Praskóvya Fëdorovna entered him at the High School. The daughter had been educated at home and had turned out well: the boy did not learn badly either.

III

So Iván Ilyich lived for seventeen years after his marriage. He was already a Public Prosecutor of long standing, and had declined several proposed transfers while awaiting a more desirable post, when an unanticipated and unpleasant occurrence quite upset the peaceful course of his life. He was expecting to be offered the post of presiding judge in a University town, but Hoppe somehow came to the front and obtained the appointment instead. Iván Ilyich became irritable, reproached Hoppe, and quarrelled both with him and with his immediate superiors—who became colder to him and again passed him over when other appointments were made.

This was in 1880, the hardest year of Iván Ilyich's life. It was then that it became evident on the one hand that his salary was insufficient for them to live on, and on the other that he had been forgotten, and not only this, but that what was for him the greatest and most cruel injustice appeared to others a quite ordinary occurrence. Even his father did not consider it his duty to help him. Iván Ilyich felt himself abandoned by everyone, and that they regarded his position with a salary of 3,500 rubles as quite normal and even fortunate. He alone knew that with the consciousness of the injustices done him, with his wife's incessant nagging, and with the debts he had contracted by living beyond his means, his position was far from normal.

In order to save money that summer he obtained leave of absence and went with his wife to live in the country at her brother's place.

In the country, without his work, he experienced *ennui* for the first time in his life, and not only *ennui* but intolerable depression, and he decided that it was impossible to go on living like that, and that it was necessary to take energetic measures.

Having passed a sleepless night pacing up and down the veranda, he decided to go to Petersburg and bestir himself, in order to punish those who had failed to appreciate him and to get transferred to another ministry.

Next day, despite many protests from his wife and her brother, he started for Petersburg with the sole object of obtaining a post with a salary of five thousand rubles a year. He was no longer bent on any particular department, or tendency, or kind of activity. All he now wanted was an appointment to another post with a salary of five thousand rubles, either in the administration, in the banks, with the railways, in one of the Empress Márya's Institutions,[6] or even in the customs—but it had to carry with it a salary of five thousand rubles and be in a ministry other than that in which they had failed to appreciate him.

And this quest of Iván Ilyich's was crowned with remarkable and unexpected success. At Kursk an acquaintance of his, F. I. Ilyín, got into the first-class carriage, sat down beside Iván Ilyich, and told him of a telegram just received by the governor of Kursk announcing that a change was about to take place in the ministry: Peter Ivánovich was to be superseded by Iván Seménovich.

The proposed change, apart from its significance for Russia, had a special significance for Iván Ilyich, because by bringing forward a new man, Peter Petróvich, and consequently his friend Zachár Ivánovich, it was

6. Charitable organization founded nearly a century earlier by the wife of Paul I.

highly favourable for Iván Ilyich, since Zachár Ivánovich was a friend and colleague of his.

In Moscow this news was confirmed, and on reaching Petersburg Iván Ilyich found Zachár Ivánovich and received a definite promise of an appointment in his former department of Justice.

A week later he telegraphed to his wife: "Zachár in Miller's place. I shall receive appointment on presentation of report."

Thanks to this change of personnel, Iván Ilyich had unexpectedly obtained an appointment in his former ministry which placed him two stages above his former colleagues besides giving him five thousand rubles salary and three thousand five hundred rubles for expenses connected with his removal.[7] All his ill humour towards his former enemies and the whole department vanished, and Iván Ilyich was completely happy.

He returned to the country more cheerful and contented than he had been for a long time. Praskóvya Fëdorovna also cheered up and a truce was arranged between them. Iván Ilyich told of how he had been fêted by everybody in Petersburg, how all those who had been his enemies were put to shame and now fawned on him, how envious they were of his appointment, and how much everybody in Petersburg had liked him.

Praskóvya Fëdorovna listened to all this and appeared to believe it. She did not contradict anything, but only made plans for their life in the town to which they were going. Iván Ilyich saw with delight that these plans were his plans, that he and his wife agreed, and that, after a stumble, his life was regaining its due and natural character of pleasant lightheartedness and decorum.

Iván Ilyich had come back for a short time only, for he had to take up his new duties on the 10th of September. Moreover, he needed time to settle into the new place, to move all his belongings from the province, and to buy and order many additional things: in a word, to make such arrangements as he had resolved on, which were almost exactly what Praskóvya Fëdorovna too had decided on.

Now that everything had happened so fortunately, and that he and his wife were at one in their aims and moreover saw so little of one another, they got on better than they had done since the first years of marriage. Iván Ilyich had thought of taking his family away with him at once, but the insistence of his wife's brother and her sister-in-law, who had suddenly become particularly amiable and friendly to him and his family, induced him to depart alone.

So he departed, and the cheerful state of mind induced by his success and by the harmony between his wife and himself, the one intensifying the other, did not leave him. He found a delightful house, just the thing both he and his wife had dreamt of. Spacious, lofty reception rooms in the old style, a convenient and dignified study, rooms for his wife and daughter, a study for his son—it might have been specially built for them. Iván Ilyich himself superintended the arrangements, chose the wallpapers, supplemented the furniture (preferably with antiques which he considered particularly *comme il faut*), and supervised the upholstering. Everything progressed and progressed and approached the ideal he had set himself: even when things were only half completed they exceeded his expectations. He saw what a refined and elegant character, free from vulgarity, it

---

7. Moving.

would all have when it was ready. On falling asleep he pictured to himself how the reception-room would look. Looking at the yet unfinished drawing-room he could see the fireplace, the screen, the what-not, the little chairs dotted here and there, the dishes and plates on the walls, and the bronzes, as they would be when everything was in place. He was pleased by the thought of how his wife and daughter, who shared his taste in this matter, would be impressed by it. They were certainly not expecting as much. He had been particularly successful in finding, and buying cheaply, antiques which gave a particularly aristocratic character to the whole place. But in his letters he intentionally understated everything in order to be able to surprise them. All this so absorbed him that his new duties—though he liked his official work—interested him less than he had expected. Sometimes he even had moments of absent-mindedness during the Court Sessions, and would consider whether he should have straight or curved cornices for his curtains. He was so interested in it all that he often did things himself, rearranging the furniture, or rehanging the curtains. Once when mounting a step-ladder to show the upholsterer, who did not understand, how he wanted the hangings draped, he made a false step and slipped, but being a strong and agile man he clung on and only knocked his side against the knob of the window frame. The bruised place was painful but the pain soon passed, and he felt particularly bright and well just then. He wrote: "I feel fifteen years younger." He thought he would have everything ready by September, but it dragged on till mid-October. But the result was charming not only in his eyes but to everyone who saw it.

In reality it was just what is usually seen in the houses of people of moderate means who want to appear rich, and therefore succeed only in resembling others like themselves: there were damasks, dark wood, plants, rugs, and dull and polished bronzes—all the things people of a certain class have in order to resemble other people of that class. His house was so like the others that it would never have been noticed, but to him it all seemed to be quite exceptional. He was very happy when he met his family at the station and brought them to the newly furnished house all lit up, where a footman in a white tie opened the door into the hall decorated with plants, and when they went on into the drawing room and the study uttering exclamations of delight. He conducted them everywhere, drank in their praises eagerly, and beamed with pleasure. At tea that evening, when Praskóvya Fëdorovna among other things asked him about his fall, he laughed, and showed them how he had gone flying and had frightened the upholsterer.

"It's a good thing I'm a bit of an athlete. Another man might have been killed, but I merely knocked myself, just here; it hurts when it's touched, but it's passing off already—it's only a bruise."

So they began living in their new home—in which, as always happens, when they got thoroughly settled in they found they were just one room short—and with the increased income, which as always was just a little (some five hundred rubles) too little, but it was all very nice.

Things went particularly well at first, before everything was finally arranged and while something had still to be done: this thing bought, that thing ordered, another thing moved, and something else adjusted. Though there were some disputes between husband and wife, they were both so well satisfied and had so much to do that it all passed off without any serious quarrels. When nothing was left to arrange it became rather dull and something seemed to be lacking, but they were then making acquaintances, forming habits, and life was growing fuller.

Iván Ilyich spent his mornings at the law court and came home to dinner, and at first he was generally in a good humour, though he occasionally became irritable just on account of his house. (Every spot on the tablecloth or the upholstery, and every broken window-blind string, irritated him. He had devoted so much trouble to arranging it all that every disturbance of it distressed him.) But on the whole his life ran its course as he believed life should do: easily, pleasantly, and decorously.

He got up at nine, drank his coffee, read the paper, and then put on his undress uniform and went to the law courts. There the harness in which he worked had already been stretched to fit him and he donned it without a hitch: petitioners, inquiries at the chancery, the chancery itself, and the sittings public and administrative. In all this the thing was to exclude everything fresh and vital, which always disturbs the regular course of official business, and to admit only official relations with people, and then only on official grounds. A man would come, for instance, wanting some information. Iván Ilyich, as one in whose sphere the matter did not lie, would have nothing to do with him: but if the man had some business with him in his official capacity, something that could be expressed on officially stamped paper, he would do everything, positively everything he could within the limits of such relations, and in doing so would maintain the semblance of friendly human relations, that is, would observe the courtesies of life. As soon as the official relations ended, so did everything else. Iván Ilyich possessed this capacity to separate his real life from the official side of affairs and not mix the two, in the highest degree, and by long practice and natural aptitude had brought it to such a pitch that sometimes, in the manner of a virtuoso, he would even allow himself to let the human and official relations mingle. He let himself do this just because he felt that he could at any time he chose resume the strictly official attitude again and drop the human relation. And he did it all easily, pleasantly, correctly, and even artistically. In the intervals between the sessions he smoked, drank tea, chatted a little about politics, a little about general topics, a little about cards, but most of all about official appointments. Tired, but with the feelings of a virtuoso—one of the first violins who has played his part in an orchestra with precision—he would return home to find that his wife and daughter had been out paying calls, or had a visitor, and that his son had been to school, had done his homework with his tutor, and was duly learning what is taught at High Schools. Everything was as it should be. After dinner, if they had no visitors, Iván Ilyich sometimes read a book that was being much discussed at the time, and in the evening settled down to work, that is, read official papers, compared the depositions of witnesses, and noted paragraphs of the Code applying to them. This was neither dull nor amusing. It was dull when he might have been playing bridge, but if no bridge was available it was at any rate better than doing nothing or sitting with his wife. Iván Ilyich's chief pleasure was giving little dinners to which he invited men and women of good social position, and just as his drawing-room resembled all other drawing-rooms so did his enjoyable little parties resemble all other such parties.

Once they even gave a dance. Iván Ilyich enjoyed it and everything went off well, except that it led to a violent quarrel with his wife about the cakes and sweets. Praskóvya Fëdorovna had made her own plans, but Iván Ilyich insisted on getting everything from an expensive confectioner and ordered too many cakes, and the quarrel occurred because some of those cakes were left over and the confectioner's bill came to forty-five rubles. It was a great and disagreeable quarrel. Praskóvya Fëdorovna called him "a fool and an imbecile," and he clutched at his head and made angry allusions to divorce.

But the dance itself had been enjoyable. The best people were there, and Iván Ilyich had danced with Princess Trúfonova, a sister of the distinguished founder of the Society "Bear my Burden."

The pleasures connected with his work were pleasures of ambition; his social pleasures were those of vanity; but Iván Ilyich's greatest pleasure was playing bridge. He acknowledged that whatever disagreeable incident happened in his life, the pleasure that beamed like a ray of light above everything else was to sit down to bridge with good players, not noisy partners, and of course to four-handed bridge (with five players it was annoying to have to stand out, though one pretended not to mind), to play a clever and serious game (when the cards allowed it) and then to have supper and drink a glass of wine. After a game of bridge, especially if he had won a little (to win a large sum was unpleasant), Iván Ilyich went to bed in specially good humour.

So they lived. They formed a circle of acquaintances among the best people and were visited by people of importance and by young folk. In their views as to their acquaintances, husband, wife, and daughter were entirely agreed, and tacitly and unanimously kept at arm's length and shook off the various shabby friends and relations who, with much show of affection, gushed into the drawing-room with its Japanese plates on the walls. Soon these shabby friends ceased to obtrude themselves and only the best people remained in the Golovíns' set.

Young men made up to Lisa, and Petríshchev, an examining magistrate and Dmítri Ivánovich Petríshchev's son and sole heir, began to be so attentive to her that Iván Ilyich had already spoken to Praskóvya Fëdorovna about it, and considered whether they should not arrange a party for them, or get up some private theatricals.

So they lived, and all went well, without change, and life flowed pleasantly.

IV

They were all in good health. It could not be called ill health if Iván Ilyich sometimes said that he had a queer taste in his mouth and felt some discomfort in his left side.

But this discomfort increased and, though not exactly painful, grew into a sense of pressure in his side accompanied by ill humour. And his irritability became worse and worse and began to mar the agreeable, easy, and correct life that had established itself in the Golovín family. Quarrels between husband and wife became more and more frequent, and soon the ease and amenity disappeared and even the decorum was barely maintained. Scenes again became frequent, and very few of those islets remained on which husband and wife could meet without an explosion. Praskóvya Fëdorovna now had good reason to say that her husband's temper was trying. With characteristic exaggeration she said he had always had a dreadful temper, and that it had needed all her good nature to put up with it for twenty years. It was true that now the quarrels were started by him. His bursts of temper always came just before dinner, often just as he began to eat his soup. Sometimes he noticed that a plate or dish was chipped, or the food was not right, or his son put his elbow on the table, or his daughter's hair was not done as he liked it, and for all this he blamed Praskóvya Fëdorovna. At first she retorted and said disagreeable things to him, but once or twice he fell into such a rage at the beginning of dinner that she realized it was due to some physical derangement brought on by taking food, and so she restrained herself and did not answer, but only hurried to get the dinner over. She regarded this self-restraint as highly praiseworthy. Having come to the conclusion that her husband had a dreadful temper and made her life miserable, she began to feel sorry for herself, and the more she pitied herself the more she hated her husband. She began to wish he would die; yet she did not want him to die because then his salary would cease. And this irritated her against him still more. She considered herself dreadfully unhappy just because not even his death could save her, and though she concealed her exasperation, that hidden exasperation of hers increased his irritation also.

After one scene in which Iván Ilyich had been particularly unfair and after which he had said in explanation that he certainly was irritable but that it was due to his not being well, she said that if he was ill it should be attended to, and insisted on his going to see a celebrated doctor.

He went. Everything took place as he had expected and as it always does. There was the usual waiting and the important air assumed by the doctor, with which he was so familiar (resembling that which he himself assumed in court), and the sounding and listening, and the questions which called for answers that were foregone conclusions and were evidently unnecessary, and the look of importance which implied that "if only you put yourself in our hands we will arrange everything—we know indubitably how it has to be done, always in the same way for everybody alike." It was all just as it was in the law courts. The doctor put on just the same air towards him as he himself put on towards an accused person.

The doctor said that so-and-so indicated that there was so-and-so inside the patient, but if the investigation of so-and-so did not confirm this, then he must assume that and that. If he assumed that and that, then ... and so on. To Iván Ilyich only one question was important: was his case serious or not? But the doctor ignored that inappropriate question. From his point of view it was not the one under consideration, the real question was to decide between a floating kidney, chronic catarrh, or appendicitis. It was not a question of Iván Ilyich's life or death, but one between a floating kidney and appendicitis. And that question the doctor solved brilliantly, as it seemed to Iván Ilyich, in favour of the appendix, with the reservation that should an examination of the urine give fresh indications the matter would be reconsidered. All this was just what Iván Ilyich had himself brilliantly accomplished a thousand times in dealing with men on trial. The doctor summed up just as brilliantly, looking over his spectacles triumphantly and even gaily at the accused. From the doctor's summing up Iván Ilyich concluded that things were bad, but that for the doctor, and perhaps for everybody else, it was a matter of indifference, though for him it was bad. And this conclusion struck him painfully, arousing in him a great feeling of pity for himself and of bitterness towards the doctor's indifference to a matter of such importance.

He said nothing of this, but rose, placed the doctor's fee on the table, and remarked with a sigh: "We sick people probably often put inappropriate questions. But tell me, in general, is this complaint dangerous, or not? . . ."

The doctor looked at him sternly over his spectacles with one eye, as if to say: "Prisoner, if you will not keep to the questions put to you, I shall be obliged to have you removed from the court."

"I have already told you what I consider necessary and proper. The analysis may show something more." And the doctor bowed.

Iván Ilyich went out slowly, seated himself disconsolately in his sledge, and drove home. All the way home he was going over what the doctor had said, trying to translate those complicated, obscure, scientific phrases into plain language and find in them an answer to the question: "Is my condition bad? Is it very bad? Or is there as yet nothing much wrong?" And it seemed to him that the meaning of what the doctor had said was that it was very bad. Everything in the streets seemed depressing. The cabmen, the houses, the passers-by, and the shops, were dismal. His ache, this dull gnawing ache that never ceased for a moment, seemed to have acquired a new and more serious significance from the doctor's dubious remarks. Iván Ilyich now watched it with a new and oppressive feeling.

He reached home and began to tell his wife about it. She listened, but in the middle of his account his daughter came in with her hat on, ready to go out with her mother. She sat down reluctantly to listen to this tedious story, but could not stand it long, and her mother too did not hear him to the end.

"Well, I am very glad," she said. "Mind now to take your medicine regularly. Give me the prescription and I'll send Gerásim to the chemist's." And she went to get ready to go out.

While she was in the room Iván Ilyich had hardly taken time to breathe, but he sighed deeply when she left it.

"Well," he thought, "perhaps it isn't so bad after all."

He began taking his medicine and following the doctor's directions, which had been altered after the examination of the urine. But then it happened that there was a contradiction between the indications drawn from the examination of the urine and the symptoms that showed themselves. It turned out that what was happening differed from what the doctor had told him, and that he had either forgotten, or blundered, or hidden something from him. He could not, however, be blamed for that, and Iván Ilyich still obeyed his orders implicitly and at first derived some comfort from doing so.

From the time of his visit to the doctor, Iván Ilyich's chief occupation was the exact fulfilment of the doctor's instructions regarding hygiene and the taking of medicine, and the observation of his pain and his excretions. His chief interests came to be people's ailments and people's health. When sickness, deaths, or recoveries were mentioned in his presence, especially when the illness resembled his own, he listened with agitation which he tried to hide, asked questions, and applied what he heard to his own case.

The pain did not grow less, but Iván Ilyich made efforts to force himself to think that he was better. And he could do this so long as nothing agitated him. But as soon as he had any unpleasantness with his wife, any lack of success in his official work, or held bad cards at bridge, he was at once acutely sensible of his disease. He had formerly borne such mischances, hoping soon to adjust what was wrong, to master it and attain success, or make a grand slam. But now every mischance upset him and plunged him into despair. He would say to himself: "There now, just as I was beginning to get better and the medicine had begun to take effect, comes this accursed misfortune, or unpleasantness . . ." And he was furious with the mishap, or with the people who were causing the unpleasantness and killing him, for he felt that this fury was killing him but could not restrain it. One would have thought that it should have been clear to him that this exasperation with circumstances and people aggravated his illness, and that he ought therefore to ignore unpleasant occurrences. But he drew the very opposite conclusion: he said that he needed peace, and he watched for everything that might disturb it and became irritable at the slightest infringement of it. His condition was rendered worse by the fact that he read medical books and consulted doctors. The progress of his disease was so gradual that he could deceive himself when comparing one day with another—the difference was so slight. But when he consulted the doctors it seemed to him that he was getting worse, and even very rapidly. Yet despite this he was continually consulting them.

That month he went to see another celebrity, who told him almost the same as the first had done but put his questions rather differently, and the interview with this celebrity only increased Iván Ilyich's doubts and fears. A friend of a friend of his, a very good doctor, diagnosed his illness again quite differently from the others, and though he predicted recovery, his questions and suppositions bewildered Iván Ilyich still more and increased his doubts. A homeopathist diagnosed the disease in yet another way, and prescribed medicine which Iván Ilyich took secretly for a week. But after a week, not feeling any improvement and having lost confidence both in the former doctor's treatment and in this one's, he became still more despondent. One day a lady acquaintance mentioned a cure effected by a wonder-working icon. Iván Ilyich caught himself listening attentively and beginning to believe that it had occurred. This incident alarmed him. "Has my mind really weakened to such an extent?" he asked himself. "Nonsense! It's all rubbish. I mustn't give way to nervous fears but having chosen a doctor must keep strictly to his treatment. That is what I will do. Now it's all settled. I won't think about it, but will follow the treatment seriously till summer, and then we shall see. From now there must be no more of this wavering!" This was easy to say but impossible to carry out. The pain in his side oppressed him and seemed to grow worse and more incessant, while the taste in his mouth grew stranger and stranger. It seemed to him that his breath had a disgusting smell, and he was conscious of a loss of appetite and strength. There was no deceiving himself: something terrible, new, and more important than anything before in his life, was taking place within him of which he alone was aware. Those about him did not understand or would not understand it, but thought everything in the world was going on as usual. That tormented Iván Ilyich more than anything. He saw that his household, especially his wife and daughter who were in a perfect whirl of visiting, did not understand anything of it and were annoyed that he was so depressed and so exacting, as if he were to blame for it. Though they tried to disguise it he saw that he was an obstacle in their path, and that his wife had adopted a definite line in regard to his illness and kept to it regardless of anything he said or did. Her attitude was this: "You know," she would say to her friends, "Iván Ilyich can't do as other people do, and keep to the treatment prescribed for him. One day he'll take his drops and keep strictly to his diet and go to bed in good time, but the next day unless I watch him he'll suddenly forget his medicine, eat sturgeon—which is forbidden—and sit up playing cards till one o'clock in the morning."

"Oh, come, when was that?" Iván Ilyich would ask in vexation. "Only once at Peter Ivánovich's."

"And yesterday with Shébek."

"Well, even if I hadn't stayed up, this pain would have kept me awake."

"Be that as it may you'll never get well like that, but will always make us wretched."

Praskóvya Fëdorovna's attitude to Iván Ilyich's illness, as she expressed it both to others and to him, was that it was his own fault and was another of the annoyances he caused her. Iván Ilyich felt that this opinion escaped her involuntarily—but that did not make it easier for him.

At the law courts too, Iván Ilyich noticed, or thought he noticed, a strange attitude towards himself. It sometimes seemed to him that people were watching him inquisitively as a man whose place might soon be vacant. Then again, his friends would suddenly begin to chaff him in a friendly way about his low spirits, as if the awful, horrible, and unheard-of thing that was going on within him, incessantly gnawing at him and irresistibly drawing him away, was a very agreeable subject for jests. Schwartz in particular irritated him by his jocularity, vivacity, and *savoir-faire*, which reminded him of what he himself had been ten years ago.

Friends came to make up a set and they sat down to cards. They dealt, bending the new cards to soften them, and he sorted the diamonds in his hand and found he had seven. His partner said "No trumps" and supported him with two diamonds. What more could be wished for? It ought to be jolly and lively. They would make a grand slam. But suddenly Iván Ilyich was conscious of that gnawing pain, that taste in his mouth, and it seemed ridiculous that in such circumstances he should be pleased to make a grand slam.

He looked at his partner Mikháil Mikháylovich, who rapped the table with his strong hand and instead of snatching up the tricks pushed the cards courteously and indulgently towards Iván Ilyich that he might have the pleasure of gathering them up without the trouble of stretching out his hand for them. "Does he think I am too weak to stretch out my arm?" thought Iván Ilyich, and forgetting what he was doing he over-trumped his partner, missing the grand slam by three tricks. And what was most awful of all was that he saw how upset Mikháil Mikháylovich was about it but did not himself care. And it was dreadful to realize why he did not care.

They all saw that he was suffering, and said: "We can stop if you are tired. Take a rest." Lie down? No, he was not at all tired, and he finished the rubber. All were gloomy and silent. Iván Ilyich felt that he had diffused this gloom over them and could not dispel it. They had supper and went away, and Iván Ilyich was left alone with the consciousness that his life was poisoned and was poisoning the lives of others, and that this poison did not weaken but penetrated more and more deeply into his whole being. With this consciousness, and with physical pain besides the terror, he must go to bed, often to lie awake the greater part of the night. Next morning he had to get up again, dress, go to the law courts, speak, and write; or if he did not go out, spend at home those twenty-four hours a day each of which was a torture. And he had to live thus all alone on the brink of an abyss, with no one who understood or pitied him.

V

So one month passed and then another. Just before the New Year his brother-in-law came to town and stayed at their house. Iván Ilyich was at the law courts and Praskóvya Fëdorovna had gone shopping. When Iván Ilyich came home and entered his study he found his brother-in-law there—a healthy, florid man—unpacking his portmanteau himself. He raised his head on hearing Iván Ilyich's footsteps and looked up at him for a moment without a word. That stare told Iván everything. His brother-in-law opened his mouth to utter an exclamation of surprise but checked himself, and that action confirmed it all.

"I have changed, eh?"

"Yes, there is a change."

And after that, try as he would to get his brother-in-law to return to the subject of his looks, the latter would say nothing about it. Praskóvya Fëdorovna came home and her brother went out to her. Iván Ilyich locked the door and began to examine himself in the glass, first full face, then in profile. He took up a portrait of himself taken with his wife, and compared it with what he saw in the glass. The change in him was immense. Then he bared his arms to the elbow, looked at them, drew the sleeves down again, sat down on an ottoman, and grew blacker than night.

"No, no, this won't do!" he said to himself, and jumped up, went to the table, took up some law papers and began to read them, but could not continue. He unlocked the door and went into the reception-room. The door leading to the drawing-room was shut. He approached it on tiptoe and listened.

"No, you are exaggerating!" Praskóvya Fëdorovna was saying.

"Exaggerating! Don't you see it? Why, he's a dead man! Look at his eyes—there's no light in them. But what is it that is wrong with him?"

"No one knows. Nikoláevich [that was another doctor] said something, but I don't know what. And Leshchetítsky [this was the celebrated specialist] said quite the contrary. . . ."

Iván Ilyich walked away, went to his own room, lay down and began musing: "The kidney, a floating kidney." He recalled all the doctors had told him of how it detached itself and swayed about. And by an effort of imagination he tried to catch that kidney and arrest it and support it. So little was needed for this, it seemed to him. "No, I'll go to see Peter Ivánovich again." [That was the friend whose friend was a doctor.] He rang, ordered the carriage, and got ready to go.

"Where are you going, Jean?"[8] asked his wife, with a specially sad and exceptionally kind look.

This exceptionally kind look irritated him. He looked morosely at her. "I must go to see Peter Ivánovich."

He went to see Peter Ivánovich, and together they went to see his friend, the doctor. He was in, and Iván Ilyich had a long talk with him. Reviewing the anatomical and physiological details of what in the doctor's opinion was going on inside him, he understood it all. There was something, a small thing, in the vermiform appendix. It might all come right. Only stimulate the energy of one organ and check the activity of another, then absorption would take place and everything would come right. He got home rather late for dinner, ate his dinner, and conversed cheerfully, but could not for a long time bring himself to go back to work in his room. At last, however, he went to his study and did what was necessary, but the consciousness that he had put something aside—an important, intimate matter which he would revert to when his work was done—never left him. When he had finished his work he remembered that this intimate matter was the thought of his vermiform appendix. But he did not give himself up to it, and went to the drawing-room for tea. There were callers there, including the examining magistrate who was a desirable match for his daughter, and they were conversing, playing the piano, and singing. Iván Ilyich, as Praskóvya Fëdorovna remarked, spent that evening more cheerfully than usual, but he never for a moment forgot that he had postponed the important matter of the appendix. At eleven o'clock he said goodnight and went to his bedroom. Since his illness he had slept alone in a small room next to his study. He undressed and took up a novel by Zola,[9] but instead of reading it he fell into thought, and in his imagination that desired improvement in the vermiform appendix occurred. There was the absorption and evacuation and the reestablishment of normal activity. "Yes, that's it!" he said to himself. "One need only assist nature, that's all." He remembered his medicine, rose, took it, and lay down on his back watching for the beneficent action of the medicine and for it to lessen the pain. "I need only take it regularly and avoid all injurious influences. I am already feeling better, much better." He began touching his side: it was not painful to the touch. "There, I really don't feel it. It's much better already." He put out the light and turned on his side . . . "The appendix is getting better, absorption is occurring." Suddenly he felt the old, familiar, dull, gnawing pain, stubborn and serious. There was the same familiar loathsome taste in his mouth. His heart sank and he felt dazed. "My God! My God!" he muttered. "Again, again! And it will never cease." And suddenly the matter presented itself in a quite different aspect. "Vermiform appendix! Kidney!" he said to himself. "It's not a question of appendix or kidney, but of life and . . . death. Yes, life was there and now it is going, going and I cannot stop it. Yes. Why deceive myself? Isn't it obvious to everyone but me that I'm dying, and that it's only a question of weeks, days . . . it may happen this moment. There was light and now there is darkness. I was here and now I'm going there! Where?" A chill came over him, his breathing ceased, and he felt only the throbbing of his heart.

8. French for Iván.
9. The French naturalistic novelist Émile Zola (1840–1902) saw human life as merely a matter of biological and mechanistic functions.

"When I am not, what will there be? There will be nothing. Then where shall I be when I am no more? Can this be dying? No, I don't want to!" He jumped up and tried to light the candle, felt for it with trembling hands, dropped candle and candlestick on the floor, and fell back on his pillow.

"What's the use? It makes no difference," he said to himself, staring with wide-open eyes into the darkness. "Death. Yes, death. And none of them know or wish to know it, and they have no pity for me. Now they are playing." (He heard through the door the distant sound of a song and its accompaniment.) "It's all the same to them, but they will die too! Fools! I first, and they later, but it will be the same for them. And now they are merry . . . the beasts!"

Anger choked him and he was agonizingly, unbearably miserable. "It is impossible that all men have been doomed to suffer this awful horror!" He raised himself.

"Something must be wrong. I must calm myself—must think it all over from the beginning." And he again began thinking. "Yes, the beginning of my illness: I knocked my side, but I was still quite well that day and the next. It hurt a little, then rather more. I saw the doctors, then followed despondency and anguish, more doctors, and I drew nearer to the abyss. My strength grew less and I kept coming nearer and nearer, and now I have wasted away and there is no light in my eyes. I think of the appendix—but this is death! I think of mending the appendix, and all the while here is death! Can it really be death?" Again terror seized him and he gasped for breath. He leant down and began feeling for the matches, pressing with his elbow on the stand beside the bed. It was in his way and hurt him, he grew furious with it, pressed on it still harder, and upset it. Breathless and in despair he fell on his back, expecting death to come immediately.

Meanwhile the visitors were leaving. Praskóvya Fëdorovna was seeing them off. She heard something fall and came in.

"What has happened?"

"Nothing. I knocked it over accidentally."

She went out and returned with a candle. He lay there panting heavily, like a man who has run a thousand yards, and stared upwards at her with a fixed look.

"What is it, *Jean*?"

"No . . . o . . . thing. I upset it." ("Why speak of it? She won't understand," he thought.)

And in truth she did not understand. She picked up the stand, lit his candle, and hurried away to see another visitor off. When she came back he still lay on his back, looking upwards.

"What is it? Do you feel worse?"

"Yes."

She shook her head and sat down.

"Do you know, *Jean*, I think we must ask Leshchetítsky to come and see you here."

This meant calling in the famous specialist, regardless of expense. He smiled malignantly and said "No." She remained a little longer and then went up to him and kissed his forehead.

While she was kissing him he hated her from the bottom of his soul and with difficulty refrained from pushing her away.

"Good-night. Please God you'll sleep."
"Yes."

VI

Iván Ilyich saw that he was dying, and he was in continual despair.

In the depth of his heart he knew he was dying, but not only was he not accustomed to the thought, he simply did not and could not grasp it.

The syllogism he had learned from Kiesewetter's *Logic:*[1] "Caius is a man, men are mortal, therefore Caius is mortal," had always seemed to him correct as applied to Caius, but certainly not as applied to himself. That Caius—man in the abstract—was mortal, was perfectly correct, but he was not Caius, not an abstract man, but a creature quite, quite separate from all others. He had been little Ványa, with a mamma and a papa, with Mítya and Volódya, with the toys, a coachman and a nurse, afterwards with Kátenka and with all the joys, griefs, and delights of childhood, boyhood, and youth. What did Caius know of the smell of that striped leather ball Ványa had been so fond of? Had Caius kissed his mother's hand like that, and did the silk of her dress rustle so for Caius? Had he rioted like that at school when the pastry was bad? Had Caius been in love like that? Could Caius preside at a session as he did? Caius really was mortal, and it was right for him to die; but for me, little Ványa, Iván Ilyich, with all my thoughts and emotions, it's altogether a different matter. It cannot be that I ought to die. That would be too terrible."

Such was his feeling.

"If I had to die like Caius I should have known it was so. An inner voice would have told me so, but there was nothing of the sort in me and I and all my friends felt that our case was quite different from that of Caius. And now here it is!" he said to himself. "It can't be. It's impossible! But here it is. How is this? How is one to understand it?"

He could not understand it, and tried to drive this false, incorrect, morbid thought away and to replace it by other proper and healthy thoughts. But that thought, and not the thought only but the reality itself, seemed to come and confront him.

And to replace that thought he called up a succession of others, hoping to find in them some support. He tried to get back into the former current of thoughts that had once screened the thought of death from him. But strange to say, all that had formerly shut off, hidden, and destroyed, his consciousness of death, no longer had that effect. Iván Ilyich now spent most of his time in attempting to re-establish that old current. He would say to himself: "I will take up my duties again—after all I used to live by them." And banishing all doubts he would go to the law courts, enter into conversation with his colleagues, and sit carelessly as was his wont, scanning the crowd with a thoughtful look and leaning both his emaciated arms on the arms of his oak chair; bending over as usual to a colleague and drawing his papers nearer he would interchange whispers with him, and then suddenly raising his eyes and sitting erect would pronounce certain words and open the proceedings. But suddenly in the midst of those proceedings the pain in his side, regardless of the stage the

---

1. Karl Kiesewetter (1766–1819), *Outline of Logic According to Kantian Principles* (1796), influential in   Russia as basis for school textbooks.

proceedings had reached, would begin its own gnawing work. Iván Ilyich would turn his attention to it and try to drive the thought of it away, but without success. It would come and stand before him and look at him, and he would be petrified and the light would die out of his eyes, and he would again begin asking himself whether It alone was true. And his colleagues and subordinates would see with surprise and distress that he, the brilliant and subtle judge, was becoming confused and making mistakes. He would shake himself, try to pull himself together, manage somehow to bring the sitting to a close, and return home with the sorrowful consciousness that his judicial labours could not as formerly hide from him what he wanted them to hide, and could not deliver him from It. And what was worst of all was that It drew his attention to itself not in order to make him take some action but only that he should look at It, look it straight in the face: look at it without doing anything, suffer inexpressibly.

And to save himself from this condition Iván Ilyich looked for consolations—new screens—and new screens were found and for a while seemed to save him, but then they immediately fell to pieces or rather became transparent, as if It penetrated them and nothing could veil It.

In these latter days he would go into the drawing-room he had arranged—that drawing-room where he had fallen and for the sake of which (how bitterly ridiculous it seemed) he had sacrificed his life—for he knew that his illness originated with that knock. He would enter and see that something had scratched the polished table. He would look for the cause of this and find that it was the bronze ornamentation of an album, that had got bent. He would take up the expensive album which he had lovingly arranged, and feel vexed with his daughter and her friends for their untidiness—for the album was torn here and there and some of the photographs turned upside down. He would put it carefully in order and bend the ornamentation back into position. Then it would occur to him to place all those things in another corner of the room, near the plants. He would call the footman, but his daughter or wife would come to help him. They would not agree, and his wife would contradict him, and he would dispute and grow angry. But that was all right, for then he did not think about It. It was invisible.

But then, when he was moving something himself, his wife would say: "Let the servants do it. You will hurt yourself again." And suddenly It would flash through the screen and he would see it. It was just a flash, and he hoped it would disappear, but he would involuntarily pay attention to his side. "It sits there as before, gnawing just the same!" And he could no longer forget It, but could distinctly see it looking at him from behind the flowers. "What is it all for?"

"It really is so! I lost my life over that curtain as I might have done when storming a fort. Is that possible? How terrible and how stupid. It can't be true! It can't, but it is."

He would go to his study, lie down, and again be alone with It: face to face with It. And nothing could be done with It except to look at it and shudder.

VII

How it happened it is impossible to say because it came about step by step, unnoticed, but in the third month of Iván Ilyich's illness, his wife, his daughter, his son, his acquaintances, the doctors, the servants, and above all he himself, were aware that the whole interest he had for other people was whether he would soon vacate his place, and at last release the living from the discomfort caused by his presence and be himself released from his sufferings.

He slept less and less. He was given opium and hypodermic injections of morphine, but this did not relieve him. The dull depression he experienced in a somnolent condition at first gave him a little relief, but only as something new, afterwards it became as distressing as the pain itself or even more so.

Special foods were prepared for him by the doctors' orders, but all those foods became increasingly distasteful and disgusting to him.

For his excretions also special arrangements had to be made, and this was a torment to him every time—a torment from the uncleanliness, the unseemliness, and the smell, and from knowing that another person had to take part in it.

But just through this most unpleasant matter, Iván Ilyich obtained comfort. Gerásim, the butler's young assistant, always came in to carry the things out. Gerásim was a clean, fresh peasant lad, grown stout on town food and always cheerful and bright. At first the sight of him, in his clean Russian peasant costume, engaged on that disgusting task embarrassed Iván Ilyich.

Once when he got up from the commode too weak to draw up his trousers, he dropped into a soft armchair and looked with horror at his bare, enfeebled thighs with the muscles so sharply marked on them.

Gerásim with a firm light tread, his heavy boots emitting a pleasant smell of tar and fresh winter air, came in wearing a clean Hessian apron,[2] the sleeves of his print shirt tucked up over his strong bare young arms; and refraining from looking at his sick master out of consideration for his feelings, and restraining the joy of life that beamed from his face, he went up to the commode.

"Gerásim!" said Iván Ilyich in a weak voice.

Gerásim started, evidently afraid he might have committed some blunder, and with a rapid movement turned his fresh, kind, simple young face which just showed the first downy signs of a beard.

"Yes, sir?"

"That must be very unpleasant for you. You must forgive me. I am helpless."

"Oh, why, sir," and Gerásim's eyes beamed and he showed his glistening white teeth, "what's a little trouble? It's a case of illness with you, sir."

And his deft strong hands did their accustomed task, and he went out of the room stepping lightly. Five minutes later he as lightly returned.

Iván Ilyich was still sitting in the same position in the armchair.

"Gerásim," he said when the latter had replaced the freshly-washed utensil. "Please come here and help me." Gerásim went up to him. "Lift me up. It is hard for me to get up, and I have sent Dmítri away."

Gerásim went up to him, grasped his master with his strong arms deftly but gently, in the same way that he stepped—lifted him, supported him with one hand, and with the other drew up his trousers and would have

2. Burlap apron.

set him down again, but Iván Ilyich asked to be led to the sofa. Gerásim, without an effort and without apparent pressure, led him, almost lifting him, to the sofa and placed him on it.

"Thank you. How easily and well you do it all!"

Gerásim smiled again and turned to leave the room. But Iván Ilyich felt his presence such a comfort that he did not want to let him go.

"One thing more, please move up that chair. No, the other one—under my feet. It is easier for me when my feet are raised."

Gerásim brought the chair, set it down gently in place, and raised Iván Ilyich's legs on to it. It seemed to Iván Ilyich that he felt better while Gerásim was holding up his legs.

"It's better when my legs are higher," he said. "Place that cushion under them."

Gerásim did so. He again lifted the legs and placed them, and again Iván Ilyich felt better while Gerásim held his legs. When he set them down Iván Ilyich fancied he felt worse.

"Gerásim," he said. "Are you busy now?"

"Not at all, sir," said Gerásim, who had learnt from the townsfolk how to speak to gentlefolk.

"What have you still to do?"

"What have I to do? I've done everything except chopping the logs for to-morrow."

"Then hold my legs up a bit higher, can you?"

"Of course I can. Why not?" and Gerásim raised his master's legs higher and Iván Ilyich thought that in that position he did not feel any pain at all.

"And how about the logs?"

"Don't trouble about that, sir. There's plenty of time."

Iván Ilyich told Gerásim to sit down and hold his legs, and began to talk to him. And strange to say it seemed to him that he felt better while Gerásim held his legs up.

After that Iván Ilyich would sometimes call Gerásim and get him to hold his legs on his shoulders, and he liked talking to him. Gerásim did it all easily, willingly, simply, and with a good nature that touched Iván Ilyich. Health, strength, and vitality in other people were offensive to him, but Gerásim's strength and vitality did not mortify but soothed him.

What tormented Iván Ilyich most was the deception, the lie, which for some reason they all accepted, that he was not dying but was simply ill, and that he only need keep quiet and undergo a treatment and then something very good would result. He however knew that do what they would nothing would come of it, only still more agonizing suffering and death. This deception tortured him—their not wishing to admit what they all knew and what he knew, but wanting to lie to him concerning his terrible condition, and wishing and forcing him to participate in that lie. Those lies—lies enacted over him on the eve of his death and destined to degrade this awful, solemn act to the level of their visitings, their curtains, their sturgeon for dinner—were a terrible agony for Iván Ilyich. And strangely enough, many times when they were going through their antics over him he had been within a hairbreadth of calling out to them: "Stop lying! You know and I know that I am dying. Then at least stop lying about it!" But he had never had the spirit to do it. The awful, terrible act of his dying was, he could see, reduced by those about him to the level of a casual, unpleasant, and almost indecorous incident (as if someone entered a drawing-room diffusing an unpleasant odour) and this was done by that very decorum which he had served all his life long. He saw that no one felt for him, because no one even wished to grasp his position. Only Gerásim recognized and pitied him. And so Iván Ilyich felt at ease only with him. He felt comforted when Gerásim supported his legs (sometimes all night long) and refused to go to bed, saying: "Don't you worry, Iván Ilyich. I'll get sleep enough later on," or when he suddenly became familiar and exclaimed: "If you weren't sick it would be another matter, but as it is, why should I grudge a little trouble?" Gerásim alone did not lie; everything showed that he alone understood the facts of the case and did not consider it necessary to disguise them, but simply felt sorry for his emaciated and enfeebled master. Once when Iván Ilyich was sending him away he even said straight out: "We shall all of us die, so why should I grudge a little trouble?"—expressing the fact that he did not think his work burdensome, because he was doing it for a dying man and hoped someone would do the same for him when his time came.

Apart from this lying, or because of it, what most tormented Iván Ilyich was that no one pitied him as he wished to be pitied. At certain moments after prolonged suffering he wished most of all (though he would have been ashamed to confess it) for someone to pity him as a sick child is pitied. He longed to be petted and comforted. He knew he was an important functionary, that he had a beard turning grey, and that therefore what he longed for was impossible, but still he longed for it. And in Gerásim's attitude towards him there was something akin to what he wished for, and so that attitude comforted him. Iván Ilyich wanted to weep, wanted to be petted and cried over, and then his colleague Shébek would come, and instead of weeping and being petted, Iván Ilyich would assume a serious, severe, and profound air, and by force of habit would express his opinion on a decision of the Court of Appeal and would stubbornly insist on that view. This falsity around him and within him did more than anything else to poison his last days.

VIII

It was morning. He knew it was morning because Gerásim had gone, and Peter the footman had come and put out the candles, drawn back one of the curtains, and begun quietly to tidy up. Whether it was morning or evening, Friday or Sunday, made no difference, it was all just the same: the gnawing, unmitigated, agonizing pain, never ceasing for an instant, the consciousness of life inexorably waning but not yet extinguished, the approach of that ever dreaded and hateful Death which was the only reality, and always the same falsity. What were days, weeks, hours, in such a case?

"Will you have some tea, sir?"

"He wants things to be regular, and wishes the gentlefolk to drink tea in the morning," thought Iván Ilyich, and only said "No."

"Wouldn't you like to move onto the sofa, sir?"

"He wants to tidy up the room, and I'm in the way. I am uncleanliness and disorder," he thought, and said only:

"No, leave me alone."

The man went on bustling about. Iván Ilyich stretched out his hand.
Peter came up, ready to help.

"What is it, sir?"

"My watch."

Peter took the watch which was close at hand and gave it to his master.

"Half-past eight. Are they up?"

"No, sir, except Vasílii Ivánich" (the son) "who has gone to school.
Praskóvya Fëdorovna ordered me to wake her if you asked for her. Shall I
do so?"

"No, there's no need to." "Perhaps I'd better have some tea," he
thought, and added aloud: "Yes, bring me some tea."

Peter went to the door, but Iván Ilyich dreaded being left alone.
"How can I keep him here? Oh yes, my medicine." "Peter, give me my
medicine." "Why not? Perhaps it may still do me some good." He took a
spoonful and swallowed it. "No, it won't help. It's all tomfoolery, all deception," he decided as soon as he became aware of the familiar, sickly,
hopeless taste. "No, I can't believe in it any longer. But the pain, why
this pain? If it would only cease just for a moment!" And he moaned.
Peter turned towards him. "It's all right. Go and fetch me some tea."

Peter went out. Left alone Iván Ilyich groaned not so much with pain,
terrible though that was, as from mental anguish. Always and forever the
same, always these endless days and nights. If only it would come
quicker! If only *what* would come quicker? Death, darkness? . . . No, no!
Anything rather than death!

When Peter returned with the tea on a tray, Iván Ilyich stared at him
for a time in perplexity, not realizing who and what he was. Peter was
disconcerted by that look and his embarrassment brought Iván Ilyich to
himself.

"Oh, tea! All right, put it down. Only help me to wash and put on a
clean shirt."

And Iván Ilyich began to wash. With pauses for rest, he washed his
hands and then his face, cleaned his teeth, brushed his hair, and looked in
the glass. He was terrified by what he saw, especially by the limp way in
which his hair clung to his pallid forehead.

While his shirt was being changed he knew that he would be still more
frightened at the sight of his body, so he avoided looking at it. Finally he
was ready. He drew on a dressing-gown, wrapped himself in a plaid, and
sat down in the armchair to take his tea. For a moment he felt refreshed,
but as soon as he began to drink the tea he was again aware of the same
taste, and the pain also returned. He finished it with an effort, and then
lay down stretching out his legs, and dismissed Peter.

Always the same. Now a spark of hope flashes up, then a sea of despair
rages, and always pain; always pain, always despair, and always the same.
When alone he had a dreadful and distressing desire to call someone, but
he knew beforehand that with others present it would be still worse. "Another dose of morphine—to lose consciousness. I will tell him, the doctor,
that he must think of something else. It's impossible, impossible, to go on
like this."

An hour and another pass like that. But now there is a ring at the door
bell. Perhaps it's the doctor? It is. He comes in fresh, hearty, plump, and
cheerful, with that look on his face that seems to say: "There now, you're

in a panic about something, but we'll arrange it all for you directly!" The doctor knows this expression is out of place here, but he has put it on once for all and can't take it off—like a man who has put on a frock-coat in the morning to pay a round of calls.

The doctor rubs his hands vigorously and reassuringly.

"Brr! How cold it is! There's such a sharp frost; just let me warm myself!" he says, as if it were only a matter of waiting till he was warm, and then he would put everything right.

"Well now, how are you?"

Iván Ilyich feels that the doctor would like to say: "Well, how are our affairs?" but that even he feels that this would not do, and says instead: "What sort of a night have you had?"

Iván Ilyich looks at him as much as to say: "Are you really never ashamed of lying?" But the doctor does not wish to understand this question, and Iván Ilyich says: "Just as terrible as ever. The pain never leaves me and never subsides. If only something . . ."

"Yes, you sick people are always like that. . . . There, now I think I'm warm enough. Even Praskóvya Fëdorovna, who is so particular, could find no fault with my temperature. Well, now I can say good-morning," and the doctor presses his patient's hand.

Then, dropping his former playfulness, he begins with a most serious face to examine the patient, feeling his pulse and taking his temperature, and then begins the sounding and auscultation.

Iván Ilyich knows quite well and definitely that all this is nonsense and pure deception, but when the doctor, getting down on his knee, leans over him, putting his ear first higher then lower, and performs various gymnastic movements over him with a significant expression on his face, Iván Ilyich submits to it all as he used to submit to the speeches of the lawyers, though he knew very well that they were all lying and why they were lying.

The doctor, kneeling on the sofa, is still sounding him when Praskóvya Fëdorovna's silk dress rustles at the door and she is heard scolding Peter for not having let her know of the doctor's arrival.

She comes in, kisses her husband, and at once proceeds to prove that she has been up a long time already, and only owing to a misunderstanding failed to be there when the doctor arrived.

Iván Ilyich looks at her, scans her all over, sets against her the whiteness and plumpness and cleanness of her hands and neck, the gloss of her hair, and the sparkle of her vivacious eyes. He hates her with his whole soul. And the thrill of hatred he feels for her makes him suffer from her touch.

Her attitude towards him and his disease is still the same. Just as the doctor had adopted a certain relation to his patient which he could not abandon, so had she formed one towards him—that he was not doing something he ought to do and was himself to blame, and that she reproached him lovingly for this—and she could not now change that attitude.

"You see he doesn't listen to me and doesn't take his medicine at the proper time. And above all he lies in a position that is no doubt bad for him—with his legs up."

She described how he made Gerásim hold his legs up.

The doctor smiled with a contemptuous affability that said: "What's to be done? These sick people do have foolish fancies of that kind, but we must forgive them."

When the examination was over the doctor looked at his watch, and then Praskóvya Fëdorovna announced to Iván Ilyich that it was of course as he pleased, but she had sent to-day for a celebrated specialist who would examine him and have a consultation with Michael Danílovich (their regular doctor).

"Please don't raise any objections. I am doing this for my own sake," she said ironically, letting it be felt that she was doing it all for his sake and only said this to leave him no right to refuse. He remained silent, knitting his brows. He felt that he was so surrounded and involved in a mesh of falsity that it was hard to unravel anything.

Everything she did for him was entirely for her own sake, and she told him she was doing for herself what she actually was doing for herself, as if that was so incredible that he must understand the opposite.

At half-past eleven the celebrated specialist arrived. Again the sounding began and the significant conversations in his presence and in another room, about the kidneys and the appendix, and the questions and answers, with such an air of importance that again, instead of the real question of life and death which now alone confronted him, the question arose of the kidney and the appendix which were not behaving as they ought to and would now be attacked by Michael Danílovich and the specialist and forced to amend their ways.

The celebrated specialist took leave of him with a serious though not hopeless look, and in reply to the timid question Iván Ilyich, with eyes glistening with fear and hope, put to him as to whether there was a chance of recovery, said that he could not vouch for it but there was a possibility. The look of hope with which Iván Ilyich watched the doctor out was so pathetic that Praskóvya Fëdorovna, seeing it, even wept as she left the room to hand the doctor his fee.

The gleam of hope kindled by the doctor's encouragement did not last long. The same room, the same pictures, curtains, wall-paper, medicine bottles, were all there, and the same aching suffering body, and Iván Ilyich began to moan. They gave him a subcutaneous injection and he sank into oblivion.

It was twilight when he came to. They brought him his dinner and he swallowed some beef tea with difficulty, and then everything was the same again and night was coming on.

After dinner, at seven o'clock, Praskóvya Fëdorovna came into the room in evening dress, her full bosom pushed up by her corset, and with traces of powder on her face. She had reminded him in the morning that they were going to the theatre. Sarah Bernhardt was visiting the town and they had a box, which he had insisted on their taking. Now he had forgotten about it and her toilet offended him, but he concealed his vexation when he remembered that he had himself insisted on their securing a box and going because it would be an instructive and aesthetic pleasure for the children.

Praskóvya Fëdorovna came in, self-satisfied but yet with a rather guilty air. She sat down and asked how he was, but, as he saw, only for the sake of asking and not in order to learn about it, knowing that there was nothing to learn—and then went on to what she really wanted to say: that she would not on any account have gone but that the box had been taken and

Helen and their daughter were going, as well as Petríshchev (the examining magistrate, their daughter's fiancé) and that it was out of the question to let them go alone; but that she would have much preferred to sit with him for a while; and he must be sure to follow the doctor's orders while she was away.

"Oh, and Fëdor Petróvich" (the fiancé) "would like to come in. May he? And Lisa?"

"All right."

Their daughter came in in full evening dress, her fresh young flesh exposed (making a show of that very flesh which in his own case caused so much suffering), strong, healthy, evidently in love, and impatient with illness, suffering, and death, because they interfered with her happiness.

Fëdor Petróvich came in too, in evening dress, his hair curled à la Capoul,[3] a tight stiff collar round his long sinewy neck, an enormous white shirt-front and narrow black trousers tightly stretched over his strong thighs. He had one white glove tightly drawn on, and was holding his opera hat in his hand.

Following him the schoolboy crept in unnoticed, in a new uniform, poor little fellow, and wearing gloves. Terribly dark shadows showed under his eyes, the meaning of which Iván Ilyich knew well.

His son had always seemed pathetic to him, and now it was dreadful to see the boy's frightened look of pity. It seemed to Iván Ilyich that Vásya was the only one besides Gerásim who understood and pitied him.

They all sat down and again asked how he was. A silence followed. Lisa asked her mother about the opera-glasses, and there was an altercation between mother and daughter as to who had taken them and where they had been put. This occasioned some unpleasantness.

Fëdor Petróvich inquired of Iván Ilyich whether he had ever seen Sarah Bernhardt. Iván Ilyich did not at first catch the question, but then replied: "No, have you seen her before?"

"Yes, in *Adrienne Lecouvreur.*"[4]

Praskóvya Fëdorovna mentioned some rôles in which Sarah Bernhardt was particularly good. Her daughter disagreed. Conversation sprang up as to the elegance and realism of her acting—the sort of conversation that is always repeated and is always the same.

In the midst of the conversation Fëdor Petróvich glanced at Iván Ilyich and became silent. The others also looked at him and grew silent. Iván Ilyich was staring with glittering eyes straight before him, evidently indignant with them. This had to be rectified, but it was impossible to do so. The silence had to be broken, but for a time no one dared to break it and they all became afraid that the conventional deception would suddenly become obvious and the truth become plain to all. Lisa was the first to pluck up courage and break that silence, but by trying to hide what everybody was feeling, she betrayed it.

"Well, if we are going it's time to start," she said, looking at her watch, a present from her father, and with a faint and significant smile at Fëdor Petróvich relating to something known only to them. She got up with a rustle of her dress.

3. With a part in the middle, hair brushed off the sides of the forehead but with two small curls over the middle of the forehead; after Joseph-Amédée-Victor Capoul (1839–1924), French singer and mati-nee idol.

4. An 1849 play by the prolific and popular French playwright Eugène Scribe (1791–1861), one of Bernhardt's most famous vehicles.

They all rose, said good-night, and went away.

When they had gone it seemed to Iván Ilyich that he felt better; the falsity had gone with them. But the pain remained—that same pain and that same fear that made everything monotonously alike, nothing harder and nothing easier. Everything was worse.

Again minute followed minute and hour followed hour. Everything remained the same and there was no cessation. And the inevitable end of it all became more and more terrible.

"Yes, send Gerásim here," he replied to a question Peter asked.

IX

His wife returned late at night. She came in on tiptoe, but he heard her, opened his eyes, and made haste to close them again. She wished to send Gerásim away and to sit with him herself, but he opened his eyes and said: "No, go away."

"Are you in great pain?"

"Always the same."

"Take some opium."

He agreed and took some. She went away.

Till about three in the morning he was in a state of stupefied misery. It seemed to him that he and his pain were being thrust into a narrow, deep black sack, but though they were pushed further and further in they could not be pushed to the bottom. And this, terrible enough in itself, was accompanied by suffering. He was frightened yet wanted to fall through the sack, he struggled but yet co-operated. And suddenly he broke through, fell, and regained consciousness. Gerásim was sitting at the foot of the bed dozing quietly and patiently, while he himself lay with his emaciated stockinged legs resting on Gerásim's shoulders; the same shaded candle was there and the same unceasing pain.

"Go away, Gerásim," he whispered.

"It's all right, sir. I'll stay a while."

"No. Go away."

He removed his legs from Gerásim's shoulders, turned sideways onto his arm, and felt sorry for himself. He only waited till Gerásim had gone into the next room and then restrained himself no longer but wept like a child. He wept on account of his helplessness, his terrible loneliness, the cruelty of man, the cruelty of God, and the absence of God.

"Why hast Thou done all this? Why hast Thou brought me here? Why dost Thou torment me so terribly?"

He did not expect an answer and yet wept because there was no answer and could be none. The pain again grew more acute, but he did not stir and did not call. He said to himself: "Go on! Strike me! But what is it for? What have I done to Thee? What is it for?"

Then he grew quiet and not only ceased weeping but even held his breath and became all attention. It was as though he were listening not to an audible voice but to a voice of his soul, to the current of thoughts arising within him.

"What is it you want?" was the first clear conception capable of expression in words, that he heard.

"What do you want? What do you want?" he repeated to himself.

"What do I want? To live and not to suffer," he answered.

And again he listened with such concentrated attention that even his pain did not distract him.

"To live? How?" asked his inner voice.

"Why, to live as I used to—well and pleasantly."

"As you lived before, well and pleasantly?" the voice repeated. And in imagination he began to recall the best moments of his pleasant life. But strange to say none of those best moments of his pleasant life now seemed at all what they had then seemed—none of them except the first recollections of childhood. There, in childhood, there had been something really pleasant with which it would be possible to live if it could return. But the child who had experienced that happiness existed no longer, it was like a reminiscence of somebody else.

As soon as the period began which had produced the present Iván Ilyich, all that had then seemed joys now melted before his sight and turned into something trivial and often nasty.

And the further he departed from childhood and the nearer he came to the present the more worthless and doubtful were the joys. This began with the School of Law. A little that was really good was still found there—there was light-heartedness, friendship, and hope. But in the upper classes there had already been fewer of such good moments. Then during the first years of his official career, when he was in the service of the Governor, some pleasant moments again occurred: they were the memories of love for a woman. Then all became confused and there was still less of what was good; later on again there was still less that was good, and the further he went the less there was. His marriage, a mere accident, then the disenchantment that followed it, his wife's bad breath and the sensuality and hypocrisy: then that deadly official life and those preoccupations about money, a year of it, and two, and ten, and twenty, and always the same thing. And the longer it lasted the more deadly it became. "It is as if I had been going downhill while I imagined I was going up. And that is really what it was. I was going up in public opinion, but to the same extent life was ebbing away from me. And now it is all done and there is only death."

"Then what does it mean? Why? It can't be that life is so senseless and horrible. But if it really has been so horrible and senseless, why must I die and die in agony? There is something wrong!"

"Maybe I did not live as I ought to have done," it suddenly occurred to him. "But how could that be, when I did everything properly?" he replied, and immediately dismissed from his mind this, the sole solution of all the riddles of life and death, as something quite impossible.

"Then what do you want now? To live? Live how? Live as you lived in the law courts when the usher proclaimed 'The judge is coming!' The judge is coming, the judge!" he repeated to himself. "Here he is, the judge. But I am not guilty!" he exclaimed angrily. "What is it for?" And he ceased crying, but turning his face to the wall continued to ponder on the same question: Why, and for what purpose, is there all this horror? But however much he pondered he found no answer. And whenever the thought occurred to him, as it often did, that it all resulted from his not having lived as he ought to have done, he at once recalled the correctness of his whole life, and dismissed so strange an idea.

X

Another fortnight passed. Iván Ilyich now no longer left his sofa. He would not lie in bed but lay on the sofa, facing the wall nearly all the time. He suffered ever the same unceasing agonies and in his loneliness pondered always on the same insoluble question: "What is this? Can it be that it is Death?" And the inner voice answered: "Yes, it is Death."

"Why these sufferings?" And the voice answered, "For no reason—they just are so." Beyond and besides this there was nothing.

From the very beginning of his illness, ever since he had first been to see the doctor, Iván Ilyich's life had been divided between two contrary and alternating moods: now it was despair and the expectation of this uncomprehended and terrible death, and now hope and an intently interested observation of the functioning of his organs. Now before his eyes there was only a kidney or an intestine that temporarily evaded its duty, and now only that incomprehensible and dreadful death from which it was impossible to escape.

These two states of mind had alternated from the very beginning of his illness, but the further it progressed the more doubtful and fantastic became the conception of the kidney, and the more real the sense of impending death.

He had but to call to mind what he had been three months before and what he was now, to call to mind with what regularity he had been going downhill, for every possibility of hope to be shattered.

Latterly during that loneliness in which he found himself as he lay facing the back of the sofa, a loneliness in the midst of a populous town and surrounded by numerous acquaintances and relations but that yet could not have been more complete anywhere—either at the bottom of the sea or under the earth—during that terrible loneliness Iván Ilyich had lived only in memories of the past. Pictures of his past rose before him one after another. They always began with what was nearest in time and then went back to what was most remote—to his childhood—and rested there. If he thought of the stewed prunes that had been offered him that day, his mind went back to the raw shrivelled French plums of his childhood, their peculiar flavour and the flow of saliva when he sucked their stones, and along with the memory of that taste came a whole series of memories of those days: his nurse, his brother, and their toys. "No, I mustn't think of that.... It is too painful," Iván Ilyich said to himself, and brought himself back to the present—to the button on the back of the sofa and the creases in its morocco. "Morocco is expensive, but it does not wear well: there had been a quarrel about it. It was a different kind of quarrel and a different kind of morocco that time when we tore father's portfolio and were punished, and mamma brought us some tarts.... " And again his thoughts dwelt on his childhood, and again it was painful and he tried to banish them and fix his mind on something else.

Then again together with that chain of memories another series passed through his mind—of how his illness had progressed and grown worse. There also the further back he looked the more life there had been. There had been more of what was good in life and more of life itself. The two merged together. "Just as the pain went on getting worse and worse, so my life grew worse and worse," he thought. "There is one bright spot there at the back, at the beginning of life, and afterwards all becomes blacker and blacker and proceeds more and more rapidly—in inverse ratio to the square of the distance from death," thought Iván Ilyich. And the example of a stone falling downwards with increasing velocity entered his mind. Life, a series of increasing sufferings, flies further and further towards its end—the most terrible suffering. "I am flying. . . . " He shuddered, shifted himself, and tried to resist, but was already aware that resistance was impossible, and again with eyes weary of gazing but unable to cease seeing what was before them, he stared at the back of the sofa and waited—awaiting that dreadful fall and shock and destruction.

"Resistance is impossible!" he said to himself. "If I could only understand what it is all for! But that too is impossible. An explanation would be possible if it could be said that I have not lived as I ought to. But it is impossible to say that," and he remembered all the legality, correctitude, and propriety of his life. "That at any rate can certainly not be admitted," he thought, and his lips smiled ironically as if someone could see that smile and be taken in by it. "There is no explanation! Agony, death. . . . What for?"

XI

Another two weeks went by in this way and during that fortnight an event occurred that Iván Ilyich and his wife had desired. Petríshchev formally proposed. It happened in the evening. The next day Praskóvya Fëdorovna came into her husband's room considering how best to inform him of it, but that very night there had been a fresh change for the worse in his condition. She found him still lying on the sofa but in a different position. He lay on his back, groaning and staring fixedly straight in front of him.

She began to remind him of his medicines, but he turned his eyes towards her with such a look that she did not finish what she was saying; so great an animosity, to her in particular, did that look express.

"For Christ's sake let me die in peace!" he said.

She would have gone away, but just then their daughter came in and went up to say good morning. He looked at her as he had done at his wife, and in reply to her inquiry about his health said dryly that he would soon free them all of himself. They were both silent and after sitting with him for a while went away.

"Is it our fault?" Lisa said to her mother. "It's as if we were to blame! I am sorry for papa, but why should we be tortured?"

The doctor came at his usual time. Iván Ilyich answered "Yes" and "No," never taking his angry eyes from him, and at last said: "You know you can do nothing for me, so leave me alone."

"We can ease your sufferings."

"You can't even do that. Let me be."

The doctor went into the drawing-room and told Praskóvya Fëdorovna that the case was very serious and that the only resource left was opium to allay her husband's sufferings, which must be terrible.

It was true, as the doctor said, that Iván Ilyich's physical sufferings were terrible, but worse than the physical sufferings were his mental sufferings which were his chief torture.

His mental sufferings were due to the fact that that night, as he looked at Gerásim's sleepy, good-natured face with its prominent cheek-bones,

the question suddenly occurred to him: "What if my whole life has really
been wrong?"

It occurred to him that what had appeared perfectly impossible before,
namely that he had not spent his life as he should have done, might after
all be true. It occurred to him that his scarcely perceptible attempts to
struggle against what was considered good by the most highly placed people, those scarcely noticeable impulses which he had immediately suppressed, might have been the real thing, and all the rest false. And his
professional duties and the whole arrangement of his life and of his family, and all his social and official interests, might all have been false. He
tried to defend all those things to himself and suddenly felt the weakness
of what he was defending. There was nothing to defend.

"But if that is so," he said to himself, "and I am leaving this life with
the consciousness that I have lost all that was given me and it is impossible to rectify it—what then?"

He lay on his back and began to pass his life in review in quite a new
way. In the morning when he saw first his footman, then his wife, then his
daughter, and then the doctor, their every word and movement confirmed
to him the awful truth that had been revealed to him during the night. In
them he saw himself—all that for which he had lived—and saw clearly
that it was not real at all, but a terrible and huge deception which had
hidden both life and death. This consciousness intensified his physical suffering tenfold. He groaned and tossed about, and pulled at his clothing
which choked and stifled him. And he hated them on that account.

He was given a large dose of opium and became unconscious, but at
noon his sufferings began again. He drove everybody away and tossed
from side to side.

His wife came to him and said:

"*Jean*, my dear, do this for me. It can't do any harm and often helps.
Healthy people often do it."

He opened his eyes wide.

"What? Take communion? Why? It's unnecessary! However . . . "

She began to cry.

"Yes, do, my dear. I'll send for our priest. He is such a nice man."

"All right. Very well," he muttered.

When the priest came and heard his confession, Iván Ilyich was softened and seemed to feel a relief from his doubts and consequently from
his sufferings, and for a moment there came a ray of hope. He again
began to think of the vermiform appendix and the possibility of correct-
ing it. He received the sacrament with tears in his eyes.

When they laid him down again afterwards he felt a moment's ease,
and the hope that he might live awoke in him again. He began to think of
the operation that had been suggested to him. "To live! I want to live!"
he said to himself.

His wife came in to congratulate him after his communion, and when
uttering the usual conventional words she added:

"You feel better, don't you?"

Without looking at her he said "Yes."

Her dress, her figure, the expression of her face, the tone of her voice,
all revealed the same thing. "This is wrong, it is not as it should be. All
you have lived for and still live for is falsehood and deception, hiding life
and death from you." And as soon as he admitted that thought, his hatred

and his agonizing physical suffering again sprang up, and with that suffering a consciousness of the unavoidable, approaching end. And to this was added a new sensation of grinding shooting pain and a feeling of suffocation.

The expression of his face when he uttered that "yes" was dreadful. Having uttered it, he looked her straight in the eyes, turned on his face with a rapidity extraordinary in his weak state and shouted: "Go away! Go away and leave me alone!"

XII

From that moment the screaming began that continued for three days, and was so terrible that one could not hear it through two closed doors without horror. At the moment he answered his wife he realized that he was lost, that there was no return, that the end had come, the very end, and his doubts were still unsolved and remained doubts.

"Oh! Oh! Oh!" he cried in various intonations. He had begun by screaming "I won't!" and continued screaming on the letter "o."

For three whole days, during which time did not exist for him, he struggled in that black sack into which he was being thrust by an invisible, resistless force. He struggled as a man condemned to death struggles in the hands of the executioner, knowing that he cannot save himself. And every moment he felt that despite all his efforts he was drawing nearer and nearer to what terrified him. He felt that his agony was due to his being thrust into that black hole and still more to his not being able to get right into it. He was hindered from getting into it by his conviction that his life had been a good one. That very justification of his life held him fast and prevented his moving forward, and it caused him most torment of all.

Suddenly some force struck him in the chest and side, making it still harder to breathe, and he fell through the hole and there at the bottom was a light. What had happened to him was like the sensation one sometimes experiences in a railway carriage when one thinks one is going backwards while one is really going forwards and suddenly becomes aware of the real direction.

"Yes, it was all not the right thing," he said to himself, "but that's no matter. It can be done. But what *is* the right thing?" he asked himself, and suddenly grew quiet.

This occurred at the end of the third day, two hours before his death. Just then his schoolboy son had crept softly in and gone up to the bedside. The dying man was still screaming desperately and waving his arms. His hand fell on the boy's head, and the boy caught it, pressed it to his lips, and began to cry.

At that very moment Iván Ilyich fell through and caught sight of the light, and it was revealed to him that though his life had not been what it should have been, this could still be rectified. He asked himself, "What *is* the right thing?" and grew still, listening. Then he felt that someone was kissing his hand. He opened his eyes, looked at his son, and felt sorry for him. His wife came up to him and he glanced at her. She was gazing at him open-mouthed, with undried tears on her nose and cheek and a despairing look on her face. He felt sorry for her too.

"Yes, I am making them wretched," he thought. "They are sorry, but it will be better for them when I die." He wished to say this but had not the strength to utter it. "Besides, why speak? I must act," he thought. With a look at his wife he indicated his son and said: "Take him away . . . sorry for him . . . sorry for you too. . . . " He tried to add, "forgive me," but said "forego" and waved his hand, knowing that He whose understanding mattered would understand.

And suddenly it grew clear to him that what had been oppressing him and would not leave him was all dropping away at once from two sides, from ten sides, and from all sides. He was sorry for them, he must act so as not to hurt them: release them and free himself from these sufferings. "How good and how simple!" he thought. "And the pain?" he asked himself. "What has become of it? Where are you, pain?"

He turned his attention to it.

"Yes, here it is. Well, what of it? Let the pain be."

"And death . . . where is it?"

He sought his former accustomed fear of death and did not find it. "Where is it? What death?" There was no fear because there was no death.

In place of death there was light.

"So that's what it is!" he suddenly exclaimed aloud. "What joy!"

To him all this happened in a single instant, and the meaning of that instant did not change. For those present his agony continued for another two hours. Something rattled in his throat, his emaciated body twitched, then the gasping and rattle became less and less frequent.

"It is finished!" said someone near him.

He heard these words and repeated them in his soul.

"Death is finished," he said to himself. "It is no more!"

He drew in a breath, stopped in the midst of a sigh, stretched out, and died.

1886

AFTERWORD

What can one expect from a story called *The Death of . . . ?* The title *Daisy Miller* is noncommital; *The Strange Case of . . .* promises mystery, arouses curiosity; *The Death of . . .* is so specific, so terminal, that it arouses little expectation and only a mild curiosity about how a novel can be made of the subject. Perhaps it will be a story in which, after adventures or trials of some sort, the main character dies at the end, or perhaps "death" will be metaphorical, ironic, somehow not literal.

But just after the very first paragraph of the novel ends, Iván's literal death is announced and our attention shifts to the *effect* of his death. By the end of the third substantial paragraph, we're pretty sure what that will be. We know what kind of society we are dealing with, or at least the tone of the narrator toward that society: all present were Iván's friends, but each first thought "of the changes and promotions it might occasion among themselves or their acquaintances." Such, then, is the governmental, bureaucratic, ruling-class world of the novel. But then, there are responses that do not seem confined to that narrow world: "Each one thought or felt, 'Well, he's dead but I'm alive' "; close friends "could not help thinking also that they would now have to fulfil the very tiresome demands of propriety," attending the funeral, visiting the widow. We join in feeling sympathy for the dead Iván and his grieving widow, distaste for the selfish and superficial others.

We follow Peter Ivánovich on his visit to the widow, which delays his bridge game, and share (or at least recognize as common, if not admirable) his fear of betraying his discomfort and lack of sincere, profound personal feeling. Even the widow, whose grief we assumed was real and deep, and with whom we sympathized, is primarily concerned, it seems, with the price of burial plots—you cannot let these practical things go just because of grief, can you? She does, in her self-centered way, try to tell Peter about his friend's suffering ("I cannot understand how I bore it," she says!), and for a moment he is terrified—for himself. Still, he just cannot put himself in Iván's place, for he is still alive. Then, no doubt to his relief, he discovers that the widow wanted to see him in order to find out if she can get more from the government than the widow's pension (about which she seems to know in detail). Iván's servant, Gerásim, whose blooming health and efficiency seem to insult poor Iván's memory, appears in his way callous—his master's death was God's will, a conventional way of not thinking about death or feeling for the dead, is it not? The first chapter ends with Peter Ivánovich leaving to join his—and Iván's—friends, finding "them just finishing the first rubber, so that it was quite convenient for him to cut in." Poor Iván is sincerely mourned only by this teenage son who himself is not "pure-minded." The first chapter seems a complete if skimpy short story or vignette in itself—a cynical portrait of the pervasive selfishness of survivors. Poor dead Iván!

This is not a 3500-word short story, however, but a novel about seven or eight times as long (and this chapter is just the first of twelve). Where can it go from here? Tolstoy could conceivably go on to show how the hard-hearted friends, and the widow herself, get their due, but the second chapter sets out to review the life of poor Iván: if his friends or wife do not pity him, we, more feeling human beings, will. About five hundred words into the chapter, however, we begin to wonder whether we should be quite so sorry for him:

> At school he had done things which had formerly seemed to him very horrid and made him feel disgusted with himself when he did them; but when later on

he saw that such actions were done by people of good position and that they did not regard them as wrong, he was able not exactly to regard them as right, but to forget about them entirely or not be at all troubled at remembering them.

Ironically, as we get to know Iván better, as his becomes the consciousness through which we see the events of his life and milieu, we feel for him less. He's just like the rest of his society; perhaps he deserves the neglect he receives. At the beginning of Chapter 3, when his luck seems to have turned for the worse and he is passed over for a promotion, we are not sure whether we are glad or sorry, and we feel equal ambivalence in his lucky, successful fishing for a job with a higher income and more prestige. That things improve for him after his hardest year we find ironic, since that year was 1880, and we know he will die at the age of forty-five in the year 1882, and our pity may return. We are therefore more apprehensive than Iván himself when he is injured "slightly" while decorating his new home. We see what he does not, what no human being can see, the future; and so we find that final sentence of the chapter ominous, moving, and a little frightening: "So they lived, and all went well, without change, and life flowed pleasantly."

In the fourth chapter Iván recognizes he is seriously ill, but others do not, and the chapter ends, as so many in this novel do, with a sentence which both summarizes and prepares us for a further stage: "And he had to live thus all alone on the brink of an abyss, with no one who understood or pitied him." Here we are almost back to the beginning of the story, the isolated and pitiable dead or dying man surrounded by the callous, on-going, unconcerned world; our sentiments too have shifted all the way back to "poor Iván." He is no longer the prideful magistrate who keeps personal feelings out of all transactions, but only a mortal man. Like ourselves? Are we mortal too? That's what Iván grapples with in the next chapter: can a syllogism be wholly accepted that concludes that an individual is mortal if the individual is Iván Ilyich? or you? . . . or *me?*

We are even yet only into the fifth of the twelve chapters, only in the middle of the novel. It seems we are in for a rather prolonged deathbed scene. Iván Ilyich is still Iván Ilyich, but hasn't our relationship to him changed? It is not that we know him better exactly, but we no longer feel the unqualified pity of Chapter 1; and gone too is the critical distance from which we viewed him as just another bureaucrat as we read Chapters 2 and 3. It is not so much that we identify with Iván, perhaps, as that (like Peter Ivánovich in Chapter 1, when told of Ivan's suffering) we now must be given pause by the syllogism: All men are mortal. Iván is (I am) a man./ Therefore Iván is (I am) mortal. That is, Iván (I) will die. (And women readers, I am sure, will not easily hide behind the word "man" in the traditional syllogism.)

We may no longer be reading simply the story of a nineteenth-century Russian bureaucrat with our entire attention, but we probably are, with some part of our minds, trying to come to terms with our own mortality. From this point on, we will be reading the story rather differently. Iván's character, his faults and virtues, become less important. The way he lived (we live) and the way he dies (we will die) become the center of the story. The sentence with which the story of his life in Chapter 2 begins may at this point come back to us: "Iván Ilyich's life had been most simple and most ordinary and therefore most terrible." We may want to back to the very beginning of the story. His surname, Golovín, is mentioned in the *Gazette* announcement of his death early in the story. Why isn't the novel called *The Death of Iván Ilyich Golovín?* Iván is the most common Russian name. Iván Ilyich is not significantly more individualizing than John Smith, or even John Doe. Are we faced with still another irony or twist? That Iván's death is not treated by his friends and loved ones as something that happened to an individual, a human being, a fellow creature, a man, was reprehensible. That Iván in his position in the government did not treat people as individuals but as cases, as abstractions, was reprehensible. But the novel seems to want us to think of him now not just as Iván Ilyich or little Ványa, but as a typical, ordinary human being like the rest of us. Our attention is directed away from Iván the individual and away from our own deaths and toward our common fate, toward the deaths of all humans, of those we love, and those we hate. But isn't dwelling on the fact that each of us is going to die "morbid"? Doesn't it keep us from living while we're living? What purpose does it serve? What can we learn about *living*—and isn't that the important thing?—by dwelling on the fact of dying?

Are there any examples of "living" in the novel? Only Iván's schoolboy son and the peasant Gerásim come off at all well. The boy is a bit soppy, but he does at least seem capable of love. Gerásim, who we understood at first to treat his master's death almost casually, really meant it when he spoke of God's will. He is willing to face Iván's illness and dying—we will all come to it someday—and do the best for him while he can at considerable cost to himself. He sees Iván Ilyich not primarily as his "master," but as a suffering mortal, like the rest of us, and while he does not deny life and sit mourning or tearing his hair, he performs the service that the living can perform for the dying. Is he merely a sentimentalized version of the unspoiled peasant, the product of the ruling class, a sort of Russian Uncle Tom?

Iván cannot understand the reason for suffering, perhaps cannot die, until he faces the truth that his life was not a proper life (though, we must remember, an ordinary one). Tolstoy does not directly tell us what *is* a proper life, though we may, through negative and positive examples in the story and through what Iván learns, piece together something of a program or rule of conduct. Gerásim clearly believes in God; but his conduct toward Iván some of us may affirm in human as well as (or aside from) religious terms. Iván communes with his soul in his direst hours; to what extent is what he discovers restricted to those who believe in the soul, God, immortality? Tolstoy himself was "converted"—though not to Orthodox or orthodox Christianity—and for several years thereafter studied theology. Why, then, does he not put his conclusions in more forthright, overt Christian terms?

In his essay "What Is Art?" he insists that art is not for art's but for society's sake, is didactic or a form of persuasion or education, but *not* in the form of overt statement or argument:

> the business of art lies just in this,—to make that understood and felt which, in the form of an argument, might be incomprehensible and inaccessible. . . .

Toward the end of that long, profound, disturbing, and exciting work (in which he "throws out" both Shakespeare and his own novels!), he specifies what the *that* is that art must communicate through the feelings:

> Art is not a pleasure, a solace, or an amusement; art is a great matter. Art is an organ of human life, transmitting man's reasonable perception into feeling. In our age the common religious perception of men is the consciousness of the brotherhood of man—we know that the well-being of man lies in union with his fellowmen. . . . Art should transform this perception into feeling.

How can a story in which men's selfish concerns are made so manifest be art, if art is the transmission of the feeling of men's fellowship? Is the feeling transmitted in the story contempt or worse for man-in-society? Or is it a sense of the brotherhood of man?

ROBERT LOUIS STEVENSON

The Strange Case of
Dr. Jekyll and Mr. Hyde

The congenital weakness of the lungs with which Stevenson was born—in Edinburgh, on November 13, 1850—hampered but did not halt his life's activity. He had to abandon the study of engineering because of ill health, but studied law and was called to the bar in 1875 (though he never practiced). In rapid succession he fell in love with two married women, each of whom was eleven years older than he, each of whom had a tubercular son. Ill health again, and his father's disapproval, caused him to leave the first for a sojourn on the continent, where he met the second, Fanny Osbourne, whom he followed in 1878 to California, where he spent a rather bad year, troubled by ill health and disapproval of friends and family. With reluctant family approval he was able to marry the divorced Mrs. Osbourne and returned to Edinburgh until the death of his father in 1887 provided him with the means of leaving Britain's damp climate. He first went to Saranac, N.Y., where there was a famous tuberculosis sanitarium, then (with money from a generous contract with the America publisher Scribners for a series of articles) sailed from the West Coast for the South Seas, where he traveled widely and where his health improved. In Samoa he bought a plantation and built a home, Vailima, where he died on December 3, 1894, not of lung disease but of a massive cerebral hemorrhage.

Stevenson's first literary accomplishments were in the form of essays written for *Cornhill* magazine in the late 1870s and collected in the volumes *Virginibus Puerisque* (1881) and *Familiar Studies of Men and Books* (1882). Though they did not in his time bring him fame nor are they much remembered now, these essays are, despite some youthful faults, accomplished and promising. The essays he wrote for Scribners a decade later fulfilled that promise. The essays as well as the novels show Stevenson for the stylist he is (Henry James said Stevenson was the only one he knew "who could write a decent English sentence"). It is the novels, however, upon which Stevenson's fame rests. *Treasure Island* appeared in book form in 1883, and both *The Strange Case of Dr. Jekyll and Mr. Hyde* and *Kidnapped* three years later. Even Stevenson's popular *A Child's Garden of Verses* appeared in this same three-year period. The mature but somewhat uneven *The Master of Ballantrae* appeared in 1889, and at his death Stevenson left a number of unfinished works, including the masterful dark fragment of a novel, *Weir of Hermiston*.

The *Doppelgänger,* or double, appears often in nineteenth- and early twentieth-century fiction, from James Hogg's *Confessions of a Justified Sinner* (1824), through Edgar Allan Poe's *William Wilson* (1839), to Joseph Conrad's *The Secret-Sharer* (1912), but *Jekyll and Hyde* is by far the most popular, the most widely known. Has anyone not read (or seen in some adaptation) *The Strange Case of Dr. Jekyll and Mr. Hyde?* Perhaps because it is so well known, we do well to be on our guard so as not to lose sight of the splendid prose and complex structure in which this compelling tale is embodied. Even Stevenson's theme cannot be satisfactorily reduced to Good vs. Evil or any other simple two-part division of the human faculties or psychological or spiritual qualities.

after every ? why is it important to your interpretation of the story?

The Strange Case
of Dr. Jekyll and Mr. Hyde

Story of the Door

MR. UTTERSON the lawyer was a man of a rugged countenance that was never lighted by a smile; cold, scanty and embarrassed in discourse; backward in sentiment; lean, long, dusty, dreary and yet somehow lovable. At friendly meetings, and when the wine was to his taste, something eminently human beaconed from his eye; something indeed which never found its way into his talk, but which spoke not only in these silent symbols of the after-dinner face, but more often and loudly in the acts of his life. He was austere with himself; drank gin when he was alone, to mortify a taste for vintages; and though he enjoyed the theatre, had not crossed the doors of one for twenty years. But he had an approved tolerance for others; sometimes wondering, almost with envy, at the high pressure of spirits involved in their misdeeds; and in any extremity inclined to help rather than to reprove. "I incline to Cain's heresy," he used to say quaintly: "I let my brother go to the devil in his own way."[1] In this character, it was frequently his fortune to be the last reputable acquaintance and the last good influence in the lives of downgoing men. And to such as these, so long as they came about his chambers, he never marked a shade of change in his demeanour.

No doubt the feat was easy to Mr. Utterson; for he was undemonstrative at the best, and even his friendship seemed to be founded in a similar catholicity of good-nature. It is the mark of a modest man to accept his friendly circle ready-made from the hands of opportunity; and that was the lawyer's way. His friends were those of his own blood or those whom he had known the longest; his affections, like ivy, were the growth of time, they implied no aptness in the object. Hence, no doubt, the bond that united him to Mr. Richard Enfield, his distant kinsman, the well-known man about town. It was a nut to crack for many, what these two could see in each other, or what subject they could find in common. It was reported by those who encountered them in their Sunday walks, that they said nothing, looked singularly dull, and would hail with obvious relief the appearance of a friend. For all that, the two men put the greatest store by these excursions, counted them the chief jewel of each week, and not only set aside occasions of pleasure, but even resisted the calls of business, that they might enjoy them uninterrupted.

It chanced on one of these rambles that their way led them down a by-street in a busy quarter of London. The street was small and what is called quiet, but it drove a thriving trade on the week-days. The inhabitants were all doing well, it seemed, and all emulously hoping to do better still, and laying out the surplus of their gains in coquetry; so that the shop fronts stood along that thoroughfare with an air of invitation, like rows of smiling saleswomen. Even on Sunday, when it veiled its more

1. Genesis 4:9. After Cain killed Abel, "the Lord said unto Cain, Where is Abel thy brother? And he said, I know not: Am I my brother's keeper?"

florid charms and lay comparatively empty of passage, the street shone out in contrast to its dingy neighbourhood, like a fire in a forest; and with its freshly painted shutters, well-polished brasses, and general cleanliness and gaiety of note, instantly caught and pleased the eye of the passenger.

Two doors from one corner, on the left hand going east, the line was broken by the entry of a court; and just at that point, a certain sinister block of building thrust forward its gable on the street. It was two storeys high; showed no window, nothing but a door on the lower storey and a blind forehead of discoloured wall on the upper; and bore in every feature, the marks of prolonged and sordid negligence. The door, which was equipped with neither bell nor knocker, was blistered and distained. Tramps slouched into the recess and struck matches on the panels; children kept shop upon the steps; the schoolboy had tried his knife on the mouldings; and for close on a generation, no one had appeared to drive away these random visitors or to repair their ravages.

Mr. Enfield and the lawyer were on the other side of the by-street; but when they came abreast of the entry, the former lifted up his cane and pointed.

"Did you ever remark that door?" he asked; and when his companion had replied in the affirmative, "It is connected in my mind," added he, "with a very odd story."

"Indeed?" said Mr. Utterson, with a slight change of voice, "and what was that?"

"Well, it was this way," returned Mr. Enfield: "I was coming home from some place at the end of the world, about three o'clock of a black winter morning, and my way lay through a part of town where there was literally nothing to be seen but lamps. Street after street, and all the folks asleep—street after street, all lighted up as if for a procession and all as empty as a church—till at last I got into that state of mind when a man listens and listens and begins to long for the sight of a policeman. All at once, I saw two figures: one a little man who was stumping along eastward at a good walk, and the other a girl of maybe eight or ten who was running as hard as she was able down a cross street. Well, sir, the two ran into one another naturally enough at the corner; and then came the horrible part of the thing; for the man trampled calmly over the child's body and left her screaming on the ground. It sounds nothing to hear, but it was hellish to see. It wasn't like a man; it was like some damned Juggernaut. I gave a view halloa,[2] took to my heels, collared my gentleman, and brought him back to where there was already quite a group about the screaming child. He was perfectly cool and made no resistance, but gave me one look, so ugly that it brought out the sweat on me like running. The people who had turned out were the girl's own family; and pretty soon, the doctor, for whom she had been sent, put in his appearance. Well, the child was not much the worse, more frightened, according to the Sawbones; and there you might have supposed would be an end to it. But there was one curious circumstance. I had taken a loathing to my gentleman at first sight. So had the child's family, which was only natural. But the doctor's case was what struck me. He was the usual cut and dry

2. Shout given by a huntsman on seeing the fox break cover.

apothecary, of no particular age and colour, with a strong Edinburgh accent, and about as emotional as a bagpipe. Well, sir, he was like the rest of us; every time he looked at my prisoner, I saw that Sawbones turn sick and white with the desire to kill him. I knew what was in his mind, just as he knew what was in mine; and killing being out of the question, we did the next best. We told the man we could and would make such a scandal out of this, as should make his name stink from one end of London to the other. If he had any friends or any credit, we undertook that he should lose them. And all the time, as we were pitching it in red hot, we were keeping the women off him as best we could, for they were as wild as harpies. I never saw a circle of such hateful faces; and there was the man in the middle, with a kind of black, sneering coolness—frightened too, I could see that—but carrying it off, sir, really like Satan. 'If you choose to make capital out of this accident,' said he, 'I am naturally helpless. No gentleman but wishes to avoid a scene,' says he. 'Name your figure.' Well, we screwed him up to a hundred pounds[3] for the child's family; he would have clearly liked to stick out; but there was something about the lot of us that meant mischief, and at last he struck. The next thing was to get the money; and where do you think he carried us but to that place with the door?—whipped out a key, went in, and presently came back with the matter of ten pounds in gold and a cheque for the balance on Coutts's,[4] drawn payable to bearer and signed with a name that I can't mention, though it's one of the points of my story, but it was a name at least very well known and often printed. The figure was stiff; but the signature was good for more than that, if it was only genuine. I took the liberty of pointing out to my gentleman that the whole business looked apocryphal, and that a man does not, in real life, walk into a cellar door at four in the morning and come out of it with another man's cheque for close upon a hundred pounds. But he was quite easy and sneering. 'Set your mind at rest,' says he, 'I will stay with you till the banks open and cash the cheque myself.' So we all set off, the doctor, and the child's father, and our friend and myself, and passed the rest of the night in my chambers; and next day, when we had breakfasted, went in a body to the bank. I gave in the cheque myself, and said I had every reason to believe it was a forgery. Not a bit of it. The cheque was genuine."

"I see you feel as I do," said Mr. Enfield. "Yes, it's a bad story. For my man was a fellow[5] that nobody could have to do with, a really damnable man; and the person that drew the cheque is the very pink[6] of the proprieties, celebrated too, and (what makes it worse) one of your fellows who do what they call good. Black mail, I suppose; an honest man paying through the nose for some of the capers of his youth. Black Mail House is what I call that place with the door, in consequence. Though even that, you know, is far from explaining all," he added, and with the words fell into a vein of musing.

From this he was recalled by Mr. Utterson asking rather suddenly: "And you don't know if the drawer of the cheque lives there?"

---

3. About $500 when purchasing power was vastly more, perhaps the equivalent of $3000–$5000 today.
4. A bank.

5. Low sort of person.
6. Highest example.

"A likely place, isn't it?" returned Mr. Enfield. "But I happen to have noticed his address; he lives in some square or other."

"And you never asked about the—place with the door?" said Mr. Utterson.

"No, sir: I had a delicacy," was the reply. "I feel very strongly about putting questions; it partakes too much of the style of the day of judgment. You start a question, and it's like starting a stone. You sit quietly on the top of a hill; and away the stone goes, starting others; and presently some bland old bird (the last you would have thought of) is knocked on the head in his own back garden and the family have to change their name. No, sir, I make it a rule of mine: the more it looks like Queer Street,[7] the less I ask."

"A very good rule, too," said the lawyer.

"But I have studied the place for myself," continued Mr. Enfield. "It seems scarcely a house. There is no other door, and nobody goes in or out of that one but, once in a great while, the gentleman of my adventure. There are three windows looking on the court on the first floor; none below; the windows are always shut but they're clean. And then there is a chimney which is generally smoking; so somebody must live there. And yet it's not so sure; for the buildings are so packed together about that court, that it's hard to say where one ends and another begins."

The pair walked on again for a while in silence; and then "Enfield," said Mr. Utterson, "that's a good rule of yours."

"Yes, I think it is," returned Enfield.

"But for all that," continued the lawyer, "there's one point I want to ask: I want to ask the name of that man who walked over the child."

"Well," said Mr. Enfield, "I can't see what harm it would do. It was a man of the name of Hyde."

"Hm," said Mr. Utterson. "What sort of a man is he to see?"

"He is not easy to describe. There is something wrong with his appearance; something displeasing, something downright detestable. I never saw a man I so disliked, and yet I scarce know why. He must be deformed somewhere; he gives a strong feeling of deformity, although I couldn't specify the point. He's an extraordinary looking man, and yet I really can name nothing out of the way. No, sir; I can make no hand of it; I can't describe him. And it's not want of memory; for I declare I can see him this moment."

Mr. Utterson again walked some way in silence and obviously under a weight of consideration. "You are sure he used a key?" he inquired at last.

"My dear sir . . ." began Enfield, surprised out of himself.

"Yes, I know," said Utterson; "I know it must seem strange. The fact is, if I do not ask you the name of the other party, it is because I know it already. You see, Richard, your tale has gone home. If you have been inexact in any point, you had better correct it."

"I think you might have warned me," returned the other with a touch of sullenness. "But I have been pedantically exact, as you call it. The fellow had a key; and what's more, he has it still. I saw him use it, not a week ago."

Mr. Utterson sighed deeply but said never a word; and the young man presently resumed. "Here is another lesson to say nothing," said he. "I am

---

7. An imaginary street where people in financial and other trouble live.

ashamed of my long tongue. Let us make a bargain never to refer to this again."

"With all my heart," said the lawyer. "I shake hands on that, Richard."

Search for Mr. Hyde

That evening Mr. Utterson came home to his bachelor house in sombre spirits and sat down to dinner without relish. It was his custom of a Sunday, when this meal was over, to sit close by the fire, a volume of some dry divinity on his reading desk, until the clock of the neighbouring church rang out the hour of twelve, when he would go soberly and gratefully to bed. On this night, however, as soon as the cloth was taken away, he took up a candle and went into his business room. There he opened his safe, took from the most private part of it a document endorsed on the envelope as Dr. Jekyll's Will, and sat down with a clouded brow to study its contents. The will was holograph, for Mr. Utterson, though he took charge of it now that it was made, had refused to lend the least assistance in the making of it; it provided not only that, in case of the decease of Henry Jekyll, M.D., D.C.L., L.L.D., F.R.S., etc., all his possessions were to pass into the hands of his "friend and benefactor Edward Hyde," but that in case of Dr. Jekyll's "disappearance or unexplained absence for any period exceeding three calendar months," the said Edward Hyde should step into the said Henry Jekyll's shoes without further delay and free from any burthen or obligation, beyond the payment of a few small sums to the members of the doctor's household. This document had long been the lawyer's eyesore. It offended him both as a lawyer and as a lover of the sane and customary sides of life, to whom the fanciful was the immodest. And hitherto it was his ignorance of Mr. Hyde that had swelled his indignation; now, by a sudden turn, it was his knowledge. It was already bad enough when the name was but a name of which he could learn no more. It was worse when it began to be clothed upon with detestable attributes; and out of the shifting, insubstantial mists that had so long baffled his eye, there leaped up the sudden, definite presentment of a fiend.

"I thought it was madness," he said, as he replaced the obnoxious paper in the safe, "and now I begin to fear it is disgrace."

With that he blew out his candle, put on a greatcoat, and set forth in the direction of Cavendish Square, that citadel of medicine, where his friend, the great Dr. Lanyon, had his house and received his crowding patients. "If anyone knows, it will be Lanyon," he had thought.

The solemn butler knew and welcomed him; he was subjected to no stage of delay, but ushered direct from the door to the dining-room where Dr. Lanyon sat alone over his wine. This was a hearty, healthy, dapper, red-faced gentleman, with a shock of hair prematurely white, and a boisterous and decided manner. At sight of Mr. Utterson, he sprang up from his chair and welcomed him with both hands. The geniality, as was the way of the man, was somewhat theatrical to the eye; but it reposed on genuine feeling. For those two were old friends, old mates both at school and college, both thorough respecters of themselves and of each other, and, what does not always follow, men who thoroughly enjoyed each other's company.

After a little rambling talk, the lawyer led up to the subject which so disagreeably preoccupied his mind.

"I suppose, Lanyon," said he, "you and I must be the two oldest friends that Henry Jekyll has?"

"I wish the friends were younger," chuckled Dr. Lanyon. "But I suppose we are. And what of that? I see little of him now."

"Indeed?" said Utterson. "I thought you had a bond of common interest."

"We had," was the reply. "But it is more than ten years since Henry Jekyll became too fanciful for me. He began to go wrong, wrong in mind; and though of course I continue to take an interest in him for old sake's sake, as they say, I see and I have seen devilish little of the man. Such unscientific balderdash," added the doctor, flushing suddenly purple, "would have estranged Damon and Pythias."

This little spirit of temper was somewhat of a relief to Mr. Utterson. "They have only differed on some point of science," he thought; and being a man of no scientific passions (except in the matter of conveyancing), he even added: "It is nothing worse than that!" He gave his friend a few seconds to recover his composure, and then approached the question he had come to put. "Did you ever come across a protégé of his—one Hyde?" he asked.

"Hyde?" repeated Lanyon. "No. Never heard of him. Since my time."

That was the amount of information that the lawyer carried back with him to the great, dark bed on which he tossed to and fro, until the small hours of the morning began to grow large. It was a night of little ease to his toiling mind, toiling in mere darkness and besieged by questions.

Six o'clock struck on the bells of the church that was so conveniently near to Mr. Utterson's dwelling, and still he was digging at the problem. Hitherto it had touched him on the intellectual side alone; but now his imagination also was engaged, or rather enslaved; and as he lay and tossed in the gross darkness of the night and the curtained room, Mr. Enfield's tale went by before his mind in a scroll of lighted pictures. He would be aware of the great field of lamps of a nocturnal city; then of the figure of a man walking swiftly; then of a child running from the doctor's; and then these met, and that human Juggernaut trod the child down and passed on regardless of her screams. Or else he would see a room in a rich house, where his friend lay asleep, dreaming and smiling at his dreams; and then the door of that room would be opened, the curtains of the bed plucked apart, the sleeper recalled, and lo! there would stand by his side a figure to whom power was given, and even at that dead hour, he must rise and do its bidding. The figure in these two phases haunted the lawyer all night; and if at any time he dozed over, it was but to see it glide more stealthily through sleeping houses, or move the more swiftly and still the more swiftly, even to dizziness, through wider labyrinths of lamplighted city, and at every street corner crush a child and leave her screaming. And still the figure had no face by which he might know it; even in his dreams, it had no face, or one that baffled him and melted before his eyes; and thus it was that there sprang up and grew apace in the lawyer's mind a singularly strong, almost an inordinate, curiosity to behold the features of the real Mr. Hyde. If he could but once set eyes on him, he thought the mystery would lighten and perhaps roll altogether away, as was the habit of mysterious things when well examined. He might see a reason for his friend's strange preference or bondage (call it which you please) and even for the startling clause of the will. At least it would be a face worth seeing: the face of a man who was without bowels of mercy: a face which had but to show itself to raise up, in the mind of the unimpressionable Enfield, a spirit of enduring hatred.

From that time forward, Mr. Utterson began to haunt the door in the by-street of shops. In the morning before office hours, at noon when business was plenty, and time scarce, at night under the face of the fogged city moon, by all lights and at all hours of solitude or concourse, the lawyer was to be found on his chosen post.

"If he be Mr. Hyde," he had thought, "I shall be Mr. Seek."

And at last his patience was rewarded. It was a fine dry night; frost in the air; the streets as clean as a ballroom floor; the lamps, unshaken by any wind, drawing a regular pattern of light and shadow. By ten o'clock, when the shops were closed, the by-street was very solitary and, in spite of the low growl of London from all round, very silent. Small sounds carried far; domestic sounds out of the houses were clearly audible on either side of the roadway; and the rumour of the approach of any passenger preceded him by a long time. Mr. Utterson had been some minutes at his post, when he was aware of an odd, light footstep drawing near. In the course of his nightly patrols, he had long grown accustomed to the quaint effect with which the footfalls of a single person, while he is still a great way off, suddenly spring out distinct from the vast hum and clatter of the city. Yet his attention had never before been so sharply and decisively arrested; and it was with a strong, superstitious prevision of success that he withdrew into the entry of the court.

The steps drew swiftly nearer, and swelled out suddenly louder as they turned the end of the street. The lawyer, looking forth from the entry, could soon see what manner of man he had to deal with. He was small and very plainly dressed, and the look of him, even at that distance, went somehow strongly against the watcher's inclination. But he made straight for the door, crossing the roadway to save time; and as he came, he drew a key from his pocket like one approaching home.

Mr. Utterson stepped out and touched him on the shoulder as he passed. "Mr. Hyde, I think?"

Mr. Hyde shrank back with a hissing intake of the breath. But his fear was only momentary; and though he did not look the lawyer in the face he answered coolly enough: "That is my name. What do you want?"

"I see you are going in," returned the lawyer. "I am an old friend of Dr. Jekyll's—Mr. Utterson of Gaunt Street—you must have heard of my name; and meeting you so conveniently, I thought you might admit me."

"You will not find Dr. Jekyll; he is from home," replied Mr. Hyde, blowing in the key. And then suddenly, but still without looking up, "How did you know me?" he asked.

"On your side," said Mr. Utterson, "will you do me a favour?"

"With pleasure," replied the other. "What shall it be?"

"Will you let me see your face?" asked the lawyer.

Mr. Hyde appeared to hesitate, and then, as if upon some sudden reflection, fronted about with an air of defiance; and the pair stared at each other pretty fixedly for a few seconds. "Now I shall know you again," said Mr. Utterson. "It may be useful."

"Yes," returned Mr. Hyde, "it is as well we have met; and *à propos,* you should have my address." And he gave a number of a street in Soho.[8]

"Good God!" thought Mr. Utterson, "can he, too, have been thinking of the will?" But he kept his feelings to himself and only grunted in acknowledgment of the address.

"And now," said the other, "how did you know me?"

"By description," was the reply.

"Whose description?"

"We have common friends," said Mr. Utterson.

"Common friends?" echoed Mr. Hyde, a little hoarsely. "Who are they?"

"Jekyll, for instance," said the lawyer.

"He never told you," cried Mr. Hyde, with a flush of anger. "I did not think you would have lied."

"Come," said Mr. Utterson, "that is not fitting language."

The other snarled aloud into a savage laugh; and the next moment, with extraordinary quickness, he had unlocked the door and disappeared into the house.

The lawyer stood awhile when Mr. Hyde had left him, the picture of disquietude. Then he began slowly to mount the street, pausing every step or two and putting his hand to his brow like a man in mental perplexity. The problem he was thus debating as he walked, was one of a class that is rarely solved. Mr. Hyde was pale and dwarfish, he gave an impression of deformity without any nameable malformation, he had a displeasing smile, he had borne himself to the lawyer with a sort of murderous mixture of timidity and boldness, and he spoke with a husky, whispering and somewhat broken voice; all these were points against him, but not all of these together could explain the hitherto unknown disgust, loathing and fear with which Mr. Utterson regarded him. "There must be something else," said the perplexed gentleman. "There *is* something more, if I could find a name for it. God bless me, the man seems hardly human! Something troglodytic, shall we say? or can it be the old story of Dr. Fell?[9] or is it the mere radiance of a foul soul that thus transpires through, and transfigures, its clay continent? The last, I think; for, O my poor old Harry Jekyll, if ever I read Satan's signature upon a face, it is on that of your new friend."

Round the corner from the by-street, there was a square of ancient, handsome houses, now for the most part decayed from their high estate and let in flats and chambers to all sorts and conditions of men; mapengravers, architects, shady lawyers and the agents of obscure enterprises. One house, however, second from the corner, was still occupied entire; and at the door of this, which wore a great air of wealth and comfort, though it was now plunged in darkness except for the fan-light, Mr. Utterson stopped and knocked. A well-dressed, elderly servant opened the door.

"Is Dr. Jekyll at home, Poole?" asked the lawyer.

"I will see, Mr. Utterson," said Poole, admitting the visitor, as he spoke, into a large, low-roofed, comfortable hall, paved with flags,

8. Section of London roughly comparable to New York's Greenwich Village: full of good continental restaurants, writers and artists, somewhat shady characters.

9. "I do not love thee, Dr. Fell./ The reason why I cannot tell."; a free translation by Tom Brown (1830–1897) of an epigram by Martial (c. 40–c. 104).

warmed (after the fashion of a country house) by a bright, open fire, and furnished with costly cabinets of oak. "Will you wait here by the fire, sir? or shall I give you a light in the dining-room?"

"Here, thank you," said the lawyer, and he drew near and leaned on the tall fender. This hall, in which he was now left alone, was a pet fancy of his friend the doctor's; and Utterson himself was wont to speak of it as the pleasantest room in London. But tonight there was a shudder in his blood; the face of Hyde sat heavy on his memory; he felt (what was rare with him) a nausea and distaste of life; and in the gloom of his spirits, he seemed to read a menace in the flickering of the firelight on the polished cabinets and the uneasy starting of the shadow on the roof. He was ashamed of his relief, when Poole presently returned to announce that Dr. Jekyll was gone out.

"I saw Mr. Hyde go in by the old dissecting-room door, Poole," he said. "Is that right, when Dr. Jekyll is from home?"

"Quite right, Mr. Utterson, sir," replied the servant. "Mr. Hyde has a key."

"Your master seems to repose a great deal of trust in that young man, Poole," resumed the other musingly.

"Yes, sir, he do indeed," said Poole. "We have all orders to obey him."

"I do not think I ever met Mr. Hyde?" asked Utterson.

"O, dear no, sir. He never *dines* here," replied the butler. "Indeed we see very little of him on this side of the house; he mostly comes and goes by the laboratory."

"Well, good-night, Poole."

"Good-night, Mr. Utterson."

And the lawyer set out homeward with a very heavy heart. "Poor Harry Jekyll," he thought, "my mind misgives me he is in deep waters! He was wild when he was young; a long while ago to be sure; but in the law of God, there is no statute of limitations. Ay, it must be that; the ghost of some old sin, the cancer of some concealed disgrace: punishment coming, *pede claudo*,[1] years after memory has forgotten and self-love condoned the fault." And the lawyer, scared by the thought, brooded awhile on his own past, groping in all the corners of memory, lest by chance some Jack-in-the-Box of an old iniquity should leap to light there. His past was fairly blameless; few men could read the rolls of their life with less apprehension; yet he was humbled to the dust by the many ill things he had done, and raised up again into a sober and fearful gratitude by the many he had come so near to doing, yet avoided. And then by a return on his former subject, he conceived a spark of hope. "This Master Hyde, if he were studied," thought he, "must have secrets of his own; black secrets, by the look of him; secrets compared to which poor Jekyll's worst would be like sunshine. Things cannot continue as they are. It turns me cold to think of this creature stealing like a thief to Harry's bedside; poor Harry, what a wakening! And the danger of it; for if this Hyde suspects the existence of the will, he may grow impatient to inherit. Ay, I must put my shoulder to the wheel—if Jekyll will but let me," he added, "if Jekyll will only let me." For once more he saw before his mind's eye, as clear as transparency, the strange clauses of the will.

1. On limping foot.

Dr. Jekyll Was Quite at Ease

A fortnight later, by excellent good fortune, the doctor gave one of his pleasant dinners to some five or six old cronies, all intelligent, reputable men and all judges of good wine; and Mr. Utterson so contrived that he remained behind after the others had departed. This was no new arrangement, but a thing that had befallen many scores of times. Where Utterson was liked, he was liked well. Hosts loved to detain the dry lawyer, when the light-hearted and loose-tongued had already their foot on the threshold; they liked to sit awhile in his unobtrusive company, practising for solitude, sobering their minds in the man's rich silence after the expense and strain of gaiety. To this rule, Dr. Jekyll was no exception; and as he now sat on the opposite side of the fire—a large, well-made, smooth-faced man of fifty, with something of a slyish cast perhaps, but every mark of capacity and kindness—you could see by his look that he cherished for Mr. Utterson a sincere and warm affection.

"I have been wanting to speak to you, Jekyll," began the latter. "You know that will of yours?"

A close observer might have gathered that the topic was distasteful; but the doctor carried it off gaily. "My poor Utterson," said he, "you are unfortunate in such a client. I never saw a man so distressed as you were by my will; unless it were that hide-bound pedant, Lanyon, at what he called my scientific heresies. O, I know he's a good fellow—you needn't frown—an excellent fellow, and I always mean to see more of him; but a hide-bound pedant for all that; an ignorant, blatant pedant. I was never more disappointed in any man than Lanyon."

"You know I never approved of it," pursued Utterson, ruthlessly disregarding the fresh topic.

"My will? Yes, certainly, I know that," said the doctor, a trifle sharply. "You have told me so."

"Well, I tell you so again," continued the lawyer. "I have been learning something of young Hyde."

The large handsome face of Dr. Jekyll grew pale to the very lips, and there came a blackness about his eyes. "I do not care to hear more," said he. "This is a matter I thought we had agreed to drop."

"What I heard was abominable," said Utterson.

"It can make no change. You do not understand my position," returned the doctor, with a certain incoherency of manner. "I am painfully situated, Utterson; my position is a very strange—a very strange one. It is one of those affairs that cannot be mended by talking."

"Jekyll," said Utterson, "you know me; I am a man to be trusted. Make a clean breast of this in confidence; and I make no doubt I can get you out of it."

"My good Utterson," said the doctor, "this is very good of you, this is downright good of you, and I cannot find words to thank you in. I believe you fully; I would trust you before any man alive, ay, before myself, if I could make the choice; but indeed it isn't what you fancy; it is not as bad as that; and just to put your good heart at rest, I will tell you one thing: the moment I choose, I can be rid of Mr. Hyde. I give you my hand upon that; and I thank you again and again; and I will just add one little word, Utterson, that I'm sure you'll take in good part: this is a private matter, and I beg of you to let it sleep."

Utterson reflected a little, looking in the fire.

"I have no doubt you are perfectly right," he said at last, getting to his feet.

"Well, but since we have touched upon this business, and for the last time I hope," continued the doctor, "there is one point I should like you to understand. I have really a very great interest in poor Hyde. I know you have seen him; he told me so; and I fear he was rude. But I do sincerely take a great, a very great interest in that young man; and if I am taken away, Utterson, I wish you to promise me that you will bear with him and get his rights for him. I think you would, if you knew all; and it would be a weight off my mind if you would promise."

"I can't pretend that I shall ever like him," said the lawyer.

"I don't ask that," pleaded Jekyll, laying his hand upon the other's arm; "I only ask for justice; I only ask you to help him for my sake, when I am no longer here."

Utterson heaved an irrepressible sigh. "Well," said he, "I promise."

The Carew Murder Case

Nearly a year later, in the month of October, 18—, London was startled by a crime of singular ferocity and rendered all the more notable by the high position of the victim. The details were few and startling. A maid servant living alone in a house not far from the river, had gone upstairs to bed about eleven. Although a fog rolled over the city in the small hours, the early part of the night was cloudless, and the lane, which the maid's window overlooked, was brilliantly lit by the full moon. It seems she was romantically given, for she sat down upon her box, which stood immediately under the window, and fell into a dream of musing. Never (she used to say, with streaming tears, when she narrated that experience), never had she felt more at peace with all men or thought more kindly of the world. And as she so sat she became aware of an aged beautiful gentleman with white hair, drawing near along the lane; and advancing to meet him, another and very small gentleman, to whom at first she paid less attention. When they had come within speech (which was just under the maid's eyes) the older man bowed and accosted the other with a very pretty manner of politeness. It did not seem as if the subject of his address were of great importance; indeed, from his pointing, it sometimes appeared as if he were only inquiring his way; but the moon shone on his face as he spoke, and the girl was pleased to watch it, it seemed to breathe such an innocent and old-world kindness of disposition, yet with something high too, as of a well-founded self-content. Presently her eye wandered to the other, and she was surprised to recognise in him a certain Mr. Hyde, who had once visited her master and for whom she had conceived a dislike. He had in his hand a heavy cane, with which he was trifling; but he answered never a word, and seemed to listen with an ill-contained impatience. And then all of a sudden he broke out in a great flame of anger, stamping with his foot, brandishing the cane, and carrying on (as the maid described it) like a madman. The old gentleman took a step back, with the air of one very much surprised and a trifle hurt; and at that Mr. Hyde broke out of all bounds and clubbed him to the earth. And next moment, with ape-like fury, he was trampling his victim under foot and hailing down a storm of blows, under which the bones were audibly shattered and the body jumped upon the roadway. At the horror of these sights and sounds, the maid fainted.

It was two o'clock when she came to herself and called for the police. The murderer was gone long ago; but there lay his victim in the middle of the lane, incredibly mangled. The stick with which the deed had been done, although it was of some rare and very tough and heavy wood, had broken in the middle under the stress of this insensate cruelty; and one splintered half had rolled in the neighbouring gutter—the other, without doubt, had been carried away by the murderer. A purse and gold watch were found upon the victim; but no cards or papers, except a sealed and stamped envelope, which he had been probably carrying to the post, and which bore the name and address of Mr. Utterson.

This was brought to the lawyer the next morning, before he was out of bed; and he had no sooner seen it, and been told the circumstances, than he shot out a solemn lip. "I shall say nothing till I have seen the body," said he; "this may be very serious. Have the kindness to wait while I dress." And with the same grave countenance he hurried through his breakfast and drove to the police station, whither the body had been carried. As soon as he came into the cell, he nodded.

"Yes," said he, "I recognise him. I am sorry to say that this is Sir Danvers Carew."

"Good God, sir," exclaimed the officer, "is it possible?" And the next moment his eye lighted up with professional ambition. "This will make a deal of noise," he said. "And perhaps you can help us to the man." And he briefly narrated what the maid had seen, and showed the broken stick.

Mr. Utterson had already quailed at the name of Hyde; but when the stick was laid before him, he could doubt no longer; broken and battered as it was, he recognised it for one that he had himself presented many years before to Henry Jekyll.

"Is this Mr. Hyde a person of small stature?" he inquired.

"Particularly small and particularly wicked-looking, is what the maid calls him," said the officer.

Mr. Utterson reflected; and then, raising his head, "If you will come with me in my cab," he said, "I think I can take you to his house."

It was by this time about nine in the morning, and the first fog of the season. A great chocolate-coloured pall lowered over heaven, but the wind was continually charging and routing these embattled vapours; so that as the cab crawled from street to street, Mr. Utterson beheld a marvelous number of degrees and hues of twilight; for here it would be dark like the back-end of evening; and there would be a glow of a rich, lurid brown, like the light of some strange conflagration; and here, for a moment, the fog would be quite broken up, and a haggard shaft of daylight would glance in between the swirling wreaths. The dismal quarter of Soho seen under these changing glimpses, with its muddy ways, and slatternly passengers, and its lamps, which had never been extinguished or had been kindled afresh to combat this mournful reinvasion of darkness, seemed, in the lawyer's eyes, like a district of some city in a nightmare. The thoughts of his mind, besides, were of the gloomiest dye; and when he glanced at the companion of his drive, he was conscious of some touch of that terror of the law and the law's officers, which may at times assail the most honest.

As the cab drew up before the address indicated, the fog lifted a little and showed him a dingy street, a gin palace, a low French eating house, a shop for the retail of penny numbers[2] and twopenny salads, many ragged children huddled in the doorways, and many women of many different nationalities passing out, key in hand, to have a morning glass; and the next moment the fog settled down again upon that part, as brown as umber, and cut him off from his blackguardly surroundings. This was the home of Henry Jekyll's favourite; of a man who was heir to a quarter of a million sterling.

An ivory-faced and silvery-haired old woman opened the door. She had an evil face, smoothed by hypocrisy: but her manners were excellent. Yes, she said, this was Mr. Hyde's, but he was not at home; he had been in that night very late, but he had gone away again in less than an hour; there was nothing strange in that; his habits were very irregular, and he was often absent; for instance, it was nearly two months since she had seen him till yesterday.

"Very well, then, we wish to see his rooms," said the lawyer; and when the woman begin to declare it was impossible, "I had better tell you who this person is," he added. "This is Inspector Newcomen of Scotland Yard."

A flash of odious joy appeared upon the woman's face. "Ah!" said she, "he is in trouble! What has he done?"

Mr. Utterson and the inspector exchanged glances. "He don't seem a very popular character," observed the latter. "And now, my good woman, just let me and this gentleman have a look about us."

In the whole extent of the house, which but for the old woman remained otherwise empty, Mr. Hyde had only used a couple of rooms; but these were furnished with luxury and good taste. A closet was filled with wine; the plate was of silver, the napery elegant; a good picture hung upon the walls, a gift (as Utterson supposed) from Henry Jekyll, who was much of a connoisseur; and the carpets were of many plies and agreeable in colour. At this moment, however, the rooms bore every mark of having been recently and hurriedly ransacked; clothes lay about the floor, with their pockets inside out; lock-fast drawers stood open; and on the hearth there lay a pile of grey ashes, as though many papers had been burned. From these embers the inspector disinterred the butt end of a green cheque book, which had resisted the action of the fire; the other half of the stick was found behind the door; and as this clinched his suspicions, the officer declared himself delighted. A visit to the bank, where several thousand pounds were found to be lying to the murderer's credit, completed his gratification.

"You may depend upon it, sir," he told Mr. Utterson: "I have him in my hand. He must have lost his head, or he never would have left the stick or, above all, burned the cheque book. Why, money's life to the man. We have nothing to do but wait for him at the bank, and get out the handbills."

This last, however, was not so easy of accomplishment; for Mr. Hyde had numbered few familiars—even the master of the servant maid had only seen him twice; his family could nowhere be traced; he had never

2. Sensational popular novels were published in small sections or numbers that sold cheaply. There were 240 pennies to the British pound sterling which was then roughly five American dollars. Though it is difficult to give exact modern equivalents, the differ- ence between two cents for the number, four cents for the salads, and a million and a quarter dollars ("a quarter of a million sterling," below) may give some idea of the proportions.

been photographed; and the few who could describe him differed widely, as common observers will. Only on one point were they agreed; and that was the haunting sense of unexpressed deformity with which the fugitive impressed his beholders.

Incident of the Letter

It was late in the afternoon, when Mr. Utterson found his way to Dr. Jekyll's door, where he was at once admitted by Poole, and carried down by the kitchen offices and across a yard which had once been a garden, to the building which was indifferently known as the laboratory or dissecting rooms. The doctor had bought the house from the heirs of a celebrated surgeon; and his own tastes being rather chemical than anatomical, had changed the destination of the block at the bottom of the garden. It was the first time that the lawyer had been received in that part of his friend's quarters; and he eyed the dingy, windowless structure with curiosity, and gazed round with a distasteful sense of strangeness as he crossed the theatre,[3] once crowded with eager students and now lying gaunt and silent, the tables laden with chemical apparatus, the floor strewn with crates and littered with packing straw, and the light falling dimly through the foggy cupola. At the further end, a flight of stairs mounted to a door covered with red baize; and through this, Mr. Utterson was at last received into the doctor's cabinet. It was a large room fitted round with glass presses,[4] furnished, among other things, with a cheval-glass and a business table, and looking out upon the court by three dusty windows barred with iron. The fire burned in the grate; a lamp was set lighted on the chimney shelf, for even in the houses the fog began to lie thickly; and there, close up to the warmth, sat Dr. Jekyll, looking deadly sick. He did not rise to meet his visitor, but held out a cold hand and bade him welcome in a changed voice.

"And now," said Mr. Utterson, as soon as Poole had left them, "you have heard the news?"

The doctor shuddered. "They were crying it in the square," he said. "I heard them in my dining-room."

"One word," said the lawyer. "Carew was my client, but so are you, and I want to know what I am doing. You have not been mad enough to hide this fellow?"

"Utterson, I swear to God," cried the doctor, "I swear to God I will never set eyes on him again. I bind my honour to you that I am done with him in this world. It is all at an end. And indeed he does not want my help; you do not know him as I do; he is safe, he is quite safe; mark my words, he will never more be heard of."

The lawyer listened gloomily; he did not like his friend's feverish manner. "You seem pretty sure of him," said he; "and for your sake, I hope you may be right. If it came to a trial, your name might appear."

"I am quite sure of him," replied Jekyll; "I have grounds for certainty that I cannot share with anyone. But there is one thing on which you may advise me. I have—I have received a letter; and I am at a loss whether I should show it to the police. I should like to leave it in your hands, Utterson; you would judge wisely, I am sure; I have so great a trust in you."

3. I.e., surgical theater, where lectures were held and autopsies and operations performed before medi-   cal students.
4. Cases, here used for holding chemicals.

"You fear, I suppose, that it might lead to his detection?" asked the lawyer.

"No," said the other. "I cannot say that I care what becomes of Hyde; I am quite done with him. I was thinking of my own character, which this hateful business has rather exposed."

Utterson ruminated awhile; he was surprised at his friend's selfishness, and yet relieved by it. "Well," said he, at last, "let me see the letter."

The letter was written in an odd, upright hand and signed "Edward Hyde": and it signified, briefly enough, that the writer's benefactor, Dr. Jekyll, whom he had long so unworthily repaid for a thousand generosities, need labour under no alarm for his safety, as he had means of escape on which he placed a sure dependence. The lawyer liked this letter well enough; it put a better colour on the intimacy than he had looked for; and he blamed himself for some of his past suspicions.

"Have you the envelope?" he asked.

"I burned it," replied Jekyll, "before I thought what I was about. But it bore no postmark. The note was handed in."

"Shall I keep this and sleep upon it?" asked Utterson.

"I wish you to judge for me entirely," was the reply. "I have lost confidence in myself."

"Well, I shall consider," returned the lawyer. "And now one word more: it was Hyde who dictated the terms in your will about that disappearance?"

The doctor seemed seized with a qualm of faintness; he shut his mouth tight and nodded.

"I knew it," said Utterson. "He meant to murder you. You had a fine escape."

"I have had what is far more to the purpose," returned the doctor solemnly; "I have had a lesson—O God, Utterson, what a lesson I have had!" And he covered his face for a moment with his hands.

On his way out, the lawyer stopped and had a word or two with Poole. "By the bye," said he, "there was a letter handed in to-day: what was the messenger like?" But Poole was positive nothing had come except by post; "and only circulars by that," he added.

This news sent off the visitor with his fears renewed. Plainly the letter had come by the laboratory door; possibly, indeed, it had been written in the cabinet; and if that were so, it must be differently judged, and handled with the more caution. The newsboys, as he went, were crying themselves hoarse along the footways: "Special edition. Shocking murder of an M.P."[5] That was the funeral oration of one friend and client; and he could not help a certain apprehension lest the good name of another should be sucked down in the eddy of the scandal. It was, at least, a ticklish decision that he had to make; and self-reliant as he was by habit, he began to cherish a longing for advice. It was not to be had directly; but perhaps, he thought, it might be fished for.

Presently after, he sat on one side of his own hearth, with Mr. Guest, his head clerk, upon the other, and midway between, at a nicely calculated distance from the fire, a bottle of a particular old wine that had long dwelt unsunned in the foundations of his house. The fog still slept on the wing above the drowned city, where the lamps glimmered like car-

5. Member of Parliament.

buncles; and through the muffle and smother of these fallen clouds, the procession of the town's life was still rolling in through the great arteries with a sound as of a mighty wind. But the room was gay with firelight. In the bottle the acids were long ago resolved; the imperial dye had softened with time, as the colour grows richer in stained windows; and the glow of hot autumn afternoons on hillside vineyards, was ready to be set free and to disperse the fogs of London. Insensibly the lawyer melted. There was no man from whom he kept fewer secrets than Mr. Guest; and he was not always sure that he kept as many as he meant. Guest had often been on business to the doctor's; he knew Poole; he could scarce have failed to hear of Mr. Hyde's familiarity about the house; he might draw conclusions: was it not as well, then, that he should see a letter which put that mystery to rights? and above all since Guest, being a great student and critic of handwriting, would consider the step natural and obliging? The clerk, besides, was a man of counsel; he could scarce read so strange a document without dropping a remark; and by that remark Mr. Utterson might shape his future course.

"This is a sad business about Sir Danvers," he said.

"Yes, sir, indeed. It has elicited a great deal of public feeling," returned Guest. "The man, of course, was mad."

"I should like to hear your views on that," replied Utterson. "I have a document here in his handwriting; it is between ourselves, for I scarce know what to do about it; it is an ugly business at the best. But there it is; quite in your way: a murderer's autograph."

Guest's eyes brightened, and he sat down at once and studied it with passion. "No sir," he said: "not mad; but it is an odd hand."

"And by all accounts a very odd writer," added the lawyer.

Just then the servant entered with a note.

"Is that from Dr. Jekyll, sir?" inquired the clerk. "I thought I knew the writing. Anything private, Mr. Utterson?"

"Only an invitation to dinner. Why? Do you want to see it?"

"One moment. I thank you, sir;" and the clerk laid the two sheets of paper alongside and sedulously compared their contents. "Thank you, sir," he said at last, returning both; "it's a very interesting autograph."

There was a pause, during which Mr. Utterson struggled with himself. "Why did you compare them, Guest?" he inquired suddenly.

"Well, sir," returned the clerk, "there's a rather singular resemblance; the two hands are in many points identical; only differently sloped."

"Rather quaint," said Utterson.

"It is, as you say, rather quaint," returned Guest.

"I wouldn't speak of this note, you know," said the master.

"No, sir," said the clerk. "I understand."

But no sooner was Mr. Utterson alone that night, than he locked the note into his safe, where it reposed from that time forward. "What!" he thought. "Henry Jekyll forge for a murderer!" And his blood ran cold in his veins.

Remarkable Incident of Dr. Lanyon

Time ran on; thousands of pounds were offered in reward, for the death of Sir Danvers was resented as a public injury; but Mr. Hyde had disappeared out of the ken of the police as though he had never existed. Much of his past was unearthed, indeed, and all disreputable: tales came out of the man's cruelty, at once so callous and violent; of his vile life, of his strange associates, of the hatred that seemed to have surrounded his career; but of his present whereabouts, not a whisper. From the time he had left the house in Soho on the morning of the murder, he was simply blotted out; and gradually, as time drew on, Mr. Utterson began to recover from the hotness of his alarm, and to grow more at quiet with himself. The death of Sir Danvers was, to his way of thinking, more than paid for by the disappearance of Mr. Hyde. Now that that evil influence had been withdrawn, a new life began for Dr. Jekyll. He came out of his seclusion, renewed relations with his friends, became once more their familiar guest and entertainer; and whilst he had always been known for charities, he was now no less distinguished for religion. He was busy, he was much in the open air, he did good; his face seemed to open and brighten, as if with an inward consciousness of service; and for more than two months, the doctor was at peace.

On the 8th of January Utterson had dined at the doctor's with a small party; Lanyon had been there; and the face of the host had looked from one to the other as in the old days when the trio were inseparable friends. On the 12th, and again on the 14th, the door was shut against the lawyer. "The doctor was confined to the house," Poole said, "and saw no one." On the 15th, he tried again, and was again refused; and having now been used for the last two months to see his friend almost daily, he found this return of solitude to weigh upon his spirits. The fifth night he had in Guest to dine with him; and the sixth he betook himself to Dr. Lanyon's.

There at least he was not denied admittance; but when he came in, he was shocked at the change which had taken place in the doctor's appearance. He had his death-warrant written legibly upon his face. The rosy man had grown pale; his flesh had fallen away; he was visibly balder and older; and yet it was not so much these tokens of a swift physical decay that arrested the lawyer's notice, as a look in the eye and quality of manner that seemed to testify to some deep-seated terror of the mind. It was unlikely that the doctor should fear death; and yet that was what Utterson was tempted to suspect. "Yes," he thought; "he is a doctor, he must know his own state and that his days are counted; and the knowledge is more than he can bear." And yet when Utterson remarked on his ill-looks, it was with an air of great firmness that Lanyon declared himself a doomed man.

"I have had a shock," he said, "and I shall never recover. It is a question of weeks. Well, life has been pleasant; I liked it; yes, sir, I used to like it. I sometimes think if we knew all, we should be more glad to get away."

"Jekyll is ill, too," observed Utterson. "Have you seen him?"

But Lanyon's face changed, and he held up a trembling hand. "I wish to see or hear no more of Dr. Jekyll," he said in a loud, unsteady voice. "I am quite done with that person; and I beg that you will spare me any allusion to one whom I regard as dead."

"Tut-tut," said Mr. Utterson; and then after a considerable pause, "Can't I do anything?" he inquired. "We are three very old friends, Lanyon; we shall not live to make others."

"Nothing can be done," returned Lanyon; "ask himself."

"He will not see me," said the lawyer.

"I am not surprised at that," was the reply. "Some day, Utterson, after I am dead, you may perhaps come to learn the right and wrong of this. I cannot tell you. And in the meantime, if you can sit and talk with me of other things, for God's sake, stay and do so; but if you cannot keep clear of this accursed topic, then in God's name, go, for I cannot bear it."

As soon as he got home, Utterson sat down and wrote to Jekyll, complaining of his exclusion from the house, and asking the cause of this unhappy break with Lanyon; and the next day brought him a long answer, often very pathetically worded, and sometimes darkly mysterious in drift. The quarrel with Lanyon was incurable. "I do not blame our old friend," Jekyll wrote, "but I share his view that we must never meet. I mean from henceforth to lead a life of extreme seclusion; you must not be surprised, nor must you doubt my friendship, if my door is often shut even to you. You must suffer me to go my own dark way. I have brought on myself a punishment and a danger that I cannot name. If I am the chief of sinners, I am the chief of sufferers also. I could not think that this earth contained a place for sufferings and terrors so unmanning; and you can do but one thing, Utterson, to lighten this destiny, and that is to respect my silence." Utterson was amazed; the dark influence of Hyde had been withdrawn, the doctor had returned to his old tasks and amities; a week ago, the prospect had smiled with every promise of a cheerful and an honoured age; and now in a moment, friendship, and peace of mind, and the whole tenor of his life were wrecked. So great and unprepared a change pointed to madness; but in view of Lanyon's manner and words, there must lie for it some deeper ground.

A week afterwards Dr. Lanyon took to his bed, and in something less than a fortnight he was dead. The night after the funeral, at which he had been sadly affected, Utterson locked the door of his business room, and sitting there by the light of a melancholy candle, drew out and set before him an envelope addressed by the hand and sealed with the seal of his dead friend. "PRIVATE: for the hands of G. J. Utterson ALONE, and in case of his predecease[6] to be destroyed unread," so it was emphatically superscribed; and the lawyer dreaded to behold the contents. "I have buried one friend to-day," he thought: "what if this should cost me another?" And then he condemned the fear as a disloyalty, and broke the seal. Within there was another enclosure, likewise sealed, and marked upon the cover as "not to be opened till the death or disappearance of Dr. Henry Jekyll." Utterson could not trust his eyes. Yes, it was disappearance; here again, as in the mad will which he had long ago restored to its author, here again were the idea of a disappearance and the name of Henry Jekyll bracketted. But in the will, that idea had sprung from the sinister suggestion of the man Hyde; it was set there with a purpose all too plain and horrible. Written by the hand of Lanyon, what should it mean? A great curiosity came on the trustee, to disregard the prohibition and dive at once to the bottom of these mysteries; but professional honour and faith to his dead friend were stringent obligations; and the packet slept in the inmost corner of his private safe.

It is one thing to mortify curiosity, another to conquer it; and it may be doubted if, from that day forth, Utterson desired the society of his surviving friend with the same eagerness. He thought of him kindly; but his

6. I.e., if Utterson were to die before Lanyon.

thoughts were disquieted and fearful. He went to call indeed; but he was perhaps relieved to be denied admittance; perhaps, in his heart, he preferred to speak with Poole upon the doorstep and surrounded by the air and sounds of the open city, rather than to be admitted into that house of voluntary bondage, and to sit and speak with its inscrutable recluse. Poole had, indeed, no very pleasant news to communicate. The doctor, it appeared, now more than ever confined himself to the cabinet over the laboratory, where he would sometimes even sleep; he was out of spirits, he had grown very silent, he did not read; it seemed as if he had something on his mind. Utterson became so used to the unvarying character of these reports, that he fell off little by little in the frequency of his visits.

Incident at the Window

It chanced on Sunday, when Mr. Utterson was on his usual walk with Mr. Enfield, that their way lay once again through the by-street; and that when they came in front of the door, both stopped to gaze on it.

"Well," said Enfield, "that story's at an end at least. We shall never see more of Mr. Hyde."

"I hope not," said Utterson. "Did I ever tell you that I once saw him, and shared your feeling of repulsion?"

"It was impossible to do the one without the other," returned Enfield. "And by the way, what an ass you must have thought me, not to know that this was a back way to Dr. Jekyll's! It was partly your own fault that I found it out, even when I did."

"So you found it out, did you?" said Utterson. "But if that be so, we may step into the court and take a look at the windows. To tell you the truth, I am uneasy about poor Jekyll; and even outside, I feel as if the presence of a friend might do him good."

The court was very cool and a little damp, and full of premature twilight, although the sky, high up overhead, was still bright with sunset. The middle one of the three windows was half-way open; and sitting close beside it, taking the air with an infinite sadness of mien, like some disconsolate prisoner, Utterson saw Dr. Jekyll.

"What! Jekyll!" he cried. "I trust you are better."

"I am very low, Utterson," replied the doctor drearily, "very low. It will not last long, thank God."

"You stay too much indoors," said the lawyer. "You should be out, whipping up the circulation like Mr. Enfield and me. (This is my cousin— Mr. Enfield—Dr. Jekyll.) Come now; get your hat and take a quick turn with us."

"You are very good," sighed the other. "I should like to very much; but no, no, no, it is quite impossible; I dare not. But indeed, Utterson, I am very glad to see you; this is really a great pleasure; I would ask you and Mr. Enfield up, but the place is really not fit."

"Why then," said the lawyer, good-naturedly, "the best thing we can do is to stay down here and speak with you from where we are."

"That is just what I was about to venture to propose," returned the doctor with a smile. But the words were hardly uttered, before the smile was struck out of his face and succeeded by an expression of such abject terror and despair, as froze the very blood of the two gentlemen below. They saw it but for a glimpse for the window was instantly thrust down;

but that glimpse had been sufficient, and they turned and left the court without a word. In silence, too, they traversed the by-street; and it was not until they had come into a neighbouring thoroughfare, where even upon a Sunday there were still some stirrings of life, that Mr. Utterson at last turned and looked at his companion. They were both pale; and there was an answering horror in their eyes.

"God forgive us, God forgive us," said Mr. Utterson.

But Mr. Enfield only nodded his head very seriously, and walked on once more in silence.

The Last Night

Mr. Utterson was sitting by his fireside one evening after dinner, when he was surprised to receive a visit from Poole.

"Bless me, Poole, what brings you here?" he cried; and then taking a second look at him, "What ails you?" he added; "is the doctor ill?"

"Mr. Utterson," said the man, "there is something wrong."

"Take a seat, and here is a glass of wine for you," said the lawyer. "Now, take your time, and tell me plainly what you want."

"You know the doctor's ways, sir," replied Poole, "and how he shuts himself up. Well, he's shut up again in the cabinet; and I don't like it sir—I wish I may die if I like it. Mr. Utterson, sir, I'm afraid."

"Now, my good man," said the lawyer, "be explicit. What are you afraid of."

"I've been afraid for about a week," returned Poole, doggedly disregarding the question, "and I can bear it no more."

The man's appearance amply bore out his words; his manner was altered for the worse; and except for the moment when he had first announced his terror, he had not once looked the lawyer in the face. Even now, he sat with the glass of wine untasted on his knee, and his eyes directed to a corner of the floor. "I can bear it no more," he repeated.

"Come," said the lawyer, "I see you have some good reason, Poole; I see there is something seriously amiss. Try to tell me what it is."

"I think there's been foul play," said Poole, hoarsely.

"Foul play!" cried the lawyer, a good deal frightened and rather inclined to be irritated in consequence. "What foul play! What does the man mean?"

"I daren't say, sir," was the answer; "but will you come along with me and see for yourself?"

Mr. Utterson's only answer was to rise and get his hat and greatcoat; but he observed with wonder the greatness of the relief that appeared upon the butler's face, and perhaps with no less, that the wine was still untasted when he set it down to follow.

It was a wild, cold, seasonable night of March, with a pale moon, lying on her back as though the wind had tilted her, and a flying wrack[7] of the most diaphanous and lawny texture. The wind made talking difficult, and flecked the blood into the face. It seemed to have swept the streets unusually bare of passengers, besides; for Mr. Utterson thought he had never seen that part of London so deserted. He could have wished it otherwise;

---

7. Mass of broken clouds driven by the wind.

never in his life had he been conscious of so sharp a wish to see and touch his fellow-creatures; for struggle as he might, there was borne in upon his mind a crushing anticipation of calamity. The square, when they got there, was full of wind and dust, and the thin trees in the garden were lashing themselves along the railing. Poole, who had kept all the way a pace or two ahead, now pulled up in the middle of the pavement, and in spite of the biting weather, took off his hat and mopped his brow with a red pocket-handkerchief. But for all the hurry of his coming, these were not the dews of exertion that he wiped away, but the moisture of some strangling anguish; for his face was white and his voice, when he spoke, harsh and broken.

"Well, sir," he said, "here we are, and God grant there be nothing wrong."

"Amen, Poole," said the lawyer.

Thereupon the servant knocked in a very guarded manner; the door was opened on the chain; and a voice asked from within, "Is that you, Poole?"

"It's all right," said Poole. "Open the door."

The hall, when they entered it, was brightly lighted up; the fire was built high; and about the hearth the whole of the servants, men and women, stood huddled together like a flock of sheep. At the sight of Mr. Utterson, the housemaid broke into hysterical whimpering; and the cook, crying out "Bless God! it's Mr. Utterson," ran forward as if to take him in her arms.

"What, what? Are you all here?" said the lawyer peevishly. "Very irregular, very unseemly; your master would be far from pleased."

"They're all afraid," said Poole.

Blank silence followed, no one protesting; only the maid lifted up her voice and now wept loudly.

"Hold your tongue!" Poole said to her, with a ferocity of accent that testified to his own jangled nerves; and indeed, when the girl had so suddenly raised the note of her lamentation, they had all started and turned towards the inner door with faces of dreadful expectation. "And now," continued the butler, addressing the knife-boy,[8] "reach me a candle, and we'll get this through hands at once." And then he begged Mr. Utterson to follow him, and led the way to the back garden.

"Now, sir," said he, "you come as gently as you can. I want you to hear, and I don't want you to be heard. And see here, sir, if by any chance he was to ask you in, don't go."

Mr. Utterson's nerves, at this unlooked-for termination, gave a jerk that nearly threw him from his balance; but he recollected his courage and followed the butler into the laboratory building and through the surgical theatre, with its lumber of crates and bottles, to the foot of the stair. Here Poole motioned him to stand on one side and listen; while he himself, setting down the candle and making a great and obvious call on his resolution, mounted the steps and knocked with a somewhat uncertain hand on the red baize of the cabinet door.

"Mr. Utterson, sir, asking to see you," he called; and even as he did so, once more violently signed to the lawyer to give ear.

8. A boy employed to clean table knives.

A voice answered from within: "Tell him I cannot see anyone," it said complainingly.

"Thank you, sir," said Poole, with a note of something like triumph in his voice; and taking up his candle, he led Mr. Utterson back across the yard and into the great kitchen, where the fire was out and the beetles were leaping on the floor.

"Sir," he said, looking Mr. Utterson in the eyes, "was that my master's voice?"

"It seems much changed," replied the lawyer, very pale, but giving look for look.

"Changed? Well, yes, I think so," said the butler. "Have I been twenty years in this man's house, to be deceived about his voice? No, sir; master's made away with; he was made away with eight days ago, when we heard him cry out upon the name of God; and who's in there instead of him, and why it stays there, is a thing that cries to Heaven, Mr. Utterson!"

"This is a very strange tale, Poole; this is rather a wild tale, my man," said Mr. Utterson, biting his finger. "Suppose it were as you suppose, supposing Dr. Jekyll to have been—well, murdered, what could induce the murderer to stay? That won't hold water; it doesn't commend itself to reason."

"Well, Mr. Utterson, you are a hard man to satisfy, but I'll do it yet," said Poole. "All this last week (you must know) him, or it, whatever it is that lives in that cabinet, has been crying night and day for some sort of medicine and cannot get it to his mind. It was sometimes his way—the master's, that is—to write his orders on a sheet of paper and throw it on the stair. We've had nothing else this week back; nothing but papers, and a closed door, and the very meals left there to be smuggled in when nobody was looking. Well, sir, every day, ay, and twice and thrice in the same day, there have been orders and complaints, and I have been sent flying to all the wholesale chemists in town. Every time I brought the stuff back, there would be another paper telling me to return it, because it was not pure, and another order to a different firm. This drug is wanted bitter bad, sir, whatever for."

"Have you any of these papers?" asked Mr. Utterson.

Poole felt in his pocket and handed out a crumpled note, which the lawyer, bending nearer to the candle, carefully examined. Its contents ran thus: "Dr. Jekyll presents his compliments to Messrs. Maw. He assures them that their last sample is impure and quite useless for his present purpose. In the year 18—, Dr. J. purchased a somewhat large quantity from Messrs. M. He now begs them to search with most sedulous care, and should any of the same quality be left, to forward it to him at once. Expense is no consideration. The importance of this to Dr. J. can hardly be exaggerated." So far the letter had run composedly enough, but here with a sudden splutter of the pen, the writer's emotion had broken loose. "For God's sake," he added, "find me some of the old."

"This is a strange note," said Mr. Utterson; and then sharply, "How do you come to have it open?"

"The man at Maw's was main angry, sir, and he threw it back to me like so much dirt," returned Poole.

"This is unquestionably the doctor's hand, do you know?" resumed the lawyer.

"I thought it looked like it," said the servant rather sulkily; and then, with another voice, "But what matters hand of write?"[9] he said. "I've seen him!"

"Seen him?" repeated Mr. Utterson. "Well?"

"That's it!" said Poole. "It was this way. I came suddenly into the theatre from the garden. It seems he had slipped out to look for this drug or whatever it is; for the cabinet door was open, and there he was at the far end of the room digging among the crates. He looked up when I came in, gave a kind of cry, and whipped upstairs into the cabinet. It was but for one minute that I saw him, but the hair stood upon my head like quills. Sir, if that was my master, why had he a mask upon his face? If it was my master, why did he cry out like a rat, and run from me? I have served him long enough. And then . . ." The man paused and passed his hand over his face.

"These are all very strange circumstances," said Mr. Utterson, "but I think I begin to see daylight. Your master, Poole, is plainly seized with one of those maladies that both torture and deform the sufferer; hence, for aught I know, the alteration of his voice; hence the mask and the avoidance of his friends; hence his eagerness to find this drug, by means of which the poor soul retains some hope of ultimate recovery—God grant that he be not deceived! There is my explanation; it is sad enough, Poole, ay, and appalling to consider; but it is plain and natural, hangs well together, and delivers us from all exorbitant alarms."

"Sir," said the butler, turning to a sort of mottled pallor, "that thing was not my master, and there's the truth. My master"—here he looked round him and began to whisper—"is a tall, fine build of a man, and this was more of a dwarf." Utterson attempted to protest. "O, sir," cried Poole, "do you think I do not know my master after twenty years? Do you think I do not know where his head comes to in the cabinet door, where I saw him every morning of my life? No, sir, that thing in the mask was never Dr. Jekyll—God knows what it was, but it was never Dr. Jekyll; and it is the belief of my heart that there was murder done."

"Poole," replied the lawyer, "if you say that, it will become my duty to make certain. Much as I desire to spare your master's feelings, much as I am puzzled by this note which seems to prove him to be still alive, I shall consider it my duty to break in that door."

"Ah, Mr. Utterson, that's talking!" cried the butler.

"And now comes the second question," resumed Utterson: "Who is going to do it?"

"Why, you and me, sir," was the undaunted reply.

"That's very well said," returned the lawyer; "and whatever comes of it, I shall make it my business to see you are no loser."

"There is an axe in the theatre," continued Poole; "and you might take the kitchen poker for yourself."

The lawyer took that rude but weighty instrument into his hand, and balanced it. "Do you know, Poole," he said, looking up, "that you and I are about to place ourselves in a position of some peril?"

"You may say so, sir, indeed," returned the butler.

"It is well, then, that we should be frank," said the other. "We both think more than we have said; let us make a clean breast. This masked figure that you saw, did you recognise it?"

9. Handwriting.

"Well, sir, it went so quick, and the creature was so doubled up, that I could hardly swear to that," was the answer. "But if you mean, was it Mr. Hyde?—why, yes, I think it was! You see, it was much of the same bigness; and it had the same quick, light way with it; and then who else could have got in by the laboratory door? You have not forgot, sir, that at the time of the murder he had still the key with him? But that's not all. I don't know, Mr. Utterson, if you ever met this Mr. Hyde?"

"Yes," said the lawyer, "I once spoke with him."

"Then you must know as well as the rest of us that there was something queer about that gentleman—something that gave a man a turn—I don't know rightly how to say it, sir, beyond this: that you felt in your marrow kind of cold and thin."

"I own I felt something of what you describe," said Mr. Utterson.

"Quite so, sir," returned Poole. "Well, when that masked thing like a monkey jumped from among the chemicals and whipped into the cabinet, it went down my spine like ice. O, I know it's not evidence, Mr. Utterson; I'm book-learned enough for that; but a man has his feelings, and I give you my bible-word it was Mr. Hyde!"

"Ay, ay," said the lawyer. "My fears incline to the same point. Evil, I fear, founded—evil was sure to come—of that connection. Ay truly, I believe you; I believe poor Harry is killed; and I believe his murderer (for what purpose, God alone can tell) is still lurking in his victim's room. Well, let our name be vengeance. Call Bradshaw."

The footman came at the summons, very white and nervous.

"Pull yourself together, Bradshaw," said the lawyer. "This suspense, I know, is telling upon all of you; but it is now our intention to make an end of it. Poole, here, and I are going to force our way into the cabinet. If all is well, my shoulders are broad enough to bear the blame. Meanwhile, lest anything should really be amiss, or any malefactor seek to escape by the back, you and the boy must go round the corner with a pair of good sticks and take your post at the laboratory door. We give you ten minutes, to get to your stations."

As Bradshaw left, the lawyer looked at his watch. "And now, Poole, let us get to ours," he said; and taking the poker under his arm, led the way into the yard. The scud had banked over the moon, and it was now quite dark. The wind, which only broke in puffs and draughts into that deep well of building, tossed the light of the candle to and fro about their steps, until they came into the shelter of the theatre, where they sat down silently to wait. London hummed solemnly all around; but nearer at hand, the stillness was only broken by the sounds of a footfall moving to and fro along the cabinet floor.

"So it will walk all day, sir," whispered Poole; "ay, and the better part of the night. Only when a new sample comes from the chemist, there's a bit of a break. Ah, it's an ill conscience that's such an enemy to rest! Ah, sir, there's blood foully shed in every step of it! But hark again, a little closer—put your heart in your ears, Mr. Utterson, and tell me, is that the doctor's foot?"

The steps fell lightly and oddly, with a certain swing, for all they went so slowly; it was different indeed from the heavy creaking tread of Henry Jekyll. Utterson sighed. "Is there never anything else?" he asked.

Poole nodded. "Once," he said. "Once I heard it weeping!"

"Weeping? how's that?" said the lawyer, conscious of a sudden chill of horror.

"Weeping like a woman or a lost soul," said the butler. "I came away with that upon my heart, and I could have wept too."

But now the ten minutes drew to an end. Poole disinterred the axe from under a stack of packing straw; the candle was set upon the nearest table to light them to the attack; and they drew near with bated breath to where that patient foot was still going up and down, up and down, in the quiet of the night. "Jekyll," cried Utterson, with a loud voice, "I demand to see you." He paused a moment, but there came no reply. "I give you fair warning, our suspicions are aroused, and I must and shall see you," he resumed; "if not by fair means, then by foul—if not of your consent, then by brute force!"

"Utterson," said the voice, "for God's sake, have mercy!"

"Ah, that's not Jekyll's voice—it's Hyde's!" cried Utterson. "Down with the door, Poole!"

Poole swung the axe over his shoulder; the blow shook the building, and the red baize door leaped against the lock and hinges. A dismal screech, as of mere animal terror, rang from the cabinet. Up went the axe again, and again the panels crashed and the frame bounded; four times the blow fell; but the wood was tough and the fittings were of excellent workmanship; and it was not until the fifth, that the lock burst and the wreck of the door fell inwards on the carpet.

The besiegers, appalled by their own riot and the stillness that had succeeded, stood back a little and peered in. There lay the cabinet before their eyes in the quiet lamplight, a good fire glowing and chattering on the hearth, the kettle singing its thin strain, a drawer or two open, papers neatly set forth on the business table, and nearer the fire, the things laid out for tea; the quietest room, you would have said, and, but for the glazed presses full of chemicals, the most commonplace that night in London.

Right in the midst there lay the body of a man sorely contorted and still twitching. They drew near on tiptoe, turned it on its back and beheld the face of Edward Hyde. He was dressed in clothes far too large for him, clothes of the doctor's bigness; the cords of his face still moved with a semblance of life, but life was quite gone: and by the crushed phial in the hand and the strong smell of kernels[1] that hung upon the air, Utterson knew that he was looking on the body of a self-destroyer.

"We have come too late," he said sternly, "whether to save or punish. Hyde is gone to his account; and it only remains for us to find the body of your master."

The far greater proportion of the building was occupied by the theatre, which filled almost the whole ground storey and was lighted from above, and by the cabinet, which formed an upper storey at one end and looked upon the court. A corridor joined the theatre to the door on the by-street; and with this the cabinet communicated separately by a second flight of stairs. There were besides a few dark closets and a spacious cellar. All these they now thoroughly examined. Each closet needed but a glance, for all were empty, and all, by the dust that fell from their doors, had

---

1. Almonds, the smell of cyanide (prussic acid).

stood long unopened. The cellar, indeed, was filled with crazy lumber, mostly dating from the times of the surgeon who was Jekyll's predecesor; but even as they opened the door they were advertised of the uselessness of further search, by the fall of a perfect mat of cobweb which had for years sealed up the entrance. Nowhere was there any trace of Henry Jekyll, dead or alive.

Poole stamped on the flags of the corridor. "He must be buried here," he said, hearkening to the sound.

"Or he may have fled," said Utterson, and he turned to examine the door in the by-street. It was locked; and lying near by on the flags, they found the key, already stained with rust.

"This does not look like use," observed the lawyer.

"Use!" echoed Poole. "Do you not see, sir, it is broken? much as if a man had stamped on it."

"Ay," continued Utterson, "and the fractures, too, are rusty." The two men looked at each other with a scare. "This is beyond me, Poole," said the lawyer. "Let us go back to the cabinet."

They mounted the stair in silence, and still with an occasional awe-struck glance at the dead body, proceeded more thoroughly to examine the contents of the cabinet. At one table, there were traces of chemical work, various measured heaps of some white salt being laid on glass saucers, as though for an experiment in which the unhappy man had been prevented.

"That is the same drug that I was always bringing him," said Poole, and even as he spoke, the kettle with a startling noise boiled over.

This brought them to the fireside, where the easychair was drawn cosily up, and the tea things stood ready to the sitter's elbow, the very sugar in the cup. There were several books on a shelf; one lay beside the tea things open, and Utterson was amazed to find it a copy of pious work, for which Jekyll had several times expressed a great esteem, annotated, in his own hand, with startling blasphemies.

Next, in the course of their review of the chamber, the searchers came to the cheval-glass, into whose depths they looked with an involuntary horror. But it was so turned as to show them nothing but the rosy glow playing on the roof, the fire sparkling in a hundred repetitions along the glazed front of the presses, and their own pale and fearful countenances stooping to look in.

"This glass has seen some strange things, sir," whispered Poole.

"And surely none stranger than itself," echoed the lawyer in the same tones. "For what did Jekyll"—he caught himself up at the word with a start, and then conquering the weakness—"what could Jekyll want with it?" he said.

"You may say that!" said Poole.

Next they turned to the business table. On the desk, among the neat array of papers, a large envelope was uppermost, and bore, in the doctor's hand, the name of Mr. Utterson. The lawyer unsealed it, and several enclosures fell to the floor. The first was a will, drawn in the same eccentric terms as the one which he had returned six months before, to serve as a testament in case of death and as a deed of gift in case of disappearance; but in place of the name of Edward Hyde, the lawyer, with indescribable amazement, read the name of Gabriel John Utterson. He looked at Poole, and then back at the paper, and last of all at the dead malefactor stretched upon the carpet.

"My head goes round," he said. "He has been all these days in possession; he had no cause to like me; he must have raged to see himself displaced; and he has not destroyed this document."

He caught up the next paper; it was a brief note in the doctor's hand and dated at the top. "O Poole!" the lawyer cried, "he was alive and here this day. He cannot have been disposed of in so short a space; he must be still alive, he must have fled! And then, why fled? and how? and in that case, can we venture to declare this suicide? O, we must be careful. I foresee that we may yet involve your master in some dire catastrophe."

"Why don't you read it, sir?" asked Poole.

"Because I fear," replied the lawyer solemnly. "God grant I have no cause for it!" And with that he brought the paper to his eyes and read as follows:

"MY DEAR UTTERSON,—When this shall fall into your hands, I shall have disappeared, under what circumstances I have not the penetration to foresee, but my instinct and all the circumstances of my nameless situation tell me that the end is sure and must be early. Go then, and first read the narrative which Lanyon warned me he was to place in your hands; and if you care to hear more, turn to the confession of

"Your unworthy and unhappy friend,
                    "HENRY JEKYLL."

"There was a third enclosure?" asked Utterson.

"Here, sir," said Poole, and gave into his hands a considerable packet sealed in several places.

The lawyer put it in his pocket. "I would say nothing of this paper. If your master has fled or is dead, we may at least save his credit. It is now ten; I must go home and read these documents in quiet; but I shall be back before midnight, when we shall send for the police."

They went out, locking the door of the theatre behind them; and Utterson, once more leaving the servants gathered about the fire in the hall, trudged back to his office to read the two narratives in which this mystery was now to be explained.

Dr. Lanyon's Narrative

On the ninth of January, now four days ago, I received by the evening delivery a registered envelope, addressed in the hand of my colleague and old school companion, Henry Jekyll. I was a good deal surprised by this; for we were by no means in the habit of correspondence; I had seen the man, dined with him, indeed, the night before; and I could imagine nothing in our intercourse that should justify formality of registration. The contents increased my wonder; for this is how the letter ran:

                    "10th December, 18—.

"DEAR LANYON,—You are one of my oldest friends; and although we may have differed at times on scientific questions, I cannot remember, at least on my side, any break in our affection. There was never a day when, if you had said to me, 'Jekyll, my life, my honour, my reason, depend upon you,' I would not have sacrificed my left hand to help you. Lanyon, my life, my honour, my reason, are all at your mercy; if you fail me tonight, I am lost. You might suppose, after this preface, that I am going to ask you for something dishonourable to grant. Judge for yourself.

"I want you to postpone all other engagements for to-night—ay, even if you were summoned to the bedside of an emperor; to take a cab, unless your carriage should be actually at the door; and with this letter in your hand for consultation, to drive straight to my house. Poole, my butler, has his orders; you will find him waiting your arrival with a locksmith. The door of my cabinet is then to be forced: and you are to go in alone; to open the glazed press (letter E) on the left hand, breaking the lock if it be shut; and to draw out, *with all its contents as they stand*, the fourth drawer from the top or (which is the same thing) the third from the bottom. In my extreme distress of mind, I have a morbid fear of misdirecting you; but even if I am in error, you may know the right drawer by its contents: some powders, a phial and a paper book. This drawer I beg of you to carry back with you to Cavendish Square exactly as it stands.

"That is the first part of the service: now for the second. You should be back, if you set out at once on the receipt of this, long before midnight; but I will leave you that amount of margin, not only in the fear of one of those obstacles that can neither be prevented nor foreseen, but because an hour when your servants are in bed is to be preferred for what will then remain to do. At midnight, then, I have to ask you to be alone in your consulting room, to admit with your own hand into the house a man who will present himself in my name, and to place in his hands the drawer that you will have brought with you from my cabinet. Then you will have played your part and earned my gratitude completely. Five minutes afterwards, if you insist upon an explanation, you will have understood that these arrangements are of capital importance; and that by the neglect of one of them, fantastic as they must appear, you might have charged your conscience with my death or the shipwreck of my reason.

"Confident as I am that you will not trifle with this appeal, my heart sinks and my hand trembles at the bare thought of such a possibility. Think of me at this hour, in a strange place, labouring under a blackness of distress that no fancy can exaggerate, and yet well aware that, if you will but punctually serve me, my troubles will roll away like a story that is told. Serve me, my dear Lanyon, and save

"Your friend,
"H. J.

"P.S.—I had already sealed this up when a fresh terror struck upon my soul. It is possible that the post-office may fail me, and this letter not come into your hands until to-morrow morning. In that case, dear Lanyon, do my errand when it shall be most convenient for you in the course of the day; and once more expect my messenger at midnight. It may then already be too late; and if that night passes without event, you will know that you have seen the last of Henry Jekyll."

Upon the reading of this letter, I made sure my colleague was insane; but till that was proved beyond the possibility of doubt, I felt bound to do as he requested. The less I understood of this farrago, the less I was in a position to judge of its importance; and an appeal so worded could not be set aside without a grave responsibility. I rose accordingly from table, got into a hansom, and drove straight to Jekyll's house. The butler was awaiting my arrival; he had received by the same post as mine a registered letter of instruction, and had sent at once for a locksmith and a carpenter. The tradesmen came while we were yet speaking; and we moved in a body to old Dr. Denman's surgical theatre, from which (as you are doubtless aware) Jekyll's private cabinet is most conveniently entered. The door was very strong, the lock excellent; the carpenter avowed he would have great trouble and have to do much damage, if force were to be used; and the locksmith was near despair. But this last was a handy fellow, and after two hours' work, the door stood open. The press marked E was unlocked; and I took out the drawer, had it filled up with straw and tied in a sheet, and returned with it to Cavendish Square.

Here I proceeded to examine its contents. The powders were neatly enough made up, but not with the nicety of the dispensing chemist; so that it was plain they were of Jekyll's private manufacture: and when I opened one of the wrappers I found what seemed to me a simple crystalline salt of a white colour. The phial, to which I next turned my attention, might have been about half full of a blood-red liquor, which was highly pungent to the sense of smell and seemed to me to contain phosphorus and some volatile ether. At the other ingredients I could make no guess. The book was an ordinary version book[2] and contained little but a series of dates. These covered a period of many years, but I observed that the entries ceased nearly a year ago and quite abruptly. Here and there a brief remark was appended to a date, usually no more than a single word: "double" occurring perhaps six times in a total of several hundred entries; and once very early in the list and followed by several marks of exclamation, "total failure!!!" All this, though it whetted my curiosity, told me little that was definite. Here were a phial of some tincture, a paper of some salt, and the record of a series of experiments that had led (like too many of Jekyll's investigations) to no end of practical usefulness. How could the presence of these articles in my house affect either the honour, the sanity, or the life of my flighty colleague? If his messenger could go to one place, why could he not go to another? And even granting some impediment, why was this gentleman to be received by me in secret? The more I reflected the more convinced I grew that I was dealing with a case of cerebral disease; and though I dismissed my servants to bed, I loaded an old revolver, that I might be found in some posture of self-defence.

Twelve o'clock had scarce rung out over London, ere the knocker sounded very gently on the door. I went myself at the summons, and found a small man crouching against the pillars of the portico.

"Are you come from Dr. Jekyll?" I asked.

He told me "yes" by a constrained gesture; and when I had bidden him enter, he did not obey me without a searching backward glance into the darkness of the square. There was a policeman not far off, advancing with his bull's eye open; and at the sight, I thought my visitor started and made greater haste.

These particulars struck me, I confess, disagreeably; and as I followed him into the bright light of the consulting room, I kept my hand ready on

2. Exercise book.

my weapon. Here, at last, I had a chance of clearly seeing him. I had never set eyes on him before, so much was certain. He was small, as I have said; I was struck besides with the shocking expression of his face, with his remarkable combination of great muscular activity and great apparent debility of constitution, and—last but not least—with the odd, subjective disturbance caused by his neighbourhood. This bore some resemblance to incipient rigour, and was accompanied by a marked sinking of the pulse. At the time, I set it down to some idiosyncratic, personal distaste, and merely wondered at the acuteness of the symptoms; but I have since had reason to believe the cause to lie much deeper in the nature of man, and to turn on some nobler hinge than the principle of hatred.

This person (who had thus, from the first moment of his entrance, struck in me what I can only describe as a disgustful curiosity) was dressed in a fashion that would have made an ordinary person laughable; his clothes, that is to say, although they were of rich and sober fabric, were enormously too large for him in every measurement—the trousers hanging on his legs and rolled up to keep them from the ground, the waist of the coat below his haunches, and the collar sprawling wide upon his shoulders. Strange to relate, this ludicrous accoutrement was far from moving me to laughter. Rather, as there was something abnormal and misbegotten in the very essence of the creature that now faced me—something seizing, surprising and revolting—this fresh disparity seemed but to fit in with and to reinforce it; so that to my interest in the man's nature and character, there was added a curiosity as to his origin, his life, his fortune and status in the world.

These observations, though they have taken so great a space to be set down in, were yet the work of a few seconds. My visitor was, indeed, on fire with sombre excitement.

"Have you got it?" he cried. "Have you got it?" And so lively was his impatience that he even laid his hand upon my arm and sought to shake me.

I put him back, conscious at his touch of a certain icy pang along my blood. "Come, sir," said I. "You forget that I have not yet the pleasure of your acquaintance. Be seated, if you please." And I showed him an example, and sat down myself in my customary seat and with as fair an imitation of my ordinary manner to a patient, as the lateness of the hour, the nature of my preoccupations, and the horror I had of my visitor, would suffer me to muster.

"I beg your pardon, Dr. Lanyon," he replied civilly enough. "What you say is very well founded; and my impatience has shown its heels to my politeness. I come here at the instance of your colleague, Dr. Henry Jekyll, on a piece of business of some moment; and I understood . . ." He paused and put his hand to his throat, and I could see, in spite of his collected manner, that he was wrestling against the approaches of the hysteria—"I understood, a drawer . . ."

But here I took pity on my visitor's suspense, and some perhaps on my own growing curiosity.

"There it is, sir," said I, pointing to the drawer, where it lay on the floor behind a table and still covered with the sheet.

He sprang to it, and then paused, and laid his hand upon his heart; I could hear his teeth grate with the convulsive action of his jaws; and his face was so ghastly to see that I grew alarmed both for his life and reason. "Compose yourself," said I.

He turned a dreadful smile to me, and as if with the decision of despair, plucked away the sheet. At sight of the contents, he uttered one loud sob of such immense relief that I sat petrified. And the next moment, in a voice that was already fairly well under control, "Have you a graduated glass?" he asked.

I rose from my place with something of an effort and gave him what he asked.

He thanked me with a smiling nod, measured out a few minims of the red tincture and added one of the powders. The mixture, which was at first of a reddish hue, began, in proportion as the crystals melted, to brighten in colour, to effervesce audibly, and to throw off small fumes of vapour. Suddenly and at the same moment, the ebullition ceased and the compound changed to a dark purple, which faded again more slowly to a watery green. My visitor, who had watched these metamorphoses with a keen eye, smiled, set down the glass upon the table, and then turned and looked upon me with an air of scrutiny.

"And now," said he, "to settle what remains. Will you be wise? will you be guided? will you suffer me to take this glass in my hand and to go forth from your house without further parley? or has the greed of curiosity too much command of you? Think before you answer, for it shall be done as you decide. As you decide, you shall be left as you were before, and neither richer nor wiser, unless the sense of service rendered to a man in mortal distress may be counted as a kind of riches of the soul. Or, if you shall so prefer to choose, a new province of knowledge and new avenues to fame and power shall be laid open to you, here, in this room, upon the instant; and your sight shall be blasted by a prodigy to stagger the unbelief of Satan."

"Sir," said I, affecting a coolness that I was far from truly possessing, "you speak enigmas, and you will perhaps not wonder that I hear you with no very strong impression of belief. But I have gone too far in the way of inexplicable services to pause before I see the end."

"It is well," replied my visitor. "Lanyon, you remember your vows: what follows is under the seal of our profession. And now, you who have so long been bound to the most narrow and material views, you who have denied the virtue of transcendental medicine, you who have derided your superiors—behold!"

He put the glass to his lips and drank at one gulp. A cry followed; he reeled, staggered, clutched at the table and held on, staring with injected[3] eyes, gasping with open mouth; and as I looked there came, I thought, a change—he seemed to swell—his face became suddenly black and the features seemed to melt and alter—and the next moment, I had sprung to my feet and leaped back against the wall, my arm raised to shield me from that prodigy, my mind submerged in terror.

"O God!" I screamed, and "O God!" again and again; for there before my eyes—pale and shaken, and half fainting, and groping before him with his hands, like a man restored from death—there stood Henry Jekyll!

What he told me in the next hour, I cannot bring my mind to set on paper. I saw what I saw, I heard what I heard, and my soul sickened at it;

3. Bloodshot.

and yet now when that sight has faded from my eyes, I ask myself if I believe it, and I cannot answer. My life is shaken to its roots; sleep has left me; the deadliest terror sits by me at all hours of the day and night; and I feel that my days are numbered, and that I must die; and yet I shall die incredulous. As for the moral turpitude that man unveiled to me, even with tears of penitence, I cannot, even in memory, dwell on it without a start of horror. I will say but one thing, Utterson, and that (if you can bring your mind to credit it) will be more than enough. The creature who crept into my house that night was, on Jekyll's own confession, known by the name of Hyde and hunted for in every corner of the land as the murderer of Carew.

HASTIE LANYON

Henry Jekyll's Full Statement of the Case

I was born in the year 18— to a large fortune, endowed besides with excellent parts[4], inclined by nature to industry, fond of the respect of the wise and good among my fellow-men, and thus, as might have been supposed, with every guarantee of an honourable and distinguished future. And indeed the worst of my faults was a certain impatient gaiety of disposition, such as has made the happiness of many, but such as I found it hard to reconcile with my imperious desire to carry my head high, and wear a more than commonly grave countenance before the public. Hence it came about that I concealed my pleasures; and that when I reached years of reflection, and began to look round me and take stock of my progress and position in the world, I stood already committed to a profound duplicity of life. Many a man would have even blazoned such irregularities as I was guilty of; but from the high views that I had set before me, I regarded and hid them with an almost morbid sense of shame. It was thus rather the exacting nature of my aspirations than any particular degradation in my faults, that made me what I was, and, with even a deeper trench than in the majority of men, severed in me those provinces of good and ill which divide and compound man's dual nature. In this case, I was driven to reflect deeply and inveterately on that hard law of life, which lies at the root of religion and is one of the most plentiful springs of distress. Though so profound a double-dealer, I was in no sense a hypocrite; both sides of me were in dead earnest; I was no more myself when I laid aside restraint and plunged in shame, than when I laboured, in the eye of day, at the furtherance of knowledge or the relief of sorrow and suffering. And it chanced that the direction of my scientific studies, which led wholly towards the mystic and the transcendental, reacted and shed a strong light on this consciousness of the perennial war among my members. With every day, and from both sides of my intelligence, the moral and the intellectual, I thus drew steadily nearer to that truth, by whose partial discovery I have been doomed to such a dreadful shipwreck: that man is not truly one, but truly two. I say two, because the state of my own knowledge does not pass beyond that point. Others will follow, others will outstrip me on the same lines; and I hazard the guess that man will be ultimately known for a mere polity of multifarious, incongruous and independent denizens. I, for my part, from the nature of

---

4. Personal and mental qualities or endowments.

my life, advanced infallibly in one direction and in one direction only. It was on the moral side, and in my own person, that I learned to recognise the thorough and primitive duality of man; I saw that, of the two natures that contended in the field of my consciousness, even if I could rightly be said to be either, it was only because I was radically both; and from an early date, even before the course of my scientific discoveries had begun to suggest the most naked possibility of such a miracle, I had learned to dwell with pleasure, as a beloved daydream, on the thought of the separation of these elements. If each, I told myself, could be housed in separate identities, life would be relieved of all that was unbearable; the unjust might go his way, delivered from the aspirations and remorse of his more upright twin; and the just could walk steadfastly and securely on his upward path, doing the good things in which he found his pleasure, and no longer exposed to disgrace and penitence by the hands of this extraneous evil. It was the curse of mankind that these incongruous faggots were thus bound together—that in the agonised womb of consciousness, these polar twins should be continuously struggling. How, then, were they dissociated?

I was so far in my reflections when, as I have said, a side light began to shine upon the subject from the laboratory table. I began to perceive more deeply than it has ever yet been stated, the trembling immateriality, the mistlike transience, of this seemingly so solid body in which we walk attired. Certain agents I found to have the power to shake and pluck back that fleshy vestment, even as a wind might toss the curtains of a pavilion. For two good reasons, I will not enter deeply into this scientific branch of my confession. First, because I have been made to learn that the doom and burthen of our life is bound for ever on man's shoulders, and when the attempt is made to cast it off, it but returns upon us with more unfamiliar and more awful pressure. Second, because, as my narrative will make, alas! too evident, my discoveries were incomplete. Enough, then, that I not only recognised my natural body from the mere aura and effulgence of certain of the powers that made up my spirit, but managed to compound a drug by which these powers should be dethroned from their supremacy, and a second form and countenance substituted, none the less natural to me because they were the expression, and bore the stamp of lower elements in my soul.

I hesitated long before I put this theory to the test of practice. I knew well that I risked death; for any drug that so potently controlled and shook the very fortress of identity, might, by the least scruple of an overdose or at the least inopportunity in the moment of exhibition,[5] utterly blot out that immaterial tabernacle which I looked to it to change. But the temptation of a discovery so singular and profound at last overcame the suggestions of alarm. I had long since prepared my tincture; I purchased at once, from a firm of wholesale chemists, a large quantity of a particular salt which I knew, from my experiments, to be the last ingredient required; and late one accursed night, I compounded the elements, watched them boil and smoke together in the glass, and when the ebullition had subsided, with a strong glow of courage, drank off the potion.

The most racking pangs succeeded: a grinding in the bones, deadly nausea, and a horror of the spirit that cannot be exceeded at the hour of

5. In medicine, administration, as of a remedy, etc. *Scruple:* 20 grains or 1/3 dram.

birth or death. Then these agonies began swiftly to subside, and I came to myself as if out of a great sickness. There was something strange in my sensations, something indescribably new and, from its very novelty, incredibly sweet. I felt younger, lighter, happier in body; within I was conscious of a heady recklessness, a current of disordered sensual images running like a millrace in my fancy, a dissolution of the bonds of obligation, an unknown but not an innocent freedom of the soul. I knew myself, at the first breath of this new life, to be more wicked, tenfold more wicked, sold a slave to my original evil; and the thought, in that moment, braced and delighted me like wine. I stretched out my hands, exulting in the freshness of these sensations; and in the act, I was suddenly aware that I had lost in stature.

There was no mirror, at that date, in my room; that which stands beside me as I write, was brought there later on and for the very purpose of these transformations. The night, however, was far gone into the morning—the morning, black as it was, was nearly ripe for the conception of the day—the inmates of my house were locked in the most rigorous hours of slumber; and I determined, flushed as I was with hope and triumph, to venture in my new shape as far as to my bedroom. I crossed the yard, wherein the constellations looked down upon me, I could have thought, with wonder, the first creature of that sort that their unsleeping vigilance had yet disclosed to them; I stole through the corridors, a stranger in my own house; and coming to my room, I saw for the first time the appearance of Edward Hyde.

I must here speak by theory alone, saying not that which I know, but that which I suppose to be most probable. The evil side of my nature, to which I had now transferred the stamping efficacy, was less robust and less developed than the good which I had just deposed. Again, in the course of my life, which had been, after all, nine tenths a life of effort, virtue and control, it had been much less exercised and much less exhausted. And hence, as I think, it came about that Edward Hyde was so much smaller, slighter and younger than Henry Jekyll. Even as good shone upon the countenance of the one, evil was written broadly and plainly on the face of the other. Evil besides (which I must still believe to be the lethal side of man) had left on that body an imprint of deformity and decay. And yet when I looked upon that ugly idol in the glass, I was conscious of no repugnance, rather of a leap of welcome. This, too, was myself. It seemed natural and human. In my eyes it bore a livelier image of the spirit, it seemed more express[6] and single, than the imperfect and divided countenance I had been hitherto accustomed to call mine. And in so far I was doubtless right. I have observed that when I wore the semblance of Edward Hyde, none could come near to me at first without a visible misgiving of the flesh. This, as I take it, was because all human beings, as we meet them, are commingled out of good and evil: and Edward Hyde, alone in the ranks of mankind, was pure evil.

I lingered but a moment at the mirror: the second and conclusive experiment had yet to be attempted; it yet remained to be seen if I had lost my identity beyond redemption and must flee before daylight from a house that was no longer mine; and hurrying back to my cabinet, I once more prepared and drank the cup, once more suffered the pangs of disso-

6. Exact.

lution, and came to myself once more with the character, the stature and the face of Henry Jekyll.

That night I had come to the fatal crossroads. Had I approached my discovery in a more noble spirit, had I risked the experiment while under the empire of generous or pious aspirations, all must have been otherwise, and from these agonies of death and birth, I had come forth an angel instead of a fiend. The drug had no discriminating action; it was neither diabolical nor divine; it but shook the doors of the prisonhouse of my disposition; and like the captives of Philippi,[7] that which stood within ran forth. At that time my virtue slumbered; my evil, kept awake by ambition, was alert and swift to seize the occasion; and the thing that was projected was Edward Hyde. Hence, although I had now two characters as well as two appearances, one was wholly evil, and the other was still the old Henry Jekyll, that incongruous compound of whose reformation and improvement I had already learned to despair. The movement was thus wholly toward the worse.

Even at that time, I had not conquered my aversion to the dryness of a life of study. I would still be merrily disposed at times; and as my pleasures were (to say the least) undignified, and I was not only well known and highly considered, but growing toward the elderly man, this incoherency of my life was daily growing more unwelcome. It was on this side that my new power tempted me until I fell in slavery. I had but to drink the cup, to doff at once the body of the noted professor, and to assume, like a thick cloak, that of Edward Hyde. I smiled at the notion; it seemed to me at the time to be humourous; and I made my preparations with the most studious care. I took and furnished that house in Soho, to which Hyde was tracked by the police; and engaged as a housekeeper a creature whom I knew well to be silent and unscrupulous. On the other side, I announced to my servants that a Mr. Hyde (whom I described) was to have full liberty and power about my house in the square; and to parry mishaps, I even called and made myself a familiar object, in my second character. I next drew up that will to which you so much objected; so that if anything befell me in the person of Dr. Jekyll, I could enter on that of Edward Hyde without pecuniary loss. And thus fortified, as I supposed, on every side, I began to profit by the strange immunities of my position.

Men have before hired bravoes to transact their crimes, while their own person and reputation sat under shelter. I was the first that ever did so for his pleasures. I was the first that could plod in the public eye with a load of genial respectability, and in a moment, like a schoolboy, strip off these lendings and spring headlong into the sea of liberty. But for me, in my impenetrable mantle, the safety was complete. Think of it—I did not even exist! Let me but escape into my laboratory door, give me but a second or two to mix and swallow the draught that I had always standing ready; and whatever he had done, Edward Hyde would pass away like the stain of breath upon a mirror; and there in his stead, quietly at home, trimming the midnight lamp in his study, a man who could afford to laugh at suspicion, would be Harry Jekyll.

The pleasures which I made haste to seek in my disguise were, as I

---

7. Acts 16:26: "And suddenly there was a great earthquake, so that the foundations of the prison were shaken: and immediately all the doors were opened, and every one's bands were loosed." The biblical captives of Philippi, however, do not flee.

have said, undignified; I would scarce use a harder term. But in the hands of Edward Hyde, they soon began to turn toward the monstrous. When I would come back from these excursions, I was often plunged into a kind of wonder at my vicarious depravity. This familiar that I called out of my own soul, and sent forth alone to do his good pleasure, was a being inherently malign and villainous; his every act and thought centered on self; drinking pleasure with bestial avidity from any degree of torture to another; relentless like a man of stone. Henry Jekyll stood at times aghast before the acts of Edward Hyde; but the situation was apart from ordinary laws, and insidiously relaxed the grasp of conscience. It was Hyde, after all, and Hyde alone, that was guilty. Jekyll was no worse; he woke again to his good qualities seemingly unimpaired; he would even make haste, where it was possible, to undo the evil done by Hyde. And thus his conscience slumbered.

Into the details of the infamy at which I thus connived (for even now I can scarce grant that I committed it) I have no design of entering; I mean but to point out the warnings and the successive steps with which my chastisement approached. I met with one accident which, as it brought on no consequence, I shall no more than mention. An act of cruelty to a child aroused against me the anger of a passerby, whom I recognised the other day in the person of your kinsman; the doctor and the child's family joined him; there were moments when I feared for my life; and at last, in order to pacify their too just resentment, Edward Hyde had to bring them to the door, and pay them in a cheque drawn in the name of Henry Jekyll. But this danger was easily eliminated from the future, by opening an account at another bank in the name of Edward Hyde himself; and when, by sloping my own hand backward, I had supplied my double with a signature, I thought I sat beyond the reach of fate.

Some two months before the murder of Sir Danvers, I had been out for one of my adventures, had returned at a late hour, and woke the next day in bed with somewhat odd sensations. It was in vain I looked about me; in vain I saw the decent furniture and tall proportions of my room in the square; in vain that I recognised the pattern of the bed curtains and the design of the mahogany frame; something still kept insisting that I was not where I was, that I had not wakened where I seemed to be, but in the little room in Soho where I was accustomed to sleep in the body of Edward Hyde. I smiled to myself, and, in my psychological way, began lazily to inquire into the elements of this illusion, occasionally, even as I did so, dropping back into a comfortable morning doze. I was still so engaged when, in one of my more wakeful moments, my eyes fell upon my hand. Now the hand of Henry Jekyll (as you have often remarked) was professional in shape and size: it was large, firm, white and comely. But the hand which I now saw, clearly enough, in the yellow light of a mid-London morning, lying half shut on the bedclothes, was lean, corded, knuckly, of a dusky pallor and thickly shaded with a swart growth of hair. It was the hand of Edward Hyde.

I must have stared upon it for near half a minute, sunk as I was in the mere stupidity of wonder, before terror woke up in my breast as sudden and startling as the crash of cymbals; and bounding from my bed, I rushed to the mirror. At the sight that met my eyes, my blood was changed into something exquisitely thin and icy. Yes, I had gone to bed Henry Jekyll, I had awakened Edward Hyde. How was this to be explained? I asked myself; and then, with another bound of terror—how was it to be remedied? It was well on in the morning; the servants were up; all my drugs were in the cabinet—a long journey down two pairs of stairs, through the back passage, across the open court and through the anatomical theatre, from where I was then standing horror-struck. It might indeed be possible to cover my face; but of what use was that, when I was unable to conceal the alteration in my stature? And then with an overpowering sweetness of relief, it came back upon my mind that the servants were already used to the coming and going of my second self. I had soon dressed, as well as I was able, in clothes of my own size; had soon passed through the house, where Bradshaw stared and drew back at seeing Mr. Hyde at such an hour and in such a strange array; and ten minutes later, Dr. Jekyll had returned to his own shape and was sitting down, with a darkened brow, to make a feint of breakfasting.

Small indeed was my appetite. This inexplicable incident, this reversal of my previous experience, seemed, like the Babylonian finger on the wall,[8] to be spelling out the letters of my judgment; and I began to reflect more seriously than ever before on the issues and possibilities of my double existence. That part of me which I had the power of projecting, had lately been much exercised and nourished; it had seemed to me of late as though the body of Edward Hyde had grown in stature, as though (when I wore that form) I were conscious of a more generous tide of blood; and I began to spy a danger that, if this were much prolonged, the balance of my nature might be permanently overthrown, the power of voluntary change be forfeited, and the character of Edward Hyde become irrevocably mine. The power of the drug had not been always equally displayed. Once, very early in my career, it had totally failed me; since then I had been obliged on more than one occasion to double, and once, with infinite risk of death, to treble the amount; and these rare uncertainties had cast hitherto the sole shadow on my contentment. Now, however, and in the light of that morning's accident, I was led to remark that whereas, in the beginning, the difficulty had been to throw off the body of Jekyll, it had of late gradually but decidedly transferred itself to the other side. All things therefore seemed to point to this: that I was slowly losing hold of my original and better self, and becoming slowly incorporated with my second and worse.

Between these two, I now felt I had to choose. My two natures had memory in common, but all other faculties were most unequally shared between them. Jekyll (who was composite) now with the most sensitive apprehensions, now with a greedy gusto, projected and shared in the pleasures and adventures of Hyde; but Hyde was indifferent to Jekyll, or but remembered him as the mountain bandit remembers the cavern in which he conceals himself from pursuit. Jekyll had more than a father's interest; Hyde had more than a son's indifference. To cast in my lot with Jekyll, was to die to those appetites which I had long secretly indulged and had of late begun to pamper. To cast it in with Hyde, was to die to a thousand interests and aspirations, and to become, at a blow and forever, despised and friendless. The bargain might appear unequal; but there was still another consideration in the scales; for while Jekyll would suffer

8. Daniel 5:25. "The handwriting on the wall" that suddenly appears ("*mene, mene, tekel, upharsin*," Aramaic for "numbered, numbered, weighed, and divided") is interpreted by Daniel as God's judgment on Belshazzar and the Babylonians.

smartingly in the fires of abstinence, Hyde would be not even conscious of all that he had lost. Strange as my circumstances were, the terms of this debate are as old and commonplace as man; much the same inducements and alarms cast the die for any tempted and trembling sinner; and it fell out with me, as it falls with so vast a majority of my fellows, that I chose the better part and was found wanting in the strength to keep to it.

Yes, I preferred the elderly and discontented doctor, surrounded by friends and cherishing honest hopes; and bade a resolute farewell to the liberty, the comparative youth, the light step, leaping impulses and secret pleasures, that I had enjoyed in the disguise of Hyde. I made this choice perhaps with some unconscious reservation, for I neither gave up the house in Soho, nor destroyed the clothes of Edward Hyde, which still lay ready in my cabinet. For two months, however, I was true to my determination; for two months, I led a life of such severity as I had never before attained to, and enjoyed the compensations of an approving conscience. But time began at last to obliterate the freshness of my alarm; the praises of conscience began to grow into a thing of course; I began to be tortured with throes and longings, as of Hyde struggling after freedom; and at last, in an hour of moral weakness, I once again compounded and swallowed the transforming draught.

I do not suppose that, when a drunkard reasons with himself upon his vice, he is once out of five hundred times affected by the dangers that he runs through his brutish, physical insensibility; neither had I, long as I had considered my position, made enough allowance for the complete moral insensibility and insensate readiness to evil, which were the leading characters of Edward Hyde. Yet it was by these that I was punished. My devil had been long caged, he came out roaring. I was conscious, even when I took the draught, of a more unbridled, a more furious propensity to ill. It must have been this, I suppose, that stirred in my soul that tempest of impatience with which I listened to the civilities of my unhappy victim; I declare, at least, before God, no man morally sane could have been guilty of that crime upon so pitiful a provocation; and that I struck in no more reasonable spirit than that in which a sick child may break a plaything. But I had voluntarily stripped myself of all those balancing instincts by which even the worst of us continues to walk with some degree of steadiness among temptations; and in my case, to be tempted, however slightly, was to fall.

Instantly the spirit of hell awoke in me and raged. With a transport of glee, I mauled the unresisting body, tasting delight from every blow; and it was not till weariness had begun to succeed, that I was suddenly, in the top fit of my delirium, struck through the heart by a cold thrill of terror. A mist dispersed; I saw my life to be forfeit; and fled from the scene of these excesses, at once glorying and trembling, my lust of evil gratified and stimulated, my love of life screwed to the topmost peg. I ran to the house in Soho, and (to make assurance doubly sure) destroyed my papers; thence I set out through the lamplit streets, in the same divided ecstasy of mind, gloating on my crime, light-headedly devising others in the future, and yet still hastening and still hearkening in my wake for the steps of the avenger. Hyde had a song upon his lips as he compounded the draught, and as he drank it, pledged the dead man. The pangs of transformation had not done tearing him, before Henry Jekyll, with streaming tears of gratitude and remorse, had fallen upon his knees and lifted his clasped hands to God. The veil of self-indulgence was rent from head to foot. I saw my life as a whole: I followed it up from the days of childhood, when I had walked with my father's hand, and through the self-denying toils of my professional life, to arrive again and again, with the same sense of unreality, at the damned horrors of the evening. I could have screamed aloud; I sought with tears and prayers to smother down the crowd of hideous images and sounds with which my memory swarmed against me; and still, between the petitions, the ugly face of my iniquity stared into my soul. As the acuteness of this remorse began to die away, it was succeeded by a sense of joy. The problem of my conduct was solved. Hyde was thenceforth impossible; whether I would or not, I was now confined to the better part of my existence; and O, how I rejoiced to think of it! with what willing humility I embraced anew the restrictions of natural life! with what sincere renunciation I locked the door by which I had so often gone and come, and ground the key under my heel!

The next day, came the news that the murder had been overlooked,[9] that the guilt of Hyde was patent to the world, and that the victim was a man high in public estimation. It was not only a crime, it had been a tragic folly. I think I was glad to know it; I think I was glad to have my better impulses thus buttressed and guarded by the terrors of the scaffold. Jekyll was now my city of refuge; let but Hyde peep out an instant, and the hands of all men would be raised to take and slay him.

I resolved in my future conduct to redeem the past; and I can say with honesty that my resolve was fruitful of some good. You know yourself how earnestly, in the last months of the last year, I laboured to relieve suffering; you know that much was done for others, and that the days passed quietly, almost happily for myself. Nor can I truly say that I wearied of this beneficent and innocent life; I think instead that I daily enjoyed it more completely; but I was still cursed with my duality of purpose; and as the first edge of my penitence wore off, the lower side of me, so long indulged, so recently chained down, began to growl for licence. Not that I dreamed of resuscitating Hyde; the bare idea of that would startle me to frenzy: no, it was in my own person that I was once more tempted to trifle with my conscience; and it was as an ordinary secret sinner that I at last fell before the assaults of temptation.

There comes an end to all things; the most capacious measure is filled at last; and this brief condescension to my evil finally destroyed the balance of my soul. And yet I was not alarmed; the fall seemed natural, like a return to the old days before I had made my discovery. It was a fine, clear, January day, wet under foot where the frost had melted, but cloudless overhead; and the Regent's Park[1] was full of winter chirrupings and sweet with spring odours. I sat in the sun on a bench; the animal within me licking the chops of memory; the spiritual side a little drowsed, promising subsequent penitence, but not yet moved to begin. After all, I reflected, I was like my neighbours; and then I smiled, comparing myself with other men, comparing my active good-will with the lazy cruelty of their neglect. And at the very moment of that vainglorious thought, a qualm came over me, a horrid nausea and the most deadly shuddering. These passed away, and left me faint; and then, as in its turn faintness subsided, I began to be aware of a change in the temper of my thoughts, a greater boldness, a contempt of danger, a solution of the bonds of obligation. I looked down; my clothes hung formlessly on my shrunken limbs; the hand that lay on my knee was corded and hairy. I was once more Edward Hyde. A moment before I had been safe of all men's respect, wealthy, beloved—the cloth laying for me in the dining-room at home; and now I was the common quarry of mankind, hunted, house-less, a known murderer, thrall to the gallows.

My reason wavered, but it did not fail me utterly. I have more than once observed that, in my second character, my faculties seemed sharpened to a point and my spirits more tensely elastic; thus it came about that, where Jekyll perhaps might have succumbed, Hyde rose to the importance of the moment. My drugs were in one of the presses of my cabinet; how was I to reach them? That was the problem that (crushing my temples in my hands) I set myself to solve. The laboratory door I had closed. If I sought to enter by the house, my own servants would consign me to the gallows. I saw I must employ another hand, and thought of Lanyon. How was he to be reached? how persuaded? Supposing that I escaped capture in the streets, how was I to make my way into his presence? and how should I, an unknown and displeasing visitor, prevail on the famous physician to rifle the study of his colleague, Dr. Jekyll? Then I remembered that of my original character, one part remained to me: I could write my own hand; and once I had conceived that kindling spark, the way that I must follow became lighted up from end to end.

Thereupon, I arranged my clothes as best I could, and summoning a passing hansom, drove to an hotel in Portland Street, the name of which I chanced to remember. At my appearance (which was indeed comical enough, however tragic a fate these garments covered) the driver could not conceal his mirth. I gnashed my teeth upon him with a gust of devilish fury; and the smile withered from his face—happily for him—yet more happily for myself, for in another instant I had certainly dragged him from his perch. At the inn, as I entered, I looked about me with so black a countenance as made the attendants tremble; not a look did they exchange in my presence; but obsequiously took my orders, led me to a private room, and brought me wherewithal to write. Hyde in danger of his life was a creature new to me; shaken with inordinate anger, strung to the pitch of murder, lusting to inflict pain. Yet the creature was astute; mastered his fury with a great effort of the will; composed his two important letters, one to Lanyon and one to Poole; and that he might receive actual evidence of their being posted, sent them out with directions that they should be registered. Thenceforward, he sat all day over the fire in the private room, gnawing his nails; there he dined, sitting alone with his fears, the waiter visibly quailing before his eye; and thence, when the night was fully come, he set forth in the corner of a closed cab, and was driven to and fro about the streets of the city. He, I say—I cannot say, I. That child of Hell had nothing human; nothing lived in him but fear and hatred. And when at last, thinking the driver had begun to grow suspicious, he discharged the cab and ventured on foot, attired in his misfitting clothes, an object marked out for observation, into the midst of the nocturnal passengers, these two base passions raged within him like a tempest. He walked fast, hunted by his fears, chattering to himself, skulking through the less frequented thoroughfares, counting the minutes that still divided him from midnight. Once a woman spoke to him, offering, I think, a box of lights. He smote her in the face, and she fled.

When I came to myself at Lanyon's, the horror of my old friend perhaps affected me somewhat: I do not know; it was at least but a drop in the sea to the abhorrence with which I looked back upon these hours. A change had come over me. It was no longer the fear of the gallows, it was the horror of being Hyde that racked me. I received Lanyon's condemnation partly in a dream; it was partly in a dream that I came home to my own house and got into bed. I slept after the prostration of the day, with a stringent and profound slumber which not even the nightmares that wrung me could avail to break. I awoke in the morning shaken, weakened, but refreshed. I still hated and feared the thought of the brute that slept within me, and I had not of course forgotten the appalling dangers of the day before; but I was once more at home, in my own house and close to my drugs; and gratitude for my escape shone so strong in my soul that it almost rivalled the brightness of hope.

I was stepping leisurely across the court after breakfast, drinking the chill of the air with pleasure, when I was seized again with those indescribable sensations that heralded the change; and I had but the time to gain the shelter of my cabinet, before I was once again raging and freezing with the passions of Hyde. It took on this occasion a double dose to recall me to myself; and alas! six hours after, as I sat looking sadly in the fire, the pangs returned, and the drug had to be re-administered. In short, from that day forth it seemed only by a great effort of gymnastics, and only under the immediate stimulation of the drug, that I was able to wear the countenance of Jekyll. At all hours of the day and night, I would be taken with the premonitory shudder; above all, if I slept, or even dozed for a moment in my chair, it was always as Hyde that I awakened. Under the strain of this continually impending doom and by the sleeplessness to which I now condemned myself, ay, even beyond what I had thought possible to man, I became, in my own person, a creature eaten up and emptied by fever, languidly weak both in body and mind, and solely occupied by one thought: the horror of my other self. But when I slept, or when the virtue of the medicine wore off, I would leap almost without transition (for the pangs of transformation grew daily less marked) into the possession of a fancy brimming with images of terror, a soul boiling with causeless hatreds, and a body that seemed not strong enough to contain the raging energies of life. The powers of Hyde seemed to have grown with the sickliness of Jekyll. And certainly the hate that now divided them was equal on each side. With Jekyll, it was a thing of vital instinct. He had now seen the full deformity of that creature that shared with him some of the phenomena of consciousness, and was co-heir with him to death: and beyond these links of community, which in themselves made the most poignant part of his distress, he thought of Hyde, for all his energy of life, as of something not only hellish but inorganic. This was the shocking thing; that the slime of the pit seemed to utter cries and voices; that the amorphous dust gesticulated and sinned; that what was dead, and had no shape, should usurp the offices of life. And this again, that that insurgent horror was knit to him closer than a wife, closer than an eye; lay caged in his flesh, where he heard it mutter and felt it struggle to be born; and at every hour of weakness, and in the confidence of slumber, prevailed against him, and deposed him out of life. The hatred of Hyde for Jekyll was of a different order. His terror of the gallows drove him continually to commit temporary suicide, and return to his subordinate station of a part instead of a person; but he loathed the necessity, he loathed the despondency into which Jekyll was now fallen, and he resented the dislike with which he was himself regarded. Hence the apelike tricks that he would play me, scrawling in my own hand blasphemies on the pages of my books, burning the letters and destroying the portrait of my father; and indeed, had it not been for his fear of death, he would long ago have ruined himself in order to involve me in the ruin. But his love of life is wonderful; I go further: I, who sicken and freeze at the mere thought of him, when I recall the abjection and passion of this attachment, and when I know how he fears my power to cut him off by suicide, I find it in my heart to pity him.

It is useless, and the time awfully fails me, to prolong this description; no one has ever suffered such torments, let that suffice; and yet even to these, habit brought—no, not alleviation—but a certain callousness of soul, a certain acquiescence of despair; and my punishment might have gone on for years, but for the last calamity which has now fallen, and which has finally severed me from my own face and nature. My provision of the salt, which had never been renewed since the date of the first experiment, began to run low. I sent out for a fresh supply and mixed the draught; the ebullition followed, and the first change of colour, not the second; I drank it and it was without efficacy. You will learn from Poole how I have had London ransacked; it was in vain; and I am now persuaded that my first supply was impure, and that it was that unknown impurity which lent efficacy to the draught.

About a week has passed, and I am now finishing this statement under the influence of the last of the old powders. This, then, is the last time, short of a miracle, that Henry Jekyll can think his own thoughts or see his own face (now how sadly altered!) in the glass. Nor must I delay too long to bring my writing to an end; for if my narrative has hitherto escaped destruction, it has been by a combination of great prudence and great good luck. Should the throes of change take me in the act of writing it, Hyde will tear it in pieces; but if some time shall have elapsed after I have laid it by, his wonderful selfishness and circumscription to the moment will probably save it once again from the action of his ape-like spite. And indeed the doom that is closing on us both has already changed and crushed him. Half an hour from now, when I shall again and forever reindue[2] that hated personality, I know how I shall sit shuddering and weeping in my chair, or continue, with the most strained and fearstruck ecstasy of listening, to pace up and down this room (my last earthly refuge) and give ear to every sound of menace. Will Hyde die upon the scaffold? or will he find courage to release himself at the last moment? God knows; I am careless;[3] this is my true hour of death, and what is to follow concerns another than myself. Here then, as I lay down the pen and proceed to seal up my confession, I bring the life of that unhappy Henry Jekyll to an end.

1886

---

2. Reassume.   3. I do not care.

AFTERWORD

This is no doubt the most widely known story, or tale, in this collection. "Tale" often refers to a narrative whose plot, outline, or situation is paramount, almost to the exclusion of its specific embodiment, structure, or words, and Stevenson's short novel has been told and retold in movies, stage and television plays, and—overtly or covertly—in other stories many, many times. There is a certain amount of irony in the fact that *Jekyll and Hyde* has been treated as a retellable tale, for Robert Louis Stevenson was one of the finest and most self-conscious stylists of his day.

For most of its length, *Jekyll and Hyde* is a mystery story: the reader who does not know the plot (are there any such readers?) is kept guessing as to who Hyde is, what hold he has on Jekyll, and how Jekyll disappears from the closed room. We are as much in the dark as Utterson, the center of consciousness through whose eyes and mind most of the early portions of the story are filtered, and our interests and fears are aroused as his are; or rather, our interest is in part aroused by his fear in the first episode, "Story of the Door," and it is only after we read the will in the second section, "Search for Mr. Hyde," that our fears take form. The possibility that Hyde is blackmailing Dr. Jekyll has been raised earlier by Enfield, but he is a cynical, worldly type whose pronouncements about life we are not disposed to take seriously. We do trust Utterson, however, and share his concern for Jekyll (whom we see surprisingly little of), his fears, and his mystification. His inferences or guesses are reasonable, and for a time convincing. When, in "The Incident of the Letter," for example, he suspects that Hyde has forged Jekyll's hand, or even, much later, when he tries to explain Jekyll's seclusion by the possibility he may have a deforming malady, his explanations seem plausible and guide our expectations—away from the truth, however, as it turns out. Utterson is not the narrator, however, and at one crucial point, in "The Incident at the Window," the narrator withholds what Utterson sees, which may not be playing entirely fair with the reader.

The narrative relies neither on Utterson nor on a narrator telling us the story, in fact. There is a good deal that comes to us through written documents of one kind or another. There is the will, for example, that Utterson dislikes and suspects; there is Hyde's letter promising he will not reappear, and Utterson's clerk, Guest, finds Hyde's and Jekyll's handwriting oddly similar; there is Lanyon's narrative, and of course Jekyll's lengthy statement at the end. Some of these serve to give information not readily available to Utterson, some give other perspectives, some mystify, and some testify or reveal. So different are their perspectives and functions that we might be led to question the validity of the written word in the novel.

The shift of perspective, like the division of the novel into ten narrative segments, each with its own title, punctuates the reading: just as we pause very briefly at a period or other end-punctuation, and a little longer at a paragraph, so we pause still longer at these "chapter" breaks—we may even use the break to take a break and return to our reading later. Even the pause without a break gives us a chance to reassess what we have read and to project more fully or question more fully what is to happen in the rest of the narrative or how the mystery is to be solved. The frequency of shifts and pauses contributes to the sense of duration, and though *Jekyll and Hyde* is only a little over 25,000 words, it has the "feel" of a novel because of the elapsed or punctuated reading time and, possibly, of the nonreading time between "chapters."

Whether we trust Stevenson's words or not, they do from time to time also make us pause, often in admiration. Look at just a single passage, say, that portion of Jekyll's statement beginning: "I hesitated long . . ." (p. 127). Look at the precision of the pharmacist's term *scruple* (20 grains or 1/3 of a dram): "I . . . might, by the least scruple of an overdose . . . utterly blot out that immaterial tabernacle which I looked to it to change." And *tabernacle,* dwelling place of the soul; or in a portion of the sentence I omitted, *exhibition*—the precise medical term for administration of something like a drug but also suggesting here its usual meaning of showing forth, for his identity will soon show forth. And *identity* occurs in another forceful phase that I have not yet quoted in the same sentence, "the fortress of identity." We might note, too, how *scruple, tabernacle, fortress,* and the areas of experience they suggest play off one another, and how the whole sentence rolls (in a way slightly foreign now to our ears, attuned as they are to the more staccato rhythms of modern American prose):

> I knew very well that I risked death; for any drug that so potently controlled and shook the very fortress of identity, might, by the least scruple of an overdose or at the least inopportunity in the moment of exhibition, utterly blot out that immaterial tabernacle which I looked to it to change.

And let your eye run down the next page or so and note the implication of stiffness in "the most *rigorous* hours of slumber," of *expressive* in the use of *express* to mean *exact.* Or read sentences aloud: "At that time my virtue slumbered; my evil, kept awake by ambition, was alert and swift to seize the occasion; and the thing that was projected was Edward Hyde"; "I was the first that could plod in the public eye with a load of genial respectability, and in a moment, like a schoolboy, strip off these lendings and spring headlong into the sea of liberty."

Perhaps the extraordinary precision of the language, its simultaneously accurate and suggestive diction, and its natural but lyrical rhythms attract our attention; perhaps they affect us unawares; certainly the language stands up to our closest scrutiny, and we have not just a tale but a written narrative, a short novel written in precise words. It is an unfortunate irony that the tale is so universal and effective in itself that we do not often enough go back to the novel in its specificity and appreciate its consummate artistry.

It is the "tale" of *Jekyll,* however, that initially connects most closely with *Daisy.* If *Daisy* raises the question of morality in terms of innocence and sinfulness, *Jekyll* does so in terms of good and evil—comparable but not identical sets of terms. If *Daisy* asks "Is she innocent or guilty?" *Jekyll* asks "Can good and evil be separated?" In *Daisy* sin is incarnate in sex; and though, interestingly enough, in most versions of *Jekyll* Mr. Hyde's career is assumed or shown to be one primarily of sexual debauchery and perversion, and though his name is related to "flesh" and so to some extent justifies that interpretation, in Stevenson's story his only specified evil-doings are those of violence (the first we see of him, he callously knocks over a little girl; later, a witness describes him brutally beating an old man to death). In post-Freudian terms, Hyde is the id, the anarchic, pleasure-seeking, amoral, instinctive portion of the psyche, and Jekyll the superego, the conscience and societal voice of the psyche. Jekyll, in pre-Freudian terms that are not inconsistent with Freud's, calls his two sides *animal* and *spiritual* as well as *good* and *evil,* and he attributes part of his fascination with evil to his repression for social and professional reasons of his natural "gayety" or love of pleasure.

"Translating" the moral into psychological terms may make the novel seem less "dated" or Victorian, and may make some of the questions it raises seem more relevant, even urgent. If the freeing of the instinctual and passional forces in the psyche does or can lead to cruelty, even murder, may this not challenge the widespread modern assumption that all "Victorian" restraints on sexual conduct are somehow wrong and reactionary? Is all freedom good? Is all "government," in the psychological as well as political sense, "bad"? Is there a definable line between liberty and license? What does Stevenson mean by "the restrictions of natural life"? (Isn't "natural" life by definition unrestricted?) These questions may seem strangely familiar to the reader of the not-so-strange "case" of *Daisy Miller* (published just eight years earlier) and may come up again in a somewhat different and even more grotesque and dramatic guise as we read a novel published not too many years later, Joseph Conrad's *Heart of Darkness*.

In most other versions of the "tale" Hyde is grossly ugly, as if monstrous evil were always readily visible. You will notice that in Stevenson's novel Hyde, though mysteriously and "spiritually" repulsive, is younger and handsomer than Jekyll. The "flesh"—Hyde—is of course stronger in youth; the superego is conventionally held to be stronger in later years. So beauty and virtue, ugliness and vice are not so intimately connected in this novel as in many versions of the tale or in our usual stereotypes. You will notice, too, that Hyde is smaller than Jekyll, for Hyde is only part of a human being, as evil or our animal nature is, while Jekyll is not merely the good, as we are sometimes prone to think, but the whole man, good and evil.

There are other significant elements in Stevenson's novel that do not often survive its transformation into the tale. Three-fourths of *The Strange Case of Dr. Jekyll and Mr. Hyde* is, like almost all of *Daisy Miller*, seen through the consciousness of someone other than the title character but is narrated through—but not by—an important observer-character. We asked whether Winterbourne's self-interest or character influenced what he saw or did not see in Daisy. Can we ask the same question of Utterson? What is he like? You might want to look back at the first sentence where he is described as "cold . . . dreary . . . lovable." Why should a story like *Jekyll and Hyde* be largely told by someone like that? He has a weakness for wine; is that the kind of consciousness through which we want to see this moral tale? But he mortifies himself for his fault—with gin! He likes the theater but never goes. (That may be a better qualification for a moralist!) He's a heretic—not his brother's keeper; but what he seems to mean by that is that he is not censorious. So lots of imperfect men or worse are his friends or acquaintances, including his man-about-town kinsman, Mr. Richard Enfield. Utterson does not become, as Winterbourne may be said to become, the objective as well as the subjective consciousness of the novel; but he is (in addition to being a convenient vehicle for the transmission of the narrative because of his role as everyone's confidant) the model, in a sense, of the mixed human being that Dr. Jekyll refuses to remain. Stevenson thus sets up from the beginning a moral perspective through the center of consciousness that is consonant with the moral values of the novel (but one that is rarely retained in its dramatization or retelling).

This is not to suggest, however, that Utterson is any more morally omniscient than he was intellectually omniscient when the "case" was still a mystery. There may be more reasons than mere narrative convenience for taking the story out of his hands toward the end. A close reading of the last quarter of the novel, "Henry Jekyll's Full Statement," seems to undercut at least some of the implications in the Utterson and other portions of the first three-quarters, and even undercuts some of Jekyll's own inferences. Though the unhappy doctor talks, for example, of the "duplicity of life" and good and evil, he also insists that man is not merely dual in nature but multifarious, that we house not merely what might be called an anarchic id but many potential beings or partial beings of various kinds. This, it seems to me, seriously undermines most of the fairly simple moral and psychological readings of the story, even if those readings are supported by Utterson's or even Jekyll's own views! Is it accidental, moreover, that in Jekyll's confession he admits that one of his fears is that Hyde can write like him and therefore might "forge" a confession? Can we trust this confession, then? Surely it is not a forgery of a diabolical Edward Hyde?

Though most adaptations of the tale, foregoing the initial mystery and often the intermediary presence of Utterson, concentrate on what is in the novel only the final quarter, the sensational elements of Jekyll's change and Hyde's indulgence in sin—usually adding sexual sins to those specified in the novel—they ignore the undermining of the dualism in Jekyll's confession and the other complications of the straightforward reading that this very portion of the novel suggests. D. H. Lawrence advises us to trust the tale and not the teller; as we have been using the term here, however, we might better warn the reader to trust the telling and not the tale.

JOSEPH CONRAD

Heart of Darkness

Jozef Teodor Konrad Nalecz Korzeniowski (1857–1924) was born in Berdyczew, Polish Ukraine; at five he accompanied his parents into exile to northern Russia and later the district near Kiev, and was left an orphan at eleven when his Polish-patriot father (and translator of Shakespeare and Hugo) died in Cracow; his mother had died four years earlier. Before he was seventeen he was off to Marseilles, making three trips from that port to the West Indies as an apprentice seaman. After some veiled troubles in France, involving gambling debts and an apparent suicide attempt, he sailed on a British ship, landed in England in 1878, and spent the next sixteen years in the British merchant service, rising to master in 1886, the same year in which he became a British subject. He began writing in 1889 but did not publish his first novel, *Almayer's Folly*, until 1895; that same year he married an Englishwoman, Jessie George.

He wrote, Conrad tells us, out of his own experience, "pushed a little (and only a very little) beyond the actual facts of the case for the perfectly legitimate . . . purpose of bringing it home to the minds and bosoms of the readers." For, he tells us, "The sustained invention of a really telling lie demands a talent which I do not possess." Much of that strange and compelling adventure of *Heart of Darkness* does come from his experience, perhaps pushed a little: Conrad did, like Marlow, go far up the Congo into the heart of Africa, in 1890, and many of the details of the trip—but not, alas, its central episode or "heart"—appear, though somewhat sketchily, in diaries he kept during the journey.

Though based on experience, art is not, for Conrad, a mere diary or transcription, but a tribute, paying "the highest kind of justice to the visible universe, . . . bringing to light the truth, . . . what is enduring and essential." Art requires more than seeing, vision; it requires execution and "should carry its justification in every line." "And it is only through complete unswerving devotion to the perfect blending of form and substance; it is only through an unremitting, never-discouraged care for the shape and ring of sentences, that . . . the light of magic suggestiveness may be brought to play for an evanescent instant over the commonplace surface of words. . . ."

Generations have testified to "the perfect blending of form and substance" in *Heart of Darkness*, to "the ring of [its] sentences," and the "magic suggestiveness" of its words. Many find in it a profoundly disturbing vision of an underlying truth, an initiation into a dark, though all too human truth. Conrad wrote to a friend that he found such a truth on that journey: "Before the Congo," he said, "I was just an animal."

Heart of Darkness

1

The *Nellie*, a cruising yawl, swung to her anchor without a flutter of the sails, and was at rest. The flood had made, the wind was nearly calm, and being bound down the river, the only thing for it was to come to and wait for the turn of the tide.

The sea-reach[1] of the Thames stretched before us like the beginning of an interminable waterway. In the offing the sea and the sky were welded together without a joint, and in the luminous space the tanned sails of the barges drifting up with the tide seemed to stand still in red clusters of canvas sharply peaked, with gleams of varnished sprits. A haze rested on the low shores that ran out to sea in vanishing flatness. The air was dark above Gravesend,[2] and farther back still seemed condensed into a mournful gloom, brooding motionless over the biggest, and the greatest, town on earth.

The Director of Companies was our captain and our host. We four affectionately watched his back as he stood in the bows looking to seaward. On the whole river there was nothing that looked half so nautical. He resembled a pilot, which to a seaman is trustworthiness personified. It was difficult to realize his work was not out there in the luminous estuary, but behind him, within the brooding gloom.

Between us there was, as I have already said somewhere, the bond of the sea. Besides holding our hearts together through long periods of separation, it had the effect of making us tolerant of each other's yarns—and even convictions. The Lawyer—the best of old fellows—had, because of his many years and many virtues, the only cushion on deck, and was lying on the only rug. The Accountant had brought out already a box of dominoes, and was toying architecturally with the bones. Marlow sat cross-legged right aft, leaning against the mizzenmast. He had sunken cheeks, a yellow complexion, a straight back, an ascetic aspect, and, with his arms dropped, the palms of hands outwards, resembled an idol. The Director, satisfied the anchor had good hold, made his way aft and sat down amongst us. We exchanged a few words lazily. Afterwards there was silence on board the yacht. For some reason or other we did not begin that game of dominoes. We felt meditative, and fit for nothing but placid staring. The day was ending in a serenity of still and exquisite brilliance. The water shone pacifically; the sky, without a speck, was a benign immensity of unstained light; the very mist on the Essex marshes was like a gauzy and radiant fabric, hung from the wooded rises inland, and draping the low shores in diaphanous folds. Only the gloom to the west, brooding over the upper reaches, became more somber every minute, as if angered by the approach of the sun.

And at last, in its curved and imperceptible fall, the sun sank low, and from glowing white changed to a dull red without rays and without heat, as if about to go out suddenly, stricken to death by the touch of that gloom brooding over a crowd of men.

---

1. Straight course of an otherwise winding river as it approaches the sea.

2. Easternmost large town on the Thames before it reaches the sea, 26 miles from London.

Forthwith a change came over the waters, and the serenity became less brilliant but more profound. The old river in its broad reach rested unruffled at the decline of day, after ages of good service done to the race that peopled its banks, spread out in the tranquil dignity of a waterway leading to the uttermost ends of the earth. We looked at the venerable stream not in the vivid flush of a short day that comes and departs forever, but in the august light of abiding memories. And indeed nothing is easier for a man who has, as the phrase goes, "followed the sea" with reverence and affection, than to evoke the great spirit of the past upon the lower reaches of the Thames. The tidal current runs to and fro in its unceasing service, crowded with memories of men and ships it has borne to the rest of home or to the battles of the sea. It had known and served all the men of whom the nation is proud, from Sir Francis Drake to Sir John Franklin,[3] knights all, titled and untitled—the great knights-errant of the sea. It had borne all the ships whose names are like jewels flashing in the night of time, from the *Golden Hind* returning with her round flanks full of treasure, to be visited by the Queen's Highness and thus pass out of the gigantic tale, to the *Erebus* and *Terror*, bound on other conquests—and that never returned. It had known the ships and the men. They had sailed from Deptford, from Greenwich, from Erith—the adventurers and the settlers; kings' ships and the ships of men on 'Change;[4] captains, admirals, the dark "interlopers" of the Eastern trade, and the commissioned "generals" of East India fleets. Hunters for gold or pursuers of fame, they all had gone out on that stream, bearing the sword, and often the torch, messengers of the might within the land, bearers of a spark from the sacred fire. What greatness had not floated on the ebb of that river into the mystery of an unknown earth! . . . The dreams of men, the seed of commonwealths, the germs of empires.

The sun set; the dusk fell on the stream, and lights began to appear along the shore. The Chapman lighthouse, a three-legged thing erect on a mudflat, shone strongly. Lights of ships moved in the fairway—a great stir of lights going up and going down. And farther west on the upper reaches the place of the monstrous town was still marked ominously on the sky, a brooding gloom in sunshine, a lurid glare under the stars.

"And this also," said Marlow suddenly, "has been one of the dark places of the earth."

He was the only man of us who still "followed the sea." The worst that could be said of him was that he did not represent his class. He was a seaman, but he was a wanderer too, while most seamen lead, if one may so express it, a sedentary life. Their minds are of the stay-at-home order, and their home is always with them—the ship; and so is their country—the sea. One ship is very much like another, and the sea is always the same. In the immutability of their surroundings the foreign shores, the foreign faces, the changing immensity of life, glide past, veiled not by a sense of mystery but by a slightly disdainful ignorance; for there is nothing mysterious to a seaman unless it be the sea itself, which is the mistress of his existence and as incrutable as Destiny. For the rest, after his hours of work, a casual stroll or a casual spree on shore suffices to unfold for him the secret of a whole continent, and generally he finds the secret not worth knowing. The yarns of seamen have a direct simplicity, the whole meaning of which lies within

---

3. Drake (1545?–1596), admiral under Elizabeth I and first Englishman to sail around the world, whose ship was the *Golden Hind*; Franklin (1786–1847) led a party in the *Erebus* and *Terror* on an ill-fated search for the Northwest Passage which none survived.
4. The Stock Exchange.

the shell of a cracked nut. But Marlow was not typical (if his propensity to spin yarns be excepted), and to him the meaning of an episode was not inside like a kernel but outside, enveloping the tale which brought it out only as a glow brings out a haze, in the likeness of one of these misty halos that sometimes are made visible by the spectral illumination of moonshine.

His remark did not seem at all surprising. It was just like Marlow. It was accepted in silence. No one took the trouble to grunt even; and presently he said, very slow:

"I was thinking of very old times, when the Romans first came here, nineteen hundred years ago—the other day. . . . Light came out of this river since—you say Knights? Yes; but it is like a running blaze on a plain, like a flash of lightning in the clouds. We live in the flicker—may it last as long as the old earth keeps rolling! But darkness was here yesterday. Imagine the feelings of a commander of a fine—what d'ye call 'em?—trireme in the Mediterranean, ordered suddenly to the north; run overland across the Gauls in a hurry; put in charge of one of these craft the legionaries—a wonderful lot of handy men they must have been too—used to build, apparently by the hundred, in a month or two, if we may believe what we read. Imagine him here—the very end of the world, a sea the color of lead, a sky the color of smoke, a kind of ship about as rigid as a concertina—and going up this river with stores, or orders, or what you like. Sandbanks, marshes, forests, savages—precious little to eat fit for a civilized man, nothing but Thames water to drink. No Falernian wine[5] here, no going ashore. Here and there a military camp lost in a wilderness, like a needle in a bundle of hay—cold, fog, tempests, disease, exile, and death—death skulking in the air, in the water, in the bush. They must have been dying like flies here. Oh yes—he did it. Did it very well, too, no doubt, and without thinking much about it either, except afterwards to brag of what he had gone through in his time, perhaps. They were men enough to face the darkness. And perhaps he was cheered by keeping his eye on a chance of promotion to the fleet at Ravenna[6] by and by, if he had good friends in Rome and survived the awful climate. Or think of a decent young citizen in a toga—perhaps too much dice, you know—coming out here in the train of some prefect, or tax-gatherer, or trader, even, to mend his fortunes. Land in a swamp, march through the woods, and in some inland post feel the savagery, the utter savagery, had closed round him—all that mysterious life of the wilderness that stirs in the forest, in the jungles, in the hearts of wild men. There's no initiation either into such mysteries. He has to live in the midst of the incomprehensible, which is also detestable. And it has a fascination, too, that goes to work upon him. The fascination of the abomination—you know. Imagine the growing regrets, the longing to escape, the powerless disgust, the surrender, the hate."

He paused.

"Mind," he began again, lifting one arm from the elbow, the palm of the hand outwards, so that, with his legs folded before him, he had the pose of a Buddha preaching in European clothes and without a lotus-flower[7]—"Mind, none of us would feel exactly like this. What saves us is efficiency—the devotion to efficiency. But these chaps were not much account, really. They

---

5. Famous ancient wine from the region of Naples.
6. Roman naval base on the Adriatic (though now inland).
7. Buddha is often depicted sitting on a lotus seat

or standing on a lotus pedestal, the lotus flower representing spirituality, perfection, immortality, divine birth, and regeneration.

were no colonists; their administration was merely a squeeze, and nothing more, I suspect. They are conquerors, and for that you want only brute force—nothing to boast of, when you have it, since your strength is just an accident arising from the weakness of others. They grabbed what they could get for the sake of what was to be got. It was just robbery with violence, aggravated murder on a great scale, and men going at it blind—as is very proper for those who tackle a darkness. The conquest of the earth, which mostly means the taking it away from those who have a different complexion or slightly flatter noses than ourselves, is not a pretty thing when you look into it too much. What redeems it is the idea only. An idea at the back of it; not a sentimental pretense but an idea; and an unselfish belief in the idea—something you can set up, and bow down before, and offer a sacrifice to. . . ."

He broke off. Flames glided in the river, small green flames, red flames, white flames, pursuing, overtaking, joining, crossing each other—then separating slowly or hastily. The traffic of the great city went on in the deepening night upon the sleepless river. We looked on, waiting patiently—there was nothing else to do till the end of the flood; but it was only after a long silence, when he said, in a hesitating voice, "I suppose you fellows remember I did once turn fresh-water sailor for a bit," that we knew we were fated, before the ebb began to run, to hear about one of Marlow's inconclusive experiences.

"I don't want to bother you much with what happened to me personally," he began, showing in this remark the weakness of many tellers of tales who seem so often unaware of what their audience would best like to hear; "yet to understand the effect of it on me you ought to know how I got out there, what I saw, how I went up that river to the place where I first met the poor chap. It was the farthest point of navigation and the culminating point of my experience. It seemed somehow to throw a kind of light on everything about me—and into my thoughts. It was somber enough too—and pitiful—not extraordinary in any way—not very clear either. No, not very clear. And yet it seemed to throw a kind of light.

"I had then, as you remember, just returned to London after a lot of Indian Ocean, Pacific, China Seas—a regular dose of the East—six years or so, and I was loafing about, hindering you fellows in your work and invading your homes, just as though I had got a heavenly mission to civilize you. It was very fine for a time, but after a bit I did get tired of resting. Then I began to look for a ship—I should think the hardest work on earth. But the ships wouldn't even look at me. And I got tired of that game too.

"Now when I was a little chap I had a passion for maps. I would look for hours at South America, or Africa, or Australia, and lose myself in all the glories of exploration. At that time there were many blank spaces on the earth, and when I saw one that looked particularly inviting on a map (but they all look that) I would put my finger on it and say, When I grow up I will go there. The North Pole was one of these places, I remember. Well, I haven't been there yet, and shall not try now. The glamour's off. Other places were scattered about the Equator, and in every sort of latitude all over the two hemispheres. I have been in some of them, and . . . well, we won't talk about that. But there was one yet—the biggest, the most blank, so to speak—that I had a hankering after.

"True, by this time it was not a blank space any more. It had got filled since my boyhood with rivers and lakes and names. It had ceased to be a blank space of delightful mystery—a white patch for a boy to dream glo-riously over. It had become a place of darkness. But there was in it one river especially, a mighty big river, that you could see on the map, resem-bling an immense snake uncoiled, with its head in the sea, its body at rest curving afar over a vast country, and its tail lost in the depths of the land. And as I looked at the map of it in a shop-window, it fascinated me as a snake would a bird—a silly little bird. Then I remembered there was a big concern, a Company for trade on that river. Dash it all! I thought to myself, they can't trade without using some kind of craft on that lot of fresh water—steamboats! Why shouldn't I try to get charge of one? I went on along Fleet Street, but could not shake off the idea. The snake had charmed me.

"You understand it was a Continental concern, that Trading Society; but I have a lot of relations living on the Continent, because it's cheap and not so nasty as it looks, they say.

"I am sorry to own I began to worry them. This was already a fresh departure for me. I was not used to get things that way, you know. I always went my own road and on my own legs where I had a mind to go. I wouldn't have believed it of myself; but, then—you see—I felt somehow I must get there by hook or by crook. So I worried them. The men said, 'My dear fellow,' and did nothing. Then—would you believe it?—I tried the women. I, Charlie Marlow, set the women to work—to get a job. Heavens! Well, you see, the notion drove me. I had an aunt, a dear enthusiastic soul. She wrote: 'It will be delightful. I am ready to do anything, anything for you. It is a glorious idea. I know the wife of a very high personage in the Admin-istration, and also a man who has lots of influence with,' etc. etc. She was determined to make no end of fuss to get me appointed skipper of a river steamboat, if such was my fancy.

"I got my appointment—of course; and I got it very quick. It appears the Company had received news that one of their captains had been killed in a scuffle with the natives. This was my chance, and it made me the more anxious to go. It was only months and months afterwards, when I made the attempt to recover what was left of the body, that I heard the original quar-rel arose from a misunderstanding about some hens. Yes, two black hens. Fresleven—that was the fellow's name, a Dane—thought himself wronged somehow in the bargain, so he went ashore and started to hammer the chief of the village with a stick. Oh, it didn't surprise me in the least to hear this, and at the same time to be told that Fresleven was the gentlest, quietest creature that ever walked on two legs. No doubt he was; but he had been a couple of years already out there engaged in the noble cause, you know, and he probably felt the need at last of asserting his self-respect in some way. Therefore he whacked the old nigger mercilessly, while a big crowd of his people watched him, thunderstruck, till some man—I was told the chief's son—in desperation at hearing the old chap yell, made a tentative jab with a spear at the white man—and of course it went quite easy between the shoulder blades. Then the whole population cleared into the forest, expecting all kinds of calamities to happen, while, on the other hand, the steamer Fresleven commanded left also in a bad panic, in charge of the engineer, I believe. Afterwards nobody seemed to trouble much about Fresleven's remains, till I got out and stepped into his shoes. I couldn't let it rest, though; but when an opportunity offered at last to meet my prede-cessor, the grass growing through his ribs was tall enough to hide his bones. They were all there. The supernatural being had not been touched after he fell. And the village was deserted, the huts gaped black, rotting, all askew within the fallen enclosures. A calamity had come to it, sure enough. The people had vanished. Mad terror had scattered them, men, women, and children, through the bush, and they had never returned. What became of the hens I don't know either. I should think the cause of progress got them, anyhow. However, through this glorious affair I got my appointment, before I had fairly begun to hope for it.

"I flew around like mad to get ready, and before forty-eight hours I was crossing the Channel to show myself to my employers, and sign the contract. In a very few hours I arrived in a city that always makes me think of a whited sepulchre.[8] Prejudice no doubt. I had no difficulty in finding the Company's offices. It was the biggest thing in the town, and everybody I met was full of it. They were going to run an oversea empire, and make no end of coin by trade.

"A narrow and deserted street in deep shadow, high houses, innumerable windows with venetian blinds, a dead silence, grass sprouting between the stones, imposing carriage archways right and left, immense double doors standing ponderously ajar. I slipped through one of these cracks, went up a swept and ungarnished staircase, as arid as a desert, and opened the first door I came to. Two women, one fat and the other slim, sat on straw-bottomed chairs, knitting black wool. The slim one got up and walked straight at me—still knitting with downcast eyes—and only just as I began to think of getting out of her way, as you would for a somnambulist, stood still, and looked up. Her dress was as plain as an umbrella-cover, and she turned round without a word and preceded me into a waiting-room. I gave my name, and looked about. Deal table in the middle, plain chairs all round the walls, on one end a large shining map, marked with all the colors of a rainbow. There was a vast amount of red—good to see at any time, because one knows that some real work is done in there, a deuce of a lot of blue, a little green, smears of orange, and, on the East Coast, a purple patch, to show where the jolly pioneers of progress drink the jolly lager-beer. However, I wasn't going into any of these. I was going into the yellow.[9] Dead in the center. And the river was there—fascinating—deadly—like a snake. Ough! A door opened, a white-haired secretarial head, but wearing a compassionate expression, appeared, and a skinny forefinger beckoned me into the sanctuary. Its light was dim, and a heavy writing-desk squatted in the middle. From behind that structure came out an impression of pale plumpness in a frock-coat. The great man himself. He was five feet six, I should judge, and had his grip on the handle-end of ever so many millions. He shook hands, I fancy, murmured vaguely, was satisfied with my French. *Bon voyage.*

"In about forty-five seconds I found myself again in the waiting room with the compassionate secretary, who, full of desolation and sympathy, made me sign some document. I believe I undertook amongst other things not to disclose any trade secrets. Well, I am not going to.

"I began to feel slightly uneasy. You know I am not used to such ceremonies, and there was something ominous in the atmosphere. It was just as though I had been let into some conspiracy—I don't know—something

8. "Whited sepulchres, which indeed appear beautiful outward, but are within full of dead men's bones." *Matthew* 23:27.

9. Though British territories or colonies are almost universally shown as red, there seems to be no fixed color system now or in the 19th century for indicating national holdings. Here the blue seems to be French; green, Portuguese; purple, German; yellow, the Congo Free State.

not quite right; and I was glad to get out. In the outer room the two women knitted black wool feverishly. People were arriving, and the younger one was walking back and forth introducing them. The old one sat on her chair. Her flat cloth slippers were propped up on a foot-warmer, and a cat reposed on her lap. She wore a starched white affair on her head, had a wart on one cheek, and silver-rimmed spectacles hung on the tip of her nose. She glanced at me above the glasses. The swift and indifferent placidity of that look troubled me. Two youths with foolish and cheery countenances were being piloted over, and she threw at them the same quick glance of unconcerned wisdom. She seemed to know all about them and about me too. An eerie feeling came over me. She seemed uncanny and fateful. Often far away there I thought of these two, guarding the door of Darkness, knitting black wool as for a warm pall, one introducing, introducing continuously to the unknown, the other scrutinizing the cheery and foolish faces with unconcerned old eyes. *Ave!* Old knitter of black wool. *Morituri te salutant.*[1] Not many of those she looked at ever saw her again—not half, by a long way.

"There was yet a visit to the doctor. 'A simple formality,' assured me the secretary, with an air of taking an immense part in all my sorrows. Accordingly a young chap wearing his hat over the left eyebrow, some clerk I suppose—there must have been clerks in the business, though the house was as still as a house in a city of the dead—came from somewhere upstairs, and led me forth. He was shabby and careless, with inkstains on the sleeves of his jacket, and his cravat was large and billowy, under a chin shaped like the toe of an old boot. It was a little too early for the doctor, so I proposed a drink, and thereupon he developed a vein of joviality. As we sat over our vermouths he glorified the Company's business, and by and by I expressed casually my surprise at him not going out there. He became very cool and collected all at once. 'I am not such a fool as I look, quoth Plato to his disciples,' he said sententiously, emptied his glass with great resolution, and we rose.

"The old doctor felt my pulse, evidently thinking of something else the while. 'Good, good for there,' he mumbled, and then with a certain eagerness asked me whether I would let him measure my head. Rather surprised, I said Yes, when he produced a thing like callipers and got the dimensions back and front and every way, taking notes carefully. He was an unshaven little man in a threadbare coat like a gaberdine, with his feet in slippers, and I thought him a harmless fool. 'I always ask leave, in the interests of science, to measure the crania of those going out there,' he said. 'And when they come back too?' I asked. 'Oh, I never see them,' he remarked; 'and, moreover, the changes take place inside, you know.' He smiled, as if at some quiet joke. 'So you are going out there. Famous.[2] Interesting too.' He gave me a searching glance, and made another note. 'Ever any madness in your family?' he asked, in a matter-of-fact tone. I felt very annoyed. 'Is that question in the interests of science too?' 'It would be,' he said, without taking notice of my irritation, 'interesting for science to watch the mental changes of individuals, on the spot, but . . .' 'Are you an alienist?'[3] I interrupted. 'Every doctor should be—a little,' answered that original imperturbably. 'I have a little theory which you Messieurs who go out there must help me to prove. This is my share in the advantages my country shall reap

---

1. Gladiators' salutation to the Roman emperor: "Hail! . . . Those who are about to die salute you."
2. Excellent, splendid.
3. Psychiatrist.

from the possession of such a magnificent dependency. The mere wealth I leave to others. Pardon my questions, but you are the first Englishman coming under my observation . . .' I hastened to assure him I was not in the least typical. 'If I were,' said I, 'I wouldn't be talking like this with you.' 'What you say is rather profound, and probably erroneous,' he said, with a laugh. 'Avoid irritation more than exposure to the sun. Adieu. How do you English say, eh? Good-bye. Ah! Good-bye. Adieu. In the tropics one must before everything keep calm.' . . . He lifted a warning forefinger. . . . 'Du calme, du calme. Adieu.'

"One thing more remained to do—say good-bye to my excellent aunt. I found her triumphant. I had a cup of tea—the last decent cup of tea for many days—and, in a room that most soothingly looked just as you would expect a lady's drawing room to look, we had a long quiet chat by the fireside. In the course of these confidences it became quite plain to me I had been represented to the wife of the high dignitary, and goodness knows to how many more people besides, as an exceptional and gifted creature—a piece of good fortune for the Company—a man you don't get hold of every day. Good Heavens! and I was going to take charge of a two-penny-halfpenny river-steamboat with a penny whistle attached! It appeared, however, I was also one of the Workers, with a capital—you know. Something like an emissary of light, something like a lower sort of apostle. There had been a lot of such rot let loose in print and talk just about that time, and the excellent woman, living right in the rush of all that humbug, got carried off her feet. She talked about 'weaning those ignorant millions from their horrid ways,' till, upon my word, she made me quite uncomfortable. I ventured to hint that the Company was run for profit.

" 'You forget, dear Charlie, that the laborer is worthy of his hire,'[4] she said brightly. It's queer how out of touch with truth women are. They live in a world of their own, and there had never been anything like it, and never can be. It is too beautiful altogether, and if they were to set it up it would go to pieces before the first sunset. Some confounded fact we men have been living contentedly with ever since the day of creation would start up and knock the whole thing over.

"After this I got embraced, told to wear flannel, be sure to write often, and so on—and I left. In the street—I don't know why—a queer feeling came to me that I was an impostor. Odd thing that I, who used to clear out for any part of the world at twenty-four hours' notice, with less thought than most men give to the crossing of a street, had a moment—I won't say of hesitation, but of startled pause, before this commonplace affair. The best way I can explain it to you is by saying that, for a second or two, I felt as though, instead of going to the center of a continent, I were about to set off for the center of the earth.

"I left in a French steamer, and she called in every blamed port they have out there, for, as far as I could see, the sole purpose of landing soldiers and customhouse officers. I watched the coast. Watching a coast as it slips by the ship is like thinking about an enigma. There it is before you—smiling, frowning, inviting, grand, mean, insipid, or savage, and always mute with an air of whispering, Come and find out. This one was almost featureless, as if still in the making, with an aspect of monotonous grimness. The edge of a colossal jungle, so dark green as to be almost black, fringed with

---

4. Words of Jesus in Luke 10:7.

white surf, ran straight, like a ruled line, far, far away along a blue sea
whose glitter was blurred by a creeping mist. The sun was fierce, the land
seemed to glisten and drip with steam. Here and there greyish-whitish
specks showed up clustered inside the white surf, with a flag flying above
them perhaps—settlements some centuries old, and still no bigger than
pinheads on the untouched expanse of their background. We pounded along,
stopped, landed soldiers; went on, landed customhouse clerks to levy toll
in what looked like a God-forsaken wilderness, with a tin shed and a flag-
pole lost in it; landed more soldiers—to take care of the customhouse clerks
presumably. Some, I heard, got drowned in the surf; but whether they did
or not, nobody seemed particularly to care. They were just flung out there,
and on we went. Every day the coast looked the same, as though we had
not moved; but we passed various places—trading places—with names like
Gran' Bassam, Little Popo; names that seemed to belong to some sordid
farce acted in front of a sinister back-cloth. The idleness of a passenger, my
isolation amongst all these men with whom I had no point of contact, the
oily and languid sea, the uniform somberness of the coast, seemed to keep
me away from the truth of things, within the toil of a mournful and senseless
delusion. The voice of the surf heard now and then was a positive pleasure,
like the speech of a brother. It was something natural, that had its reason,
that had a meaning. Now and then a boat from the shore gave one a
momentary contact with reality. It was paddled by black fellows. You could
see from afar the white of their eyeballs glistening. They shouted, sang;
their bodies streamed with perspiration; they had faces like grotesque masks—
these chaps; but they had bone, muscle, a wild vitality, an intense energy
of movement, that was as natural and true as the surf along their coast.
They wanted no excuse for being there. They were a great comfort to look
at. For a time I would feel I belonged still to a world of straightforward
facts; but the feeling would not last long. Something would turn up to scare
it away. Once, I remember, we came upon a man-of-war anchored off the
coast. There wasn't even a shed there, and she was shelling the bush. It
appears the French had one of their wars going on thereabouts. Her ensign
dropped limp like a rag; the muzzles of the long six-inch guns stuck out all
over the low hull; the greasy, slimy swell swung her up lazily and let her
down, swaying her thin masts. In the empty immensity of earth, sky, and
water, there she was, incomprehensible, firing into a continent. Pop, would
go one of the six-inch guns; a small flame would dart and vanish, a little
white smoke would disappear, a tiny projectile would give a feeble screech—
and nothing happened. Nothing could happen. There was a touch of insanity in the proceeding, a sense of lugubrious drollery in the sight; and it was
not dissipated by somebody on board assuring me earnestly there was a
camp of natives—he called them enemies!—hidden out of sight somewhere.

"We gave her her letters (I heard the men in that lonely ship were dying
of fever at the rate of three a day) and went on. We called at some more
places with farcical names, where the merry dance of death and trade goes
on in a still and earthy atmosphere as of an overheated catacomb; all along
the formless coast bordered by dangerous surf, as if Nature herself had tried
to ward off intruders; in and out of rivers, streams of death in life, whose
banks were rotting into mud, whose waters, thickened into slime, invaded
the contorted mangroves, that seemed to writhe at us in the extremity of
an impotent despair. Nowhere did we stop long enough to get a particular-

ized impression, but the general sense of vague and oppressive wonder grew upon me. It was like a weary pilgrimage amongst hints for nightmares.

"It was upward of thirty days before I saw the mouth of the big river. We anchored off the seat of the government. But my work would not begin till some two hundred miles farther on. So as soon as I could I made a start for a place thirty miles higher up.

"I had my passage on a little sea-going steamer. Her captain was a Swede, and knowing me for a seaman, invited me on the bridge. He was a young man, lean, fair, and morose, with lanky hair and a shuffling gait. As we left the miserable little wharf, he tossed his head contemptuously at the shore. 'Been living there?' he asked. I said, 'Yes.' 'Fine lot these government chaps— are they not?' he went on, speaking English with great precision and considerable bitterness. 'It is funny what some people will do for a few francs a month. I wonder what becomes of that kind when it goes up country?' I said to him I expected to see that soon. 'So-o-o!' he exclaimed. He shuffled athwart, keeping one eye ahead vigilantly. 'Don't be too sure,' he continued. 'The other day I took up a man who hanged himself on the road. He was a Swede, too.' 'Hanged himself! Why, in God's name?' I cried. He kept on looking out watchfully. 'Who knows? The sun too much for him, or the country perhaps.'

"At last we opened a reach. A rocky cliff appeared, mounds of turned-up earth by the shore, houses on a hill, others with iron roofs, amongst a waste of excavations, or hanging to the declivity. A continuous noise of the rapids above hovered over this scene of inhabited devastation. A lot of people, mostly black and naked, moved about like ants. A jetty projected into the river. A blinding sunlight drowned all this at times in a sudden recrudescence of glare. 'There's your Company's station,' said the Swede, pointing to three wooden barrack-like structures on the rocky slope. 'I will send your things up. Four boxes did you say? So. Farewell.'

"I came upon a boiler wallowing in the grass, then found a path leading up the hill. It turned aside for the boulders, and also for an undersized railway truck lying there on its back with its wheels in the air. One was off. The thing looked as dead as the carcass of some animal. I came upon more pieces of decaying machinery, a stack of rusty rails. To the left a clump of trees made a shady spot, where dark things seemed to stir feebly. I blinked, the path was steep. A horn tooted to the right, and I saw the black people run. A heavy and dull detonation shook the ground, a puff of smoke came out of the cliff, and that was all. No change appeared on the face of the rock. They were building a railway. The cliff was not in the way or anything; but this objectless blasting was all the work going on.

"A slight clinking behind me made me turn my head. Six black men advanced in a file, toiling up the path. They walked erect and slow, balancing small baskets full of earth on their heads, and the clink kept time with their footsteps. Black rags were wound round their loins, and the short ends behind waggled to and fro like tails. I could see every rib, the joints of their limbs were like knots in a rope; each had an iron collar on his neck, and all were connected together with a chain whose bights swung between them, rhythmically clinking. Another report from the cliff made me think suddenly of that ship of war I had seen firing into a continent. It was the same kind of ominous voice; but these men could by no stretch of imagination be called enemies. They were called criminals, and the outraged law, like the bursting shells, had come to them, an insoluble mystery from the sea. All their meager breasts panted together, the violently dilated nostrils quivered, the eyes stared stonily uphill. They passed me within six inches, without a glance, with that complete, deathlike indifference of unhappy savages. Behind this raw matter one of the reclaimed, the product of the new forces at work, strolled despondently, carrying a rifle by its middle. He had a uniform jacket with one button off, and seeing a white man on the path, hoisted his weapon to his shoulder with alacrity. This was simple prudence, white men being so much alike at a distance that he could not tell who I might be. He was speedily reassured, and with a large, white, rascally grin, and a glance at his charge, seemed to take me into partnership in his exalted trust. After all, I also was a part of the great cause of these high and just proceedings.

"Instead of going up, I turned and descended to the left. My idea was to let that chain gang get out of sight before I climbed the hill. You know I am not particularly tender; I've had to strike and to fend off. I've had to resist and to attack sometimes—that's only one way of resisting—without counting the exact cost, according to the demands of such sort of life as I had blundered into. I've seen the devil of violence, and the devil of greed, and the devil of hot desire; but, by all the stars! these were strong, lusty, red-eyed devils, that swayed and drove men—men, I tell you. But as I stood on this hillside, I foresaw that in the blinding sunshine of that land I would become acquainted with a flabby, pretending, weak-eyed devil of a rapacious and pitiless folly. How insidious he could be, too, I was only to find out several months later and a thousand miles farther. For a moment I stood appalled, as though by a warning. Finally I descended the hill, obliquely, towards the trees I had seen.

"I avoided a vast artificial hole somebody had been digging on the slope, the purpose of which I found it impossible to divine. It wasn't a quarry or a sandpit, anyhow. It was just a hole. It might have been connected with the philanthropic desire of giving the criminals something to do. I don't know. Then I nearly fell into a very narrow ravine, almost no more than a scar in the hillside. I discovered that a lot of imported drainage-pipes for the settlement had been tumbled in there. There wasn't one that was not broken. It was a wanton smashup. At last I got under the trees. My purpose was to stroll into the shade for a moment; but no sooner within than it seemed to me I had stepped into the gloomy circle of some Inferno. The rapids were near, and an uninterrupted, uniform, headlong, rushing noise filled the mournful stillness of the grove, where not a breath stirred, not a leaf moved, with a mysterious sound—as though the tearing pace of the launched earth had suddenly become audible.

"Black shapes crouched, lay, sat between the trees, leaning against the trunks, clinging to the earth, half coming out, half effaced within the dim light, in all the attitudes of pain, abandonment, and despair. Another mine on the cliff went off, followed by a slight shudder of the soil under my feet. The work was going on. The work! And this was the place where some of the helpers had withdrawn to die.

"They were dying slowly—it was very clear. They were not enemies, they were not criminals, they were nothing earthly now—nothing but black shadows of disease and starvation, lying confusedly in the greenish gloom. Brought from all the recesses of the coast in all the legality of time contracts, lost in uncongenial surroundings, fed on unfamiliar food, they sickened, became inefficient, and were then allowed to crawl away and rest. These moribund shapes were free as air—and nearly as thin. I began to distinguish the gleam of eyes under the trees. Then, glancing down, I saw a face near my hand. The black bones reclined at full length with one shoulder against the tree, and slowly the eyelids rose and the sunken eyes looked up at me, enormous and vacant, a kind of blind, white flicker in the depths of the orbs, which died out slowly. The man seemed young—almost a boy—but you know with them it's hard to tell. I found nothing else to do but to offer him one of my good Swede's ship's biscuits I had in my pocket. The fingers closed slowly on it and held—there was no other movement and no other glance. He had tied a bit of white worsted round his neck—Why? Where did he get it? Was it a badge—an ornament—a charm—a propitiatory act? Was there any idea at all connected with it? It looked startling round his black neck, this bit of white thread from beyond the seas.

"Near the same tree two more bundles of acute angles sat with their legs drawn up. One, with his chin propped on his knees, stared at nothing, in an intolerable and appalling manner: his brother phantom rested its forehead, as if overcome with a great weariness; and all about others were scattered in every pose of contorted collapse, as in some picture of a massacre or a pestilence. While I stood horror-struck, one of these creatures rose to his hands and knees, and went off on all-fours towards the river to drink. He lapped out of his hand, then sat up in the sunlight, crossing his shins in front of him, and after a time let his woolly head fall on his breastbone.

"I didn't want any more loitering in the shade, and I made haste towards the station. When near the buildings I met a white man, in such an unexpected elegance of getup that in the first moment I took him for a sort of vision. I saw a high starched collar, white cuffs, a light alpaca jacket, snowy trousers, a clear necktie, and varnished boots. No hat. Hair parted, brushed, oiled, under a green-lined parasol held in a big white hand. He was amazing, and had a pen-holder behind his ear.

"I shook hands with this miracle, and I learned he was the Company's chief accountant, and that all the bookkeeping was done at this station. He had come out for a moment, he said, 'to get a breath of fresh air.' The expression sounded wonderfully odd, with its suggestion of sedentary desk-life. I wouldn't have mentioned the fellow to you at all, only it was from his lips that I first heard the name of the man who is so indissolubly connected with the memories of that time. Moreover, I respected the fellow. Yes; I respected his collars, his vast cuffs, his brushed hair. His appearance was certainly that of a hairdresser's dummy; but in the great demoralization of the land he kept up his appearance. That's backbone. His starched collars and got-up shirtfronts were achievements of character. He had been out nearly three years; and, later, I could not help asking him how he managed to sport such linen. He had just the faintest blush, and said modestly, 'I've been teaching one of the native women about the station. It was difficult. She had a distaste for the work.' Thus this man had verily accomplished something. And he was devoted to his books, which were in apple-pie order.

"Everything else in the station was in a muddle,—heads, things, buildings. Strings of dusty niggers with splay feet arrived and departed; a stream of manufactured goods, rubbishy cottons, beads, and brass-wire set into the depths of darkness, and in return came a precious trickle of ivory.

"I had to wait in the station for ten days—an eternity. I lived in a hut in the yard, but to be out of the chaos I would sometimes get into the accountant's office. It was built of horizontal planks, and so badly put together that, as he bent over his high desk, he was barred from neck to heels with narrow strips of sunlight. There was no need to open the big shutter to see. It was hot there too; big flies buzzed fiendishly, and did not sting, but stabbed. I sat generally on the floor, while, of faultless appearance (and even slightly scented), perching on a high stool, he wrote, he wrote. Sometimes he stood up for exercise. When a truckle bed with a sick man (some invalided agent from up-country) was put in there, he exhibited a gentle annoyance. 'The groans of this sick person' he said, 'distract my attention. And without that it is extremely difficult to guard against clerical errors in this climate.'

"One day he remarked, without lifting his head, 'In the interior you will no doubt meet Mr. Kurtz.' On my asking who Mr. Kurtz was, he said he was a first-class agent; and seeing my disappointment at this information, he added slowly, laying down his pen, 'He is a very remarkable person.' Further questions elicited from him that Mr. Kurtz was at present in charge of a trading post, a very important one, in the true ivory-country, at 'the very bottom of there. Sends in as much ivory as all the others put together . . .' He began to write again. The sick man was too ill to groan. The flies buzzed in a great peace.

"Suddenly there was a growing murmur of voices and a great tramping of feet. A caravan had come in. A violent babble of uncouth sounds burst out on the other side of the planks. All the carriers were speaking together, and in the midst of the uproar the lamentable voice of the chief agent was heard 'giving it up'[5] tearfully for the twentieth time that day. . . . He rose slowly. 'What a frightful row,' he said. He crossed the room gently to look at the sick man, and returning, said to me, 'He does not hear.' 'What! Dead?' I asked, startled. 'No, not yet,' he answered, with great composure. Then, alluding with a toss of the head to the tumult in the station-yard, 'When one has got to make correct entries, one comes to hate those savages—hate them to the death.' He remained thoughtful for a moment. 'When you see Mr. Kurtz,' he went on, 'tell him from me that everything here'— he glanced at the desk—'is very satisfactory. I don't like to write to him— with those messengers of ours you never know who may get hold of your letter—at that Central Station.' He stared at me for a moment with his mild, bulging eyes. 'Oh, he will go far, very far,' he began again. 'He will be a somebody in the Administration before long. They, above—the Council in Europe, you know—mean him to be.'

"He turned to his work. The noise outside had ceased, and presently in going out I stopped at the door. In the steady buzz of flies the homeward-bound agent was lying flushed and insensible; the other, bent over his books, was making correct entries of perfectly correct transactions; and fifty feet below the doorstep I could see the still treetops of the grove of death.

"Next day I left that station at last, with a caravan of sixty men, for a two-hundred-mile tramp.

"No use telling you much about that. Paths, paths, everywhere; a stamped-in network of paths spreading over the empty land, through long grass, through burnt grass, through thickets, down and up chilly ravines, up and down stony hills ablaze with heat; and a solitude, a solitude, nobody, not a hut. The population had cleared out a long time ago. Well, if a lot of mysterious niggers armed with all kinds of fearful weapons suddenly took to

5. Uttering a cry.

traveling on the road between Deal[6] and Gravesend, catching the yokels right and left to carry heavy loads for them, I fancy every farm and cottage thereabouts would get empty very soon. Only here the dwellings were gone too. Still, I passed through several abandoned villages. There's something pathetically childish in the ruins of grass walls. Day after day, with the stamp and shuffle of sixty pair of bare feet behind me, each pair under a 60-lb. load. Camp, cook, sleep; strike camp, march. Now and then a carrier dead in harness, at rest in the long grass near the path, with an empty water-gourd and his long staff lying by his side. A great silence around and above. Perhaps on some quiet night the tremor of far-off drums, sinking, swelling, a tremor vast, faint; a sound weird, appealing, suggestive, and wild—and perhaps with as profound a meaning as the sound of bells in a Christian country. Once a white man in an unbuttoned uniform, camping on the path with an armed escort of lank Zanzibaris,[7] very hospitable and festive—not to say drunk. Was looking after the upkeep of the road, he declared. Can't say I saw any road or any upkeep, unless the body of a middle-aged negro, with a bullet hole in the forehead, upon which I absolutely stumbled three miles farther on, may be considered as a permanent improvement. I had a white companion too, not a bad chap, but rather too fleshy and with the exasperating habit of fainting on the hot hillsides, miles away from the least bit of shade and water. Annoying, you know, to hold your own coat like a parasol over a man's head while he is coming to. I couldn't help asking him once what he meant by coming there at all. 'To make money, of course. What do you think?' he said scornfully. Then he got fever, and had to be carried in a hammock slung under a pole. As he weighed sixteen stone.[8] I had no end of rows with the carriers. They jibbed, ran away, sneaked off with their loads in the night—quite a mutiny. So, one evening, I made a speech in English with gestures, not one of which was lost to the sixty pairs of eyes before me, and the next morning I started the hammock off in front all right. An hour afterwards I came upon the whole concern wrecked in a bush—man, hammock, groans, blankets, horrors. The heavy pole had skinned his poor nose. He was very anxious for me to kill somebody, but there wasn't the shadow of a carrier near. I remembered the old doctor—'It would be interesting for science to watch the mental changes of individuals, on the spot.' I felt I was becoming scientifically interesting. However, all that is to no purpose. On the fifteenth day I came in sight of the big river again, and hobbled into the Central Station. It was on a backwater surrounded by scrub and forest, with a pretty border of smelly mud on one side, and on the three others enclosed by a crazy[9] fence of rushes. A neglected gap was all the gate it had, and the first glance at the place was enough to let you see the flabby devil was running that show. White men with long staves in their hands appeared languidly from amongst the buildings, strolling up to take a look at me, and then retired out of sight somewhere. One of them, a stout, excitable chap with black moustaches, informed me with great volubility and many digressions, as soon as I told him who I was, that my steamer was at the bottom of the river. I was thunderstruck. What, how, why? Oh, it was 'all right.' The 'manager himself' was there. All quite correct. 'Everybody had behaved

6. Port near Dover.
7. Zanzibar, then a British-controlled region of East Africa (now part of Tanzania), supplied mercenaries for service throughout the continent.
8. I.e., 224 pounds; a stone, 14 pounds, is a standard British measure.
9. Irregular and/or shaky.

splendidly! splendidly!'—'You must,' he said in agitation, 'go and see the general manager at once. He is waiting.'

"I did not see the real significance of that wreck at once. I fancy I see it now, but I am not sure—not at all. Certainly the affair was too stupid—when I think of it—to be altogether natural. Still . . . But at the moment it presented itself simply as a confounded nuisance. The steamer was sunk. They had started two days before in a sudden hurry up the river with the manager on board, in charge of some volunteer skipper, and before they had been out three hours they tore the bottom out of her on stones, and she sank near the south bank. I asked myself what I was to do there, now my boat was lost. As a matter of fact, I had plenty to do in fishing my command out of the river. I had to set about it the very next day. That, and the repairs when I brought the pieces to the station, took some months.

"My first interview with the manager was curious. He did not ask me to sit down after my twenty-mile walk that morning. He was commonplace in complexion, in feature, in manners, and in voice. He was of middle size and of ordinary build. His eyes, of the usual blue, were perhaps remarkably cold, and he certainly could make his glance fall on one as trenchant and heavy as an axe. But even at these times the rest of his person seemed to disclaim the intention. Otherwise there was only an indefinable, faint expression of his lips, something stealthy—a smile—not a smile—I remember it, but I can't explain. It was unconscious, this smile was, though just after he had said something it got intensified for an instant. It came at the end of his speeches like a seal applied on the words to make the meaning of the commonest phrase appear absolutely inscrutable. He was a common trader, from his youth up employed in these parts—nothing more. He was obeyed, yet he inspired neither love nor fear, nor even respect. He inspired uneasiness. That was it! Uneasiness. Not a definite mistrust—just uneasiness—nothing more. You have no idea how effective such a . . . a . . . faculty can be. He had no genius for organizing, for initiative, or for order even. That was evident in such things as the deplorable state of the station. He had no learning, and no intelligence. His position had come to him—why? Perhaps because he was never ill . . . He had served three terms of three years out there . . . Because triumphant health in the general rout of constitutions is a kind of power in itself. When he went home on leave he rioted on a large scale—pompously. Jack[1] ashore—with a difference—in externals only. This one could gather from his casual talk. He originated nothing, he could keep the routine going—that's all. But he was great. He was great by this little thing that it was impossible to tell what could control such a man. He never gave that secret away. Perhaps there was nothing within him. Such a suspicion made one pause—for out there there were no external checks. Once when various tropical diseases had laid low almost every 'agent' in the station, he was heard to say, 'Men who come out here should have no entrails.' He sealed the utterance with that smile of his, as though it had been a door opening into a darkness he had in his keeping. You fancied you had seen things—but the seal was on. When annoyed at mealtimes by the constant quarrels of the white men about precedence, he ordered an immense round table to be made, for which a special house had to be built. This was the station's mess room. Where he sat was the first place—the rest were nowhere. One felt this to be his unalterable con-

1. Sailor.

viction. He was neither civil nor uncivil. He was quiet. He allowed his 'boy'—an overfed young negro from the coast—to treat the white men, under his very eyes, with provoking insolence.

"He began to speak as soon as he saw me. I had been very long on the road. He could not wait. Had to start without me. The up-river stations had to be relieved. There had been so many delays already that he did not know who was dead and who was alive, and how they got on—and so on, and so on. He paid no attention to my explanations, and, playing with a stick of sealing wax, repeated several times that the situation was 'very grave, very grave.' There were rumors that a very important station was in jeopardy, and its chief, Mr. Kurtz, was ill. Hoped it was not true. Mr. Kurtz was . . . I felt weary and irritable. Hang Kurtz, I thought. I interrupted him by saying I had heard of Mr. Kurtz on the coast. 'Ah! So they talk of him down there,' he murmured to himself. Then he began again, assuring me Mr. Kurtz was the best agent he had, an exceptional man, of the greatest importance to the Company; therefore I could understand his anxiety. He was, he said, 'very, very uneasy.' Certainly he fidgeted on his chair a good deal, exclaimed, 'Ah, Mr. Kurtz!' broke the stick of sealing wax and seemed dumbfounded by the accident. Next thing he wanted to know 'how long it would take to' . . . I interrupted him again. Being hungry, you know, and kept on my feet too, I was getting savage. 'How can I tell?' I said. 'I haven't even seen the wreck yet—some months, no doubt.' All this talk seemed to me so futile. 'Some months,' he said. 'Well, let us say three months before we can make a start. Yes. That ought to do the affair.' I flung out of his hut (he lived all alone in a clay hut with a sort of verandah) muttering to myself my opinion of him. He was a chattering idiot. Afterwards I took it back when it was borne in upon me startlingly with what extreme nicety he had estimated the time requisite for the 'affair.'

"I went to work the next day, turning, so to speak, my back on that station. In that way only it seemed to me I could keep my hold on the redeeming facts of life. Still, one must look about sometimes; and then I saw this station, these men strolling aimlessly about in the sunshine of the yard. I asked myself sometimes what it all meant. They wandered here and there with their absurd long staves in their hands, like a lot of faithless pilgrims bewitched inside a rotten fence. The word 'ivory' rang in the air, was whispered, was sighed. You would think they were praying to it. A taint of imbecile rapacity blew through it all, like a whiff from some corpse. By Jove! I've never seen anything so unreal in my life. And outside, the silent wilderness surrounding this cleared speck on the earth struck me as something great and invincible, like evil or truth, waiting patiently for the passing away of this fantastic invasion.

"Oh, these months! Well, never mind. Various things happened. One evening a grass shed full of calico, cotton prints, beads, and I don't know what else, burst into a blaze so suddenly that you would have thought the earth had opened to let an avenging fire consume all that trash. I was smoking my pipe quietly by my dismantled steamer, and saw them all cutting capers in the light, with their arms lifted high, when the stout man with moustaches came tearing down to the river, a tin pail in his hand, assured me that everybody was 'behaving splendidly, splendidly,' dipped about a quart of water and tore back again. I noticed there was a hole in the bottom of his pail.

"I strolled up. There was no hurry. You see the thing had gone off like a box of matches. It had been hopeless from the very first. The flame had leaped high, driven everybody back, lighted up everything—and collapsed. The shed was already a heap of embers glowing fiercely. A nigger was being beaten near by. They said he had caused the fire in some way; be that as it may, he was screeching most horribly. I saw him, later, for several days, sitting in a bit of shade looking very sick and trying to recover himself: afterwards he arose and went out—and the wilderness without a sound took him into its bosom again. As I approached the glow from the dark I found myself at the back of two men, talking. I heard the name of Kurtz pronounced, then the words, 'take advantage of this unfortunate accident.' One of the men was the manager. I wished him a good evening. 'Did you ever see anything like it—eh? it is incredible,' he said, and walked off. The other man remained. He was a first-class agent, young, gentlemanly, a bit reserved, with a forked little beard and a hooked nose. He was standoffish with the other agents, and they on their side said he was the manager's spy upon them. As to me, I had hardly ever spoken to him before. We got into talk, and by and by we strolled away from the hissing ruins. Then he asked me to his room, which was in the main building of the station. He struck a match, and I perceived that this young aristocrat had not only a silver-mounted dressing case but also a whole candle all to himself. Just at that time the manager was the only man supposed to have any right to candles. Native mats covered the clay walls; a collection of spears, assegais, shields, knives, was hung up in trophies. The business entrusted to this fellow was the making of bricks—so I had been informed; but there wasn't a fragment of a brick anywhere in the station, and he had been there more than a year—waiting. It seems he could not make bricks without something, I don't know what—straw² maybe. Anyway, it could not be found there, and as it was not likely to be sent from Europe, it did not appear clear to me what he was waiting for. An act of special creation perhaps. However, they were all waiting—all the sixteen or twenty pilgrims of them—for something; and upon my word it did not seem an uncongenial occupation, from the way they took it, though the only thing that ever came to them was disease—as far as I could see. They beguiled the time by backbiting and intriguing against each other in a foolish kind of way. There was an air of plotting about that station, but nothing came of it, of course. It was as unreal as everything else—as the philanthropic pretense of the whole concern, as their talk, as their government, as their show of work. The only real feeling was a desire to get appointed to a trading post where ivory was to be had, so that they could earn percentages. They intrigued and slandered and hated each other only on that account—but as to effectually lifting a little finger—oh no. By Heavens! there is something after all in the world allowing one man to steal a horse while another must not look at a halter. Steal a horse straight out. Very well. He has done it. Perhaps he can ride. But there is a way of looking at a halter that would provoke the most charitable of saints into a kick.

"I had no idea why he wanted to be sociable, but as we chatted in there it suddenly occurred to me the fellow was trying to get at something—in fact, pumping me. He alluded constantly to Europe, to the people I was

---

2. In *Exodus* 5, the Hebrews, slaves of the Egyptians, had to make a certain number of bricks daily, the straw for the process supplied by the Egyptians, but the Pharaoh ordered the supplying of straw stopped while keeping the daily quota the same; not only was a good deal of time lost searching for straw, but little else than stubble could be found.

supposed to know there—putting leading questions as to my acquaintances in the sepulchral city, and so on. His little eyes glittered like mica discs—with curiosity—though he tried to keep up a bit of superciliousness. At first I was astonished, but very soon I became awfully curious to see what he would find out from me. I couldn't possibly imagine what I had in me to make it worth his while. It was very pretty to see how he baffled himself, for in truth my body was full only of chills, and my head had nothing in it but that wretched steamboat business. It was evident he took me for a perfectly shameless prevaricator. At last he got angry, and, to conceal a movement of furious annoyance, he yawned. I rose. Then I noticed a small sketch in oils, on a panel, representing a woman, draped and blindfolded, carrying a lighted torch. The background was somber—almost black. The movement of the woman was stately, and the effect of the torchlight on the face was sinister.

"It arrested me, and he stood by civilly, holding an empty half-pint champagne bottle (medical comforts) with the candle stuck in it. To my question he said Mr. Kurtz had painted this—in this very station more than a year ago—while waiting for means to go to his trading-post. 'Tell me, pray,' said I, 'who is this Mr. Kurtz?'

" 'The chief of the Inner Station,' he answered in a short tone, looking away. 'Much obliged,' I said, laughing. 'And you are the brickmaker of the Central Station. Everyone knows that.' He was silent for a while. 'He is a prodigy,' he said at last. 'He is an emissary of pity, and science, and progress, and devil knows what else. We want,' he began to declaim suddenly, 'for the guidance of the cause entrusted to us by Europe, so to speak, higher intelligence, wide sympathies, a singleness of purpose.' 'Who says that?' I asked. 'Lots of them,' he replied. 'Some even write that; and so *he* comes here, a special being, as you ought to know.' 'Why ought I to know?' I interrupted, really surprised. He paid no attention. 'Yes. Today he is chief of the best station, next year he will be assistant-manager, two years more and . . . but I daresay you know what he will be in two years' time. You are of the new gang—the gang of virtue. The same people who sent him specially also recommended you. Oh, don't say no. I've my own eyes to trust.' Light dawned upon me. My dear aunt's influential acquaintances were producing an unexpected effect upon that young man. I nearly burst into a laugh. 'Do you read the Company's confidential correspondence?' I asked. He hadn't a word to say. It was great fun. 'When Mr. Kurtz,' I continued severely, 'is General Manager, you won't have the opportunity.'

"He blew the candle out suddenly, and we went outside. The moon had risen. Black figures strolled about listlessly, pouring water on the glow, whence proceeded a sound of hissing; steam ascended in the moonlight; the beaten nigger groaned somewhere. 'What a row the brute makes!' said the indefatigable man with the moustaches, appearing near us. 'Serve him right. Transgression—punishment—bang! Pitiless, pitiless. That's the only way. This will prevent all conflagrations for the future. I was just telling the manager . . .' He noticed my companion, and became crestfallen all at once. 'Not in bed yet,' he said, with a kind of servile heartiness; 'it's so natural. Ha! Danger—agitation.' He vanished. I went on to the riverside, and the other followed me. I heard a scathing murmur at my ear, 'Heap of muffs—go to.' The pilgrims could be seen in knots gesticulating, discussing. Several had still their staves in their hands. I verily believe they took these sticks to bed with them. Beyond the fence the forest stood up spectrally in the moonlight, and through the dim stir, through the faint sounds of that lamentable courtyard, the silence of the land went home to one's very heart— its mystery, its greatness, the amazing reality of its concealed life. The hurt nigger moaned feebly somewhere near by, and then fetched a deep sigh that made me mend my pace away from there. I felt a hand introducing itself under my arm. 'My dear sir,' said the fellow, 'I don't want to be misunderstood, and especially by you, who will see Mr. Kurtz long before I can have that pleasure. I wouldn't like him to get a false idea of my disposition. . . .'

"I let him run on, this papier-mâché Mephistopheles, and it seemed to me that if I tried I could poke my forefinger through him, and would find nothing inside but a little loose dirt, maybe. He, don't you see, had been planning to be assistant manager by and by under the present man, and I could see that the coming of that Kurtz had upset them both not a little. He talked precipitately, and I did not try to stop him. I had my shoulders against the wreck of my steamer, hauled up on the slope like a carcass of some big river animal. The smell of mud, of primeval mud, by Jove! was in my nostrils, the high stillness of primeval forest was before my eyes; there were shiny patches on the black creek. The moon had spread over everything a thin layer of silver—over the rank grass, over the mud, upon the wall of matted vegetation standing higher than the wall of a temple, over the great river I could see through a somber gap glittering, glittering, as it flowed broadly by without a murmur. All this was great, expectant, mute, while the man jabbered about himself. I wondered whether the stillness on the face of the immensity looking at us two were meant as an appeal or as a menace. What were we who had strayed in here? Could we handle that dumb thing, or would it handle us? I felt how big, how confoundedly big, was that thing that couldn't talk and perhaps was deaf as well. What was in there? I could see a little ivory coming out from there, and I had heard Mr. Kurtz was in there. I had heard enough about it too—God knows! Yet somehow it didn't bring any image with it—no more than if I had been told an angel or a fiend was in there. I believed it in the same way one of you might believe there are inhabitants in the planet Mars. I knew once a Scotch sailmaker who was certain, dead sure, there were people in Mars. If you asked him for some idea how they looked and behaved, he would get shy and mutter something about 'walking on all-fours.' If you as much as smiled, he would—though a man of sixty—offer to fight you. I would not have gone so far as to fight for Kurtz, but I went for him near enough to a lie. You know I hate, detest, and can't bear a lie, not because I am straighter than the rest of us, but simply because it appals me. There is a taint of death, a flavor of mortality in lies—which is exactly what I hate and detest in the world—what I want to forget. It makes me miserable and sick, like biting something rotten would do. Temperament, I suppose. Well, I went near enough to it by letting the young fool there believe anything he liked to imagine as to my influence in Europe. I became in an instant as much of a pretense as the rest of the bewitched pilgrims. This simply because I had a notion it somehow would be of help to that Kurtz whom at the time I did not see—you understand. He was just a word for me. I did not see the man in the name any more than you do. Do you see him? Do you see the story? Do you see anything? It seems to me I am trying to tell you a dream— making a vain attempt, because no relation of a dream can convey the dream-sensation, that commingling of absurdity, surprise, and bewilderment in a tremor of struggling revolt, that notion of being captured by the incredible which is of the very essence of dreams. . . ."

He was silent for a while.

". . . No, it is impossible; it is impossible to convey the life-sensation of any given epoch of one's existence—that which makes its truth, its meaning—its subtle and penetrating essence. It is impossible. We live, as we dream—alone. . . ."

He paused again as if reflecting, then added:

"Of course in this you fellows see more than I could then. You see me, whom you know. . . ."

It had become so pitch dark that we listeners could hardly see one another. For a long time already he, sitting apart, had been no more to us than a voice. There was not a word from anybody. The others might have been asleep, but I was awake. I listened, I listened on the watch for the sentence, for the word, that would give me the clue to the faint uneasiness inspired by this narrative that seemed to shape itself without human lips in the heavy night air of the river.

". . . Yes—I let him run on," Marlow began again, "and think what he pleased about the powers that were behind me. I did! And there was nothing behind me! There was nothing but that wretched, old, mangled steamboat I was leaning against, while he talked fluently about 'the necessity for every man to get on.' 'And when one comes out here, you conceive, it is not to gaze at the moon.' Mr. Kurtz was a 'universal genius,' but even a genius would find it easier to work with 'adequate tools—intelligent men.' He did not make bricks—why, there was a physical impossibility in the way—as I was well aware; and if he did secretarial work for the manager, it was because 'no sensible man rejects wantonly the confidence of his superiors.' Did I see it? I saw it. What more did I want? What I really wanted was rivets, by Heaven! Rivets. To get on with the work—to stop the hole. Rivets I wanted. There were cases of them down at the coast—cases—piled up—burst—split! You kicked a loose rivet at every second step in that station yard on the hillside. Rivets had rolled into the grove of death. You could fill your pockets with rivets for the trouble of stooping down—and there wasn't one rivet to be found where it was wanted. We had plates that would do, but nothing to fasten them with. And every week the messenger, a lone negro, letterbag on shoulder and staff in hand, left our station for the coast. And several times a week a coast caravan came in with trade goods—ghastly glazed calico that made you shudder only to look at it, glass beads value about a penny a quart, confounded spotted cotton handkerchiefs. And no rivets. Three carriers could have brought all that was wanted to set that steamboat afloat.

"He was becoming confidential now, but I fancy my unresponsive attitude must have exasperated him at last, for he judged it necessary to inform me he feared neither God nor devil, let alone any mere man. I said I could see that very well, but what I wanted was a certain quantity of rivets—and rivets were what really Mr. Kurtz wanted, if he had only known it. Now letters went to the coast every week. . . . 'My dear sir,' he cried, 'I write from dictation.' I demanded rivets. There was a way—for an intelligent man. He changed his manner; became very cold, and suddenly began to talk about a hippopotamus; wondered whether sleeping on board the steamer (I stuck to my salvage night and day) I wasn't disturbed. There was an old hippo that had the bad habit of getting out on the bank and roaming at night over the station grounds. The pilgrims used to turn out in a body and empty every rifle they could lay hands on at him. Some even had sat up o' nights for him. All his energy was wasted, though. 'That animal has a charmed life,' he said; 'but you can say this only of brutes in this country. No man— you apprehend me?—no man here bears a charmed life.' He stood there for a moment in the moonlight with his delicate hooked nose set a little askew, and his mica eyes glittering without a wink, then, with a curt Goodnight, he strode off. I could see he was disturbed and considerably puzzled, which made me feel more hopeful than I had been for days. It was a great comfort to turn from that chap to my influential friend, the battered, twisted, ruined, tin-pot steamboat. I clambered on board. She rang under my feet like an empty Huntley & Palmer biscuit tin kicked along a gutter; she was nothing so solid in make, and rather less pretty in shape, but I had expended enough hard work on her to make me love her. No influential friend would have served me better. She had given me a chance to come out a bit—to find out what I could do. No, I don't like work. I had rather laze about and think of all the fine things that can be done. I don't like work—no man does—but I like what is in the work—the chance to find yourself. Your own reality—for yourself, not for others—what no other man can ever know. They can only see the mere show, and never can tell what it really means.

"I was not surprised to see somebody sitting aft, on the deck, with his legs dangling over the mud. You see I rather chummed with the few mechanics there were in that station, whom the other pilgrims naturally despised—on account of their imperfect manners, I suppose. This was the foreman—a boilermaker by trade—a good worker. He was a lank, bony, yellow-faced man, with big intense eyes. His aspect was worried, and his head was as bald as the palm of my hand; but his hair in falling seemed to have stuck to his chin, and had prospered in the new locality, for his beard hung down to his waist. He was a widower with six young children (he had left them in charge of a sister of his to come out there), and the passion of his life was pigeon-flying. He was an enthusiast and a connoisseur. He would rave about pigeons. After work hours he used sometimes to come over from his hut for a talk about his children and his pigeons; at work, when he had to crawl in the mud under the bottom of the steamboat, he would tie up that beard of his in a kind of white serviette he brought for the purpose. It had loops to go over his ears. In the evening he could be seen squatted on the bank rinsing that wrapper in the creek with great care, then spreading it solemnly on a bush to dry.

"I slapped him on the back and shouted 'We shall have rivets!' He scrambled to his feet exclaiming 'No! Rivets!' as though he couldn't believe his ears. Then in a low voice, 'You . . . eh?' I don't know why we behaved like lunatics. I put my finger to the side of my nose and nodded mysteriously. 'Good for you!' he cried, snapped his fingers above his head, lifting one foot. I tried a jig. We capered on the iron deck. A frightful clatter came out of that hulk, and the virgin forest on the other bank of the creek sent it back in a thundering roll upon the sleeping station. It must have made some of the pilgrims sit up in their hovels. A dark figure obscured the lighted doorway of the manager's hut, vanished, then, a second or so after, the doorway itself vanished too. We stopped, and the silence driven away by the stamping of our feet flowed back again from the recesses of the land. The great wall of vegetation, an exuberant and entangled mass of trunks, branches, leaves, boughs, festoons, motionless in the moonlight, was like a rioting invasion of soundless life, a rolling wave of plants, piled up, crested, ready to topple over the creek, to sweep every little man of us out of his little existence. And it moved not. A deadened burst of mighty splashes and snorts reached us from afar, as though an ichthyosaurus had been taking a bath of glitter in the great river. 'After all,' said the boilermaker in a reasonable tone, 'why shouldn't we get the rivets?' Why not, indeed! I did not know of any reason why we shouldn't. 'They'll come in three weeks,' I said confidently.

"But they didn't. Instead of rivets there came an invasion, an infliction, a visitation. It came in sections during the next three weeks, each section headed by a donkey carrying a white man in new clothes and tan shoes, bowing from that elevation right and left to the impressed pilgrims. A quarrelsome band of footsore sulky niggers trod on the heels of the donkey; a lot of tents, camp-stools, tin boxes, white cases, brown bales would be shot down in the courtyard, and the air of mystery would deepen a little over the muddle of the station. Five such instalments came, with their absurd air of disorderly flight with the loot of innumerable outfit shops and provision stores, that, one would think, they were lugging, after a raid, into the wilderness for equitable division. It was an inextricable mess of things decent in themselves but that human folly made look like the spoils of thieving.

"This devoted band called itself the Eldorado Exploring Expedition, and I believe they were sworn to secrecy. Their talk, however, was the talk of sordid buccaneers: it was reckless without hardihood, greedy without audacity, and cruel without courage; there was not an atom of foresight or of serious intention in the whole batch of them, and they did not seem aware these things are wanted for the work of the world. To tear treasure out of the bowels of the land was their desire, with no more moral purpose at the back of it than there is in burglars breaking into a safe. Who paid the expenses of the noble enterprise I don't know; but the uncle of our manager was leader of that lot.

"In exterior he resembled a butcher in a poor neighborhood, and his eyes had a look of sleepy cunning. He carried his fat paunch with ostentation on his short legs, and during the time his gang infested the station spoke to no one but his nephew. You could see these two roaming about all day long with their heads close together in an everlasting confab.

"I had given up worrying myself about the rivets. One's capacity for that kind of folly is more limited than you would suppose. I said Hang!—and let things slide. I had plenty of time for meditation, and now and then I would give some thought to Kurtz. I wasn't very interested in him. No. Still, I was curious to see whether this man, who had come out equipped with moral ideas of some sort, would climb to the top after all, and how he would set about his work when there."

2

"One evening as I was lying flat on the deck of my steamboat, I heard voices approaching—and there were the nephew and the uncle strolling along the bank. I laid my head on my arm again, and had nearly lost myself in a doze, when somebody said in my ear, as it were: 'I am as harmless as a little child, but I don't like to be dictated to. Am I the manager—or am I not? I was ordered to send him there. It's incredible.' . . . I became aware that the two were standing on the shore alongside the forepart of the steamboat, just below my head. I did not move; it did not occur to me to move; I was sleepy. 'It *is* unpleasant,' grunted the uncle. 'He has asked the Administration to be sent there,' said the other, 'with the idea of showing what he could do; and I was instructed accordingly. Look at the influence that man must have. Is it not frightful?' They both agreed it was frightful, then made several bizarre remarks: 'Make rain and fine weather—one man—the Council—by the nose'—bits of absurd sentences that got the better of my drowsiness, so that I had pretty near the whole of my wits about me when the uncle said, 'The climate may do away with this difficulty for you. Is he alone there?' 'Yes,' answered the manager; 'he sent his assistant down the river with a note to me in these terms: "Clear this poor devil out of the country, and don't bother sending more of that sort. I had rather be alone than have the kind of men you can dispose of with me." It was more than a year ago. Can you imagine such impudence?' 'Anything since then?' asked the other hoarsely. 'Ivory,' jerked the nephew; 'lots of it—prime sort—lots,—most annoying, from him.' 'And with that?' questioned the heavy rumble. 'Invoice,' was the reply fired out, so to speak. Then silence. They had been talking about Kurtz.

"I was broad awake by this time, but, lying perfectly at ease, remained still, having no inducement to change my position. 'How did that ivory come all this way?' growled the elder man, who seemed very vexed. The other explained that it had come with a fleet of canoes in charge of an English half-caste clerk Kurtz had with him; that Kurtz had apparently intended to return himself, the station being by that time bare of goods and stores, but after coming three hundred miles, had suddenly decided to go back, which he started to do alone in a small dugout with four paddlers, leaving the half-caste to continue down the river with the ivory. The two fellows there seemed astounded at anybody attempting such a thing. They were at a loss for an adequate motive. As for me, I seemed to see Kurtz for the first time. It was a distinct glimpse: the dugout, four paddling savages, and the lone white man turning his back suddenly on the headquarters, on relief, on thoughts of home—perhaps; setting his face towards the depths of the wilderness, towards his empty and desolate station. I did not know the motive. Perhaps he was just simply a fine fellow who stuck to his work for its own sake. His name, you understand, had not been pronounced once. He was 'that man.' The half-caste, who, as far as I could see, had conducted a difficult trip with great prudence and pluck, was invariably alluded to as 'that scoundrel.' The 'scoundrel' had reported that the 'man' had been very ill—had recovered imperfectly. . . . The two below me moved away then a few paces, and strolled back and forth at some little distance. I heard: 'Military post—doctor—two hundred miles—quite alone now—unavoidable delays—nine months—no news—strange rumours.' They approached again, just as the manager was saying, 'No one, as far as I know, unless a species of wandering trader—a pestilential fellow, snapping ivory from the natives.' Who was it they were talking about now? I gathered in snatches that this was some man supposed to be in Kurtz's district, and of whom the manager did not approve. 'We will not be free from unfair competition till one of these fellows is hanged for an example,' he said. 'Certainly,' grunted the other; 'get him hanged! Why not? Anything—anything can be done in this country. That's what I say; nobody here, you understand, *here*, can endanger your position. And why? You stand the climate—you outlast them all. The danger is in Europe; but there before I left I took

care to—' They moved off and whispered, then their voices rose again. 'The
extraordinary series of delays is not my fault. I did my possible.' The fat
man sighed, 'Very sad.' 'And the pestiferous absurdity of his talk,' continued the other; 'he bothered me enough when he was here. "Each station
should be like a beacon on the road towards better things, a center for trade
of course, but also for humanizing, improving, instructing." Conceive you—
that ass! And he wants to be manager! No, it's—' Here he got choked by
excessive indignation, and I lifted my head the least bit. I was surprised to
see how near they were—right under me. I could have spat upon their hats.
They were looking on the ground, absorbed in thought. The manager was
switching his leg with a slender twig: his sagacious relative lifted his head.
'You have been well since you came out this time?' he asked. The other
gave a start. 'Who? I? Oh! Like a charm—like a charm. But the rest—oh,
my goodness! All sick. They die so quick, too, that I haven't the time to
send them out of the country—it's incredible!' 'H'm. Just so,' grunted the
uncle. 'Ah! my boy, trust to this—I say, trust to this.' I saw him extend his
short flipper of an arm for a gesture that took in the forest, the creek, the
mud, the river—seemed to beckon with a dishonoring flourish before the
sunlit face of the land a treacherous appeal to the lurking death, to the
hidden evil, to the profound darkness of its heart. It was so startling that I
leaped to my feet and looked back at the edge of the forest, as though I had
expected an answer of some sort to that black display of confidence. You
know the foolish notions that come to one sometimes. The high stillness
confronted these two figures with its ominous patience, waiting for the passing
away of a fantastic invasion.

"They swore aloud together—out of sheer fright, I believe—then, pretending not to know anything of my existence, turned back to the station.
The sun was low; and leaning forward side by side, they seemed to be
tugging painfully uphill their two ridiculous shadows of unequal length, that
trailed behind them slowly over the tall grass without bending a single
blade.

"In a few days the Eldorado Expedition went into the patient wilderness,
that closed upon it as the sea closes over a diver. Long afterwards the news
came that all the donkeys were dead. I know nothing as to the fate of the
less valuable animals. They, no doubt, like the rest of us, found what they
deserved. I did not inquire. I was then rather excited at the prospect of
meeting Kurtz very soon. When I say very soon I mean it comparatively.
It was just two months from the day we left the creek when we came to the
bank below Kurtz's station.

"Going up that river was like travelling back to the earliest beginnings of
the world, when vegetation rioted on the earth and the big trees were
kings. An empty stream, a great silence, an impenetrable forest. The air
was warm, thick, heavy, sluggish. There was no joy in the brilliance of
sunshine. The long stretches of the waterway ran on, deserted, into the
gloom of overshadowed distances. On silvery sandbanks hippos and alliga-
tors sunned themselves side by side. The broadening waters flowed through
a mob of wooded islands; you lost your way on that river as you would in a
desert, and butted all day long against shoals, trying to find the channel,
till you thought yourself bewitched and cut off forever from everything you
had known once—somewhere—far away—in another existence perhaps.
There were moments when one's past came back to one, as it will some-

times when you have not a moment to spare to yourself; but it came in the
shape of an unrestful and noisy dream, remembered with wonder amongst
the overwhelming realities of this strange world of plants, and water, and
silence. And this stillness of life did not in the least resemble a peace. It
was the stillness of an implacable force brooding over an inscrutable intention. It looked at you with a vengeful aspect. I got used to it afterwards; I
did not see it any more; I had no time. I had to keep guessing at the channel; I had to discern, mostly by inspiration, the signs of hidden banks; I
watched for sunken stones; I was learning to clap my teeth smartly before
my heart flew out, when I shaved by a fluke some infernal sly old snag that
would have ripped the life out of the tin-pot steamboat and drowned all the
pilgrims; I had to keep a lookout for the signs of dead wood we could cut
up in the night for next day's steaming. When you have to attend to things
of that sort, to the mere incidents of the surface, the reality—the reality, I
tell you—fades. The inner truth is hidden—luckily, luckily. But I felt it all
the same; I felt often its mysterious stillness watching me at my monkey
tricks, just as it watches you fellows performing on your respective tight-
ropes for—what is it? half a crown a tumble—"

"Try to be civil, Marlow," growled a voice, and I knew there was at least
one listener awake besides myself.

"I beg your pardon. I forgot the heartache which makes up the rest of
the price. And indeed what does the price matter, if the trick be well done?
You do your tricks very well. And I didn't do badly either, since I managed
not to sink that steamboat on my first trip. It's a wonder to me yet. Imagine
a blindfolded man set to drive a van over a bad road. I sweated and shivered
over that business considerably, I can tell you. After all, for a seaman, to
scrape the bottom of the thing that's supposed to float all the time under
his care is the unpardonable sin. No one may know of it, but you never
forget the thump—eh? A blow on the very heart. You remember it, you
dream of it, you wake up at night and think of it—years after—and go hot
and cold all over. I don't pretend to say that steamboat floated all the time.
More than once she had to wade for a bit, with twenty cannibals splashing
around and pushing. We had enlisted some of these chaps on the way for a
crew. Fine fellows—cannibals—in their place. They were men one could
work with, and I am grateful to them. And, after all, they did not eat each
other before my face: they had brought along a provision of hippo-meat
which went rotten, and made the mystery of the wilderness stink in my
nostrils. Phoo! I can sniff it now. I had the manager on board and three or
four pilgrims with their staves—all complete. Sometimes we came upon a
station close by the bank, clinging to the skirts of the unknown, and the
white men rushing out of a tumbledown hovel, with great gestures of joy
and surprise and welcome, seemed very strange—had the appearance of
being held there captive by a spell. The word 'ivory' would ring in the air
for a while—and on we went again into the silence, along empty reaches,
round the still bends, between the high walls of our winding way, reverberating in hollow claps the ponderous beat of the stern-wheel. Trees, trees,
millions of trees, massive, immense, running up high; and at their foot,
hugging the bank against the stream, crept the little begrimed steamboat,
like a sluggish beetle crawling on the floor of a lofty portico. It made you
feel very small, very lost, and yet it was not altogether depressing, that
feeling. After all, if you were small, the grimy beetle crawled on—which

was just what you wanted it to do. Where the pilgrims imagined it crawled to I don't know. To some place where they expected to get something, I bet! For me it crawled towards Kurtz—exclusively; but when the steam-pipes started leaking we crawled very slow. The reaches opened before us and closed behind, as if the forest had stepped leisurely across the water to bar the way for our return. We penetrated deeper and deeper into the heart of darkness. It was very quiet there. At night sometimes the roll of drums behind the curtain of trees would run up the river and remain sustained faintly, as if hovering in the air high over our heads, till the first break of day. Whether it meant war, peace, or prayer we could not tell. The dawns were heralded by the descent of a chill stillness; the woodcutters slept, their fires burned low; the snapping of a twig would make you start. We were wanderers on a prehistoric earth, on an earth that wore the aspect of an unknown planet. We could have fancied ourselves the first of men taking possession of an accursed inheritance, to be subdued at the cost of profound anguish and of excessive toil. But suddenly, as we struggled round a bend, there would be a glimpse of rush walls, of peaked grass roofs, a burst of yells, a whirl of black limbs, a mass of hands clapping, of feet stamping, of bodies swaying, of eyes rolling, under the droop of heavy and motionless foliage. The steamer toiled along slowly on the edge of a black and incomprehensible frenzy. The prehistoric man was cursing us, praying to us, welcoming us—who could tell? We were cut off from the comprehension of our surroundings; we glided past like phantoms, wondering and secretly appalled, as sane men would be before an enthusiastic outbreak in a madhouse. We could not understand because we were too far and could not remember, because we were traveling in the night of first ages, of those ages that are gone, leaving hardly a sign—and no memories.

"The earth seemed unearthly. We are accustomed to look upon the shackled form of a conquered monster, but there—there you could look at a thing monstrous and free. It was unearthly, and the men were— No, they were not inhuman. Well, you know, that was the worst of it—this suspicion of their not being inhuman. It would come slowly to one. They howled and leaped, and spun, and made horrid faces; but what thrilled you was just the thought of their humanity—like yours—the thought of your remote kinship with this wild and passionate uproar. Ugly. Yes, it was ugly enough; but if you were man enough you would admit to yourself that there was in you just the faintest trace of a response to the terrible frankness of that noise, a dim suspicion of there being a meaning in it which you—you so remote from the night of first ages—could comprehend. And why not? The mind of man is capable of anything—because everything is in it, all the past as well as all the future. What was there after all? Joy, fear, sorrow, devotion, valor, rage—who can tell?—but truth—truth stripped of its cloak of time. Let the fool gape and shudder—the man knows, and can look on without a wink. But he must at least be as much of a man as these on the shore. He must meet that truth with his own true stuff—with his own inborn strength. Principles? Principles won't do. Acquisitions, clothes, pretty rags—rags that would fly off at the first good shake. No; you want a deliberate belief. An appeal to me in this fiendish row—is there? Very well; I hear; I admit, but I have a voice too, and for good or evil mine is the speech that cannot be silenced. Of course, a fool, what with sheer fright and fine sentiments, is always safe. Who's that grunting? You wonder I didn't go ashore for a howl and a dance? Well, no—I didn't. Fine sentiments, you say? Fine senti-

ments be hanged! I had no time. I had to mess about with white-lead[3] and
strips of woollen blanket helping to put bandages on those leaky steam-
pipes—I tell you. I had to watch the steering, and circumvent those snags,
and get the tin-pot along by hook or by crook. There was surface-truth
enough in these things to save a wiser man. And between whiles I had to
look after the savage who was fireman. He was an improved specimen; he
could fire up a vertical boiler.[4] He was there below me, and, upon my
word, to look at him was as edifying as seeing a dog in a parody of breeches
and a feather hat, walking on his hind legs. A few months of training had
done for that really fine chap. He squinted at the steam-gauge and at the
water-gauge with an evident effort of intrepidity—and he had filed teeth
too, the poor devil, and the wool of his pate shaved into queer patterns,
and three ornamental scars on each of his cheeks. He ought to have been
clapping his hands and stamping his feet on the bank, instead of which he
was hard at work, a thrall to strange witchcraft, full of improving knowledge. He was useful because he had been instructed; and what he knew
was this—that should the water in that transparent thing disappear, the evil
spirit inside the boiler would get angry through the greatness of his thirst,
and take a terrible vengeance. So he sweated and fired up and watched the
glass fearfully (with an impromptu charm, made of rags, tied to his arm,
and a piece of polished bone, as big as a watch, stuck flatways through his
lower lip), while the wooded banks slipped past us slowly, the short noise
was left behind, the interminable miles of silence—and we crept on, towards
Kurtz. But the snags were thick, the water was treacherous and shallow,
the boiler seemed indeed to have a sulky devil in it, and thus neither that
fireman nor I had any time to peer into our creepy thoughts.

"Some fifty miles below the Inner Station we came upon a hut of reeds,
an inclined and melancholy pole, with the unrecognizable tatters of what
had been a flag of some sort flying from it, and a neatly stacked woodpile.
This was unexpected. We came to the bank, and on the stack of firewood
found a flat piece of board with some faded pencil-writing on it. When
deciphered it said: 'Wood for you. Hurry up. Approach cautiously.' There
was a signature, but it was illegible—not Kurtz—a much longer word. 'Hurry
up.' Where? Up the river? 'Approach cautiously.' We had not done so. But
the warning could not have been meant for the place where it could be only
found after approach. Something was wrong above. But what—and how
much? That was the question. We commented adversely upon the imbecil-
ity of that telegraphic style. The bush around said nothing, and would not
let us look very far, either. A torn curtain of red twill hung in the doorway
of the hut, and flapped sadly in our faces. The dwelling was dismantled; but
we could see a white man had lived there not very long ago. There remained
a rude table—a plank on two posts; a heap of rubbish reposed in a dark
corner, and by the door I picked up a book. It had lost its covers, and the
pages had been thumbed into a state of extremely dirty softness; but the
back had been lovingly stitched afresh with white cotton thread, which
looked clean yet. It was an extraordinary find. Its title was *An Inquiry into
Some Points of Seamanship,* by a man Towser, Towson—some such name—
Master in His Majesty's Navy. The matter looked dreary reading enough,
with illustrative diagrams and repulsive tables of figures, and the copy was
sixty years old. I handled this amazing antiquity with the greatest possible

3. Putty.   4. An upright, simple, easily fired boiler.

tenderness, lest it should dissolve in my hands. Within, Towson or Towser was inquiring earnestly into the breaking strain of ships' chains and tackle, and other such matters. Not a very enthralling book; but at the first glance you could see there a singleness of intention, an honest concern for the right way of going to work, which made these humble pages, thought out so many years ago, luminous with another than a professional light. The simple old sailor, with his talk of chains and purchases,[5] made me forget the jungle and the pilgrims in a delicious sensation of having come upon something unmistakably real. Such a book being there was wonderful enough; but still more astounding were the notes penciled in the margin, and plainly referring to the text. I couldn't believe my eyes! They were in cipher! Yes, it looked like cipher. Fancy a man lugging with him a book of that description into this nowhere and studying it—and making notes—in cipher at that! It was an extravagant mystery.

"I had been dimly aware for some time of a worrying noise, and when I lifted my eyes I saw the woodpile was gone, and the manager, aided by all the pilgrims, was shouting at me from the riverside. I slipped the book into my pocket. I assure you to leave off reading was like tearing myself away from the shelter of an old and solid friendship.

"I started the lame engine ahead. 'It must be this miserable trader—this intruder,' exclaimed the manager, looking back malevolently at the place we had left. 'He must be English,' I said. 'It will not save him from getting into trouble if he is not careful,' muttered the manager darkly. I observed with assumed innocence that no man was safe from trouble in this world.

"The current was more rapid now, the steamer seemed at her last gasp, the stern-wheel flopped languidly, and I caught myself listening on tiptoe for the next beat of the float,[6] for in sober truth I expected the wretched thing to give up every moment. It was like watching the last flickers of a life. But still we crawled. Sometimes I would pick out a tree a little way ahead to measure our progress towards Kurtz by, but I lost it invariably before we got abreast. To keep the eyes so long on one thing was too much for human patience. The manager displayed a beautiful resignation. I fretted and fumed and took to arguing with myself whether or no I would talk openly with Kurtz; but before I could come to any conclusion it occurred to me that my speech or my silence, indeed any action of mine, would be a mere futility. What did it matter what anyone knew or ignored? What did it matter who was manager? One gets sometimes such a flash of insight. The essentials of this affair lay deep under the surface, beyond my reach, and beyond my power of meddling.

"Towards the evening of the second day we judged ourselves about eight miles from Kurtz's station. I wanted to push on; but the manager looked grave, and told me the navigation up there was so dangerous that it would be advisable, the sun being very low already, to wait where we were till next morning. Moreover, he pointed out that if the warning to approach cautiously were to be followed, we must approach in daylight—not at dusk, or in the dark. This was sensible enough. Eight miles meant nearly three hours' steaming for us, and I could also see suspicious ripples at the upper end of the reach. Nevertheless, I was annoyed beyond expression at the delay, and most unreasonably too, since one night more could not matter much after so many months. As we had plenty of wood, and caution was

5. Levers, or system of pulleys.   closing a water-supply valve.
6. Automatic water-level regulator opening and

the word, I brought up in the middle of the stream. The reach was narrow, straight, with high sides like a railway cutting. The dusk came gliding into it long before the sun had set. The current ran smooth and swift, but a dumb immobility sat on the banks. The living trees, lashed together by the creepers and every living bush of the undergrowth, might have been changed into stone, even to the slenderest twig, to the lightest leaf. It was not sleep—it seemed unnatural, like a state of trance. Not the faintest sound of any kind could be heard. You looked on amazed, and began to suspect yourself of being deaf—then the night came suddenly, and struck you blind as well. About three in the morning some large fish leaped, and the loud splash made me jump as though a gun had been fired. When the sun rose there was a white fog, very warm and clammy, and more blinding than the night. It did not shift or drive; it was just there, standing all round you like something solid. At eight or nine, perhaps, it lifted as a shutter lifts. We had a glimpse of the towering multitude of trees, of the immense matted jungle, with the blazing little ball of the sun hanging over it—all perfectly still—and then the white shutter came down again, smoothly, as if sliding in greased grooves. I ordered the chain, which we had begun to heave in, to be paid out again. Before it stopped running with a muffled rattle, a cry, a very loud cry, as of infinite desolation, soared slowly in the opaque air. It ceased. A complaining clamour, modulated in savage discords, filled our ears. The sheer unexpectedness of it made my hair stir under my cap. I don't know how it struck the others: to me it seemed as though the mist itself had screamed, so suddenly, and apparently from all sides at once, did this tumultuous and mournful uproar arise. It culminated in a hurried outbreak of almost intolerably excessive shrieking, which stopped short, leaving us stiffened in a variety of silly attitudes, and obstinately listening to the nearly as appalling and excessive silence. 'Good God! What is the meaning—?' stammered at my elbow one of the pilgrims—a little fat man, with sandy hair and red whiskers, who wore side-spring boots, and pink pajamas tucked into his socks. Two others remained openmouthed a whole minute, then dashed into the little cabin, to rush out incontinently and stand darting scared glances, with Winchesters at 'ready' in their hands. What we could see was just the steamer we were on, her outlines blurred as though she had been on the point of dissolving, and a misty strip of water, perhaps two feet broad, around her—and that was all. The rest of the world was nowhere, as far as our eyes and ears were concerned. Just nowhere. Gone, disappeared; swept off without leaving a whisper or a shadow behind.

"I went forward, and ordered the chain to be hauled in short, so as to be ready to trip the anchor and move the steamboat at once if necessary. 'Will they attack?' whispered an awed voice. 'We will all be butchered in this fog,' murmured another. The faces twitched with the strain, the hands trembled slightly, the eyes forgot to wink. It was very curious to see the contrast of expressions of the white men and of the black fellows of our crew, who were as much strangers to that part of the river as we, though their homes were only eight hundred miles away. The whites, of course greatly discomposed, had besides a curious look of being painfully shocked by such an outrageous row. The others had an alert, naturally interested expression; but their faces were essentially quiet, even those of the one or two who grinned as they hauled at the chain. Several exchanged short, grunting phrases, which seemed to settle the matter to their satisfaction. Their head man, a young, broad-chested black, severely draped in dark-blue fringed cloths, with fierce nostrils and his hair all done up artfully in oily ringlets, stood near me. 'Aha!' I said, just for good fellowship's sake. 'Catch 'im,' he snapped, with a bloodshot widening of his eyes and a flash of sharp teeth—'catch 'im. Give 'im to us.' 'To you, eh?' I asked; 'what would you do with them?' 'Eat 'im!' he said curtly, and, leaning his elbow on the rail, looked out into the fog in a dignified and profoundly pensive attitude. I would no doubt have been properly horrified, had it not occurred to me that he and his chaps must be very hungry: that they must have been growing increasingly hungry for at least this month past. They had been engaged for six months (I don't think a single one of them had any clear idea of time, as we at the end of countless ages have. They still belonged to the beginnings of time—had no inherited experience to teach them, as it were), and of course, as long as there was a piece of paper written over in accordance with some farcical law or other made down the river, it didn't enter anybody's head to trouble how they would live. Certainly they had brought with them some rotten hippo-meat, which couldn't have lasted very long, anyway, even if the pilgrims hadn't, in the midst of a shocking hullabaloo, thrown a considerable quantity of it overboard. It looked like a high-handed proceeding; but it was really a case of legitimate self-defense. You can't breathe dead hippo waking, sleeping, and eating, and at the same time keep your precarious grip on existence. Besides that, they had given them every week three pieces of brass wire, each about nine inches long; and the theory was they were to buy their provisions with that currency in riverside villages. You can see how *that* worked. There were either no villages, or the people were hostile, or the director, who like the rest of us fed out of tins, with an occasional old he-goat thrown in, didn't want to stop the steamer for some more or less recondite reason. So, unless they swallowed the wire itself, or made loops of it to snare the fishes with, I don't see what good their extravagant salary could be to them. I must say it was paid with a regularity worthy of a large and honorable trading company. For the rest, the only thing to eat—though it didn't look eatable in the least—I saw in their possession was a few lumps of some stuff like half-cooked dough, of a dirty lavender color, they kept wrapped in leaves, and now and then swallowed a piece of, but so small that it seemed done more for the look of the thing than for any serious purpose of sustenance. Why in the name of all the gnawing devils of hunger they didn't go for us—they were thirty to five—and have a good tuck-in[7] for once, amazes me now when I think of it. They were big powerful men, with not much capacity to weigh the consequences, with courage, with strength, even yet, though their skins were no longer glossy and their muscles no longer hard. And I saw that something restraining, one of those human secrets that baffle probability, had come into play there. I looked at them with a swift quickening of interest—not because it occurred to me I might be eaten by them before very long, though I own to you that just then I perceived—in a new light, as it were—how unwholesome the pilgrims looked, and I hoped, yes, I positively hoped, that my aspect was not so—what shall I say?—so—unappetizing: a touch of fantastic vanity which fitted well with the dream-sensation that pervaded all my days at that time. Perhaps I had a little fever too. One can't live with one's finger everlastingly on one's pulse. I had often 'a little fever,' or a little touch of other things—the playful paw-strokes of

7. Meal.

the wilderness, the preliminary trifling before the more serious onslaught
which came in due course. Yes; I looked at them as you would on any
human being, with a curiosity of their impulses, motives, capacities, weak-
nesses, when brought to the test of an inexorable physical necessity. Restraint!
What possible restraint? Was it superstition, disgust, patience, fear—or
some kind of primitive honor? No fear can stand up to hunger, no patience
can wear it out, disgust simply does not exist where hunger is; and as to
superstition, beliefs, and what you may call principles, they are less than
chaff in a breeze. Don't you know the devilry of lingering starvation, its
exasperating torment, its black thoughts, its somber and brooding ferocity?
Well, I do. It takes a man all his inborn strength to fight hunger properly.
It's really easier to face bereavement, dishonor, and the perdition of one's
soul—than this kind of prolonged hunger. Sad, but true. And these chaps
too had no earthly reason for any kind of scruple. Restraint! I would just as
soon have expected restraint from a hyena prowling amongst the corpses of
a battlefield. But there was the fact facing me—the fact dazzling, to be seen,
like the foam on the depths of the sea, like a ripple on an unfathomable
enigma, a mystery greater—when I thought of it—than the curious, inexplicable note of desperate grief in this savage clamor that had swept by us
on the riverbank, behind the blind whiteness of the fog.
      "Two pilgrims were quarreling in hurried whispers as to which bank.
'Left.' 'No, no; how can you? Right, right, of course.' 'It is very serious,'
said the manager's voice behind me; 'I would be desolated if anything should
happen to Mr. Kurtz before we came up.' I looked at him, and had not the
slightest doubt he was sincere. He was just the kind of man who would wish
to preserve appearances. That was his restraint. But when he muttered
something about going on at once, I did not even take the trouble to answer
him. I knew, and he knew, that it was impossible. Were we to let go our
hold of the bottom, we would be absolutely in the air—in space. We wouldn't
be able to tell where we were going to—whether up or down stream, or
across—till we fetched against one bank or the other—and then we wouldn't
know at first which it was. Of course I made no move. I had no mind for a
smashup. You couldn't imagine a more deadly place for a shipwreck. Whether
drowned at once or not, we were sure to perish speedily in one way or
another. 'I authorize you to take all the risks,' he said, after a short silence.
'I refuse to take any,' I said shortly; which was just the answer he expected,
though its tone might have surprised him. 'Well, I must defer to your judgment. You are captain,' he said, with marked civility. I turned my shoulder
to him in sign of my appreciation, and looked into the fog. How long would
it last? It was the most hopeless lookout. The approach to this Kurtz grub-
bing for ivory in the wretched bush was beset by as many dangers as though
he had been an enchanted princess sleeping in a fabulous castle. 'Will they
attack, do you think?' asked the manager, in a confidential tone.
      "I did not think they would attack, for several obvious reasons. The thick
fog was one. If they left the bank in their canoes they would get lost in it,
as we would be if we attempted to move. Still, I had also judged the jungle
of both banks quite impenetrable—and yet eyes were in it, eyes that had
seen us. The river-side bushes were certainly very thick; but the undergrowth behind was evidently penetrable. However, during the short lift I
had seen no canoes anywhere in the reach—certainly not abreast of the
steamer. But what made the idea of attack inconceivable to me was the
nature of the noise—of the cries we had heard. They had not the fierce

character boding of immediate hostile intention. Unexpected, wild, and violent as they had been, they had given me an irresistible impression of sorrow. The glimpse of the steamboat had for some reason filled those savages with unrestrained grief. The danger, if any, I expounded, was from our proximity to a great human passion let loose. Even extreme grief may ultimately vent itself in violence—but more generally takes the form of apathy. . . .

"You should have seen the pilgrims stare! They had no heart to grin, or even to revile me; but I believe they thought me gone mad—with fright, maybe. I delivered a regular lecture. My dear boys, it was no good bothering. Keep a lookout? Well, you may guess I watched the fog for the signs of lifting as a cat watches a mouse; but for anything else our eyes were of no more use to us than if we had been buried miles deep in a heap of cotton wool. It felt like it too—choking, warm, stifling. Besides, all I said, though it sounded extravagant, was absolutely true to fact. What we afterwards alluded to as an attack was really an attempt at repulse. The action was very far from being aggressive—it was not even defensive, in the usual sense: it was undertaken under the stress of desperation, and in its essence was purely protective.

"It developed itself, I should say, two hours after the fog lifted, and its commencement was at a spot, roughly speaking, about a mile and a half below Kurtz's station. We had just floundered and flopped round a bend, when I saw an islet, a mere grassy hummock of bright green, in the middle of the stream. It was the only thing of the kind; but as we opened the reach more, I perceived it was the head of a long sandbank, or rather of a chain of shallow patches stretching down the middle of the river. They were discolored, just awash, and the whole lot was seen just under the water, exactly as a man's backbone is seen running down the middle of his back under the skin. Now, as far as I did see, I could go to the right or to the left of this. I didn't know either channel, of course. The banks looked pretty well alike, the depth appeared the same; but as I had been informed the station was on the west side, I naturally headed for the western passage.

"No sooner had we fairly entered it than I became aware it was much narrower than I had supposed. To the left of us there was the long uninterrupted shoal, and to the right a high steep bank heavily overgrown with bushes. Above the bush the trees stood in serried ranks. The twigs overhung the current thickly, and from distance to distance a large limb of some tree projected rigidly over the steam. It was then well on in the afternoon, the face of the forest was gloomy, and a broad strip of shadow had already fallen on the water. In this shadow we steamed up—very slowly, as you may imagine. I sheered her well inshore—the water being deepest near the bank, as the sounding pole informed me.

"One of my hungry and forbearing friends was sounding in the bows just below me. This steamboat was exactly like a decked scow. On the deck there were two little teakwood houses, with doors and windows. The boiler was in the fore-end, and the machinery right astern. Over the whole there was a light roof, supported on stanchions. The funnel projected through that roof, and in front of the funnel a small cabin built of light planks served for a pilothouse. It contained a couch, two camp-stools, a loaded Martini-Henry[8] leaning in one corner, a tiny table, and the steering wheel. It had a

8. Breech-action rifle.

wide door in front and a broad shutter at each side. All these were always thrown open, of course. I spent my days perched up there on the extreme fore-end of that roof, before the door. At night I slept, or tried to, on the couch. An athletic black belonging to some coast tribe, and educated by my poor predecessor, was the helmsman. He sported a pair of brass earrings, wore a blue cloth wrapper from the waist to the ankles, and thought all the world of himself. He was the most unstable kind of fool I had ever seen. He steered with no end of a swagger while you were by; but if he lost sight of you, he became instantly the prey of an abject funk, and would let that cripple of a steamboat get the upper hand of him in a minute.

"I was looking down at the sounding pole, and feeling much annoyed to see at each try a little more of it stick out of that river, when I saw my poleman give up the business suddenly, and stretch himself flat on the deck, without even taking the trouble to haul his pole in. He kept hold on it though, and it trailed in the water. At the same time the fireman, whom I could also see below me, sat down abruptly before his furnace and ducked his head. I was amazed. Then I had to look at the river mighty quick, because there was a snag in the fairway. Sticks, little sticks, were flying about—thick; they were whizzing before my nose, dropping below me, striking behind me against my pilothouse. All this time the river, the shore, the woods, were very quiet—perfectly quiet. I could only hear the heavy splashing thump of the stern-wheel and the patter of these things. We cleared the snag clumsily. Arrows, by Jove! We were being shot at! I stepped in quickly to close the shutter on the land-side. That fool helmsman, his hands on the spokes, was lifting his knees high, stamping his feet, champing his mouth, like a reined-in horse. Confound him! And we were staggering within ten feet of the bank. I had to lean right out to swing the heavy shutter, and I saw a face amongst the leaves on the level with my own, looking at me very fierce and steady; and then suddenly, as though a veil had been removed from my eyes, I made out, deep in the tangled gloom, naked breasts, arms, legs, glaring eyes—the bush was swarming with human limbs in movement, glistening, of bronze color. The twigs shook, swayed and rustled, the arrows flew out of them, and then the shutter came to. 'Steer her straight,' I said to the helmsman. He held his head rigid, face forward; but his eyes rolled, he kept on lifting and setting down his feet gently, his mouth foamed a little. 'Keep quiet!' I said in a fury. I might just as well have ordered a tree not to sway in the wind. I darted out. Below me there was a great scuffle of feet on the iron deck; confused exclamations; a voice screamed, 'Can you turn back?' I caught sight of a V-shaped ripple on the water ahead. What? Another snag! A fusillade burst out under my feet. The pilgrims had opened with their Winchesters, and were simply squirting lead into that bush. A deuce of a lot of smoke came up and drove slowly forward. I swore at it. Now I couldn't see the ripple or the snag either. I stood in the doorway, peering, and the arrows came in swarms. They might have been poisoned, but they looked as though they wouldn't kill a cat. The bush began to howl. Our woodcutters raised a warlike whoop; the report of a rifle just at my back deafened me. I glanced over my shoulder, and the pilothouse was yet full of noise and smoke when I made a dash at the wheel. The fool nigger had dropped everything, to throw the shutter open and let off that Martini-Henry. He stood before the wide opening, glaring, and I yelled at him to come back, while I straightened the sudden twist out of that steamboat. There was no room to turn even if I had wanted to, the snag was somewhere very near ahead in that confounded smoke, there was no time to lose, so I just crowded her into the bank—right into the bank, where I knew the water was deep.

"We tore slowly along the overhanging bushes in a whirl of broken twigs and flying leaves. The fusillade below stopped short, as I had foreseen it would when the squirts got empty. I threw my head back to a glinting whiz that traversed the pilothouse, in at one shutter-hole and out at the other. Looking past that mad helmsman, who was shaking the empty rifle and yelling at the shore, I saw vague forms of men running bent double, leaping, gliding, distinct, incomplete, evanescent. Something big appeared in the air before the shutter, the rifle went overboard, and the man stepped back swiftly, looked at me over his shoulder in an extraordinary, profound, familiar manner, and fell upon my feet. The side of his head hit the wheel twice, and the end of what appeared a long cane clattered round and knocked over a little camp-stool. It looked as though after wrenching that thing from somebody ashore he had lost his balance in the effort. The thin smoke had blown away, we were clear of the snag, and looking ahead I could see that in another hundred yards or so I would be free to sheer off, away from the bank; but my feet felt so very warm and wet that I had to look down. The man had rolled on his back and stared straight up at me; both his hands clutched that cane. It was the shaft of a spear that, either thrown or lunged through the opening, had caught him in the side just below the ribs; the blade had gone in out of sight, after making a frightful gash; my shoes were full; a pool of blood lay very still, gleaming dark red under the wheel; his eyes shone with an amazing luster. The fusillade burst out again. He looked at me anxiously, gripping the spear like something precious, with an air of being afraid I would try to take it away from him. I had to make an effort to free my eyes from his gaze and attend to the steering. With one hand I felt above my head for the line of the steam whistle, and jerked out screech after screech hurriedly. The tumult of angry and warlike yells was checked instantly, and then from the depths of the woods went out such a tremulous and prolonged wail of mournful fear and utter despair as may be imagined to follow the flight of the last hope from the earth. There was a great commotion in the bush; the shower of arrows stopped, a few dropping shots rang out sharply—then silence, in which the languid beat of the stern-wheel came plainly to my ears. I put the helm hard a-starboard at the moment when the pilgrim in pink pajamas, very hot and agitated, appeared in the doorway. 'The manager sends me—' he began in an official tone, and stopped short. 'Good God!' he said, glaring at the wounded man.

"We two whites stood over him, and his lustrous and inquiring glance enveloped us both. I declare it looked as though he would presently put to us some question in an understandable language; but he died without uttering a sound, without moving a limb, without twitching a muscle. Only in the very last moment, as though in response to some sign we could not see, to some whisper we could not hear, he frowned heavily, and that frown gave to his black death mask an inconceivably somber, brooding, and menacing expression. The luster of inquiring glance faded swiftly into vacant glassiness. 'Can you steer?' I asked the agent eagerly. He looked very dubious; but I made a grab at his arm, and he understood at once I meant him to steer whether or no. To tell you the truth, I was morbidly anxious to change my shoes and socks. 'He is dead,' murmured the fellow, immensely impressed. 'No doubt about it,' said I, tugging like mad at the shoelaces. 'And by the way, I suppose Mr. Kurtz is dead as well by this time.'

"For the moment that was the dominant thought. There was a sense of extreme disappointment, as though I had found out I had been striving after something altogether without a substance. I couldn't have been more disgusted if I had traveled all this way for the sole purpose of talking with Mr. Kurtz. Talking with . . . I flung one shoe overboard, and became aware that that was exactly what I had been looking forward to—a talk with Kurtz. I made the strange discovery that I had never imagined him as doing, you know, but as discoursing. I didn't say to myself, 'Now I will never see him,' or 'Now I will never shake him by the hand,' but, 'Now I will never hear him.' The man presented himself as a voice. Not of course that I did not connect him with some sort of action. Hadn't I been told in all the tones of jealousy and admiration that he had collected, bartered, swindled, or stolen more ivory than all the other agents together? That was not the point. The point was in his being a gifted creature, and that of all his gifts the one that stood out pre-eminently, that carried with it a sense of real presence, was his ability to talk, his words—the gift of expression, the bewildering, the illuminating, the most exalted and the most contemptible, the pulsating stream of light, or the deceitful flow from the heart of an impenetrable darkness.

"The other shoe went flying unto the devil-god of that river. I thought, By Jove! it's all over. We are too late; he has vanished—the gift has vanished, by means of some spear, arrow, or club. I will never hear that chap speak after all—and my sorrow had a startling extravagance of emotion, even such as I had noticed in the howling sorrow of these savages in the bush. I couldn't have felt more of lonely desolation somehow, had I been robbed of a belief or had missed my destiny in life. . . . Why do you sigh in this beastly way, somebody? Absurd? Well, absurd. Good Lord! mustn't a man ever— Here, give me some tobacco."

There was a pause of profound stillness, then a match flared, and Marlow's lean face appeared, worn, hollow, with downward folds and dropped eyelids, with an aspect of concentrated attention; and as he took vigorous draws at his pipe, it seemed to retreat and advance out of the night in the regular flicker of the tiny flame. The match went out.

"Absurd!" he cried. "This is the worst of trying to tell . . . Here you all are, each moored with two good addresses, like a hulk with two anchors, a butcher round one corner, a policeman round another, excellent appetites, and temperature normal—you hear—normal from year's end to year's end. And you say, Absurd! Absurd be—exploded! Absurd! My dear boys, what can you expect from a man who out of sheer nervousness had just flung overboard a pair of new shoes? Now I think of it, it is amazing I did not shed tears. I am, upon the whole, proud of my fortitude. I was cut to the quick at the idea of having lost the inestimable privilege of listening to the gifted Kurtz. Of course I was wrong. The privilege was waiting for me. Oh yes, I heard more than enough. And I was right, too. A voice. He was very little more than a voice. And I heard—him—it—this voice—other voices—all of them were so little more than voices—and the memory of that time itself lingers around me, impalpable, like a dying vibration of one immense jabber, silly, atrocious, sordid, savage, or simply mean, without any kind of sense. Voices, voices—even the girl herself—now—"

He was silent for a long time.

"I laid the ghost of his gifts at last with a lie," he began suddenly. "Girl! What? Did I mention a girl? Oh, she is out of it—completely. They—the women I mean—are out of it—should be out of it. We must help them to stay in that beautiful world of their own, lest ours gets worse. Oh, she had to be out of it. You should have heard the disinterred body of Mr. Kurtz saying, 'My Intended.' You would have perceived directly then how completely she was out of it. And the lofty frontal bone of Mr. Kurtz! They say the hair goes on growing sometimes, but this—ah—specimen was impressively bald. The wilderness had patted him on the head, and, behold, it was like a ball—an ivory ball; it had caressed him, and—lo!—he had withered; it had taken him, loved him, embraced him, got into his veins, consumed his flesh, and sealed his soul to its own by the inconceivable ceremonies of some devilish initiation. He was its spoiled and pampered favorite. Ivory? I should think so. Heaps of it, stacks of it. The old mud shanty was bursting with it. You would think there was not a single tusk left either above or below the ground in the whole country. 'Mostly fossil,' the manager had remarked disparagingly. It was no more fossil than I am; but they call it fossil when it is dug up. It appears these niggers do bury the tusks sometimes—but evidently they couldn't bury this parcel deep enough to save the gifted Mr. Kurtz from his fate. We filled the steamboat with it, and had to pile a lot on the deck. Thus he could see and enjoy as long as he could see, because the appreciation of this favor had remained with him to the last. You should have heard him say, 'My ivory.' Oh yes, I heard him. 'My Intended, my ivory, my station, my river, my—' everything belonged to him. It made me hold my breath in expectation of hearing the wilderness burst into a prodigious peal of laughter that would shake the fixed stars in their places. Everything belonged to him—but that was a trifle. The thing was to know what he belonged to, how many powers of darkness claimed him for their own. That was the reflection that made you creepy all over. It was impossible—it was not good for one either—trying to imagine. He had taken a high seat amongst the devils of the land—I mean literally. You can't understand. How could you?—with solid pavement under your feet, surrounded by kind neighbors ready to cheer you or to fall on you, stepping delicately between the butcher and the policeman, in the holy terror of scandal and gallows and lunatic asylums—how can you imagine what particular region of the first ages a man's untrammeled feet may take him into by the way of solitude—utter solitude without a policeman—by the way of silence—utter silence, where no warning voice of a kind neighbor can be heard whispering of public opinion? These little things make all the great difference. When they are gone you must fall back upon your own innate strength, upon your own capacity for faithfulness. Of course you may be too much of a fool to go wrong—too dull even to know you are being assaulted by the powers of darkness. I take it, no fool ever made a bargain for his soul with the devil: the fool is too much of a fool, or the devil too much of a devil—I don't know which. Or you may be such a thunderingly exalted creature as to be altogether deaf and blind to anything but heavenly sights and sounds. Then the earth for you is only a standing place—and whether to be like this is your loss or your gain I won't pretend to say. But most of us are neither one nor the other. The earth for us is a place to live in, where we must put up with sights, with sounds, with smells, too, by Jove!—breathe dead hippo, so to speak, and not be contaminated. And there, don't you see? your strength comes in, the faith in your ability for the digging of unostentatious holes to bury the stuff in—your power of devotion, not to yourself, but to an obscure, backbreaking business. And that's difficult enough. Mind, I am not trying to excuse or even explain—I am trying to account to myself for—for—Mr. Kurtz—for the shade of Mr. Kurtz. This initiated wraith from the back of Nowhere honored me with its amazing confidence before it vanished altogether. This was because it could speak English to me. The original Kurtz had been educated partly in England, and—as he was good enough to say himself—his sympathies were in the right place. His mother was half-English, his father was half-French. All Europe contributed to the making of Kurtz; and by and by I learned that, most appropriately, the International Society for the Suppression of Savage Customs had entrusted him with the making of a report, for its future guidance. And he had written it too. I've seen it. I've read it. It was eloquent, vibrating with eloquence, but too high-strung, I think. Seventeen pages of close writing he had found time for! But this must have been before his— let us say—nerves went wrong, and caused him to preside at certain midnight dances ending with unspeakable rites, which—as far as I reluctantly gathered from what I heard at various times—were offered up to him—do you understand?—to Mr. Kurtz himself. But it was a beautiful piece of writing. The opening paragraph, however, in the light of later information, strikes me now as ominous. He began with the argument that we whites, from the point of development we had arrived at, 'must necessarily appear to them [savages] in the nature of supernatural beings—we approach them with the might as of a deity,' and so on, and so on. 'By the simple exercise of our will we can exert a power for good practically unbounded,' etc. etc. From that point he soared and took me with him. The peroration was magnificent, though difficult to remember, you know. It gave me the notion of an exotic Immensity ruled by an august Benevolence. It made me tingle with enthusiasm. This was the unbounded power of eloquence—of words— of burning noble words. There were no practical hints to interrupt the magic current of phrases, unless a kind of note at the foot of the last page, scrawled evidently much later, in an unsteady hand, may be regarded as the exposition of a method. It was very simple, and at the end of that moving appeal to every altruistic sentiment it blazed at you, luminous and terrifying, like a flash of lightning in a serene sky: 'Exterminate all the brutes!' The curious part was that he had apparently forgotten all about that valuable postscriptum, because, later on, when he in a sense came to himself, he repeatedly entreated me to take good care of 'my pamphlet' (he called it), as it was sure to have in the future a good influence upon his career. I had full information about all these things, and, besides, as it turned out, I was to have the care of his memory. I've done enough for it to give me the indisputable right to lay it, if I choose, for an everlasting rest in the dustbin of progress, amongst all the sweepings and, figuratively speaking, all the dead cats of civilization. But then, you see, I can't choose. He won't be forgotten. Whatever he was, he was not common. He had the power to charm or frighten rudimentary souls into an aggravated witch-dance in his honor; he could also fill the small souls of the pilgrims with bitter misgivings: he had one devoted friend at least, and he had conquered one soul in the world that was neither rudimentary nor tainted with self-seeking. No; I can't forget him, though I am not prepared to affirm the fellow was exactly worth the life we lost in getting to him. I missed my late helmsman awfully—I missed him even while his body was still lying in the pilothouse. Perhaps you will think it passing strange this regret for a savage who was no more account than a grain of sand in a black Sahara. Well, don't you see, he had done something, he had steered; for months I had him at my back—a help—an instrument. It was a kind of partnership. He steered for me—I had to look after him, I worried about his deficiencies, and thus a subtle bond had been created, of which I only became aware when it was suddenly broken. And the intimate profundity of that look he gave me when he received his hurt remains to this day in my memory—like a claim of distant kinship affirmed in a supreme moment.

"Poor fool! If he had only left that shutter alone. He had no restraint, no restraint—just like Kurtz—a tree swayed by the wind. As soon as I had put on a dry pair of slippers, I dragged him out, after first jerking the spear out of his side, which operation I confess I performed with my eyes shut tight. His heels leaped together over the little door-step; his shoulders were pressed to my breast; I hugged him from behind desperately. Oh! he was heavy, heavy; heavier than any man on earth, I should imagine. Then without more ado I tipped him overboard. The current snatched him as though he had been a wisp of grass, and I saw the body roll over twice before I lost sight of it for ever. All the pilgrims and the manager were then congregated on the awning-deck about the pilothouse, chattering at each other like a flock of excited magpies, and there was a scandalized murmur at my heartless promptitude. What they wanted to keep that body hanging about for I can't guess. Embalm it, maybe. But I had also heard another, and a very ominous, murmur on the deck below. My friend the woodcutters were likewise scandalized, and with a better show of reason—though I admit that the reason itself was quite inadmissible. Oh, quite! I had made up my mind that if my late helmsman was to be eaten, the fishes alone should have him. He had been a very second-rate helmsman while alive, but now he was dead he might have become a first-class temptation, and possibly cause some startling trouble. Besides, I was anxious to take the wheel, the man in pink pajamas showing himself a hopeless duffer at the business.

"This I did directly the simple funeral was over. We were going half-speed, keeping right in the middle of the stream, and I listened to the talk about me. They had given up Kurtz, they had given up the station; Kurtz was dead, and the station had been burnt—and so on, and so on. The red-haired pilgrim was beside himself with the thought that at least this poor Kurtz had been properly revenged. 'Say! We must have made a glorious slaughter of them in the bush. Eh? What do you think? Say?' He positively danced, the bloodthirsty little gingery beggar.[9] And he had nearly fainted when he saw the wounded man! I could not help saying, 'You made a glorious lot of smoke, anyhow.' I had seen, from the way the tops of the bushes rustled and flew, that almost all the shots had gone too high. You can't hit anything unless you take aim and fire from the shoulder; but these chaps fired from the hip with their eyes shut. The retreat, I maintained—and I was right—was caused by the screeching of the steam-whistle. Upon this they forgot Kurtz, and began to howl at me with indignant protests.

"The manager stood by the wheel murmuring confidentially about the necessity of getting well away down the river before dark at all events, when I saw in the distance a clearing on the riverside and the outlines of

9. Reed-haired scoundrel.

some sort of building. 'What's this?' I asked. He clapped his hands in wonder. 'The station!' he cried. I edged in at once, still going half-speed.
"Through my glasses I saw the slope of a hill interspersed with rare trees and perfectly free from undergrowth. A long decaying building on the summit was half buried in the high grass; the large holes in the peaked roof gaped black from afar; the jungle and the woods made a background. There was no enclosure or fence of any kind; but there had been one apparently, for near the house half a dozen slim posts remained in a row, roughly trimmed, and with their upper ends ornamented with round carved balls. The rails, or whatever there had been between, had disappeared. Of course the forest surrounded all that. The river-bank was clear, and on the water side I saw a white man under a hat like a cart-wheel beckoning persistently with his whole arm. Examining the edge of the forest above and below, I was almost certain I could see movements—human forms gliding here and there. I steamed past prudently, then stopped the engines and let her drift down. The man on the shore began to shout, urging us to land. 'We have been attacked,' screamed the manager. 'I know—I know. It's all right,' yelled back the other, as cheerful as you please. 'Come along. It's all right. I am glad.'

"His aspect reminded me of something I had seen—something funny I had seen somewhere. As I maneuvered to get alongside, I was asking myself, 'What does this fellow look like?' Suddenly I got it. He looked like a harlequin. His clothes had been made of some stuff that was brown holland probably, but it was covered with patches all over, with bright patches, blue, red, and yellow—patches on the back, patches on the front, patches on elbows, on knees; colored binding round his jacket, scarlet edging at the bottom of his trousers; and the sunshine made him look extremely gay and wonderfully neat withal, because you could see how beautifully all this patching had been done. A beardless, boyish face, very fair, no features to speak of, nose peeling, little blue eyes, smiles and frowns chasing each other over that open countenance like sunshine and shadow on a windswept plain. 'Look out, captain!' he cried; 'there's a snag lodged in here last night.' What! Another snag? I confess I swore shamefully. I had nearly holed my cripple, to finish off that charming trip. The harlequin on the bank turned his little pug-nose up to me. 'You English?' he asked, all smiles. 'Are you?' I shouted from the wheel. The smiles vanished, and he shook his head as if sorry for my disappointment. Then he brightened up. 'Never mind!' he cried encouragingly. 'Are we in time?' I asked. 'He is up there,' he replied, with a toss of the head up the hill, and becoming gloomy all of a sudden. His face was like the autumn sky, overcast one moment and bright the next.

"When the manager, escorted by the pilgrims, all of them armed to the teeth, had gone to the house, this chap came on board. 'I say, I don't like this. These natives are in the bush,' I said. He assured me earnestly it was all right. 'They are simple people,' he added; 'well, I am glad you came. It took me all my time to keep them off.' 'But you said it was all right,' I cried. 'Oh, they meant no harm,' he said; and as I stared he corrected himself, 'Not exactly.' Then vivaciously, 'My faith, your pilothouse wants a clean up!' In the next breath he advised me to keep enough steam on the boiler to blow the whistle in case of any trouble. 'One good screech will do more for you than all your rifles. They are simple people,' he repeated. He rattled away at such a rate he quite overwhelmed me. He seemed to be trying to make up for lots of silence, and actually hinted, laughing, that such was the case. 'Don't you talk with Mr. Kurtz?' I said. 'You don't talk with that man— you listen to him,' he exclaimed with severe exaltation. 'But now—' He waved his arm, and in the twinkling of an eye was in the uttermost depths of despondency. In a moment he came up again with a jump, possessed himself of both my hands, shook them continuously, while he gabbled: 'Brother sailor . . . honor . . . pleasure . . . delight . . . introduce myself . . . Russian . . . son of an archpriest . . . Government of Tambov . . . What? Tobacco! English tobacco; the excellent English tobacco! Now, that's brotherly. Smoke? Where's a sailor that does not smoke?'

"The pipe soothed him, and gradually I made out he had run away from school, had gone to sea in a Russian ship; ran away again; served some time in English ships; was now reconciled with the archpriest. He made a point of that. 'But when one is young one must see things, gather experience, ideas; enlarge the mind.' 'Here!' I interrupted. 'You can never tell! Here I met Mr. Kurtz,' he said, youthfully solemn and reproachful. I held my tongue after that. It appears he had persuaded a Dutch tradinghouse on the coast to fit him out with stores and goods, and had started for the interior with a light heart, and no more idea of what would happen to him than a baby. He had been wandering about that river for nearly two years alone, cut off from everybody and everything. 'I am not so young as I look. I am twenty-five,' he said. 'At first old Van Shuyten would tell me to go to the devil,' he narrated with keen enjoyment; 'but I stuck to him, and talked and talked, till at last he got afraid I would talk the hind-leg off his favorite dog, so he gave me some cheap things and a few guns, and told me he hoped he would never see my face again. Good old Dutchman, Van Shuyten. I sent him one small lot of ivory a year ago, so that he can't call me a little thief when I get back. I hope he got it. And for the rest, I don't care. I had some wood stacked for you. That was my old house. Did you see?'

"I gave him Towson's book. He made as though he would kiss me, but restrained himself. 'The only book I had left, and I thought I had lost it,' he said, looking at it ecstatically. 'So many accidents happen to a man going about alone, you know. Canoes get upset sometimes—and sometimes you've got to clear out so quick when the people get angry.' He thumbed the pages. 'You made notes in Russian?' I asked. He nodded. 'I thought they were written in cipher,' I said. He laughed, then became serious. 'I had lots of trouble to keep these people off,' he said. 'Did they want to kill you?' I asked. 'Oh no!' he cried, and checked himself. 'Why did they attack us?' I pursued. He hesitated, then said shamefacedly, 'They don't want him to go.' 'Don't they?' I said curiously. He nodded a nod full of mystery and wisdom. 'I tell you,' he cried, 'this man has enlarged my mind.' He opened his arms wide, staring at me with his little blue eyes that were perfectly round."

3

"I looked at him, lost in astonishment. There he was before me, in motley, as though he had absconded from a troupe of mimes, enthusiastic, famulous.[1] His very existence was improbable, inexplicable, and altogether bewildering. He was an insoluble problem. It was inconceivable how he

1. Like a famulus, a sorcerer's assistant.

had existed, how he had succeeded in getting so far, how he had managed to remain—why he did not instantly disappear. 'I went a little farther,' he said, 'then still a little farther—till I had gone so far that I don't know how I'll ever get back. Never mind. Plenty time. I can manage. You take Kurtz away quick—quick—I tell you.' The glamour of youth enveloped his parti-colored rags, his destitution, his loneliness, the essential desolation of his futile wanderings. For months—for years—his life hadn't been worth a day's purchase; and there he was gallantly, thoughtlessly alive, to all appearance indestructible solely by the virtue of his few years and of his unreflecting audacity. I was seduced into something like admiration—like envy. Glamour urged him on, glamour kept him unscathed. He surely wanted nothing from the wilderness but space to breathe in and to push on through. His need was to exist, and to move onwards at the greatest possible risk, and with a maximum of privation. If the absolutely pure, uncalculating, unpractical spirit of adventure had ever ruled a human being, it ruled this be-patched youth. I almost envied him the possession of this modest and clear flame. It seemed to have consumed all thought of self so completely, that, even while he was talking to you, you forgot that it was he—the man before your eyes—who had gone through these things. I did not envy him his devotion to Kurtz, though. He had not meditated over it. It came to him, and he accepted it with a sort of eager fatalism. I must say that to me it appeared about the most dangerous thing in every way he had come upon so far.

"They had come together unavoidably, like two ships becalmed near each other, and lay rubbing sides at last. I suppose Kurtz wanted an audience, because on a certain occasion, when encamped in the forest, they had talked all night, or more probably Kurtz had talked. 'We talked of everything,' he said, quite transported at the recollection. 'I forgot there was such a thing as sleep. The night did not seem to last an hour. Everything! Everything! . . . Of love too.' 'Ah, he talked to you of love!' I said, much amused. 'It isn't what you think,' he cried, almost passionately. 'It was in general. He made me see things—things.'

"He threw his arms up. We were on deck at the time, and the headman of my woodcutters, lounging near by, turned upon him his heavy and glittering eyes. I looked around, and I don't know why, but I assure you that never, never before, did this land, this river, this jungle, the very arch of this blazing sky, appear to me so hopeless and so dark, so impenetrable to human thought, so pitiless to human weakness. 'And, ever since, you have been with him, of course?' I said.

"On the contrary. It appears their intercourse had been very much broken by various causes. He had, as he informed me proudly, managed to nurse Kurtz through two illnesses (he alluded to it as you would to some risky feat), but as a rule Kurtz wandered alone, far in the depths of the forest. 'Very often coming to this station, I had to wait days and days before he would turn up,' he said. 'Ah, it was worth waiting for!—sometimes.' 'What was he doing? exploring or what?' I asked. 'Oh yes, of course'; he had discovered lots of villages, a lake too—he did not know exactly in what direction; it was dangerous to inquire too much—but mostly his expeditions had been for ivory. 'But he had no goods to trade with by that time,' I objected. 'There's a good lot of cartridges left even yet,' he answered, looking away. 'To speak plainly, he raided the country,' I said. He nodded. 'Not alone, surely!' He muttered something about the villages round that lake. 'Kurtz got the tribe to follow him, did he?' I suggested. He fidgeted a little.

'They adored him,' he said. The tone of these words was so extraordinary that I looked at him searchingly. It was curious to see his mingled eagerness and reluctance to speak of Kurtz. The man filled his life, occupied his thoughts, swayed his emotions. 'What can you expect?' he burst out; 'he came to them with thunder and lightning, you know—and they had never seen anything like it—and very terrible. He could be very terrible. You can't judge Mr. Kurtz as you would an ordinary man. No, no, no! Now—just to give you an idea—I don't mind telling you, he wanted to shoot me too one day—but I don't judge him.' 'Shoot you!' I cried. 'What for?' 'Well, I had a small lot of ivory the chief of that village near my house gave me. You see I used to shoot game for them. Well, he wanted it, and wouldn't hear reason. He declared he would shoot me unless I gave him the ivory and then cleared out of the country, because he could do so, and had a fancy for it, and there was nothing on earth to prevent him killing whom he jolly well pleased. And it was true too. I gave him the ivory. What did I care! But I didn't clear out. No, no. I couldn't leave him. I had to be careful, of course, till we got friendly again for a time. He had his second illness then. Afterwards I had to keep out of the way; but I didn't mind. He was living for the most part in those villages on the lake. When he came down to the river, sometimes he would take to me, and sometimes it was better for me to be careful. This man suffered too much. He hated all this, and somehow he couldn't get away. When I had a chance I begged him to try and leave while there was time; I offered to go back with him. And he would say yes, and then he would remain; go off on another ivory hunt; disappear for weeks; forget himself amongst these people—forget himself—you know.' 'Why! he's mad,' I said. He protested indignantly. Mr. Kurtz couldn't be mad. If I had heard him talk, only two days ago, I wouldn't dare hint at such a thing. . . . I had taken up my binoculars while we talked, and was looking at the shore, sweeping the limit of the forest at each side and at the back of the house. The consciousness of there being people in that bush, so silent, so quiet—as silent and quiet as the ruined house on the hill—made me uneasy. There was no sign on the face of nature of this amazing tale that was not so much told as suggested to me in desolate exclamations, completed by shrugs, in interrupted phrases, in hints ending in deep sighs. The woods were unmoved, like a mask—heavy, like the closed door of a prison—they looked with their air of hidden knowledge, of patient expectation, of unapproachable silence. The Russian was explaining to me that it was only lately that Mr. Kurtz had come down to the river, bringing along with him all the fighting men of that lake tribe. He had been absent for several months—getting himself adored, I suppose—and had come down unexpectedly, with the intention to all appearance of making a raid either across the river or down stream. Evidently the appetite for more ivory had got the better of the—what shall I say?—less material aspirations. However, he had got much worse suddenly. 'I heard he was lying helpless, and so I came up—took my chance,' said the Russian. 'Oh, he is bad, very bad.' I directed my glass to the house. There were no signs of life, but there were the ruined roof, the long mud wall peeping above the grass, with three little square window-holes, no two of the same size; all this brought within reach of my hand, as it were. And then I made a brusque movement, and one of the remaining posts of that vanished fence leaped up in the field of my glass. You remember I told you I had been struck at the distance by certain attempts at ornamentation, rather remarkable in the ruinous aspect of the place.

Now I had suddenly a nearer view, and its first result was to make me throw my head back as if before a blow. Then I went carefully from post to post with my glass, and I saw my mistake. These round knobs were not ornamental but symbolic; they were expressive and puzzling, striking and disturbing—food for thought and also for the vultures if there had been any looking down from the sky; but at all events for such ants as were industrious enough to ascend the pole. They would have been even more impressive, those heads on the stakes, if their faces had not been turned to the house. Only one, the first I had made out, was facing my way. I was not so shocked as you may think. The start back I had given was really nothing but a movement of surprise. I had expected to see a knob of wood there, you know. I returned deliberately to the first I had seen—and there it was, black, dried, sunken, with closed eyelids—a head that seemed to sleep at the top of that pole, and, with the shrunken dry lips showing a narrow white line of the teeth, was smiling too, smiling continuously at some endless and jocose dream of that eternal slumber.

"I am not disclosing any trade secrets. In fact the manager said afterwards that Mr. Kurtz's methods had ruined the district. I have no opinion on that point, but I want you clearly to understand that there was nothing exactly profitable in these heads being there. They only showed that Mr. Kurtz lacked restraint in the gratification of his various lusts, that there was something wanting in him—some small matter which, when the pressing need arose, could not be found under his magnificent eloquence. Whether he knew of this deficiency himself I can't say. I think the knowledge came to him at last—only at the very last. But the wilderness had found him out early, and had taken on him a terrible vengeance for the fantastic invasion. I think it had whispered to him things about himself which he did not know, things of which he had no conception till he took counsel with this great solitude—and the whisper had proved irresistibly fascinating. It echoed loudly within him because he was hollow at the core. . . . I put down the glass, and the head that had appeared near enough to be spoken to seemed at once to have leaped away from me into inaccessible distance.

"The admirer of Mr. Kurtz was a bit crestfallen. In a hurried, indistinct voice he began to assure me he had not dared to take these—say, symbols—down. He was not afraid of the natives; they would not stir till Mr. Kurtz gave the word. His ascendancy was extraordinary. The camps of these people surrounded the place, and the chiefs came every day to see him. They would crawl . . . 'I don't want to know anything of the ceremonies used when approaching Mr. Kurtz,' I shouted. Curious, this feeling that came over me that such details would be more intolerable than those heads drying on the stakes under Mr. Kurtz's windows. After all, that was only a savage sight, while I seemed at one bound to have been transported into some lightless region of subtle horrors, where pure, uncomplicated savagery was a positive relief, being something that had a right to exist—obviously—in the sunshine. The young man looked at me with surprise. I suppose it did not occur to him that Mr. Kurtz was no idol of mine. He forgot I hadn't heard any of these splendid monologues on, what was it? on love, justice, conduct of life—or what not. If it had come to crawling before Mr. Kurtz, he crawled as much as the veriest savage of them all. I had no idea of the conditions, he said: these heads were the heads of rebels. I shocked him excessively by laughing. Rebels! What would be the next definition I was to hear? There had been enemies, criminals, workers—and these were reb-

els. Those rebellious heads looked very subdued to me on their sticks. 'You
don't know how such a life tries a man like Kurtz,' cried Kurtz's last disci-
ple. 'Well, and you?' I said. 'I! I! I am a simple man. I have no great thoughts.
I want nothing from anybody. How can you compare me to . . . ?' His
feelings were too much for speech, and suddenly he broke down. 'I don't
understand,' he groaned. 'I've been doing my best to keep him alive, and
that's enough. I had no hand in all this. I have no abilities. There hasn't
been a drop of medicine or a mouthful of invalid food for months here. He
was shamefully abandoned. A man like this, with such ideas. Shamefully!
Shamefully! I—I—haven't slept for the last ten nights. . . .

"His voice lost itself in the calm of the evening. The long shadows of the
forest had slipped down hill while we talked, had gone far beyond the ruined
hovel, beyond the symbolic row of stakes. All this was in the gloom, while
we down there were yet in the sunshine, and the stretch of the river abreast
of the clearing glittered in a still and dazzling splendor, with a murky and
overshadowed bend above and below. Not a living soul was seen on the
shore. The bushes did not rustle.

"Suddenly round the corner of the house a group of men appeared, as
though they had come up from the ground. They waded waist-deep in the
grass, in a compact body, bearing an improvised stretcher in their midst.
Instantly, in the emptiness of the landscape, a cry arose whose shrillness
pierced the still air like a sharp arrow flying straight to the very heart of the
land; and, as if by enchantment, streams of human beings—of naked human
beings—with spears in their hands, with bows, with shields, with wild glances
and savage movements, were poured into the clearing by the dark-faced
and pensive forest. The bushes shook, the grass swayed for a time, and then
everything stood still in attentive immobility.

" 'Now, if he does not say the right thing to them we are all done for,'
said the Russian at my elbow. The knot of men with the stretcher had
stopped too, half-way to the steamer, as if petrified. I saw the man on the
stretcher sit up, lank and with an uplifted arm, above the shoulders of the
bearers. 'Let us hope that the man who can talk so well of love in general
will find some particular reason to spare us this time,' I said. I resented
bitterly the absurd danger of our situation, as if to be at the mercy of that
atrocious phantom had been a dishonoring necessity. I could not hear a
sound, but through my glasses I saw the thin arm extended commandingly,
the lower jaw moving, the eyes of that apparition shining darkly far in its
bony head that nodded with grotesque jerks. Kurtz—Kurtz—that means
'short' in German—don't it? Well, the name was as true as everything else
in his life—and death. He looked at least seven feet long. His covering had
fallen off, and his body emerged from it pitiful and appalling as from a
winding-sheet. I could see the cage of his ribs all astir, the bones of his arm
waving. It was as though an animated image of death carved out of old ivory
had been shaking its hand with menaces at a motionless crowd of men made
of dark and glittering bronze. I saw him open his mouth wide—it gave him
a weirdly voracious aspect, as though he had wanted to swallow all the air,
all the earth, all the men before him. A deep voice reached me faintly. He
must have been shouting. He fell back suddenly. The stretcher shook as
the bearers staggered forward again, and almost at the same time I noticed
that the crowd of savages was vanishing without any perceptible movement
of retreat, as if the forest that had ejected these beings so suddenly had
drawn them in again as the breath is drawn in a long aspiration.

"Some of the pilgrims behind the stretcher carried his arms—two shot-guns, a heavy rifle, and a light revolver-carbine—the thunderbolts of that pitiful Jupiter. The manager bent over him murmuring as he walked beside his head. They laid him down in one of the little cabins—just a room for a bed-place and a camp-stool or two, you know. We had brought his belated correspondence, and a lot of torn envelopes and open letters littered his bed. His hand roamed feebly amongst these papers. I was struck by the fire of his eyes and the composed languor of his expression. It was not so much the exhaustion of disease. He did not seem in pain. This shadow looked satiated and calm, as though for the moment it had had its fill of all the emotions.

"He rustled one of the letters, and looking straight in my face said, 'I am glad.' Somebody had been writing to him about me. These special recom-mendations were turning up again. The volume of tone he emitted without effort, almost without the trouble of moving his lips, amazed me. A voice! a voice! It was grave, profound, vibrating, while the man did not seem capable of a whisper. However, he had enough strength in him—factitious no doubt—to very nearly make an end of us, as you shall hear directly.

"The manager appeared silently in the doorway; I stepped out at once and he drew the curtain after me. The Russian, eyed curiously by the pil-grims, was staring at the shore. I followed the direction of his glance.

"Dark human shapes could be made out in the distance, flitting indis-tinctly against the gloomy border of the forest, and near the river two bronze figures, leaning on tall spears, stood in the sunlight under fantastic head-dresses of spotted skins, warlike and still in statuesque repose. And from right to left along the lighted shore moved a wild and gorgeous apparition of a woman.

"She walked with measured steps, draped in striped and fringed cloths, treading the earth proudly, with a slight jingle and flash of barbarous orna-ments. She carried her head high; her hair was done in the shape of a helmet; she had brass leggings to the knees, brass wire gauntlets to the elbow, a crimson spot on her tawny cheek, innumerable necklaces of glass beads on her neck; bizarre things, charms, gifts of witch-men, that hung about her, glittered and trembled at every step. She must have had the value of several elephant tusks upon her. She was savage and superb, wild-eyed and magnificent; there was something ominous and stately in her deliberate progress. And in the hush that had fallen suddenly upon the whole sorrowful land, the immense wilderness, the colossal body of the fecund and mysterious life seemed to look at her, pensive, as though it had been looking at the image of its own tenebrous and passionate soul.

"She came abreast of the steamer, stood still, and faced us. Her long shadow fell to the water's edge. Her face had a tragic and fierce aspect of wild sorrow and of dumb pain mingled with the fear of some struggling, half-shaped resolve. She stood looking at us without a stir, and like the wilderness itself, with an air of brooding over an inscrutable purpose. A whole minute passed, and then she made a step forward. There was a low jingle, a glint of yellow metal, a sway of fringed draperies, and she stopped as if her heart had failed her. The young fellow by my side growled. The pilgrims murmured at my back. She looked at us all as if her life had depended upon the unswerving steadiness of her glance. Suddenly she opened her bared arms and threw them up rigid above her head, as though in an uncon-trollable desire to touch the sky, and at the same time the swift shadows darted out on the earth, swept around on the river, gathering the steamer into a shadowy embrace. A formidable silence hung over the scene.

"She turned away slowly, walked on, following the bank, and passed into the bushes to the left. Once only her eyes gleamed back at us in the dusk of the thickets before she disappeared.

" 'If she had offered to come aboard I really think I would have tried to shoot her,' said the man of patches nervously. 'I had been risking my life every day for the last fortnight to keep her out of the house. She got in one day and kicked up a row about those miserable rags I picked up in the storeroom to mend my clothes with. I wasn't decent. At least it must have been that, for she talked like a fury to Kurtz for an hour, pointing at me now and then. I don't understand the dialect of this tribe. Luckily for me, I fancy Kurtz felt too ill that day to care, or there would have been mischief. I don't understand. . . . No—it's too much for me. Ah, well, it's all over now.'

"At this moment I heard Kurtz's deep voice behind the curtain: 'Save me!—save the ivory, you mean. Don't tell me. Save me! Why, I've had to save you. You are interrupting my plans now. Sick! Sick! Not so sick as you would like to believe. Never mind. I'll carry my ideas out yet—I will return. I'll show you what can be done. You with your little peddling notions—you are interfering with me. I will return. I . . . '

"The manager came out. He did me the honor to take me under the arm and lead me aside. 'He is very low, very low,' he said. He considered it necessary to sigh, but neglected to be consistently sorrowful. 'We have done all we could for him—haven't we? But there is no disguising the fact, Mr. Kurtz has done more harm than good to the Company. He did not see the time was not ripe for vigorous action. Cautiously, cautiously—that's my principle. We must be cautious yet. The district is closed to us for a time. Deplorable! Upon the whole, the trade will suffer. I don't deny there is a remarkable quantity of ivory—mostly fossil. We must save it, at all events—but look how precarious the position is—and why? Because the method is unsound.' 'Do you,' said I, looking at the shore, 'call it "unsound method"?' 'Without doubt,' he exclaimed hotly, 'Don't you?' . . . 'No method at all,' I murmured after a while. 'Exactly,' he exulted. 'I anticipated this. Shows a complete want of judgment. It is my duty to point it out in the proper quarter.' 'Oh,' said I, 'that fellow—what's his name?—the brickmaker, will make a readable report for you.' He appeared confounded for a moment. It seemed to me I had never breathed an atmosphere so vile, and I turned mentally to Kurtz for relief—positively for relief. 'Nevertheless, I think Mr. Kurtz is a remarkable man,' I said with emphasis. He started, dropped on me a cold heavy glance, said very quietly, 'He was,' and turned his back on me. My hour of favor was over; I found myself lumped along with Kurtz as a partisan of methods for which the time was not ripe: I was unsound! Ah! but it was something to have at least a choice of nightmares.

"I had turned to the wilderness really, not to Mr. Kurtz, who, I was ready to admit, was as good as buried. And for a moment it seemed to me as if I also were buried in a vast grave full of unspeakable secrets. I felt an intolerable weight oppressing my breast, the smell of the damp earth, the unseen presence of victorious corruption, the darkness of an impenetrable night. . . . The Russian tapped me on the shoulder. I heard him mumbling and stammering something about 'brother seaman—couldn't conceal—knowledge of matters that would affect Mr. Kurtz's reputation.' I waited. For him evidently Mr. Kurtz was not in his grave; I suspect that for him Mr. Kurtz was one of the immortals. 'Well!' said I at last, 'speak out. As it happens, I am Mr. Kurtz's friend—in a way.'

"He stated with a good deal of formality that had we not been 'of the same profession,' he would have kept the matter to himself without regard to consequences. He suspected 'there was an active ill will towards him on the part of these white men that—' 'You are right,' I said, remembering a certain conversation I had overheard. 'The manager thinks you ought to be hanged.' He showed a concern at this intelligence which amused me at first. 'I had better get out of the way quietly,' he said earnestly. 'I can do no more for Kurtz now, and they would soon find some excuse. What's to stop them? There's a military post three hundred miles from here.' 'Well, upon my word,' said I, 'perhaps you had better go if you have any friends amongst the savages near by.' 'Plenty,' he said. 'They are simple people—and I want nothing, you know.' He stood biting his lip, then: 'I don't want any harm to happen to these whites here, but of course I was thinking of Mr. Kurtz's reputation—but you are a brother seaman and—' 'All right,' said I, after a time. 'Mr. Kurtz's reputation is safe with me.' I did not know how truly I spoke.

"He informed me, lowering his voice, that it was Kurtz who had ordered the attack to be made on the steamer. 'He hated sometimes the idea of being taken away—and then again . . . But I don't understand these matters. I am a simple man. He thought it would scare you away—that you would give it up, thinking him dead. I could not stop him. Oh, I had an awful time of it this last month.' 'Very well,' I said. 'He is all right now.' 'Ye-e-es,' he muttered, not very convinced apparently. 'Thanks,' said I; 'I shall keep my eyes open.' 'But quiet—eh?' he urged anxiously. 'It would be awful for his reputation if anybody here—' I promised a complete discretion with great gravity. 'I have a canoe and three black fellows waiting not very far. I am off. Could you give me a few Martini-Henry cartridges?' I could, and did, with proper secrecy. He helped himself, with a wink at me, to a handful of my tobacco. 'Between sailors—you know—good English tobacco.' At the door of the pilothouse he turned round—'I say, haven't you a pair of shoes you could spare?' He raised one leg. 'Look.' The soles were tied with knotted strings sandal-wise under his bare feet. I rooted out an old pair, at which he looked with admiration before tucking it under his left arm. One of his pockets (bright red) was bulging with cartridges, from the other (dark blue) peeped 'Towson's Inquiry,' etc. etc. He seemed to think himself excellently well equipped for a renewed encounter with the wilderness. 'Ah! I'll never, never meet such a man again. You ought to have heard him recite poetry—his own too it was, he told me. Poetry!' He rolled his eyes at the recollection of these delights. 'Oh, he enlarged my mind!' 'Goodbye,' said I. He shook hands and vanished in the night. Sometimes I ask myself whether I had ever really seen him—whether it was possible to meet such a phenomenon! . . .

"When I woke up shortly after midnight his warning came to my mind with its hint of danger that seemed, in the starred darkness, real enough to make me get up for the purpose of having a look round. On the hill a big fire burned, illuminating fitfully a crooked corner of the station house. One of the agents with a picket of a few of our blacks, armed for the purpose, was keeping guard over the ivory; but deep within the forest, red gleams that wavered, that seemed to sink and rise from the ground amongst confused columnar shapes of intense blackness, showed the exact position of the camp where Mr. Kurtz's adorers were keeping their uneasy vigil. The monotonous beating of a big drum filled the air with muffled shocks and a lingering vibration. A steady droning sound of many men chanting each to himself some weird incantation came out from the black, flat wall of the woods as the humming of bees comes out of a hive, and had a strange narcotic effect upon my half-awake senses. I believe I dozed off leaning over the rail, till an abrupt burst of yells, an overwhelming outbreak of a pent-up and mysterious frenzy, woke me up in a bewildered wonder. It was cut short all at once, and the low droning went on with an effect of audible and soothing silence. I glanced casually into the little cabin. A light was burning within, but Mr. Kurtz was not there.

"I think I would have raised an outcry if I had believed my eyes. But I didn't believe them at first—the thing seemed so impossible. The fact is, I was completely unnerved by a sheer blank fright, pure abstract terror, unconnected with any distinct shape of physical danger. What made this emotion so overpowering was—how shall I define it?—the moral shock I received, as if something altogether monstrous, intolerable to thought and odious to the soul, had been thrust upon me unexpectedly. This lasted of course the merest fraction of a second, and then the usual sense of commonplace, deadly danger, the possibility of a sudden onslaught and massacre, or something of the kind, which I saw impending, was positively welcome and composing. It pacified me, in fact, so much, that I did not raise an alarm.

"There was an agent buttoned up inside an ulster and sleeping on a chair on deck within three feet of me. The yells had not awakened him; he snored very slightly; I left him to his slumbers and leaped ashore. I did not betray Mr. Kurtz—it was ordered I should never betray him—it was written I should be loyal to the nightmare of my choice. I was anxious to deal with this shadow by myself alone—and to this day I don't know why I was so jealous of sharing with anyone the peculiar blackness of that experience.

"As soon as I got on the bank I saw a trail—a broad trail through the grass. I remember the exultation with which I said to myself, 'He can't walk—he is crawling on all fours—I've got him.' The grass was wet with dew. I strode rapidly with clenched fists. I fancy I had some vague notion of falling upon him and giving him a drubbing. I don't know. I had some imbecile thoughts. The knitting old woman with the cat obtruded herself upon my memory as a most improper person to be sitting at the other end of such an affair. I saw a row of pilgrims squirting lead in the air out of Winchesters held to the hip. I thought I would never get back to the steamer, and imagined myself living alone and unarmed in the woods to an advanced age. Such silly things—you know. And I remember I confounded the beat of the drum with the beating of my heart, and was pleased at its calm regularity.

"I kept to the track though—then stopped to listen. The night was very clear; a dark blue space, sparkling with dew and starlight, in which black things stood very still. I thought I could see a kind of motion ahead of me. I was strangely cocksure of everything that night. I actually left the track and ran in a wide semicircle (I verily believe chuckling to myself) so as to get in front of that stir, of that motion I had seen—if indeed I had seen anything. I was circumventing Kurtz as though it had been a boyish game.

"I came upon him, and, if he had not heard me coming, I would have fallen over him too, but he got up in time. He rose, unsteady, long, pale, indistinct, like a vapour exhaled by the earth, and swayed slightly, misty and silent before me; while at my back the fires loomed between the trees, and the murmur of many voices issued from the forest. I had cut him off cleverly; but when actually confronting him I seemed to come to my senses, I saw the danger in its right proportion. It was by no means over yet. Suppose he began to shout? Though he could hardly stand, there was still plenty of vigor in his voice. 'Go away—hide yourself,' he said, in that profound tone. It was very awful. I glanced back. We were within thirty yards of the nearest fire. A black figure stood up, strode on long black legs, waving long black arms, across the glow. It had horns—antelope horns, I think—on its head. Some sorcerer, some witch-man no doubt: it looked fiend-like enough. 'Do you know what you are doing?' I whispered. 'Perfectly,' he answered, raising his voice for that single word: it sounded to me far off and yet loud, like a hail through a speaking-trumpet. If he makes a row we are lost, I thought to myself. This clearly was not a case for fisticuffs, even apart from the very natural aversion I had to beat that Shadow—this wandering and tormented thing. 'You will be lost,' I said—'utterly lost.' One gets sometimes such a flash of inspiration, you know. I did say the right thing, though indeed he could not have been more irretrievably lost than he was at this very moment, when the foundations of our intimacy were being laid—to endure—to endure—even to the end—even beyond.

" 'I had immense plans,' he muttered irresolutely. 'Yes,' said I; 'but if you try to shout I'll smash your head with—' There was not a stick or a stone near. 'I will throttle you for good,' I corrected myself. 'I was on the threshold of great things,' he pleaded, in a voice of longing, with a wistfulness of tone that made my blood run cold. 'And now for this stupid scoundrel—' 'Your success in Europe is assured in any case,' I affirmed steadily. I did not want to have the throttling of him, you understand—and indeed it would have been very little use for any practical purpose. I tried to break the spell—the heavy, mute spell of the wilderness—that seemed to draw him to its pitiless breast by the awakening of forgotten and brutal instincts, by the memory of gratified and monstrous passions. This alone, I was convinced, had driven him out to the edge of the forest, to the bush, towards the gleam of fires, the throb of drums, the drone of weird incantations; this alone had beguiled his unlawful soul beyond the bounds of permitted aspirations. And, don't you see, the terror of the position was not in being knocked on the head—though I had a very lively sense of that danger too—but in this, that I had to deal with a being to whom I could not appeal in the name of anything high or low. I had, even like the niggers, to invoke him—himself—his own exalted and incredible degradation. There was nothing either above or below him, and I knew it. He had kicked himself loose of the earth. Confound the man! he had kicked the very earth to pieces. He was alone, and I before him did not know whether I stood on the ground or floated in the air. I've been telling you what we said—repeating the phrases we pronounced—but what's the good? They were common everyday words—the familiar, vague sounds exchanged on every waking day of life. But what of that? They had behind them, to my mind, the terrific suggestiveness of words heard in dreams, of phrases spoken in nightmares. Soul! If anybody had ever struggled with a soul, I am the man. And I wasn't arguing with a lunatic either. Believe me or not, his intelligence was perfectly clear—concentrated, it is true, upon himself with horrible intensity, yet clear; and therein was my only chance—barring, of course, the killing him there and then, which wasn't so good, on account of unavoidable noise. But his soul was mad. Being alone in the wilderness, it had looked within itself, and, by Heavens! I tell you, it had gone mad. I had—for my sins, I suppose, to go through the ordeal of looking into it myself. No eloquence could have been so withering to one's belief in mankind as his final burst of sincerity. He struggled with himself too. I saw it— I heard it. I saw the inconceivable mystery of a soul that knew no restraint, no faith, and no fear, yet struggling blindly with itself. I kept my head pretty well; but when I had him at last stretched on the couch, I wiped my forehead, while my legs shook under me as though I had carried half a ton on my back down that hill. And yet I had only supported him, his bony arm clasped round my neck—and he was not much heavier than a child.

"When next day we left at noon, the crowd, of whose presence behind the curtain of trees I had been acutely conscious all the time, flowed out of the woods again, filled the clearing, covered the slope with a mass of naked, breathing, quivering, bronze bodies. I steamed up a bit, then swung downstream, and two thousand eyes followed the evolutions of the splashing, thumping, fierce river-demon beating the water with its terrible tail and breathing black smoke into the air. In front of the first rank, along the river, three men, plastered with bright red earth from head to foot, strutted to and fro restlessly. When we came abreast again, they faced the river, stamped their feet, nodded their horned heads, swayed their scarlet bodies; they shook towards the fierce river-demon a bunch of black feathers, a mangy skin with a pendent tail—something that looked like a dried gourd; they shouted periodically together strings of amazing words that resembled no sounds of human language; and the deep murmurs of the crowd, interrupted suddenly, were like the responses of some satanic litany.

"We had carried Kurtz into the pilothouse: there was more air there. Lying on the couch, he stared through the open shutter. There was an eddy in the mass of human bodies, and the woman with helmeted head and tawny cheeks rushed out to the very brink of the stream. She put out her hands, shouted something, and all that wild mob took up the shout in a roaring chorus of articulated, rapid, breathless utterance.

" 'Do you understand this?' I asked.

"He kept on looking out past me with fiery, longing eyes, with a mingled expression of wistfulness and hate. He made no answer, but I saw a smile, a smile of indefinable meaning, appear on his colorless lips that a moment after twitched convulsively. 'Do I not?' he said slowly, gasping, as if the words had been torn out of him by a supernatural power.

"I pulled the string of the whistle, and I did this because I saw the pilgrims on deck getting out their rifles with an air of anticipating a jolly lark. At the sudden screech there was a movement of abject terror through that wedged mass of bodies. 'Don't! don't you frighten them away,' cried someone on deck disconsolately. I pulled the string time after time. They broke and ran, they leaped, they crouched, they swerved, dodged the flying terror of the sound. The three red chaps had fallen flat, face down on the shore, as though they had been shot dead. Only the barbarous and superb woman did not so much as flinch, and stretched tragically her bare arms after us over the somber and glittering river.

"And then that imbecile crowd down on the deck started their little fun, and I could see nothing more for smoke.

"The brown current ran swiftly out of the heart of darkness, bearing us down towards the sea with twice the speed of our upward progress; and Kurtz's life was running swiftly too, ebbing, ebbing out of his heart into the sea of inexorable time. The manager was very placid, he had no vital anxieties now, he took us both in with a comprehensive and satisfied glance: the 'affair' had come off as well as could be wished. I saw the time approaching when I would be left alone of the party of 'unsound method.' The pilgrims looked upon me with disfavor. I was, so to speak, numbered with the dead. It is strange how I accepted this unforeseen partnership, this choice of nightmares forced upon me in the tenebrous land invaded by these mean and greedy phantoms.

"Kurtz discoursed. A voice! a voice! It rang deep to the very last. It survived his strength to hide in the magnificent folds of eloquence the barren darkness of his heart. Oh, he struggled! he struggled! The wastes of his weary brain were haunted by shadowy images now—images of wealth and fame revolving obsequiously round his unextinguishable gift of noble and lofty expression. My Intended, my station, my career, my ideas—these were the subjects for the occasional utterances of elevated sentiments. The shade of the original Kurtz frequented the bedside of the hollow sham, whose fate it was to be buried presently in the mould of primeval earth. But both the diabolic love and the unearthly hate of the mysteries it had penetrated fought for the possession of that soul satiated with primitive emotions, avid of lying fame, of sham distinction, of all the appearances of success and power.

"Sometimes he was contemptibly childish. He desired to have kings meet him at railway stations on his return from some ghastly Nowhere, where he intended to accomplish great things. 'You show them you have in you something that is really profitable, and then there will be no limits to the recognition of your ability,' he would say. 'Of course you must take care of the motives—right motives—always.' The long reaches that were like one and the same reach, monotonous bends that were exactly alike, slipped past the steamer with their multitude of secular[2] trees looking patiently after this grimy fragment of another world, the forerunner of change, of conquest, of trade, of massacres, of blessings. I looked ahead—piloting. 'Close the shutter,' said Kurtz suddenly one day; 'I can't bear to look at this.' I did so. There was a silence. 'Oh, but I will wring your heart yet!' he cried at the invisible wilderness.

"We broke down—as I had expected—and had to lie up for repairs at the head of an island. This delay was the first thing that shook Kurtz's confidence. One morning he gave me a packet of papers and a photograph—the lot tied together with a shoe-string. 'Keep this for me,' he said. 'This noxious fool' (meaning the manager) 'is capable of prying into my boxes when I am not looking.' In the afternoon I saw him. He was lying on his back with closed eyes, and I withdrew quietly, but I heard him mutter, 'Live rightly, die, die . . .' I listened. There was nothing more. Was he rehearsing some speech in his sleep, or was it a fragment of a phrase from some newspaper article? He had been writing for the papers and meant to do so again, 'for the furthering of my ideas. It's a duty.'

"His was an impenetrable darkness. I looked at him as you peer down at a man who is lying at the bottom of a precipice where the sun never shines.

___

2. Ancient.

But I had not much time to give him, because I was helping the engine-driver to take to pieces the leaky cylinders, to straighten a bent connecting rod, and in other such matters. I lived in an infernal mess of rust, filings, nuts, bolts, spanners, hammers, ratchet drills—things I abominate, because I don't get on with them. I tended the little forge we fortunately had aboard; I toiled wearily in a wretched scrap heap—unless I had the shakes too bad to stand.

"One evening coming in with a candle I was startled to hear him say a little tremulously, 'I am lying here in the dark waiting for death.' The light was within a foot of his eyes. I forced myself to murmur, 'Oh, nonsense!' and stood over him as if transfixed.

"Anything approaching the change that came over his features I have never seen before, and hope never to see again. Oh, I wasn't touched. I was fascinated. It was as though a veil had been rent. I saw on that ivory face the expression of somber pride, of ruthless power, of craven terror—of an intense and hopeless despair. Did he live his life again in every detail of desire, temptation, and surrender during that supreme moment of complete knowledge? He cried in a whisper at some image, at some vision—he cried out twice, a cry that was no more than a breath:

" 'The horror! The horror!'

"I blew the candle out and left the cabin. The pilgrims were dining in the mess room, and I took my place opposite the manager, who lifted his eyes to give me a questioning glance, which I successfully ignored. He leaned back, serene, with that peculiar smile of his sealing the unexpressed depths of his meanness. A continuous shower of small flies streamed upon the lamp, upon the cloth, upon our hands and faces. Suddenly the manager's boy put his insolent black head in the doorway, and said in a tone of scathing contempt:

" 'Mistah Kurtz—he dead.'

"All the pilgrims rushed out to see. I remained, and went on with my dinner. I believe I was considered brutally callous. However, I did not eat much. There was a lamp in there—light, don't you know—and outside it was so beastly, beastly dark. I went no more near the remarkable man who had pronounced a judgment upon the adventures of his soul on this earth. The voice was gone. What else had been there? But I am of course aware that next day the pilgrims buried something in a muddy hole.

"And then they very nearly buried me.

"However, as you see, I did not go to join Kurtz there and then. I did not. I remained to dream the nightmare out to the end, and to show my loyalty to Kurtz once more. Destiny. My destiny! Droll thing life is—that mysterious arrangement of merciless logic for a futile purpose. The most you can hope from it is some knowledge of yourself—that comes too late—a crop of unextinguishable regrets. I have wrestled with death. It is the most unexciting contest you can imagine. It takes place in an impalpable grayness, with nothing underfoot, with nothing around, without spectators, without clamour, without glory, without the great desire of victory, without the great fear of defeat, in a sickly atmosphere of tepid skepticism, without much belief in your own right, and still less in that of your adversary. If such is the form of ultimate wisdom, then life is a greater riddle than some of us think it to be. I was within a hair's breadth of the last opportunity for pronouncement, and I found with humiliation that probably I would have nothing to say. This is the reason why I affirm that Kurtz was a remarkable man. He had something to say. He said it. Since I had peeped over the edge myself, I understand better the meaning of his stare, that could not see the flame of the candle, but was wide enough to embrace the whole universe, piercing enough to penetrate all the hearts that beat in the darkness. He had summed up—he had judged. 'The horror!' He was a remarkable man. After all, this was the expression of some sort of belief; it had candour, it had conviction, it had a vibrating note of revolt in its whisper, it had the appalling face of a glimpsed truth—the strange commingling of desire and hate. And it is not my own extremity I remember best—a vision of grayness without form filled with physical pain, and a careless contempt for the evanescence of all things—even of this pain itself. No! It is his extremity that I seem to have lived through. True, he had made that last stride, he had stepped over the edge, while I had been permitted to draw back my hesitating foot. And perhaps in this is the whole difference; perhaps all the wisdom, and all truth, and all sincerity, are just compressed into that inappreciable moment of time in which we step over the threshold of the invisible. Perhaps! I like to think my summing-up would not have been a word of careless contempt. Better his cry—much better. It was an affirmation, a moral victory paid for by innumerable defeats, by abominable terrors, by abominable satisfactions. But it was a victory! That is why I have remained loyal to Kurtz to the last, and even beyond, when a long time after I heard once more, not his own voice, but the echo of his magnificent eloquence thrown to me from a soul as translucently pure as a cliff of crystal.

"No, they did not bury me, though there is a period of time which I remember mistily, with a shuddering wonder, like a passage through some inconceivable world that had no hope in it and no desire. I found myself back in the sepulchral city resenting the sight of people hurrying through the streets to filch a little money from each other, to devour their infamous cookery, to gulp their unwholesome beer, to dream their insignificant and silly dreams. They trespassed upon my thoughts. They were intruders whose knowledge of life was to me an irritating pretense, because I felt so sure they could not possibly know the things I knew. Their bearing, which was simply the bearing of commonplace individuals going about their business in the assurance of perfect safety, was offensive to me like the outrageous flauntings of folly in the face of a danger it is unable to comprehend. I had no particular desire to enlighten them, but I had some difficulty in restraining myself from laughing in their faces, so full of stupid importance. I daresay I was not very well at that time. I tottered about the streets—there were various affairs to settle—grinning bitterly at perfectly respectable persons. I admit my behavior was inexcusable, but then my temperature was seldom normal in these days. My dear aunt's endeavors to 'nurse up my strength' seemed altogether beside the mark. It was not my strength that wanted nursing, it was my imagination that wanted soothing. I kept the bundle of papers given me by Kurtz, not knowing exactly what to do with it. His mother had died lately, watched over, as I was told, by his Intended. A clean-shaven man, with an official manner and wearing gold-rimmed spectacles, called on me one day and made inquiries, at first circuitous, afterwards suavely pressing, about what he was pleased to denominate certain 'documents.' I was not surprised, because I had had two rows with the manager on the subject out there. I had refused to give up the smallest scrap out of that package, and I took the same attitude with the spectacled man. He became darkly menacing at last, and with much heat argued that the Company had the right to every bit of information about its 'territories.' And, said he, 'Mr. Kurtz's knowledge of unexplored regions must have been necessarily extensive and peculiar—owing to his great abilities and to the deplorable circumstances in which he had been placed: therefore—' I assured him Mr. Kurtz's knowledge, however extensive, did not bear upon the problems of commerce or administration. He invoked then the name of science. 'It would be an incalculable loss if,' etc. etc. I offered him the report on the 'Suppression of Savage Customs,' with the postscriptum torn off. He took it up eagerly, but ended by sniffing at it with an air of contempt. 'This is not what we had a right to expect,' he remarked. 'Expect nothing else,' I said. 'There are only private letters.' He withdrew upon some threat of legal proceedings, and I saw him no more; but another fellow, calling himself Kurtz's cousin, appeared two days later, and was anxious to hear all the details about his dear relative's last moments. Incidentally he gave me to understand that Kurtz had been essentially a great musician. 'There was the making of an immense success,' said the man, who was an organist, I believe, with lank grey hair flowing over a greasy coat collar. I had no reason to doubt his statement; and to this day I am unable to say what was Kurtz's profession, whether he ever had any—which was the greatest of his talents. I had taken him for a painter who wrote for the papers, or else for a journalist who could paint—but even the cousin (who took snuff during the interview) could not tell me what he had been— exactly. He was a universal genius—on that point I agreed with the old chap, who thereupon blew his nose noisily into a large cotton handkerchief and withdrew in senile agitation, bearing off some family letters and memoranda without importance. Ultimately a journalist anxious to know something of the fate of his 'dear colleague' turned up. This visitor informed me Kurtz's proper sphere ought to have been politics 'on the popular side.' He had furry straight eyebrows, bristly hair cropped short, an eyeglass on a broad ribbon, and, becoming expansive, confessed his opinion that Kurtz really couldn't write a bit—'but Heavens! how that man could talk! He electrified large meetings. He had faith—don't you see?—he had the faith. He could get himself to believe anything—anything. He would have been a splendid leader of an extreme party.' 'What party?' I asked. 'Any party,' answered the other. 'He was an—an—extremist.' Did I not think so? I assented. Did I know, he asked, with a sudden flash of curiosity, 'what it was that had induced him to go out there?' 'Yes,' said I, and forthwith handed him the famous Report for publication, if he thought fit. He glanced through it hurriedly, mumbling all the time, judged 'it would do,' and took himself off with this plunder.

"Thus I was left at last with a slim packet of letters and the girl's portrait. She struck me as beautiful—I mean she had a beautiful expression. I know that the sunlight can be made to lie too, yet one felt that no manipulation of light and pose could have conveyed the delicate shade of truthfulness upon those features. She seemed ready to listen without mental reservation, without suspicion, without a thought for herself. I concluded I would go and give her back her portrait and those letters myself. Curiosity? Yes; and also some other feeling perhaps. All that had been Kurtz's had passed out of my hands: his soul, his body, his station, his plans, his ivory, his career. There remained only his memory and his Intended—and I wanted to give that up too to the past, in a way—to surrender personally all that remained of him with me to that oblivion which is the last word of our common fate. I don't defend myself. I had no clear perception of what it was I really wanted. Perhaps it was an impulse of unconscious loyalty, or the fulfilment of one of those ironic necessities that lurk in the facts of human existence. I don't know. I can't tell. But I went.

"I thought his memory was like the other memories of the dead that accumulate in every man's life—a vague impress on the brain of shadows that had fallen on it in their swift and final passage; but before the high and ponderous door, between the tall houses of a street as still and decorous as a well-kept alley in a cemetery, I had a vision of him on the stretcher, opening his mouth voraciously, as if to devour all the earth with all its mankind. He lived then before me; he lived as much as he had ever lived— a shadow insatiable of splendid appearances, of frightful realities; a shadow darker than the shadow of the night, and draped nobly in the folds of a gorgeous eloquence. The vision seemed to enter the house with me—the stretcher, the phantom-bearers, the wild crowd of obedient worshippers, the gloom of the forests, the glitter of the reach between the murky bends, the beat of the drum, regular and muffled like the beating of a heart—the heart of a conquering darkness. It was a moment of triumph for the wilderness, an invading and vengeful rush which, it seemed to me, I would have to keep back alone for the salvation of another soul. And the memory of what I had heard him say afar there, with the horned shapes stirring at my back, in the glow of fires, within the patient woods, those broken phrases came back to me, were heard again in their ominous and terrifying simplicity. I remembered his abject pleading, his abject threats, the colossal scale of his vile desires, the meanness, the torment, the tempestuous anguish of his soul. And later on I seemed to see his collected languid manner, when he said one day, 'This lot of ivory now is really mine. The Company did not pay for it. I collected it myself at a very great personal risk. I am afraid they will try to claim it as theirs though. H'm. It is a difficult case. What do you think I ought to do—resist? Eh? I want no more than justice.' . . . He wanted no more than justice—no more than justice. I rang the bell before a mahogany door on the first floor, and while I waited he seemed to stare at me out of the glassy panel—stare with that wide and immense stare embracing, condemning, loathing all the universe. I seemed to hear the whispered cry, 'The horror! The horror!'

"The dusk was falling. I had to wait in a lofty drawing room with three long windows from floor to ceiling that were like three luminous and bedraped columns. The bent gilt legs and backs of the furniture shone in indistinct curves. The tall marble fireplace had a cold and monumental whiteness. A grand piano stood massively in a corner; with dark gleams on the flat surfaces like a somber and polished sarcophagus. A high door opened—closed. I rose.

"She came forward, all in black, with a pale head, floating towards me in the dusk. She was in mourning. It was more than a year since his death, more than a year since the news came; she seemed as though she would remember and mourn forever. She took both my hands in hers and murmured, 'I had heard you were coming.' I noticed she was not very young— I mean not girlish. She had a mature capacity for fidelity, for belief, for suffering. The room seemed to have grown darker, as if all the sad light of the cloudy evening had taken refuge on her forehead. This fair hair, this pale visage, this pure brow, seemed surrounded by an ashy halo from which the dark eyes looked out at me. Their glance was guileless, profound, confident, and trustful. She carried her sorrowful head as though she were proud of that sorrow, as though she would say, I—I alone know how to mourn for him as he deserves. But while we were still shaking hands, such a look of awful desolation came upon her face that I perceived she was one of those creatures that are not the playthings of Time. For her he had died only yesterday. And, by Jove! the impression was so powerful that for me too he seemed to have died only yesterday—nay, this very minute. I saw her and him in the same instant of time—his death and her sorrow—I saw her sorrow in the very moment of his death. Do you understand? I saw them together—I heard them together. She had said, with a deep catch of the breath, 'I have survived'; while my strained ears seemed to hear distinctly, mingled with her tone of despairing regret, the summing-up whisper of his eternal condemnation. I asked myself what I was doing there, with a sensation of panic in my heart as though I had blundered into a place of cruel and absurd mysteries not fit for a human being to behold. She motioned me to a chair. We sat down. I laid the packet gently on the little table, and she put her hand over it. . . . 'You knew him well,' she murmured, after a moment of mourning silence.

" 'Intimacy grows quickly out there,' I said. 'I knew him as well as it is possible for one man to know another.'

" 'And you admired him,' she said. 'It was impossible to know him and not to admire him. Was it?'

" 'He was a remarkable man,' I said unsteadily. Then before the appealing fixity of her gaze, that seemed to watch for more words on my lips, I went on, 'It was impossible not to—'

" 'Love him,' she finished eagerly, silencing me into an appalled dumbness. 'How true! how true! But when you think that no one knew him so well as I! I had all his noble confidence. I knew him best.'

" 'You knew him best,' I repeated. And perhaps she did. But with every word spoken the room was growing darker, and only her forehead, smooth and white, remained illumined by the unextinguishable light of belief and love.

" 'You were his friend,' she went on. 'His friend,' she repeated, a little louder. 'You must have been, if he had given you this, and sent you to me. I feel I can speak to you—and oh! I must speak. I want you—you who have heard his last words—to know I have been worthy of him. . . . It is not pride. . . . Yes! I am proud to know I understood him better than anyone on earth—he told me so himself. And since his mother died I have had no one—no one—to—to—'

"I listened. The darkness deepened. I was not even sure whether he had given me the right bundle. I rather suspect he wanted me to take care of another batch of his papers which, after his death, I saw the manager examining under the lamp. And the girl talked, easing her pain in the certitude of my sympathy; she talked as thirsty men drink. I had heard that her engagement with Kurtz had been disapproved by her people. He wasn't rich enough or something. And indeed I don't know whether he had not been a pauper all his life. He had given me some reason to infer that it was his impatience of comparative poverty that drove him out there.

" '. . . Who was not his friend who had heard him speak once?' she was saying. 'He drew men towards him by what was best in them.' She looked at me with intensity. 'It is the gift of the great,' she went on, and the sound of her low voice seemed to have the accompaniment of all the other sounds, full of mystery, desolation, and sorrow, I had ever heard—the ripple of the river, the soughing of the trees swayed by the wind, the murmurs of the crowds, the faint ring of incomprehensible words cried from afar, the whisper of a voice speaking from beyond the threshold of an eternal darkness. 'But you have heard him! You know!' she cried.

" 'Yes, I know,' I said with something like despair in my heart, but bowing my head before the faith that was in her, before that great and saving illusion that shone with an unearthly glow in the darkness, in the triumphant darkness from which I could not have defended her—from which I could not even defend myself.

" 'What a loss to me—to us!'—she corrected herself with beautiful generosity; then added in a murmur, 'To the world.' By the last gleams of twilight I could see the glitter of her eyes, full of tears—of tears that would not fall.

" 'I have been very happy—very fortunate—very proud,' she went on. 'Too fortunate. Too happy for a little while. And now I am unhappy for—for life.'

"She stood up; her fair hair seemed to catch all the remaining light in a glimmer of gold. I rose too.

" 'And of all this,' she went on mournfully, 'of all his promise, and of all his greatness, of his generous mind, of his noble heart, nothing remains—nothing but a memory. You and I—'

" 'We shall always remember him,' I said hastily.

" 'No!' she cried. 'It is impossible that all this should be lost—that such a life should be sacrificed to leave nothing—but sorrow. You know what vast plans he had. I knew of them too—I could not perhaps understand—but others knew of them. Something must remain. His words, at least, have not died.'

" 'His words will remain,' I said.

" 'And his example,' she whispered to herself. 'Men looked up to him—his goodness shone in every act. His example—'

" 'True,' I said; 'his example too. Yes, his example. I forgot that.'

" 'But I do not. I cannot—I cannot believe—not yet. I cannot believe that I shall never see him again, that nobody will see him again, never, never, never.'

"She put out her arms as if after a retreating figure, stretching them back and with clasped pale hands across the fading and narrow sheen of the window. Never see him! I saw him clearly enough then. I shall see this eloquent phantom as long as I live, and I shall see her too, a tragic and familiar Shade, resembling in this gesture another one, tragic also, and bedecked with powerless charms, stretching bare brown arms over the glitter of the infernal stream, the stream of darkness. She said suddenly very low, 'He died as he lived.'

" 'His end,' said I, with dull anger stirring in me, 'was in every way worthy of his life.'

" 'And I was not with him,' she murmured. My anger subsided before a feeling of infinite pity.

" 'Everything that could be done—' I mumbled.

" 'Ah, but I believed in him more than anyone on earth—more than his own mother, more than—himself. He needed me! Me! I would have treasured every sigh, every word, every sign, every glance.'

"I felt like a chill grip on my chest. 'Don't,' I said, in a muffled voice.

" 'Forgive me. I—I—have mourned so long in silence—in silence. . . . You were with him—to the last? I think of his loneliness. Nobody near to understand him as I would have understood. Perhaps no one to hear . . .'

" 'To the very end,' I said shakily. 'I heard his very last words. . . .' I stopped in a fright.

" 'Repeat them,' she murmured in a heartbroken tone. 'I want—I want—something—something—to—to live with.'

"I was on the point of crying at her, 'Don't you hear them?' The dusk was repeating them in a persistent whisper all around us, in a whisper that seemed to swell menacingly like the first whisper of a rising wind. 'The horror! The horror!'

" 'His last word—to live with,' she insisted. 'Don't you understand I loved him—I loved him—I loved him!'

"I pulled myself together and spoke slowly.

" 'The last word he pronounced was—your name.'

"I heard a light sigh and then my heart stood still, stopped dead short by an exulting and terrible cry, by the cry of inconceivable triumph and of unspeakable pain. 'I knew it—I was sure!' . . . She knew. She was sure. I heard her weeping; she had hidden her face in her hands. It seemed to me that the house would collapse before I could escape, that the heavens would fall upon my head. But nothing happened. The heavens do not fall for such a trifle. Would they have fallen, I wonder, if I had rendered Kurtz that justice which was his due? Hadn't he said he wanted only justice? But I couldn't. I could not tell her. It would have been too dark—too dark altogether. . . ."

Marlow ceased, and sat apart, indistinct and silent, in the pose of a meditating Buddha. Nobody moved for a time. "We have lost the first of the ebb," said the Director suddenly. I raised my head. The offing was barred by a black bank of clouds, and the tranquil waterway leading to the uttermost ends of the earth flowed somber under an overcast sky—seemed to lead into the heart of an immense darkness.

1902

AFTERWORD

You can't say that Conrad doesn't warn us that he has "intentions." Even if we gloss over the title (why not *The Heart of Darkness?* or *A Heart of Darkness?* or *The Heart of the Darkness?*), it is difficult to ignore the narrator's "directions for interpreting a Marlow tale":

> The yarns of seamen have a direct simplicity, the whole meaning of which lies within the shell of a cracked nut. But . . . to him the meaning of an episode was not inside like a kernel but outside, enveloping the tale which brought it out only as a glow brings out a haze . . .

So, it seems, we are to look for meaning, and to look for it not just at the climax or denouement of the novel, not even entirely within the episode itself, but outside. And, we are warned, the meaning or illumination that emerges will not be a bright light, but a suggestion, a hint, a haze. Later, Marlow himself will talk of his tale as like a dream, and he will struggle with the difficulty of communicating the dreamlike sensation of his experience:

> It seems to me I am trying to tell you a dream . . . [but] no relation of a dream can convey the dream-sensation, that commingling of absurdity, surprise, and bewilderment in a tremor of struggling revolt, that notion of being captured by the incredible . . .

But, he says, it is just as difficult to communicate the precise nature and meaning of any experience, dream or not:

> it is impossible to convey the life-sensation of any given epoch of one's exis-tence—that which makes its truth, its meaning—its subtle and penetrating essence.

For he tells us, "We live, as we dream, alone."

At this discouraging point there is a break in Marlow's story, almost as if he despairs of going on because he has recognized the hopelessness of trying to convey to others one's significant experiences. But the narrator of our story, *Heart of Darkness*—who, we must remember, is not Marlow, for Marlow's words are always in quotation marks, but a narrator who can speak in the first person without putting what he says in quotation marks and who has been sitting on the deck listening to Marlow's story—that narrator has not given up. He is determined to pay even closer attention in order to get at the dark heart of Marlow's story. He says, "I listened on the watch for the sentence, for the word, that would give me the clue to the faint uneasiness inspired by this narrative." So we, too, if we are to have any chance of understanding, must be on the watch for clues in the words and sentences of Marlow's narration. Some of us, if not uneasy, are at least slightly puzzled at this point and want to find our way through the haze. Perhaps we should be uneasy as well as puzzled, however, for, Marlow suggests, the ultimate reality, which is not the apparent reality of "the mere incidents of the surface," is not very pleasant: "The inner truth is hidden—luckily, luckily."

There are "inner truths" in the novel that are, luckily, hidden but that do not seem quite so hazy or incommunicable as Marlow makes out. The more obvious, perhaps an "incident of the surface," is the inner evil of the imperialist project. Regardless of the fine, hypocritical words—the announced mission of bringing the benefits of civ-ilization (and Christianity) to the "savages," of bringing light to the dark heart of

Africa—imperialism is, indeed, cruel and savage, and its true motive is greed and the lust for power. *Heart of Darkness* was thus a "relevant," socially significant fiction when it was first published, when Belgium was exploiting the riches of the Congo—and is so, no doubt, now, when there is still subtle and unsubtle imperial exploitation of what we now call "the Third World." Without significant distortion, Conrad's novel was read in its own time—and can be read now—as an anti-imperialist work.

If such a reading does not distort, it may not sufficiently penetrate the heart of the story to satisfy all readers, however. These may seek and, quite readily discover another "inner truth"—the "darkness" in the individual human heart, something like innate evil or Original Sin. At the heart of the darkness of the Congo, in darkest Africa, is Kurtz, an intelligent, humane, and well-intentioned reformer, who has come out to Africa to bring the light of civilization but gets caught up in . . . what? Is he enthralled by the game, the enterprise of bringing out as much ivory as possible? by the temptations of material wealth? the even more thrilling opportunity of exercising absolute power? Or is he betrayed by strange, savage appetites in his own heart? Or all of the above . . . or none? Whatever the explanation, Kurtz, the most noble, becomes the most depraved. If Kurtz, even he, can be so corrupted (or is innately so corrupt) then what about the rest of us? What are we really like? What is the "inner truth" of our natures? How much temptation would we be able to resist?

If the temptation is greatest when the veneer of civilization and its restraints are stripped away, it is also when that veneer of civilization and its falsifying words are stripped away that the "inner truth" of reality and of our natures is most apparent. It is Kurtz, then, who, in the heart of darkest Africa, the region at that time the most remote from civilization, is subject to the least restraint and who is thus most bedeviled by temptation. And so it would also seem to be Kurtz who must have the clearest understanding of the true nature of human reality. And what does he tell us? "Exterminate all the brutes"? What does that mean? Who are the brutes? Are they the "savages" who live in darkest Africa and who worship the strange white god who lives among them and engage in unspeakable rites? Has Kurtz made a beginning by beheading a number of them and affixing their severed heads to poles around his lodge? Or is this one of his indulgences or one of the savage rites? On the other hand, hasn't the novel, or at least Marlow's story, shown us that the colonists at the Central Station, for example, are as savage as the savages and as brutal as the brutes? Who should be exterminated? savages? colonists? mankind? The kernel of the story seems clear, and if this were a yarn by an ordinary seaman, its meaning would be clear by now as well. But the narrator has told us that the meaning of a story by Marlow is not a kernel but a surrounding "glow."

Marlow has told us that we live, as we dream, alone, and that conveying life-sensations and the subtle, penetrating essence or meaning of our experiences is impossible. Kurtz has certainly been "alone" (if we mean away from civilization) and his experiences are at the heart of the darkness of Africa, of his self, and of Marlow's story. Marlow, unlike the narrator and even more unlike us, has been up the Congo and into that dark heart. He has met Kurtz, seen his surroundings and some of the results of his work in the bush. He even seems to sympathize with him. Next to Kurtz, who is in any case, dead, Marlow is best equipped to tell his story and to extract something like its meaning. But it is not necessarily Kurtz's meaning, is it? We live, as we dream, alone, and the essence of experience is incommunicable, Marlow has told us, so Marlow's story and Marlow's meaning are not Kurtz's, then, but Marlow's. Kurtz may have penetrated the heart of darkness, Marlow merely illuminated the haze around that truth, but he has been there, has known Kurtz, and has at least "illuminated" truth with a glow from within its dark heart.

Then it is the narrator who listens on the deck of the ship in the Thames and the others who listen with him—those who are now Lawyers, and Accountants, and so on, but who have been to sea and thus away from Europe and the falsifying glitter of its civilization—who may be able to approximately understand the approximate truth that Marlow is recounting, or who at least may be able to see the glow within the haze. Those who can understand least are those who live wholly within the flickering circle of light we call civilization, the flattering but artificial gaslights of the European home. Thus those to whom it is impossible to show the darkness at the heart of natural and human reality are those who are most confined within the limits of civilized society: that is, civilized European women who are bound to the home. As Marlow says, "They—the women I mean—are out of it—should be out of it. We must help them to stay in that beautiful world of their own, lest ours gets worse." (I'll come back to that final phrase in a bit, but we need even at this point to recognize that this lack of understanding is not wholly gender related—note the magnificent savage woman at the very heart of the Inner Station—but culture-specific.). So, while Marlow tries to tell his version of Kurtz's truth to his fellow seafarers—those who, if they have not been into the heart of darkness, have at least been away from the lights of London and the land—he tells the Intended, that is, Kurtz's fiancée, despite everything in him that hates dishonesty, a lie, a huge and ironic lie. He does so, apparently, to prevent "our" (masculine) world from getting even worse than it already is.

Then where do we, the readers, come in? Marlow's audience is all male and all seamen. To whom is the narrator telling the tale? Is his audience, too, meant to be all male, European (and American) landlubbers? To what extent can we—even if we are lucky enough to be male—penetrate the "misty halo . . . made visible by the spectral illumination of [the] moonshine" of Marlow's story?

Or is the first-person narrator more confident than Marlow that the essence of an experience can be communicated? (Or more confident in his own ability as a storyteller than in Marlow's? Or more confident in us as readers?)

As you can see, though I have picked at a couple of kernels in the story, I have not been able to penetrate, perhaps not even illuminate, the haze. Just what does Marlow think of civilization, for example? It is clear he hates the claptrap of the self-seeking colonials and considers them as cruel as the savages, if not more so. (He has considerable respect for the cannibals, for example.) If we are tempted to think of the Europeans as rational and see at the heart of darkness the Freudian "Id" elsewhere restrained by the "Superego" of civilization, what do we make of their absurdity, the mysterious but almost comic picture of the women knitting in the outer office of the Company? the haphazard firing of shells into the vast continent of Africa? the comic chaos of the Central Station?

The most civilized of men, Kurtz, succumbs to the darkness, yet somehow the ancient Romans, conquering Britain, which was then also "one of the dark places of the earth," were not defeated by it:

> Imagine him [a Roman commander of a ship, a sort of "Marlow," as it were] here—the very end of the world, a sea the color of lead, a sky the color of smoke . . . —and going up the river with stores, or orders, or what you like. Sandbanks, marshes, forests, savages—precious little to eat fit for a civilized man. . . . Here and there a military camp lost in a wilderness . . . death skulking in the air, in the water, in the bush. They must have been dying like flies here. Oh yes—he did it. Did it very well, too. . . . They were men enough to face the darkness.

Was Kurtz, then, not man enough to face the darkness? If so, why is Marlow so sympathetic toward him? And though it is only a flicker, according to Marlow, "we" live in a flicker of *light*. If the imperialists are hypocritical in professing to bring "light" to the darkness of Africa, is there not nonetheless "light" in Europe? And aren't we the better for it—until we get greedy for material wealth or power? If, unrestrained, we can be as cruel as savages or worse, is there not some value in restraint, in neighbors or policemen? Or in the false but beautiful world of the women at home, without whose illusions we would be worse? Marlow himself seems saved by having to pay attention to snags and other dangers of the river—"When you have to attend to things of that sort, to the mere incidents of the surface, the reality fades. The inner truth is hidden—luckily, luckily." Is this "good" or admirable? He seems to admire the accountant at the Central Station for keeping the books straight and keeping up the front of civilization despite the rot and ruin of the surroundings, and despite the apparent triviality of his bookkeeping and even its share in the imperial enterprise. Marlow says that man

> must meet that truth [truth stripped of its cloak of time] with his own true stuff— with his own inborn strength. . . . Principles won't do. Acquisitions . . . No; you want a deliberate belief.

Kurtz had only principles, apparently? But didn't he "believe" in those humanistic principles? What, then, should he have believed in? Work? Civilization? Order? God? The Beauty of Life? His experience, his corruption, his life—and death—are, to be sure, a "nightmare," but why does Marlow choose Kurtz's nightmare? and over what other nightmares?

What glows through the haze? What illuminates the heart of darkness? Is it only moonshine?

Moonshine or marshlight—the false light that misleads travelers, the *ignis fatuus*— we are led from the Thames to the Congo and up the Congo to the heart of darkness in a breathtaking journey. We are enthralled by the adventure and by the mystery, not just the mystery of Kurtz and the conspiracy that surrounds him, but the mystery of the haze that floats on the surface of the Thames and shines mistily, misty but glowing, through every incident, every sentence of this rich and justly renowned novel.

Heart of Darkness is as challenging and problematic in its narration as *Daisy Miller,* as exciting as *Dr. Jekyll and Mr. Hyde,* as soul-searching and as socially "subversive" as *The Death of Iván Ilyich.* It penetrates beneath the surface of existence and challenges our ordinary, almost thoughtless belief in the ability of words to represent reality even more than do all these others. Story, structure, significance—it's got it all. We may not "like" it; it may make us—should make us?—uneasy, perhaps even repulse us in some ways, but it communicates the experience of the incommunicability of experience that lies at the heart of—perhaps is the darkness at the heart of— the literary or reading experience.

EDITH WHARTON

Ethan Frome

Born into an aristocratic New York City family, Edith Newbold Jones (1862–1937) married, in 1885, an aristocratic Bostonian, Edward Wharton. Both suffered from nervous illnesses. The marriage was an unhappy one and ended in divorce. . . . But not until 1913.

Edith Wharton wrote early and often and all through her trials, at first satiric, even acerbic, or desolate works. In her first volume of stories, published in 1899, for example, there were stories like "Souls Belated," which treated broken marriage and adultery sympathetically but that acknowledged the overwhelming force of society arrayed against those who openly broke with social convention.

Her second novel, *The House of Mirth* (1905)—like much of her work, it was about social pressures on the individual in New York society—was a great success and established her place in the world of letters. Her best-known work, the short novel *Ethan Frome*, began as a French exercise, and an eight-page version of it in French still exists (it was published in a scholarly journal in 1952).

This early version, if it may be called that, was written in 1907, before the watershed experience in Edith Jones Wharton's life, an affair with Morton Fullerton. Her diary testifies to the depth and power of her sexual "awakening" at the age of forty-six. The relationship was deep and meaningful, yet it somehow gradually faded after two years, and three more years would pass before the conventional person and unconventional writer would get a divorce.

Her subsequent works were softer, and tended to deal more with passion than with desolation. *The Age of Innocence* won the Pulitzer Prize for 1920. Though she continued writing—some fifty books in all—she never reached such heights again, and perhaps this decline has contributed to the unjustified neglect, which, despite a splendid biography by R.W.B Lewis and some critical attention, has prevented her being accorded the high place in American letters that she would seem to deserve.

What is at the heart of fiction (and life?), Edith Wharton found, was not darkness but that ancient legendary emblem of passion that lived in fire, the salamander:

> It is useless to box your reader's ear unless you have a salamander to show him. If the heart of your blaze is not animated by a living, moving *something* no shouting and shaking will fix the anecdote in your reader's memory.

In the frozen depths of the Starkfield winter, in the tight-lipped Ethan Frome, and in the conventional lady of New York, Newport, and Paris, there glows somewhat darkly in the blaze a salamandrine fire.

Ethan Frome

I had the story, bit by bit, from various people, and, as generally happens in such cases, each time it was a different story.

If you know Starkfield, Massachusetts, you know the post office. If you know the post office you must have seen Ethan Frome drive up to it, drop the reins on his hollow-backed bay and drag himself across the brick pavement to the white colonnade: and you must have asked who he was.

It was there that, several years ago, I saw him for the first time; and the sight pulled me up sharp. Even then he was the most striking figure in Starkfield, though he was but the ruin of a man. It was not so much his great height that marked him, for the "natives" were easily singled out by their lank longitude from the stockier foreign breed: it was the careless powerful look he had, in spite of a lameness checking each step like the jerk of a chain. There was something bleak and unapproachable in his face, and he was so stiffened and grizzled that I took him for an old man and was surprised to hear that he was not more than fifty-two. I had this from Harmon Gow, who had driven the stage from Bettsbridge to Starkfield in pretrolley days and knew the chronicle of all the families on his line.

"He's looked that way ever since he had his smashup; and that's twenty-four years ago come next February," Harmon threw out between reminiscent pauses.

The "smashup" it was—I gathered from the same informant—which, besides drawing the red gash across Ethan Frome's forehead, had so shortened and warped his right side that it cost him a visible effort to take the few steps from his buggy to the post office window. He used to drive in from his farm every day at about noon, and as that was my own hour for fetching my mail I often passed him in the porch or stood beside him while we waited on the motions of the distributing hand behind the grating. I noticed that, though he came so punctually, he seldom received anything but a copy of the *Bettsbridge Eagle*, which he put without a glance into his sagging pocket. At intervals, however, the postmaster would hand him an envelope addressed to Mrs. Zenobia—or Mrs. Zeena—Frome, and usually bearing conspicuously in the upper left-hand corner the address of some manufacturer of patent medicine and the name of his specific. These documents my neighbor would also pocket without a glance, as if too much used to them to wonder at their number and variety, and would then turn away with a silent nod to the postmaster.

Every one in Starkfield knew him and gave him a greeting tempered to his own grave mien; but his taciturnity was respected and it was only on rare occasions that one of the older men of the place detained him for a word. When this happened he would listen quietly, his blue eyes on the speaker's face, and answer in so low a tone that his words never reached me; then he would climb stiffly into his buggy, gather up the reins in his left hand and drive slowly away in the direction of his farm.

"It was a pretty bad smashup?" I questioned Harmon, looking after Frome's retreating figure, and thinking how gallantly his lean brown head, with its shock of light hair, must have sat on his strong shoulders before they were bent out of shape.

"Wust kind," my informant assented. "More'n enough to kill most men. But the Fromes are tough. Ethan'll likely touch a hundred."

"Good God!" I exclaimed. At the moment Ethan Frome, after climbing to his seat, had leaned over to assure himself of the security of a wooden box—also with a druggist's label on it—which he had placed in the back of the buggy, and I saw his face as it probably looked when he thought himself alone. "*That* man touch a hundred? He looks as if he was dead and in hell now!"

Harmon drew a slab of tobacco from his pocket, cut off a wedge and pressed it into the leather pouch of his cheek. "Guess he's been in Starkfield too many winters. Most of the smart ones get away."

"Why didn't *he*?"

"Somebody had to stay and care for the folks. There warn't ever anybody but Ethan. Fust his father—then his mother—then his wife."

"And then the smashup?"

Harmon chuckled sardonically. "That's so. He *had* to stay then."

"I see. And since then they've had to care for him?"

Harmon thoughtfully passed his tobacco to the other cheek. "Oh, as to that: I guess it's always Ethan done the caring."

Though Harmon Gow developed the tale as far as his mental and moral reach permitted there were perceptible gaps between his facts, and I had the sense that the deeper meaning of the story was in the gaps. But one phrase stuck in my memory and served as the nucleus about which I grouped my subsequent inferences: "Guess he's been in Starkfield too many winters."

Before my own time there was up I had learned to know what that meant. Yet I had come in the degenerate day of trolley, bicycle and rural delivery, when communication was easy between the scattered mountain villages, and the bigger towns in the valleys, such as Bettsbridge and Shadd's Falls, had libraries, theaters and Y.M.C.A. halls to which the youth of the hills could descend for recreation. But when winter shut down on Starkfield, and the village lay under a sheet of snow perpetually renewed from the pale skies, I began to see what life there—or rather its negation—must have been in Ethan Frome's young manhood.

I had been sent up by my employers on a job connected with the big powerhouse at Corbury Junction, and a long-drawn carpenters' strike had so delayed the work that I found myself anchored at Starkfield—the nearest habitable spot—for the best part of the winter. I chafed at first, and then, under the hypnotizing effect of routine, gradually began to find a grim satisfaction in the life. During the early part of my stay I had been struck by the contrast between the vitality of the climate and the deadness of the community. Day by day, after the December snows were over, a blazing blue sky poured down torrents of light and air on the white landscape, which gave them back in an intenser glitter. One would have supposed that such an atmosphere must quicken the emotions as well as the blood; but it seemed to produce no change except that of retarding still more the sluggish pulse of Starkfield. When I had been there a little longer, and had seen this phase of crystal clearness followed by long stretches of sunless cold; when the storms of February had pitched their white tents about the devoted village and the wild cavalry of March winds had charged down to their support, I began to understand why Starkfield emerged from its six months'

siege like a starved garrison capitulating without quarter. Twenty years earlier the means of resistance must have been far fewer, and the enemy in
command of almost all the lines of access between the beleaguered villages;
and, considering these things, I felt the sinister force of Harmon's phrase:
"Most of the smart ones get away." But if that were the case, how could
any combination of obstacles have hindered the flight of a man like Ethan
Frome?

During my stay at Starkfield I lodged with a middle-aged widow collo-
quially known as Mrs. Ned Hale. Mrs. Hale's father had been the village
lawyer of the previous generation, and "lawyer Varnum's house," where
my landlady still lived with her mother, was the most considerable mansion
in the village. It stood at one end of the main street, its classic portico and
small-paned windows looking down a flagged path between Norway spruces
to the slim white steeple of the Congregational church. It was clear that the
Varnum fortunes were at the ebb, but the two women did what they could
to preserve a decent dignity; and Mrs. Hale, in particular, had a certain
wan refinement not out of keeping with her pale old-fashioned house.

In the "best parlor," with its black horse-hair and mahogany weakly illuminated by a gurgling Carcel lamp,[1] I listened every evening to another
and more delicately shaded version of the Starkfield chronicle. It was not
that Mrs. Ned Hale felt, or affected, any social superiority to the people
about her; it was only that the accident of a finer sensibility and a little more
education had put just enough distance between herself and her neighbors
to enable her to judge them with detachment. She was not unwilling to
exercise this faculty, and I had great hopes of getting from her the missing
facts of Ethan Frome's story, or rather such a key to his character as should
coordinate the facts I knew. Her mind was a storehouse of innocuous anec-
dote and any question about her acquaintances brought forth a volume of
detail; but on the subject of Ethan Frome I found her unexpectedly reti-
cent. There was no hint of disapproval in her reserve; I merely felt in her
an insurmountable reluctance to speak of him or his affairs, a low "Yes, I
knew them both . . . it was awful . . ." seeming to be the utmost concession
that her distress could make to my curiosity.

So marked was the change in her manner, such depths of sad initiation
did it imply, that, with some doubts as to my delicacy, I put the case anew
to my village oracle, Harmon Gow; but got for my pains only an uncompre-
hending grunt.

"Ruth Varnum was always as nervous as a rat; and, come to think of it,
she was the first one to see 'em after they was picked up. It happened right
below lawyer Varnum's, down at the bend of the Corbury road, just round
about the time that Ruth got engaged to Ned Hale. The young folks was all
friends, and I guess she just can't bear to talk about it. She's had troubles
enough of her own."

All the dwellers in Starkfield, as in more notable communities, had had
troubles enough of their own to make them comparatively indifferent to
those of their neighbors; and though all conceded that Ethan Frome's had
been beyond the common measure, no one gave me an explanation of the
look in his face which, as I persisted in thinking, neither poverty nor physical suffering could have put there. Nevertheless, I might have contented

1. A lamp in which the oil is pumped up to the   cal" lamp).
wick by clockwork (also called "French" or "mechani-

myself with the story pieced together from these hints had it not been for the provocation of Mrs. Hale's silence, and—a little later—for the accident of personal contact with the man.

On my arrival at Starkfield, Denis Eady, the rich Irish grocer, who was the proprietor of Starkfield's nearest approach to a livery stable, had entered into an agreement to send me over daily to Corbury Flats, where I had to pick up my train for the Junction. But about the middle of the winter Eady's horses fell ill of a local epidemic. The illness spread to the other Starkfield stables and for a day or two I was put to it to find a means of transport. Then Harmon Gow suggested that Ethan Frome's bay was still on his legs and that his owner might be glad to drive me over.

I stared at the suggestion. "Ethan Frome? But I've never even spoken to him. Why on earth should he put himself out for me?"

Harmon's answer surprised me still more. "I don't know as he would; but I know he wouldn't be sorry to earn a dollar."

I had been told that Frome was poor, and that the sawmill and the arid acres of his farm yielded scarcely enough to keep his household through the winter; but I had not supposed him to be in such want as Harmon's words implied, and I expressed my wonder.

"Well, matters ain't gone any too well with him," Harmon said. "When a man's been setting round like a hulk for twenty years or more, seeing things that want doing, it eats inter him, and he loses his grit. That Frome farm was always 'bout as bare's a milkpan when the cat's been round; and you know what one of them old watermills is wuth nowadays. When Ethan could sweat over 'em both from sunup to dark he kinder choked a living out of 'em; but his folks ate up most everything, even then, and I don't see how he makes out now. Fust his father got a kick, out haying, and went soft in the brain, and gave away money like Bible texts afore he died. Then his mother got queer and dragged along for years as weak as a baby; and his wife Zeena, she's always been the greatest hand at doctoring in the county. Sickness and trouble: that's what Ethan's had his plate full up with, ever since the very first helping."

The next morning, when I looked out, I saw the hollow-backed bay between the Varnum spruces, and Ethan Frome, throwing back his worn bearskin, made room for me in the sleigh at his side. After that, for a week, he drove me over every morning to Corbury Flats, and on my return in the afternoon met me again and carried me back through the icy night to Starkfield. The distance each way was barely three miles, but the old bay's pace was slow, and even with firm snow under the runners we were nearly an hour on the way. Ethan Frome drove in silence, the reins loosely held in his left hand, his brown seamed profile, under the helmetlike peak of the cap, relieved against the banks of snow like the bronze image of a hero. He never turned his face to mine, or answered, except in monosyllables, the questions I put, or such slight pleasantries as I ventured. He seemed a part of the mute melancholy landscape, an incarnation of its frozen woe, with all that was warm and sentient in him fast bound below the surface; but there was nothing unfriendly in his silence. I simply felt that he lived in a depth of moral isolation too remote for casual access, and I had the sense that his loneliness was not merely the result of his personal plight, tragic as I guessed that to be, but had in it, as Harmon Gow had hinted, the profound accumulated cold of many Starkfield winters.

Only once or twice was the distance between us bridged for a moment;

and the glimpses thus gained confirmed my desire to know more. Once I happened to speak of an engineering job I had been on the previous year in Florida, and of the contrast between the winter landscape about us and that in which I had found myself the year before; and to my surprise Frome said suddenly: "Yes: I was down there once, and for a good while afterward I could call up the sight of it in winter. But now it's all snowed under."

He said no more, and I had to guess the rest from the inflection of his voice and his sharp relapse into silence.

Another day, on getting into my train at the Flats, I missed a volume of popular science—I think it was on some recent discoveries in biochemistry—which I had carried with me to read on the way. I thought no more about it till I got into the sleigh again that evening, and saw the book in Frome's hand.

"I found it after you were gone," he said.

I put the volume into my pocket and we dropped back into our usual silence; but as we began to crawl up the long hill from Corbury Flats to the Starkfield ridge I became aware in the dusk that he had turned his face to mine.

"There are things in that book that I didn't know the first word about," he said.

I wondered less at his words than at the queer note of resentment in his voice. He was evidently surprised and slightly aggrieved at his own ignorance.

"Does that sort of thing interest you?" I asked.

"It used to."

"There are one or two rather new things in the book: there have been some big strides lately in that particular line of research." I waited a moment for an answer that did not come; then I said: "If you'd like to look the book through I'd be glad to leave it with you."

He hesitated, and I had the impression that he felt himself about to yield to a stealing tide of inertia; then, "Thank you—I'll take it," he answered shortly.

I hoped that this incident might set up some more direct communication between us. Frome was so simple and straightforward that I was sure his curiosity about the book was based on a genuine interest in its subject. Such tastes and acquirements in a man of his condition made the contrast more poignant between his outer situation and his inner needs, and I hoped that the chance of giving expression to the latter might at least unseal his lips. But something in his past history, or in his present way of living, had apparently driven him too deeply into himself for any casual impulse to draw him back to his kind. At our next meeting he made no allusion to the book, and our intercourse seemed fated to remain as negative and one-sided as if there had been no break in his reserve.

Frome had been driving me over to the Flats for about a week when one morning I looked out of my window into a thick snowfall. The height of the white waves massed against the garden fence and along the wall of the church showed that the storm must have been going on all night, and that the drifts were likely to be heavy in the open. I thought it probable that my train would be delayed; but I had to be at the powerhouse for an hour or two that afternoon, and I decided, if Frome turned up, to push through to the Flats and wait there till my train came in. I don't know why I put it in the conditional, however, for I never doubted that Frome would appear.

He was not the kind of man to be turned from his business by any commotion of the elements; and at the appointed hour his sleigh glided up through the snow like a stage apparition behind thickening veils of gauze.

I was getting to know him too well to express either wonder or gratitude at his keeping his appointment; but I exclaimed in surprise as I saw him turn his horse in a direction opposite to that of the Corbury road.

"The railroad's blocked by a freight train that got stuck in a drift below the Flats," he explained, as we jogged off into the stinging whiteness.

"But look here—where are you taking me, then?"

"Straight to the Junction, by the shortest way," he answered, pointing up School House Hill with his whip.

"To the Junction—in this storm? Why, it's a good ten miles!"

"The bay'll do it if you give him time. You said you had some business there this afternoon. I'll see you get there."

He said it so quietly that I could only answer: "You're doing me the biggest kind of favor."

"That's all right," he rejoined.

Abreast of the schoolhouse the road forked, and we dipped down a lane to the left, between hemlock boughs bent inward to their trunks by the weight of the snow. I had often walked that way on Sundays, and knew that the solitary roof showing through bare branches near the bottom of the hill was that of Frome's sawmill. It looked exanimate enough, with its idle wheel looming above the black stream dashed with yellow-white spume, and its cluster of sheds sagging under their white load. Frome did not even turn his head as we drove by, and still in silence we began to mount the next slope. About a mile farther, on a road I had never traveled, we came to an orchard of starved apple trees writhing over a hillside among outcroppings of slate that nuzzled up through the snow like animals pushing out their noses to breathe. Beyond the orchard lay a field or two, their boundaries lost under drifts; and above the fields, huddled against the white immensities of land and sky, one of those lonely New England farmhouses that make the landscape lonelier.

"That's my place," said Frome, with a sideway jerk of his lame elbow; and in the distress and oppression of the scene I did not know what to answer. The snow had ceased, and a flash of watery sunlight exposed the house on the slope above us in all its plaintive ugliness. The black wraith of a deciduous creeper flapped from the porch, and the thin wooden walls, under their worn coat of paint, seemed to shiver in the wind that had risen with the ceasing of the snow.

"The house was bigger in my father's time: I had to take down the 'L,' a while back," Frome continued, checking with a twitch of the left rein the bay's evident intention of turning in through the broken-down gate.

I saw then that the unusually forlorn and stunted look of the house was partly due to the loss of what is known in New England as the "L": that long deep-rooted adjunct usually built at right angles to the main house, and connecting it, by way of storerooms and toolhouse, with the woodshed and cowbarn. Whether because of its symbolic sense, the image it presents of a life linked with the soil, and enclosing in itself the chief sources of warmth and nourishment, or whether merely because of the consolatory thought that it enables the dwellers in that harsh climate to get to their morning's work without facing the weather, it is certain that the "L" rather than the house itself seems to be the center, the actual hearthstone of the

New England farm. Perhaps this connection of ideas, which had often occurred to me in my rambles about Starkfield, caused me to hear a wistful note in Frome's words, and to see in the diminished dwelling the image of his own shrunken body.

"We're kinder sidetracked here now," he added, "but there was considerable passing before the railroad was carried through to the Flats." He roused the lagging bay with another twitch; then, as if the mere sight of the house had let me too deeply into his confidence for any farther pretense of reserve, he went on slowly: "I've always set down the worst of mother's trouble to that. When she got the rheumatism so bad she couldn't move around she used to sit up there and watch the road by the hour; and one year, when they was six months mending the Bettsbridge pike after the floods, and Harmon Gow had to bring his stage round this way, she picked up so that she used to get down to the gate most days to see him. But after the trains begun running nobody ever come by here to speak of, and mother never could get it through her head what had happened, and it preyed on her right along till she died."

As we turned into the Corbury road the snow began to fall again, cutting off our last glimpse of the house; and Frome's silence fell with it, letting down between us the old veil of reticence. This time the wind did not cease with the return of the snow. Instead, it sprang up to a gale which now and then, from a tattered sky, flung pale sweeps of sunlight over a landscape chaotically tossed. But the bay was as good as Frome's word, and we pushed on to the Junction through the wild white scene.

In the afternoon the storm held off, and the clearness in the west seemed to my inexperienced eye the pledge of a fair evening. I finished my business as quickly as possible, and we set out for Starkfield with a good chance of getting there for supper. But at sunset the clouds gathered again, bringing an earlier night, and the snow began to fall straight and steadily from a sky without wind, in a soft universal diffusion more confusing than the gusts and eddies of the morning. It seemed to be a part of the thickening darkness, to be the winter night itself descending on us layer by layer.

The small ray of Frome's lantern was soon lost in this smothering medium, in which even his sense of direction, and the bay's homing instinct, finally ceased to serve us. Two or three times some ghostly landmark sprang up to warn us that we were astray, and then was sucked back into the mist; and when we finally regained our road the old horse began to show signs of exhaustion. I felt myself to blame for having accepted Frome's offer, and after a short discussion I persuaded him to let me get out of the sleigh and walk along through the snow at the bay's side. In this way we struggled on for another mile or two, and at last reached a point where Frome, peering into what seemed to me formless night, said: "That's my gate down yonder."

The last stretch had been the hardest part of the way. The bitter cold and the heavy going had nearly knocked the wind out of me, and I could feel the horse's side ticking like a clock under my hand.

"Look here, Frome," I began, "there's no earthly use in your going any farther—" but he interrupted me: "Nor you neither. There's been about enough of this for anybody."

I understood that he was offering me a night's shelter at the farm, and without answering I turned into the gate at his side, and followed him to the barn, where I helped him to unharness and bed down the tired horse.

When this was done he unhooked the lantern from the sleigh, stepped out again into the night, and called to me over his shoulder: "This way."

Far off above us a square of light trembled through the screen of snow. Staggering along in Frome's wake I floundered toward it, and in the darkness almost fell into one of the deep drifts against the front of the house. Frome scrambled up the slippery steps of the porch, digging a way through the snow with his heavily booted foot. Then he lifted his lantern, found the latch, and led the way into the house. I went after him into a low unlit passage, at the back of which a ladderlike staircase rose into obscurity. On our right a line of light marked the door of the room which had sent its ray across the night; and behind the door I heard a woman's voice droning querulously.

Frome stamped on the worn oilcloth to shake the snow from his boots, and set down his lantern on a kitchen chair which was the only piece of furniture in the hall. Then he opened the door.

"Come in," he said; and as he spoke the droning voice grew still . . .

It was that night that I found the clue to Ethan Frome, and began to put together this vision of his story. . . .

Chapter I

The village lay under two feet of snow, with drifts at the windy corners. In a sky of iron the points of the Dipper hung like icicles and Orion flashed his cold fires. The moon had set, but the night was so transparent that the white house fronts between the elms looked gray against the snow, clumps of bushes made black stains on it, and the basement windows of the church sent shafts of yellow light far across the endless undulations.

Young Ethan Frome walked at a quick pace along the deserted street, past the bank and Michael Eady's new brick store and Lawyer Varnum's house with the two black Norway spruces at the gate. Opposite the Varnum gate, where the road fell away toward the Corbury valley, the church reared its slim white steeple and narrow peristyle. As the young man walked toward it the upper windows drew a black arcade along the side wall of the building, but from the lower openings, on the side where the ground sloped steeply down to the Corbury road, the light shot its long bars, illuminating many fresh furrows in the track leading to the basement door, and showing, under an adjoining shed, a line of sleighs with heavily blanketed horses.

The night was perfectly still, and the air so dry and pure that it gave little sensation of cold. The effect produced on Frome was rather of a complete absence of atmosphere, as though nothing less tenuous than ether intervened between the white earth under his feet and the metallic dome overhead. "It's like being in an exhausted receiver,"[2] he thought. Four or five years earlier he had taken a year's course at a technological college at Worcester, and dabbled in the laboratory with a friendly professor of physics; and the images supplied by that experience still cropped up, at unexpected moments, through the totally different associations of thought in which he had since been living. His father's death, and the misfortunes following it, had put a premature end to Ethan's studies; but though they had not gone far enough to be of much practical use they had fed his fancy

2. Vessel to receive and contain gases that has been emptied.

and made him aware of huge cloudy meanings behind the daily face of things.

As he strode along through the snow the sense of such meanings glowed in his brain and mingled with the bodily flush produced by his sharp tramp. At the end of the village he paused before the darkened front of the church. He stood there a moment, breathing quickly, and looking up and down the street, in which not another figure moved. The pitch of the Corbury road, below lawyer Varnum's spruces, was the favorite coasting ground of Starkfield, and on clear evenings the church corner rang till late with the shouts of the coasters; but tonight not a sled darkened the whiteness of the long declivity. The hush of midnight lay on the village, and all its waking life was gathered behind the church windows, from which strains of dance music flowed with the broad bands of yellow light.

The young man, skirting the side of the building, went down the slope toward the basement door. To keep out of range of the revealing rays from within he made a circuit through the untrodden snow and gradually approached the farther angle of the basement wall. Thence, still hugging the shadow, he edged his way cautiously forward to the nearest window, holding back his straight spare body and craning his neck till he got a glimpse of the room.

Seen thus, from the pure and frosty darkness in which he stood, it seemed to be seething in a mist of heat. The metal reflectors of the gas-jet sent crude waves of light against the whitewashed walls, and the iron flanks of the stove at the end of the hall looked as though they were heaving with volcanic fires. The floor was thronged with girls and young men. Down the side wall facing the window stood a row of kitchen chairs from which the older women had just risen. By this time the music had stopped, and the musicians—a fiddler, and the young lady who played the harmonium on Sundays—were hastily refreshing themselves at one corner of the supper table which aligned its devastated pie dishes and ice-cream saucers on the platform at the end of the hall. The guests were preparing to leave, and the tide had already set toward the passage where coats and wraps were hung, when a young man with a sprightly foot and a shock of black hair shot into the middle of the floor and clapped his hands. The signal took instant effect. The musicians hurried to their instruments, the dancers—some already half-muffled for departure—fell into line down each side of the room, the older spectators slipped back to their chairs, and the lively young man, after diving about here and there in the throng, drew forth a girl who had already wound a cherry-colored "fascinator" about her head, and, leading her up to the end of the floor, whirled her down its length to the bounding tune of a Virginia reel.

Frome's heart was beating fast. He had been straining for a glimpse of the dark head under the cherry-colored scarf and it vexed him that another eye should have been quicker than his. The leader of the reel, who looked as if he had Irish blood in his veins, danced well, and his partner caught his fire. As she passed down the line, her light figure swinging from hand to hand in circles of increasing swiftness, the scarf flew off her head and stood out behind her shoulders, and Frome, at each turn, caught sight of her laughing panting lips, the cloud of dark hair about her forehead, and the dark eyes which seemed the only fixed points in a maze of flying lines.

The dancers were going faster and faster, and the musicians, to keep up with them, belabored their instruments like jockeys lashing their mounts on the homestretch; yet it seemed to the young man at the window that the reel would never end. Now and then he turned his eyes from the girl's face to that of her partner, which, in the exhilaration of the dance, had taken on a look of almost impudent ownership. Denis Eady was the son of Michael Eady, the ambitious Irish grocer, whose suppleness and effrontery had given Starkfield its first notion of "smart" business methods, and whose new brick store testified to the success of the attempt. His son seemed likely to follow in his steps, and was meanwhile applying the same arts to the conquest of the Starkfield maidenhood. Hitherto Ethan Frome had been content to think him a mean fellow; but now he positively invited a horsewhipping. It was strange that the girl did not seem aware of it: that she could lift her rapt face to her dancer's, and drop her hands into his, without appearing to feel the offense of his look and touch.

Frome was in the habit of walking into Starkfield to fetch home his wife's cousin, Mattie Silver, on the rare evenings when some chance of amusement drew her to the village. It was his wife who had suggested, when the girl came to live with them, that such opportunities should be put in her way. Mattie Silver came from Stamford, and when she entered the Fromes' household to act as her cousin Zeena's aid it was thought best, as she came without pay, not to let her feel too sharp a contrast between the life she had left and the isolation of a Starkfield farm. But for this—as Frome sardonically reflected—it would hardly have occurred to Zeena to take any thought for the girl's amusement.

When his wife first proposed that they should give Mattie an occasional evening out he had inwardly demurred at having to do the extra two miles to the village and back after his hard day on the farm; but not long afterward he had reached the point of wishing that Starkfield might give all its nights to revelry.

Mattie Silver had lived under his roof for a year, and from early morning till they met at supper he had frequent chances of seeing her; but no moments in her company were comparable to those when, her arm in his, and her light step flying to keep time with his long stride, they walked back through the night to the farm. He had taken to the girl from the first day, when he had driven over to the Flats to meet her, and she had smiled and waved to him from the train, crying out, "You must be Ethan!" as she jumped down with her bundles, while he reflected, looking over her slight person: "She don't look much on housework, but she ain't a fretter, anyhow." But it was not only that the coming to his house of a bit of hopeful young life was like the lighting of a fire on a cold hearth. The girl was more than the bright serviceable creature he had thought her. She had an eye to see and an ear to hear: he could show her things and tell her things, and taste the bliss of feeling that all he imparted left long reverberations and echoes he could wake at will.

It was during their night walks back to the farm that he felt most intensely the sweetness of this communion. He had always been more sensitive than the people about him to the appeal of natural beauty. His unfinished studies had given form to this sensibility and even in his unhappiest moments field and sky spoke to him with a deep and powerful persuasion. But hitherto the emotion had remained in him as a silent ache, veiling with sadness the beauty that evoked it. He did not even know whether any one else in the world felt as he did, or whether he was the sole victim of this mournful privilege. Then he learned that one other spirit had trembled with the same touch of wonder: that at his side, living under his roof and eating his bread, was a creature to whom he could say: "That's Orion down yonder; the big fellow to the right is Aldebaran, and the bunch of little ones—like bees swarming—they're the Pleiades . . ." or whom he could hold entranced before a ledge of granite thrusting up through the fern while he unrolled the huge panorama of the ice age, and the long dim stretches of succeeding time. The fact that admiration for his learning mingled with Mattie's wonder at what he taught was not the least part of his pleasure. And there were other sensations, less definable but more exquisite, which drew them together with a shock of silent joy: the cold red of sunset behind winter hills, the flight of cloud-flocks over slopes of golden stubble, or the intensely blue shadows of hemlocks on sunlit snow. When she said to him once: "It looks just as if it was painted!" it seemed to Ethan that the art of definition could go no farther, and that words had at last been found to utter his secret soul. . . .

As he stood in the darkness outside the church these memories came back with the poignancy of vanished things. Watching Mattie whirl down the floor from hand to hand he wondered how he could ever have thought that his dull talk interested her. To him, who was never gay but in her presence, her gaiety seemed plain proof of indifference. The face she lifted to her dancers was the same which, when she saw him, always looked like a window that has caught the sunset. He even noticed two or three gestures which, in his fatuity, he had thought she kept for him: a way of throwing her head back when she was amused, as if to taste her laugh before she let it out, and a trick of sinking her lids slowly when anything charmed or moved her.

The sight made him unhappy, and his unhappiness roused his latent fears. His wife had never shown any jealousy of Mattie, but of late she had grumbled increasingly over the housework and found oblique ways of attracting attention to the girl's inefficiency. Zeena had always been what Starkfield called "sickly," and Frome had to admit that, if she were as ailing as she believed, she needed the help of a stronger arm than the one which lay so lightly in his during the night walks to the farm. Mattie had no natural turn for housekeeping, and her training had done nothing to remedy the defect. She was quick to learn, but forgetful and dreamy, and not disposed to take the matter seriously. Ethan had an idea that if she were to marry a man she was fond of the dormant instinct would wake, and her pies and biscuits become the pride of the county; but domesticity in the abstract did not interest her. At first she was so awkward that he could not help laughing at her; but she laughed with him and that made them better friends. He did his best to supplement her unskilled efforts, getting up earlier than usual to light the kitchen fire, carrying in the wood overnight, and neglecting the mill for the farm that he might help her about the house during the day. He even crept down on Saturday nights to scrub the kitchen floor after the women had gone to bed; and Zeena, one day, had surprised him at the churn and had turned away silently, with one of her queer looks.

Of late there had been other signs of her disfavor, as intangible but more disquieting. One cold winter morning, as he dressed in the dark, his candle flickering in the draught of the ill-fitting window, he had heard her speak from the bed behind him.

"The doctor don't want I should be left without anybody to do for me," she said in her flat whine.

He had supposed her to be asleep, and the sound of her voice had startled him, though she was given to abrupt explosions of speech after long intervals of secretive silence.

He turned and looked at her where she lay indistinctly outlined under the dark calico quilt, her high-boned face taking a grayish tinge from the whiteness of the pillow.

"Nobody to do for you?" he repeated.

"If you say you can't afford a hired girl when Mattie goes."

Frome turned away again, and taking up his razor stooped to catch the reflection of his stretched cheek in the blotched looking glass above the washstand.

"Why on earth should Mattie go?"

"Well, when she gets married, I mean," his wife's drawl came from behind him.

"Oh, she'd never leave us as long as you needed her," he returned, scraping hard at his chin.

"I wouldn't ever have it said that I stood in the way of a poor girl like Mattie marrying a smart fellow like Denis Eady," Zeena answered in a tone of plaintive self-effacement.

Ethan, glaring at his face in the glass, threw his head back to draw the razor from ear to chin. His hand was steady, but the attitude was an excuse for not making an immediate reply.

"And the doctor don't want I should be left without anybody," Zeena continued. "He wanted I should speak to you about a girl he's heard about, that might come—"

Ethan laid down the razor and straightened himself with a laugh.

"Denis Eady! If that's all, I guess there's no such hurry to look round for a girl."

"Well, I'd like to talk to you about it," said Zeena obstinately.

He was getting into his clothes in fumbling haste. "All right. But I haven't got the time now; I'm late as it is," he returned, holding his old silver turnip-watch to the candle.

Zeena, apparently accepting this as final, lay watching him in silence while he pulled his suspenders over his shoulders and jerked his arms into his coat; but as he went toward the door she said, suddenly and incisively: "I guess you're always late, now you shave every morning."

That thrust had frightened him more than any vague insinuations about Denis Eady. It was a fact that since Mattie Silver's coming he had taken to shaving every day; but his wife always seemed to be asleep when he left her side in the winter darkness, and he had stupidly assumed that she would not notice any change in his appearance. Once or twice in the past he had been faintly disquieted by Zenobia's way of letting things happen without seeming to remark them, and then, weeks afterward, in a casual phrase, revealing that she had all along taken her notes and drawn her inferences. Of late, however, there had been no room in his thoughts for such vague apprehensions. Zeena herself, from an oppressive reality, had faded into an insubstantial shade. All his life was lived in the sight and sound of Mattie Silver, and he could no longer conceive of its being otherwise. But now, as he stood outside the church, and saw Mattie spinning down the floor with Denis Eady, a throng of disregarded hints and menaces wove their cloud about his brain. . . .

Chapter II

As the dancers poured out of the hall, Frome, drawing back behind the projecting storm door, watched the segregation of the grotesquely muffled groups, in which a moving lantern ray now and then lit up a face flushed with food and dancing. The villagers, being afoot, were the first to climb the slope to the main street, while the country neighbors packed themselves more slowly into the sleighs under the shed.

"Ain't you riding, Mattie?" a woman's voice called back from the throng about the shed, and Ethan's heart gave a jump. From where he stood he could not see the persons coming out of the hall till they had advanced a few steps beyond the wooden sides of the storm door; but through its cracks he heard a clear voice answer: "Mercy no! Not on such a night."

She was there, then, close to him, only a thin board between. In another moment she would step forth into the night, and his eyes, accustomed to the obscurity, would discern her as clearly as though she stood in daylight. A wave of shyness pulled him back into the dark angle of the wall, and he stood there in silence instead of making his presence known to her. It had been one of the wonders of their intercourse that from the first, she, the quicker, finer, more expressive, instead of crushing him by the contrast, had given him something of her own ease and freedom; but now he felt as heavy and loutish as in his student days, when he had tried to "jolly" the Worcester girls at a picnic.

He hung back, and she came out alone and paused within a few yards of him. She was almost the last to leave the hall, and she stood looking uncertainly about her as if wondering why he did not show himself. Then a man's figure approached, coming so close to her that under their formless wrappings they seemed merged in one dim outline.

"Gentleman friend gone back on you? Say, Matt, that's tough! No, I wouldn't be mean enough to tell the other girls. I ain't as lowdown as that." (How Frome hated his cheap banter!) "But look a here, ain't it lucky I got the old man's cutter down there waiting for us?"

Frome heard the girl's voice, gaily incredulous:

"What on earth's your father's cutter doin' down there?"

"Why, waiting for me to take a ride. I got the roan colt, too. I kinder knew I'd want to take a ride tonight." Eady, in his triumph, tried to put a sentimental note into his bragging voice.

The girl seemed to waver, and Frome saw her twirl the end of her scarf irresolutely about her fingers. Not for the world would he have made a sign to her, though it seemed to him that his life hung on her next gesture.

"Hold on a minute while I unhitch the colt," Denis called to her, springing toward the shed.

She stood perfectly still, looking after him, in an attitude of tranquil expectancy torturing to the hidden watcher. Frome noticed that she no longer turned her head from side to side, as though peering through the night for another figure. She let Denis Eady lead out the horse, climb into the cutter and fling back the bearskin to make room for her at his side; then, with a swift motion of flight, she turned about and darted up the slope toward the front of the church.

"Good-bye! Hope you'll have a lovely ride!" she called back to him over her shoulder.

Denis laughed, and gave the horse a cut that brought him quickly abreast of her retreating figure.

"Come along! Get in quick! It's as slippery as thunder on this turn," he cried, leaning over to reach out a hand to her.

She laughed back at him: "Goodnight! I'm not getting in."

By this time they had passed beyond Frome's earshot and he could only follow the shadowy pantomime of their silhouettes as they continued to move along the crest of the slope above him. He saw Eady, after a moment, jump from the cutter and go toward the girl with the reins over one arm. The other he tried to slip through hers; but she eluded him nimbly, and Frome's heart, which had swung out over a black void, trembled back to safety. A moment later he heard the jingle of departing sleigh bells and discerned a figure advancing alone toward the empty expanse of snow before the church.

In the black shade of the Varnum spruces he caught up with her and she turned with a quick "Oh!"

"Think I'd forgotten you, Matt?" he asked with sheepish glee.

She answered seriously: "I thought maybe you couldn't come back for me."

"Couldn't? What on earth could stop me?"

"I knew Zeena wasn't feeling any too good today."

"Oh, she's in bed long ago." He paused, a question struggling in him. "Then you meant to walk home all alone?"

"Oh, I ain't afraid!" she laughed.

The stood together in the gloom of the spruces, an empty world glimmering about them wide and gray under the stars. He brought his question out.

"If you thought I hadn't come, why didn't you ride back with Denis Eady?"

"Why, where *were* you? How did you know? I never saw you!"

Her wonder and his laughter ran together like spring rills in a thaw. Ethan had the sense of having done something arch and ingenious. To prolong the effect he groped for a dazzling phrase, and brought out, in a growl of rapture: "Come along."

He slipped an arm through hers, as Eady had done, and fancied it was faintly pressed against her side; but neither of them moved. It was so dark under the spruces that he could barely see the shape of her head beside his shoulder. He longed to stoop his cheek and rub it against her scarf. He would have liked to stand there with her all night in the blackness. She moved forward a step or two and then paused again above the dip of the Corbury road. Its icy slope, scored by innumerable runners, looked like a mirror scratched by travellers at an inn.

"There was a whole lot of them coasting before the moon set," she said.

"Would you like to come in and coast with them some night?" he asked.

"Oh, *would* you, Ethan? It would be lovely!"

"We'll come tomorrow if there's a moon."

She lingered, pressing closer to his side. "Ned Hale and Ruth Varnum came just as *near* running into the big elm at the bottom. We were all sure they were killed." Her shiver ran down his arm. "Wouldn't it have been too awful? They're so happy!"

"Oh, Ned ain't much at steering. I guess I can take you down all right!" he said disdainfully.

He was aware that he was "talking big," like Denis Eady; but his reaction of joy had unsteadied him, and the inflection with which she had said of the engaged couple "They're so happy!" made the words sound as if she had been thinking of herself and him.

"The elm *is* dangerous, though. It ought to be cut down," she insisted.

"Would you be afraid of it, with me?"

"I told you I ain't the kind to be afraid," she tossed back, almost indifferently; and suddenly she began to walk on with a rapid step.

These alterations of mood were the despair and joy of Ethan Frome. The motions of her mind were as incalculable as the flit of a bird in the branches. The fact that he had no right to show his feelings, and thus provoke the expression of hers, made him attach a fantastic importance to every change in her look and tone. Now he thought she understood him, and feared; now he was sure she did not, and despaired. Tonight the pressure of accumulated misgivings sent the scale drooping toward despair, and her indifference was the more chilling after the flush of joy into which she had plunged him by dismissing Denis Eady. He mounted School House Hill at her side and walked on in silence till they reached the lane leading to the sawmill; then the need of some definite assurance grew too strong for him.

"You'd have found me right off if you hadn't gone back to have the last reel with Denis," he brought out awkwardly. He could not pronounce the name without a stiffening of the muscles of his throat.

"Why, Ethan, how could I tell you were there?"

"I suppose what folks say is true," he jerked out at her, instead of answering.

She stopped short, and he felt, in the darkness, that her face was lifted quickly to his. "Why, what do folks say?"

"It's natural enough you should be leaving us," he floundered on, following his thought.

"Is that what they say?" she mocked back at him; then, with a sudden drop of her sweet treble: "You mean that Zeena—ain't suited with me any more?" she faltered.

Their arms had slipped apart and they stood motionless, each seeking to distinguish the other's face.

"I know I ain't anything like as smart as I ought to be," she went on, while he vainly struggled for expression. "There's lots of things a hired girl could do that come awkward to me still—and I haven't got much strength in my arms. But if she'd only tell me I'd try. You know she hardly ever says anything, and sometimes I can see she ain't suited, and yet I don't know why." She turned on him with a sudden flash of indignation. "You'd ought to tell me, Ethan Frome—you'd ought to! Unless *you* want me to go too—"

Unless he wanted her to go too! The cry was balm to his raw wound. The iron heavens seemed to melt and rain down sweetness. Again he struggled for the all-expressive word, and again, his arm in hers, found only a deep "Come along."

They walked on in silence through the blackness of the hemlock-shaded lane, where Ethan's sawmill gloomed through the night, and out again into the comparative clearness of the fields. On the farther side of the hemlock belt the open country rolled away before them gray and lonely under the stars. Sometimes their way led them under the shade of an overhanging bank or through the thin obscurity of a clump of leafless trees. Here and there a farmhouse stood far back among the fields, mute and cold as a gravestone. The night was so still that they heard the frozen snow crackle under

their feet. The crash of a loaded branch falling far off in the woods rever-
berated like a musket shot, and once a fox barked, and Mattie shrank closer
to Ethan, and quickened her steps.

At length they sighted the group of larches at Ethan's gate, and as they
drew near it the sense that the walk was over brought back his words.

"Then you don't want to leave us, Matt?"

He had to stoop his head to catch her stifled whisper: "Where'd I go, if I
did?"

The answer sent a pang through him but the tone suffused him with joy.
He forgot what else he had meant to say and pressed her against him so
closely that he seemed to feel her warmth in his veins.

"You ain't crying are you, Matt?"

"No, of course I'm not," she quavered.

They turned in at the gate and passed under the shaded knoll where,
enclosed in a low fence, the Frome gravestones slanted at crazy angles
through the snow. Ethan looked at them curiously. For years that quiet
company had mocked his restlessness, his desire for change and freedom.
"We never got away—how should you?" seemed to be written on every
headstone; and whenever he went in or out of his gate he thought with a
shiver: "I shall just go on living here till I join them." But now all desire for
change had vanished, and the sight of the little enclosure gave him a warm
sense of continuance and stability.

"I guess we'll never let you go, Matt," he whispered, as though even the
dead, lovers once, must conspire with him to keep her; and brushing by
the graves, he thought: "We'll always go on living here together, and some
day she'll lie there beside me."

He let the vision possess him as they climbed the hill to the house. He
was never so happy with her as when he abandoned himself to these dreams.
Halfway up the slope Mattie stumbled against some unseen obstruction and
clutched his sleeve to steady herself. The wave of warmth that went through
him was like the prolongation of his vision. For the first time he stole his
arm about her, and she did not resist. They walked on as if they were
floating on a summer stream.

Zeena always went to bed as soon as she had had her supper, and the
shutterless windows of the house were dark. A dead cucumber vine dangled
from the porch like the crape streamer tied to the door for a death, and the
thought flashed through Ethan's brain: "If it was there for Zeena—" Then
he had a distinct sight of his wife lying in their bedroom asleep, her mouth
slightly open, her false teeth in a tumbler by the bed . . .

They walked around to the back of the house, between the rigid goose-
berry bushes. It was Zeena's habit, when they came back late from the
village, to leave the key of the kitchen door under the mat. Ethan stood
before the door, his head heavy with dreams, his arm still about Mattie.
"Matt—" he began, not knowing what he meant to say.

She slipped out of his hold without speaking, and he stooped down and
felt for the key.

"It's not there!" he said, straightening himself with a start.

They strained their eyes at each other through the icy darkness. Such a
thing had never happened before.

"Maybe she's forgotten it," Mattie said in a tremulous whisper; but both
of them knew that it was not like Zeena to forget.

"It might have fallen off into the snow," Mattie continued, after a pause during which they had stood intently listening.

"It must have been pushed off, then," he rejoined in the same tone. Another wild thought tore through him. What if tramps had been there— what if . . .

Again he listened, fancying he heard a distant sound in the house; then he felt in his pocket for a match, and kneeling down, passed its light slowly over the rough edges of snow about the doorstep.

He was still kneeling when his eyes, on a level with the lower panel of the door, caught a faint ray beneath it. Who could be stirring in that silent house? He heard a step on the stairs, and again for an instant the thought of tramps tore through him. Then the door opened and he saw his wife.

Against the dark background of the kitchen she stood up tall and angular, one hand drawing a quilted counterpane to her flat breast, while the other held a lamp. The light, on a level with her chin, drew out of the darkness her puckered throat and the projecting wrist of the hand that clutched the quilt, and deepened fantastically the hollows and prominences of her high-boned face under its ring of crimping-pins. To Ethan, still in the rosy haze of his hour with Mattie, the sight came with the intense precision of the last dream before waking. He felt as if he had never before known what his wife looked like.

She drew aside without speaking, and Mattie and Ethan passed into the kitchen, which had the deadly chill of a vault after the dry cold of the night.

"Guess you forgot about us, Zeena," Ethan joked, stamping the snow from his boots.

"No. I just felt so mean³ I couldn't sleep."

Mattie came forward, unwinding her wraps, the color of the cherry scarf in her fresh lips and cheeks. "I'm so sorry, Zeena! Isn't there anything I can do?"

"No; there's nothing." Zeena turned away from her. "You might 'a' shook off that snow outside," she said to her husband.

She walked out of the kitchen ahead of them and pausing in the hall raised the lamp at arm's length, as if to light them up the stairs.

Ethan paused also, affecting to fumble for the peg on which he hung his coat and cap. The doors of the two bedrooms faced each other across the narrow upper landing, and tonight it was peculiarly repugnant to him that Mattie should see him follow Zeena.

"I guess I won't come up yet awhile," he said, turning as if to go back to the kitchen.

Zeena stopped short and looked at him. "For the land's sake—what you going to do down here?"

"I've got the mill accounts to go over."

She continued to stare at him, the flame of the unshaded lamp bringing out with microscopic cruelty the fretful lines of her face.

"At this time o' night? You'll ketch your death. The fire's out long ago."

Without answering he moved away toward the kitchen. As he did so his glance crossed Mattie's and he fancied that a fugitive warning gleamed through her lashes. The next moment they sank to her flushed cheeks and she began to mount the stairs ahead of Zeena.

3. Ill.

"That's so. It *is* powerful cold down here," Ethan assented; and with lowered head he went up in his wife's wake, and followed her across the threshold of their room.

Chapter III

There was some hauling to be done at the lower end of the woodlot, and Ethan was out early the next day.

The winter morning was as clear as crystal. The sunrise burned red in a pure sky, the shadows on the rim of the woodlot were darkly blue, and beyond the white and scintillating fields patches of far-off forest hung like smoke.

It was in the early morning stillness, when his muscles were swinging to their familiar task and his lungs expanding with long draughts of mountain air, that Ethan did his clearest thinking. He and Zeena had not exchanged a word after the door of their room had closed on them. She had measured out some drops from a medicine bottle on a chair by the bed and, after swallowing them, and wrapping her head in a piece of yellow flannel, had lain down with her face turned away. Ethan undressed hurriedly and blew out the light so that he should not see her when he took his place at her side. As he lay there he could hear Mattie moving about in her room, and her candle, sending its small ray across the landing, drew a scarcely perceptible line of light under his door. He kept his eyes fixed on the light till it vanished. Then the room grew perfectly black, and not a sound was audible but Zeena's asthmatic breathing. Ethan felt confusedly that there were many things he ought to think about, but through his tingling veins and tired brain only one sensation throbbed: the warmth of Mattie's shoulder against his. Why had he not kissed her when he held her there? A few hours earlier he would not have asked himself the question. Even a few minutes earlier, when they had stood alone outside the house, he would not have dared to think of kissing her. But since he had seen her lips in the lamplight he felt that they were his.

Now, in the bright morning air, her face was still before him. It was part of the sun's red and of the pure glitter on the snow. How the girl had changed since she had come to Starkfield! He remembered what a colorless slip of a thing she had looked the day he had met her at the station. And all the first winter, how she had shivered with cold when the northerly gales shook the thin clapboards and the snow beat like hail against the loose-hung windows!

He had been afraid that she would hate the hard life, the cold and loneliness; but not a sign of discontent escaped her. Zeena took the view that Mattie was bound to make the best of Starkfield since she hadn't any other place to go to; but this did not strike Ethan as conclusive. Zeena, at any rate, did not apply the principle in her own case.

He felt all the more sorry for the girl because misfortune had, in a sense, indentured her to them. Mattie Silver was the daughter of a cousin of Zenobia Frome's who had inflamed his clan with mingled sentiments of envy and admiration by descending from the hills to Connecticut, where he had married a Stamford girl and succeeded to her father's thriving "drug" business. Unhappily Orin Silver, a man of far-reaching aims, had died too soon to prove that the end justifies the means. His accounts revealed merely what the means had been; and these were such that it was fortunate for his wife and daughter that his books were examined only after his impressive funeral. His wife died of the disclosure, and Mattie, at twenty, was left alone to make her way on the fifty dollars obtained from the sale of her piano. For this purpose her equipment, though varied, was inadequate. She could trim a hat, make molasses candy, recite "Curfew shall not ring tonight," and play "The Lost Chord" and a pot-pourri from "Carmen."[4] When she tried to extend the field of her activities in the direction of stenography and bookkeeping her health broke down, and six months on her feet behind the counter of a department store did not tend to restore it. Her nearest relations had been induced to place their savings in her father's hands, and though, after his death, they ungrudgingly acquitted themselves of the Christian duty of returning good for evil by giving his daughter all the advice at their disposal, they could hardly be expected to supplement it by material aid. But when Zenobia's doctor recommended her looking about for someone to help her with the housework, the clan instantly saw the chance of exacting a compensation from Mattie. Zenobia, though doubtful of the girl's efficiency, was tempted by the freedom to find fault without much risk of losing her; and so Mattie came to Starkfield.

Zenobia's fault-finding was of the silent kind, but not the less penetrating for that. During the first months Ethan alternately burned with the desire to see Mattie defy her and trembled with fear of the result. Then the situation grew less strained. The pure air, and the long summer hours in the open, gave back life and elasticity to Mattie, and Zeena, with more leisure to devote to her complex ailments, grew less watchful of the girl's omissions; so that Ethan, struggling on under the burden of his barren farm and failing sawmill, could at least imagine that peace reigned in his house.

There was really, even now, no tangible evidence to the contrary; but since the previous night a vague dread had hung on his skyline. It was formed of Zeena's obstinate silence, of Mattie's sudden look of warning, of the memory of just such fleeting imperceptible signs as those which told him, on certain stainless mornings, that before night there would be rain.

His dread was so strong that, manlike, he sought to postpone certainty. The hauling was not over till midday, and as the lumber was to be delivered to Andrew Hale, the Starkfield builder, it was really easier for Ethan to send Jotham Powell, the hired man, back to the farm on foot, and drive the load down to the village himself. He had scrambled up on the logs, and was sitting astride of them, close over his shaggy grays, when, coming between him and their streaming necks, he had a vision of the warning look that Mattie had given him the night before.

"If there's going to be any trouble I want to be there," was his vague reflection, as he threw to Jotham the unexpected order to unhitch the team and lead them back to the barn.

It was a slow trudge home through the heavy fields, and when the two men entered the kitchen Mattie was lifting the coffee from the stove and Zeena was already at the table. Her husband stopped short at sight of her. Instead of her usual calico wrapper and knitted shawl she wore her best dress of brown merino, and above her thin strands of hair, which still preserved the tight undulations of the crimping-pins, rose a hard perpendicu-

---

4. Popular opera (1875) by Georges Bizet (1838–1875) based on Prosper Merimée's 1847 Romantic novel dealing with gypsy life; "Curfew Must Not Ring Tonight": sentimental song (1882) by Rose Hartwick Thorpe (1850–1939); "The Lost Chord": an archetypal Victorian drawing-room song written by Sir Arthur Sullivan (1842–1900) on the occasion of his brother's death.

lar bonnet, as to which Ethan's clearest notion was that he had to pay five dollars for it at the Bettsbridge Emporium. On the floor beside her stood his old valise and a bandbox wrapped in newspapers.

"Why, where are you going, Zeena?" he exclaimed.

"I've got my shooting pains so bad that I'm going over to Bettsbridge to spend the night with Aunt Martha Pierce and see that new doctor," she answered in a matter-of-fact tone, as if she had said she was going into the storeroom to take a look at the preserves, or up to the attic to go over the blankets.

In spite of her sedentary habits such abrupt decisions were not without precedent in Zeena's history. Twice or thrice before she had suddenly packed Ethan's valise and started off to Bettsbridge, or even Springfield, to seek the advice of some new doctor, and her husband had grown to dread these expeditions because of their cost. Zeena always came back laden with expensive remedies, and her last visit to Springfield had been commemorated by her paying twenty dollars for an electric battery of which she had never been able to learn the use. But for the moment his sense of relief was so great as to preclude all other feelings. He had now no doubt that Zeena had spoken the truth in saying, the night before, that she had sat up because she felt "too mean" to sleep: her abrupt resolve to seek medical advice showed that, as usual, she was wholly absorbed in her health.

As if expecting a protest, she continued plaintively; "if you're too busy with the hauling I presume you can let Jotham Powell drive me over with the sorrel in time to ketch the train at the Flats."

Her husband hardly heard what she was saying. During the winter months there was no stage between Starkfield and Bettsbridge, and the trains which stopped at Corbury Flats were slow and infrequent. A rapid calculation showed Ethan that Zeena could not be back at the farm before the following evening. . . .

"If I'd supposed you'd 'a' made any objection to Jotham Powell's driving me over—" she began again, as though his silence had implied refusal. On the brink of departure she was always seized with a flux of words. "All I know is," she continued, "I can't go on the way I am much longer. The pains are clear away down to my ankles now, or I'd 'a' walked in to Starkfield on my own feet, sooner'n put you out, and asked Michael Eady to let me ride over on his wagon to the Flats, when he sends to meet the train that brings his groceries. I'd 'a' had two hours to wait in the station, but I'd sooner 'a' done it, even with this cold, than to have you say—"

"Of course Jotham'll drive you over," Ethan roused himself to answer. He became suddenly conscious that he was looking at Mattie while Zeena talked to him, and with an effort he turned his eyes to his wife. She sat opposite the window, and the pale light reflected from the banks of snow made her face look more than usually drawn and bloodless, sharpened the three parallel creases between ear and cheek, and drew querulous lines from her thin nose to the corners of her mouth. Though she was but seven years her husband's senior, and he was only twenty-eight, she was already an old woman.

Ethan tried to say something befitting the occasion, but there was only one thought in his mind: the fact that, for the first time since Mattie had come to live with them, Zeena was to be away for a night. He wondered if the girl were thinking of it too. . . .

He knew that Zeena must be wondering why he did not offer to drive her to the Flats and let Jotham Powell take the lumber to Starkfield, and at first he could not think of a pretext for not doing so; then he said: "I'd take you over myself, only I've got to collect the cash for the lumber."

As soon as the words were spoken he regretted them, not only because they were untrue—there being no prospect of his receiving cash payment from Hale—but also because he knew from experience the imprudence of letting Zeena think he was in funds on the eve of one of her therapeutic excursions. At the moment, however, his one desire was to avoid the long drive with her behind the ancient sorrel who never went out of a walk.

Zeena made no reply: she did not seem to hear what he had said. She had already pushed her plate aside, and was measuring out a draught from a large bottle at her elbow.

"It ain't done me a speck of good, but I guess I might as well use it up," she remarked; adding, as she pushed the empty bottle toward Mattie: "If you can get the taste out it'll do for pickles."

Chapter IV

As soon as his wife had driven off Ethan took his coat and cap from the peg. Mattie was washing up the dishes, humming one of the dance tunes of the night before. He said "So long, Matt," and she answered gaily "So long, Ethan"; and that was all.

It was warm and bright in the kitchen. The sun slanted through the south window on the girl's moving figure, on the cat dozing in a chair, and on the geraniums brought in from the doorway, where Ethan had planted them in the summer to "make a garden" for Mattie. He would have liked to linger on, watching her tidy up and then settle down to her sewing; but he wanted still more to get the hauling done and be back at the farm before night.

All the way down to the village he continued to think of his return to Mattie. The kitchen was a poor place, not "spruce" and shining as his mother had kept it in his boyhood; but it was surprising what a homelike look the mere fact of Zeena's absence gave it. And he pictured what it would be like that evening, when he and Mattie were there after supper. For the first time they would be alone together indoors, and they would sit there, one on each side of the stove, like a married couple, he in his stocking feet and smoking his pipe, she laughing and talking in that funny way she had, which was always as new to him as if he had never heard her before.

The sweetness of the picture, and the relief of knowing that his fears of "trouble" with Zeena were unfounded, sent up his spirits with a rush, and he, who was usually so silent, whistled and sang aloud as he drove through the snowy fields. There was in him a slumbering spark of sociability which the long Starkfield winters had not yet extinguished. By nature grave and inarticulate, he admired recklessness and gaiety in others and was warmed to the marrow by friendly human intercourse. At Worcester, though he had the name of keeping to himself and not being much of a hand at a good time, he had secretly gloried in being clapped on the back and hailed as "Old Ethe" or "Old Stiff"; and the cessation of such familiarities had increased the chill of his return to Starkfield.

There the silence had deepened about him year by year. Left alone, after his father's accident, to carry the burden of farm and mill, he had had no time for convivial loiterings in the village; and when his mother fell ill the loneliness of the house grew more oppressive than that of the fields. His mother had been a talker in her day, but after her "trouble" the sound of her voice was seldom heard, though she had not lost the power of speech. Sometimes, in the long winter evenings, when in desperation her son asked her why she didn't "say something," she would lift a finger and answer: "Because I'm listening"; and on stormy nights, when the loud wind was about the house, she would complain, if he spoke to her: "They're talking so out there that I can't hear you."

It was only when she drew toward her last illness, and his cousin Zenobia Pierce came over from the next valley to help him nurse her, that human speech was heard again in the house. After the mortal silence of his long imprisonment Zeena's volubility was music in his ears. He felt that he might have "gone like his mother" if the sound of a new voice had not come to steady him. Zeena seemed to understand his case at a glance. She laughed at him for not knowing the simplest sickbed duties and told him to "go right along out" and leave her to see to things. The mere fact of obeying her orders, of feeling free to go about his business again and talk with other men, restored his shaken balance and magnified his sense of what he owed her. Her efficiency shamed and dazzled him. She seemed to possess by instinct all the household wisdom that his long apprenticeship had not instilled in him. When the end came it was she who had to tell him to hitch up and go for the undertaker, and she thought it "funny" that he had not settled beforehand who was to have his mother's clothes and the sewing machine. After the funeral, when he saw her preparing to go away, he was seized with an unreasoning dread of being left alone on the farm; and before he knew what he was doing he had asked her to stay there with him. He had often thought since that it would not have happened if his mother had died in spring instead of winter . . .

When they married it was agreed that, as soon as he could straighten out the difficulties resulting from Mrs. Frome's long illness, they would sell the farm and sawmill and try their luck in a large town. Ethan's love of nature did not take the form of a taste for agriculture. He had always wanted to be an engineer, and to live in towns, where there were lectures and big libraries and "fellows doing things." A slight engineering job in Florida, put in his way during his period of study at Worcester, increased his faith in his ability as well as his eagerness to see the world; and he felt sure that, with a "smart" wife like Zeena, it would not be long before he had made himself a place in it.

Zeena's native village was slightly larger and nearer to the railway than Starkfield, and she had let her husband see from the first that life on an isolated farm was not what she had expected when she married. But purchasers were slow in coming, and while he waited for them Ethan learned the impossibility of transplanting her. She chose to look down on Starkfield, but she could not have lived in a place which looked down on her. Even Bettsbridge or Shadd's Falls would not have been sufficiently aware of her, and in the greater cities which attracted Ethan she would have suffered a complete loss of identity. And within a year of their marriage she developed the "sickliness" which had since made her notable even in a community rich in pathological instances. When she came to take care of his mother she had seemed to Ethan like the very genius of health, but he soon saw that her skill as a nurse had been acquired by the absorbed observation of her own symptoms.

Then she too fell silent. Perhaps it was the inevitable effect of life on the farm, or perhaps, as she sometimes said, it was because Ethan "never listened." The charge was not wholly unfounded. When she spoke it was only to complain, and to complain of things not in his power to remedy; and to check a tendency to impatient retort he had first formed the habit of not answering her, and finally of thinking of other things while she talked. Of late, however, since he had had reasons for observing her more closely, her silence had begun to trouble him. He recalled his mother's growing taciturnity, and wondered if Zeena were also turning "queer." Women did, he knew. Zeena, who had at her fingers' ends the pathological chart of the whole region, had cited many cases of the kind while she was nursing his mother; and he himself knew of certain lonely farmhouses in the neighborhood where striken creatures pined, and of others where sudden tragedy had come of their presence. At times, looking at Zeena's shut face, he felt the chill of such forebodings. At other times her silence seemed deliberately assumed to conceal far-reaching intentions, mysterious conclusions drawn from suspicions and resentments impossible to guess. That supposition was even more disturbing than the other; and it was the one which had come to him the night before, when he had seen her standing in the kitchen door.

Now her departure for Bettsbridge had once more eased his mind, and all his thoughts were on the prospect of his evening with Mattie. Only one thing weighed on him, and that was his having told Zeena that he was to receive cash for the lumber. He foresaw so clearly the consequences of this imprudence that with considerable reluctance he decided to ask Andrew Hale for a small advance on his load.

When Ethan drove into Hale's yard the builder was just getting out of his sleigh.

"Hello, Ethe!" he said "This comes handy."

Andrew Hale was a ruddy man with a big gray mustache and a stubbly double chin unconstrained by a collar; but his scrupulously clean shirt was always fastened by a small diamond stud. This display of opulence was misleading, for though he did a fairly good business it was known that his easygoing habits and the demands of his large family frequently kept him what Starkfield called "behind." He was an old friend of Ethan's family, and his house one of the few to which Zeena occasionally went, drawn there by the fact that Mrs. Hale, in her youth, had done more "doctoring" than any other woman in Starkfield, and was still a recognized authority on symptoms and treatment.

Hale went up to the grays and patted their sweating flanks.

"Well, sir," he said, "you keep them two as if they was pets."

Ethan set about unloading the logs and when he had finished his job he pushed open the glazed door of the shed which the builder used as his office. Hale sat with his feet up on the stove, his back propped against a battered desk strewn with papers: the place, like the man, was warm, genial and untidy.

"Sit right down and thaw out," he greeted Ethan.

The latter did not know how to begin, but at length he managed to bring out his request for an advance of fifty dollars. The blood rushed to his thin skin under the sting of Hale's astonishment. It was the builder's custom to pay at the end of three months, and there was no precedent between the two men for a cash settlement.

Ethan felt that if he had pleaded an urgent need Hale might have made shift to pay him; but pride, and an instinctive prudence, kept him from resorting to this argument. After his father's death it had taken time to get his head above water, and he did not want Andrew Hale, or anyone else in Starkfield, to think he was going under again. Besides, he hated lying; if he wanted the money he wanted it, and it was nobody's business to ask why. He therefore made his demand with the awkwardness of a proud man who will not admit to himself that he is stooping; and he was not much surprised at Hale's refusal.

The builder refused genially, as he did everything else: he treated the matter as something in the nature of a practical joke, and wanted to know if Ethan meditated buying a grand piano or adding a "cupolo" to his house, offering, in the latter case, to give his services free of cost.

Ethan's arts were soon exhausted, and after an embarrassed pause he wished Hale good day and opened the door of the office. As he passed out the builder suddenly called after him: "See here—you ain't in a tight place, are you?"

"Not a bit," Ethan's pride retorted before his reason had time to intervene.

"Well, that's good! Because I *am*, a shade. Fact is, I was going to ask you to give me a little extra time on that payment. Business is pretty slack, to begin with, and then I'm fixing up a little house for Ned and Ruth when they're married. I'm glad to do it for 'em, but it costs." His look appealed to Ethan for sympathy. "The young people like things nice. You know how it is yourself: it's not so long ago since you fixed up your own place for Zeena."

Ethan left the grays in Hale's stable and went about some other business in the village. As he walked away the builder's last phrase lingered in his ears, and he reflected grimly that his seven years with Zeena seemed to Starkfield "not so long."

The afternoon was drawing to an end, and here and there a lighted pane spangled the cold gray dusk and made the snow look whiter. The bitter weather had driven every one indoors and Ethan had the long rural street to himself. Suddenly he heard the brisk play of sleigh bells and a cutter passed him, drawn by a free-going horse. Ethan recognized Michael Eady's roan colt, and young Denis Eady, in a handsome new fur cap, leaned forward and waved a greeting. "Hello, Ethe!" he shouted and spun on.

The cutter was going in the direction of the Frome farm, and Ethan's heart contracted as he listened to the dwindling bells. What more likely than that Denis Eady had heard of Zeena's departure for Bettsbridge, and was profiting by the opportunity to spend an hour with Mattie? Ethan was ashamed of the storm of jealousy in his breast. It seemed unworthy of the girl that his thoughts of her should be so violent.

He walked on to the church corner and entered the shade of the Varnum spruces, where he had stood with her the night before. As he passed into their gloom he saw an indistinct outline just ahead of him. At his approach it melted for an instant into two separate shapes and then conjoined again, and he heard a kiss, and a half-laughing "Oh!" provoked by the discovery of his presence. Again the outline hastily disunited and the Varnum gate slammed on one half while the other hurried on ahead of him. Ethan smiled at the discomfiture he had caused. What did it matter to Ned Hale and Ruth Varnum if they were caught kissing each other? Everybody in Starkfield knew they were engaged. It pleased Ethan to have surprised a pair of lovers on the spot where he and Mattie had stood with such a thirst for each other in their hearts; but he felt a pang at the thought that these two need not hide their happiness.

He fetched the grays from Hale's stable and started on his long climb back to the farm. The cold was less sharp than earlier in the day and a thick fleecy sky threatened snow for the morrow. Here and there a star pricked through, showing behind it a deep well of blue. In an hour or two the moon would push over the ridge behind the farm, burn a gold-edged rent in the clouds, and then be swallowed by them. A mournful peace hung on the fields, as though they felt the relaxing grasp of the cold and stretched themselves in their long winter sleep.

Ethan's ears were alert for the jingle of sleighbells, but not a sound broke the silence of the lonely road. As he drew near the farm he saw, through the thin screen of larches at the gate, a light twinkling in the house above him. "She's up in her room," he said to himself, "fixing herself up for supper"; and he remembered Zeena's sarcastic stare when Mattie, on the evening of her arrival, had come down to supper with smoothed hair and a ribbon at her neck.

He passed by the graves on the knoll and turned his head to glance at one of the older headstones, which had interested him deeply as a boy because it bore his name.

SACRED TO THE MEMORY OF
ETHAN FROME AND ENDURANCE HIS WIFE,
WHO DWELLED TOGETHER IN PEACE
FOR FIFTY YEARS.

He used to think that fifty years sounded like a long time to live together, but now it seemed to him that they might pass in a flash. Then, with a sudden dart of irony, he wondered if, when their turn came, the same epitaph would be written over him and Zeena.

He opened the barn door and craned his head into the obscurity, half-fearing to discover Denis Eady's roan colt in the stall beside the sorrel. But the old horse was there alone, mumbling his crib with toothless jaws, and Ethan whistled cheerfully while he bedded down the grays and shook an extra measure of oats into their mangers. His was not a tuneful throat, but harsh melodies burst from it as he locked the barn and sprang up the hill to the house. He reached the kitchen porch and turned the door-handle; but the door did not yield to his touch.

Startled at finding it locked he rattled the handle violently; then he reflected that Mattie was alone and that it was natural she should barricade herself at nightfall. He stood in the darkness expecting to hear her step. It did not come, and after vainly straining his ears he called out in a voice that shook with joy: "Hello, Matt!"

Silence answered; but in a minute or two he caught a sound on the stairs and saw a line of light about the doorframe, as he had seen it the night before. So strange was the precision with which the incidents of the previous evening were repeating themselves that he half expected, when he heard the key turn, to see his wife before him on the threshold; but the door opened, and Mattie faced him.

She stood just as Zeena had stood, a lifted lamp in her hand, against the black background of the kitchen. She held the light at the same level, and it drew out with the same distinctness her slim young throat and the brown wrist no bigger than a child's. Then, striking upward, it threw a lustrous fleck on her lips, edged her eyes with velvet shade, and laid a milky whiteness above the black curve of her brows.

She wore her usual dress of darkish stuff, and there was no bow at her neck; but through her hair she had run a streak of crimson ribbon. This tribute to the unusual transformed and glorified her. She seemed to Ethan taller, fuller, more womanly in shape and motion. She stood aside, smiling silently, while he entered, and then moved away from him with something soft and flowing in her gait. She set the lamp on the table, and he saw that it was carefully laid for supper, with fresh doughnuts, stewed blueberries, and his favorite pickles in a dish of gay red glass. A bright fire glowed in the stove and the cat lay stretched before it, watching the table with a drowsy eye.

Ethan was suffocated with the sense of well-being. He went out into the passage to hang up his coat and pull off his wet boots. When he came back Mattie had set the teapot on the table and the cat was rubbing itself persuasively against her ankles.

"Why, Puss! I nearly tripped over you," she cried, the laughter sparkling through her lashes.

Again Ethan felt a sudden twinge of jealousy. Could it be his coming that gave her such a kindled face?

"Well, Matt, any visitors?" he threw off, stooping down carelessly to examine the fastening of the stove.

She nodded and laughed "Yes, one," and he felt a blackness settling on his brows.

"Who was that?" he questioned, raising himself up to slant a glance at her beneath his scowl.

Her eyes danced with malice. "Why, Jotham Powell. He came in after he got back, and asked for a drop of coffee before he went down home."

The blackness lifted and light flooded Ethan's brain. "That all? Well, I hope you made out to let him have it." And after a pause he felt it right to add: "I suppose he got Zeena over to the Flats all right?"

"Oh, yes; in plenty of time."

The name threw a chill between them, and they stood a moment looking sideways at each other before Mattie said with a sly laugh. "I guess it's about time for supper."

They drew their seats up to the table, and the cat, unbidden, jumped between them into Zeena's empty chair. "Oh, Puss!" said Mattie, and they laughed again.

Ethan, a moment earlier, had felt himself on the brink of eloquence; but the mention of Zeena had paralyzed him. Mattie seemed to feel the contagion of his embarrassment, and sat with downcast lids, sipping her tea, while he feigned an insatiable appetite for doughnuts and sweet pickles. At last, after casting about for an effective opening, he took a long gulp of tea, cleared his throat, and said: "Looks as if there'd be more snow."

She feigned great interest. "Is that so? Do you suppose it'll interfere with Zeena's getting back?" She flushed red as the question escaped her, and hastily set down the cup she was lifting.

Ethan reached over for another helping of pickles. "You never can tell, this time of year, it drifts so bad on the Flats." The name had benumbed him again, and once more he felt as if Zeena were in the room between them.

"Oh, Puss, you're too greedy!" Mattie cried.

The cat, unnoticed, had crept up on muffled paws from Zeena's seat to the table, and was stealthily elongating its body in the direction of the milk jug, which stood between Ethan and Mattie. The two leaned forward at the same moment and their hands met on the handle of the jug. Mattie's hand was underneath, and Ethan kept his clasped on it a moment longer than was necessary. The cat, profiting by this unusual demonstration, tried to effect an unnoticed retreat, and in doing so backed into the pickle dish, which fell to the floor with a crash.

Mattie, in an instant, had sprung from her chair and was down on her knees by the fragments.

"Oh, Ethan, Ethan—it's all to pieces! What will Zeena say?"

But this time his courage was up. "Well, she'll have to say it to the cat, anyway!" he rejoined with a laugh, kneeling down at Mattie's side to scrape up the swimming pickles.

She lifted stricken eyes to him. "Yes, but, you see, she never meant it should be used, not even when there was company; and I had to get up on the stepladder to reach it down from the top shelf of the china closet, where she keeps it with all her best things, and of course she'll want to know why I did it—"

The case was so serious that it called forth all of Ethan's latent resolution.

"She needn't know anything about it if you keep quiet. I'll get another just like it tomorrow. Where did it come from? I'll go to Shadd's Falls for it if I have to!"

"Oh, you'll never get another even there! It was a wedding present— don't you remember? It came all the way from Philadelphia, from Zeena's aunt that married the minister. That's why she wouldn't ever use it. Oh, Ethan, Ethan, what in the world shall I do?"

She began to cry, and he felt as if every one of her tears were pouring over him like burning lead. "Don't, Matt, don't—oh, *don't!*" he implored her.

She struggled to her feet, and he rose and followed her helplessly while she spread out the pieces of glass on the kitchen dresser. It seemed to him as if the shattered fragments of their evening lay there.

"Here, give them to me," he said in a voice of sudden authority.

She drew aside, instinctively obeying his tone. "Oh, Ethan, what are you going to do?"

Without replying he gathered the pieces of glass into his broad palm and walked out of the kitchen to the passage. There he lit a candle end, opened the china closet, and, reaching his long arm up to the highest shelf, laid the pieces together with such accuracy of touch that a close inspection convinced him of the impossibility of detecting from below that the dish was broken. If he glued it together the next morning months might elapse before his wife noticed what had happened, and meanwhile he might after all be able to match the dish at Shadd's Falls or Bettsbridge. Having satisfied himself that there was no risk of immediate discovery he went back to the kitchen with a lighter step, and he found Mattie disconsolately removing the last scraps of pickle from the floor.

"It's all right, Matt. Come back and finish supper," he commanded her.

Completely reassured she shone on him through tear-hung lashes, and his soul swelled with pride as he saw how his tone subdued her. She did not even ask what he had done. Except when he was steering a big log down the mountain to his mill he had never known such a thrilling sense of mastery.

Chapter V

They finished supper, and while Mattie cleared the table Ethan went to look at the cows and then took a last turn about the house. The earth lay dark under a muffled sky and the air was so still that now and then he heard a lump of snow come thumping down from a tree far off on the edge of the woodlot.

When he returned to the kitchen Mattie had pushed up his chair to the stove and seated herself near the lamp with a bit of sewing. The scene was just as he had dreamed of it that morning. He sat down, drew his pipe from his pocket and stretched his feet to the glow. His hard day's work in the keen air made him feel at once lazy and light of mood, and he had a confused sense of being in another world, where all was warmth and harmony and time could bring no change. The only drawback to his complete well-being was the fact that he could not see Mattie from where he sat; but he was too indolent to move and after a moment he said: "Come over here and sit by the stove."

Zeena's empty rocking chair stood facing him. Mattie rose obediently, and seated herself in it. As her young brown head detached itself against the patchwork cushion that habitually framed his wife's gaunt countenance, Ethan had a momentary shock. It was almost as if the other face, the face of the superseded woman, had obliterated that of the intruder. After a moment Mattie seemed to be affected by the same sense of constraint. She changed her position, leaning forward to bend her head above her work, so that he saw only the foreshortened tip of her nose and the streak of red in her hair; then she slipped to her feet, saying, "I can't see to sew," and went back to her chair by the lamp.

Ethan made a pretext of getting up to replenish the stove, and when he returned to his seat he pushed it sideways that he might get a view of her profile and of the lamplight falling on her hands. The cat, who had been a puzzled observer of these unusual movements, jumped up into Zeena's chair, rolled itself into a ball, and lay watching them with narrowed eyes.

Deep quiet sank on the room. The clock ticked above the dresser, a piece of charred wood fell now and then in the stove, and the faint sharp scent of the geraniums mingled with the odor of Ethan's smoke, which began to throw a blue haze about the lamp and to hang its grayish cobwebs in the shadowy corners of the room.

All constraint had vanished between the two, and they began to talk easily and simply. They spoke of everyday things, of the prospect of snow, of the next church sociable, of the loves and quarrels of Starkfield. The commonplace nature of what they said produced in Ethan an illusion of long-established intimacy which no outburst of emotion could have given, and he set his imagination adrift on the fiction that they had always spent their evenings thus and would always go on doing so . . .

"This is the night we were to have gone coasting, Matt," he said at length, with the rich sense, as he spoke, that they could go on any other night they chose, since they had all time before them.

She smiled back at him. "I guess you forgot!"

"No, I didn't forget; but it's as dark as Egypt outdoors. We might go tomorrow if there's a moon."

She laughed with pleasure, her head tilted back, the lamplight sparkling on her lips and teeth. "That would be lovely, Ethan!"

He kept his eyes fixed on her, marveling at the way her face changed with each turn of their talk, like a wheatfield under a summer breeze. It was intoxicating to find such magic in his clumsy words, and he longed to try new ways of using it.

"Would you be scared to go down the Corbury road with me on a night like this?" he asked.

Her cheeks burned redder. "I ain't any more scared than you are!"

"Well, I'd be scared, then; I wouldn't do it. That's an ugly corner down by the big elm. If a fellow didn't keep his eyes open he'd go plumb into it." He luxuriated in the sense of protection and authority which his words conveyed. To prolong and intensify the feeling he added: "I guess we're well enough here."

She let her lids sink slowly, in the way he loved. "Yes, we're well enough here," she sighed.

Her tone was so sweet that he took the pipe from his mouth and drew his chair up to the table. Leaning forward, he touched the farther end of the strip of brown stuff that she was hemming. "Say, Matt," he began with a smile, "what do you think I saw under the Varnum spruces, coming along home just now? I saw a friend of yours getting kissed."

The words had been on his tongue all the evening, but now that he had spoken them they struck him as inexpressibly vulgar and out of place.

Mattie blushed to the roots of her hair and pulled her needle rapidly twice or thrice through her work, insensibly drawing the end of it away from him. "I suppose it was Ruth and Ned," she said in a low voice, as though he had suddenly touched on something grave.

Ethan had imagined that his allusion might open the way to the accepted pleasantries, and these perhaps in turn to a harmless caress, if only a mere touch on her hand. But now he felt as if her blush had set a flaming guard about her. He supposed it was his natural awkwardness that made him feel so. He knew that most young men made nothing at all of giving a pretty girl a kiss, and he remembered that the night before, when he had put his arm about Mattie, she had not resisted. But that had been out-of-doors, under the open irresponsible night. Now, in the warm lamp-lit room, with all its ancient implications of conformity and order, she seemed infinitely farther away from him and more unapproachable.

To ease his constraint he said: "I suppose they'll be setting a date before long."

"Yes. I shouldn't wonder if they got married some time along in the summer." She pronounced the word *married* as if her voice caressed it. It seemed a rustling covert leading to enchanted glades. A pang shot through Ethan, and he said, twisting away from her in his chair: "It'll be your turn next, I wouldn't wonder."

She laughed a little uncertainly. "Why do you keep on saying that?"

He echoed her laugh. "I guess I do it to get used to the idea."

He drew up to the table again and she sewed on in silence, with dropped lashes, while he sat in fascinated contemplation of the way in which her hands went up and down above the strip of stuff, just as he had seen a pair of birds make short perpendicular flights over a nest they were building. At length, without turning her head or lifting her lids, she said in a low tone: "It's not because you think Zeena's got anything against me, is it?"

His former dread started up full-armed at the suggestion. "Why, what do you mean?" he stammered.

She raised distressed eyes to his, her work dropping on the table between them. "I don't know. I thought last night she seemed to have."

"I'd like to know what," he growled.

"Nobody can tell with Zeena." It was the first time they had ever spoken so openly of her attitude toward Mattie, and the repetition of the name seemed to carry it to the farther corners of the room and send it back to them in long repercussions of sound. Mattie waited, as if to give the echo time to drop, and then went on: "She hasn't said anything to *you?*"

He shook his head. "No, not a word."

She tossed the hair back from her forehead with a laugh. "I guess I'm just nervous, then. I'm not going to think about it any more."

"Oh, no—don't let's think about it, Matt!"

The sudden heat of his tone made her color mount again, not with a rush, but gradually, delicately, like the reflection of a thought stealing slowly across her heart. She sat silent, her hands clasped on her work, and it seemed to him that a warm current flowed toward him along the strip of stuff that still lay unrolled between them. Cautiously he slid his hand palm downward along the table till his fingertips touched the end of the stuff. A faint vibration of her lashes seemed to show that she was aware of his gesture, and that it had sent a countercurrent back to her; and she let her hands lie motionless on the other end of the strip.

As they sat thus he heard a sound behind him and turned his head. The cat had jumped from Zeena's chair to dart at a mouse in the wainscot, and as a result of the sudden movement the empty chair had set up a spectral rocking.

"She'll be rocking in it herself this time tomorrow," Ethan thought, "I've been in a dream, and this is the only evening we'll ever have together." The return to reality was as painful as the return to consciousness after taking an anesthetic. His body and brain ached with indescribable weariness, and he could think of nothing to say or to do that should arrest the mad flight of the moments.

His alteration of mood seemed to have communicated itself to Mattie. She looked up at him languidly, as though her lids were weighted with sleep and it cost her an effort to raise them. Her glance fell on his hand, which now completely covered the end of her work and grasped it as if it were a part of herself. He saw a scarcely perceptible tremor cross her face, and without knowing what he did he stooped his head and kissed the bit of stuff in his hold. As his lips rested on it he felt it glide slowly from beneath them, and saw that Mattie had risen and was silently rolling up her work. She fastened it with a pin, and then, finding her thimble and scissors, put them with the roll of stuff into the box covered with fancy paper which he had once brought to her from Bettsbridge.

He stood up also, looking vaguely about the room. The clock above the dresser struck eleven.

"Is the fire all right?" she asked in a low voice.

He opened the door of the stove and poked aimlessly at the embers. When he raised himself again he saw that she was dragging toward the stove the old soapbox lined with carpet in which the cat made its bed. Then she recrossed the floor and lifted two of the geranium pots in her arms, moving them away from the cold window. He followed her and brought the other geraniums, the hyacinth bulbs in a cracked custard bowl and the German ivy trained over an old croquet hoop.

When these nightly duties were performed there was nothing left to do but to bring in the tin candlestick from the passage, light the candle and blow out the lamp. Ethan put the candlestick in Mattie's hand and she went out of the kitchen ahead of him, the light that she carried before her making her dark hair look like a drift of mist on the moon.

"Good night, Matt," he said as she put her foot on the first step of the stairs.

She turned and looked at him a moment. "Good night, Ethan," she answered, and went up.

When the door of her room had closed on her he remembered that he had not even touched her hand.

Chapter VI

The next morning at breakfast Jotham Powell was between them, and Ethan tried to hide his joy under an air of exaggerated indifference, lounging back in his chair to throw scraps to the cat, growling at the weather, and not so much as offering to help Mattie when she rose to clear away the dishes.

He did not know why he was so irrationally happy, for nothing was changed in his life or hers. He had not even touched the tip of her fingers or looked her full in the eyes. But their evening together had given him a vision of what life at her side might be, and he was glad now that he had done nothing to trouble the sweetness of the picture. He had a fancy that she knew what had restrained him . . .

There was a last load of lumber to be hauled to the village, and Jotham Powell—who did not work regularly for Ethan in winter—had "come round" to help with the job. But a wet snow, melting to sleet, had fallen in the night and turned the roads to glass. There was more wet in the air and it seemed likely to both men that the weather would "milden" toward afternoon and make the going safer. Ethan therefore proposed to his assistant that they should load the sledge at the woodlot, as they had done on the previous morning, and put off the "teaming" to Starkfield till later in the day. This plan had the advantage of enabling him to send Jotham to the Flats after dinner to meet Zenobia, while he himself took the lumber down to the village.

He told Jotham to go out and harness up the grays, and for a moment he and Mattie had the kitchen to themselves. She had plunged the breakfast dishes into a tin dishpan and was bending above it with her slim arms bared to the elbow, the steam from the hot water beading her forehead and tightening her rough hair into little brown rings like the tendrils on the traveler's joy.

Ethan stood looking at her, his heart in his throat. He wanted to say: "We shall never be alone again like this." Instead, he reached down his tobacco pouch from a shelf of the dresser, put it into his pocket and said: "I guess I can make out to be home for dinner."

She answered: "All right, Ethan," and he heard her singing over the dishes as he went.

As soon as the sledge was loaded he meant to send Jotham back to the farm and hurry on foot into the village to buy the glue for the pickle dish. With ordinary luck he should have had time to carry out this plan; but everything went wrong from the start. On the way over to the woodlot one of the grays slipped on a glare of ice and cut his knee; and when they got him up again Jotham had to go back to the barn for a strip of rag to bind the cut. Then, when the loading finally began, a sleety rain was coming down once more, and the tree trunks were so slippery that it took twice as long as usual to lift them and get them in place on the sledge. It was what Jotham called a sour morning for work, and the horses, shivering and stamping under their wet blankets, seemed to like it as little as the men. It was long past the dinner hour when the job was done, and Ethan had to give up going to the village because he wanted to lead the injured horse home and wash the cut himself.

He thought that by starting out again with the lumber as soon as he had finished his dinner he might get back to the farm with the glue before Jotham and the old sorrel had had time to fetch Zenobia from the Flats; but he knew the chance was a slight one. It turned on the state of the roads and on the possible lateness of the Bettsbridge train. He remembered afterward, with a grim flash of self-derision, what importance he had attached to the weighing of these probabilities . . .

As soon as dinner was over he set out again for the woodlot, not daring to linger till Jotham Powell left. The hired man was still drying his wet feet at the stove, and Ethan could only give Mattie a quick look as he said beneath his breath: "I'll be back early."

He fancied that she nodded her comprehension; and with that scant solace he had to trudge off through the rain.

He had driven his load halfway to the village when Jotham Powell overtook him, urging the reluctant sorrel toward the Flats. "I'll have to hurry up to do it," Ethan mused, as the sleigh dropped down ahead of him over the dip of the schoolhouse hill. He worked like ten at the unloading, and when it was over hastened on to Michael Eady's for the glue. Eady and his assistant were both "down street," and young Denis, who seldom deigned to take their place, was lounging by the stove with a knot of the golden youth of Starkfield. They hailed Ethan with ironic compliment and offers of conviviality; but no one knew where to find the glue. Ethan, consumed with the longing for a last moment alone with Mattie, hung about impatiently while Denis made an ineffectual search in the obscurer corners of the store.

"Looks as if we were all sold out. But if you'll wait around till the old man comes along maybe he can put his hand on it."

"I'm obliged to you, but I'll try if I can get it down at Mrs. Homan's," Ethan answered, burning to be gone.

Denis's commercial instinct compelled him to aver on oath that what Eady's store could not produce would never be found at the widow Homan's; but Ethan, heedless of this boast, had already climbed to the sledge and was driving on to the rival establishment. Here, after considerable search, and sympathetic questions as to what he wanted it for, and whether ordinary flour paste wouldn't do as well if she couldn't find it, the widow Homan finally hunted down her solitary bottle of glue to its hiding place in a medley of cough lozenges and corset laces.

"I hope Zeena ain't broken anything she sets store by," she called after him as he turned the grays toward home.

The fitful bursts of sleet had changed into a steady rain and the horses had heavy work even without a load behind them. Once or twice, hearing sleigh bells, Ethan turned his head, fancying that Zeena and Jotham might overtake him; but the old sorrel was not in sight, and he set his face against the rain and urged on his ponderous pair.

The barn was empty when the horses turned into it and, after giving them the most perfunctory ministrations they had ever received from him, he strode up to the house and pushed open the kitchen door.

Mattie was there alone, as he had pictured her. She was bending over a pan on the stove; but at the sound of his step she turned with a start and sprang to him.

"See, here, Matt, I've got some stuff to mend the dish with! Let me get at it quick," he cried, waving the bottle in one hand while he put her lightly aside; but she did not seem to hear him.

"Oh, Ethan—Zeena's come," she said in a whisper, clutching his sleeve.

They stood and stared at each other, pale as culprits.

"But the sorrel's not in the barn!" Ethan stammered.

"Jotham Powell brought some goods over from the Flats for his wife, and he drove right on home with them," she explained.

He gazed blankly about the kitchen, which looked cold and squalid in the rainy winter twilight.

"How is she?" he asked, dropping his voice to Mattie's whisper.

She looked away from him uncertainly. "I don't know. She went right up to her room."

"She didn't say anything?"

"No."

Ethan let out his doubts in a low whistle and thrust the bottle back into his pocket. "Don't fret; I'll come down and mend it in the night," he said. He pulled on his wet coat again and went back to the barn to feed the grays.

While he was there Jotham Powell drove up with the sleigh, and when the horses had been attended to Ethan said to him: "You might as well come back up for a bite." He was not sorry to assure himself of Jotham's neutralizing presence at the supper table, for Zeena was always "nervous" after a journey. But the hired man, though seldom loth to accept a meal not included in his wages, opened his stiff jaws to answer slowly: "I'm obliged to you, but I guess I'll go along back."

Ethan looked at him in surprise. "Better come up and dry off. Looks as if there'd be something hot for supper."

Jotham's facial muscles were unmoved by this appeal and, his vocabulary being limited, he merely repeated: "I guess I'll go along back."

To Ethan there was something vaguely ominous in this stolid rejection of free food and warmth, and he wondered what had happened on the drive to nerve Jotham to such stoicism. Perhaps Zeena had failed to see the new doctor or had not liked his counsels: Ethan knew that in such cases the first person she met was likely to be held responsible for her grievance.

When he reentered the kitchen the lamp lit up the same scene of shining comfort as on the previous evening. The table had been as carefully laid, a clear fire glowed in the stove, the cat dozed in its warmth, and Mattie came forward carrying a plate of doughnuts.

She and Ethan looked at each other in silence; then she said, as she had said the night before: "I guess it's about time for supper."

Chapter VII

Ethan went out into the passage to hang up his wet garments. He listened for Zeena's step and, not hearing it, called her name up the stairs. She did not answer, and after a moment's hesitation he went up and opened her door. The room was almost dark, but in the obscurity he saw her sitting by the window, bolt upright, and knew by the rigidity of the outline projected against the pane that she had not taken off her traveling dress.

"Well, Zeena," he ventured from the threshold.

She did not move, and he continued: "Supper's about ready. Ain't you coming?"

She replied: "I don't feel as if I could touch a morsel."

It was the consecrated formula, and he expected it to be followed, as usually, by her rising and going down to supper. But she remained seated, and he could think of nothing more felicitous than: "I presume you're tired after the long ride."

Turning her head at this, she answered solemnly: "I'm a great deal sicker than you think."

Her words fell on his ear with a strange shock of wonder. He had often heard her pronounce them before—what if at last they were true?

He advanced a step or two into the dim room. "I hope that's not so, Zeena," he said.

She continued to gaze at him through the twilight with a mien of wan authority, as of one consciously singled out for a great fate. "I've got complications," she said.

Ethan knew the word for one of exceptional import. Almost everybody in the neighborhood had "troubles," frankly localized and specified; but only the chosen had "complications." To have them was in itself a distinction, though it was also, in most cases, a death warrant. People struggled on for years with "troubles," but they almost always succumbed to "complications."

Ethan's heart was jerking to and fro between two extremities of feeling, but for the moment compassion prevailed. His wife looked so hard and lonely, sitting there in the darkness with such thoughts.

"Is that what the new doctor told you?" he asked, instinctively lowering his voice.

"Yes. He says any regular doctor would want me to have an operation."

Ethan was aware that, in regard to the important question of surgical intervention, the female opinion of the neighborhood was divided, some glorying in the prestige conferred by operations while others shunned them as indelicate. Ethan, from motives of economy, had always been glad that Zeena was of the latter faction.

In the agitation caused by the gravity of her announcement he sought a consolatory short cut. "What do you know about this doctor anyway? Nobody ever told you that before."

He saw his blunder before she could take it up: she wanted sympathy, not consolation.

"I didn't need to have anybody tell me I was losing ground every day. Everybody but you could see it. And everybody in Bettsbridge knows about Dr. Buck. He has his office in Worcester, and comes over once a fortnight to Shadd's Falls and Bettsbridge for consultations. Eliza Spears was wasting away with kidney trouble before she went to him, and now she's up and around, and singing in the choir."

"Well, I'm glad of that. You must do just what he tells you," Ethan answered sympathetically.

She was still looking at him. "I mean to," she said. He was struck by a new note in her voice. It was neither whining nor reproachful, but drily resolute.

"What does he want you should do?" he asked, with a mounting vision of fresh expenses.

"He wants I should have a hired girl. He says I oughtn't to have to do a single thing around the house."

"A hired girl?" Ethan stood transfixed.

"Yes. And Aunt Martha found me one right off. Everybody said I was lucky to get a girl to come away out here, and I agreed to give her a dollar extry to make sure. She'll be over tomorrow afternoon."

Wrath and dismay contended in Ethan. He had foreseen an immediate demand for money, but not a permanent drain on his scant resources. He no longer believed what Zeena had told him of the supposed seriousness of her state: he saw in her expedition to Bettsbridge only a plot hatched between herself and her Pierce relations to foist on him the cost of a servant; and for the moment wrath predominated.

"If you meant to engage a girl you ought to have told me before you started," he said.

"How could I tell you before I started? How did I know what Dr. Buck would say?"

"Oh, Dr. Buck—" Ethan's incredulity escaped in a short laugh. "Did Dr. Buck tell you how I was to pay her wages?"

Her voice rose furiously with his. "No, he didn't. For I'd 'a' been ashamed to tell *him* that you grudged me the money to get back my health, when I lost it nursing your own mother!"

"*You* lost your health nursing mother?"

"Yes; and my folks all told me at the time you couldn't do no less than marry me after—"

"Zeena!"

Through the obscurity which hid their faces their thoughts seemed to dart at each other like serpents shooting venom. Ethan was seized with horror of the scene and shame at his own share in it. It was as senseless and savage as a physical fight between two enemies in the darkness.

He turned to the shelf above the chimney, groped for matches and lit the one candle in the room. At first its weak flame made no impression on the shadows; then Zeena's face stood grimly out against the uncurtained pane, which had turned from gray to black.

It was the first scene of open anger between the couple in their sad seven years together, and Ethan felt as if he had lost an irretrievable advantage in descending to the level of recrimination. But the practical problem was there and had to be dealt with.

"You know I haven't got the money to pay for a girl, Zeena. You'll have to send her back: I can't do it."

"The doctor says it'll be my death if I go on slaving the way I've had to. He doesn't understand how I've stood it as long as I have."

"Slaving!—" He checked himself again, "You sha'n't lift a hand, if he says so. I'll do everything round the house myself—"

She broke in: "You're neglecting the farm enough already," and this being true, he found no answer, and left her time to add ironically: "Better send me over to the almshouse and done with it . . . I guess there's been Fromes there afore now."

The taunt burned into him, but he let it pass. "I haven't got the money. That settles it."

There was a moment's pause in the struggle, as though the combatants were testing their weapons. Then Zeena said in a level voice: "I thought you were to get fifty dollars from Andrew Hale for that lumber."

"Andrew Hale never pays under three months." He had hardly spoken when he remembered the excuse he had made for not accompanying his wife to the station the day before; and the blood rose to his frowning brows.

"Why, you told me yesterday you'd fixed it up with him to pay cash down. You said that was why you couldn't drive me over to the Flats."

Ethan had no suppleness in deceiving. He had never before been convicted of a lie, and all the resources of evasion failed him. "I guess that was a misunderstanding," he stammered.

"You ain't got the money?"

"No."

"And you ain't going to get it?"

"No."

"Well, I couldn't know that when I engaged the girl, could I?"

"No." He paused to control his voice. "But you know it now. I'm sorry, but it can't be helped. You're a poor man's wife, Zeena; but I'll do the best I can for you."

For a while she sat motionless, as if reflecting, her arms stretched along the arms of her chair, her eyes fixed on vacancy. "Oh, I guess we'll make out," she said mildly.

The change in her tone reassured him. "Of course we will! There's a whole lot more I can do for you, and Mattie—"

Zeena, while he spoke, seemed to be following out some elaborate mental calculation. She emerged from it to say: "There'll be Mattie's board less, anyhow—"

Ethan, supposing the discussion to be over, had turned to go down to supper. He stopped short, not grasping what he heard. "Mattie's board less—?" he began.

Zeena laughed. It was an odd unfamiliar sound—he did not remember ever having heard her laugh before. "You didn't suppose I was going to keep two girls, did you? No wonder you were scared at the expense!"

He still had but a confused sense of what she was saying. From the beginning of the discussion he had instinctively avoided the mention of Mattie's name, fearing he hardly knew what: criticism, complaints, or vague allusions to the imminent probability of her marrying. But the thought of a definite rupture had never come to him, and even now could not lodge itself in his mind.

"I don't know what you mean," he said. "Mattie Silver's not a hired girl. She's your relation."

"She's a pauper that's hung onto us all after her father'd done his best to ruin us. I've kep' her here a whole year: it's somebody else's turn now."

As the shrill words shot out Ethan heard a tap on the door, which he had drawn shut when he turned back from the threshold.

"Ethan—Zeena!" Mattie's voice sounded gaily from the landing, "do you know what time it is? Supper's been ready half an hour."

Inside the room there was a moment's silence; then Zeena called out from her seat: "I'm not coming down to supper."

"Oh, I'm sorry! Aren't you well? Sha'n't I bring you up a bite of something?"

Ethan roused himself with an effort and opened the door. "Go along down, Matt. Zeena's just a little tired. I'm coming."

He heard her "All right!" and her quick step on the stairs; then he shut the door and turned back into the room. His wife's attitude was unchanged, her face inexorable, and he was seized with the despairing sense of his helplessness.

"You ain't going to do it, Zeena?"

"Do what?" she emitted between flattened lips.

"Send Mattie away—like this?"

"I never bargained to take her for life!"

He continued with rising vehemence: "You can't put her out of the house like a thief—a poor girl without friends or money. She's done her best for you and she's got no place to go to. You may forget she's your kin but everybody else'll remember it. If you do a thing like that what do you suppose folks'll say of you?"

Zeena waited a moment, as if giving him time to feel the full force of the contrast between his own excitement and her composure. Then she replied in the same smooth voice: "I know well enough what they say of my having kep' her here as long as I have."

Ethan's hand dropped from the doorknob, which he had held clenched since he had drawn the door shut on Mattie. His wife's retort was like a knife cut across the sinews and he felt suddenly weak and powerless. He had meant to humble himself, to argue that Mattie's keep didn't cost much, after all, that he could make out to buy a stove and fix up a place in the attic for the hired girl—but Zeena's words revealed the peril of such pleadings.

"You mean to tell her she's got to go—at once?" he faltered out, in terror of letting his wife complete her sentence.

As if trying to make him see reason she replied impartially: "The girl will go over from Bettsbridge tomorrow, and I presume she's got to have somewheres to sleep."

Ethan looked at her with loathing. She was no longer the listless creature who had lived at his side in a state of sullen self-absorption, but a mysterious alien presence, an evil energy secreted from the long years of silent brooding. It was the sense of his helplessness that sharpened his antipathy. There had never been anything in her that one could appeal to; but as long as he could ignore and command her he had remained indifferent. Now she had mastered him and he abhorred her. Mattie was her relation, not his: there were no means by which he could compel her to keep the girl under her roof. All the long misery of his baffled past, of his youth of failure, hardship and vain effort, rose up in his soul in bitterness and seemed to take shape before him in the woman who at every turn had barred his way. She had taken everything else from him; and now she meant to take the one thing that made up for all the others. For a moment such a flame of hate rose in him that it ran down his arm and clenched his fist against her. He took a wild step forward and then stopped.

"You're—you're not coming down?" he said in a bewildered voice.

"No. I guess I'll lay down on the bed a little while," she answered mildly; and he turned and walked out of the room.

In the kitchen Mattie was sitting by the stove, the cat curled up on her knees. She sprang to her feet as Ethan entered and carried the covered dish of meat pie to the table.

"I hope Zeena isn't sick?" she asked.

"No."

She shone at him across the table. "Well, sit right down then. You must be starving." She uncovered the pie and pushed it over to him. So they were to have one more evening together, her happy eyes seemed to say!

He helped himself mechanically and began to eat; then disgust took him by the throat and he laid down his fork.

Mattie's tender gaze was on him and she marked the gesture.

"Why, Ethan, what's the matter? Don't it taste right?"

"Yes—it's first-rate. Only I—" He pushed his plate away, rose from his chair, and walked around the table to her side. She started up with frightened eyes.

"Ethan, there's something wrong? I *knew* there was!"

She seemed to melt against him in her terror, and he caught her in his arms, held her fast there, felt her lashes beat his cheek like netted butterflies.

"What is it—what is it?" she stammered; but he had found her lips at last and was drinking unconsciousness of everything but the joy they gave him.

She lingered a moment, caught in the same strong current; then she slipped from him and drew back a step or two, pale and troubled. Her look smote him with compunction, and he cried out, as if he saw her drowning in a dream: "You can't go, Matt! I'll never let you!"

"Go—go?" she stammered. "Must I go?"

The words went on sounding between them as though a torch of warning flew from hand to hand through a black landscape.

Ethan was overcome with shame at his lack of self-control in flinging the news at her so brutally. His head reeled and he had to support himself against the table. All the while he felt as if he were still kissing her, and yet dying of thirst for her lips.

"Ethan, what has happened? Is Zeena mad with me?"

Her cry steadied him, though it deepened his wrath and pity. "No, no," he assured her, "it's not that. But this new doctor has scared her about herself. You know she believes all they say the first time she sees them. And this one's told her she won't get well unless she lays up and don't do a thing about the house—not for months—"

He paused, his eyes wandering from her miserably. She stood silent a moment, drooping before him like a broken branch. She was so small and weak-looking that it wrung his heart; but suddenly she lifted her head and looked straight at him. "And she wants somebody handier in my place? Is that it?"

"That's what she says tonight."

"If she says it tonight she'll say it tomorrow."

Both bowed to the inexorable truth: they knew that Zeena never changed her mind, and that in her case a resolve once taken was equivalent to an act performed.

There was a long silence between them; then Mattie said in a low voice: "Don't be too sorry, Ethan."

"Oh, God—oh, God," he groaned. The glow of passion he had felt for her had melted to an aching tenderness. He saw her quick lids beating back the tears, and longed to take her in his arms and soothe her.

"You're letting your supper get cold," she admonished him with a pale gleam of gaiety.

"Oh, Matt—Matt—where'll you go to?"

Her lids sank and a tremor crossed her face. He saw that for the first time the thought of the future came to her distinctly. "I might get something to do over at Stamford," she faltered, as if knowing that he knew she had no hope.

He dropped back into his seat and hid his face in his hands. Despair seized him at the thought of her setting out alone to renew the weary quest for work. In the only place where she was known she was surrounded by indifference or animosity; and what chance had she, inexperienced and untrained, among the million breadseekers of the cities? There came back to him miserable tales he had heard at Worcester, and the faces of girls whose lives had begun as hopefully as Mattie's. . . . It was not possible to think of such things without a revolt of his whole being. He sprang up suddenly.

"You can't go, Matt! I won't let you! She's always had her way, but I mean to have mine now—"

Mattie lifted her hand with a quick gesture, and he heard his wife's step behind him.

Zeena came into the room with her dragging down-at-the-heel step, and quietly took her accustomed seat between them.

"I felt a little mite better, and Dr. Buck says I ought to eat all I can to keep my strength up, even if I ain't got any appetite," she said in her flat whine, reaching across Mattie for the teapot. Her "good" dress had been replaced by the black calico and brown knitted shawl which formed her daily wear, and with them she had put on her usual face and manner. She poured out her tea, added a great deal of milk to it, helped herself largely to pie and pickles, and made the familiar gesture of adjusting her false teeth before she began to eat. The cat rubbed itself ingratiatingly against her, and she said "Good Pussy," stooped to stoke it and gave it a scrap of meat from her plate.

Ethan sat speechless, not pretending to eat, but Mattie nibbled valiantly at her food and asked Zeena one or two questions about her visit to Betts-bridge. Zeena answered in her everyday tone and, warming to the theme, regaled them with several vivid descriptions of intestinal disturbances among her friends and relatives. She looked straight at Mattie as she spoke, a faint smile deepening the vertical lines between her nose and chin.

When supper was over she rose from her seat and pressed her hand to the flat surface over the region of her heart. "That pie of yours always sets a mite heavy, Matt," she said, not ill-naturedly. She seldom abbreviated the girl's name, and when she did so it was always a sign of affability.

"I've a good mind to go and hunt up those stomach powders I got last year over in Springfield," she continued. "I ain't tried them for quite a while, and maybe they'll help the heartburn."

Mattie lifted her eyes. "Can't I get them for you, Zeena?" she ventured.

"No. They're in a place you don't know about," Zeena answered darkly, with one of her secret looks.

She went out of the kitchen and Mattie, rising, began to clear the dishes from the table. As she passed Ethan's chair their eyes met and clung together desolately. The warm still kitchen looked as peaceful as the night before. The cat had sprung to Zeena's rocking chair, and the heat of the fire was beginning to draw out the faint sharp scent of the geraniums. Ethan dragged himself wearily to his feet.

"I'll go out and take a look around," he said, going toward the passage to get his lantern.

As he reached the door he met Zeena coming back into the room, her lips twitching with anger, a flush of excitement on her sallow face. The shawl had slipped from her shoulders and was dragging at her downtrodden heels, and in her hands she carried the fragments of the red glass pickle dish.

"I'd like to know who done this," she said, looking sternly from Ethan to Mattie.

There was no answer, and she continued in a trembling voice: "I went to get those powders I'd put away in father's old spectacle case, top of the china closet, where I keep the things I set store by, so's folks sha'n't meddle with them—" Her voice broke, and two small tears hung on her lashless lids and ran slowly down her cheeks. "It takes the stepladder to get at the top shelf, and I put Aunt Philura Maple's pickle dish up there o' purpose when we was married, and it's never been down since, 'cept for the spring cleaning, and then I always lifted it with my own hands, so's 't shouldn't get broke." She laid the fragments reverently on the table. "I want to know who done this," she quavered.

At the challenge Ethan turned back into the room and faced her. "I can tell you, then. The cat done it."

"The *cat?*"

"That's what I said."

She looked at him hard, and then turned her eyes to Mattie, who was carrying the dishpan to the table.

"I'd like to know how the cat got into my china closet," she said.

"Chasin' mice, I guess," Ethan rejoined. "There was a mouse round the kitchen all last evening."

Zeena continued to look from one to the other; then she emitted her small strange laugh. "I knew the cat was a smart cat," she said in a high voice, "but I didn't know he was smart enough to pick up the pieces of my pickle dish and lay 'em edge to edge on the very shelf he knocked 'em off of."

Mattie suddenly drew her arms out of the steaming water. "It wasn't Ethan's fault, Zeena! The cat *did* break the dish; but I got it down from the china closet, and I'm the one to blame for its getting broken."

Zeena stood beside the ruin of her treasure, stiffening into a stony image of resentment, "*You* got down my pickle dish—what for?"

A bright flush flew to Mattie's cheeks. "I wanted to make the supper table pretty," she said.

"You wanted to make the supper table pretty; and you waited till my back was turned, and took the thing I set most store by of anything I've got, and wouldn't never use it, not even when the minister come to dinner, or Aunt Martha Pierce come over from Bettsbridge—" Zeena paused with a gasp, as if terrified by her own evocation of the sacrilege. "You're a bad girl, Mattie Silver, and I always known it. It's the way your father begun, and I was warned of it when I took you, and I tried to keep my things where you couldn't get at 'em—and now you've took from me the one I cared for most of all—" She broke off in a short spasm of sobs that passed and left her more than ever like a shape of stone.

"If I'd 'a' listened to folks, you'd 'a' gone before now, and this wouldn't 'a' happened," she said; and gathering up the bits of broken glass she went out of the room as if she carried a dead body . . .

Chapter VIII

When Ethan was called back to the farm by his father's illness his mother gave him, for his own use, a small room behind the untenanted "best parlor." Here he had nailed up shelves for his books, built himself a box-sofa out of boards and a mattress, laid out his papers on a kitchen table, hung on the rough plaster wall an engraving of Abraham Lincoln and a calender with "Thoughts from the Poets," and tried, with these meager properties, to produce some likeness of the study of a "minister" who had been kind to him and lent him books when he was at Worcester. He still took refuge there in summer, but when Mattie came to live at the farm he had had to give her his stove, and consequently the room was uninhabitable for several months of the year.

To this retreat he descended as soon as the house was quiet, and Zeena's steady breathing from the bed had assured him that there was to be no sequel to the scene in the kitchen. After Zeena's departure he and Mattie had stood speechless, neither seeking to approach the other. Then the girl had returned to her task of clearing up the kitchen for the night and he had taken his lantern and gone on his usual round outside the house. The kitchen was empty when he came back to it; but his tobacco pouch and pipe had been laid on the table, and under them was a scrap of paper torn from the back of a seedsman's catalogue, on which three words were written: "Don't trouble, Ethan."

Going into his cold dark "study" he placed the lantern on the table and, stooping to its light, read the message again and again. It was the first time that Mattie had ever written to him, and the possession of the paper gave him a strange new sense of her nearness; yet it deepened his anguish by reminding him that henceforth they would have no other way of communicating with each other. For the life of her smile, the warmth of her voice, only cold paper and dead words!

Confused motions of rebellion stormed in him. He was too young, too strong, too full of the sap of living, to submit so easily to the destruction of his hopes. Must he wear out all his years at the side of a bitter querulous woman? Other possibilities had been in him, possibilities sacrificed, one by one, to Zeena's narrow-mindedness and ignorance. And what good had come of it? She was a hundred times bitterer and more discontented than when he had married her: the one pleasure left her was to inflict pain on him. All the healthy instincts of self-defense rose up in him against such waste. . .

He bundled himself into his old coonskin coat and lay down on the box-sofa to think. Under his cheek he felt a hard object with strange protuberances. It was a cushion which Zeena had made for him when they were engaged—the only piece of needlework he had ever seen her do. He flung it across the floor and propped his head against the wall. . .

He knew a case of a man over the mountain—a young fellow of about his own age—who had escaped from just such a life of misery by going West with the girl he cared for. His wife had divorced him, and he had married the girl and prospered. Ethan had seen the couple the summer before at Shadd's Falls, where they had come to visit relatives. They had a little girl with fair curls, who wore a gold locket and was dressed like a princess. The deserted wife had not done badly either. Her husband had given her the farm and she had managed to sell it, and with that and the alimony she had started a lunchroom at Bettsbridge and bloomed into activity and importance. Ethan was fired by the thought. Why should he not leave with Mattie the next day, instead of letting her go alone? He would hide his valise under the seat of the sleigh, and Zeena would suspect nothing till she went upstairs for her afternoon nap and found a letter on the bed. . .

His impulses were still near the surface, and he sprang up, relit the lantern, and sat down at the table. He rummaged in the drawer for a sheet of paper, found one, and began to write.

"Zeena, I've done all I could for you, and I don't see as it's been any use. I don't blame you, nor I don't blame myself. Maybe both of us will do better separate. I'm going to try my luck West, and you can sell the farm and mill, and keep the money—"

His pen paused on the word, which brought home to him the relentless conditions of his lot. If he gave the farm and mill to Zeena what would be left him to start his own life with? Once in the West he was sure of picking up work—he would not have feared to try his chance alone. But with Mattie depending on him the case was different. And what of Zeena's fate? Farm and mill were mortgaged to the limit of their value, and even if she found a purchaser—in itself an unlikely chance—it was doubtful if she could clear a thousand dollars on the sale. Meanwhile, how could she keep the farm going? It was only by incessant labor and personal supervision that Ethan drew a meager living from his land, and his wife, even if she were in better health than she imagined, could never carry such a burden alone.

Well, she could go back to her people, then, and see what they would do for her. It was the fate she was forcing on Mattie—why not let her try it herself? By the time she had discovered his whereabouts, and brought suit for divorce, he would probably—wherever he was—be earning enough to pay her a sufficient alimony. And the alternative was to let Mattie go forth alone, with far less hope of ultimate provision. . .

He had scattered the contents of the table drawer in his search for a sheet of paper, and as he took up his pen his eye fell on an old copy of the *Bettsbridge Eagle*. The advertising sheet was folded uppermost, and he read the seductive words: "Trips to the West: Reduced Rates."

He drew the lantern nearer and eagerly scanned the fares; then the paper fell from his hand and he pushed aside his unfinished letter. A moment ago he had wondered what he and Mattie were to live on when they reached the West; now he saw that he had not even the money to take her there. Borrowing was out of the question: six months before he had given his only security to raise funds for necessary repairs to the mill, and he knew that without security no one at Starkfield would lend him ten dollars. The inexorable facts closed in on him like prison warders handcuffing a convict. There was no way out—none. He was a prisoner for life, and now his one ray of light was to be extinguished.

He crept back heavily to the sofa, stretching himself out with limbs so leaden that he felt as if they would never move again. Tears rose in his throat and slowly burned their way to his lids.

As he lay there, the windowpane that faced him, growing gradually lighter, inlaid upon the darkness a square of moon-suffused sky. A crooked tree branch crossed it, a branch of the apple tree under which, on summer evenings, he had sometimes found Mattie sitting when he came up from the mill. Slowly the rim of the rainy vapors caught fire and burnt away, and a pure moon swung into the blue. Ethan, rising on his elbow, watched the landscape whiten and shape itself under the sculpture of the moon. This was the night on which he was to have taken Mattie coasting, and there hung the lamp to light them! He looked out at the slopes bathed in luster, the silveredged darkness of the woods, the spectral purple of the hills against the sky, and it seemed as though all the beauty of the night had been poured out to mock his wretchedness. . .

He fell asleep, and when he woke the chill of the winter dawn was in the room. He felt cold and stiff and hungry, and ashamed of being hungry. He rubbed his eyes and went to the window. A red sun stood over the gray rim of the fields, behind trees that looked black and brittle. He said to himself: "This is Matt's last day," and tried to think what the place would be without her.

As he stood there he heard a step behind him and she entered.

"Oh, Ethan—were you here all night?"

She looked so small and pinched, in her poor dress, with the red scarf wound about her, and the cold light turning her paleness sallow, that Ethan stood before her without speaking.

"You must be frozen," she went on, fixing lusterless eyes on him.

He drew a step nearer. "How did you know I was here?"

"Because I heard you go downstairs again after I went to bed, and I listened all night, and you didn't come up."

All his tenderness rushed to his lips. He looked at her and said: "I'll come right along and make up the kitchen fire."

They went back to the kitchen, and he fetched the coal and kindlings and cleared out the stove for her, while she brought in the milk and the cold remains of the meat pie. When warmth began to radiate from the stove, and the first ray of sunlight lay on the kitchen floor, Ethan's dark thoughts melted in the mellower air. The sight of Mattie going about her work as he had seen her on so many mornings made it seem impossible that she should ever cease to be a part of the scene. He said to himself that he had doubtless exaggerated the significance of Zeena's threats, and that she too, with the return of daylight, would come to a saner mood.

He went up to Mattie as she bent above the stove, and laid his hand on her arm. "I don't want you should trouble either," he said, looking down into her eyes with a smile.

She flushed up warmly and whispered back: "No, Ethan, I ain't going to trouble."

"I guess things'll straighten out," he added.

There was no answer but a quick throb of her lids, and he went on: "She ain't said anything this morning?"

"No. I haven't seen her yet."

"Don't you take any notice when you do."

With this injunction he left her and went out to the cow barn. He saw Jotham Powell walking up the hill through the morning mist, and the familiar sight added to his growing conviction of security.

As the two men were clearing out the stalls Jotham rested on his pitchfork to say: "Dan'l Byrne's goin' over to the Flats today noon, an' he c'd take Mattie's trunk along, and make it easier ridin' when I take her over in the sleigh."

Ethan looked at him blankly, and he continued: "Mis' Frome said the new girl'd be at the Flats at five, and I was to take Mattie then, so's 't she could ketch the six o'clock train for Stamford."

Ethan felt the blood drumming in his temples. He had to wait a moment before he could find voice to say: "Oh, it ain't so sure about Mattie's going—"

"That so?" said Jotham indifferently; and they went on with their work.

When they returned to the kitchen the two women were already at breakfast. Zeena had an air of unusual alertness and activity. She drank two cups of coffee and fed the cat with the scraps left in the pie dish; then she rose from her seat and, walking over to the window, snipped two or three yellow leaves from the geraniums. "Aunt Martha's ain't got a faded leaf on 'em; but they pine away when they ain't cared for," she said reflectively. Then she turned to Jotham and asked: "What time'd you say Dan'l Byrne'd be along?"

The hired man threw a hesitating glance at Ethan. "Round about noon," he said.

Zeena turned to Mattie. "That trunk of yours is too heavy for the sleigh, and Dan'l Byrne'll be round to take it over to the Flats," she said.

"I'm much obliged to you, Zeena," said Mattie.

"I'd like to go over things with you first," Zeena continued in an unperturbed voice. "I know there's a huckaback towel missing; and I can't make out what you done with that match-safe[5] 't used to stand behind the stuffed owl in the parlor."

She went out, followed by Mattie, and when the men were alone Jotham said to his employer: "I guess I better let Dan'l come round, then."

Ethan finished his usual morning tasks about the house and barn; then he said to Jotham: "I'm going down to Starkfield. Tell them not to wait dinner."

The passion of rebellion had broken out in him again. That which had seemed incredible in the sober light of day had really come to pass, and he was to assist as a helpless spectator at Mattie's banishment. His manhood was humbled by the part he was compelled to play and by the thought of what Mattie must think of him. Confused impulses struggled in him as he strode along to the village. He had made up his mind to do something, but he did not know what it would be.

---

5. Matchbox.

The early mist had vanished and the fields lay like a silver shield under the sun. It was one of the days when the glitter of winter shines through a pale haze of spring. Every yard of the road was alive with Mattie's presence, and there was hardly a branch against the sky or tangle of brambles on the bank in which some bright shred of memory was not caught. Once, in the stillness, the call of a bird in a mountain ash was so like her laughter that his heart tightened and then grew large; and all these things made him see that something must be done at once.

Suddenly it occurred to him that Andrew Hale, who was a kindhearted man, might be induced to reconsider his refusal and advance a small sum on the lumber if he were told that Zeena's ill health made it necessary to hire a servant. Hale, after all, knew enough of Ethan's situation to make it possible for the latter to renew his appeal without too much loss of pride; and, moreover, how much did pride count in the ebullition of passions in his breast?

The more he considered his plan the more hopeful it seemed. If he could get Mrs. Hale's ear he felt certain of success, and with fifty dollars in his pocket nothing could keep him from Mattie. . .

His first object was to reach Starkfield before Hale had started for his work; he knew the carpenter had a job down the Corbury road and was likely to leave his house early. Ethan's long strides grew more rapid with the accelerated beat of his thoughts, and as he reached the foot of School House Hill he caught sight of Hale's sleigh in the distance. He hurried forward to meet it, but as it drew nearer he saw that it was driven by the carpenter's youngest boy and that the figure at his side, looking like a large upright cocoon in spectacles, was that of Mrs. Hale. Ethan signed to them to stop, and Mrs. Hale leaned forward, her pink wrinkles twinkling with benevolence.

"Mr. Hale? Why, yes, you'll find him down home now. He ain't going to work this forenoon. He woke up with a touch o' lumbago, and I just made him put on one of old Dr. Kidder's plasters and set right up into the fire."

Beaming maternally on Ethan, she bent over to add: "I on'y just heard from Mr. Hale 'bout Zeena's going over to Bettsbridge to see that new doctor. I'm real sorry she's feeling so bad again! I hope he thinks he can do something for her. I don't know anybody round here's had more sickness than Zeena. I always tell Mr. Hale I don't know what she'd 'a' done if she hadn't 'a' had you to look after her; and I used to say the same thing 'bout your mother. You've had an awful mean time, Ethan Frome."

She gave him a last nod of sympathy while her son chirped to the horse; and Ethan, as she drove off, stood in the middle of the road and stared after the retreating sleigh.

It was a long time since any one had spoken to him as kindly as Mrs. Hale. Most people were either indifferent to his troubles, or disposed to think it natural that a young fellow of his age should have carried without repining the burden of three crippled lives. But Mrs. Hale had said, "You've had an awful mean time, Ethan Frome," and he felt less alone with his misery. If the Hales were sorry for him they would surely respond to his appeal. . .

He started down the road toward their house, but at the end of a few yards he pulled up sharply, the blood in his face. For the first time, in the light of the words he had just heard, he saw what he was about to do. He was planning to take advantage of the Hales' sympathy to obtain money from them on false pretenses. That was a plain statement of the cloudy purpose which had driven him in headlong to Starkfield.

With the sudden perception of the point to which his madness had carried him, the madness fell and he saw his life before him as it was. He was a poor man, the husband of a sickly woman, whom his desertion would leave alone and destitute; and even if he had had the heart to desert her he could have done so only by deceiving two kindly people who had pitied him.

He turned and walked slowly back to the farm.

Chapter IX

At the kitchen door Daniel Byrne sat in his sleigh behind a big-boned gray who pawed the snow and swung his long head restlessly from side to side.

Ethan went into the kitchen and found his wife by the stove. Her head was wrapped in her shawl, and she was reading a book called "Kidney Troubles and Their Cure" on which he had had to pay extra postage only a few days before.

Zeena did not move or look up when he entered, and after a moment he asked: "Where's Mattie?"

Without lifting her eyes from the page she replied: "I presume she's getting down her trunk."

The blood rushed to his face. "Getting down her trunk—alone?"

"Jotham Powell's down in the woodlot, and Dan'l Byrne says he darsn't leave that horse," she returned.

Her husband, without stopping to hear the end of the phrase, had left the kitchen and sprung up the stairs. The door of Mattie's room was shut, and he wavered a moment on the landing. "Matt," he said in a low voice; but there was no answer, and he put his hand on the doorknob.

He had never been in her room except once, in the early summer, when he had gone there to plaster up a leak in the eaves, but he remembered exactly how everything had looked: the red-and-white quilt on her narrow bed, the pretty pincushion on the chest of drawers, and over it the enlarged photograph of her mother, in an oxydized frame, with a bunch of dyed grasses at the back. Now these and all other tokens of her presence had vanished and the room looked as bare and comfortless as when Zeena had shown her into it on the day of her arrival. In the middle of the floor stood her trunk, and on the trunk she sat in her Sunday dress, her back turned to the door and her face in her hands. She had not heard Ethan's call because she was sobbing and she did not hear his step till he stood close behind her and laid his hands on her shoulders.

"Matt—oh, don't—oh, *Matt!*"

She started up, lifting her wet face to his. "Ethan—I thought I wasn't ever going to see you again!"

He took her in his arms, pressing her close, and with a trembling hand smoothed away the hair from her forehead.

"Not see me again? What do you mean?"

She sobbed out: "Jotham said you told him we wasn't to wait dinner for you, and I thought—"

"You thought I meant to cut it?" he finished for her grimly.

She clung to him without answering, and he laid his lips on her hair, which was soft yet springy, like certain mosses on warm slopes, and had the faint woody fragrance of fresh sawdust in the sun.

Through the door they heard Zeena's voice calling out from below: "Dan'l Byrne says you better hurry up if you want him to take that trunk."

They drew apart with stricken faces. Words of resistance rushed to Ethan's lips and died there. Mattie found her handkerchief and dried her eyes; then, bending down, she took hold of a handle of the trunk.

Ethan put her aside. "You let go, Matt," he ordered her.

She answered: "It takes two to coax it round the corner"; and submitting to this argument he grasped the other handle, and together they maneuvered the heavy trunk out to the landing.

"Now let go," he repeated; then he shouldered the trunk and carried it down the stairs and across the passage to the kitchen. Zeena, who had gone back to her seat by the stove, did not lift her head from her book as he passed. Mattie followed him out of the door and helped him to lift the trunk into the back of the sleigh. When it was in place they stood side by side on the doorstep, watching Daniel Byrne plunge off behind his fidgety horse.

It seemed to Ethan that his heart was bound with cords which an unseen hand was tightening with every tick of the clock. Twice he opened his lips to speak to Mattie and found no breath. At length, as she turned to reenter the house, he laid a detaining hand on her.

"I'm going to drive you over, Matt," he whispered.

She murmured back: "I think Zeena wants I should go with Jotham."

"I'm going to drive you over," he repeated; and she went into the kitchen without answering.

At dinner Ethan could not eat. If he lifted his eyes they rested on Zeena's pinched face, and the corners of her straight lips seemed to quiver away into a smile. She ate well, declaring that the mild weather made her feel better, and pressed a second helping of beans on Jotham Powell, whose wants she generally ignored.

Mattie, when the meal was over, went about her usual task of clearing the table and washing up the dishes. Zeena, after feeding the cat, had returned to her rocking chair by the stove, and Jotham Powell, who always lingered last, reluctantly pushed back his chair and moved toward the door.

On the threshold he turned back to say to Ethan: "What time'll I come round for Mattie?"

Ethan was standing near the window, mechanically filling his pipe while he watched Mattie move to and fro. He answered: "You needn't come round; I'm going to drive her over myself."

He saw the rise of the color in Mattie's averted cheek, and the quick lifting of Zeena's head.

"I want you should stay here this afternoon, Ethan," his wife said. "Jotham can drive Mattie over."

Mattie flung an imploring glance at him, but he repeated curtly: "I'm going to drive her over myself."

Zeena continued in the same even tone: "I wanted you should stay and fix up that stove in Mattie's room afore the girl gets here. It ain't been drawing right for nigh on a month now."

Ethan's voice rose indignantly. "If it was good enough for Mattie I guess it's good enough for a hired girl."

"That girl that's coming told me she was used to a house where they had a furnace," Zeena persisted with the same monotonous mildness.

"She'd better ha' stayed there then," he flung back at her; and turning to Mattie he added in a hard voice: "You be ready by three, Matt; I've got business at Corbury."

Jotham Powell had started for the barn, and Ethan strode down after him aflame with anger. The pulses in his temples throbbed and a fog was in his eyes. He went about his task without knowing what force directed him, or whose hands and feet were fulfilling its orders. It was not till he led out the sorrel and backed him between the shafts of the sleigh that he once more became conscious of what he was doing. As he passed the bridle over the horse's head, and wound the traces around the shafts, he remembered the day when he had made the same preparations in order to drive over and meet his wife's cousin at the Flats. It was little more than a year ago, on just such a soft afternoon, with a "feel" of spring in the air. The sorrel, turning the same big ringed eye on him, nuzzled the palm of his hand in the same way; and one by one all the days between rose up and stood before him. . .

He flung the bearskin into the sleigh, climbed to the seat, and drove up to the house. When he entered the kitchen it was empty, but Mattie's bag and shawl lay ready by the door. He went to the foot of the stairs and listened. No sound reached him from above, but presently he thought he heard some one moving about in his deserted study, and pushing open the door he saw Mattie, in her hat and jacket, standing with her back to him near the table.

She started at his approach and turning quickly said: "Is it time?"

"What are you doing here, Matt?" he asked her.

She looked at him timidly. "I was just taking a look round—that's all," she answered, with a wavering smile.

They went back into the kitchen without speaking, and Ethan picked up her bag and shawl.

"Where's Zeena?" he asked.

"She went upstairs right after dinner. She said she had those shooting pains again, and didn't want to be disturbed."

"Didn't she say good-bye to you?"

"No. That was all she said."

Ethan, looking slowly about the kitchen, said to himself with a shudder that in a few hours he would be returning to it alone. Then the sense of unreality overcame him once more, and he could not bring himself to believe that Mattie stood there for the last time before him.

"Come on," he said almost gaily, opening the door and putting her bag into the sleigh. He sprang to his seat and bent over to tuck the rug about her as she slipped into the place at his side. "Now then, go 'long," he said, with a shake of the reins that sent the sorrel placidly jogging down the hill.

"We got lots of time for a good ride, Matt!" he cried seeking her hand beneath the fur and pressing it in his. His face tingled and he felt dizzy, as if he had stopped in at the Starkfield saloon on a zero day for a drink.

At the gate, instead of making for Starkfield, he turned the sorrel to the right, up the Bettsbridge road. Mattie sat silent, giving no sign of surprise; but after a moment she said: "Are you going round by Shadow Pond?"

He laughed and answered: "I knew you'd know!"

She drew closer under the bearskin, so that, looking sideways around his coat sleeve, he could just catch the tip of her nose and a blown brown wave of hair. They drove slowly up the road between fields glistening under the pale sun, and then bent to the right down a lane edged with spruce and larch. Ahead of them, a long way off, a range of hills stained by mottlings of black forest flowed away in round white curves against the sky. The lane passed into a pine wood with boles reddening in the afternoon sun and delicate blue shadows on the snow. As they entered it the breeze fell and a warm stillness seemed to drop from the branches with the dropping needles. Here the snow was so pure that the tiny tracks of wood-animals had left on it intricate lacelike patterns, and the bluish cones caught in its surface stood out like ornaments of bronze.

Ethan drove on in silence till they reached a part of the wood where the pines were more widely spaced, then he drew up and helped Mattie to get out of the sleigh. They passed between the aromatic trunks, the snow breaking crisply under their feet, till they came to a small sheet of water with steep wooded sides. Across its frozen surface, from the farther bank, a single hill rising against the western sun threw the long conical shadow which gave the lake its name. It was a shy secret spot, full of the same dumb melancholy that Ethan felt in his heart.

He looked up and down the little pebbly beach till his eye lit on a fallen tree trunk half submerged in snow.

"There's where we sat at the picnic," he reminded her.

The entertainment of which he spoke was one of the few that they had taken part in together: a "church picnic" which, on a long afternoon of the preceding summer, had filled the retired place with merrymaking. Mattie had begged him to go with her but he had refused. Then, toward sunset, coming down from the mountain where he had been felling timber, he had been caught by some strayed revellers and drawn into the group by the lake, where Mattie, encircled by facetious youths, and bright as a blackberry under her spreading hat, was brewing coffee over a gipsy fire. He remembered the shyness he had felt at approaching her in his uncouth clothes, and then the lighting up of her face, and the way she had broken through the group to come to him with a cup in her hand. They had sat for a few minutes on the fallen log by the pond, and she had missed her gold locket, and set the young men searching for it; and it was Ethan who had spied it in the moss. . . . That was all; but all their intercourse had been made up of just such inarticulate flashes, when they seemed to come suddenly upon happiness as if they had surprised a butterfly in the winter woods. . .

"It was right there I found your locket," he said, pushing his foot into a dense tuft of blueberry bushes.

"I never saw anybody with such sharp eyes!" she answered.

She sat down on the tree trunk in the sun and he sat down beside her.

"You were as pretty as a picture in that pink hat," he said.

She laughed with pleasure. "Oh, I guess it was the hat!" she rejoined.

They had never before avowed their inclination so openly, and Ethan, for a moment, had the illusion that he was a free man, wooing the girl he meant to marry. He looked at her hair and longed to touch it again, and to tell her that it smelt of the woods; but he had never learned to say such things.

Suddenly she rose to her feet and said: "We mustn't stay here any longer."

He continued to gaze at her vaguely, only half-roused from his dream. "There's plenty of time," he answered.

They stood looking at each other as if the eyes of each were straining to absorb and hold fast the other's image. There were things he had to say to her before they parted, but he could not say them in that place of summer memories, and he turned and followed her in silence to the sleigh. As they drove away the sun sank behind the hill and the pine boles turned from red to gray.

By a devious track between the fields they wound back to the Starkfield road. Under the open sky the light was still clear, with a reflection of cold red on the eastern hills. The clumps of trees in the snow seemed to draw together in ruffled lumps, like birds with their heads under their wings; and the sky, as it paled, rose higher, leaving the earth more alone.

As they turned into the Starkfield road Ethan said: "Matt, what do you mean to do?"

She did not answer at once, but at length she said: "I'll try to get a place in a store."

"You know you can't do it. The bad air and the standing all day nearly killed you before."

"I'm a lot stronger than I was before I came to Starkfield."

"And now you're going to throw away all the good it's done you!"

There seemed to be no answer to this, and again they drove on for a while without speaking. With every yard of the way some spot where they had stood and laughed together or been silent clutched at Ethan and dragged him back.

"Isn't there any of your father's folks could help you?"

"There isn't any of 'em I'd ask."

He lowered his voice to say: "You know there's nothing I wouldn't do for you if I could."

"I know there isn't."

"But I can't—"

She was silent, but he felt a slight tremor in the shoulder against his.

"Oh, Matt," he broke out, "if I could ha' gone with you now I'd ha' done it—"

She turned to him, pulling a scrap of paper from her breast. "Ethan—I found this," she stammered. Even in the failing light he saw it was the letter to his wife that he had begun the night before and forgotten to destroy. Through his astonishment there ran a fierce thrill of joy. "Matt—" he cried; "if I could ha' done it, would you?"

"Oh, Ethan, Ethan—what's the use?" With a sudden movement she tore the letter in shreds and sent them fluttering off into the snow.

"Tell me, Matt! Tell me!" he adjured her.

She was silent for a moment; then she said, in such a low tone that he had to stoop his head to hear her: "I used to think of it sometimes, summer nights, when the moon was so bright I couldn't sleep."

His heart reeled with the sweetness of it. "As long ago as that?"

She answered, as if the date had long been fixed for her: "The first time was at Shadow Pond."

"Was that why you gave me my coffee before the others?"

"I don't know. Did I? I was dreadfully put out when you wouldn't go to the picnic with me; and then, when I saw you coming down the road, I thought maybe you'd gone home that way o' purpose; and that made me glad."

They were silent again. They had reached the point where the road dipped to the hollow by Ethan's mill and as they descended the darkness descended with them, dropping down like a black veil from the heavy hemlock boughs.

"I'm tied hand and foot, Matt. There isn't a thing I can do," he began again.

"You must write to me sometimes, Ethan."

"Oh, what good'll writing do? I want to put my hand out and touch you. I want to do for you and care for you. I want to be there when you're sick and when you're lonesome."

"You mustn't think but what I'll do all right."

"You won't need me, you mean? I suppose you'll marry!"

"Oh, Ethan!" she cried.

"I don't know how it is you make me feel, Matt. I'd a'most rather have you dead than that!"

"Oh, I wish I was, I wish I was!" she sobbed.

The sound of her weeping shook him out of his dark anger, and he felt ashamed.

"Don't let's talk that way," he whispered.

"Why shouldn't we, when it's true? I've been wishing it every minute of the day."

"Matt! You be quiet! Don't you say it."

"There's never anybody been good to me but you."

"Don't say that either, when I can't lift a hand for you!"

"Yes, but it's true just the same."

They had reached the top of School House Hill and Starkfield lay below them in the twilight. A cutter, mounting the road from the village, passed them by in a joyous flutter of bells, and they straightened themselves and looked ahead with rigid faces. Along the main street lights had begun to shine from the house fronts and stray figures were turning in here and there at the gates. Ethan, with a touch of his whip, roused the sorrel to a languid trot.

As they drew near the end of the village the cries of children reached them, and they saw a knot of boys, with sleds behind them, scattering across the open space before the church.

"I guess this'll be their last coast for a day or two," Ethan said, looking up at the mild sky.

Mattie was silent, and he added: "We were to have gone down last night."

Still she did not speak and, prompted by an obscure desire to help himself and her through their miserable last hour, he went on discursively: "Ain't it funny we haven't been down together but just that once last winter?"

She answered: "It wasn't often I got down to the village."

"That's so," he said.

They had reached the crest of the Corbury road, and between the indistinct white glimmer of the church and the black curtain of the Varnum spruces the slope stretched away below them without a sled on its length. Some erratic impulse prompted Ethan to say: "How'd you like me to take you down now?"

She forced a laugh. "Why, there isn't time!"

"There's all the time we want. Come along!" His one desire now was to postpone the moment of turning the sorrel toward the Flats.

"But the girl," she faltered. "The girl'll be waiting at the station."

"Well, let her wait. You'd have to if she didn't. Come!"

The note of authority in his voice seemed to subdue her, and when he had jumped from the sleigh she let him help her out, saying only, with a vague feint of reluctance: "But there isn't a sled round anywheres."

"Yes, there is! Right over there under the spruces."

He threw the bearskin over the sorrel, who stood passively by the roadside, hanging a meditative head. Then he caught Mattie's hand and drew her after him toward the sled.

She seated herself obediently and he took his place behind her, so close that her hair brushed his face. "All right, Matt?" he called out, as if the width of the road had been between them.

She turned her head to say: "It's dreadfully dark. Are you sure you can see?"

He laughed contemptuously: "I could go down this coast with my eyes tied!" and she laughed with him, as if she liked his audacity. Nevertheless he sat still a moment, straining his eyes down the long hill, for it was the most confusing hour of the evening, the hour when the last clearness from the upper sky is merged with the rising night in a blur that disguises landmarks and falsifies distances.

"Now!" he cried.

The sled started with a bound, and they flew on through the dusk, gathering smoothness and speed as they went, with the hollow night opening out below them and the air singing by like an organ. Mattie sat perfectly still, but as they reached the bend at the foot of the hill, where the big elm thrust out a deadly elbow, he fancied that she shrank a little closer.

"Don't be scared, Matt!" he cried exultantly, as they spun safely past it and flew down the second slope; and when they reached the level ground beyond, and the speed of the sled began to slacken, he heard her give a little laugh of glee.

They sprang off and started to walk back up the hill. Ethan dragged the sled with one hand and passed the other through Mattie's arm.

"Were you scared I'd run you into the elm?" he asked with a boyish laugh.

"I told you I was never scared with you," she answered.

The strange exaltation of his mood had brought on one of his rare fits of boastfulness. "It is a tricky place, though. The least swerve, and we'd never ha' come up again. But I can measure distances to a hair's-breadth—always could."

She murmured: "I always say you've got the surest eye . . ."

Deep silence had fallen with the starless dusk, and they leaned on each other without speaking; but at every step of their climb Ethan said to himself: "It's the last time we'll ever walk together."

They mounted slowly to the top of the hill. When they were abreast of the church he stooped his head to her to ask: "Are you tired?" and she answered, breathing quickly: "It was splendid!"

With a pressure of his arm he guided her toward the Norway spruces. "I guess this sled must be Ned Hale's. Anyhow I'll leave it where I found it." He drew the sled up to the Varnum gate and rested it against the fence. As he raised himself he suddenly felt Mattie close to him among the shadows.

"Is this where Ned and Ruth kissed each other?" she whispered breathlessly, and flung her arms about him. Her lips, groping for his, swept over his face, and he held her fast in a rapture of surprise.

"Good-bye—good-bye," she stammered, and kissed him again.

"Oh, Matt, I can't let you go!" broke from him in the same old cry.

She freed herself from his hold and he heard her sobbing. "Oh, I can't go either!" she wailed.

"Matt! What'll we do? What'll we do?"

They clung to each others' hands like children, and her body shook with desperate sobs.

Through the stillness they heard the church clock striking five.

"Oh, Ethan, it's time!" she cried.

He drew her back to him. "Time for what? You don't suppose I'm going to leave you now?"

"If I missed my train where'd I go?"

"Where are you going if you catch it?"

She stood silent, her hand lying cold and relaxed in his.

"What's the good of either of us going anywheres without the other one now?" he said.

She remained motionless, as if she had not heard him. Then she snatched her hands from his, threw her arms around his neck, and pressed a sudden drenched cheek against his face. "Ethan! Ethan! I want you to take me down again!"

"Down where?"

"The coast. Right off," she panted. "So 't we'll never come up any more."

"Matt! What on earth do you mean?"

She put her lips close against his ear to say: "Right into the big elm. You said you could. So 't we'd never have to leave each other any more."

"Why, what are you talking of? You're crazy!"

"I'm not crazy; but I will be if I leave you."

"Oh, Matt, Matt—" he groaned.

She tightened her fierce hold about his neck. Her face lay close to his face.

"Ethan, where'll I go if I leave you? I don't know how to get along alone. You said so yourself just now. Nobody but you was ever good to me. And there'll be that strange girl in the house . . . and she'll sleep in my bed, where I used to lay nights and listen to hear you come up the stairs . . ."

The words were like fragments torn from his heart. With them came the hated vision of the house he was going back to—of the stairs he would have to go up every night, of the woman who would wait for him there. And the sweetness of Mattie's avowal, the wild wonder of knowing at last that all that had happened to him had happened to her too, made the other vision more abhorrent, the other life more intolerable to return to. . .

Her pleadings still came to him between short sobs, but he no longer heard what she was saying. Her hat had slipped back and he was stroking her hair. He wanted to get the feeling of it into his hand, so that it would sleep there like a seed in winter. Once he found her mouth again, and they seemed to be by the pond together in the burning August sun. But his cheek touched hers, and it was cold and full of weeping, and he saw the road to the Flats under the night and heard the whistle of the train up the line.

The spruces swathed them in blackness and silence. They might have been in their coffins underground. He said to himself: "Perhaps it'll feel like this . . ." and then again: "After this I sha'n't feel anything . . ."

Suddenly he heard the old sorrel whinny across the road, and thought: "He's wondering why he doesn't get his supper . . ."

"Come," Mattie whispered, tugging at his hand.

Her somber violence constrained him: she seemed the embodied instrument of fate. He pulled the sled out, blinking like a nightbird as he passed from the shade of the spruces into the transparent dusk of the open. The slope below them was deserted. All Starkfield was at supper, and not a figure crossed the open space before the church. The sky, swollen with the clouds that announce a thaw, hung as low as before a summer storm. He strained his eyes through the dimness, and they seemed less keen, less capable than usual.

He took his seat on the sled and Mattie instantly placed herself in front of him. Her hat had fallen into the snow and his lips were in her hair. He stretched out his legs, drove his heels into the road to keep the sled from slipping forward, and bent her head back between his hands. Then suddenly he sprang up again.

"Get up," he ordered her.

It was the tone she always heeded, but she cowered down in her seat, repeating vehemently: "No, no, no!"

"Get up!"

"Why?"

"I want to sit in front."

"No, no! How can you steer in front?"

"I don't have to. We'll follow the track."

They spoke in smothered whispers, as though the night were listening.

"Get up! Get up!" he urged her; but she kept on repeating: "Why do you want to sit in front?"

"Because I—because I want to feel you holding me," he stammered, and dragged her to her feet.

The answer seemed to satisfy her, or else she yielded to the power of his voice. He bent down, feeling in the obscurity for the glassy slide worn by preceding coasters, and placed the runners carefully between its edges. She waited while he seated himself with crossed legs in the front of the sled; then she crouched quickly down at his back and clasped her arms about him. Her breath in his neck set him shuddering again, and he almost sprang from his seat. But in a flash he remembered the alternative. She was right: this was better than parting. He leaned back and drew her mouth to his. . .

Just as they started he heard the sorrel's whinny again, and the familiar wistful call, and all the confused images it brought with it, went with him down the first reach of the road. Halfway down there was a sudden drop, then a rise, and after that another long delirious descent. As they took wing for this it seemed to him that they were flying indeed, flying far up into the cloudy night, with Starkfield immeasurably below them, falling away like a speck in space. . . . Then the big elm shot up ahead, lying in wait for them at the bend of the road, and he said between his teeth: "We can fetch it; I know we can fetch it—"

As they flew toward the tree Mattie pressed her arms tighter, and her blood seemed to be in his veins. Once or twice the sled swerved a little under them. He slanted his body to keep it headed for the elm, repeating to himself again and again: "I know we can fetch it"; and little phrases she had spoken ran through his head and danced before him on the air. The big tree loomed bigger and closer, and as they bore down on it he thought: "It's waiting for us: it seems to know." But suddenly his wife's face, with twisted monstrous lineaments, thrust itself between him and his goal, and he made an instinctive movement to brush it aside. The sled swerved in response, but he righted it again, kept it straight, and drove down on the black projecting mass. There was a last instant when the air shot past him like millions of fiery wires; and then the elm. . .

The sky was still thick, but looking straight up he saw a single star, and tried vaguely to reckon whether it was Sirius, or—or— The effort tired him too much, and he closed his heavy lids and thought that he would sleep. . . . The stillness was so profound that he heard a little animal twittering somewhere near by under the snow. It made a small frightened *cheep* like a field mouse, and he wondered languidly if it were hurt. Then he understood that it must be in pain: pain so excruciating that he seemed, mysteriously, to feel it shooting through his own body. He tried in vain to roll over in the direction of the sound, and stretched his left arm out across the snow. And now it was as though he felt rather than heard the twittering; it seemed to be under his palm, which rested on something soft and springy. The thought of the animal's suffering was intolerable to him and he struggled to raise himself, and could not because a rock, or some huge mass, seemed to be lying on him. But he continued to finger about cautiously with his left hand, thinking he might get hold of the little creature and help it; and all at once he knew that the soft thing he had touched was Mattie's hair and that his hand was on her face.

He dragged himself to his knees, the monstrous load on him moving with him as he moved, and his hand went over and over her face, and he felt that the twittering came from her lips. . .

He got his face down close to hers, with his ear to her mouth, and in the darkness he saw her eyes open and heard her say his name.

"Oh, Matt, I thought we'd fetched it," he moaned; and far off, up the hill, he heard the sorrel whinny, and thought: "I ought to be getting him his feed . . ."

Chapter X

The querulous drone ceased as I entered Frome's kitchen, and of the two women sitting there I could not tell which had been the speaker.

One of them, on my appearing, raised her tall bony figure from her seat, not as if to welcome me—for she threw me no more than a brief glance of surprise—but simply to set about preparing the meal which Frome's absence had delayed. A slatternly calico wrapper hung from her shoulders and the wisps of her thin gray hair were drawn away from a high forehead and fastened at the back by a broken comb. She had pale opaque eyes which revealed nothing and reflected nothing, and her narrow lips were of the same sallow color as her face.

The other woman was much smaller and slighter. She sat huddled in an armchair near the stove, and when I came in she turned her head quickly toward me, without the least corresponding movement of her body. Her hair was as gray as her companion's, her face as bloodless and shrivelled, but amber-tinted, with swarthy shadows sharpening the nose and hollowing the temples. Under her shapeless dress her body kept its limp immobility, and her dark eyes had the bright witchlike stare that disease of the spine sometimes gives.

Even for that part of the country the kitchen was a poor looking place. With the exception of the dark-eyed woman's chair, which looked like a soiled relic of luxury bought at a country auction, the furniture was of the roughest kind. Three coarse china plates and a broken-nosed milk jug had been set on a greasy table scored with knife cuts, and a couple of straw-bottomed chairs and a kitchen dresser of unpainted pine stood meagerly against the plaster walls.

"My, it's cold here! The fire must be 'most out," Frome said, glancing about him apologetically as he followed me in.

The tall woman, who had moved away from us toward the dresser, took no notice; but the other, from her cushioned niche, answered complainingly, in a high thin voice. "It's on'y just been made up this very minute. Zeena fell asleep and slep' ever so long, and I though I'd be frozen stiff before I could wake her up and get her to 'tend to it."

I knew then that it was she who had been speaking when we entered.

Her companion, who was just coming back to the table with the remains of a cold mince pie in a battered pie dish, set down her unappetizing burden without appearing to hear the accusation brought against her.

Frome stood hesitatingly before her as she advanced; then he looked at me and said: "This is my wife, Mis' Frome." After another interval he added, turning toward the figure in the armchair: "And this is Miss Mattie Silver . . ."

.   .   .   .

Mrs. Hale, tender soul, had pictured me as lost in the Flats and buried under a snowdrift; and so lively was her satisfaction on seeing me safely restored to her the next morning that I felt my peril had caused me to advance several degrees in her favor.

Great was her amazement, and that of old Mrs. Varnum, on learning that Ethan Frome's old horse had carried me to and from Corbury Junction through the worst blizzard of the winter; greater still their surprise when they heard that his master had taken me in for the night.

Beneath their wondering exclamations I felt a secret curiosity to know what impressions I had received from my night in the Frome household, and divined that the best way of breaking down their reserve was to let them try to penetrate mine. I therefore confined myself to saying, in a matter-of-fact tone, that I had been received with great kindness, and that Frome had made a bed for me in a room on the ground floor which seemed in happier days to have been fitted up as a kind of writing room or study.

"Well," Mrs. Hale mused, "in such a storm I suppose he felt he couldn't do less than take you in—but I guess it went hard with Ethan. I don't believe but what you're the only stranger has set foot in that house for over twenty years. He's that proud he don't even like his oldest friends to go there; and I don't know as any do, any more, except myself and the doctor . . ."

"You still go there, Mrs. Hale?" I ventured.

"I used to go a good deal after the accident, when I was first married; but after awhile I got to think it made 'em feel worse to see us. And then one thing and another came, and my own troubles. . . . But I generally make out to drive over there round about New Year's, and once in the summer. Only I always try to pick a day when Ethan's off somewheres. It's bad enough to see the two women sitting there—but *his* face, when he looks round that bare place, just kills me. . . . You see, I can look back and call it up in his mother's day, before their troubles."

Old Mrs. Varnum, by this time, had gone up to bed, and her daughter and I were sitting alone, after supper, in the austere seclusion of the horsehair parlor. Mrs. Hale glanced at me tentatively, as though trying to see how much footing my conjectures gave her; and I guessed that if she had kept silence till now it was because she had been waiting, through all the years, for some one who should see what she alone had seen.

I waited to let her trust in me gather strength before I said: "Yes, it's pretty bad, seeing all three of them there together."

She drew her mild brows into a frown of pain. "It was just awful from the beginning. I was here in the house when they were carried up—they laid Mattie Silver in the room you're in. She and I were great friends, and she was to have been my bridesmaid in the spring. . . . When she came to I went up to her and stayed all night. They gave her things to quiet her, and she didn't know much till to'rd morning, and then all of a sudden she woke up just like herself, and looked straight at me out of her big eyes, and said . . . . Oh, I don't know why I'm telling you all this," Mrs. Hale broke off, crying.

She took off her spectacles, wiped the moisture from them, and put them on again with an unsteady hand. "It got about the next day," she went on, "that Zeena Frome had sent Mattie off in a hurry because she had a hired girl coming, and the folks here could never rightly tell what she and Ethan were doing that night coasting, when they'd ought to have been on their way to the Flats to ketch the train. . . . I never knew myself what Zeena thought—I don't to this day. Nobody knows Zeena's thoughts. Anyhow, when she heard o' the accident she came right in and stayed with Ethan over to the minister's, where they'd carried him. And as soon as the doctors said that Mattie could be moved, Zeena sent for her and took her back to the farm."

"And there she's been ever since?"

Mrs. Hale answered simply: "There was nowhere else for her to go"; and my heart tightened at the thought of the hard compulsions of the poor.

"Yes, there she's been," Mrs. Hale continued, "and Zeena's done for her, and done for Ethan, as good as she could. It was a miracle, considering how sick she was—but she seemed to be raised right up just when the call came to her. Not as she's ever given up doctoring, and she's had sick spells right along; but she's had the strength given her to care for those two for over twenty years, and before the accident came she thought she couldn't even care for herself."

Mrs. Hale paused a moment, and I remained silent, plunged in the vision of what her words evoked. "It's horrible for them all," I murmured.

"Yes: it's pretty bad. And they ain't any of 'em easy people either. Mattie *was*, before the accident; I never knew a sweeter nature. But she's suffered too much—that's what I always say when folks tell me how she's soured. And Zeena, she was always cranky. Not but what she bears with Mattie wonderful—I've seen that myself. But sometimes the two of them get going at each other, and then Ethan's face'd break your heart. . . . When I see that, I think it's *him* that suffers most . . . anyhow it ain't Zeena, because she ain't got the time. . . . It's a pity, though," Mrs. Hale ended, sighing, "that they're all shut up there'n that one kitchen. In the summertime, on pleasant days, they move Mattie into the parlor, or out in the dooryard, and that makes it easier . . . but winters there's the fires to be thought of; and there ain't a dime to spare up at the Fromes'."

Mrs. Hale drew a deep breath, as though her memory were eased of its long burden, and she had no more to say; but suddenly an impulse of complete avowal seized her.

She took off her spectacles again, leaned toward me across the beadwork table cover, and went on with lowered voice: "There was one day, about a week after the accident, when they all thought Mattie couldn't live. Well, I say it's a pity she *did*. I said it right out to our minister once, and he was shocked at me. Only he wasn't with me that morning when she first came to. . . . And I say, if she'd ha' died, Ethan might ha' lived; and the way they are now, I don't see's there's much difference between the Fromes up at the farm and the Fromes down in the graveyard; 'cept that down there they're all quiet, and the women have got to hold their tongues."

1911

AFTERWORD

This is a novel of pent-up passion; of feeling frustrated by the cold, stony countryside of New England and its long hard winters, the stark field of life for the citizens of Starkfield; of desire repressed by conventional morality, and a tight-knit, narrow, restrictive society, and, perhaps worst of all, by one's own inarticulateness, one's own inability to express turbulence, yearning, desire.

What first strikes the narrator about Ethan Frome, he tells us, is this sense of power confined, "the careless powerful look he had, in spite of a lameness checking each step like the jerk of a chain." It is to solve the mystery of this look, which, he is sure, "neither poverty nor physical suffering could have put there," that the narrator tries to find out as much as he can about Ethan Frome, and for a while we follow his progress step by step. From Harmon Gow he learns that Ethan was confined initially to Starkfield by having to take care of his parents and his wife, and then, twenty-four years ago, came the "smashup," which not only crippled him but, somewhat mysteriously, meant that he had to continue doing the "caring." "Guess he's been in Starkfield too many winters," Gow says.

Despite the narrator's own subsequent experience of the imprisoning power of the Starkfield winters, he is not quite satisfied, and his curiosity is further piqued by the reticence of his landlady, Mrs. Hale, on the subject, though she was more than willing to talk about everyone and everything else. " 'Yes, I knew them both . . . it was awful . . .' seeming to be the utmost concession that her distress could make to my curiosity." (Who does she mean by both?) The narrator meets Frome, learns that he had once been to Florida, that he is interested in popular science, "But something in his past history, or in his present way of living, had apparently driven him too deeply into himself for any casual impulse to draw him back to his kind." By now, we are thoroughly hooked, our curiosity, detective sense, and expectations are aroused, and we are grateful that the narrator, on entering Frome's house, drops the step-by-step accumulation of information and interpretations, as well as the narrative frame, and reconstructs the story for us. What he is about to tell us he carefully qualifies as only his "vision" of Frome's story. But we are ready for the story to begin, and so to Chapter 1.

Young Ethan Frome is stimulated by a brisk walk through the snow on a winter night and the sense that there is meaning "behind the daily face of things." The narrator tells us this, but the words he chooses—remember, it is *his* vision of Frome's story—suggest a darker, more confining reality. The winter night sky above is like a *metallic* dome; Ethan feels he is in an *exhausted* receiver; his interrupted education has "fed his fancy" and made him aware of meanings beyond the surface of things, but those "huge meanings" are *cloudy*.

There is a dance going on in the church basement, and Ethan looks in through the window. Standing alone in the dark and cold, looking in at the gaiety, the light, and heat seems an emblem of Ethan's situation, though at the moment he does not seem conscious of that fact. It is not until he sees his wife's cousin, Mattie Silver, whom he has come to fetch home, dancing with the despicable Denis Eady—"He even noticed two or three gestures which, in his fatuity, he had thought she kept for him . . ."—that he feels unhappy and fearful. (Could Mrs. Hale's "Both" meant Ethan and Mattie?) Mattie, with her "cherry-colored 'fascinator' about her head"; the look of "impudent ownership" on the face of Denis Eady as he dances with her; Ethan, and Zeena, his wife: all the elements of a love story, a triangle or quadrangle, are in place. "Both" is foremost in our minds; too many winters, smashup, "lameness checking each step like the jerk of a chain," lurk darkly somewhere in the back of our mind. We know, with some part of our mind, how it will end, more or less. But we push the knowledge away, empathizing with the trapped young lovers, sharing their joy and unspoken hopes—speaking those hopes for them, perhaps, in the form of expectations. We *know* those expectations cannot be fulfilled, however. It's almost as if we're suffering through a great dramatic irony, but the ironic joke is on us: what we want to happen, what our wishful expectations try to make happen, will not happen. And we know it. There is, however, against all odds, a surprise ending, and one of the surprises is that there can be, in a story like this, in which we already know part of the ending—the smashup, the crippled Ethan—a surprise.

The structure of *Ethan Frome* is not typical of a narrative with a surprise or twist at the end. Most such stories proceed chronologically, leading up to some unexpected conclusion. Here, we know from the beginning that Ethan is crippled, and that his life has contained some great pain that is even worse than his physical pain. The stark tone of the story, the seemingly cold, unpassionate people, the setting, the deadly dullness of life in Starkfield—that which Harmon Gow tries to express in the term "winter"—all seem to prepare the reader for a somber, inevitable ending, one without any surprises: we have to get in the end, after all, to the crippled Ethan. If we are warned in the very first paragraph that "each time it was a different story," we know that this does not mean that the outcome could be different, but only that its meaning, the inferred events or motives leading up to the ending can be different. The "interpretation"—not the ending—depends upon the narrator. Surely it is impossible for the Ethan-Mattie story to have anything but a tragic ending, and we know Ethan's state twenty years later, so what kind of a surprise can there be?

Yet, as we now know, there is to be a surprise, not just in the immediate outcome of the death-seeking ride down the hill and into the tree—for though the result of the crash is not entirely expected, neither is it a very great surprise—but in the eventual outcome, the transformation of lovely and lively and life-enhancing Mattie into something quite different. That transformation also transforms the story and its meaning into something quite different. What would be the difference in meaning and effect if Mattie had died in the smashup? Or if Ethan had simply tried to kill himself when Mattie left, and failed? Or accidentally crippled himself before Mattie left, and she then left him (perhaps for Denis Eady)? Endings have more than narrative or technical significance: they bear interpretations of human character, motives, reality.

What do we know, for sure, about the ending? How much is fact, and how much is the narrator's "vision"? We know that Ethan is lame, that he was injured in the same smashup (why isn't it referred to as an accident?) as was Mattie, and that the querulously droning voice heard before we entered the Frome farmhouse is Mattie's. We know a little, but very little, from Harmon Gow and Mrs. Ned Hale. The narrator has told us, "I had the story, bit by bit, from various people, and, as generally happens in such cases, each time it was a different story." But we really do not hear the different stories. What, if anything, did Ethan tell him that night? or Mattie? or Zenobia? We do not know. The main body of the story, chapters 1 through 9, is in the third person, told to us by the narrator, who was not in Starkfield at the time, but who has apparently reconstructed or invented the central situation and episodes leading up to the desperate crash into the elm. Though it is true that often in the narrative that follows the only source—for Ethan's thoughts or perceptions, for example—would seem to be Ethan, we are not allowed to hear Ethan tell anything of his story, and we do not know how much of it the narrator has simply made up.

Remember, he told us that every time you hear a story it is a different story. Though perhaps he did not intend it that way, this gives us license not only to judge the fragmentary version of Harmon Gow and the somewhat more sympathetic and fuller version of Mrs. Hale, but to look critically at the version he himself gives us. Indeed, he seems to recognize the tentativeness of his own rendition of the tale. As he was about to drop the first-person narration and go back twenty years to the events leading up to the crash, he has told us, remember, that this is only his "vision of the story," a vision based on "the clue to Ethan Frome" that he discovered that night he spent with the three main protagonists. But he says "clue," not "evidence," not the story as told to him by Ethan.

Not only what he sees or tells, but the way he tells it is also the narrator's, for what follows is not "the whole" or "true" story, the unmediated events offered in "natural"—that is, strictly chronological—order. It is a narrative structured or manipulated by the narrator to best embody what he has called his "vision." In the very first chapter, for example, we stand with Ethan outside the church where a dance is in progress and learn by exposition and flashback of his education and its interruption, of Mattie's first arrival, Zeena's growing jealousy, and other prior details. The hand of the narrator in the presentation of events, though not obtrusive, is clear enough if we watch for it.

If we watch the narrative strategy carefully, there are also some questions we might have about the narrator's "authority." He tells us that Ethan "had always been more sensitive than the people about him to the appeal of natural beauty"; the sensitivity may be confirmed by Mattie's having had the same sense of wonder, but how do we know, how does the narrator know, for that matter, that she did indeed have such sensitivity? Even if she did or does, how do we know that this kind of sensitivity is not common to many, most, perhaps all young people in love, even in Starkfield, so that it is not so much rare among those New Englanders but almost always confined to those who are in love? May this not also be an expression of Ethan's pride—for clearly the narrator's source, if he has one, must be Ethan himself—or of his sense of alienation from others in Starkfield? Perhaps, however, Ethan is not the source, and this is only the projection of the narrator, his vision of how it must have been.

And are there not some questions of tone? Again, no doubt on what is supposed to appear to be Ethan's authority, we are told that Mattie "said to him once: 'It [the scene] looks just as if it was painted!' " and that "it seemed to Ethan that the art of definition could go no farther, and that words had at last been found to utter his secret soul . . ." What are we to think of Mattie's expression and of Ethan's judgment of it? Are we to understand that it is the intensity of his love that makes him blind—or, rather, deaf—to the banality of the remark? Or does the narrator look down and want or expect us to look down from the heights of our literary and worldly sophistication with pity on these passionate but limited souls who can rudely feel but hardly express their feelings? Perhaps only an English teacher would hesitate over Mattie's use of the indicative "was" where the subjunctive "were" would be more appropriate, but surely the narrator must be distanced from the naiveté of Ethan's response. Or are we to distance ourselves from the narrator himself and see a certain amount of snobbery or condescension in him even as he tries to sympathize with these hardy but suffering provincial folk?

In our officially democratic society it is not acceptable to speak publically of the sophisticated people and the simple people (unless it is to denigrate sophistication), and it is not good public manners to say of someone, as the narrator does of Harmon Gow, that he "developed the tale as far as his mental and moral reach permitted," but that "there were perceptible gaps between his facts, and I had a sense that the deeper meaning of the story was in the gaps." It may be this unabashed frankness in making distinctions that tempts us to search out the story for traces of condescension or snobbery. Mattie's description of the scene is banal, but it is only her alleged description and not necessarily her response that is being judged, and the story is profoundly compassionate toward and profoundly frustrated by the characters' inability to express their very real and very deep feelings. They come up only with common-places—or nothing at all. Often, indeed, the narrator seems to be supplying the words that the characters cannot supply themselves, and these passages are among the most moving in the story, beyond the reach of the protagonists' language but not foreign to their feelings and experience.

In chapter 2, for example, Mattie expresses her fear that Ethan may want her to leave his house, and he realizes how much she wants to stay:

> Unless he wanted her to go too! The cry was balm to his raw wound. The iron heavens seemed to melt and rain down sweetness. Again he struggled for the all-expressive word, and again, his arm in hers, found only a deep "Come along."

Mattie and Ethan are trapped in the narrow confines of their language as they are in the stark, confining landscape. They are so restricted by their environment that they seem almost to be part of it, and it is in this identification of the human and inhuman that the narrator's language again approaches the agonizingly poetic. Early on he describes Ethan sitting in the sleigh in the snow as if he were

> a part of the mute melancholy landscape, an incarnation of its frozen woe, with all that was warm and sentient in him fast bound below the surface; but there was nothing unfriendly in his silence. . . . I had the sense that his loneliness was not merely the result of his personal plight, tragic as I guessed that to be, but had in it, as Harmon Gow had hinted, the profound accumulated cold of many Starkfield winters.

When the narrator sees that the "L"—which, on a New England farm usually links farmhouse to barns, toolsheds, etc., and links the house to the life of the soil—has been taken down on the Frome farm, he sees "in the diminished dwelling the image of his [Ethan's] own shrunken body." The narrator is clearly sympathetic toward Ethan, is agonized, as we are, by his multiple entrapment—by marriage, custom, poverty, environment, inarticulateness—and he seems to want to express for him the beauty he saw, the love he felt, the frustration he endured, all that Ethan could not express for himself, and thereby to make his life, his tragedy, "count," to ennoble him and make his suffering meaningful. A nagging question may remain, however, whether he is telling the story of Ethan for Ethan's sake or for his own, not merely to ennoble the victim but to denounce the trap, not of language, for the narrator is in control of language. What trap, then: the New England winter, small town morality, marriage bonds?

The narrator's sense of the oneness of the land and its inhabitants he shares with Edith Wharton herself. She tells us that *Ethan Frome* originated from and may for some be justified by her feeling that "the outcropping granite" of New England, the harshness that goes with its beauty, had been omitted from previous fiction set in that region, and that the protagonists of the novel are "in truth, these figures, my *granite outcroppings; but half-merged from the soil, and scarcely more articulate."

But why, then, does the narrator need a "clue" to understand Ethan Frome? What do we learn beyond Gow's contention (which the narrator to some degree confirms), that Frome spent too many winters in Starkfield and Mrs. Hale's contention that Ethan and the rest of his household are not much different from "the Fromes down in the graveyard; 'cept that down there they're all quiet, and the women have got to hold their tongues"?

We seem to be back to the powerful irony of the ending. Why is it so powerful, and what does it mean to us? It is powerful largely, perhaps, because of the over-whelming feeling of entrapment that the story communicates—or creates. Ethan and Mattie are entrapped by his marriage; the straitened economic circumstances that don't even allow them the opportunity to buy a train ticket out of town much less the opportunity to support themselves should they run off together; the equally con-fining traditional society with the façade—or perhaps the actuality—of passionless-ness or of passions so repressed as to seem not to exist; the limited sense of space or variety made even worse by the severe winter weather, the limited experience of other worlds, lives, possibilities; and the entrapment of their souls inside themselves, without the ability to make their thoughts and feelings known to each other. The only way out they can imagine is death, and even that escapes them; they seem to give new and tragic meaning to the expression "a fate worse than death."

But why is the story called *Ethan Frome* and not *Mattie and Ethan* or *Starkfield* or *Granite Outcroppings*, or some such descriptive or poetic title? After all, Mattie is more severely injured than Ethan, if it comes to that. Why is the tragedy primarily Ethan's? Why is he compared to "the bronzed image of a hero" and why is it only the "key" to Ethan's character and to his look of tragic pain that the narrator leads us to seek out?

Mattie has of course "become" Zeena; hers is the querulous drone we hear as we are about to step into Ethan's house with the narrator. She has been, according to the narrator's "vision" of the story, in Zeena's "place" before: on the night that Zenobia is away Mattie stands in the doorway as Zeena had done the night before and the contrast between the aging, soured face of the one and the youthful, lively, desirable face of the other makes Ethan's plight poignant, and his marriage bonds almost unbearable, even for the reader. When, later that evening, Mattie sits in Zeena's rocking chair she seems to be taken over by the spirit of the older woman (prophet-ically, it turns out, though neither they nor we know it at the time); she feels it, and has to move. Now, at the end of the story, she has, ironically, taken over Zenobia's place—what both she and Ethan had wished for—but the gods play tricks on us, and just as Tithonus in wishing for immortality forgot to ask for eternal youth, so Mattie and Ethan got their wish in a way they did not anticipate and could not desire.

That, at least, is the story the narrator has so artfully structured in beautifully ren-dered language.

What, then, does the story "mean"? Are Ethan and Mattie being punished for the sin of "adultery in their hearts"? Is the story an attack, as *Jane Eyre* was said by some to be, on the unqualified assumption of the sacredness of marriage? Can the novel be, as Edith Wharton seemed to suggest in her "Introduction," primarily "intertex-tual," an antidote to earlier fiction that makes life in the small towns and rural areas of New England among the moral, simple, straight-talking Yankees seem idyllic, the epitome of the "American way"? Is it, as words like "hero" and "tragedy" suggest, "an American tragedy" (as one of Wharton's contemporaries, Theodore Dreiser, would call one of his novels), a tragedy with the ironic overtones and sense of fatality of its Greek predecessors? All of the above? None of the above? Wharton, if we can assume it is Wharton, through the narrator, tells us that Ethan's studies "made him aware of huge cloudy meanings behind the daily face of things," and her novel surely suggests such meanings.

FRANZ KAFKA

The Metamorphosis

His father a butcher, Hermann Kafka worked his way up from peddlar to owner of a wholesale women's-wear company. The story of the life and work of his only son, Franz (born on July 3, 1883, in Prague, then part of the Austro-Hungarian Empire), begins and in a sense virtually ends with the Father. This overbearing, powerful, aggressive, worldly man terrified his rather sickly intellectual son, so that even at thirty-six years of age the "boy" was writing a long, long letter (never delivered) to his father explaining why he was afraid of him, and the son's strange fiction is dominated by a powerful father-figure—father of the family, of the political state, or Father of the Universe. This fear, and guilt at the fear and lack of love, this smouldering rebellion and sense of both helplessness and unworthiness, whatever its cause, and however we read it—psychologically, politically, religiously—seems to speak to our experience of the modern world, to reflect how we sometimes see ourselves. Many other writers have reflected this aspect of the modern world, but Kafka, perhaps because his works both contain, yet are not reducible to, any of the interpretive modes or systems, seems to stand as *the* symbol—the irreducible embodiment—of that vision.

Franz Kafka, whatever his inner fears, was not an insect or an ineffectual angel, however. He earned a doctorate in law from Karl-Ferdinand University in Prague, entered the Austrian civil service, rising in the government's Workers' Accident Insurance Company in fourteen years as far as his training would permit, to the post of senior secretary. No doubt in opposition to his father's secularism and identification with the dominant German culture, Franz studied Judaism, Hebrew, and Czech. Though he never married, he was often enough engaged—three times between 1912 and 1917 to Felice Bauer of Belin, for example; he had an equally inconclusive relationship with another Jewish girl, Julie Wohryzek, from 1918 to 1920, a stormy love affair with a married Czech woman, Melenia Jesenska, who was translating part of his unfinished novel *Amerika*, and, toward the very end of his life, he lived with a very young Hasidic girl, Dora Dymant, whom he had met in a tuberculosis sanitorium and who nursed him through his last illness.

Though his full-length novels, *The Trial, The Castle,* and *Amerika* (published in 1925, 1926, and 1927, respectively), which he had been working on during the last decade of his life, were all left incomplete and had to be pieced together posthumously by his best friend and literary executor Max Brod (who had been ordered by Kafka to burn his work but didn't), Kafka had published *The Metamorphosis* in 1915, a volume of short stories called *The Country Doctor* the following year, a longish story (about 12,500 words), "In the Penal Colony," published as a separate work in 1919, and had fully prepared for publication before his death a second volume of short stories, *A Hunger Artist* (1924).

The fragmentary novels and the fragmentary love affairs were no doubt indicative of a deep psychological disturbance evident in his work, but Franz Kafka died on his forty-first birthday, had a law degree, a full-time job from the age of twenty-five, poor health throughout his life and was known to have tuberculosis as early as 1917, so his published work, though far from voluminous, was not negligible in quantity, and is certainly monumental in quality.

The Metamorphosis*

A S GREGOR SAMSA awoke one morning from uneasy dreams he found himself transformed in his bed into a gigantic insect. He was lying on his hard, as it were armor-plated, back and when he lifted his head a little he could see his dome-like brown belly divided into stiff arched segments on top of which the bed quilt could hardly keep in position and was about to slide off completely. His numerous legs, which were pitifully thin compared to the rest of his bulk, waved helplessly before his eyes.

What has happened to me? he thought. It was no dream. His room, a regular human bedroom, only rather too small, lay quiet between the four familiar walls. Above the table on which a collection of cloth samples was unpacked and spread out—Samsa was a commercial traveler—hung the picture which he had recently cut out of an illustrated magazine and put into a pretty gilt frame. It showed a lady, with a fur cap on and a fur stole, sitting upright and holding out to the spectator a huge fur muff into which the whole of her forearm had vanished!

Gregor's eyes turned next to the window, and the overcast sky—one could hear rain drops beating on the window gutter—made him quite melancholy. What about sleeping a little longer and forgetting all this nonsense, he thought, but it could not be done, for he was accustomed to sleep on his right side and in his present condition he could not turn himself over. However violently he forced himself towards his right side he always rolled on to his back again. He tried it at least a hundred times, shutting his eyes to keep from seeing his struggling legs, and only desisted when he began to feel in his side a faint dull ache he had never experienced before.

Oh God, he thought, what an exhausting job I've picked on! Traveling about day in, day out. It's much more irritating work than doing the actual business in the office, and on top of that there's the trouble of constant traveling, of worrying about train connections, the bed and irregular meals, casual acquaintances that are always new and never become intimate friends. The devil take it all! He felt a slight itching up on his belly; slowly pushed himself on his back near to the top of the bed so that he could lift his his head more easily; identified the itching place which was surrounded by many small white spots the nature of which he could not understand and made to touch it with a leg, but drew the leg back immediately, for the contact made a cold shiver run through him.

He slid down again into his former position. This getting up early, he thought, makes one quite stupid. A man needs his sleep. Other commercials live like harem women. For instance, when I come back to the hotel of a morning to write up the orders I've got, these others are only sitting down to breakfast. Let me just try that with my chief; I'd be sacked on the spot. Anyhow, that might be quite a good thing for me, who can tell? If I didn't have to hold my hand because of my parents I'd have given notice long ago, I'd have gone to the chief and told him exactly what I

* Translated by Willa and Edwin Muir.

think of him. That would knock him endways from his desk! It's a queer way of doing, too, this sitting on high at a desk and talking down to employees, especially when they have to come quite near because the chief is hard of hearing. Well, there's still hope; once I've saved enough money to pay back my parents' debts to him—that should take another five or six years—I'll do it without fail. I'll cut myself completely loose then. For the moment, though, I'd better get up, since my train goes at five.

He looked at the alarm clock ticking on the chest. Heavenly Father! he thought. It was half-past six o'clock and the hands were quickly moving on, it was even past the half-hour, it was getting on toward a quarter to seven. Had the alarm clock not gone off? From the bed one could see that it had been properly set for four o'clock; of course it must have gone off. Yes, but was it possible to sleep quietly through that ear-splitting noise? Well, he had not slept quietly, yet apparently all the more soundly for that. But what was he to do now? The next train went at seven o'clock; to catch that he would need to hurry like mad and his samples weren't even packed up, and he himself wasn't feeling particularly fresh and active. And even if he did catch the train he wouldn't avoid a row with the chief, since the firm's porter would have been waiting for the five o'clock train and would have long since reported his failure to turn up. The porter was a creature of the chief's, spineless and stupid. Well, supposing he were to say he was sick? But that would be most unpleasant and would look suspicious, since during his five years' employment he had not been ill once. The chief himself would be sure to come with the sick-insurance doctor, and reproach his parents with their son's laziness and would cut all excuses short by referring to the insurance doctor, who of course regarded all mankind as perfectly healthy malingerers. And would he be so far wrong on this occasion? Gregor really felt quite well, apart from a drowsiness that was utterly superfluous after such a long sleep, and he was even unusually hungry.

As all this was running through his mind at top speed without his being able to decide to leave his bed—the alarm clock had just struck a quarter to seven—there came a cautious tap at the door behind the head of his bed. "Gregor," said a voice—it was his mother's—"it's a quarter to seven. Hadn't you a train to catch?" That gentle voice! Gregor had a shock as he heard his own voice answering hers, unmistakably his own voice, it was true, but with a persistent horrible twittering squeak behind it like an undertone, that left the words in their clear shape only for the first moment and then rose up reverberating around them to destroy their sense, so that one could not be sure one had heard them rightly. Gregor wanted to answer at length and explain everything, but in the circumstances he confined himself to saying: "Yes, yes, thank you, Mother, I'm getting up now." The wooden door between them must have kept the change in his voice from being noticeable outside, for his mother contented herself with this statement and shuffled away. Yet this brief exchange of words had made the other members of the family aware that Gregor was still in the house, as they had not expected, and at one of the side doors his father was already knocking, gently, yet with his fist. "Gregor, Gregor," he called, "what's the matter with you?" And after a little while he called again in a deeper voice: "Gregor! Gregor!" At the other side door his sister was saying in a low, plaintive tone: "Gregor? Aren't you well? Are you needing anything?" He answered them both at once: "I'm just ready," and did his best to make his voice sound as normal as possible by enunciating the words very clearly and leaving long pauses between them. So his father went back to his breakfast, but his sister whispered: "Gregor, open the door, do." However, he was not thinking of opening the door, and felt thankful for the prudent habit he had acquired in traveling of locking all doors during the night, even at home.

His immediate intention was to get up quietly without being disturbed, to put on his clothes and above all eat his breakfast, and only then to consider what else was to be done, since in bed, he was well aware, his meditations would come to no sensible conclusion. He remembered that often enough in bed he had felt small aches and pains, probably caused by awkward postures, which had proved purely imaginary once he got up, and he looked forward eagerly to seeing this morning's delusions gradually fall away. That the change in his voice was nothing but the precursor of a severe chill, a standing ailment of commercial travelers, he had not the least possible doubt.

To get rid of the quilt was quite easy; he had only to inflate himself a little and it fell off by itself. But the next move was difficult, especially because he was so uncommonly broad. He would have needed arms and hands to hoist himself up; instead he had only the numerous little legs which never stopped waving in all directions and which he could not control in the least. When he tried to bend one of them it was the first to stretch itself straight; and did he succeed at last in making it do what he wanted, all the other legs meanwhile waved the more wildly in a high degree of unpleasant agitation. "But what's the use of lying idle in bed," said Gregor to himself.

He thought that he might get out of bed with the lower part of his body first, but this lower part, which he had not yet seen and of which he could form no clear conception, proved too difficult to move; it shifted so slowly; and when finally, almost wild with annoyance, he gathered his forces together and thrust out recklessly, he had miscalculated the direction and bumped heavily against the lower end of the bed, and the stinging pain he felt informed him that precisely this lower part of his body was at the moment probably the most sensitive.

So he tried to get the top part of himself out first, and cautiously moved his head towards the edge of the bed. That proved easy enough, and despite its breadth and mass the bulk of his body at last slowly followed the movement of his head. Still, when he finally got his head free over the edge of the bed he felt too scared to go on advancing, for after all if he let himself fall in this way it would take a miracle to keep his head from being injured. And at all costs he must not lose consciousness now, precisely now; he would rather stay in bed.

But when after a repetition of the same efforts he lay in his former position again, sighing, and watched his little legs struggling against each other more wildly than ever, if that were possible, and saw no way of bringing any order into this arbitrary confusion, he told himself again that it was impossible to stay in bed and that the most sensible course was to risk everything for the smallest hope of getting away from it. At the same time he did not forget meanwhile to remind himself that cool reflection, the coolest possible, was much better than desperate resolves. In such moments he focused his eyes as sharply as possible on the window, but, unfortunately, the prospect of the morning fog, which muffled even the other side of the narrow street, brought him little encouragement and comfort. "Seven o'clock already," he said to himself when the alarm clock chimed again, "seven o'clock already and still such a thick fog." And for a little while he lay quiet, breathing lightly, as if perhaps expecting such complete repose to restore all things to their real and normal condition. But then he said to himself: "Before it strikes a quarter past seven I must be quite out of this bed, without fail. Anyhow, by that time someone will have come from the office to ask for me, since it opens before seven." And he set himself to rocking his whole body at once in a regular rhythm, with the idea of swinging it out of the bed. If he tipped himself out in that way he could keep his head from injury by lifting it at an acute angle when he fell. His back seemed to be hard and was not likely to suffer from a fall on the carpet. His biggest worry was the loud crash he would not be able to help making, which would probably cause anxiety, if not terror, behind all the doors. Still, he must take the risk.

When he was already half out of the bed—the new method was more a game than an effort, for he needed only to hitch himself across by rocking to and fro—it struck him how simple it would be if he could get help. Two strong people—he thought of his father and the servant girl—would be amply sufficient; they would only have to thrust their arms under his convex back, lever him out of the bed, bend down with their burden and then be patient enough to let him turn himself right over on the floor, where it was to be hoped his legs would then find their proper function. Well, ignoring the fact that the doors were all locked, ought he really to call for help? In spite of his misery he could not suppress a smile at the very idea of it.

He had got so far that he could barely keep his equilibrium when he rocked himself strongly, and he would have to nerve himself very soon for the final decision since in five minutes' time it would be a quarter past seven—when the front door bell rang. "That's someone from the office," he said to himself, and grew almost rigid, while his little legs only jigged about all the faster. For a moment everything stayed quiet. "They're not going to open the door," said Gregor to himself, catching at some kind of irrational hope. But then of course the servant girl went as usual to the door with her heavy tread and opened it. Gregor needed only to hear the first good morning of the visitor to know immediately who it was—the chief clerk himself. What a fate, to be condemned to work for a firm where the smallest omission at once gave rise to the gravest suspicion! Were all employees in a body nothing but scoundrels, was there not among them one single loyal devoted man who, had he wasted only an hour or so of the firm's time in a morning, was so tormented by conscience as to be driven out of his mind and actually incapable of leaving his bed? Wouldn't it really have been sufficient to send an apprentice to inquire—if any inquiry were necessary at all—did the chief clerk himself have to come and thus indicate to the entire family, an innocent family, that this suspicious circumstance could be investigated by no one less versed in affairs than himself? And more through the agitation caused by these reflections than through any act of will Gregor swung himself out of bed with all his strength. There was a loud thump, but it was not really a crash. His fall was broken to some extent by the carpet, his back, too, was less stiff than he thought, and so there was merely a dull thud, not so very startling. Only he had not lifted his head carefully enough and had hit it; he turned it and rubbed it on the carpet in pain and irritation.

"That was something falling down in there," said the chief clerk in the next room to the left. Gregor tried to suppose to himself that something like what had happened to him today might some day happen to the chief clerk; one really could not deny that it was possible. But as if in brusque reply to this supposition the chief clerk took a couple of firm steps in the next-door room and his patent leather boots creaked. From the right-hand room his sister was whispering to inform him of the situation: "Gregor, the chief clerk's here." "I know," muttered Gregor to himself; but he didn't dare to make his voice loud enough for his sister to hear it.

"Gregor," said his father now from the left-hand room, "the chief clerk has come and wants to know why you didn't catch the early train. We don't know what to say to him. Besides, he wants to talk to you in person. So open the door, please. He will be good enough to excuse the untidiness of your room." "Good morning. Mr. Samsa," the chief clerk was calling amiably meanwhile. "He's not well," said his mother to the visitor, while his father was still speaking through the door, "he's not well, sir, believe me. What else would make him miss a train! The boy thinks about nothing but his work. It makes me almost cross the way he never goes out in the evenings; he's been here the last eight days and has stayed at home every single evening. He just sits there quietly at the table reading a newspaper or looking through railway timetables. The only amusement he gets is doing fretwork. For instance, he spent two or three evenings cutting out a little picture frame; you would be surprised to see how pretty it is; it's hanging in his room; you'll see it in a minute when Gregor opens the door. I must say I'm glad you've come, sir; we should never have got him to unlock the door by ourselves; he's so obstinate; and I'm sure he's unwell, though he wouldn't have it to be so this morning." "I'm just coming," said Gregor slowly and carefully, not moving an inch for fear of losing one word of the conversation. "I can't think of any other explanation, madam," said the chief clerk, "I hope it's nothing serious. Although on the other hand I must say that we men of business—fortunately or unfortunately—very often simply have to ignore any slight indisposition, since business must be attended to." "Well, can the chief clerk come in now?" asked Gregor's father impatiently, again knocking on the door. "No," said Gregor. In the left-hand room a painful silence followed this refusal, in the right-hand room his sister began to sob.

Why didn't his sister join the others? She was probably newly out of bed and hadn't even begun to put on her clothes yet. Well, why was she crying? Because he wouldn't get up and let the chief clerk in, because he was in danger of losing his job, and because the chief would begin dunning his parents again for the old debts? Surely these were things one didn't need to worry about for the present. Gregor was still at home and not in the least thinking of deserting the family. At the moment, true, he was lying on the carpet and no one who knew the condition he was in could seriously expect him to admit the chief clerk. But for such a small discourtesy, which could plausibly be explained away somehow later on, Gregor could hardly be dismissed on the spot. And it seemed to Gregor that it would be much more sensible to leave him in peace for the present than to trouble him with tears and entreaties. Still, of course, their uncertainty bewildered them all and excused their behavior.

"Mr. Samsa," the chief clerk called now in a louder voice, "what's the matter with you? Here you are, barricading yourself in your room, giving only 'yes' and 'no' for answers, causing your parents a lot of unnecessary trouble and neglecting—I mention this only in passing—neglecting your business duties in an incredible fashion. I am speaking here in the name of your parents and of your chief, and I beg you quite seriously to give me an immediate and precise explanation. You amaze me, you amaze me. I thought you were a quiet, dependable person, and now all at once you seem bent on making a disgraceful exhibition of yourself. The chief did hint to me early this morning a possible explanation for your disappearance—with reference to the cash payments that were entrusted to you recently—but I almost pledged my solemn word of honor that this could not be so. But now that I see how incredibly obstinate you are, I no longer have the slightest desire to take your part at all. And your position in the firm is not so unassailable. I came with the intention of telling you all this in private, but since you are wasting my time so needlessly I don't see why your parents shouldn't hear it too. For some time past your work has been most unsatisfactory; this is not the season of the year for a business boom, of course, we admit that, but a season of the year for doing no business at all, that does not exist, Mr. Samsa, must not exist."

"But, sir," cried Gregor, beside himself and in his agitation forgetting everything else, "I'm just going to open the door this very minute. A slight illness, an attack of giddiness, has kept me from getting up. I'm still lying in bed. But I feel all right again. I'm getting out of bed now. Just give me a moment or two longer! I'm not quite so well as I thought. But I'm all right, really. How a thing like that can suddenly strike one down! Only last night I was quite well, my parents can tell you, or rather I did have a slight presentiment. I must have showed some sign of it. Why didn't I report it at the office! But one always thinks that an indisposition can be got over without staying in the house. Oh sir, do spare my parents! All that you're reproaching me with now has no foundation; no one has ever said a word to me about it. Perhaps you haven't looked at the last orders I sent in. Anyhow, I can still catch the eight o'clock train, I'm much the better for my few hours' rest. Don't let me detain you here, sir; I'll be attending to business very soon, and do be good enough to tell the chief so and to make my excuses to him!"

And while all this was tumbling out pell-mell and Gregor hardly knew what he was saying, he had reached the chest quite easily, perhaps because of the practice he had had in bed, and was now trying to lever himself upright by means of it. He meant actually to open the door, actually to show himself and speak to the chief clerk; he was eager to find out what the others, after all their insistence, would say at the sight of him. If they were horrified then the responsibility was no longer his and he could stay quiet. But if they took it calmly, then he had no reason either to be upset, and could really get to the station for the eight o'clock train if he hurried. At first he slipped down a few times from the polished surface of the chest, but at length with a last heave he stood upright; he paid no more attention to the pains in the lower part of his body, however they smarted. Then he let himself fall against the back of a near-by chair, and clung with his little legs to the edges of it. That brought him into control of himself again and he stopped speaking, for now he could listen to what the chief clerk was saying.

"Did you understand a word of it?" the chief clerk was asking; "surely he can't be trying to make fools of us?" "Oh dear," cried his mother, in tears, "perhaps he's terribly ill and we're tormenting him. Grete! Grete!" she called out then. "Yes Mother?" called his sister from the other side. They were calling to each other across Gregor's room. "You must go this minute for the doctor, quick. Did you hear how he was speaking?" "That was no human voice," said the chief clerk in a voice noticeably low beside the shrillness of the mother's. "Anna! Anna!" his father was calling through the hall to the kitchen, clapping his hands, "get a locksmith at once!" And the two girls were already running through the hall with a swish of skirts—how could his sister have got dressed so quickly?—and were tearing the front door open. There was no sound of its closing again; they had evidently left it open, as one does in houses where some great misfortune has happened.

But Gregor was now much calmer. The words he uttered were no longer understandable, apparently, although they seemed clear enough to him, even clearer than before, perhaps because his ear had grown accustomed to the sound of them. Yet at any rate people now believed that something was wrong with him, and were ready to help him. The positive certainty with which these first measures had been taken comforted him. He felt himself drawn once more into the human circle and hoped for great and remarkable results from both the doctor and the locksmith, without really distinguishing precisely between them. To make his voice as clear as possible for the decisive conversation that was now imminent he coughed a little, as quietly as he could, of course, since this noise too might not sound like a human cough for all he was able to judge. In the next room meanwhile there was complete silence. Perhaps his parents were sitting at the table with the chief clerk, whispering, perhaps they were all leaning against the door and listening.

Slowly Gregor pushed the chair towards the door, then let go of it, caught hold of the door for support—the soles at the end of his little legs were somewhat sticky—and rested against it for a moment after his efforts. Then he set himself to turning the key in the lock with his mouth. It seemed, unhappily, that he hadn't really any teeth—what could he grip the key with?—but on the other hand his jaws were certainly very strong; with their help he did manage to set the key in motion, heedless of the fact that he was undoubtedly damaging them somewhere, since a brown fluid issued from his mouth, flowed over the key and dripped on the floor. "Just listen to that," said the chief clerk next door; "he's turning the key." That was a great encouragement to Gregor; but they should all have shouted encouragement to him, his father and mother too: "Go on, Gregor," they should have called out, "keep going, hold on to that key!" And in the belief that they were all following his efforts intently, he clenched his jaws recklessly on the key with all the force at his command. As the turning of the key progressed he circled round the lock, holding on now only with his mouth, pushing on the key, as required, or pulling it down again with all the weight of his body. The louder click of the finally yielding lock literally quickened Gregor. With a deep breath of relief he said to himself: "So I didn't need the locksmith," and laid his head on the handle to open the door wide.

Since he had to pull the door towards him, he was still invisible when it was really wide open. He had to edge himself slowly round the near half of the double door, and to do it very carefully if he was not to fall plump upon his back just on the threshold. He was still carrying out this difficult manoeuvre, with no time to observe anything else, when he heard the chief clerk utter a loud "Oh!"—it sounded like a gust of wind—and now he could see the man, standing as he was nearest to the door, clapping one hand before his open mouth and slowly backing away as if driven by some invisible steady pressure. His mother—in spite of the chief clerk's being there her hair was still undone and sticking up in all directions—first clasped her hands and looked at his father, then took two steps towards Gregor and fell on the floor among her outspread skirts, her face quite hidden on her breast. His father knotted his fist with a fierce expression on his face as if he meant to knock Gregor back into his room, then looked uncertainly round the living room, covered his eyes with his hands and wept till his great chest heaved.

Gregor did not go now into the living room, but leaned against the inside of the firmly shut wing of the door, so that only half his body was visible and his head above it bending sideways to look at the others. The light had meanwhile strengthened; on the other side of the street one could see clearly a section of the endlessly long, dark gray building opposite—it was a hospital—abruptly punctuated by its row of regular windows; the rain was still falling, but only in large singly discernible and literally singly splashing drops. The breakfast dishes were set out on the table lavishly, for breakfast was the most important meal of the day to Gregor's father, who lingered it out for hours over various newspapers. Right opposite Gregor on the wall hung a photograph of himself on military service, as a lieutenant, hand on sword, a carefree smile on his face, inviting one to respect his uniform and military bearing. The door leading to the hall was open, and one could see that the front door stood open too, showing the landing beyond and the beginning of the stairs going down.

"Well," said Gregor, knowing perfectly that he was the only one who had retained any composure, "I'll put my clothes on at once, pack up my samples and start off. Will you only let me go? You see, sir, I'm not obstinate, and I'm willing to work; traveling is a hard life, but I couldn't live without it. Where are you going, sir? To the office? Yes? Will you give a true account of all this? One can be temporarily incapacitated, but that's just the moment for remembering former services and bearing in mind that later on, when the incapacity has been got over, one will certainly work with all the more industry and concentration. I'm loyally bound to serve the chief, you know that very well. Besides, I have to provide for my parents and my sister. I'm in great difficulties, but I'll get out of them again. Don't make things any worse for me than they are. Stand up for me in the firm. Travelers are not popular there, I know. People think they earn sacks of money and just have a good time. A prejudice there's no particular reason for revising. But you, sir, have a more comprehensive view of affairs than the rest of the staff, yes, let me tell you in confidence, a more comprehensive view than the chief himself, who, being the owner, lets his judgment easily be swayed against one of his employees. And you know very well that the traveler, who is never seen in the office almost the whole year round, can so easily fall a victim to gossip and ill luck and unfounded complaints, which he mostly knows nothing about, except when he comes back exhausted from his rounds, and only then suffers in person from their evil consequences, which he can no longer trace back to the original causes. Sir, sir, don't go away without a word to me to show that you think me in the right at least to some extent!"

But at Gregor's very first words the chief clerk had already backed away and only stared at him with parted lips over one twitching shoulder. And while Gregor was speaking he did not stand still one moment but stole away towards the door, without taking his eyes off Gregor, yet only an inch at a time, as if obeying some secret injunction to leave the room. He was already at the hall, and the suddenness with which he took his last step out of the living room would have made one believe he had burned the sole of his foot. Once in the hall he stretched his right arm before him towards the staircase, as if some supernatural power were waiting there to deliver him.

Gregor perceived that the chief clerk must on no account be allowed to go away in this frame of mind if his position in the firm were not to be endangered to the utmost. His parents did not understand this so well; they had convinced themselves in the course of years that Gregor was settled for life in this firm, and besides they were so preoccupied with their immediate troubles that all foresight had forsaken them. Yet Gregor had this foresight. The chief clerk must be detained, soothed, persuaded and finally won over; the whole future of Gregor and his family depended on it! If only his sister had been there! She was intelligent; she had begun to cry while Gregor was still lying quietly on his back. And no doubt the chief clerk, so partial to ladies, would have been guided by her; she would have shut the door of the flat and in the hall talked him out of his horror. But she was not there, and Gregor would have to handle the situation himself. And without remembering that he was still unaware what powers of movement he possessed, without even remembering that his words in all possibility, indeed in all likelihood, would again be unintelligible, he let go the wing of the door, pushed himself through the opening, started to walk towards the chief clerk, who was already ridiculously clinging with both hands to the railing on the landing; but immediately, as he was feeling for a support, he fell down with a little cry upon all his numerous legs. Hardly was he down when he experienced for the first time this morning a sense of physical comfort; his legs had firm ground under them; they were completely obedient, as he noted with joy; they even strove to carry him forward in whatever direction he chose; and he was inclined to believe that a final relief from all his sufferings was at hand. But in the same moment as he found himself on the floor, rocking with suppressed eagerness to move, not far from his mother, indeed just in front of her, she, who had seemed so completely crushed, sprang all at once to her feet, her arms and fingers outspread, cried: "Help, for God's sake, help!" bent her head down as if to see Gregor better, yet on the contrary kept backing senselessly away; had quite forgotten that the laden table stood behind her; sat upon it hastily, as if in absence of mind, when she bumped into it; and seemed altogether unaware that the big coffee pot beside her was upset and pouring coffee in a flood over the carpet.

"Mother, Mother," said Gregor in a low voice, and looked up at her. The chief clerk, for the moment, had quite slipped from his mind; instead, he could not resist snapping his jaws together at the sight of the streaming coffee. That made his mother scream again, she fled from the table and fell into the arms of his father, who hastened to catch her. But

Gregor had now no time to spare for his parents; the chief clerk was already on the stairs; with his chin on the banisters he was taking one last backward look. Gregor made a spring, to be as sure as possible of overtaking him; the chief clerk must have divined his intention, for he leaped down several steps and vanished; he was still yelling "Ugh!" and it echoed through the whole staircase.

Unfortunately, the flight of the chief clerk seemed completely to upset Gregor's father, who had remained relatively calm until now, for instead of running after the man himself, or at least not hindering Gregor in his pursuit, he seized in his right hand the walking stick which the chief clerk had left behind on a chair, together with a hat and greatcoat, snatched in his left hand a large newspaper from the table and began stamping his feet and flourishing the stick and the newspaper to drive Gregor back into his room. No entreaty of Gregor's availed, indeed no entreaty was even understood, however humbly he bent his head his father only stamped on the floor the more loudly. Behind his father his mother had torn open a window, despite the cold weather, and was leaning far out of it with her face in her hands. A strong draught set in from the street to the staircase, the window curtains blew in, the newspapers on the table fluttered, stray pages whisked over the floor. Pitilessly Gregor's father drove him back, hissing and crying "Shoo!" like a savage. But Gregor was quite unpracticed in walking backwards, it really was a slow business. If he only had a chance to turn round he could get back to his room at once, but he was afraid of exasperating his father by the slowness of such a rotation and at any moment the stick in his father's hand might hit him a fatal blow on the back or on the head. In the end, however, nothing else was left for him to do since to his horror he observed that in moving backwards he could not even control the direction he took; and so, keeping an anxious eye on his father all the time over his shoulder, he began to turn round as quickly as he could, which was in reality very slowly. Perhaps his father noted his good intentions, for he did not interfere except every now and then to help him in the manoeuvre from a distance with the point of the stick. If only he would have stopped making that unbearable hissing noise! It made Gregor quite lose his head. He had turned almost completely round when the hissing noise so distracted him that he even turned a little the wrong way again. But when at last his head was fortunately right in front of the doorway, it appeared that his body was too broad simply to get through the opening. His father, of course in his present mood was far from thinking of such a thing as opening the other half of the door, to let Gregor have enough space. He had merely the fixed idea of driving Gregor back into his room as quickly as possible. He would never have suffered Gregor to make the circumstantial preparations for standing up on end and perhaps slipping his way through the door. Maybe he was now making more noise than ever to urge Gregor forward, as if no obstacle impeded him; to Gregor, anyhow, the noise in his rear sounded no longer like the voice of one single father; this was really no joke, and Gregor thrust himself—come what might—into the doorway. One side of his body rose up, he was tilted at an angle in the doorway, his flank was quite bruised, horrid blotches stained the white door, soon he was stuck fast and, left to himself, could not have moved at all, his legs on one side fluttered trembling in the air, those on the other were crushed painfully to the floor—when from behind his father gave him a strong push which was literally a deliverance and he flew far into the room, bleeding freely. The door was slammed behind him with the stick, and then at last there was silence.

II

Not until it was twilight did Gregor awake out of a deep sleep, more like a swoon than a sleep. He would certainly have waked up of his own accord not much later, for he felt himself sufficiently rested and well-slept, but it seemed to him as if a fleeting step and a cautious shutting of the door leading into the hall had aroused him. The electric lights in the street cast a pale sheen here and there on the ceiling and the upper surfaces of the furniture, but down below, where he lay, it was dark. Slowly, awkwardly trying out his feelers, which he now first learned to appreciate, he pushed his way to the door to see what had been happening there. His left side felt like one single long, unpleasantly tense scar, and he had actually to limp on his two rows of legs. One little leg, moreover, had been severely damaged in the course of that morning's events—it was almost a miracle that only one had been damaged—and trailed uselessly behind him.

He had reached the door before he discovered what had really drawn him to it: the smell of food. For there stood a basin filled with fresh milk in which floated little sops of white bread. He could almost have laughed with joy, since he was now still hungrier than in the morning, and he dipped his head almost over the eyes straight into the milk. But soon in disappointment he withdrew it again; not only did he find it difficult to feed because of his tender left side—and he could only feed with the palpitating collaboration of his whole body—he did not like the milk either, although milk had been his favorite drink and that was certainly why his sister had set it there for him, indeed it was almost with repulsion that he turned away from the basin and crawled back to the middle of the room.

He could see through the crack of the door that the gas was turned on in the living room, but while usually at this time his father made a habit of reading the afternoon newspaper in a loud voice to his mother and occasionally to his sister as well, not a sound was now to be heard. Well, perhaps his father had recently given up this habit of reading aloud, which his sister had mentioned so often in conversation and in her letters. But there was the same silence all around, although the flat was certainly not empty of occupants. "What a quiet life our family has been leading," said Gregor to himself, and as he sat there motionless staring into the darkness he felt great pride in the fact that he had been able to provide such a life for his parents and sister in such a fine flat. But what if all the quiet, the comfort, the contentment were now to end in horror? To keep himself from being lost in such thoughts Gregor took refuge in movement and crawled up and down the room.

Once during the long evening one of the side doors was opened a little and quickly shut again, later the other side door too; someone had apparently wanted to come in and then thought better of it. Gregor now stationed himself immediately before the living room door, determined to persuade any hesitating visitor to come in or at least to discover who it might be; but the door was not opened again and he waited in vain. In the early morning, when the doors were locked, they had all wanted to come in, now that he had opened one door and the other had apparently been opened during the day, no one came in and even the keys were on the other side of the doors.

It was late at night before the gas went out in the living room, and Gregor could easily tell that his parents and his sister had all stayed awake until then, for he could clearly hear the three of them stealing away on tiptoe. No one was likely to visit him, not until the morning, that was certain; so he had plenty of time to meditate at his leisure on how he was to arrange his life afresh. But the lofty, empty room in which he had to lie flat on the floor filled him with an apprehension he could not account for, since it had been his very own room for the past five years—and with a half-unconscious action, not without a slight feeling of shame, he scuttled under the sofa, where he felt comfortable at once, although his back was a little cramped and he could not lift his head up, and his only regret was that his body was too broad to get the whole of it under the sofa.

He stayed there all night, spending the time partly in a light slumber, from which his hunger kept waking him up with a start, and partly in worrying and sketching vague hopes, which all led to the same conclusion, that he must lie low for the present and, by exercising patience and the utmost consideration, help the family to bear the inconvenience he was bound to cause them in his present condition.

Very early in the morning, it was still almost night, Gregor had the chance to test the strength of his new resolutions, for his sister, nearly fully dressed, opened the door from the hall and peered in. She did not see him at once, yet when she caught sight of him under the sofa—well, he had to be somewhere, he couldn't have flown away, could he?—she was so startled that without being able to help it she slammed the door shut again. But as if regretting her behavior she opened the door again immediately and came in on tiptoe, as if she were visiting an invalid or even a stranger. Gregor had pushed his head forward to the very edge of the sofa and watched her. Would she notice that he had left the milk standing, and not for lack of hunger, and would she bring in some other kind of food more to his taste? If she did not do it of her own accord, he would rather starve than draw her attention to the fact, although he felt a wild impulse to dart out from under the sofa, throw himself at her feet and beg her for something to eat. But his sister at once noticed, with surprise, that the basin was still full, except for a little milk that had been spilt all around it, she lifted it immediately, not with her bare hands, true, but with a cloth and carried it away. Gregor was wildly curious to know what she would bring instead, and made various speculations about it. Yet what she actually did next, in the goodness of her heart, he could never have guessed at. To find out what he liked she brought him a whole selection of food, all set on an old newspaper. There were old, half-decayed vegetables, bones from last night's supper covered with a white sauce that had thickened; some raisins and almonds; a piece of cheese that Gregor would have called uneatable two days ago; a dry roll of bread, a buttered roll, and a roll both buttered and salted. Besides all that, she set down again the same basin, into which she had poured some water, and which was apparently to be reserved for his exclusive use. And with fine tact, knowing that Gregor would not eat in her presence, she withdrew quickly and even turned the key, to let him understand that he could take his ease as much as he liked. Gregor's legs all whizzed towards the food. His wounds must have healed completely, moreover, for he felt no disability, which amazed him and made him reflect how more than a month ago he had cut one finger a little with a knife and had still suffered pain from the wound only the day before yesterday. Am I less sensitive now? he thought, and sucked greedily at the cheese, which above all the other edibles attracted him at once and strongly. One after another and with tears of satisfaction in his eyes he quickly devoured the cheese, the vegetables and the sauce; the fresh food, on the other hand, had no charms for him, he could not even stand the smell of it and actually dragged away to some little distance the things he could eat. He had long finished his meal and was only lying lazily on the same spot when his sister turned the key slowly as a sign for him to retreat. That roused him at once, although he was nearly asleep, and he hurried under the sofa again. But it took considerable self-control for him to stay under the sofa, even for the short time his sister was in the room, since the large meal had swollen his body somewhat and he was so cramped he could hardly breathe. Slight attacks of breathlessness afflicted him and his eyes were starting a little out of his head as he watched his unsuspecting sister sweeping together with a broom not only the remains of what he had eaten but even the things he had not touched, as if these were now of no use to anyone, and hastily shoveling it all into a bucket, which she covered with a wooden lid and carried away. Hardly had she turned her back when Gregor came from under the sofa and stretched and puffed himself out.

In this manner Gregor was fed, once in the early morning while his parents and the servant girl were still asleep, and a second time after they had all had their midday dinner, for then his parents took a short nap and the servant girl could be sent out on some errand or other by his sister. Not that they would have wanted him to starve, of course, but perhaps they could not have borne to know more about his feeding than from hearsay, perhaps too his sister wanted to spare them such little anxieties wherever possible, since they had quite enough to bear as it was.

Under what pretext the doctor and the locksmith had been got rid of on that first morning Gregor could not discover, for since what he said was not understood by the others it never struck any of them, not even his sister, that he could understand what they said, and so whenever his sister came into his room he had to content himself with hearing her utter only a sigh now and then and an occasional appeal to the saints. Later on, when she had got a little used to the situation—of course she could never get completely used to it—she sometimes threw out a remark which was kindly meant or could be so interpreted. "Well, he liked his dinner today," she would say when Gregor had made a good clearance of his food; and when he had not eaten, which gradually happened more and more often, she would say almost sadly: "Everything's been left standing again."

But although Gregor could get no news directly, he overheard a lot from the neighboring rooms, and as soon as voices were audible, he would run to the door of the room concerned and press his whole body against it. In the first few days especially there was no conversation that did not refer to him somehow, even if only indirectly. For two whole days there were family consultations at every mealtime about what should be done;

but also between meals the same subject was discussed, for there were always at least two members of the family at home, since no one wanted to be alone in the flat and to leave it quite empty was unthinkable. And on the very first of these days the household cook—it was not quite clear what and how much she knew of the situation—went down on her knees to his mother and begged leave to go, and when she departed, a quarter of an hour later, gave thanks for her dismissal with tears in her eyes as if for the greatest benefit that could have been conferred on her, and without any prompting swore a solemn oath that she would never say a single word to anyone about what had happened.

Now Gregor's sister had to cook too, helping her mother; true, the cooking did not amount to much, for they ate scarcely anything. Gregor was always hearing one of the family vainly urging another to eat and getting no answer but: "Thanks, I've had all I want," or something similar. Perhaps they drank nothing either. Time and again his sister kept asking his father if he wouldn't like some beer and offered kindly to go and fetch it herself, and when he made no answer suggested that she could ask the concierge to fetch it, so that he need feel no sense of obligation, but then a round "No" came from his father and no more was said about it.

In the course of that very first day Gregor's father explained the family's financial position and prospects to both his mother and his sister. Now and then he rose from the table to get some voucher or memorandum out of the small safe he had rescued from the collapse of his business five years earlier. One could hear him opening the complicated lock and rustling papers out and shutting it again. This statement made by his father was the first cheerful information Gregor had heard since his imprisonment. He had been of the opinion that nothing at all was left from his father's business, at least his father had never said anything to the contrary, and of course he had not asked him directly. At that time Gregor's sole desire was to do his utmost to help the family to forget as soon as possible the catastrophe which had overwhelmed the business and thrown them all into a state of complete despair. And so he had set to work with unusual ardor and almost overnight had become a commercial traveler instead of a little clerk, with of course much greater chances of earning money, and his success was immediately translated into good round coin which he could lay on the table for his amazed and happy family. These had been fine times, and they had never recurred, at least not with the same sense of glory, although later on Gregor had earned so much money that he was able to meet the expenses of the whole household and did so. They had simply got used to it, both the family and Gregor; the money was gratefully accepted and gladly given, but there was no special uprush of warm feeling. With his sister alone had he remained intimate, and it was a secret plan of his that she, who loved music, unlike himself, and could play movingly on the violin, should be sent next year to study at the Conservatorium, despite the great expense that would entail, which must be made up in some other way. During his brief visits home the Conservatorium was often mentioned in the talks he had with his sister, but always merely as a beautiful dream which could never come true, and his parents discouraged even these innocent references to it; yet Gregor had made up his mind firmly about it and meant to announce the fact with due solemnity on Christmas Day.

Such were the thoughts, completely futile in his present condition, that went through his head as he stood clinging upright to the door and listening. Sometimes out of sheer weariness he had to give up listening and let his head fall negligently against the door, but he always had to pull himself together again at once, for even the slight sound his head made was audible next door and brought all conversation to a stop. "What can he be doing now?" his father would say after a while, obviously turning towards the door, and only then would the interrupted conversation gradually be set going agian.

Gregor was now informed as amply as he could wish—for his father tended to repeat himself in his explanations, partly because it was a long time since he had handled such matters and partly because his mother could not always grasp things at once—that a certain amount of investments, a very small amount it was true, had survived the wreck of their fortunes and had even increased a little because the dividends had not been touched meanwhile. And besides that, the money Gregor brought home every month—he had kept only a few dollars for himself—had never been quite used up and now amounted to a small capital sum. Behind the door Gregor nodded his head eagerly, rejoiced at this evidence of unexpected thrift and foresight. True, he could really have paid off some more of his father's debts to the chief with this extra money, and so brought much nearer the day on which he could quit his job, but doubtless it was better the way his father had arranged it.

Yet this capital was by no means sufficient to let the family live on the interest of it; for one year, perhaps, or at the most two, they could live on the principal, that was all. It was simply a sum that ought not to be touched and should be kept for a rainy day; money for living expenses would have to be earned. Now his father was still hale enough but an old man, and he had done no work for the past five years and could not be expected to do much; during these five years, the first years of leisure in his laborious though unsuccessful life, he had grown rather fat and become sluggish. And Gregor's old mother, how was she to earn a living with her asthma, which troubled her even when she walked through the flat and kept her lying on a sofa every other day panting for breath beside an open window? And was his sister to earn her bread, she who was still a child of seventeen and whose life hitherto had been so pleasant, consisting as it did in dressing herself nicely, sleeping long, helping in the housekeeping, going out to a few modest entertainments and above all playing the violin? At first whenever the need for earning money was mentioned Gregor let go his hold on the door and threw himself down on the cool leather sofa beside it, he felt so hot with shame and grief.

Often he just lay there the long nights through without sleeping at all, scrabbling for hours on the leather. Or he nerved himself to the great effort of pushing an armchair to the window, then crawled up over the window sill and, braced against the chair, leaned against the window panes, obviously in some recollection of the sense of freedom that looking out of a window always used to give him. For in reality day by day things that were even a little way off were growing dimmer to his sight; the hospital across the street, which he used to execrate for being all too often before his eyes, was now quite beyond his range of vision, and if he had not known that he lived in Charlotte Street, a quiet street but still a city street, he might have believed that his window gave on a desert waste where gray sky and gray land blended indistinguishably into each other. His quick-witted sister only needed to observe twice that the armchair stood by the window; after that whenever she had tidied the room she always pushed the chair back to the same place at the window and even left the inner casements open.

If he could have spoken to her and thanked her for all she had to do for him, he could have borne her ministrations better; as it was, they oppressed him. She certainly tried to make as light as possible of whatever was disagreeable in her task, and as time went on she succeeded, of course, more and more, but time brought more enlightenment to Gregor too. The very way she came in distressed him. Hardly was she in the room when she rushed to the window, without even taking time to shut the door, careful as she was usually to shield the sight of Gregor's room from the others, and as if she were almost suffocating tore the casements open with hasty fingers, standing then in the open draught for a while even in the bitterest cold and drawing deep breaths. This noisy scurry of hers upset Gregor twice a day; he would crouch trembling under the sofa all the time, knowing quite well that she would certainly have spared him such a disturbance had she found it at all possible to stay in his presence without opening the window.

On one occasion, about a month after Gregor's metamorphosis, when there was surely no reason for her to be still startled at his appearance, she came a little earlier than usual and found him gazing out of the window, quite motionless, and thus well placed to look like a bogey. Gregor would not have been surprised had she not come in at all, for she could not immediately open the window while he was there, but not only did she retreat, she jumped back as if in alarm and banged the door shut; a stranger might have thought that he had been lying in wait for her there meaning to bite her. Of course he hid himself under the sofa at once, but he had to wait until midday before she came again, and she seemed more ill at ease than usual. This made him realize how repulsive the sight of him still was to her, and that it was bound to go on being repulsive, and what an effort it must cost her not to run away even from the sight of the small portion of his body that stuck out from under the sofa. In order to spare her that, therefore, one day he carried a sheet on his back to the sofa—it cost him four hours' labor—and arranged it there in such a way as to hide him completely, so that even if she were to bend down she could not see him. Had she considered the sheet unnecessary, she would certainly have stripped it off the sofa again, for it was clear enough that this curtaining and confining of himself was not likely to conduce to Gregor's comfort, but she left it where it was, and Gregor even fancied that he caught a thankful glance from her eye when he lifted the sheet carefully a very little with his head to see how she was taking the new arrangement.

For the first fortnight his parents could not bring themselves to the point of entering his room, and he often heard them expressing their appreciation of his sister's activities, whereas formerly they had frequently scolded her for being as they thought a somewhat useless daughter. But now, both of them waited outside the door, his father and his mother, while his sister tidied his room, and as soon as she came out she had to tell them exactly how things were in the room, what Gregor had eaten, how he had conducted himself this time and whether there was not perhaps some slight improvement in his condition. His mother, moreover, began relatively soon to want to visit him, but his father and sister dissuaded her at first with arguments which Gregor listened to very attentively and altogether approved. Later, however, she had to be held back by main force, and when she cried out: "Do let me in to Gregor, he is my unfortunate son! Can't you understand that I must go to him?" Gregor thought that it might be well to have her come in, not every day, of course, but perhaps once a week; she understood things, after all, much better than his sister, who was only a child despite the efforts she was making and had perhaps taken on so difficult a task merely out of childish thoughtlessness.

Gregor's desire to see his mother was soon fulfilled. During the daytime he did not want to show himself at the window, out of consideration for his parents, but he could not crawl very far around the few square yards of floor space he had, nor could he bear lying quietly at rest all during the night, while he was fast losing any interest he had ever taken in food, so that for mere recreation he had formed the habit of crawling crisscross over the walls and ceiling. He especially enjoyed hanging suspended from the ceiling; it was much better than lying on the floor; one could breathe more freely; one's body swung and rocked lightly; and in the almost blissful absorption induced by this suspension it could happen to his own surprise that he let go and fell plump on the floor. Yet he now had his body much better under control than formerly, and even such a big fall did him no harm. His sister had once remarked the new distraction Gregor had found for himself—he left traces behind him of the sticky stuff on his soles wherever he crawled—and she got the idea in her head of giving him as wide a field as possible to crawl in and of removing the pieces of furniture that hindered him, above all the chest of drawers and the writing desk. But that was more than she could manage all by herself; she did not dare ask her father to help her; and as for the servant girl, a young creature of sixteen who had had the courage to stay on after the cook's departure, she could not be asked to help, for she had begged as an especial favor that she might keep the kitchen door locked and open it only on a definite summons; so there was nothing left but to apply to her mother at an hour when her father was out. And the old lady did come, with exclamations of joyful eagerness, which, however, died away at the door of Gregor's room. Gregor's sister, of course, went in first, to see that everything was in order before letting his mother enter. In great haste Gregor pulled the sheet lower and rucked it more in folds so that it really looked as if it had been thrown accidentally over the sofa. And this time he did not peer out from under it; he renounced the pleasure of seeing his mother on this occasion and was only glad she had come at all. "Come in, he's out of sight," said his sister, obviously leading her mother in by the hand. Gregor could now hear the two women struggling to shift the heavy old chest from its place, and his sister claiming the greater part of the labor for herself, without listening to the admonitions of her mother who feared she might overstrain herself. It took a long time. After at least a quarter of an hour's tugging his mother objected that the chest had better be left where it was, for in the first place it was too heavy and could never be got out before his father came home, and standing in the middle of the room like that it would only hamper Gregor's movements, while in the second place it was not at all certain that removing the furniture would be doing a service to Gregor. She was inclined to think to the contrary; the sight of the naked walls made her own heart heavy and why shouldn't Gregor have the same feeling, considering that he had been used to his furniture for so long and might feel forlorn without it. "And doesn't it look," she concluded in a low voice—in fact she had been almost whispering all the time as if to avoid letting Gregor, whose exact whereabouts she did not know, hear even the tones of her voice, for she was convinced that he could not understand her words—"doesn't it look as if we were showing him, by taking away his furniture, that we have given up hope of his ever getting better and are just leaving him coldly to himself? I think it would be best to keep his room exactly as it has always been, so that when he comes back to us he will find everything unchanged and be able all the more easily to forget what has happened in between."

On hearing these words from his mother Gregor realized that the lack of all direct human speech for the past two months together with the monotony of family life must have confused his mind, otherwise he could not account for the fact that he had quite earnestly looked forward to having his room emptied of furnishing. Did he really want his warm room, so comfortably fitted with old family furniture, to be turned into a naked den in which he would certainly be able to crawl unhampered in all directions but at the price of shedding simultaneously all recollection of his human background? He had indeed been so near the brink of forgetfulness that only the voice of his mother, which he had not heard for so long, had drawn him back from it. Nothing should be taken out of his room; everything must stay as it was; he could not dispense with the good influence of the furniture on his state of mind; and even if the furniture did hamper him in his senseless crawling round and round, that was no drawback but a great advantage.

Unfortunately his sister was of the contrary opinion; she had grown accustomed, and not without reason, to consider herself an expert in Gregor's affairs as against her parents, and so her mother's advice was now enough to make her determined on the removal not only of the chest and the writing desk, which had been her first intention, but of all the furniture except the indispensable sofa. This determination was not, of course, merely the outcome of childish recalcitrance and of the self-confidence she had recently developed so unexpectedly and at such cost; she had in fact perceived that Gregor needed a lot of space to crawl about in, while on the other hand he never used the furniture at all, so far as could be seen. Another factor might have been also the enthusiastic temperament of an adolescent girl, which seeks to indulge herself on every opportunity and which now tempted Grete to exaggerate the horror of her brother's circumstances in order that she might do all the more for him. In a room where Gregor lorded it all alone over empty walls no one save herself was likely ever to set foot.

And so she was not to be moved from her resolve by her mother, who seemed moreover to be ill at ease in Gregor's room and therefore unsure of herself, was soon reduced to silence and helped her daughter as best she could to push the chest outside. Now, Gregor could do without the chest, if need be, but the writing desk he must retain. As soon as the two women had got the chest out of his room, groaning as they pushed it, Gregor stuck his head out from under the sofa to see how he might intervene as kindly and cautiously as possible. But as bad luck would have it, his mother was the first to return, leaving Grete clasping the chest in the room next door where she was trying to shift it all by herself, without of course moving it from the spot. His mother however was not accustomed to the sight of him, it might sicken her and so in alarm Gregor backed quickly to the other end of the sofa, yet could not prevent the sheet from swaying a little in front. That was enough to put her on the alert. She paused, stood still for a moment and then went back to Grete.

Although Gregor kept reassuring himself that nothing out of the way was happening, but only a few bits of furniture were being changed around, he soon had to admit that all this trotting to and fro of the two women, their little ejaculations and the scraping of furniture along the floor affected him like a vast disturbance coming from all sides at once, and however much he tucked in his head and legs and cowered to the very floor he was bound to confess that he would not be able to stand it for long. They were clearing his room out; taking away everything he loved; the chest in which he kept his fret saw and other tools was already dragged off; they were now loosening the writing desk which had almost sunk into the floor, the desk at which he had done all his homework when he was at the commercial academy, at the grammar school before that, and, yes, even at the primary school—he had no more time to waste in weighing the good intentions of the two women, whose existence he had by now almost forgotten, for they were so exhausted that they were laboring in silence and nothing could be heard but the heavy scuffling of their feet.

And so he rushed out—the women were just leaning against the writing desk in the next room to give themselves a breather—and four times changed his direction, since he really did not know what to rescue first, then on the wall opposite, which was already otherwise cleared, he was struck by the picture of the lady muffled in so much fur and quickly crawled up to it and pressed himself to the glass, which was a good surface to hold on to and comforted his hot belly. This picture at least, which was entirely hidden beneath him, was going to be removed by nobody. He turned his head towards the door of the living room so as to observe the women when they came back.

They had not allowed themselves much of a rest and were already coming; Grete had twined her arm round her mother and was almost supporting her. "Well, what shall we take now?" said Grete, looking round. Her eyes met Gregor's from the wall. She kept her composure, presumably because of her mother, bent her head down to her mother, to keep her from looking up, and said, although in a fluttering, unpremeditated voice: "Come, hadn't we better go back to the living room for a moment?" Her intentions were clear enough to Gregor, she wanted to bestow her mother in safety and then chase him down from the wall. Well, just let her try it! He clung to his picture and would not give it up. He would rather fly in Grete's face.

But Grete's words had succeeded in disquieting her mother, who took a step to one side, caught sight of the huge brown mass on the flowered wallpaper, and before she was really conscious that what she saw was Gregor screamed in a loud, hoarse voice: "Oh God, oh God!" fell with outspread arms over the sofa as if giving up and did not move. "Gregor!"

cried his sister, shaking her fist and glaring at him. This was the first time she had directly addressed him since his metamorphosis. She ran into the next room for some aromatic essence with which to rouse her mother from her fainting fit. Gregor wanted to help too—there was still time to rescue the picture—but he was stuck fast to the glass and had to tear himself loose; he then ran after his sister into the next room as if he could advise her, as he used to do; but then had to stand helplessly behind her; she meanwhile searched among various small bottles and when she turned round started in alarm at the sight of him; one bottle fell on the floor and broke; a splinter of glass cut Gregor's face and some kind of corrosive medicine splashed him; without pausing a moment longer Grete gathered up all the bottles she could carry and ran to her mother with them; she banged the door shut with her foot. Gregor was now cut off from his mother, who was perhaps nearly dying because of him; he dared not open the door for fear of frightening away his sister, who had to stay with her mother; there was nothing he could do but wait; and harassed by self-reproach and worry he began now to crawl to and fro, over everything, walls, furniture and ceiling, and finally in his despair, when the whole room seemed to be reeling round him, fell down on the middle of the big table.

A little while elapsed, Gregor was still lying there feebly and all around was quiet, perhaps that was a good omen. Then the doorbell rang. The servant girl was of course locked in her kitchen, and Grete would have to open the door. It was his father. "What's been happening?" were his first words; Grete's face must have told him everything. Grete answered in a muffled voice, apparently hiding her head on his breast: "Mother has been fainting, but she's better now. Gregor's broken loose." "Just what I expected," said his father, "just what I've been telling you, but you women would never listen." It was clear to Gregor that his father had taken the worst interpretation of Grete's all too brief statement and was assuming that Gregor had been guilty of some violent act. Therefore Gregor must now try to propitiate his father, since he had neither time nor means for an explanation. And so he fled to the door of his own room and crouched against it, to let his father see as soon as he came in from the hall that his son had the good intention of getting back into his room immediately and that it was not necessary to drive him there, but that if only the door were opened he would disappear at once.

Yet his father was not in the mood to perceive such fine distinctions. "Ah!" he cried as soon as he appeared, in a tone which sounded at once angry and exultant. Gregor drew his head back from the door and lifted it to look at his father. Truly, this was not the father he had imagined to himself; admittedly he had been too absorbed of late in his new recreation of crawling over the ceiling to take the same interest as before in what was happening elsewhere in the flat, and he ought really to be prepared for some changes. And yet, and yet, could that be his father? The man who used to lie wearily sunk in bed whenever Gregor set out on a business journey; who welcomed him back of an evening lying in a long chair in a dressing gown; who could not really rise to his feet but only lifted his arms in greeting, and on the rare occasions when he did go out with his family, on one or two Sundays a year and on high holidays, walked between Gregor and his mother, who were slow walkers anyhow, even more slowly than they did, muffled in his old greatcoat, shuffling laboriously forward with the help of his crook-handled stick which he set down most cautiously at every step and, whenever he wanted to say anything, nearly always came to a full stop and gathered his escort around him? Now he was standing there in fine shape; dressed in a smart blue uniform with gold buttons, such as bank messengers wear; his strong double chin bulged over the stiff high collar of his jacket; from under his bushy eyebrows his black eyes darted fresh and penetrating glances; his onetime tangled white hair had been combed flat on either side of a shining and carefully exact parting. He pitched his cap, which bore a gold monogram, probably the badge of some bank, in a wide sweep across the whole room on to a sofa and with the tail-ends of his jacket thrown back, his hands in his trouser pockets, advanced with a grim visage towards Gregor. Likely enough he did not himself know what he meant to do, at any rate he lifted his feet uncommonly high, and Gregor was dumbfounded at the enormous size of his shoe soles. But Gregor could not risk standing up to him, aware as he had been from the very first day of his new life that his father believed only the severest measures suitable for dealing with him. And so he ran before his father, stopping when he stopped and scuttling forward again when his father made any kind of move. In this way they circled the room several times without anything decisive happening, indeed the whole operation did not even look like a pursuit because it was carried out so slowly. And so Gregor did not leave the floor, for he feared that his father might take as a piece of peculiar wickedness any excursion of his over the walls or the ceiling. All the same, he could not stay this course much longer, for while his father took one step he had to carry out a whole series of movements. He was already beginning to feel breathless, just as in his former life his lungs had not been very dependable. As he was staggering along, trying to concentrate his energy on running, hardly keeping his eyes open; in his dazed state never even thinking of any other escape than simply going forward; and having almost forgotten that the walls were free to him, which in this room were well provided with finely carved pieces of furniture full of knobs and crevices—suddenly something lightly flung landed close behind him and rolled before him. It was an apple; a second apple followed immediately; Gregor came to a stop in alarm; there was no point in running on, for his father was determined to bombard him. He had filled his pockets with fruit from the dish on the sideboard and was now shying apple after apple, without taking particularly good aim for the moment. The small red apples rolled about the floor as if magnetized and cannoned into each other. An apple thrown without much force grazed Gregor's back and glanced off harmlessly. But another following immediately landed right on his back and sank in; Gregor wanted to drag himself forward, as if this startling, incredible pain could be left behind him; but he felt as if nailed to the spot and flattened himself out in a complete derangement of all his senses. With his last conscious look he saw the door of his room being torn open and his mother rushing out ahead of his screaming sister, in her underbodice, for her daughter had loosened her clothing to let her breathe more freely and recover from her swoon, he saw his mother rushing towards his father, leaving one after another behind her on the floor her loosened petticoats, stumbling over her petticoats straight to his father and embracing him, in complete union with him—but here Gregor's sight began to fail—with her hands clasped round his father's neck as she begged for her son's life.

III

The serious injury done to Gregor, which disabled him for more than a month—the apple went on sticking in his body as a visible reminder, since no one ventured to remove it—seemed to have made even his father recollect that Gregor was a member of the family, despite his present unfortunate and repulsive shape, and ought not to be treated as an enemy, that, on the contrary, family duty required the suppression of disgust and the exercise of patience, nothing but patience.

And although his injury had impaired, probably for ever, his powers of movement, and for the time being it took him long, long minutes to creep across his room like an old invalid—there was no question now of crawling up the wall—yet in his opinion he was sufficiently compensated for this worsening of his condition by the fact that towards evening the living-room door, which he used to watch intently for an hour or two beforehand, was always thrown open, so that lying in the darkness of his room, invisible to the family, he could see them all at the lamp-lit table and listen to their talk, by general consent as it were, very different from his earlier eavesdropping.

True, their intercourse lacked the lively character of former times, which he had always called to mind with a certain wistfulness in the small hotel bedrooms where he had been wont to throw himself down, tired out, on damp bedding. They were now mostly very silent. Soon after supper his father would fall asleep in his armchair; his mother and sister would admonish each other to be silent; his mother, bending low over the lamp, stitched at fine sewing for an underwear firm; his sister, who had taken a job as a salesgirl, was learning shorthand and French in the evenings on the chance of bettering herself. Sometimes his father woke up, and as if quite unaware that he had been sleeping said to his mother: "What a lot of sewing you're doing today!" and at once fell asleep again, while the two women exchanged a tired smile.

With a kind of mulishness his father persisted in keeping his uniform on even in the house; his dressing gown hung uselessly on its peg and he slept fully dressed where he sat, as if he were ready for service at any moment and even here only at the beck and call of his superior. As a result, his uniform, which was not brand-new to start with, began to look dirty, despite all the loving care of the mother and sister to keep it clean, and Gregor often spent whole evenings gazing at the many greasy spots on the garment, gleaming with gold buttons always in a high state of polish, in which the old man sat sleeping in extreme discomfort and yet quite peacefully.

As soon as the clock struck ten his mother tried to rouse his father with gentle words and to persuade him after that to get into bed, for sitting there he could not have a proper sleep and that was what he needed most, since he had to go on duty at six. But with the mulishness that had obsessed him since he became a bank messenger he always insisted on staying longer at the table, although he regularly fell asleep again and in the end only with the greatest trouble could be got out of his armchair and into his bed. However insistently Gregor's mother and sister kept urging him with gentle reminders, he would go on slowly shaking his head for a quarter of an hour, keeping his eyes shut, and refuse to get to his feet. The mother plucked at his sleeve, whispering endearments in his ear, the sister left her lessons to come to her mother's help, but Gregor's father was not to be caught. He would only sink down deeper in his chair. Not until the two women hoisted him up by the armpits did he open his eyes and look at them both, one after the other, usually with the remark: "This is a life. This is the peace and quiet of my old age." And leaning on the two of them he would heave himself up, with difficulty, as if he were a great burden to himself, suffer them to lead him as far as the door and then wave them off and go on alone, while the mother abandoned her needlework and the sister her pen in order to run after him and help him farther.

Who could find time, in this overworked and tired-out family, to bother about Gregor more than was absolutely needful? The household was reduced more and more; the servant girl was turned off; a gigantic bony charwoman with white hair flying round her head came in morning and evening to do the rough work; everything else was done by Gregor's mother, as well as great piles of sewing. Even various family ornaments, which his mother and sister used to wear with pride at parties and celebrations, had to be sold, as Gregor discovered of an evening from hearing them all discuss the prices obtained. But what they lamented most was the fact that they could not leave the flat which was much too big for their present circumstances, because they could not think of any way to shift Gregor. Yet Gregor saw well enough that consideration for him was not the main difficulty preventing the removal, for they could have easily shifted him in some suitable box with a few air holes in it; what really kept them from moving into another flat was rather their own complete hopelessness and the belief that they had been singled out for a misfortune such as had never happened to any of their relations or acquaintances. They fulfilled to the uttermost all that the world demands of poor people, the father fetched breakfast for the small clerks in the bank, the mother devoted her energy to making underwear for strangers, the sister trotted to and fro behind the counter at the behest of customers, but more than this they had not the strength to do. And the wound in Gregor's back began to nag at him afresh when his mother and sister, after getting his father into bed, came back again, left their work lying, drew close to each other and sat cheek to cheek; when his mother, pointing towards his room, said: "Shut that door now, Grete," and he was left again in darkness, while next door the women mingled their tears or perhaps sat dry-eyed staring at the table.

Gregor hardly slept at all by night or by day. He was often haunted by the idea that next time the door opened he would take the family's affairs in hand again just as he used to do; once more, after this long interval, there appeared in his thoughts the figures of the chief and the chief clerk, the commercial travelers and the apprentices, the porter who was so dull-witted, two or three friends in other firms, a chambermaid in one of the rural hotels, a sweet and fleeting memory, a cashier in a milliner's shop, whom he had wooed earnestly but too slowly—they all appeared, together with strangers or people he had quite forgotten, but instead of helping him and his family they were one and all unapproachable and he was glad when they vanished. At other times he would not be in the mood to bother about his family, he was only filled with rage at the way they were neglecting him, and although he had no clear idea of what he might care to eat he would make plans for getting into the larder to take the food that was after all his due, even if he were not hungry. His sister no longer took thought to bring him what might especially please him, but in the morning and at noon before she went to business hurriedly pushed into his room with her foot any food that was available, and in the evening cleared it out again with one sweep of the broom, heedless of whether it had been merely tasted, or—as most frequently happened—left untouched. The cleaning of his room, which she now did always in the evenings, could not have been more hastily done. Streaks of dirt stretched along the walls, here and there lay balls of dust and filth. At first Gregor used to station himself in some particularly filthy corner when his sister arrived, in order to reproach her with it, so to speak. But he could have sat there for weeks without getting her to make any improvement; she could see the dirt as well as he did, but she had simply made up her mind to leave it alone. And yet, with a touchiness that was new to her, which seemed anyhow to have infected the whole family, she jealously guarded her claim to be the sole caretaker of Gregor's room. His mother once subjected his room to a thorough cleaning, which was achieved only by means of several buckets of water—all this dampness of course upset Gregor too and he lay widespread, sulky and motionless on the sofa—but she was well punished for it. Hardly had his sister noticed the changed aspect of his room that evening than she rushed in high dudgeon into the living room and, despite the imploringly raised hands of her mother, burst into a storm of weeping, while her parents—her father had of course been startled out of his chair—looked on at first in helpless amazement; then they too began to go into action; the father reproached the mother on his right for not having left the cleaning of Gregor's room to his sister; shrieked at the sister on his left that never again was she to be allowed to clean Gregor's room; while the mother tried to pull the father into his bedroom, since he was beyond himself with agitation; the sister, shaken with sobs, then beat upon the table with her small fists; and Gregor hissed loudly with rage because not one of them thought of shutting the door to spare him such a spectacle and so much noise.

Still, even if the sister, exhausted by her daily work, had grown tired of looking after Gregor as she did formerly, there was no need for his mother's intervention or for Gregor's being neglected at all. The charwoman was there. This old widow, whose strong bony frame had enabled her to survive the worst a long life could offer, by no means recoiled from Gregor. Without being in the least curious she had once by chance opened the door of his room and at the sight of Gregor, who, taken by surprise, began to rush to and fro although no one was chasing him, merely stood there with her arms folded. From that time she never failed to open his door a little for a moment, morning and evening, to have a look at him. At first she even used to call him to her, with words which apparently she took to be friendly, such as: "Come along, then, you old dung beetle!" or "Look at the old dung beetle, then!" To such allocutions Gregor made no answer, but stayed motionless where he was, as if the door had never been opened. Instead of being allowed to disturb him so senselessly whenever the whim took her, she should rather have been ordered to clean out his room daily, that charwoman! Once, early in the morning—heavy rain was lashing on the windowpanes, perhaps a sign that spring was on the way—Gregor was so exasperated when she began addressing him again that he ran at her, as if to attack her, although slowly and feebly enough. But the charwoman instead of showing fright merely lifted high a chair that happened to be beside the door, and as she stood there with her mouth wide open it was clear that she meant to shut it only when she brought the chair down on Gregor's back. "So you're not coming any nearer?" she asked, as Gregor turned away again, and quietly put the chair back into the corner.

Gregor was now eating hardly anything. Only when he happened to pass the food laid out for him did he take a bit of something in his mouth as a pastime, kept it there for an hour at a time and usually spat it out again. At first he thought it was chagrin over the state of his room that prevented him from eating, yet he soon got used to the various changes in his room. It had become a habit in the family to push into his room things there was no room for elsewhere, and there were plenty of these now, since one of the rooms had been let to three lodgers. These serious gentlemen—all three of them with full beards, as Gregor once observed through a crack in the door—had a passion for order, not only in their own room but, since they were now members of the household, in all its arrangements, especially in the kitchen. Superfluous, not to say dirty, objects they could not bear. Besides, they had brought with them most of the furnishings they needed. For this reason many things could be dispensed with that it was no use trying to sell but that should not be thrown away either. All of them found their way into Gregor's room. The ash can likewise and the kitchen garbage can. Anything that was not needed for the moment was simply flung into Gregor's room by the charwoman, who did everything in a hurry; fortunately Gregor usually saw only the object, whatever it was, and the hand that held it. Perhaps she intended to take the things away again as time and opportunity offered, or to collect them until she could throw them all out in a heap, but in fact they just lay wherever she happened to throw them, except when Gregor pushed his way through the junk heap and shifted it somewhat, at first out of necessity, because he had not room enough to crawl, but later with increasing enjoyment, although after such excursions, being sad and weary to death, he would lie motionless for hours. And since the lodgers often ate their supper at home in the common living room, the living-room door stayed shut many an evening, yet Gregor reconciled himself quite easily to the shutting of the door, for often enough on evenings when it was opened he had disregarded it entirely and lain in the darkest corner of his room, quite unnoticed by the family. But on one occasion the charwoman left the door open a little and it stayed ajar even when the lodgers came in for supper and the lamp was lit. They set themselves at the top end of the table where formerly Gregor and his father and mother had eaten their meals, unfolded their napkins and took knife and fork in hand. At once his mother appeared in the other doorway with a dish of meat and close behind her his sister with a dish of potatoes piled high. The food steamed with a thick vapor. The lodgers bent over the food set before them as if to scrutinize it before eating, in fact the man in the middle, who seemed to pass for an authority with the other two, cut a piece of meat as it lay on the dish, obviously to discover if it were tender or should be sent back to the kitchen. He showed satisfaction, and Gregor's mother and sister, who had been watching anxiously, breathed freely and began to smile. The family itself took its meals in the kitchen. None the less, Gregor's father came into the living room before going into the kitchen and with one prolonged bow, cap in hand, made a round of the table. The lodgers all stood up and murmured something in their beards. When they were alone again they ate their food in almost complete silence. It seemed remarkable to Gregor that among the various noises coming from the table he could always distinguish the sound of their masticating teeth, as if this were a sign to Gregor that one needed teeth in order to eat, and that with toothless jaws even of the finest make one could do nothing. "I'm hungry enough," said Gregor sadly to himself, "but not for that kind of food. How these lodgers are stuffing themselves, and here am I dying of starvation!"

On that very evening—during the whole of his time there Gregor could not remember ever having heard the violin—the sound of violin-playing came from the kitchen. The lodgers had already finished their supper, the one in the middle had brought out a newspaper and given the other two a page apiece, and now they were leaning back at ease reading and smoking. When the violin began to play they pricked up their ears, got to their feet, and went on tiptoe to the hall door where they stood huddled together. Their movements must have been heard in the kitchen, for Gregor's father called out: "Is the violin-playing disturbing you, gentlemen? It can be stopped at once." "On the contrary," said the middle lodger, "could not Fräulein Samsa come and play in this room, beside us, where it is much more convenient and comfortable?" "Oh certainly," cried Gregor's father, as if he were the violin-player. The lodgers came back into the living room and waited. Presently Gregor's father arrived with the music stand, his mother carrying the music and his sister with the violin. His sister quietly made everything ready to start playing; his parents, who had never let rooms before and so had an exaggerated idea of the courtesy due to lodgers, did not venture to sit down on their own chairs; his father leaned against the door, the right hand thrust between two buttons of his livery coat, which was formally buttoned up; but his mother was offered a chair by one of the lodgers and, since she left the chair just where he had happened to put it, sat down in a corner to one side.

Gregor's sister began to play; the father and mother, from either side, intently watched the movements of her hands. Gregor, attracted by the playing, ventured to move forward a little until his head was actually inside the living room. He felt hardly any surprise at his growing lack of consideration for the others; there had been a time when he prided himself on being considerate. And yet just on this occasion he had more reason than ever to hide himself, since owing to the amount of dust which lay thick in his room and rose into the air at the slightest movement, he too was covered with dust; fluff and hair and remnants of food trailed with him, caught on his back and along his sides; his indifference to everything was much too great for him to turn on his back and scrape himself clean on the carpet, as once he had done several times a day. And in spite of his condition, no shame deterred him from advancing a little over the spotless floor in the living room.

To be sure, no one was aware of him. The family was entirely absorbed in the violin-playing; the lodgers, however, who first of all had stationed themselves, hands in pockets, much too close behind the music stand so that they could all have read the music, which must have bothered his sister, had soon retreated to the window, half-whispering with downbent heads, and stayed there while his father turned an anxious eye on them. Indeed, they were making it more than obvious that they had been disappointed in their expectation of hearing good or enjoyable violin-playing, that they had had more than enough of the performance and only out of courtesy suffered a continued disturbance of their peace. From the way they all kept blowing the smoke of their cigars high in the air through nose and mouth one could divine their irritation. And yet Gregor's sister was playing so beautifully. Her face leaned sideways, intently and sadly her eyes followed the notes of music. Gregor crawled a little farther forward and lowered his head to the ground so that it might be possible for his eyes to meet hers. Was he an animal, that music had such an effect upon him? He felt as if the way were opening before him to the unknown nourishment he craved. He was determined to push forward till he reached his sister, to pull at her skirt and so let her know that she was to come into his room with her violin, for no one here appreciated her playing as he could appreciate it. He would never let her out of his room, at least, not so long as he lived; his frightful appearance would become, for the first time, useful to him; he would watch all the doors of his room at once and spit at intruders; but his sister should need no constraint, she should stay with him of her own free will; she should sit beside him on the sofa; bend down her ear to him and hear him confide that he had had the firm intention of sending her to the Conservatorium, and that, but for his mishap, last Christmas—surely Christmas was long past?—he would have announced it to everybody without allowing a single objection. After this confession his sister would be so touched that she would burst into tears, and Gregor would then raise himself to her shoulder and kiss her on the neck, which, now that she went to business, she kept free of any ribbon or collar.

"Mr. Samsa!" cried the middle lodger, to Gregor's father, and pointed, without wasting any more words, at Gregor, now working himself slowly forwards. The violin fell silent, the middle lodger first smiled at his friends with a shake of the head and then looked at Gregor again. Instead of driving Gregor out, his father seemed to think it more needful to begin by soothing down the lodgers, although they were not at all agitated and apparently found Gregor more entertaining than the violin-playing. He hurried towards them and spreading out his arms, tried to urge them back into their own room and at the same time to block their view of Gregor. They now began to be really a little angry, one could not tell whether because of the old man's behavior or because it had just dawned on them that all unwittingly they had such a neighbor as Gregor next door. They demanded explanations of his father, they waved their arms like him, tugged uneasily at their beards, and only with reluctance backed towards their room. Meanwhile Gregor's sister, who stood there as if lost when her playing was so abruptly broken off, came to life again, pulled herself together all at once after standing for a while holding violin and bow in nervelessly hanging hands and staring at her music, pushed her violin into the lap of her mother, who was still sitting in her chair fighting asthmatically for breath, and ran into the lodgers' rooms to which they were now being shepherded by her father rather more quickly than before. One could see the pillows and blankets on the beds flying under her accustomed fingers and being laid in order. Before the lodgers had actually reached their rooms she had finished making the beds and slipped out. The old man seemed once more to be so possessed by his mulish self-assertiveness that he was forgetting all the respect he should show to his lodgers. He kept driving them on and driving them on until in the very door of the bedroom the middle lodger stamped his foot loudly on the floor and so brought him to a halt. "I beg to announce," said the lodger, lifting one hand and looking also at Gregor's mother and sister, "that because of the disgusting conditions prevailing in this household and family"—here he spat on the floor with emphatic brevity—"I give you notice on the spot. Naturally I won't pay you a penny for the days I have lived here, on the contrary I shall consider bringing an action for damages against you, based on claims—believe me—that will be easily susceptible of proof." He ceased and stared straight in front of him, as if he expected something. In fact his two friends at once rushed into the breach with these words: "And we too give notice on the spot." On that he seized the door-handle and shut the door with a slam.

Gregor's father, groping with his hands, staggered forward and fell into his chair; it looked as if he were stretching himself there for his ordinary evening nap, but the marked jerkings of his head, which was as if uncontrollable, showed that he was far from asleep. Gregor had simply stayed quietly all the time on the spot where the lodgers had espied him. Disappointment at the failure of his plan, perhaps also the weakness arising from extreme hunger, made it impossible for him to move. He feared, with a fair degree of certainty, that at any moment the general tension would discharge itself in a combined attack upon him, and he lay waiting. He did not react even to the noise made by the violin as it fell off his mother's lap from under her trembling fingers and gave out a resonant note.

"My dear parents," said his sister, slapping her hand on the table by way of introduction, "things can't go on like this. Perhaps you don't realize that, but I do. I won't utter my brother's name in the presence of this creature, and so all I say is: we must try to get rid of it. We've tried to look after it and to put up with it as far as is humanly possible, and I don't think anyone could reproach us in the slightest."

"She is more than right," said Gregor's father to himself. His mother, who was still choking for lack of breath, began to cough hollowly into her hand with a wild look in her eyes.

His sister rushed over to her and held her forehead. His father's thoughts seemed to have lost their vagueness at Grete's words, he sat more upright, fingering his service cap that lay among the plates still lying on the table from the lodgers' supper, and from time to time looked at the still form of Gregor.

"We must try to get rid of it," his sister now said explicitly to her father, since her mother was coughing too much to hear a word, "it will be the death of both of you, I can see that coming. When one has to work as hard as we do, all of us, one can't stand this continual torment at home on top of it. At least I can't stand it any longer." And she burst into such a passion of sobbing that her tears dropped on her mother's face, where she wiped them off mechanically.

"My dear," said the old man sympathetically, and with evident understanding, "but what can we do?"

Gregor's sister merely shrugged her shoulders to indicate the feeling of helplessness that had now overmastered her during her weeping fit, in contrast to her former confidence.

"If he could understand us," said her father, half questioningly; Grete, still sobbing, vehemently waved a hand to show how unthinkable that was.

"If he could understand us," repeated the old man, shutting his eyes to consider his daughter's conviction that understanding was impossible, "then perhaps we might come to some agreement with him. But as it is—"

"He must go," cried Gregor's sister, "that's the only solution, Father. You must just try to get rid of the idea that this is Gregor. The fact that we've believed it for so long is the root of all our trouble. But how can it be Gregor? If this were Gregor, he would have realized long ago that human beings can't live with such a creature, and he'd have gone away on his own accord. Then we wouldn't have any brother, but we'd be able to go on living and keep his memory in honor. As it is, this creature persecutes us, drives away our lodgers, obviously wants the whole apartment to himself and would have us all sleep in the gutter. Just look, Father," she shrieked all at once, "he's at it again!" And in an access of panic that was quite incomprehensible to Gregor she even quitted her mother, literally thrusting the chair from her as if she would rather sacrifice her mother than stay so near to Gregor, and rushed behind her father, who also rose up, being simply upset by her agitation, and half-spread his arms out as if to protect her.

Yet Gregor had not the slightest intention of frightening anyone, far less his sister. He had only begun to turn round in order to crawl back to his room, but it was certainly a startling operation to watch, since because of his disabled condition he could not execute the difficult turning movements except by lifting his head and then bracing it against the floor over and over again. He paused and looked round. His good intentions seemed to have been recognized; the alarm had only been momentary. Now they were all watching him in melancholy silence. His mother lay in her chair, her legs stiffly outstretched and pressed together, her eyes almost closing for sheer weariness; his father and his sister were sitting beside each other, his sister's arm around the old man's neck.

Perhaps I can go on turning round now, thought Gregor, and began his labors again. He could not stop himself from panting with the effort, and had to pause now and then to take breath. Nor did anyone harass him, he was left entirely to himself. When he had completed the turn-round he began at once to crawl straight back. He was amazed at the distance separating him from his room and could not understand how in his weak state he had managed to accomplish the same journey so recently, almost without remarking it. Intent on crawling as fast as possible, he barely noticed that not a single word, not an ejaculation from his family, interfered with his progress. Only when he was already in the doorway did he turn his head round, not completely, for his neck muscles were getting stiff, but enough to see that nothing had changed behind him except that his sister had risen to her feet. His last glance fell on his mother, who was not quite overcome by sleep.

Hardly was he well inside his room when the door was hastily pushed shut, bolted and locked. The sudden noise in his rear startled him so much that his little legs gave beneath him. It was his sister who had shown such haste. She had been standing ready waiting and had made a light spring forward, Gregor had not even heard her coming, and she cried "At last!" to her parents as she turned the key in the lock.

"And what now?" said Gregor to himself, looking round in the darkness. Soon he made the discovery that he was now unable to stir a limb. This did not surprise him, rather it seemed unnatural that he should ever actually have been able to move on these feeble little legs. Otherwise he felt relatively comfortable. True, his whole body was aching, but it seemed that the pain was gradually growing less and would finally pass away. The rotting apple in his back and the inflamed area around it, all covered with soft dust, already hardly troubled him. He thought of his family with tenderness and love. The decision that he must disappear was one that he held to even more strongly than his sister, if that were possible. In this state of vacant and peaceful meditation he remained until the tower clock struck three in the morning. The first broadening of light in the world outside the window entered his consciousness once more. Then his head sank to the floor of its own accord and from his nostrils came the last faint flicker of his breath.

When the charwoman arrived early in the morning—what between her strength and her impatience she slammed all the doors so loudly, never mind how often she had been begged not to do so, that no one in the whole apartment could enjoy any quiet sleep after her arrival—she noticed nothing unusual as she took her customary peep into Gregor's room. She thought he was lying motionless on purpose, pretending to be in the sulks; she credited him with every kind of intelligence. Since she happened to have the long-handled broom in her hand she tried to tickle him up with it from the doorway. When that too produced no reaction she felt provoked and poked at him a little harder, and only when she had pushed him along the floor without meeting any resistance was her attention aroused. It did not take her long to establish the truth of the matter, and her eyes widened, she let out a whistle, yet did not waste much time over it but tore open the door of the Samsas' bedroom and yelled into the darkness at the top of her voice: "Just look at this, it's dead; it's lying here dead and done for!"

Mr. and Mrs. Samsa started up in their double bed and before they realized the nature of the charwoman's announcement had some difficulty in overcoming the shock of it. But then they got out of bed quickly, one on either side, Mr. Samsa throwing a blanket over his shoulders, Mrs. Samsa in nothing but her nightgown; in this array they entered Gregor's room. Meanwhile the door of the living room opened, too, where Grete had been sleeping since the advent of the lodgers; she was completely dressed as if she had not been to bed, which seemed to be confirmed also by the paleness of her face. "Dead?" said Mrs. Samsa, looking questioningly at the charwoman, although she could have investigated for herself, and the fact was obvious enough without investigation. "I should say so," said the charwoman, proving her words by pushing Gregor's corpse a long way to one side with her broomstick. Mrs. Samsa made a movement as if to stop her, but checked it. "Well," said Mr. Samsa, "now thanks be to God." He crossed himself, and the three women followed his example. Grete, whose eyes never left the corpse, said: "Just see how thin he was. It's such a long time since he's eaten anything. The food came out again just as it went in." Indeed, Gregor's body was completely flat and dry, as could only now be seen when it was no longer supported by the legs and nothing prevented one from looking closely at it. "Come in beside us, Grete, for a little while," said Mrs. Samsa with a tremulous smile, and Grete, not without looking back at the corpse, followed her parents into their bedroom. The charwoman shut the door and opened the window wide. Although it was so early in the morning a certain softness was perceptible in the fresh air. After all, it was already the end of March.

The three lodgers emerged from their room and were surprised to see no breakfast; they had been forgotten. "Where's our breakfast?" said the middle lodger peevishly to the charwoman. But she put her finger to her lips and hastily, without a word, indicated by gestures that they should go into Gregor's room. They did so and stood, their hands in the pockets of their somewhat shabby coats, around Gregor's corpse in the room where it was now fully light.

At that the door of the Samsas' bedroom opened and Mr. Samsa appeared in his uniform, his wife on one arm, his daughter on the other. They all looked a little as if they had been crying; from time to time Grete hid her face on her father's arm.

"Leave my house at once!" said Mr. Samsa, and pointed to the door without disengaging himself from the women. "What do you mean by that?" said the middle lodger, taken somewhat aback, with a feeble smile. The two others put their hands behind them and kept rubbing them together, as if in gleeful expectation of a fine set-to in which they were bound to come off the winners. "I mean just what I say," answered Mr. Samsa, and advanced in a straight line with his two companions towards the lodger. He stood his ground at first quietly, looking at the floor as if his thoughts were taking a new pattern in his head. "Then let us go, by all means," he said, and looked up at Mr. Samsa as if in a sudden access of humility he were expecting some renewed sanction for this decision. Mr. Samsa merely nodded briefly once or twice with meaning eyes. Upon that the lodger really did go with long strides into the hall, his two friends had been listening and had quite stopped rubbing their hands for some moments and now went scuttling after him as if afraid that Mr. Samsa might get into the hall before them and cut them off from their leader. In the hall they all three took their hats from the rack, their sticks from the umbrella stand, bowed in silence and quitted the apartment. With a suspiciousness which proved quite unfounded Mr. Samsa and the two women followed them out to the landing; leaning over the banister they watched the three figures slowly but surely going down the long stairs, vanishing from sight at a certain turn of the staircase on every floor and coming into view again after a moment or so; the more they dwindled, the more the Samsa family's interest in them dwindled, and when a butcher's boy met them and passed them on the stairs coming up proudly with a tray on his head, Mr. Samsa and the two women soon left the landing and as if a burden had been lifted from them went back into their apartment.

They decided to spend this day in resting and going for a stroll; they had not only deserved such a respite from work, but absolutely needed it. And so they sat down at the table and wrote three notes of excuse, Mr. Samsa to his board of management, Mrs. Samsa to her employer and Grete to the head of her firm. While they were writing, the charwoman came in to say that she was going now, since her morning's work was finished. At first they only nodded without looking up, but as she kept hovering there they eyed her irritably. "Well?" said Mr. Samsa. The charwoman stood grinning in the doorway as if she had good news to impart to the family but meant not to say a word unless properly questioned. The small ostrich feather standing upright on her hat, which had annoyed Mr. Samsa ever since she was engaged, was waving gaily in all directions. "Well, what is it then?" asked Mrs. Samsa, who obtained more respect from the charwoman than the others. "Oh," said the charwoman, giggling so amiably that she could not at once continue, "just this, you don't need to bother about how to get rid of the thing next door. It's been seen to already." Mrs. Samsa and Grete bent over their letters again, as if preoccupied; Mr. Samsa, who perceived that she was eager to begin describing it all in detail, stopped her with a decisive hand. But since she was not allowed to tell her story, she remembered the great hurry she was in, being obviously deeply huffed: "Bye, everybody," she said, whirling off violently, and departed with a frightful slamming of doors.

"She'll be given notice tonight," said Mr. Samsa, but neither from his wife nor his daughter did he get any answer, for the charwoman seemed to have shattered again the composure they had barely achieved. They rose, went to the window and stayed there, clasping each other tight. Mr. Samsa turned in his chair to look at them and quietly observed them for a little. Then he called out: "Come along, now, do. Let bygones be bygones. And you might have some consideration for me." The two of them complied at once, hastened to him, caressed him and quickly finished their letters.

Then they all three left the apartment together, which was more than they had done for months, and went by tram into the open country outside the town. The tram, in which they were the only passengers, was filled with warm sunshine. Leaning comfortably back in their seats they canvassed their prospects for the future, and it appeared on closer inspection that these were not at all bad, for the jobs they had got, which so far they had never really discussed with each other, were all three admirable and likely to lead to better things later on. The greatest immediate improvement in their condition would of course arise from moving to another house; they wanted to take a smaller and cheaper but also better situated and more easily run apartment than the one they had, which Gregor had selected. While they were thus conversing, it struck both Mr. and Mrs. Samsa, almost at the same moment, as they became aware of their daughter's increasing vivacity, that in spite of all the sorrow of recent times, which had made her cheeks pale, she had bloomed into a pretty girl with a good figure. They grew quieter and half unconsciously exchanged glances of complete agreement, having come to the conclusion that it would soon be time to find a good husband for her. And it was like a confirmation of their new dreams and excellent intentions that at the end of their journey their daughter sprang to her feet first and stretched her young body.

1915

AFTERWORD

"As Gregor Samsa awoke one morning from uneasy dreams he found himself transformed in his bed into a gigantic insect." Not how you would expect one of the great short novels of the twentieth century to begin. But of course, the canny reader notices, "awoke . . . from uneasy dreams"; he didn't really wake? and this is just another dream? Suppose not: in the second paragraph Samsa says it is no dream. Suppose he stays a giant insect, a beetle or bedbug, say, throughout the story? How do we come to terms with it? How can we take it seriously? Indeed, if the protagonist—usually the person we like to identify with—is going to remain a bug the whole time, how can we even be interested enough to read the story? The adventures, survival, sex life of bugs just don't seem all that fascinating.

Gregor Samsa was, when he went to bed, a human being, and still thinks he's human; but he has awakened to find himself transformed. He both believes and does not believe he is an insect. His mind is still functioning as a human mind and his feelings are human, so we can relate to him there. From time to time he even seems to forget about his predicament—if it is a real one—and complains to himself about his job and his boss, worries about catching his train. Interwoven with these half-awake thoughts are Gregor's attempts to roll over, to get out of bed, to control his voice, which is becoming a kind of "twittering squeak" and less and less comprehensible to others. So mixed are the human and realistic with the inhuman and fantastic, most readers find themselves fully engaged with Gregor Samsa's consciousness, his worries, likes, and dislikes, despite his new, distasteful form. For the sake of his human self we accept his insect self.

Meanwhile, there's another question about the reader's relation to the story, especially in the early passages. Is the story supposed to be funny? Because of the manner in which the human and insect concerns are mixed or juxtaposed, it sometimes seems that way. While Gregor is struggling to turn over, for example, his legs kicking uncontrollably in the air, he thinks, "Oh God . . . what an exhausting job I've picked on!" He doesn't mean turning over, but his job as a traveling salesman, "Traveling about day in, day out. It's much more irritating work than doing the actual business in the office . . ." And in the midst of going on about his job his belly begins to itch. Isn't there something ludicrous about the infiltrating of the real and the fantastic, the fantastic and the real? He even sees something comic in the situation himself. When he cannot get out of bed he thinks, "Well, ignoring the fact that the doors were all locked, ought he really to call for help? In spite of his misery he could not suppress a smile at the very idea of it." Later, he tries to stand up and open the door; there's a kind of Hitchcock suspense and absurdity in the posture and possibility: the door seems to separate the worlds of fantasy and reality, and the imminence of their mingling seems frightening and funny.

At times, too, the confusion of those outside the room seems comic—their failure to understand his increasingly insectlike speech, for example. This is, of course, another means by which the reader is engaged with Gregor: we begin to feel impatient with the chief clerk and the members of the family because they do not understand that behind that door is not an obstinate, rebellious Gregor Samsa but a giant bug struggling to move, to speak, to come to terms with his metamorphosis. The "outsiders," those outside the room, here seem as lacking in understanding and sympathy as Iván Ilyich's circle of friends when they hear of his death. And just as Iván's widow seeks out his friend not for consolation but to discover if she can get more from the government than a widow's pension, so Gregor's sister is concerned for Gregor because she fears he will lose his job and the family will be dunned for debts; and so, too, Gregor's boss suspects that Gregor's absence has something to do with his having some of the customers' cash in his hands.

When Gregor manages to open the door there is another slapstick scene as the horrified witnesses fall all over each other. The comedy is reinforced by Gregor's trying to speak to the terrified chief clerk, to get him to speak up for Gregor in the firm, not for his having been transformed into a repulsive insect, but because "Travelers are not popular there, I know." When the chief clerk eludes Gregor, Gregor's father is "upset." The tone begins to change. His father tries to drive him back into his room, and when Gregor gets stuck in the doorway, pushes him violently from behind, a "push which was literally a deliverance and he flew far into the room, bleeding freely." It is still ludicrous but doesn't seem quite so funny any more; it's a little frightening.

So ends the first chapter. We are more than likely not so concerned any longer about whether this story is fantasy or reality as we are about whether it is comic or tragic, whether Gregor will successfully reassume his human shape, or . . .? Escape into the insect world seems as unlikely as returning to the human world while in this form; all other possibilities seem rather dreadful.

Our sympathies for Gregor are further reinforced by the evidence in the second chapter of his sweetness of temper—or is it his naïveté or passivity?—when it is disclosed that his father has been holding out from him some money he has salvaged from the ruin of his business, money that could have shortened Gregor's virtual indentured servitude had it been paid to the chief. Though we learn of this with Gregor and through his consciousness, we see more in it than he does, understand the callousness of his father and indeed of the family, and how they all have taken advantage of him. His father has not worked for five years and has grown fat; his mother complains of asthma; his sister is only seventeen: the whole burden for supporting the family has been on Gregor's shoulders, and to make matters even worse—though Gregor does not think so—his father has actually been saving money from the sums Gregor had given him for support.

While our pity has been deepened, Gregor is sinking more deeply into his insect state: he uses his feelers, does not like milk or fresh food or the spaciousness of his room; he has learned how to crawl over the walls and ceiling; his eyesight is dimming. Less and less is said about his occupation. Still, he does not want to part with the encumbering furniture, for it preserves his memories of his human state, and that he wants to cling to. He even turns a little hostile to his sister Grete as she comes to take the picture out of the room.

Despite the decline in his condition, then, we are led to expect that he might indeed regain his former identity. But toward the end of the chapter, after his resistance to Grete, things take a serious turn for the worse and a less happy eventuality seems the more likely. Another metamorphosis has taken place: his father, now a bank guard, has flourished and become more authoritative. He tries to force Gregor back into his room and throws apples at him. One sticks in Gregor's insect back. If his mother had not intervened Gregor might well have been killed right then and there.

There is still one more up and a final down in Gregor's fortunes and our hopes before what we must have known all along was the inevitable end. Rather surprisingly, Grete, the one who from the beginning seemed to understand him best, is the one who turns against him—or as she says, "it." What are we to feel about her "betrayal"? There is even a final indignity: after Gregor's death, the new charwoman is eager but unable to tell the family and us how "it" was disposed of. It is astonishing how, through the repellent and the comic, our sympathies have been engaged on the side of Gregor, and how moving and pathetic the end of his story is.

But that is not the end of *The Metamorphosis*. Gregor's consciousness and plight removed, we see the family better off than they were—not just better off than when the insect loomed in the inner room, but better off than when Gregor, working as a traveling salesman, supported them. They are all in reasonably good jobs and hopeful of improvement in the future. Grete has grown up to be a pretty young lady during the ordeal; her parents plan to find a husband for her. The story ends, "And it was like a confirmation of their new dreams and excellent intentions that at the end of their journey their daughter sprang to her feet first and stretched her young body." Have they forgotten already? have we? Is this an affirmation of life? a condemnation of Gregor? a tribute to his "sacrifice"? a cynical view of human selfishness and separateness? The ambivalence or mixture of mode and tone continues right to the end. We are not even absolutely certain which "metamorphosis" the title is referring to.

When we close the book and think about what we have read and how we have responded to what we have read, how do we answer the unanswered question we asked at the beginning? We know that it is no dream, no comedy, so how do we come to terms with a story that tells us that a traveling salesman woke one morning to find he was an insect? It's a delicate operation at best. On the one hand, you probably need to bring it into "ordinary" terms: Gregor is not *really* turned into a bug—cockroach, bedbug, dung beetle, whatever—but falls ill or falls in love or he just wakes up one morning and says to hell with it all and decides not to go to work (even though he's frightened not to), or in some other way separates himself from his family and his job, his role as provider, and he becomes repulsive, or unnecessary. He is rejected, and the family, which seemed dependent on him, survives and even flourishes. Or can it be Gregor's revulsion at himself and at the role forced upon him by the family, the feeling that they are exploiting him and will exploit him until he dies, but that they can, if they want, get along very well without him and without exploiting him? Some such reductive "realistic" or psychological reading is possible and in a sense perhaps necessary so that we can connect the story to our own lives or world.

But we cannot exterminate the bug without destroying the story. The preservation of the narrative surface is not just homage to some icon sacred to art or literature but necessary to preserve the emotional and imaginative impact of the story, the feelings—repulsion, frustration, horror, contempt, pity, impatience, humor—all mixed and separate, simultaneous and alternating which *define the experience* more accurately than the reductive realistic or psychological interpretation can. As Tolstoy might have it, art is a more effective form of transmission of perception through feeling than is any argument or statement into which we can translate (or metamorphose) it. Gregor Samsa is a traveling salesman who supports his family, *and* an insect, a mutant of the imagination essential for understanding the world of human experience.

D. H. LAWRENCE

The Fox

His father a coal miner, his mother middle class, young "Bertie" Lawrence won a scholarship to Nottingham High School in 1898 when he was thirteen, but had to leave school a few years later when his elder brother died. He worked for a surgical-appliance manufacturer, became a pupil-teacher, and attended Nottingham College, where in 1906 he earned his certificate; he left Nottinghamshire for Croydon, near London, where he taught school. When, in 1911, his first novel, *The White Peacock*, was published, he left teaching to devote his time to writing. The next year he eloped to the continent with Frieda, wife of Prof. Ernest Weekley and daughter of Baron von Richthofen; in 1914, after her divorce, they were married. During World War I both his novels and the fact that his wife was German gave him trouble: *The Rainbow* was published in September 1915 and suppressed in November; in 1917 he and his wife were ordered away from the Cornish coast, suspected of spying for the Germans. Understandably, in November 1919 the Lawrences left England. Their years of wandering began: first Italy, then Ceylon and Australia, Mexico and New Mexico, then back to England and Italy. His troubles with publishers were not ended by his exile, however: *Women in Love* was published in a subscription edition in New York in 1920, and *Lady Chatterley's Lover* in a similar edition eight years later, but even that was not enough to stem the outrage that lasted for more than a quarter-century after his death; even a volume of his poems was seized in the mails. Through it all he suffered from tuberculosis, the disease from which he finally died, in France in 1930. His other major novels include *Sons and Lovers, Aaron's Rod, The Plumed Serpent;* he is as well an acknowledged twentieth-century master of the short novel and of the short story; his poetry, long neglected, is gaining greater and greater recognition; even his plays have been revived in London, and he is a brilliant, profound, eccentric, and disturbing critic. He seems to speak for and to recent generations even more directly than does his rival as the greatest British fiction writer of the twentieth century, James Joyce.

He believed the novel the highest form of knowing, dealing with the whole living human being. "And being a novelist, I consider myself superior to the saint, the scientist, the philosopher, and the poet, who are all great masters of different bits of man alive, but never get the whole thing." Because he felt novels dealt with particulars, lived life at a specific time and place, he did not believe in the "well-made novel," or rules for writing narrative: "all rules of construction hold good only for novels which are copies of other novels," he wrote. His great subject was, of course, heterosexual love, not because it made great novels, but because it was *the* important human relationship and art is, he thought, "the relation between man and his circumambient universe, at the living moment. . . . The great relationship for humanity will always be the relation between man and woman. The relation between man and man, woman and woman, parent and child, will always be subsidiary."

The Fox was written not long after World War I, which Lawrence, along with most others of his generation, found a cataclysmic upheaval, changing life forever. It is, characteristically, a love story—a Lawrencian love story, which means like no other.

The Fox

THE TWO GIRLS were usually known by their surnames, Banford and March. They had taken the farm together, intending to work it all by themselves: that is, they were going to rear chickens, make a living by poultry, and add to this by keeping a cow, and raising one or two young beasts. Unfortunately things did not turn out well.

Banford was a small, thin, delicate thing with spectacles. She, however, was the principal investor, for March had little or no money. Banford's father, who was a tradesman in Islington,[1] gave his daughter the start, for her health's sake, and because he loved her, and because it did not look as if she would marry. March was more robust. She had learned carpentry and joinery at the evening classes in Islington. She would be the man about the place. They had, moreover, Banford's old grandfather living with them at the start. He had been a farmer. But unfortunately the old man died after he had been at Bailey Farm for a year. Then the two girls were left alone.

They were neither of them young: that is, they were near thirty. But they certainly were not old. They set out quite gallantly with their enterprise. They had numbers of chickens, black Leghorns and white Leghorns, Plymouths and Wyandots; also some ducks; also two heifers in the fields. One heifer, unfortunately, refused absolutely to stay in the Bailey Farm closes. No matter how March made up the fences, the heifer was out, wild in the woods, or trespassing on the neighbouring pasture, and March and Banford were away, flying after her, with more haste than success. So this heifer they sold in despair. And just before the other beast was expecting her first calf, the old man died, and the girls, afraid of the coming event, sold her in a panic, and limited their attentions to fowls and ducks.

In spite of a little chagrin, it was a relief to have no more cattle on hand. Life was not made merely to be slaved away. Both girls agreed in this. The fowls were quite enough trouble. March had set up her carpenter's bench at the end of the open shed. Here she worked, making coops and doors and other appurtenances. The fowls were housed in the bigger building, which had served as barn and cowshed in old days. They had a beautiful home, and should have been perfectly content. Indeed, they looked well enough. But the girls were disgusted at their tendency to strange illnesses, at their exacting way of life, and at their refusal, obstinate refusal, to lay eggs.

March did most of the outdoor work. When she was out and about, in her puttees and breeches, her belted coat and her loose cap, she looked almost like some graceful, loose-balanced young man, for her shoulders were straight, and her movements easy and confident, even tinged with a little indifference, or irony. But her face was not a man's face, ever. The wisps of her crisp dark hair blew about her as she stooped, her eyes were big and wide and dark, when she looked up again, strange, startled, shy and sardonic at once. Her mouth, too, was almost pinched as if in pain

---

1. Heavily populated, residential borough of London with some commerce and light industry.

and irony. There was something odd and unexplained about her. She would stand balanced on one hip, looking at the fowls pottering about in the obnoxious fine mud of the sloping yard, and calling to her favourite white hen, which came in answer to her name. But there was an almost satirical flicker in March's big, dark eyes as she looked at her three-toed flock pottering about under her gaze, and the same slight dangerous satire in her voice as she spoke to the favoured Patty, who pecked at March's boot by way of friendly demonstration.

Fowls did not flourish at Bailey Farm, in spite of all that March did for them. When she provided hot food for them, in the morning, according to rule, she noticed that it made them heavy and dozy for hours. She expected to see them lean against the pillars of the shed in their languid processes of digestion. And she knew quite well that they ought to be busily scratching and foraging about, if they were to come to any good. So she decided to give them their hot food at night, and let them sleep on it. Which she did. But it made no difference.

War conditions, again, were very unfavourable to poultry keeping. Food was scarce and bad. And when the Daylight Saving Bill was passed, the fowls obstinately refused to go to bed as usual, about nine o'clock in the summer time. That was late enough, indeed, for there was no peace till they were shut up and asleep. Now they cheerfully walked around, without so much as glancing at the barn, until ten o'clock or later. Both Banford and March disbelieved in living for work alone. They wanted to read or take a cycle-ride in the evening, or perhaps March wished to paint curvilinear swans on porcelain, with green background, or else make a marvellous fire-screen by processes of elaborate cabinet work. For she was a creature of odd whims and unsatisfied tendencies. But from all these things she was prevented by the stupid fowls.

One evil there was greater than any other. Bailey Farm was a little homestead, with ancient wooden barn and low gabled farm-house, lying just one field removed from the edge of the wood. Since the War[2] the fox was a demon. He carried off the hens under the very noses of March and Banford. Banford would start and stare through her big spectacles with all her eyes, as another squawk and flutter took place at her heels. Too late! Another white Leghorn gone. It was disheartening.

They did what they could to remedy it. When it became permitted to shoot foxes, they stood sentinel with their guns, the two of them, at the favoured hours. But it was no good. The fox was too quick for them. So another year passed, and another, and they were living on their losses, as Banford said. They let their farm-house one summer, and retired to live in a railway-carriage that was deposited as a sort of out-house in a corner of the field. This amused them, and helped their finances. None the less, things looked dark.

Although they were usually the best of friends, because Banford, though nervous and delicate, was a warm, generous soul, and March, though so odd and absent in herself, had a strange magnanimity, yet, in the long solitude, they were apt to become a little irritable with one another, tired of one another. March had four-fifths of the work to do, and though she did not mind, there seemed no relief, and it made her eyes flash curiously sometimes. Then Banford, feeling more nerve-worn than ever, would become despondent, and March would speak sharply to her. They seemed to be losing ground, somehow, losing hope as the months went by. There alone in the fields by the wood, with the wide country stretching hollow and dim to the round hills of the White Horse,[3] in the far distance, they seemed to have to live too much off themselves. There was nothing to keep them up—and no hope.

The fox really exasperated them both. As soon as they had let the fowls out, in the early summer mornings, they had to take their guns and keep guard: and then again, as soon as evening began to mellow, they must go once more. And he was so sly. He slid along in the deep grass, he was difficult as a serpent to see. And he seemed to circumvent the girls deliberately. Once or twice March had caught sight of the white tip of his brush, or the ruddy shadow of him in the deep grass, and she had let fire at him. But he made no account of this.

One evening March was standing with her back to the sunset, her gun under her arm, her hair pushed under her cap. She was half watching, half musing. It was her constant state. Her eyes were keen and observant, but her inner mind took no notice of what she saw. She was always lapsing into this odd, rapt state, her mouth rather screwed up. It was a question, whether she was there, actually consciously present, or not.

The trees on the wood-edge were a darkish, brownish green in the full light—for it was the end of August. Beyond, the naked, copper-like shafts and limbs of the pine-trees shone in the air. Nearer, the rough grass, with its long brownish stalks all agleam, was full of light. The fowls were round about—the ducks were still swimming on the pond under the pine-trees. March looked at it all, saw it all, and did not see it. She heard Banford speaking to the fowls, in the distance—and she did not hear. What was she thinking about? Heaven knows. Her consciousness was, as it were, held back.

She lowered her eyes, and suddenly saw the fox. He was looking up at her. His chin was pressed down, and his eyes were looking up. They met her eyes. And he knew her. She was spell-bound—she knew he knew her. So he looked into her eyes, and her soul failed her. He knew her, he was not daunted.

She struggled, confusedly she came to herself, and saw him making off, with slow leaps over some fallen boughs, slow, impudent jumps. Then he glanced over his shoulder, and ran smoothly away. She saw his brush held smooth like a feather, she saw his white buttocks twinkle. And he was gone, softly, soft as the wind.

She put her gun to her shoulder, but even then pursed her mouth, knowing it was nonsense to pretend to fire. So she began to walk slowly after him, in the direction he had gone, slowly, pertinaciously. She expected to find him. In her heart she was determined to find him. What she would do when she saw him again she did not consider. But she was determined to find him. So she walked abstractedly about on the edge of the wood, with wide, vivid dark eyes, and a faint flush in her cheeks. She did not think. In strange mindlessness she walked hither and thither.

At last she became aware that Banford was calling her. She made an effort of attention, turned, and gave some sort of screaming call in an-

---

3. Hills fifty to seventy-five miles west of London; the White Horse is a large figure (over 350 feet long) made by cutting away the turf on an escarpment of the Chalk Downs in Berkshire.

swer. Then again she was striding off towards the homestead. The red sun was setting, the fowls were retiring towards their roost. She watched them, white creatures, black creatures, gathering to the barn. She watched them spell-bound, without seeing them. But her automatic intelligence told her when it was time to shut the door.

She went indoors to supper, which Banford had set on the table. Banford chatted easily. March seemed to listen, in her distant, manly way. She answered a brief word now and then. But all the time she was as if spell-bound. And as soon as supper was over, she rose again to go out, without saying why.

She took her gun again and went to look for the fox. For he had lifted his eyes upon her, and his knowing look seemed to have entered her brain. She did not so much think of him: she was possessed by him. She saw his dark, shrewd, unabashed eye looking into her, knowing her. She felt him invisibly master her spirit. She knew the way he lowered his chin as he looked up, she knew his muzzle, the golden brown, and the greyish white. And again, she saw him glance over his shoulder at her, half-inviting, half-contemptuous and cunning. So she went, with her great startled eyes glowing, her gun under her arm, along the wood-edge. Meanwhile the night fell, and a great moon rose above the pine-trees. And again Banford was calling.

So she went indoors. She was silent and busy. She examined her gun, and cleaned it, musing abstractedly by the lamp-light. Then she went out again, under the great moon, to see if everything was right. When she saw the dark crests of the pine-trees against the blood-red sky, again her heart beat to the fox, the fox. She wanted to follow him, with her gun.

It was some days before she mentioned the affair to Banford. Then suddenly, one evening, she said:

"The fox was right at my feet on Saturday night."

"Where?" said Banford, her eyes opening behind her spectacles.

"When I stood just above the pond."

"Did you fire?" cried Banford.

"No, I didn't."

"Why not?"

"Why, I was too much surprised, I suppose."

It was the same old, slow, laconic way of speech March always had. Banford stared at her friend for a few moments.

"You saw him?" she cried.

"Oh, yes! He was looking up at me, cool as anything."

"I tell you," cried Banford—"the cheek!—They're not afraid of us, Nellie."

"Oh, no," said March.

"Pity you didn't get a shot at him," said Banford.

"Isn't it a pity! I've been looking for him ever since. But I don't suppose he'll come so near again."

"I don't suppose he will," said Banford.

And she proceeded to forget about it, except that she was more indignant than ever at the impudence of the beggar. March also was not conscious that she thought of the fox. But whenever she fell into her half-musing, when she was half-rapt, and half-intelligently aware of what passed under her vision, then it was the fox which somehow dominated her unconsciousness, possessed the blank half of her musing. And so it was

for weeks, and months. No matter whether she had been climbing the
trees for the apples, or beating down the last of the damsons, or whether
she had been digging out the ditch from the duck-pond, or clearing out
the barn, when she had finished, or when she straightened herself, and
pushed the wisps of hair away again from her forehead, and pursed up
her mouth again in an odd, screwed fashion, much too old for her years,
there was sure to come over her mind the old spell of the fox, as it came
when he was looking at her. It was as if she could smell him at these
times. And it always recurred, at unexpected moments, just as she was
going to sleep at night, or just as she was pouring the water into the
tea-pot, to make tea—it was the fox, it came over her like a spell.

So the months passed. She still looked for him unconsciously when
she went towards the wood. He had become a settled effect in her spirit,
a state permanently established, not continuous, but always recurring. She
did not know what she felt or thought: only the state came over her, as
when he looked at her.

The months passed, the dark evenings came, heavy, dark November,
when March went about in high boots, ankle deep in mud, when the
night began to fall at four o'clock, and the day never properly dawned.
Both girls dreaded these times. They dreaded the almost continuous darkness that enveloped them on their desolate little farm near the wood.
Banford was physically afraid. She was afraid of tramps, afraid lest someone should come prowling round. March was not so much afraid, as uncomfortable, and disturbed. She felt discomfort and gloom in all her
physique.

Usually the two girls had tea in the sitting room. March lighted a fire
at dusk, and put on the wood she had chopped and sawed during the day.
Then the long evening was in front, dark, sodden, black outside, lonely
and rather oppressive inside, a little dismal. March was content not to
talk, but Banford could not keep still. Merely listening to the wind in the
pines outside, or the drip of water, was too much for her.

One evening the girls had washed up the tea-things in the kitchen, and
March had put on her house-shoes, and taken up a roll of crochet-work,
which she worked at slowly from time to time. So she lapsed into silence.
Banford stared at the red fire, which, being of wood, needed constant
attention. She was afraid to begin to read too early, because her eyes
would not bear any strain. So she sat staring at the fire, listening to the
distant sounds, sound of cattle lowing, of a dull, heavy moist wind, of the
rattle of the evening train on the little railway not far off. She was almost
fascinated by the red glow of the fire.

Suddenly both girls started, and lifted their heads. They heard a footstep—distinctly a footstep. Banford recoiled in fear. March stood listening.
Then rapidly she approached the door that led into the kitchen. At the
same time they heard the footsteps approach the back door. They waited
a second. The back door opened softly. Banford gave a loud cry. A man's
voice said softly:

"Hello!"

March recoiled, and took a gun from a corner.

"What do you want?" she cried, in a sharp voice.

Again the soft, softly-vibrating man's voice said:

"Hello! What's wrong?"

"I shall shoot!" cried March. "What do you want?"

"Why, what's wrong? What's wrong?" came the soft, wondering, rather scared voice: and a young soldier, with his heavy kit on his back, advanced into the dim light. "Why," he said, "who lives here then?"

"We live here," said March. "What do you want?"

"Oh!" came the long, melodious, wonder-note from the young soldier. "Doesn't William Grenfel live here then?"

"No—you know he doesn't."

"Do I?—Do I? I don't, you see.—He *did* live here, because he was my grandfather, and I lived here myself five years ago. What's become of him then?"

The young man—or youth, for he would not be more than twenty, now advanced and stood in the inner doorway. March, already under the influence of his strange, soft, modulated voice, stared at him spell-bound. He had a ruddy, roundish face, with fairish hair, rather long, flattened to his forehead with sweat. His eyes were blue, and very bright and sharp. On his cheeks, on the fresh ruddy skin were fine, fair hairs, like a down, but sharper. It gave him a slightly glistening look. Having his heavy sack on his shoulders, he stooped, thrusting his head forward. His hat was loose in one hand. He stared brightly, very keenly from girl to girl, particularly at March, who stood pale, with great dilated eyes, in her belted coat and puttees, her hair knotted in a big crisp knot behind. She still had the gun in her hand. Behind her, Banford, clinging to the sofa-arm, was shrinking away, with half-averted head.

"I thought my grandfather still lived here?—I wonder if he's dead."

"We've been here for three years," said Banford, who was beginning to recover her wits, seeing something boyish in the round head with its rather long sweaty hair.

"Three years! you don't say so!—And you don't know who was here before you?"

"I know it was an old man, who lived by himself."

"Ay! Yes, that's him!—And what became of him then?"

"He died.—I know he died—"

"Ay! He's dead then!"

The youth stared at them without changing colour or expression. If he had any expression, besides a slight baffled look of wonder, it was one of sharp curiosity concerning the two girls; sharp impersonal curiosity, the curiosity of that round young head.

But to March he was the fox. Whether it was the thrusting forward of his head, or the glisten of fine whitish hairs on the ruddy cheek-bones, or the bright, keen eyes, that can never be said: but the boy was to her the fox, and she could not see him otherwise.

"How is it you didn't know if your grandfather was alive or dead?" asked Banford, recovering her natural sharpness.

"Ay, that's it," replied the softly-breathing youth. "You see I joined up in Canada, and I hadn't heard for three or four years.—I ran away to Canada."

"And now have you just come from France?"

"Well—from Salonika really."

There was a pause, nobody knowing quite what to say.

"So you've nowhere to go now?" said Banford rather lamely.

"Oh, I know some people in the village. Anyhow, I can go to the Swan."

"You came on the train, I suppose.—Would you like to sit down a bit?"

"Well—I don't mind."

He gave an odd little groan as he swung off his kit. Banford looked at March.

"Put the gun down," she said. "We'll make a cup of tea."

"Ay," said the youth. "We've seen enough of rifles."

He sat down rather tired on the sofa, leaning forward.

March recovered her presence of mind, and went into the kitchen. There she heard the soft young voice musing:

"Well, to think I should come back and find it like this!" He did not seem sad, not at all—only rather interestedly surprised.

"And what a difference in the place, eh?" he continued, looking round the room.

"You see a difference, do you?" said Banford.

"Yes,—don't I!"

His eyes were unnaturally clear and bright, though it was the brightness of abundant health.

March was busy in the kitchen preparing another meal. It was about seven o'clock. All the time, while she was active, she was attending to the youth in the sitting-room, not so much listening to what he said, as feeling the soft run of his voice. She primmed up her mouth tighter and tighter, puckering it as if it was sewed, in her effort to keep her will uppermost. Yet her large eyes dilated and glowed in spite of her; she lost herself. Rapidly and carelessly she prepared the meal, cutting large chunks of bread and margarine—for there was no butter. She racked her brain to think of something else to put on the tray—she had only bread, margarine, and jam, and the larder was bare. Unable to conjure anything up, she went into the sitting-room with her tray.

She did not want to be noticed. Above all, she did not want him to look at her. But when she came in, and was busy setting the table just behind him, he pulled himself up from his sprawling, and turned and looked over his shoulder. She became pale and wan.

The youth watched her as she bent over the table, looked at her slim, well-shapen legs, at the belted coat dropping around her thighs, at the knot of dark hair, and his curiosity, vivid and widely alert, was again arrested by her.

The lamp was shaded with a dark-green shade, so that the light was thrown downwards, the upper half of the room was dim. His face moved bright under the light, but March loomed shadowy in the distance.

She turned round, but kept her eyes sideways, dropping and lifting her dark lashes. Her mouth unpuckered as she said to Banford:

"Will you pour out?"

Then she went into the kitchen again.

"Have your tea where you are, will you?" said Banford to the youth—"unless you'd rather come to the table."

"Well," said he, "I'm nice and comfortable here, aren't I? I will have it here, if you don't mind."

"There's nothing but bread and jam," she said. And she put his plate on a stool by him. She was very happy now, waiting on him. For she loved company. And now she was no more afraid of him than if he were her own younger brother. He was such a boy.

"Nellie," she cried. "I've poured you a cup out."

March appeared in the doorway, took her cup, and sat down in a corner, as far from the light as possible. She was very sensitive in her knees. Having no skirts to cover them, and being forced to sit with them boldly exposed, she suffered. She shrank and shrank, trying not to be seen. And the youth, sprawling low on the couch, glanced up at her, with long, steady, penetrating looks, till she was almost ready to disappear. Yet she held her cup balanced, she drank her tea, screwed up her mouth and held her head averted. Her desire to be invisible was so strong that it quite baffled the youth. He felt he could not see her distinctly. She seemed like a shadow within the shadow. And ever his eyes came back to her, searching, unremitting, with unconscious fixed attention.

Meanwhile he was talking softly and smoothly to Banford, who loved nothing so much as gossip, and who was full of perky interest, like a bird. Also he ate largely and quickly and voraciously, so that March had to cut more chunks of bread and margarine, for the roughness of which Banford apologized.

"Oh, well," said March, suddenly speaking, "if there's no butter to put on it, it's no good trying to make dainty pieces."

Again the youth watched her, and he laughed, with a sudden, quick laugh, showing his teeth and wrinkling his nose.

"It isn't, is it?" he answered, in his soft, near voice.

It appeared he was Cornish by birth and upbringing. When he was twelve years old he had come to Bailey Farm with his grandfather, with whom he had never agreed very well. So he had run away to Canada, and worked far away in the West. Now he was here—and that was the end of it.

He was very curious about the girls, to find out exactly what they were doing. His questions were those of a farm youth; acute, practical, a little mocking. He was very much amused by their attitude to their losses: for they were amusing on the score of heifers and fowls.

"Oh, well," broke in March, "we don't believe in living for nothing but work."

"Don't you?" he answered. And again the quick young laugh came over his face. He kept his eyes steadily on the obscure woman in the corner.

"But what will you do when you've used up all your capital?" he said.

"Oh, I don't know," answered March laconically. "Hire ourselves out for landworkers, I suppose."

"Yes, but there won't be any demand for women landworkers, now the war's over," said the youth.

"Oh, we'll see. We shall hold on a bit longer yet," said March, with a plangent, half-sad, half-ironical indifference.

"There wants a man about the place," said the youth softly. Banford burst out laughing.

"Take care what you say," she interrupted. "We consider ourselves quite efficient."

"Oh," came March's slow, plangent voice, "It isn't a case of efficiency, I'm afraid. If you're going to do farming you must be at it from morning till night, and you might as well be a beast yourself."

"Yes, that's it," said the youth. "You aren't willing to put yourselves into it."

"We aren't," said March, "and we know it."

"We want some of our time for ourselves," said Banford.

The youth threw himself back on the sofa, his face tight with laughter, and laughed silently but thoroughly. The calm scorn of the girls tickled him tremendously.

"Yes," he said, "but why did you begin then?"

"Oh," said March, "we had a better opinion of the nature of fowls then, than we have now."

"Of Nature altogether, I'm afraid," said Banford. "Don't talk to me about Nature."

Again the face of the youth tightened with delighted laughter.

"You haven't a very high opinion of fowls and cattle, have you?" he said.

"Oh, no—quite a low one," said March.

He laughed out.

"Neither fowls nor heifers," said Banford, "nor goats nor the weather."

The youth broke into a sharp yap of laughter, delighted. The girls began to laugh too, March turning aside her face and wrinkling her mouth in amusement.

"Oh, well," said Banford, "we don't mind, do we, Nellie?"

"No," said March, "we don't mind."

The youth was very pleased. He had eaten and drunk his fill. Banford began to question him. His name was Henry Grenfel—no, he was not called Harry, always Henry. He continued to answer with courteous simplicity, grave and charming. March, who was not included, cast long, slow glances at him from her recess, as he sat there on the sofa, his hands clasping his knees, his face under the lamp bright and alert, turned to Banford. She became almost peaceful, at last. He was identified with the fox—and he was here in full presence. She need not go after him any more. There in the shadow of her corner she gave herself up to a warm, relaxed peace, almost like sleep, accepting the spell that was on her. But she wished to remain hidden. She was only fully at peace whilst he forgot her, talking with Banford. Hidden in the shadow of the corner, she need not any more be divided in herself, trying to keep up two planes of consciousness. She could at last lapse into the odour of the fox.

For the youth, sitting before the fire in his uniform, sent a faint but distinct odour into the room, indefinable, but something like a wild creature. March no longer tried to reserve herself from it. She was still and soft in her corner like a passive creature in its cave.

At last the talk dwindled. The youth relaxed his clasp of his knees, pulled himself together a little, and looked round. Again he became aware of the silent, half-invisible woman in the corner.

"Well," he said, unwillingly, "I suppose I'd better be going, or they'll be in bed at the Swan."

"I'm afraid they're in bed anyhow," said Banford. "They've all got this influenza."

"Have they!" he exclaimed. And he pondered. "Well," he continued, "I shall find a place somewhere."

"I'd say you could stay here, only—" Banford began.

He turned and watched her, holding his head forward.

"What—?" he asked.

"Oh, well," she said, "propriety, I suppose—" She was rather confused.

"It wouldn't be improper, would it?" he said, gently surprised.

"Not as far as we're concerned," said Banford.

"And not as far as I'm concerned," he said, with grave naïveté. "After all, it's my own home, in a way."

Banford smiled at this.

"It's what the village will have to say," she said.

There was a moment's blank pause.

"What do you say, Nellie?" asked Banford

"I don't mind," said March, in her distinct tone. "The village doesn't matter to me, anyhow."

"No," said the youth, quick and soft. "Why should it?—I mean, what should they say?"

"Oh, well," came March's plangent, laconic voice, "they'll easily find something to say. But it makes no difference, what they say. We can look after ourselves."

"Of course you can," said the youth.

"Well then, stop if you like," said Banford. "The spare room is quite ready."

His face shone with pleasure.

"If you're quite sure it isn't troubling you too much," he said, with that soft courtesy which distinguished him.

"Oh, it's no trouble," they both said.

He looked, smiling with delight, from one to another.

"It's awfully nice not to have to turn out again, isn't it?" he said gratefully.

"I suppose it is," said Banford.

March disappeared to attend to the room. Banford was as pleased and thoughtful as if she had her own young brother home from France. It gave her just the same kind of gratification to attend on him, to get out the bath for him, and everything. Her natural warmth and kindliness had now an outlet. And the youth luxuriated in her sisterly attention. But it puzzled him slightly to know that March was silently working for him too. She was so curiously silent and obliterated. It seemed to him he had not really seen her. He felt he should not know her if he met her in the road.

That night March dreamed vividly. She dreamed she heard a singing outside, which she could not understand, a singing that roamed round the house, in the fields and in the darkness. It moved her so, that she felt she must weep. She went out, and suddenly she knew it was the fox singing. He was very yellow and bright, like corn. She went nearer to him, but he ran away and ceased singing. He seemed near, and she wanted to touch him. She stretched out her hand, but suddenly he bit her wrist, and at the same instant, as she drew back, the fox, turning round to bound away, whisked his brush across her face, and it seemed his brush was on fire, for it seared and burned her mouth with a great pain. She awoke with the pain of it, and lay trembling as if she were really seared.

In the morning, however, she only remembered it as a distant memory. She arose and was busy preparing the house and attending to the fowls. Banford flew into the village on her bicycle, to try and buy food. She was a hospitable soul. But alas in the year 1918 there was not much food to buy. The youth came downstairs in his shirt-sleeves. He was young and fresh, but he walked with his head thrust forward, so that his shoulders seemed raised and rounded, as if he had a slight curvature of the spine. It must have been only a manner of bearing himself, for he was young and vigorous. He washed himself and went outside, whilst the women were preparing breakfast.

He saw everything, and examined everything. His curiosity was quick and insatiable. He compared the state of things with that which he remembered before, and cast over in his mind the effect of the changes. He watched the fowls and the ducks, to see their condition, he noticed the flight of wood-pigeons overhead: they were very numerous; he saw the few apples high up, which March had not been able to reach; he remarked that they had borrowed a draw-pump, presumably to empty the big soft-water cistern which was on the north side of the house.

"It's a funny, dilapidated old place," he said to the girls, as he sat at breakfast.

His eyes were wise and childish, with thinking about things. He did not say much, but ate largely. March kept her face averted. She, too, in the early morning, could not be aware of him, though something about the glint of his khaki reminded her of the brilliance of her dream-fox.

During the day the girls went about their business. In the morning, he attended to the guns, shot a rabbit and a wild duck that was flying high, towards the wood. That was a great addition to the empty larder. The girls felt that already he had earned his keep. He said nothing about leaving, however. In the afternoon he went to the village. He came back at tea-time. He had the same alert, forward-reaching look on his roundish face. He hung his hat on a peg with a little swinging gesture. He was thinking about something.

"Well," he said to the girls, as he sat at table. "What am I going to do?"

"How do you mean—what are you going to do?" said Banford.

"Where am I going to find a place in the village to stay?" he said.

"I don't know," said Banford. "Where do you think of staying?"

"Well—" he hesitated—"at the Swan they've got this flu, and at the Plough and Harrow they've got the soldiers who are collecting the hay for the army: besides in the private houses, there's ten men and a corporal altogether billeted in the village, they tell me. I'm not sure where I could get a bed."

He left the matter to them. He was rather calm about it. March sat with her elbows on the table, her two hands supporting her chin, looking at him unconsciously. Suddenly he lifted his clouded blue eyes, and unthinking looked straight into March's eyes. He was startled as well as she. He, too, recoiled a little. March felt the same sly, taunting, knowing spark leap out of his eyes as he turned his head aside, and fall into her soul, as it had fallen from the dark eyes of the fox. She pursed her mouth as if in pain, as if asleep too.

"Well, I don't know—" Banford was saying. She seemed reluctant, as if she were afraid of being imposed upon. She looked at March. But, with her weak, troubled sight, she only saw the usual semi-abstraction on her friend's face. "Why don't you speak, Nellie?" she said.

But March was wide-eyed and silent, and the youth, as if fascinated, was watching her without moving his eyes.

"Go on—answer something," said Banford. And March turned her head slightly aside, as if coming to consciousness, or trying to come to consciousness.

"What do you expect me to say?" she asked automatically.

"Say what you think," said Banford.

"It's all the same to me," said March.

And again there was silence. A pointed light seemed to be on the boy's eyes, penetrating like a needle.

"So it is to me," said Banford. "You can stop on here if you like."

A smile like a cunning little flame came over his face, suddenly and involuntarily. He dropped his head quickly to hide it, and remained with his head dropped, his face hidden.

"You can stop on here if you like. You can please yourself, Henry," Banford concluded.

Still he did not reply, but remained with his head dropped. Then he lifted his face. It was bright with a curious light, as if exultant, and his eyes were strangely clear as he watched March. She turned her face aside, her mouth suffering as if wounded, and her consciousness dim.

Banford became a little puzzled. She watched the steady, pellucid gaze of the youth's eyes, as he looked at March, with the invisible smile gleaming on his face. She did not know how he was smiling, for no feature moved. It seemed only in the gleam, almost the glitter of the fine hairs on his cheeks. Then he looked with quite a changed look, at Banford.

"I'm sure," he said in his soft, courteous voice, "you're awfully good. You're too good. You don't want to be bothered with me, I'm sure."

"Cut a bit of bread, Nellie," said Banford uneasily; adding: "It's no bother, if you like to stay. It's like having my own brother here for a few days. He's a boy like you are."

"That's awfully kind of you," the lad repeated. "I should like to stay, ever so much, if you're sure I'm not a trouble to you."

"No, of course you're no trouble. I tell you, it's a pleasure to have somebody in the house besides ourselves," said warm-hearted Banford.

"But Miss March?" he said in his soft voice, looking at her.

"Oh, it's quite all right as far as I'm concerned," said March vaguely.

His face beamed, and he almost rubbed his hands with pleasure.

"Well, then," he said, "I should love it, if you'd let me pay my board and help with the work."

"You've no need to talk about board," said Banford.

One or two days went by, and the youth stayed on at the farm. Banford was quite charmed by him. He was so soft and courteous in speech, not wanting to say much himself, preferring to hear what she had to say, and to laugh in his quick, half-mocking way. He helped readily with the work—but not too much. He loved to be out alone with the gun in his hands, to watch, to see. For his sharp-eyed, impersonal curiosity was insatiable, and he was most free when he was quite alone, half-hidden, watching.

Particularly he watched March. She was a strange character to him. Her figure, like a graceful young man's, piqued him. Her dark eyes made something rise in his soul, with a curious elate excitement, when he looked into them, an excitement he was afraid to let be seen, it was so keen and secret. And then her odd, shrewd speech made him laugh outright. He felt he must go further, he was inevitably impelled. But he put away the thought of her, and went off towards the wood's edge with the gun.

The dusk was falling as he came home, and with the dusk, a fine, late November rain. He saw the fire-light leaping in the window of the sitting-room, a leaping light in the little cluster of the dark buildings. And he thought to himself, it would be a good thing to have this place for his own. And then the thought entered him shrewdly: why not marry March? He stood still in the middle of the field for some moments, the dead rabbit hanging still in his hand, arrested by this thought. His mind waited in amazement—it seemed to calculate . . . then he smiled curiously to himself in acquiescence. Why not? Why not, indeed? It was a good idea. What if it was rather ridiculous? What did it matter? What if she was older than he? It didn't matter. When he thought of her dark, startled, vulnerable eyes he smiled subtly to himself. He was older than she, really. He was master of her.

He scarcely admitted his intention even to himself. He kept it as a secret even from himself. It was all too uncertain as yet. He would have to see how things went. Yes, he would have to see how things went. If he wasn't careful, she would just simply mock at the idea. He knew, sly and subtle as he was, that if he went to her plainly and said: "Miss March, I love you and want you to marry me," her inevitable answer would be: "Get out. I don't want any of that tomfoolery." This was her attitude to men and their "tomfoolery." If he was not careful, she would turn round on him with her savage, sardonic ridicule, and dismiss him from the farm and from her own mind, for ever. He would have to go gently. He would have to catch her as you catch a deer or a wood-cock when you go out shooting. It's no good walking out into the forest and saying to the deer: "Please fall to my gun." No, it is a slow, subtle battle. When you really go out to get a deer, you gather yourself together, you coil yourself inside yourself, and you advance secretly, before dawn, into the mountains. It is not so much what you do, when you go out hunting, as how you feel. You have to be subtle and cunning and absolutely fatally ready. It becomes like a fate. Your own fate overtakes and determines the fate of the deer you are hunting. First of all, even before you come in sight of your quarry, there is a strange battle, like mesmerism. Your own soul, as a hunter, has gone out to fasten on the soul of the deer, even before you see any deer. And the soul of the deer fights to escape. Even before the deer has any wind of you, it is so. It is a subtle, profound battle of wills, which takes place in the invisible. And it is a battle never finished till your bullet goes home. When you are *really* worked up to the true pitch, and you come at last into range, you don't then aim as you do when you are firing at a bottle. It is your own *will* which carries the bullet into the heart of your quarry. The bullet's flight home is a sheer projection of your own fate into the fate of the deer. It happens like a supreme wish, a supreme act of volition, not as a dodge of cleverness.

He was a huntsman in spirit, not a farmer, and not a soldier stuck in a regiment. And it was as a young hunter, that he wanted to bring down March as his quarry, to make her his wife. So he gathered himself subtly together, seemed to withdraw into a kind of invisibility. He was not quite sure how he would go on. And March was suspicious as a hare. So he remained in appearance just the nice, odd stranger-youth, staying for a fortnight on the place.

He had been sawing logs for the fire, in the afternoon. Darkness came very early. It was still a cold, raw mist. It was getting almost too dark to see. A pile of short sawed logs lay beside the trestle. March came to carry them indoors, or into the shed, as he was busy sawing the last log. He was working in his shirt-sleeves, and did not notice her approach. She came unwillingly, as if shy. He saw her stooping to the bright-ended logs, and he stopped sawing. A fire like lightning flew down his legs in the nerves.

"March?" he said, in his quiet young voice.

She looked up from the logs she was piling.

"Yes!" she said.

He looked down on her in the dusk. He could see her not too distinctly.

"I wanted to ask you something," he said.

"Did you? What was it?" she said. Already the fright was in her voice. But she was too much mistress of herself.

"Why—" his voice seemed to draw out soft and subtle, it penetrated her nerves—"why, what do you think it is?"

She stood up, placed her hands on her hips, and stood looking at him transfixed, without answering. Again he burned with a sudden power.

"Well," he said, and his voice was so soft it seemed rather like a subtle touch, like the merest touch of a cat's paw, a feeling rather than a sound. "Well—I wanted to ask you to marry me."

March felt rather than heard him. She was trying in vain to turn aside her face. A great relaxation seemed to have come over her. She stood silent, her head slightly on one side. He seemed to be bending towards her, invisibly smiling. It seemed to her fine sparks came out of him.

Then very suddenly, she said:

"Don't try any of your tomfoolery on me."

A quiver went over his nerves. He had missed. He waited a moment to collect himself again. Then he said, putting all the strange softness into his voice, as if he were imperceptibly stroking her:

"Why, it's not tomfoolery. It's not tomfoolery. I mean it. I mean it. What makes you disbelieve me?"

He sounded hurt. And his voice had such a curious power over her; making her feel loose and relaxed. She struggled somewhere for her own power. She felt for a moment that she was lost—lost—lost. The word seemed to rock in her as if she were dying. Suddenly again she spoke.

"You don't know what you are talking about," she said, in a brief and transient stroke of scorn. "What nonsense! I'm old enough to be your mother."

"Yes, I do know what I'm talking about. Yes, I do," he persisted softly, as if he were producing his voice in her blood. "I know quite well what I'm talking about. You're not old enough to be my mother. That isn't true. And what does it matter even if it was? You can marry me whatever age we are. What is age to me? And what is age to you! Age is nothing."

A swoon went over her as he concluded. He spoke rapidly—in the rapid Cornish fashion—and his voice seemed to sound in her somewhere where she was helpless against it. "Age is nothing!" The soft, heavy insistence of it made her sway dimly out there in the darkness. She could not answer.

A great exultance leaped like fire over his limbs. He felt he had won.

"I want to marry you, you see. Why shouldn't I?" he proceeded, soft and rapid. He waited for her to answer. In the dusk he saw her almost phosphorescent. Her eyelids were dropped, her face half-averted and unconscious. She seemed to be in his power. But he waited, watchful. He dared not yet touch her.

"Say then," he said. "Say then you'll marry me. Say—say!" He was softly insistent.

"What?" she asked, faint, from a distance, like one in pain. His voice was now unthinkably near and soft. He drew very near to her.

"Say yes."

"Oh, I can't," she wailed helplessly, half articulate, as if semi-conscious, and as if in pain, like one who dies. "How can I?"

"You can," he said softly, laying his hand gently on her shoulder as she stood with her head averted and dropped, dazed. "You can. Yes, you can. What makes you say you can't? You can. You can." And with awful softness he bent forward and just touched her neck with his mouth and his chin.

"Don't!" she cried, with a faint mad cry like hysteria, starting away and facing round on him. "What do you mean?" But she had no breath to speak with. It was as if she were killed.

"I mean what I say," he persisted softly and cruelly. "I want you to marry me. I want you to marry me. You know that, now, don't you? You know that, now? Don't you? Don't you?"

"What?" she said.

"Know," he replied.

"Yes," she said. "I know you say so."

"And you know I mean it, don't you?"

"I know you say so."

"You believe me?" he said.

She was silent for some time. Then she pursed her lips.

"I don't know what I believe," she said.

"Are you out there?" came Banford's voice, calling from the house.

"Yes, we're bringing in the logs," he answered.

"I thought you'd gone lost," said Banford disconsolately. "Hurry up, do, and come and let's have tea. The kettle's boiling."

He stooped at once, to take an armful of little logs and carry them into the kitchen, where they were piled in a corner. March also helped, filling her arms and carrying the logs on her breast as if they were some heavy child. The night had fallen cold.

When the logs were all in, the two cleaned their boots noisily on the scraper outside, then rubbed them on the mat. March shut the door and took off her old felt hat—her farm-girl hat. Her thick, crisp black hair was loose, her face was pale and strained. She pushed back her hair vaguely, and washed her hands. Banford came hurrying into the dimly-lighted kitchen, to take from the oven the scones she was keeping hot.

"Whatever have you been doing all this time?" she asked fretfully. "I thought you were never coming in. And it's ages since you stopped sawing. What were you doing out there?"

"Well," said Henry, "we had to stop that hole in the barn, to keep the rats out."

"Why, I could see you standing there in the shed. I could see your shirt-sleeves," challenged Banford.

"Yes, I was just putting the saw away."

They went in to tea. March was quite mute. Her face was pale and strained and vague. The youth, who always had the same ruddy, self-contained look on his face, as though he were keeping himself to himself, had come to tea in his shirt-sleeves as if he were at home. He bent over his plate as he ate his food.

"Aren't you cold?" said Banford spitefully. "In your shirt-sleeves."

He looked up at her, with his chin near his plate, and his eyes very clear, pellucid, and unwavering as he watched her.

"No, I'm not cold," he said with his usual soft courtesy. "It's much warmer in here than it is outside, you see."

"I hope it is," said Banford, feeling nettled by him. He had a strange suave assurance, and a wide-eyed bright look that got on her nerves this evening.

"But perhaps," he said softly and courteously, "you don't like me coming to tea without my coat. I forgot that."

"Oh, I don't mind," said Banford: although she *did*.

"I'll go and get it, shall I?" he said.

March's dark eyes turned slowly down to him.

"No, don't you bother," she said in her queer, twanging tone. "If you feel all right as you are, stop as you are." She spoke with a crude authority.

"Yes," said he, "I *feel* all right, if I'm not rude."

"It's usually considered rude," said Banford. "But we don't mind."

"Go along, 'considered rude,'" ejaculated March. "Who considers it rude?"

"Why you do, Nellie, in anybody else," said Banford, bridling a little behind her spectacles, and feeling her food stick in her throat.

But March had again gone vague and unheeding, chewing her food as if she did not know she was eating at all. And the youth looked from one to another, with bright, watchful eyes.

Banford was offended. For all his suave courtesy and soft voice, the youth seemed to her impudent. She did not like to look at him. She did not like to meet his clear, watchful eyes, she did not like to see the strange glow in his face, his cheeks with their delicate fine hair, and his ruddy skin that was quite dull and yet which seemed to burn with a curious heat of life. It made her feel a little ill to look at him: the quality of his physical presence was too penetrating, too hot.

After tea the evening was very quiet. The youth rarely went into the village. As a rule he read: he was a great reader, in his own hours. That is, when he did begin, he read absorbedly. But he was not very eager to begin. Often he walked about the fields and along the hedges alone in the dark at night, prowling with a queer instinct for the night, and listening to the wild sounds.

To-night, however, he took a Captain Mayne Reid[4] book from Banford's shelf and sat down with knees wide apart and immersed himself in his story. His brownish fair hair was long, and lay on his head like a thick cap, combed sideways. He was still in his shirt-sleeves, and bending forward under the lamp-light, with his knees stuck wide apart and the book in his hand and his whole figure absorbed in the rather strenuous business of reading, he gave Banford's sitting-room the look of a lumber-camp. She resented this. For on her sitting-room floor she had a red Turkey rug and dark stain round, the fire-place had fashionable green tiles, the piano stood open with the latest dance-music—she played quite well—and on the walls were March's hand-painted swans and water-lilies. Moreover, with the logs nicely, tremulously burning in the grate, the thick curtains drawn,

---

4. A British novelist (1818–1883) who served as captain in the U.S. Army in the Mexican war, and wrote such tales of adventure as *The Rifle Rangers* (1850), *The Scalp-Hunters* (1851), and *The Boy Hunters* (1852).

the doors all shut, and the pine-trees hissing and shuddering in the wind outside, it was cosy, it was refined and nice. She resented the big, raw, long-legged youth sticking his khaki knees out and sitting there with his soldier's shirt-cuffs buttoned on his thick red wrists. From time to time he turned a page, and from time to time he gave a sharp look at the fire, settling the logs. Then he immersed himself again in the intense and isolated business of reading.

March, on the far side of the table, was spasmodically crochetting. Her mouth was pursed in an odd way, as when she had dreamed the fox's brush burned it, her beautiful, crisp black hair strayed in wisps. But her whole figure was absorbed in its bearing, as if she herself were miles away. In a sort of semi-dream she seemed to be hearing the fox singing round the house in the wind, singing wildly and sweetly and like a madness. With red but well-shaped hands she slowly crochetted the white cotton, very slowly, awkwardly.

Banford was also trying to read, sitting in her low chair. But between those two she felt fidgety. She kept moving and looking round and listening to the wind and glancing secretly from one to the other of her companions. March, seated on a straight chair, with her knees in their close breeches crossed, and slowly, laboriously crochetting, was also a trial.

"Oh, dear!" said Banford. "My eyes are bad tonight." And she pressed her fingers on her eyes.

The youth looked up at her with his clear bright look, but did not speak.

"Are they, Jill?" said March absently.

Then the youth began to read again, and Banford perforce returned to her book. But she could not keep still. After a while she looked up at March, and a queer, almost malignant little smile was on her thin face.

"A penny for them, Nell," she said suddenly.

March looked round with big, startled black eyes, and went pale as if with terror. She had been listening to the fox singing so tenderly, so tenderly, as he wandered round the house.

"What?" she said vaguely.

"A penny for them," said Banford sarcastically. "Or twopence, if they're as deep as all that."

The youth was watching with bright clear eyes from beneath the lamp.

"Why," came March's vague voice, "what do you want to waste your money for?"

"I thought it would be well spent," said Branford.

"I wasn't thinking of anything except the way the wind was blowing," said March.

"Oh, dear," replied Banford. "I could have had as original thoughts as that myself. I'm afraid I *have* wasted my money this time."

"Well, you needn't pay," said March.

The youth suddenly laughed. Both women looked at him: March rather surprised-looking, as if she had hardly known he was there.

"Why, do you ever pay up on these occasions?" he asked.

"Oh, yes," said Banford. "We always do. I've sometimes had to pass a shilling[5] a week to Nellie, in the winter time. It costs much less in summer."

5. Twelve pence.

"What, paying for each other's thoughts?" he laughed.

"Yes, when we've absolutely come to the end of everything else."

He laughed quickly, wrinkling his nose sharply like a puppy and laughing with quick pleasure, his eyes shining.

"It's the first time I ever heard of that," he said.

"I guess you'd hear of it often enough if you stayed a winter on Bailey Farm," said Banford lamentably.

"Do you get so tired, then?" he asked.

"So bored," said Banford.

"Oh!" he said gravely. "But why should you be bored?"

"Who wouldn't be bored?" said Banford.

"I'm sorry to hear that," he said gravely.

"You must be, if you were hoping to have a lively time here," said Banford.

He looked at her long and gravely.

"Well," he said, with his odd young seriousness, "it's quite lively enough for me."

"I'm glad to hear it," said Banford.

And she returned to her book. In her thin, frail hair were already many threads of grey, though she was not yet thirty. The boy did not look down, but turned his eyes to March, who was sitting with pursed mouth laboriously crochetting, her eyes wide and absent. She had a warm, pale, fine skin, and a delicate nose. Her pursed mouth looked shrewish. But the shrewish look was contradicted by the curious lifted arch of her dark brows, and the wideness of her eyes; a look of startled wonder and vagueness. She was listening again for the fox, who seemed to have wandered farther off into the night.

From under the edge of the lamp-light the boy sat with his face looking up, watching her silently, his eyes round and very clear and intent. Banford, biting her fingers irritably, was glancing at him under her hair. He sat there perfectly still, his ruddy face tilted up from the low level under the light, on the edge of the dimness, and watching with perfect abstract intentness. March suddenly lifted her great dark eyes from her crochetting, and saw him. She started, giving a little exclamation.

"There he is!" she cried, involuntarily, as if terribly startled.

Banford looked around in amazement, sitting up straight.

"Whatever has got you, Nellie?" she cried.

But March, her face flushed a delicate rose colour, was looking away to the door.

"Nothing! Nothing!" she said crossly. "Can't one speak?"

"Yes, if you speak sensibly," said Banford. "Whatever did you mean?"

"I don't know what I meant," cried March testily.

"Oh, Nellie, I hope you aren't going jumpy and nervy. I feel I can't stand another *thing!*—Whoever did you mean? Did you mean Henry?" cried poor frightened Banford.

"Yes, I suppose so," said March laconically. She would never confess to the fox.

"Oh, dear, my nerves are all gone for to-night," wailed Banford.

At nine o'clock March brought in a tray with bread and cheese and tea—Henry had confessed that he liked a cup of tea. Banford drank a glass of milk, and ate a little bread. And soon she said:

"I'm going to bed, Nellie. I'm all nerves to-night. Are you coming?"

"Yes, I'm coming the minute I've taken the tray away," said March.

"Don't be long then," said Banford fretfully. "Good-night, Henry. You'll see the fire is safe, if you come up last, won't you?"

"Yes, Miss Banford, I'll see it's safe," he replied in his reassuring way.

March was lighting the candle to go to the kitchen. Banford took her candle and went upstairs. When March came back to the fire she said to him:

"I suppose we can trust you to put out the fire and everything?" She stood there with her hand on her hip, and one knee loose, her head averted shyly, as if she could not look at him. He had his face lifted, watching her.

"Come and sit down a minute," he said softly.

"No, I'll be going. Jill will be waiting, and she'll get upset if I don't come."

"What made you jump like that this evening?" he asked.

"When did I jump?" she retorted, looking at him.

"Why, just now you did," he said. "When you cried out."

"Oh!" she said. "Then!—Why, I thought you were the fox!" And her face screwed into a queer smile, half ironic.

"The fox! Why the fox?" he asked softly.

"Why, one evening last summer when I was out with the gun I saw the fox in the grass nearly at my feet, looking straight up at me. I don't know—I suppose he made an impression on me." She turned aside her head again, and let one foot stray loose, self-consciously.

"And did you shoot him?" asked the boy.

"No, he gave me such a start, staring straight at me as he did, and then stopping to look back at me over his shoulder with a laugh on his face."

"A laugh on his face!" repeated Henry, also laughing. "He frightened you, did he?"

"No, he didn't frighten me. He made an impression on me, that's all."

"And you thought I was the fox, did you?" he laughed, with the same queer quick little laugh, like a puppy wrinkling its nose.

"Yes, I did, for the moment," she said. "Perhaps he'd been in my mind without my knowing."

"Perhaps you think I've come to steal your chickens or something," he said, with the same young laugh.

But she only looked at him with a wide, dark, vacant eye.

"It's the first time," he said, "that I've ever been taken for a fox. Won't you sit down for a minute?" His voice was very soft and cajoling.

"No," she said. "Jill will be waiting." But still she did not go, but stood with one foot loose and her face turned aside, just outside the circle of light.

"But won't you answer my question?" he said, lowering his voice still more.

"I don't know what question you mean."

"Yes, you do. Of course you do. I mean the question of you marrying me."

"No, I shan't answer that question," she said flatly.

"Won't you?" The queer young laugh came on his nose again. "Is it because I'm like the fox? Is that why?" And still he laughed.

She turned and looked at him with a long, slow look.

"I wouldn't let that put you against me," he said. "Let me turn the lamp low, and come and sit down a minute."

He put his red hand under the glow of the lamp, and suddenly made the light very dim. March stood there in the dimness quite shadowy, but unmoving. He rose silently to his feet, on his long legs. And now his voice was extraordinarily soft and suggestive, hardly audible.

"You'll stay a moment," he said. "Just a moment." And he put his hand on her shoulder.—She turned her face from him. "I'm sure you don't really think I'm like the fox," he said, with the same softness and with a suggestion of laughter in his tone, a subtle mockery. "Do you now?"—And he drew her gently towards him and kissed her neck, softly. She winced and trembled and hung away. But his strong young arm held her, and he kissed her softly again, still on the neck, for her face was averted.

"Won't you answer my question? Won't you now?" came his soft, lingering voice. He was trying to draw her near to kiss her face. And he kissed her cheek softly, near the ear.

At that moment Banford's voice was heard calling fretfully, crossly, from upstairs.

"There's Jill!" cried March, starting and drawing erect.

And as she did so, quick as lightning he kissed her on the mouth, with a quick brushing kiss. It seemed to burn through her every fibre. She gave a queer little cry.

"You will, won't you? You will?" he insisted softly.

"Nellie! *Nellie!* Whatever are you so long for?" came Banford's faint cry from the outer darkness.

But he held her fast, and was murmuring with that intolerable softness and insistency:

"You will, won't you? Say yes! Say yes!"

March, who felt as if the fire had gone through her and scathed her, and as if she could do no more, murmured:

"Yes! Yes! Anything you like! Anything you like! Only let me go! Only let me go! Jill's calling."

"You know you've promised," he said insidiously.

"Yes! Yes! I do!—" Her voice suddenly rose into a shrill cry. "All right, Jill, I'm coming."

Startled, he let her go, and she went straight upstairs.

In the morning at breakfast, after he had looked round the place and attended to the stock and thought to himself that one could live easily enough here, he said to Banford:

"Do you know what, Miss Banford?"

"Well, what?" said the good-natured, nervy Banford.

He looked at March, who was spreading jam on her bread.

"Shall I tell?" he said to her.

She looked up at him, and a deep pink colour flushed over her face.

"Yes, if you mean Jill," she said. "I hope you won't go talking all over the village, that's all." And she swallowed her dry bread with difficulty.

"Whatever's coming?" said Banford, looking up with wide, tired, slightly reddened eyes. She was a thin, frail little thing, and her hair, which was delicate and thin, was bobbed, so it hung softly by her worn face in its faded brown and grey.

"Why, what do you think?" he said, smiling like one who has a secret.

"How do I know!" said Banford.

"Can't you guess?" he said, making bright eyes, and smiling, pleased with himself.

"I'm sure I can't. What's more, I'm not going to try."

"Nellie and I are going to be married."

Banford put down her knife, out of her thin, delicate fingers, as if she would never take it up to eat any more. She stared with blank, reddened eyes.

"You what?" she exclaimed.

"We're going to get married. Aren't we, Nellie?" and he turned March.

"You say so, anyway," said March laconically. But again she flushed with an agonized flush. She, too, could swallow no more.

Banford looked at her like a bird that has been shot: a poor little sick bird. She gazed at her with all her wounded soul in her face, at the deep-flushed March.

"Never!" she exclaimed, helpless.

"It's quite right," said the bright and gloating youth.

Banford turned aside her face, as if the sight of the food on the table made her sick. She sat like this for some moments, as if she were sick. Then, with one hand on the edge of the table, she rose to her feet.

"I'll *never* believe it, Nellie," she cried. "It's absolutely impossible!"

Her plaintive, fretful voice had a thread of hot anger and despair.

"Why? Why shouldn't you believe it?" asked the youth, with all his soft, velvety impertinence in his voice.

Banford looked at him from her wide vague eyes, as if he were some creature in a museum.

"Oh," she said languidly, "because she can never be such a fool. She can't lose her self-respect to such an extent." Her voice was cold and plaintive, drifting.

"In what way will she lose her self-respect?" asked the boy.

Banford looked at him with vague fixity from behind her spectacles.

"If she hasn't lost it already," she said.

He became very red, vermilion, under the slow vague stare from behind the spectacles.

"I don't see it at all," he said.

"Probably you don't. I shouldn't expect you would," said Banford, with that straying mild tone of remoteness which made her words even more insulting.

He sat stiff in his chair, staring with hot blue eyes from his scarlet face. An ugly look had come on his brow.

"My word, she doesn't know what she's letting herself in for," said Banford, in her plaintive, drifting, insulting voice.

"What has it got to do with you, anyway?" said the youth in a temper.

"More than it has to do with you, probably," she replied, plaintive and venomous.

"Oh, has it! I don't see that at all," he jerked out.

"No, you wouldn't," she answered, drifting.

"Anyhow," said March, pushing back her chair and rising uncouthly, "it's no good arguing about it." And she seized the bread and the tea-pot, and strode away to the kitchen.

Banford let her fingers stray across her brow and along her hair, like one bemused. Then she turned and went away upstairs.

Henry sat stiff and sulky in his chair, with his face and his eyes on fire. March came and went, clearing the table. But Henry sat on, stiff with temper. He took no notice of her. She had regained her composure and her soft, even, creamy complexion. But her mouth was pursed up. She glanced at him each time as she came to take things from the table, glanced from her large, curious eyes, more in curiosity than anything. Such a long, red-faced sulky boy! That was all he was. He seemed as remote from her as if his red face were a red chimney-pot on a cottage across the fields, and she looked at him just as objectively, as remotely.

At length he got up and stalked out into the fields with the gun. He came in only at dinner-time, with the devil still in his face, but his manners quite polite. Nobody said anything particular: they sat each one at the sharp corner of a triangle, in obstinate remoteness. In the afternoon he went out again at once with the gun. He came in at nightfall with a rabbit and a pigeon. He stayed in all evening, but hardly opened his mouth. He was in the devil of a temper, feeling he had been insulted.

Banford's eyes were red, she had evidently been crying. But her manner was more remote and supercilious than ever; the way she turned her head if he spoke at all, as if he were some tramp or inferior intruder of that sort, made his blue eyes go almost black with rage. His face looked sulkier. But he never forgot his polite intonation, if he opened his mouth to speak.

March seemed to flourish in this atmosphere. She seemed to sit between the two antagonists with a little wicked smile on her face, enjoying herself. There was even a sort of complacency in the way she laboriously crochetted this evening.

When he was in bed, the youth could hear the two women talking and arguing in their room. He sat up in bed and strained his ears to hear what they said. But he could hear nothing, it was too far off. Yet he could hear the soft, plaintive drip of Banford's voice, and March's deeper note.

The night was quiet, frosty. Big stars were snapping outside, beyond the ridge-tops of the pine-trees. He listened and listened. In the distance he heard a fox yelping: and the dogs from the farms barking in answer. But it was not that he wanted to hear. It was what the two women were saying.

He got stealthily out of bed, and stood by his door. He could hear no more than before. Very, very carefully he began to lift the door-latch. After quite a time he had his door open. Then he stepped stealthily out into the passage. The old oak planks were cold under his feet, and they creaked preposterously. He crept very, very gently up the one step, and along by the wall, till he stood outside their door. And there he held his breath and listened. Banford's voice:

"No, I simply couldn't stand it. I should be dead in a month. Which is just what he would be aiming at, of course. That would just be his game, to see me in the churchyard. No, Nellie, if you were to do such a thing as to marry him, you could never stop here. I couldn't, I couldn't live in the same house with him. Oh-h! I feel quite sick with the smell of his clothes. And his red face simply turns me over. I can't eat my food when he's at the table. What a fool I was ever to let him stop. One ought *never* to try to do a kind action. It always flies back in your face like a boomerang."

"Well, he's only got two more days," said March.

"Yes, thank heaven. And when he's gone he'll never come in this house again. I feel so bad while he's here. And I know, I know he's only counting what he can get out of you. I know that's all it is. He's just a good-for-nothing, who doesn't want to work, and who thinks he'll live on us. But he won't live on me. If you're such a fool, then it's your own lookout. Mrs. Burgess knew him all the time he was here. And the old man could never get him to do any steady work. He was off with the gun on every occasion, just as he is now. Nothing but the gun! Oh, I do hate it. You don't know what you're doing, Nellie, you don't. If you marry him he'll just make a fool of you. He'll go off and leave you stranded. I know he will. If he can't get Bailey Farm out of us—and he's not going to, while I live. While I live he's never going to set foot here. I know what it would be. He'd soon think he was master of both of us, as he thinks he's master of you already."

"But he isn't," said Nellie.

"He thinks he is, anyway. And that's what he wants: to come and be master here. Yes, imagine it! That's what we've got the place together for, is it, to be bossed and bullied by a hateful red-faced boy, a beastly labourer? Oh, we *did* make a mistake when we let him stop. We ought never to have lowered ourselves. And I've had such a fight with all the people here, not to be pulled down to their level. No, he's not coming here.—And then you see—if he can't have the place, he'll run off to Canada or somewhere again, as if he'd never known you. And here you'll be, absolutely ruined and made a fool of. I know I shall never have any peace of mind again."

"We'll tell him he can't come here. We'll tell him that," said March.

"Oh, don't you bother; I'm going to tell him that, and other things as well, before he goes. He's not going to have all his own way, while I've got the strength left to speak. Oh, Nellie, he'll despise you, he'll despise you like the awful little beast he is, if you give way to him. I'd no more trust him than I'd trust a cat not to steal. He's deep, he's deep, and he's bossy, and he's selfish through and through, as cold as ice. All he wants is to make use of you. And when you're no more use to him, then I pity you."

"I don't think he's as bad as all that," said March.

"No, because he's been playing up to you. But you'll find out, if you see much more of him. Oh, Nellie, I can't bear to think of it."

"Well, it won't hurt you, Jill darling."

"Won't it! Won't it! I shall never know a moment's peace again while I live, nor a moment's happiness. No, Nellie—" and Banford began to weep bitterly.

The boy outside could hear the stifled sound of the woman's sobbing, and could hear March's soft, deep, tender voice comforting, with wonderful gentleness and tenderness, the weeping woman.

His eyes were so round and wide that he seemed to see the whole night, and his ears were almost jumping off his head. He was frozen stiff. He crept back to bed, but felt as if the top of his head were coming off. He could not sleep. He could not keep still. He rose, quietly dressed himself, and crept out on to the landing once more. The women were silent. He went softly downstairs and out to the kitchen.

Then he put on his boots and his overcoat, and took the gun. He did not think to go away from the farm. No, he only took the gun. As softly as possible he unfastened the door and went out into the frosty December night. The air was still, the stars bright, the pine-trees seemed to bristle audibly in the sky. He went stealthily away down a fence-side, looking for something to shoot. At the same time he remembered that he ought not to shoot and frighten the women.

So he prowled round the edge of the gorse cover, and through the grove of tall old hollies, to the woodside. There he skirted the fence, peering through the darkness with dilated eyes that seemed to be able to grow black and full of sight in the dark, like a cat's. An owl was slowly and mournfully whooing round a great oak tree. He stepped stealthily with his gun, listening, listening, watching.

As he stood under the oaks of the wood-edge he heard the dogs from the neighbouring cottage, up the hill, yelling suddenly and startlingly, and the wakened dogs from the farms around barking answer. And suddenly, it seemed to him England was little and tight, he felt the landscape was constricted even in the dark, and that there were too many dogs in the night, making a noise like a fence of sound, like the network of English hedges netting the view. He felt the fox didn't have a chance. For it must be the fox that had started all this hullabaloo.

Why not watch for him, anyhow! He would no doubt be coming sniffing round. The lad walked downhill to where the farmstead with its few pine-trees crouched blackly. In the angle of the long shed, in the black dark, he crouched down. He knew the fox would be coming. It seemed to him it would be the last of the foxes in this loudly-barking, thick-voiced England, tight with innumerable little houses.

He sat a long time with his eyes fixed unchanging upon the open gateway, where a little light seemed to fall from the stars or from the horizon, who knows? He was sitting on a log in a dark corner with the gun across his knees. The pine-trees snapped. Once a chicken fell off its perch in the barn, with a loud crawk and cackle and commotion that startled him, and he stood up, watching with all his eyes, thinking it might be a rat. But he *felt* it was nothing. So he sat down again with the gun on his knees and his hands tucked in to keep them warm, and his eyes fixed unblinking on the pale reach of the open gateway. He felt he could smell the hot, sickly, rich smell of live chickens on the cold air.

And then—a shadow. A sliding shadow in the gateway. He gathered all his vision into a concentrated spark, and saw the shadow of the fox, the fox creeping on his belly through the gate. There he went, on his belly like a snake. The boy smiled to himself and brought the gun to his shoulder. He knew quite well what would happen. He knew the fox would go to where the fowl-door was boarded up, and sniff there. He knew he would lie there for a minute, sniffing the fowls within. And then he would start again prowling under the edge of the old barn, waiting to get in.

The fowl-door was at the top of a slight incline. Soft, soft as a shadow the fox slid up this incline, and crouched with his nose to the boards. And at the same moment there was the awful crash of a gun reverberating between the old buildings, as if all the night had gone smash. But the boy watched keenly. He saw even the white belly of the fox as the beast beat his paws in death. So he went forward.

There was a commotion everywhere. The fowls were scuffling and crawling, the ducks were quark-quarking, the pony had stamped wildly to his feet. But the fox was on his side, struggling in his last tremors. The boy bent over him and smelt his foxy smell.

There was a sound of a window opening upstairs, then March's voice calling:

"Who is it?"

"It's me," said Henry; "I've shot the fox."

"Oh, goodness! You nearly frightened us to death."

"Did I? I'm awfully sorry."

"Whatever made you get up?"

"I heard him about."

"And have you shot him?"

"Yes, he's here," and the boy stood in the yard holding up the warm, dead brute. "You can't see, can you? Wait a minute." And he took his flash-light from his pocket, and flashed it on to the dead animal. He was holding it by the brush. March saw, in the middle of the darkness, just the reddish fleece and the white belly and the white underneath of the pointed chin, and the queer, dangling paws. She did not know what to say.

"He's a beauty," he said. "He will make you a lovely fur."

"You don't catch me wearing a fox fur," she replied.

"Oh!" he said. And he switched off the light.

"Well, I should think you'd come in and go to bed again now," she said.

"Probably I shall. What time is it?"

"What time is it, Jill?" called March's voice. It was a quarter to one.

That night March had another dream. She dreamed that Banford was dead, and that she, March, was sobbing her heart out. Then she had to put Banford into her coffin. And the coffin was the rough wood-box in which the bits of chopped wood were kept in the kitchen, by the fire. This was the coffin, and there was no other, and March was in agony and dazed bewilderment, looking for something to line the box with, something to make it soft with, something to cover up the poor dead darling. Because she couldn't lay her in there just in her white thin nightdress, in the horrible wood-box. So she hunted and hunted, and picked up thing after thing, and threw it aside in the agony of dream-frustration. And in her dream-despair all she could find that would do was a fox-skin. She knew that it wasn't right, that this was not what she should have. But it was all she could find. And so she folded the brush of the fox, and laid her darling Jill's head on this, and she brought round the skin of the fox and laid it on the top of the body, so that it seemed to make a whole ruddy, fiery coverlet, and she cried and cried and woke to find the tears streaming down her face.

The first thing that both she and Banford did in the morning was to go out to see the fox. He had hung it up by the heels in the shed, with its poor brush falling backwards. It was a lovely dog-fox in its prime, with a handsome thick winter coat: a lovely golden-red colour, with grey as it passed to the belly, and belly all white, and a great full brush with a delicate black and grey and pure white tip.

"Poor brute!" said Banford. "If it wasn't such a thieving wretch, you'd feel sorry for it."

March said nothing, but stood with her foot trailing aside, one hip out; her face was pale and her eyes big and black, watching the dead animal that was suspended upside down. White and soft as snow his belly: white and soft as snow. She passed her hand softly down it. And his wonderful black-glinted brush was full and frictional, wonderful. She passed her hand down this also, and quivered. Time after time she took the full fur of that thick tail between her hand, and passed her hand slowly downwards. Wonderful sharp thick splendour of a tail! And he was dead! She pursed her lips, and her eyes went black and vacant. Then she took the head in her hand.

Henry was sauntering up, so Banford walked rather pointedly away. March stood there bemused, with the head of the fox in her hand. She was wondering, wondering, wondering over his long fine muzzle. For some reason it reminded her of a spoon or a spatula. She felt she could not understand it. The beast was a strange beast to her, incomprehensible, out of her range. Wonderful silver whiskers he had, like ice-threads. And pricked ears with hair inside.—But that long, long slender spoon of a nose!—and the marvellous white teeth beneath! It was to thrust forward and bite with,—deep, deep into the living prey, to bite and bite the blood.

"He's a beauty, isn't he?" said Henry, standing by.

"Oh, yes, he's a fine big fox. I wonder how many chickens he's responsible for," she replied.

"A good many. Do you think he's the same one you saw in the summer?"

"I should think very likely he is," she replied.

He watched her, but he could make nothing of her. Partly she was so shy and virgin, and partly she was so grim, matter-of-fact, shrewish. What she said seemed to him so different from the look of her big, queer dark eyes.

"Are you going to skin him?" she asked.

"Yes, when I've had breakfast, and got a board to peg him on."

"My word, what a strong smell he's got! Pooo!—It'll take some washing off one's hands. I don't know why I was so silly as to handle him."—And she looked at her right hand, that had passed down his belly and along his tail, and had even got a tiny streak of blood from one dark place in his fur.

"Have you seen the chickens when they smell him, how frightened they are?" he said.

"Yes, aren't they!"

"You must mind you don't get some of his fleas."

"Oh, fleas!" she replied, nonchalant.

Later in the day she saw the fox's skin nailed flat on a board, as if crucified. It gave her an uneasy feeling.

The boy was angry. He went about with his mouth shut, as if he had swallowed part of his chin. But in behaviour he was polite and affable. He did not say anything about his intentions. And he left March alone.

That evening they sat in the dining-room. Banford wouldn't have him in her sitting-room any more. There was a very big log on the fire. And everybody was busy. Banford had letters to write, March was sewing a dress, and he was mending some little contrivance.

Banford stopped her letter-writing from time to time to look round and rest her eyes. The boy had his head down, his face hidden over his job.

"Let's see," said Banford. "What train do you go by, Henry?"

He looked up straight at her.

"The morning train. In the morning," he said.

"What, the eight-ten or the eleven-twenty?"

"The eleven-twenty, I suppose," he said.

"That is the day after to-morrow?" said Banford.

"Yes, the day after to-morrow."

"Mmm!" murmured Banford, and she returned to her writing. But as she was licking her envelope, she asked:

"And what plans have you made for the future, if I may ask?"

"Plans?" he said, his face very bright and angry.

"I mean about you and Nellie, if you are going on with this business. When do you expect the wedding to come off?" She spoke in a jeering tone.

"Oh, the wedding!" he replied. "I don't know."

"Don't you know anything?" said Banford. "Are you going to clear out on Friday and leave things no more settled than they are?"

"Well, why shouldn't I? We can always write letters."

"Yes, of course you can. But I wanted to know because of this place. If Nellie is going to get married all of a sudden, I shall have to be looking round for a new partner."

"Couldn't she stay on here if she was married?" he said. He knew quite well what was coming.

"Oh," said Banford, "this is no place for a married couple. There's not enough work to keep a man going, for one thing. And there's no money to be made. It's quite useless your thinking of staying on here if you marry. Absolutely!"

"Yes, but I wasn't thinking of staying on here," he said.

"Well, that's what I want to know. And what about Nellie, then? How long is *she* going to be here with me, in that case?"

The two antagonists looked at one another.

"That I can't say," he answered.

"Oh, go along," she cried petulantly. "You must have some idea what you are going to do, if you ask a woman to marry you. Unless it's all a hoax."

"Why should it be a hoax?—I am going back to Canada."

"And taking her with you?"

"Yes, certainly."

"You hear that, Nellie?" said Banford.

March, who had had her head bent over her sewing, now looked up with a sharp pink blush on her face and a queer, sardonic laugh in her eyes and on her twisted mouth.

"That's the first time I've heard that I was going to Canada," she said.

"Well, you have to hear it for the first time, haven't you?" said the boy.

"Yes, I suppose I have," she said nonchalantly. And she went back to her sewing.

"You're quite ready, are you, to go to Canada? Are you, Nellie?" asked Banford.

March looked up again. She let her shoulders go slack, and let her hand that held the needle lie loose in her lap.

"It depends on *how* I'm going," she said. "I don't think I want to go jammed up in the steerage, as a soldier's wife. I'm afraid I'm not used to that way."

The boy watched her with bright eyes.

"Would you rather stay over here while I go first?" he asked.

"I would, if that's the only alternative," she replied.

"That's much the wisest. Don't make it any fixed engagement," said Banford. "Leave yourself free to go or not after he's got back and found you a place, Nellie. Anything else is madness, madness."

"Don't you think," said the youth, "we ought to get married before I go—and then go together, or separate, according to how it happens?"

"I think it's a terrible idea," cried Banford.

But the boy was watching March.

"What do you think?" he asked her.

She let her eyes stray vaguely into space.

"Well, I don't know," she said. "I shall have to think about it."

"Why?" he asked, pertinently.

"Why?"—She repeated his question in a mocking way, and looked at him laughing, though her face was pink again. "I should think there's plenty of reasons why."

He watched her in silence. She seemed to have escaped him. She had got into league with Banford against him. There was again the queer sardonic look about her; she would mock stoically at everything he said or which life offered.

"Of course," he said, "I don't want to press you to do anything you don't wish to do."

"I should think not, indeed," cried Banford indignantly.

At bedtime Banford said plaintively to March:

"You take my hot bottle up for me, Nellie, will you?"

"Yes, I'll do it," said March, with the kind of willing unwillingness she so often showed towards her beloved but uncertain Jill.

The two women went upstairs. After a time March called from the top of the stairs: "Good-night, Henry. I shan't be coming down. You'll see to the lamp and the fire, won't you?"

The next day Henry went about with the cloud on his brow and his young cub's face shut up tight. He was cogitating all the time. He had wanted March to marry him and go back to Canada with him. And he had been sure she would do it. Why he wanted her he didn't know. But he did want her. He had set his mind on her. And he was convulsed with a youth's fury at being thwarted. To be thwarted, to be thwarted! It made him so furious inside, that he did not know what to do with himself. But he kept himself in hand. Because even now things might turn out differently. She might come over to him. Of course she might. It was her business to do so.

Things drew to a tension again towards evening. He and Banford had avoided each other all day. In fact Banford went in to the little town by the 11.20 train. It was market day. She arrived back on the 4.25. Just as the night was falling Henry saw her little figure in a dark-blue coat and a dark-blue tam-o'-shanter hat crossing the first meadow from the station. He stood under one of the wild pear-trees, with the old dead leaves round his feet. And he watched the little blue figure advancing persistently over the rough winter-ragged meadow. She had her arms full of parcels, and advanced slowly, frail thing she was, but with that devilish little certainty which he so detested in her. He stood invisible under the pear-tree, watching her every step. And if looks could have affected her, she would have felt a log of iron on each of her ankles as she made her way forward.

"You're a nasty little thing, you are," he was saying softly, across the distance. "You're a nasty little thing. I hope you'll be paid back for all the harm you've done me for nothing. I hope you will—you nasty little thing. I hope you'll have to pay for it. You will, if wishes are anything. You nasty little creature that you are."

She was toiling slowly up the slope. But if she had been slipping back at every step towards the Bottomless Pit, he would not have gone to help her with her parcels. Aha! there went March, striding with her long, land stride in her breeches and her short tunic! Striding down hill at a great pace, and even running a few steps now and then, in her great solicitude and desire to come to the rescue of the little Banford. The boy watched her with rage in his heart. See her leap a ditch, and run, run as if a house was on fire, just to get to that creeping dark little object down there! So, the Banford just stood still and waited. And March strode up and took *all* the parcels except a bunch of yellow chrysanthemums. These the Banford still carried—yellow chrysanthemums!

"Yes, you look well, don't you," he said softly into the dusk air. "You look well, pottering up there with a bunch of flowers, you do. I'd make you eat them for your tea, if you hug them so tight. And I'd give them you for breakfast again, I would. I'd give you flowers. Nothing but flowers."

He watched the progress of the two women. He could hear their voices: March always outspoken and rather scolding in her tenderness, Banford murmuring rather vaguely. They were evidently good friends. He could not hear what they said till they came to the fence of the home meadow, which they must climb. Then he saw March manfully climbing over the bars with all her packages in her arms, and on the still air he heard Banford's fretful:

"Why don't you let me help you with the parcels?" She had a queer plaintive hitch in her voice.—Then came March's robust and reckless:

"Oh, I can manage. Don't you bother about me. You've all you can do to get yourself over."

"Yes, that's all very well," said Banford fretfully. "You say '*Don't you bother about me*' and then all the while you feel injured because nobody thinks of you."

"When do I feel injured?" said March.

"Always. You always feel injured. Now you're feeling injured because I won't have that boy to come and live on the farm."

"I'm not feeling injured at all," said March.

"I know you are. When he's gone you'll sulk over it. I know you will."

"Shall I?" said March. "We'll see."

"Yes, we *shall* see, unfortunately.—I can't think how you can make yourself so cheap. I can't *imagine* how you can lower yourself like it."

"I haven't lowered myself," said March.

"I don't know what you call it, then. Letting a boy like that come so cheeky and impudent and make a mug of you. I don't know what you think of yourself. How much respect do you think he's going to have for you afterwards?—My word, I wouldn't be in your shoes, if you married him."

"Of course you wouldn't. My boots are a good bit too big for you, and not half dainty enough," said March, with rather a miss-fire sarcasm.

"I thought you had too much pride, really I did. A woman's got to hold herself high, especially with a youth like that. Why, he's impudent. Even the way he forced himself on us at the start."

"We asked him to stay," said March.

"Not till he'd almost forced us to.—And then he's so cocky and self-assured. My word, he puts my back up. I simply can't imagine how you can let him treat you so cheaply."

"I don't let him treat me cheaply," said March. "Don't you worry yourself, nobody's going to treat me cheaply. And even you aren't, either." She had a tender defiance, and a certain fire in her voice.

"Yes, it's sure to come back to me," said Banford bitterly. "That's always the end of it. I believe you only do it to spite me."

They went now in silence up the steep grassy slope and over the brow through the gorse bushes. On the other side of the hedge the boy followed in the dusk, at some little distance. Now and then, through the huge ancient hedge of hawthorn, risen into trees, he saw the two dark figures creeping up the hill. As he came to the top of the slope he saw the homestead dark in the twilight, with a huge old pear-tree leaning from the near gable, and a little yellow light twinkling in the small side windows of the kitchen. He heard the clink of the latch and saw the kitchen door open into light as the two women went indoors. So, they were at home.

And so!—this was what they thought of him. It was rather in his nature to be a listener, so he was not at all suprised whatever he heard. The things people said about him always missed him personally. He was only rather surprised at the women's way with one another. And he disliked the Banford with an acid dislike. And he felt drawn to the March again. He felt again irresistibly drawn to her. He felt there was a secret bond, a secret thread between him and her, something very exclusive, which shut out everybody else and made him and her possess each other in secret.

He hoped again that she would have him. He hoped with his blood suddenly firing up that she would agree to marry him quite quickly: at Christmas, very likely. Christmas was not far off. He wanted, whatever else happened, to snatch her into a hasty marriage and a consummation with him. Then for the future, they could arrange later. But he hoped it would happen as he wanted it. He hoped that to-night she would stay a little while with him, after Banford had gone upstairs. He hoped he could touch her soft, creamy cheek, her strange, frightened face. He hoped he could look into her dilated, frightened dark eyes, quite near. He hoped he might even put his hand on her bosom and feel her soft breasts under her tunic. His heart beat deep and powerful as he thought of that. He wanted very much to do so. He wanted to make sure of her soft woman's breasts under her tunic. She always kept the brown linen coat buttoned so close up to her throat. It seemed to him like some perilous secret, that her soft woman's breasts must be buttoned up in that uniform. It seemed to him moreover that they were so much softer, tenderer, more lovely and lovable, shut up in that tunic, than were the Banford's breasts, under her soft blouses and chiffon dresses. The Banford would have little iron breasts, he said to himself. For all her frailty and fretfulness and delicacy, she would have tiny iron breasts. But March under her crude, fast, workman's tunic, would have soft white breasts, white and unseen. So he told himself, and his blood burned.

When he went in to tea, he had a surprise. He appeared at the inner door, his face very ruddy and vivid and his blue eyes shining, dropping his head forward as he came in, in his usual way, and hesitating in the doorway to watch the inside of the room, keenly and cautiously, before he entered. He was wearing a long-sleeved waistcoat. His face seemed extraordinarily like a piece of the out-of-doors come indoors: as holly-berries do. In his second of pause in the doorway he took in the two women sitting at table, at opposite ends, saw them sharply. And to his amazement March was dressed in a dress of dull, green silk crêpe. His mouth came open in surprise. If she had suddenly grown a moustache he could not have been more surprised.

"Why," he said, "do you wear a dress, then?"

She looked up, flushing a deep rose colour, and twisting her mouth with a smile, said:

"Of course I do. What else do you expect me to wear, but a dress?"

"A land girl's uniform, of course," said he.

"Oh," she cried nonchalant, "that's only for this dirty mucky work about here."

"Isn't it your proper dress, then?" he said.

"No, not indoors it isn't," she said. But she was blushing all the time as she poured out his tea. He sat down in his chair at table, unable to take his eyes off her. Her dress was a perfectly simple slip of bluey-green crêpe, with a line of gold stitching round the top and round the sleeves, which came to the elbow. It was cut just plain and round at the top, and showed her white soft throat. Her arms he knew, strong and firm muscled, for he had often seen her with her sleeves rolled up. But he looked her up and down, up and down.

Banford, at the other end of the table, said not a word, but piggled with[6] the sardine on her plate. He had forgotten her existence. He just simply stared at March, while he ate his bread and margarine in huge mouthfuls, forgetting even his tea.

"Well, I never knew anything make such a difference!" he murmured, across he mouthfuls.

"Oh, goodness!" cried March, blushing still more. "I might be a pink monkey!"

And she rose quickly to her feet and took the tea-pot to the fire, to the kettle. And as she crouched on the hearth with her green slip about her, the boy stared more wide-eyed than ever. Through the crêpe her woman's form seemed soft and womanly. And when she stood up and walked he saw her legs move soft within her modernly short skirt. She had on black silk stockings and small, patent-leather shoes with little gold buckles.

No, she was another being. She was something quite different. Seeing her always in the hard-cloth breeches, wide on the hips, buttoned on the knee, strong as armour, and in the brown puttees and thick boots, it had never occurred to him that she had a woman's legs and feet. Now it came upon him. She had a woman's soft, skirted legs, and she was accessible. He blushed to the roots of his hair, shoved his nose in his teacup and drank his tea with a little noise that made Banford simply squirm: and strangely, suddenly he felt a man, no longer a youth. He felt a man, with

6. Picked at; touched continually.

all a man's grave weight of responsibility. A curious quietness and gravity came over his soul. He felt a man, quiet, with a little of the heaviness of male destiny upon him.

She was soft and accessible in her dress. The thought went home in him like an everlasting responsibility.

"Oh, for goodness sake, say something, somebody," cried Banford fretfully. "It might be a funeral." The boy looked at her, and she could not bear his face.

"A funeral!" said March, with a twisted smile. "Why, that breaks my dream."

Suddenly she had thought of Banford in the wood-box for a coffin.

"What, have you been dreaming of a wedding?" said Banford sarcastically.

"Must have been," said March.

"Whose wedding?" asked the boy.

"I can't remember," said March.

She was shy and rather awkward that evening, in spite of the fact that, wearing a dress, her bearing was much more subdued than in her uniform. She felt unpeeled and rather exposed. She felt almost improper.

They talked desultorily about Henry's departure next morning, and made the trivial arrangement. But of the matter on their minds, none of them spoke. They were rather quiet and friendly this evening; Banford had practically nothing to say. But inside herself she seemed still, perhaps kindly.

At nine o'clock March brought in the tray with the everlasting tea and a little cold meat which Banford had managed to procure. It was the last supper, so Banford did not want to be disagreeable. She felt a bit sorry for the boy, and felt she must be as nice as she could.

He wanted her to go to bed. She was usually the first. But she sat on in her chair under the lamp, glancing at her book now and then, and staring into the fire. A deep silence had come into the room. It was broken by March asking, in a rather small tone:

"What time is it, Jill?"

"Five past ten," said Banford, looking at her wrist.

And then not a sound. The boy had looked up from the book he was holding between his knees. His rather wide, cat-shaped face had its obstinate look, his eyes were watchful.

"What about bed?" said March at last.

"I'm ready when you are," said Banford.

"Oh, very well," said March. "I'll fill your bottle."

She was as good as her word. When the hot-water bottle was ready, she lit a candle and went upstairs with it. Banford remained in her chair, listening acutely. March came downstairs again.

"There you are then," she said. "Are you going up?"

"Yes, in a minute," said Banford. But the minute passed, and she sat on in her chair under the lamp.

Henry, whose eyes were shining like a cat's as he watched from under his brows, and whose face seemed wider, more chubbed[7] and cat-like with unalterable obstinacy, now rose to his feet to try his throw.

---

7. Rounded.

"I think I'll go and look if I can see the she-fox," he said. "She may be creeping round. Won't you come as well for a minute, Nellie, and see if we see anything?"

"Me!" cried March, looking up with her startled, wondering face.

"Yes. Come on," he said. It was wonderful how soft and warm and coaxing his voice could be, how near. The very sound of it made Banford's blood boil.

"Come on for a minute," he said, looking down into her uplifted, unsure face.

And she rose to her feet as if drawn up by his young, ruddy face that was looking down on her.

"I should think you're never going out at this time of night, Nellie!" cried Banford.

"Yes, just for a minute," said the boy, looking round on her, and speaking with an odd sharp yelp in his voice.

March looked from one to the other, as if confused, vague. Banford rose to her feet for a battle.

"Why, it's ridiculous. It's bitter cold. You'll catch your death in that thin frock. And in those slippers. You're not going to do any such thing."

There was a moment's pause. Banford turtled up like a little fighting cock, facing March and the boy.

"Oh, I don't think you need worry yourself," he replied. "A moment under the stars won't do anybody any damage. I'll get the rug off the sofa in the dining-room. You're coming, Nellie."

His voice had so much anger and contempt and fury in it as he spoke to Banford: and so much tenderness and proud authority as he spoke to March, that the latter answered:

"Yes, I'm coming."

And she turned with him to the door.

Banford, standing there in the middle of the room, suddenly burst into a long wail and a spasm of sobs. She covered her face with her poor thin hands, and her thin shoulders shook in an agony of weeping. March looked back from the door.

"Jill!" she cried in a frantic tone, like someone just coming awake. And she seemed to start towards her darling.

But the boy had March's arm in his grip, and she could not move. She did not know why she could not move. It was as in a dream when the heart strains and the body cannot stir.

"Never mind," said the boy, softly. "Let her cry. Let her cry. She will have to cry sooner or later. And the tears will relieve her feelings. They will do her good."

So he drew March slowly through the door-way. But her last look was back to the poor little figure which stood in the middle of the room with covered face and thin shoulders shaken with bitter weeping.

In the dining-room he picked up the rug and said:

"Wrap yourself up in this."

She obeyed—and they reached the kitchen door, he holding her soft and firm by the arm, though she did not know it. When she saw the night outside she started back.

"I must go back to Jill," she said. "I *must!* Oh, yes, I must!"

Her tone sounded final. The boy let go of her and she turned indoors.

But he seized her again and arrested her.

"Wait a minute," he said. "Wait a minute. Even if you go you're not going yet."

"Leave go! Leave go!" she cried. "My place is at Jill's side. Poor little thing, she's sobbing her heart out."

"Yes," said the boy bitterly. "And your heart, too, and mine as well."

"Your heart?" said March. He still gripped her and detained her.

"Isn't it as good as her heart?" he said. "Or do you think it's not?"

"Your heart?" she said again, incredulous.

"Yes, mine! Mine! Do you think I haven't *got* a heart?"—And with his hot grasp he took her hand and pressed it under his left breast. "There's my heart," he said, "if you don't believe in it."

It was wonder which made her attend. And then she felt the deep, heavy, powerful stroke of his heart, terrible, like something from beyond. It was like something from beyond, something awful from outside, signalling to her. And the signal paralysed her. It beat upon her very soul, and made her helpless. She forgot Jill. She could not think of Jill any more. She could not think of her. That terrible signalling from outside!

The boy put his arm round her waist.

"Come with me," he said gently. "Come and let us say what we've got to say."

And he drew her outside, closed the door. And she went with him darkly down the garden path. That he should have a beating heart! And that he should have his arm round her, outside the blanket! She was too confused to think who he was or what he was.

He took her to a dark corner of the shed, where there was a tool-box with a lid, long and low.

"We'll sit here a minute," he said.

And obediently she sat down by his side.

"Give me your hand," he said.

She gave him both her hands, and he held them between his own. He was young, and it made him tremble.

"You'll marry me. You'll marry me before I go back, won't you?" he pleaded.

"Why, aren't we both a pair of fools!" she said.

He had put her in the corner, so that she should not look out and see the lighted window of the house, across the dark yard and garden. He tried to keep her all there inside the shed with him.

"In what way a pair of fools?" he said. "If you go back to Canada with me, I've got a job and a good wage waiting for me, and it's a nice place, near the mountains. Why shouldn't you marry me? Why shouldn't we marry? I should like to have you there with me. I should like to feel I'd got somebody there, at the back of me, all my life."

"You'd easily find somebody else, who'd suit you better," she said.

"Yes, I might easily find another girl. I know I could. But not one I really wanted. I've never met one I really wanted, for good. You see, I'm thinking of all my life. If I marry, I want to feel it's for all my life. Other girls: well, they're just girls, nice enough to go a walk with now and then. Nice enough for a bit of play. But when I think of my life, then I should be very sorry to have to marry one of them, I should indeed."

"You mean they wouldn't make you a good wife."

"Yes, I mean that. But I don't mean they wouldn't do their duty by me.

I mean—I don't know what I mean. Only when I think of my life, and of you, then the two things go together."

"And what if they didn't?" she said, with her odd sardonic touch.

"Well, I think they would."

They sat for some time silent. He held her hands in his, but he did not make love to her. Since he had realized that she was a woman, and vulnerable, accessible, a certain heaviness had possessed his soul. He did not want to make love to her. He shrank from any such performance, almost with fear. She was a woman, and vulnerable, accessible to him finally, and he held back from that which was ahead, almost with dread. It was a kind of darkness he knew he would enter finally, but of which he did not want as yet even to think. She was the woman, and he was responsible for the strange vulnerability he had suddenly realized in her.

"No," she said at last, "I'm a fool. I know I'm a fool."

"What for?" he asked.

"To go on with this business."

"Do you mean me?" he asked.

"No, I mean myself. I'm making a fool of myself, and a big one."

"Why, because you don't want to marry me, really?"

"Oh, I don't know whether I'm against it, as a matter of fact. That's just it. I don't know."

He looked at her in the darkness, puzzled. He did not in the least know what she meant.

"And don't you know whether you like to sit here with me this minute, or not?" he asked.

"No, I don't, really. I don't know whether I wish I was somewhere else, or whether I like being here. I don't know, really."

"Do you wish you were with Miss Banford? Do you wish you'd gone to bed with her?" he asked, as a challenge.

She waited a long time before she answered:

"No," she said at last. "I don't wish that."

"And do you think you would spend all your life with her—when your hair goes white, and you are old?" he said.

"No," she said, without much hesitation. "I don't see Jill and me two old women together."

"And don't you think, when I'm an old man, and you're an old woman, we might be together still, as we are now?" he said.

"Well, not as we are now," she replied. "But I could imagine—no, I can't. I can't imagine you an old man. Besides, it's dreadful!"

"What, to be an old man?"

"Yes, of course."

"Not when the time comes," he said. "But it hasn't come. Only it will. And when it does, I should like to think you'd be there as well."

"Sort of old age pensions," she said drily.

Her kind of witless humour always startled him. He never knew what she meant. Probably she didn't quite know herself.

"No," he said, hurt.

"I don't know why you harp on old age," she said. "I'm not ninety."

"Did anybody ever say you were?" he asked, offended.

They were silent for some time, pulling different ways in the silence.

"I don't want you to make fun of me," he said.

"Don't you?" she replied, enigmatic.

"No, because just this minute I'm serious. And when I'm serious, I believe in not making fun of it."

"You mean nobody else must make fun of you," she replied.

"Yes, I mean that. And I mean I don't believe in making fun of it myself. When it comes over me so that I'm serious, then—there it is, I don't want it to be laughed at."

She was silent for some time. Then she said, in a vague, almost pained voice:

"No, I'm not laughing at you."

A hot wave rose in his heart.

"You believe me, do you?" he asked.

"Yes, I believe you," she replied, with a twang of her old tired nonchalance, as if she gave in because she was tired.—But he didn't care. His heart was hot and clamorous.

"So you agree to marry me before I go?—perhaps at Christmas?"

"Yes, I agree."

"There!" he exclaimed. "That's settled it."

And he sat silent, unconscious, with all the blood burning in all his veins, like fire in all the branches and twigs of him. He only pressed her two hands to his chest, without knowing. When the curious passion began to die down, he seemed to come awake to the world.

"We'll go in, shall we?" he said: as if he realized it was cold.

She rose without answering.

"Kiss me before we go, now you've said it," he said.

And he kissed her gently on the mouth, with a young, frightened kiss. It made her feel so young, too, and frightened, and wondering: and tired, tired, as if she were going to sleep.

They went indoors. And in the sitting-room, there, crouched by the fire like a queer little witch, was Banford. She looked round with reddened eyes as they entered, but did not rise. He thought she looked frightening, unnatural, crouching there and looking round at them. Evil he thought her look was, and he crossed his fingers.

Banford saw the ruddy, elate face of the youth: he seemed strangely tall and bright and looming. And March had a delicate look on her face; she wanted to hide her face, to screen it, to let it not be seen.

"You've come at last," said Banford uglily.

"Yes, we've come," said he.

"You've been long enough for anything," she said.

"Yes, we have. We've settled it. We shall marry as soon as possible," he replied.

"Oh, you've settled it, have you! Well, I hope you won't live to repent it," said Banford.

"I hope so too," he replied.

"Are you going to bed *now*, Nellie?" said Banford.

"Yes, I'm going now."

"Then for goodness sake come along."

March looked at the boy. He was glancing with his very bright eyes at her and at Banford. March looked at him wistfully. She wished she could stay with him. She wished she had married him already, and it was all over. For oh, she felt suddenly so safe with him. She felt so strangely safe and peaceful in his presence. If only she could sleep in his shelter, and not with Jill. She felt afraid of Jill. In her dim, tender state, it was agony to have to go with Jill and sleep with her. She wanted the boy to save her. She looked again at him.

And he, watching with bright eyes, divined something of what she felt. It puzzled and distressed him that she must go with Jill.

"I shan't forget what you've promised," he said, looking clear into her eyes, right into her eyes, so that he seemed to occupy all her self with his queer, bright look.

She smiled to him, faintly, gently. She felt safe again—safe with him.

But in spite of all the boy's precautions, he had a set-back. The morning he was leaving the farm he got March to accompany him to the market-town, about six miles away, where they went to the registrar and had their names stuck up as two people who were going to marry. He was to come at Christmas, and the wedding was to take place then. He hoped in the spring to be able to take March back to Canada with him, now the war was really over. Though he was so young, he had saved some money.

"You never have to be without *some* money at the back of you, if you can help it," he said.

So she saw him off in the train that was going West: his camp was on Salisbury plains. And with big dark eyes she watched him go, and it seemed as if everything real in life was retreating as the train retreated with his queer, chubby, ruddy face, that seemed so broad across the cheeks, and which never seemed to change its expression, save when a cloud of sulky anger hung on the brow, or the bright eyes fixed themselves in their stare. This was what happened now. He leaned there out of the carriage window as the train drew off, saying good-bye and staring back at her, but his face quite unchanged. There was no emotion on his face. Only his eyes tightened and became fixed and intent in their watching, as a cat when suddenly she sees something and stares. So the boy's eyes stared fixedly as the train drew away, and she was left feeling intensely forlorn. Failing his physical presence, she seemed to have nothing of him. And she had nothing of anything. Only his face was fixed in her mind: the full, ruddy, unchanging cheeks, and the straight snout of a nose, and the two eyes staring above. All she could remember was how he suddenly wrinkled his nose when he laughed, as a puppy does when he is playfully growling. But him, himself, and what he was—she knew nothing, she had nothing of him when he left her.

On the ninth day after he had left her he received this letter:

"DEAR HENRY,

"I have been over it all again in my mind, this business of me and you, and it seems to me impossible. When you aren't there I see what a fool I am. When you are there you seem to blind me to things as they actually are. You make me see things all unreal and I don't know what. Then when I am alone again with Jill I seem to come to my own senses and realize what a fool I am making of myself and how I am treating you unfairly. Because it must be unfair to you for me to go on with this affair when I can't feel in my heart that I really love you. I know people talk a lot of stuff and nonsense about love, and I don't want to do that. I want to keep to plain facts and act in a sensible way. And that seems to me what I'm not doing. I don't see on what grounds I am going to marry you. I know I am not head over heels in love with you, as I have fancied myself to be with fellows when I was a young fool of a girl. You are an absolute stranger to me, and it seems to me you will always be one. So on what grounds am I going to marry you? When I think of Jill, she is ten times more real to me. I know her and I'm awfully fond of her and I hate myself for a beast if I ever hurt her little finger. We have a life together. And even if it can't last for ever, it is a life while it does last. And it might last as long as either of us lives. Who knows how long we've got to live? She is a delicate little thing, perhaps nobody but me knows how delicate. And as for me, I feel I might fall down the well any day. What I don't seem to see at all is you. When I think of what I've been and what I've done with you, I'm afraid I am a few screws loose. I should be sorry to think that softening of the brain is setting in so soon, but that is what it seems like. You are such an absolute stranger and so different from what I'm used to and we don't seem to have a thing in common. As for love, the very word seems impossible. I know what love means even in Jill's case, and I know that in this affair with you it's an absolute impossibility. And then going to Canada. I'm sure I must have been clean off my chump when I promised such a thing. It makes me feel fairly frightened of myself. I feel I might do something really silly, that I wasn't responsible for. And end my days in a lunatic asylum. You may think that's all I'm fit for after the way I've gone on, but it isn't a very nice thought for me. Thank goodness Jill is here and her being here makes me feel sane again, else I don't know what I might do; I might have an accident with the gun one evening. I love Jill and she makes me feel safe and sane, with her loving anger against me for being such a fool. Well, what I want to say is, won't you let us cry the whole thing off? I can't marry you, and really, I won't do such a thing if it seems to me wrong. It is all a great mistake. I've made a complete fool of myself, and all I can do is to apologize to you and ask you please to forget it and please to take no further notice of me. Your fox skin is nearly ready and seems all right. I will post it to you if you will let me know if this address is still right, and if you will accept my apology for the awful and lunatic way I have behaved with you, and then let the matter rest.

"Jill sends her kindest regards. Her mother and father are staying with us over Christmas.

"Yours very sincerely,
"ELLEN MARCH."

The boy read this letter in camp as he was cleaning his kit. He set his teeth and for a moment went almost pale, yellow round the eyes with fury. He said nothing and saw nothing and felt nothing but a livid rage that was quite unreasoning. Balked! Balked again! Balked! He wanted the woman, he had fixed like doom upon having her. He felt that was his doom, his destiny, and his reward, to have this woman. She was his heaven and hell on earth, and he would have none elsewhere. Sightless with rage and thwarted madness he got through the morning. Save that in his mind he was lurking and scheming towards an issue, he would have committed some insane act. Deep in himself he felt like roaring and howling and gnashing his teeth and breaking things. But he was too intelligent. He knew society was on top of him, and he must scheme. So with his teeth bitten together and his nose curiously slightly lifted, like some creature that is vicious, and his eyes fixed and staring, he went through the morning's affairs drunk with anger and suppression. In his mind was one thing—Banford. He took no heed of all March's outpouring: none. One thorn rankled, stuck in his mind. Banford. In his mind, in his soul, in his whole being, one thorn rankling to insanity. And he would have to get it out. He would have to get the thorn of Banford out of his life, if he died for it.

With this one fixed idea in his mind, he went to ask for twenty-four hours' leave of absence. He knew it was not due to him. His consciousness was supernaturally keen. He knew where he must go—he must go to the captain. But how could he get at the captain? In that great camp of wooden huts and tents, he had no idea where his captain was.

But he went to the officers' canteen. There was his captain standing talking with three other officers. Henry stood in the door-way at attention.

"May I speak to Captain Berryman?"—The captain was Cornish like himself.

"What do you want?" called the captain.

"May I speak to you, Captain?"

"What do you want?" replied the captain, not stirring from among his group of fellow officers.

Henry watched his superior for a minute without speaking.

"You won't refuse me, sir, will you?" he asked gravely.

"It depends what it is."

"Can I have twenty-four hours' leave?"

"No, you've no business to ask."

"I know I haven't. But I must ask you."

"You've had your answer."

"Don't send me away, Captain."

There was something strange about the boy as he stood there so everlasting in the door-way. The Cornish captain felt the strangeness at once, and eyed him shrewdly.

"Why, what's afoot?" he said, curious.

"I'm in trouble about something. I must go to Blewbury," said the boy.

"Blewbury, eh? After the girls?"

"Yes, it is a woman, Captain." And the boy, as he stood there with his head reaching forward a little, went suddenly terribly pale, or yellow, and his lips seemed to give off pain. The captain saw and paled a little also. He turned aside.

"Go on then," he said. "But for God's sake don't cause any trouble of any sort."

"I won't, Captain, thank you."

He was gone. The captain, upset, took a gin and bitters. Henry managed to hire a bicycle. It was twelve o'clock when he left the camp. He had sixty miles of wet and muddy cross-roads to ride. But he was in the saddle and down the road without a thought of food.

At the farm, March was busy with a work she had had some time in hand. A bunch of Scotch fir-trees stood at the end of the open shed, on a little bank where ran the fence between two of the gorse-shaggy meadows. The furthest of these trees was dead—it had died in the summer and stood with all its needles brown and sere in the air. It was not a very big tree. And it was absolutely dead. So March determined to have it, although they were not allowed to cut any of the timber. But it would make such splendid firing, in these days of scarce fuel.

She had been giving a few stealthy chops at the trunk for a week or more, every now and then hacking away for five minutes, low down, near the ground, so no one should notice. She had not tried the saw, it was such hard work, alone. Now the tree stood with a great yawning gap in his base, perched as it were on one sinew, and ready to fall. But he did not fall.

It was late in the damp December afternoon, with cold mists creeping out of the woods and up the hollows, and darkness waiting to sink in from above. There was a bit of yellowness where the sun was fading away beyond the low woods of the distance. March took her axe and went to the tree. The small thud-thud of her blows resounded rather ineffectual about the wintry homestead. Banford came out wearing her thick coat, but with no hat on her head, so that her thin, bobbed hair blew on the uneasy wind that sounded in the pines and in the wood.

"What I'm afraid of," said Banford, "is that it will fall on the shed and we'll have another job repairing that."

"Oh, I don't think so," said March, straightening herself and wiping her arm over her hot brow. She was flushed red, her eyes were very wide-open and queer, her upper lip away from her two white front teeth with a curious, almost rabbit-look.

A little stout man in a black overcoat and a bowler hat came pottering across the yard. He had a pink face and a white beard and smallish, pale-blue eyes. He was not very old, but nervy, and he walked with little short steps.

"What do you think, father?" said Banford. "Don't you think it might hit the shed in falling?"

"Shed, no!" said the old man. "Can't hit the shed. Might as well say the fence."

"The fence doesn't matter," said March, in her high voice.

"Wrong as usual, am I?" said Banford, wiping her straying hair from her eyes.

The tree stood as it were on one spelch[8] of itself, leaning, and creaking in the wind. It grew on the bank of a little dry ditch between the two meadows. On the top of the bank straggled one fence, running to the bushes uphill. Several trees clustered there in the corner of the field near the shed and near the gate which led into the yard. Towards this gate, horizontal across the weary meadows, came the grassy, rutted approach from the highroad. There trailed another rickety fence, long split poles joining the short, thick, wide-apart uprights. The three people stood at the back of the tree, in the corner of the shed meadow, just above the yard gate. The house with its two gables and its porch stood tidy in a little grassed garden across the yard. A little stout rosy-faced woman in a little red woollen shoulder shawl had come and taken her stand in the porch.

"Isn't it down yet?" she cried, in a high little voice.

"Just thinking about it," called her husband. His tone towards the two girls was always rather mocking and satirical. March did not want to go

8. Spelk, splinter.

on with her hitting while he was there. As for him, he wouldn't lift a stick from the ground if he could help it, complaining, like his daughter, of rheumatics in his shoulder. So the three stood there a moment silent in the cold afternoon, in the bottom corner near the yard.

They heard the far-off taps of a gate, and craned to look. Away across, on the green horizontal approach, a figure was just swinging on to a bicycle again, and lurching up and down over the grass, approaching.

"Why it's one of our boys—it's Jack," said the old man.

"Can't be," said Banford.

March craned her head to look. She alone recognized the khaki figure. She flushed, but said nothing.

"No, it isn't Jack, I don't think," said the old man, staring with little round blue eyes under his white lashes.

In another moment the bicycle lurched into sight, and the rider dropped off at the gate. It was Henry, his face wet and red and spotted with mud. He was altogether a muddy sight.

"Oh!" cried Banford, as if afraid. "Why, it's Henry!"

"What!" muttered the old man. He had a thick, rapid, muttering way of speaking, and was slightly deaf. "What? What? Who is it? Who is it, do you say? That young fellow? That young fellow of Nellie's? Oh! Oh!" And the satiric smile came on his pink face and white eyelashes.

Henry, pushing the wet hair off his steaming brow, had caught sight of them and heard what the old man said. His hot young face seemed to flame in the cold light.

"Oh, are you all there!" he said, giving his sudden, puppy's little laugh. He was so hot and dazed with cycling he hardly knew where he was. He leaned the bicycle against the fence and climbed over into the corner on to the bank, without going in to the yard.

"Well, I must say, we weren't expecting *you*," said Banford laconically.

"No, I suppose not," said he, looking at March.

She stood aside, slack, with one knee drooped and the axe resting its head loosely on the ground. Her eyes were wide and vacant, and her upper lip lifted from her teeth in that helpless, fascinated rabbit-look. The moment she saw his glowing red face it was all over with her. She was as helpless as if she had been bound. The moment she saw the way his head seemed to reach forward.

"Well, who is it? Who is it, anyway?" asked the smiling, satiric old man in his muttering voice.

"Why, Mr. Grenfel, whom you've heard us tell about, father," said Banford coldly.

"Heard you tell about, I should think so. Heard of nothing else practically," muttered the elderly man with his queer little jeering smile on his face. "How do you do," he added, suddenly reaching out his hand to Henry.

The boy shook hands just as startled. Then the two men fell apart.

"Cycled over from Salisbury Plain have you?" asked the old man.

"Yes."

"Ha! Longish ride. How long d'it take you, eh? Some time, eh? Several hours, I suppose."

"About four."

"Eh? Four! Yes, I should have thought so. When are you going back then?"

"I've got till to-morrow evening."

"Till to-morrow evening, eh? Yes. Ha! Girls weren't expecting you, were they?"

And the old man turned his pale-blue, round little eyes under their white lashes mockingly towards the girls. Henry also looked round. He had become a little awkward. He looked at March, who was still staring away into the distance as if to see where the cattle were. Her hand was on the pommel of the axe, whose head rested loosely on the ground.

"What were you doing there?" he asked in his soft, courteous voice. "Cutting a tree down?"

March seemed not to hear, as if in a trance.

"Yes," said Banford. "We've been at it for over a week."

"Oh! And have you done it all by yourselves, then?"

"Nellie's done it all, I've done nothing," said Banford.

"Really!—You must have worked quite hard," he said, addressing himself in a curious gentle tone direct to March. She did not answer, but remained half averted, staring away towards the woods above as if in a trance.

"*Nellie!*" cried Banford sharply. "Can't you answer?"

"What—me?" cried March, starting round, and looking from one to the other. "Did anyone speak to me?"

"Dreaming!" muttered the old man, turning aside to smile. "Must be in love, eh, dreaming in the day-time!"

"Did you say anything to me?" said March, looking at the boy as from a strange distance, her eyes wide and doubtful, her face delicately flushed.

"I said you must have worked hard at the tree," he replied courteously.

"Oh, that! Bit by bit. I thought it would have come down by now."

"I'm thankful it hasn't come down in the night, to frighten us to death," said Banford.

"Let me just finish it for you, shall I?" said the boy.

March slanted the axe-shaft in his direction.

"Would you like to?" she said.

"Yes, if you wish it," he said.

"Oh, I'm thankful when the thing's down, that's all," she replied, nonchalant.

"Which way is it going to fall?" said Banford. "Will it hit the shed?"

"No, it won't hit the shed," he said. "I should think it will fall there— quite clear. Though it might give a twist and catch the fence."

"Catch the fence!" cried the old man. "What, catch the fence! When it's leaning at that angle?—Why it's further off than the shed. It won't catch the fence."

"No," said Henry, "I don't suppose it will. It has plenty of room to fall quite clear, and I suppose it will fall clear."

"Won't tumble backwards on top of *us*, will it?" asked the old man sarcastic.

"No, it won't do that," said Henry, taking off his short overcoat and his tunic. "Ducks! Ducks! Go back!"

A line of four brown-speckled ducks led by a brown-and-green drake were stemming away downhill from the upper meadow, coming like boats running on a ruffled sea, cackling their way top speed downwards towards the fence and towards the little group of people, and cackling as excitedly as if they brought news of the Spanish Armada.

"Silly things! Silly things!" cried Banford going forward to turn them off. But they came eagerly towards her, opening their yellow-green beaks and quacking as if they were so excited to say something.

"There's no food. There's nothing here. You must wait a bit," said Banford to them. "Go away. Go away. Go round to the yard."

They didn't go, so she climbed the fence to swerve them round under the gate and into the yard. So off they waggled in an excited string once more, wagging their rumps like the sterns of little gondolas ducking under the bar of the gate. Banford stood on the top of the bank, just over the fence, looking down on the other three.

Henry looked up at her, and met her queer, round-pupilled, weak eyes staring behind her spectacles. He was perfectly still. He looked away, up at the weak, leaning tree. And as he looked into the sky, like a huntsman who is watching a flying bird, he thought to himself: "If the tree falls in just such a way, and spins just so much as it falls, then the branch there will strike her exactly as she stands on top of that bank."

He looked at her again. She was wiping the hair from her brow again, with that perpetual gesture. In his heart he had decided her death. A terrible still force seemed in him, and a power that was just his. If he turned even a hair's breadth in the wrong direction, he would lose the power.

"Mind yourself, Miss Banford," he said. And his heart held perfectly still, in the terrible pure will that she should not move.

"Who me, mind myself?" she cried, her father's jeering tone in her voice. "Why, do you think you might hit me with the axe?"

"No, it's just possible the tree might, though," he answered soberly. But the tone of his voice seemed to her to imply that he was only being falsely solicitous and trying to make her move because it was his will to move her.

"Absolutely impossible," she said.

He heard her. But he held himself icy still, lest he should lose his power.

"No, it's just possible. You'd better come down this way."

"Oh, all right. Let us see some crack Canadian tree felling," she retorted.

"Ready then," he said, taking the axe, looking round to see he was clear.

There was a moment of pure, motionless suspense, when the world seemed to stand still. Then suddenly his form seemed to flash up enormously tall and fearful, he gave two swift, flashing blows, in immediate succession, the tree was severed, turning slowly, spinning strangely in the air and coming down like a sudden darkness on the earth. No one saw what was happening except himself. No one heard the strange little cry which the Banford gave as the dark end of the bough swooped down, down on her. No one saw her crouch a little and receive the blow on the back of the neck. No one saw her flung outwards and laid, a little twitching heap, at the foot of the fence. No one except the boy. And he watched with intense bright eyes, as he would watch a wild goose he had shot. Was it winged, or dead? Dead!

Immediately he gave a loud cry. Immediately March gave a wild shriek that went far, far down the afternoon. And the father started a strange bellowing sound.

The boy leapt the fence and ran to the figure. The back of the neck and head was a mass of blood, of horror. He turned it over. The body was quivering with little convulsions. But she was dead really. He knew it, that it was so. He knew it in his soul and his blood. The inner necessity of his life was fulfilling itself, it was he who was to live. The thorn was drawn out of his bowels. So, he put her down gently. She was dead.

He stood up. March was standing there petrified and absolutely motionless. Her face was dead white, her eyes big black pools. The old man was scrambling horribly over the fence.

"I'm afraid it's killed her," said the boy.

The old man was making curious, blubbering noises as he huddled over the fence.

"What!" cried March, starting electric.

"Yes, I'm afraid," repeated the boy.

March was coming forward. The boy was over the fence before she reached it.

"What do you say, killed her?" she asked in a sharp voice.

"I'm afraid so," he answered softly.

She went still whiter, fearful. The two stood facing each other. Her black eyes gazed on him with the last look of resistance. And then in a last agonized failure she began to grizzle, to cry in a shivery little fashion of a child that doesn't want to cry, but which is beaten from within, and gives that little first shudder of sobbing which is not yet weeping, dry and fearful.

He had won. She stood there absolutely helpless, shuddering her dry sobs and her mouth trembling rapidly. And then, as in a child, with a little crash came the tears and the blind agony of sightless weeping. She sank down on the grass and sat there with her hands on her breast and her face lifted in sightless, convulsed weeping. He stood above her, looking down on her, mute, pale, and everlasting seeming. He never moved, but looked down on her. And among all the torture of the scene, the torture of his own heart and bowels, he was glad, he had won.

After a long time he stooped to her and took her hands.

"Don't cry," he said softly. "Don't cry."

She looked up at him with tears running from her eyes, a senseless look of helplessness and submission. So she gazed on him as if sightless, yet looking up to him. She would never leave him again. He had won her. And he knew it and was glad, because he wanted her for his life. His life must have her. And now he had won her. It was what his life must have.

But if he had won her, he had not yet got her. They were married at Christmas as he had planned, and he got again ten days' leave. They went to Cornwall, to his own village, on the sea. He realized that it was awful for her to be at the farm any more.

But though she belonged to him, though she lived in his shadow, as if she could not be away from him, she was not happy. She did not want to leave him: and yet she did not feel free with him. Everything around her seemed to watch her, seemed to press on her. He had won her, he had her with him, she was his wife. And she—she belonged to him, she knew it. But she was not glad. And he was still foiled. He realized that though he was married to her and possessed her in every possible way, apparently, and though she *wanted* him to possess her, she wanted it, she wanted nothing else, now, still he did not quite succeed.

Something was missing. Instead of her soul swaying with new life, it seemed to droop, to bleed, as if it were wounded. She would sit for a long time with her hand in his, looking away at the sea. And in her dark, vacant eyes was a sort of wound, and her face looked a little peaked. If he spoke to her, she would turn to him with a faint new smile, the strange, quivering little smile of a woman who has died in the old way of love, and can't quite rise to the new way. She still felt she ought to *do* something, to strain herself in some direction. And there was nothing to do, and no direction in which to strain herself. And she could not quite accept the submergence which his new love put upon her. If she was in love, she ought to *exert* herself, in some way, loving. She felt the weary need of our day to *exert* herself in love. But she knew that in fact she must no more exert herself in love. He would not have the love which exerted itself towards him. It made his brow go black. No, he wouldn't let her exert her love towards him. No, she had to be passive, to acquiesce, and to be submerged under the surface of love. She had to be like the seaweed she saw as she peered down from the boat, swaying for ever delicately under water, with all their delicate fibrils put tenderly out upon the flood, sensitive, utterly sensitive and receptive within the shadowy sea, and never, never rising and looking forth above water while they lived. Never. Never looking forth from the water until they died, only then washing corpses, upon the surface. But while they lived, always submerged, always beneath the wave. Beneath the wave they might have powerful roots, stronger than iron, they might be tenacious and dangerous in their soft waving within the flood. Beneath the water they might be stronger, more indestructible than resistant oak trees are on land. But it was always under-water, always under-water. And she, being a woman, must be like that.

And she had been so used to the very opposite. She had had to take all the thought for love and for life, and all the responsibility. Day after day she had been responsible for the coming day, for the coming year: for her dear Jill's health and happiness and well-being. Verily, in her own small way, she had felt herself responsible for the well-being of the world. And this had been her great stimulant, this grand feeling that, in her own small sphere, she was responsible for the well-being of the world.

And she had failed. She knew that, even in her small way, she had failed. She had failed to satisfy her own feeling of responsibility. It was so difficult. It seemed so grand and easy at first. And the more you tried, the more difficult it became. It had seemed so easy to make one beloved creature happy. And the more you tried, the worse the failure. It was terrible. She had been all her life reaching, reaching, and what she reached for seemed so near, until she had stretched to her utmost limit. And then it was always beyond her.

Always beyond her, vaguely, unrealizably beyond her, and she was left with nothingness at last. The life she reached for, the happiness she reached for, the well-being she reached for, all slipped back, became unreal, the further she stretched her hand. She wanted some goal, some finality—and there was none. Always this ghastly reaching, reaching, striving for something that might be just beyond. Even to make Jill happy.

She was glad Jill was dead. For she had realized that she could never make her happy. Jill would always be fretting herself thinner and thinner, weaker and weaker. Her pains grew worse instead of less. It would be so for ever. She was glad she was dead.

And if she had married a man it would have been just the same. The woman striving, striving to make the man happy, striving within her own limits for the well-being of her world. And always achieving failure. Little, foolish successes in money or in ambition. But at the very point where she most wanted success, in the anguished effort to make some one beloved human being happy and perfect, there the failure was almost catastrophic. You wanted to make your beloved happy, and his happiness seemed always achievable. If only you did just this, that and the other. And you did this, that, and the other, in all good faith, and every time the failure became a little more ghastly. You could love yourself to ribbons, and strive and strain yourself to the bone, and things would go from bad to worse, bad to worse, as far as happiness went. The awful mistake of happiness.

Poor March, in her goodwill and her responsibility, she had strained herself till it seemed to her that the whole of life and everything was only a horrible abyss of nothingness. The more you reached after the fatal flower of happiness, which trembles so blue and lovely in a crevice just beyond your grasp, the more fearfully you become aware of the ghastly and awful gulf of the precipice below you, into which you will inevitably plunge, as into the bottomless pit, if you reach any further. You pluck flower after flower—it is never *the* flower. The flower itself—its calyx is a horrible gulf, it is the bottomless pit.

That is the whole history of the search for happiness, whether it be your own or somebody else's that you want to win. It ends, and it always ends, in the ghastly sense of the bottomless nothingness into which you will inevitably fall if you strain any further.

And women?—what goal can any woman conceive, except happiness? Just happiness, for herself and the whole world. That, and nothing else. And so, she assumes the responsibility, and sets off towards her goal. She can see it there, at the foot of the rainbow. Or she can see it a little way beyond, in the blue distance. Not far, not far.

But the end of the rainbow is a bottomless gulf down which you can fall for ever without arriving, and the blue distance is a void pit which can swallow you and all your efforts into its emptiness, and still be no emptier. You and all your efforts. So, the illusion of attainable happiness!

Poor March, she had set off so wonderfully, towards the blue goal. And the further and further she had gone, the more fearful had become the realization of emptiness. An agony, an insanity at last.

She was glad it was over. She was glad to sit on the shore and look westwards over the sea, and know the great strain had ended. She would never strain for love and happiness any more. And Jill was safely dead. Poor Jill, poor Jill. It must be sweet to be dead.

For her own part, death was not her destiny. She would have to leave her destiny to the boy. But then, the boy. He wanted more than that. He wanted her to give herself without defences, to sink and become submerged in him. And she—she wanted to sit still, like a woman on the last milestone, and watch. She wanted to see, to know, to understand. She wanted to be alone: with him at her side.

And he! He did not want her to watch any more, to see any more, to understand any more. He wanted to veil her woman's spirit, as Orientals veil the woman's face. He wanted her to commit herself to him, and to put her independent spirit to sleep. He wanted to take away from her all her effort, all that seemed her very *raison d'être*. He wanted to make her submit, yield, blindly pass away out of all her strenuous consciousness. He wanted to take away her consciousness, and make her just his woman. Just his woman.

And she was so tired, so tired, like a child that wants to go to sleep, but which fights against sleep as if sleep were death. She seemed to stretch her eyes wider in the obstinate effort and tension of keeping awake. She *would* keep awake. She *would* know. She *would* consider and judge and decide. She *would* have the reins of her own life between her own hands. She *would* be an independent woman, to the last. But she was so tired, so tired of everything. And sleep seemed near. And there was such rest in the boy.

Yet there, sitting in a niche of the high wild cliffs of West Cornwall, looking over the westward sea, she stretched her eyes wider and wider. Away to the West, Canada, America. She *would* know and she *would* see what was ahead. And the boy, sitting beside her staring down at the gulls, had a cloud between his brows and the strain of discontent in his eyes. He wanted her asleep, at peace in him. He wanted her at peace, asleep in him. And *there* she was, dying with the strain of her own wakefulness. Yet she would not sleep: no, never. Sometimes he thought bitterly that he ought to have left her. He ought never to have killed Banford. He should have left Banford and March to kill one another.

But that was only impatience: and he knew it. He was waiting, waiting to go west. He was aching almost in torment to leave England, to go west, to take March away. To leave this shore! He believed that as they crossed the seas, as they left this England which he so hated, because in some way it seemed to have stung him with poison, she would go to sleep. She would close her eyes at last, and give in to him.

And then he would have her and he would have his own life at last. He chafed, feeling he hadn't got his own life. He would never have it till she yielded and slept in him. Then he would have all his own life as a young man and a male, and she would have all her own life as a woman and a female. There would be no more of this awful straining. She would not be a man any more, an independent woman with a man's responsibility. Nay, even the responsibility for her own soul she would have to commit to him. He knew it was so, and obstinately held out against her, waiting for the surrender.

"You'll feel better when once we get over the seas, to Canada, over there," he said to her as they sat among the rocks on the cliff.

She looked away to the sea's horizon, as if it were not real. Then she looked round at him, with the strained, strange look of a child that is struggling against sleep.

"Shall I?" she said.

"Yes," he answered quietly.

And her eyelids dropped with the slow motion, sleep weighing them unconscious. But she pulled them open again to say:

"Yes, I may. I can't tell. I can't tell what it will be like over there."

"If only we could go soon!" he said, with pain in his voice.

1923

AFTERWORD

> She heard Banford speaking to the fowls, in the distance—and she did not hear.
> What was she thinking about? Heaven knows. Her consciousness was, as it
> were, held back.
>   She lowered her eyes, and suddenly saw the fox. He was looking up at her.
> His chin was pressed down, and his eyes were looking up. They met her eyes.
> And he knew her. She was spell-bound—she knew he knew her. So he looked
> into her eyes, and her soul failed her. He knew her, he was not daunted.

This is Lawrence country: easy to parody, easy to misunderstand, but difficult to
deny.

It is August 1918, World War I is drawing to an end at long last. Nellie March and
Jill Banford have been living on the farm for the last three years of the war, at first
with Banford's grandfather, who died after the first year. At first they had cattle too,
but one heifer turned wild, another got pregnant and troublesome, so they since have
had only chickens and ducks. March, looselimbed, graceful, like a young man, "did
most of the outside work." Banford—like March, nearly thirty—tends the house,
pours the tea, likes company and gossip; it is her money that runs the farm. But the
farm is not flourishing. The hens won't lay. The two women, generally compatible,
are starting to get irritated with one another. A fox preys on the chickens.

"There was something odd and unexplained about [March]," with her boy's figure, her woman's face, her mouth "almost pinched as if in pain and irony," her eyes
big, wide, deep, "strange, startled, shy and sardonic at once." What is this odd and
unexplained element? What does the fox know about her? What is the "she" the fox
knows? Why does her soul fail in looking at the fox? Is it because he knows her and
she knows he knows her? And what does that mean? How can a fox know a person,
whatever 'know" means? And what does Lawrence mean by March's soul? And how
does a soul "fail"?

The incident is clearly important to March, and whenever she goes into one of her
rapt or trancelike states thereafter she thinks of the fox. About three months (but only
a few pages) later, a twenty-year-old soldier shows up. He used to live on the farm
with his grandfather. He ran away to Canada, joined the army, and has been serving
in Greece, but the war is over now. He has a "ruddy, roundish face, with fairish
hair" and bright blue eyes.

> But to March he was the fox. Whether it was the thrusting forward of his head,
> or the glisten of fine whitish hairs on the ruddy cheek-bones, or the bright, keen
> eyes, that can never be said: but the boy was to her the fox, and she could not
> see him otherwise.

The narrative focus is rather odd if you think about it. We seem to know what is
going on inside March (and the other characters) to some degree, more, certainly,
than we or the narrator could learn merely by observing. Yet "Heaven knows" what
she was thinking about when the fox first appeared; there's something about her
"unexplained," and just what makes her think the boy is the fox "can never be said."
The depth yet limitation of the narrator's knowledge is rather puzzling. Is it a mere
awkwardness or arbitrariness in the narration, or does it have some significance in
the world of the fiction, in Lawrence's vision of reality?

Other things are beginning to clear up, however, or so it seems. This is to be a love story, of sorts, or at least a story about sex. The fox is male (a dog-fox, as we learn) and what he "knows" about her—having caught her unawares, with her defenses of intelligence and consciousness down—is that she needs a male, a man. She needs a man to help run the farm; she needs a man to protect her—and the "other" chickens—from the marauders, the hunters, the male foxes—she has a rifle with her but cannot shoot, she's so startled and absorbed. She needs a man sexually; she's nearly thirty, very womanly despite her boyish grace, and has been living with another woman for three years. There's something unnatural about her life, her role; Nature, in the form of the fox, can sense it. When Henry Grenfel the soldier shows up, it all falls into place. He is the fox, the male, what March wants (both in the sense of "desires" and "needs"). She identifies him with the fox. She dreams the fox is bright yellow and singing; he bites her on the wrist and flicks his brush across her face, burning her mouth. Henry's khaki uniform, glinting in the sun, reminds her of the fox's yellowness. When, later, Henry kisses her on the mouth, the kiss burns like the fox's brush.

It's all very simple, not to say crude. March and Banford have a lesbian or lesbianlike arrangement. That's "unnatural." March is cast in the role of the male and that perverts her natural self. She needs to be dominated by a male, sexually and otherwise. Henry Grenfel fills the bill perfectly: he's young and vigorous—only twenty; he's a soldier and natural-born "hunter" or predator (that is, macho male); he knows how to put food on the table and run the farm. The fox is a literary symbol, crude, perhaps as crude as the theme, but an obvious symbol, and the coincidence of the fox scene and the advent of Henry is almost ludicrous. (The heavy-handedness of the symbol may lead us to believe that the problematical focus is, too, mere awkwardness.) *Voilà!* The Lawrence we all know: all about sex; sexist; formally negligent or nearly inept; simple, obvious, and repetitive (we're less than halfway into the story) in theme, narration, and language (why is the fox described as looking up in two consecutive sentences: "He was looking up at her. His chin was pressed down, and his eyes were looking up"?).

This is a great writer? This a great short novel?

Still, even thus far there are items difficult to explain away as merely Lawrence's ineptitude. The schema we (or, let me take the blame, I) have rigged casts Banford in something of the villain's role. She's not going to marry, her family has decided, so that's where she got the money that set up the farm and put March in the role of "husband." She's the "unnatural" one, one would think. Shouldn't she then resent Henry from the beginning? consciously or unconsciously try to get rid of him even before he makes a move toward March? She *is* a bit concerned about the propriety of his staying with them at first, but seems as reluctantly agreeable as March. She enjoys waiting on him, enjoys the company and the gossip, treats him as if he were her brother and is "naturally warm and kind." She will fight March's intention to marry the boy, but she is not instinctively, unnaturally, bitchily hostile—yet. But perhaps that's just Lawrence's chauvinist way of making her more womanly—warm, kind, accommodating, that sort of sexist palaver.

What about Henry, the soldier, the hunter, the macho male, the fox? Are we not supposed to admire him, the natural one fulfilling his natural role and offering March the opportunity to live a natural, fulfilled life? How or why does he fall in love with March? Or is "love" too soft and feminine an emotion? Given the schema he should probably just want her, want to possess her, dominate her sexually. That's not exactly how Lawrence presents his "courtship." Henry has noticed March all right, but we do not know too much about what he thinks of her. Then one evening he's returning from hunting and sees the cozy home:

And he thought to himself, it would be a good thing to have this place for his own. And then the thought entered him shrewdly: why not marry March? . . . His mind . . . seemed to calculate. . .

He scarcely admitted his intentions even to himself. He kept it as a secret even from himself [repetition again]. It was all too uncertain as yet. He would have to see how things went. Yes, he would have to see how things went [and again].

Is this our macho hero? Well, he is the fox. Foxes are cunning, aren't they? But calculation seems somehow a bit less admirable than "cunning," especially putting profit or at least economic security or domesticity before sex. He doesn't even say, "Yeah, this farm and cozy house, and wow! March too," and go off into scenes of love and such. Too cool, Henry is, for the perfect hero in our Lawrencian scheme, isn't he? What's Lawrence up to?

Henry does not identify himself with the fox. " 'Perhaps you think I've come to steal your chickens or something,' he said . . ." This is the first time anyone has ever identified him with a fox (and he is often described here in terms of a cat or puppy). He, with his Canadian sense of space, sympathizes with the fox in constricted England; the fox doesn't have a chance. But it is Henry who shoots the fox, kills him. It is only the middle of the story, the fox is dead, and after March fondles the pelt for a bit, the creature gets scarcely a mention. The fox is shot and Henry is leaving the farm; the predators—or is there only one?—are going. But March dreams that it is Banford who is dead, not Henry; it's Banford who is put in the wood-box coffin, with the fox's brush beneath her head and the skin on top of the body.

The battle between Banford and Henry over March is now intense. It is his last day. He watches the two women return from shopping. March carrying all the packages, acting "the male." His hatred for Banford wells.

Then, in the middle of the scene there is a break on the page, like this one, the first in the novel; the scene does not change, nor the time, nor the focus, but there is a break. Nothing is said or implied that explains the break. The new section simply begins, "He watched the progress of the two women. He could hear their voices . . ." He eavesdrops. Banford is trying to talk March out of marrying him.

And he disliked the Banford with an acid dislike. And he felt drawn to the March again. He felt again irresistibly drawn to her. He felt there was a secret bond, a secret thread between him and her, something very exclusive, which shut out everybody else and made him and her possess each other in secret.

There is another change, a costume change—March that evening wears a dress. And still another—Henry changes from boy to man, feeling "a little of the heaviness of male destiny upon him." His battle with Banford over March is now overt. When March goes out into the night with Henry, Banford sobs. Her heart is breaking, March says, but Henry says theirs—March's and his—are breaking too. She never thought of Henry's having a heart—and we have had little reason to think so either—but he puts her hand on his chest and she feels his heart "like a thing far beyond . . . signalling to her." He tells her he had never before met a woman " 'I really wanted, for good. You see, I'm thinking of all my life.' " In his new maturity he does not take advantage of her vulnerability; he feels responsible for her. He is born into a new world. She is "his heaven and hell on earth, and he would have none elsewhere."

There is another break on the page; Henry leaves the farm for camp; March, out from under the influence of his presence, reneges on her promise to marry him; and the final dramatic act in the struggle of Henry against Banford for March ensues. We see the struggle largely through Henry and his consciousness or subconsciousness—

he feels winning March is the "inner necessity of his life fulfilling itself," or "His life must have her. And now he had won her. It was what his life must have." March must "submit"; she must not, as she has been doing, "exert herself." We see little that is going on inside her. The story ends but the struggle does not. (This indecisiveness is typical of a Lawrence conclusion.)

Surely this is a male chauvinist story, the kind of thing popularly believed to be characteristic of Lawrence. Nellie—not March, androgynous name—must be saved from being (an ineffectual) male, running things (the farm), exerting (or asserting) herself; she must submit to the superior and protective and responsible male predator or hunter. Even though the story is left unresolved, surely its vision (or "message") is clear. We may think we see in this single work a global world or vision or position that we take to be Lawrence's own, but we ought to remember that if he, like the later Tolstoy, believes in art as essentially truth-telling, the irresolution of the ending is as honest and uncontrived as the internal argument. That is, Lawrence does not know precisely how to extrapolate the "contest" between March and Henry, does not know precisely how to conclude. His fiction is a progress or pilgrimage, seeking and testing, trying and adjusting his vision and its articulation.

It seems clear from such short stories as "Tickets, Please" and novels as *Aaron's Rod,* written in the war and postwar years, as was *The Fox,* that Lawrence saw a disruption or perversion of the relationship between the sexes generated or intensified by the Great War. Aaron's wife Lottie, he thinks, believes "that she, as woman, was the centre of creation, the man was but an adjunct. She, as woman, and particularly as mother, was the first great source of life and being, and also of culture. . . . It is the substantial and professed belief of the whole white world: . . . the life-centrality of woman. Woman, the life-bearer, the life-source." If Henry Grenfel had been able to think or even feel in general terms, this could have been what he might have said he was fighting against in March. But Aaron also says that love is not a goal but a process, and that "The completion of the process of love is the arrival at a state of simple, pure self-possession, *for man and woman."* Would Henry have said this? Did Lawrence see this in the years 1918–1921 when he was writing *The Fox?* Could Henry and March have come to see this after their novel-time was over, in Canada perhaps? When we read *The Fox* are we getting a global view of Lawrence's whole vision, or even his vision of man-woman relationships? or even his vision of man-woman relationships during or just after World War I? Or are we seeing how the conditions of the war and of relationships, of their individual lives and their states of growth, make things appear to Henry, perhaps to March, or to one within the confines of their time and place? What was March thinking before she saw the fox? Heaven knows? *Is* Henry the fox or only in March's eyes? Or is Banford the fox? Should woman submit,

> be submerged under the surface of love . . . like the seaweed she saw as she peered down from the boat, swaying for ever delicately under water, with all their delicate fibrils put tenderly out upon the flood, sensitive, utterly sensitive and receptive within the shadowy sea, and never, never rising and looking forth above water while they lived?

Or should she be an eagle, bearing herself on her own wings, consummating love in mid-air, as Aaron puts it:

> Two eagles in mid-air, grappling, whirling, coming to their intensification of love-oneness there in mid-air. In mid-air the love consummation. But all the time each lifted on its own wings: each bearing itself on its own wings at every moment of the mid-air love consummation. That is the splendid love-way.

WILLIAM FAULKNER

As I Lay Dying

If there is any American author who truly needs no introduction, it is Nobel Laureate William Faulkner (1897–1962), perhaps the greatest of twentieth-century American writers of fiction.

He was not always recognized as such. In 1945, almost twenty years after he began publishing novels, none of his seventeen books was in print, a neglect that could not be entirely accounted for by the war-related paper shortage. His two volumes of poetry—*The Marble Faun* (1924) and *A Green Bough* (1931)—were not, perhaps, a great loss, and neither *Soldiers' Pay* (1926) nor *Mosquitoes* (1927) was greatly missed, but the novels of 1929–30—*Sartoris, The Sound and the Fury,* and *As I Lay Dying*—are now part of the great tradition of twentieth-century American fiction, the first introducing Yoknapatawpha County, the other two great novels in their own right. Among his novels of the 1930s were *Sanctuary, Light in August,* and *Absalom, Absalom!* and early in the 1940s came *The Hamlet* and *Go Down, Moses,* so that by the end of World War II the heart of the Faulkner canon was, if not in print, at least written and published. There were other volumes, too, and there would be more to come, but the greatest of the works were done, and largely unavailable, by 1945.

In some ways, it's no wonder, for William Faulkner was always one to do it his way (except, perhaps, for the pot-boiler version of *Sanctuary,* later revised, and for his movie scripts that he wrote or worked on during his many trips to Hollywood during the years 1932–36, 1942–45, 1951, and 1954). He dropped out of high school in Oxford, Mississippi, without a diploma, and after he was admitted to the University of Mississippi as a veteran (he had enlisted in the Canadian Royal Air Force during World War I and had pilot training), he left after a year, of course without a degree. When he was in New Orleans in the mid-1920s, though he was aided and influenced by Sherwood Anderson, he never mixed with the literary crowd (and satirized them in his 1927 novel *Mosquitoes,* as he did Anderson himself in a book he collaborated on in 1926 entitled *Sherwood Anderson and Other Famous Creoles*). He never courted other writers, critics, or even—except as noted—the public. He once wrote a friend, "I think I have written a lot and sent it off to print before I actually realized strangers might read it." Indeed, he had to rely on the kindness, or at least the close attention, of strangers, for his works did not leap off the page and into the mind without some concentration on the part of the reader.

Though he visited New Haven and New Orleans, France, and elsewhere (including Stockholm to receive the Nobel Prize), and died in Charlottesville, where he was on the faculty of the University of Virginia, he is always remembered as a citizen of the land of his own creation, Yoknapatawpha County, of Mississippi—and of the world.

As I Lay Dying

Darl

Jewel and I come up from the field, following the path in single file. Although I am fifteen feet ahead of him, anyone watching us from the cottonhouse can see Jewel's frayed and broken straw hat a full head above my own.

The path runs straight as a plumb-line, worn smooth by feet and baked brick-hard by July, between the green rows of laidby cotton, to the cottonhouse in the center of the field, where it turns and circles the cottonhouse at four soft right angles and goes on across the field again, worn so by feet in fading precision.

The cottonhouse is of rough logs, from between which the chinking has long fallen. Square, with a broken roof set at a single pitch, it leans in empty and shimmering dilapidation in the sunlight, a single broad window in two opposite walls giving onto the approaches of the path. When we reach it I turn and follow the path which circles the house. Jewel, fifteen feet behind me, looking straight ahead, steps in a single stride through the window. Still staring straight ahead, his pale eyes like wood set into his wooden face, he crosses the floor in four strides with the rigid gravity of a cigar store Indian dressed in patched overalls and endued with life from the hips down, and steps in a single stride through the opposite window and into the path again just as I come around the corner. In single file and five feet apart and Jewel now in front, we go on up the path toward the foot of the bluff.

Tull's wagon stands beside the spring, hitched to the rail, the reins wrapped about the seat stanchion. In the wagon bed are two chairs. Jewel stops at the spring and takes the gourd from the willow branch and drinks. I pass him and mount the path, beginning to hear Cash's saw.

When I reach the top he has quit sawing. Standing in a litter of chips, he is fitting two of the boards together. Between the shadow spaces they are yellow as gold, like soft gold, bearing on their flanks in smooth undulations the marks of the adze blade: a good carpenter, Cash is. He holds the two planks on the trestle, fitted along the edges in a quarter of the finished box. He kneels and squints along the edge of them, then he lowers them and takes up the adze. A good carpenter. Addie Bundren could not want a better one, a better box to lie in. It will give her confidence and comfort. I go on to the house, followed by the

Chuck.   Chuck.   Chuck.

of the adze.

Cora

So I saved out the eggs and baked yesterday. The cakes turned out right well. We depend a lot on our chickens. They are good layers, what few we have left after the possums and such. Snakes too, in the summer. A snake will break up a hen-house quicker than anything. So after they were going to cost so much more than Mr Tull thought, and after I promised that the difference in the number of eggs would make it up, I had to be more careful than ever because it was on my final say-so we took them. We could have stocked cheaper chickens, but I gave my promise as Miss Lawington said when she advised me to get a good breed, because Mr Tull himself admits that a good breed of cows or hogs pays in the long run. So when we lost so many of them we couldn't afford to use the eggs ourselves, because I could not have had Mr Tull chide me when it was on my say-so we took them. So when Miss Lawington told me about the cakes I thought that I could bake them and earn enough at one time to increase the net value of the flock the equivalent of two head. And that by saving the eggs out one at a time, even the eggs wouldn't be costing anything. And that week they laid so well that I not only saved out enough eggs above what we had engaged to sell, to bake the cakes with, I had saved enough so that the flour and the sugar and the stove wood would not be costing anything. So I baked yesterday, more careful than ever I baked in my life, and the cakes turned out right well. But when we got to town this morning Miss Lawington told me the lady had changed her mind and was not going to have the party after all.

"She ought to taken those cakes anyway," Kate says.

"Well," I say, "I reckon she never had no use for them now."

"She ought to taken them," Kate says. "But those rich town ladies can change their minds. Poor folks cant."

Riches is nothing in the face of the Lord, for He can see into the heart. "Maybe I can sell them at the bazaar Saturday," I say. They turned out real well.

"You cant get two dollars a piece for them," Kate says.

"Well, it isn't like they cost me anything," I say. I saved them out and swapped a dozen of them for the sugar and flour. It isn't like the cakes cost me anything, as Mr Tull himself realises that the eggs I saved were over and beyond what we had engaged to sell, so it was like we had found the eggs or they had been given to us.

"She ought to taken those cakes when she same as gave you her word," Kate says. The Lord can see into the heart. If it is His will that some folks has different ideas of honesty from other folks, it is not my place to question His decree.

"I reckon she never had any use for them," I say. They turned out real well, too.

The quilt is drawn up to her chin, hot as it is, with only her two hands and her face outside. She is propped on the pillow, with her head raised so she can see out the window, and we can hear him every time he takes up the adze or the saw. If we were deaf we could almost watch her face and hear him, see him. Her face is wasted away so that the bones draw just under the skin in white lines. Her eyes are like two candles when you watch them gutter down into the sockets of iron candlesticks. But the eternal and the everlasting salvation and grace is not upon her.

"They turned out real nice," I say. "But not like the cakes Addie used to bake." You can see that girl's washing and ironing in the pillowslip, if ironed it ever was. Maybe it will reveal her blindness to her, laying there at the mercy and the ministration of four men and a tom-boy girl. "There's not a woman in this section could ever bake with Addie Bundren," I say. "First thing we know she'll be up and baking again, and then we wont have any sale for ours at all." Under the quilt she makes no more of a hump than a rail would, and the only way you can tell she is breathing is by the sound of the mattress shucks. Even the hair at her cheek does not move, even with that girl standing right over her, fanning her with the fan. While we watch she swaps the fan to the other hand without stopping it.

"Is she sleeping?" Kate whispers.

"She's just watching Cash yonder," the girl says. We can hear the saw in the board. It sounds like snoring. Eula turns on the trunk and looks out the window. Her necklace looks real nice with her red hat. You wouldn't think it only cost twenty-five cents.

"She ought to taken those cakes," Kate says.

I could have used the money real well. But it's not like they cost me anything except the baking. I can tell him that anybody is likely to make a miscue, but it's not all of them that can get out of it without loss, I can tell him. It's not everybody can eat their mistakes, I can tell him.

Someone comes through the hall. It is Darl. He does not look in as he passes the door. Eula watches him as he goes on and passes from sight again toward the back. Her hand rises and touches her beads lightly, and then her hair. When she finds me watching her, her eyes go blank.

Darl

Pa and Vernon are sitting on the back porch. Pa is tilting snuff from the lid of his snuff-box into his lower lip, holding the lip outdrawn between thumb and finger. They look around as I cross the porch and dip the gourd into the water bucket and drink.

"Where's Jewel?" pa says. When I was a boy I first learned how much better water tastes when it has set a while in a cedar bucket. Warmish-cool, with a faint taste like the hot July wind in cedar trees smells. It has to set at least six hours, and be drunk from a gourd. Water should never be drunk from metal.

And at night it is better still. I used to lie on the pallet in the hall, waiting until I could hear them all asleep, so I could get up and go back to the bucket. It would be black, the shelf black, the still surface of the water a round orifice in nothingness, where before I stirred it awake with the dipper I could see maybe a star or two in the bucket, and maybe in the dipper a star or two before I drank. After that I was bigger, older. Then I would wait until they all went to sleep so I could lie with my shirttail up, hearing them asleep, feeling myself without touching myself, feeling the cool silence blowing upon my parts and wondering if Cash was yonder in the darkness doing it too, had been doing it perhaps for the last two years before I could have wanted to or could have.

Pa's feet are badly splayed, his toes cramped and bent and warped, with no toenail at all on his little toes, from working so hard in the wet in home-made shoes when he was a boy. Beside his chair his brogans sit. They look as though they had been hacked with a blunt axe out of pig-iron. Vernon has been to town. I have never seen him go to town in overalls. His wife, they say. She taught school too, once.

I fling the dipper dregs to the ground and wipe my mouth on my sleeve. It is going to rain before morning. Maybe before dark. "Down to the barn," I say. "Harnessing the team."

Down there fooling with that horse. He will go on through the barn, into the pasture. The horse will not be in sight: he is up there among the pine seedlings, in the cool. Jewel whistles, once and shrill. The horse snorts, then Jewel sees him, glinting for a gaudy instant among the blue shadows. Jewel whistles again; the horse comes dropping down the slope, stiff-legged, his ears cocking and flicking, his mismatched eyes rolling, and fetches up twenty feet away, broadside on, watching Jewel over his shoulder in an attitude kittenish and alert.

"Come here, sir," Jewel says. He moves. Moving that quick his coat, bunching, tongues swirling like so many flames. With tossing mane and tail and rolling eye the horse makes another short curvetting rush and stops again, feet bunched, watching Jewel. Jewel walks steadily toward him, his hands at his sides. Save for Jewel's legs they are like two figures carved for a tableau savage in the sun.

When Jewel can almost touch him, the horse stands on his hind legs and slashes down at Jewel. Then Jewel is enclosed by a glittering maze of hooves as by an illusion of wings; among them, beneath the upreared chest, he moves with the flashing limberness of a snake. For an instant before the jerk comes onto his arms he sees his whole body earth-free, horizontal, whipping snake-limber, until he finds the horse's nostrils and touches earth again. Then they are rigid, motionless, terrific, the horse back-thrust on stiffened, quivering legs, with lowered head; Jewel with dug heels, shutting off the horse's wind with one hand, with the other patting the horse's neck in short strokes myriad and caressing, cursing the horse with obscene ferocity.

They stand in rigid terrific hiatus, the horse trembling and groaning. Then Jewel is on the horse's back. He flows upward in a stooping swirl like the lash of a whip, his body in midair shaped to the horse. For another moment the horse stands spraddled, with lowered head, before it bursts into motion. They descend the hill in a series of spine-jolting jumps, Jewel high, leech-like on the withers, to the fence where the horse bunches to a scuttering halt again.

"Well," Jewel says, "you can quit now, if you got a-plenty."

Inside the barn Jewel slides running to the ground before the horse stops. The horse enters the stall, Jewel following. Without looking back the horse kicks at him, slamming a single hoof into the wall with a pistol-like report. Jewel kicks him in the stomach; the horse arches his neck back, crop-toothed; Jewel strikes him across the face with his fist and slides on to the trough and mounts upon it. Clinging to the hay-rack he lowers his head and peers out across the stall tops and through the doorway. The path is empty; from here he cannot even hear Cash sawing. He reaches up and drags down hay in hurried armsful and crams it into the rack.

"Eat," he says. "Get the goddamn stuff out of sight while you got a chance, you pussel-gutted[1] bastard. You sweet son of a bitch," he says.

Jewel

It's because he stays out there, right under the window, hammering and sawing on that goddamn box. Where she's got to see him. Where every breath she draws is full of his knocking and sawing where she can see him saying See. See what a good one I am making for you. I told him to go somewhere else. I said Good God do you want to see her in it. It's like when he was a little boy and she says if she had some fertilizer she would try to raise some flowers and he taken the bread pan and brought it back from the barn full of dung.

And now them others sitting there, like buzzards. Waiting, fanning

1. Fat.

themselves. Because I said If you wouldn't keep on sawing and nailing at it until a man cant sleep even and her hands laying on the quilt like two of them roots dug up and tried to wash and you couldn't get them clean. I can see the fan and Dewey Dell's arm. I said if you'd just let her alone. Sawing and knocking, and keeping the air always moving so fast on her face that when you're tired and you cant breathe it, and that goddamn adze going One lick less. One lick less. One lick less until everybody that passes in the road will have to stop and see it and say what a fine carpenter he is. If it had just been me when Cash fell off of that church and if it had just been me when pa laid sick with that load of wood fell on him, it would not be happening with every bastard in the country coming in to stare at her because if there is a God what the hell is He for. It would just be me and her on a high hill and me rolling the rocks down the hill at their faces, picking them up and throwing them down the hill faces and teeth and all by God until she was quiet and not that goddamn adze going One lick less. One lick less and we could be quiet.

Darl

We watch him come around the corner and mount the steps. He does not look at us. "You ready?" he says.

"If you're hitched up," I say. I say "Wait." He stops, looking at pa. Vernon spits, without moving. He spits with decorous and deliberate precision into the pocked dust below the porch. Pa rubs his hands slowly on his knees. He is gazing out beyond the crest of the bluff, out across the land. Jewel watches him a moment, then he goes on to the pail and drinks again.

"I mislike undecision as much as ere a man," pa says.

"It means three dollars," I say. The shirt across pa's hump is faded lighter than the rest of it. There is no sweat stain on his shirt. I have never seen a sweat stain on his shirt. He was sick once from working in the sun when he was twenty-two years old, and he tells people that if he ever sweats, he will die. I suppose he believes it.

"But if she dont last until you get back," he says. "She will be disappointed."

Vernon spits into the dust. But it will rain before morning.

"She's counted on it," pa says. "She'll want to start right away. I know her. I promised her I'd keep the team here and ready, and she's counting on it."

"We'll need that three dollars then, sure," I say. He gazes out over the land, rubbing his hands on his knees. Since he lost his teeth his mouth collapses in slow repetition when he dips. The stubble gives his lower face that appearance that old dogs have. "You'd better make up your mind soon, so we can get there and get a load on before dark," I say.

"Ma aint that sick," Jewel says. "Shut up, Darl."

"That's right," Vernon says. "She seems more like herself today than she has in a week. Time you and Jewel get back, she'll be setting up."

"You ought to know," Jewel says. "You been here often enough looking at her. You or your folks." Vernon looks at him. Jewel's eyes look like pale wood in his high-blooded face. He is a head taller than any of the rest of us, always was. I told them that's why ma always whipped him and petted him more. Because he was peakling around the house more. That's why she named him Jewel I told them.

"Shut up, Jewel," pa says, but as though he is not listening much. He gazes out across the land, rubbing his knees.

"You could borrow the loan of Vernon's team and we could catch up with you," I say. "If she didn't wait for us."

"Ah, shut your goddamn mouth," Jewel says.

"She'll want to go in ourn," pa says. He rubs his knees. "Dont ere a man mislike it more."

"It's laying there, watching Cash whittle on that damn. . . . . . ." Jewel says. He says it harshly, savagely, but he does not say the word. Like a little boy in the dark to flail his courage and suddenly aghast into silence by his own noise.

"She wanted that like she wants to go in our own wagon," pa says. "She'll rest easier for knowing it's a good one, and private. She was ever a private woman. You know it well."

"Then let it be private," Jewel says. "But how the hell can you expect it to be——" he looks at the back of pa's head, his eyes like pale wooden eyes.

"Sho," Vernon says, "she'll hold on till it's finished. She'll hold on till everything's ready, till her own good time. And with the roads like they are now, it wont take you no time to get her to town."

"It's fixing up to rain," pa says. "I am a luckless man. I have ever been." He rubs his hands on his knees. "It's that durn doctor, liable to come at any time. I couldn't get word to him till so late. If he was to come tomorrow and tell her the time was nigh, she wouldn't wait. I know her. Wagon or no wagon, she wouldn't wait. Then she'd be upset, and I wouldn't upset her for the living world. With that family burying-ground in Jefferson and them of her blood waiting for her there, she'll be impatient. I promised my word me and the boys would get her there quick as mules could walk it, so she could rest quiet." He rubs his hands on his knees. "No man ever misliked it more."

"If everybody wasn't burning hell to get her there," Jewel says in that harsh, savage voice. "With Cash all day along right under the window, hammering and sawing at that——"

"It was her wish," pa says. "You got no affection nor gentleness for her. You never had. We would be beholden to no man," he says, "me and her. We have never yet been, and she will rest quieter for knowing it and that it was her own blood sawed out the boards and drove the nails. She was ever one to clean up after herself."

"It means three dollars," I say. "Do you want us to go, or not?" Pa rubs his knees. "We'll be back by tomorrow sundown."

"Well . . . ." pa says. He looks out over the land, awry-haired, mouthing the snuff slowly against his gums.

"Come on," Jewel says. He goes down the steps. Vernon spits neatly into the dust.

"By sundown, now," pa says. "I would not keep her waiting."

Jewel glances back, then he goes on around the house. I enter the hall, hearing the voices before I reach the door. Tilting a little down the hill, as our house does, a breeze draws through the hall all the time, upslanting. A feather dropped near the front door will rise and brush along the ceiling, slanting backward, until it reaches the down-turning current at the back door: so with voices. As you enter the hall, they sound as though they were speaking out of the air about your head.

Cora

It was the sweetest thing I ever saw. It was like he knew he would never see her again, that Anse Bundren was driving him from his mother's death bed, never to see her in this world again. I always said Darl was different from those others. I always said he was the only one of them that had his mother's nature, had any natural affection. Not that Jewel, the one she labored so to bear and coddled and petted so and him flinging into tantrums or sulking spells, inventing devilment to devil her until I would have frailed him time and time. Not him to come and tell her goodbye. Not him to miss a chance to make that extra three dollars at the price of his mother's goodbye kiss. A Bundren through and through, loving nobody, caring for nothing except how to get something with the least amount of work. Mr Tull says Darl asked them to wait. He said Darl almost begged them on his knees not to force him to leave her in her condition. But nothing would do but Anse and Jewel must make that three dollars. Nobody that knows Anse could have expected different, but to think of that boy, that Jewel, selling all those years of self-denial and down-right partiality—they couldn't fool me: Mr Tull says Mrs Bundren liked Jewel the least of all, but I knew better. I knew she was partial to him, to the same quality in him that let her put up with Anse Bundren when Mr Tull said she ought to poisoned him—for three dollars, denying his dying mother the goodbye kiss.

Why, for the last three weeks I have been coming over every time I could, coming sometimes when I shouldn't have, neglecting my own family and duties so that somebody would be with her in her last moments and she would not have to face the Great Unknown without one familiar face to give her courage. Not that I deserve credit for it: I will expect the same for myself. But thank God it will be the faces of my loved kin, my blood and flesh, for in my husband and children I have been more blessed than most, trials though they have been at times.

She lived, a lonely woman, lonely with her pride, trying to make folks believe different, hiding the fact that they just suffered her, because she was not cold in the coffin before they were carting her forty miles away to bury her, flouting the will of God to do it. Refusing to let her lie in the same earth with those Bundrens.

"But she wanted to go," Mr Tull said. "It was her own wish to lie among her own people."

"Then why didn't she go alive?" I said. "Not one of them would have stopped her, with even that little one almost old enough now to be selfish and stone-hearted like the rest of them."

"It was her own wish," Mr Tull said. "I heard Anse say it was."

"And you would believe Anse, of course," I said. "A man like you would. Dont tell me."

"I'd believe him about something he couldn't expect to make anything off of me by not telling," Mr Tull said.

"Dont tell me," I said. "A woman's place is with her husband and children, alive or dead. Would you expect me to want to go back to Alabama and leave you and the girls when my time comes, that I left of my own will to cast my lot with yours for better and worse, until death and after?"

"Well, folks are different," he said.

I should hope so. I have tried to live right in the sight of God and man, for the honor and comfort of my Christian husband and the love and respect of my Christian children. So that when I lay me down in the consciousness of my duty and reward I will be surrounded by loving faces, carrying the farewell kiss of each of my loved ones into my reward. Not like Addie Bundren dying alone, hiding her pride and her broken heart. Glad to go. Lying there with her head propped up so she could watch Cash building the coffin, having to watch him so he would not skimp on it, like as not, with those men not worrying about anything except if there was time to earn another three dollars before the rain come and the river got too high to get across it. Like as not, if they hadn't decided to make that last load, they would have loaded her into the wagon on a quilt and crossed the river first and then stopped and give her time to die what Christian death they would let her.

Except Darl. It was the sweetest thing I ever saw. Sometimes I lose faith in human nature for a time; I am assailed by doubt. But always the Lord restores my faith and reveals to me His bounteous love for His creatures. Not Jewel, the one she had always cherished, not him. He was after that three extra dollars. It was Darl, the one that folks say is queer, lazy, pottering about the place no better than Anse, with Cash a good carpenter and always more building than he can get around to, and Jewel always doing something that made him some money or got him talked about, and that near-naked girl always standing over Addie with a fan so that every time a body tried to talk to her and cheer her up, would answer for her right quick, like she was trying to keep anybody from coming near her at all.

It was Darl. He come to the door and stood there, looking at his dying mother. He just looked at her, and I felt the bounteous love of the Lord again and His mercy. I saw that with Jewel she had just been pretending, but that it was between her and Darl that the understanding and the true love was. He just looked at her, not even coming in where she could see him and get upset, knowing that Anse was driving him away and he would never see her again. He said nothing, just looking at her.

"What you want, Darl?" Dewey Dell said, not stopping the fan, speaking up quick, keeping even him from her. He didn't answer. He just stood and looked at his dying mother, his heart too full for words.

Dewey Dell

The first time me and Lafe picked on down the row. Pa dassent[2] sweat because he will catch his death from the sickness so that everybody comes to help us. And Jewel dont care about anything he is not kin to us in caring, not carekin. And Cash like sawing the long hot sad yellow days up into planks and nailing them to something. And pa thinks because neighbors will always treat one another that way because he has always been too busy letting neighbors do for him to find out. And I did not think that Darl would, that sits at the supper table with his eyes gone further than the food and the lamp, full of the land dug out of his skull and the holes filled with distance beyond the land.

We picked on down the row, the woods getting closer and closer and the secret shade, picking on into the secret shade with my sack and Lafe's sack. Because I said will I or wont I when the sack was half full because I said if

---

2. Dares not.

the sack is full when we get to the woods it wont be me. I said if it dont mean for me to do it the sack will not be full and I will turn up the next row but if the sack is full, I cannot help it. It will be that I had to do it all the time and I cannot help it. And we picked on toward the secret shade and our eyes would drown together touching on his hands and my hands and I didn't say anything. I said "What are you doing?" and he said "I am picking into your sack." And so it was full when we came to the end of the row and I could not help it.

And so it was because I could not help it. It was then, and then I saw Darl and he knew. He said he knew without the words like he told me that ma is going to die without words, and I knew he knew because if he had said he knew with the words I would not have believed that he had been there and saw us. But he said he did know and I said "Are you going to tell pa are you going to kill him?" without the words I said it and he said "Why?" without the words. And that's why I can talk to him with knowing with hating because he knows.

He stands in the door, looking at her.

"What you want, Darl?" I say.

"She is going to die," he says. And old turkey-buzzard Tull coming to watch her die but I can fool them.

"When is she going to die?" I say.

"Before we get back," he says.

"Then why are you taking Jewel?" I say.

"I want him to help me load," he says.

Tull

Anse keeps on rubbing his knees. His overalls are faded; on one knee a serge patch cut out of a pair of Sunday pants, wore iron-slick. "No man mislikes it more than me," he says.

"A fellow's got to guess ahead now and then," I say. "But, come long and short, it wont be no harm done neither way."

"She'll want to get started right off," he says. "It's far enough to Jefferson at best."

"But the roads is good now," I say. It's fixing to rain tonight, too. His folks buries at New Hope, too, not three miles away. But it's just like him to marry a woman born a day's hard ride away and have her die on him.

He looks out over the land, rubbing his knees. "No man so mislikes it," he says.

"They'll get back in plenty of time," I say. "I wouldn't worry none."

"It means three dollars," he says.

"Might be it wont be no need for them to rush back, no ways," I say. "I hope it."

"She's a-going," he says. "Her mind is set on it."

It's a hard life on women, for a fact. Some women. I mind my mammy lived to be seventy and more. Worked every day, rain or shine; never a sick day since her last chap was born until one day she kind of looked around her and then she went and taken that lace-trimmed night gown she had had forty-five years and never wore out of the chest and put it on and laid down on the bed and pulled the covers up and shut her eyes. "You all will have to look out for pa the best you can," she said. "I'm tired."

Anse rubs his hands on his knees. "The Lord giveth," he says. We can hear Cash a-hammering and sawing beyond the corner.

It's true. Never a truer breath was ever breathed. "The Lord giveth," I say.

That boy comes up the hill. He is carrying a fish nigh long as he is. He slings it to the ground and grunts "Hah" and spits over his shoulder like a man. Durn nigh long as he is.

"What's that?" I say. "A hog? Where'd you get it?"

"Down to the bridge," he says. He turns it over, the under side caked over with dust where it is wet, the eye coated over, humped under the dirt.

"Are you aiming to leave it laying there?" Anse says.

"I aim to show it to ma," Vardaman says. He looks toward the door. We can hear the talking, coming out on the draft. Cash too, knocking and hammering at the boards. "There's company in there," he says.

"Just my folks," I say. "They'd enjoy to see it too."

He says nothing, watching the door. Then he looks down at the fish laying in the dust. He turns it over with his foot and prods at the eye-bump with his toe, gouging at it. Anse is looking out over the land. Vardaman looks at Anse's face, then at the door. He turns, going toward the corner of the house, when Anse calls him without looking around.

"You clean that fish," Anse says.

Vardaman stops. "Why cant Dewey Dell clean it?" he says.

"You clean that fish," Anse says.

"Aw, pa," Vardaman says.

"You clean it," Anse says. He dont look around. Vardaman comes back and picks up the fish. It slides out of his hands, smearing wet dirt onto him, and flops down, dirtying itself again, gapmouthed, goggle-eyed, hiding into the dust like it was ashamed of being dead, like it was in a hurry to get back hid again. Vardaman cusses it. He cusses it like a grown man, standing a-straddle of it. Anse dont look around. Vardaman picks it up again. He goes on around the house, toting it in both arms like a armful of wood, it overlapping him on both ends, head and tail. Durn nigh big as he is.

Anse's wrists dangle out of his sleeves: I never see him with a shirt on that looked like it was his in all my life. They all looked like Jewel might have give him his old ones. Not Jewel, though. He's long-armed, even if he is spindling. Except for the lack of sweat. You could tell they aint been nobody else's but Anse's that way without no mistake. His eyes look like pieces of burnt-out cinder fixed in his face, looking out over the land.

When the shadow touches the steps he says "It's five oclock."

Just as I get up Cora comes to the door and says it's time to get on. Anse reaches for his shoes. "Now, Mr Bundren," Cora says, "dont you get up now." He puts his shoes on, stomping into them, like he does everything, like he is hoping all the time he really cant do it and can quit trying to. When we go up the hall we can hear them clumping on the floor like they was iron shoes. He comes toward the door where she is, blinking his eyes, kind of looking ahead of hisself before he sees, like he is hoping to find her setting up, in a chair maybe or maybe sweeping, and looks into the door in that surprised way like he looks in and finds her still in bed every time and Dewey Dell still a-fanning her with the fan. He stands there, like he dont aim to move again nor nothing else.

"Well, I reckon we better get on," Cora says. "I got to feed the chickens." It's fixing to rain, too. Clouds like that dont lie, and the cotton making every day the Lord sends. That'll be something else for him. Cash is still trimming at the boards. "If there's ere a thing we can do," Cora says.

"Anse'll let us know," I say.

Anse dont look at us. He looks around, blinking, in that surprised way, like he had wore hisself down being surprised and was even surprised at that. If Cash just works that careful on my barn.

"I told Anse it likely wont be no need," I say. "I so hope it."

"Her mind is set on it," he says. "I reckon she's bound to go."

"It comes to all of us," Cora says. "Let the Lord comfort you."

"About that corn," I say. I tell him again I will help him out if he gets into a tight, with her sick and all. Like most folks around here, I done holp him so much already I cant quit now.

"I aimed to get to it today," he says. "Seems like I cant get my mind on nothing."

"Maybe she'll hold out till you are laid-by," I say.

"If God wills it," he says.

"Let Him comfort you," Cora says.

If Cash just works that careful on my barn. He looks up when we pass. "Don reckon I'll get to you this week," he says.

"'Taint no rush," I say. "Whenever you get around to it."

We get into the wagon. Cora sets the cake box on her lap. It's fixing to rain, sho.

"I dont know what he'll do," Cora says. "I just dont know."

"Poor Anse," I say. "She kept him at work for thirty-odd years. I reckon she is tired."

"And I reckon she'll be behind him for thirty years more," Kate says. "Or if it aint her, he'll get another one before cotton-picking."

"I reckon Cash and Darl can get married now," Eula says.

"That poor boy," Cora says. "The poor little tyke."

"What about Jewel?" Kate says.

"He can, too," Eula says.

"Hmph," Kate says. "I reckon he will. I reckon so. I reckon there's more gals than one around here that dont want to see Jewel tied down. Well, they needn't to worry."

"Why, Kate!" Cora says. The wagon begins to rattle. "The poor little tyke," Cora says.

It's fixing to rain this night. Yes, sir. A rattling wagon is mighty dry weather, for a Birdsell. But that'll be cured. It will for a fact.

"She ought to taken them cakes after she said she would," Kate says.

Anse

Durn that road. And it fixing to rain, too. I can stand here and same as see it with second-sight, a-shutting down behind them like a wall, shutting down betwixt them and my given promise. I do the best I can, much as I can get my mind on anything, but durn them boys.

A-laying there, right up to my door, where every bad luck that comes and goes is bound to find it. I told Addie it want[3] any luck living on a road when it come by here, and she said, for the world like a woman, "Get up and move, then." But I told her it want no luck in it, because the Lord put

3. Wasn't.

roads for travelling: why He laid them down flat on the earth. When He aims for something to be always a-moving, He makes it long ways, like a road or a horse or a wagon, but when He aims for something to stay put, He makes it up-and-down ways, like a tree or a man. And so He never aimed for folks to live on a road, because which gets there first, I says, the road or the house? Did you ever know Him to set a road down by a house? I says. No you never, I says, because it's always men cant rest till they gets the house set where everybody that passes in a wagon can spit in the doorway, keeping the folks restless and wanting to get up and go somewheres else when He aimed for them to stay put like a tree or a stand of corn. Because if He'd a aimed for man to be always a-moving and going somewheres else, wouldn't He a put him longways on his belly, like a snake? It stands to reason He would.

Putting it where every bad luck prowling can find it and come straight to my door, charging me taxes on top of it. Making me pay for Cash having to get them carpenter notions when if it hadn't been no road come there, he wouldn't a got them; falling off of churches and lifting no hand in six months and me and Addie slaving and a-slaving, when there's plenty of sawing on this place he could do if he's got to saw.

And Darl too. Talking me out of him, durn them. It aint that I am afraid of work; I always is fed me and mine and kept a roof above us: it's that they would short-hand me just because he tends to his own business, just because he's got his eyes full of the land all the time. I says to them, he was alright at first, with his eyes full of the land, because the land laid up-and-down ways then; it wasn't till that ere road come and switched the land around longways and his eyes still full of the land, that they begun to threaten me out of him, trying to short-hand me with the law.

Making me pay for it. She was well and hale as ere a woman ever were, except for that road. Just laying down, resting herself in her own bed, asking naught of none. "Are you sick, Addie?" I said.

"I am not sick," she said.

"You lay you down and rest you," I said. "I knowed you are not sick. You're just tired. You lay you down and rest."

"I am not sick," she said. "I will get up."

"Lay still and rest," I said. "You are just tired. You can get up tomorrow." And she was laying there, well and hale as ere a woman ever were, except for that road.

"I never sent for you," I said. "I take you to witness I never sent for you."

"I know you didn't," Peabody said. "I bound that. Where is she?"

"She's a-laying down," I said. "She's just a little tired, but she'll——"

"Get outen here, Anse," he said. "Go set on the porch a while."

And now I got to pay for it, me without a tooth in my head, hoping to get ahead enough so I could get my mouth fixed where I could eat God's own victuals as a man should, and her hale and well as ere a woman in the land until that day. Got to pay for being put to the need of that three dollars. Got to pay for the way for them boys to have to go away to earn it. And now I can see same as second sight the rain shutting down betwixt us, a-coming up that road like a durn man, like it want ere a other house to rain on in all the living land.

I have heard men cuss their luck, and right, for they were sinful men. But I do not say it's a curse on me, because I have done no wrong to be cussed by. I am not religious, I reckon. But peace is in my heart: I know it is. I have done things but neither better nor worse than them that pretend otherlike, and I know that Old Marster will care for me as for ere a sparrow that falls. But it seems hard that a man in his need could be so flouted by a road.

Vardaman comes around the house, bloody as a hog to his knees, and that ere fish chopped up with the axe like as not, or maybe throwed away for him to lie about the dogs et it. Well, I reckon I aint no call to expect no more of him than of his man-growed brothers. He comes along, watching the house, quiet, and sits on the steps. "Whew," he says, "I'm pure tired."

"Go wash them hands," I say. But couldn't no woman strove harder than Addie to make them right, man and boy: I'll say that for her.

"It was full of blood and guts as a hog," he says. But I just cant seem to get no heart into anything, with this here weather sapping me, too. "Pa," he says, "is ma sick some more?"

"Go wash them hands," I say. But I just cant seem to get no heart into it.

Darl

He has been to town this week: the back of his neck is trimmed close, with a white line between hair and sunburn like a joint of white bone. He has not once looked back.

"Jewel," I say. Back running, tunnelled between the two sets of bobbing mule ears, the road vanishes beneath the wagon as though it were a ribbon and the front axle were a spool. "Do you know she is going to die, Jewel?"

It takes two people to make you, and one people to die. That's how the world is going to end.

I said to Dewey Dell: "You want her to die so you can get to town: is that it?" She wouldn't say what we both knew. "The reason you will not say it is, when you say it, even to yourself, you will know it is true: is that it? But you know it is true now. I can almost tell you the day when you knew it is true. Why wont you say it, even to yourself?" She will not say it. She just keeps on saying Are you going to tell pa? Are you going to kill him? "You cannot believe it is true because you cannot believe that Dewey Dell, Dewey Dell Bundren, could have such bad luck: is that it?"

The sun, an hour above the horizon, is poised like a bloody egg upon a crest of thunderheads; the light has turned copper: in the eye portentous, in the nose sulphurous, smelling of lightning. When Peabody comes, they will have to use the rope. He has pussel-gutted himself eating cold greens. With the rope they will haul him up the path, balloon-like up the sulphurous air.

"Jewel," I say, "do you know that Addie Bundren is going to die? Addie Bundren is going to die?"

Peabody

When Anse finally sent for me of his own accord, I said "He has wore her out at last." And I said a damn good thing, and at first I would not go because there might be something I could do and I would have to haul her back, by God. I thought maybe they have the same sort of fool ethics in heaven they have in the Medical College and that it was maybe Vernon Tull sending for me again, getting me there in the nick of time, as Vernon always does things, getting the most for Anse's money like he does for his own. But when it got far enough into the day for me to read weather sign I knew it couldn't have been anybody but Anse that sent. I knew that nobody but a luckless man could ever need a doctor in the face of a cyclone. And I knew that if it had finally occurred to Anse himself that he needed one, it was already too late.

When I reach the spring and get down and hitch the team, the sun has gone down behind a bank of black cloud like a topheavy mountain range, like a load of cinders dumped over there, and there is no wind. I could hear Cash sawing for a mile before I got there. Anse is standing at the top of the bluff above the path.

"Where's the horse?" I say.

"Jewel's taken and gone," he says. "Cant nobody else ketch hit. You'll have to walk up, I reckon."

"Me, walk up, weighing two hundred and twenty-five pounds?" I say. "Walk up that durn wall?" He stands there beside a tree. Too bad the Lord made the mistake of giving trees roots and giving the Anse Bundrens He makes feet and legs. If He'd just swapped them, there wouldn't ever be a worry about this country being deforested someday. Or any other country. "What do you aim for me to do?" I say. "Stay here and get blowed clean out of the country when that cloud breaks?" Even with the horse it would take me fifteen minutes to ride up across the pasture to the top of the ridge and reach the house. The path looks like a crooked limb blown against the bluff. Anse has not been in town in twelve years. And how his mother ever got up there to bear him, he being his mother's son.

"Vardaman's gittin the rope," he says.

After a while Vardaman appears with the plowline. He gives the end of it to Anse and comes down the path, uncoiling it.

"You hold it tight," I say. "I done already wrote this visit onto my books, so I'm going to charge you just the same, whether I get there or not."

"I got hit," Anse says. "You kin come on up."

I'll be damned if I can see why I dont quit. A man seventy years old, weighing two hundred and odd pounds, being hauled up and down a damn mountain on a rope. I reckon it's because I must reach the fifty thousand dollar mark of dead accounts on my books before I can quit. "What the hell does your wife mean," I say, "taking sick on top of a durn mountain?"

"I'm right sorry," he says. He let the rope go, just dropped it, and he has turned toward the house. There is a little daylight up here still, of the color of sulphur matches. The boards look like strips of sulphur. Cash does not look back. Vernon Tull says he brings each board up to the window for her to see it and say it is all right. The boy overtakes us. Anse looks back at him. "Wher's the rope?" he says.

"It's where you left it," I say. "But never you mind that rope. I got to get back down that bluff. I dont aim for that storm to catch me up here. I'd blow too durn far once I got started."

The girl is standing by the bed, fanning her. When we enter she turns her head and looks at us. She has been dead these ten days. I suppose it's having been a part of Anse for so long that she cannot even make that change, if change it be. I can remember how when I was young I believed death to be a phenomenon of the body; now I know it to be merely a function of the mind—and that of the minds of the ones who suffer the bereavement. The nihilists say it is the end; the fundamentalists, the beginning;

when in reality it is no more than a single tenant or family moving out of a tenement or a town.

She looks at us. Only her eyes seem to move. It's like they touch us, not with sight or sense, but like the stream from a hose touches you, the stream at the instant of impact as dissociated from the nozzle as though it had never been there. She does not look at Anse at all. She looks at me, then at the boy. Beneath the quilt she is no more than a bundle of rotten sticks.

"Well, Miss Addie," I say. The girl does not stop the fan. "How are you, sister?" I say. Her head lies gaunt on the pillow, looking at the boy. "You picked out a fine time to get me out here and bring up a storm." Then I send Anse and the boy out. She watches the boy as he leaves the room. She has not moved save her eyes.

He and Anse are on the porch when I come out, the boy sitting on the steps, Anse standing by a post, not even leaning against it, his arms dangling, the hair pushed and matted up on his head like a dipped rooster. He turns his head, blinking at me.

"Why didn't you send for me sooner?" I say.

"Hit was jest one thing and then another," he says. "That ere corn me and the boys was aimin to git up with, and Dewey Dell a-takin good keer of her, and folks comin in, a-offerin to help and sich, till I jest thought . . . . . ."

"Damn the money," I say. "Did you ever hear of me worrying a fellow before he was ready to pay?"

"Hit aint begrudgin the money," he says. "I jest kept a-thinking. . . . . . She's goin, is she?" The durn little tyke is sitting on the top step, looking smaller than ever in the sulphur-colored light. That's the one trouble with this country: everything, weather, all, hangs on too long. Like our rivers, our land: opaque, slow, violent; shaping and creating the life of man in its implacable and brooding image. "I knowed hit," Anse says. "All the while I made sho. Her mind is sot on hit."

"And a damn good thing, too," I say. "With a trifling——" He sits on the top step, small, motionless in faded overalls. When I came out he looked up at me, then at Anse. But now he has stopped looking at us. He just sits there.

"Have you told her yit?" Anse says.

"What for?" I say. "What the devil for?"

"She'll know hit. I knowed that when she see you she would know hit, same as writing. You wouldn't need to tell her. Her mind——"

Behind us the girl says, "Paw." I look at her, at her face.

"You better go quick," I say.

When we enter the room she is watching the door. She looks at me. Her eyes look like lamps blaring up just before the oil is gone. "She wants you to go out," the girl says.

"Now, Addie," Anse says, "when he come all the way from Jefferson to git you well?" She watches me: I can feel her eyes. It's like she was shoving at me with them. I have seen it before in women. Seen them drive from the room them coming with sympathy and pity, with actual help, and clinging to some trifling animal to whom they never were more than pack-horses. That's what they mean by the love that passeth understanding: that pride, that furious desire to hide that abject nakedness which we bring here with us, carry with us into operating rooms, carry stubbornly and furiously with us into the earth again. I leave the room. Beyond the porch Cash's saw snores steadily into the board. A minute later she calls his name, her voice harsh and strong.

"Cash," she says; "you, Cash!"

Darl

Pa stands beside the bed. From behind his leg Vardaman peers, with his round head and his eyes round and his mouth beginning to open. She looks at pa; all her failing life appears to drain into her eyes, urgent, irremediable. "It's Jewel she wants," Dewey Dell says.

"Why, Addie," pa says, "him and Darl went to make one more load. They thought there was time. That you would wait for them, and that three dollars and all. . . . . . ." He stoops laying his hand on hers. For a while yet she looks at him, without reproach, without anything at all, as if her eyes alone are listening to the irrevocable cessation of his voice. Then she raises herself, who has not moved in ten days. Dewey Dell leans down, trying to press her back.

"Ma," she says; "ma."

She is looking out the window, at Cash stooping steadily at the board in the failing light, laboring on toward darkness and into it as though the stroking of the saw illumined its own motion, board and saw engendered.

"You, Cash," she shouts, her voice harsh, strong, and unimpaired. "You, Cash!"

He looks up at the gaunt face framed by the window in the twilight. It is a composite picture of all time since he was a child. He drops the saw and lifts the board for her to see, watching the window in which the face has not moved. He drags a second plank into position and slants the two of them into their final juxtaposition, gesturing toward the ones yet on the ground, shaping with his empty hand in pantomime the finished box. For a while still she looks down at him from the composite picture, neither with censure nor approbation. Then the face disappears.

She lies back and turns her head without so much as glancing at pa. She looks at Vardaman; her eyes, the life in them, rushing suddenly upon them; the two flames glare up for a steady instant. Then they go out as though someone had leaned down and blown upon them.

"Ma," Dewey Dell says; "ma!" Leaning above the bed, her hands lifted a little, the fan still moving like it has for ten days, she begins to keen. Her voice is strong, young, tremulous and clear, rapt with its own timbre and volume, the fan still moving steadily up and down, whispering the useless air. Then she flings herself across Addie Bundren's knees, clutching her, shaking her with the furious strength of the young before sprawling suddenly across the handful of rotten bones that Addie Bundren left, jarring the whole bed into a chattering sibilance of mattress shucks, her arms outflung and the fan in one hand still beating with expiring breath into the quilt.

From behind pa's leg Vardaman peers, his mouth full open and all color draining from his face into his mouth, as though he has by some means fleshed his own teeth in himself, sucking. He begins to move slowly backward from the bed, his eyes round, his pale face fading into the dusk like a piece of paper pasted on a failing wall, and so out of the door.

Pa leans above the bed in the twilight, his humped silhouette partaking of that owl-like quality of awry-feathered, disgruntled outrage within which lurks a wisdom too profound or too inert for even thought.

"Durn them boys," he says.

Jewel, I say. Overhead the day drives level and gray, hiding the sun by a flight of gray spears. In the rain the mules smoke a little, splashed yellow with mud, the off[4] one clinging in sliding lunges to the side of the road above the ditch. The tilted lumber gleams dull yellow, water-soaked and heavy as lead, tilted at a steep angle into the ditch above the broken wheel; about the shattered spokes and about Jewel's ankles a runnel of yellow neither water nor earth swirls, curving with the yellow road neither of earth nor water, down the hill dissolving into a streaming mass of dark green neither of earth nor sky. Jewel, I say

Cash comes to the door, carrying the saw. Pa stands beside the bed, humped, his arms dangling. He turns his head, his shabby profile, his chin collapsing slowly as he works the snuff against his gums.

"She's gone," Cash says.

"She taken and left us," pa says. Cash does not look at him. "How nigh are you done?" pa says. Cash does not answer. He enters, carrying the saw. "I reckon you better get at it," pa says. "You'll have to do the best you can, with them boys gone off that-a-way." Cash looks down at her face. He is not listening to pa at all. He does not approach the bed. He stops in the middle of the floor, the saw against his leg, his sweating arms powdered lightly with sawdust, his face composed. "If you get in a tight, maybe some of them'll get here tomorrow and help you," pa says. "Vernon could." Cash is not listening. He is looking down at her peaceful, rigid face fading into the dusk as though darkness were a precursor of the ultimate earth, until at last the face seems to float detached upon it, lightly as the reflection of a dead leaf. "There is Christians enough to help you," pa says. Cash is not listening. After a while he turns without looking at pa and leaves the room. Then the saw begins to snore again. "They will help us in our sorrow," pa says.

The sound of the saw is steady, competent, unhurried, stirring the dying light so that at each stroke her face seems to wake a little into an expression of listening and of waiting, as though she were counting the strokes. Pa looks down at the face, at the black sprawl of Dewey Dell's hair, the outflung arms, the clutched fan now motionless on the fading quilt. "I reckon you better get supper on," he says.

Dewey Dell does not move.

"Git up, now, and put supper on," pa says. "We got to keep our strength up. I reckon Doctor Peabody's right hungry, coming all this way. And Cash'll need to eat quick and get back to work so he can finish it in time."

Dewey Dell rises, heaving to her feet. She looks down at the face. It is like a casting of fading bronze upon the pillow, the hands alone still with any semblance of life: a curled, gnarled inertness; a spent yet alert quality from which weariness, exhaustion, travail has not yet departed, as though they doubted even yet the actuality of rest, guarding with horned and penurious alertness the cessation which they know cannot last.

Dewey Dell stoops and slides the quilt from beneath them and draws it up over them to the chin, smoothing it down, drawing it smooth. Then without looking at pa she goes around the bed and leaves the room.

4. Right.

She will go out where Peabody is, where she can stand in the twilight and look at his back with such an expression that, feeling her eyes and turning, he will say: I would not let it grieve me, now. She was old, and sick too. Suffering more than we knew. She couldn't have got well. Vardaman's getting big now, and with you to take good care of them all. I would try not to let it grieve me. I expect you'd better go and get some supper ready. It dont have to be much. But they'll need to eat, and she looking at him, saying You could do so much for me if you just would. If you just knew. I am I and you are you and I know it and you dont know it and you could do so much for me if you just would and if you just would then I could tell you and then nobody would have to know it except you and me and Darl

Pa stands over the bed, dangle-armed, humped, motionless. He raises his hand to his head, scouring his hair, listening to the saw. He comes nearer and rubs his hand, palm and back, on his thigh and lays it on her face and then on the hump of quilt where her hands are. He touches the quilt as he saw Dewey Dell do, trying to smoothe it up to the chin, but disarranging it instead. He tries to smoothe it again, clumsily, his hand awkward as a claw, smoothing at the wrinkles which he made and which continue to emerge beneath his hand with perverse ubiquity, so that at last he desists, his hand falling to his side and stroking itself again, palm and back, on his thigh. The sound of the saw snores steadily into the room. Pa breathes with a quiet, rasping sound, mouthing the snuff against his gums. "God's will be done," he says. "Now I can get them teeth."

Jewel's hat droops limp about his neck, channelling water onto the soaked towsack tied about his shoulders as, ankle-deep in the running ditch, he pries with a slipping two-by-four, with a piece of rotting log for fulcrum, at the axle. Jewel, I say, she is dead, Jewel. Addie Bundren is dead

Vardaman

Then I begin to run. I run toward the back and come to the edge of the porch and stop. Then I begin to cry. I can feel where the fish was in the dust. It is cut up into pieces of not-fish now, not-blood on my hands and overalls. Then it wasn't so. It hadn't happened then. And now she is getting so far ahead I cannot catch her.

The trees look like chickens when they ruffle out into the cool dust on the hot days. If I jump off the porch I will be where the fish was, and it all cut up into a not-fish now. I can hear the bed and her face and them and I can feel the floor shake when he walks on it that came and did it. That came and did it when she was all right but he came and did it.

"The fat son of a bitch."

I jump from the porch, running. The top of the barn comes swooping up out of the twilight. If I jump I can go through it like the pink lady in the circus, into the warm smelling, without having to wait. My hands grab at the bushes; beneath my feet the rocks and dirt go rubbling down.

Then I can breathe again, in the warm smelling. I enter the stall, trying to touch him, and then I can cry then I vomit the crying. As soon as he gets through kicking I can and then I can cry, the crying can.

"He kilt her. He kilt her."

The life in him runs under the skin, under my hand, running through the splotches, smelling up into my nose where the sickness is beginning to

cry, vomiting the crying, and then I can breathe, vomiting it. It makes a lot
of noise. I can smell the life running up from under my hands, up my arms,
and then I can leave the stall.

I cannot find it. In the dark, along the dust, the walls I cannot find it.
The crying makes a lot of noise. I wish it wouldn't make so much noise.
Then I find it in the wagon shed, in the dust, and I run across the lot and
into the road, the stick jouncing on my shoulder.

They watch me as I run up, beginning to jerk back, their eyes rolling,
snorting, jerking back on the hitch-rein. I strike. I can hear the stick striking; I can see it hitting their heads, the breast-yoke, missing altogether
sometimes as they rear and plunge, but I am glad.

"You kilt my maw!"

The stick breaks, they rearing and snorting, their feet popping loud on
the ground; loud because it is going to rain and the air is empty for the rain.
But it is still long enough. I run this way and that as they rear and jerk at
the hitch-rein, striking.

"You kilt her!"

I strike at them, striking, they wheeling in a long lunge, the buggy wheeling
onto two wheels and motionless like it is nailed to the ground and the horses
motionless like they are nailed by the hind feet to the center of a whirling
plate.

I run in the dust. I cannot see, running in the sucking dust where the
buggy vanishes tilted on two wheels. I strike, the stick hitting into the
ground, bouncing, striking into the dust and then into the air again and the
dust sucking on down the road faster than if a car was in it. And then I can
cry, looking at the stick. It is broken down to my hand, not longer than
stove wood that was a long stick. I throw it away and I can cry. It does not
make so much noise now.

The cow is standing in the barn door, chewing. When she sees me come
into the lot she lows, her mouth full of flopping green, her tongue flopping.

"I aint a-goin to milk you. I aint a-goin to do nothing for them."

I hear her turn when I pass. When I turn she is just behind me with her
sweet, hot, hard breath.

"Didn't I tell you I wouldn't?"

She nudges me, snuffing. She moans deep inside, her mouth closed. I
jerk my hand, cursing her like Jewel does.

"Git, now."

I stoop my hand to the ground and run at her. She jumps back and whirls
away and stops, watching me. She moans. She goes on to the path and
stands there, looking up the path.

It is dark in the barn, warm, smelling, silent. I can cry quietly, watching
the top of the hill.

Cash comes to the hill, limping where he fell off of the church. He looks
down at the spring, then up the road and back toward the barn. He comes
down the path stiffly and looks at the broken hitch-rein and at the dust in
the road and then up the road, where the dust is gone.

"I hope they've got clean past Tull's by now. I so hope hit."

Cash turns and limps up the path.

"Durn him. I showed him. Durn him."

I am not crying now. I am not anything. Dewey Dell comes to the hill
and calls me. Vardaman. I am not anything. I am quiet. You, Vardaman. I
can cry quiet now, feeling and hearing my tears.

"Then hit want. Hit hadn't happened then. Hit was a-layin right there on the ground. And now she's gittin ready to cook hit."

It is dark. I can hear wood, silence: I know them. But not living sounds, not even him. It is as though the dark were resolving him out of his integrity, into an unrelated scattering of components—snuffings and stampings; smells of cooling flesh and ammoniac hair; an illusion of a co-ordinated whole of splotched hide and strong bones within which, detached and secret and familiar, an *is* different from my *is*. I see him dissolve—legs, a rolling eye, a gaudy splotching like cold flames—and float upon the dark in fading solution; all one yet neither; all either yet none. I can see hearing coil toward him, caressing, shaping his hard shape—fetlock, hip, shoulder and head; smell and sound. I am not afraid.

"Cooked and et. Cooked and et."

Dewey Dell

He could do so much for me if he just would. He could do everything for me. It's like everything in the world for me is inside a tub full of guts, so that you wonder how there can be any room in it for anything else very important. He is a big tub of guts and I am a little tub of guts and if there is not any room for anything else important in a big tub of guts, how can it be room in a little tub of guts. But I know it is there because God gave women a sign when something has happened bad.

It's because I am alone. If I could just feel it, it would be different, because I would not be alone. But if I were not alone, everybody would know it. And he could do so much for me, and then I would not be alone. Then I could be all right alone.

I would let him come in between me and Lafe, like Darl came in between me and Lafe, and so Lafe is alone too. He is Lafe and I am Dewey Dell, and when mother died I had to go beyond and outside of me and Lafe and Darl to grieve because he could do so much for me and he dont know it. He dont even know it.

From the back porch I cannot see the barn. Then the sound of Cash's sawing comes in from that way. It is like a dog outside the house, going back and forth around the house to whatever door you come to, waiting to come in. He said I worry more than you do and I said You dont know what worry is so I cant worry. I try to but I cant think long enough to worry.

I light the kitchen lamp. The fish, cut into jagged pieces, bleeds quietly in the pan. I put it into the cupboard quick, listening into the hall, hearing. It took her ten days to die; maybe she dont know it is yet. Maybe she wont go until Cash. Or maybe until Jewel. I take the dish of greens from the cupboard and the bread pan from the cold stove, and I stop, watching the door.

"Where's Vardaman?" Cash says. In the lamp his sawdusted arms look like sand.

"I dont know. I aint seen him."

"Peabody's team run away. See if you can find Vardaman. The horse will let him catch him."

"Well. Tell them to come to supper."

I cannot see the barn. I said, I dont know how to worry. I dont know how to cry. I tried, but I cant. After a while the sound of the saw comes around, coming dark along the ground in the dust-dark. Then I can see him, going up and down above the plank.

"You come in to supper," I say. "Tell him." He could do everything for me. And he dont know it. He is his guts and I am my guts. And I am Lafe's guts. That's it. I dont see why he didn't stay in town. We are country people, not as good as town people. I dont see why he didn't. Then I can see the top of the barn. The cow stands at the foot of the path, lowing. When I turn back, Cash is gone.

I carry the buttermilk in. Pa and Cash and he are at the table.

"Where's that big fish Bud caught, sister?" he says.

I set the milk on the table. "I never had no time to cook it."

"Plain turnip greens is mighty spindling eating for a man my size," he says. Cash is eating. About his head the print of his hat is sweated into his hair. His shirt is blotched with sweat. He has not washed his hands and arms.

"You ought to took time," pa says. "Where's Vardaman?"

I go toward the door. "I cant find him."

"Here, sister," he says; "never mind about the fish. It'll save, I reckon. Come on and sit down."

"I aint minding it," I say. "I'm going to milk before it sets in to rain."

Pa helps himself and pushes the dish on. But he does not begin to eat. His hands are halfclosed on either side of his plate, his head bowed a little, his awry hair standing into the lamplight. He looks like right after the maul hits the steer and it no longer alive and dont yet know that it is dead.

But Cash is eating, and he is too. "You better eat something," he says. He is looking at pa. "Like Cash and me. You'll need it."

"Ay," pa says. He rouses up, like a steer that's been kneeling in a pond and you run at it. "She would not begrudge me it."

When I am out of sight of the house, I go fast. The cow lows at the foot of the bluff. She nuzzles at me, snuffing, blowing her breath in a sweet, hot blast, through my dress, against my hot nakedness, moaning. "You got to wait a little while. Then I'll tend to you." She follows me into the barn where I set the bucket down. She breathes into the bucket, moaning. "I told you. You just got to wait, now. I got more to do than I can tend to." The barn is dark. When I pass, he kicks the wall a single blow. I go on. The broken plank is like a pale plank standing on end. Then I can see the slope, feel the air moving on my face again, slow, pale with lesser dark and with empty seeing, the pine clumps blotched up the tilted slope, secret and waiting.

The cow in silhouette against the door nuzzles at the silhouette of the bucket, moaning.

Then I pass the stall. I have almost passed it. I listen to it saying for a long time before it can say the word and the listening part is afraid that there may not be time to say it. I feel my body, my bones and flesh beginning to part and open upon the alone, and the process of coming unalone is terrible. Lafe. Lafe. "Lafe" Lafe. Lafe. I lean a little forward, one foot advanced with dead walking. I feel the darkness rushing past my breast, past the cow; I begin to rush upon the darkness but the cow stops me and the darkness rushes on upon the sweet blast of her moaning breath, filled with wood and with silence.

"Vardaman. You, Vardaman."

He comes out of the stall. "You durn little sneak! You durn little sneak!"
He does not resist; the last of rushing darkness flees whistling away. "What?
I aint done nothing."

"You durn little sneak!" My hands shake him, hard. Maybe I couldn't
stop them. I didn't know they could shake so hard. They shake both of us,
shaking.

"I never done it," he says. "I never touched them."

My hands stop shaking him, but I still hold him. "What are you doing
here? Why didn't you answer when I called you?"

"I aint doing nothing."

"You go on to the house and get your supper."

He draws back. I hold him. "You quit now. You leave me be."

"What were you doing down here? You didn't come down here to sneak
after me?"

"I never. I never. You quit, now. I didn't even know you was down here.
You leave me be."

I hold him, leaning down to see his face, feel it with my eyes. He is about
to cry. "Go on, now. I done put supper on and I'll be there soon as I milk.
You better go on before he eats everything up. I hope that team runs clean
back to Jefferson."

"He kilt her," he says. He begins to cry.

"Hush."

"She never hurt him and he come and kilt her."

"Hush." He struggles. I hold him. "Hush."

"He kilt her." The cow comes up behind us, moaning. I shake him again.

"You stop it, now. Right this minute. You're fixing to make yourself sick
and then you cant go to town. You go on to the house and eat your supper."

"I dont want no supper. I dont want to go to town."

"We'll leave you here, then. Lessen you behave, we will leave you. Go
on, now, before that old green-eating tub of guts eats everything up from
you." He goes on, disappearing slowly into the hill. The crest, the trees,
the roof of the house stand against the sky. The cow nuzzles at me, moaning. "You'll just have to wait. What you got in you aint nothing to what I
got in me, even if you are a woman too." She follows me, moaning. Then
the dead, hot, pale air breathes on my face again. He could fix it all right,
if he just would. And he dont even know it. He could do everything for me
if he just knowed it. The cow breathes upon my hips and back, her breath
warm, sweet, stertorous, moaning. The sky lies flat down the slope, upon
the secret clumps. Beyond the hill sheet-lightning stains upward and fades.
The dead air shapes the dead earth in the dead darkness, further away than
seeing shapes the dead earth. It lies dead and warm upon me, touching me
naked through my clothes. I said You dont know what worry is. I dont know
what it is. I dont know whether I am worrying or not. Whether I can or
not. I dont know whether I can cry or not. I dont know whether I have
tried to or not. I feel like a wet seed wild in the hot blind earth.

Vardaman

When they get it finished they are going to put her in it and then for a long
time I couldn't say it. I saw the dark stand up and go whirling away and I
said "Are you going to nail her up in it, Cash? Cash? Cash?" I got shut up
in the crib the new door it was too heavy for me it went shut I couldn't

breathe because the rat was breathing up all the air, I said "Are you going
to nail it shut, Cash? Nail it? *Nail* it?"

Pa walks around. His shadow walks around, over Cash going up and down
above the saw, at the bleeding plank.

Dewey Dell said we will get some bananas. The train is behind the glass,
red on the track. When it runs the track shines on and off. Pa said flour and
sugar and coffee costs so much. Because I am a country boy because boys
in town. Bicycles. Why do flour and sugar and coffee cost so much when he
is a country boy. "Wouldn't you ruther have some bananas instead?" Bananas
are gone, eaten. Gone. When it runs on the track shines again. "Why aint
I a town boy, pa?" I said. God made me. I did not said to God to made me
in the country. If He can make the train, why cant He make them all in the
town because flour and sugar and coffee. "Wouldn't you ruther have bananas?"

He walks around. His shadow walks around.

It was not her. I was there, looking. I saw. I thought it was her, but it
was not. It was not my mother. She went away when the other one laid
down in her bed and drew the quilt up. She went away. "Did she go as far
as town?" "She went further than town." "Did all those rabbits and possums
go further than town?" God made the rabbits and possums. He made the
train. Why must He make a different place for them to go if she is just like
the rabbit.

Pa walks around. His shadow does. The saw sounds like it is asleep.

And so if Cash nails the box up, she is not a rabbit. And so if she is not a
rabbit I couldn't breathe in the crib and Cash is going to nail it up. And so
if she lets him it is not her. I know. I was there. I saw when it did not be
her. I saw. They think it is and Cash is going to nail it up.

It was not her because it was laying right yonder in the dirt. And now it's
all chopped up. I chopped it up. It's laying in the kitchen in the bleeding
pan, waiting to be cooked and et. Then it wasn't and she was, and now it is
and she wasn't. And tomorrow it will be cooked and et and she will be him
and pa and Cash and Dewey Dell and there wont be anything in the box
and so she can breathe. It was laying right yonder on the ground. I can get
Vernon. He was there and he seen it, and with both of us it will be and
then it will not be.

Tull

It was nigh to midnight and it had set in to rain when he woke us. It had
been a misdoubtful night, with the storm making; a night when a fellow
looks for most anything to happen before he can get the stock fed and himself to the house and supper et and in bed with the rain starting, and when
Peabody's team come up, lathered, with the broke harness dragging and
the neck-yoke betwixt the off critter's legs, Cora says "It's Addie Bundren.
She's gone at last."

"Peabody mought have been to ere a one of a dozen houses hereabouts,"
I says. "Besides, how do you know it's Peabody's team?"

"Well, aint it?" she says. "You hitch up, now."

"What for?" I says. "If she is gone, we cant do nothing till morning. And
it fixing to storm, too."

"It's my duty," she says. "You put the team in."

But I wouldn't do it. "It stands to reason they'd send for us if they needed
us. You dont even know she's gone yet."

"Why, dont you know that's Peabody's team? Do you claim it aint? Well, then." But I wouldn't go. When folks wants a fellow, it's best to wait till they sends for him, I've found. "It's my Christian duty," Cora says. "Will you stand between me and my Christian duty?"

"You can stay there all day tomorrow, if you want," I says.

So when Cora waked me it had set in to rain. Even while I was going to the door with the lamp and it shining on the glass so he could see I am coming, it kept on knocking. Not loud, but steady, like he might have gone to sleep thumping, but I never noticed how low down on the door the knocking was till I opened it and never seen nothing. I held the lamp up, with the rain sparkling across it and Cora back in the hall saying "Who is it, Vernon?" but I couldn't see nobody a-tall at first until I looked down and around the door, lowering the lamp.

He looked like a drowned puppy, in them overalls, without no hat, splashed up to his knees where he had walked them four miles in the mud. "Well, I'll be durned," I says.

"Who is it, Vernon?" Cora says.

He looked at me, his eyes round and black in the middle like when you throw a light in a owl's face. "You mind[5] that ere fish," he says.

"Come in the house," I says. "What is it? Is your maw——"

"Vernon," Cora says.

He stood kind of around behind the door, in the dark. The rain was blowing onto the lamp, hissing on it so I am scared every minute it'll break. "You was there," he says. "You seen it."

Then Cora come to the door. "You come right in outen the rain," she says, pulling him in and him watching me. He looked just like a drownded puppy. "I told you," Cora says. "I told you it was a-happening. You go and hitch."

"But he aint said——" I says.

He looked at me, dripping onto the floor. "He's a-ruining the rug," Cora says. "You go get the team while I take him to the kitchen."

But he hung back, dripping, watching me with them eyes. "You was there. You seen it laying there. Cash is fixing to nail her up, and it was a-laying right there on the ground. You seen it. You seen the mark in the dirt. The rain never come up till after I was a-coming here. So we can get back in time."

I be durn if it didn't give me the creeps, even when I didn't know yet. But Cora did. "You get that team quick as you can," she says. "He's outen his head with grief and worry."

I be durn if it didn't give me the creeps. Now and then a fellow gets to thinking. About all the sorrow and afflictions in this world; how it's liable to strike anywhere, like lightning. I reckon it does take a powerful trust in the Lord to guard a fellow, though sometimes I think that Cora's a mite over-cautious, like she was trying to crowd the other folks away and get in closer than anybody else. But then, when something like this happens, I reckon she is right and you got to keep after it and I reckon I am blessed in having a wife that ever strives for sanctity and well-doing like she says I am.

Now and then a fellow gets to thinking about it. Not often, though. Which is a good thing. For the Lord aimed for him to do and not to spend too much time thinking, because his brain it's like a piece of machinery: it wont

5. Remember.

stand a whole lot of racking. It's best when it all runs along the same, doing the day's work and not no one part used no more than needful. I have said and I say again, that's ever living thing the matter with Darl: he just thinks by himself too much. Cora's right when she says all he needs is a wife to straighten him out. And when I think about that, I think that if nothing but being married will help a man, he's durn nigh hopeless. But I reckon Cora's right when she says the reason the Lord had to create women is because man dont know his own good when he sees it.

When I come back to the house with the team, they was in the kitchen. She was dressed on top of her nightgown, with a shawl over her head and her umbrella and her bible wrapped up in the oilcloth, and him sitting on a up-turned bucket on the stove-zinc where she had put him, dripping onto the floor. "I cant get nothing outen him except about a fish," she says. "It's a judgment on them. I see the hand of the Lord upon this boy for Anse Bundren's judgment and warning."

"The rain never come up till after I left," he says. "I had done left. I was on the way. And so it was there in the dust. You seen it. Cash is fixing to nail her, but you seen it."

When we got there it was raining hard, and him sitting on the seat between us, wrapped up in Cora's shawl. He hadn't said nothing else, just sitting there with Cora holding the umbrella over him. Now and then Cora would stop singing long enough to say "It's a judgment on Anse Bundren. May it show him the path of sin he is a-trodding." Then she would sing again, and him sitting there between us, leaning forward a little like the mules couldn't go fast enough to suit him.

"It was laying right yonder," he says, "but the rain come up after I taken and left. So I can go and open the windows, because Cash aint nailed her yet."

It was long a-past midnight when we drove the last nail, and almost dust-dawn when I got back home and taken the team out and got back in bed, with Cora's nightcap laying on the other pillow. And be durned if even then it wasn't like I could still hear Cora singing and feel that boy leaning forward between us like he was ahead of the mules, and still see Cash going up and down with that saw, and Anse standing there like a scarecrow, like he was a steer standing knee-deep in a pond and somebody come by and set the pond up on edge and he aint missed it yet.

It was nigh toward daybreak when we drove the last nail and toted it into the house, where she was laying on the bed with the window open and the rain blowing on her again. Twice he did it, and him so dead for sleep that Cora says his face looked like one of these here Christmas masts[6] that had done been buried a while and then dug up, until at last they put her into it and nailed it down so he couldn't open the window on her no more. And the next morning they found him in his shirt tail, laying asleep on the floor like a felled steer, and the top of the box bored clean full of holes and Cash's new auger broke off in the last one. When they taken the lid off they found that two of them had bored on into her face.

If it's a judgment, it aint right. Because the Lord's got more to do than that. He's bound to have. Because the only burden Anse Bundren's ever had is himself. And when folks talks him low, I think to myself he aint that less of a man or he couldn't a bore himself this long.

6. Masks.

It aint right. I be durn if it is. Because He said Suffer little children to come unto Me dont make it right, neither. Cora said, "I have bore you what the Lord God sent me. I faced it without fear nor terror because my faith was strong in the Lord, a-bolstering and sustaining me. If you have no son, it's because the Lord has decreed otherwise in His wisdom. And my life is and has ever been a open book to ere a man or woman among His creatures because I trust in my God and my reward."

I reckon she's right. I reckon if there's ere a man or woman anywhere that He could turn it all over to and go away with His mind at rest, it would be Cora. And I reckon she would make a few changes, no matter how He was running it. And I reckon they would be for man's good. Leastways, we would have to like them. Leastways, we might as well go on and make like we did.

Darl

The lantern sits on a stump. Rusted, grease-fouled, its cracked chimney smeared on one side with a soaring smudge of soot, it sheds a feeble and sultry glare upon the trestles and the boards and the adjacent earth. Upon the dark ground the chips look like random smears of soft pale paint on a black canvas. The boards look like long smooth tatters torn from the flat darkness and turned backside out.

Cash labors about the trestles, moving back and forth, lifting and placing the planks with long clattering reverberations in the dead air as though he were lifting and dropping them at the bottom of an invisible well, the sounds ceasing without departing, as if any movement might dislodge them from the immediate air in reverberant repetition. He saws again, his elbow flashing slowly, a thin thread of fire running along the edge of the saw, lost and recovered at the top and bottom of each stroke in unbroken elongation, so that the saw appears to be six feet long, into and out of pa's shabby and aimless silhouette. "Give me that plank," Cash says. "No; the other one." He puts the saw down and comes and picks up the plank he wants, sweeping pa away with the long swinging gleam of the balanced board.

The air smells like sulphur. Upon the impalpable plane of it their shadows form as upon a wall, as though like sound they had not gone very far away in falling but had merely congealed for a moment, immediate and musing. Cash works on, half turned into the feeble light, one thigh and one pole-thin arm braced, his face sloped into the light with a rapt dynamic immobility above his tireless elbow. Below the sky sheet-lightning slumbers lightly; against it the trees, motionless, are ruffled out to the last twig, swollen, increased as though quick with young.

It begins to rain. The first harsh, sparse, swift drops rush through the leaves and across the ground in a long sigh, as though relief from intolerable suspense. They are big as buckshot, warm as though fired from a gun; they sweep across the lantern in a vicious hissing. Pa lifts his face, slack-mouthed, the wet black rim of snuff plastered close along the base of his gums; from behind his slack-faced astonishment he muses as though from beyond time, upon the ultimate outrage. Cash looks once at the sky, then at the lantern. The saw has not faltered, the running gleam of its pistoning edge unbroken. "Get something to cover the lantern," he says.

Pa goes to the house. The rain rushes suddenly down, without thunder, without warning of any sort; he is swept onto the porch upon the edge of it and in an instant Cash is wet to the skin. Yet the motion of the saw has not faltered, as though it and the arm functioned in a tranquil conviction that rain was an illusion of the mind. Then he puts down the saw and goes and crouches above the lantern, shielding it with his body, his back shaped lean and scrawny by his wet shirt as though he had been abruptly turned wrong-side out, shirt and all.

Pa returns. He is wearing Jewel's raincoat and carrying Dewey Dell's. Squatting over the lantern, Cash reaches back and picks up four sticks and drives them into the earth and takes Dewey Dell's raincoat from pa and spreads it over the sticks, forming a roof above the lantern. Pa watches him. "I dont know what you'll do," he says. "Darl taken his coat with him."

"Get wet," Cash says. He takes up the saw again; again it moves up and down, in and out of that unhurried imperviousness as a piston moves in the oil; soaked, scrawny, tireless, with the lean light body of a boy or an old man. Pa watches him, blinking, his face streaming; again he looks up at the sky with that expression of dumb and brooding outrage and yet of vindication, as though he had expected no less; now and then he stirs; moves, gaunt and streaming, picking up a board or a tool and then laying it down. Vernon Tull is there now, and Cash is wearing Mrs Tull's raincoat and he and Vernon are hunting the saw. After a while they find it in pa's hand.

"Why don't you go on to the house, out of the rain?" Cash says. Pa looks at him, his face streaming slowly. It is as though upon a face carved by a savage caricaturist a monstrous burlesque of all bereavement flowed. "You go on in," Cash says. "Me and Vernon can finish it."

Pa looks at them. The sleeves of Jewel's coat are too short for him. Upon his face the rain streams, slow as cold glycerin. "I dont begrudge her the wetting," he says. He moves again and falls to shifting the planks, picking them up, laying them down again carefully, as though they are glass. He goes to the lantern and pulls at the propped raincoat until he knocks it down and Cash comes and fixes it back.

"You get on to the house," Cash says. He leads pa to the house and returns with the raincoat and folds it and places it beneath the shelter where the lantern sits. Vernon has not stopped. He looks up, still sawing.

"You ought to done that at first," he says. "You knowed it was fixing to rain."

"It's his fever," Cash says. He looks at the board.

"Ay," Vernon says. "He'd a come, anyway."

Cash squints at the board. On the long flank of it the rain crashes steadily, myriad, fluctuant. "I'm going to bevel it," he says.

"It'll take more time," Vernon says. Cash sets the plank on edge; a moment longer Vernon watches him, then he hands him the plane.

Vernon holds the board steady while Cash bevels the edge of it with the tedious and minute care of a jeweler. Mrs Tull comes to the edge of the porch and calls Vernon. "How near are you done?" she says.

Vernon does not look up. "Not long. Some, yet."

She watches Cash stooping at the plank, the turgid savage gleam of the lantern slicking on the raincoat as he moves. "You go down and get some planks off the barn and finish it and come in out of the rain," she says. "You'll both catch your death." Vernon does not move. "Vernon," she says.

"We wont be long," he says. "We'll be done after a spell." Mrs Tull watches them a while. Then she reenters the house.

"If we get in a tight, we could take some of them planks," Vernon says. "I'll help you put them back."

Cash ceases the plane and squints along the plank, wiping it with his palm. "Give me the next one," he says.

Some time toward dawn the rain ceases. But it is not yet day when Cash drives the last nail and stands stiffly up and looks down at the finished coffin, the others watching him. In the lantern light his face is calm, musing; slowly he strokes his hands on his raincoated thighs in a gesture deliberate, final and composed. Then the four of them—Cash and pa and Vernon and Peabody—raise the coffin to their shoulders and turn toward the house. It is light, yet they move slowly; empty, yet they carry it carefully; lifeless, yet they move with hushed precautionary words to one another, speaking of it as though, complete, it now slumbered lightly alive, waiting to come awake. On the dark floor their feet clump awkwardly, as though for a long time they have not walked on floors.

They set it down by the bed. Peabody says quietly: "Let's eat a snack. It's almost daylight. Where's Cash?"

He has returned to the trestles, stooped again in the lantern's feeble glare as he gathers up his tools and wipes them on a cloth carefully and puts them into the box with its leather sling to go over the shoulder. Then he takes up box, lantern and raincoat and returns to the house, mounting the steps into faint silhouette against the paling east.

In a strange room you must empty yourself for sleep. And before you are emptied for sleep, what are you. And when you are emptied for sleep, you are not. And when you are filled with sleep, you never were. I dont know what I am. I dont know if I am or not. Jewel knows he is, because he does not know that he does not know whether he is or not. He cannot empty himself for sleep because he is not what he is and he is what he is not. Beyond the unlamped wall I can hear the rain shaping the wagon that is ours, the load that is no longer theirs that felled and sawed it nor yet theirs that bought it and which is not ours either, lie on our wagon though it does, since only the wind and the rain shape it only to Jewel and me, that are not asleep. And since sleep is is-not and rain and wind are *was*, it is not. Yet the wagon *is*, because when the wagon is *was*, Addie Bundren will not be. And Jewel *is*, so Addie Bundren must be. And then I must be, or I could not empty myself for sleep in a strange room. And so if I am not emptied yet, I am *is*.

How often have I lain beneath rain on a strange roof, thinking of home.

Cash

I made it on the bevel.

1. There is more surface for the nails to grip.
2. There is twice the gripping-surface to each seam.
3. The water will have to seep into it on a slant. Water moves easiest up and down or straight across.
4. In a house people are upright two thirds of the time. So the seams and joints are made up-and-down. Because the stress is up-and-down.
5. In a bed where people lie down all the time, the joints and seams are made sideways, because the stress is sideways.

6. Except.
7. A body is not square like a crosstie.
8. Animal magnetism.
9. The animal magnetism of a dead body makes the stress come slanting, so the seams and joints of a coffin are made on the bevel.
10. You can see by an old grave that the earth sinks down on the bevel.
11. While in a natural hole it sinks by the center, the stress being up-and-down.
12. So I made it on the bevel.
13. It makes a neater job.

Vardaman

My mother is a fish.

Tull

It was ten oclock when I got back, with Peabody's team hitched on to the back of the wagon. They had already dragged the buckboard back from where Quick found it upside down straddle of the ditch about a mile from the spring. It was pulled out of the road at the spring, and about a dozen wagons was already there. It was Quick found it. He said the river was up and still rising. He said it had already covered the highest water-mark on the bridge-piling he had ever seen. "That bridge wont stand a whole lot of water," I said. "Has somebody told Anse about it?"

"I told him," Quick said. "He says he reckons them boys has heard and unloaded and are on the way back by now. He says they can load up and get across."

"He better go on and bury her at New Hope," Armstid said. "That bridge is old. I wouldn't monkey with it."

"His mind is set on taking her to Jefferson," Quick said.

"Then he better get at it soon as he can," Armstid said.

Anse meets us at the door. He has shaved, but not good. There is a long cut on his jaw, and he is wearing his Sunday pants and a white shirt with the neckband buttoned. It is drawn smooth over his hump, making it look bigger than ever, like a white shirt will, and his face is different too. He looks folks in the eye now, dignified, his face tragic and composed, shaking us by the hand as we walk up onto the porch and scrape our shoes, a little stiff in our Sunday clothes, our Sunday clothes rustling, not looking full at him as he meets us.

"The Lord giveth," we say.

"The Lord giveth."

That boy is not there. Peabody told about how he come into the kitchen, hollering, swarming and clawing at Cora when he found her cooking that fish, and how Dewey Dell taken him down to the barn. "My team all right?" Peabody says.

"All right," I tell him. "I give them a bait this morning. Your buggy seems all right too. It aint hurt."

"And no fault of somebody's," he says. "I'd give a nickel to know where that boy was when that team broke away."

"If it's broke anywhere, I'll fix it," I say.

The women folks go on into the house. We can hear them, talking and fanning. The fans go whish. whish. whish and them talking, the talking sounding kind of like bees murmuring in a water bucket. The men stop on the porch, talking some, not looking at one another.

"Howdy, Vernon," they say. "Howdy, Tull."

"Looks like more rain."

"It does for a fact."

"Yes, sir. It will rain some more."

"It come up quick."

"And going away slow. It dont fail."

I go around to the back. Cash is filling up the holes he bored in the top of it. He is trimming out plugs for them, one at a time, the wood wet and hard to work. He could cut up a tin can and hide the holes and nobody wouldn't know the different. Wouldn't mind, anyway. I have seen him spend a hour trimming out a wedge like it was glass he was working, when he could have reached around and picked up a dozen sticks and drove them into the joint and made it do.

When we finished I go back to the front. The men have gone a little piece from the house, sitting on the ends of the boards and on the saw-horses where we made it last night, some sitting and some squatting. Whitfield aint come yet.

They look up at me, their eyes asking.

"It's about," I say. "He's ready to nail."

While they are getting up Anse comes to the door and looks at us and we return to the porch. We scrape our shoes again, careful, waiting for one another to go in first, milling a little at the door. Anse stands inside the door, dignified, composed. He waves us in and leads the way into the room.

They had laid her in it reversed. Cash made it clock-shape, like this with every joint and seam bevelled and scrubbed with the plane, tight as a drum and neat as a sewing basket, and they had laid her in it head to foot so it wouldn't crush her dress. It was her wedding dress and it had a flare-out bottom, and they had laid her head to foot in it so the dress could spread out, and they had made her a veil out of a mosquito bar so the auger holes in her face wouldn't show.

When we are going out, Whitfield comes. He is wet and muddy to the waist, coming in. "The Lord comfort this house," he says. "I was late because the bridge has gone. I went down to the old ford and swum my horse over, the Lord protecting me. His grace be upon this house."

We go back to the trestles and plank-ends and sit or squat.

"I knowed it would go," Armstid says.

"It's been there a long time, that ere bridge," Quick says.

"The Lord has kept it there, you mean," Uncle Billy says. "I dont know ere a man that's touched hammer to it in twenty-five years."

"How long has it been there, Uncle Billy?" Quick says.

"It was built in . . . . . . let me see. . . . . . It was in the year 1888," Uncle Billy says. "I mind it because the first man to cross it was Peabody coming to my house when Jody was born."

"If I'd a crossed it every time your wife littered since, it'd a been wore out long before this, Billy," Peabody says.

We laugh, suddenly loud, then suddenly quiet again. We look a little aside at one another.

"Lots of folks has crossed it that wont cross no more bridges," Houston says.

"It's a fact," Littlejohn says. "It's so."

"One more aint, no ways," Armstid says. "It'd taken them two-three days to get her to town in the wagon. They'd be gone a week, getting her to Jefferson and back."

"What's Anse so itching to take her to Jefferson for, anyway?" Houston says.

"He promised her," I say. "She wanted it. She come from there. Her mind was set on it."

"And Anse is set on it, too," Quick says.

"Ay," Uncle Billy says. "It's like a man that's let everything slide all his life to get set on something that will make the most trouble for everybody he knows."

"Well, it'll take the Lord to get her over that river now," Peabody says. "Anse cant do it."

"And I reckon He will," Quick says. "He's took care of Anse a long time, now."

"It's a fact," Littlejohn says.

"Too long to quit now," Armstid says.

"I reckon He's like everybody else around here," Uncle Billy says. "He's done it so long now He cant quit."

Cash comes out. He has put on a clean shirt, his hair, wet, is combed smooth down on his brow, smooth and black as if he had painted it onto his head. He squats stiffly among us, we watching him.

"You feeling this weather, aint you?" Armstid says.

Cash says nothing.

"A broke bone always feels it," Littlejohn says. "A fellow with a broke bone can tell it a-coming."

"Lucky Cash got off with just a broke leg," Armstid says. "He might have hurt himself bed-rid. How far'd you fall, Cash?"

"Twenty-eight foot, four and a half inches, about," Cash says. I move over beside him.

"A fellow can sho slip quick on wet planks," Quick says.

"It's too bad," I say. "But you couldn't a holp it."

"It's them durn women," he says. "I made it to balance with her. I made it to her measure and weight."

If it takes wet boards for folks to fall, it's fixing to be lots of falling before this spell is done.

"You couldn't have holp it," I say.

I dont mind the folks falling. It's the cotton and corn I mind.

Neither does Peabody mind the folks falling. How bout it, Doc?

It's a fact. Washed clean outen the ground it will be. Seems like something is always happening to it.

Course it does. That's why it's worth anything. If nothing didn't happen and everybody made a big crop, do you reckon it would be worth the raising?

Well, I be durn if I like to see my work washed outen the ground, work I sweat over.

It's a fact. A fellow wouldn't mind seeing it washed up if he could just turn on the rain himself.

Who is that man can do that? Where is the color of his eyes?

Ay. The Lord made it to grow. It's Hisn to wash up if He sees it fitten so.

"You couldn't have holp it," I say.

"It's them durn women," he says.

In the house the women begin to sing. We hear the first line commence, beginning to swell as they take hold, and we rise and move toward the door, taking off our hats and throwing our chews away. We do not go in. We stop at the steps, clumped, holding our hats between our lax hands in front or behind, standing with one foot advanced and our heads lowered, looking aside, down at our hats in our hands and at the earth or now and then at the sky and at one another's grave, composed face.

The song ends; the voices quaver away with a rich and dying fall. Whit-field begins. His voice is bigger than him. It's like they are not the same. It's like he is one, and his voice is one, swimming on two horses side by side across the ford and coming into the house, the mud-splashed one and the one that never even got wet, triumphant and sad. Somebody in the house begins to cry. It sounds like her eyes and her voice were turned back inside her, listening; we move, shifting to the other leg, meeting one anoth-er's eye and making like they hadn't touched.

Whitfield stops at last. The women sing again. In the thick air it's like their voices come out of the air, flowing together and on in the sad, com-forting tunes. When they cease it's like they hadn't gone away. It's like they had just disappeared into the air and when we moved we would loose them again out of the air around us, sad and comforting. Then they finish and we put on our hats, our movements stiff, like we hadn't never wore hats before.

On the way home Cora is still singing. "I am bounding toward my God and my reward," she sings, sitting on the wagon, the shawl around her shoulders and the umbrella open over her, though it is not raining.

"She has hern," I say. "Wherever she went, she has her reward in being free of Anse Bundren." *She laid there three days in that box, waiting for Darl and Jewel to come clean back home and get a new wheel and go back to where the wagon was in the ditch. Take my team, Anse, I said.*

We'll wait for ourn, he said. She'll want it so. She was ever a particular woman.

On the third day they got back and they loaded her into the wagon and started and it already too late. You'll have to go all the way round by Sam-son's bridge. It'll take you a day to get there. Then you'll be forty miles from Jefferson. Take my team, Anse.

We'll wait for ourn. She'll want it so.

It was about a mile from the house we saw him, sitting on the edge of the slough. It hadn't had a fish in it never that I knowed. He looked around at us, his eyes round and calm, his face dirty, the pole across his knees. Cora was still singing.

"This aint no good day to fish," I said. "You come on home with us and me and you'll go down to the river first thing in the morning and catch some fish."

"It's one in here," he said. "Dewey Dell seen it."

"You come on with us. The river's the best place."

"It's in here," he said. "Dewey Dell seen it."

"I'm bounding toward my God and my reward," Cora sung.

Darl

"It's not your horse that's dead, Jewel," I say. He sits erect on the seat, leaning a little forward, wooden-backed. The brim of his hat has soaked free of the crown in two places, drooping across his wooden face so that, head lowered, he looks through it like through the visor of a helmet, looking long across the valley to where the barn leans against the bluff, shaping the invisible horse. "See them?" I say. High above the house, against the quick thick sky, they hang in narrowing circles. From here they are no more than specks, implacable, patient, portentous. "But it's not your horse that's dead." "Goddamn you," he says. "Goddamn you."

I cannot love my mother because I have no mother. Jewel's mother is a horse.

Motionless, the tall buzzards hang in soaring circles, the clouds giving them an illusion of retrograde.

Motionless, wooden-backed, wooden-faced, he shapes the horse in a rigid stoop like a hawk, hook-winged. They are waiting for us, ready for the moving of it, waiting for him. He enters the stall and waits until it kicks at him so that he can slip past and mount onto the trough and pause, peering out across the intervening stall-tops toward the empty path, before he reaches into the loft.

"Goddamn him. Goddamn him."

Cash

"It wont balance. If you want it to tote and ride on a balance, we will have——"

"Pick up. Goddamn you, pick up."

"I'm telling you it wont tote and it wont ride on a balance unless——"

"Pick up! Pick up, goddamn your thick-nosed soul to hell, pick up!"

It wont balance. If they want it to tote and ride on a balance, they will have

Darl

He stoops among us above it, two of the eight hands. In his face the blood goes in waves. In between them his flesh is greenish looking, about that smooth, thick, pale green of cow's cud; his face suffocated, furious, his lip lifted upon his teeth. "Pick up!" he says. "Pick up, goddamn your thick-nosed soul!"

He heaves, lifting one whole side so suddenly that we all spring into the lift to catch and balance it before he hurls it completely over. For an instant it resists, as though volitional, as though within it her pole-thin body clings furiously, even though dead, to a sort of modesty, as she would have tried to conceal a soiled garment that she could not prevent her body soiling. Then it breaks free, rising suddenly as though the emaciation of her body had added buoyancy to the planks or as though, seeing that the garment was about to be torn from her, she rushes suddenly after it in a passionate reversal that flouts its own desire and need. Jewel's face goes completely green and I can hear teeth in his breath.

We carry it down the hall, our feet harsh and clumsy on the floor, moving with shuffling steps, and through the door.

"Steady it a minute, now," pa says, letting go. He turns back to shut and lock the door, but Jewel will not wait.

"Come on," he says in that suffocating voice. "Come on."

We lower it carefully down the steps. We move, balancing it as though it were something infinitely precious, our faces averted, breathing through our teeth to keep our nostrils closed. We go down the path, toward the slope.

"We better wait," Cash says. "I tell you it aint balanced now. We'll need another hand on the hill."

"Then turn loose," Jewel says. He will not stop. Cash begins to fall behind, hobbling to keep up, breathing harshly; then he is distanced and Jewel carries the entire front end alone, so that, tilting as the path begins to slant, it begins to rush away from me and slip down the air like a sled upon invisible snow, smoothly evacuating atmosphere in which the sense of it is still shaped.

"Wait, Jewel," I say. But he will not wait. He is almost running now and Cash is left behind. It seems to me that the end which I now carry alone has no weight, as though it coasts like a rushing straw upon the furious tide of Jewel's despair. I am not even touching it when, turning, he lets it overshoot him, swinging, and stops it and sloughs it into the wagon bed in the same motion and looks back at me, his face suffused with fury and despair.

"Goddamn you. Goddamn you."

Vardaman

We are going to town. Dewey Dell says it wont be sold because it belongs to Santa Claus and he taken it back with him until next Christmas. Then it will be behind the glass again, shining with waiting.

Pa and Cash are coming down the hill, but Jewel is going to the barn. "Jewel," pa says. Jewel does not stop. "Where you going?" pa says. But Jewel does not stop. "You leave that horse here," pa says. "We'll all go in the wagon with ma, like she wanted."

But my mother is a fish. Vernon seen it. He was there.

"Jewel's mother is a horse," Darl said.

"Then mine can be a fish, cant it, Darl?" I said.

Jewel is my brother.

"Then mine will have to be a horse, too," I said.

"Why?" Darl said. "If pa is your pa, why does your ma have to be a horse just because Jewel's is?"

"Why does it?" I said. "Why does it, Darl?"

Darl is my brother.

"Then what is your ma, Darl?" I said.

"I haven't got ere one," Darl said. "Because if I had one, it is *was*. And if it is was, it cant be *is*. Can it?"

"No," I said.

"Then I am not," Darl said. "Am I?"

"No," I said.

I am. Darl is my brother.

"But you *are*, Darl," I said.

"I know it," Darl said. "That's why I am not *is*. *Are* is too many for one woman to foal."

Cash is carrying his tool box. Pa looks at him. "I'll stop at Tull's on the way back," Cash says. "Get on that barn roof."

"It aint respectful," pa says. "It's a deliberate flouting of her and of me."

"Do you want him to come all the way back here and carry them up to

Tull's afoot?" Darl says. Pa looks at Darl, his mouth chewing. Pa shaves every day now because my mother is a fish.

"It aint right," pa says.

Dewey Dell has the package in her hand. She has the basket with our dinner too.

"What's that?" pa says.

"Mrs Tull's cakes," Dewey Dell says, getting into the wagon. "I'm taking them to town for her."

"It aint right," pa says. "It's a flouting of the dead."

It'll be there. It'll be there come Christmas, she says, shining on the track. She says he wont sell it to no town boys.

Darl

He goes on toward the barn, entering the lot, woodenbacked.

Dewey Dell carries the basket on one arm, in the other hand something wrapped square in a newspaper. Her face is calm and sullen, her eyes brooding and alert; within them I can see Peabody's back like two round peas in two thimbles: perhaps in Peabody's back two of those worms which work surreptitious and steady through you and out the other side and you waking suddenly from sleep or from waking, with on your face an expression sudden, intent, and concerned. She sets the basket into the wagon and climbs in, her leg coming long from beneath her tightening dress: that lever which moves the world; one of that caliper which measures the length and breadth of life. She sits on the seat beside Vardaman and sets the parcel on her lap.

Then he enters the barn. He has not looked back.

"It aint right," pa says. "It's little enough for him to do for her."

"Go on," Cash says. "Leave him stay if he wants. He'll be all right here. Maybe he'll go up to Tull's and stay."

"He'll catch us," I say. "He'll cut across and meet us at Tull's lane."

"He would have rid that horse, too," pa says, "if I hadn't a stopped him. A durn spotted critter wilder than a cattymount.[7] A deliberate flouting of her and of me."

The wagon moves; the mules' ears begin to bob. Behind us, above the house, motionless in tall and soaring circles, they diminish and disappear.

Anse

I told him not to bring that horse out of respect for his dead ma, because it wouldn't look right, him prancing along on a durn circus animal and her wanting us all to be in the wagon with her that sprung from her flesh and blood, but we hadn't no more than passed Tull's lane when Darl begun to laugh. Setting back there on the plank seat with Cash, with his dead ma laying in her coffin at his feet, laughing. How many times I told him it's doing such things as that that makes folks talk about him, I dont know. I says I got some regard for what folks says about my flesh and blood even if you haven't, even if I have raised such a durn passel of boys, and when you fixes it so folks can say such about you, it's a reflection on your ma, I says, not me: I am a man and I can stand it; it's on your womenfolks, your ma

7. Mountain lion.

and sister that you should care for, and I turned and looked back at him and him setting there, laughing.

"I dont expect you to have no respect for me," I says. "But with your own ma not cold in her coffin yet."

"Yonder," Cash says, jerking his head toward the lane. The horse is still a right smart piece away, coming up at a good pace, but I dont have to be told who it is. I just looked back at Darl, setting there laughing.

"I done my best," I says. "I tried to do as she would wish it. The Lord will pardon me and excuse the conduct of them He sent me." And Darl setting on the plank seat right above her where she was laying, laughing.

Darl

He comes up the lane fast, yet we are three hundred yards beyond the mouth of it when he turns into the road, the mud flying beneath the flicking drive of the hooves. Then he slows a little, light and erect in the saddle, the horse mincing through the mud.

Tull is in his lot. He looks at us, lifts his hand. We go on, the wagon creaking, the mud whispering on the wheels. Vernon still stands there. He watches Jewel as he passes, the horse moving with a light, high-kneed driving gait, three hundred yards back. We go on, with a motion so soporific, so dreamlike as to be uninferant of progress, as though time and not space were decreasing between us and it.

It turns off at right angles, the wheel-marks of last Sunday healed away now: a smooth, red scoriation curving away into the pines; a white signboard with faded lettering: New Hope Church. 3 mi. It wheels up like a motionless hand lifted above the profound desolation of the ocean; beyond it the red road lies like a spoke of which Addie Bundren is the rim. It wheels past, empty, unscarred, the white signboard turns away its fading and tranquil assertion. Cash looks up the road quietly, his head turning as we pass it like an owl's head, his face composed. Pa looks straight ahead, humped. Dewey Dell looks at the road too, then she looks back at me, her eyes watchful and repudiant, not like that question which was in those of Cash, for a smoldering while. The signboard passes; the unscarred road wheels on. Then Dewey Dell turns her head. The wagon creaks on.

Cash spits over the wheel. "In a couple of days now it'll be smelling," he says.

"You might tell Jewel that," I say.

He is motionless now, sitting the horse at the junction, upright, watching us, no less still than the signboard that lifts its fading capitulation opposite him.

"It aint balanced right for no long ride," Cash says.

"Tell him that, too," I say. The wagon creaks on.

A mile further along he passes us, the horse, archnecked, reined back to a swift singlefoot. He sits lightly, poised, upright, wooden-faced in the saddle, the broken hat raked at a swaggering angle. He passes us swiftly, without looking at us, the horse driving, its hooves hissing in the mud. A gout of mud, backflung, plops onto the box. Cash leans forward and takes a tool from his box and removes it carefully. When the road crosses Whiteleaf, the willows leaning near enough, he breaks off a branch and scours at the stain with the wet leaves.

Anse

It's a hard country on man; it's hard. Eight miles of the sweat of his body washed up outen the Lord's earth, where the Lord Himself told him to put it. Nowhere in this sinful world can a honest, hardworking man profit. It takes them that runs the stores in the towns, doing no sweating, living off of them that sweats. It aint the hardworking man, the farmer. Sometimes I wonder why we keep at it. It's because there is a reward for us above, where they cant take their autos and such. Every man will be equal there and it will be taken from them that have and give to them that have not by the Lord.

But it's a long wait, seems like. It's bad that a fellow must earn the reward of his right-doing by flouting hisself and his dead. We drove all the rest of the day and got to Samson's at dusk-dark and then that bridge was gone, too. They hadn't never see the river so high, and it not done raining yet. There was old men that hadn't never see nor hear of it being so in the memory of man. I am the chosen of the Lord, for who He loveth, so doeth He chastiseth. But I be durn if He dont take some curious ways to show it, seems like.

But now I can get them teeth. That will be a comfort. It will.

Samson

It was just before sundown. We were sitting on the porch when the wagon came up the road with the five of them in it and the other one on the horse behind. One of them raised his hand, but they was going on past the store without stopping.

"Who's that?" MacCallum says: I cant think of his name: Rafe's twin; that one it was.

"It's Bundren, from down beyond New Hope," Quick says. "There's one of them Snopes horses Jewel's riding."

"I didn't know there was ere a one of them horses left," MacCallum says. "I thought you folks down there finally contrived to give them all away."

"Try and get that one," Quick says. The wagon went on.

"I bet old man Lon never gave it to him," I says.

"No," Quick says. "He bought it from pappy." The wagon went on. "They must not a heard about the bridge," he says.

"What're they doing up here, anyway?" MacCallum says.

"Taking a holiday since he got his wife buried, I reckon," Quick says. "Heading for town, I reckon, with Tull's bridge gone too. I wonder if they aint heard about the bridge."

"They'll have to fly, then," I says. "I dont reckon there's ere a bridge between here and Mouth of Ishatawa."

They had something in the wagon. But Quick had been to the funeral three days ago and we naturally never thought anything about it except that they were heading away from home mighty late and that they hadn't heard about the bridge. "You better holler at them," MacCallum says. Durn it, the name is right on the tip of my tongue. So Quick hollered and they stopped and he went to the wagon and told them.

He come back with them. "They're going to Jefferson," he says. "The bridge at Tull's is gone, too." Like we didn't know it, and his face looked funny, around the nostrils, but they just sat there, Bundren and the girl and the chap on the seat, and Cash and the second one, the one folks talks about, on a plank across the tail-gate, and the other one on that spotted horse. But I reckon they was used to it by then, because when I said to Cash that they'd have to pass by New Hope again and what they'd better do, he just says,

"I reckon we can get there."

I aint much for meddling. Let every man run his own business to suit himself, I say. But after I talked to Rachel about them not having a regular man to fix her and it being July and all, I went back down to the barn and tried to talk to Bundren about it.

"I give her my promise," he says. "Her mind was set on it."

I notice how it takes a lazy man, a man that hates moving, to get set on moving once he does get started off, the same as he was set on staying still, like it aint the moving he hates so much as the starting and the stopping. And like he would be kind of proud of whatever come up to make the moving or the setting still look hard. He set there on the wagon, hunched up, blinking, listening to us tell about how quick the bridge went and how high the water was, and I be durn if he didn't act like he was proud of it, like he had made the river rise himself.

"You say it's higher than you ever see it before?" he says. "God's will be done," he says. "I reckon it wont go down much by morning, neither," he says.

"You better stay here tonight," I says, "and get a early start for New Hope tomorrow morning." I was just sorry for them bone-gaunted mules. I told Rachel, I says, "Well, would you have had me turn them away at dark, eight miles from home? What else could I do," I says. "It wont be but one night, and they'll keep it in the barn, and they'll sholy get started by daylight." And so I says, "You stay here tonight and early tomorrow you can go back to New Hope. I got tools enough, and the boys can go on right after supper and have it dug and ready if they want" and then I found that girl watching me. If her eyes had a been pistols, I wouldn't be talking now. I be dog[8] if they didn't blaze at me. And so when I went down to the barn I come on them, her talking so she never noticed when I come up.

"You promised her," she says. "She wouldn't go until you promised. She thought she could depend on you. If you dont do it, it will be a curse on you."

"Cant no man say I dont aim to keep my word," Bundren says. "My heart is open to ere a man."

"I dont care what your heart is," she says. She was whispering, kind of, talking fast. "You promised her. You've got to. You——" then she seen me and quit, standing there. If they'd been pistols, I wouldn't be talking now. So when I talked to him about it, he says,

"I give her my promise. Her mind is set on it."

"But seems to me she'd rather have her ma buried close by, so she could——"

"It's Addie I give the promise to," he says. "Her mind is set on it."

So I told them to drive it into the barn, because it was threatening rain again, and that supper was about ready. Only they didn't want to come in.

---

8. Doggone, or darned.

"I thank you," Bundren says. "We wouldn't discommode you. We got a little something in the basket. We can make out."

"Well," I says, "since you are so particular about your womenfolks, I am too. And when folks stops with us at meal time and wont come to the table, my wife takes it as a insult."

So the girl went on to the kitchen to help Rachel. And then Jewel come to me.

"Sho," I says. "Help yourself outen the loft. Feed him when you bait the mules."

"I rather pay you for him," he says.

"What for?" I says. "I wouldn't begrudge no man a bait for his horse."

"I rather pay you," he says; I thought he said extra.

"Extra for what?" I says. "Wont he eat hay and corn?"

"Extra feed," he says. "I feed him a little extra and I dont want him beholden to no man."

"You cant buy no feed from me, boy," I says. "And if he can eat that loft clean, I'll help you load the barn onto the wagon in the morning."

"He aint never been beholden to no man," he says. "I rather pay you for it."

And if I had my rathers, you wouldn't be here a-tall, I wanted to say. But I just says, "Then it's high time he commenced. You cant buy no feed from me."

When Rachel put supper on, her and the girl went and fixed some beds. But wouldn't any of them come in. "She's been dead long enough to get over that sort of foolishness," I says. Because I got just as much respect for the dead as ere a man, but you've got to respect the dead themselves, and a woman that's been dead in a box four days, the best way to respect her is to get her into the ground as quick a you can. But they wouldn't do it.

"It wouldn't be right," Bundren says. "Course, if the boys wants to go to bed, I reckon I can set up with her. I dont begrudge her it."

So when I went back down there they were squatting on the ground around the wagon, all of them. "Let that chap come to the house and get some sleep, anyway," I says. "And you better come too," I says to the girl. I wasn't aiming to interfere with them. And I sholy hadn't done nothing to her that I knowed.

"He's done already asleep," Bundren says. They had done put him to bed in the trough in a empty stall.

"Well, you come on, then," I says to her. But still she never said nothing. They just squatted there. You couldn't hardly see them. "How about you boys?" I says. "You got a full day tomorrow." After a while Cash says, "I thank you. We can make out."

"We wouldn't be beholden," Bundren says. "I thank you kindly."

So I left them squatting there. I reckon after four days they was used to it. But Rachel wasn't.

"It's a outrage," she says. "A outrage."

"What could he a done?" I says. "He give her his promised word."

"Who's talking about him?" she says. "Who cares about him?" she says, crying. "I just wish that you and him and all the men in the world that torture us alive and flout us dead, dragging us up and down the country——"

"Now, now," I says. "You're upset."

"Dont you touch me!" she says. "Dont you touch me!"

A man cant tell nothing about them. I lived with the same one fifteen years and I be durn if I can. And I imagined a lot of things coming up between us, but I be durn if I ever thought it would be a body four days dead and that a woman. But they make life hard on them, not taking it as it comes up, like a man does.

So I laid there, hearing it commence to rain, thinking about them down there, squatting around the wagon and the rain on the roof, and thinking about Rachel crying there until after a while it was like I could still hear her crying even after she was asleep, and smelling it even when I knowed I couldn't. I couldn't decide even then whether I could or not, or if it wasn't just knowing it was what it was.

So next morning I never went down there. I heard them hitching up and then when I knowed they must be about ready to take out, I went out the front and went down the road toward the bridge until I heard the wagon come out of the lot and go back toward New Hope. And then when I come back to the house, Rachel jumped on me because I wasn't there to make them come in to breakfast. You cant tell about them. Just about when you decide they mean one thing, I be durn if you not only haven't got to change your mind, like as not you got to take a rawhiding for thinking they meant it.

But it was still like I could smell it. And so I decided then that it wasn't smelling it, but it was just knowing it was there, like you will get fooled now and then. But when I went to the barn I knew different. When I walked into the hallway I saw something. It kind of hunkered up when I come in and I thought at first it was one of them got left, then I saw what it was. It was a buzzard. It looked around and saw me and went on down the hall, spraddle-legged, with its wings kind of hunkered out, watching me first over one shoulder and then over the other, like a old baldheaded man. When it got outdoors it begun to fly. It had to fly a long time before it ever got up into the air, with it thick and heavy and full of rain like it was.

If they was bent on going to Jefferson, I reckon they could have gone around up by Mount Vernon, like MacCallum did. He'll get home about day after tomorrow, horseback. Then they'd be just eighteen miles from town. But maybe this bridge being gone too has learned him the Lord's sense and judgment.

That MacCallum. He's been trading with me off and on for twelve years. I have known him from a boy up; know his name as well as I do my own. But be durn if I can say it.

Dewey Dell

The signboard comes in sight. It is looking out at the road now, because it can wait. New Hope. 3 mi. it will say. New Hope. 3 mi. And then the road will begin, curving away into the trees, empty with waiting, saying New Hope three miles.

I heard that my mother is dead. I wish I had time to let her die. I wish I had time to wish I had. It is because in the wild and outraged earth too soon too soon too soon. It's not that I wouldn't and will not it's that it is too soon too soon too soon.

Now it begins to say it. New Hope three miles. New Hope three miles. *That's what they mean by the womb of time: the agony and the despair of spreading bones, the hard girdle in which lie the outraged entrails of events*

Cash's head turns slowly as we approach, his pale empty sad composed and questioning face following the red and empty curve; beside the back wheel Jewel sits the horse, gazing straight ahead.

The land runs out of Darl's eyes; they swim to pin points. They begin at my feet and rise along my body to my face, and then my dress is gone: I sit naked on the seat above the unhurrying mules, above the travail. *Suppose I tell him to turn. He will do what I say. Dont you know he will do what I say?* Once I waked with a black void rushing under me. I could not see. I saw Vardaman rise and go to the window and strike the knife into the fish, the blood gushing, hissing like steam but I could not see. *He'll do as I say. He always does. I can persuade him to anything. You know I can. Suppose I say Turn here.* That was when I died that time. *Suppose I do. We'll go to New Hope. We wont have to go to town.* I rose and took the knife from the streaming fish still hissing and I killed Darl.

When I used to sleep with Vardaman I had a nightmare once I thought I was awake but I couldn't see and couldn't feel I couldn't feel the bed under me and I couldn't think what I was I couldn't think of my name I couldn't even think I am a girl I couldn't even think I nor even think I want to wake up nor remember what was opposite to awake so I could do that I knew that something was passing but I couldn't even think of time then all of a sudden I knew that something was it was wind blowing over me it was like the wind came and blew me back from where it was I was not blowing the room and Vardaman asleep and all of them back under me again and going on like a piece of cool silk dragging across my naked legs

It blows cool out of the pines, a sad steady sound. New Hope. Was 3 mi. Was 3 mi. I believe in God I believe in God.

"Why didn't we go to New Hope, pa?" Vardaman says. "Mr Samson said we was, but we done passed the road."

Darl says, "Look, Jewel." But he is not looking at me. He is looking at the sky. The buzzard is as still as if he were nailed to it.

We turn into Tull's lane. We pass the barn and go on, the wheels whispering in the mud, passing the green rows of cotton in the wild earth, and Vernon little across the field behind the plow. He lifts his hand as we pass and stands there looking after us for a long while.

"Look, Jewel," Darl says. Jewel sits on his horse like they were both made out of wood, looking straight ahead.

I believe in God, God. God, I believe in God.

Tull

After they passed I taken the mule out and looped up the trace chains and followed. They was setting in the wagon at the end of the levee. Anse was setting there, looking at the bridge where it was swagged down into the river with just the two ends in sight. He was looking at it like he had believed all the time that folks had been lying to him about it being gone, but like he was hoping all the time it really was. Kind of pleased astonishment he looked, setting on the wagon in his Sunday pants, mumbling his mouth. Looking like a uncurried horse dressed up: I don't know.

The boy was watching the bridge where it was mid-sunk and logs and such drifted up over it and it swagging and shivering like the whole thing would go any minute, big-eyed he was watching it, like he was to a circus. And the gal too. When I come up she looked around at me, her eyes kind of blaring up and going hard like I had made to touch her. Then she looked at Anse again and then back at the water again.

It was nigh up to the levee on both sides, the earth hid except for the tongue of it we was on going out to the bridge and then down into the water, and except for knowing how the road and the bridge used to look, a fellow couldn't tell where was the river and where the land. It was just a tangle of yellow and the levee not less wider than a knife-back kind of, with us setting in the wagon and on the horse and the mule.

Darl was looking at me, and then Cash turned and looked at me with that look in his eyes like when he was figuring on whether the planks would fit her that night, like he was measuring them inside of him and not asking you to say what you thought and not even letting on he was listening if you did say it, but listening all right. Jewel hadn't moved. He sat there on the horse, leaning a little forward, with that same look on his face when him and Darl passed the house yesterday, coming back to get her.

"If it was just up, we could drive across," Anse says. "We could drive right on across it."

Sometimes a log would get shoved over the jam and float on, rolling and turning, and we could watch it go on to where the ford used to be. It would slow up and whirl crossways and hang out of water for a minute, and you could tell by that that the ford used to be there.

"But that dont show nothing," I say. "It could be a bar of quicksand built up there." We watch the log. Then the gal is looking at me again.

"Mr Whitfield crossed it," she says.

"He was a horse-back," I say. "And three days ago. It's a riz five foot since."

"If the bridge was just up," Anse says.

The log bobs up and goes on again. There is a lot of trash and foam, and you can hear the water.

"But it's down," Anse says.

Cash says, "A careful fellow could walk across yonder on the planks and logs."

"But you couldn't tote nothing," I say. "Likely time you set foot on that mess, it'll all go, too. What you think, Darl?"

He is looking at me. He dont say nothing; just looks at me with them queer eyes of hisn that makes folks talk. I always say it aint never been what he done so much or said or anything so much as how he looks at you. It's like he had got into the side of you, someway. Like somehow you was looking at yourself and your doings outen his eyes. Then I can feel that gal watching me like I had made to touch her. She says something to Anse.

". . . . . . Mr. Whitfield. . . ." she says.

"I give her my promised word in the presence of the Lord," Anse says. "I reckon it aint no need to worry."

But still he does not start the mules. We set there above the water. Another log bobs up over the jam and goes on; we watch it check up and swing slow for a minute where the ford used to be. Then it goes on.

"It might start falling tonight," I say. "You could lay over one more day."

Then Jewel turns sideways on the horse. He has not moved until then, and he turns and looks at me. His face is kind of green, then it would go red and then green again. "Get to hell on back to your damn plowing," he says. "Who the hell asked you to follow us here?"

"I never meant no harm," I say.

"Shut up, Jewel," Cash says. Jewel looks back at the water, his face gritted, going red and green and then red. "Well," Cash says after a while, "what you want to do?"

Anse dont say nothing. He sets humped up, mumbling his mouth. "If it was just up, we could drive across it," he says.

"Come on," Jewel says, moving the horse.

"Wait," Cash says. He looks at the bridge. We look at him, except Anse and the gal. They are looking at the water. "Dewey Dell and Vardaman and pa better walk across on the bridge," Cash says.

"Vernon can help them," Jewel says. "And we can hitch his mule ahead of ourn."

"You ain't going to take my mule into that water," I say.

Jewel looks at me. His eyes look like pieces of a broken plate. "I'll pay for your damn mule. I'll buy it from you right now."

"My mule aint going into that water," I say.

"Jewel's going to use his horse," Darl says. "Why wont you risk your mule, Vernon?"

"Shut up, Darl," Cash says. "You and Jewel both."

"My mule aint going into that water," I say.

Darl

He sits the horse, glaring at Vernon, his lean face suffused up to and beyond the pale rigidity of his eyes. The summer when he was fifteen, he took a spell of sleeping. One morning when I went to feed the mules the cows were still in the tie-up and then I heard pa going back to the house and call him. When we came on back to the house for breakfast he passed us, carrying the milk buckets, stumbling along like he was drunk, and he was milking when we put the mules in and went on to the field without him. We had been there an hour and still he never showed up. When Dewey Dell came with our lunch, pa sent her back to find Jewel. They found him in the tie-up, sitting on the stool, asleep.

After that, every morning pa would go in and wake him. He would go to sleep at the supper table and soon as supper was finished he would go to bed, and when I came in to bed he would be lying there like a dead man. Yet still pa would have to wake him in the morning. He would get up, but he wouldn't hardly have half sense: he would stand for pa's jawing and complaining without a word and take the milk buckets and go to the barn, and once I found him asleep at the cow, the bucket in place and half full and his hands up to the wrists in the milk and his head against the cow's flank.

After that Dewey Dell had to do the milking. He still got up when pa waked him, going about what we told him to do in that dazed way. It was like he was trying hard to do them; that he was as puzzled as anyone else.

"Are you sick?" ma said. "Dont you feel all right?"

"Yes," Jewel said. "I feel all right."

"He's just lazy, trying me," pa said, and Jewel standing there, asleep on his feet like as not. "Ain't you?" he said, waking Jewel up again to answer.

"No," Jewel said.

"You take off and stay in the house today," ma said.

"With that whole bottom piece to be busted out?" pa said. "If you aint sick, what's the matter with you?"

"Nothing," Jewel said. "I'm all right."

"All right?" pa said. "You're asleep on your feet this minute."

"No," Jewel said. "I'm all right."

"I want him to stay at home today," ma said.

"I'll need him," pa said. "It's tight enough, with all of us to do it."

"You'll just have to do the best you can with Cash and Darl," ma said. "I want him to stay in today."

But he wouldn't do it. "I'm all right," he said, going on. But he wasn't all right. Anybody could see it. He was losing flesh, and I have seen him go to sleep chopping; watched the hoe going slower and slower up and down, with less and less of an arc, until it stopped and he leaning on it motionless in the hot shimmer of the sun.

Ma wanted to get the doctor, but pa didn't want to spend the money without it was needful, and Jewel did seem all right except for his thinness and his way of dropping off to sleep at any moment. He ate hearty enough, except for his way of going to sleep in his plate, with a piece of bread half way to his mouth and his jaws still chewing. But he swore he was all right.

It was ma that got Dewey Dell to do his milking, paid her somehow, and the other jobs around the house that Jewel had been doing before supper she found some way for Dewey Dell and Vardaman to do them. And doing them herself when pa wasn't there. She would fix him special things to eat and hide them for him. And that may have been when I first found it out, that Addie Bundren should be hiding anything she did, who had tried to teach us that deceit was such that, in a world where it was, nothing else could be very bad or very important, not even poverty. And at times when I went in to go to bed she would be sitting in the dark by Jewel where he was asleep. And I knew that she was hating herself for that deceit and hating Jewel because she had to love him so that she had to act the deceit.

One night she was taken sick and when I went to the barn to put the team in and drive to Tull's, I couldn't find the lantern. I remembered noticing it on the nail the night before, but it wasn't there now at midnight. So I hitched in the dark and went on and came back with Mrs Tull just after daylight. And there the lantern was, hanging on the nail where I remembered it and couldn't find it before. And then one morning while Dewey Dell was milking just before the sunup, Jewel came into the barn from the back, through the hole in the back wall, with the lantern in his hand.

I told Cash, and Cash and I looked at one another.

"Rutting," Cash said.

"Yes," I said. "But why the lantern? And every night, too. No wonder he's losing flesh. Are you going to say anything to him?"

"Wont do any good," Cash said.

"What he's doing now wont do any good, either."

"I know. But he'll have to learn that himself. Give him time to realise that it'll save, that there'll be just as much more tomorrow, and he'll be all right. I wouldn't tell anybody, I reckon."

"No," I said. "I told Dewey Dell not to. Not ma, anyway."

"No. Not ma."

After that I thought it was right comical: he acting so bewildered and willing and dead for sleep and gaunt as a beanpole, and thinking he was so smart with it. And I wondered who the girl was. I thought of all I knew that it might be, but I couldn't say for sure.

" 'Taint any girl," Cash said. "It's a married woman somewhere. Aint any young girl got that much daring and staying power. That's what I dont like about it."

"Why?" I said. "She'll be safer for him that a girl would. More judgment."

He looked at me, his eyes fumbling, the words fumbling at what he was trying to say. "It aint always the safe things in this world that a fellow. . . . . . ."

"You mean, the safe things are not always the best things?"

"Ay; best," he said, fumbling again. "It aint the best things, the things that are good for him. . . . . . A young boy. A fellow kind of hates to see. . . . . . .wallowing in somebody else's mire. . . . . . ." That's what he was trying to say. When something is new and hard and bright, there ought to be something a little better for it than just being safe, since the safe things are just the things that folks have been doing so long they have worn the edges off and there's nothing to the doing of them that leaves a man to say, That was not done before and it cannot be done again.

So we didn't tell, not even when after a while he'd appear suddenly in the field beside us and go to work, without having had time to get home and make out he had been in bed all night. He would tell ma that he hadn't been hungry at breakfast or that he had eaten a piece of bread while he was hitching up the team. But Cash and I knew that he hadn't been home at all on those nights and he had come up out of the woods when we got to the field. But we didn't tell. Summer was almost over then; we knew that when the nights began to get cool, she would be done if he wasn't.

But when fall came and the nights began to get longer, the only difference was that he would always be in bed for pa to wake him, getting him up at last in that first state of semi-idiocy like when it first started, worse than when he had stayed out all night.

"She's sure a stayer," I told Cash. "I used to admire her, but I downright respect her now."

"It ain't a woman," he said.

"You know," I said. But he was watching me. "What is it, then?"

"That's what I aim to find out," he said.

"You can trail him through the woods all night if you want to," I said. "I'm not."

"I aint trailing him," he said.

"What do you call it, then?"

"I aint trailing him," he said. "I dont mean it that way."

And so a few nights later I heard Jewel get up and climb out the window, and then I heard Cash get up and follow him. The next morning when I went to the barn, Cash was already there, the mules fed, and he was helping Dewey Dell milk. And when I saw him I knew that he knew what it was. Now and then I would catch him watching Jewel with a queer look, like having found out where Jewel went and what he was doing had given him something to really think about at last. But it was not a worried look; it was the kind of look I would see on him when I would find him doing some of Jewel's work around the house, work that pa still thought Jewel was doing and that ma thought Dewey Dell was doing. So I said nothing to him, believing that when he got done digesting it in his mind, he would tell me. But he never did.

One morning—it was November then, five months since it started—Jewel was not in bed and he didn't join us in the field. That was the first time ma learned anything about what had been going on. She went Vardaman down to find where Jewel was, and after a while she came down too. It was as though, so long as the deceit ran along quiet and monotonous, all of us let ourselves be deceived, abetting it unawares or maybe through cowardice, since all people are cowards and naturally prefer any kind of treachery because it was a bland outside. But now it was like we had all—and by a kind of telepathic agreement of admitted fear—flung the whole thing back like covers on the bed and we all sitting bolt upright in our nakedness, staring at one another and saying "Now is the truth. He hasn't come home. Something has happened to him. We let something happen to him."

Then we saw him. He came up along the ditch and then turned straight across the field, riding the horse. Its mane and tail were going, as though in motion they were carrying out the splotchy pattern of its coat: he looked like he was riding on a big pinwheel, barebacked, with a rope bridle, and no hat on his head. It was a descendant of those Texas ponies Flem Snopes brought here twenty-five years ago and auctioned off for two dollars a head and nobody but old Lon Quick ever caught his and still owned some of the blood because he could never give it away.

He galloped up and stopped, his heels in the horse's ribs and it dancing and swirling like the shape of its mane and tail and the splotches of its coat had nothing whatever to do with the flesh-and-bone horse inside them, and he sat there, looking at us.

"Where did you get that horse?" pa said.

"Bought it," Jewel said. "From Mr Quick."

"Bought it?" pa said. "With what? Did you buy that thing on my word?"

"It was my money," Jewel said. "I earned it. You wont need to worry about it."

"Jewel," ma said; "Jewel."

"It's all right," Cash said. "He earned the money. He cleaned up that forty acres of new ground Quick laid out last spring. He did it single handed, working at night by lantern. I saw him. So I dont reckon that horse cost anybody anything except Jewel. I dont reckon we need worry."

"Jewel," ma said. "Jewel——" Then she said: "You come right to the house and go to bed."

"Not yet," Jewel said. "I aint got time. I got to get me a saddle and bridle. Mr Quick says he——"

"Jewel," ma said, looking at him. "I'll give——I'll give——give——" Then she began to cry. She cried hard, not hiding her face, standing there in her faded wrapper, looking at him and him on the horse, looking down at her, his face growing cold and a little sick looking, until he looked away quick and Cash came and touched her.

"You go on to the house," Cash said. "This here ground is too wet for you. You go on, now." She put her hands to her face then and after a while she went on, stumbling a little on the plow-marks. But pretty soon she straightened up and went on. She didn't look back. When she reached the ditch she stopped and called Vardaman. He was looking at the horse, kind of dancing up and down by it.

"Let me ride, Jewel," he said. "Let me ride, Jewel."

Jewel looked at him, then he looked away again, holding the horse reined back. Pa watched him, mumbling his lip.

"So you bought a horse," he said. "You went behind my back and bought a horse. You never consulted me; you know how tight it is for us to make by, yet you bought a horse for me to feed. Taken the work from your flesh and blood and bought a horse with it."

Jewel looked at pa, his eyes paler than ever. "He wont never eat a mouthful of yours," he said. "Not a mouthful. I'll kill him first. Dont you never think it. Dont you never."

"Let me ride, Jewel," Vardaman said. "Let me ride, Jewel." He sounded like a cricket in the grass, a little one. "Let me ride, Jewel."

That night I found ma sitting beside the bed where he was sleeping, in the dark. She cried hard, maybe because she had to cry so quiet; maybe because she felt the same way about tears she did about deceit, hating herself for doing it, hating him because she had to. And then I knew that I knew. I knew that as plain on that day as I knew about Dewey Dell on that day.

Tull

So they finally got Anse to say what he wanted to do, and him and the gal and the boy got out of the wagon. But even when we were on the bridge Anse kept on looking back, like he thought maybe, once he was outen the wagon, the whole thing would kind of blow up and he would find himself back yonder in the field again and her laying up there in the house, waiting to die and it to do all over again.

"You ought to let them taken your mule," he says, and the bridge shaking and swaying under us, going down into the moiling water like it went clean through to the other side of the earth, and the other end coming up outen the water like it wasn't the same bridge a-tall and that them that would walk up outen the water on that side must come from the bottom of the earth. But it was still whole; you could tell that by the way when this end swagged, it didn't look like the other end swagged at all: just like the other trees and the bank yonder were swinging back and forth slow like on a big clock. And them logs scraping and bumping at the sunk part and tilting end-up and shooting clean outen the water and tumbling on toward the fore and the waiting, slick, whirling, and foamy.

"What good would that a done?" I says. "If your team cant find the ford and haul it across, what good would three mules or even ten mules do?"

"I aint asking it of you," he says. "I can always do for me and mine. I aint asking you to risk your mule. It aint your dead; I am not blaming you."

"They ought to went back and laid over until tomorrow," I says. The water was cold. It was thick, like slush ice. Only it kind of lived. One part of you knowed it was just water, the same thing that had been running under this same bridge for a long time yet when them logs would come spewing up outen it, you were not surprised, like they was a part of water, of the waiting and the threat.

It was like when we was across, up out of the water again and the hard earth under us, that I was surprised. It was like we hadn't expected the bridge to end on the other bank, on something tame like the hard earth again that we had tromped on before this time and knowed well. Like it couldn't be me here, because I'd have had better sense than to done what I just done. And when I looked back and saw the other bank and saw my mule standing there where I used to be and knew that I'd have to get back there someway, I knew it couldn't be, because I just couldn't think of anything that could make me cross that bridge ever even once. Yet here I was, and the fellow that could make himself cross it twice, couldn't be me, not even if Cora told him to.

It was that boy. I said "Here; you better take a holt of my hand" and he waited and held to me. I be durn if it wasn't like he come back and got me; like he was saying They wont nothing hurt you. Like he was saying about a fine place he knowed where Christmas come twice with Thanksgiving and lasts on through the winter and the spring and the summer, and if I just stayed with him I'd be all right too.

When I looked back at my mule it was like he was one of these here spy-glasses and I could look at him standing there and see all the broad land and my house sweated outen it like it was the more the sweat, the broader the land; the more the sweat, the tighter the house because it would take a tight house for Cora, to hold Cora like a jar of milk in the spring: you've got to have a tight jar or you'll need a powerful spring, so if you have a big spring, why then you have the incentive to have tight, wellmade jars, because it is your milk, sour or not, because you would rather have milk that will sour than to have milk that wont, because you are a man.

And him holding to my hand, his hand that hot and confident, so that I was like to say: Look-a-here. Cant you see that mule yonder? He never had no business over here, so he never come, not being nothing but a mule. Because a fellow can see ever now and then that children have more sense than him. But he dont like to admit it to them until they have beards. After they have a beard, they are too busy because they dont know if they'll ever quite make it back to where they were in sense before they was haired, so you dont mind admitting then to folks that are worrying about the same thing that aint worth the worry that you are yourself.

Then we was over and we stood there, looking at Cash turning the wagon around. We watched them drive back down the road to where the trail turned off into the bottom. After a while the wagon was out of sight.

"We better get on down to the ford and git ready to help," I said.

"I give her my word," Anse says. "It is sacred on me. I know you begrudge it, but she will bless you in heaven."

"Well, they got to finish circumventing the land before they can dare the water," I said. "Come on."

"It's the turning back," he said. "It ain't no luck in turning back."

He was standing there, humped, mournful, looking at the empty road beyond the swagging and swaying bridge. And that gal, too, with the lunch basket on one arm and that package under the other. Just going to town. Bent on it. They would risk the fire and the earth and the water and all just to eat a sack of bananas. "You ought to laid over a day," I said. "It would a fell some by morning. It mought not a rained tonight. And it cant get no higher."

"I give my promise," he says. "She is counting on it."

Darl

Before us the thick dark current runs. It talks up to us in a murmur become ceaseless and myriad, the yellow surface dimpled monstrously into fading swirls travelling along the surface for an instant, silent, impermanent and profoundly significant, as though just beneath the surface something huge and alive waked for a moment of lazy alertness out of and into light slumber again.

It clucks and murmurs among the spokes and about the mules' knees, yellow, skummed with flotsam and with thick soiled gouts of foam as though it had sweat, lathering, like a driven horse. Through the undergrowth it goes with a plaintive sound, a musing sound; in it the unwinded cane and saplings lean as before a little gale, swaying without reflections as though suspended on invisible wires from the branches overhead. Above the ceaseless surface they stand—trees, cane, vines—rootless, severed from the earth, spectral above a scene of immense yet circumscribed desolation filled with the voice of the waste and mournful water.

Cash and I sit in the wagon; Jewel sits the horse at the off rear wheel. The horse is trembling, its eye rolling wild and baby-blue in its long pink face, its breathing stertorous like groaning. He sits erect, poised, looking quietly and steadily and quickly this way and that, his face calm, a little pale, alert. Cash's face is also gravely composed; he and I look at one another with long probing looks, looks that plunge unimpeded through one another's eyes and into the ultimate secret place where for an instant Cash and Darl crouch flagrant and unabashed in all the old terror and the old foreboding, alert and secret and without shame. When we speak our voices are quiet, detached.

"I reckon we're still in the road, all right."

"Tull taken and cut them two big whiteoaks. I heard tell how at high water in the old days they used to line up the ford by them trees."

"I reckon he did that two years ago when he was logging down here. I reckon he never thought that anybody would ever use this ford again."

"I reckon not. Yes, it must have been then. He cut a sight of timber outen here then. Payed off that mortgage with it, I hear tell."

"Yes. Yes, I reckon so. I reckon Vernon could have done that."

"That's a fact. Most folks that logs in this here country, they need a durn good farm to support the sawmill. Or maybe a store. But I reckon Vernon could."

"I reckon so. He's a sight."

"Ay. Vernon is. Yes, it must still be here. He never would have got that timber out of here if he hadn't cleaned out that old road. I reckon we are still on it." He looks about quietly, at the position of the trees, leaning this way and that, looking back along the floorless road shaped vaguely high in air by the position of the lopped and felled trees, as if the road too had been soaked free of earth and floated upward, to leave in its spectral tracing a monument to a still more profound desolation than this above which we now sit, talking quietly of old security and old trivial things. Jewel looks at him, then at me, then his face turns in in that quiet, constant, questing about the scene, the horse trembling quietly and steadily between his knees.

"He could go on ahead slow and sort of feel it out," I say.

"Yes," Cash says, not looking at me. His face is in profile as he looks forward where Jewel has moved on ahead.

"He cant miss the river," I say. "He couldn't miss seeing it fifty yards ahead."

Cash does not look at me, his face in profile. "If I'd just suspicioned it, I could a come down last week and taken a sight on it."

"The bridge was up then," I say. He does not look at me. "Whitfield crossed it a-horseback."

Jewel looks at us again, his expression sober and alert and subdued. His voice is quiet. "What you want me to do?"

"I ought to come down last week and taken a sight on it," Cash says.

"We couldn't have known," I say. "There wasn't any way for us to know."

"I'll ride on ahead," Jewel says. "You can follow where I am." He lifts the horse. It shrinks, bowed; he leans to it, speaking to it, lifting it forward almost bodily, it setting its feet down with gingerly splashings, trembling, breathing harshly. He speaks to it, murmurs to it. "Go on," he says. "I aint going to let nothing hurt you. Go on, now."

"Jewel," Cash says. Jewel does not look back. He lifts the horse on.

"He can swim," I say. "If he'll just give the horse time, any-how. . . . . . ." When he was born, he had a bad time of it. Ma would sit in the lamp-light, holding him on a pillow on her lap. We would wake and find her so. There would be no sound from them.

"That pillow was longer than him," Cash says. He is leaning a little forward. "I ought to come down last week and sighted. I ought to done it."

"That's right," I say. "Neither his feet nor his head would reach the end of it. You couldn't have known," I say.

"I ought to done it," he says. He lifts the reins. The mules move, into the traces; the wheels murmur alive in the water. He looks back and down at Addie. "It aint on a balance," he says.

At last the trees open; against the open river Jewel sits the horse, half turned, it belly deep now. Across the river we can see Vernon and pa and Vardaman and Dewey Dell. Vernon is waving at us, waving us further down stream.

"We are too high up," Cash says. Vernon is shouting too, but we cannot make out what he says for the noise of the water. It runs steady and deep now, unbroken, without sense of motion until a log comes along, turning slowly. "Watch it," Cash says. We watch it and see it falter and hang for a moment, the current building up behind it in a thick wave, submerging it for an instant before it shoots up and tumbles on.

"There it is," I say.

"Ay," Cash says. "It's there." We look at Vernon again. He is now flapping his arms up and down. We move on down stream, slowly and carefully, watching Vernon. He drops his hands. "This is the place," Cash says.

"Well, goddamn it, let's get across, then," Jewel says. He moves the horse on.

"You wait," Cash says. Jewel stops again.

"Well, by God——" he says. Cash looks at the water, then he looks back at Addie. "It aint on a balance," he says.

"Then go on back to the goddamn bridge and walk across," Jewel says. "You and Darl both. Let me on that wagon."

Cash does not pay him any attention. "It aint on a balance," he says. "Yes, sir. We got to watch it."

"Watch it, hell," Jewel says. "You get out of that wagon and let me have it. By God, if you're afraid to drive it over. . . . . . ." His eyes are pale as two bleached chips in his face. Cash is looking at him.

"We'll get it over," he says. "I tell you what you do. You ride on back and walk across the bridge and come down the other bank and meet us with the rope. Vernon'll take your horse home with him and keep it till we get back."

"You go to hell," Jewel says.

"You take the rope and come down the bank and be ready with it," Cash

says. "Three cant do no more than two can—one to drive and one to steady
it."

"Goddamn you," Jewel says.

"Let Jewel take the end of the rope and cross upstream of us and brace
it," I say. "Will you do that, Jewel?"

Jewel watches me, hard. He looks quick at Cash, then back at me, his
eyes alert and hard. "I dont give a damn. Just so we do something. Setting
here, not lifting a goddamn hand. . . ."

"Let's do that, Cash," I say.

"I reckon we'll have to," Cash says.

The river itself is not a hundred yards across, and pa and Vernon and
Vardaman and Dewey Dell are the only things in sight not of that single
monotony of desolation leaning with that terrific quality a little from right
to left, as though we had reached the place where the motion of the wasted
world accelerates just before the final precipice. Yet they appear dwarfed.
It is as though the space between us were time: an irrevocable quality. It is
as though time, no longer running straight before us in a diminishing line,
now runs parallel between us like a looping string, the distance between
the doubling accretion of the thread and not the interval between. The
mules stand, their fore quarters already sloped a little, their rumps high.
They too are breathing now with a deep groaning sound; looking back once,
their gaze sweeps across us with in their eyes a wild, sad, profound and
despairing quality as though they had already seen in the thick water the
shape of the disaster which they could not speak and we could not see.

Cash turns back into the wagon. He lays his hands flat on Addie, rocking
her a little. His face is calm, down-sloped, calculant, concerned. He lifts
his box of tools and wedges it forward under the seat; together we shove
Addie forward, wedging her between the tools and the wagon bed. Then
he looks at me.

"No," I say. "I reckon I'll stay. Might take both of us."

From the tool box he takes his coiled rope and carries the end twice
around the seat stanchion and passes the end to me without tying it. The
other end he pays out to Jewel, who takes a turn about his saddle horn.

He must force the horse down into the current. It moves, highkneed,
archnecked, boring and chafing. Jewel sits lightly forward, his knees lifted
a little; again his swift alert calm gaze sweeps upon us and on. He lowers
the horse into the stream, speaking to it in a soothing murmur. The horse
slips, goes under to the saddle, surges to its feet again, the current building
up against Jewel's thighs.

"Watch yourself," Cash says.

"I'm on it now," Jewel says. "You can come ahead now."

Cash takes the reins and lowers the team carefully and skillfully into the
stream.

*I felt the current take us and I knew we were on the ford by that reason,
since it was only by means of that slipping contact that we could tell that
we were in motion at all. What had once been a flat surface was now a
succession of troughs and hillocks lifting and falling about us, shoving at
us, teasing at us with light lazy touches in the vain instants of solidity
underfoot. Cash looked back at me, and then I knew that we were gone.
But I did not realize the reason for the rope until I saw the log. It surged
up out of the water and stood for an instant upright upon that surging and*

*heaving desolation like Christ. Get out and let the current take you down
to the bend, Cash said, You can make it all right. No, I said, I'd get just as
wet that way as this*

The log appears suddenly between two hills, as if it had rocketed suddenly from the bottom of the river. Upon the end of it a long gout of foam hangs like the beard of an old man or a goat. When Cash speaks to me I know that he has been watching it all the time, watching it and watching Jewel ten feet ahead of us. "Let the rope go," he says. With his other hand he reaches down and reeves the two turns from the stanchion. "Ride on, Jewel," he says; "see if you can pull us ahead of the log."

Jewel shouts at the horse; again he appears to lift it bodily between his knees. He is just above the top of the ford and the horse has a purchase of some sort for it surges forward, shining wetly half out of water, crashing on in a succession of lunges. It moves unbelievably fast; by that token Jewel realises at last that the rope is free, for I can see him sawing back on the reins, his head turned, as the log rears in a long sluggish lunge between us, bearing down upon the team. They see it too; for a moment they also shine black out of water. Then the downstream one vanishes, dragging the other with him; the wagon sheers crosswise, poised on the crest of the ford as the log strikes it, tilting it up and on. Cash is half turned, the reins running taut from his hand and disappearing into the water, the other hand reached back upon Addie, holding her jammed over against the high side of the wagon. "Jump clear," he says quietly. "Stay away from the team and dont try to fight it. It'll swing you into the bend all right."

"You come too," I say. Vernon and Vardaman are running along the bank, pa and Dewey Dell stand watching us, Dewey Dell with the basket and the package in her arms. Jewel is trying to fight the horse back. The head of one mule appears, its eyes wide; it looks back at us for an instant, making a sound almost human. The head vanishes again.

"Back, Jewel," Cash shouts. "Back, Jewel." For another instant I see him leaning to the tilting wagon, his arm braced back against Addie and his tools; I see the bearded head of the rearing log strike up again, and beyond it Jewel holding the horse upreared, its head wrenched around, hammering its head with his fist. I jump from the wagon on the downstream side. Between two hills I see the mules once more. They roll up out of the water in succession, turning completely over, their legs stiffly extended as when they had lost contact with the earth.

Vardaman

Cash tried but she fell off and Darl jumped going under he went under and Cash hollering to catch her and I hollering running and hollering and Dewey Dell hollering at me Vardaman you vardaman you vardaman and Vernon passed me because he was seeing her come up and she jumped into the water again and Darl hadn't caught her yet

He came up to see and I hollering catch her Darl catch her and he didn't come back because she was too heavy he had to go on catching at her and I hollering catch her darl catch her darl because in the water she could go faster than a man and Darl had to grabble for her so I knew he could catch her because he is the best grabber even with the mules in the way again they dived up rolling their feet stiff rolling down again and their backs up now and Darl had to again because in the water she could go faster than a man or a woman and I passed Vernon and he wouldn't get in the water and help Darl he wouldn't grabble for her with Darl he knew but he wouldn't help

The mules dived up again diving their legs stiff their stiff legs rolling slow and then Darl again and I hollering catch her darl catch her head her into the bank darl and Vernon wouldn't help and then Darl dodged past the mules where he could he had her under the water coming in to the bank coming in slow because in the water she fought to stay under the water but Darl is strong and he was coming in slow and so I knew he had her because he came slow and I ran down into the water to help and I couldn't stop hollering because Darl was strong and steady holding her under the water even if she did fight he would not let her go he was seeing me and he would hold her and it was all right now it was all right now it was all right

Then he comes up out of the water. He comes a long way up slow before his hands do but he's got to have her got to so I can bear it. Then his hands come up and all of him above the water. I cant stop. I have not got time to try. I will try to when I can but his hands came empty out of the water emptying the water emptying away

"Where is ma, Darl?" I said. "You never got her. You knew she is a fish but you let her get away. You never got her. Darl. Darl. Darl." I began to run along the bank, watching the mules dive up slow again and then down again.

Tull

When I told Cora how Darl jumped out of the wagon and left Cash sitting there trying to save it and the wagon turning over, and Jewel that was almost to the bank fighting that horse back where it had more sense than to go, she says "And you're one of the folks that says Darl is the queer one, the one that aint bright, and him the only one of them that had sense enough to get off that wagon. I notice Anse was too smart to been on it a-tall."

"He couldn't a done no good, if he'd been there," I said. "They was going about it right and they would have made it if it hadn't a been for that log."

"Log, fiddlesticks," Cora said. "It was the hand of God."

"Then how can you say it was foolish?" I said. "Nobody cant guard against the hand of God. It would be sacrilege to try to."

"Then why dare it?" Cora says. "Tell me that."

"Anse didn't," I said. "That's just what you faulted him for."

"His place was there," Cora said. "If he had been a man, he would a been there instead of making his sons do what he dursn't."

"I dont know what you want, then," I said. "One breath you say they was daring the hand of God to try it, and the next breath you jump on Anse because he wasn't with them." Then she begun to sing again, working at the washtub, with that singing look in her face like she had done give up folks and all their foolishness and had done went on ahead of them, marching up the sky, singing.

The wagon hung for a long time while the current built up under it, shoving it off the ford, and Cash leaning more and more, trying to keep the coffin braced so it wouldn't slip down and finish tilting the wagon over. Soon as the wagon got tilted good, to where the current could finish it, the log went on. It headed around the wagon and went on good as a swimming man could have done. It was like it had been sent there to do a job and done it and went on.

When the mules finally kicked loose, it looked for a minute like maybe Cash would get the wagon back. It looked like him and the wagon wasn't moving at all, and just Jewel fighting that horse back to the wagon. Then that boy passed me, running and hollering at Darl and the gal trying to catch him, and then I see the mules come rolling slow up out of the water, their legs spraddled stiff like they had balked upside down, and roll on into the water again.

Then the wagon tilted over and then it and Jewel and the horse was all mixed up together. Cash went outen sight, still holding the coffin braced, and then I couldn't tell anything for the horse lunging and splashing. I thought that Cash had give up then and was swimming for it and I was yelling at Jewel to come on back and then all of a sudden him and the horse went under too and I thought they was all going. I knew that the horse had got dragged off the ford too, and with that wild drowning horse and that wagon and that loose box, it was going to be pretty bad, and there I was, standing knee deep in the water, yelling at Anse behind me: "See what you done now? See what you done now?"

The horse come up again. It was headed for the bank now, throwing its head up, and then I saw one of them holding to the saddle on the downstream side, so I started running along the bank, trying to catch sight of Cash because he couldn't swim, yelling at Jewel where Cash was like a durn fool, bad as that boy that was on down the bank still hollering at Darl.

So I went down into the water so I could still keep some kind of a grip in the mud, when I saw Jewel. He was middle deep, so I knew he was on the ford, anyway, leaning hard upstream, and then I see the rope, and then I see the water building up where he was holding the wagon snubbed just below the ford.

So it was Cash holding to the horse when it come splashing and scrambling up the bank, moaning and groaning like a natural man. When I come to it it was just kicking Cash loose from his holt on the saddle. His face turned up a second when he was sliding back into the water. It was gray, with his eyes closed and a long swipe of mud across his face. Then he let go and turned over in the water. He looked just like a old bundle of clothes kind of washing up and down against the bank. He looked like he was laying there in the water on his face, rocking up and down a little, looking at something on the bottom.

We could watch the rope cutting down into the water, and we could feel the weight of the wagon kind of blump and lunge lazy like, like it just as soon as not, and that rope cutting down into the water hard as a iron bar. We could hear the water hissing on it like it was red hot. Like it was a straight iron bar stuck into the bottom and us holding the end of it, and the wagon lazing up and down, kind of pushing and prodding at us like it had come around and got behind us, lazy like, like it just as soon as not when it made up its mind. There was a shoat come by, blowed up like a balloon: one of them spotted shoats of Lon Quick's. It bumped against the rope like it was a iron bar and bumped off and went on, and us watching that rope slanting down into the water. We watched it.

Darl

Cash lies on his back on the earth, his head raised on a rolled garment. His eyes are closed, his face is gray, his hair plastered in a smooth smear across his forehead as though done with a paint brush. His face appears sunken a little, sagging from the bony ridges of eye sockets, nose, gums, as though the wetting had slacked the firmness which had held the skin full; his teeth, set in pale gums, are parted a little as if he had been laughing quietly. He lies pole-thin in his wet clothes, a little pool of vomit at his head and a thread of it running from the corner of his mouth and down his cheek where he couldn't turn his head quick or far enough, until Dewey Dell stoops and wipes it away with the hem of her dress.

Jewel approaches. He has the plane. "Vernon just found the square," he says. He looks down at Cash, dripping too. "Aint he talked none yet?"

"He had his saw and hammer and chalk-line and rule," I say. "I know that."

Jewel lays the square down. Pa watches him. "They cant be far away," pa says. "It all went together. Was there ere a such misfortunate man."

Jewel does not look at pa. "You better call Vardaman back here," he says. He looks at Cash. Then he turns and goes away. "Get him to talk soon as he can," he says, "so he can tell us what else there was."

We return to the river. The wagon is hauled clear, the wheels chocked (carefully: we all helped; it is as though upon the shabby, familiar, inert shape of the wagon there lingered somehow, latent yet still immediate, that violence which had slain the mules that drew it not an hour since) above the edge of the flood. In the wagon bed it lies profoundly, the long pale planks hushed a little with wet yet still yellow, like gold seen through water, save for two long muddy smears. We pass it and go on to the bank.

One end of the rope is made fast to a tree. At the edge of the stream, knee-deep, Vardaman stands, bent forward a little, watching Vernon with rapt absorption. He has stopped yelling and he is wet to the armpits. Vernon is at the other end of the rope, shoulder-deep in the river, looking back at Vardaman. "Further back than that," he says. "You git back by the tree and hold the rope for me, so it cant slip."

Vardaman backs along the rope, to the tree, moving blindly, watching Vernon. When we come up he looks at us once, his eyes round and a little dazed. Then he looks at Vernon again in that posture of rapt alertness.

"I got the hammer too," Vernon says. "Looks like we ought to done already got that chalk-line. It ought to floated."

"Floated clean away," Jewel says. "We wont get it. We ought to find the saw, though."

"I reckon so," Vernon says. He looks at the water. "That chalk-line, too. What else did he have?"

"He aint talked yet," Jewel says, entering the water. He looks back at me. "You go back and get him roused up to talk," he says.

"Pa's there," I say. I follow Jewel into the water, along the rope. It feels alive in my hand, bellied faintly in a prolonged and resonant arc. Vernon is watching me.

"You better go," he says. "You better be there."

"Let's see what else we can get before it washes down," I say.

We hold to the rope, the current curling and dimpling about our shoulders. But beneath that false blandness the true force of it leans against us lazily. I had not thought that water in July could be so cold. It is like hands molding and prodding at the very bones. Vernon is still looking back toward the bank.

"Reckon it'll hold us all?" he says. We too look back, following the rigid bar of the rope as it rises from the water to the tree and Vardaman crouched a little beside it, watching us. "Wish my mule wouldn't strike out for home," Vernon says.

"Come on," Jewel says. "Let's get outen here."

We submerge in turn, holding to the rope, being clutched by one another while the cold wall of the water sucks the slanting mud backward and upstream from beneath our feet and we are suspended so, groping along the cold bottom. Even the mud there is not still. It has a chill, scouring quality, as though the earth under us were in motion too. We touch and fumble at one another's extended arms, letting ourselves go cautiously against the rope; or, erect in turn, watch the water suck and boil where one of the other two gropes beneath the surface. Pa has come down to the shore, watching us.

Vernon comes up, streaming, his face sloped down into his pursed blowing mouth. His mouth is bluish, like a circle of weathered rubber. He has the rule.

"He'll be glad of that," I say. "It's right new. He bought it just last month out of the catalogue."

"If we just knowed for sho what else," Vernon says, looking over his shoulder and then turning to face where Jewel had disappeared. "Didn't he go down fore me?" Vernon says.

"I dont know," I say. "I think so. Yes. Yes, he did."

We watch the thick curling surface, streaming away from us in slow whorls.

"Give him a pull on the rope," Vernon says.

"He's on your end of it," I say.

"Aint nobody on my end of it," he says.

"Pull it in," I say. But he has already done that, holding the end above the water; and then we see Jewel. He is ten yards away; he comes up, blowing, and looks at us, tossing his long hair back with a jerk of his head, then he looks toward the bank; we can see him filling his lungs.

"Jewel," Vernon says, not loud, but his voice going full and clear along the water, peremptory yet tactful. "It'll be back here. Better come back."

Jewel dives again. We stand there, leaning back against the current, watching the water where he disappeared, holding the dead rope between us like two men holding the nozzle of a fire hose, waiting for the water. Suddenly Dewey Dell is behind us in the water. "You make him come back," she says. "Jewel!" she says. He comes up again, tossing his hair back from his eyes. He is swimming now, toward the bank, the current sweeping him downstream quartering. "You, Jewel!" Dewey Dell says. We stand holding the rope and see him gain the bank and climb out. As he rises from the water, he stoops and picks up something. He comes back along the bank. He has found the chalk-line. He comes opposite us and stands there, looking about as if he were seeking something. Pa goes on down the bank. He is going to look at the mules again where their round bodies float and rub quietly together in the slack water within the bend.

"What did you do with the hammer, Vernon?" Jewel says.

"I give it to him," Vernon says, jerking his head at Vardaman. Vardaman is looking after pa. Then he looks at Jewel. "With the square." Vernon is

watching Jewel. He moves toward the bank, passing Dewey Dell and me.
"You get on out of here," I say. She says nothing, looking at Jewel and
Vernon.
"Where's the hammer?" Jewel says. Vardaman scuttles up the bank and
fetches it.
"It's heavier than the saw," Vernon says. Jewel is tying the end of the
chalk-line about the hammer shaft.
"Hammer's got the most wood in it," Jewel says. He and Vernon face
one another, watching Jewel's hands.
"And flatter, too," Vernon says, "It'd float three to one, almost. Try the
plane."
Jewel looks at Vernon. Vernon is tall, too; long and lean, eye to eye they
stand in their close wet clothes. Lon Quick could look even at a cloudy sky
and tell the time to ten minutes. Big Lon I mean, not little Lon.
"Why dont you get out of the water?" I say.
"It wont float like a saw," Jewel says.
"It'll float nigher to a saw than a hammer will," Vernon says.
"Bet you," Jewel says.
"I wont bet," Vernon says.
They stand there, watching Jewel's still hands.
"Hell," Jewel says. "Get the plane, then."
So they get the plane and tie it to the chalk-line and enter the water
again. Pa comes back along the bank. He stops for a while and looks at us,
hunched, mournful, like a failing steer or an old tall bird.
Vernon and Jewel return, leaning against the current. "Get out of the
way," Jewel says to Dewey Dell. "Get out of the water."
She crowds against me a little so they can pass, Jewel holding the plane
high as though it were perishable, the blue string trailing back over his
shoulder. They pass us and stop; they fall to arguing quietly about just
where the wagon went over.
"Darl ought to know," Vernon says. They look at me.
"I dont know," I says. "I wasn't there that long."
"Hell," Jewel says. They move on, gingerly, leaning against the current,
reading the ford with their feet.
"Have you got a holt of the rope?" Vernon says. Jewel does not answer.
He glances back at the shore, calculant, then at the water. He flings the
plane outward, letting the string run through his fingers, his fingers turning
blue where it runs over them. When the line stops, he hands it back to
Vernon.
"Better let me go this time," Vernon says. Again Jewel does not answer;
we watch him duck beneath the surface.
"Jewel," Dewey Dell whimpers.
"It aint so deep there," Vernon says. He does not look back. He is watch-
ing the water where Jewel went under.
When Jewel comes up he has the saw.
When we pass the wagon pa is standing beside it, scrubbing at the two
mud smears with a handful of leaves. Against the jungle Jewel's horse looks
like a patchwork quilt hung on a line.
Cash has not moved. We stand above him, holding the plane, the saw,
the hammer, the square, the rule, the chalkline, while Dewey Dell squats
and lifts Cash's head. "Cash," she says; "Cash."
He opens his eyes, staring profoundly up at our inverted faces.

"If ever was such a misfortunate man," pa says.

"Look, Cash," we say, holding the tools up so he can see; "what else did you have?"

He tries to speak, rolling his head, shutting his eyes.

"Cash," we say; "Cash."

It is to vomit he is turning his head. Dewey Dell wipes his mouth on the wet hem of her dress; then we can speak.

"It's his saw-set," Jewel says. "The new one he bought when he bought the rule." He moves, turning away. Vernon looks up after him, still squatting. Then he rises and follows Jewel down to the water.

"If ever was such a misfortunate man," pa says. He looms tall above us as we squat; he looks like a figure carved clumsily from tough wood by a drunken caricaturist. "It's a trial," he says. "But I dont begrudge her it. No man can say I begrudge her it." Dewey Dell has laid Cash's head back on the folded coat, twisting his head a little to avoid the vomit. Beside him his tools lie. "A fellow might call it lucky it was the same leg he broke when he fell offen that church," pa says. "But I dont begrudge her it."

Jewel and Vernon are in the river again. From here they do not appear to violate the surface at all; it is as though it had severed them both at a single blow, the two torsos moving with infinitesimal and ludicrous care upon the surface. It looks peaceful, like machinery does after you have watched it and listened to it for a long time. As though the clotting which is you had dissolved into the myriad original motion, and seeing and hearing in themselves blind and deaf; fury in itself quiet with stagnation. Squatting, Dewey Dell's wet dress shapes for the dead eyes of three blind men those mammalian ludicrosities which are the horizons and the valleys of the earth.

Cash

It wasn't on a balance. I told them that if they wanted it to tote and ride on a balance, they would have to

Cora

One day we were talking. She had never been pure religious, not even after that summer at the camp meeting when Brother Whitfield wrestled with her spirit, singled her out and strove with the vanity in her mortal heart, and I said to her many a time, "God gave you children to comfort your hard human lot and for a token of His own suffering and love, for in love you conceived and bore them." I said that because she took God's love and her duty to Him too much as a matter of course, and such conduct is not pleasing to Him. I said, "He gave us the gift to raise our voices in His undying praise" because I said there is more rejoicing in heaven over one sinner than over a hundred that never sinned. And she said "My daily life is an acknowledgment and expiation of my sin" and I said "Who are you, to say what is sin and what is not sin? It is the Lord's part to judge; ours to praise His mercy and His holy name in the hearing of our fellow mortals" because He alone can see into the heart, and just because a woman's life is right in the sight of man, she cant know if there is no sin in her heart without she opens her heart to the Lord and receives His grace. I said, "Just because you have been a faithful wife is no sign that there is no sin in your heart, and just because your life is hard is no sign that the Lord's grace is absolving you." And she said, "I know my own sin. I know that I deserve my punishment. I do not begrudge it." And I said, "It is out of your vanity that you would judge sin and salvation in the Lord's place. It is our mortal lot to suffer and to raise our voices in praise of Him who judges the sin and offers the salvation through our trials and tribulations time out of mind amen. Not even after Brother Whitfield, a godly man if ever one breathed God's breath, prayed for you and strove as never a man could except him," I said.

Because it is not us that can judge our sins or know what is sin in the Lord's eyes. She has had a hard life, but so does every woman. But you'd think from the way she talked that she knew more about sin and salvation than the Lord God Himself, than them who have strove and labored with the sin in this human world. When the only sin she ever committed was being partial to Jewel that never loved her and was its own punishment, in preference to Darl that was touched by God Himself and considered queer by us mortals and that did love her. I said, "There is your sin. And your punishment too. Jewel is your punishment. But where is your salvation? And life is short enough," I said, "to win eternal grace in. And God is a jealous God. It is His to judge and to mete; not yours."

"I know," she said. "I——" Then she stopped, and I said, "Know what?"

"Nothing," she said. "He is my cross and he will be my salvation. He will save me from the water and from the fire. Even though I have laid down my life, he will save me."

"How do you know, without you open your heart to Him and lift your voice in His praise?" I said. Then I realised that she did not mean God. I realised that out of the vanity of her heart she had spoken sacrilege. And I went down on my knees right there. I begged her to kneel and open her heart and cast from it the devil and of vanity and cast herself upon the mercy of the Lord. But she wouldn't. She just sat there, lost in her vanity and her pride, that had closed her heart to God and set that selfish mortal boy in His place. Kneeling there I prayed for her. I prayed for that poor blind woman as I had never prayed for me and mine.

Addie

In the afternoon when school was out and the last one had left with his little dirty snuffling nose, instead of going home I would go down the hill to the spring where I could be quiet and hate them. It would be quiet there then, with the water bubbling up and away and the sun slanting quiet in the trees and the quiet smelling of damp and rotting leaves and new earth; especially in the early spring, for it was worst then.

I could just remember how my father used to say that the reason for living was to get ready to stay dead a long time. And when I would have to look at them day after day, each with his and her secret and selfish thought, and blood strange to each other blood and strange to mine, and think that this seemed to be the only way I could get ready to stay dead, I would hate my father for having ever planted me. I would look forward to the times when they faulted, so I could whip them. When the switch fell I could feel it upon my flesh; when it welted and ridged it was my blood that ran, and I would think with each blow of the switch: Now you are aware of me! Now I am something in your secret and selfish life, who have marked your blood with my own for ever and ever.

And so I took Anse. I saw him pass the school house three or four times before I learned that he was driving four miles out of his way to do it. I noticed then how he was beginning to hump—a tall man and young—so that he looked already like a tall bird hunched in the cold weather, on the wagon seat. He would pass the school house, the wagon creaking slow, his head turning slow to watch the door of the school house as the wagon passed, until he went on around the curve and out of sight. One day I went to the door and stood there when he passed. When he saw me he looked quickly away and did not look back again.

In the early spring it was worst. Sometimes I thought that I could not bear it, lying in bed at night, with the wild geese going north and their honking coming faint and high and wild out of the wild darkness, and during the day it would seem as though I couldn't wait for the last one to go so I could go down to the spring. And so when I looked up that day and saw Anse standing there in his Sunday clothes, turning his hat round and round in his hands, I said:

"If you've got any womenfolks, why in the world dont they make you get your hair cut?"

"I aint got none," he said. Then he said suddenly, driving his eyes at me like two hounds in a strange yard: "That's what I come to see you about."

"And make you hold your shoulders up," I said. "You haven't got any? But you've got a house. They tell me you've got a house and a good farm. And you live there alone, doing for yourself, do you?" He just looked at me, turning the hat in his hands. "A new house," I said. "Are you going to get married?"

And he said again, holding his eyes to mine: "That's what I come to see you about."

Later he told me, "I aint got no people. So that wont be no worry to you. I dont reckon you can say the same."

"No. I have people. In Jefferson."

His face fell a little. "Well, I got a little property. I'm forehanded; I got a good honest name. I know how town folks are, but maybe when they talk to me. . . . . . ."

"They might listen," I said. "But they'll be hard to talk to." He was watching my face. "They're in the cemetery."

"But your living kin," he said. "They'll be different."

"Will they?" I said. "I dont know. I never had any other kind."

So I took Anse. And when I knew that I had Cash, I knew that living was terrible and that this was the answer to it. That was when I learned that words are no good; that words dont ever fit even what they are trying to say at. When he was born I knew that motherhood was invented by someone who had to have a word for it because the ones that had the children didn't care whether there was a word for it or not. I knew that fear was invented by someone that had never had the fear; pride, who never had the pride. I knew that it had been, not that they had dirty noses, but that we had had to use one another by words like spiders dangling by their mouths from a beam, swinging and twisting and never touching, and that only through the blows of the switch could my blood and their blood flow as one stream. I knew that it had been, not that my aloneness had to be violated over and over each day, but that it had never been violated until Cash came. Not even by Anse in the nights.

He had a word, too. Love, he called it. But I had been used to words for a long time. I knew that that word was like the others: just a shape to fill a lack; that when the right time came, you wouldn't need a word for that anymore than for pride or fear. Cash did not need to say it to me nor I to him, and I would say, Let Anse use it, if he wants to. So that it was Anse or love; love or Anse: it didn't matter.

I would think that even while I lay with him in the dark and Cash asleep in the cradle within the swing of my hand. I would think that if he were to wake and cry, I would suckle him, too. Anse or love: it didn't matter. My aloneness had been violated and then made whole again by the violation: time, Anse, love, what you will, outside the circle.

Then I found that I had Darl. At first I would not believe it. Then I believed that I would kill Anse. It was as though he had tricked me, hidden within a word like within a paper screen and struck me in the back through it. But then I realised that I had been tricked by words older than Anse or love, and that the same word had tricked Anse too, and that my revenge would be that he would never know I was taking revenge. And when Darl was born I asked Anse to promise to take me back to Jefferson when I died, because I knew that father had been right, even when he couldn't have known he was right anymore than I could have known I was wrong.

"Nonsense," Anse said; "you and me aint nigh done chapping yet, with just two."

He did not know that he was dead, then. Sometimes I would lie by him in the dark, hearing the land that was now of my blood and flesh, and I would think: Anse. Why Anse. Why are you Anse. I would think about his name until after a while I could see the word as a shape, a vessel, and I would watch him liquify and flow into it like cold molasses flowing out of the darkness into the vessel, until the jar stood full and motionless: a significant shape profoundly without life like an empty door frame; and then I would find that I had forgotten the name of the jar. I would think: The shape of my body where I used to be a virgin is in the shape of a and I couldn't think Anse, couldn't remember Anse. It was not that I could think of myself as no longer unvirgin, because I was three now. And when I would think Cash and Darl that way until their names would die and solidify into a shape and then fade away, I would say, All right. It doesn't matter. It doesn't matter what they call them.

And so when Cora Tull would tell me I was not a true mother, I would think how words go straight up in a thin line, quick and harmless, and how terribly doing goes along the earth, clinging to it, so that after a while the two lines are too far apart for the same person to straddle from one to the other; and that sin and love and fear are just sounds that people who never sinned nor loved nor feared have for what they never had and cannot have until they forget the words. Like Cora, who could never even cook.

She would tell me what I owed to my children and to Anse and to God. I gave Anse the children. I did not ask for them. I did not even ask him for what he could have given me: not-Anse. That was my duty to him, to not ask that, and that duty I fulfilled. I would be I; I would let him be the shape and echo of his word. That was more than he asked, because he could not have asked for that and been Anse, using himself so with a word.

And then he died. He did not know he was dead. I would lie by him in the dark, hearing the dark land talking of God's love and His beauty and His sin; hearing the dark voicelessness in which the words are the deeds, and the other words that are not deeds, that are just the gaps in people's lacks, coming down like the cries of the geese out of the wild darkness in the old terrible nights, fumbling at the deeds like orphans to whom are pointed out in a crowd two faces and told, That is your father, your mother.

I believed that I had found it. I believed that the reason was the duty to the alive, to the terrible blood, the red bitter flood boiling through the land. I would think of sin as I would think of the clothes we both wore in the world's face, of the circumspection necessary because he was he and I was I; the sin the more utter and terrible since he was the instrument ordained by God who created the sin, to sanctify that sin He had created. While I waited for him in the woods, waiting for him before he saw me, I would think of him as dressed in sin. I would think of him as thinking of me as dressed also in sin, he the more beautiful since the garment which he had exchanged for sin was sanctified. I would think of the sin as garments which we would remove in order to shape and coerce the terrible blood to the forlorn echo of the dead word high in the air. Then I would lay with Anse again—I did not lie to him: I just refused, just as I refused my breast to Cash and Darl after their time was up—hearing the dark land talking the voiceless speech.

I hid nothing. I tried to deceive no one. I would not have cared. I merely took the precautions that he thought necessary for his sake, not for my safety, but just as I wore clothes in the world's face. And I would think then when Cora talked to me, of how the high dead words in time seemed to lose even the significance of their dead sound.

Then it was over. Over in the sense that he was gone and I knew that, see him again though I would, I would never again see him coming swift and secret to me in the woods dressed in sin like a gallant garment already blowing aside with the speed of his secret coming.

But for me it was not over. I mean, over in the sense of beginning and ending, because to me there was no beginning nor ending to anything then. I even held Anse refraining still, not that I was holding him recessional, but as though nothing else had ever been. My children were of me alone, of the wild blood boiling along the earth, of me and of all that lived; of none and of all. Then I found that I had Jewel. When I waked to remember to discover it, he was two months gone.

My father said that the reason for living is getting ready to stay dead. I knew at last what he meant and that he could not have known what he meant himself, because a man cannot know anything about cleaning up the house afterward. And so I have cleaned my house. With Jewel—I lay by the lamp, holding up my own head, watching him cap and suture it before he breathed—the wild blood boiled away and the sound of it ceased. Then there was only the milk, warm and calm, and I lying calm in the slow silence, getting ready to clean my house.

I gave Anse Dewey Dell to negative Jewel. Then I gave him Vardaman to replace the child I had robbed him of. And now he has three children that are his and not mine. And then I could get ready to die.

One day I was talking to Cora. She prayed for me because she believed I was blind to sin, wanting me to kneel and pray too, because people to whom sin is just a matter of words, to them salvation is just words too.

Whitfield

When they told me she was dying, all that night I wrestled with Satan, and I emerged victorious. I woke to the enormity of my sin; I saw the true light at last, and I fell on my knees and confessed to God and asked His guidance and received it. "Rise," He said; "repair it to that home in which you have put a living lie, among those people with whom you have outraged My Word; confess your sin aloud. It is for them, for that deceived husband, to forgive you: not I."

So I went. I heard that Tull's bridge was gone; I said "Thanks, O Lord, O Mighty Ruler of all;" for by those dangers and difficulties which I should have to surmount I saw that He had not abandoned me; that my reception again into His holy peace and love would be the sweeter for it. "Just let me not perish before I have begged the forgiveness of the man whom I betrayed," I prayed; "let me not be too late; let not the tale of mine and her transgression come from her lips instead of mine. She had sworn then that she would never tell it, but eternity is a fearsome thing to face: have I not wrestled thigh to thigh with Satan myself? let me not have also the sin of her broken vow upon my soul. Let not the waters of Thy Mighty Wrath encompass me until I have cleansed my soul in the presence of them whom I injured."

It was His hand that bore me safely above the flood, that fended from me the dangers of the waters. My horse was frightened, and my own heart failed me as the logs and the uprooted trees bore down upon my littleness. But not my soul: time after time I saw them averted at destruction's final instant, and I lifted my voice above the noise of the flood: "Praise to Thee, O Mighty Lord and King. By this token shall I cleanse my soul and gain again into the fold of Thy undying love."

I knew then that forgiveness was mine. The flood, the danger, behind, and as I rode on across the firm earth again and the scene of my Gethsemane drew closer and closer, I framed the words which I should use. I would enter the house; I would stop her before she had spoken; I would say to her husband: "Anse, I have sinned. Do with me as you will."

It was already as though it were done. My soul felt freer, quieter than it had in years; already I seemed to dwell in abiding peace again as I rode on. To either side I saw His hand; in my heart I could hear His voice: "Courage. I am with thee."

Then I reached Tull's house. His youngest girl came out and called to me as I was passing. She told me that she was already dead.

I have sinned, O Lord. Thou knowest the extent of my remorse and the will of my spirit. But He is merciful; He will accept the will for the deed, Who knew that when I framed the words of my confession it was to Anse I spoke them, even though he was not there. It was He in His infinite wisdom that restrained the tale from her dying lips as she lay surrounded by those who loved and trusted her; mine the travail by water which I sustained by the strength of His hand. Praise to Thee in Thy bounteous and omnipotent love; O praise.

I entered the house of bereavement, the lowly dwelling where another erring mortal lay while her soul faced the awful and irrevocable judgment, peace to her ashes.

"God's grace upon this house," I said.

Darl

On the horse he rode up to Armstid's and *came back on the horse,* leading Armstid's team. We hitched up and laid Cash on top of Addie. When we laid him down he vomited again, but he got his head over the wagon bed in time.

"He taken a lick in the stomach, too," Vernon said.

"The horse may have kicked him in the stomach too," I said. "Did he kick you in the stomach, Cash?"

He tried to say something. Dewey Dell wiped his mouth again.

"What's he say?" Vernon said.

"What is it, Cash?" Dewey Dell said. She leaned down. "His tools," she said. Vernon got them and put them into the wagon. Dewey Dell lifted Cash's head so he could see. We drove on, Dewey Dell and I sitting beside Cash to steady him *and he riding on ahead on the horse.* Vernon stood watching us for a while. Then he turned and went back toward the bridge. He walked gingerly, beginning to flap the wet sleeves of his shirt as though he had just got wet.

He was sitting the horse before the gate. Armstid was waiting at the gate. We stopped *and he got down* and we lifted Cash down and carried him into the house, where Mrs Armstid had the bed ready. We left her and Dewey Dell undressing him.

We followed pa out to the wagon. He went back and got into the wagon and drove on, we following on foot, into the lot. The wetting had helped, because Armstid said, "You're welcome to the house. You can put it there." *He followed, leading the horse, and stood beside the wagon, the reins in his hand.*

"I thank you," pa said. "We'll use in the shed yonder. I know it's a imposition on you."

"You're welcome to the house," Armstid said. *He had that wooden look on his face again; that bold, surly, high-colored rigid look like his face and eyes were two colors of wood, the wrong one pale and the wrong one dark. His shirt was beginning to dry, but it still clung close upon him when he moved.*

"She would appreciate it," pa said.

We took the team out and rolled the wagon back under the shed. One side of the shed was open.

"It wont rain under," Armstid said. "But if you'd rather. . . . . . ."

Back of the barn was some rusted sheets of tin roofing. We took two of them and propped them against the open side.

"You're welcome to the house," Armstid said.

"I thank you," pa said. "I'd take it right kind if you'd give them a little snack."

"Sho," Armstid said. "Lula'll have supper ready soon as she gets Cash comfortable." *He had gone back to the horse and he was taking the saddle off, his damp shirt lapping flat to him when he moved.*

Pa wouldn't come in the house.

"Come in and eat," Armstid said. "It's nigh ready."

"I wouldn't crave nothing," pa said. "I thank you."

"You come in and dry and eat," Armstid said. "It'll be all right here."

"It's for her," pa said. "It's for her sake I am taking the food. I got no team, no nothing. But she will be grateful to ere a one of you."

"Sho," Armstid said. "You folks come in and dry."

But after Armstid gave pa a drink, he felt better, and when we went in to see about Cash *he hadn't come in with us. When I looked back he was leading the horse into the barn* he was already talking about getting another team, and by supper time he had good as bought it. *He is down there in the barn, sliding fluidly past the gaudy lunging swirl, into the stall with it. He climbs onto the manger and drags the hay down and leaves the stall and seeks and finds the curry-comb. Then he returns and slips quickly past the single crashing thump and up against the horse, where it cannot overreach. He applies the curry-comb, holding himself within the horse's striking radius with the agility of an acrobat, cursing the horse in a whisper of obscene caress. Its head flashes back, tooth-cropped; its eyes roll in the dusk like marbles on a gaudy velvet cloth as he strikes it upon the face with the back of the curry-comb.*

Armstid

But time I give him another sup of whisky and supper was about ready, he had done already bought a team from somebody, on a credit. Picking and choosing he were by then, saying how he didn't like this span and wouldn't put his money in nothing so-and-so owned, not even a hen coop.

"You might try Snopes," I said. "He's got three-four span. Maybe one of them would suit you."

Then he begun to mumble his mouth, looking at me like it was me that owned the only span of mules in the county and wouldn't sell them to him, when I knew that like as not it would be my team that would ever get them out of the lot at all. Only I dont know what they would do with them, if they had a team. Littlejohn had told me that the levee through Haley bottom had done gone for two miles and that the only way to get to Jefferson would be to go around by Mottson. But that was Anse's business.

"He's a close man to trade with," he says, mumbling his mouth. But when I give him another sup after supper, he cheered up some. He was aiming to go back to the barn and set up with her. Maybe he thought that if he just stayed down there ready to take out, Santa Claus would maybe bring him a span of mules. "But I reckon I can talk him around," he says. "A man'll always help a fellow in a tight, if he's got ere a drop of Christian blood in him."

"Of course you're welcome to use the use of mine," I said, me knowing how much he believed that was the reason.

"I thank you," he said. "She'll want to go in ourn," and him knowing how much I believed that was the reason.

After supper Jewel rode over to the Bend to get Peabody. I heard he was to be there today at Varner's. Jewel come back about midnight. Peabody had gone down below Inverness somewhere, but Uncle Billy come back with him, with his satchel of horse-physic. Like he says, a man aint so different from a horse or a mule, come long come short, except a mule or a horse has got a little more sense. "What you been into now, boy?" he says, looking at Cash. "Get me a mattress and a chair and a glass of whisky," he says.

He made Cash drink the whisky, then he run Anse out of the room. "Lucky it was the same leg he broke last summer," Anse says, mournful, mumbling and blinking. "That's something."

We folded the mattress across Cash's legs and set the chair on the mattress and me and Jewel set on the chair and the gal held the lamp and Uncle Billy taken a chew of tobacco and went to work. Cash fought pretty hard for a while, until he fainted. Then he laid still, with big balls of sweat standing on his face like they had started to roll down and then stopped to wait for him.

When we waked up, Uncle Billy had done packed up and left. He kept on trying to say something until the gal leaned down and wiped his mouth. "It's his tools," she said.

"I brought them in," Darl said. "I got them."

He tried to talk again; she leaned down. "He wants to see them," she said. So Darl brought them in where he could see them. They shoved them under the side of the bed, where he could reach his hand and touch them when he felt better. Next morning Anse taken that horse and rode over to the Bend to see Snopes. Him and Jewel stood in the lot talking a while, then Anse got on the horse and rode off. I reckon that was the first time Jewel ever let anybody ride that horse, and until Anse come back he hung around in that swole-up way, watching the road like he was half a mind to take out after Anse and get the horse back.

Along toward nine oclock it begun to get hot. That was when I see the first buzzard. Because of the wetting, I reckon. Anyway it wasn't until well into the day that I see them. Lucky the breeze was setting away from the house, so it wasn't until well into the morning. But soon as I see them it was like I could smell it in the field a mile away from just watching them, and them circling and circling for everybody in the county to see what was in my barn.

I was still a good half a mile from the house when I heard that boy yelling. I thought maybe he might have fell into the well or something, so I whipped up and come into the lot on the lope.

There must have been a dozen of them setting along the ridge-pole of the barn, and that boy was chasing another one around the lot like it was a turkey and it just lifting enough to dodge him and go flopping back to the roof of the shed again where he had found it setting on the coffin. It had got hot then, right, and the breeze had dropped or changed or something, so I went and found Jewel, but Lula come out.

"You got to do something," she said. "It's a outrage."

"That's what I aim to do," I said.

"It's a outrage," she said. "He should be lawed for treating her so."

"He's getting her into the ground the best he can," I said. So I found Jewel and asked him if he didn't want to take one of the mules and go over to the Bend and see about Anse. He didn't say nothing. He just looked at me with his jaws going bone-white and them bone-white eyes of hisn, then he went and begun to call Darl.

"What you fixing to do?" I said.

He didn't answer. Darl come out. "Come on," Jewel said.

"What you aim to do?" Darl said.

"Going to move the wagon," Jewel said over his shoulder.

"Dont be a fool," I said. "I never meant nothing. You couldn't help it." And Darl hung back too, but nothing wouldn't suit Jewel.

"Shut your goddamn mouth," he says.

"It's got to be somewhere," Darl said. "We'll take out soon as pa gets back."

"You wont help me?" Jewel says, them white eyes of hisn kind of blaring and his face shaking like he had a aguer.

"No," Darl said. "I wont. Wait till pa gets back."

So I stood in the door and watched him push and haul at that wagon. It was on a downhill, and once I thought he was fixing to beat out the back end of the shed. Then the dinner bell rung. I called him, but he didn't look around. "Come on to dinner," I said. "Tell that boy." But he didn't answer, so I went on to dinner. The gal went down to get that boy, but she come back without him. About half through dinner we heard him yelling again, running that buzzard out.

"It's a outrage," Lula said; "a outrage."

"He's doing the best he can," I said. "A fellow dont trade with Snopes in thirty minutes. They'll set in the shade all afternoon to dicker."

"Do?" she says. "Do? He's done too much, already."

And I reckon he had. Trouble is, his quitting was just about to start our doing. He couldn't buy no team from nobody, let alone Snopes, withouten he had something to mortgage he didn't know would mortgage yet. And so when I went back to the field I looked at my mules and same as told them goodbye for a spell. And when I come back that evening and the sun shining all day on that shed, I wasn't so sho I would regret it.

He come riding up just as I went out to the porch, where they all was. He looked kind of funny: kind of more hangdog than common, and kind of proud too. Like he had done something he thought was cute but wasn't so sho now how other folks would take it.

"I got a team," he said.

"You bought a team from Snopes?" I said.

"I reckon Snopes aint the only man in this country that can drive a trade," he said.

"Sho," I said. He was looking at Jewel, with that funny look, but Jewel had done got down from the porch and was going toward the horse. To see what Anse had done to it, I reckon.

"Jewel," Anse says. Jewel looked back. "Come here," Anse says. Jewel come back a little and stopped again.

"What you want?" he said.

"So you got a team from Snopes," I said. "He'll send them over tonight, I reckon? You'll want a early start tomorrow, long as you'll have to go by Mottson."

Then he quit looking like he had been for a while. He got that badgered look like he used to have, mumbling his mouth.

"I do the best I can," he said. "Fore God, if there were ere a man in the living world suffered the trials and floutings I have suffered."

"A fellow that just beat Snopes in a trade ought to feel pretty good," I said. "What did you give him, Anse?"

He didn't look at me. "I give a chattel mortgage on my cultivator and seeder," he said.

"But they aint worth forty dollars. How far do you aim to get with a forty dollar team?"

They were all watching him now, quiet and steady. Jewel was stopped, halfway back, waiting to go on to the horse. "I give other things," Anse said. He begun to mumble his mouth again, standing there like he was waiting for somebody to hit him and him with his mind already made up not to do nothing about it.

"What other things?" Darl said.

"Hell," I said. "You take my team. You can bring them back. I'll get along someway."

"So that's what you were doing in Cash's clothes last night," Darl said. He said it just like he was reading it outen the paper. Like he never give a durn himself one way or the other. Jewel had come back now, standing there, looking at Anse with them marble eyes of hisn. "Cash aimed to buy that talking machine from Suratt with that money," Darl said.

Anse stood there, mumbling his mouth. Jewel watched him. He ain't never blinked yet.

"But that's just eight dollars more," Darl said, in that voice like he was just listening and never give a durn himself. "That still wont buy a team."

Anse looked at Jewel, quick, kind of sliding his eyes that way, then he looked down again. "God knows, if there were ere a man," he says. Still they didn't say nothing. They just watched him, waiting, and him sliding his eyes toward their feet and up their legs but no higher. "And the horse," he says.

"What horse?" Jewel said. Anse just stood there. I be durn, if a man cant keep the upper hand of his sons, he ought to run them away from home, no matter how big they are. And if he cant do that, I be durn if he oughtn't to leave himself. I be durn if I wouldn't. "You mean, you tried to swap my horse?" Jewel says.

Anse stands there, dangle-armed. "For fifteen years I aint had a tooth in my head," he says. "God knows it. He knows in fifteen years I aint et the victuals" He aimed for man to eat to keep his strength up, and me saving a nickel here and a nickel there so my family wouldn't suffer it, to buy them teeth so I could eat God's appointed food. I give that money. I thought that if I could do without eating, my sons could do without riding. God knows I did."

Jewel stands with his hands on his hips, looking at Anse. Then he looks away. He looked out across the field, his face still as a rock. Like it was somebody else talking about somebody else's horse and him not even listening. Then he spit, slow, and said "Hell" and he turned and went on to the gate and unhitched the horse and got on it. It was moving when he come into the saddle and by the time he was on it they was tearing down the road like the Law might have been behind them. They went out of sight that way, the two of them looking like some kind of a spotted cyclone.

"Well," I says. "You take my team," I said. But he wouldn't do it. And they wouldn't even stay, and that boy chasing them buzzards all day in the hot sun until he was nigh as crazy as the rest of them. "Leave Cash here, anyway," I said. But they wouldn't do that. They made a pallet for him with quilts on top of the coffin and laid him on it and set his tools by him, and we put my team in and hauled the wagon about a mile down the road.

"If we'll bother you here," Anse says, "just say so."

"Sho," I said. "It'll be fine here. Safe, too. Now let's go back and eat supper."

"I thank you," Anse said. "We got a little something in the basket. We can make out."

"Where'd you get it?" I said.

"We brought it from home."

"But it'll be stale now," I said. "Come and get some hot victuals."

But they wouldn't come. "I reckon we can make out," Anse said. So I went home and et and taken a basket back to them and tried again to make them come back to the house.

"I thank you," he said. "I reckon we can make out." So I left them there, squatting around a little fire, waiting; God knows what for.

I come on home. I kept thinking about them there, and about that fellow tearing away on that horse. And that would be the last they would see of him. And I be durn if I could blame him. Not for wanting to not give up his horse, but for getting shut of such a durn fool as Anse.

Or that's what I thought then. Because be durn if there aint something about a durn fellow like Anse that seems to make a man have to help him, even when he knows he'll be wanting to kick himself next minute. Because about a hour after breakfast next morning Eustace Grimm that works Snopes' place come up with a span of mules, hunting Anse.

"I thought him and Anse never traded," I said.

"Sho," Eustace said. "All they liked was the horse. Like I said to Mr Snopes, he was letting his team go for fifty dollars, because if his uncle Flem had just kept them Texas horses when he owned them, Anse wouldn't a never——"

"The horse?" I said. "Anse's boy taken that horse and cleared out last night, probably half way to Texas by now, and Anse——"

"I didn't know who brung it," Eustace said. "I never see them. I just found the horse in the barn this morning when I went to feed, and I told Mr Snopes and he said to bring the team on over here."

Well, that'll be the last they'll ever see of him now, sho enough. Come Christmas time they'll maybe get a postal card from him in Texas, I reckon. And if it hadn't been Jewel, I reckon it'd a been me; I owe him that much, myself. I be durn if Anse dont conjure a man, some way. I be durn if he aint a sight.

Vardaman

Now there are seven of them, in little tall black circles. "Look, Darl," I say; "see?"

He looks up. We watch them in little tall black circles of not-moving.

"Yesterday there were just four," I say.

There were more than four on the barn.

"Do you know what I would do it he tries to light on the wagon again?" I say.

"What would you do?" Darl says.

"I wouldn't let him light on her," I say. "I wouldn't let him light on Cash, either."

Cash is sick. He is sick on the box. But my mother is a fish.

"We got to get some medicine in Mottson," pa says. "I reckon we'll just have to."

"How do you feel, Cash?" Darl says.

"It dont bother none," Cash says.

"Do you want it propped a little higher?" Darl says.

Cash has a broken leg. He has had two broken legs. He lies on the box with a quilt rolled under his head and a piece of wood under his knee.

"I reckon we ought to left him at Armstid's," pa says.

I haven't got a broken leg and pa hasn't and Darl hasn't and "It's just the bumps," Cash says. "It kind of grinds together a little on a bump. It dont bother none." *Jewel has gone away. He and his horse went away one supper time*

"It's because she wouldn't have us beholden," pa says. "Fore God, I do the best that ere a man" *Is it because Jewel's mother is a horse Darl? I said.*

"Maybe I can draw the ropes a little tighter," Darl says. *"That's why Jewel and I were both in the shed and she was in the wagon because the horse lives in the barn and I had to keep on running the buzzard away from*

"If you just would," Cash says. And Dewey Dell hasn't got a broken leg and I haven't. Cash is my brother.

We stop. When Darl loosens the rope Cash begins to sweat again. His teeth look out.

"Hurt?" Darl says.

"I reckon you better put it back," Cash says.

Darl puts the rope back, pulling hard. Cash's teeth look out.

"Hurt?" Darl says.

"It dont bother none," Cash says.

"Do you want pa to drive slower?" Darl says.

"No," Cash says. "Aint no time to hang back. It dont bother none."

"We'll have to get some medicine at Mottson," pa says. "I reckon we'll have to."

"Tell him to go on," Cash says. We go on. Dewey Dell leans back and wipes Cash's face. Cash is my brother. *But Jewel's mother is a horse. My mother is a fish. Darl says that when we come to the water again I might see her and Dewey Dell said, She's in the box; how could she have got out? She got out through the holes I bored, into the water I said, and when we come to the water again I am going to see her. My mother is not in the box. My mother does not smell like that. My mother is a fish*

"Those cakes will be in fine shape by the time we get to Jefferson," Darl says.

Dewey Dell does not look around.

"You better try to sell them in Mottson," Darl says.

"When will we get to Mottson, Darl?" I say.

"Tomorrow," Darl says. "If this team dont rack to pieces. Snopes must have fed them on sawdust."

"Why did he feed them on sawdust, Darl?" I say.

"Look," Darl says. "See?"

Now there are nine of them, tall in little tall black circles.

When we come to the foot of the hill pa stops and Darl and Dewey Dell and I get out. Cash cant walk because he has a broken leg. "Come up, mules," pa says. The mules walk hard; the wagon creaks. Darl and Dewey Dell and I walk behind the wagon, up the hill. When we come to the top of the hill pa stops and we get back into the wagon.

Now there are ten of them, tall in little tall black circles on the sky.

Moseley

I happened to look up, and saw her outside the window, looking in. Not close to the glass, and not looking at anything in particular; just standing there with her head turned this way and her eyes full on me and kind of blank too, like she was waiting for a sign. When I looked up again she was moving toward the door.

She kind of bumbled at the screen door a minute, like they do, and came in. She had on a stiff-brimmed straw hat setting on the top of her head and she was carrying a package wrapped in newspaper: I thought that she had a quarter or a dollar at the most, and that after she stood around a while she would maybe buy a cheap comb or a bottle of nigger toilet water, so I never disturbed her for a minute or so except to notice that she was pretty in a kind of sullen, awkward way, and that she looked a sight better in her gingham dress and her own complexion than she would after she bought whatever she would finally decide on. Or tell that she wanted. I knew that she had already decided before she came in. But you have to let them take their time. So I went on with what I was doing, figuring to let Albert wait on her when he caught up at the fountain, when he came back to me.

"That woman," he said. "You better see what she wants."

"What does she want?" I said.

"I dont know. I cant get anything out of her. You better wait on her."

So I went around the counter. I saw that she was barefooted, standing with her feet flat and easy on the floor, like she was used to it. She was looking at me, hard, holding the package; I saw she had about as black a pair of eyes as ever I saw, and she was a stranger. I never remembered seeing her in Mottson before. "What can I do for you?" I said.

Still she didn't say anything. She stared at me without winking. Then she looked back at the folks at the fountain. Then she looked past me, toward the back of the store.

"Do you want to look at some toilet things?" I said. "Or is it medicine you want?"

"That's it," she said. She looked quick back at the fountain again. So I thought maybe her ma or somebody had sent her in for some of this female dope and she was ashamed to ask for it. I knew she couldn't have a complexion like hers and use it herself, let alone not being much more than old enough to barely know what it was for. It's a shame, the way they poison themselves with it. But a man's got to stock it or go out of business in this country.

"Oh," I said. "What do you use? We have——" She looked at me again, almost like she had said hush, and looked toward the back of the store again.

"I'd liefer go back there," she said.

"All right," I said. You have to humor them. You save time by it. I followed her to the back. She put her hand on the gate. "There's nothing back there but the prescription case," I said. "What do you want?" She stopped and looked at me. It was like she had taken some kind of a lid off her face, her eyes. It was her eyes: kind of dumb and hopeful and sullenly willing to be disappointed all at the same time. But she was in trouble of some sort; I could see that. "What's your trouble?" I said. "Tell me what it is you want. I'm pretty busy." I wasn't meaning to hurry her, but a man just hasn't got the time they have out there.

"It's the female trouble," she said.

"Oh," I said. "Is that all?" I thought maybe she was younger than she looked, and her first one had scared her, or maybe one had been a little abnormal as it will in young women. "Where's your ma?" I said. "Haven't you got one?"

"She's out yonder in the wagon," she said.

"Why not talk to her about it before you take any medicine," I said. "Any woman would have told you about it." She looked at me, and I looked at her again and said, "How old are you?"

"Seventeen," she said.

"Oh," I said. "I thought maybe you were. .‥ . . . ." She was watching me. But then, in the eyes all of them look like they had no age and knew everything in the world, anyhow. "Are you too regular, or not regular enough?"

She quit looking at me but she didn't move. "Yes," she said. "I reckon so. Yes."

"Well, which?" I said. "Dont you know?" It's a crime and a shame; but after all, they'll buy it from somebody. She stood there, not looking at me. "You want something to stop it?" I said. "Is that it?"

"No," she said. "That's it. It's already stopped."

"Well, what——" Her face was lowered a little, still, like they do in all their dealings with a man so he dont ever know just where the lightning will strike next. "You are not married, are you?" I said.

"No."

"Oh," I said. "And how long has it been since it stopped? about five months maybe?"

"It aint been but two," she said.

"Well, I haven't got anything in my store you want to buy," I said, "unless it's a nipple. And I'd advise you to buy that and go back home and tell your pa, if you have one, and let him make somebody buy you a wedding license. Was that all you wanted?"

But she just stood there, not looking at me.

"I got the money to pay you," she said.

"Is it your own, or did he act enough of a man to give you the money?"

"He give it to me. Ten dollars. He said that would be enough."

"A thousand dollars wouldn't be enough in my store and ten cents wouldn't be enough," I said. "You take my advice and go home and tell your pa or your brothers if you have any or the first man you come to in the road."

But she didn't move. "Lafe said I could get it at the drugstore. He said to tell you me and him wouldn't never tell nobody you sold it to us."

"And I just wish your precious Lafe had come for it himself; that's what I wish. I dont know: I'd have had a little respect for him then. And you can go back and tell him I said so—if he aint halfway to Texas by now, which I dont doubt. Me, a respectable druggist, that's kept store and raised a family and been a church-member for fifty-six years in this town. I'm a good mind to tell your folks myself, if I can just find who they are."

She looked at me now, her eyes and face kind of blank again like when I first saw her through the window. "I didn't know," she said. "He told me I could get something at the drugstore. He said they might not want to sell it to me, but if I had ten dollars and told them I wouldn't never tell nobody. . . ."

"He never said this drug-store," I said. "If he did or mentioned my name, I defy him to prove it. I defy him to repeat it or I'll prosecute him to the full extent of the law, and you can tell him so."

"But maybe another drugstore would," she said.

"Then I dont want to know it. Me, that's——" Then I looked at her. But it's a hard life they have; sometimes a man. . . . . . .if there can ever be any excuse for sin, which it cant be. And then, life wasn't made to be easy on folks: they wouldn't ever have any reason to be good and die. "Look here," I said. "You get that notion out of your head. The Lord gave you what you have, even if He did use the devil to do it; you let Him take it

away from you if it's His will to do so. You go on back to Lafe and you and
him take that ten dollars and get married with it."

"Lafe said I could get something at the drugstore," she said.

"Then go and get it," I said. "You wont get it here."

She went out, carrying the package, her feet making a little hissing on
the floor. She bumbled again at the door and went out. I could see her
through the glass going on down the street.

It was Albert told me about the rest of it. He said the wagon was stopped
in front of Grummet's hardware store, with the ladies all scattering up and
down the street with handkerchiefs to their noses, and a crowd of hard-
nosed men and boys standing around the wagon, listening to the marshal
arguing with the man. He was a kind of tall, gaunted man sitting on the
wagon, saying it was a public street and he reckoned he had as much right
there as anybody, and the marshal telling him he would have to move on;
folks couldn't stand it. It had been dead eight days, Albert said. They came
from some place out in Yoknapatawpha county, trying to get to Jefferson
with it. It must have been like a piece of rotten cheese coming into an ant-
hill, in that ramshackle wagon that Albert said folks were scared would fall
all to pieces before they could get it out of town, with that home-made box
and another fellow with a broken leg lying on a quilt on top of it, and the
father and a little boy sitting in the seat and the marshal trying to make
them get out of town.

"It's a public street," the man says. "I reckon we can stop to buy something same as airy other man. We got the money to pay for hit, and hit aint
airy law that says a man cant spend his money where he wants."

They had stopped to buy some cement. The other son was in Grummet's,
trying to make Grummet break a sack and let him have ten cents' worth,
and finally Grummet broke the sack to get him out. They wanted the cement
to fix the fellow's broken leg, someway.

"Why, you'll kill him," the marshal said. "You'll cause him to lose his leg.
You take him on to the doctor, and you get this thing buried soon as you
can. Dont you know you're liable to jail for endangering the public health?"

"We're doing the best we can," the father said. Then he told a long tale
about how they had to wait for the wagon to come back and how the bridge
was washed away and how they went eight miles to another bridge and it
was gone too so they came back and swum the ford and the mules got
drowned and how they got another team and found that the road was washed
out and they had to come clean around by Mottson, and then the one with
the cement came back and told him to shut up.

"We'll be gone in a minute," he told the marshal.

"We never aimed to bother nobody," the father said.

"You take that fellow to a doctor," the marshal told the one with the
cement.

"I reckon he's all right," he said.

"It aint that we're hard-hearted," the marshal said. "But I reckon you can
tell yourself how it is."

"Sho," the other said. "We'll take out soon as Dewey Dell comes back.
She went to deliver a package."

So they stood there with the folks backed off with handkerchiefs to their
faces, until in a minute the girl came up with that newspaper package.

"Come on," the one with the cement said, "we've lost too much time."

So they go in the wagon and went on. And when I went to supper it still seemed like I could smell it. And the next day I met the marshal and I begun to sniff and said,

"Smell anything?"

"I reckon they're in Jefferson by now," he said.

"Or in jail. Well, thank the Lord it's not our jail."

"That's a fact," he said.

Darl

"Here's a place," pa says. He pulls the team up and sits looking at the house. "We could get some water over yonder."

"All right," I say. "You'll have to borrow a bucket from them, Dewey Dell."

"God knows," pa says. "I wouldn't be beholden, God knows."

"If you see a good-sized can, you might bring it," I say. Dewey Dell gets down from the wagon, carrying the package. "You had more trouble than you expected, selling those cakes in Mottson," I say. How do our lives ravel out into the no-wind, no-sound, the weary gestures wearily recapitulant: echoes of old compulsions with no-hand on no-strings: in sunset we fall into furious attitudes, dead gestures of dolls. Cash broke his leg and now the sawdust is running out. He is bleeding to death is Cash.

"I wouldn't be beholden," pa says. "God knows."

"Then make some water yourself," I say. "We can use Cash's hat."

When Dewey Dell comes back the man comes with her. Then he stops and she comes on and he stands there and after a while he goes back to the house and stands on the porch, watching us.

"We better not try to lift him down," pa says. "We can fix it here."

"Do you want to be lifted down, Cash?" I say.

"Wont we get to Jefferson tomorrow?" he says. He is watching us, his eyes interrogatory, intent, and sad. "I can last it out."

"It'll be easier on you," pa says. "It'll keep it from rubbing together."

"I can last it," Cash says. "We'll lose time stopping."

"We done bought the cement, now," pa says.

"I could last it," Cash says. "It ain't but one more day. It don't bother to speak of." He looks at us, his eyes wide in his thin gray face, questioning. "It sets up so," he says.

"We done bought it now," pa says.

I mix the cement in the can, stirring the slow water into the pale green thick coils. I bring the can to the wagon where Cash can see. He lies on his back, his thin profile in silhouette, ascetic and profound against the sky. "Does that look about right?" I say.

"You dont want too much water, or it wont work right," he says.

"Is this too much?"

"Maybe if you could get a little sand," he says. "It aint but one more day," he says. "It dont bother me none."

Vardaman goes back down the road to where we crossed the branch and returns with sand. He pours it slowly into the thick coiling in the can. I go to the wagon again.

"Does that look all right?"

"Yes," Cash says. "I could have lasted. It dont bother me none."

We loosen the splints and pour the cement over his leg, slow.

"Watch out for it," Cash says. "Dont get none on it if you can help."

"Yes," I say. Dewey Dell tears a piece of paper from the package and wipes the cement from the top of it as it drips from Cash's leg.

"How does that feel?"

"It feels fine," he says. "It's cold. It feels fine."

"If it'll just help you," pa says. "I asks your forgiveness. I never foreseen it no more than you."

"It feels fine," Cash says.

If you could just ravel out into time. That would be nice. It would be nice if you could just ravel out into time.

We replace the splints, the cords, drawing them tight, the cement in thick pale green slow surges among the cords. Cash watching us quietly with that profound questioning look.

"That'll steady it," I say.

"Ay," Cash says. "I'm obliged."

Then we all turn on the wagon and watch him. He is coming up the road behind us, wooden-backed, wooden-faced, moving only from his hips down. He comes up without a word, with his pale rigid eyes in his high sullen face, and gets into the wagon.

"Here's a hill," pa says. "I reckon you'll have to get out and walk."

Vardaman

Darl and Jewel and Dewey Dell and I are walking up the hill, behind the wagon. Jewel came back. He came up the road and got into the wagon. He was walking. Jewel hasn't got a horse anymore. Jewel is my brother. Cash is my brother. Cash has a broken leg. We fixed Cash's leg so it doesn't hurt. Cash is my brother. Jewel is my brother too, but he hasn't got a broken leg.

Now there are five of them, tall in little tall black circles.

"Where do they stay at night, Darl?" I say. "When we stop at night in the barn, where do they stay?"

The hill goes off into the sky. Then the sun comes up from behind the hill and the mules and the wagon and pa walk on the sun. You cannot watch them, walking slow on the sun. In Jefferson it is red on the track behind the glass. The track goes shining round and round. Dewey Dell says so.

Tonight I am going to see where they stay while we are in the barn.

Darl

"Jewel," I say, "whose son are you?"

The breeze was setting up from the barn, so we put her under the apple tree, where the moonlight can dapple the apple tree upon the long slumbering flanks within which now and then she talks in little trickling bursts of secret and murmurous bubbling. I took Vardaman to listen. When we came up the cat leaped down from it and flicked away with silver claw and silver eye into the shadow.

"Your mother was a horse, but who was your father, Jewel?"

"You goddamn lying son of a bitch."

"Dont call me that," I say.

"You goddamn lying son of a bitch."

"Dont you call me that, Jewel." In the tall moonlight his eyes look like spots of white paper pasted on a high small football.

After supper Cash began to sweat a little. "It's getting a little hot," he said. "It was the sun shining on it all day, I reckon."

"You want some water poured on it?" we say. "Maybe that will ease it some."

"I'd be obliged," Cash said. "It was the sun shining on it, I reckon. I ought to thought and kept it covered."

"We ought to thought," we said. "You couldn't have suspicioned."

"I never noticed it getting hot," Cash said. "I ought to minded it."

So we poured the water over it. His leg and foot below the cement looked like they had been boiled. "Does that feel better?" we said.

"I'm obliged," Cash said. "It feels fine."

Dewey Dell wipes his face with the hem of her dress.

"See if you can get some sleep," we say.

"Sho," Cash says. "I'm right obliged. It feels fine now."

Jewel, I say, Who was your father, Jewel?

Goddamn you. Goddamn you.

Vardaman

She was under the apple tree and Darl and I go across the moon and the cat jumps down and runs and we can hear her inside the wood.

"Hear?" Darl says. "Put your ear close."

I put my ear close and I can hear her. Only I cant tell what she is saying.

"What is she saying, Darl?" I say. "Who is she talking to?"

"She's talking to God," Darl says. "She is calling on Him to help her."

"What does she want Him to do?" I say.

"She wants Him to hide her away from the sight of man," Darl says.

"Why does she want to hide her away from the sight of man, Darl?"

"So she can lay down her life," Darl says.

"Why does she want to lay down her life, Darl?"

"Listen," Darl says. We hear her. We hear her turn over on her side. "Listen," Darl says.

"She's turned over," I say. "She's looking at me through the wood."

"Yes," Darl says.

"How can she see through the wood, Darl?"

"Come," Darl says. "We must let her be quiet. Come."

"She cant see out there, because the holes are in the top," I say. "How can she see, Darl?"

"Let's go see about Cash," Darl says.

And I saw something Dewey Dell told me not to tell nobody

Cash is sick in his leg. We fixed his leg this afternoon, but he is sick in it again, lying on the bed. We pour water on his leg and then he feels fine.

"I feel fine," Cash says. "I'm obliged to you."

"Try to get some sleep," we say.

"I feel fine," Cash says. "I'm obliged to you."

And I saw something Dewey Dell told me not to tell nobody. It is not about pa and it is not about Cash and it is not about Jewel and it is not about Dewey Dell and it is not about me

Dewey Dell and I are going to sleep on the pallet. It is on the back porch, where we can see the barn, and the moon shines on half of the pallet and we will lie half in the white and half in the black, with the moonlight on our legs. And then I am going to see where they stay at night while we are in the barn. We are not in the barn tonight but I can see the barn and so I am going to find where they stay at night.

We lie on the pallet, with our legs in the moon.

"Look," I say, "my legs look black. Your legs look black, too."

"Go to sleep," Dewey Dell says.

Jefferson is a far piece.

"Dewey Dell."

"What."

"If it's not Christmas now, how will it be there?"

It goes round and round on the shining track. Then the track goes shining round and round.

"Will what be there?"

"That train. In the window."

"You go to sleep. You can see tomorrow if it's there."

Maybe Santa Claus wont know they are town boys.

"Dewey Dell."

"You go to sleep. He aint going to let none of them town boys have it."

It was behind the window, red on the track, the track shining round and round. It made my heart hurt. And then it was pa and Jewel and Darl and Mr Gillespie's boy. Mr Gillespie's boy's legs come down under his nightshirt. When he goes into the moon, his legs fuzz. They go on around the house toward the apple tree.

"What are they going to do, Dewey Dell?"

They went around the house toward the apple tree.

"I can smell her," I say. "Can you smell her, too?"

"Hush," Dewey Dell says. "The wind's changed. Go to sleep."

And so I am going to know where they stay at night soon. They come around the house, going across the yard in the moon, carrying her on their shoulders. They carry her down to the barn, the moon shining flat and quiet on her. Then they come back and go into the house again. While they were in the moon, Mr Gillespie's boy's legs fuzzed. And then I waited and I said Dewey Dell? and then I waited and then I went to find where they stay at night and I saw something that Dewey Dell told me not to tell nobody.

Darl

Against the dark doorway he seems to materialise out of the darkness, lean as a race horse in his underclothes in the beginning of the glare. He leaps to the ground with on his face an expression of furious unbelief. He has seen me without even turning his head or his eyes in which the glare swims like two small torches. "Come on," he says, leaping down the slope toward the barn.

For an instant longer he runs silver in the moonlight, then he springs out like a flat figure cut leanly from tin against an abrupt and soundless explosion as the whole loft of the barn takes fire at once, as though it had been stuffed with powder. The front, the conical façade with the square orifice of doorway broken only by the square squat shape of the coffin on the sawhorses like a cubistic bug, comes into relief. Behind me pa and Gillespie and Mack and Dewey Dell and Vardaman emerge from the house.

He pauses at the coffin, stooping, looking at me, his face furious. Overhead the flames sound like thunder; across us rushes a cool draft: there is no heat in it at all yet, and a handful of chaff lifts suddenly and sucks swiftly along the stalls where a horse is screaming. "Quick," I say; "the horses."

He glares a moment longer at me, then at the roof overhead, then he leaps toward the stall where the horse screams. It plunges and kicks, the sound of the crashing blows sucking up into the sound of the flames. They sound like an interminable train crossing an endless trestle. Gillespie and Mack pass me, in knee-length nightshirts, shouting, their voices thin and high and meaningless and at the same time profoundly wild and sad: ". . . . . .cow. . . . . .stall. . . . . ." Gillespie's nightshirt rushes ahead of him on the draft, ballooning about his hairy thighs.

The stall door has swung shut. Jewel thrusts it back with his buttocks and he appears, his back arched, the muscles ridged through his garment as he drags the horse out by its head. In the glare its eyes roll with soft, fleet, wild opaline fire; its muscles bunch and run as it flings its head about, lifting Jewel clear of the ground. He drags it on, slowly, terrifically; again he gives me across his shoulder a single glare furious and brief. Even when they are clear of the barn the horse continues to fight and lash backward toward the doorway until Gillespie passes me, stark-naked, his nightshirt wrapped about the mule's head, and beats the maddened horse on out of the door.

Jewel returns, running; again he looks down at the coffin. But he comes on. "Where's cow?" he cries, passing me. I follow him. In the stall Mack is struggling with the other mule. When its head turns into the glare I can see the wild rolling of its eye too, but it makes no sound. It just stands there, watching Mack over its shoulder, swinging its hind quarters toward him whenever he approaches. He looks back at us, his eyes and mouth three round holes in his face on which the freckles look like english peas on a plate. His voice is thin, high, faraway.

"I cant do nothing. . . . . ." It is as though the sound had been swept from his lips and up and away, speaking back to us from an immense distance of exhaustion. Jewel slides past us; the mule whirls and lashes out, but he has already gained its head. I lean to Mack's ear:

"Nightshirt. Around his head."

Mack stares at me. Then he rips the nightshirt off and flings it over the mule's head, and it becomes docile at once. Jewel is yelling at him: "Cow? Cow?"

"Back," Mack cries. "Last stall."

The cow watches us as we enter. She is backed into the corner, head lowered, still chewing though rapidly. But she makes no move. Jewel has paused, looking up, and suddenly we watch the entire floor to the loft dissolve. It just turns to fire; a faint litter of sparks rains down. He glances about. Back under the trough is a three-legged milking stool. He catches it up and swings it into the planking of the rear wall. He splinters a plank, then another, a third; we tear the fragments away. While we are stooping at the opening something charges into us from behind. It is the cow; with a single whistling breath she rushes between us and through the gap and into the outer glare, her tail erect and rigid as a broom nailed upright to the end of her spine.

Jewel turns back into the barn. "Here," I say; "Jewel!" I grasp at him; he strikes my hand. "You fool," I say, "dont you see you cant make it back yonder?" The hallway looks like a searchlight turned into rain. "Come on," I say, "around this way."

When we are through the gap he begins to run. "Jewel," I say, running. He darts around the corner. When I reach it he has almost reached the next one, running against the glare like that figure cut from tin. Pa and Gillespie and Mack are some distance away, watching the barn, pink against the darkness where for the time the moonlight has been vanquished. "Catch him!" I cry; "stop him!"

When I reach the front, he is struggling with Gillespie; the one lean in underclothes, the other stark naked. They are like two figures in a Greek frieze, isolated out of all reality by the red glare. Before I can reach them he has struck Gillespie to the ground and turned and run back into the barn.

The sound of it has become quite peaceful now, like the sound of the river did. We watch through the dissolving proscenium of the doorway as Jewel runs crouching to the far end of the coffin and stoops to it. For an instant he looks up and out at us through the rain of burning hay like a portière of flaming beads, and I can see his mouth shape as he calls my name.

"Jewel!" Dewey Dell cries; "Jewel!" It seems to me that I now hear the accumulation of her voice through the last five minutes, and I hear her scuffling and struggling as pa and Mack hold her, screaming "Jewel! Jewel!" But he is no longer looking at us. We see his shoulders strain as he upends the coffin and slides it single-handed from the saw horses. It looms unbelievably tall, hiding him: I would not have believed that Addie Bundren would have needed that much room to lie comfortable in; for another instant it stands upright while the sparks rain on it in scattering bursts as though they engendered other sparks from the contact. Then it topples forward, gaining momentum, revealing Jewel and the sparks raining on him too in engendering gusts, so that he appears to be enclosed in a thin nimbus of fire. Without stopping it overends and rears again, pauses, then crashes slowly forward and through the curtain. This time Jewel is riding upon it, clinging to it, until it crashes down and flings him forward and clear and Mack leaps forward into the thin smell of scorching meat and slaps at the widening crimson-edged holes that bloom like flowers in his undershirt.

Vardaman

When I went to find where they stay at night, I saw something They said, "Where is Darl? Where did Darl go?"

They carried her back under the apple tree.

The barn was still red, but it wasn't a barn now. It was sunk down, and the red went swirling up. The barn went swirling up in little red pieces, against the sky and the stars so that the stars moved backward.

And then Cash was still awake. He turned his head from side to side, with sweat on his face.

"Do you want some more water on it, Cash?" Dewey Dell said.

Cash's leg and foot turned black. We held the lamp and looked at Cash's foot and leg where it was black.

"Your foot looks like a nigger's foot, Cash," I said.

"I reckon we'll have to bust it off," pa said.

"What in the tarnation you put it on there for," Mr Gillespie said.

"I thought it would steady it some," pa said. "I just aimed to help him."

They got the flat iron and the hammer. Dewey Dell held the lamp. They had to hit it hard. And then Cash went to sleep.

"He's asleep now," I said. "It cant hurt him while he's asleep."

It just cracked. It wouldn't come off.

"It'll take the hide, too," Mr Gillespie said. "Why in the tarnation you put it on there. Didn't none of you think to grease his leg first?"

"I just aimed to help him," pa said. "It was Darl put it on."

"Where is Darl?" they said.

"Didn't none of you have more sense that that?" Mr Gillespie said. "I'd a thought he would, anyway."

Jewel was lying on his face. His back was red. Dewey Dell put the medicine on it. The medicine was made out of butter and soot, to draw out the fire. Then his back was black.

"Does it hurt, Jewel?" I said. "Your back looks like a nigger's, Jewel," I said. Cash's foot and leg looked like a nigger's. Then they broke it off. Cash's leg bled.

"You go on back and lay down," Dewey Dell said. "You ought to be asleep."

"Where is Darl?" they said.

He is out there under the apple tree with her, lying on her. He is there so the cat wont come back. I said, "Are you going to keep the cat away, Darl?"

The moonlight dappled on him too. On her it was still, but on Darl it dappled up and down.

"You needn't to cry," I said. "Jewel got her out. You needn't to cry, Darl."

The barn is still red. It used to be redder than this. Then it went swirling, making the stars run backward without falling. It hurt my heart like the train did.

When I went to find where they stay at night, I saw something that Dewey Dell says I mustn't never tell nobody

Darl

We have been passing the signs for sometime now: the drug stores, the clothing stores, the patent medicine and the garages and cafés, and the mile-boards diminishing, becoming more starkly reaccruent: 3 mi. 2 mi. From the crest of a hill, as we get into the wagon again, we can see the smoke low and flat, seemingly unmoving in the unwinded afternoon.

"Is that it, Darl?" Vardaman says. "Is that Jefferson?" He too has lost flesh; like ours, his face has an expression strained, dreamy and gaunt.

"Yes," I say. He lifts his head and looks at the sky. High against it they hang in narrowing circles, like the smoke, with an outward semblance of form and purpose, but with no inference of motion, progress or retrograde. We mount the wagon again where Cash lies on the box, the jagged shards of cement cracked about his leg. The shabby mules droop rattling and clanking down the hill.

"We'll have to take him to the doctor," pa says. "I reckon it aint no way around it." The back of Jewel's shirt, where it touches him, stains slow and black with grease. Life was created in the valleys. It blew up onto the hills on the old terrors, the old lusts, the old despairs. That's why you must walk up the hills so you can ride down.

Dewey Dell sits on the seat, the newspaper package on her lap. When we reach the foot of the hill where the road flattens between close walls of trees, she begins to look about quietly from one side of the road to the other. At last she says,

"I got to stop."

Pa looks at her, his shabby profile that of anticipant and disgruntled annoyance. He does not check the team. "What for?"

"I got to go to the bushes," Dewey Dell says.

Pa does not check the team. "Cant you wait till we get to town? It aint over a mile now."

"Stop," Dewey Dell says. "I got to go to the bushes."

Pa stops in the middle of the road and we watch Dewey Dell descend, carrying the package. She does not look back.

"Why not leave your cakes here?" I say. "We'll watch them."

She descends steadily, not looking at us.

"How would she know where to go if she waited till we get to town?" Vardaman says. "Where would you go to do it in town, Dewey Dell?"

She lifts the package down and turns and disappears among the trees and undergrowth.

"Dont be no longer than you can help," pa says. "We aint got no time to waste." She does not answer. After a while we cannot hear her even. "We ought to done like Armstid and Gillespie said and sent word to town and had it dug and ready," he says.

"Why didn't you?" I say. "You could have telephoned."

"What for?" Jewel says. "Who the hell can't dig a hole in the ground?"

A car comes over the hill. It begins to sound the horn, slowing. It runs along the roadside in low gear, the outside wheels in the ditch, and passes us and goes on. Vardaman watches it until it is out of sight.

"How far is it now, Darl?" he says.

"Not far," I say.

"We ought to done it," pa says. "I just never wanted to be beholden to none except her flesh and blood."

"Who the hell cant dig a damn hole in the ground?" Jewel says.

"It aint respectful, talking that way about her grave," pa says. "You all dont know what it is. You never pure loved her, none of you." Jewel does not answer. He sits a little stiffly erect, his body arched away from his shirt. His high-colored jaw juts.

Dewey Dell returns. We watch her emerge from the bushes, carrying the package, and climb into the wagon. She now wears her Sunday dress, her beads, her shoes and stockings.

"I thought I told you to leave them clothes to home," pa says. She does not answer, does not look at us. She sets the package in the wagon and gets in. The wagon moves on.

"How many more hills now, Darl?" Vardaman says.

"Just one," I say. "The next one goes right up into town."

This hill is red sand, bordered on either hand by negro cabins; against the sky ahead the massed telephone lines run, and the clock on the courthouse lifts among the trees. In the sand the wheels whisper, as though the very earth would hush our entry. We descend as the hill commences to rise.

We follow the wagon, the whispering wheels, passing the cabins where faces come suddenly to the doors, white-eyed. We hear sudden voices, ejaculant. Jewel has been looking from side to side; now his head turns forward and I can see his ears taking on a still deeper tone of furious red. Three negroes walk beside the road ahead of us; ten feet ahead of them a white man walks. When we pass the negroes their heads turn suddenly with that expression of shock and instinctive outrage. "Great God," one says; "what they got in that wagon?"

Jewel whirls. "Son of a bitches," he says. As he does so he is abreast of the white man, who has paused. It is as though Jewel had gone blind for the moment, for it is the white man toward whom he whirls.

"Darl!" Cash says from the wagon. I grasp at Jewel. The white man has fallen back a pace, his face still slack-jawed; then his jaw tightens, claps to. Jewel leans above him, his jaw muscles gone white.

"What did you say?" he says.

"Here," I say. "He dont mean anything, mister. Jewel," I say. When I touch him he swings at the man. I grasp his arm; we struggle. Jewel has never looked at me. He is trying to free his arm. When I see the man again he has an open knife in his hand.

"Hold up, mister," I say; "I've got him, Jewel," I say.

"Thinks because he's a goddamn town fellow," Jewel says, panting, wrenching at me. "Son of a bitch," he says.

The man moves. He begins to edge around me, watching Jewel, the knife low against his flank. "Cant no man call me that," he says. Pa has got down, and Dewey Dell is holding Jewel, pushing at him. I release him and face the man.

"Wait," I say. "He dont mean nothing. He's sick; got burned in a fire last night, and he aint himself."

"Fire or no fire," the man says, "cant no man call me that."

"He thought you said something to him," I say.

"I never said nothing to him. I never seen him before."

"Fore God," pa says; "fore God."

"I know," I say. "He never meant anything. He'll take it back."

"Let him take it back, then."

"Put up your knife, and he will."

The man looks at me. He looks at Jewel. Jewel is quiet now.

"Put up your knife," I say.

The man shuts the knife.

"Fore God," pa says. "Fore God."

"Tell him you didn't mean anything, Jewel," I say.

"I thought he said something," Jewel says. "Just because he's——"

"Hush," I say. "Tell him you didn't mean it."

"I didn't mean it," Jewel says.

"He better not," the man says. "Calling me a——"

"Do you think he's afraid to call you that?" I say.

The man looks at me. "I never said that," he said.

"Dont think it, neither," Jewel says.

"Shut up," I say. "Come on. Drive on, pa."

The wagon moves. The man stands watching us. Jewel does not look back. "Jewel would a whipped him," Vardaman says.

We approach the crest, where the street runs, where cars go back and forth; the mules haul the wagon up and onto the crest and the street. Pa stops them. The street runs on ahead, where the square opens and the monument stands before the courthouse. We mount again while the heads turn with that expression which we know; save Jewel. He does not get on, even though the wagon has started again. "Get in, Jewel," I say. "Come on. Let's get away from here." But he does not get in. Instead he sets his foot on the turning hub of the rear wheel, one hand grasping the stanchion, and with the hub turning smoothly under his sole he lifts the other foot and squats there, staring straight ahead, motionless, lean, wooden-backed, as though carved squatting out of the lean wood.

Cash

It wasn't nothing else to do. It was either send him to Jackson, or have Gillespie sue us, because he knowed some way that Darl set fire to it. I dont know how he knowed, but he did. Vardaman seen him do it, but he swore he never told nobody but Dewey Dell and that she told him not to tell nobody. But Gillespie knowed it. But he would a suspicioned it sooner or later. He could have done it that night just watching the way Darl acted.

And so pa said, "I reckon there aint nothing else to do," and Jewel said, "You want to fix him now?"

"Fix him?" pa said.

"Catch him and tie him up," Jewel said. "Goddamn it, do you want to wait until he sets fire to the goddamn team and wagon?"

But there wasn't no use in that. "There aint no use in that," I said. "We can wait till she is underground." A fellow that's going to spend the rest of his life locked up, he ought to be let to have what pleasure he can have before he goes.

"I reckon he ought to be there," pa says. "God knows, it's a trial on me. Seems like it aint no end to bad luck when once it starts."

Sometimes I aint so sho who's got ere a right to say when a man is crazy and when he aint. Sometimes I think it aint none of us pure crazy and aint none of us pure sane until the balance of us talks him that-a-way. It's like it aint so much what a fellow does, but it's the way the majority of folks is looking at him when he does it.

Because Jewel is too hard on him. Of course it was Jewel's horse was traded to get her that nigh to town, and in a sense it was the value of his horse Darl tried to burn up. But I thought more than once before we crossed the river and after, how it would be God's blessing if He did take her outen our hands and get shut of her in some clean way, and it seemed to me that when Jewel worked so to get her outen the river, he was going against God in a way, and then when Darl seen that it looked like one of us would have to do something, I can almost believe he done right in a way. But I dont reckon nothing excuses setting fire to a man's barn and endangering his stock and destroying his property. That's how I reckon a man is crazy. That's how he cant see eye to eye with other folks. And I reckon they aint nothing else to do with him but what the most folks says is right.

But it's a shame, in a way. Folks seems to get away from the olden right teaching that says to drive the nails down and trim the edges well always like it was for your own use and comfort you were making it. It's like some folks has the smooth, pretty boards to build a courthouse with and others dont have no more than rough lumber fitten to build a chicken coop. But it's better to build a tight chicken coop than a shoddy courthouse, and when they both build shoddy or build well, neither because it's one or tother is going to make a man feel the better nor the worse.

So we went up the street, toward the square, and he said, "We better take Cash to the doctor first. We can leave him there and come back for him." That's it. It's because me and him was born close together, and it nigh ten years before Jewel and Dewey Dell and Vardaman begun to come along. I feel kin to them, all right, but I dont know. And me being the oldest, and thinking already the very thing that he done: I dont know.

Pa was looking at me, then at him, mumbling his mouth.

"Go on," I said. "We'll get it done first."

"She would want us all there," pa says.

"Let's take Cash to the doctor first," Darl said. "She'll wait. She's already waited nine days."

"You all dont know," pa says. "The somebody you was young with and you growed old in her and she growed old in you, seeing the old coming on and it was the one somebody you could hear say it dont matter and know it was the truth outen the hard world and all a man's grief and trials. You all dont know."

"We got the digging to do, too," I said.

"Armstid and Gillespie both told you to send word ahead," Darl said. "Dont you want to go to Peabody's now, Cash?"

"Go on," I said. "It feels right easy now. It's best to get things done in the right place."

"If it was just dug," pa says. "We forgot our spade, too."

"Yes," Darl said. "I'll go to the hardware store. We'll have to buy one."

"It'll cost money," pa says.

"Do you begrudge her it?" Darl says.

"Go on and get a spade," Jewel said. "Here. Give me the money."

But pa didn't stop. "I reckon we can get a spade," he said. "I reckon there are Christians here." So Darl set still and we went on, with Jewel squatting on the tail-gate, watching the back of Darl's head. He looked like one of these bull dogs, one of these dogs that dont bark none, squatting against the rope, watching the thing he was waiting to jump at.

He set that way all the time we was in front of Mrs Bundren's house, hearing the music, watching the back of Darl's head with them hard white eyes of hisn.

The music was playing in the house. It was one of them graphophones. It was natural as a music-band.

"Do you want to go to Peabody's?" Darl said. "They can wait here and tell pa, and I'll drive you to Peabody's and come back for them."

"No," I said. It was better to get her underground, now we was this close, just waiting until pa borrowed the shovel. He drove along the street until we could hear the music.

"Maybe they got one here," he said. He pulled up at Mrs Bundren's. It was like he knowed. Sometimes I think that if a working man could see work as far ahead as a lazy man can see laziness. So he stopped there like he knowed, before that little new house, where the music was. We waited there, hearing it. I believe I could have dickered Suratt down to five dollars on that one of his. It's a comfortable thing, music is. "Maybe they got one here," pa says.

"You want Jewel to go," Darl says, "or do you reckon I better?"

"I reckon I better," pa says. He got down and went up the path and around the house to the back. The music stopped, then it started again.

"He'll get it, too," Darl said.

"Ay," I said. It was just like he knowed, like he could see through the walls and into the next ten minutes.

Only it was more than ten minutes. The music stopped and never commenced again for a good spell, where her and pa was talking at the back. We waited in the wagon.

"You let me take you back to Peabody's," Darl said.

"No," I said. "We'll get her underground."

"If he ever gets back," Jewel said. He begun to cuss. He started to get down from the wagon. "I'm going," he said.

Then we saw pa coming back. He had two spades, coming around the house. He laid them in the wagon and got in and we went on. The music never started again. Pa was looking back at the house. He kind of lifted his hand a little and I saw the shade pulled back a little at the window and her face in it.

But the curiousest thing was Dewey Dell. It surprised me. I see all the while how folks could say he was queer, but that was the very reason couldn't nobody hold it personal. It was like he was outside of it too, same as you, and getting mad at it would be kind of like getting mad at a mud-puddle that splashed you when you stepped in it. And then I always kind of had a idea that him and Dewey Dell kind of knowed things betwixt them. If I'd a said it was ere a one of us she liked better than ere a other, I'd a said it was Darl. But when we got it filled and covered and drove out the gate and turned into the lane where them fellows was waiting, when they come out and come on him and he jerked back, it was Dewey Dell that was on him before even Jewel could get at him. And then I believed I knowed how Gillespie knowed about how his barn taken fire.

She hadn't said a word, hadn't even looked at him, but when them fellows told him what they wanted and that they had come to get him and he throwed back, she jumped on him like a wild cat so that one of the fellows had to quit and hold her and her scratching and clawing at him like a wild cat, while the other one and pa and Jewel throwed Darl down and held him lying on his back, looking up at me.

"I thought you would have told me," he said. "I never thought you wouldn't have."

"Darl," I said. But he fought again, him and Jewel and the fellow, and the other one holding Dewey Dell and Vardaman yelling and Jewel saying,

"Kill him. Kill the son of a bitch."

It was bad so. It was bad. A fellow cant get away from a shoddy job. He cant do it. I tried to tell him, but he just said, "I thought you'd a told me. It's not that I," he said, then he begun to laugh. The other fellow pulled Jewel off of him and he sat there on the ground, laughing.

I tried to tell him. If I could have just moved, even set up. But I tried to tell him and he quit laughing, looking up at me.

"Do you want me to go?" he said.

"It'll be better for you," I said. "Down there it'll be quiet, with none of the bothering and such. It'll be better for you, Darl," I said.

"Better," he said. He begun to laugh again. "Better," he said. He couldn't hardly say it for laughing. He sat on the ground and us watching him, laughing and laughing. It was bad. It was bad so. I be durn if I could see anything to laugh at. Because there just aint nothing justifies the deliberate destruction of what a man has built with his own sweat and stored the fruit of his sweat into.

But I aint so sho that ere a man has the right to say what is crazy and what aint. It's like there was a fellow in every man that's done a-past the sanity or the insanity, that watches the sane and the insane doings of that man with the same horror and the same astonishment.

Peabody

I said, "I reckon a man in a tight might let Bill Varner patch him up like a damn mule, but I be damned if the man that'd let Anse Bundren treat him with raw cement aint got more spare legs than I have."

"They just aimed to ease hit some," he said.

"Aimed, hell," I said. "What in hell did Armstid mean by even letting them put you on that wagon again?"

"Hit was gittin right noticeable," he said. "We never had time to wait." I just looked at him. "Hit never bothered me none," he said.

"Dont you lie there and try to tell me you rode six days on a wagon without springs, with a broken leg and it never bothered you."

"It never bothered me much," he said.

"You mean, it never bothered Anse much," I said. "No more than it bothered him to throw that poor devil down in the public street and hand-cuff him like a damn murderer. Dont tell me. And dont tell me it aint going to bother you to lose sixty-odd square inches of skin to get that concrete off. And dont tell me it aint going to bother you to have to limp around on one short leg for the balance of your life—if you walk at all again. Concrete," I said. "God Amighty, why didn't Anse carry you to the nearest sawmill and stick your leg in the saw? That would have cured it. Then you all could have stuck his head into the saw and cured a whole family. . . . . . Where is Anse, anyway? What's he up to now?"

"He's takin back them spades he borrowed," he said.

"That's right," I said. "Of course he'd have to borrow a spade to bury his wife with. Unless he could borrow a hole in the ground. Too bad you all didn't put him in it too. . . . . . Does that hurt?"

"Not to speak of," he said, and the sweat big as marbles running down his face and his face about the color of blotting paper.

"Course not," I said. "About next summer you can hobble around fine on this leg. Then it wont bother you, not to speak of. . . . . . If you had anything you could call luck, you might say it was lucky this is the same leg you broke before," I said.

"Hit's what paw says," he said.

MacGowan

It happened I am back of the prescription case, pouring up some chocolate sauce, when Jody comes back and says, "Say, Skeet, there's a woman up front that wants to see the doctor and when I said What doctor you want to see, she said she wants to see the doctor that works here and when I said There aint any doctor works here, she just stood there, looking back this way."

"What kind of a woman is it?" I says. "Tell her to go upstairs to Alford's office."

"Country woman," he says.

"Send her to the courthouse," I says. "Tell her all the doctors have gone to Memphis to a Barbers' Convention."

"All right," he says, going away. "She looks pretty good for a country girl," he says.

"Wait," I says. He waited and I went and peeped through the crack. But I couldn't tell nothing except she had a good leg against the light. "Is she young, you say?" I says.

"She looks like a pretty hot mamma, for a country girl," he says.

"Take this," I says, giving him the chocolate. I took off my apron and went up there. She looked pretty good. One of them black eyed ones that look like she'd as soon put a knife in you as not if you two-timed her. She looked pretty good. There wasn't nobody else in the store; it was dinner time.

"What can I do for you?" I says.

"Are you the doctor?" she says.

"Sure," I says. She quit looking at me and was kind of looking around.

"Can we go back yonder?" she says.

It was just a quarter past twelve, but I went and told Jody to kind of watch out and whistle if the old man come in sight, because he never got back before one.

"You better lay off of that," Jody says. "He'll fire your stern out of here so quick you cant wink."

"He dont never get back before one," I says. "You can see him go into the postoffice. You keep your eye peeled, now, and give me a whistle."

"What you going to do?" he says.

"You keep your eye out. I'll tell you later."

"Aint you going to give me no seconds on it?" he says.

"What the hell do you think this is?" I says; "a stud-farm? You watch out for him. I'm going into conference."

So I go on to the back. I stopped at the glass and smoothed my hair, then I went behind the prescription case, where she was waiting. She is looking at the medicine cabinet, then she looks at me.

"Now, madam," I says; "what is your trouble?"

"It's the female trouble," she says, watching me. "I got the money," she says.

"Ah," I says. "Have you got female troubles or do you want female troubles? If so, you come to the right doctor." Them country people. Half the time they dont know what they want, and the balance of the time they cant tell it to you. The clock said twenty past twelve.

"No," she says.

"No which?" I says.

"I aint had it," she says. "That's it." She looked at me. "I got the money," she says.

So I knew what she was talking about.

"Oh," I says. "You got something in your belly you wish you didn't have." She looks at me. "You wish you had a little more or a little less, huh?"

"I got the money," she says. "He said I could git something at the drugstore for hit."

"Who said so?" I says.

"He did," she says, looking at me.

"You dont want to call no names," I says. "The one that put the acorn in your belly? He the one that told you?" She dont say nothing. "You aint married, are you?" I says. I never saw no ring. But like as not, they aint heard yet out there that they use rings.

"I got the money," she says. She showed it to me, tied up in her handkerchief: a ten spot.

"I'll swear you have," I says. "He give it to you?"

"Yes," she says.

"Which one?" I says. She looks at me. "Which one of them give it to you?"

"It aint but one," she says. She looks at me.

"Go on," I says. She dont say nothing. The trouble about the cellar is, it aint but one way out and that's back up the inside stairs. The clock says twenty-five to one. "A pretty girl like you," I says.

She looks at me. She begins to tie the money back up in the handkerchief. "Excuse me a minute," I says. I go around the prescription case. "Did you hear about that fellow sprained his ear?" I says. "After that he couldn't even hear a belch."

"You better get her out from back there before the old man comes," Jody says.

"If you'll stay up there in front where he pays you to stay, he wont catch nobody but me," I says.

He goes on, slow, toward the front. "What you doing to her, Skeet?" he says.

"I cant tell you," I says. "It wouldn't be ethical. You go on up there and watch."

"Say, Skeet," he says.

"Ah, go on," I says. "I aint doing nothing but filling a prescription."

"He may not do nothing about that woman back there, but if he finds you monkeying with that prescription case, he'll kick your stern clean down them cellar stairs."

"My stern has been kicked by bigger bastards than him," I says. "Go back and watch out for him, now."

So I come back. The clock said fifteen to one. She is tying the money in the handkerchief. "You aint the doctor," she says.

"Sure I am," I says. She watches me. "Is it because I look too young, or am I too handsome?" I says. "We used to have a bunch of old water-jointed doctors here," I says; "Jefferson used to be a kind of Old Doctors' Home for them. But business started falling off and folks stayed so well until one day they found out that the women wouldn't never get sick at all. So they run all the old doctors out and got us young good-looking ones that the women would like and then the women begun to get sick again and so business picked up. They're doing that all over the country. Hadn't you heard about it? Maybe it's because you aint never needed a doctor."

"I need one now," she says.

"And you come to the right one," I says. "I already told you that."

"Have you got something for it?" she says. "I got the money."

"Well," I says, "of course a doctor has to learn all sorts of things while he's learning to roll calomel; he cant help himself. But I dont know about your trouble."

"He told me I could get something. He told me I could get it at the drugstore."

"Did he tell you the name of it?" I says. "You better go back and ask him."

She quit looking at me, kind of turning the handkerchief in her hands. "I got to do something," she says.

"How bad do you want to do something?" I says. She looks at me. "Of course, a doctor learns all sorts of things folks dont think he knows. But he aint supposed to tell all he knows. It's against the law."

Up front Jody says, "Skeet."

"Excuse me a minute," I says. I went up front. "Do you see him?" I says.

"Aint you done yet?" he says. "Maybe you better come up here and watch and let me do that consulting."

"Maybe you'll lay a egg," I says. I come back. She is looking at me. "Of course you realise that I could be put in the penitentiary for doing what you want," I says. "I would lose my license and then I'd have to go to work. You realise that?"

"I aint got but ten dollars," she says. "I could bring the rest next month, maybe."

"Pooh," I says, "ten dollars? You see, I cant put no price on my knowledge and skill. Certainly not for no little paltry sawbuck."

She looks at me. She dont even blink. "What you want, then?"

The clock said four to one. So I decided I better get her out. "You guess three times and then I'll show you," I says.

She dont even blink her eyes. "I got to do something," she says. She looks behind her and around, then she looks toward the front. "Gimme the medicine first," she says.

"You mean, you're ready to right now?" I says. "Here?"

"Gimme the medicine first," she says.

So I took a graduated glass and kind of turned my back to her and picked out a bottle that looked all right, because a man that would keep poison setting around in a unlabelled bottle ought to be in jail, anyway. It smelled like turpentine. I poured some into the glass and give it to her. She smelled it, looking at me across the glass.

"Hit smells like turpentine," she says.

"Sure," I says. "That's just the beginning of the treatment. You come back at ten oclock tonight and I'll give you the rest of it and perform the operation."

"Operation?" she says.

"It wont hurt you. You've had the same operation before. Ever hear about the hair of the dog?"

She looks at me. "Will it work?" she says.

"Sure it'll work. If you come back and get it."

So she drunk whatever it was without batting a eye, and went out. I went up front.

"Didn't you get it?" Jody says.

"Get what?" I says.

"Ah, come on," he says. "I aint going to try to beat your time."

"Oh, her," I says. "She just wanted a little medicine. She's got a bad case of dysentery and she's a little ashamed about mentioning it with a stranger there."

It was my night, anyway, so I helped the old bastard check up and I got his hat on him and got him out of the store by eight-thirty. I went as far as the corner with him and watched him until he passed under two street lamps and went on out of sight. Then I come back to the store and waited until nine-thirty and turned out the front lights and locked the door and left just one light burning at the back, and I went back and put some talcum powder into six capsules and kind of cleared up the cellar and then I was all ready.

She come in just at ten, before the clock had done striking. I let her in and she come in, walking fast. I looked out the door, but there wasn't nobody but a boy in overalls sitting on the curb. "You want something?" I says. He never said nothing, just looking at me. I locked the door and turned off the light and went on back. She was waiting. She didn't look at me now.

"Where is it?" she said.

I gave her the box of capsules. She held the box in her hand, looking at the capsules.

"Are you sure it'll work?" she says.

"Sure," I says. "When you take the rest of the treatment."

"Where do I take it?" she says.

"Down in the cellar," I says.

Vardaman

Now it is wider and lighter, but the stores are dark because they have all gone home. The stores are dark, but the lights pass on the windows when we pass. The lights are in the trees around the courthouse. They roost in the trees, but the courthouse is dark. The clock on it looks four ways, because it is not dark. The moon is not dark too. Not very dark. *Darl he went to Jackson is my brother Darl is my brother*   Only it was over that way, shining on the track.

"Let's go that way, Dewey Dell," I say.

"What for?" Dewey Dell says. The track went shining around the window, it red on the track. But she said he would not sell it to the town boys. "But it will be there Christmas," Dewey Dell says. "You'll have to wait till then, when he brings it back."

Darl went to Jackson. Lots of people didn't go to Jackson. Darl is my brother. My brother is going to Jackson

While we walk the lights go around, roosting in the trees. On all sides it is the same. They go around the courthouse and then you cannot see them. But you can see them in the black windows beyond. They have all gone home to bed except me and Dewey Dell.

Going on the train to Jackson. My brother

There is a light in the store, far back. In the window are two big glasses of soda water, red and green. Two men could not drink them. Two mules could not. Two cows could not. *Darl*

A man comes to the door. He looks at Dewey Dell.

"You wait out here," Dewey Dell says.

"Why cant I come in?" I say. "I want to come in, too."

"You wait out here," she says.

"All right," I say.

Dewey Dell goes in.

Darl is my brother. Darl went crazy

The walk is harder than sitting on the ground. He is in the open door.

He looks at me. "You want something?" he says. His head is slick. Jewel's head is slick sometimes. Cash's head is not slick. *Darl he went to Jackson my brother Darl* In the street he ate a banana. *Wouldn't you rather have bananas? Dewey Dell said. You wait till Christmas. It'll be there then. Then you can see it. So we are going to have some bananas. We are going to have a bag full, me and Dewey Dell.* He locks the door. Dewey Dell is inside. Then the light winks out.

He went to Jackson. He went crazy and went to Jackson both. Lots of people didn't go crazy. Pa and Cash and Jewel and Dewey Dell and me didn't go crazy. We never did go crazy. We didn't go to Jackson either. Darl

I hear the cow a long time, clopping   on the street. Then she comes into the square. She goes across the square, her head down   clopping   . She lows. There was nothing in the square before she lowed, but it wasn't empty. Now it is empty after she lowed. She goes on,   clopping   . She lows. *My brother is Darl. He went to Jackson on the train. He didn't go on the train to go crazy. He went crazy in our wagon. Darl* She has been in there a long time. And the cow is gone too. A long time. She has been in there longer than the cow was. But not as long as empty. *Darl is my brother. My brother Darl*

Dewey Dell comes out. She looks at me.

"Let's go around that way now," I say.

She looks at me. "It aint going to work," she says. "That son of a bitch."

"What aint going to work, Dewey Dell?"

"I just know it wont," she says. She is not looking at anything. "I just know it."

"Let's go that way," I say.

"We got to go back to the hotel. It's late. We got to slip back in."

"Cant we go by and see, anyway?"

"Hadn't you rather have bananas? Hadn't you rather?"

"All right." *My brother he went crazy and he went to Jackson too. Jackson is further away than crazy*

"It wont work," Dewey Dell says. "I just know it wont."

"What wont work?" I say. *He had to get on the train to go to Jackson. I have not been on the train, but Darl has been on the train. Darl. Darl is my brother. Darl. Darl*

Darl

Darl has gone to Jackson. They put him on the train, laughing, down the long car laughing, the heads turning like the heads of owls when he passed. "What are you laughing at?" I said.

"Yes yes yes yes yes."

Two men put him on the train. They wore mismatched coats, bulging behind over their right hip pockets. Their necks were shaved to a hairline, as though the recent and simultaneous barbers had had a chalk-line like Cash's. "Is it the pistols you're laughing at?" I said. "Why do you laugh?" I said. "Is it because you hate the sound of laughing?"

They pulled two seats together so Darl could sit by the window to laugh. One of them sat beside him, the other sat on the seat facing him, riding backward. One of them had to ride backward because the state's money has a face to each backside and a backside to each face, and they are riding on the state's money which is incest. A nickel has a woman on one side and a buffalo on the other; two faces and no back.[9] I dont know what that is. Darl had a little spy-glass he got in France at the war. In it it had a woman and a pig with two backs and no face. I know what that is. "Is that why you are laughing, Darl?"

"Yes yes yes yes yes yes."

The wagon stands on the square, hitched, the mules motionless, the reins wrapped about the seat-spring, the back of the wagon toward the court-house. It looks no different from a hundred other wagons there; Jewel standing beside it and looking up the street like any other man in town that day, yet there is something different, distinctive. There is about it that unmistakable air of definite and imminent departure that trains have, perhaps due to the fact that Dewey Dell and Vardaman on the seat and Cash on a pallet in the wagon bed are eating bananas from a paper bag. "Is that why you are laughing, Darl?"

Darl is our brother, our brother Darl. Our brother Darl in a cage in Jackson where, his grimed hands lying light in the quiet interstices, looking out he foams.

"Yes yes yes yes yes yes yes yes."

Dewey Dell

When he saw the money I said, "It's not my money, it doesn't belong to me."

"Whose is it, then?"

"It's Cora Tull's money. It's Mrs Tull's. I sold the cakes for it."

"Ten dollars for two cakes?"

"Dont you touch it. It's not mine."

"You never had them cakes. It's a lie. It was them Sunday clothes you had in that package."

"Dont you touch it! If you take it you are a thief."

"My own daughter accuses me of being a thief. My own daughter."

"Pa. Pa."

"I have fed you and sheltered you. I give you love and care, yet my own daughter, the daughter of my dead wife, calls me a thief over her mother's grave."

"It's not mine, I tell you. If it was, God knows you could have it."

"Where did you get ten dollars?"

"Pa. Pa."

"You wont tell me. Did you come by it so shameful you dare not?"

"It's not mine, I tell you. Cant you understand it's not mine?"

"It's not like I wouldn't pay it back. But she calls her own father a thief."

"I cant, I tell you. I tell you it's not my money. God knows you could have it."

"I wouldn't take it. My own born daughter that has et my food for seventeen years, begrudges me the loan of ten dollars."

"It's not mine. I cant."

9. The buffalo or Indian head nickel, 1913–1938, has an Indian brave's head in profile, not a woman's; the Liberty nickel, 1833–1913, which overlapped with the Indian head, had a woman's (Liberty's) head on one side but a V in a wreath, not a buffalo, on the other. In any case, the buffalo is in profile and his back or hump is as much in evidence as is his head.

"Whose is it, then?"

"It was give to me. To buy something with."

"To buy what with?"

"Pa. Pa."

"It's just a loan. God knows, I hate for my blooden children to reproach me. But I give them what was mine without stint. Cheerful I give them, without stint. And now they deny me. Addie. It was lucky for you you died, Addie."

"Pa. Pa."

"God knows it is."

He took the money and went out.

Cash

So when we stopped there to borrow the shovels we heard the graphophone playing in the house, and so when we got done with the shovels pa says, "I reckon I better take them back."

So we went back to the house. "We better take Cash on to Peabody's," Jewel said.

"It wont take but a minute," pa said. He got down from the wagon. The music was not playing now.

"Let Vardaman do it," Jewel said. "He can do it in half the time you can. Or here, you let me——"

"I reckon I better do it," pa says. "Long as it was me that borrowed them."

So we set in the wagon, but the music wasn't playing now. I reckon it's a good thing we aint got ere a one of them. I reckon I wouldn't never get no work done a-tall for listening to it. I dont know if a little music aint about the nicest thing a fellow can have. Seems like when he comes in tired of a night, it aint nothing could rest him like having a little music played and him resting. I have seen them that shuts up like a hand-grip, with a handle and all, so a fellow can carry it with him wherever he wants.

"What you reckon he's doing?" Jewel says. "I could a toted them shovels back and forth ten times by now."

"Let him take his time," I said. "He aint as spry as you, remember."

"Why didn't he let me take them back, then? We got to get your leg fixed up so we can start home tomorrow."

"We got plenty of time," I said. "I wonder what them machines cost on the installment."

"Installment of what?" Jewel said. "What you got to buy it with?"

"A fellow cant tell," I said. "I could a bought that one from Suratt for five dollars, I believe."

And so pa come back and we went to Peabody's. While we was there pa said he was going to the barbershop and get a shave. And so that night he said he had some business to tend to, kind of looking away from us while he said it, with his hair combed wet and slick and smelling sweet with perfume, but I said leave him be; I wouldn't mind hearing a little more of that music myself.

And so next morning he was gone again, then he come back and told us to get hitched up and ready to take out and he would meet us and when they was gone he said,

"I dont reckon you got no more money."

"Peabody just give me enough to pay the hotel with," I said. "We dont need nothing else, do we?"

"No," pa said; "no. We dont need nothing." He stood there, not looking at me.

"If it is something we got to have, I reckon maybe Peabody," I said.

"No," he said; "it aint nothing else. You all wait for me at the corner."

So Jewel got the team and come for me and they fixed me a pallet in the wagon and we drove across the square to the corner where pa said, and we was waiting there in the wagon, with Dewey Dell and Vardaman eating bananas, when we see them coming up the street. Pa was coming along with that kind of daresome and hangdog look all at once like when he has been up to something he knows ma aint going to like, carrying a grip in his hand, and Jewel says,

"Who's that?"

Then we see it wasn't the grip that made him look different; it was his face, and Jewel says, "He got them teeth."

It was a fact. It made him look a foot taller, kind of holding his head up, hangdog and proud too, and then we see her behind him, carrying the other grip—a kind of duck-shaped woman all dressed up, with them kind of hard-looking pop eyes like she was daring ere a man to say nothing. And there we set watching them, with Dewey Dell's and Vardaman's mouth half open and half-et bananas in their hands and her coming around from behind pa, looking at us like she dared ere a man. And then I see that the grip she was carrying was one of them little graphophones. It was for a fact, all shut up as pretty as a picture, and everytime a new record would come from the mail order and us setting in the house in the winter, listening to it, I would think what a shame Darl couldn't be to enjoy it too. But it is better so for him. This world is not his world; this life his life.

"It's Cash and Jewel and Vardaman and Dewey Dell," pa says, kind of hangdog and proud too, with his teeth and all, even if he wouldn't look at us. "Meet Mrs Bundren," he says.

1930

AFTERWORD

Reading a traditional narrative, we expect to begin more or less at the beginning, to have the action move forward more or less regularly, or to have time changes signaled to us by words like "later," or "six years passed," or even, perhaps, to be warned that though the reading time was going forward the narrative time was not: "meanwhile, back at the ranch." We expect to stay within the mind or vision of one character either in the first-person or the third, or to be accompanied by a narrator who can guide us in and out of character's minds or fields of vision.

As I Lay Dying begins at the beginning. The first word we read is "Darl," in big bold letters, and we soon recognize that we are in the mind of a character with that rather strange name or nickname (for Darrell, presumably). So far, so good. But in a few hundred words—a minute or two of reading time—there's a blank space, and then, in big, bold letters, "Cora," and without benefit of a narrator to tell us who Darl was or who Cora is, we are listening to someone—Cora, no doubt—talking, though her words are not in quotation marks and she's answered by someone named Kate—called Kate four times in a row, as a matter of fact, and never referred to by a pronoun (Cora is always "I"). At first what Cora is saying seems to have nothing to do with Darl's thoughts or his walking with Jewel or his going into some house or other, as he did at the end of the part called "Darl." He has referred to someone named Cash making a box and has referred to someone named Addie Bundren who "could not want a better one." It does not take the reader long to figure out that Cash is making a coffin and Addie Bundren is the one who is lying dying, what with the title and all.

Then, after Cora and Kate are talking about eggs and making cakes and some rich lady who had seemed to want them refusing to take them, the next paragraph begins,

> The quilt is drawn up to her chin, hot as it is, with only her two hands and her face outside. She is propped on the pillow, with her head raised so she can see out the window, and we can hear him every time he takes up the adze or the saw.

We know the "he" must be Cash, who, Darl has told us, has been working with an adze, but the only grammatical antecedent for "she" is Kate, for, as we noted, Cora is always "I," and, so far as we know, Kate is the only other person in the room. Not so. We figure it out sooner or later, if not by the time we read the second sentence quoted above, then at least by the time we read the second sentence that follows: "Her face is wasted away so that the bones draw just under the skin in white lines." A couple of paragraphs later Kate asks, "Is she sleeping?" so we know for sure "she" is not Kate, and given the description of her wasted form and all, we infer that it is Addie. But, note, we infer; Faulkner does not tell us—we have to figure it out for ourselves. Now we are made aware that there's at least one other person in the room—"that girl standing right over her [Addie], fanning her with the fan." But a couple of sentences later "that girl" says something, and someone named Eula "turns on the trunk and looks out the window." Is "that girl" Eula? No one tells us, but we should be able to figure it out, because "that girl" is standing over Addie and Eula seems to be sitting on a trunk. Once again, however, the key point is that we figure it out; there is no author or narrator to tell us for sure.

A few sentences later, "Someone comes through the hall. It is Darl." We can assume, then, that this is the house Darl was entering at the end of his brief section, and that the time is almost immediately after the action—if we can call it that—of that first "Darl" section.

So time and sequence, setting and situation, the presence and nature of the characters—we pretty much have to figure all these out by ourselves, even though we are privy first to Darl's thoughts and then to Cora's within the first thousand words or so.

This is how we are drawn into the novel, almost as if we were the proverbial fly on the wall (except that we can sometimes see inside someone's head). We have to do so much inferring that it is as if we are virtually writing—or at least helping to write—the novel ourselves. These gaps and implications help get us involved in the story then, put us on a plane with the characters, and, perhaps as important, make us *pay close attention.*

From the very beginning, however, we may suspect that the ghost of the author is lurking between the walls or somewhere. Of course, we know that we didn't write the novel, nor is it just happening in front of our eyes or on the other side of the page. It takes less perspicacity than does inferring sequence, setting, and situation, to know that this is a novel by William Faulkner—even if we have never read a word of Faulkner before: after all, doesn't it say so on the cover and in the table of contents and at the head of the story? Now, we don't want to be snobbish or prejudiced or anything like that, but can we imagine anyone like Darl saying that the circle around the cottonhouse was "worn so by feet in fading precision"? Or that Jewel "crosses the floor in four strides with the rigid gravity of a cigar store Indian dressed in patched overalls and endued with life from the hips down . . ."? ("Endued," indeed.) What's going on here? Is Darl, despite some of our prejudices or assumptions, somehow capable of that language? Is the language out of control, running away with Faulkner, who is intoxicated with the sound of his own words? Is this just still another device to make us pay attention? This "double-voiced" language, this character's voice imbued with a second voice, that of the author, takes us deeper into the nature of this narrative than we can explore staying within the first few pages.

The story that comes to us from about fifteen different voices, one of them speaking as many as seventeen times, some only once, involves the death of Addie Bundren, mother of Cash, Darl, Jewel, Dewey Dell, and Vardaman, and wife of Anse, who has promised her that when she dies he will take her body to Jefferson to be buried. There is a delay, a flood, bridges washed out, and various other impediments and disasters, as the family persists in taking the corpse, latterly shadowed by vultures and putrefying in the July heat, to Jefferson for burial. Cash rebreaks a leg; Dewey Dell, pregnant, tries in Jefferson to get a drug to abort the baby; Darl finally is committed to an asylum—i.e., mental hospital—and a good deal of the history and character of the family and of the individual members comes out, including the fact that Addie had had an affair with the preacher, Whitfield. Most of this we piece together from the conversations and internal monologues or thoughts or reports of some sort that make up the "chapters." The characters do not speak to us or pamper our ignorance but run the disconnected details through their heads or out of their mouths in speech as they would were there no reader reading. Still, the characters' thoughts read more like reports to party or parties unknown; for example, on p. 442, Darl says or thinks,

> We have been passing signs for sometime now: the drug stores, the clothing stores, the patent medicine and the garages and cafés, and the mile-boards diminishing, becoming more starkly reaccruent: 3 mi. 2 mi. From the crest of a hill, as we get into the wagon again, we can see the smoke low and flat, seemingly unmoving in the unwinded afternoon.

It is not exactly what he is thinking, not exactly what he would say aloud; it is more like a report of some sort.

Just before this Darl section, little Vardaman has "reported": *"When I went to find where they stay at night, I saw something that Dewey Dell says I mustn't never tell nobody"* The Vardaman section or chapter then ends, without so much as a period, and we do not know exactly what it is that he saw. We infer that it must be fairly important, however, for not only is it in the climactic position at the end of the section, but he had "reported" even earlier that he ". . . saw something Dewey Dell told me not to tell nobody." (p. 439). Finally, several pages later, Cash reports,

> It wasn't nothing else to do. It was either send him to Jackson, or have Gillespie sue us, because he knowed some way that Darl set fire to it [the barn]. I dont know how he knowed, but he did. Vardaman seen him do it, but he swore he never told nobody but Dewey Dell and that she told him not to tell nobody.

While that one mystery is solved, we now have to figure out what Cash means by sending "him" (there's no antecedent) to Jackson.

With patience and close attention, we have no serious difficulty in figuring out the main line of the action, the basic nature of the characters, and much of the history and context. Depending on our home and upbringing, perhaps our age and reading experience, we will get more or fewer of the specific details—of exactly how they crossed the river, for example, or why Gillespie is stark naked when he leads the mule out of the burning barn (mules and horses will run right into a fire or will freeze; Gillespie—and then Mack—puts his nightshirt over the mule's head and eyes to keep him from panicking). This active, involved reading does more than mystify, interest, or even involve; it also affects or helps constitute the nature of the narrative. That is, though the story moves chronologically forward in more or less a straight line (there is one section in which Addie, who is already dead, reports, apparently out of time sequence) and in the same direction as our reading, this presenting of details, whose significance will become clear only later, makes us hold these unexplained items in our minds and hark back to them when the explanation does at last come. This has the effect of making our reading "vertical" rather than "horizontal" (some would say "spatial" rather than "temporal"), putting separated hunks of the story together at a specific moment of reading time. So just as Darl enters a house and disappears in the first section and then enters the house "later," when we are reading the Cora section (both entrances are the same and so we know no time has passed in the narrative though it has in our reading), so we keep collapsing episodes throughout the novel. Further, we reconstruct the history of the family in much the same way: it is offered to us piece by mysterious piece and *we* are the ones who put it together, not just having the thrill of creation or re-creation, but also collapsing time so that the historical past permeates the present as the history of the family permeates the narrative action.

Readers familiar with Faulkner will fit even more pieces into the pattern or jigsaw: Jewel's wild spotted horse is, as the novel tells us, descended from the horses Flem Snopes brought into Yoknapatawpha some twenty-five years earlier. Those who know Faulkner's short story "Spotted Horses" or his novel *The Hamlet*, where the story of the horses is told, will have that story brought back into their consciousnesses and the Armstids and others will be conjured up. This is just one example of how the whole Faulkner world is—despite occasional discrepancies of dates or details—made potentially present in every corner of that world, how all the stories contribute to the whole, reflect on each other, and make a three-dimensional, or perhaps a four-dimensional world, in which past, present, and future are all eternally present.

Faulkner has by narrative means created two kinds of suspense or forward-thrust to our attention. He makes us wonder whether the Bundrens will be able to bury Addie in Jefferson as Anse has promised her he would. And he makes us cast our mind forward in hopes of finding out which pronouns refer to whom, who Cora is and what she has to do with Darl and the others, or what Vardaman saw that he cannot tell about. He has also created characters in depth by showing us what they are thinking and doing—what things look like from their own perspective—and showing us how they are seen and understood by several other characters, as well as supplying us in many cases with their individual and family history.

The function of the narrative technique, if that's what it is—that is, if "technique" can be separated from "vision"—is not to complicate, to obscure, or merely to "document" a way of life, though it does, perhaps, all three. The documentation and depth are necessary to support the vision, the truth of an Anse who will stubbornly risk life and limb against overwhelming odds to fulfill the promise to his dead wife, and, within hours after burying her as he had promised, take to himself another "Mrs. Bundren." Does the surprise—I assume it is as surprising to you as it was to me—ending seem gratuitous? Is it a happy ending? It would seem so, on the surface at least; a story called *As I Lay Dying*, about the death and burial of a Mrs. Bundren, ends with a marriage and the words, " 'Meet Mrs Bundren,' he says." Surely, it's a happier surprise than the seemingly happy surprise of Mattie's survival in *Ethan Frome*. Surely, the tone is lighter than that of *The Death of Iván Ilyich*, though the religion of Faulkner's characters seems narrow and superficial compared to the religious vision of the dying Iván. Is it funny, this story of death and decay, unwanted pregnancy, arson, madness, flood and injury, and the revelation of old sins of the flesh on the part of the decaying flesh of one Mrs. Bundren and the suggestions of the dubious morality of the recent profession of the new Mrs. Bundren? We laugh, at the end and elsewhere in the story, laughter punctuating the wrenching pity and hopeless narrowness of some of these lives and expectations. Is the laughter life-affirming? Do Anse's new store-bought teeth and the new Mrs. Bundren tell us that life goes on? that in the midst of death we are in life? Or is there a catch to it—and in our laughing throats? Within the haze of laughter and irony is there a fire-eating salamander of life and passion or a heart of darkness? Faulkner's world, Yoknapatawpha County, is even more difficult to characterize definitively and accurately than it is to pronounce or spell. Not because it is obscure, not because Faulkner withholds information we need, but because it is so rich and complex, invulnerable to reductive generalizations or easy characterizations, to words like "funny" or "tragic" or "real" or "fantastic," or even "good" or "evil."

KATHERINE ANNE PORTER

Old Mortality

It took Katherine Anne Porter about twenty-five years to write her only lengthy novel, *The Ship of Fools*, parts of which (when it was to have been called *No Safe Harbor*) appeared from time to time in literary magazines. Even her short novels, such as *Pale Horse, Pale Rider* and *Old Mortality*, are at the shorter rather than longer end of the short novel spectrum. Yet this is not because the range of experience or vision in her works is narrow or thin, but because her diction and style are precise, concise, pure, and resonant; deftly, with few but sufficient details and no wasted words, she can capture a character with its contradictions, strata of a culture, life and its chaos. So beautifully wrought and perfect are her stories and short novels that she has assured herself a high and permanent place among the writers of her generation, and in America alone her generation includes Faulkner, Fitzgerald, and Hemingway. Indeed, in 1967 the National Institute of Arts and Letters gave her fiction its Gold Medal, an award it offers only every five years and had given five years earlier to Faulkner.

"Human life is mostly pure chaos," she once said, and her own life she once described as "jumbled." Part of the jumble, no doubt, was her three marriages (the first when she was sixteen), each of which lasted only three or four years. Part was the variety of occupations she engaged in to keep herself afloat: journalism, hack writing, acting, lecturing. Part was travel: she reached Mexico in 1920 in the middle of a revolution, stayed for two years, during which time she managed to get a Los Angeles dealer to exhibit huge quantities of Mexican art on behalf of the Mexican government, and wrote several of her early stories. She returned to Mexico almost ten years later (on a Guggenheim Fellowship) and sailed from there to Europe for five or six years. She lectured in Mexico, Trinidad, Belgium, and in Asia, taught and lectured in universities all over the United States, and received a number of honorary degrees (though she never attended college). Besides the Guggenheim Fellowship and Fulbright and Department of State grants, and the Gold Medal, she won many other awards, including both the Pulitzer and National Book Awards in 1966 for *The Collected Stories of Katherine Anne Porter*. She translated from French and Spanish, wrote nonfiction as well as essays and autobiography; but she wrote rather little fiction, given her long life and great fame and accomplishment.

Her early stories were published in the *Century Magazine* in the early 1920s, her first volume, *Flowering Judas*, in 1930 (to critical acclaim). Her last volume of stories (except for the *Collected Stories*, which included some unpublished early works and others) was *The Leaning Tower* in 1944, in bulk what a Dickens or a Henry James might turn out in a year or eighteen months. These stories are the order she distilled from the jumble and chaos of her experience.

"My one aim is to tell a straight story and give true testimony," she said, but "true" did not mean "actual" or "autobiographical." Though Miranda in *Old Mortality*, who also appears in *Pale Horse, Pale Rider*, admittedly resembles her author rather closely, Katherine Anne Porter, with her usual nicety of distinction, warned that "the reviewers are much mistaken when they insist on identifying me with any and every woman that appears in my stories. . . . I am a considerably more complicated person than they. They were not writers."

Old Mortality

Part I: 1885-1902

SHE WAS a spirited-looking young woman, with dark curly hair cropped and parted on the side, a short oval face with straight eyebrows, and a large curved mouth. A round white collar rose from the neck of her tightly buttoned black basque, and round white cuffs set off lazy hands with dimples in them, lying at ease in the folds of her flounced skirt which gathered around to a bustle. She sat thus, forever in the pose of being photographed, a motionless image in her dark walnut frame with silver oak leaves in the corners, her smiling gray eyes following one about the room. It was a reckless indifferent smile, rather disturbing to her nieces Maria and Miranda. Quite often they wondered why every older person who looked at the picture said, "How lovely"; and why everyone who had known her thought her so beautiful and charming.

There was a kind of faded merriment in the background, with its vase of flowers and draped velvet curtains, the kind of vase and the kind of curtains no one would have any more. The clothes were not even romantic looking, but merely most terribly out of fashion, and the whole affair was associated, in the minds of the little girls, with dead things: the smell of Grandmother's medicated cigarettes and her furniture that smelled of beeswax, and her old-fashioned perfume, Orange Flower. The woman in the picture had been Aunt Amy, but she was only a ghost in a frame, and a sad, pretty story from old times. She had been beautiful, much loved, unhappy, and she had died young.

Maria and Miranda, aged twelve and eight years, knew they were young, though they felt they had lived a long time. They had lived not only their own years; but their memories, it seemed to them, began years before they were born, in the lives of the grown-ups around them, old people above forty, most of them, who had a way of insisting that they too had been young once. It was hard to believe.

Their father was Aunt Amy's brother Harry. She had been his favorite sister. He sometimes glanced at the photograph and said, "It's not very good. Her hair and her smile were her chief beauties, and they aren't shown at all. She was much slimmer than that, too. There were never any fat women in the family, thank God."

When they heard their father say things like that, Maria and Miranda simply wondered, without criticism, what he meant. Their grandmother was thin as a match; the pictures of their mother, long since dead, proved her to have been a candle-wick, almost. Dashing young ladies, who turned out to be, to Miranda's astonishment, merely more of Grandmother's grandchildren, like herself, came visiting from school for the holidays, boasting of their eighteen-inch waists. But how did their father account for great-aunt Eliza, who quite squeezed herself through doors, and who, when seated, was one solid pyramidal monument from floor to neck? What about great-aunt Keziah, in Kentucky? Her husband, great-uncle John Jacob, had refused to allow her to ride his good horses after she had achieved two hundred and twenty pounds. "No," said great-uncle

John Jacob, "my sentiments of chivalry are not dead in my bosom; but neither is my common sense, to say nothing of charity to our faithful dumb friends. And the greatest of these is charity."[1] It was suggested to great-uncle John Jacob that charity should forbid him to wound great-aunt Keziah's female vanity by such a comment on her figure. "Female vanity will recover," said great-uncle John Jacob, callously, "but what about my horses' backs? And if she had the proper female vanity in the first place, she would never have got into such shape." Well, great-aunt Keziah was famous for her heft, and wasn't she in the family? But something seemed to happen to their father's memory when he thought of the girls he had known in the family of his youth, and he declared steadfastly they had all been, in every generation without exception, as slim as reeds and graceful as sylphs.

This loyalty of their father's in the face of evidence contrary to his ideal had its springs in family feeling, and a love of legend that he shared with the others. They loved to tell stories, romantic and poetic, or comic with a romantic humor; they did not gild the outward circumstance, it was the feeling that mattered. Their hearts and imaginations were captivated by their past, a past in which worldly considerations had played a very minor role. Their stories were almost always love stories against a bright blank heavenly blue sky.

Photographs, portraits by inept painters who meant earnestly to flatter, and the festival garments folded away in dried herbs and camphor were disappointing when the little girls tried to fit them to the living beings created in their minds by the breathing words of their elders. Grandmother, twice a year compelled in her blood by the change of seasons, would sit nearly all of one day beside old trunks and boxes in the lumber room, unfolding layers of garments and small keepsakes; she spread them out on sheets on the floor around her, crying over certain things, nearly always the same things, looking again at pictures in velvet cases, unwrapping locks of hair and dried flowers, crying gently and easily as if tears were the only pleasure she had left.

If Maria and Miranda were very quiet, and touched nothing until it was offered, they might sit by her at these times, or come and go. There was a tacit understanding that her grief was strictly her own, and must not be noticed or mentioned. The little girls examined the objects, one by one, and did not find them, in themselves, impressive. Such dowdy little wreaths and necklaces, some of them made of pearly shells; such moth-eaten bunches of pink ostrich feathers for the hair; such clumsy big breast pins and bracelets of gold and colored enamel; such silly-looking combs, standing up on tall teeth capped with seed pearls and French paste.[2] Miranda, without knowing why, felt melancholy. It seemed such a pity that these faded things, these yellowed long gloves and misshapen satin slippers, these broad ribbons cracking where they were folded, should have been all those vanished girls had to decorate themselves with. And where were they now, those girls, and the boys in the odd-looking collars? The young men seemed even more unreal than the girls, with their high-buttoned coats, their puffy neckties, their waxed mustaches, their waving

---

1. 1 Corinthians 13:12—"And now abideth faith, hope, charity, these three; but the greatest of these is charity."
2. Lead-glass compound used for imitation jewelry, perfected in France in the eighteenth century; seed pearls are very small, often irregularly shaped, and used decoratively.

thick hair combed carefully over their foreheads. Who could have taken them seriously, looking like that?

No, Maria and Miranda found it impossible to sympathize with those young persons, sitting rather stiffly before the camera, hopelessly out of fashion; but they were drawn and held by the mysterious love of the living, who remembered and cherished these dead. The visible remains were nothing; they were dust, perishable as the flesh; the features stamped on paper and metal were nothing, but their living memory enchanted the little girls. They listened, all ears and eager minds, picking here and there among the floating ends of narrative, patching together as well as they could fragments of tales that were like bits of poetry or music, indeed were associated with the poetry they had heard or read, with music, with the theater.

"Tell me again how Aunt Amy went away when she was married." "She ran into the gray cold and stepped into the carriage and turned and smiled with her face as pale as death, and called out 'Good-by, good-by,' and refused her cloak, and said, 'Give me a glass of wine.' And none of us saw her alive again." "Why wouldn't she wear her cloak, Cousin Cora?" "Because she was not in love, my dear." Ruin hath taught me thus to ruminate, that time will come and take my love away.[3] "Was she really beautiful, Uncle Bill?" "As an angel, my child." There were golden-haired angels with long blue pleated skirts dancing around the throne of the Blessed Virgin. None of them resembled Aunt Amy in the least, nor the type of beauty they had been brought up to admire. There were points of beauty by which one was judged severely. First, a beauty must be tall; whatever color the eyes, the hair must be dark, the darker the better; the skin must be pale and smooth. Lightness and swiftness of movement were important points. A beauty must be a good dancer, superb on horseback, with a serene manner, an amiable gaiety tempered with dignity at all hours. Beautiful teeth and hands, of course, and over and above all this, some mysterious crown of enchantment that attracted and held the heart. It was all very exciting and discouraging.

Miranda persisted through her childhood in believing, in spite of her smallness, thinness, her little snubby nose saddled with freckles, her speckled gray eyes and habitual tantrums, that by some miracle she would grow into a tall, cream-colored brunette, like cousin Isabel; she decided always to wear a trailing white satin gown. Maria, born sensible, had no such illusions. "We are going to take after Mamma's family," she said. "It's no use, we are. We'll never be beautiful, we'll always have freckles. And *you*," she told Miranda, "haven't even a good disposition."

Miranda admitted both truth and justice in this unkindness, but still secretly believed that she would one day suddenly receive beauty, as by inheritance, riches laid suddenly in her hands through no deserts of her own. She believed for quite a while that she would one day be like Aunt Amy, not as she appeared in the photograph, but as she was remembered by those who had seen her.

When Cousin Isabel came out in her tight black riding habit, surrounded by young men, and mounted gracefully, drawing her horse up and around so that he pranced learnedly on one spot while the other riders sprang to their saddles in the same sedate flurry, Miranda's heart

3. Shakespeare, Sonnet 64.

would close with such a keen dart of admiration, envy, vicarious pride it was almost painful; but there would always be an elder present to lay a cooling hand upon her emotions. "She rides almost as well as Amy, doesn't she? But Amy had the pure Spanish style, she could bring out paces in a horse no one else knew he had." Young namesake Amy, on her way to a dance, would swish through the hall in ruffled white taffeta, glimmering like a moth in the lamplight, carrying her elbows pointed backward stiffly as wings, sliding along as if she were on rollers, in the fashionable walk of her day. She was considered the best dancer at any party, and Maria, sniffing the wave of perfume that followed Amy, would clasp her hands and say, "Oh, I can't *wait* to be grown up." But the elders would agree that the first Amy had been lighter, more smooth and delicate in her waltzing; young Amy would never equal her. Cousin Molly Parrington, far past her youth, indeed she belonged to the generation before Aunt Amy, was a noted charmer. Men who had known her all her life still gathered about her; now that she was happily widowed for the second time there was no doubt that she would yet marry again. But Amy, said the elders, had the same high spirits and wit without boldness, and you really could not say that Molly had ever been discreet. She dyed her hair, and made jokes about it. She had a way of collecting the men around her in a corner, where she told them stories. She was an unnatural mother to her ugly daughter Eva, an old maid past forty while her mother was still the belle of the ball. "Born when I was fifteen, you remember," Molly would say shamelessly, looking an old beau straight in the eye, both of them remembering that he had been best man at her first wedding when she was past twenty-one. "Everyone said I was like a little girl with her doll."

Eva, shy and chinless, straining her upper lip over two enormous teeth, would sit in corners watching her mother. She looked hungry, her eyes were strained and tired. She wore her mother's old clothes, made over, and taught Latin in a Female Seminary. She believed in votes for women, and had traveled about, making speeches. When her mother was not present, Eva bloomed out a little, danced prettily, smiled, showing all her teeth, and was like a dry little plant set out in a gentle rain. Molly was merry about her ugly duckling. "It's lucky for me my daughter is an old maid. She's not so apt," said Molly naughtily, "to make a grandmother of me." Eva would blush as if she had been slapped.

Eva was a blot, no doubt about it, but the little girls felt she belonged to their everyday world of dull lessons to be learned, stiff shoes to be limbered up, scratchy flannels to be endured in cold weather, measles and disappointed expectations. Their Aunt Amy belonged to the world of poetry. The romance of Uncle Gabriel's long, unrewarded love for her, her early death, was such a story as one found in old books: unworldly books, but true, such as the Vita Nuova, the Sonnets of Shakespeare and the Wedding Song of Spenser; and poems by Edgar Allan Poe. "Her tantalized spirit now blandly reposes, Forgetting or never regretting its roses. . . ."[4] Their father read that to them, and said, "He was our greatest poet," and they knew that "our" meant he was Southern. Aunt Amy was real as the pictures in the old Holbein and Dürer books were real. The little girls lay flat on their stomachs and peered into a world of wonder,

---

4. Slightly altered from Poe's "For Annie" (1849); *Epithalamion* by Edmund Spenser (1552-1599). *Vita Nuova*, by Dante Alighiere (1265-1321); *The*

turning the shabby leaves that fell apart easily, not surprised at the sight of the Mother of God sitting on a hollow log nursing her Child; not doubting either Death or the Devil riding at the stirrups of the grim knight;[5] not questioning the propriety of the stiffly dressed ladies of Sir Thomas More's household, seated in dignity on the floor, or seeming to be. They missed all the dog and pony shows, and lantern-slide entertainments, but their father took them to see "Hamlet," and "The Taming of the Shrew," and "Richard the Third," and a long sad play with Mary, Queen of Scots, in it. Miranda thought the magnificent lady in black velvet was truly the Queen of Scots, and was pained to learn that the real Queen had died long ago, and not at all on the night she, Miranda, had been present.

The little girls loved the theater, that world of personages taller than human beings, who swept upon the scene and invested it with their presences, their more than human voices, their gestures of gods and goddesses ruling a universe. But there was always a voice recalling other and greater occasions. Grandmother in her youth had heard Jenny Lind, and thought that Nellie Melba was much overrated.[6] Father had seen Bernhardt, and Madame Modjeska was no sort of rival. When Paderewski played for the first time in their city, cousins came from all over the state and went from the grandmother's house to hear him. The little girls were left out of this great occasion. They shared the excitement of the going away, and shared the beautiful moment of return, when cousins stood about in groups, with coffee cups and glasses in their hands, talking in low voices, awed and happy. The little girls, struck with the sense of a great event, hung about in their nightgowns and listened, until someone noticed and hustled them away from the sweet nimbus of all that glory. One old gentleman, however, had heard Rubinstein frequently. He could not but feel that Rubinstein had reached the final height of musical interpretation, and, for him, Paderewski had been something of an anticlimax. The little girls heard him muttering on, holding up one hand, patting the air as if he were calling for silence. The others looked at him, and listened, without any disturbance of their grave tender mood. They had never heard Rubinstein; they had, one hour since, heard Paderewski, and why should anyone need to recall the past? Miranda, dragged away, half understanding the old gentleman, hated him. She felt that she too had heard Paderewski.

There was then a life beyond a life in this world, as well as in the next; such episodes confirmed for the little girls the nobility of human feeling, the divinity of man's vision of the unseen, the importance of life and death, the depths of the human heart, the romantic value of tragedy. Cousin Eva, on a certain visit, trying to interest them in the study of Latin, told them the story of John Wilkes Booth, who, handsomely garbed in a long black cloak, had leaped to the stage after assassinating President Lincoln. "Sic semper tyrannis,"[7] he had shouted superbly, in spite of his broken leg. The little girls never doubted that it had happened in just that way, and the moral seemed to be that one should always have Latin, or at least a good classical poetry quotation, to depend upon in great or

5. *Death and the Devil*, print by Albrecht Dürer (1471-1528); following is a description of a painting by Hans Holbein (1465-1524).
6. Two nineteenth-century sopranos. Father compares two actresses, and the old gentleman (below) two pianists.
7. "Thus always to tyrants."

desperate moments. Cousin Eva reminded them that no one, not even a
good Southerner, could possibly approve of John Wilkes Booth's deed. It
was murder, after all. They were to remember that. But Miranda, used to
tragedy in books and in family legends—two great-uncles had committed
suicide and a remote ancestress had gone mad for love—decided that,
without the murder, there would have been no point to dressing up and
leaping to the stage shouting in Latin. So how could she disapprove of the
deed? It was a fine story. She knew a distantly related old gentleman who
had been devoted to the art of Booth, had seen him in a great many
plays, but not, alas, at his greatest moment. Miranda regretted this; it
would have been so pleasant to have the assassination of Lincoln in the
family.

Uncle Gabriel, who had loved Aunt Amy so desperately, still lived
somewhere, though Miranda and Maria had never seen him. He had gone
away, far away, after her death. He still owned racehorses, and ran them
at famous tracks all over the country, and Miranda believed there could
not possibly be a more brilliant career. He had married again, quite soon,
and had written to Grandmother, asking her to accept his new wife as a
daughter in place of Amy. Grandmother had written coldly, accepting,
inviting them for a visit, but Uncle Gabriel had somehow never brought
his bride home. Harry had visited them in New Orleans, and reported
that the second wife was a very good-looking well-bred blonde girl who
would undoubtedly be a good wife for Gabriel. Still, Uncle Gabriel's heart
was broken. Faithfully once a year he wrote a letter to someone of the
family, sending money for a wreath for Amy's grave. He had written a
poem for her gravestone, and had come home, leaving his second wife in
Atlanta, to see that it was carved properly. He could never account for
having written this poem; he had certainly never tried to write a single
rhyme since leaving school. Yet one day when he had been thinking about
Amy, the verse occurred to him, out of the air. Maria and Miranda had
seen it, printed in gold on a mourning card. Uncle Gabriel had sent a
great number of them to be handed around among the family.

> "She lives again who suffered life,
> Then suffered death, and now set free
> A singing angel, she forgets
> The griefs of old mortality."

"Did she really sing?" Maria asked her father.

"Now what has that to do with it?" he asked. "It's a poem."

"I think it's very pretty," said Miranda, impressed. Uncle Gabriel was
second cousin to her father and Aunt Amy. It brought poetry very near.

"Not so bad for tombstone poetry," said their father, "but it should be
better."

Uncle Gabriel had waited five years to marry Aunt Amy. She had been
ill, her chest was weak; she was engaged twice to other young men and
broke her engagements for no reason; and she laughed at the advice of
older and kinder-hearted persons who thought it very capricious of her
not to return the devotion of such a handsome and romantic young man
as Gabriel, her second cousin, too; it was not as if she would be marrying
a stranger. Her coldness was said to have driven Gabriel to a wild life and
even to drinking. His grandfather was wealthy and Gabriel was his favor-

ite; they had quarreled over the racehorses, and Gabriel had shouted, "By God, I must have *something*." As if he had not everything already: youth, health, good looks, the prospect of riches, and a devoted family circle. His grandfather pointed out to him that he was little better than an ingrate, and showed signs of being a wastrel as well. Gabriel said, "You had racehorses, and made a good thing of them." "I never depended upon them for a livelihood, sir," said his grandfather.

Gabriel wrote letters about this and many other things to Amy from Saratoga[8] and from Kentucky and from New Orleans, sending her presents, and flowers packed in ice, and telegrams. The presents were amusing, such as a huge cage full of small green lovebirds; or, as an ornament for her hair, a full-petaled enameled rose with paste dewdrops, with an enameled butterfly in brilliant colors suspended quivering on a gold wire about it; but the telegrams always frightened her mother, and the flowers, after a journey by train and then by stage into the country, were much the worse for wear. He would send roses when the rose garden at home was in full bloom. Amy could not help smiling over it, though her mother insisted it was touching and sweet of Gabriel. It must prove to Amy that she was always in his thoughts.

"That's no place for me," said Amy, but she had a way of speaking, a tone of voice, which made it impossible to discover what she meant by what she said. It was possible always that she might be serious. And she would not answer questions.

"Amy's wedding dress," said the grandmother, unfurling an immense cloak of dove-colored cut velvet, spreading beside it a silvery-gray watered-silk frock, and a small gray velvet toque with a dark red breast of feathers. Cousin Isabel, the beauty, sat with her. They talked to each other, and Miranda could listen if she chose.

"She would not wear white, nor a veil," said Grandmother. "I couldn't oppose her, for I had said my daughters should each have exactly the wedding dress they wanted. But Amy surprised me. 'Now what would I look like in white satin?' she asked. It's true she was pale, but she would have been angelic in it, and all of us told her so, 'I shall wear mourning if I like,' she said, 'it is *my* funeral, you know.' I reminded her that Lou and your mother had worn white with veils and it would please me to have my daughters all alike in that. Amy said, 'Lou and Isabel are not like me,' but I could not persuade her to explain what she meant. One day when she was ill she said, 'Mammy, I'm not long for this world,' but not as if she meant it. I told her, 'You might live as long as anyone, if only you will be sensible.' 'That's the whole trouble,' said Amy. 'I feel sorry for Gabriel,' she told me. 'He doesn't know what he's asking for.'

"I tried to tell her once more," said the grandmother, "that marriage and children would cure her of everything. 'All women of our family are delicate when they are young,' I said. 'Why, when I was your age no one expected me to live a year. It was called greensickness, and everybody knew there was only one cure.' 'If I live for a hundred years and turn green as grass,' said Amy, 'I still shan't want to marry Gabriel,' So I told her very seriously that if she truly felt that way she must never do it, and Gabriel must be told once for all, and sent away. He would get over it. 'I have told him, and I have sent him away,' said Amy. 'He just doesn't listen.' We both laughed at that, and I told her young girls found a hundred ways to deny they wished to be married, and a thousand more to test their power over men, but that she had more than enough of that, and now it was time for her to be entirely sincere and make her decision. As for me," said the grandmother, "I wished with all my heart to marry your grandfather, and if he had not asked me, I should have asked him most certainly. Amy insisted that she could not imagine wanting to marry anybody. She would be, she said, a nice old maid like Eva Parrington. For even then it was pretty plain that Eva was an old maid, born. Harry said, 'Oh, Eva—Eva has no chin, that's her trouble. If you had no chin, Amy, you'd be in the same fix as Eva, no doubt.' Your Uncle Bill would say, 'When women haven't anything else, they'll take a vote for consolation. A pretty thin bed-fellow,' said your Uncle Bill. 'What I really need is a good dancing partner to guide me through life,' said Amy, 'that's the match I'm looking for,' It was no good trying to talk to her."

Her brothers remembered her tenderly as a sensible girl. After listening to their comments on her character and ways, Maria decided that they considered her sensible because she asked their advice about her apprearance when she was going out to dance. If they found fault in any way, she would change her dress or her hair until they were pleased, and say, "You are an angel not to let your poor sister go out looking like a freak." But she would not listen to her father, nor to Gabriel. If Gabriel praised the frock she was wearing, she was apt to disappear and come back in another. He loved her long black hair, and once, lifting it up from her pillow when she was ill, said, "I love your hair, Amy, the most beautiful hair in the world." When he returned on his next visit, he found her with her hair cropped and curled close to her head. He was horrified, as if she had willfully mutilated herself. She would not let it grow again, not even to please her brothers. The photograph hanging on the wall was one she had made at that time to send to Gabriel, who sent it back without a word. This pleased her, and she framed the photograph. There was a thin inky scrawl low in one corner, "To dear brother Harry, who likes my hair cut."

This was a mischievous reference to a very grave scandal. The little girls used to look at their father, and wonder what would have happened if he had really hit the young man he shot at. The young man was believed to have kissed Aunt Amy, when she was not in the least engaged to him. Uncle Gabriel was supposed to have had a duel with the young man, but Father had got there first. He was a pleasant, everyday sort of father, who held his daughters on his knee if they were prettily dressed and well behaved, and pushed them away if they had not freshly combed hair and nicely scrubbed fingernails. "Go away, you're disgusting," he would say, in a matter-of-fact voice. He noticed if their stocking seams were crooked. He caused them to brush their teeth with a revolting mixture of prepared chalk, powdered charcoal and salt. When they behaved stupidly he could not endure the sight of them. They understood dimly that all this was for their own future good; and when they were snively with colds, he prescribed delicious hot toddy for them, and saw that it was given them. He was always hoping they might not grow up to be so silly as they seemed to him at any given moment, and he had a disconcerting way of inquiring, "How do you *know?*" when they forgot and made dogmatic statements in his presence. It always came out embarrassingly that they did not know at all, but were repeating something they had heard. This made conversation with him difficult, for he laid traps and they fell into them, but it became important to them that their father should not believe them to be fools. Well, this very father had gone to Mexico once and stayed there for nearly a year, because he had shot at a man with whom Aunt Amy had flirted at a dance. It had been very wrong of him, because he should have challenged the man to a duel, as Uncle Gabriel had done. Instead, he just took a shot at him, and this was the lowest sort of manners. It had caused great disturbance in the whole community and had almost broken up the affair between Aunt Amy and Uncle Gabriel for good. Uncle Gabriel insisted that the young man had kissed Aunt Amy, and Aunt Amy insisted that the young man had merely paid her a compliment on her hair.

During the Mardi Gras holidays there was to be a big gay fancy-dress ball. Harry was going as a bull-fighter because his sweetheart, Mariana, had a new black lace mantilla and high comb from Mexico. Maria and Miranda had seen a photograph of their mother in this dress, her lovely face without a trace of coquetry looking gravely out from under a tremendous fall of lace from the peak of the comb, a rose tucked firmly over her ear. Amy copied her costume from a small Dresden-china shepherdess which stood on the mantelpiece in the parlor; a careful copy with ribboned hat, gilded crook, very low-laced bodice, short basket skirts, green slippers and all. She wore it with a black half-mask, but it was no disguise. "You would have known it was Amy at any distance," said Father. Gabriel, six feet three in height as he was, had got himself up to match, and a spectacle he provided in pale blue satin knee breeches and a blond curled wig with a hair ribbon. "He felt a fool, and he looked like one," said Uncle Bill, "and he behaved like one before the evening was over."

Everything went beautifully until the party gathered downstairs to leave for the ball. Amy's father—he must have been born a grandfather, thought Miranda—gave one glance at his daughter, her white ankles shining, bosom deeply exposed, two round spots of paint on her cheeks, and fell into a frenzy of outraged propriety. "It's disgraceful," he pronounced, loudly. "No daughter of mine is going to show herself in such a rig-out. It's bawdy," he thundered. "Bawdy!"

Amy had taken off her mask to smile at him. "Why, Papa," she said very sweetly, "what's wrong with it? Look on the mantelpiece. She's been there all along, and you were never shocked before."

"There's all the difference in the world," said her father, "all the difference, young lady, and you know it. You go upstairs this minute and pin up that waist in front and let down those skirts to a decent length before you leave this house. *And wash your face!*"

"I see nothing wrong with it," said Amy's mother, firmly, "and you shouldn't use such language before innocent young girls." She and Amy sat down with several females of the household to help, and they made short work of the business. In ten minutes Amy returned, face clean, bodice filled in with lace, shepherdess skirt modestly sweeping the carpet behind her.

When Amy appeared from the dressing room for her first dance with Gabriel, the lace was gone from her bodice, her skirts were tucked up more daringly than before, and the spots on her cheeks were like pomegranates. "Now Gabriel, tell me truly, wouldn't it have been a pity to spoil my costume?" Gabriel, delighted that she had asked his opinion, declared it was perfect. They agreed with kindly tolerance that old people were often tiresome, but one need not upset them by open disobedience: their youth was gone, what had they to live for?

Harry, dancing with Mariana who swung a heavy train around her expertly at every turn of the waltz, began to be uneasy about his sister Amy. She was entirely too popular. He saw young men make beelines across the floor, eyes fixed on those white silk ankles. Some of the young men he did not know at all, others he knew too well and could not approve of for his sister Amy. Gabriel, unhappy in his lyric satin and wig, stood about holding his ribboned crook as though it had sprouted thorns. He hardly danced at all with Amy, he did not enjoy dancing with anyone else, and he was having a thoroughly wretched time of it.

There appeared late, alone, got up as Jean Lafitte,[9] a young Creole gentleman who had, two years before, been for a time engaged to Amy. He came straight to her, with the manner of a happy lover, and said, clearly enough for everyone near by to hear him, "I only came because I knew you were to be here. I only want to dance with you and I shall go again." Amy, with a face of delight, cried out, "Raymond!" as if to a lover. She had danced with him four times, and had then disappeared from the floor on his arm.

Harry and Mariana, in conventional disguise of romance, irreproachably betrothed, safe in their happiness, were waltzing slowly to their favorite song, the melancholy farewell of the Moorish King on leaving Granada. They sang in whispers to each other, in their uncertain Spanish, a song of love and parting and that sword's point of grief that makes the heart tender towards all other lost and disinherited creatures: Oh, mansion of love, my earthly paradise ... that I shall see no more ... whither flies the poor swallow, weary and homeless, seeking for shelter where no shelter is? I too am far from home without the power to fly.... Come to my heart, sweet bird, beloved pilgrim, build your nest near my bed, let me listen to your song, and weep for my lost land of joy....

Into this bliss broke Gabriel. He had thrown away his shepherd's crook and he was carrying his wig. He wanted to speak to Harry at once, and before Mariana knew what was happening she was sitting beside her mother and the two excited young men were gone. Waiting, disturbed and displeased, she smiled at Amy who waltzed past with a young man in Devil costume, including ill-fitting scarlet cloven hoofs. Almost at once, Harry and Gabriel came back, with serious faces, and Harry darted on the dance floor, returning with Amy. The girls and the chaperones were asked to come at once, they must be taken home. It was all mysterious and sudden, and Harry said to Mariana, "I will tell you what is happening, but not now—"

The grandmother remembered of this disgraceful affair only that Gabriel brought Amy home alone and that Harry came in somewhat later. The other members of the party straggled in at various hours, and the story came out piecemeal. Amy was silent and, her mother discovered later, burning with fever. "I saw at once that something was very wrong.

'What has happened, Amy?' 'Oh, Harry goes about shooting at people at a party,' she said, sitting down as if she were exhausted. 'It was on your account, Amy,' said Gabriel. 'Oh, no, it was not,' said Amy. 'Don't believe him, Mammy.' So I said, 'Now enough of this. Tell me what happened, Amy.' And Amy said, 'Mammy, this is it. Raymond came in, and you know I like Raymond, and he is a good dancer. So we danced together, too much, maybe. We went on the gallery for a breath of air, and stood there. He said, "How well your hair looks. I like this new shingled style." ' She glanced at Gabriel. 'And then another young man came out and said, "I've been looking everywhere. This is our dance, isn't it?" And I went in to dance. And now it seems that Gabriel went out at once and challenged Raymond to a duel about something or other, but Harry doesn't wait for that. Raymond had already gone out to have his horse brought, I suppose one doesn't duel in fancy dress,' she said, looking at Gabriel, who fairly shriveled in his blue satin shepherd's costume, 'and Harry simply went out and shot at him. I don't think that was fair,' said Amy."

Her mother agreed that indeed it was not fair; it was not even decent, and she could not imagine what her son Harry thought he was doing. "It isn't much of a way to defend your sister's honor," she said to him afterward. "I didn't want Gabriel to go fighting duels," said Harry. "That wouldn't have helped much, either."

Gabriel had stood before Amy, leaning over, asking once more the question he had apparently been asking her all the way home. "Did he kiss you, Amy?"

Amy took off her shepherdess hat and pushed her hair back. "Maybe he did," she answered, "and maybe I wished him to."

"Amy, you must not say such things," said her mother. "Answer Gabriel's question."

"He hasn't the right to ask it," said Amy, but without anger.

"Do you love him, Amy?" asked Gabriel, the sweat standing out on his forehead.

"It doesn't matter," answered Amy, leaning back in her chair.

"Oh, it does matter; it matters terribly," said Gabriel. "You must answer me now." He took both of her hands and tried to hold them. She drew her hands away firmly and steadily so that he had to let go.

"Let her alone, Gabriel," said Amy's mother. "You'd better go now. We are all tired. Let's talk about it tomorrow."

She helped Amy to undress, noticing the changed bodice and the shortened skirt. "You shouldn't have done that, Amy. That was not wise of you. It was better the other way."'

Amy said, "Mammy, I'm sick of this world. I don't like anything in it. It's so *dull*," she said, and for a moment she looked as if she might weep. She had never been tearful, even as a child, and her mother was alarmed. It was then she discovered that Amy had fever.

"Gabriel is dull, Mother—he sulks," she said. "I could see him sulking every time I passed. It spoils things," she said. "Oh, I want to go to sleep."

Her mother sat looking at her and wondering how it had happened she had brought such a beautiful child into the world. "Her face," said her mother, "was angelic in sleep."

Some time during that fevered night, the projected duel between Gabriel and Raymond was halted by the offices of friends on both sides.

There remained the open question of Harry's impulsive shot, which was not so easily settled. Raymond seemed vindictive about that, it was possible he might choose to make trouble. Harry, taking the advice of Gabriel, his brothers and friends, decided that the best way to avoid further scandal was for him to disappear for a while. This being decided upon, the young men returned about daybreak, saddled Harry's best horse and helped him pack a few things; accompanied by Gabriel and Bill, Harry set out for the border, feeling rather gay and adventurous.

Amy, being wakened by the stirring in the house, found out the plan. Five minutes after they were gone, she came down in her riding dress, had her own horse saddled, and struck out after them. She rode almost every morning; before her parents had time to be uneasy over her prolonged absence, they found her note.

What had threatened to be a tragedy became a rowdy lark. Amy rode to the border, kissed her brother Harry good-bye, and rode back again with Bill and Gabriel. It was a three days' journey, and when they arrived Amy had to be lifted from the saddle. She was really ill by now, but in the gayest of humors. Her mother and father had been prepared to be severe with her, but, at sight of her, their feelings changed. They turned on Bill and Gabriel. "Why did you let her do this?" they asked.

"You know we could not stop her," said Gabriel helplessly, "and she did enjoy herself so much!"

Amy laughed. "Mammy, it was splendid, the most delightful trip I ever had. And if I am to be the heroine of this novel, why shouldn't I make the most of it?"

The scandal, Maria and Miranda gathered, had been pretty terrible. Amy simply took to bed and stayed there, and Harry had skipped out blithely to wait until the little affair blew over. The rest of the family had to receive visitors, write letters, go to church, return calls, and bear the whole brunt, as they expressed it. They sat in the twilight of scandal in their little world, holding themselves very rigidly, in a shared tension as if all their nerves began at a common center. This center had received a blow, and family nerves shuddered, even into the farthest reaches of Kentucky. From whence in due time great-great-aunt Sally Rhea addressed a letter to *Mifs*[1] *Amy Rhea*. In deep brown ink like dried blood, in a spidery hand adept at archaic symbols and abbreviations, great-great-aunt Sally informed Amy that she was fairly convinced that this calamity was only the forerunner of a series shortly to be visited by the Almighty God upon a race already condemned through its own wickedness, a warning that man's time was short, and that they must all prepare for the end of the world. For herself, she had long expected it, she was entirely resigned to the prospect of meeting her Maker; and Amy, no less than her wicked brother Harry, must likewise place herself in God's hands and prepare for the worst. "*Oh, my dear unfortunate young relative,*" twittered great-great-aunt Sally, "*we must in our Extremty join hands and appr before ye Dread Throne of Jdgmnt a United Fmly, if One is Mssg from ye Flock, what will Jesus say?*"

Great-great-aunt Sally's religious career had become comic legend. She

---

1. Old-fashioned double *s*; the *y* in *ye*, below, is old-fashioned *th*.

had forsaken her Catholic rearing for a young man whose family were Cumberland Presbyterians. Unable to accept their opinions, however, she was converted to the Hard-Shell Baptists,[2] a sect as loathsome to her husband's family as the Catholic could possibly be. She had spent a life of vicious self-indulgent martyrdom to her faith; as Harry commented: "Religion put claws on Aunt Sally and gave her a post to whet them on." She had out-argued, out-fought, and out-lived her entire generation, but she did not miss them. She bedeviled the second generation without ceasing, and was beginning hungrily on the third.

Amy, reading this letter, broke into her gay full laugh that always caused everyone around her to laugh too, even before they knew why, and her small green lovebirds in their cage turned and eyed her solemnly. "Imagine drawing a pew in heaven beside Aunt Sally," she said. "What a prospect."

"Don't laugh too soon," said her father. "Heaven was made to order for Aunt Sally. She'll be on her own territory there."

"For my sins," said Amy, "I must go to heaven with Aunt Sally."

During the uncomfortable time of Harry's absence, Amy went on refusing to marry Gabriel. Her mother could hear their voices going on in their endless colloquy, during many long days. One afternoon Gabriel came out, looking very sober and discouraged. He stood looking down at Amy's mother as she sat sewing, and said, "I think it is all over, I believe now that Amy will never have me." The grandmother always said afterward, "Never have I pitied anyone as I did poor Gabriel at that moment. But I told him, very firmly, 'Let her alone, then, she is ill.'" So Gabriel left, and Amy had no word from him for more than a month.

The day after Gabriel was gone, Amy rose looking extremely well, went hunting with her brothers Bill and Stephen, bought a velvet wrap, had her hair shingled and curled again, and wrote long letters to Harry, who was having a most enjoyable exile in Mexico City.

After dancing all night three times in one week, she woke one morning in a hemorrhage. She seemed frightened and asked for the doctor, promising to do whatever he advised. She was quiet for a few days, reading. She asked for Gabriel. No one knew where he was. "You should write him a letter; his mother will send it on." "Oh, no," she said. "I miss him coming in with his sour face. Letters are no good."

Gabriel did come in, only a few days later, with a very sour face and unpleasant news. His grandfather had died, after a day's illness. On his death bed, in the name of God, being of a sound and disposing mind, he had cut off his favorite grandchild Gabriel with one dollar. "In the name of God, Amy," said Gabriel, "the old devil has ruined me in one sentence."

It was the conduct of his immediate family in the matter that had embittered him, he said. They could hardly conceal their satisfaction. They had known and envied Gabriel's quite just, well-founded expectations. Not one of them offered to make any private settlement. No one even thought of repairing this last-minute act of senile vengeance. Privately they blessed their luck. "I have been cut off with a dollar," said Gabriel,

---

2. Or Primitive Baptists, extreme Calvinists who split from the church in the middle of the nineteenth century. The Cumberland Presbyterians originated in revival preaching in Cumberland County, Kentucky, in 1810.

"and they are all glad of it. I think they feel somehow that this justifies every criticism they ever made against me. They were right about me all along. I am a worthless poor relation," said Gabriel. "My God, I wish you could see them."

Amy said, "I wonder how you will ever support a wife, now."

Gabriel said, "Oh, it isn't so bad as that. If you would, Amy—"

Amy said, "Gabriel, if we get married now there'll be just time to be in New Orleans for Mardi Gras. If we wait until after Lent, it may be too late."

"Why, Amy," said Gabriel, "how could it ever be too late?"

"You might change your mind," said Amy. "You know how fickle you are."

There were two letters in the grandmother's many packets of letters that Maria and Miranda read after they were grown. One of them was from Amy. It was dated ten days after her marriage.

"Dear Mammy, New Orleans hasn't changed as much as I have since we saw each other last. I am now a staid old married woman, and Gabriel is very devoted and kind. Footlights won a race for us yesterday, she was the favorite, and it was wonderful. I go to the races every day, and our horses are doing splendidly; I had my choice of Erin Go Bragh[3] or Miss Lucy, and I chose Miss Lucy. She is mine now, she runs like a streak. Gabriel says I made a mistake, Erin Go Bragh will stay better. I think Miss Lucy will stay my time.

"We are having a lovely visit. I'm going to put on a domino and take to the streets with Gabriel sometime during Mardi Gras. I'm tired of watching the show from a balcony. Gabriel says it isn't safe. He says he'll take me if I insist, but I doubt it. Mammy, he's very nice. Don't worry about me. I have a beautiful black-and-rose-colored velvet gown for the Proteus Ball.[4] Madame, my new mother-in-law, wanted to know if it wasn't a little dashing. I told her I hoped so or I had been cheated. It is fitted perfectly smooth in the bodice, very low in the shoulders—Papa would not approve—and the skirt is looped with wide silver ribbons between the waist and knees in front, and then it surges around and is looped enormously in the back, with a train just one yard long. I now have an eighteen-inch waist, thanks to Madame Duré. I expect to be so dashing that my mother-in-law will have an attack. She has them quite often. Gabriel sends love. Please take good care of Graylie and Fiddler. I want to ride them again when I come home. We're going to Saratoga, I don't know just when. Give everybody my dear dear love. It rains all the time here, of course. . . .

"P.S. Mammy, as soon as I get a minute to myself, I'm going to be terribly homesick. Good-by, my darling Mammy."

The other was from Amy's nurse, dated six weeks after Amy's marriage.

"I cut off the lock of hair because I was sure you would like to have it. And I do not want you to think I was careless, leaving her medicine where she could get it, the doctor has written and explained. It would not have done her any harm except that her heart was weak. She did not know how much she was taking, often she said to me, one more of those little capsules wouldn't do any harm, and so I told her to be careful and not take anything except what I gave her. She begged me for them sometimes but I would not give her more than the doctor said. I slept during the night because she did not seem to be so sick as all that and the doctor did not order me to sit up with her. Please accept my regrets for your great loss and please do not think that anybody was careless with your dear daughter. She suffered a great deal and now she is at rest. She could not get well but she might have lived longer. Yours respectfully. . . . "

The letters and all the strange keepsakes were packed away and forgotten for a great many years. They seemed to have no place in the world.

Part II: 1904

During vacation on their grandmother's farm, Maria and Miranda, who read as naturally and constantly as ponies crop grass, and with much the same kind of pleasure, had by some happy chance laid hold of some forbidden reading matter, brought in and left there with missionary intent, no doubt, by some Protestant cousin. It fell into the right hands if enjoyment had been its end. The reading matter was printed in poor type on spongy paper, and was ornamented with smudgy illustrations all the more exciting to the little girls because they could not make head or tail of them. The stories were about beautiful but unlucky maidens, who for mysterious reasons had been trapped by nuns and priests in dire collusion; they were then "immured" in convents, where they were forced to take the veil—an appalling rite during which the victims shrieked dreadfully— and condemned forever after to most uncomfortable and disorderly existences. They seemed to divide their time between lying chained in dark cells and assisting other nuns to bury throttled infants under stones in moldering rat-infested dungeons.

Immured! It was the word Maria and Miranda had been needing all along to describe their condition at the Convent of the Child Jesus, in New Orleans, where they spent the long winters trying to avoid an education. There were no dungeons at the Child Jesus, and this was only one of numerous marked differences between convent life as Maria and Miranda knew it and the thrilling paper-backed version. It was no good at all trying to fit the stories to life, and they did not even try. They had long since learned to draw the lines between life, which was real and earnest, and the grave was not its goal;[5] poetry, which was true but not real; and stories, or forbidden reading matter, in which things happened as nowhere else, with the most sublime irrelevance and unlikelihood, and one need not turn a hair, because there was not a word of truth in them.

It was true the little girls were hedged and confined, but in a large garden with trees and a grotto; they were locked at night into a long cold dormitory, with all the windows open, and a sister sleeping at either end. Their beds were curtained with muslin, and small night-lamps were so arranged that the sisters could see through the curtains, but the children could not see the sisters. Miranda wondered if they ever slept, or did they sit there all night quietly watching the sleepers through the muslin? She tried to work up a little sinister thrill about this, but she found it impossi-

5. "Life is real! Life is earnest!/ And the grave is not its goal"; from A Psalm of Life by Henry Wads-   worth Longfellow (1807–1882).

ble to care much what either of the sisters did. They were very dull good-natured women who managed to make the whole dormitory seem dull. All days and all things in the Convent of the Child Jesus were dull, in fact, and Maria and Miranda lived for Saturdays.

No one had even hinted that they should become nuns. On the contrary Miranda felt that the discouraging attitude of Sister Claude and Sister Austin and Sister Ursula towards her expressed ambition to be a nun barely veiled a deeply critical knowledge of her spiritual deficiencies. Still Maria and Miranda had got a fine new word out of their summer reading, and they referred to themselves as "immured." It gave a romantic glint to what was otherwise a very dull life for them, except for blessed Saturday afternoons during the racing season.

If the nuns were able to assure the family that the deportment and scholastic achievements of Maria and Miranda were at least passable, some cousin or other always showed up smiling, in holiday mood, to take them to the races, where they were given a dollar each to bet on any horse they chose. There were black Saturdays now and then, when Maria and Miranda sat ready, hats in hand, curly hair plastered down and slicked behind their ears, their stiffly pleated navy-blue skirts spread out around them, waiting with their hearts going down slowly into their high-topped laced-up black shoes. They never put on their hats until the last minute, for somehow it would have been too horrible to have their hats on, when, after all, Cousin Henry and Cousin Isabel, or Uncle George and Aunt Polly, were not coming to take them to the races. When no one appeared, and Saturday came and went a sickening waste, they were then given to understand that it was a punishment for bad marks during the week. They never knew until it was too late to avoid the disappointment. It was very wearing.

One Saturday they were sent down to wait in the visitor's parlor, and there was their father. He had come all the way from Texas to see them. They leaped at sight of him, and then stopped short, suspiciously. Was he going to take them to the races? If so, they were happy to see him.

"Hello," said father, kissing their cheeks. "Have you been good girls? Your Uncle Gabriel is running a mare at the Crescent City[6] today, so we'll all go and bet on her. Would you like that?"

Maria put on her hat without a word, but Miranda stood and addressed her father sternly. She had suffered many doubts about this day. "Why didn't you send word yesterday? I could have been looking forward all this time."

"We didn't know," said father, in his easiest paternal manner, "that you were going to deserve it. Remember Saturday before last?"

Miranda hung her head and put on her hat, with the round elastic under the chin. She remembered too well. She had, in midweek, given way to despair over her arithmetic and had fallen flat on her face on the classroom floor, refusing to rise until she was carried out. The rest of the week had been a series of novel deprivations, and Saturday a day of mourning; secret mourning, for if one mourned too noisily, it simply meant another bad mark against deportment.

"Never mind," said father, as if it were the smallest possible matter, "today you're going. Come along now. We've barely time."

---

6. Nickname for New Orleans, here the name of a horse race.

These expeditions were all joy, every time, from the moment they stepped into a closed one-horse cab, a treat in itself with its dark, thick upholstery, soaked with strange perfumes and tobacco smoke, until the thrilling moment when they walked into a restaurant under big lights and were given dinner with things to eat they never had at home, much less at the convent. They felt worldly and grown up, each with her glass of water colored pink with claret.

The great crowd was always exciting as if they had never seen it before, with the beautiful, incredibly dressed ladies, all plumes and flowers and paint, and the elegant gentlemen with yellow gloves. The bands played in turn with thundering drums and brasses, and now and then a wild beautiful horse would career around the track with a tiny, monkey-shaped boy on his back, limbering up for his race.

Miranda had a secret personal interest in all this which she knew better than to confide to anyone, even Maria. Least of all to Maria. In ten minutes the whole family would have known. She had lately decided to be a jockey when she grew up. Her father had said one day that she was going to be a little thing all her life, she would never be tall; and this meant, of course, that she would never be a beauty like Aunt Amy, or Cousin Isabel. Her hope of being a beauty died hard, until the notion of being a jockey came suddenly and filled all her thoughts. Quietly, blissfully, at night before she slept, and too often in the daytime when she should have been studying, she planned her career as jockey. It was dim in detail, but brilliant at the right distance. It seemed too silly to be worried about arithmetic at all, when what she needed for her future was to ride better—much better. "You ought to be ashamed of yourself," said father, after watching her gallop full tilt down the lane at the farm, on Trixie, the mustang mare. "I can see the sun, moon and stars between you and the saddle every jump." Spanish style meant that one sat close to the saddle, and did all kinds of things with the knees and reins. Jockeys bounced lightly, their knees almost level with the horse's back, rising and falling like a rubber ball. Miranda felt she could do that easily. Yes, she would be a jockey, like Tod Sloan,[7] winning every other race at least. Meantime, while she was training, she would keep it a secret, and one day she would ride out, bouncing lightly, with the other jockeys, and win a great race, and surprise everybody, her family most of all.

On that particular Saturday, her idol, the great Tod Sloan, was riding, and he won two races. Miranda longed to bet her dollar on Tod Sloan, but father said, "Not now, honey. Today you must bet on Uncle Gabriel's horse. Save your dollar for the fourth race, and put it on Miss Lucy. You've got a hundred to one shot. Think if she wins."

Miranda knew well enough that a hundred to one shot was no bet at all. She sulked, the crumpled dollar in her hand grew damp and warm. She could have won three dollars already on Tod Sloan. Maria said virtuously, "It wouldn't be nice not to bet on Uncle Gabriel. That way, we keep the money in the family." Miranda put out her under lip at her sister. Maria was too prissy for words. She wrinkled her nose back at Miranda.

They had just turned their dollar over to the bookmaker for the fourth race when a vast bulging man with a red face and immense tan ragged

---

7. James Foreman Sloan (1874–1933), known for his "monkey crouch" riding form.

mustaches fading into gray hailed them from a lower level of the grandstand, over the heads of the crowd, "Hey, there, Harry?" Father said, "Bless my soul, there's Gabriel." He motioned to the man, who came pushing his way heavily up the shallow steps. Maria and Miranda stared, first at him, then at each other. "Can that be our Uncle Gabriel?" their eyes asked. "Is that Aunt Amy's handsome romantic beau? Is that the man who wrote the poem about our Aunt Amy?" Oh, what did grown-up people *mean* when they talked, anyway?

He was a shabby fat man with bloodshot blue eyes, sad beaten eyes, and a big melancholy laugh, like a groan. He towered over them shouting to their father, "Well, for God's sake, Harry, it's been a coon's age. You ought to come out and look 'em over. You look just like yourself, Harry, how are you?"

The band struck up "Over the River" and Uncle Gabriel shouted louder. "Come on, let's get out of this. What are you doing up here with the pikers?"

"Can't," shouted Father. "Brought my little girls. Here they are."

Uncle Gabriel's bleared eyes beamed blindly upon them. "Fine looking set, Harry," he bellowed, "pretty as pictures, how old are they?"

"Ten and fourteen now," said Father; "awkward ages. Nest of vipers," he boasted, "perfect batch of serpent's teeth.[8] Can't do a thing with 'em." He fluffed up Miranda's hair, pretending to tousle it.

"Pretty as pictures," bawled Uncle Gabriel, "but rolled into one they don't come up to Amy, do they?"

"No, they don't," admitted their father at the top of his voice, "but they're only half-baked." *Over the river, over the river,* moaned the band, *my sweetheart's waiting for me.*

"I've got to get back now," yelled Uncle Gabriel. The little girls felt quite deaf and confused. "Got the God-damnedest jockey in the world, Harry, just my luck. Ought to tie him on. Fell off Fiddler yesterday, just plain fell off on his tail—Remember Amy's mare, Miss Lucy? Well, this is her namesake, Miss Lucy IV. None of 'em ever came up to the first one, though. Stay right where you are, I'll be back."

Maria spoke up boldly. "Uncle Gabriel, tell Miss Lucy we're betting on her." Uncle Gabriel bent down and it looked as if there were tears in his swollen eyes. "God bless your sweet heart," he bellowed, "I'll tell her." He plunged down through the crowd again, his fat back bowed slightly in his loose clothes, his thick neck rolling over his collar.

Miranda and Maria, disheartened by the odds, by their first sight of their romantic Uncle Gabriel, whose language was so coarse, sat listlessly without watching, their chances missed, their dollars gone, their hearts sore. They didn't even move until their father leaned over and hauled them up. "Watch your horse," he said, in a quick warning voice, "watch Miss Lucy come home."

They stood up, scrambled to their feet on the bench, every vein in them suddenly beating so violently they could hardly focus their eyes, and saw a thin little mahogany-colored streak flash by the judges' stand, only a neck ahead, but their Miss Lucy, oh, their darling, their lovely—oh, Miss Lucy, their Uncle Gabriel's Miss Lucy, had won, had won. They

---

8. Shakespeare, *King Lear* I, iv, 371–72—"How sharper than a serpent's tooth it is/ To have a thankless child."

leaped up and down screaming and clapping their hands, their hats falling back on their shoulders, their hair flying wild. *Whoa, you heifer,* squalled the band with snorting brasses, and the crowd broke into a long roar like the falling of the walls of Jericho.[9]

The little girls sat down, feeling quite dizzy, while their father tried to pull their hats straight, and taking out his handkerchief held it to Miranda's face, saying very gently, "Here, blow your nose," and he dried her eyes while he was about it. He stood up then and shook them out of their daze. He was smiling with deep laughing wrinkles around his eyes, and spoke to them as if they were grown young ladies he was squiring around.

"Let's go out and pay our respects to Miss Lucy," he said. "She's the star of the day."

The horses were coming in, looking as if their hides had been drenched and rubbed with soap, their ribs heaving, their nostrils flaring and closing. The jockeys sat bowed and relaxed, their faces calm, moving a little at the waist with the movement of their horses. Miranda noted this for future use; that was the way you came in from a race, easy and quiet, whether you had won or lost. Miss Lucy came last, and a little handful of winners applauded her and cheered the jockey. He smiled and lifted his whip, his eyes and shriveled brown face perfectly serene. Miss Lucy was bleeding at the nose, two thick red rivulets were stiffening her tender mouth and chin, the round velvet chin that Miranda thought the nicest kind of chin in the world. Her eyes were wild and her knees were trembling, and she snorted when she drew her breath.

Miranda stood staring. That was winning, too. Her heart clinched tight; that was winning, for Miss Lucy. So instantly and completely did her heart reject that victory, she did not know when it happened, but she hated it, and was ashamed that she had screamed and shed tears for joy when Miss Lucy, with her bloodied nose and bursting heart had gone past the judges' stand a neck ahead. She felt empty and sick and held to her father's hand so hard that he shook her off a little impatiently and said, "What is the matter with you? Don't be so fidgety."

Uncle Gabriel was standing there waiting, and he was completely drunk. He watched the mare go in, then leaned against the fence with its white-washed posts and sobbed openly. "She's got the nosebleed, Harry," he said. "Had it since yesterday. We thought we had her all fixed up. But she did it, all right. She's got a heart like a lion. I'm going to breed her, Harry. Her heart's worth a million dollars, by itself, God bless her." Tears ran over his brick-colored face and into his straggling mustaches. "If anything happens to her now I'll blow my brains out. She's my last hope. She saved my life. I've had a run," he said, groaning into a large handkerchief and mopping his face all over, "I've had a run of luck that would break a brass billy goat. God, Harry, let's go somewhere and have a drink."

"I must get the children back to school first, Gabriel," said their father, taking each by a hand.

"No, no, don't go yet," said Uncle Gabriel desperately. "Wait here a minute, I want to see the vet and take a look at Miss Lucy, and I'll be

---

9. Joshua 6:20—"So the people shouted when the priests blew the trumpets: and it came to pass, when the people heard the sound of the trumpet, and the people shouted with a great shout, that the wall fell down flat, so that the people went up into the city, every man straight before him, and they took the city."

right back. Don't go, Harry, for God's sake. I want to talk to you a few
minutes."

Maria and Miranda, watching Uncle Gabriel's lumbering, unsteady
back, were thinking that this was the first time they had ever seen a man
that they knew to be drunk. They had seen pictures and read descriptions, and had heard descriptions, so they recognized the symptoms at
once. Miranda felt it was an important moment in a great many ways.

"Uncle Gabriel's a drunkard, isn't he?" she asked her father, rather
proudly.

"Hush, don't say such things," said father with a heavy frown, "or I'll
never bring you here again." He looked worried and unhappy, and, above
all, undecided. The little girls stood stiff with resentment against such
obvious injustice. They loosed their hands from his and moved away
coldly, standing together in silence. Their father did not notice, watching
the place where Uncle Gabriel had disappeared. In a few minutes he
came back, still wiping his face, as if there were cobwebs on it, carrying
his big black hat. He waved at them from a short distance, calling out in
a cheerful way, "She's going to be all right, Harry. It's stopped now.
Lord, this will be good news for Miss Honey. Come on, Harry, let's all go
home and tell Miss Honey. She deserves some good news."

Father said, "I'd better take the children back to school first, then we'll
go."

"No, no," said Uncle Gabriel, fondly. "I want her to see the girls. She'll
be tickled pink to see them, Harry. Brimg 'em along."

"Is it another race horse we're going to see?" whispered Miranda in her
sister's ear.

"Don't be silly," said Maria. "It's Uncle Gabriel's second wife."

"Let's find a cab, Harry," said Uncle Gabriel, "and take your little girls
out to cheer up Miss Honey. Both of 'em rolled into one look a lot like
Amy, I swear they do. I want Miss Honey to see them. She's always liked
our family, Harry, though of course she's not what you'd call an expansive
kind of woman."

Maria and Miranda sat facing the driver, and Uncle Gabriel squeezed
himself in facing them beside their father. The air became at once bitter
and sour with his breathing. He looked sad and poor. His necktie was on
crooked and his shirt was rumpled. Father said, "You're going to see
Uncle Gabriel's second wife, children," exactly if they had not heard everything; and to Gabriel, "How *is* your wife nowadays? It must be twenty
years since I saw her last."

"She's pretty gloomy, and that's a fact," said Uncle Gabriel. "She's
been pretty gloomy for years now, and nothing seems to shake her out of
it. She never did care for horses, Harry, if you remember; she hasn't been
near the track three times since we were married. When I think how
Amy wouldn't have missed a race for anything . . . She's very different
from Amy, Harry, a very different kind of woman. As fine a woman as
ever lived in her own way, but she hates change and moving around, and
she just lives in the boy."

"Where is Gabe now?" asked father.

"Finishing college," said Uncle Gabriel; "a smart boy, but awfully like
his mother. Awfully like," he said, in a melancholy way. "She hates being
away from him. Just wants to sit down in the same town and wait for him
to get through with his education. Well, I'm sorry it can't be done if

that's what she wants, but God Almighty—And this last run of luck has
about got her down. I hope you'll be able to cheer her up a little, Harry,
she needs it."

The little girls sat watching the streets grow duller and dingier and
narrower, and at last the shabbier and shabbier white people gave way to
dressed-up Negroes, and then to shabby Negroes, and after a long way the
cab stopped before a desolate-looking little hotel in Elysian Fields.[1] Their
father helped Maria and Miranda out, told the cabman to wait, and they
followed Uncle Gabriel through a dirty damp-smelling patio, down a long
gas-lighted hall full of a terrible smell, Miranda couldn't decide what it
was made of but it had a bitter taste even, and up a long staircase with a
ragged carpet. Uncle Gabriel pushed open a door without warning, saying, "Come in, here we are."

A tall pale-faced woman with faded straw-colored hair and pink-
rimmed eyelids rose suddenly from a squeaking rocking chair. She wore a
stiff blue-and-white striped shirtwaist and a still black skirt of some hard
shiny material. Her large knuckled hands rose to her round, neat pompa-
dour at sight of her visitors.

"Honey," said Uncle Gabriel, with large false heartiness, "you'll never
guess who's come to see you." He gave her a clumsy hug. Her face did
not change and her eyes rested steadily on the three strangers. "Amy's
brother Harry, Honey, you remember, don't you?"

"Of course," said Miss Honey, putting out her hand straight as a pad-
dle, "of course I remember you, Harry." She did not smile.

"And Amy's two little nieces," went on Uncle Gabriel, bringing them
forward. They put out their hands limply, and Miss Honey gave each one
a slight flip and dropped it. "And we've got good news for you," went
on Uncle Gabriel, trying to bolster up the painful situation. "Miss Lucy
stepped out and showed 'em today, Honey. We're rich again, old girl,
cheer up."

Miss Honey turned her long, despairing face towards her visitors. "Sit
down," she said with a heavy sigh, seating herself and motioning towards
various rickety chairs. There was a big lumpy bed, with a grayish-white
counterpane on it, a marble-topped washstand, grayish coarse lace curtains on strings at the two small windows, a small closed fireplace with a
hole in it for a stovepipe, and two trunks, standing at odds as if somebody
were just moving in, or just moving out. Everything was dingy and soiled
and neat and bare; not a pin out of place.

"We'll move to the St. Charles[2] tomorrow," said Uncle Gabriel, as
much to Harry as to his wife. "Get your best dresses together, Honey, the
long dry spell is over."

Miss Honey's nostrils pinched together and she rocked slightly, with
her arms folded. "I've lived in the St. Charles before, and I've lived here
before," she said, in a tight deliberate voice, "and this time I'll just stay
where I am, thank you. I prefer it to moving back here in three months.
I'm settled now, I feel at home here," she told him, glancing at Harry,
her pale eyes kindling with blue fire, a stiff white line around her mouth.

The little girls sat trying not to stare, miserably ill at ease. Their grandmother had pronounced Harry's children to be the most unteachable she
had ever seen in her long experience with the young; but they had

1. Run-down section of New Orleans.   2. Expensive New Orleans hotel.

learned by indirection one thing well—nice people did not carry on quarrels before outsiders. Family quarrels were sacred, to be waged privately in fierce hissing whispers, low choked mutters and growls. If they did yell and stamp, it must be behind closed doors and windows. Uncle Gabriel's second wife was hopping mad and she looked ready to fly out at Uncle Gabriel any second, with him sitting there like a hound when someone shakes a whip at him.

"She loathes and despises everybody in this room," thought Miranda, coolly, "and she's afraid we won't know it. She needn't worry, we knew it when we came in." With all her heart she wanted to go, but her father, though his face was a study, made no move. He seemed to be trying to think of something pleasant to say. Maria, feeling guilty, though she couldn't think why, was calculating rapidly, "Why, she's only Uncle Gabriel's second wife, and Uncle Gabriel was only married before to Aunt Amy, why, why, she's no kin at all, and I'm glad of it." Sitting back easily, she let her hands fall open in her lap; they would be going in a few minutes, undoubtedly, and they need never come back.

Then father said, "We mustn't be keeping you, we just dropped in for a few minutes. We wanted to see how you are."

Miss Honey said nothing, but she made a little gesture with her hands, from the wrist, as if to say, "Well, you see how I am, and now what next?"

"I must take these young ones back to school," said father, and Uncle Gabriel said stupidly, "Look, Honey, don't you think they resemble Amy a little? Especially around the eyes, especially Maria, don't you think, Harry?"

Their father glanced at them in turn. "I really couldn't say," he decided, and the little girls saw he was more monstrously embarrassed than ever. He turned to Miss Honey, "I hadn't seen Gabriel for so many years," he said, "we thought of getting out for a talk about old times together. You know how it is."

"Yes, I know," said Miss Honey, rocking a little, and all that she knew gleamed forth in a pallid, unquenchable hatred and bitterness that seemed enough to bring her long body straight up out of the chair in a fury, "I know," and she sat staring at the floor. Her mouth shook and straightened. There was a terrible silence, which was broken when the little girls saw their father rise. They got up, too, and it was all they could do to keep from making a dash for the door.

"I must get the young ones back," said their father. "They've had enough excitement for one day. They each won a hundred dollars on Miss Lucy. It was a good race," he said, in complete wretchedness, as if he simply could not extricate himself from the situation. "Wasn't it, Gabriel?"

"It was a grand race," said Gabriel, brokenly, "a grand race."

Miss Honey stood up and moved a step towards the door. "Do you take them to the races, actually?" she asked, and her lids flickered towards them as if they were loathsome insects, Maria felt.

"If I feel they deserve a little treat, yes," said their father, in an easy tone but with wrinkled brow.

"I had rather, much rather," said Miss Honey clearly, "see my son dead at my feet than hanging around a race track."

The next few moments were rather a blank, but at last they were out of it, going down the stairs, across the patio, with Uncle Gabriel seeing them back into the cab. His face was sagging, the features had fallen as if the flesh had slipped from the bones, and his eyelids were puffed and blue. "Good-by, Harry," he said soberly. "How long you expect to be here?" "Starting back tomorrow," said Harry. "Just dropped in on a little business and to see how the girls were getting along."

"Well," said Uncle Gabriel, "I may be dropping into your part of the country one of these days. Good-by, children," he said, taking their hands one after the other in his big warm paws. "They're nice children, Harry. I'm glad you won on Miss Lucy," he said to the little girls, tenderly. "Don't spend your money foolishly, now. Well, so long, Harry." As the cab jolted away he stood there fat and sagging, holding up his arm and wagging his hand at them.

"Goodness," said Maria, in her most grown-up manner, taking her hat off and hanging it over her knee, "I'm glad that's over."

"What I want to know is," said Miranda, "is Uncle Gabriel a real drunkard?"

"Oh, hush," said their father, sharply, "I've got the heartburn."

There was a respectful pause, as before a public monument. When their father had the heartburn it was time to lay low. The cab rumbled on, back to clean gay streets, with the lights coming on in the early February darkness, past shimmering shop windows, smooth pavements, on and on, past beautiful old houses set in deep gardens, on, on back to the dark walls with the heavy-topped trees hanging over them. Miranda sat thinking so hard she forgot and spoke out in her thoughtless way: "I've decided I'm not going to be a jockey, after all." She could as usual have bitten her tongue, but as usual it was too late.

Father cheered up and twinkled at her knowingly, as if that didn't surprise him in the least. "Well, well," said he, "so you aren't going to be a jockey! That's very sensible of you. I think she ought to be a lion-tamer, don't you, Maria? That's a nice, womanly profession."

Miranda, seeing Maria from the height of her fourteen years suddenly joining with their father to laugh at her, made an instant decision and laughed with them at herself. That was better. Everybody laughed and it was such a relief.

"Where's my hundred dollars?" asked Maria, anxiously.

"It's going in the bank," said their father, "and yours too," he told Miranda. "That is your nest-egg."

"Just so they don't buy my stockings with it," said Miranda, who had long resented the use of her Christmas money by their grandmother. "I've got enough stockings to last me a year."

"I'd like to buy a racehorse," said Maria, "but I know it's not enough." The limitations of wealth oppressed her. "What could you buy with a hundred dollars?" she asked fretfully.

"Nothing, nothing at all," said their father, "a hundred dollars is just something you put in the bank."

Maria and Miranda lost interest. They had won a hundred dollars on a horse race once. It was already in the far past. They began to chatter about something else.

The lay sister opened the door on a long cord, from behind the grille; Maria and Miranda walked in silently to their familiar world of shining bare floors and insipid wholesome food and cold-water washing and regular prayers; their world of poverty, chastity and obedience, of early to bed and early to rise, of sharp little rules and tittle-tattle. Resignation was in their childish faces as they held them up to be kissed.

"Be good girls," said their father, in the strange serious, rather helpless way he always had when he told them good-by. "Write to your daddy, now, nice long letters," he said, holding their arms firmly for a moment before letting go for good. Then he disappeared, and the sister swung the door closed after him.

Maria and Miranda went upstairs to the dormitory to wash their faces and hands and slick down their hair again before supper.

Miranda was hungry. "We didn't have a thing to eat, after all," she grumbled. "Not even a chocolate nut bar. I think that's mean. We didn't even get a quarter to spend," she said.

"Not a living bite," said Maria. "Not a nickel." She poured out cold water into the bowl and rolled up her sleeves.

Another girl about her own age came in and went to a washbowl near another bed. "Where have you been?" she asked. "Did you have a good time?"

"We went to the races, with our father," said Maria, soaping her hands.

"Our uncle's horse won," said Miranda.

"My goodness," said the other girl, vaguely, "that must have been grand."

Maria looked at Miranda, who was rolling up her own sleeves. She tried to feel martyred, but it wouldn't go. "Immured for another week," she said, her eyes sparkling over the edge of her towel.

Part III: 1912

Miranda followed the porter down the stuffy aisle of the sleeping-car, where the berths were nearly all made down and the dusty green curtains buttoned, to a seat at the further end. "Now yo' berth's ready any time, Miss," said the porter.

"But I want to sit up a while," said Miranda. A very thin old lady raised choleric black eyes and fixed upon her a regard of unmixed disapproval. She had two immense front teeth and a receding chin, but she did not lack character. She had piled her luggage around her like a barricade, and she glared at the porter when he picked some of it up to make room for his new passenger. Miranda sat, saying mechanically, "May I?"

"You may, indeed," said the old lady, for she seemed old in spite of a certain brisk, rustling energy. Her taffeta petticoats creaked like hinges every time she stirred. With ferocious sarcasm, after a half second's pause, she added, "You may be so good as to get off my hat!"

Miranda rose instantly in horror, and handed to the old lady a wilted contrivance of black horsehair braid and shattered white poppies. "I'm dreadfully sorry," she stammered, for she had been brought up to treat ferocious old ladies respectfully, and this one seemed capable of spanking her, then and there. "I didn't dream it was your hat."

"And whose hat did you dream it might be?" inquired the old lady, baring her teeth and twirling the hat on a forefinger to restore it.

"I didn't think it was a hat at all," said Miranda with a touch of hysteria.

"Oh, you didn't think it was a hat? Where on earth are your eyes, child?" and she proved the nature and function of the object by placing it on her head at a somewhat tipsy angle, though still it did not much resemble a hat. "Now can you see what it is?"

"Yes, oh, yes," said Miranda, with a meekness she hoped was disarming. She ventured to sit again after a careful inspection of the narrow space she was to occupy.

"Well, well," said the old lady, "let's have the porter remove some of these encumbrances," and she stabbed the bell with a lean sharp forefinger. There followed a flurry of rearrangements, during which they both stood in the aisle, the old lady giving a series of impossible directions to the Negro which he bore philosophically while he disposed of the luggage exactly as he had meant to do. Seated again, the old lady asked in a kindly, authoritative tone, "And what might your name be, child?"

At Miranda's answer, she blinked somewhat, unfolded her spectacles, straddled them across her high nose competently, and took a good long look at the face beside her.

"If I'd had my spectacles on," she said, in an astonishingly changed voice, "I might have known. I'm Cousin Eva Parrington," she said, "Cousin Molly Parrington's daughter, remember? I knew you when you were a little girl. You were a lively little girl," she added as if to console her, "and very opinionated. The last thing I heard about you, you were planning to be a tight-rope walker. You were going to play the violin and walk the tight rope at the same time."

"I must have seen it at the vaudeville show," said Miranda. "I couldn't have invented it. Now I'd like to be an air pilot!"

"I used to go to dances with your father," said Cousin Eva, busy with her own thoughts, "and to big holiday parties at your grandmother's house, long before you were born. Oh, indeed, yes, a long time before."

Miranda remembered several things at once. Aunt Amy had threatened to be an old maid like Eva. Oh, Eva, the trouble with her is she has no chin. Eva has given up, and is teaching Latin in a Female Seminary. Eva's gone out for votes for women, God help her. The nice thing about an ugly daughter is, she's not apt to make me a grandmother.... "They didn't do you much good, those parties, dear Cousin Eva," thought Miranda.

"They didn't do me much good, those parties," said Cousin Eva aloud as if she were a mind-reader, and Miranda's head swam for a moment with fear that she had herself spoken aloud. "Or at least, they didn't serve their purpose, for I never got married; but I enjoyed them, just the same. I had a good time at those parties, even if I wasn't a belle. And so you are Harry's child, and here I was quarreling with you. You do remember me, don't you?"

"Yes," said Miranda, and thinking that even if Cousin Eva had been really an old maid ten years before, still she couldn't be much past fifty now, and she looked so withered and tired, so famished and sunken in the cheeks, so *old*, somehow. Across the abyss separating Cousin Eva from her own youth, Miranda looked with painful premonition. "Oh, must I ever be like that?" She said aloud, "Yes, you used to read Latin to me, and tell me not to bother about the sense, to get the sound in my mind, and it would come easier later."

"Ah, so I did," said Cousin Eva, delighted. "So I did. You don't happen to remember that I once had a beautiful sapphire velvet dress with a train on it?"

"No, I don't remember that dress," said Miranda.

"It was an old dress of my mother's made over and cut down to fit," said Eva, "and it wasn't in the least becoming to me, but it was the only really good dress I ever had, and I remember it as if it were yesterday. Blue was never my color." She sighed with a humorous bitterness. The humor seemed momentary, but the bitterness was a constant state of mind.

Miranda, trying to offer the sympathy of fellow suffering, said, "I know. I've had Maria's dresses made over for me, and they were never right. It was dreadful."

"Well," said Cousin Eva, in the tone of one who did not wish to share her unique disappointments. "How is your father? I always liked him. He was one of the finest-looking young men I ever saw. Vain, too, like all his family. He wouldn't ride any but the best horses he could buy, and I used to say he made them prance and then watched his own shadow. I used to tell this on him at dinner parties, and he hated me for it. I feel pretty certain he hated me." An overtone of complacency in Cousin Eva's voice explained better than words that she had her own method of commanding attention and arousing emotion. "How *is* your father, I asked you, my dear?"

"I haven't seen him for nearly a year," answered Miranda, quickly, before Cousin Eva could get ahead again. "I'm going home now to Uncle Gabriel's funeral; you know, Uncle Gabriel died in Lexington[3] and they have brought him back to be buried beside Aunt Amy."

"So that's how we meet," said Cousin Eva. "Yes, Gabriel drank himself to death at last. I'm going to the funeral, too. I haven't been home since I went to Mother's funeral, it must be, let's see, yes, it will be nine years next July. I'm going to Gabriel's funeral, though. I wouldn't miss that. Poor fellow, what a life he had. Pretty soon, they'll all be gone."

Miranda said, "We're left, Cousin Eva," meaning those of her own generation, the young, and Cousin Eva said, "Pshaw, you'll live forever, and you won't bother to come to our funerals." She didn't seem to think this was a misfortune, but flung the remark from her like a woman accustomed to saying what she thought.

Miranda sat thinking, "Still, I suppose it would be pleasant if I could say something to make her believe that she and all of them would be lamented, but—but—" With a smile which she hoped would be her denial of Cousin Eva's cynicism about the younger generation, she said, "You were right about the Latin, Cousin Eva, your reading did help when I began with it. I still study," she said. "Latin, too."

"And why shouldn't you?" asked Cousin Eva, sharply, adding at once mildly, "I'm glad you are going to use your mind a little, child. Don't let yourself rust away. Your mind outwears all sorts of things you may set your heart upon; you can enjoy it when all other things are taken away." Miranda was chilled by her melancholy. Cousin Eva went on: "In our part of the country, in my time, we were so provincial—a woman didn't dare to think or act for herself. The whole world was a little that way,"

---

3. The center of Kentucky horse country.

she said, "but we were the worst, I believe. I suppose you must know how I fought for votes for women when it almost made a pariah of me—I was turned out of my chair at the Seminary, but I'm glad I did it and I would do it again. You young things don't realize. You'll live in a better world because we worked for it."

Miranda knew something of Cousin Eva's career. She said sincerely, "I think it was brave of you, and I'm glad you did it, too. I loved your courage."

"It wasn't just showing off, mind you," said Cousin Eva, rejecting praise, fretfully. "Any fool can be brave. We were working for something we knew was right, and it turned out that we needed a lot of courage for it. That was all. I didn't expect to go to jail, but I went three times, and I'd go three times three more if it were necessary. We aren't voting yet," she said, "but we will be."

Miranda did not venture any answer, but she felt convinced that indeed women would be voting soon if nothing fatal happened to Cousin Eva. There was something in her manner which said such things could be left safely to her. Miranda was dimly fired for the cause herself; it seemed heroic and worth suffering for, but discouraging, too, to those who came after: Cousin Eva so plainly had swept the field clear of opportunity.

They were silent for a few minutes, while Cousin Eva rummaged in her handbag, bringing up odds and ends: peppermint drops, eye drops, a packet of needles, three handkerchiefs, a little bottle of violet perfume, a book of addresses, two buttons, one black, one white, and, finally, a packet of headache powders.

"Bring me a glass of water, will you, my dear?" she asked Miranda. She poured the headache powder on her tongue, swallowed the water, and put two peppermints in her mouth.

"So now they're going to bury Gabriel near Amy," she said after a while, as if her eased headache had started her on a new train of thought. "Miss Honey would like that, poor dear, if she could know. After listening to stories about Amy for twenty-five years, she must lie alone in her grave in Lexington while Gabriel sneaks off to Texas to make his bed with Amy again. It was a kind of life-long infidelity, Miranda, and now an eternal infidelity on top of that. He ought to be ashamed of himself."

"It was Aunt Amy he loved," said Miranda, wondering what Miss Honey could have been like before her long troubles with Uncle Gabriel. "First, anyway."

"Oh, that Amy," said Cousin Eva, her eyes glittering. "Your Aunt Amy was a devil and a mischief-maker, but I loved her dearly. I used to stand up for Amy when her reputation wasn't worth that." Her fingers snapped like castanets. "She used to say to me, in that gay soft way she had, 'Now, Eva, don't go talking votes for women when the lads ask you to dance. Don't recite Latin poems to 'em,' she would say, 'they got sick of that in school. Dance and say nothing, Eva,' she would say, her eyes perfectly devilish, 'and hold your chin up, Eva.' My chin was my weak point, you see. 'You'll never catch a husband if you don't look out,' she would say. Then she would laugh and fly away, and where did she fly to?" demanded Cousin Eva, her sharp eyes pinning Miranda down to the bitter facts of the case, "To scandal and to death, nowhere else."

"She was joking, Cousin Eva," said Miranda, innocently, "and everybody loved her."

"Not everybody, by a long shot," said Cousin Eva in triumph. "She had enemies. If she knew, she pretended she didn't. If she cared, she never said. You couldn't make her quarrel. She was sweet as a honeycomb to everybody. *Everybody*," she added, "that was the trouble. She went through life like a spoiled darling, doing as she pleased and letting other people suffer for it, and pick up the pieces after her. I never believed for one moment," said Cousin Eva, putting her mouth close to Miranda's ear and breathing peppermint hotly into it, "that Amy was an impure woman. Never! But let me tell you, there were plenty who did believe it. There were plenty to pity poor Gabriel for being so completely blinded by her. A great many persons were not suprised when they heard that Gabriel was perfectly miserable all the time, on their honeymoon, in New Orleans. Jealousy. And why not? But I used to say to such persons that, no matter what the appearances were, I had faith in Amy's virtue. Wild, I said, indiscreet, I said, heartless, I said, but *virtuous*, I feel certain. But you could hardly blame anyone for being mystified. The way she rose up suddenly from death's door to marry Gabriel Breaux, after refusing him and treating him like a dog for years, looked odd, to say the least. To say the very least," she added, after a moment, "odd is a mild word for it. And there was something very mysterious about her death, only six weeks after marriage."

Miranda roused herself. She felt she knew this part of the story and could set Cousin Eva right about one thing. "She died of a hemorrhage from the lungs," said Miranda. "She had been ill for five years, don't you remember?"

Cousin Eva was ready for that. "Ha, that was the story, indeed. The official account, you might say. Oh, yes, I heard that often enough. But did you ever hear about that fellow Raymond somebody-or-other from Calcasieu Parish,[4] almost a stranger, who persuaded Amy to elope with him from a dance one night, and she just ran out into the darkness without even stopping for her cloak, and your poor dear nice father Harry— you weren't even thought of then—had to run him down to earth and shoot him?"

Miranda leaned back from the advancing flood of speech. "Cousin Eva, my father shot *at* him, don't you remember? He didn't hit him. . . . "

"Well, that's a pity."

" . . . and they had only gone out for a breath of air between dances. It was Uncle Gabriel's jealousy. And my father shot at the man because he thought that was better than letting Uncle Gabriel fight a duel about Aunt Amy. There was *nothing* in the whole affair except Uncle Gabriel's jealousy."

"You poor baby," said Cousin Eva, and pity gave a light like daggers to her eyes, "you dear innocent, you—do you believe that? How old are you, anyway?"

"Just past eighteen," said Miranda.

"If you don't understand what I tell you," said Cousin Eva portentously, "you will later. Knowledge can't hurt you. You mustn't live in a romantic haze about life. You'll understand when you're married, at any rate."

"I'm marrried now, Cousin Eva," said Miranda, feeling for almost the

4. Parish (county) about 200 miles due west of New Orleans, on the Texas border.

first time that it might be an advantage, "nearly a year. I eloped from school." It seemed very unreal even as she said it, and seemed to have nothing at all to do with the future; still, it was important, it must be declared, it was a situation in life which people seemed to be most exacting about, and the only feeling she could rouse in herself about it was an immense weariness as if it were an illness that she might one day hope to recover from.

"Shameful, shameful," cried Cousin Eva, genuinely repelled. "If you had been my child I should have brought you home and spanked you."

Miranda laughed out. Cousin Eva seemed to believe things could be arranged like that. She was so solemn and fierce, so comic and baffled.

"And you must know I should have just gone straight out again, through the nearest window," she taunted her. "If I went the first time, why not the second?"

"Yes, I suppose so," said Cousin Eva. "I hope you married rich."

"Not so very," said Miranda. "Enough." As if anyone could have stopped to think of such a thing!

Cousin Eva adjusted her spectacles and sized up Miranda's dress, her luggage, examined her engagement ring and wedding ring, with her nostrils fairly quivering as if she might smell out wealth on her.

"Well, that's better than nothing," said Cousin Eva. "I thank God every day of my life that I have a small income. It's a Rock of Ages.[5] What would have become of me if I hadn't a cent of my own? Well, you'll be able now to do something for your family."

Miranda remembered what she had always heard about the Parringtons. They were money-hungry, they loved money and nothing else, and when they had got some they kept it. Blood was thinner than water between the Parringtons where money was concerned.

"We're pretty poor," said Miranda, stubbornly allying herself with her father's family instead of her husband's, "but a rich marriage is no way out," she said, with the snobbishness of poverty. She was thinking, "You don't know my branch of the family, dear Cousin Eva, if you think it is."

"Your branch of the family," said Cousin Eva, with that terrifying habit she had of lifting phrases out of one's mind, "has no more practical sense than so many children. Everything for love," she said, with a face of positive nausea, "that was it. Gabriel would have been rich if his grandfather had not disinherited him, but would Amy be sensible and marry him and make him settle down so the old man would have been pleased with him? No. And what could Gabriel do without money? I wish you could have seen the life he led Miss Honey, one day buying her Paris gowns and the next day pawning her earrings. It just depended on how the horses ran, and they ran worse and worse, and Gabriel drank more and more."

Miranda did not say, "I saw a little of it." She was trying to imagine Miss Honey in a Paris gown. She said, "But Uncle Gabriel was so mad about Aunt Amy, there was no question of her not marrying him at last, money or no money."

Cousin Eva strained her lips tightly over her teeth, let them fly again and leaned over, gripping Miranda's arm. "What I ask myself, what I ask myself over and over again," she whispered, "is, what connection did this

<hr />

5. Solid support; the 1775 hymn of that title by Augustus Montague Toplady (1740–1778) begins, "Rock of Ages, cleft for me,/ Let me hide myself in thee."

man Raymond from Calcasieu have with Amy's sudden marriage to Gabriel, and *what* did Amy do to make away with herself so soon afterward? For mark my words, child, Amy wasn't so ill as all that. She'd been flying around for years after the doctors said her lungs were weak. Amy did away with herself to escape some disgrace, some exposure that she faced."

The beady black eyes glinted; Cousin Eva's face was quite frightening, so near and so intent. Miranda wanted to say, "Stop. Let her rest. What harm did she ever do you?" but she was timid and unnerved, and deep in her was a horrid fascination with the terrors and the darkness Cousin Eva had conjured up. What was the end of this story?

"She was a bad, wild girl, but I was fond of her to the last," said Cousin Eva. "She got into trouble somehow, and she couldn't get out again, and I have every reason to believe she killed herself with the drug they gave her to keep her quiet after a hemorrhage. If she didn't, what happened, what happened?"

"I don't know," said Miranda. "How should I know? She was very beautiful," she said, as if this explained everything. "Everybody said she was very beautiful."

"Not everybody," said Cousin Eva, firmly, shaking her head. "I for one never thought so. They made entirely too much fuss over her. She was good-looking enough, but why did they think she was beautiful? I cannot understand it. She was too thin when she was young, and later I always thought she was too fat, and again in her last year she was altogether too thin. She always got herself up to be looked at, and so people looked, of course. She rode too hard, and she danced too freely, and she talked too much, and you'd have to be blind, deaf and dumb not to notice her. I don't mean she was loud or vulgar, she wasn't, but she was *too free*," said Cousin Eva. She stopped for breath and put a peppermint in her mouth. Miranda could see Cousin Eva on the platform, making her speeches, stopping to take a peppermint. But why did she hate Aunt Amy so, when Aunt Amy was dead and she alive? Wasn't being alive enough?

"And her illness wasn't romantic either," said Cousin Eva, "though to hear them tell it she faded like a lily. Well, she coughed blood, if that's romantic. If they had made her take proper care of herself, if she had been nursed sensibly, she might have been alive today. But no, nothing of the kind. She lay wrapped in beautiful shawls on a sofa with flowers around her, eating as she liked or not eating, getting up after a hemorrhage and going out to ride or dance, sleeping with the windows closed; with crowds coming in and out laughing and talking at all hours, and Amy sitting up so her hair wouldn't get out of curl. And why wouldn't that sort of thing kill a well person in time? I have almost died twice in my life," said Cousin Eva, "and both times I was sent to a hospital where I belonged and left there until I came out. And I came out," she said, her voice deepening to a bugle note, "and I went to work again."

"Beauty goes, character stays," said the small voice of axiomatic morality in Miranda's ear. It was a dreary prospect; why was a strong character so deforming? Miranda felt she truly wanted to be strong, but how could she face it, seeing what it did to one?

"She had a lovely complexion," said Cousin Eva, "perfectly transparent with a flush on each cheekbone. But it was tuberculosis, and is disease beautiful? And she brought it on herself by drinking lemon and salt to stop her periods when she wanted to go to dances. There was a superstition among young girls about that. They fancied that young men could tell what ailed them by touching their hands, or even by looking at them. As if it mattered? But they were terribly self-conscious and they had immense respect for man's worldly wisdom in those days. My own notion is that a man couldn't—but anyway, the whole thing was stupid."

"I should have thought they'd have stayed at home if they couldn't manage better than that," said Miranda, feeling very knowledgeable and modern.

"They didn't dare. Those parties and dances were their market, a girl couldn't afford to miss out, there were always rivals waiting to cut the ground from under her. The rivalry—" said Cousin Eva, and her head lifted, she arched like a cavalry horse getting a whiff of the battlefield—"you can't imagine what the rivalry was like. The way those girls treated each other—nothing was too mean, nothing too false—"

Cousin Eva wrung her hands. "It was just sex," she said in despair; "their minds dwelt on nothing else. They didn't call it that, it was all smothered under pretty names, but that's all it was, sex." She looked out of the window into the darkness, her sunken cheek near Miranda flushed deeply. She turned back. "I took to the soap box and the platform when I was called upon," she said proudly, "and I went to jail when it was necessary, and my condition didn't make any difference. I was booed and jeered and shoved around just as if I had been in perfect health. But it was part of our philosophy not to let our physical handicaps make any difference to our work. You know what I mean," she said, as if until now it was all mystery. "Well, Amy carried herself with more spirit than the others, and she didn't seem to be making any sort of fight, but she was simply sex-ridden, like the rest. She behaved as if she hadn't a rival on earth, and she pretended not to know what marriage was about, but I know better. None of them had, and they didn't want to have, anything else to think about, and they didn't really know anything about that, so they simply festered inside—they festered—"

Miranda found herself deliberately watching a long procession of living corpses, festering women stepping gaily towards the charnel house, their corruption concealed under laces and flowers, their dead faces lifted smiling, and thought quite coldly, "Of course it was not like that. This is no more true than what I was told before, it's every bit as romantic," and she realized that she was tired of her intense Cousin Eva, she wanted to go to sleep, she wanted to be at home, she wished it were tomorrow and she could see her father and her sister, who were so alive and solid; who would mention her freckles and ask her if she wanted something to eat.

"My mother was not like that," she said, childishly. "My mother was a perfectly natural woman who liked to cook. I have seen some of her sewing," she said. "I have read her diary."

"Your mother was a saint," said Cousin Eva, automatically.

Miranda sat silent, outraged. "My mother was nothing of the sort," she wanted to fling in Cousin Eva's big front teeth. But Cousin Eva had been gathering bitterness until more speech came of it.

" 'Hold your chin up, Eva,' Amy used to tell me," she began, doubling up both her fists and shaking them a little. "All my life the whole family bedeviled me about my chin. My entire girlhood was spoiled by it. Can you imagine," she asked, with a ferocity that seemed much too deep for this one cause, "people who call themselves civilized spoiling life for a young girl because she had one unlucky feature? Of course, you understand perfectly it was all in the very best humor, everybody was very amusing about it, no harm meant—oh, no, no harm at all. That is the hellish thing about it. It is that I can't forgive," she cried out, and she twisted her hands together as if they were rags. "Ah, the family," she said, releasing her breath and sitting back quietly, "the whole hideous institution should be wiped from the face of the earth. It is the root of all human wrongs," she ended, and relaxed, and her face became calm. She was trembling. Miranda reached out and took Cousin Eva's hand and held it. The hand fluttered and lay still, and Cousin Eva said, "You've not the faintest idea what some of us went through, but I wanted you to hear the other side of the story. And I'm keeping you up when you need your beauty sleep," she said grimly, stirring herself with an immense rustle of petticoats.

Miranda pulled herself together, feeling limp, and stood up. Cousin Eva put out her hand again, and drew Miranda down to her. "Good night, you dear child," she said, "to think you're grown up." Miranda hesitated, then quite suddenly kissed her Cousin Eva on the cheek. The black eyes shown brightly through water for an instant, and Cousin Eva said with a warm note in her sharp clear orator's voice, "Tomorrow we'll be at home again. I'm looking forward to it, aren't you? Good night."

Miranda fell asleep while she was getting off her clothes. Instantly it was morning again. She was still trying to close her suitcase when the train pulled into the small station, and there on the platform she saw her father, looking tired and anxious, his hat pulled over his eyes. She rapped on the window to catch his attention, then ran out and threw herself upon him. He said, "Well, here's my big girl," as if she were still seven, but his hands on her arms held her off, the tone was forced. There was no welcome for her, and there had not been since she had run away. She could not persuade herself to remember how it would be; between one home-coming and the next her mind refused to accept its own knowledge. Her father looked over her head and said, without surprise, "Why, hello, Eva, I'm glad somebody sent you a telegram." Miranda, rebuffed again, let her arms fall away again, with the same painful dull jerk of the heart.

"No one in my family," said Eva, her face framed in the thin black veil she reserved, evidently, for family funerals, "ever sent me a telegram in my life. I had the news from young Keziah who had it from young Gabriel. I suppose Gabe is here?"

"Everybody seems to be here," said Father. "The house is getting full."

"I'll go to the hotel if you like," said Cousin Eva.

"Damnation, no," said Father. "I didn't mean that. You'll come with us where you belong."

Skid, the handy man, grabbed the suitcases and started down the rocky village street. "We've got the car," said Father. He took Miranda by the hand, then dropped it again, and reached for Cousin Eva's elbow.

"I'm perfectly able, thank you," said Cousin Eva, shying away.

"If you're so independent now, said Father, "God help us when you get that vote."

Cousin Eva pushed back her veil. She was smiling merrily. She liked Harry, she always had liked him, he could tease as much as he liked. She slipped her arm through his. "So it's all over with poor Gabriel, isn't it?"

"Oh, yes," said Father, "it's all over, all right. They're pegging out pretty regularly now. It will be our turn next, Eva?"

"I don't know, and I don't care," said Eva, recklessly. "It's good to be back now and then, Harry, even if it is only for funerals. I feel sinfully cheerful."

"Oh, Gabriel wouldn't mind, he'd like seeing you cheerful. Gabriel was the cheerfulest cuss I ever saw, when we were young. Life for Gabriel," said Father, "was just one perpetual picnic."

"Poor fellow," said Cousin Eva.

"Poor old Gabriel," said Father, heavily.

Miranda walked along beside her father, feeling homeless, but not sorry for it. He had not forgiven her, she knew that. When would he? She could not guess, but she felt it would come of itself, without words and without acknowledgment on either side, for by the time it arrived neither of them would need to remember what had caused their division, nor why it had seemed so important. Surely old people cannot hold their grudges forever because the young want to live, too, she thought, in her arrogance, her pride. I will make my own mistakes, not yours; I cannot depend upon you beyond a certain point, why depend at all? There was something more beyond, but this was a first step to take, and she took it, walking in silence beside her elders who were no longer Cousin Eva and Father, since they had forgotten her presence, but had become Eva and Harry, who knew each other well, who were comfortable with each other, being contemporaries on equal terms, who occupied by right their place in this world, at the time of life to which they had arrived by paths familiar to them both. They need not play their roles of daughter, of son, to aged persons who did not understand them; nor of father and elderly female cousin to young persons whom they did not understand. They were precisely themselves; their eyes cleared, their voices relaxed into perfect naturalness, they need not weigh their words or calculate the effect of their manner. "It is I who have no place," thought Miranda. "Where are my own people and my own time?" She resented, slowly and deeply and in profound silence, the presence of these aliens who lectured and admonished her, who loved her with bitterness and denied her the right to look at the world with her own eyes, who demanded that she accept their version of life and yet could not tell her the truth, not in the smallest thing. "I hate them both," her most inner and secret mind said plainly, "*I will be free of them, I shall not even remember them.*"

She sat in the front seat with Skid, the Negro boy. "Come back with us, Miranda," said Cousin Eva, with the sharp little note of elderly command, "there is plenty of room."

"No, thank you," said Miranda, in a firm cold voice. "I'm quite comfortable. Don't disturb yourself."

Neither of them noticed her voice or her manner. They sat back and went on talking steadily in their friendly family voices, talking about their dead, their living, their affairs, their prospects, their common memories, interrupting each other, catching each other up on small points of dispute, laughing with a gaiety and freshness Miranda had not known they were capable of, going over old stories and finding new points of interest in them.

Miranda could not hear the stories above the noisy motor, but she felt she knew them well, or stories like them. She knew too many stories like

them, she wanted something new of her own. The language was familiar
to them, but not to her, not any more. The house, her father had said, was
full. It would be full of cousins, many of them strangers. Would there be
any young cousins there, to whom she could talk about things they both
knew? She felt a vague distaste for seeing cousins. There were too many
of them and her blood rebelled against the ties of blood. She was sick to
death of cousins. She did not want any more ties with this house, she was
going to leave it, and she was not going back to her husband's family
either. She would have no more bonds that smothered her in love and
hatred. She knew now why she had run away to marriage, and she knew
that she was going to run away from marriage, and she was not going to
stay in any place, with anyone, that threatened to forbid her making her
own discoveries, that said "No" to her. She hoped no one had taken her
old room, she would like to sleep there once more, she would say good-by
there where she had loved sleeping once, sleeping and waking and waiting to be grown, to begin to live. Oh, what is life, she asked herself in
desperate seriousness, in those childish unanswerable words, and what
shall I do with it? It is something of my own, she thought in a fury of
jealous possessiveness, what shall I make of it? She did not know that she
asked herself this because all her earliest training had argued that life was
a substance, a material to be used, it took shape and direction and meaning only as the possessor guided and worked it; living was a progress of
continuous and varied acts of the will directed towards a definite end. She
had been assured that there were good and evil ends, one must make a
choice. But what was good, and what was evil? I hate love, she thought,
as if this were the answer, I hate loving and being loved, I hate it. And
her disturbed and seething mind received a shock of comfort from this
sudden collapse of an old painful structure of distorted images and mis-
conceptions. "You don't know anything about it," said Miranda to herself,
with extraordinary clearness as if she were an elder admonishing some
younger misguided creature. "You have to find out about it." But nothing
in her prompted her to decide, "I will now do this, I will be that, I will
go yonder, I will take a certain road to a certain end." There are questions to be asked first, she thought, but who will answer them? No one, or
there will be too many answers, none of them right. What is the truth,
she asked herself as intently as if the question had never been asked, the
truth, even about the smallest, the least important of all the things I must
find out? and where shall I begin to look for it? Her mind closed stubbornly against remembering, not the past but the legend of the past,
other people's memory of the past, at which she had spent her life peering in wonder like a child at a magic-lantern show. Ah, but there is my
own life to come yet, she thought, my own life now and beyond. I don't
want any promises, I won't have false hopes, I won't be romantic about
myself. I can't live in their world any longer, she told herself, listening to
the voices back of her. Let them tell their stories to each other. Let them
go on explaining how things happened. I don't care. At least I can know
the truth about what happens to me, she assured herself silently, making
a promise to herself, in her hopefulness, her ignorance.

1937

AFTERWORD

Reading this anthology in isolation, you would have to believe that Katherine Anne Porter wrote *Old Mortality* with *Daisy Miller* in mind. Both novels concern themselves with the reality behind the unconventional behavior of a beautiful American girl. In both, that "reality" has to do more or less directly with the girl's sexual conduct, her "purity"; in both, the "threat" comes from a "Latin lover," someone outside her own (and therefore "proper") society. Both girls die soon after, both possibly as a result of their "misconduct." Both narratives are presented through centers of consciousness which learn or believe they learn something about themselves and their own lives from the stories of the girls.

Katherine Anne Porter may indeed have had the James novel in mind, and since her conclusions are so different, may have been "answering" it. Even if she were not consciously responding to James, by comparing the two stories we may bring out depths and nuances in each that might otherwise be missed. We must remember, however, that in the sixty years between the two there were not only drastic changes in American society and mores, but that there were a significant number of narratives by writers such as Edith Wharton and F. Scott Fitzgerald, centering on just such American girls as Daisy and Amy.

The change in social customs and mores from roughly the Civil War to the eve of World War I (seen by an author writing on the eve of World War II) underlies the structure of the story. The three chapters have, instead of verbal titles, dates: "1885–1902," "1904," "1912." And not long after the scandal represented by the first date, Amy receives a letter from Great-great-aunt Sally, a representative of the moral values and mores (including handwriting and abbreviations) of two generations earlier, the generation that fought the Civil War. So, whereas James uses space or geography to indicate moral attitudes—Winterbourne lives in Geneva, center of Calvinism; he meets Daisy in Vevey, where a romantic hero had been imprisoned; Daisy's "scandal" and death take place in "corrupt" Rome—Porter does so historically or chronologically. The audience for which the novels were written may be presumed to be close to the centers of consciousness in the novels—American Protestant for James, twentieth rather than nineteenth century for Porter. If this is so, then both novels may be intentionally instructive, teaching their readers something, for both centers of consciousness learn not only about "reality" but about themselves.

The focus in Porter's novel is on a somewhat Jamesian center of consciousness, that of Miranda, though in the first two chapters Maria and Miranda seem to share the focus of the narration. In the third section, the consciousness is for the most part Miranda's alone, until very near the end of the novel, when the focus seems to pull back from her and we are warned more explicitly than in the James novel that the central, focal consciousness may not be entirely reliable. At the end of *Old Mortality*, we see that Miranda's way of looking at things, her "truth," is limited by her youth and inexperience: "I won't be romantic about myself. I can't live in their world any longer. . . . At least I can know the truth about what happens to me, she assured herself silently, making a promise to herself in her hopefulness, her ignorance."

What does Miranda learn, then? What is the truth? What is the story?

The story seems to be about telling stories. At the very beginning, though Maria and Miranda cannot see in the old-fashioned picture of their Aunt Amy why all the "old" people think she was so beautiful and so charming, they do share their father's and their family's love of legend, love of romantic stories, that were like poetry, music, theater. "Their Aunt Amy belonged to the world of poetry. The romance of Uncle Gabriel's long, unrewarded love for her, her early death, was such a story as one found in old books. . . ." The first chapter tells the story of this romantic tragedy more or less according to how the twelve-year-old Maria and eight-year-old Miranda, nieces of Amy's, reconstruct it from family tradition. The second chapter narrates the encounter of the fourteen-year-old Maria and ten-year-old Miranda with their Uncle Gabriel, Amy's husband. The girls are in a convent school in New Orleans, and

> had long since learned to draw the lines between life, which was real and earnest, and the grave was not its goal; poetry, which was true but not real; and stories, or forbidden reading matter, in which things happened as nowhere else, with the most sublime irrelevance and unlikelihood, and one need not turn a hair, because there was not a word of truth in them.

That life's reality is described in terms of Longfellow's rather pietistic poem suggests that the girls have yet a way to go toward seeing things as they really are, and the central incident in this chapter does reveal that the romantic hero of Amy's story, Gabriel, is now a fat, sentimental, hard-drinking, seedy horseowner and gambler. Their experience at the track and after cures Miranda of her childish fantasy of becoming a jockey, and reveals, through the horse Miss Lucy (named after Amy's horse), that even the reality of winning may mean not glamour and joy but pain and bleeding. Gabriel's romanticizing of Amy and the past has ruined him and embittered his second wife.

Though the romance of remembering is undercut by the damage it does to the living, the memory itself, Amy's story, is not reviewed or revised in this chapter; but it is in the final chapter, however. Miranda, eighteen and having herself been through an unhappy marriage, is alone on a train, on her way home to Uncle Gabriel's funeral, when she meets her chinless, feminist, Latin-teaching, spinster Aunt Eva. From her she hears that Amy was no innocent romantic heroine; that she and all her friends thought of nothing but sex; that Amy, everyone's darling, was spoiled, but not an "impure" woman; that the scandal was not that the outsider had complimented Amy on her looks or even that he had kissed her (as in the family's versions) but that he had persuaded her to elope with him; that her death was mysterious, that it was not the result of her weak lungs, may have had something to do with pills, and that Eva believes " 'Amy did away with herself to escape some disgrace, some exposure that she faced.' "

What's this, now? Pregnancy and suicide? Abortion, perhaps? We are now in the modern world, the harsh world of twentieth-century reality. We have had a familiar enlightenment: in the good old days before the First World War, especially in such already anachronistic societies as that of the Old South, people lived by romantic myths, covering up unpalatable or embarrassing truths—from slavery to sex, from drunkenness to death—with poetry, fiction, lies. The title of the novel comes from the one poem the prosaic Gabriel wrote in which he sentimentally transforms the saucy, headstrong reality of Amy to a saccharine angel:

> She lives again who suffered life,
> Then suffered death, and now set free
> A singing angel, she forgets
> The griefs of old mortality.

> "Did she really sing?" Maria asked her father.
> "Now what has that to do with it?" he asked. "It's a poem."

We might also note that *Old Mortality* is the title of one of Sir Walter Scott's finest historical novels, itself a mixture of the barbarous putting down of the Scottish Covenanters by the forces of Charles II and a sentimental romantic plot in which the hero returns from supposed death just in the nick of time, etc. Mark Twain, in one of those truth-bearing comic extravagances of his, blamed the Civil War on Scott's novels: the romantic sense of the chivalry of combat and the inevitable triumph of the well-born good over whatever odds led the South, where every gentleman's library had a set of Scott's Waverley novels, to undertake an unrealistic war for a sentimentalized cause.

Most short stories and some novels would have been content with this "epiphany" or moment of illumination, fulfilling one of the most common functions of fiction— to say, "You have been told reality is like this, but I say it is otherwise." Even our imagined response to James is complete: you call "her" Daisy, the innocent; I call her Amy, the loved. Miranda, however, finds Eva's version "no more true than what I was told before, it's every bit as romantic." Is it Eva, then, who is obsessed with sex? Or is she merely driven by a bitterness toward the beautiful Amy, loved by all, who used to tell her with unwitting cruelty how to minimize her chinlessness? She transforms Miranda's mother into a saint—which Miranda rejects as a lie, loving her human mother too much—just as Gabriel transformed Amy into an angel. And though Eva wishes, she says, to do away with the family as an institution, she has not only come to Gabriel's funeral, but she sinks back into her old relationship with Miranda's father.

Miranda's father greets Miranda herself somewhat coolly because she ran away from the family to marry, and as he talks comfortably to his contemporary, Eva, both of them "precisely themselves," not needing to play the roles of son or daughter, of father or elderly cousin, Miranda rejects them both. They are the ones who have "denied her the right to look at the world with her own eyes, who demanded that she accept their version of life and yet could not tell her the truth, not in the smallest thing. 'I hate them both,' her innermost and secret mind said plainly, '*I will be free of them, I shall not even remember them.*'"

That's it, then. There is the romance of chivalry, and the romance of the sex-starved "festering women stepping gaily toward the charnel house, their corruption concealed under laces and flowers, their dead faces lifted smiling. . . ." Miranda will be free of their memory, will live her own life, find her own truths, if not about the past, at least about her own life. Youth, freedom, seeing things for oneself, that's what Miranda comes up with in rejection of the past her family has created in its stories.

But what about Miranda's own story? She has given up as childish her ambition to be a jockey—she wants to be an airline pilot instead (or is she kidding?). She says she will not even remember her family, but isn't this story a testimonial to the fact that she has not forgotten them? Eva tells her that her branch of the family " 'has no more practical sense than so many children. Everything for love. . . .' " Has Miranda escaped her family? Has she no practical sense, eloping, everything for love? Has she reenacted Amy's mistake, *mutatis mutandis*? The date *in* the story is 1912, the date *of* the story is 1937. How far removed from the eighteen-year-old Miranda is the focus of the story?

> Surely old people cannot hold their grudges forever because the young want to live, too, she thought, in her arrogance, her pride. I will make my own mistakes, not yours; I cannot depend upon you beyond a certain point, why depend at all?

What is arrogant and proud about Miranda's wanting to live her own life? declaring her independence? awakening?

> At least I can know the truth about what happens to me, she assured herself silently, making a promise to herself, in her hopefulness, her ignorance.

That's the last word in the story, "ignorance." In the eyes of the narrator of 1937, Miranda is telling herself stories too. Is she as romantic as Gabriel? her father? Eva? And while the truth recedes still farther, who *is* that narrator of 1937, whose voice is telling us the story? Is it Miranda looking back at her youthfully arrogant and innocent self? a member of a still newer generation, Miranda's son or daughter or niece, perhaps? And what myth, what "chinlessness" distorts that narrator's vision, writing out of the depths of a world-shaking depression, the earth, even in America, echoing to the sound of marching boots and rumbling tanks in central Europe?

PHILIP ROTH

Goodbye, Columbus

Neil — unreliable narrator

It is difficult to write a biographical note about a living, indeed relatively young, author without its sounding like an obituary, so let's begin with Philip Roth (born 1933) at twenty-three, about the same age as his protagonist, Neil Klugman, in *Goodbye, Columbus*. Roth, like Klugman, is Jewish, was also born in Newark, attended Rutgers, and was in the army in 1955–56. Unlike Neil, he had graduated from Bucknell University (not Rutgers, Newark), and before he entered the army he had earned a master's degree from the University of Chicago. After getting out of the army he did more graduate work at Chicago and taught there. But the big difference between Philip and Neil was that in 1956 Roth published his first short story, "Defender of the Faith," in the *New Yorker*. And he went on very soon thereafter to write *Goodbye, Columbus*, which won the National Book Award in 1959. Ten years and two books later, *Portnoy's Complaint* brought him fame, fortune, and plenty to complain about. His early work had been criticized for being anti-Semitic in its portrayal of the humor and the agonies of being a second- or third-generation American Jew: after a half-century of striving for subsistence, success, and acceptance, American Jews just after the defeat of Hitler and the "liberation" of the living and dead bones from the concentration camps almost literally did not know which way to turn. Alienated from what they felt was a clannish, claustrophobic tradition, ashamed of their survival and Americanization, they added to the sardonic self-deprecating humor of the ghetto a new bitterness and shame, a sense of being betrayed by history and betraying their own past. Roth's humor and thrashing around between defiance and self-hatred was too close to the bone. With *Portnoy*, the complaint was different: it was that Roth had not lived up to his early promise. His response seems to have been to move to Connecticut and seclusion, and to publish seven books in the next eight years, including *The Great American Novel, My Life as a Man,* and *The Professor of Desire*. Nor has he slowed down since: in 1985, *Zuckerman Bound*, a trilogy made up of *The Ghost Writer* (1979), *Zuckerman Unbound* (1981), and *The Anatomy Lesson* (1983), along with an epilogue, *The Prague Orgy,* appeared to considerable critical acclaim.

Roth told an interviewer that in recent years he has been struck by "the uses to which literature is put in this country. The writer in his isolation publishes a book, the book goes out into the world, and the strangest things begin to happen. . . . What I write has a particular purpose and use for me, but I've learned that what it means to me isn't what it means to others. When you publish a book, it's the world's book. The world edits it."

Perhaps Roth's purpose in writing *Goodbye, Columbus* was no more than to exorcise his own painful experience of being a young Jew caught in the identity crisis of the 1950s, but sympathetic readers will see in it both that experience and more; they will "edit" it into a novel about a more universal American experience—coming to terms with American myth and American reality—a novel in its way not unlike *The Great Gatsby*.

Goodbye, Columbus

THE FIRST TIME I saw Brenda she asked me to hold her glasses. Then she stepped out to the edge of the diving board and looked foggily into the pool; it could have been drained, myopic Brenda would never have known it. She dove beautifully, and a moment later she was swimming back to the side of the pool, her head of short clipped auburn hair held up, straight ahead of her, as though it were a rose on a long stem. She glided to the edge and then was beside me. "Thank you," she said, her eyes watery though not from the water. She extended a hand for her glasses but did not put them on until she turned and headed away. I watched her move off. Her hands suddenly appeared behind her. She caught the bottom of her suit between thumb and index finger and flicked what flesh had been showing back where it belonged. My blood jumped.

That night, before dinner, I called her.

"Who are you calling?" my Aunt Gladys asked.

"Some girl I met today."

"Doris introduced you?"

"Doris wouldn't introduce me to the guy who drains the pool, Aunt Gladys."

"Don't criticize all the time. A cousin's a cousin. How did you meet her?"

"I didn't really meet her. I saw her."

"Who is she?"

"Her last name is Patimkin."

"Patimkin I don't know," Aunt Gladys said, as if she knew anybody who belonged to the Green Lane Country Club. "You're going to call her you don't know her?"

"Yes," I explained. "I'll introduce myself."

"Casanova," she said, and went back to preparing my uncle's dinner. None of us ate together: my Aunt Gladys ate at five o'clock, my cousin Susan at five-thirty, me at six, and my uncle at six-thirty. There is nothing to explain this beyond the fact that my aunt is crazy.

"Where's the suburban phone book?" I asked after pulling out all the books tucked under the telephone table.

"What?"

"The suburban phone book. I want to call Short Hills."[1]

"That skinny book? What, I gotta clutter my house with that, I never use it?"

"Where is it?"

"Under the dresser where the leg came off."

"For God's sake," I said.

"Call information better. You'll go yanking around there, you'll mess up my drawers. Don't bother me, you see your uncle'll be home soon. I haven't even fed *you* yet."

---

1. Posh New Jersey suburb of New York City.

503

"Aunt Gladys, suppose tonight we all eat together. It's hot, it'll be easier for you."

"Sure, I should serve four different meals at once. You eat pot roast, Susan with the cottage cheese, Max has steak. Friday night is his steak night, I wouldn't deny him. And I'm having a little cold chicken. I should jump up and down twenty different times? What am I, a workhorse?"

"Why don't we all have steak, or cold chicken—"

"Twenty years I'm running a house. Go call your girl friend."

But when I called, Brenda Patimkin wasn't home. She's having dinner at the club, a woman's voice told me. Will she be home after (my voice was two octaves higher than a choirboy's)? I don't know, the voice said, she may go driving golf balls. Who is this? I mumbled some words—nobody she wouldn't know I'll call back no message thank you sorry to bother . . . I hung up somewhere along in there. Then my aunt called me and I steeled myself for dinner.

She pushed the black whirring fan up to *High* and that way it managed to stir the cord that hung from the kitchen light.

"What kind of soda you want? I got ginger ale, plain seltzer, black raspberry, and a bottle cream soda I could open up."

"None, thank you."

"You want water?"

"I don't drink with my meals. Aunt Gladys, I've told you that every day for a year already—"

"Max could drink a whole case with his chopped liver only. He works hard all day. If you worked hard you'd drink more."

At the stove she heaped up a plate with pot roast, gravy, boiled potatoes, and peas and carrots. She put it in front of me and I could feel the heat of the food in my face. Then she cut two pieces of rye bread and put that next to me, on the table.

I forked a potato in half and ate it, while Aunt Gladys, who had seated herself across from me, watched. "You don't want bread," she said, "I wouldn't cut it it should go stale."

"I *want* bread," I said.

"You don't like with seeds, do you?"

I tore a piece of bread in half and ate it.

"How's the meat?" she said.

"Okay. Good."

"You'll fill yourself with potatoes and bread, the meat you'll leave over I'll have to throw it out."

Suddenly she leaped up from the chair. "Salt!" When she returned to the table she plunked a salt shaker down in front of me—pepper wasn't served in her home: she'd heard on Galen Drake[2] that it was not absorbed by the body, and it was disturbing to Aunt Gladys to think that anything she served might pass through a gullet, stomach, and bowel just for the pleasure of the trip.

"You're going to pick the peas out is all? You tell me that, I wouldn't buy with the carrots."

"I love carrots," I said, "I love them." And to prove it, I dumped half of them down my throat and the other half onto my trousers.

"Pig," she said.

---

2. Host of daytime radio talk show of interest primarily to housewives.

Though I am very fond of desserts, especially fruit, I chose not to have any. I wanted, this hot night, to avoid the conversation that revolved around my choosing fresh fruit over canned fruit, or canned fruit over fresh fruit; whichever I preferred, Aunt Gladys always had an abundance of the other jamming her refrigerator like stolen diamonds. "He wants canned peaches, I have a refrigerator full of grapes I have to get rid of ..." Life was a throwing off for poor Aunt Gladys, her greatest joys were taking out the garbage, emptying her pantry, and making threadbare bundles for what she still referred to as the Poor Jews in Palestine. I only hope she dies with an empty refrigerator, otherwise she'll ruin eternity for everyone else, what with her Velveeta turning green, and her navel oranges growing fuzzy jackets down below.

My Uncle Max came home and while I dialed Brenda's number once again, I could hear soda bottles being popped open in the kitchen. The voice that answered this time was high, curt, and tired. "Hullo."

I launched into my speech. "Hello-Brenda-Brenda-you-don't-know-me-that-is-you-don't-know-my-name-but-I-held-your-glasses-for-you-this-afternoon-at-the-club . . . You-asked-me-to-I'm-not-a-member-my-cousin-Doris-is-Doris-Klugman-I-asked-who-you-were ..." I breathed, gave her a chance to speak, and then went ahead and answered the silence on the other end. "Doris? She's the one who's always reading *War and Peace*. That's how I know it's the summer, when Doris is reading *War and Peace*." Brenda didn't laugh; right from the start she was a practical girl.

"What's your name?" she said.

"Neil Klugman. I held your glasses at the board, remember?"

She answered me with a question of her own, one, I'm sure, that is an embarrassment to both the homely and the fair. "What do you look like?"

"I'm ... dark."

"Are you a Negro?"

"No," I said.

"What *do* you look like?"

"May I come see you tonight and show you?"

"That's nice," she laughed. "I'm playing tennis tonight."

"I thought you were driving golf balls."

"I drove them already."

"How about after tennis?"

"I'll be sweaty after," Brenda said.

It was not to warn me to clothespin my nose and run in the opposite direction, it was a fact; it apparently didn't bother Brenda, but she wanted it recorded.

"I don't mind," I said, and hoped by my tone to earn a niche somewhere between the squeamish and the grubby. "Can I pick you up?"

She did not answer a minute; I heard her muttering, "Doris Klugman, Doris Klugman ..." Then she said, "Yes, Briarpath Hills, eight-fifteen."

"I'll be driving a—" I hung back with the year, "a tan Plymouth. So you'll know me. How will I know you?" I said with a sly, awful laugh.

"I'll be sweating," she said and hung up.

Once I'd driven out of Newark, past Irvington and the packed-in tangle of railroad crossings, switchmen shacks, lumberyards, Dairy Queens, and used-car lots, the night grew cooler. It was, in fact, as though the hundred and eighty feet that the suburbs rose in altitude above Newark brought one closer to heaven, for the sun itself became bigger, lower, and rounder, and soon I was driving past long lawns which seemed to be twirling water on themselves, and past houses where no one sat on stoops, where lights were on but no windows open, for those inside, refusing to share the very texture of life with those of us outside, regulated with a dial the amounts of moisture that were allowed access to their skin. It was only eight o'clock, and I did not want to be early, so I drove up and down the streets whose names were those of eastern colleges, as though the township, years ago, when things were named, had planned the destinies of the sons of its citizens. I thought of my Aunt Gladys and Uncle Max sharing a Mounds bar in the cindery darkness of their alley, on beach chairs, each cool breeze sweet to them as the promise of afterlife, and after a while I rolled onto the gravel roads of the small park where Brenda was playing tennis. Inside my glove compartment it was as though the map of *The City Streets of Newark* had metamorphosed into crickets, for those mile-long tarry streets did not exist for me any longer, and the night noises sounded loud as the blood whacking at my temples.

I parked the car under the black-green canopy of three oaks, and walked towards the sound of the tennis balls. I heard an exasperated voice say, "Deuce *again*." It was Brenda and she sounded as though she was sweating considerably. I crackled slowly up the gravel and heard Brenda once more. "My ad," and then just as I rounded the path, catching a cuff full of burrs, I heard, "Game!" Her racket went spinning up in the air and she caught it neatly as I came into sight.

"Hello," I called.

"Hello, Neil. One more game," she called. Brenda's words seemed to infuriate her opponent, a pretty brown-haired girl, not quite so tall as Brenda, who stopped searching for the ball that had been driven past her, and gave both Brenda and myself a dirty look. In a moment I learned the reason why: Brenda was ahead five games to four, and her cocksureness about there being just one game remaining aroused enough anger in her opponent for the two of us to share.

As it happened, Brenda finally won, though it took more games than she'd expected. The other girl, whose name sounded like Simp, seemed happy to end it at six all, but Brenda, shifting, running, up on her toes, would not stop, and finally all I could see moving in the darkness were her glasses, a glint of them, the clasp of her belt, her socks, her sneakers, and, on occasion, the ball. The darker it got the more savagely did Brenda rush the net, which seemed curious, for I had noticed that earlier, in the light, she had stayed back, and even when she had had to rush, after smashing back a lob, she didn't look entirely happy about being so close to her opponent's racket. Her passion for winning a point seemed outmatched by an even stronger passion for maintaining her beauty as it was. I suspected that the red print of a tennis ball on her cheek would pain her more than losing all the points in the world. Darkness pushed her in, however, and she stroked harder, and at last Simp seemed to be running on her ankles. When it was all over, Simp refused my offer of a ride home and indicated with a quality of speech borrowed from some old Katharine Hepburn movie that she could manage for herself; apparently her manor lay no further than the nearest briar patch. She did not like me and I her, though I worried about it, I'm sure, more than she did.

"Who is *she?*"

"Laura Simpson Stolowitch."

"Why don't you call her Stolo?" I asked.

"Simp is her Bennington[3] name. The ass."

"Is that where you go to school?" I asked.

She was pushing her shirt up against her skin to dry the perspiration.

"No. I go to school in Boston."

I disliked her for the answer. Whenever anyone asks me where I went to school I come right out with it: Newark Colleges of Rutgers University. I may say it a bit too ringingly, too fast, too up-in-the-air, but I say it. For an instant Brenda reminded me of the pug-nosed little bastards from Montclair who come down to the library during vacations, and while I stamp out their books, they stand around tugging their elephantine scarves until they hang to their ankles, hinting all the while at "Boston" and "New Haven."

"Boston University?" I asked, looking off at the trees.

"Radcliffe."[4]

We were still standing on the court, bounded on all sides by white lines. Around the bushes back of the court, fireflies were cutting figure eights in the thorny-smelling air and then, as the night suddenly came all the way in, the leaves on the trees shone for an instant, as though they'd just been rained upon. Brenda walked off the court, with me a step behind her. Now I had grown accustomed to the dark, and as she ceased being merely a voice and turned into a sight again, some of my anger at her "Boston" remark floated off and I let myself appreciate her. Her hands did not twitch at her bottom, but the form revealed itself, covered or not, under the closeness of her khaki Bermudas. There were two wet triangles on the back of her tiny-collared white polo shirt, right where her wings would have been if she'd had a pair. She wore, to complete the picture, a tartan belt, white socks, and white tennis sneakers.

As she walked she zipped the cover on her racket.

"Are you anxious to get home?" I said.

"No."

"Let's sit here. It's pleasant."

"Okay."

We sat down on a bank of grass slanted enough for us to lean back without really leaning; from the angle it seemed as though we were preparing to watch some celestial event, the christening of a new star, the inflation to full size of a half-ballooned moon. Brenda zipped and unzipped the cover while she spoke; for the first time she seemed edgy. Her edginess coaxed mine back, and so we were ready now for what, magically, it seemed we might be able to get by without: a meeting.

"What does your cousin Doris look like?" she asked.

"She's dark—"

"Is she—"

"No," I said. "She has freckles and dark hair and she's very tall."

"Where does she go to school?"

"Northampton."[5]

3. Prestigious Vermont college, at the time exclusively for women.
4. The woman's college of Harvard University. Rutgers is the state university of New Jersey. Montclair, like Short Hills and (below) Livingston, is a suburb for the well-to-do.
5. Massachusetts site of Smith College, a prestigious college for women.

She did not answer and I don't know how much of what I meant she had understood.

"I guess I don't know her," she said after a moment. "Is she a new member?"

"I think so. They moved to Livingston only a couple of years ago."

"Oh."

No new star appeared, at least for the next five minutes.

"Did you remember me from holding your glasses?" I said.

"Now I do," she said. "Do you live in Livingston too?"

"No. Newark."

"We lived in Newark when I was a baby," she offered.

"Would you like to go home?" I was suddenly angry.

"No. Let's walk though."

Brenda kicked a stone and walked a step ahead of me.

"Why is it you rush the net only after dark?" I said.

She turned to me and smiled. "You noticed? Old Simp the Simpleton doesn't."

"Why do you?"

"I don't like to be up too close, unless I'm sure she won't return it."

"Why?"

"My nose."

"What?"

"I'm afraid of my nose. I had it bobbed."

"What?"

"I had my nose fixed."

"What was the matter with it?"

"It was bumpy."

"A lot?"

"No," she said, "I was pretty. Now I'm prettier. My brother's having his fixed in the fall."

"Does he want to be prettier?"

She didn't answer and walked ahead of me again.

"I don't mean to sound facetious. I mean why's he doing it?"

"He *wants* to . . . unless he becomes a gym teacher . . . but he won't," she said. "We all look like my father."

"Is he having his fixed?"

"Why are you so nasty?"

"I'm not. I'm sorry." My next question was prompted by a desire to sound interested and thereby regain civility; it didn't quite come out as I'd expected—I said it too loud. "How much does it cost?"

Brenda waited a moment but then she answered. "A thousand dollars. Unless you go to a butcher."

"Let me see if you got your money's worth."

She turned again; she stood next to a bench and put the racket down on it. "If I let you kiss me would you stop being nasty?"

We had to take about two too many steps to keep the approach from being awkward, but we pursued the impulse and kissed. I felt her hand on the back of my neck and so I tugged her towards me, too violently perhaps, and slid my own hands across the side of her body and around to her back. I felt the wet spots on her shoulder blades, and beneath them, I'm sure of it, a faint fluttering, as though something stirred so deep in her breasts, so far back it could make itself felt through her shirt. It was like the fluttering of wings, tiny wings no bigger than her breasts. The smallness of the wings did not bother me—it would not take an eagle to carry me up those lousy hundred and eighty feet to make summer nights so much cooler in Short Hills than they are in Newark.

2

The next day I held Brenda's glasses for her once again, this time not as momentary servant but as afternoon guest; or perhaps as both, which still was an improvement. She wore a black tank suit and went barefooted, and among the other women, with their Cuban heels and boned-up breasts, their knuckle-sized rings, their straw hats, which resembled immense wicker pizza plates and had been purchased, as I heard one deeply tanned woman rasp, "from the cutest little *shvartze*[6] when we docked at Barbados," Brenda among them was elegantly simple, like a sailor's dream of a Polynesian maiden, albeit one with prescription sun glasses and the last name of Patimkin. She brought a little slurp of water with her when she crawled back towards the pool's edge, and at the edge she grabbed up with her hands and held my ankles, tightly and wet.

"Come in," she said up to me, squinting. "We'll play."

"Your glasses," I said.

"Oh break the goddam things. I hate them."

"Why don't you have your eyes fixed?"

"There you go again."

"I'm sorry," I said. "I'll give them to Doris."

Doris, in the surprise of the summer, had gotten past Prince Andrey's departure from his wife, and now sat brooding, not, it turned out, over the lonely fate of poor Princess Liza,[7] but at the skin which she had lately discovered to be peeling off her shoulders.

"Would you watch Brenda's glasses?" I said.

"Yes." She fluffed little scales of translucent flesh into the air. "Damn it."

I handed her the glasses.

"Well, for God's sake," she said, "I'm not going to hold them. Put them down. *I'm* not her slave."

"You're a pain in the ass, you know that, Doris?" Sitting there, she looked a little like Laura Simpson Stolowitch, who was, in fact, walking somewhere off at the far end of the pool, avoiding Brenda and me because (I liked to think) of the defeat Brenda had handed her the night before; or maybe (I didn't like to think) because of the strangeness of my presence. Regardless, Doris had to bear the weight of my indictment of both Simp and herself.

"Thank you," she said. "After I invite you up for the day."

"That was yesterday."

"What about last year?"

"That's right, your mother told you last year too—invite Esther's boy so when he writes his parents they won't complain we don't look after him. Every summer I get my day."

"You should have gone with them. That's not our fault. You're not our charge," and when she said it, I could just tell it was something she'd

6. A black.
7. Events at the end of the first of the fifteen sections, or "books," of *War and Peace*.

heard at home, or received in a letter one Monday mail, after she'd returned to Northampton from Stowe, or Dartmouth, or perhaps from that
weekend when she'd taken a shower with her boyfriend in Lowell House.[8]
"Tell your father not to worry. Uncle Aaron, the sport. I'll take care of
myself," and I ran on back to the pool, ran into a dive, in fact, and came
up like a dolphin beside Brenda, whose legs I slid upon with my own.

"How's Doris?" she said.

"Peeling," I said. "She's going to have her skin fixed."

"*Stop* it," she said, and dove down beneath us till I felt her clamping
her hands on the soles of my feet. I pulled back and then down too, and
then, at the bottom, no more than six inches above the wiggling black
lines that divided the pool into lanes for races, we bubbled a kiss into
each other's lips. She was smiling there, at *me*, down at the bottom of the
swimming pool of the Green Lane Country Club. Way above us, legs
shimmied in the water and a pair of fins skimmed greenly by: my cousin
Doris could peel away to nothing for all I cared, my Aunt Gladys have
twenty feedings every night, my father and mother could roast away their
asthma down in the furnace of Arizona, those penniless deserters—I didn't
care for anything but Brenda. I went to pull her towards me just as she
started fluttering up; my hand hooked on to the front of her suit and the
cloth pulled away from her. Her breasts swam towards me like two pink-
nosed fish and she let me hold them. Then, in a moment, it was the sun
who kissed us both, and we were out of the water, too pleased with each
other to smile. Brenda shook the wetness of her hair onto my face and
with the drops that touched me I felt she had made a promise to me
about the summer, and, I hoped, beyond.

"Do you want your sun glasses?"

"You're close enough to see," she said. We were under a big blue umbrella, side-by-side on two chaise longues, whose plastic covers sizzled
against out suits and flesh; I turned my head to look at Brenda and
smelled that pleasant little burning odor in the skin of my shoulders. I
turned back up to the sun, as did she, and as we talked, and it grew
hotter and brighter, the colors splintered under my closed eyelids.

"This is all very fast," she said.

"Nothing's happened," I said softly.

"No. I guess not. I sort of feel something has."

"In eighteen hours?"

"Yes. I feel . . . pursued," she said after a moment.

"*You* invited *me*, Brenda."

"Why do you always sound a little nasty to me?"

"Did I sound nasty? I don't mean to. Truly."

"You do! *You* invited *me*, Brenda. So what?" she said. "That isn't what
I mean anyway."

"I'm sorry."

"Stop apologizing. You're so automatic about it, you don't even mean
it."

"Now you're being nasty to me," I said.

"No. Just stating the facts. Let's not argue. I like you." She turned her
head and looked as though she too paused a second to smell the summer

---

8. A Harvard College residence for upperclassmen.   college in New Hampshire.
Stowe: Vermont ski resort. Dartmouth: Ivy League

on her own flesh. "I like the way you look." She saved it from embarrassing me with that factual tone of hers.

"Why?" I said.

"Where did you get those fine shoulders? Do you play something?"

"No," I said. "I just grew up and they came with me."

"I like your body. It's fine."

"I'm glad," I said.

"You like mine, don't you?"

"No," I said.

"Then it's denied you," she said.

I brushed her hair flat against her ear with the back of my hand and then we were silent a while.

"Brenda," I said, "you haven't asked me anything about me."

"How you feel? Do you want me to ask you how you feel?"

"Yes," I said, accepting the back door she gave me, though probably not for the same reasons she had offered it.

"How *do* you feel?"

"I want to swim."

"Okay," she said.

We spent the rest of the afternoon in the water. There were eight of those long lines painted down the length of the pool and by the end of the day I think we had parked for a while in every lane, close enough to the dark stripes to reach out and touch them. We came back to the chairs now and then and sang hesitant, clever, nervous, gentle dithyrambs about how we were beginning to feel towards one another. Actually we did not have the feelings we said we had until we spoke them—at least I didn't; to phrase them was to invent them and own them. We whipped our strangeness and newness into a froth that resembled love, and we dared not play too long with it, talk too much of it, or it would flatten and fizzle away. So we moved back and forth from chairs to water, from talk to silence, and considering my unshakable edginess with Brenda, and the high walls of ego that rose, buttresses and all, between her and her knowledge of herself, we managed pretty well.

At about four o'clock, at the bottom of the pool, Brenda suddenly wrenched away from me and shot up to the surface. I shot up after her.

"What's the matter?" I said.

First she whipped the hair off her forehead. Then she pointed a hand down towards the base of the pool. "My brother," she said, coughing some water free inside her.

And suddenly, like a crew-cut Proteus rising from the sea, Ron Patimkin emerged from the lower depths we'd just inhabited and his immensity was before us.

"Hey, Bren," he said, and pushed a palm flat into the water so that a small hurricane beat up against Brenda and me.

"What are you so happy about?" she said.

"The Yankees took two."

"Are we going to have Mickey Mantle for dinner?" she said. "When the Yankees win," she said to me, treading so easily she seemed to have turned the chlorine to marble beneath her, "we set an extra place for Mickey Mantle."

"You want to race?" Ron asked.

"No, Ronald. Go race alone."

Nobody had as yet said a word about me. I treaded unobtrusively as I could, as a third party, unintroduced, will step back and say nothing, awaiting the amenities. I was tired, however, from the afternoon's sport, and wished to hell brother and sister would not tease and chat much longer. Fortunately Brenda introduced me. "Ronald, this is Neil Klugman. This is my brother, Ronald Patimkin."

Of all things there in the fifteen feet water, Ron reached out his hand to shake. I returned the shake, not quite as monumentally as he apparently expected; my chin slipped an inch into the water and all at once I was exhausted.

"Want to race?" Ron asked me good-naturedly.

"Go ahead, Neil, race with him. I want to call home and tell them you're coming to dinner."

"Am I? I'll have to call my aunt. You didn't say anything. My clothes—"

"We dine *au naturel.*"

"What?" Ronald said.

"Swim, baby," Brenda said to him and it ached me some when she kissed him on the face.

I begged out of the race, saying I had to make a phone call myself, and once upon the tiled blue border of the pool, looked back to see Ron taking the length in sleek, immense strokes. He gave one the feeling that after swimming the length of the pool a half dozen times he would have earned the right to drink its contents; I imagined he had, like my Uncle Max, a colossal thirst and a gigantic bladder.

Aunt Gladys did not seem relieved when I told her she'd have only three feedings to prepare that night. "Fancy-shmancy" was all she said to me on the phone.

We did not eat in the kitchen; rather, the six of us—Brenda, myself, Ron, Mr. and Mrs. Patimkin, and Brenda's little sister, Julie—sat around the dining room table, while the maid, Carlota, a Navaho-faced Negro who had little holes in her ears but no earrings, served us the meal. I was seated next to Brenda, who was dressed in what was *au naturel* for her: Bermudas, the close ones, white polo shirt, tennis sneakers and white socks. Across from me was Julie, ten, round-faced, bright, who before dinner, while the other little girls on the street had been playing with jacks and boys and each other, had been on the back lawn putting golf balls with her father. Mr. Patimkin reminded me of my father, except that when he spoke he did not surround each syllable with a wheeze. He was tall, strong, ungrammatical, and a ferocious eater. When he attacked his salad—after drenching it in bottled French dressing—the veins swelled under the heavy skin of his forearm. He ate three helpings of salad, Ron had four, Brenda and Julie had two, and only Mrs. Patimkin and I had one each. I did not like Mrs. Patimkin, though she was certainly the handsomest of all of us at the table. She was disastrously polite to me, and with her purple eyes, her dark hair, and large, persuasive frame, she gave me the feeling of some captive beauty, some wild princess, who has been tamed and made the servant to the king's daughter—who was Brenda.

Outside, through the wide picture window, I could see the back lawn with its twin oak trees. I say oaks, though fancifully, one might call them sporting-goods trees. Beneath their branches, like fruit dropped from their limbs, were two irons, a golf ball, a tennis can, a baseball bat, a basketball, a first-baseman's glove, and what was apparently a riding crop. Further back, near the scrubs that bounded the Patimkin property and in front of the small basketball court, a square red blanket, with a white O stitched in the center, looked to be on fire against the green grass. A breeze must have blown outside, for the net on the basket moved; inside we ate in the steady coolness of air by Westinghouse. It was a pleasure, except that eating among those Brobdingnags,[9] I felt for quite a while as though four inches had been clipped from my shoulders, three inches from my height, and for good measure, someone had removed my ribs and my chest had settled meekly in towards my back.

There was not much dinner conversation; eating was heavy and methodical and serious, and it would be just as well to record all that was said in one swoop, rather than indicate the sentences lost in the passing of food, the words gurgled into mouthfuls, the syntax chopped and forgotten in heapings, spillings, and gorgings.

To RON: When's Harriet calling?

RON: Five o'clock.

JULIE: It *was* five o'clock.

RON: Their time.

JULIE: Why is it that it's earlier in Milwaukee? Suppose you took a plane back and forth all day. You'd never get older.

BRENDA: That's right, sweetheart.

MRS. P.: What do you give the child misinformation for? Is that why she goes to school?

BRENDA: I don't know why she goes to school.

MR. P. *(lovingly)*: College girl.

RON: Where's Carlota? Carlota!

MRS. P.: Carlota, give Ronald more.

CARLOTA *(calling)*: More what?

RON: Everything.

MR. P.: Me too.

MRS. P.: They'll have to *roll* you on the links.

MR. P. *(pulling his shirt up and slapping his black, curved belly)*: What are you talking about? Look at that.

RON *(yanking his T-shirt up)*: Look at *this*.

BRENDA *(to me)*: Would you care to bare your middle?

ME *(the choir boy again)*: No.

MRS. P.: That's right, Neil.

ME: Yes. Thank you.

CARLOTA *(over my shoulder, like an unsummoned spirit)*: Would *you* like more?

ME: No.

MR. P.: He eats like a bird.

JULIE: Certain birds eat a lot.

BRENDA: Which ones?

MRS. P.: Let's not talk about animals at the dinner table. Brenda, why do you encourage her?

RON: Where's Carlota, I gotta play tonight.

MR. P.: Tape your wrist, don't forget.

MRS. P.: Where do you live, Bill?

BRENDA: Neil.

9. The giants in Jonathan Swift's *Gulliver's Travels* (1726).

MRS. P.: Didn't I say Neil?

JULIE: You said "Where do you live, *Bill?*"

MRS. P.: I must have been thinking of something else.

RON: I hate tape. How the hell can I play in tape?

JULIE: Don't curse.

MRS. P.: That's right.

MR. P.: What is Mantle batting now?

JULIE: Three twenty-eight.

RON: Three twenty-five.

JULIE: Eight!

RON: Five, jerk! He got three for four in the second game.

JULIE: *Four* for four.

RON: That was an error, Minoso[1] should have had it.

JULIE: *I* didn't think so.

BRENDA *(to me)*: See?

MRS. P.: See what?

BRENDA: I was talking to Bill.

JULIE: Neil.

MR. P.: Shut up and eat.

MRS. P.: A little less talking, young lady.

JULIE: *I* didn't say anything.

BRENDA: She was talking to me, sweetie.

MR. P.: What's this *she* business. Is that how you call your mother? What's dessert?

The phone rings, and though we are awaiting dessert, the meal seems at a formal end, for Ron breaks for his room, Julie shouts "Harriet!" and Mr. Patimkin is not wholly successful in stifling a belch, though the failure even more than the effort ingratiates him to me. Mrs. Patimkin is directing Carlota not to mix the milk silverware and the meat silverware[2] again, and Carlota is eating a peach while she listens; under the table I feel Brenda's fingers tease my calf. I am full.

We sat under the biggest of the oak trees while out on the basketball court Mr. Patimkin played five and two[3] with Julie. In the driveway Ron was racing the motor of the Volkswagen. "Will somebody *please* move the Chrysler out from behind me?" he called angrily. "I'm late as it is."

"Excuse me," Brenda said, getting up.

"I think I'm behind the Chrysler," I said.

"Let's go," she said.

We backed the cars out so that Ron could hasten on to his game. Then we reparked them and went back to watching Mr. Patimkin and Julie.

"I like your sister," I said.

"So do I," she said. "I wonder what she'll turn out to be."

"Like you," I said.

"I don't know," she said. "Better probably." And then she added, "Or maybe worse. How can you tell? My father's nice to her, but I'll give her another three years with my mother . . . Bill," she said, musingly.

"I didn't mind that," I said. "She's very beautiful, your mother."

---

1. Minnie Minoso, then left fielder for the Chicago White Sox.

2. According to Jewish dietary laws, meat and dairy products may not be eaten together, and their respective dishes and utensils are kept separate.

3. Basketball game played by shooting longer (set) shots from the foul line for five points each and shorter (lay-up) shots for two points each.

"I can't even think of her as my mother. She hates me. Other girls, when they pack in September, at least their mothers help them. Not mine. She'll be busy sharpening pencils for Julie's pencil box while I'm carrying my trunk around upstairs. And it's so obvious why. It's practically a case study."

"Why?"

"She's jealous. It's so corny I'm ashamed to say it. Do you know my mother had the best back-hand in New Jersey? Really, she was the best tennis player in the state, man or woman. You ought to see the pictures of her when she was a girl. She was so healthy-looking. But not chubby or anything. She was soulful, truly. I love her in those pictures. Sometimes I say to her how beautiful the pictures are. I even asked to have one blown up so I could have it at school. 'We have other things to do with our money, young lady, than spend it on old photographs.' Money! My father's up to here with it, but whenever I buy a coat you should hear her. 'You don't have to go to Bonwit's, young lady, Ohrbach's[4] has the strongest fabrics of any of them.' Who *wants* a strong fabric! Finally I get what I want, but not till she's had a chance to aggravate me. Money is a waste for her. She doesn't even know how to enjoy it. She still thinks we live in Newark."

"But you get what you want," I said.

"Yes. Him," and she pointed out to Mr. Patimkin who had just swished his third straight set shot through the basket to the disgruntlement, apparently, of Julie, who stamped so hard at the ground that she raised a little dust storm around her perfect young legs.

"He's not too smart but he's sweet at least. He doesn't treat my brother the way she treats me. Thank God, for that. Oh, I'm tired of talking about them. Since my freshman year I think every conversation I've ever had has always wound up about my parents and how awful it is. It's universal. The only trouble is they don't know it."

From the way Julie and Mr. Patimkin were laughing now, out on the court, no problem could ever have seemed less universal; but, of course, it was universal for Brenda, more than that, cosmic—it made every cashmere sweater a battle with her mother, and her life, which, I was certain, consisted to a large part of cornering the market on fabrics that felt soft to the skin, took on the quality of a Hundred Years' War . . .

I did not intend to allow myself such unfaithful thoughts, to line up with Mrs. Patimkin while I sat beside Brenda, but I could not shake from my elephant's brain that she-still-thinks-we-live-in-Newark remark. I did not speak, however, fearful that my tone would shatter our post-dinner ease and intimacy. It had been so simple to be intimate with water pounding and securing all our pores, and later, with the sun heating them and drugging our senses, but now, in the shade and the open, cool and clothed on her own grounds, I did not want to voice a word that would lift the cover and reveal that hideous emotion I always felt for her, and is the underside of love. It will not always *stay* the underside—but I am skipping ahead.

Suddenly, little Julie was upon us. "Want to play?" she said to me. "Daddy's tired."

"C'mon," Mr. Patimkin called. "Finish for me."

I hesitated—I hadn't held a basketball since high school—but Julie was dragging at my hand, and Brenda said, "Go ahead."

Mr. Patimkin tossed the ball towards me while I wasn't looking and it bounced off my chest, leaving a round dust spot, like the shadow of a moon, on my shirt. I laughed, insanely.

"Can't you catch?" Julie said.

Like her sister, she seemed to have a knack for asking practical, infuriating questions.

"Yes."

"Your turn," she said. "Daddy's behind forty-seven to thirty-nine. Two hundred wins."

For an instant, as I placed my toes in the little groove that over the years had been nicked into a foul line, I had one of those instantaneous waking dreams that plague me from time to time, and send, my friends tell me, deadly cataracts over my eyes: the sun had sunk, crickets had come and gone, the leaves had blackened, and still Julie and I stood alone on the lawn, tossing the ball at the basket; "Five hundred wins," she called, and then when she beat me to five hundred she called, "Now *you* have to reach it," and I did, and the night lengthened, and she called, "*Eight* hundred wins," and we played on and then it was eleven hundred that won and we played on and it never was morning.

"Shoot," Mr. Patimkin said. "You're me."

That puzzled me, but I took my set shot and, of course, missed. With the Lord's blessing and a soft breeze, I made the lay-up.

"You have forty-one. I go," Julie said.

Mr. Patimkin sat on the grass at the far end of the court. He took his shirt off, and in his undershirt, and his whole day's growth of beard, looked like a trucker. Brenda's old nose fitted him well. There was a bump in it, all right; up at the bridge it seemed as though a small eight-sided diamond had been squeezed in under the skin. I knew Mr. Patimkin would never bother to have that stone cut from his face, and yet, with joy and pride, no doubt, had paid to have Brenda's diamond removed and dropped down some toilet in Fifth Avenue Hospital.

Julie missed her set shot, and I admit to a slight, gay, flutter of heart.

"Put a little spin on it," Mr. Patimkin told her.

"Can I take it again?" Julie asked me.

"Yes." What with paternal directions from the sidelines and my own grudging graciousness on the court, there did not seem much of a chance for me to catch up. And I wanted to, suddenly, I wanted to win, to run little Julie into the ground. Brenda was back on one elbow, under the tree, chewing on a leaf, watching. And up in the house, at the kitchen window, I could see that the curtain had swished back—the sun too low now to glare off electrical appliances—and Mrs. Patimkin was looking steadily out at the game. And then Carlota appeared on the back steps, eating a peach and holding a pail of garbage in her free hand. She stopped to watch too.

It was my turn again. I missed the set shot and laughingly turned to Julie and said, "Can I take it again?"

"No!"

So I learned how the game was played. Over the years Mr. Patimkin had taught his daughters that free throws were theirs for the asking; he

could afford to. However, with the strange eyes of Short Hills upon me,
matrons, servants, and providers, I somehow felt I couldn't. But I had to
and I did.

"Thanks a lot, Neil," Julie said when the game was ended—at 100—and
the crickets had come.

"You're welcome."

Under the trees, Brenda smiled. "Did you let her win?"

"I think so," I said. "I'm not sure."

There was something in my voice that prompted Brenda to say, com-
fortingly, "Even Ron lets her win."

"It's all nice for Julie," I said.

3

The next morning I found a parking space on Washington Street directly across from the library. Since I was twenty minutes early I decided
to stroll in the park rather than cross over to work; I didn't particularly
care to join my colleagues, who I knew would be sipping early morning
coffee in the binding room, smelling still of all the orange crush they'd
drunk that weekend at Asbury Park.[5] I sat on a bench and looked out
towards Broad Street and the morning traffic. The Lackawanna commuter
trains were rumbling in a few blocks to the north and I could hear them,
I thought—the sunny green cars, old and clean, with windows that opened
all the way. Some mornings, with time to kill before work, I would walk
down to the tracks and watch the open windows roll in, on their sills the
elbows of tropical suits and the edges of briefcases, the properties of businessmen arriving in town from Maplewood, the Oranges, and the suburbs
beyond.

The park, bordered by Washington Street on the west and Broad on
the east, was empty and shady and smelled of trees, night, and dog leav-
ings; and there was a faint damp smell too, indicating that the huge rhino
of a water cleaner had passed by already, soaking and whisking the downtown streets. Down Washington Street, behind me, was the Newark Museum—I could see it without even looking: two oriental vases in front like
spittoons for a rajah, and next to it the little annex to which we had
traveled on special buses as schoolchildren. The annex was a brick building, old and vine-covered, and always reminded me of New Jersey's link
with the beginning of the country, with George Washington, who had
trained his scrappy army—a little bronze tablet informed us children—in
the very park where I now sat. At the far end of the park, beyond the
Museum, was the bank building where I had gone to college. It had been
converted some years before into an extension of Rutgers University; in
fact, in what once had been the bank president's waiting room I had
taken a course called Contemporary Moral Issues. Though it was summer
now, and I was out of college three years, it was not hard for me to
remember the other students, my friends, who had worked evenings in
Bamberger's and Kresge's and had used the commissions they'd earned
pushing ladies' out-of-season shoes to pay their laboratory fees. And then I
looked out to Broad Street again. Jammed between a grimy-windowed
bookstore and a cheesy luncheonette was the marquee of a tiny art the-

5. New Jersey seaside resort.

ater—how many years had passed since I'd stood beneath that marquee, lying about the year of my birth so as to see Hedy Lamarr swim naked in *Ecstasy;* and then, having slipped the ticket taker an extra quarter, what disappointment I had felt at the frugality of her Slavic charm . . .[6] Sitting there in the park, I felt a deep knowledge of Newark, an attachment so rooted that it could not help but branch out into affection.

Suddenly it was nine o'clock and everything was scurrying. Wobbly-heeled girls revolved through the doors of the telephone building across the way, traffic honked desperately, policemen barked, whistled, and waved motorists to and fro. Over at St. Vincent's Church the huge dark portals swung back and those bleary-eyes that had risen early for Mass now blinked at the light. Then the worshipers had stepped off the church steps and were racing down the streets towards desks, filing cabinets, secretaries, bosses, and—if the Lord had seen fit to remove a mite of harshness from their lives—to the comfort of air-conditioners pumping at their windows. I got up and crossed over to the library, wondering if Brenda was awake yet.

The pale cement lions stood unconvincing guard on the library steps, suffering their usual combination of elephantiasis and arteriosclerosis, and I was prepared to pay them as little attention as I had for the past eight months were it not for a small colored boy who stood in front of one of them. The lion had lost all of its toes the summer before to a safari of juvenile delinquents, and now a new tormentor stood before him, sagging a little in his knees, and growling. He would growl, low and long, drop back, wait, then growl again. Then he would straighten up, and, shaking his head, he would say to the lion, "Man, you's a coward . . . " Then, once again, he'd growl.

The day began the same as any other. From behind the desk on the main floor, I watched the hot high-breasted teen-age girls walk twitchingly up the wide flight of marble stairs that led to the main reading room. The stairs were an imitation of a staircase somewhere in Versailles, though in their toreador pants and sweaters these young daughters of Italian leatherworkers, Polish brewery hands, and Jewish furriers were hardly duchesses. They were not Brenda either, and any lust that sparked inside me through the dreary day was academic and time-passing. I looked at my watch occasionally, thought of Brenda, and waited for lunch and then for after lunch, when I would take over the Information Desk upstairs and John McKee, who was only twenty-one but wore elastic bands around his sleeves, would march starchily down the stairs to work assiduously at stamping books in and out. John McRubberbands was in his last year at Newark State Teachers College where he was studying at the Dewey Decimal System[7] in preparation for his lifework. The library was not going to be my lifework, I knew it. Yet, there had been some talk—from Mr. Scapello, an old eunuch who had learned somehow to disguise his voice as a man's—that when I returned from my summer vacation I would be put in charge of the Reference Room, a position that had been empty ever since that morning when Martha Winney had fallen off a high stool in the Encyclopedia Room and shattered all those frail bones that come together to form what in a woman half her age we would call the hips.

6. In this 1933 Czech film the slim beauty Hedy Lamarr (b. 1913) appears, though rather indistinctly, nude.

7. Method for cataloguing and shelving library books.

I had strange fellows at the library and, in truth, there were many hours when I never quite knew how I'd gotten there or why I stayed. But I did stay and after a while waited patiently for that day when I would go into the men's room on the main floor for a cigarette and, studying myself as I expelled smoke into the mirror, would see that at some moment during the morning I had gone pale, and that under my skin, as under McKee's and Scapello's and Miss Winney's, there was a thin cushion of air separating the blood from the flesh. Someone had pumped it there while I was stamping out a book, and so life from now on would be not a throwing off, as it was for Aunt Gladys, and not a gathering in, as it was for Brenda, but a bouncing off, a numbness. I began to fear this, and yet, in my muscleless devotion to my work, seemed edging towards it, silently, as Miss Winney used to edge up to the *Britannica*. Her stool was empty now and awaited me.

Just before lunch the lion tamer came wide-eyed into the library. He stood still for a moment, only his fingers moving, as though he were counting the number of marble stairs before him. Then he walked creepily about on the marble floor, snickering at the clink of his taps and the way his little noise swelled up to the vaulted ceiling. Otto, the guard at the door, told him to make less noise with his shoes, but that did not seem to bother the little boy. He clacked on his tiptoes, high, secretively, delighted at the opportunity Otto had given him to practice this posture. He tiptoed up to me.

"Hey," he said, "where's the heart section?"

"The what?" I said.

"The heart section. Ain't you got no heart section?"

He had the thickest sort of southern Negro dialect and the only word that came clear to me was the one that sounded like heart.

"How do you spell it?" I said.

"*Heart*. Man, pictures. Drawing books. Where you got them?"

"You mean art books? Reproductions?"

He took my polysyllabic word for it. "Yea, they's them."

"In a couple of places," I told him. "Which artist are you interested in?"

The boy's eyes narrowed so that his whole face seemed black. He started backing away, as he had from the lion. "All of them . . ." he mumbled.

"That's okay," I said. "You go look at whichever ones you want. The next flight up. Follow the arrow to where it says Stack Three. You remember that? Stack Three. Ask somebody upstairs."

He did not move; he seemed to be taking my curiosity about his taste as a kind of poll-tax investigation.[8] "Go ahead," I said, slashing my face with a smile, "right up there . . ."

And like a shot he was scuffling and tapping up towards the heart section.

After lunch I came back to the in-and-out desk and there was John McKee, waiting, in his pale blue slacks, his black shoes, his barber-cloth shirt with the elastic bands, and a great knit tie, green, wrapped into a Windsor knot, that was huge and jumped when he talked. His breath smelled of hair oil and his hair of breath and when he spoke, spittle cob-

<hr/>

8. A voting eligibility tax used for years in some states to keep blacks from voting; outlawed for federal elections by the Twenty-fourth Amendment (1964).

webbed the corners of his mouth. I did not like him and at times had the urge to yank back on his armbands and slingshoot him out past Otto and the lions into the street.

"Has a little Negro boy passed the desk? With a thick accent? He's been hiding in the art books all morning. You know what those boys *do* in there."

"I saw him come in, John."

"So did I. Has he gone *out* though?"

"I haven't noticed. I guess so."

"Those are *very* expensive books."

"Don't be so nervous, John. People are supposed to touch them."

"There is touching," John said sententiously, "and there is touching. Someone should check on him. I was afraid to leave the desk here. You know the way they treat the housing projects we give them."

"*You* give them?"

"The city. Have you seen what they do at Seth Boyden? They threw *beer* bottles, those big ones, on the *lawn*. They're taking over the city."

"Just the Negro sections."

"It's easy to laugh, you don't live near them. I'm going to call Mr. Scapello's office to check the Art Section. Where did he ever find out about art?"

"You'll give Mr. Scapello an ulcer, so soon after his egg-and-pepper sandwich. I'll check, I have to go upstairs anyway."

"You know what they do in there," John warned me.

"Don't worry, Johnny, *they're* the ones who'll get warts on their dirty little hands."

"Ha ha. Those books happen to cost—"

So that Mr. Scapello would not descend upon the boy with his chalky fingers, I walked up the three flights to Stack Three, past the receiving room where rheumy-eyed Jimmy Boylen, our fifty-one-year-old boy, unloaded books from a cart; past the reading room, where bums off Mulberry Street slept over *Popular Mechanics;* past the smoking corridor where damp-browed summer students from the law school relaxed, some smoking, others trying to rub the colored dye from their tort texts off their fingertips; and finally, past the periodical room, where a few ancient ladies who'd been motored down from Upper Montclair now huddled in their chairs, pince-nezing over yellowed, fraying society pages in old old copies of the Newark *News.* Up on Stack Three I found the boy. He was seated on the glass-brick floor holding an open book in his lap, a book, in fact, that was bigger than his lap and had to be propped up by his knees. By the light of the window behind him I could see the hundreds of spaces between the hundreds of tiny black corkscrews that were his hair. He was very black and shiny, and the flesh of his lips did not so much appear to be a different color as it looked to be unfinished and awaiting another coat. The lips were parted, the eyes wide, and even the ears seemed to have a heightened receptivity. He looked ecstatic—until he saw me, that is. For all he knew I was John McKee.

"That's okay," I said before he could even move, "I'm just passing through. You read."

"Ain't nothing *to* read. They's pictures."

"Fine." I fished around the lowest shelves a moment, playing at work.

"Hey, mister," the boy said after a minute, "where is this?"

"Where is what?"

"Where is these pictures? These people, man, they sure does look cool. They ain't no yelling or shouting here, you could just see it."

He lifted the book so I could see. It was an expensive large-sized edition of Gauguin reproductions. The page he had been looking at showed an 8½ x 11 print, in color, of three native women standing knee-high in a rose-colored stream. It *was* a silent picture, he was right.

"That's Tahiti. That's an island in the Pacific Ocean."

"That ain't no place you could go, is it? Like a ree-*sort?*"

"You could go there, I suppose. It's very far. People live there . . ."

"Hey, *look,* look here at this one." He flipped back to a page where a young brown-skinned maid was leaning forward on her knees, as though to dry her hair. "Man," the boy said, "that's the fuckin life." The euphoria of his diction would have earned him eternal banishment from the Newark Public Library and its branches had John or Mr. Scapello—or, God forbid, the hospitalized Miss Winney—come to investigate.

"Who took these pictures?" he asked me.

"Gauguin. He didn't take them, he painted them. Paul Gauguin. He was a Frenchman."

"Is he a white man or a colored man?"

"He's white."

"Man," the boy smiled, chuckled almost, "I knew that. He don't *take* pictures like no colored men would. He's a good picture taker . . . *Look, look,* look here at this one. Ain't that the fuckin *life?*"

I agreed it was and left.

Later I sent Jimmy Boylen hopping down the stairs to tell McKee that everything was all right. The rest of the day was uneventful. I sat at the Information Desk thinking about Brenda and reminding myself that that evening I would have to get gas before I started up to Short Hills, which I could see now, in my mind's eye, at dusk, rose-colored, like a Gauguin stream.

When I pulled up to the Patimkin house that night, everybody but Julie was waiting for me on the front porch: Mr. and Mrs., Ron, and Brenda, wearing a dress. I had not seen her in a dress before and for an instant she did not look like the same girl. But that was only half the surprise. So many of those Lincolnesque college girls turn out to be limbed for shorts alone. Not Brenda. She looked, in a dress, as though she'd gone through life so attired, as though she'd never worn shorts, or bathing suits, or pajamas, or anything but that pale linen dress. I walked rather bouncingly up the lawn, past the huge weeping willow, towards the waiting Patimkins, wishing all the while that I'd had my car washed. Before I'd even reached them, Ron stepped forward and shook my hand, vigorously, as though he hadn't seen me since the Diaspora. Mrs. Patimkin smiled and Mr. Patimkin grunted something and continued twitching his wrists before him, then raising an imaginary golf club and driving a ghost of a golf ball up and away towards the Orange Mountains, that are called Orange, I'm convinced, because in that various suburban light that's the *only* color they do not come dressed in.

"We'll be right back," Brenda said to me. "You have to sit with Julie. Carlota's off."

"Okay," I said.

"We're taking Ron to the airport."

"Okay."

"Julie doesn't want to go. She says Ron pushed her in the pool this afternoon. We've been waiting for you, so we don't miss Ron's plane. Okay?"

"*Okay.*"

Mr. and Mrs. Patimkin and Ron moved off, and I flashed Brenda just the hint of a glare. She reached out and took my hand a moment.

"How do you like me?" she said.

"You're great to baby-sit for. Am I allowed all the milk and cake I want?"

"Don't be angry, baby. We'll be right back." Then she waited a moment, and when I failed to deflate the pout from my mouth, she gave *me* a glare, no hints about it. "I *meant* how do you like me in a dress!" Then she ran off towards the Chrysler, trotting in her high heels like a colt.

When I walked into the house, I slammed the screen door behind me.

"Close the other door too," a little voice shouted. "The air-conditioning."

I closed the other door, obediently.

"Neil?" Julie called.

"Yes."

"Hi. Want to play five and two?"

"No."

"Why not?"

I did not answer.

"I'm in the television room," she called.

"Good."

"Are you supposed to stay with me?"

"Yes."

She appeared unexpectedly through the dining room. "Want to read a book report I wrote?"

"Not now."

"What do you want to do?" she said.

"Nothing, honey. Why don't you watch TV?"

"All right," she said disgustedly, and kicked her way back to the television room.

For a while I remained in the hall, bitten with the urge to slide quietly out of the house, into my car, and back to Newark, where I might even sit in the alley and break candy with my own. I felt like Carlota; no, not even as comfortable as that. At last I left the hall and began to stroll in and out of rooms on the first floor. Next to the living room was the study, a small knotty-pine room jammed with cater-cornered leather chairs and a complete set of *Information Please Almanacs*. On the wall hung three colored photo-paintings; they were the kind which, regardless of the subjects, be they vital or infirm, old or youthful, are characterized by bud-cheeks, wet lips, pearly teeth, and shiny, metallized hair. The subjects in this case were Ron, Brenda, and Julie at about ages fourteen, thirteen, and two. Brenda had long auburn hair, her diamond-studded nose, and no glasses; all combined to make her look a regal thirteen-year-old who'd just gotten smoke in her eyes. Ron was rounder and his hairline was lower, but that love of spherical objects and lined courts twinkled in his boyish eyes. Poor little Julie was lost in the photo-painter's Platonic idea of childhood; her tiny humanity was smothered somewhere back of gobs of pink and white.

There were other pictures about, smaller ones, taken with a Brownie Reflex before photo-paintings had become fashionable. There was a tiny picture of Brenda on a horse; another of Ron in bar mitzvah suit, *yamal-kah*, and *tallas;*[9] and two pictures framed together—one of a beautiful, faded woman, who must have been, from the eyes, Mrs. Patimkin's mother, and the other of Mrs. Patimkin herself, her hair in a halo, her eyes joyous and not those of a slowly aging mother with a quick and lovely daughter.

I walked through the archway into the dining room and stood a moment looking out at the sporting goods tree. From the television room that winged off the dining room, I could hear Julie listening to *This Is Your Life.*[1] The kitchen, which winged off the other side, was empty, and apparently, with Carlota off, the Patimkins had had dinner at the club. Mr. and Mrs. Patimkin's bedroom was in the middle of the house, down the hall, next to Julie's, and for a moment I wanted to see what size bed those giants slept in—I imagined it wide and deep as a swimming pool— but I postponed my investigation while Julie was in the house, and instead opened the door in the kitchen that led down to the basement.

The basement had a different kind of coolness from the house, and it had a smell, which was something the upstairs was totally without. It felt cavernous down there, but in a comforting way, like the simulated caves children make for themselves on rainy days, in hall closets, under blankets, or in between the legs of dining room tables. I flipped on the light at the foot of the stairs and was not surprised at the pine paneling, the bamboo furniture, the ping-pong table, and the mirrored bar that was stocked with every kind and size of glass, ice bucket, decanter, mixer, swizzle stick, shot glass, pretzel bowl—all the bacchanalian paraphernalia, plentiful, orderly, and untouched, as it can be only in the bar of a wealthy man who never entertains drinking people, who himself does not drink, who, in fact, gets a fishy look from his wife when every several months he takes a shot of schnapps before dinner. I went behind the bar where there was an aluminum sink that had not seen a dirty glass, I'm sure, since Ron's bar mitzvah party, and would not see another, probably, until one of the Patimkin children was married or engaged. I would have poured myself a drink—just as a wicked wage for being forced into servantry—but I was uneasy about breaking the label on a bottle of whiskey. You had to break a label to get a drink. On the shelf back of the bar were two dozen bottles—twenty-three to be exact—of Jack Daniels, each with a little booklet tied to its collared neck informing patrons how patrician of them it was to drink the stuff. And over the Jack Daniels were more photos: there was a blown-up newspaper photo of Ron palming a basketball in one hand like a raisin; under the picture it said, "Center, Ronald Patimkin, Milburn High School, 6'4", 217 pounds." And there was another picture of Brenda on a horse, and next to that, a velvet mounting board with ribbons and medals clipped to it: Essex County Horse Show 1949, Union County Horse Show 1950, Garden State Fair 1952, Morris-

9. Prayer shawl. *Yamalkah:* skullcap worn by Jews in synagogue and at prayers (and by the very orthodox in and out of doors).

1. Popular television program in which the guest was surprised by a review of the highlights of his or her life and the presence of old friends, colleagues, relatives.

town Horse Show 1953, and so on—all for Brenda, for jumping and running or galloping or whatever else young girls receive ribbons for. In the entire house I hadn't seen one picture of Mr. Patimkin.

The rest of the basement, back of the wide pine-paneled room, was gray cement walls and linoleum floor and contained innumerable electrical appliances, including a freezer big enough to house a family of Eskimos. Beside the freezer, incongruously, was a tall old refrigerator; its ancient presence was a reminder to me of the Patimkin roots in Newark. This same refrigerator had once stood in the kitchen of an apartment in some four-family house, probably in the same neighborhood where I had lived all my life, first with my parents and then, when the two of them went wheezing off to Arizona, with my aunt and uncle. After Pearl Harbor the refrigerator had made the move up to Short Hills; Patimkin Kitchen and Bathroom Sinks had gone to war: no new barracks was complete until it had a squad of Patimkin sinks lined up in its latrine.

I opened the door of the old refrigerator; it was not empty. No longer did it hold butter, eggs, herring in cream sauce, ginger ale, tuna fish salad, an occasional corsage—rather it was heaped with fruit, shelves swelled with it, every color, every texture, and hidden within, every kind of pit. There were greengage plums, black plums, red plums, apricots, nectarines, peaches, long horns of grapes, black, yellow, red, and cherries, cherries flowing out of boxes and staining everything scarlet. And there were melons—cantaloupes and honeydews—and on the top shelf, half of a huge watermelon, a thin sheet of wax paper clinging to its bare red face like a wet lip. Oh Patimkin! Fruit grew in their refrigerator and sporting goods dropped from their trees!

I grabbed a handful of cherries and then a nectarine, and I bit right down to its pit.

"You better wash that or you'll get diarrhea."

Julie was standing behind me in the pine-paneled room. She was wearing *her* Bermudas and *her* white polo shirt which was unlike Brenda's only in that it had a little dietary history of its own.

"What?" I said.

"They're not washed yet," Julie said, and in such a way that it seemed to place the refrigerator itself out-of-bounds, if only for me.

"That's all right," I said, and devoured the nectarine and put the pit in my pocket and stepped out of the refrigerator room, all in one second. I still didn't know what to do with the cherries. "I was just looking around," I said.

Julie didn't answer.

"Where's Ron going?" I asked, dropping the cherries into my pocket, among my keys and change.

"Milwaukee."

"For long?"

"To see Harriet. They're in love."

We looked at each other for longer than I could bear. "Harriet?" I asked.

"Yes."

Julie was looking at me as though she were trying to look behind me, and then I realized that I was standing with my hands out of sight. I brought them around to the front, and, I swear it, she did peek to see if they were empty.

We confronted one another again; she seemed to have a threat in her face.

Then she spoke. "Want to play ping-pong?"

"God, yes," I said, and made for the table with two long, bounding steps. "You can serve."

Julie smiled and we began to play.

I have no excuses to offer for what happened next. I began to win and I liked it.

"Can I take that one over?" Julie said. "I hurt my finger yesterday and it just hurt when I served."

"No."

I continued to win.

"That wasn't fair, Neil. My shoelace came untied. Can I take it—"

"No."

We played, I ferociously.

"Neil, you leaned over the table. That's illegal—"

"I didn't lean and it's not illegal."

I felt the cherries hopping among my nickels and pennies.

"Neil, you gypped me out of a point. You have nineteen and I have eleven—"

"Twenty and *ten*," I said. "Serve!"

She did and I smashed my return past her—it zoomed off the table and skittered into the refrigerator room.

"You're a cheater!" she screamed at me. "You cheat!" Her jaw was trembling as though she carried a weight on top of her pretty head. "*I hate* you!" And she threw the racket across the room and it clanged off the bar, just as, outside, I heard the Chrysler crushing gravel in the drive-way.

"The game isn't over," I said to her.

"You cheat! And you were stealing fruit!" she said, and ran away before I had my chance to win.

Later that night, Brenda and I made love, our first time. We were sit-ting on the sofa in the television room and for some ten minutes had not spoken a word to each other. Julie had long since gone to a weepy bed, and though no one had said anything to me about her crying, I did not know if the child had mentioned my fistful of cherries, which, some time before, I had flushed down the toilet.

The television set was on and though the sound was off and the house quiet, the gray pictures still wiggled at the far end of the room. Brenda was quiet and her dress circled her legs, which were tucked back beneath her. We sat there for some while and did not speak. Then she went into the kitchen and when she came back she said that it sounded as though everyone was asleep. We sat a while longer, watching the soundless bodies on the screen eating a silent dinner in someone's silent restaurant. When I began to unbutton her dress she resisted me, and I like to think it was because she knew how lovely she looked in it. But she looked lovely, my Brenda, anyway, and we folded it carefully and held each other close and soon there we were, Brenda falling, slowly but with a smile, and me rising.

How can I describe loving Brenda? It was so sweet, as though I'd fi-nally scored that twenty-first point.

When I got home I dialed Brenda's number, but not before my aunt heard and rose from her bed.

"Who are you calling at this hour? The doctor?"

"No."

"What kind phone calls, one o'clock at night?"

"Shhh!" I said.

"He tells *me* shhh. Phone calls one o'clock at night, we haven't got a big enough bill," and then she dragged herself back into bed, where with a martyr's heart and bleary eyes she had resisted the downward tug of sleep until she'd heard my key in the door.

Brenda answered the phone.

"Neil?" she said.

"Yes," I whispered. "You didn't get out of bed, did you?"

"No," she said, "the phone is next to the bed."

"Good. How is it in bed?"

"Good. Are you in bed?"

"Yes," I lied, and tried to right myself by dragging the phone by its cord as close as I could to my bedroom.

"I'm in bed with you," she said.

"That's right," I said, "and I'm with you."

"I have the shades down, so it's dark and I don't see you."

"I don't see you either."

"That was so nice, Neil."

"Yes. Go to sleep, sweet, I'm here," and we hung up without goodbyes. In the morning, as planned, I called again, but I could hardly hear Brenda or myself for that matter, for Aunt Gladys and Uncle Max were going on a Workmen's Circle[2] picnic in the afternoon, and there was some trouble about grape juice that had dripped all night from a jug in the refrigerator and by morning had leaked out onto the floor. Brenda was still in bed and so could play our game with some success, but I had to pull down all the shades of my senses to imagine myself beside her. I could only pray our nights and mornings would come, and soon enough they did.

4

Over the next week and a half there seemed to be only two people in my life: Brenda and the little colored kid who liked Gauguin. Every morning before the library opened, the boy was waiting; sometimes he seated himself on the lion's back, sometimes under his belly, sometimes he just stood around throwing pebbles at his mane. Then he would come inside, tap around the main floor until Otto stared him up on tiptoes, and finally headed up the long marble stairs that led to Tahiti. He did not always stay to lunch time, but one very hot day he was there when I arrived in the morning and went through the door behind me when I left at night. The next morning, it was, that he did not show up, and as though in his place, a very old man appeared, white, smelling of Life Savers, his nose and jowls showing erupted veins beneath them. "Could you tell me where I'd find the art section?"

"Stack Three," I said.

In a few minutes, he returned with a big brown-covered book in his

2. A predominantly but not exclusively Jewish fra-ternal benefit life insurance society with many social and educational activities.

hand. He placed it on my desk, withdrew his card from a long moneyless billfold and waited for me to stamp out the book.

"Do you want to take this book *out?*" I said.

He smiled.

I took his card and jammed the metal edge into the machine; but I did not stamp down. "Just a minute," I said. I took a clipboard from under the desk and flipped through a few pages, upon which were games of battleship and tick-tack-toe that I'd been playing through the week with myself. "I'm afraid there's a hold on this book."

"A what?"

"A hold. Someone's called up and asked that we hold it for them. Can I take your name and address and drop a card when it's free . . ."

And so I was able, not without flushing once or twice, to get the book back in the stacks. When the colored kid showed up later in the day, it was just where he'd left it the afternoon before.

As for Brenda, I saw her every evening and when there was not a night game that kept Mr. Patimkin awake and in the TV room, or a Hadassah[3] card party that sent Mrs. Patimkin out of the house and brought her in at unpredictable hours, we made love before the silent screen. One muggy, low-skied night Brenda took me swimming at the club. We were the only ones in the pool, and all the chairs, the cabañas, the lights, the diving boards, the very water seemed to exist only for our pleasure. She wore a blue suit that looked purple in the lights and down beneath the water it flashed sometimes green, sometimes black. Late in the evening a breeze came up off the golf course and we wrapped ourselves in one huge towel, pulled two chaise lounges together, and despite the bartender, who was doing considerable pacing back and forth by the bar window, which over-looked the pool, we rested side by side on the chairs. Finally the bar light itself flipped off, and then, in a snap, the lights around the pool went down and out. My heart must have beat faster, or something, for Brenda seemed to guess my sudden doubt—*we should go,* I thought.

She said: "That's okay."

It was very dark, the sky was low and starless, and it took a while for me to see, once again, the diving board a shade lighter than the night, and to distinguish the water from the chairs that surrounded the far side of the pool.

I pushed the straps of her bathing suit down but she said no and rolled an inch away from me, and for the first time in the two weeks I'd known her she asked me a question about me.

"Where are your parents?" she said.

"Tucson," I said. "Why?"

"My mother asked me."

I could see the life guard's chair now, white almost.

"Why are you still here? Why aren't you with them?" she asked.

"I'm not a child any more, Brenda," I said, more sharply than I'd in-tended. "I just can't go wherever my parents are."

"But then why do you stay with your aunt and uncle?"

"They're not my parents."

"They're better?"

"No. Worse. I don't *know* why I stay with them."

3. Women's Zionist organization, which in the United States engages in educational and charitable   work.

"Why?" she said.

"Why don't I know?"

"Why do you stay? You do know, don't you?"

"My job, I suppose. It's convenient from there, and it's cheap, and it pleases my parents. My aunt's all right really ... Do I really have to explain to your mother why I live where I do?"

"It's not for my mother. I want to know. I wondered why you weren't with your parents, that's all."

"Are you cold?" I asked.

"No."

"Do you want to go home?"

"No, not unless you do. Don't you feel well, Neil?"

"I feel all right," and to let her know that I was still me, I held her to me, though that moment I was without desire.

"Neil?"

"What?"

"What about the library?"

"Who wants to know that?"

"My father," she laughed.

"And you?"

She did not answer a moment. "And me," she said finally.

"Well, what about it? Do I like it? It's okay. I sold shoes once and like the library better. After the Army they tried me for a couple of months at Uncle Aaron's real estate company—Doris' father—and I like the library better than that ..."

"How did you get a job *there?*"

"I worked there for a little while when I was in college, then when I quit Uncle Aaron's, oh, I don't know ..."

"What did you take in college?"

"At Newark Colleges of Rutgers University I majored in philosophy. I am twenty-three years old. I—"

"Why do you sound nasty again?"

"Do I?"

"Yes."

I didn't say I was sorry.

"Are you planning on making a career of the library?"

"Bren, I'm not planning anything. I haven't planned a thing in three years. At least for the year I've been out of the Army. In the Army I used to plan to go away weekends. I'm—I'm not a planner." After all the truth I'd suddenly given her, I shouldn't have ruined it for myself with that final lie. I added, "I'm a liver."

"I'm a pancreas," she said.

"I'm a—"

And she kissed the absurd game away; she wanted to be serious.

"Do you love me, Neil?"

I did not answer.

"I'll sleep with you whether you do or not, so tell me the truth."

"That was pretty crude."

"Don't be prissy," she said.

"No, I mean a crude thing to say about me."

"I don't understand," she said, and she didn't, and that she didn't pained me; I allowed myself the minor subterfuge, however, of forgiving

Brenda her obtuseness. "Do you?" she said.

"No."

"I want you to."

"What about the library?"

"What about it?" she said.

Was it obtuseness again? I thought not—and it wasn't, for Brenda said, "When you love me, there'll be nothing to worry about."

"Then of course I'll love you." I smiled.

"I know you will," she said. "Why don't you go in the water, and I'll wait for you and close my eyes, and when you come back you'll surprise me with the wet. Go ahead."

"You like games, don't you?"

"Go ahead. I'll close my eyes."

I walked down to the edge of the pool and dove in. The water felt colder than it had earlier, and when I broke through and was headed blindly down I felt a touch of panic. At the top again, I started to swim the length of the pool and then turned at the end and started back, but suddenly I was sure that when I left the water Brenda would be gone. I'd be alone in this damn place. I started for the side and pulled myself up and ran to the chairs and Brenda was there and I kissed her.

"God," she shivered, "you didn't stay long."

"I know."

"My turn," she said, and then she was up and a second later I heard a little crack of water and then nothing. Nothing for quite a while.

"Bren," I called softly, "are you all right?" but no one answered.

I found her glasses on the chair beside me and held them in my hands. "Brenda?"

Nothing.

"Brenda?"

"No fair calling," she said and gave me her drenched self. "Your turn," she said.

This time I stayed below the water for a long while and when I surfaced again my lungs were ready to pop. I threw my head back for air and above me saw the sky, low like a hand pushing down, and I began to swim as though to move out from under its pressure. I wanted to get back to Brenda, for I worried once again—and there was no evidence, was there?—that if I stayed away too long she would not be there when I returned. I wished that I had carried her glasses away with me, so she would have to wait for me to lead her back home. I was having crazy thoughts, I knew, and yet they did not seem uncalled for in the darkness and strangeness of that place. Oh how I wanted to call out to her from the pool, but I knew she would not answer and I forced myself to swim the length a third time, and then a fourth, but midway through the fifth I felt a weird fright again, had momentary thoughts of my own extinction, and that time when I came back I held her tighter than either of us expected.

"Let go, let go," she laughed, "my turn—"

"But Brenda—"

But Brenda was gone and this time it seemed as though she'd never come back. I settled back and waited for the sun to dawn over the ninth hole, prayed it would if only for the comfort of its light, and when Brenda finally returned to me I would not let her go, and her cold wetness crept

into me somehow and made me shiver. "That's it, Brenda. Please, no
more games," I said, and then when I spoke again I held her so tightly I
almost dug my body into hers, "I love you," I said, "I do."

So the summer went on. I saw Brenda every evening: we went swimming, we went for walks, we went for rides, up through the mountains so
far and so long that by the time we started back the fog had begun to
emerge from the trees and push out into the road, and I would tighten
my hands on the wheel and Brenda would put on her glasses and watch
the white line for me. And we would eat—a few nights after my discovery
of the fruit refrigerator Brenda led me to it herself. We would fill huge
soup bowls with cherries, and in serving dishes for roast beef we would
heap slices of watermelon. Then we would go up and out the back doorway of the basement and onto the back lawn and sit under the sporting-
goods tree, the light from the TV room the only brightness we had out
there. All we would hear for a while were just the two of us spitting pits.
"I wish they would take root overnight and in the morning there'd just be
watermelons and cherries."

"If they took root in this yard, sweetie, they'd grow refrigerators and
Westinghouse Preferred. I'm not being nasty," I'd add quickly, and
Brenda would laugh, and say she felt like a greengage plum, and I would
disappear down into the basement and the cherry bowl would now be a
greengage plum bowl, and then a nectarine bowl, and then a peach bowl,
until, I have to admit it, I cracked my frail bowel, and would have to
spend the following night, sadly, on the wagon. And then too we went
out for corned beef sandwiches, pizza, beer and shrimp, ice cream sodas,
and hamburgers. We went to the Lions Club Fair one night and Brenda
won a Lions Club ashtray by shooting three baskets in a row. And when
Ron came home from Milwaukee we went from time to time to see him
play basketball in the semi-pro summer league, and it was those evenings
that I felt a stranger with Brenda, for she knew all the players' names,
and though for the most part they were gawky-limbed and dull, there was
one named Luther Ferrari who was neither, and whom Brenda had dated
for a whole year in high school. He was Ron's closest friend and I remembered his name from the Newark *News:* he was one of the great Ferrari
brothers, All State all of them in at least two sports. It was Ferrari who
called Brenda Buck, a nickname which apparently went back to her
ribbon-winning days. Like Ron, Ferrari was exceedingly polite, as though
it were some affliction of those over six feet three; he was gentlemanly
towards me and gentle towards Brenda, and after a while I balked when
the suggestion was made that we go to see Ron play. And then one night
we discovered that at eleven o'clock the cashier of the Hilltop Theatre
went home and the manager disappeared into his office, and so that summer we saw the last quarter of at least fifteen movies, and then when we
were driving home—driving Brenda home, that is—we would try to reconstruct the beginnings of the films. Our favorite last quarter of a movie was
Ma and Pa Kettle in the City,[4] our favorite fruit, greengage plums, and
our favorite, our only, people, each other. Of course we ran into others
from time to time, some of Brenda's friends, and occasionally, one or two
of mine. One night in August we even went to a bar out on Route 6 with

4. One of the nine comic Ma and Pa Kettle films
made between 1949 and 1957 starring salty Marjorie   Main (1890–1975) and peppery Percy Kilbride (1888–
1964) as earthy rural characters.

Laura Simpson Stolowitch and her fiancé, but it was a dreary evening. Brenda and I seemed untrained in talking to others, and so we danced a great deal, which we realized was one thing we'd never done before. Laura's boyfriend drank stingers pompously and Simp—Brenda wanted me to call her Stolo but I didn't—Simp drank a tepid combination of something like ginger ale and soda. Whenever we returned to the table, Simp would be talking about "the dance" and her fiancé about "the film," until finally Brenda asked him "Which film?" and then we danced till closing time. And when we went back to Brenda's we filled a bowl with cherries which we carried into the TV room and ate sloppily for a while; and later, on the sofa, we loved each other and when I moved from the darkened room to the bathroom I could always feel cherry pits against my bare soles. At home, undressing for the second time that night, I would find red marks on the undersides of my feet.

And how did her parents take all of this? Mrs. Patimkin continued to smile at me and Mr. Patimkin continued to think I ate like a bird. When invited to dinner I would, for his benefit, eat twice what I wanted, but the truth seemed to be that after he'd characterized my appetite that first time, he never really bothered to look again. I might have eaten ten times my normal amount, have finally killed myself with food, he would still have considered me not a man but a sparrow. No one seemed distressed by my presence, though Julie had cooled considerably; consequently, when Brenda suggested to her father that at the end of August I spend a week of my vacation at the Patimkin house, he pondered a moment, decided on the five iron, made his approach shot, and said yes. And when she passed on to her mother the decision of Patimkin Sink, there wasn't much Mrs. Patimkin could do. So, through Brenda's craftiness, I was invited.

On that Friday morning that was to be my last day of work, my Aunt Gladys saw me packing my bag and she asked where I was going. I told her. She did not answer and I thought I saw awe in those red-rimmed hysterical eyes—I had come a long way since that day she'd said to me on the phone, "Fancy-shmancy."

"How long you going, I should know how to shop I wouldn't buy too much. You'll leave me with a refrigerator full of milk it'll go bad it'll stink up the refrigerator—"

"A week," I said.

"A *week?*" she said. "They got room for a week?"

"Aunt Gladys, they don't live over the store."

"I lived over a store I wasn't ashamed. Thank God we always had a roof. We never went begging in the streets," she told me as I packed the Bermudas I'd just bought, "and your cousin Susan we'll put through college, Uncle Max should live and be well. We didn't send her away to camp for August, she doesn't have shoes when she wants them, sweaters she doesn't have a drawerful—"

"I didn't say anything, Aunt Gladys."

"You don't get enough to eat here? You leave over sometimes I show your Uncle Max your plate it's a shame. A child in Europe could make a four-course meal from what you leave over."

"Aunt Gladys." I went over to her. "I get everything I want here. I'm just taking a vacation. Don't I deserve a vacation?"

She held herself to me and I could feel her trembling. "I told your mother I would take care of her Neil she shouldn't worry. And now you go running—"

I put my arms around her and kissed her on the top of her head. "C'mon," I said, "you're being silly. I'm not running away. I'm just going away for a week, on a vacation."

"You'll leave their telephone number God forbid you should get sick."

"Okay."

"Milburn they live?"

"Short Hills. I'll leave the number."

"Since when do Jewish people live in Short Hills? They couldn't be real Jews believe me."

"They're real Jews," I said.

"I'll see it I'll believe it." She wiped her eyes with the corner of her apron, just as I was zipping up the sides of the suitcase. "Don't close the bag yet. I'll make a little package with some fruit in it, you'll take with you."

"Okay, Aunt Gladys," and on the way to work that morning I ate the orange and the two peaches that she'd put in a bag for me.

A few hours later Mr. Scapello informed me that when I returned from my vacation after Labor Day, I would be hoisted up onto Martha Winney's stool. He himself, he said, had made the same move some twelve years ago, and so it appeared that if I could manage to maintain my balance I might someday be Mr. Scapello. I would also get an eight-dollar increase in salary which was five dollars more than the increase Mr. Scapello had received years before. He shook my hand and then started back up the long flight of marble stairs, his behind barging against his suit jacket like a hoop. No sooner had he left my side then I smelled spearmint and looked up to see the old man with veiny nose and jowls.

"Hello, young man," he said pleasantly. "Is the book back?"

"What book?"

"The Gauguin. I was shopping and I thought I'd stop by to ask. I haven't gotten the card yet. It's two weeks already."

"No," I said, and as I spoke I saw that Mr. Scapello had stopped midway up the stairs and turned as though he'd forgotten to tell me something. "Look," I said to the old man, "it should be back any day." I said it with a finality that bordered on rudeness, and I alarmed myself, for suddenly I saw what would happen: the old man making a fuss, Mr. Scapello gliding down the stairs, Mr. Scapello scampering up to the stacks, Scapello scandalized, Scapello profuse, Scapello presiding at the ascension of John McKee to Miss Winney's stool. I turned to the old man, "Why don't you leave your phone number and I'll try to get a hold of it this afternoon—" but my attempt at concern and courtesy came too late, and the man growled some words about public servants, a letter to the Mayor, snotty kids, and left the library, thank God, only a second before Mr. Scapello returned to my desk to remind me that everyone was chipping in for a present for Miss Winney and that if I liked I should leave a half dollar on his desk during the day.

After lunch the colored kid came in. When he headed past the desk for the stairs, I called over to him. "Come here," I said. "Where are you going?"

"The heart section."

"What book are you reading?"

"That Mr. Go-again's book. Look, man, I ain't doing nothing wrong. I didn't do *no* writing in *any*thing. You could search me—"

"I know you didn't. Listen, if you like that book so much why don't you please take it home? Do you have a library card?"

"No, sir, I didn't take *nothing.*"

"No, a library card is what we give to you so you can take books home. Then you won't have to come down here every day. Do you go to school?"

"Yes, sir. Miller Street School. But this here's summertime. It's okay I'm not in school. I ain't *supposed* to be in school."

"I know. As long as you go to school you can *have* a library card. You could take the book home."

"What you keep telling me take that book home for? At home somebody dee-*stroy* it."

"You could hide it someplace, in a desk—"

"Man," he said, squinting at me, "why don't you want me to come round here?"

"I didn't say you shouldn't."

"I *likes* to come here. I likes them stairs."

"I like them too," I said. "But the trouble is that someday somebody's going to take that book out."

He smiled. "Don't you worry," he said to me. "Ain't nobody done that yet," and he tapped off to the stairs and Stack Three.

Did I perspire that day! It was the coolest of the summer, but when I left work in the evening my shirt was sticking to my back. In the car I opened my bag, and while the rush-hour traffic flowed down Washington Street, I huddled in the back and changed into a clean shirt so that when I reached Short Hills I'd look as though I was deserving of an interlude in the suburbs. But driving up Central Avenue I could not keep my mind on my vacation, or for that matter on my driving: to the distress of pedestrians and motorists, I ground gears, overshot crosswalks, hesitated at green and red lights alike. I kept thinking that while I was on vacation that jowly bastard would return to the library, that the colored kid's book would disappear, that my new job would be taken away from me, that, in fact my old job—but then why should I worry about all that: the library wasn't going to be my life.

5

"Ron's getting married!" Julie screamed at me when I came through the door. "Ron's getting married!"

"Now?" I said.

"Labor Day! He's marrying Harriet, he's marrying Harriet." She began to sing it like a jump-rope song, nasal and rhythmic. "I'm going to be a sister-in-law!"

"Hi," Brenda said, "I'm going to be a sister-in-law."

"So I hear. When did it happen?"

"This afternoon he told us. They spoke long distance for forty minutes last night. She's flying here next week, and there's going to be a *huge* wedding. My parents are flittering all over the place. They've got to arrange everything in about a day or two. And my father's taking Ron in the business—but he's going to have to start at two hundred a week and then work himself up. That'll take till October."

"I thought he was going to be a gym teacher."

"He was. But now he has responsibilities . . ."

And at dinner Ron expanded on the subject of responsibilities and the future.

"We're going to have a boy," he said, to his mother's delight, "and when he's about six months old I'm going to sit him down with a basketball in front of him, and a football, and a baseball, and then whichever one he reaches for, that's the one we're going to concentrate on."

"Suppose he doesn't reach for any of them," Brenda said.

"Don't be funny, young lady," Mrs. Patimkin said.

"I'm going to be an aunt," Julie sang, and she stuck her tongue out at Brenda.

"When is Harriet coming?" Mr. Patimkin breathed through a mouthful of potatoes.

"A week from yesterday."

"Can she sleep in my room?" Julie cried. "*Can* she?"

"No, the guest room—" Mrs. Patimkin began, but then she remembered me—with a crushing side glance from those purple eyes, and said, "Of course."

Well, I did eat like a bird. After dinner my bag was carried—by me—up to the guest room which was across from Ron's room and right down the hall from Brenda. Brenda came along to show me the way.

"Let me see your bed, Bren."

"Later," she said.

"Can we? Up here?"

"I think so," she said. "Ron sleeps like a log."

"Can I stay the night?"

"I don't know."

"I could get up early and come back in here. We'll set the alarm."

"It'll wake everybody up."

"I'll remember to get up. I can do it."

"I better not stay up here with you too long," she said. "My mother'll have a fit. I think she's nervous about your being here."

"So am I. I hardly know them. Do you think I should really stay a whole week?"

"A whole week? Once Harriet gets here it'll be so chaotic you can probably stay two months."

"You think so?"

"Yes."

"Do you want me to?"

"Yes," she said, and went down the stairs so as to ease her mother's conscience.

I unpacked my bag and dropped my clothes into a drawer that was empty except for a packet of dress shields and a high school yearbook. In the middle of my unpacking, Ron came clunking up the stairs.

"Hi," he called into my room.

"Congratulations," I called back. I should have realized that any word of ceremony would provoke a handshake from Ron; he interrupted whatever it was he was about to do in his room, and came into mine.

"Thanks." He pumped me. "Thanks."

Then he sat down on my bed and watched me as I finished unpacking. I have one shirt with a Brooks Brothers label and I let it linger on the bed a while; the Arrows[5] I heaped in the drawer. Ron sat there rubbing his forearm and grinning. After a while I was thoroughly unsettled by the silence.

"Well," I said, "that's something."

He agreed, to *what* I don't know.

"How does it feel?" I asked, after another longer silence.

"Better. Ferrari smacked it under the boards."

"Oh. Good," I said. "How does getting married feel?"

"Ah, okay, I guess."

I leaned against the bureau and counted stitches in the carpet.

Ron finally risked a journey into language. "Do you know anything about music?" he asked.

"Something, yes."

"You can listen to my phonograph if you want."

"Thanks, Ron. I didn't know you were interested in music."

"Sure. I got all the Andre Kostelanetz records ever made. You like Mantovani?[6] I got all of him too. I like semi-classical a lot. You can hear my Columbus record if you want . . ." he dwindled off. Finally he shook my hand and left.

Downstairs I could hear Julie singing. "I'm going to be an a-a-aunt," and Mrs. Patimkin saying to her, "No, honey, you're going to be a sister-in-law. Sing that, sweetheart," but Julie continued to sing, "I'm going to be an a-a-aunt," and then I heard Brenda's voice joining hers, singing, "We're going to be an a-a-aunt," and then Julie joined that, and finally Mrs. Patimkin called to Mr. Patimkin, "Will you make her stop encouraging her . . ." and soon the duet ended.

And then I heard Mrs. Patimkin again. I couldn't make out the words but Brenda answered her. Their voices grew louder; finally I could hear perfectly. "I need a houseful of company at a time like this?" It was Mrs. Patimkin. "I asked you, Mother." "You asked your father. I'm the one you should have asked first. He doesn't know how much extra work this is for me . . ." "My God, Mother, you'd think we didn't have Carlota and Jenny." "Carlota and Jenny can't do everything. This is not the Salvation Army!" "What the hell does that mean?" "Watch your tongue, young lady. That may be very well for your college friends." "Oh, *stop* it, Mother!" "Don't raise your voice to me. When's the last time you lifted a finger to help around here?" "I'm not a slave . . . I'm a daughter." "You ought to learn what a day's work means." "Why?" Brenda said. "*Why?*" "Because you're lazy," Mrs. Patimkin answered, "and you think the world owes you a living." "Whoever said *that?*" "You ought to earn some money and buy your own clothes." "Why? Good God, Mother, Daddy could live off the stocks alone, for God's sake. What are you complaining about?" "When's the last time you washed the dishes!" "Jesus Christ!" Brenda flared, "Carlota washes the dishes!" "Don't Jesus Christ me!" "Oh, Mother!" and Brenda was crying. "Why the hell are you like this!" "That's it," Mrs. Patimkin said, "cry in front of your company . . ." "My

5. An ordinary label; Brooks Brothers is an exclusive one.
6. Both the Russian-born American conductor, pianist, composer Andre Kostelanetz (1901-1980) and the Italian-born English bandleader Annunzio Paulo

Mantovani (b. 1908) are best known for their radio broadcasts and recordings; both Kostelanetz's arrangements of semiclassical music and Mantovani's large orchestra, dominated by strings, have been described as "lush."

company . . ." Brenda wept, "why don't you go yell at him too . . . why is everyone so nasty to me . . ."

From across the hall I heard Andre Kostelanetz let several thousand singing violins loose on "Night and Day." Ron's door was open and I saw he was stretched out, colossal, on his bed; he was singing along with the record. The words belonged to "Night and Day," but I didn't recognize Ron's tune. In a minute he picked up the phone and asked the operator for a Milwaukee number. While she connected him, he rolled over and turned up the volume on the record player, so that it would carry the nine hundred miles west.

I heard Julie downstairs. "Ha, ha, Brenda's crying, ha, ha, Brenda's crying."

And then Brenda was running up the stairs. "Your day'll come, you little bastard!" she called.

"Brenda!" Mrs. Patimkin called.

"Mommy!" Julie cried. "Brenda cursed at me!"

"What's going *on* here!" Mr. Patimkin shouted.

"You call *me*, Mrs. P?" Carlota shouted.

And Ron, in the other room, said, "Hello, Har, I told them . . ."

I sat down on my Brooks Brothers shirt and pronounced my own name out loud.

"Goddam her!" Brenda said to me as she paced up and down my room.

"Bren, do you think I should go—"

"Shhh . . ." She went to the door of my room and listened. "They're going visiting, thank God."

"Brenda—"

"Shhh . . . They've gone."

"Julie too?"

"Yes," she said. "Is Ron in his room? His door is closed."

"He went out."

"You can't hear anybody move around here. They all creep around in *sneakers*. Oh Neil."

"Bren, I asked you, maybe I should just stay through tomorrow and then go."

"Oh, it isn't you she's angry about."

"I'm not helping any."

"It's Ron, really. That he's getting married just has her flipped. And me. Now with that goody-good Harriet around she'll just forget I ever exist."

"Isn't that okay with you?"

She walked off to the window and looked outside. It was dark and cool; the trees rustled and flapped as though they were sheets that had been hung out to dry. Everything outside hinted at September, and for the first time I realized how close we were to Brenda's departure for school.

"Is it, Bren?" but she was not listening to me.

She walked across the room to a door at the far end of the room. She opened it.

"I thought it was a closet," I said.

"Come here."

She held the door back and we leaned into the darkness and could hear the strange wind hissing in the eaves of the house.

"What's in here?" I said.

"Money."

Brenda went into the room. When the puny sixty-watt bulb was twisted on, I saw that the place was full of old furniture—two wing chairs with hair-oil lines at the back, a sofa with a paunch in its middle, a bridge table, two bridge chairs with their stuffing showing, a mirror whose backing had peeled off, shadeless lamps, lampless shades, a coffee table with a cracked glass top, and a pile of rolled up shades.

"What is this?" I said.

"A storeroom. Our old furniture."

"How old?"

"From Newark," she said. "Come here." She was on her hands and knees in front of the sofa and was holding up its paunch to peek beneath.

"Brenda, what the hell are we doing here? You're getting filthy."

"It's not here."

"*What?*"

"The money. I told you."

I sat down on a wing chair, raising some dust. It had begun to rain outside, and we could smell the fall dampness coming through the vent that was outlined at the far end of the storeroom. Brenda got up from the floor and sat down on the sofa. Her knees and Bermudas were dirty and when she pushed her hair back she dirtied her forehead. There among the disarrangement and dirt I had the strange experience of seeing us, *both* of us, placed among disarrangement and dirt: we looked like a young couple who had just moved into a new apartment; we had suddenly taken stock of our furniture, finances, and future, and all we could feel any pleasure about was the clean smell of outside, which reminded us we were alive, but which, in a pinch, would not feed us.

"What money?" I said again.

"The hundred-dollar bills. From when I was a little girl . . ." and she breathed deeply. "When I was little and we'd just moved from Newark, my father took me up here one day. He took me into this room and told me that if anything should ever happen to him, he wanted me to know where there was some money that I should have. He said it wasn't for anybody else but me, and that I should never tell anyone about it, not even Ron. Or my mother."

"How much was it?"

"Three hundred-dollar bills. I'd never seen them before. I was nine, around Julie's age. I don't think we'd been living here a month. I remember I used to come up here about once a week, when no one was home but Carlota, and crawl under the sofa and make sure it was still here. And it always was. He never mentioned it once again. Never."

"Where is it? Maybe someone stole it."

"I don't know, Neil. I suppose he took it back."

"When it was gone," I said, "my God, didn't you tell him? Maybe Carlota—"

"I never knew it was gone, until just now. I guess I stopped looking at one time or another . . . And then I forgot about it. Or just didn't think about it. I mean I always had enough, I didn't need this. I guess one day *he* figured I wouldn't need it."

Brenda paced up to the narrow, dust-covered window and drew her initials on it.

"Why did you want it now?" I said.

"I don't know . . ." she said and went over and twisted the bulb off.

I didn't move from the chair and Brenda, in her tight shorts and shirt, seemed naked standing there a few feet away. Then I saw her shoulders shaking. "I wanted to find it and tear it up in little pieces and put the goddam pieces in her purse! If it was there, I swear it, I would have done it."

"I wouldn't have let you, Bren."

"Wouldn't you have?"

"No."

"Make love to me, Neil. Right now."

"Where?"

"Do it! *Here*. On this cruddy cruddy cruddy sofa."

And I obeyed her.

The next morning Brenda made breakfast for the two of us. Ron had gone off to his first day of work—I'd heard him singing in the shower only an hour after I'd returned to my own room; in fact, I had still been awake when the Chrysler had pulled out of the garage, carrying boss and son down to the Patimkin works in Newark. Mrs. Patimkin wasn't home either; she had taken her car and had gone off to the Temple to talk to Rabbi Kranitz about the wedding. Julie was on the back lawn playing at helping Carlota hang the clothes.

"You know what I want to do this morning?" Brenda said. We were eating a grapefruit, sharing it rather sloppily, for Brenda couldn't find a paring knife, and so we'd decided to peel it down like an orange and eat the segments separately.

"What?" I said.

"Run," she said. "Do you ever run?"

"You mean on a track? God, yes. In high school we had to run a mile every month. So we wouldn't be Momma's boys. I think the bigger your lungs get the more you're supposed to hate your mother."

"I want to run," she said, "and I want you to run. Okay?"

"Oh, Brenda . . ."

But an hour later, after a breakfast that consisted of another grapefruit, which apparently is all a runner is supposed to eat in the morning, we had driven the Volkswagen over to the high school, behind which was a quarter-mile track. Some kids were playing with a dog out in the grassy center of the track, and at the far end, near the woods, a figure in white shorts with slits in the side, and no shirt, was twirling, twirling, and then flinging a shot put as far as he could. After it left his hand he did a little eagle-eyed tap dance while he watched it arch and bend and land in the distance.

"You know," Brenda said, "you look like me. Except bigger."

We were dressed similarly, sneakers, sweat socks, khaki Bermudas, and sweat shirts, but I had the feeling that Brenda was not talking about the accidents of our dress—if they were accidents. She meant, I was sure, that I was somehow beginning to look the way she wanted me to. Like herself.

"Let's see who's faster," she said, and then we started along the track. Within the first eighth of a mile the three little boys and their dog were following us. As we passed the corner where the shot putter was, he waved at us; Brenda called "Hi!" and I smiled, which, as you may or may not know, makes one engaged in serious running feel inordinately silly. At the quarter mile the kids dropped off and retired to the grass, the dog turned and started the other way, and I had a tiny knife in my side. Still I was abreast of Brenda, who as we started on the second lap, called "Hi!" once again to the lucky shot putter, who was reclining in the grass now, watching us, and rubbing his shot like a crystal ball. Ah, I thought, there's the sport.

"How about us throwing the shot put?" I panted.

"After," she said, and I saw beads of sweat clinging to the last strands of hair that shagged off her ear. When we approached the half mile Brenda suddenly swerved off the track onto the grass and tumbled down; her departure surprised me and I was still running.

"Hey, Bob Mathias,"[7] she called, "let's lie in the sun . . ."

But I acted as though I didn't hear her and though my heart pounded in my throat and my mouth was dry as a drought, I made my legs move, and swore I would not stop until I'd finished one more lap. As I passed the shot putter for the third time, I called "Hi!"

She was excited when I finally pulled up alongside of her. "You're good," she said. My hands were on my hips and I was looking at the ground and sucking air—rather, air was sucking me, I didn't have much to say about it.

"Uh-huh," I breathed.

"Let's do this every morning," she said. "We'll get up and have two grapefruit, and then you'll come out here and run. I'll time you. In two weeks you'll break four minutes, won't you sweetie? I'll get Ron's stop watch." She was so excited—she'd slid over on the grass and was pushing my socks up against my wet ankles and calves. She bit my kneecap.

"Okay," I said.

"Then we'll go back and have a real breakfast."

"Okay."

"You drive back," she said, and suddenly she was up and running ahead of me, and then we were headed back in the car.

And the next morning, my mouth still edgy from the grapefruit segments, we were at the track. We had Ron's stop watch and a towel for me, for when I was finished.

"My legs are a little sore," I said.

"Do some exercises," Brenda said. "I'll do them with you." She heaped the towel on the grass and together we did deep knee bends, and sit-ups, and push-ups, and some high-knee raising in place. I felt overwhelmingly happy.

"I'm just going to run a half today, Bren. We'll see what I do . . ." and I heard Brenda click the watch, and then when I was on the far side of the track, the clouds trailing above me like my own white, fleecy tail, I saw that Brenda was on the ground, hugging her knees, and alternately checking the watch and looking out at me. We were the only ones there, and it all reminded me of one of those scenes in race-horse movies, where an old trainer like Walter Brennan[8] and a young handsome man clock the beautiful girl's horse in the early Kentucky morning, to see if it really is the fastest two-year-old alive. There were differences all right—one being sim-

---

7. American athlete (b. 1930), Olympic decathlon champion in 1948 and 1952.
8. A famous Hollywood character actor, Brennan (1894–1974) played a horse-trainer in the film *Kentucky* (1938).

ply that at the quarter mile Brenda shouted out to me, "A minute and fourteen seconds," but it was pleasant and exciting and clean and when I was finished Brenda was standing up and waiting for me. Instead of a tape to break I had Brenda's sweet flesh to meet, and I did, and it was the first time she said that she loved me.

We ran—I ran—every morning, and by the end of the week I was running a 7:02 mile, and always at the end there was the little click of the watch and Brenda's arms.

At night, I would read in my pajamas, while Brenda, in her room, read, and we would wait for Ron to go to sleep. Some nights we had to wait longer than others, and I would hear the leaves swishing outside, for it had grown cooler at the end of August, and the air-conditioning was turned off at night and we were all allowed to open our windows. Finally Ron would be ready for bed. He would stomp around his room and then he would come to the door in his shorts and T-shirt and go into the bathroom where he would urinate loudly and brush his teeth. After he brushed his teeth I would go in to brush mine. We would pass in the hall and I would give him a hearty and sincere "Goodnight." Once in the bathroom, I would spend a moment admiring my tan in the mirror; behind me I could see Ron's jock straps hanging out to dry on the Hot and Cold knobs of the shower. Nobody ever questioned their tastefulness as adornment, and after a few nights I didn't even notice them.

While Ron brushed his teeth and I waited in my bed for my turn, I could hear the record player going in his room. Generally, after coming in from basketball, he would call Harriet—who was now only a few days away from us—and then would lock himself up with *Sports Illustrated* and Mantovani; however, when he emerged from his room for his evening toilet, it was not a Mantovani record I would hear playing, but something else, apparently what he'd once referred to as his Columbus record. I *imagined* that was what I heard, for I could not tell much from the last moments of sound. All I heard were bells moaning evenly and soft patriotic music behind them, and riding over it all, a deep kind of Edward R. Murrow[9] gloomy voice: "*And so goodbye, Columbus,*" the voice intoned, "*. . . goodbye, Columbus . . . goodbye . . .*" Then there would be silence and Ron would be back in his room; the light would switch off and in only a few minutes I would hear him rumbling down into that exhilarating, restorative, vitamin-packed sleep that I imagined athletes to enjoy.

One morning near sneaking-away time I had a dream and when I awakened from it, there was just enough dawn coming into the room for me to see the color of Brenda's hair. I touched her in her sleep, for the dream had unsettled me: it had taken place on a ship, an old sailing ship like those you see in pirate movies. With me on the ship was the little colored kid from the library—I was the captain and he my mate, and we were the only crew members. For a while it was a pleasant dream; we were anchored in the harbor of an island in the Pacific and it was very sunny. Upon the beach there were beautiful bare-skinned Negresses, and none of them moved; but suddenly *we* were moving, our ship, out of the harbor, and the Negresses moved slowly down to the shore and began to throw leis at us and say "Goodbye, Columbus . . . goodbye, Columbus . . . good-

9. Murrow (1908–1965) formed and headed the CBS radio news-reporting team that in the World War II years revolutionized news broadcasting; after the war he had his own news and documentary programs on both radio and television.

bye . . ." and though we did not want to go, the little boy and I, the boat was moving and there was nothing we could do about it, and he shouted at me that it was my fault and I shouted it was his for not having a library card, but we were wasting our breath, for we were further and further from the island, and soon the natives were nothing at all. Space was all out of proportion in the dream, and things were sized and squared in no way I'd ever seen before, and I think it was that more than anything else that steered me into consciousness. I did not want to leave Brenda's side that morning, and for a while I played with the little point at the nape of her neck, where she'd had her hair cut. I stayed longer than I should have, and when finally I returned to my room I almost ran into Ron who was preparing for his day at Patimkin Kitchen and Bathroom Sinks.

6

That morning was supposed to have been my last at the Patimkin house; however, when I began to throw my things into my bag late in the day, Brenda told me I could unpack—somehow she'd managed to inveigle another week out of her parents, and I would be able to stay right through till Labor Day, when Ron would be married; then, the following morning Brenda would be off to school and I would go back to work. So we would be with each other until the summer's last moment. This should have made me overjoyed, but as Brenda trotted back down the stairs to accompany her family to the airport—where they were to pick up Harriet—I was not joyful but disturbed, as I had been more and more with the thought that when Brenda went back to Radcliffe, that would be the end for me. I was convinced that even Miss Winney's stool was not high enough for me to see clear up to Boston. Nevertheless, I tossed my clothing back into the drawer and was able, finally, to tell myself that there'd been no hints of ending our affair from Brenda, and any suspicions I had, any uneasiness, was spawned in my own uncertain heart. Then I went into Ron's room to call my aunt.

"Hello?" she said.

"Aunt Gladys," I said, "how are you?"

"You're sick."

"No, I'm having a fine time. I wanted to call you, I'm going to stay another week."

"Why?"

"I told you. I'm having a good time. Mrs. Patimkin asked me to stay until Labor Day."

"You've got clean underwear?"

"I'm washing it at night. I'm okay, Aunt Gladys."

"By hand you can't get it clean."

"It's clean enough. Look, Aunt Gladys, I'm having a wonderful time."

"*Shmutz*[1] he lives in and I shouldn't worry."

"How's Uncle Max?" I asked.

"What should he be? Uncle Max is Uncle Max. You, I don't like the way your voice sounds."

"Why? Do I sound like I've got on dirty underwear?"

---

1. Dirt.

"Smart guy. Someday you'll learn."

"What?"

"What do you mean *what?* You'll find out. You'll stay there too long you'll be too good for us."

"Never, sweetheart," I said.

"I'll see it I'll believe it."

"Is it cool in Newark, Aunt Gladys?"

"It's snowing," she said.

"Hasn't it been cool all week?"

"You sit around all day it's cool. For me it's not February, believe me."

"Okay, Aunt Gladys. Say hello to everybody."

"You got a letter from your mother."

"Good. I'll read it when I get home."

"You couldn't take a ride down you'll read it?"

"It'll wait. I'll drop them a note. Be a good girl," I said.

"What about your socks?"

"I go barefoot. Goodbye, honey." And I hung up.

Down in the kitchen Carlota was getting dinner ready. I was always amazed at how Carlota's work never seemed to get in the way of her life. She made household chores seem like illustrative gestures of whatever it was she was singing, even, if as now, it was "I Get a Kick out of You."[2] She moved from the oven to the automatic dishwasher—she pushed buttons, turned dials, peeked in the glass-doored oven, and from time to time picked a big black grape out of a bunch that lay on the sink. She chewed and chewed, humming all the time, and then, with a deliberated casualness, shot the skin and the pit directly into the garbage disposal unit. I said hello to her as I went out the back door, and though she did not return the greeting, I felt a kinship with one who, like me, had been partially wooed and won on Patimkin fruit.

Out on the lawn I shot baskets for a while; then I picked up an iron and drove a cotton golf ball limply up into the sunlight; then I kicked a soccer ball towards the oak tree; then I tried shooting foul shots again. Nothing diverted me—I felt open-stomached, as though I hadn't eaten for months, and though I went back inside and came out with my own handful of grapes, the feeling continued, and I knew it had nothing to do with my caloric intake; it was only a rumor of the hollowness that would come when Brenda was away. The fact of her departure had, of course, been on my mind for a while, but overnight it had taken on a darker hue. Curiously, the darkness seemed to have something to do with Harriet, Ron's intended, and I thought for a time that it was simply the reality of Harriet's arrival that had dramatized the passing of time: we had been talking about it and now suddenly it was here—just as Brenda's departure would be here before we knew it.

But it was more than that: the union of Harriet and Ron reminded me that separation need not be a permanent state. People could marry each other, even if they were young! And yet Brenda and I had never mentioned marriage, except perhaps for that night at the pool when she'd said, "When you love me, everything will be all right." Well, I loved her, and she me, and things didn't seem all right at all. Or was I inventing troubles again? I supposed I should really have thought my lot improved

2. Song (1934) by Cole Porter (1893–1964) from the musical *Anything Goes;* the second movie version of the play was released in 1956.

considerably; yet, there on the lawn, the August sky seemed too beautiful and temporary to bear, and I wanted Brenda to marry me. Marriage, though, was not what I proposed to her when she drove the car up the driveway, alone, some fifteen minutes later. That proposal would have taken a kind of courage that I did not think I had. I did not feel myself prepared for any answer but "Hallelujah!" Any other kind of yes wouldn't have satisfied me, and any kind of no, even one masked behind the words, "Let's wait, sweetheart," would have been my end. So I imagine that's why I proposed the surrogate, which turned out finally to be far more daring than I knew it to be at the time.

"Harriet's plane is late, so I drove home," Brenda called.

"Where's everyone else?"

"They're going to wait for her and have dinner at the airport. I have to tell Carlota," and she went inside.

In a few minutes she appeared on the porch. She wore a yellow dress that cut a wide-bottomed U across her shoulders and neck, and showed where the tanned flesh began above her breasts. On the lawn she stepped out of her heels and walked barefoot over to where I was sitting under the oak tree.

"Women who wear high heels all the time get tipped ovaries," she said.

"Who told you that?"

"I don't remember. I like to think everything's shipshape in there."

"Brenda, I want to ask you something . . ."

She yanked the blanket with the big O on it over to us and sat down. "What?" she said.

"I know this is out of the blue, though really it's not . . . I want you to buy a diaphragm. To go to a doctor and get one."

She smiled. "Don't worry, sweetie, we're careful. Everything is okay."

"But that's the safest."

"We're safe. It'd be a waste."

"Why take chances?"

"But we *aren't?* How many things do you need."

"Honey, it isn't bulk I'm interested in. It's not even safety," I added.

"You just want me to own one, is that it? Like a walking stick, or a pith helmet—"

"Brenda, I want you to own one for . . . for the sake of pleasure."

"Pleasure? Whose? The doctor's?"

"Mine," I said.

She did not answer me, but rubbed her fingers along the ridge of her collarbone to wipe away the tiny globes of perspiration that had suddenly formed there.

"No, Neil, it's silly."

"Why?"

"Why? It just is."

"You know why it's silly, Brenda—because *I* asked you to do it?"

"That's sillier."

"If you asked *me* to buy a diaphragm we'd have to go straight to the Yellow Pages and find a gynecologist open on Saturday afternoon."

"I would never ask you to do that, baby."

"It's the truth," I said, though I was smiling. "It's the truth."

"It's not," she said, and got up and walked over to the basketball court, where she walked on the white lines that Mr. Patimkin had laid the day before.

"Come back here," I said.

"Neil, it's silly and I don't want to talk about it."

"Why are you being so selfish?"

"Selfish? You're the one who's being selfish. It's your pleasure ... "

"That's right. My pleasure. Why not!"

"Don't raise your voice. Carlota."

"Then get the hell over here," I said.

She walked over to me, leaving white footprints on the grass. "I didn't think you were such a creature of the flesh," she said.

"Didn't you?" I said. "I'll tell you something that you ought to know. It's not even the pleasures of the flesh I'm talking about."

"Then frankly, I don't know *what* you're talking about. Why you're even bothering. Isn't what we use sufficient?"

"I'm bothering just because I want you to go to a doctor and get a diaphragm. That's all. No explanation. Just do it. Do it because I asked you to."

"You're not being reasonable—"

"Goddamit, Brenda!"

"Goddamit yourself!" she said and went up into the house.

I closed my eyes and leaned back and in fifteen minutes, or maybe less, I heard somebody stroking at the cotton golf ball. She had changed into shorts and a blouse and was still barefoot.

We didn't speak with each other, but I watched her bring the club back of her ear, and then swing through, her chin tilted up with the line of flight a regular golf ball would have taken.

"That's five hundred yards," I said.

She didn't answer but walked after the cotton ball and then readied for another swing.

"Brenda. Please come here."

She walked over, dragging the club over the grass.

"What?"

"I don't want to argue with you."

"Nor I with you," she said. "It was the first time."

"Was it such an awful thing for me to ask?"

She nodded.

"Bren, I know it was probably a surprise. It was for me. But we're not children."

"Neil, I just don't want to. It's not because you asked me to, either. I don't know where you get that from. That's not it."

"Then why is it?"

"Oh everything. I just don't feel *old* enough for all that equipment."

"What does age have to do with it?"

"I don't mean age. I just mean—well, *me*. I mean it's so conscious a thing to do."

"Of course it's conscious. That's exactly it. Don't you see? It would change us."

"It would change me."

"Us. Together."

"Neil, how do you think I'd feel lying to some doctor."

"You can go to Margaret Sanger,[3] in New York. They don't ask any questions."

"You've done this before?"

"No, I said. "I just know. I read Mary McCarthy."[4]

"That's exactly right. That's just what I'd feel like, somebody out of *her.*"

"Don't be dramatic," I said.

"You're the one who's being dramatic. You think there would be something affairish about it, then. Last summer I went with this whore who I sent out to buy—"

"Oh, Brenda, you're a selfish egotistical bitch! You're the one who's thinking about 'last summer,' about an end for us. In fact, that's the whole thing, isn't it—"

"That's right, I'm a bitch. I want this to end. That's why I ask you to stay another week, that's why I let you sleep with me in my own house. What's the *matter* with you! Why don't you and my mother take turns— one day she can plague me, the next you—"

"Stop it!"

"Go to hell, all of you!" Brenda said, and now she was crying and I knew when she ran off I would not see her, as I didn't, for the rest of the afternoon.

Harriet Ehrlich impressed me as a young lady singularly unconscious of a motive in others or herself. All was surfaces, and she seemed a perfect match for Ron, and too for the Patimkins. Mrs. Patimkin, in fact, did just as Brenda prophesied: Harriet appeared, and Brenda's mother lifted one wing and pulled the girl in towards the warm underpart of her body, where Brenda herself would have liked to nestle. Harriet was built like Brenda, although a little chestier, and she nodded her head insistently whenever anyone spoke. Sometimes she would even say the last few words of your sentence with you, though that was infrequent; for the most part she nodded and kept her hands folded. All evening, as the Patimkins planned where the newlyweds should live, what furniture they should buy, how soon they should have a baby—all through this I kept thinking that Harriet was wearing white gloves, but she wasn't.

Brenda and I did not exchange a word or a glance; we sat, listening, Brenda somewhat more impatient than me. Near the end Harriet began calling Mrs. Patimkin "Mother," and once, "Mother Patimkin," and that was when Brenda went to sleep. I stayed behind, mesmerized almost by the dissection, analysis, reconsideration, and finally, the embracing of the trivial. At last Mr. and Mrs. Patimkin tumbled off to bed, and Julie, who had fallen asleep on her chair, was carried into her room by Ron. That left us two non-Patimkins together.

"Ron tells me you have a very interesting job."

"I work in the library."

"I've always liked reading."

"That'll be nice, married to Ron."

3. Clinic named for Sanger (1883–1966), longtime advocate of birth control education.
4. Though her most notorious work, *The Group,* was not published until 1963, McCarthy (b. 1912) was already well known in the 1950s for her explicit autobiographical fiction, such as *Cast a Cold Eye* (1950), and nonfiction, such as *Memories of a Catholic Girlhood* (1959), which, though it appeared in book form the same year as *Goodbye, Columbus,* had been appearing in the *New Yorker.*

"Ron likes music."

"Yes," I said. What had I *said?*

"You must get first crack at the best-sellers," she said.

"Sometimes," I said.

"Well," she said, flapping her hands on her knees, "I'm sure we'll all have a good time together. Ron and I hope you and Brenda will double with us soon."

"Not tonight." I smiled. "Soon. Will you excuse me?"

"Good night. I like Brenda very much."

"Thank you," I said as I started up the stairs.

I knocked gently on Brenda's door.

"I'm sleeping."

"Can I come in?" I asked.

Her door opened an inch and she said, "Ron will be up soon."

"We'll leave the door open. I only want to talk."

She let me in and I sat in the chair that faced the bed.

"How do you like your sister-in-law?"

"I've met her before."

"Brenda, you don't have to sound so damn terse."

She didn't answer and I just sat there yanking the string on the shade up and down.

"Are you still angry?" I asked at last.

"Yes."

"Don't be," I said. "You can forget about my suggestion. It's not worth it if this is what's going to happen."

"What did you expect to happen?"

"Nothing. I didn't think it would be so horrendous."

"That's because you can't understand my side."

"Perhaps."

"No perhaps about it."

"*Okay,*" I said. "I just wish you'd realize what it is you're getting angry about. It's not my suggestion, Brenda."

"No? What is it?"

"It's me."

"Oh don't start that again, will you? I can't win, no matter what I say."

"Yes, you can," I said. "You have."

I walked out of her room, closing the door behind me for the night.

When I got downstairs the following morning there was a great deal of activity. In the living room I heard Mrs. Patimkin reading a list to Harriet while Julie ran in and out of rooms in search of a skate key. Carlota was vacuuming the carpet; every appliance in the kitchen was bubbling, twisting, and shaking. Brenda greeted me with a perfectly pleasant smile and in the dining room, where I walked to look out at the back lawn and the weather, she kissed me on the shoulder.

"Hello," she said.

"Hello."

"I have to go with Harriet this morning," Brenda told me. "So we can't run. Unless you want to go alone."

"No. I'll read or something. Where are you going?"

"We're going to New York. Shopping. She's going to buy a wedding dress. For after the wedding. To go away in."

"What are *you* going to buy?"

"A dress to be maid of honor in. If I go with Harriet then I can go to Bergdorf's[5] without all that Ohrbach's business with my mother."

"Get me something, will you?" I said.

"Oh, Neil, are you going to bring that up again!"

"I was only *fooling*. I wasn't even thinking about that."

"Then why did you say it?"

"Oh Jesus!" I said, and went outside and drove my car down into Millburn Center where I had some eggs and coffee.

When I came back, Brenda was gone, and there were only Carlota, Mrs. Patimkin, and myself in the house. I tried to stay out of whichever rooms they were in, but finally Mrs. Patimkin and I wound up sitting opposite each other in the TV room. She was checking off names on a long sheet of paper she held; next to her, on the table, were two thin phone books which she consulted from time to time.

"No rest for the weary," she said to me.

I smiled hugely, embracing the proverb as though Mrs. Patimkin had just then coined it. "Yes. Of course," I said. "Would you like some help? Maybe I could help you check something."

"Oh, no," she said with a little head-shaking dismissal, "it's for Hadassah."

"Oh," I said.

I sat and watched her until she asked, "Is your mother in Hadassah?"

"I don't know if she is now. She was in Newark."

"Was she an active member?"

"I guess so, she was always planting trees in Israel for someone."[6]

"Really?" Mrs. Patimkin said. "What's her name?"

"Esther Klugman. She's in Arizona now. Do they have Hadassah there?"

"Wherever there are Jewish women."

"Then I guess she is. She's with my father. They went there for their asthma. I'm staying with my aunt in Newark. She's not in Hadassah. My Aunt Sylvia is, though. Do you know her, Aaron Klugman and Sylvia? They belong to your club. They have a daughter, my cousin Doris—" I couldn't stop myself "—They live in Livingston. Maybe it isn't Hadassah my Aunt Sylvia belongs to. I think it's some TB organization. Or cancer. Muscular dystrophy, maybe. I know she's interested in *some* disease."

"That's very nice," Mrs. Patimkin said.

"Oh yes."

"They do very good work."

"I know."

Mrs. Patimkin, I thought, had begun to warm to me; she let the purple eyes stop peering and just look out at the world for a while without judging. "Are you interested in B'nai B'rith?"[7] she asked me. "Ron is joining, you know, as soon as he gets married."

"I think I'll wait till then," I said.

Petulantly, Mrs. Patimkin went back to her lists, and I realized it had been foolish of me to risk lightheartedness with her about Jewish affairs. "You're active in the Temple, aren't you?" I asked with all the interest I could muster.

5. Bergdorf Goodman, exclusive Fifth Avenue clothing store.
6. The Hadassah (mentioned earlier) does indeed collect money for planting memorial trees in Israel in the name of a loved one.
7. A Jewish fraternity founded in New York in 1843, now international.

"Yes," she said.

"What Temple do *you* belong to?" she asked in a moment.

"We used to belong to Hudson Street Synagogue. Since my parents left, I haven't had much contact."

I didn't know whether Mrs. Patimkin caught a false tone in my voice. Personally I thought I had managed my rueful confession pretty well, especially when I recalled the decade of paganism prior to my parents' departure. Regardless, Mrs. Patimkin asked immediately—and strategically it seemed—"We're all going to Temple Friday night. Why don't you come with us? I mean, are you orthodox or conservative?"

I considered. "Well, I haven't gone in a long time . . . I sort of switch . . ." I smiled. "I'm just Jewish," I said well-meaningly, but that too sent Mrs. Patimkin back to her Hadassah work. Desperately I tried to think of something that would convince her I wasn't an infidel. Finally I asked: "Do you know Martin Buber's[8] work?"

"Buber . . . Buber," she said, looking at her Hadassah list. "Is he orthodox or conservative?" she asked.

" . . . He's a philosopher."

"Is he *reformed*?" she asked, piqued either at my evasiveness or at the possibility that Buber attended Friday night services without a hat, and Mrs. Buber had only one set of dishes in her kitchen.

"Orthodox," I said faintly.

"That's very nice," she said.

"Yes."

"Isn't Hudson Street Synagogue orthodox?" she asked.

"I don't know."

"I thought you belonged."

"I was bar-mitzvahed there."

"And you don't know that it's orthodox?"

"Yes. I do. It is."

"Then *you* must be."

"Oh, yes, I am," I said. "What are you?" I popped, flushing.

"Orthodox. My husband is conservative," which meant, I took it, that he didn't care. "Brenda is nothing, as you probably know."

"Oh?" I said. "No, I didn't know that."

"She was the best Hebrew student I've ever seen," Mrs. Patimkin said, "but then, of course, she got too big for her britches."

Mrs. Patimkin looked at me, and I wondered whether courtesy demanded that I agree. "Oh, I don't know," I said at last, "I'd say Brenda is conservative. Maybe a little reformed . . ."

The phone rang, rescuing me, and I spoke a silent orthodox prayer to the Lord.

"Hello," Mrs. Patimkin said. " . . . no . . . I can *not*, I have all the Hadassah calls to make . . ."

I acted as though I were listening to the birds outside, though the closed windows let no natural noises in.

"Have Ronald drive them up . . . But we can't wait, not if we want it on time . . ."

Mrs. Patimkin glanced up at me; then she put one hand over the mouthpiece. "Would you ride down to Newark for me?"

---

8. Eminent Jewish philosopher and biblical commentator (1878–1965), best known for his book *I and Thou* (1923; 2nd ed. 1958), in which he describes the relation between God and man as a direct and personal dialogue, not a matter of "It," or institutions.

I stood. "Yes. Surely."

"Dear?" she said back into the phone, "Neil will come for it ... No, *Neil*, Brenda's friend ... Yes ... Goodbye.

"Mr. Patimkin has some silver patterns I have to see. Would you drive down to his place and pick them up?"

"Of course."

"Do you know where the shop is?"

"Yes."

"Here," she said, handing a key ring to me, "take the Volkswagen."

"My car is right outside."

"Take these," she said.

Patimkin Kitchen and Bathroom Sinks was in the heart of the Negro section of Newark. Years ago, at the time of the great immigration, it had been the Jewish section, and still one could see the little fish stores, the kosher delicatessens, the Turkish baths, where my grandparents had shopped and bathed at the beginning of the century. Even the smells had lingered: whitefish, corned beef, sour tomatoes—but now, on top of these, was the grander greasier smell of auto wrecking shops, the sour stink of a brewery, the burning odor from a leather factory; and on the streets, instead of Yiddish, one heard the shouts of Negro children playing at Willie Mays with a broom handle and half a rubber ball.[9] The neighborhood had changed: the old Jews like my grandparents had struggled and died, and their offspring had struggled and prospered, and moved further and further west, towards the edge of Newark, then out of it, and up the slope of the Orange Mountains, until they had reached the crest and started down the other side, pouring into Gentile territory as the Scotch-Irish had poured through the Cumberland Gap. Now, in fact, the Negroes were making the same migration, following the steps of the Jews, and those who remained in the Third Ward lived the most squalid of lives and dreamed in their fetid mattresses of the piny smell of Georgia nights.

I wondered, for an instant only, if I would see the colored kid from the library on the streets here. I didn't, of course, though I was sure he lived in one of the scabby, peeling buildings out of which dogs, children, and aproned women moved continually. On the top floors, windows were open, and the very old, who could no longer creak down the long stairs to the street, sat where they had been put, in the screenless windows, their elbows resting on fluffless pillows, and their heads tipping forward on their necks, watching the push of the young and the pregnant and the unemployed. Who would come after the Negroes? Who was left? No one, I thought, and someday these streets, where my grandmother drank hot tea from an old *jahrzeit* glass,[1] would be empty and we would all of us have moved to the crest of the Orange Mountains, and wouldn't the dead stop kicking at the slats in their coffins then?

I pulled the Volkswagen up in front of a huge garage door that said across the front of it:

PATIMKIN KITCHEN AND BATHROOM SINKS
"Any Size—Any Shape"

Inside I could see a glass-enclosed office; it was in the center of an im-

---

9. The great centerfielder (b. 1931) for the New York and San Francisco Giants developed his skills as a child playing stickball in the New York streets.

1. Glass for holding a candle that memorializes the anniversary of a loved one's death.

mense warehouse. Two trucks were being loaded in the rear, and Mr. Patimkin, when I saw him, had a cigar in his mouth and was shouting at someone. It was Ron, who was wearing a white T-shirt that said Ohio State Athletic Association across the front. Though he was taller than Mr. Patimkin, and almost as stout, his hands hung weakly at his sides like a small boy's; Mr. Patimkin's cigar locomoted in his mouth. Six Negroes were loading one of the trucks feverishly, tossing—my stomach dropped—sink bowls at one another.

Ron left Mr. Patimkin's side and went back to directing the men. He thrashed his arms about a good deal, and though on the whole he seemed rather confused, he didn't appear to be at all concerned about anybody dropping a sink. Suddenly I could see myself directing the Negroes—I would have an ulcer in an hour. I could almost hear the enamel surfaces shattering on the floor. And I could hear myself: "Watch it, you guys. Be careful, will you? *Whoops!* Oh, please be—*watch* it! Watch! Oh!" Suppose Mr. Patimkin should come up to me and say, "Okay, boy, you want to marry my daughter, let's see what you can do." Well, he would see: in a moment that floor would be a shattered mosaic, a crunchy path of enamel. "Klugman, what kind of worker are you? You work like you eat!" "That's right, that's right, I'm a sparrow, let me go." "Don't you even know how to load and unload?" "Mr. Patimkin, even breathing gives me trouble, sleep tires me out, let me go, let me go . . ."

Mr. Patimkin was headed back to the fish bowl to answer a ringing phone, and I wrenched myself free of my reverie and headed towards the office too. When I entered, Mr. Patimkin looked up from the phone with his eyes; the sticky cigar was in his free hand—he moved it at me, a greeting. From outside I heard Ron call in a high voice, "You can't all go to lunch at the same time. We haven't got all day!"

"Sit down," Mr. Patimkin shot at me, though when he went back to his conversation I saw there was only one chair in the office, his. People did not sit at Patimkin Sink—here you earned your money the hard way, standing up. I busied myself looking at the several calendars that hung from filing cabinets; they showed illustrations of women so dreamy, so fantastically thighed and uddered, that one could not think of them as pornographic. The artist who had drawn the calendar girls for "Lewis Construction Company," and "Earl's Truck and Auto Repair," and "Grossman and Son, Paper Box" had been painting some third sex I had never seen.

"Sure, sure, sure," Mr. Patimkin said into the phone. "Tomorrow, don't tell me tomorrow. Tomorrow the world could blow up."

At the other end someone spoke. Who was it? Lewis from the construction company? Earl from truck repair?

"I'm running a business, Grossman, not a charity."

So it was Grossman being browbeaten at the other end.

"Shit on that," Mr. Patimkin said. "You're not the only one in town, my good friend," and he winked at me.

Ah-ha, a conspiracy against Grossman. Me and Mr. Patimkin. I smiled as collusively as I knew how.

"All right then, we're here till five . . . No later."

He wrote something on a piece of paper. It was only a big X.

"My kid'll be here," he said. "Yea, he's in the business."

Whatever Grossman said on the other end, it made Mr. Patimkin laugh.

Mr. Patimkin hung up without a goodbye.

He looked out the back to see how Ron was doing. "Four years in college he can't unload a truck."

I didn't know what to say but finally chose the truth. "I guess I couldn't either."

"You could learn. What am I, a genius? I learned. Hard work never killed anybody."

To that I agreed.

Mr. Patimkin looked at his cigar. "A man works hard he's got something. You don't get anywhere sitting on your behind, you know . . . The biggest men in the country worked hard, believe me. Even Rockefeller. Success don't come easy . . ." He did not say this so much as he mused it out while he surveyed his dominion. He was not a man enamored of words, and I had the feeling that what had tempted him into this barrage of universals was probably the combination of Ron's performance and my presence—me, the outsider who might one day be an insider. But did Mr. Patimkin even consider that possibility? I did not know; I only knew that these few words he did speak could hardly transmit all the satisfaction and surprise he felt about the life he had managed to build for himself and his family.

He looked out at Ron again. "Look at him, if he played basketball like that they'd throw him the hell off the court." But he was smiling when he said it.

He walked over to the door. "Ronald, let them go to lunch."

Ron shouted back, "I thought I'd let some go now, and some later."

"Why?"

"Then somebody'll always be—"

"No fancy deals here," Mr. Patimkin shouted. "We all go to lunch at once."

Ron turned back. "All right, boys, lunch!"

His father smiled at me. "Smart boy? Huh?" He tapped his head. "That took brains, huh? He ain't got the stomach for business. He's an idealist," and then I think Mr. Patimkin suddenly realized who I was, and eagerly corrected himself so as not to offend. "That's all right, you know, if you're a schoolteacher, or like you, you know, a student or something like that. Here you need a little of the *gonif* in you. You know what that means? *Gonif?*"

"Thief," I said.

"You know more than my own kids. They're *goyim,*[2] my kids, that's how much they understand." He watched the Negro loading gang walk past the office and shouted out to them, "You guys know how long an hour is? All right, you'll be back in an hour!"

Ron came into the office and of course shook my hand.

"Do you have that stuff for Mrs. Patimkin?" I asked.

"Ronald, get him the silver patterns." Ron turned away and Mr. Patimkin said, "When I got married we had forks and knives from the five and ten. This kid needs gold to eat off," but there was no anger; far from it.

I drove to the mountains in my own car that afternoon, and stood for a while at the wire fence watching the deer lightly prance, coyly feed,

2. Gentiles.

under the protection of signs that read, DO NOT FEED THE DEER, *By Order of South Mountain Reservation.* Alongside me at the fence were dozens of kids; they giggled and screamed when the deer licked the popcorn from their hands, and then were sad when their own excitement sent the young loping away towards the far end of the field where their tawny-skinned mothers stood regally watching the traffic curl up the mountain road. Young white-skinned mothers, hardly older than I, and in many instances younger, chatted in their convertibles behind me, and looked down from time to time to see what their children were about. I had seen them before, when Brenda and I had gone out for a bite in the afternoon, or had driven up here for lunch: in clotches of three and four they sat in the rustic hamburger joints that dotted the Reservation area while their children gobbled hamburgers and malteds and were given dimes to feed the jukebox. Though none of the little ones were old enough to read the song titles, almost all of them could holler out the words, and they did, while the mothers, a few of whom I recognized as high school mates of mine, compared suntans, supermarkets, and vacations. They looked immortal sitting there. Their hair would always stay the color they desired, their clothes the right texture and shade; in their homes they would have simple Swedish modern when that was fashionable, and if huge, ugly baroque ever came back, out would go the long, midget-legged marble coffee table and in would come Louis Quatorze. These were the goddesses, and if I were Paris I could not have been able to choose among them,[3] so microscopic were the differences. Their fates had collapsed them into one. Only Brenda shone. Money and comfort would not erase her singleness—they hadn't yet, or had they? What was I loving, I wondered, and since I am not one to stick scalpels into myself, I wiggled my hands in the fence and allowed a tiny-nosed buck to lick my thoughts away.

When I returned to the Patimkin house, Brenda was in the living room looking more beautiful than I had ever seen her. She was modeling her new dress for Harriet and her mother. Even Mrs. Patimkin seemed softened by the sight of her; it looked as though some sedative had been injected into her, and so relaxed the Brenda-hating muscles around her eyes and mouth.

Brenda, without glasses, modeled in place; when she looked at me it was a kind of groggy, half-waking look I got, and though others might have interpreted it as sleepiness it sounded in my veins as lust. Mrs. Patimkin told her finally that she'd bought a very nice dress and I told her she looked lovely and Harriet told her she was very beautiful and that *she* ought to be the bride, and then there was an uncomfortable silence while all of us wondered who ought to be the groom.

Then when Mrs. Patimkin had led Harriet out to the kitchen, Brenda came up to me and said, "I *ought* to be the bride."

"You ought, sweetheart." I kissed her, and suddenly she was crying.

"What is it, honey?" I said.

"Let's go outside."

On the lawn, Brenda was no longer crying but her voice sounded very tired.

"Neil, I called Margaret Sanger Clinic," she said. "When I was in New York."

---

3. In Greek myth Paris had to choose the fairest of goddesses from among Hera, Athena, and Aphrodite.

I didn't answer.

"Neil, they *did* ask if I was married. God, the woman sounded like my mother . . ."

"What did you say?"

"I said *no*."

"What did she say?"

"I don't know. I hung up." She walked away and around the oak tree. When she appeared again she'd stepped out of her shoes and held one hand on the tree, as though it were a Maypole she were circling.

"You can call them back," I said.

She shook her head. "No, I can't. I don't even know why I called in the first place. We were shopping and I just walked away, looked up the number, and called."

"Then you can go to a doctor."

She shook again.

"Look, Bren," I said, rushing to her, "we'll go together, to a doctor. In New York—"

"I don't want to go to some dirty little office—"

"We won't. We'll go to the most posh gynecologist in New York. One who gets *Harper's Bazaar* for the reception room. How does that sound?"

She bit her lower lip.

"You'll come with me?" she asked.

"I'll come with you."

"To the office?"

"Sweetie, your husband wouldn't come to the office."

"No?"

"He'd be working."

"But you're not," she said.

"I'm on vacation," I said, but I had answered the wrong question. "Bren, I'll wait and when you're all done we'll buy a drink. We'll go out to dinner."

"Neil, I shouldn't have called Margaret Sanger—it's not right."

"It is, Brenda. It's the most right thing we can do." She walked away and I was exhausted from pleading. Somehow I felt I could have convinced her had I been a bit more crafty; and yet I did not want it to be craftiness that changed her mind. I was silent when she came back, and perhaps it was just that, my *not* saying anything, that prompted her finally to say, "I'll ask Mother Patimkin if she wants us to take Harriet too . . ."

7

I shall never forget the heat and mugginess of that afternoon we drove into New York. It was four days after the day she'd called Margaret Sanger—she put it off and put it off, but finally on Friday, three days before Ron's wedding and four before her departure, we were heading through the Lincoln Tunnel, which seemed longer and fumier than ever, like Hell with tiled walls. Finally we were in New York and smothered again by the thick day. I pulled around the policeman who directed traffic in his shirt sleeves and up onto the Port Authority[4] roof to park the car.

4. Bus terminal at the Manhattan end of the Lincoln Tunnel.

"Do you have cab fare?" I said.

"Aren't you going to come with me?"

"I thought I'd wait in the bar. Here, downstairs."

"You can wait in Central Park. His office is right across the street."

"Bren, what's the diff—" But when I saw the look that invaded her eyes I gave up the air-conditioned bar to accompany her across the city. There was a sudden shower while our cab went crosstown, and when the rain stopped the streets were sticky and shiny, and below the pavement was the rumble of the subways, and in all it was like entering the ear of a lion.

The doctor's office was in the Squibb Building, which is across from Bergdorf Goodman's and so was a perfect place for Brenda to add to her wardrobe. For some reason we had never once considered her going to a doctor in Newark, perhaps because it was too close to home and might allow for possiblities of discovery. When Brenda got to the revolving door she looked back at me; her eyes were very watery, even with her glasses, and I did not say a word, afraid what a word, any word, might do. I kissed her hair and motioned that I would be across the street by the Plaza fountain, and then I watched her revolve through the doors. Out on the street the traffic moved slowly as though the humidity were a wall holding everything back. Even the fountain seemed to be bubbling boiling water on the people who sat at its edge, and in an instant I decided against crossing the street, and turned south on Fifth and began to walk the steaming pavement towards St. Patrick's. On the north steps a crowd was gathered; everyone was watching a model being photographed. She was wearing a lemon-colored dress and had her feet pointed like ballerina, and as I passed into the church I heard some lady say, "If I ate cottage cheese *ten* times a day, I couldn't be that skinny."

It wasn't much cooler inside the church, though the stillness and the flicker of the candles made me think it was. I took a seat at the rear and while I couldn't bring myself to kneel, I did lean forward onto the back of the bench before me, and held my hands together and closed my eyes. I wondered if I looked like a Catholic, and in my wonderment I began to make a little speech to myself. Can I call the self-conscious words I spoke prayer? At any rate, I called my audience God. God, I said, I am twenty-three years old. I want to make the best of things. Now the doctor is about to wed Brenda to me, and I am not entirely certain this is all for the best. What is it I love, Lord? Why have I chosen? Who is Brenda? The race is to the swift.[5] Should I have stopped to think?

I was getting no answers, but I went on. If we meet You at all, God, it's that we're carnal, and acquisitive, and thereby partake of You. I am carnal, and I know You approve, I just know it. But how carnal can I get? I am acquisitive. Where do I turn now in my acquisitiveness? Where do we meet? Which prize is You?

It was an ingenious meditation, and suddenly I felt ashamed. I got up and walked outside, and the noise of Fifth Avenue met me with an answer:

Which prize do you think, *schmuck*?[6] Gold dinnerware, sporting-goods trees, nectarines, garbage disposals, bumpless noses, Patimkin Sink, Bonwit Teller—

---

5. Cp. Ecclesiastes 9:11—"The race is not to the swift, nor the battle to the strong."

6. *Jerk* or *dope*, but somewhat obscene.

But damn it, God, that *is* You!

And God only laughed, that clown.

On the steps around the fountain I sat in a small arc of a rainbow that the sun had shot through the spray of the water. And then I saw Brenda coming out of the Squibb Building. She carried nothing with her, like a woman who's only been window shopping, and for a moment I was glad that in the end she had disobeyed my desire.

As she crossed the street, though, that little levity passed, and then I was myself again.

She walked up before me and looked down at where I sat; when she inhaled she filled her entire body, and then let her breath out with a "Whew!"

"Where is it?" I said.

My answer, at first, was merely that victorious look of hers, the one she'd given Simp the night she'd beaten her, the one I'd gotten the morning I finished the third lap alone. At last she said, "I'm wearing it."

"Oh, Bren."

"He said shall I wrap it or will you take it with you?"

"Oh Brenda, I love you."

We slept together that night, and so nervous were we about our new toy that we performed like kindergartners, or (in the language of that country) like a lousy double-play combination. And then the next day we hardly saw one another at all, for with the last-minute wedding preparations came scurrying, telegramming, shouting, crying, rushing—in short, lunacy. Even the meals lost their Patimkin fullness, and were tortured out of Kraft cheese, stale onion rolls, dry salami, a little chopped liver, and fruit cocktail. It was hectic all weekend, and I tried as best I could to keep clear of the storm, at whose eye, Ron, clumsy and smiling, and Harriet, flittering and courteous, were being pulled closer and closer together. By Sunday night fatigue had arrested hysteria and all of the Patimkins, Brenda included, had gone off to an early sleep. When Ron went into the bathroom to brush his teeth I decided to go in and brush mine. While I stood over the sink he checked his supports for dampness; then he hung them on the shower knobs and asked me if I would like to listen to his records for a while. It was not out of boredom and loneliness that I accepted; rather a brief spark of locker-room comradery had been struck there among the soap and the water and the tile, and I thought that perhaps Ron's invitation was prompted by a desire to spend his last moments as a Single Man with another Single Man. If I was right, then it was the first real attestation he'd given to my masculinity. How could I refuse?

I sat on the unused twin bed.

"You want to hear Mantovani?"

"Sure," I said.

"Who do you like better, him or Kostelanetz?"

"It's a toss-up."

Ron went to his cabinet. "Hey, how about the Columbus record? Brenda ever play it for you?"

"No. I don't think so."

He extracted a record from its case, and like a giant with a sea shell, placed it gingerly on the phonograph. Then he smiled at me and leaned back onto his bed. His arms were behind his head and his eyes fixed on the ceiling. "They give this to all the seniors. With the yearbook—" but he hushed as soon as the sound began. I watched Ron and listened to the record.

At first there was just a roll of drums, then silence, then another drum roll—and then softly, a marching song, the melody of which was very familiar. When the song ended, I heard the bells, soft, loud, then soft again. And finally there came a Voice, bowel-deep and historic, the kind one associates with documentaries about the rise of Fascism.

"The year, 1956. The season, fall. The place, Ohio State University . . . "

Blitzkrieg! Judgment Day! The Lord had lowered his baton and the Ohio State Glee Club were lining out the Alma Mater as if their souls depended on it. After one desperate chorus, they fell, still screaming, into bottomless oblivion, and the Voice resumed:

"The leaves had begun to turn and redden on the trees. Smoky fires line Fraternity Row, as pledges rake the leaves and turn them to a misty haze. Old faces greet new ones, new faces meet old, and another year has begun . . . "

Music. Glee Club in great comeback. Then the Voice: "The place, the banks of the Olentangy. The event, Homecoming Game, 1956. The opponent, the ever dangerous Illini . . . "

Roar of crowd. New voice—Bill Stern:[7] "Illini over the ball. The snap. Linday fading to pass, he finds a receiver, he passes long *long* down field— and IT'S INTERCEPTED BY NUMBER 43, HERB CLARK OF OHIO STATE! Clark evades one tackler, he evades another as he comes up to midfield. Now he's picking up blockers, he's down to the 45, the 40, the 35—"

And as Bill Stern egged on Clark, and Clark, Bill Stern, Ron, on his bed, with just a little body-english, eased Herb Clark over the goal.

"And it's the Buckeyes ahead now, 21 to 19. *What a game!*"

The Voice of History baritoned in again: "But the season was up and down, and by the time the first snow had covered the turf, it was the sound of dribbling and the cry *Up and In!* that echoed through the field-house . . . "

Ron closed his eyes.

"The Minnesota game," a new, high voice announced, "and for some of our seniors, their last game for the red and white . . . The players are ready to come out on the floor and into the spotlight. There'll be a big hand of appreciation from this capacity crowd for some of the boys who won't be back next year. Here comes Larry Gardner, big Number 7, out onto the floor, Big Larry from Akron, Ohio . . . "

"Larry—" announced the P.A. system; "Larry," the crowd roared back.

"And here comes Ron Patimkin dribbling out. Ron, Number 11, from Short Hills, New Jersey. Big Ron's last game, and it'll be some time before Buckeye fans forget him . . . "

Big Ron tightened on his bed as the loudspeaker called his name; his ovation must have set the nets to trembling. Then the rest of the players were announced, and then basketball season was over, and it was Religious Emphasis Week, the Senior Prom (Billy May[8] blaring at the gymna-

---

7. Famous radio sportcaster, Stern (1907–1971) was noted for his "embroidering" both sports history and play-by-play accounts.
8. Trumpeter, and arranger for Glenn Miller, Les

Brown, and Frank Sinatra, Williams E. ("Billy") May (b. 1916) had a studio and touring band in the early fifties, before going to Hollywood as a freelance arranger for films and television.

sium roof), Fraternity Skit Night, E. E. Cummings reading to students
(verse, silence, applause); and then, finally, commencement:
"The campus is hushed this day of days. For several thousand young
men and women it is a joyous yet a solemn occasion. And for their
parents a day of laughter and a day of tears. It is a bright green day, it is
June the seventh of the year one thousand nine hundred and fifty-seven
and for these young Americans the most stirring day of their lives. For
many this will be their last glimpse of the campus, of Columbus, for many
many years. Life calls us, and anxiously if not nervously we walk out into
the world and away from the pleasures of these ivied walls. But not from
its memories. They will be the concomitant, if not the fundament, of our
lives. We shall choose husbands and wives, we shall choose jobs and
homes, we shall sire children and grandchildren, but we will not forget
you, Ohio State. In the years ahead we will carry with us always memories of thee, Ohio State . . . "
Slowly, softly, the OSU band begins the Alma Mater, and then the bells
chime that last hour. Soft, very soft, for it is spring.
There was goose flesh on Ron's veiny arms as the Voice continued. "We
offer ourselves to you then, world, and come at you in search of Life. And
to you, Ohio State, to you Columbus, we say thank you, thank you and
goodbye. We will miss you, in the fall, in the winter, in the spring, but
some day we shall return. Till then, goodbye, Ohio State, goodbye, red
and white, goodbye, Columbus . . . goodbye, Columbus . . . goodbye . . . "
Ron's eyes were closed. The band was upending its last truckload of
nostalgia, and I tiptoed from the room, in step with the 2163 members of
the Class of '57.
I closed my door, but then opened it and looked back at Ron: he was
still humming on his bed. Thee! I thought, my brother-in-law!

The wedding.
Let me begin with the relatives.
There was Mrs. Patimkin's side of the family: her sister Molly, a tiny
buxom hen whose ankles swelled and ringed her shoes, and who would
remember Ron's wedding if for no other reason than she'd martyred her
feet in three-inch heels, and Molly's husband, the butter and egg man,
Harry Grossbart, who had earned his fortune with barley and corn in the
days of Prohibition. Now he was active in the Temple and whenever he
saw Brenda he swatted her on the can; it was a kind of physical bootleg-
ging that passed, I guess, for familial affection. Then there was Mrs. Patimkin's brother, Marty Kreiger, the Kosher Hot-Dog King, an immense
man, as many stomachs as he had chins, and already, at fifty-five, with as
many heart attacks as chins and stomachs combined. He had just come
back from a health cure in the Catskills,[9] where he said he'd eaten nothing but All-Bran and had won $1500 at gin rummy. When the photogra-
pher came by to take pictures, Marty put his hand on his wife's pancake
breasts and said, "Hey, how about a picture of this!" His wife, Sylvia, was
a frail, spindly woman with bones like a bird's. She had cried throughout
the ceremony and sobbed openly, in fact, when the rabbi had pronounced
Ron and Harriet "man and wife in the eyes of God and the State of New
Jersey." Later, at dinner, she had hardened enough to slap her husband's

9. Mountains in southern New York State, site of
numerous, primarily Jewish resorts well known for
their generous quantities of food and their entertainment (the "Borscht Belt").

hand as it reached out for a cigar. However, when he reached across to hold her breast she just looked aghast and said nothing.

Also there were Mrs. Patimkin's twin sisters, Rose and Pearl, who both had white hair, the color of Lincoln convertibles, and nasal voices, and husbands who followed after them but talked only to each other, as though, in fact, sister had married sister, and husband had married husband. The husbands, named Earl Klein and Manny Kartzman, sat next to each other during the ceremony, then at dinner, and once, in fact, while the band was playing between courses, they rose, Klein and Kartzman, as though to dance, but instead walked to the far end of the hall where together they paced off the width of the floor. Earl, I learned later, was in the carpet business, and apparently he was trying to figure how much money he would make if the Hotel Pierre[1] favored him with a sale.

On Mr. Patimkin's side there was only Leo, his half-brother. Leo was married to a woman named Bea whom nobody seemed to talk to. Bea kept hopping up and down during the meal and running over to the kiddie table to see if her little girl, Sharon, was being taken care of. "I told her not to take the kid. Get a baby-sitter, I said." Leo told me this while Brenda danced with Ron's best man, Ferrari. "She says what are we, millionaires? No, for Christ sake, but my brother's kids gets married, I can have a little celebration. No, we gotta *shelp*[2] the kid with us. Aah, it gives her something to do! ..." He looked around the hall. Upon the stage Harry Winters (né Weinberg) was leading his band in a medley from *My Fair Lady*; on the floor, all ages, all sizes, all shapes were dancing. Mr. Patimkin was dancing with Julie, whose dress had slipped down from her shoulders to reveal her soft small back, and long neck, like Brenda's. He danced in little squares and was making considerable effort not to step on Julie's toes. Harriet, who was, as everyone said, a beautiful bride, was dancing with her father. Ron danced with Harriet's mother, Brenda with Ferrari, and I had sat down for a while in the empty chair beside Leo so as not to get maneuvered into dancing with Mrs. Patimkin, which seemed to be the direction towards which things were moving.

"You're Brenda's boy friend? Huh?" Leo said.

I nodded—earlier in the evening I'd stopped giving blushing explanations. "You gotta deal there, boy," Leo said, "you don't louse it up."

"She's very beautiful," I said.

Leo poured himself a glass of champagne, and then waited as though he expected a head to form on it; when one didn't, he filled the glass to the brim.

"Beautiful, not beautiful, what's the difference. I'm a practical man. I'm on the bottom, so I gotta be. You're Aly Khan[3] you worry about marrying movie stars. I wasn't born yesterday ... You know how old I was when I got married? Thirty-five years old. I don't know what the hell kind of hurry I was in." He drained his glass and refilled it. "I'll tell you something, one good thing happened to me in my whole life. Two maybe. Before I came back from overseas I got a letter from my wife—she wasn't my wife then. My mother-in-law found an apartment for us in Queens. Sixty-two fifty a month it cost. That's the last good thing that happened."

1. Very posh New York hotel.
2. Drag.
3. Playboy son of Moslem spiritual leader who in 1949, after a courtship conducted rather publicly while he was still married, wed Rita Hayworth (b. 1918), torrid Hollywood dancer, movie star, and sex symbol.

"What was the first?"

"What first?"

"You said *two* things," I said.

"I don't remember. I say two because my wife tells me I'm sarcastic and a cynic. That way maybe she won't think I'm such a wise guy."

I saw Brenda and Ferrari separate, and so excused myself and started for Brenda, but just then Mr. Patimkin separated from Julie and it looked as though the two men were going to switch partners. Instead the four of them stood on the dance floor and when I reached them they were laughing and Julie was saying, "What's so funny!" Ferrari said "Hi" to me and whisked Julie away, which sent her into peals of laughter.

Mr. Patimkin had one hand on Brenda's back and suddenly the other one was on mine. "You kids having a good time?" he said.

We were sort of swaying, the three of us, to "Get Me to the Church on Time."

Brenda kissed her father. "Yes," she said. "I'm so drunk my head doesn't even need my neck."

"It's a fine wedding, Mr. Patimkin."

"You want anything just ask me . . . " he said, a little drunken himself. "You're two good kids . . . How do you like that brother of yours getting married? . . . Huh? . . . Is that a girl or is that a girl?"

Brenda smiled, and though she apparently thought her father had spoken of her, I was sure he'd been referring to Harriet.

"You like weddings, Daddy?" Brenda said.

"I like my kids' weddings . . . " He slapped me on the back. "You two kids, you want anything? Go have a good time. Remember," he said to Brenda, "you're my honey . . . " Then he looked at me. "Whatever my Buck wants is good enough for me. There's no business too big it can't use another head."

I smiled, though not directly at him, and beyond I could see Leo sopping up champagne and watching the three of us; when he caught my eye he made a sign with his hand, a circle with his thumb and forefinger, indicating, "That a boy, that a boy!"

After Mr. Patimkin departed, Brenda and I danced closely, and we only sat down when the waiters began to circulate with the main course. The head table was noisy, particularly at our end where the men were almost all teammates of Ron's, in one sport or another; they ate a fantastic number of rolls. Tank Feldman, Ron's roommate, who had flown in from Toledo, kept sending the waiter back for rolls, for celery, for olives, and always to the squealing delight of Gloria Feldman, his wife, a nervous, undernourished girl who continually looked down the front of her gown as though there was some sort of construction project going on under her clothes. Gloria and Tank, in fact, seemed to be self-appointed precinct captains at our end. They proposed toasts, burst into wild song, and continually referred to Brenda and me as "love birds." Brenda smiled at this with her eyeteeth and I brought up a cheery look from some fraudulent auricle of my heart.

And the night continued: we ate, we drank, we danced—Rose and Pearl did the Charleston with one another (while their husbands examined woodwork and chandeliers), and then I did the Charleston with none other than Gloria Feldman, who made coy, hideous faces at me all the time we danced. Near the end of the evening, Brenda, who'd been drinking champagne like her Uncle Leo, did a Rita Hayworth tango with herself, and Julie fell asleep on some ferns she'd whisked off the head table and made into a mattress at the far end of the hall. I felt a numbness creep into my hard palate, and by three o'clock people were dancing in their coats, shoeless ladies were wrapping hunks of wedding cake in napkins for their children's lunch, and finally Gloria Feldman made her way over to our end of the table and said, freshly, "Well, our little Radcliffe smarty, what have *you* been doing all summer?"

"Growing a penis."

Gloria smiled and left as quickly as she'd come, and Brenda without another word headed shakily away for the ladies' room and the rewards of overindulgence. No sooner had she left than Leo was beside me, a glass in one hand, a new bottle of champagne in the other.

"No sign of the bride and groom?" he said, leering. He'd lost most of his consonants by this time and was doing the best he could with long, wet vowels. "Well, you're next, kid, I see it in the cards ... You're nobody's sucker ... " And he stabbed me in the side with the top of the bottle, spilling champagne onto the side of my rented tux. He straightened up, poured more onto his hand and glass, but then suddenly he stopped. He was looking into the lights which were hidden beneath a long bank of flowers that adorned the front of the table. He shook the bottle in his hand as though to make it fizz. "The son of a bitch who invented the fluorescent bulb should drop dead!" He set the bottle down and drank.

Up on the stage Harry Winters brought his musicians to a halt. The drummer stood up, stretched, and they all began to open up cases and put their instruments away. On the floor, relatives, friends, associates, were holding each other around the waists and the shoulders, and small children huddled around their parents' legs. A couple of kids ran in and out of the crowd, screaming at tag, until one was grabbed by an adult and slapped soundly on the behind. He began to cry, and couple by couple the floor emptied. Our table was a tangle of squashed everything: napkins, fruits, flowers; there were empty whiskey bottles, droopy ferns, and dishes puddled with unfinished cherry jubilee, gone sticky with the hours. At the end of the table Mr. Patimkin was sitting next to his wife, holding her hand. Opposite them, on two bridge chairs that had been pulled up, sat Mr. and Mrs. Ehrlich. They spoke quietly and evenly, as though they had known each other for years and years. Everything had slowed down now, and from time to time people would come up to the Patimkins and Ehrlichs, wish them *mazel tov*,[4] and then drag themselves and their families out into the September night, which was cool and windy, someone said, and reminded me that soon would come winter and snow.

"They never wear out, those things, you know that." Leo was pointing to the fluorescent lights that shone through the flowers. "They last for years. They could make a car like that if they wanted, that could never wear out. It would run on water in the summer and snow in the winter. But they wouldn't do it, the big boys ... Look at me," Leo said, splashing his suit front with champagne, "I sell a good bulb. You can't get the kind of bulb I sell in the drugstores. It's a quality bulb. But I'm the little guy. I don't even own a car. His brother, and I don't even own an automobile. I

---

4. Congratulations.

take a train wherever I go. I'm the only guy I know who wears out three pairs of rubbers every winter. Most guys get new ones when they lose the old ones. I wear them out, like shoes. Look," he said, leaning into me, "I could sell a crappy bulb, it wouldn't break my heart. But it's not good business."

The Ehrlichs and Patimkins scraped back their chairs and headed away, all except Mr. Patimkin who came down the table towards Leo and me.

He slapped Leo on the back. "Well, how you doing, *shtarke*?"[5]

"All right, Ben. All right . . ."

"You have a good time?"

"You had a nice affair, Ben, it must've cost a pretty penny, believe me . . ."

Mr. Patimkin laughed. "When I make out my income tax I go to see Leo. He knows just how much money I spent . . . You need a ride home?" he asked me.

"No, thanks. I'm waiting for Brenda. We have my car."

"Good night," Mr. Patimkin said.

I watched him step down off the platform that held the head table, and then start towards the exit. Now the only people in the hall—the shambles of a hall—were myself, Leo, and his wife and child who slept, both of them, with their heads pillowed on a crumpled tablecloth at a table down on the floor before us. Brenda still wasn't around.

"When you got it," Leo said, rubbing his fingers together, "you can afford to talk like a big shot. Who needs a guy like me any more? Salesmen, you spit on them. You can go to the supermarket and buy anything. Where my wife shops you can buy sheets and pillowcases. Imagine, a grocery store! Me, I sell to gas stations, factories, small businesses, all up and down the east coast. Sure, you can sell a guy in a gas station a crappy bulb that'll burn out in a week. For inside the pumps I'm talking, it takes a certain kind of bulb. A utility bulb. All right, so you sell him a crappy bulb, and then a week later he puts in a new one, and while he's screwing it in he still remembers your name. Not me. I sell a quality bulb. It lasts a month, five weeks, before it even flickers, then it gives you another couple days, dim maybe, but so you shouldn't go blind. It hangs on, it's a quality bulb. Before it even burns out you notice it's getting darker, so you put a new one in. What people don't like is when one minute it's sunlight and the next dark. Let it glimmer a few days and they don't feel so bad. Nobody ever throws out my bulb—they figure they'll save them, can always use them in a pinch. Sometimes I say to a guy, you ever throw out a bulb you bought from Leo Patimkin? You gotta use psychology. That's why I'm sending my kid to college. You don't know a little psychology these days, you're licked . . ."

He lifted an arm and pointed out to his wife; then he slumped down in his seat. "Aaach!" he said, and drank off half a glass of champagne. "I'll tell you, I go as far as New London, Connecticut.[6] That's as far as I'll go, and when I come home at night I stop first for a couple drinks. Martinis. Two I have, sometimes three. That seems fair, don't it? But to her a little sip or a bathtubful, it smells the same. She says it's bad for the kid if I come home smelling. The kid's a baby, for God's sake, she thinks that's the way I'm *supposed* to smell. A forty-eight-year-old man with a three-year-old kid! She'll give me a thrombosis that kid. My wife, she wants me to come home early and play with the kid before she goes to bed. Come home, she says, and *I'll* make you a drink. Hah! I spend all day sniffing gas, leaning under hoods with grimy *poilishehs*[7] in New London, trying to force a lousy bulb into a socket—I'll screw it in myself, I tell them—and she thinks I want to come home and drink a martini from a jelly glass! How long are you going to stay in bars, she says. Till a Jewish girl is Miss Rheingold![8]

"Look," he went on after another drink, "I love my kid like Ben loves his Brenda. It's not that I don't want to play with her. But if I play with the kid and then at night get into bed with my wife, then she can't expect fancy things from me. It's one or the other. I'm no movie star."

Leo looked at his empty glass and put it on the table; he tilted the bottle up and drank the champagne like soda water. "How much do you think I make a week?" he said.

"I don't know."

"Take a guess."

"A hundred dollars."

"Sure, and tomorrow they're gonna let the lions out of the cage in Central Park. What do you think I make?"

"I can't tell."

"A cabdriver makes more than me. That's a fact. My wife's brother is a cabdriver, *he* lives in Kew Gardens.[9] And he don't take no crap, no sir, not those cabbies. Last week it was raining one night and I said the hell with it, I'm taking a cab. I'd been all day in Newton, Mass.[1] I don't usually go so far, but on the train in the morning I said to myself, stay on, go further, it'll be a change. And I know all the time I'm kidding myself. I wouldn't even make up the extra fare it cost me. But I stay on. And at night I still had a couple boxes with me, so when the guy pulls up at Grand Central there's like a genie inside me says get in. I even threw the bulbs in, not caring if they broke. And this cabbie says, Whatya want to do, buddy, rip the leather? Those are brand new seats I got. No, I said. Jesus Christ, he says, some goddam people. I get in and give him a Queens address which ought to shut him up, but no, all the way up the Drive he was Jesus Christing me. It's hot in the cab, so I open a window and *then* he turns around and says, Whatya want to do, give me a cold in the neck? I just got over a goddam cold . . ." Leo looked at me, bleary-eyed. "This city is crazy! If I had a little money I'd get out of here in a minute. I'd go to California. They don't need bulbs out there it's so light. I went to New Guinea during the war from San Francisco. *There*," he burst, "there is the other good thing that happened to me, that night in San Francisco with this Hannah Schreiber. That's the both of them, you asked me I'm telling you—the apartment my mother-in-law got us, and this Hannah Schreiber. One night was all. I went to a B'nai B'rith dance for servicemen in the basement of some big temple, and I met her. I wasn't married then, so don't make faces."

"I'm not."

"She had a nice little room by herself. She was going to school to be a

7. Poles.
8. Rheingold Beer commercials, subway posters, etc., featured a series of beautiful girls, each called in turn "Miss Rheingold."
9. A middle-class section of Queens.
1. Near Boston, some 220 miles from New York.

teacher. Already I knew something was up because she let me feel inside
her slip in the cab. Listen to me, I sound like I'm always in cabs. Maybe
two other times in my life. To tell the truth I don't even enjoy it. All the
time I'm riding I'm watching the meter. Even the pleasures I can't
enjoy!"

"What about Hannah Schreiber?"

He smiled, flashing some gold in his mouth. "How do you like that
name? She was only a girl, but she had an old lady's name. In the room
she says to me she believes in oral love. I can still hear her: Leo Patimkin,
I believe in oral love. I don't know what the hell she means. I figure she
was one of those Christian Scientists or some cult or something. So I said,
But what about for soldiers, guys going overseas who may get killed, God
forbid." He shrugged his shoulders. "The smartest guy in the world I
wasn't. But that's twenty years almost, I was still wet behind the ears. I'll
tell you, every once in a while my wife—you know, she does for me what
Hannah Schreiber did. I don't like to force her, she works hard. That to
her is like a cab to me. I wouldn't force her. I can remember every time,
I'll bet. Once after a Seder, my mother was still living, she should rest in
peace. My wife was up to here with Mogen David.[2] In fact, *twice* after
Seders. Aachhh! Everything good in my life I can count on my fingers!
God forbid some one should leave me a million dollars, I wouldn't even
have to take off my shoes. I got a whole other hand yet."

He pointed to the fluorescent bulbs with the nearly empty champagne
bottle. "You call that a light? That's a light to *read* by? It's purple, for
God's sake! Half the blind men in the world ruined themselves by those
damn things. You know who's behind them? The optometrists! I'll tell
you, if I could get a couple hundred for all my stock and the territory, I'd
sell tomorrow. That's right, Leo A. Patimkin, one semester accounting,
City College nights, will sell equipment, territory, good name. I'll buy
two inches in the *Times*. The territory is from here to everywhere. I go
where I want, my own boss, no one tells me what to do. You know the
Bible? 'Let there be light—and there's Leo Patimkin!'[3] That's my trade-
mark, I'll sell that too. I tell them that slogan, the *poilishehs*, they think
I'm making it up. What good is it to be smart unless you're in on the
ground floor! I got more brains in my pinky than Ben got in his whole
head. Why is it he's on top and I'm on the bottom! *Why!* Believe me, if
you're born lucky, you're lucky!" And then he exploded into silence.

I had the feeling that he was going to cry, so I leaned over and whispered to him, "You better go home." He agreed, but I had to raise him
out of his seat and steer him by one arm down to his wife and child. The
little girl could not be awakened, and Leo and Bea asked me to watch
her while they went out into the lobby to get their coats. When they
returned, Leo seemed to have dragged himself back to the level of human
communication. He shook my hand with real feeling. I was very touched.

"You'll go far," he said to me. "You're a smart boy, you'll play it safe.
Don't louse things up."

"I won't."

"Next time we see you it'll be *your* wedding," and he winked at me.
Bea stood alongside, muttering goodbye all the while he spoke. He shook

2. A wine (literally, Star of David). Seder: Passover
ritual meal.

3. Genesis 1:3—"And God said, Let there be light:
and there was light."

my hand again and then picked the child out of her seat, and they turned towards the door. From the back, round-shouldered, burdened, child-carrying, they looked like people fleeing a captured city.

Brenda, I discovered, was asleep on a couch in the lobby. It was almost four o'clock and the two of us and the desk clerk were the only ones in the hotel lobby. At first I did not waken Brenda, for she was pale and wilted and I knew she had been sick. I sat beside her, smoothing her hair back off her ears. How would I ever come to know her, I wondered, for as she slept I felt I knew no more of her than what I could see in a photograph. I stirred her gently and in a half-sleep she walked beside me out to the car.

It was almost dawn when we came out of the Jersey side of the Lincoln Tunnel. I switched down to my parking lights, and drove on to the Turnpike, and there out before me I could see the swampy meadows that spread for miles and miles, watery, blotchy, smelly, like an oversight of God. I thought of that other oversight, Leo Patimkin, half-brother to Ben. In a few hours he would be on a train heading north, and as he passed Scarsdale and White Plains, he would belch and taste champagne and let the flavor linger in his mouth. Alongside him on the seat, like another passenger, would be cartons of bulbs. He would get off at New London, or maybe, inspired by the sight of his half-brother, he would stay on again, hoping for some new luck further north. For the world was Leo's territory, every city, every swamp, every road and highway. He could go on to Newfoundland if he wanted, Hudson Bay, and on up to Thule, and then slide down the other side of the globe and rap on frosted windows on the Russian steppes, if he wanted. But he wouldn't. Leo was forty-eight years old and he had learned. He pursued discomfort and sorrow, all right, but if you had a heartful by the time you reached New London, what new awfulness could you look forward to in Vladivostok?

The next day the wind was blowing the fall in and the branches of the weeping willow were fingering at the Patimkin front lawn. I drove Brenda to the train at noon, and she left me.

8

Autumn came quickly. It was cold and in Jersey the leaves turned and fell overnight. The following Saturday I took a ride up to see the deer, and did not even get out of the car, for it was too brisk to be standing at the wire fence, and so I watched the animals walk and run in the dimness of the late afternoon, and after a while everything, even the objects of nature, the trees, the clouds, the grass, the weeds, reminded me of Brenda, and I drove back down to Newark. Already we had sent our first letters and I had called her late one night, but in the mail and on the phone we had some difficulty discovering one another; we had not the style yet. That night I tried her again, and someone on her floor said she was out and would not be in till late.

Upon my return to the library I was questioned by Mr. Scapello about the Gauguin book. The jowly gentleman *had* sent a nasty letter about my discourtesy, and I was only able to extricate myself by offering a confused story in an indignant tone. In fact, I even managed to turn it around so that Mr. Scapello was apologizing to me as he led me up to my new post, there among the encyclopedias, the bibliographies, the indexes and guides. My bullying surprised me, and I wondered if some of it had not been learned from Mr. Patimkin that morning I'd heard him giving Grossman an earful on the phone. Perhaps I was more of a businessman than I thought. Maybe I could learn to become a Patimkin with ease . . .

Days passed slowly; I never did see the colored kid again, and when, one noon, I looked in the stacks, Gauguin was gone, apparently charged out finally by the jowly man. I wondered what it had been like that day the colored kid had discovered the book was gone. Had he cried? For some reason I imagined that he had blamed it on me, but then I realized that I was confusing the dream I'd had with reality. Chances were he had discovered someone else, Van Gogh, Vermeer . . . But no, they were not his kind of artists. What had probably happened was that he'd given up on the library and gone back to playing Willie Mays in the streets. He was better off, I thought. No sense carrying dreams of Tahiti in your head, if you can't afford the fare.

Let's see, what else did I do? I ate, I slept, I went to the movies, I sent broken-spined books to the bindery—I did everything I'd ever done before, but now each activity was surrounded by a fence, existed alone, and my life consisted of jumping from one fence to the next. There was no flow, for that had been Brenda.

And then Brenda wrote saying that she would be coming in for the Jewish holidays which were only a week away. I was so overjoyed I wanted to call Mr. and Mrs. Patimkin, just to tell them of my pleasure. However, when I got to the phone and had actually dialed the first two letters, I knew that at the other end there would be silence; if there was anything said, it would only be Mrs. Patimkin asking, "What is it you want?" Mr. Patimkin had probably forgotten my name.

That night, after dinner, I gave Aunt Gladys a kiss and told her she shouldn't work so hard.

"In less than a week it's Rosh Hashana and he thinks I should take a vacation. Ten people I'm having. What do you think, a chicken cleans itself? Thank God, the holidays come once a year, I'd be an old woman before my time."

But then it was only nine people Aunt Gladys was having, for only two days after her letter Brenda called.

"Oy, Gut!"[4] Aunt Gladys called. "Long *distance!*"

"Hello?" I said.

"Hello, sweetie?"

"Yes," I said.

"What *is* it?" Aunt Gladys tugged at my shirt. "What is it?"

"It's for me."

"Who?" Aunt Gladys said, pointing into the receiver.

"Brenda," I said.

"Yes?" Brenda said.

"Brenda?" Aunt Gladys said. "What does she call long distance, I almost had a heart attack."

"Because she's in Boston," I said. "Please, Aunt Gladys . . ."

And Aunt Gladys walked off, mumbling, "These kids . . ."

"Hello," I said again into the phone.

"Neil, how are you?"

4. *O, God!*

"I love you."

"Neil, I have bad news. I can't come in this week."

"But, honey, it's the Jewish holidays."

"Sweet*heart*," she laughed.

"Can't you say that, for an excuse?"

"I have a test Saturday, and a paper, and you know if I went home I wouldn't get anything done ... "

"You would."

"Neil, I just *can't*. My mother'd make me go to Temple, and I wouldn't even have enough time to see *you*."

"Oh God, Brenda."

"Sweetie?"

"Yes?"

"Can't you come up here?" she asked.

"I'm working."

"The Jewish holidays," she said.

"Honey, I can't. Last year I didn't take them off, I can't all—"

"You can say you had a conversion."

"Besides, my aunt's having all the family for dinner, and you know what with my parents—"

"Come up, Neil."

"I can't just take two days off, Bren. I just got promoted and a raise—"

"The hell with the raise."

"Baby, it's my job."

"Forever?" she said.

"No."

"Then come. I've got a hotel room."

"For me?"

"For us."

"Can you do that?"

"No and yes. People do it."

"Brenda, you tempt me."

"Be tempted."

"I could take a train Wednesday right from work."

"You could stay till Sunday night."

"Bren, I can't. I still have to be back to work on Saturday."

"Don't you ever get a day *off?*" she said.

"Tuesdays," I said glumly.

"God."

"And Sunday," I added.

Brenda said something but I did not hear her, for Aunt Gladys called, "You talk all day long distance?"

"Quiet!" I shouted back to her.

"Neil, will you?"

"Damn it, yes," I said.

"Are you angry?"

"I don't think so. I'm going to come up."

"Till Sunday."

"We'll see."

"Don't feel upset, Neil. You sound upset. It is the Jewish holidays. I mean you *should* be off."

"That's right," I said. "I'm an orthodox Jew, for God's sake, I ought to take advantage of it."

"That's right," she said.

"Is there a train around six?"

"Every hour, I think."

"Then I'll be on the one that leaves at six."

"I'll be at the station," she said. "How will I know you?"

"I'll be disguised as an orthodox Jew."

"Me too," she said.

"Good night, love," I said.

Aunt Gladys cried when I told her I was going away for Rosh Hashana.

"And I was preparing a big meal," she said.

"You can still prepare it."

"What will I tell your mother?"

"I'll tell her, Aunt Gladys. Please. You have no right to get upset . . . "

"Someday you'll have a family you'll know what it's like."

"I have a family now."

"What's a matter," she said, blowing her nose. "That girl couldn't come home to see her family it's the holidays?"

"She's in school, she just can't—"

"If she loved her family she'd find time. We don't live six hundred years."

"She does love her family."

"Then one day a year you could break your heart and pay a visit."

"Aunt Gladys, you don't understand."

"Sure," she said, "when I'm twenty-three years old I'll understand everything."

I went to kiss her and she said, "Go away from me, go run to Boston . . . "

The next morning I discovered that Mr. Scapello didn't want me to leave on Rosh Hashana either, but I unnerved him, I think, by hinting that his coldness about my taking the two days off might just be so much veiled anti-Semitism, so on the whole he was easier to manage. At lunch time I took a walk down to Penn Station and picked up a train schedule to Boston. That was my bedtime reading for the next three nights.

She did not look like Brenda, at least for the first minute. And probably to her I did not look like me. But we kissed and held each other, and it was strange to feel the thickness of our coats between us.

"I'm letting my hair grow," she said in the cab, and that in fact was all she said. Not until I helped her out of the cab did I notice the thin gold band shining on her left hand.

She hung back, strolling casually about the lobby while I signed the register "Mr. and Mrs. Neil Klugman," and then in the room we kissed again.

"Your heart's pounding," I said to her.

"I know," she said.

"Are you nervous?"

"No."

"Have you done this before?" I said.

"I read Mary McCarthy."

She took off her coat and instead of putting it in the closet, she tossed it across the chair. I sat down on the bed; she didn't.

"What's the matter?"

Brenda took a deep breath and walked over to the window, and I thought that perhaps it would be best for me to ask nothing—for us to get used to each other's presence in quiet. I hung her coat and mine in the empty closet, and left the suitcases—mine and hers—standing by the bed.

Brenda was kneeling backwards in the chair, looking out the window as though out the window was where she'd rather be. I came up behind her and put my hands around her body and held her breasts, and when I felt the cool draft that swept under the sill, I realized how long it had been since that first warm night when I had put my arms around her and felt the tiny wings beating in her back. And then I realized why I'd really come to Boston—it had been long enough. It was time to stop kidding about marriage.

"Is something the matter?" I said.

"Yes."

It wasn't the answer I'd expected; I wanted no answer really, only to soothe her nervousness with my concern.

But I asked, "What is it? Why didn't you mention it on the phone?"

"It only happened today."

"School?"

"Home. They found out about us."

I turned her face up to mine. "That's okay. I told my aunt I was coming here too. What's the difference?"

"About the summer. About our sleeping together."

"Oh?"

"Yes."

" . . . Ron?"

"No."

"That night, you mean, did Julie—"

"No," she said, "it wasn't *anybody*."

"I don't get it."

Brenda got up and walked over to the bed where she sat down on the edge. I sat in the chair.

"My mother found the thing."

"The diaphragm?"

She nodded.

"When?" I asked.

"The other day, I guess." She walked to the bureau and opened her purse. "Here, you can read them in the order I got them." She tossed an envelope at me; it was dirty-edged and crumpled, as though it had been in and out of her pockets a good many times. "I got this one this morning," she said. "Special delivery."

I took out the letter and read:

PATIMKIN KITCHEN AND BATHROOM SINKS
"Any Size—Any Shape"

Dear Brenda—

Don't pay any Attention to your Mother's Letter when you get it. I love you honey if you want a coat I'll buy You a coat. You could always have anything you wanted. We have every faith in you so you won't be too upset by what your mother says in her Letter. Of course she is a little hysterical because of the shock and she has been Working so hard for Hadassah. She is a Woman and it is hard for her to understand some of the Shocks in life. Of course I can't say We weren't all surprised because from the beginning I was nice to him and Thought he would appreciate the nice vacation we supplied for him. Some People never turn out the way you hope and pray but I am willing to forgive and call Buy Gones, Buy Gones, You have always up till now been a good Buck and got good scholastic Grades and Ron has always been what we wanted a Good Boy, most important, and a Nice boy. This late in my life believe me I am not going to start hating my own flesh and blood. As for your mistake it takes Two to make a mistake and now that you will be away at school and from him and what you got involved in you will probably do all right I have every faith you will. You have to have faith in your children like in a Business or any serious undertaking and there is nothing that is so bad that we can't forgive especially when Our own flesh and blood is involved. We have a nice close nitt family and why not???? Have a nice Holiday and in Temple I will say a Prayer for you as I do every year. On Monday I want you to go into Boston and buy a coat. Whatever you need because I know how Cold it gets up where you are . . . Give my regards to Linda and remember to bring her home with you on Thanksgiving like last year. You two had such a nice time. I have always never said bad things about any of your friends or Rons and that this should happen is only the exception that proves the rule. Have a Happy Holiday.

YOUR FATHER

And then it was signed BEN PATIMKIN, but that was crossed out and written beneath "Your Father" were again, like an echo, the words, "Your Father."

"Who's Linda?" I asked.

"My roommate, last year." She tossed another envelope to me. "Here. I got this one in the afternoon. Air Mail."

The letter was from Brenda's mother. I started to read it and then put it down a moment. "You got this *after?*"

"Yes," she said. "When I got his I didn't know what was happening. Read hers."

I began again.

Dear Brenda:

I don't even know how to begin. I have been crying all morning and have had to skip my board meeting this afternoon because my eyes are so red. I never thought this would happen to a daughter of mine. I wonder if you know what I mean, if it is at least on your conscience, so I won't have to degrade either of us with a description. All I can say is that this morning when I was cleaning out the drawers and putting away your summer clothing I came upon something in your bottom drawer, *under* some sweaters which you probably remember leaving there. I cried the minute I saw it and I haven't stopped crying yet. Your father called a while ago and now he is driving home because he heard how upset I was on the phone.

I don't know what we ever did that you should reward us this way. We gave you a nice home and all the love and respect a child needs. I always was proud when you were a little girl that you could take care of yourself so well. You took care of Julie so beautifully it was a treat to see, when you were only fourteen years old. But you drifted away from your family, even though we sent you to the best schools and gave you the best money could buy. Why you should reward us this way is a question I'll carry with me to the grave.

About your friend I have no words. He is his parents' responsibility and I cannot imagine what kind of home life he had that he could act that way. Certainly that was a fine way to repay us for the hospitality we were nice enough to show to him, a perfect stranger. That the two of you should be carrying on like that in our very house I will never in my life be able to understand. Times certainly have changed since I was a girl that this kind of thing could go on. I keep asking myself if at least you didn't think of us while you were doing that. If not for me, how could you do this to your father? God forbid Julie should ever learn of this.

God only knows what you have been doing all these years we put our trust in you.

You have broken your parents' hearts and you should know that. This is some thank you for all we gave you.

MOTHER

She only signed "Mother" once, and that was in an extraordinarily miniscule hand, like a whisper.

"Brenda," I said.

"What?"

"Are you starting to cry?"

"No. I cried already."

"Don't start again."

"I'm trying not to, for God's sake."

"Okay . . . Brenda, can I ask you one question?"

"What?"

"Why did you leave it home?"

"Because I didn't plan on using it here, that's why."

"Suppose I'd come up. I mean I have come up, what about that?"

"I thought I'd come down first."

"So then couldn't you have carried it down then? Like a toothbrush?"

"Are you trying to be funny?"

"No. I'm just asking you why you left it home."

"I told you," Brenda said. "I thought I'd come home."

"But, Brenda, that doesn't make any sense. Suppose you did come home, and then you came back again. Wouldn't you have taken it with you then?"

"I don't *know*."

"Don't get angry," I said.

"You're the one who's angry."

"I'm upset, I'm not angry."

"I'm upset then too."

I did not answer but walked to the window and looked out. The stars and moon were out, silver and hard, and from the window I could see over to the Harvard campus where lights burned and then seemed to flicker when the trees blew across them.

"Brenda . . . "

"What?"

"Knowing how your mother feels about you, wasn't it silly to leave it home? Risky?"

"What does how she feels about me have to do with it?"

"You can't trust her."

"Why can't I?"

"Don't you see. You *can't.*"

"Neil, she was only cleaning out the drawers."

"Didn't you know she would?"

"She never did before. Or maybe she did. Neil, I couldn't think of everything. We slept together night after night and nobody heard or noticed—"

"Brenda, why the hell are you willfully confusing things?"

"I'm not!"

"Okay," I said softly. "All right."

"It's you who's confusing things," Brenda said. "You act as though I wanted her to find it."

I didn't answer.

"Do you believe *that?*" she said, after neither of us had spoken for a full minute.

"I don't know."

"Oh, Neil, you're *crazy.*"

"What was crazier than leaving that damn thing around?"

"It was an oversight."

"Now it's an oversight, before it was deliberate."

"It was an oversight about the drawer. It wasn't an oversight about leaving it," she said.

"Brenda, sweetheart, wouldn't the safest, smartest, easiest, simplest thing been to have taken it with you? Wouldn't it?"

"It didn't make any difference either way."

"Brenda, this is the most frustrating argument of my life!"

"You keep making it seem as though I *wanted* her to find it. Do you think I need this? Do you? I can't even go home any more."

"Is that so?"

"Yes!"

"No," I said. "You can go home—your father will be waiting with two coats and a half-dozen dresses."

"What about my mother?"

"It'll be the same with her."

"Don't be absurd. How can I face them!"

"Why can't you face them? Did you do anything wrong?"

"Neil, look at the reality of the thing, will you?"

"*Did* you do anything wrong?"

"Neil, *they* think it's wrong. They're my parents."

"But do you think it's wrong—"

"That doesn't *matter.*"

"It does to me, Brenda . . ."

"Neil, why are *you* confusing things? You keep accusing me of things."

"Damn it, Brenda, you're guilty of some things."

"*What?*"

"Of leaving that damn diaphragm there. How can you call it an oversight!"

"Oh, Neil, don't start any of that psychoanalytic crap!"

"Then why else did you do it? You wanted her to find it!"

"Why?"

"I don't know, Brenda, *why?*"

"Oh!" she said, and she picked up the pillow and threw it back on to the bed.

"What happens now, Bren?" I said.

"What does that mean?"

"Just that. What happens now?"

She rolled over on to the bed and buried her head in it.

"Don't start crying," I said.

"I'm *not.*"

I was still holding the letters and took Mr. Patimkin's from its envelope.

"Why does your father capitalize all these letters?"

She didn't answer.

" 'As for your mistake,' " I read aloud to Brenda, " 'it takes Two to make a mistake and now that you will be away at school and from him and what you got involved in you will probably do all right I have every faith you will. Your father. Your father.' "

She turned and looked at me; but silently.

" 'I have always never said bad things about any of your friends or Rons and that this should happen is only the exception that proves the rule. Have a Happy Holiday.' " I stopped; in Brenda's face there was positively no threat of tears; she looked, suddenly, solid and decisive. "Well, what are you going to do?" I asked.

"Nothing."

"Who are you going to bring home Thanksgiving—Linda?" I said, "or me?"

"Who *can* I bring home, Neil?"

"I don't know, who can you?"

"Can I bring you home?"

"I don't know," I said, "can you?"

"Stop repeating the question!"

"I sure as hell can't give you the answer."

"Neil, be realistic. After this, can I bring you home? Can you see us all sitting around the table?"

"I can't if you can't, and I can if you can."

"Are you going to speak Zen,[5] for God's sake!"

"Brenda, the choices aren't mine. You can bring Linda or me. You can go home or not go home. That's another choice. Then you don't even have to worry about choosing between me and Linda."

"Neil, you don't understand. They're still my parents. They did send me to the best schools, didn't they? They have given me everything I've wanted, haven't they?"

"Yes."

"Then how can I not go home? I *have* to go home."

"Why?"

"You don't understand. Your parents don't bother you any more. You're lucky."

"Oh, sure. I live with my crazy aunt, that's a real bargain."

"Families are different. You don't understand."

"Goddamit, I understand more than you think. I understand why the hell you left that thing lying around. Don't you? Can't you put two and two together?"

"Neil, what are you talking about! You're the one who doesn't understand. You're the one who from the very beginning was accusing me of things? Remember? Isn't it so? Why don't you have your eyes fixed? Why don't you have this fixed, that fixed? As if it were my fault that I *could* have them fixed. You kept acting as if I was going to run away from you every minute. And now you're doing it again, telling me I planted that thing on purpose."

"I loved you, Brenda, so I cared."

"I loved *you*. That's why I got that damn thing in the first place."

And then we heard the tense in which we'd spoken and we settled back into ourselves and silence.

A few minutes later I picked up my bag and put on my coat. I think Brenda was crying too when I went out the door.

Instead of grabbing a cab immediately, I walked down the street and out towards the Harvard Yard which I had never seen before. I entered one of the gates and then headed out along a path, under the tired autumn foliage and the dark sky. I wanted to be alone, in the dark; not because I wanted to think about anything, but rather because, for just a while, I wanted to think about nothing. I walked clear across the Yard and up a little hill and then I was standing in front of the Lamont Library, which, Brenda had once told me, had Patimkin Sinks in its rest rooms. From the light of the lamp on the path behind me I could see my reflection in the glass front of the building. Inside, it was dark and there were no students to be seen, no librarians. Suddenly, I wanted to set down my suitcase and pick up a rock and heave it right through the glass, but of course I didn't. I simply looked at myself in the mirror the light made of the window. I was only that substance, I thought, those limbs, that face that I saw in front of me. I looked, but the outside of me gave up little information about the inside of me. I wished I could scoot around to the other side of the window, faster than light or sound or Herb Clark on Homecoming Day, to get behind that image and catch whatever it was that looked through those eyes. What was it inside me that had turned pursuit and clutching into love, and then turned it inside out again? What was it that had turned winning into losing, and losing—who knows—into winning? I was sure I had loved Brenda, though standing there, I knew I couldn't any longer. And I knew it would be a long while before I made love to anyone the way I had made love to her. With anyone else, could I summon up such a passion? Whatever spawned my love for her, had that spawned such lust too? If she had only been slightly *not* Brenda ... but then would I have loved her? I looked hard at the image of me, at that darkening of the glass, and then my gaze pushed through it, over the cool floor, to a broken wall of books, imperfectly shelved.

I did not look very much longer, but took a train that got me into Newark just as the sun was rising on the first day of the Jewish New Year. I was back in plenty of time for work.

1959

AFTERWORD

This is a love story, or, I guess you could say, the story of what turns out to have been just a summer romance. It spans the summer and a bit of the fall, so there's enough time to warrant a narrative the length of a novel, at least a short novel. There are eight chapters and the chapters are often divided by white space into discrete scenes, giving a reading pace and sense of time and space sufficient to make the reading feel like the reading of a novel. There are a number of settings: Aunt Gladys's apartment in Newark, the city library, the Short Hills Country Club, the Patimkin house, Central Park in New York City, the hotel in Boston, Harvard Yard. So there's certainly enough development and detail, scene and setting, to meaningfully fill out a novel about a young couple's brief love affair.

But there's more, and perhaps we ought to look at what else is here before focusing on the central story. Though the novel begins, as we would expect a love story to, when boy (Neil) meets girl (Brenda), after the first fairly brief paragraph the scene shifts to a Newark apartment and the boy's conversation with his aunt. Though the topic is chiefly the girl, the reader's attention is likely to be diverted from the romance by the brilliantly mimetic and characterizing dialogue. There is, first of all, Aunt Gladys's Yiddish-American accent (or rather, syntax and rhythm): not "Did Doris introduce you?" but "Doris introduced you?"; not "I don't know the Patimkins," but "Patimkin I don't know" (without even a comma); not "Are you going to call her even though you don't know her?" but "You're going to call her you don't know her?"

There's more to this than mere delight in mimicry, for, it becomes clear, the love story is also about social class and climbing, about second- and third-generation Jewish immigrant families climbing not only from the lower to the middle class but from the urban ghetto to the suburban one and, tentatively, into the American "mainstream." Aunt Gladys's language identifies her as a first-generation lower- or lower-middle-class Jewish housewife. Compare her language to Mrs. Patimkin's standard American (with pretensions to culture). Though we are not specifically told, her tennis-playing youth does suggest that she's at least second generation and middle class (the "masses" did not play tennis forty or fifty years ago, when she was a girl). Though she is as least as religious as Aunt Gladys, she's not as "Jewish"—in the ethnic sense, that is—just as her husband, a "self-made man" (that is, one who made lots of money during the Second World War), is economically but not socially middle class.

Class differences and their social and psychological nuances are an important element in the love story itself. Though Neil is first attracted to Brenda sexually (by her snapping her bathing-suit back into place), her relative gentility and sensibility, the absence of vulgarity in any obvious sense, are also a major part of her attraction for him. It is his half-conscious sense that this is true that generates his jokes, or what Brenda somewhat justifiably calls his "nastiness," about such things as her ostentatiously wealthy bourgeois surroundings, her and her friends' swanky schools, her "nose-job." He is also inordinately sensitive to real or imagined references to his lower social and economic status. We applaud his puncturing pretentiousness, but he is sometimes guilty of what has been called "working-class snobbery," and his own awareness and sense of guilt that his is a love-hate relationship to higher social status gives his humor an aftertaste of bitterness that more or less justifies Brenda's criticism.

Lovers separated by or in conflict with social stratification are not rare in love stories. In *Goodbye, Columbus*, however, the social theme is so pervasive we may question whether this is a love story in which social distinctions play an important part, or whether it is a story of ethnic social movement into the American "mainstream" embodied in a love story. The "Americanization" of the sons and daughters, grandsons and granddaughters of Jewish immigrants is not treated here through intermarriage or "mixing." All the major characters are Jewish, both lovers are Jewish, and even Ronald's Harriet from Milwaukee is Jewish. This could, then, just be the anatomy or portrait of eastern Jewish society soon after World War II. But that is a society on the move, and the move is into Establishment schools like Radcliffe and Smith, and into "gentile" living areas—Aunt Gladys wants to know if Jews live in Short Hills: they didn't used to.

Roth, like James, uses geography to suggest different ways of life as well as mere setting. Newark and Short Hills function here much as Geneva and Vevey in *Daisy Miller*, and Columbus, Ohio, we might say, is the "Rome" in this novel. This is not to suggest that they "stand for" the same things: Roth's counters are more economic and social than moral. Newark is lower or lower middle class, just a step above the old Jewish ghetto where Neil's grandparents lived; Short Hills is upper middle class Jewish suburban; Columbus is America. (If there are those who think there's nothing much west of the Hudson until you get to California, there are others who believe that America only begins west of the Appalachians.) Though the novel never leaves the East Coast and Ron is not one of the major characters, the title comes from a record of Ron's bidding farewell to Ohio State University (where he played varsity basketball) in Columbus, Ohio. Why should that extraneous detail serve as the title of this novel?

The last scene of the novel *is* a farewell, but not in Columbus: it takes place in the Harvard Yard in Cambridge, Massachusetts, and the farewell is not to Columbus or Cambridge, but to Brenda and Neil's love for her. The novel begins and ends with the love story, and so clearly *is* the love story, isn't it? Why, then, *Goodbye, Columbus*? Is it a Rothian joke? Is the love affair being judged as mawkishly sentimental like Ron's record? Perhaps, but Neil, though he no longer loves Brenda, affirms in the last scene that what he felt that summer *was* love. It was love, and lust, and both had been generated in him by something in Brenda, but also something in her that spoke to something he cannot identify in himself. And it seems to be a flaw of some sort that doomed as well as generated the love and lust:

> Whatever spawned my love for her, had that spawned such lust too? If she had only been slightly *not* Brenda . . . but then would I have loved her?

What does Neil—what do we?—want to be different in Brenda? Her faults all seem associated with her bourgeois surrounding, her being spoiled by her father, her irresponsibility and lack of commitment. But, then, would he have loved her if she had not been so surrounded, so spoiled, so irresponsible, and therefore not Brenda?

The story is not quite at an end. Neil looks through the Lamont Library window, "to a broken wall of books, imperfectly shelved." Though he is only three years out of college where he majored in philosophy, and a year out of the army, he is—only for a time, he has been insisting—a librarian. He is on his way back to the library in Newark, and the last word of the novel is "work."

Is the farewell only to Brenda, then, and is the ending only the ending of the love story? Hasn't Neil been almost as irresponsible as Brenda? If he is not a librarian, what is he? To what has he made a commitment? Wasn't his love at least in part the love of the bourgeois life? Perhaps the social theme is broader than eastern American Jewish society in the 1950s. Perhaps even the town named after the wealth-seeking discoverer of our country, and that country and its postwar materialist culture are also being bid farewell. Work is certainly not un-American; even working in a library may not be wholly un-American, but Neil does seem at the end to be saying goodbye to the scramble for wealth and status. He's even going back to Newark!

Novels that are both love stories and stories about America or the American Way of Life are not uncommon, as readers of *Daisy Miller*, *The Great Gatsby*, *An American Tragedy* well know. Reading *Goodbye, Columbus* as such a novel helps explain not only the somewhat puzzling title but also the apparently extraneous story of the black boy and the art books that threads through the novel. The boy is not only divorced from the love story but also from the whole Short Hills section of the novel, except at one point of intersection: when Neil visits Mr. Patimkin's sink business in the black ghetto, he wonders whether he will see the boy. That strand is, however, more tightly connected to the larger social theme: that section of Newark was, in Neil's grandfather's time, the Jewish ghetto, and the movement from there to Aunt Gladys's apartment in Newark, to Short Hills, and beyond, is the same journey Neil foresees American blacks will now be undertaking, and that, presumably, Americans have undertaken before the Jewish journey: at the very beginning, George Washington had trained his scraggly army on the site of the park in front of where the Newark library now stands. (There is also some suggestion that the climb is not necessarily aided by those who have recently made the same effort: remember the rather derogatory reference of one of the women at the country club to having bought her straw hat in Barbados from "the cutest little *shvartze*"?)

The other librarians' racism, their suspicion that the boy will do something nasty or destructive in the art section, and Neil's passive resistance to their racism, his protection of the black boy's right to look at Gauguin prints, and even his "affirmative action" on the boy's behalf by not letting the book be withdrawn from the library, establish Neil as a "good guy" and his conduct as something of a norm or yardstick for measuring social, or rather human, relations. To show a first-person narrator to be good, more moral and sensitive than the other characters, poses difficulties for an author. We accept Dickens's Pip in *Great Expectations* not only because he's small and put-upon, but because as he grows up he becomes an ungrateful snob and has to learn his lesson; we accept David Copperfield more readily when we recognize that his innocence is a fault once he grows up. If we read *Goodbye, Columbus* believing that Neil is telling us that he is the intelligent, sensitive, human, faultless hero, doesn't he seem a bit of a prig (like Winterbourne), or a bit too self-righteous? Do we feel his smugness about not being a racist (or bourgeois, or a fat or unvirile librarian, or old, or ugly) off-putting, or do we so identify with him that it makes us feel good all over to think how good we are, just like Neil-baby? Is it okay to be nasty if you're funny? Do we ever believe Neil truly loves Brenda? When does he fall in love with her? when she flicks her bathing suit? when he's lying by the pool at night and fears she will not come back to him?

Henry, in *The Fox*, seems to set out to marry March to get the farm, and we never know exactly why or how he falls in love with her, but somehow, as he watches her bringing packages home with Banford, he, and we, realize he does, or at least that his life and hers are tied to each other, that he's committed. Is Neil "committed"? The diaphragm is to him a symbol that Brenda will commit herself; how does he? Do you think we could find him if we were to go to the Newark library?

We get no indication just who Neil is or what he will become. Now he can take only the first step, go back to work, be for a time at least the librarian; when he looks for himself in the mirroring window of Lamont Library, he sees not into the outer image of himself, but through himself to his "duty":

> I looked hard at the image of me, at that darkening of the glass, and then my gaze pushed through it, over the cool floor, to a broken wall of books, imperfectly shelved.

GABRIEL GARCÍA MÁRQUEZ

The Incredible and Sad Tale
of Innocent Eréndira and
Her Heartless Grandmother

Gabriel García Márquez was born on March 6, 1928, in Aracataca near the Caribbean coast of Colombia, and he was reared there by his maternal grandparents until he went to school near Bogotá at the age of eight. (His parents were alive and living in Riohacha, but they were too poor and had too many children apparently—eleven more after Gabriel—to be able to care for him themselves.) Aracataca is the basis for his Macondo where so much of his fiction is set, and the stories of his grandfather, a retired colonel, about war, and of his grandmother about ancestors and ghosts, as well as the realities of Colombian dictatorships, civil wars, and banana companies pervade that mythic world. "Surrealism comes from the reality of Latin America," García Márquez has said.

Though he studied law and journalism and worked for some time as a journalist, and during his "dry" period in the early 1960s as copywriter, editor, and screenwriter, he says he has been trying to tell stories ever since he can remember. He was, indeed, only nineteen when his first story was published. La hojarasca, a short novel (translated in 1972 as Leaf Storm), was written in 1948, or shortly thereafter, but was not published until 1955. Whether because he was published so early or because he had such difficulty with Leaf Storm, García Márquez is rather careless about publishing; El Colonel no tiene quien le escriba (translated as No One Writes to the Colonel, 1968), a short novel, appeared in a magazine in Colombia in 1958, as a book in Bogotá in 1961, in a mutilated version in Madrid in 1962, and finally in an authorized version in Mexico City in 1966. His most famous work, a novel that has had such extravagant, world-wide praise that to call it a masterpiece might seem understatement, is Cien años de soledad (1967; translated as One Hundred Years of Solitude in 1970), a surreal century-long saga of the Buendias family of Macondo, which has been read as everything from a history of Latin America to a history of the human race, readings not fully undercut by the author's insistence that he is merely a storyteller: "The writer is not here to make declarations but to tell about things," he has said. Another novel, El otono del patriarca, appeared in 1975 and was almost immediately translated into English as The Autumn of the Patriarch (1976); a novel of 1962, La mala hora was finally translated in 1979 (In Evil Hour), and the 1981 novel Crónica de una muerte anunciada was translated in 1982 (Chronicle of a Death Foretold). In 1982, García Márquez was awarded the Nobel Prize for literature.

La increible y triste historia de la candida Eréndira y de su abuela desalmada (1972, translated as The Incredible and Sad Tale of Innocent Eréndira and Her Heartless Grandmother in 1973, and first published in book form in English in 1978) was the first work García Márquez published after Solitude and, indeed, a brief version of the story appears in that novel. Eréndira is in his mature style, not so flamboyant as Leaf Storm nor so terse as the style of the stories of the 1950s but rich and ranging, with a wealth of natural detail in strange juxtapositions and interpenetrated by the supernatural or surreal.

The Incredible and Sad Tale
of Innocent Eréndira and
Her Heartless Grandmother[*]

ERÉNDIRA[1] WAS BATHING her grandmother when the wind of her misfortune began to blow. The enormous mansion of moonlike concrete lost in the solitude of the desert trembled down to its foundations with the first attack. But Eréndira and her grandmother were used to the risks of the wild nature there, and in the bathroom decorated with a series of peacocks and childish mosaics of Roman baths they scarcely paid any attention to the caliber of the wind.

The grandmother, naked and huge in the marble tub, looked like a handsome white whale. The granddaughter had just turned fourteen and was languid, soft-boned, and too meek for her age. With a parsimony that had something like sacred rigor about it, she was bathing her grandmother with water in which purifying herbs and aromatic leaves had been boiled, the latter clinging to the succulent back, the flowing metal-colored hair, and the powerful shoulders which were so mercilessly tattooed as to put sailors to shame.

"Last night I dreamt I was expecting a letter," the grandmother said.

Eréndira, who never spoke except when it was unavoidable, asked:

"What day was it in the dream?"

"Thursday."

"Then it was a letter with bad news," Eréndira said, "but it will never arrive."

When she had finished bathing her grandmother, she took her to her bedroom. The grandmother was so fat that she could only walk by leaning on her granddaughter's shoulder or on a staff that looked like a bishop's crosier, but even during her most difficult efforts the power of an antiquated grandeur was evident. In the bedroom, which had been furnished with an excessive and somewhat demented taste, like the whole house, Eréndira needed two more hours to get her grandmother ready. She untangled her hair strand by strand, perfumed and combed it, put an equatorially flowered dress on her, put talcum powder on her face, bright red lipstick on her mouth, rouge on her cheeks, musk on her eyelids, and mother-of-pearl polish on her nails, and when she had her decked out like a larger than life-size doll, she led her to an artificial garden with suffocating flowers that were like the ones on the dress, seated her in a large chair that had the foundation and the pedigree of a throne, and left her listening to elusive records on a phonograph that had a speaker like a megaphone.

While the grandmother floated through the swamps of the past, Eréndira busied herself sweeping the house, which was dark and motley, with bizarre furniture and statues of invented Caesars, chandeliers of teardrops and alabaster angels, a gilded piano, and numerous clocks of unthinkable

---

[*] Translated by Gregory Rabassa.
1. The name suggests the Spanish verb *rendir*, meaning "to surrender."

sizes and shapes. There was a cistern in the courtyard for the storage of
water carried over many years from distant springs on the backs of Indians, and hitched to a ring on the cistern wall was a broken-down ostrich,
the only feathered creature who could survive the torment of that accursed climate. The house was far away from everything, in the heart of
the desert, next to a settlement with miserable and burning streets where
the goats committed suicide from desolation when the wind of misfortune
blew.

That incomprehensible refuge had been built by the grandmother's husband, a legendary smuggler whose name was Amadís,[2] by whom she had a
son whose name was also Amadís and who was Eréndira's father. No one
knew either the origins or the motivations of that family. The best known
version in the language of the Indians was that Amadís the father had
rescued his beautiful wife from a house of prostitution in the Antilles,
where he had killed a man in a knife fight, and that he had transplanted
her forever in the impunity of the desert. When the Amadíses died, one
of melancholy fevers and the other riddled with bullets in a fight over a
woman, the grandmother buried their bodies in the courtyard, sent away
the fourteen barefoot servant girls, and continued ruminating on her
dreams of grandeur in the shadows of the furtive house, thanks to the
sacrifices of the bastard granddaughter whom she had reared since birth.

Eréndira needed six hours just to set and wind the clocks. The day
when her misfortune began she didn't have to do that because the clocks
had enough winding left to last until the next morning, but on the other
hand, she had to bathe and overdress her grandmother, scrub the floors,
cook lunch, and polish the crystalware. Around eleven o'clock, when she
was changing the water in the ostrich's bowl and watering the desert
weeds around the twin graves of the Amadíses, she had to fight off the
anger of the wind, which had become unbearable, but she didn't have the
slightest feeling that it was the wind of her misfortune. At twelve o'clock
she was wiping the last champagne glasses when she caught the smell of
broth and had to perform the miracle of running to the kitchen without
leaving a disaster of Venetian glass in her wake.

She just managed to take the pot off the stove as it was beginning to
boil over. Then she put on a stew she had already prepared and took
advantage of a chance to sit down and rest on a stool in the kitchen. She
closed her eyes, opened them again with an unfatigued expression, and
began pouring the soup into the tureen. She was working as she slept.

The grandmother had sat down alone at the head of a banquet table
with silver candlesticks set for twelve people. She shook her little bell
and Eréndira arrived almost immediately with the steaming tureen. As
Eréndira was serving the soup, her grandmother noticed the somnambulist look and passed her hand in front of her eyes as if wiping an invisible
pane of glass. The girl didn't see the hand. The grandmother followed her
with her look and when Eréndira turned to go back to the kitchen, she
shouted at her:

"Eréndira!"

Having been awakened all of a sudden, the girl dropped the tureen
onto the rug.

2. Echoing *Amadís de Gaula,* a thirteenth- or four-
teenth-century Spanish or Portuguese chivalric prose
romance and model for its code of honor and knightly
perfection.

"That's all right, child," the grandmother said to her with assuring tenderness. "You fell asleep while you were walking about again."

"My body has that habit," Eréndira said by way of an excuse.

Still hazy with sleep, she picked up the tureen, and tried to clean the stain on the rug.

"Leave it," he grandmother dissuaded her. "You can wash it this afternoon."

So in addition to her regular afternoon chores, Eréndira had to wash the dining room rug, and she took advantage of her presence at the washtub to do Monday's laundry as well, while the wind went around the house looking for a way in. She had so much to do that night came upon her without her realizing it, and when she put the dining room rug back in its place it was time to go to bed.

The grandmother had been fooling around on the piano all afternoon, singing the songs of her times to herself in a falsetto, and she had stains of musk and tears on her eyelids. But when she lay down on her bed in her muslin nightgown, the bitterness of fond memories returned.

"Take advantage of tomorrow to wash the living room rug too," she told Eréndira. "It hasn't seen the sun since the days of all the noise."

"Yes, Grandmother," the girl answered.

She picked up a feather fan and began to fan the implacable matron, who recited the list of nighttime orders to her as she sank into sleep.

"Iron all the clothes before you go to bed so you can sleep with a clear conscience."

"Yes, Grandmother."

"Check the clothes closets carefully, because moths get hungrier on windy nights."

"Yes, Grandmother."

"With the time you have left, take the flowers out into the courtyard so they can get a breath of air."

"Yes, Grandmother."

"And feed the ostrich."

She had fallen asleep but she was still giving orders, for it was from her that the granddaughter had inherited the ability to be alive while sleeping. Eréndira left the room without making any noise and did the final chores of the night, still replying to the sleeping grandmother's orders.

"Give the graves some water."

"Yes, Grandmother."

"And if the Amadíses arrive, tell them not to come in," the grandmother said, "because Porfirio Galán's gang is waiting to kill them."

Eréndira didn't answer her any more because she knew that the grandmother was getting lost in her delirium, but she didn't miss a single order. When she finished checking the window bolts and put out the last lights, she took a candlestick from the dining room and lighted her way to her bedroom as the pauses in the wind were filled with the peaceful and enormous breathing of her sleeping grandmother.

Her room was also luxurious, but not so much as her grandmother's, and it was piled high with the rag dolls and wind-up animals of her recent childhood. Overcome by the barbarous chores of the day, Eréndira didn't have the strength to get undressed and she put the candlestick on the night table and fell onto the bed. A short while later the wind of her misfortune came into the bedroom like a pack of hounds and knocked the candle over against the curtain.

At dawn, when the wind finally stopped, a few thick and scattered drops of rain began to fall, putting out the last embers and hardening the smoking ashes of the mansion. The people in the village, Indians for the most part, tried to rescue the remains of the disaster: the charred corpse of the ostrich, the frame of the gilded piano, the torso of a statue. The grandmother was contemplating the residue of her fortune with an impenetrable depression. Eréndira, sitting between the two graves of the Amadíses, had stopped weeping. When the grandmother was convinced that very few things remained intact among the ruins, she looked at her granddaughter with sincere pity.

"My poor child," she sighed. "Life won't be long enough for you to pay me back for this mishap."

She began to pay it back that very day, beneath the noise of the rain, when she was taken to the village storekeeper, a skinny and premature widower who was quite well known in the desert for the good price he paid for virginity. As the grandmother waited undauntedly, the widower examined Eréndira with scientific austerity: he considered the strength of her thighs, the size of her breasts, the diameter of her hips. He didn't say a word until he had some calculation of what she was worth.

"She's still quite immature," he said then. "She has the teats of a bitch."

Then he had her get on a scale to prove his decision with figures. Eréndira weighed ninety pounds.

"She isn't worth more than a hundred pesos," the widower said.

The grandmother was scandalized.

"A hundred pesos for a girl who's completely new!" she almost shouted. "No, sir, that shows a great lack of respect for virtue on your part."

"I'll make it a hundred and fifty," the widower said.

"This girls caused me damages amounting to more than a million pesos," the grandmother said. "At this rate she'll need two hundred years to pay me back."

"You're lucky that the only good feature she has is her age," the widower said.

The storm threatened to knock the house down, and there were so many leaks in the roof that it was raining almost as much inside as out. The grandmother felt all alone in a world of disaster.

"Just raise it to three hundred," she said.

"Two hundred and fifty."

Finally they agreed on two hundred and twenty pesos in cash and some provisions. The grandmother then signaled Eréndira to go with the widower and he led her by the hand to the back room as if he were taking her to school.

"I'll wait for you here," the grandmother said.

"Yes, Grandmother," said Eréndira.

The back room was a kind of shed with four brick columns, a roof of rotted palm leaves, and an adobe wall three feet high, through which outdoor disturbances got into the building. Placed on top of the adobe wall were pots with cacti and other plants of aridity. Hanging between two columns and flapping like the free sail of a drifting sloop was a faded hammock. Over the whistle of the storm and the lash of the water one could hear distant shouts, the howling of far-off animals, the cries of a shipwreck.

When Eréndira and the widower went into the shed they had to hold on so as not to be knocked down by a gust of rain which left them soaked. Their voices could not be heard but their movements became clear in the roar of the squall. At the widower's first attempt, Eréndira shouted something inaudible and tried to get away. The widower answered her without any voice, twisted her arm by the wrist, and dragged her to the hammock. She fought him off with a scratch on the face and shouted in silence again, but he replied with a solemn slap which lifted her off the ground and suspended her in the air for an instant with her long Medusa hair[3] floating in space. He grabbed her about the waist before she touched ground again, flung her into the hammock with a brutal heave, and held her down with his knees. Eréndira then succumbed to terror, lost consciousness, and remained as if fascinated by the moonbeams from a fish that was floating through the storm air, while the widower undressed her, tearing off her clothes with a methodical clawing, as if he were pulling up grass, scattering them with great tugs of color that waved like streamers and went off with the wind.

When there was no other man left in the village who could pay anything for Eréndira's love, her grandmother put her on a truck to go where the smugglers were. They made the trip on the back of the truck in the open, among sacks of rice and buckets of lard and what had been left by the fire: the headboard of the viceregal bed, a warrior angel, the scorched throne, and other pieces of useless junk. In a trunk with two crosses painted in broad strokes they carried the bones of the Amadíses.

The grandmother protected herself from the sun with a tattered umbrella and it was hard for her to breathe because of the torment of sweat and dust, but even in that unhappy state she kept control of her dignity. Behind the pile of cans and sacks of rice Eréndira paid for the trip and the cartage by making love for twenty pesos a turn with the truck's loader. At first her system of defense was the same as she had used against the widower's attack, but the loader's approach was different, slow and wise, and he ended up taming her with tenderness. So when they reached the first town after a deadly journey, Eréndira and the loader were relaxing from good love behind the parapet of cargo. The driver shouted to the grandmother:

"Here's where the world begins."

The grandmother observed with disbelief the miserable and solitary streets of a town somewhat larger but just as sad as the one they had abandoned.

"It doesn't look like it to me," she said.

"It's mission country," the driver said.

"I'm not interested in charity, I'm interested in smugglers," said the grandmother.

Listening to the dialogue from behind the load, Eréndira dug into a sack of rice with her finger. Suddenly she found a string, pulled on it, and drew out a necklace of genuine pearls. She looked at it amazed, holding it

---

3. In Greek mythology, Medusa had snakes for hair.

between her fingers like a dead snake, while the driver answered her grandmother:

"Don't be daydreaming, ma'am. There's no such thing as smugglers."

"Of course not," the grandmother said. "I've got your word for it."

"Try to find one and you'll see," the driver bantered. "Everybody talks about them, but no one's ever seen one."

The loader realized that Eréndira had pulled out the necklace and hastened to take it away from her and stick it back into the sack of rice. The grandmother, who had decided to stay in spite of the poverty of the town, then called to her granddaughter to help her out of the truck. Eréndira said good-bye to the loader with a kiss that was hurried but spontaneous and true.

The grandmother waited, sitting on her throne in the middle of the street, until they finished unloading the goods. The last item was the trunk with the remains of the Amadíses.

"This thing weighs almost as much as a dead man," said the driver, laughing.

"There are two of them," the grandmother said, "so treat them with the proper respect."

"I bet they're marble statues." The driver laughed again.

He put the trunk with bones down carelessly among the singed furniture and held out his open hand to the grandmother.

"Fifty pesos," he said.

"Your slave has already paid on the right-hand side."

The driver looked at his helper with surprise and the latter made an affirmative sign. The driver then went back to the cab, where a woman in mourning was riding, in her arms a baby who was crying from the heat. The loader, quite sure of himself, told the grandmother:

"Eréndira is coming with me, if it's all right by you. My intentions are honorable."

The girl intervened, surprised:

"I didn't say anything!"

"The idea was all mine," the loader said.

The grandmother looked him up and down, not to make him feel small but trying to measure the true size of his guts.

"It's all right by me," she told him, "provided you pay me what I lost because of her carelessness. It's eight hundred seventy-two thousand three hundred fifteen pesos, less the four hundred and twenty she's already paid me, making it eight hundred seventy-one thousand eight hundred ninety-five."

The truck started up.

"Believe me, I'd give you that pile of money if I had it," the loader said seriously. "The girl is worth it."

The grandmother was pleased with the boy's decision.

"Well, then, come back when you have it, son," she answered in a sympathetic tone. "But you'd better go now, because if we figure out accounts again you'll end up owing me ten pesos."

The loader jumped onto the back of the truck and it went off. From there he waved good-bye to Eréndira, but she was still so surprised that she didn't answer him.

In the same vacant lot where the truck had left them, Eréndira and her grandmother improvised a shelter to live in from sheets of zinc and the remains of Oriental rugs. They laid two mats on the ground and slept as well as they had in the mansion until the sun opened holes in the ceiling and burned their faces.

Just the opposite of what normally happened, it was the grandmother who busied herself that morning fixing up Eréndira. She made up her face in the style of sepulchral beauty that had been the vogue in her youth and touched her up with artificial fingernails and an organdy bow that looked like a butterfly on her head.

"You look awful," she admitted, "but it's better that way: men are quite stupid when it comes to female matters."

Long before they saw them they both recognized the sound of two mules walking on the flint of the desert. At a command from her grandmother, Eréndira lay down on the mat the way an amateur actress might have done at the moment when the curtain was about to go up. Leaning on her bishop's crosier, the grandmother went out of the shelter and sat down on the throne to wait for the mules to pass.

The mailman was coming. He was only twenty years old, but his work had aged him, and he was wearing a khaki uniform, leggings, a pith helmet, and had a military pistol on his cartridge belt. He was riding a good mule and leading by the halter another, more timeworn one, on whom the canvas mailbags were piled.

As he passed by the grandmother he saluted her and kept on going, but she signaled him to look inside the shelter. The man stopped and saw Eréndira lying on the mat in her posthumous make-up and wearing a purple-trimmed dress.

"Do you like it?" the grandmother asked.

The mailman hadn't understood until then what the proposition was.

"It doesn't look bad to someone who's been on a diet," he said, smiling.

"Fifty pesos," the grandmother said.

"Boy, you're asking a mint!" he said. "I can eat for a whole month on that."

"Don't be a tightwad," the grandmother said. "The airmail pays even better than being a priest."

"I'm the domestic mail," the man said. "The airmail man travels in a pickup truck."

"In any case, love is just as important as eating," the grandmother said.

"But it doesn't feed you."

The grandmother realized that a man who lived from what other people were waiting for had more than enough time for bargaining.

"How much have you got?" she asked him.

The mailman dismounted, took some chewed-up bills from his pocket, and showed them to the grandmother. She snatched them up all together with a rapid hand just as if they had been a ball.

"I'll lower the price for you," she said, "but on one condition: that you spread the word all around."

"All the way to the other side of the world," the mailman said. "That's what I'm for."

Eréndira, who had been unable to blink, then took off her artificial eyelashes and moved to one side of the mat to make room for the chance boyfriend. As soon as he was in the shelter, the grandmother closed the entrance with an energetic tug on the sliding curtain.

It was an effective deal. Taken by the words of the mailman, men came from very far away to become acquainted with the newness of Eréndira. Behind the men came gambling tables and food stands, and behind them all came a photographer on a bicycle, who, across from the encampment, set up a camera with a mourning sleeve on a tripod and a backdrop of a lake with listless swans.

The grandmother, fanning herself on her throne, seemed alien to her own bazaar. The only thing that interested her was keeping order in the line of customers who were waiting their turn and checking the exact amount of money they paid in advance to go in to Eréndira. At first she had been so strict that she refused a good customer because he was five pesos short. But with the passage of months she was assimilating the lessons of reality and she ended up letting people in who completed their payment with religious medals, family relics, wedding rings, and anything her bite could prove was bona-fide gold even if it didn't shine.

After a long stay in that first town, the grandmother had sufficient money to buy a donkey, and she went off into the desert in search of places more propitious for the payment of the debt. She traveled on a litter that had been improvised on top of the donkey and she was protected from the motionless sun by the half-spoked umbrella that Eréndira held over her head. Behind them walked four Indian bearers with the remnants of the encampment: the sleeping mats, the restored throne, the alabaster angel, and the trunks with the remains of the Amadíses. The photographer followed the caravan on his bicycle, but never catching up, as if he were going to a different festival.

Six months had passed since the fire when the grandmother was able to get a complete picture of the business.

"If things go on like this," she told Eréndira, "you will have paid me the debt inside of eight years, seven months, and eleven days."

She went back over her calculations with her eyes closed, fumbling with the seeds she was taking out of a cord pouch where she also kept the money, and she corrected herself:

"All that, of course, not counting the pay and board of the Indians and other minor expenses."

Eréndira, who was keeping in step with the donkey, bowed down by the heat and dust, did not reproach her grandmother for her figures, but she had to hold back her tears.

"I've got ground glass in my bones," she said.

"Try to sleep."

"Yes, Grandmother."

She closed her eyes, took in a deep breath of scorching air, and went on walking in her sleep.

A small truck loaded with cages appeared, frightening goats in the dust of the horizon, and the clamor of the birds was like a splash of cool water for the Sunday torpor of San Miguel del Desierto. At the wheel was a corpulent Dutch farmer, his skin splintered by the outdoors, and with a squirrel-colored mustache he had inherited from some great-grandfather. His son Ulises,[4] who was riding in the other seat, was a gilded adolescent with lonely maritime eyes and with the appearance of a furtive angel. The Dutchman noticed a tent in front of which all the soldiers of the

4. Ulysses. *San Miguel del Desierto:* Saint Michael of the Desert.

local garrison were awaiting their turn. They were sitting on the ground, drinking out of the same bottle, which passed from mouth to mouth, and they had almond branches on their heads as if camouflaged for combat. The Dutchman asked in his language:

"What the devil can they be selling there?"

"A woman," his son answered quite naturally. "Her name is Eréndira."

"How do you know?"

"Everybody in the desert knows," Ulises answered.

The Dutchman stopped at the small hotel in town and got out. Ulises stayed in the truck. With agile fingers he opened a briefcase that his father had left on the seat, took out a roll of bills, put several in his pocket, and left everything just the way it had been. That night, while his father was asleep, he climbed out the hotel window and went to stand in line in front of Eréndira's tent.

The festivities were at their height. The drunken recruits were dancing by themselves so as not to waste the free music, and the photographer was taking nighttime pictures with magnesium papers. As she watched over her business, the grandmother counted the bank notes in her lap, dividing them into equal piles and arranging them in a basket. There were only twelve soldiers at that time, but the evening line had grown with civilian customers. Ulises was the last one.

It was the turn of a soldier with a woeful appearance. The grandmother not only blocked his way but avoided contact with his money.

"No, son," she told him. "You couldn't go in for all the gold in the world. You bring bad luck."

The soldier, who wasn't from those parts, was puzzled.

"What do you mean?"

"You bring down the evil shadows," the grandmother said. "A person only has to look at your face."

She waved him off with her hand, but without touching him, and made way for the next soldier.

"Go right in, handsome," she told him good-naturedly, "but don't take too long, your country needs you."

The soldier went in but he came right out again because Eréndira wanted to talk to her grandmother. She hung the basket of money on her arm and went into the tent, which wasn't very roomy, but which was neat and clean. In the back, on an army cot, Eréndira was unable to repress the trembling in her body, and she was in sorry shape, all dirty with soldier sweat.

"Grandmother," she sobbed, "I'm dying."

The grandmother felt her forehead and when she saw she had no fever, she tried to console her.

"There are only ten soldiers left," she said.

Eréndira began to weep with the shrieks of a frightened animal. The grandmother realized then that she had gone beyond the limits of horror and, stroking her head, she helped her calm down.

"The trouble is that you're weak," she told her. "Come on, don't cry any more, take a bath in sage water to get your blood back into shape."

She left the tent when Eréndira was calmer and she gave the soldier waiting his money back. "That's all for today," she told him. "Come back tomorrow and I'll give you the first place in line." Then she shouted to those lined up:

"That's all, boys. Tomorrow morning at nine."

Soldiers and civilians broke ranks with shouts of protest. The grand-mother confronted them, in a good mood but brandishing the devastating crosier in earnest.

"You're an inconsiderate bunch of slobs!" she shouted. "What do you think the girl is made of, iron? I'd like to see you in her place. You perverts! You shitty bums!"

The men answered her with even cruder insults, but she ended up con-trolling the revolt and stood guard with her staff until they took away the snack tables and dismantled the gambling stands. She was about to go back into the tent when she saw Ulises, as large as life, all by himself in the dark and empty space where the line of men had been before. He had an unreal aura about him and he seemed to be visible in the shadows because of the very glow of his beauty.

"You," the grandmother asked him. "What happened to your wings?"

"The one who had wings was my grandfather,"[5] Ulises answered in his natural way, "but nobody believed it."

The grandmother examined him again with fascination. "Well, I do," she said. "Put them on and come back tomorrow." She went into the tent and left Ulises burning where he stood.

Eréndira felt better after her bath. She had put on a short, lace-trimmed slip and she was drying her hair before going to bed, but she was still making an effort to hold back her tears. Her grandmother was asleep.

Behind Eréndira's bed, very slowly, Ulises' head appeared. She saw the anxious and diaphanous eyes, but before saying anything she rubbed her head with the towel in order to prove that it wasn't an illusion. When Ulises blinked for the first time, Eréndira asked him in a very low voice:

"Who are you?"

Ulises showed himself down to his shoulders. "My name is Ulises," he said. He showed her the bills he had stolen and added:

"I've got money."

Eréndira put her hands on the bed, brought her face close to that of Ulises, and went on talking to him as if in a kindergarten game.

"You were supposed to get in line," she told him.

"I waited all night long," Ulises said.

"Well, now you have to wait until tomorrow," Eréndira said. "I feel as if someone had been beating me on the kidneys."

At that instant the grandmother began to talk in her sleep.

"It's going on twenty years since it rained last," she said. "It was such a terrible storm that the rain was all mixed in with sea water, and the next morning the house was full of fish and snails and your grandfather Amadís, may he rest in peace, saw a glowing manta ray floating through the air."

Ulises hid behind the bed again. Eréndira showed an amused smile.

"Take it easy," she told him. "She always acts kind of crazy when she's asleep, but not even an earthquake can wake her up."

Ulises reappeared. Eréndira looked at him with a smile that was naughty and even a little affectionate and took the soiled sheet off the mattress.

"Come," she said. "Help me change the sheet."

5. See García Márquez's story "A Very Old Man with Enormous Wings" for a possible reference. Márquez often refers to other works from his fictional world of Macondo.

Then Ulises came from behind the bed and took one end of the sheet. Since the sheet was much larger than the mattress, they had to fold it several times. With every fold Ulises drew closer to Eréndira. "I was going crazy wanting to see you," he suddenly said. "Everybody says you're very pretty and they're right."

"But I'm going to die," Eréndira said.

"My mother says that people who die in the desert don't go to heaven but to the sea," Ulises said.

Eréndira put the dirty sheet aside and covered the mattress with another, which was clean and ironed.

"I never saw the sea," she said.

"It's like the desert but with water," said Ulises.

"Then you can't walk on it."

"My father knew a man who could," Ulises said, "but that was a long time ago."

Eréndira was fascinated but she wanted to sleep.

"If you come very early tomorrow you can be first in line," she said.

"I'm leaving with my father at dawn," said Ulises.

"Won't you be coming back this way?"

"Who can tell?" Ulises said. "We just happened along now because we got lost on the road to the border."

Eréndira looked thoughtfully at her sleeping grandmother.

"All right," she decided. "Give me the money."

Ulises gave it to her. Eréndira lay down on the bed but he remained trembling where he was: at the decisive moment his determination had weakened. Eréndira took him by the hand to hurry him up and only then did she notice his tribulation. She was familiar with that fear.

"Is it the first time?" she asked him.

Ulises didn't answer but he smiled in desolation. Eréndira became a different person.

"Breathe slowly," she told him. "That's the way it always is the first time. Afterwards you won't even notice."

She laid him down beside her and while she was taking his clothes off she was calming him maternally.

"What's your name?"

"Ulises."

"That's a gringo name," Eréndira said.

"No, a sailor name."

Eréndira uncovered his chest, gave a few little orphan kisses, sniffed him.

"It's like you were made of gold all over," she said, "but you smell of flowers."

"It must be the oranges," Ulises said.

Calmer now, he gave a smile of complicity.

"We carry a lot of birds along to throw people off the track," he added, "but what we're doing is smuggling a load of oranges across the border."

"Oranges aren't contraband," Eréndira said.

"These are," said Ulises. "Each one is worth fifty thousand pesos."

Eréndira laughed for the first time in a long while.

"What I like about you," she said, "is the serious way you make up nonsense."

She had become spontaneous and talkative again, as if Ulises' innocence had changed not only her mood but her character. The grand-mother, such a short distance away from misfortune, was still talking in her sleep.

"Around those times, at the beginning of March, they brought you home," she said. "You looked like a lizard wrapped in cotton. Amadís, your father, who was young and handsome, was so happy that afternoon that he sent for twenty carts loaded with flowers and arrived strewing them along the street until the whole village was gold with flowers like the sea."

She ranted on with great shouts and with a stubborn passion for several hours. But Ulises couldn't hear her because Eréndira had loved him so much and so truthfully that she loved him again for half price while her grandmother was raving and kept on loving him for nothing until dawn.

A group of missionaries holding up their crucifixes stood shoulder to shoulder in the middle of the desert. A wind as fierce as the wind of misfortune shook their burlap habits and their rough beards and they were barely able to stand on their feet. Behind them was the mission, a colonial pile of stone with a tiny belfry on top of the harsh whitewashed walls.

The youngest missionary, who was in charge of the group, pointed to a natural crack in the glazed clay ground.

"You shall not pass beyond this line!" he shouted.

The four Indian bearers carrying the grandmother in a litter made of boards stopped when they heard the shout. Even though she was uncomfortable sitting on the planks of the litter and her spirit was dulled by the dust and sweat of the desert, the grandmother maintained her haughtiness intact. Eréndira was on foot. Behind the litter came a file of eight Indians carrying the baggage and at the very end the photographer on his bicycle.

"The desert doesn't belong to anyone," the grandmother said.

"It belongs to God," the missionary said, "and you are violating his sacred laws with your filthy business."

The grandmother then recognized the missionary's peninsular[6] usage and diction and avoided a head-on confrontation so as not to break her head against his intransigence. She went back to being herself.

"I don't understand your mysteries, son."

The missionary pointed at Eréndira.

"That child is underage."

"But she's my granddaughter."

"So much the worse," the missionary replied. "Put her under our care willingly or we'll have to seek recourse in other ways."

The grandmother had not expected them to go so far.

"All right, if that's how it is." She surrendered in fear. "But sooner or later I'll pass, you'll see."

Three days after the encounter with the missionaries, the grandmother and Eréndira were sleeping in a village near the mission when a group of stealthy, mute bodies, creeping along like an infantry patrol, slipped into the tent. They were six Indian novices, strong and young, their rough cloth habits seeming to glow in the moonlight. Without making a sound

---

6. Colombia's Península de la Guajira.

they cloaked Eréndira in a mosquito netting, picked her up without waking her, and carried her off wrapped like a large, fragile fish caught in a lunar net.

There were no means left untried by the grandmother in an attempt to rescue her granddaughter from the protection of the missionaries. Only when they had all failed, from the most direct to the most devious, did she turn to the civil authority, which was vested in a military man. She found him in the courtyard of his home, his chest bare, shooting with an army rifle at a dark and solitary cloud in the burning sky. He was trying to perforate it to bring on rain, and his shots were furious and useless, but he did take the necessary time out to listen to the grandmother.

"I can't do anything," he explained to her when he had heard her out. "The priesties, according to the concordat, have the right to keep the girl until she comes of age. Or until she gets married."

"Then why do they have you here as mayor?" the grandmother asked.

"To make it rain," was the mayor's answer.

Then, seeing that the cloud had moved out of range, he interrupted his official duties and gave his full attention to the grandmother.

"What you need is someone with a lot of weight who will vouch for you," he told her. "Someone who can swear to your moral standing and your good behavior in a signed letter. Do you know Senator Onésimo Sánchez?"

Sitting under the naked sun on a stool that was too narrow for her astral buttocks, the grandmother answered with a solemn rage:

"I'm just a poor woman all alone in the vastness of the desert."

The mayor, his right eye twisted from the heat, looked at her with pity.

"Then don't waste your time, ma'am," he said. "You'll rot in hell."

She didn't rot, of course. She set up her tent across from the mission and sat down to think, like a solitary warrior besieging a fortified city. The wandering photographer, who knew her quite well, loaded his gear onto the carrier of his bicycle and was ready to leave all alone when he saw her in the full sun with her eyes fixed on the mission.

"Let's see who gets tired first," the grandmother said, "they or I."

"They've been here for three hundred years and they can still take it," the photographer said. "I'm leaving."

Only then did the grandmother notice the loaded bicycle.

"Where are you going?"

"Wherever the wind takes me," the photographer said, and he left. "It's a big world."

The grandmother sighed.

"Not as big as you think, you ingrate."

But she didn't move her head in spite of her anger so as not to lose sight of the mission. She didn't move it for many, many days of mineral heat, for many, many nights of wild winds, for all the time she was meditating and no one came out of the mission. The Indians built a lean-to of palm leaves beside the tent and hung their hammocks there, but the grandmother stood watch until very late, nodding on her throne and chewing the uncooked grain in her pouch with the invincible laziness of a resting ox.

One night a convoy of slow covered trucks passed very close to her and the only lights they carried were wreaths of colored bulbs which gave them the ghostly size of sleepwalking altars. The grandmother recognized them at once because they were just like the trucks of the Amadíses. The last truck in the convoy slowed, stopped, and a man got out of the cab to adjust something in back. He looked like a replica of the Amadíses, wearing a hat with a turned-up brim, high boots, two crossed cartridge belts across his chest, an army rifle, and two pistols. Overcome by an irresistible temptation, the grandmother called to the man.

"Don't you know who I am?" she asked him.

The man lighted her pitilessly with a flashlight. For an instant he studied the face worn out by vigil, the eyes dim from fatigue, the withered hair of the woman who, even at her age, in her sorry state, and with that crude light on her face, could have said that she had been the most beautiful woman in the world. When he examined her enough to be sure that he had never seen her before, he turned out the light.

"The only thing I know for sure is that you're not the Virgin of Perpetual Help."

"Quite the contrary," the grandmother said with a very sweet voice. "I'm the Lady."

The man put his hand to his pistol out of pure instinct.

"What lady?"

"Big Amadís's."

"Then you're not of this world," he said, tense. "What is it you want?"

"For you to help me rescue my granddaughter, Big Amadís's granddaughter, the daughter of our son Amadís, held captive in that mission."

The man overcame his fear.

"You knocked on the wrong door," he said. "If you think we're about to get mixed up in God's affairs, you're not the one you say you are, you never knew the Amadíses, and you haven't got the whoriest notion of what smuggling's all about."

Early that morning the grandmother slept less than before. She lay awake pondering things, wrapped in a wool blanket while the early hour got her memory all mixed up and the repressed raving struggled to get out even though she was awake, and she had to tighten her heart with her hand so as not to be suffocated by the memory of a house by the sea with great red flowers where she had been happy. She remained that way until the mission bell rang and the first lights went on in the windows and the desert became saturated with the smell of the hot bread of matins. Only then did she abandon her fatigue, tricked by the illusion that Eréndira had got up and was looking for a way to escape and come back to her.

Eréndira, however, had not lost a single night's sleep since they had taken her to the mission. They had cut her hair with pruning shears until her head was like a brush, they put a hermit's rough cassock on her and gave her a bucket of whitewash and a broom so that she could whitewash the stairs every time someone went up or down. It was mule work because there was an incessant coming and going of muddied missionaries and novice carriers, but Eréndira felt as if every day were Sunday after the fearsome galley that had been her bed. Besides, she wasn't the only one worn out at night, because the mission was dedicated to fighting not against the devil but against the desert. Eréndira had seen the Indian novices bulldogging cows in the barn in order to milk them, jumping up and down on planks for days on end in order to press cheese, helping a

goat through a difficult birth. She had seen them sweat like tanned steve-
dores hauling water from the cistern, watering by hand a bold garden that
other novices cultivated with hoes in order to plant vegetables in the
flintstone of the desert. She had seen the earthly inferno of the ovens for
baking bread and the rooms for ironing clothes. She had seen a nun chase
a pig through the courtyard, slide along holding the runaway animal by
the ears, and roll in a mud puddle without letting go until two novices in
leather aprons helped her get it under control and one of them cut its
throat with a butcher knife as they all became covered with blood and
mire. In the isolation ward of the infirmary she had seen tubercular nuns
in their nightgown shrouds, waiting for God's last command as they embroidered bridal sheets on the terraces while the men preached in the
desert. Eréndira was living in her shadows and discovering other forms of
beauty and horror that she had never imagined in the narrow world of
her bed, but neither the coarsest nor the most persuasive of the novices
had managed to get her to say a word since they had taken her to the
mission. One morning, while she was preparing the whitewash in her
bucket, she heard string music that was like a light even more diaphanous
than the light of the desert. Captivated by the miracle, she peeped into
an immense and empty salon with bare walls and large windows through
which the dazzling June light poured in and remained still, and in the
center of the room she saw a very beautiful nun whom she had never seen
before playing an Easter oratorio on the clavichord. Eréndira listened to
the music without blinking, her heart hanging by a thread, until the
lunch bell rang. After eating, while she whitewashed the stairs with her
reed brush, she waited until all the novices had finished going up and
coming down, and she was alone, with no one to hear her, and then she
spoke for the first time since she had entered the mission.

"I'm happy," she said.

So that put an end to the hopes the grandmother had that Eréndira
would run away to rejoin her, but she maintained her granite siege without having made any decision until Pentecost. During that time the missionaries were combing the desert in search of pregnant concubines in
order to get them married. They traveled all the way to the most remote
settlements in a broken-down truck with four well-armed soldiers and a
chest of cheap cloth. The most difficult part of that Indian hunt was to
convince the women, who defended themselves against divine grace with
the truthful argument that men, sleeping in their hammocks with legs
spread, felt they had the right to demand much heavier work from legitimate wives than from concubines. It was necessary to seduce them with
trickery, dissolving the will of God in the syrup of their own language so
that it would seem less harsh to them, but even the most crafty of them
ended up being convinced by a pair of flashy earrings. The men, on the
other hand, once the women's acceptance had been obtained, were
routed out of their hammocks with rifle butts, bound, and hauled away in
the back of the truck to be married by force.

For several days the grandmother saw the little truck loaded with pregnant Indian women heading for the mission, but she failed to recognize
her opportunity. She recognized it on Pentecost Sunday itself, when she
heard the rockets and the ringing of the bells and saw the miserable and
merry crowd that was going to the festival, and she saw that among the

crowds there were pregnant women with the veil and crown of a bride holding the arms of their casual mates, whom they would legitimize in the collective wedding.

Among the last in the procession a boy passed, innocent of heart, with gourd-cut Indian hair and dressed in rags, carrying an Easter candle with a silk bow in his hand. The grandmother called him over.

"Tell me something, son," she asked with her smoothest voice. "What part do you have in this affair?"

The boy felt intimidated by the candle and it was hard for him to close his mouth because of his donkey teeth.

"The priests are going to give me my first communion," he said.

"How much did they pay you?"

"Five pesos."

The grandmother took a roll of bills from her pouch and the boy looked at them with surprise.

"I'm going to give you twenty," the grandmother said. "Not for you to make your first communion, but for you to get married."

"Who to?"

"My granddaughter."

So Eréndira was married in the courtyard of the mission in her hermit's cassock and a silk shawl that the novices gave her, and without even knowing the name of the groom her grandmother had bought for her. With uncertain hope she withstood the torment of kneeling on the saltpeter ground, the goat-hair stink of the two hundred pregnant brides, the punishment of the Epistle of Saint Paul hammered out in Latin under the motionless and burning sun, because the missionaries had found no way to oppose the wile of that unforeseen marriage, but had given her a promise as a last attempt to keep her in the mission. Nevertheless, after the ceremony in the presence of the apostolic prefect, the military mayor who shot at the clouds, her recent husband, and her impassive grandmother, Eréndira found herself once more under the spell that had dominated her since birth. When they asked her what her free, true, and definitive will was, she didn't even give a sigh of hesitation.

"I want to leave," she said. And she clarified things by pointing at her husband. "But not with him, with my grandmother."

Ulises had wasted a whole afternoon trying to steal an orange from his father's grove, because the older man wouldn't take his eyes off him while they were pruning the sick trees, and his mother kept watch from the house. So he gave up his plan, for that day at least, and grudgingly helped his father until they had pruned the last orange trees.

The extensive grove was quiet and hidden, and the wooden house with a tin roof had copper grating over the windows and a large porch set on pilings, with primitive plants bearing intense flowers. Ulises' mother was on the porch sitting back in a Viennese rocking chair[7] with smoked leaves on her temples to relieve her headache, and her full-blooded-Indian look followed her son like a beam of invisible light to the most remote corners of the orange grove. She was quite beautiful, much younger than her husband, and not only did she still wear the garb of her tribe, but she knew the most ancient secrets of her blood.

---

7. One with back and seat made of tied straw.

When Ulises returned to the house with the pruning tools, his mother asked him for her four o'clock medicine, which was on a nearby table. As soon as he touched them, the glass and the bottle changed color. Then, out of pure play, he touched a glass pitcher that was on the table beside some tumblers and the pitcher also turned blue. His mother observed him while she was taking her medicine and when she was sure that it was not a delirium of her pain, she asked him in the Guajiro Indian language:

"How long has that been happening to you?"

"Ever since we came back from the desert," Ulises said, also in Guajiro. "It only happens with glass things."

In order to demonstrate, one after the other he touched the glasses that were on the table and they all turned different colors.

"Those things happen only because of love," his mother said. "Who is it?"

Ulises didn't answer. His father, who couldn't understand the Guajiro language, was passing by the porch at that moment with a cluster of oranges.

"What are you two talking about?" he asked Ulises in Dutch.

"Nothing special," Ulises answered.

Ulises' mother didn't know any Dutch. When her husband went into the house, she asked her son in Guajiro:

"What did he say?"

"Nothing special," Ulises answered.

He lost sight of his father when he went into the house, but he saw him again through a window of the office. The mother waited until she was alone with Ulises and then repeated:

"Tell me who it is."

"It's nobody," Ulises said.

He answered without paying attention because he was hanging on his father's movements in the office. He had seen him put the oranges on top of the safe when he worked out the combination. But while he was keeping an eye on his father, his mother was keeping an eye on him.

"You haven't eaten any bread for a long time," she observed.

"I don't like it."

The mother's face suddenly took on an unaccustomed liveliness. "That's a lie," she said. "It's because you're lovesick and people who are lovesick can't eat bread." Her voice, like her eyes, had passed from entreaty to threat.

"It would be better if you told me who it was," she said, "or I'll make you take some purifying baths."

In the office the Dutchman opened the safe, put the oranges inside, and closed the armoured door. Ulises moved away from the window then and answered his mother impatiently.

"I already told you there wasn't anyone," he said. "If you don't believe me, ask Papa."

The Dutchman appeared in the office doorway lighting his sailor's pipe and carrying his threadbare Bible under his arm. His wife asked him in Spanish:

"Who did you meet in the desert?"

"Nobody," her husband answered, a little in the clouds. "If you don't believe me, ask Ulises."

He sat down at the end of the hall and sucked on his pipe until the tobacco was used up. Then he opened the Bible at random and recited spot passages for almost two hours in flowing and ringing Dutch. At midnight Ulises was still thinking with such intensity that he couldn't sleep. He rolled about in his hammock for another hour, trying to overcome the pain of memories until the very pain gave him the strength he needed to make a decision. Then he put on his cowboy pants, his plaid shirt, and his riding boots, jumped through the window, and fled from the house in the truck loaded with birds. As he went through the groves he picked the three ripe oranges he had been unable to steal that afternoon.

He traveled across the desert for the rest of the night and at dawn he asked in towns and villages about the whereabouts of Eréndira, but no one could tell him. Finally they informed him that she was traveling in the electoral campaign retinue of Senator Onésimo Sánchez and that on that day he was probably in Nueva Castilla.[8] He didn't find him there but in the next town and Eréndira was no longer with him, for the grandmother had managed to get the senator to vouch for her morality in a letter written in his own hand, and with it she was going about opening the most tightly barred doors in the desert. On the third day he came across the domestic mailman and the latter told him what direction to follow.

"They're heading toward the sea," he said, "and you'd better hurry because the goddamned old woman plans to cross over to the island of Aruba."[9]

Following that direction, after half a day's journey Ulises spotted the broad, stained tent that the grandmother had bought from a bankrupt circus. The wandering photographer had come back to her, convinced that the world was really not as large as he had thought, and he had set up his idyllic backdrops near the tent. A band of brass-blowers was captivating Eréndira's clientele with a taciturn waltz.

Ulises waited for his turn to go in, and the first thing that caught his attention was the order and cleanliness of the inside of the tent. The grandmother's bed had recovered its viceregal splendor, the statue of the angel was in its place beside the funerary trunk of the Amadíses, and in addition, there was a pewter bathtub with lion's feet. Lying on her new canopied bed, Eréndira was naked and placid, irradiating a childlike glow under the light that filtered through the tent. She was sleeping with her eyes open. Ulises stopped beside her, the oranges in his hand, and he noticed that she was looking at him without seeing him. Then he passed his hand over her eyes and called her by the name he had invented when he wanted to think about her:

"Arídnere."[1]

Eréndira woke up. She felt naked in front of Ulises, let out a squeak, and covered herself with the sheet up to her neck.

"Don't look at me," she said. "I'm horrible."

"You're the color of an orange all over," Ulises said. He raised the fruits to her eyes so that she could compare. "Look."

---

8. New Castile (after the province in Spain).
9. Off the coast of Venezuela, and about eighty miles from the Península de la Guajira.

1. *Eréndira* backwards; the root of the name means "dryness, aridity."

Eréndira uncovered her eyes and saw that indeed the oranges did have her color.

"I don't want you to stay now," she said.

"I only came to show you this," Ulises said. "Look here."

He broke open an orange with his nails, split it in two with his hands, and showed Eréndira what was inside: stuck in the heart of the fruit was a genuine diamond.

"These are the oranges we take across the border," he said.

"But they're living oranges!" Eréndira exclaimed.

"Of course." Ulises smiled. "My father grows them."

Eréndira couldn't believe it. She uncovered her face, took the diamond in her fingers and contemplated it with surprise.

"With three like these we can take a trip around the world," Ulises said.

Eréndira gave him back the diamond with a look of disappointment. Ulises went on:

"Besides, I've got a pickup truck," he said. "And besides that . . . Look!"

From underneath his shirt he took an ancient pistol.

"I can't leave for ten years," Eréndira said.

"You'll leave," Ulises said. "Tonight, when the white whale falls asleep, I'll be outside there calling like an owl."

He made such a true imitation of the call of an owl that Eréndira's eyes smiled for the first time.

"It's my grandmother," she said.

"The owl?"

"The whale."

They both laughed at the mistake, but Eréndira picked up the thread again.

"No one can leave for anywhere without her grandmother's permission."

"There's no reason to say anything."

"She'll find out in any case," Eréndira said. "She can dream things."

"When she starts to dream that you're leaving we'll already be across the border. We'll cross over like smugglers," Ulises said.

Grasping the pistol with the confidence of a movie gunfighter, he imitated the sounds of the shots to excite Eréndira with his audacity. She didn't say yes or no, but her eyes gave a sigh and she sent Ulises away with a kiss. Ulises, touched, whispered:

"Tomorrow we'll be watching the ships go by."

That night, a little after seven o'clock, Eréndira was combing her grandmother's hair when the wind of her misfortune blew again. In the shelter of the tent were the Indian bearers and the leader of the brass band, waiting to be paid. The grandmother finished counting out the bills on a chest she had within reach, and after consulting a ledger she paid the oldest of the Indians.

"Here you are," she told him. "Twenty pesos for the week, less eight for meals, less three for water, less fifty cents on account for the new shirts, that's eight fifty. Count it."

The oldest Indian counted the money and they all withdrew with a bow.

"Thank you, white lady."

Next came the leader of the band. The grandmother consulted her ledger and turned to the photographer, who was trying to repair the bellows of his camera with wads of gutta-percha.

"What's it going to be?" she asked him. "Will you or won't you pay a quarter of the cost of the music?"

The photographer didn't even raise his head to answer.

"Music doesn't come out in pictures."

"But it makes people want to have their pictures taken," the grandmother answered.

"On the contrary," said the photographer. "It reminds them of the dead and then they come out in the picture with their eyes closed."

The bandleader intervened.

"What makes them close their eyes isn't the music," he said. "It's the lightning you make taking pictures at night."

"It's the music," the photographer insisted.

The grandmother put an end to the dispute. "Don't be a cheapskate," she said to the photographer. "Look how well things have been going for Senator Onésimo Sánchez and it's thanks to the musicians he has along." Then, in a harsh tone, she concluded:

"So pay what you ought to or go follow your fortune by yourself. It's not right for that poor child to carry the whole burden of expenses."

"I'll follow my fortune by myself," the photographer said. "After all, an artist is what I am."

The grandmother shrugged her shoulders and took care of the musician. She handed him a bundle of bills that matched the figure written in her ledger.

"Two hundred and fifty-four numbers," she told him. "At fifty cents apiece, plus thirty-two on Sundays and holidays at sixty cents apiece, that's one hundred fifty-six twenty."

The musician wouldn't accept the money.

"It's one hundred eighty-two forty," he said. "Waltzes cost more."

"Why is that?"

"Because they're sadder," the musician said.

The grandmother made him take the money.

"Well, this week you'll play us two happy numbers for each waltz I owe you for and we'll be even."

The musician didn't understand the grandmother's logic, but he accepted the figures while he unraveled the tangle. At that moment the fearsome wind threatened to uproot the tent, and in the silence that it left in its wake, outside, clear and gloomy, the call of an owl was heard.

Eréndira didn't know what to do to disguise her upset. She closed the chest with the money and hid it under the bed, but the grandmother recognized the fear in her hand when she gave her the key. "Don't be frightened," she told her. "There are always owls on windy nights." Still she didn't seem so convinced when she saw the photographer go out with the camera on his back.

"Wait till tomorrow if you'd like," she told him. "Death is on the loose tonight."

The photographer had also noticed the call of the owl, but he didn't change his intentions.

"Stay, son," the grandmother insisted. "Even if it's just because of the liking I have for you."

"But I won't pay for the music," the photographer said.

"Oh, no," the grandmother said. "Not that."

"You see?" the photographer said. "You've got no love for anybody." The grandmother grew pale with rage.

"Then beat it!" she said. "You lowlife!"

She felt so outraged that she was still venting her rage on him while Eréndira helped her go to bed. "Son of an evil mother," she muttered. "What does that bastard know about anyone else's heart?" Eréndira paid no attention to her, because the owl was calling her with tenacious insistence during the pauses in the wind and she was tormented by uncertainty. The grandmother finally went to bed with the same ritual that had been *de rigueur* in the ancient mansion, and while her granddaughter fanned her she overcame her anger and once more breathed her sterile breath.

"You have to get up early," she said then, "so you can boil the infusion for my bath before the people get here."

"Yes, Grandmother."

"With the time you have left, wash the Indians' dirty laundry and that way we'll have something else to take off their pay next week."

"Yes, Grandmother," Eréndira said.

"And sleep slowly so that you won't get tired, because tomorrow is Thursday, the longest day of the week."

"Yes, Grandmother."

"And feed the ostrich."

"Yes, Grandmother," Eréndira said.

She left the fan at the head of the bed and lighted two altar candles in front of the chest with their dead. The grandmother, asleep now, was lagging behind with her orders.

"Don't forget to light the candles for the Amadíses."

"Yes, Grandmother."

Eréndira knew then that she wouldn't wake up, because she had begun to rave. She heard the wind barking about the tent, but she didn't recognize it as the wind of her misfortune that time either. She looked out into the night until the owl called again and her instinct for freedom in the end prevailed over her grandmother's spell.

She hadn't taken five steps outside the tent when she came across the photographer, who was lashing his equipment to the carrier of his bicycle. His accomplice's smile calmed her down.

"I don't know anything," the photographer said, "I haven't seen anything, and I won't pay for the music."

He took his leave with a blessing for all. Then Eréndira ran toward the desert, having decided once and for all, and she was swallowed up in the shadows of the wind where the owl was calling.

That time the grandmother went to the civil authorities at once. The commandment of the local detachment leaped out of his hammock at six in the morning when she put the senator's letter before his eyes. Ulises' father was waiting at the door.

"How in hell do you expect me to know what it says!" the commandant shouted. "I can't read."

"It's a letter of recommendation from Senator Onésimo Sánchez," the grandmother said.

Without further questions, the commandant took down a rifle he had near his hammock and began to shout orders to his men. Five minutes later they were all in a military truck flying toward the border against a contrary wind that had erased all trace of the fugitives. The commandant rode in the front seat beside the driver. In back were the Dutchman and the grandmother, with an armed policeman on each running board.

Close to town they stopped a convoy of trucks covered with waterproof canvases. Several men who were riding concealed in the rear raised the canvas and aimed at the small vehicle with machine guns and army rifles. The commandant asked the driver of the first truck how far back they had passed a farm truck loaded with birds.

The driver started up before he answered.

"We're not stool pigeons," he said indignantly, "we're smugglers."

The commandant saw the sooty barrels of the machine guns pass close to his eyes and he raised his arms and smiled.

"At least," he shouted at them, "you could have the decency not to go around in broad daylight."

The last truck had a sign on its rear bumper: I THINK OF YOU, ERÉNDIRA.

The wind became drier as they headed north and the sun was fiercer than the wind. It was hard to breathe because of the heat and dust inside the closed-in truck.

The grandmother was the first to spot the photographer: he was pedaling along in the same direction in which they were flying, with no protection against the sun except for a handkerchief tied around his head.

"There he is." She pointed. "He was their accomplice, the lowlife."

The commandant ordered one of the policemen on the running board to take charge of the photographer.

"Grab him and wait for us here," he said. "We'll be right back."

The policeman jumped off the running board and shouted twice for the photographer to halt. The photographer didn't hear him because of the wind blowing in the opposite direction. When the truck went on, the grandmother made an enigmatic gesture to him, but he confused it with a greeting, smiled, and waved. He didn't hear the shot. He flipped into the air and fell dead on top of his bicycle, his head blown apart by a rifle bullet, and he never knew where it came from.

Before noon they began to see feathers. They were passing by in the wind and they were feathers from young birds. The Dutchman recognized them because they were from his birds, plucked out by the wind. The driver changed direction, pushed the gas pedal to the floor, and in half an hour they could make out the pickup truck on the horizon.

When Ulises saw the military vehicle appear in the rear-view mirror, he made an effort to increase the distance between them, but the motor couldn't do any better. They had traveled with no sleep and were done in from fatigue and thirst. Eréndira, who was dozing on Ulises' shoulder, woke up in fright. She saw the truck that was about to overtake them and with innocent determination she took the pistol from the glove compartment.

"It's no good," Ulises said. "It used to belong to Sir Francis Drake."

She pounded it several times and threw it out the window. The military patrol passed the broken-down truck loaded with birds plucked by the wind, turned sharply, and cut it off.

It was around that time that I came to know them, their moment of greatest splendor, but I wouldn't look into the details of their lives until many years later when Rafael Escalona, in a song, revealed the terrible ending of the drama and I thought it would be good to tell the tale. I was traveling about selling encyclopedias and medical books in the province of Riohacha.[2] Álvaro Cepeda Samudio, who was also traveling in the region, selling beer-cooling equipment, took me through the desert towns in his truck with the intention of talking to me about something and we talked so much about nothing and drank so much beer that without knowing when or where we crossed the entire desert and reached the border. There was the tent of wandering love under hanging canvas signs: ERÉNDIRA IS BEST; LEAVE AND COME BACK—ERÉNDIRA WAITS FOR YOU; THERE'S NO LIFE WITHOUT ERÉNDIRA. The endless wavy line composed of men of diverse races and ranks looked like a snake with human vertebrae dozing through vacant lots and squares, through gaudy bazaars and noisy marketplaces, coming out of the streets of that city, which was noisy with passing merchants. Every street was a public gambling den, every house a saloon, every doorway a refuge for fugitives. The many undecipherable songs and the shouted offerings of wares formed a single roar of panic in the hallucinating heat.

Among the throng of men without a country and sharpers was Blacamán the Good, up on a table and asking for a real serpent in order to test an antidote of his invention on his own flesh. There was the woman who had been changed into a spider[3] for having disobeyed her parents, who would let herself be touched for fifty cents so that people would see there was no trick, and she would answer questions of those who might care to ask about her misfortune. There was an envoy from the eternal life who announced the imminent coming of the fearsome astral bat, whose burning brimstone breath would overturn the order of nature and bring the mysteries of the sea to the surface.

The one restful backwater was the red-light district, reached only by the embers of the urban din. Women from the four quadrants of the nautical rose[4] yawned with boredom in the abandoned cabarets. They had slept their siestas sitting up, unawakened by people who wanted them, and they were still waiting for the astral bat under the fans that spun on the ceilings. Suddenly one of them got up and went to a balcony with pots of pansies that overlooked the street. Down there the rows of Eréndira's suitors was passing.

"Come on," the woman shouted at them. "What's that one got that we don't have?"

"A letter from a senator," someone shouted.

Attracted by the shouts and the laughter, other women came out onto the balcony.

"The line's been like that for days," one of them said. "Just imagine, fifty pesos apiece."

2. Capital of the province of La Guajira, in northeastern Colombia. Rafael Escalona: Not identified, possibly fictitious.
3. The spider woman, Blacamán, and other ele-
ments appear elsewhere in García Márquez's fictional works, in the world of Macondo.
4. Compass card.

The one who had come out first made a decision:

"Well, I'm going to go find out what jewel that seven-month baby has got."

"Me, too," another said. "It'll be better than sitting here warming our chairs for free."

On the way others joined them and when they got to Eréndira's tent they made up a rowdy procession. They went in without any announcement, used pillows to chase away the man they found spending himself as best he could for his money, and they picked up Eréndira's bed and carried it out into the street like a litter.

"This is an outrage!" the grandmother shouted. "You pack of traitors, you bandits!" And then, turning to the men in line: "And you, you sissies, where do you keep your balls, letting this attack against a poor defenseless child go on? Damned fags!"

She kept on shouting as far as her voice would carry, distributing whacks with her crosier against all who came within reach, but her rage was inaudible amongst the shouts and mocking whistles of the crowd.

Eréndira couldn't escape the ridicule because she was prevented by the dog chain that the grandmother used to hitch her to a slat of the bed ever since she had tried to run away. But they didn't harm her. They exhibited her on the canopied altar along the noisiest streets like the allegorical passage of the enchained penitent and finally they set her down like a catafalque in the center of the main square. Eréndira was all coiled up, her face hidden, but not weeping, and she stayed that way under the terrible sun in the square, biting with shame and rage at the dog chain of her evil destiny until someone was charitable enough to cover her with a shirt.

That was the only time I saw them, but I found out that they had stayed in that border town under the protection of the public forces until the grandmother's chests were bursting and then they left the desert and headed toward the sea. Never had such opulence been seen gathered together in that realm of poor people. It was a procession of ox-drawn carts on which cheap replicas of the paraphernalia lost in the disaster of the mansion were piled, not just the imperial busts and rare clocks, but also a secondhand piano and a Victrola with a crank and the records of nostalgia. A team of Indians took care of the cargo and a band of musicians announced their triumphal arrival in the villages.

The grandmother traveled on a litter with paper wreaths, chomping on the grains in her pouch, in the shadow of a church canopy. Her monumental size had increased, because under her blouse she was wearing a vest of sailcloth in which she kept the gold bars the way one keeps cartridges in a bandoleer. Eréndira was beside her, dressed in gaudy fabrics and with trinkets hanging, but with the dog chain still on her ankle.

"You've got no reason to complain," her grandmother had said to her when they left the border town. "You've got the clothes of a queen, a luxurious bed, a musical band of your own, and fourteen Indians at your service. Don't you think that's splendid?"

"Yes, Grandmother."

"When you no longer have me," the grandmother went on, "you won't be left to the mercy of men because you'll have your own home in an important city. You'll be free and happy."

It was a new and unforeseen vision of the future. On the other hand, she no longer spoke about the original debt, whose details had become twisted and whose installments had grown as the costs of the business became more complicated. Still Eréndira didn't let slip any sigh that would have given a person a glimpse of her thoughts. She submitted in silence to the torture of the bed in the saltpeter pits, in the torpor of the lakeside towns, in the lunar craters of the talcum mines, while her grandmother sang the vision of the future to her as if she were reading cards. One afternoon, as they came out of an oppressive canyon, they noticed a wind of ancient laurels and they caught snatches of Jamaica conversations and felt an urge to live and a knot in their hearts. They had reached the sea.

"There it is," the grandmother said, breathing in the glassy light of the Caribbean after half a lifetime of exile. "Don't you like it?"

"Yes, Grandmother."

They pitched the tent there. The grandmother spent the night talking without dreaming and sometimes she mixed up her nostalgia with clairvoyance of the future. She slept later than usual and awoke relaxed by the sound of the sea. Nevertheless, when Eréndira was bathing her she again made predictions of the future and it was such a feverish clairvoyance that it seemed like the delirium of a vigil.

"You'll be a noble lady," she told her. "A lady of quality, venerated by those under your protection and favored and honored by the highest authorities. Ships' captains will send you postcards from every port in the world."

Eréndira wasn't listening to her. The warm water perfumed with oregano was pouring into the bathtub through a tube fed from outside. Eréndira picked it up in a gourd, impenetrable, not even breathing, and poured it over her grandmother with one hand while she soaped her with the other.

"The prestige of your house will fly from mouth to mouth from the string of the Antilles to the realm of Holland," the grandmother was saying. "And it will be more important than the presidential palace, because the affairs of government will be discussed there and the fate of the nation will be decided."

Suddenly the water in the tube stopped. Eréndira left the tent to find out what was going on and saw the Indian in charge of pouring water into the tube chopping wood by the kitchen.

"It ran out," the Indian said. "We have to cool more water."

Eréndira went to the stove, where there was another large pot with aromatic herbs boiling. She wrapped her hands in a cloth and saw that she could lift the pot without the help of the Indian.

"You can go," she told him. "I'll pour the water."

She waited until the Indian had left the kitchen. Then she took the boiling pot off the stove, lifted it with great effort to the height of the tube, and was about to pour the deadly water into the conduit to the bathtub when the grandmother shouted from inside the tent:

"Eréndira!"

It was as if she had seen. The granddaughter, frightened by the shout, repented at the last minute.

"Coming, Grandmother," she said. "I'm cooling off the water."

That night she lay thinking until quite late while her grandmother sang in her sleep, wearing the golden vest. Eréndira looked at her from her bed with intense eyes that in the shadows resembled those of a cat. Then she went to bed like a person who had drowned, her arms on her breast and her eyes open, and she called with all the strength of her inner voice: "Ulises!"

Ulises woke up suddenly in the house on the orange plantation. He had heard Eréndira's voice so clearly that he was looking for her in the shadows of the room. After an instant of reflection, he made a bundle of his clothing and shoes and left the bedroom. He had crossed the porch when his father's voice surprised him:

"Where are you going?"

Ulises saw him blue in the moonlight.

"Into the world," he answered.

"This time I won't stop you," the Dutchman said. "But I warn you of one thing: wherever you go your father's curse will follow you."

"So be it," said Ulises.

Surprised and even a little proud of his son's resolution, the Dutchman followed him through the orange grove with a look that slowly began to smile. His wife was behind him with her beautiful Indian woman's way of standing. The Dutchman spoke when Ulises closed the gate.

"He'll be back," he said, "beaten down by life, sooner than you think."

"You're so stupid," she sighed. "He'll never come back."

On that occasion Ulises didn't have to ask anyone where Eréndira was. He crossed the desert hiding in passing trucks, stealing to eat and sleep and stealing many times for the pure pleasure of the risk until he found the tent in another seaside town which the glass buildings gave the look of an illuminated city and where resounded the nocturnal farewells of ships weighing anchor for the island of Aruba. Eréndira was asleep chained to the slat and in the same position of a drowned person on the beach from which she had called him. Ulises stood looking at her for a long time without waking her up, but he looked at her with such intensity that Eréndira awoke. Then they kissed in the darkness, caressed each other slowly, got undressed wearily, with a silent tenderness and a hidden happiness that was more than ever like love.

At the other end of the tent the sleeping grandmother gave a monumental turn and began to rant.

"That was during the time the Greek ship arrived," she said. "It was a crew of madmen who made the women happy and didn't pay them with money but with sponges, living sponges that later on walked about the houses moaning like patients in a hospital and making the children cry so that they could drink the tears."

She made a subterranean movement and sat up in bed.

"That was when he arrived, my God," she shouted, "stronger, taller, and much more of a man than Amadís."

Ulises, who until then had not paid any attention to the raving, tried to hide when he saw the grandmother sitting up in bed. Eréndira calmed him.

"Take it easy," she told him. "Every time she gets to that part she sits up in bed, but she doesn't wake up."

Ulises leaned on her shoulder.

"I was singing with the sailors that night and I thought it was an earthquake," the grandmother went on. "They all must have thought the same thing because they ran away shouting, dying with laughter, and only he remained under the starsong canopy. I remember as if it had been yesterday that I was singing the song that everyone was singing those days. Even the parrots in the courtyard sang it."

Flat as a mat, as one can sing only in dreams, she sang the lines of her bitterness:

Lord, oh, Lord, give me back the innocence I had
So I can feel his love all over again from the start.

Only then did Ulises become interested in the grandmother's nostalgia.

"There he was," she was saying, "with a macaw on his shoulder and a cannibal-killing blunderbuss, the way Guatarral arrived in the Guianas,[5] and I felt his breath of death when he stood opposite me and said: 'I've been around the world a thousand times and seen women of every nation, so I can tell you on good authority that you are the haughtiest and the most obliging, the most beautiful woman on earth.'"

She lay down again and sobbed on her pillow. Ulises and Eréndira remained silent for a long time, rocked in the shadows by the sleeping old woman's great breathing. Suddenly Eréndira, without the slightest quiver in her voice, asked:

"Would you dare to kill her?"

Taken by surprise, Ulises didn't know what to answer.

"Who knows," he said. "Would you dare?"

"I can't," Eréndira said. "She's my grandmother."

Then Ulises looked once more at the enormous sleeping body as if measuring its quantity of life and decided:

"For you I'd be capable of anything."

Ulises bought a pound of rat poison, mixed it with whipped cream and raspberry jam, and poured that fatal cream into a piece of pastry from which he had removed the original filling. Then he put some thicker cream on top, smoothing it with a spoon until there was no trace of his sinister maneuver, and he completed the trick with seventy-two little pink candles.

The grandmother sat up on her throne waving her threatening crosier when she saw him come into the tent with the birthday cake.

"You brazen devil!" she shouted. "How dare you set foot in this place?"

Ulises hid behind his angel face.

"I've come to ask your forgiveness," he said, "on this day, your birthday."

Disarmed by his lie, which had hit its mark, the grandmother had the table set as if for a wedding feast. She sat Ulises down on her right while Eréndira served them, and after blowing out the candles with one devastating gust, she cut the cake into two equal parts. She served Ulises.

"A man who knows how to get himself forgiven has earned half of heaven," she said. "I give you the first piece, which is the piece of happiness."

"I don't like sweet things," he said. "You take it."

The grandmother offered Eréndira a piece of cake. She took it into the kitchen and threw it in the garbage.

The grandmother ate the rest all by herself. She put whole pieces into

5. Not identified, possibly fictitious.

her mouth and swallowed them without chewing, moaning with delight and looking at Ulises from the limbo of her pleasure. When there was no more on her plate she also ate what Ulises had turned down. While she was chewing the last bit, with her fingers she picked up the crumbs from the tablecloth and put them into her mouth.

She had eaten enough arsenic to exterminate a whole generation of rats. And yet she played the piano and sang until midnight, went to bed happy, and was able to have a normal sleep. The only thing new was a rocklike scratch in her breathing.

Eréndira and Ulises kept watch over her from the other bed, and they were only waiting for her death rattle. But the voice was as alive as ever when she began to rave.

"I went crazy, my God, I went crazy!" she shouted. "I put two bars on the bedroom door so he couldn't get in; I put the dresser and table against the door and the chairs on the table, and all he had to do was give a little knock with his ring for the defenses to fall apart, the chairs to fall off the table by themselves, the table and dresser to separate by themselves, the bars to move out of their slots by themselves."

Eréndira and Ulises looked at her with growing surprise as the delirium became more profound and dramatic and the voice more intimate.

"I felt I was going to die, soaked in the sweat of fear, begging inside for the door to open without opening, for him to enter without entering, for him never to go away but never to come back either so I wouldn't have to kill him!"

She went on repeating her drama for several hours, even the most intimate details, as if she had lived it again in her dream. A little before dawn she rolled over in bed with a movement of seismic accommodation and the voice broke with the imminence of sobs.

"I warned him and he laughed," she shouted. "I warned him again and he laughed again, until he opened his eyes in terror, saying, 'Agh, queen! Agh, queen!' and his voice wasn't coming out of his mouth but through the cut the knife had made in his throat."

Ulises, terrified at the grandmother's fearful evocation, grabbed Eréndira's hand.

"Murdering old woman!" he exclaimed.

Eréndira didn't pay any attention to him because at that instant dawn began to break. The clocks struck five.

"Go!" Eréndira said. "She's going to wake up now."

"She's got more life in her than an elephant," Ulises exclaimed. "It can't be!"

Eréndira cut him with a knifing look.

"The whole trouble," she said, "is that you're no good at all for killing anybody."

Ulises was so affected by the crudeness of the reproach that he left the tent. Eréndira kept on looking at the sleeping grandmother with her secret hate, with the rage of her frustration, as the sun rose and the bird air awakened. Then the grandmother opened her eyes and looked at her with a placid smile.

"God be with you, child."

The only noticeable change was a beginning of disorder in the daily routine. It was Wednesday, but the grandmother wanted to put on a Sunday dress, decided that Eréndira would receive no customers before eleven o'clock, and asked her to paint her nails garnet and give her a pontifical coiffure.

"I never had so much of an urge to have my picture taken," she exclaimed.

Eréndira began to comb her grandmother's hair, but as she drew the comb through the tangles a clump of hair remained between the teeth. She showed it to her grandmother in alarm. The grandmother examined it, pulled on another clump with her fingers, and another bush of hair was left in her hand. She threw it on the ground, tried again and pulled out a larger lock. Then she began to pull her hair with both hands, dying with laughter, throwing the handfuls into the air with an incomprehensible jubliation until her head looked like a peeled coconut.

Eréndira had no more news of Ulises until two weeks later when she caught the call of the owl outside the tent. The grandmother had begun to play the piano and was so absorbed in her nostalgia that she was unaware of reality. She had a wig of radiant feathers on her head.

Eréndira answered the call and only then did she notice the wick that came out of the piano and went on through the underbrush and was lost in the darkness. She ran to where Ulises was, hid next to him among the bushes, and with tight hearts they both watched the little blue flame that crept along the wick, crossed the dark space, and went into the tent.

"Cover your ears," Ulises said.

They both did, without any need, for there was no explosion. The tent lighted up inside with a radiant glow, burst in silence, and disappeared in a whirlwind of wet powder. When Eréndira dared enter, thinking that her grandmother was dead, she found her with her wig singed and her nightshirt in tatters, but more alive than ever, trying to put out the fire with a blanket.

Ulises slipped away under the protection of the shouts of the Indians, who didn't know what to do, confused by the grandmother's contradictory orders. When they finally managed to conquer the flames and get rid of the smoke, they were looking at a shipwreck.

"It's like the work of the evil one," the grandmother said. "Pianos don't explode just like that."

She made all kinds of conjectures to establish the causes of the new disaster, but Eréndira's evasions and her impassive attitude ended up confusing her. She couldn't find the slightest crack in her granddaughter's behavior, nor did she consider the existence of Ulises. She was awake until dawn, threading suppositions together and calculating the loss. She slept little and poorly. On the following morning, when Eréndira took the vest with the gold bars off her grandmother, she found fire blisters on her shoulders and raw flesh on her breast. "I had good reason to be turning over in my sleep," she said as Eréndira put egg whites on the burns. "And besides, I had a strange dream." She made an effort at concentration to evoke the image until it was as clear in her memory as in the dream.

"It was a peacock in a white hammock," she said.

Eréndira was surprised but she immediately assumed her everyday expression once more.

"It's a good sign," she lied. "Peacocks in dreams are animals with long lives."

"May God hear you," the grandmother said, "because we're back where we started. We have to begin all over again."

Eréndira didn't change her expression. She went out of the tent with the plate of compresses and left her grandmother with her torso soaked in egg white and her skull daubed with mustard. She was putting more egg whites in the plate under the palm shelter that served as a kitchen when she saw Ulises' eyes appear behind the stove as she had seen them the first time behind the bed. She wasn't startled, but told him in a weary voice:

"The only thing you've managed to do is increase my debt."

Ulises' eyes clouded over with anxiety. He was motionless, looking at Eréndira in silence, watching her crack the eggs with a fixed expression of absolute disdain, as if he didn't exist. After a moment the eyes moved, looked over the things in the kitchen, the hanging pots, the strings of annatto, the carving knife. Ulises stood up, still not saying anything, went in under the shelter, and took down the knife.

Eréndira didn't look at him again, but when Ulises left the shelter she told him in a very low voice:

"Be careful, because she's already had a warning of death. She dreamed about a peacock in a white hammock."

The grandmother saw Ulises come in with the knife, and making a supreme effort, she stood up without the aid of her staff and raised her arms.

"Boy!" she shouted. "Have you gone mad?"

Ulises jumped on her and plunged the knife into her naked breast. The grandmother moaned, fell on him, and tried to strangle him with her powerful bear arms.

"Son of a bitch," she growled. "I discovered too late that you have the face of a traitor angel."

She was unable to say anything more because Ulises managed to free the knife and stab her a second time in the side. The grandmother let out a hidden moan and hugged her attacker with more strength. Ulises gave her a third stab, without pity, and a spurt of blood, released by high pressure, sprinkled his face: it was oily blood, shiny and green, just like mint honey.

Eréndira appeared at the entrance with the plate in her hand and watched the struggle with criminal impassivity.

Huge, monolithic, roaring with pain and rage, the grandmother grasped Ulises' body. Her arms, her legs, even her hairless skull were green with blood. Her enormous bellows-breathing, upset by the first rattles of death, filled the whole area. Ulises managed to free his arm with the weapon once more, opened a cut in her belly, and an explosion of blood soaked him in green from head to toe. The grandmother tried to reach the open air which she needed in order to live now and fell face down. Ulises got away from the lifeless arms and without pausing a moment gave the vast fallen body a final thrust.

Eréndira then put the plate on a table and leaned over her grandmother, scrutinizing her without touching her. When she was convinced that she was dead her face suddenly acquired all the maturing of an older person which her twenty years of misfortune had not given her. With quick and precise movements she grabbed the gold vest and left the tent.

Ulises remained sitting by the corpse, exhausted by the fight, and the more he tried to clean his face the more it was daubed with the green and living matter that seemed to be flowing from his fingers. Only when he saw Eréndira go out with the gold vest did he become aware of his state. He shouted to her but got no answer. He dragged himself to the entrance to the tent and he saw Eréndira starting to run along the shore away from the city. Then he made a last effort to chase her, calling her with painful shouts that were no longer those of a lover but of a son, yet he was overcome by the terrible drain of having killed a woman without anybody's help. The grandmother's Indians caught up to him lying face down on the beach, weeping from solitude and fear.

Eréndira had not heard him. She was running into the wind, swifter than a deer, and no voice of this world could stop her. Without turning her head she ran past the saltpeter pits, the talcum craters, the torpor of the shacks, until the natural science of the sea ended and the desert began, but she still kept on running with the gold vest beyond the arid winds and the never-ending sunsets and she was never heard of again nor was the slightest trace of her misfortune ever found.

1972

AFTERWORD

The title warns us that García Márquez's story will be incredible, and that it certainly is. Unlike Kafka's novel, which began with the fantastic proposition that the protagonist woke one morning to find he was an insect, there is nothing fantastic or clearly surreal in the first sentence, paragraph, or "chapter"—that is, to the break on page 584 after the knocking over of the candle (I shall call the sections marked by breaks "Chapters"). This is not to say that all is ordinary. The concrete mansion in the desert, complete with ostrich, marble tub, statues of fictional Caesars, and so many clocks of all shapes and sizes that it takes six hours just to wind them; the grandmother huge as a whale, grossly tattooed, decked out like a doll, dining alone at a banquet table for twelve with silver candlesticks, giving orders even in her sleep and dreaming deliriously; even Eréndira's working in her sleep, are not your run-of-the-mill everyday setting, situation, and cast of characters, exactly. Still, there is nothing here so improbable as to be "incredible." (The reference to the goats' committing suicide may be taken as hyperbolic or figurative.)

The second chapter (to the appearance of Ulises) is also bizarre, a bit more surreal, but not yet fantastic. Still, how do you read this sentence: "Over the whistle of the storm and the lash of the water one could hear distant shouts, the howling of far-off animals, the cries of a shipwreck"? Or this passage: "Eréndira then succumbed to terror, lost consciousness, and remained as if fascinated by the moonbeams from a fish that was floating through the storm air . . ."? Does she merely remain as if fascinated at a fish really flying through the air, or fascinated as if by a fish flying . . . ? By the end of the third chapter we are at or over the border of fantasy: Ulises looks like a furtive angel and the grandmother asks him where his wings are; it isn't he, he says, but his grandfather who is the winged one; he cannot walk on water, but his father knew a man who could. Still, like the oranges that Ulises says are worth 50,000 pesos, these are all reports or superstitions; nothing incredible has yet happened on the literal surface in the action of the story.

Perhaps we've all heard of mayors who have done rather less reasonable things than shoot at clouds to bring rain (Chapter 4), but in Chapter 5, Ulises the angel is changing the color of everything glass that he touches. Perhaps we find that fantastic, but his Indian mother accepts it as a familiar symptom of being in love. This first bit of "on-stage," verified fantasy on the surface of the narrative occurs in the middle of the novel; in the next chapter (the sixth of seven) the fantastic comes to the fore: the woman who has been turned into a spider (or is this just a carnival stunt?); Eréndira calling Ulises in the night across miles and miles, summoning him to her (but remember Jane Eyre); the sponges that walk around the house moaning, making the children cry and drinking their tears (but that's just the crazy grandmother remembering—or fantasizing—in her dreams again); the grandmother's surviving the huge dose of arsenic and the dynamite blast (almost like the coyote or cat in cartoons); and then the final horrible scene with its torrents of green blood. That, surely, is incredible.

Kafka proceeds logically, even realistically after his opening sentence: if we accept Gregor Samsa's metamorphosis, all else in the story follows. Here we begin with the extraordinary, with what seems like exaggeration or distortion of reality but not with the wholly impossible or incredible, and we are led deeper and deeper into the fantastic world of García Márquez's Macondo.

How do we take such a story? As a fairy tale with an innocent heroine, wicked grand- (not step-) mother, and occasional "magic"? As a folk tale or legend? If we want to reduce Kafka to the mundane and rational we treat his world as allegorically or psychologically symbolic. I don't think many readers do this sort of thing with García Márquez. We either reject it, or we accept it as an imaginative creation without any paraphrasable or interpretable meaning, as something outside the rules or "physics" of phenomenal reality. It is enough, perhaps, that it is the creation of a human mind and therefore part of human reality in the largest sense. The characters, moreover, have human traits, emotions, and, usually, responses, and the story creates in most readers feelings of considerable intensity.

What are those feelings, precisely? The title says the tale is "sad," and there's certainly enough unhappiness in the story to justify that part of the title. The heartless grandmother's exploitation of Eréndira even before the "misfortune" is pitiable. The list of Eréndira duties, so overwhelming that she works even in her sleep, surely moves us despite—or perhaps more so because of—the girl's stoic acceptance of her lot. The grandmother's plan for making Eréndira pay her back for the losses incurred in the fire is disgusting; the image of Eréndira being led by the storekeeper who has bought her virginity "to the back room as if he were taking her to school" is wrenchingly pathetic. Eréndira endures her rape in a daze, benumbed, so we are spared the detailed account of her feelings; just as her first "misfortune," the burning-down of the mansion, occurs in the white space between the first two chapters, so the details of her sale to and use by all the men in the village passes in the silent space between paragraphs. Are our horror and pity made more or less intense by these stoic silences?

We do not get the full sense of Eréndira's pain until, in Chapter 3, she tells her grandmother she is dying, and when her heartless grandmother "consoles" her with the information that there are only ten more soldiers in line, "Eréndira began to weep with the shrieks of a frightened animal." When, later, the "mule work" endlessly whitewashing the busy stairs of the mission feels to her "as if every day were Sunday after the fearsome galley that had been her bed," we get a rare glimpse into her consciousness of her earlier oppression. During this "interlude," when she hears a nun playing an Easter oratorio on the clavichord, she speaks for the first time since leaving her grandmother: she says aloud that she's happy! Is this just inexpressibly sad? Does it make us furious at what has been done to her by emphasizing her "innocence"? Is it, possibly, exhilarating, a tribute to human endurance and the resiliency of the human spirit? Pathos, anger, horror, even exultation seem as commingled as the realistic, the extraordinary, and the fantastic in this novel.

As in *The Metamorphosis*, alternating and even mixed with the horror there also runs a bizarre streak of humor. The terrible and comic are mixed in the grandmother's shrewd wit in bargaining with the village shopkeeper over Eréndira's virginity: his low offer, she says, shows a lack of respect for virtue. More purely humorous is the musician's attempt to outwit the grandmother by claiming that waltzes cost more because they're sadder, only to be vanquished by her dizzying calculations. The grotesqueness of the moaning sponges and even of the grandmother's surviving the explosion is ludicrous, but the mixture of fantasy and humor has a tinge of feelings more sinister. The nun wrestling the pig begins as slapstick but ends with the pig's throat being cut. The horror of the photographer's head being blown apart is presented like a scene from a slapstick comedy in a silent film.

All of this, perhaps, prepares us for the climactic events of the story and its conclusion. Eréndira can stand her life no longer and calls Ulises to kill her grandmother but the heartless one seems invulnerable—arsenic results only in her loss of hair (compensated for by a wig of feathers!), the piano blast is ineffective. Finally, however, she and the story come to an end in a fantastic sea of green blood. Does that make the scene more horrible or less? funnier or nauseating? And how about Eréndira's taking off with the gold at the very end, skipping out on the angelic murderer

Ulises? What are we to think of that? of her? of the novel? Is she no longer "innocent"? Is she now (has she always been?) like her grandmother (who was also a prostitute in her youth)? Where do you imagine she is? Is she off somewhere living a life of luxury? growing old and fat and being bathed in exotic and decadent surroundings by an overworked girl? Is she wandering in the desert laden with the vest of gold, mad and screaming? Has she died, or will she die there? We'll never know.

Why do we care? Is Eréndira a "real" person to us, despite the fantasy, the bewildering mix of emotional stimuli, the challenge to (if not an attack on) our sense of psychological and phenomenal reality, the orderliness of the universe? There is even an affront to conventional narrative decorum: Who is the book salesman who wanders into the story in the next-to-last chapter as a momentary first-person narrator and takes authority for reconstructing the story? It is from this narrator that we get some of the details from other García Márquez stories of Macondo—the spiderwoman, for example. Does this remind us of the actual author and so undermine the authenticity of the story, or does it verify or substantiate that fictional world? If it is the first-person narrator's function to make the incredible a bit more credible, to "authenticate" it, why does he wander off again? Does this brief appearance not raise questions about the narration and thus call our attention to the novel as a fiction? Do we somehow find it wonderful (in the literal sense) and moving? Do we, because of its unreality, its fictionality, reduce it to the status of a fairy tale—"just a story"—or to a clever manipulation of narrative devices, a spoof on story-telling? García Márquez's fiction seems to raise some of the same questions that have been raised from time to time about the paintings of Picasso (or Salvador Dali, or perhaps Andy Warhol). Are modern audiences too sophisticated to believe fictions to be real or to be fooled by what Henry James called "the illusion of reality," or has modern reality become so bizarre, the actions of supposedly sane and civilized men and nations so irrational, that only fantasy seems real?

TONI MORRISON

Sula

When you are enthusiastic about a writer who is still in mid-career, who is known but whose name is not yet a household word, whose third novel, *Song of Solomon*, won the National Book Critics' Award as the best work of fiction in 1977, but who is not yet an inevitable part of the college curriculum, subject for doctoral dissertations, or fixture in anthologies, it is difficult not to sound as if you are writing a blurb for a dust-jacket.

Toni Morrison was born on February 18, 1931, in Lorain, Ohio, as Chloe Anthony Wofford. She has a B.A. from Howard University and an M.A. from Cornell, has taught at Texas Southern University, Howard, Yale, and Bard College, and is now Albert Schweitzer Professor of Humanitics at the State University of New York at Albany. She has been a senior editor at Random House, having worked as a textbook editor for one of their subsidiaries soon after she left Howard and her marriage in 1964. Her first novel, *The Bluest Eye* (1970), was well received by the critics and *Sula* (1974) was widely acclaimed. Though she was taken seriously by the critics—being compared to such established writers as Vladimir Nabokov and Doris Lessing—her first truly popular success was *Song of Solomon* (1977). The eagerly awaited *Tar Baby* was published in 1981, and her play *Dreaming Emmett* was first performed in 1986.

Sula was named an alternate Book-of-the-Month Club selection, was condensed in *Redbook*, and was nominated for the 1975 National Book Award in fiction. Like all her novels to date, *Sula* is about the experience of black Americans—their history and mythology, their contemporary reality, mores, and methods of coping as a visible and exploited minority. *Sula* is also about Sula, an individual—black, female, growing up in the Midwest between the World Wars: all of these, but also herself. It is also about her friend Nel—black, female, growing up in the Midwest between the wars, but as different from Sula in the life she chooses and the values she holds as two people can be. Or is she?

Just as *Daisy Miller* is the object of that short novel and, as it turns out, Winterbourne the subject, so Sula moves from subject to object and toward the end it is Nel whose examined life we are closer to. Are Nel and Sula doubles? mirror images? Jekyll and Hyde? As in *Old Mortality*, the chapters are dated rather than titled and the action spreads over years; both novels are one woman's quest to understand another woman, and herself, and are images of complex, traditional societies seen changing and enduring over time. Sula even has an awakening in New Orleans, coincidentally the site Katherine Anne Porter uses in *Old Mortality*. Like *Goodbye, Columbus*, this is a novel of cultural transition. Is the price of survival, much less success, worth the cost? Toni Morrison explores not only the cost of rebellion or difference for Sula—as James does for Daisy and Porter for Amy—but the hidden cost few explore: that of living according to traditional values. In this splendid short novel, many of the themes, issues, and structures represented in the earlier selections emerge from rich new experiences and are embodied in a supple lyric prose with compelling narrative interest to create a new vision. When an interviewer recently asked her to describe what is distinctive about her fiction, Toni Morrison replied: "The language, only the language. The language must be careful and must appear effortless. It must not sweat."

Sula

"Nobody knew my rose of the world
but me. . . . I had too much glory.
They don't want glory like that
in nobody's heart."
—The Rose Tattoo[1]

Part One

I N THAT PLACE, where they tore the nightshade
and blackberry patches from their roots to make room
for the Medallion City Golf Course, there was once a
neighborhood. It stood in the hills above the valley town of Medallion
and spread all the way to the river. It is called the suburbs now, but
when black people lived there it was called the Bottom. One road, shaded
by beeches, oaks, maples and chestnuts, connected it to the valley. The
beeches are gone now, and so are the pear trees where children sat and
yelled down through the blossoms to passersby. Generous funds have been
allotted to level the stripped and faded buildings that clutter the road
from Medallion up to the golf course. They are going to raze the Time
and a Half Pool Hall, where feet in long tan shoes once pointed down
from chair rungs. A steel ball will knock to dust Irene's Palace of Cosmetology, where women used to lean their heads back on sink trays and
doze while Irene lathered Nu Nile into their hair. Men in khaki work
clothes will pry loose the slats of Reba's Grill, where the owner cooked in
her hat because she couldn't remember the ingredients without it.

There will be nothing left of the Bottom (the footbridge that crossed
the river is already gone), but perhaps it is just as well, since it wasn't a
town anyway: just a neighborhood where on quiet days people in valley
houses could hear singing sometimes, banjos sometimes, and, if a valley
man happened to have business up in those hills—collecting rent or insurance payments—he might see a dark woman in a flowered dress doing a
bit of cakewalk, a bit of black bottom,[2] a bit of "messing around" to the
lively notes of a mouth organ. Her bare feet would raise the saffron dust
that floated down on the coveralls and bunion-split shoes of the man
breathing music in and out of his harmonica. The black people watching
her would laugh and rub their knees, and it would be easy for the valley
man to hear the laughter and not notice the adult pain that rested somewhere under the eyelids, somewhere under their head rags and soft felt
hats, somewhere in the palm of the hand, somewhere behind the frayed
lapels, somewhere in the sinew's curve. He'd have to stand in the back of
Greater Saint Matthew's and let the tenor's voice dress him in silk, or
touch the hands of the spoon carvers (who had not worked in eight years)
and let the fingers that danced on wood kiss his skin. Otherwise the pain
would escape him even though the laughter was part of the pain.

A shucking, knee-slapping, wet-eyed laughter that could even describe

1. 1951 play by Tennessee Williams (b. 1911).
2. The cakewalk was a syncopated dance that originated among southern blacks in the 1890s and was
popular through the 1920s, the black bottom from the
1920s through the 1930s.

and explain how they came to be where they were.

A joke. A nigger joke. That was the way it got started. Not the town, of course, but that part of town where the Negroes lived, the part they called the Bottom in spite of the fact that it was up in the hills. Just a nigger joke. The kind white folks tell when the mill closes down and they're looking for a little comfort somewhere. The kind colored folks tell on themselves when the rain doesn't come, or comes for weeks, and they're looking for a little comfort somehow.

A good white farmer promised freedom and a piece of bottom land to his slave if he would perform some very difficult chores. When the slave completed the work, he asked the farmer to keep his end of the bargain. Freedom was easy—the farmer had no objection to that. But he didn't want to give up any land. So he told the slave that he was very sorry that he had to give him valley land. He had hoped to give him a piece of the Bottom. The slave blinked and said he thought valley land was bottom land. The master said, "Oh, no! See those hills? That's bottom land, rich and fertile."

"But it's high up in the hills," said the slave.

"High up from us," said the master, "but when God looks down, it's the bottom. That's why we call it so. It's the bottom of heaven—best land there is."

So the slave pressed his master to try to get him some. He preferred it to the valley. And it was done. The nigger got the hilly land, where planting was backbreaking, where the soil slid down and washed away the seeds, and where the wind lingered all through the winter.

Which accounted for the fact that white people lived on the rich valley floor in that little river town in Ohio, and the blacks populated the hills above it, taking small consolation in the fact that every day they could literally look down on the white folks.

Still, it was lovely up in the Bottom. After the town grew and the farm land turned into a village and the village into a town and the streets of Medallion were hot and dusty with progress, those heavy trees that sheltered the shacks up in the Bottom were wonderful to see. And the hunters who went there sometimes wondered in private if maybe the white farmer was right after all. Maybe it was the bottom of heaven.

The black people would have disagreed, but they had no time to think about it. They were mightily preoccupied with earthly things—and each other, wondering even as early as 1920 what Shadrack was all about, what that little girl Sula who grew into a woman in their town was all about, and what they themselves were all about, tucked up there in the Bottom.

1919

Except for World War II, nothing ever interfered with the celebration of National Suicide Day. It had taken place every January third since 1920, although Shadrack, its founder, was for many years the only celebrant. Blasted and permanently astonished by the events of 1917, he had returned to Medallion handsome but ravaged, and even the most fastidious people in the town sometimes caught themselves dreaming of what he must have been like a few years back before he went off to war. A young man of hardly twenty, his head full of nothing and his mouth recalling the taste of lipstick, Shadrack had found himself in December,

1917, running with his comrades across a field in France. It was his first encounter with the enemy and he didn't know whether his company was running toward them or away. For several days they had been marching, keeping close to a stream that was frozen at its edges. At one point they crossed it, and no sooner had he stepped foot on the other side than the day was adangle with shouts and explosions. Shellfire was all around him, and though he knew that this was something called *it*, he could not muster up the proper feeling—the feeling that would accommodate *it*. He expected to be terrified or exhilarated—to feel *something* very strong. In fact, he felt only the bite of a nail in his boot, which pierced the ball of his foot whenever he came down on it. The day was cold enough to make his breath visible, and he wondered for a moment at the purity and whiteness of his own breath among the dirty, gray explosions surrounding him. He ran, bayonet fixed, deep in the great sweep of men flying across this field. Wincing at the pain in his foot, he turned his head a little to the right and saw the face of a soldier near him fly off. Before he could register shock, the rest of the soldier's head disappeared under the inverted soup bowl of his helmet. But stubbornly, taking no direction from the brain, the body of the headless soldier ran on, with energy and grace, ignoring altogether the drip and slide of brain tissue down its back.

When Shadrack opened his eyes he was propped up in a small bed. Before him on a tray was a large tin plate divided into three triangles. In one triangle was rice, in another meat, and in the third stewed tomatoes. A small round depression held a cup of whitish liquid. Shadrack stared at the soft colors that filled these triangles: the lumpy whiteness of rice, the quivering blood tomatoes, the grayish-brown meat. All their repugnance was contained in the neat balance of the triangles—a balance that soothed him, transferred some of its equilibrium to him. Thus reassured that the white, the red and the brown would stay where they were—would not explode or burst forth from their restricted zones—he suddenly felt hungry and looked around for his hands. His glance was cautious at first, for he had to be very careful—anything could be anywhere. Then he noticed two lumps beneath the beige blanket on either side of his hips. With extreme care he lifted one arm and was relieved to find his hand attached to his wrist. He tried the other and found it also. Slowly he directed one hand toward the cup and, just as he was about to spread his fingers, they began to grow in higgledy-piggledy fashion like Jack's beanstalk all over the tray and the bed. With a shriek he closed his eyes and thrust his huge growing hands under the covers. Once out of sight they seemed to shrink back to their normal size. But the yell had brought a male nurse.

"Private? We're not going to have any trouble today, are we? Are we, Private?"

Shadrack looked up at a balding man dressed in a green-cotton jacket and trousers. His hair was parted low on the right side so that some twenty or thirty yellow hairs could discreetly cover the nakedness of his head.

"Come on. Pick up that spoon. Pick it up, Private. Nobody is going to feed you forever."

Sweat slid from Shadrack's armpits down his sides. He could not bear to see his hands grow again and he was frightened of the voice in the apple-green suit.

"Pick it up, I said. There's no point to this . . ." The nurse reached under the cover for Shadrack's wrist to pull out the monstrous hand. Shadrack jerked it back and overturned the tray. In panic he raised himself to his knees and tried to fling off and away his terrible fingers, but succeeded only in knocking the nurse into the next bed.

When they bound Shadrack into a straitjacket, he was both relieved and grateful, for his hands were at last hidden and confined to whatever size they had attained.

Laced and silent in his small bed, he tried to tie the loose cords in his mind. He wanted desperately to see his own face and connect it with the word "private"—the word the nurse (and the others who helped bind him) had called him. "Private" he thought was something secret, and he wondered why they looked at him and called him a secret. Still, if his hands behaved as they had done, what might he expect from his face? The fear and longing were too much for him, so he began to think of other things. That is, he let his mind slip into whatever cave mouths of memory it chose.

He saw a window that looked out on a river which he knew was full of fish. Someone was speaking softly just outside the door . . .

Shadrack's earlier violence had coincided with a memorandum from the hospital executive staff in reference to the distribution of patients in high-risk areas. There was clearly a demand for space. The priority or the violence earned Shadrack his release, $217 in cash, a full suit of clothes and copies of very official-looking papers.

When he stepped out of the hospital door the grounds overwhelmed him: the cropped shrubbery, the edged lawns, the undeviating walks. Shadrack looked at the cement stretches: each one leading clearheadedly to some presumably desirable destination. There were no fences, no warnings, no obstacles at all between concrete and green grass, so one could easily ignore the tidy sweep of stone and cut out in another direction—a direction of one's own.

Shadrack stood at the foot of the hospital steps watching the heads of trees tossing ruefully but harmlessly, since their trunks were rooted too deeply in the earth to threaten him. Only the walks made him uneasy. He shifted his weight, wondering how he could get to the gate without stepping on the concrete. While plotting his course—where he would have to leap, where to skirt a clump of bushes—a loud guffaw startled him. Two men were going up the steps. Then he noticed that there were many people about, and that he was just now seeing them, or else they had just materialized. They were thin slips, like paper dolls floating down the walks. Some were seated in chairs with wheels, propelled by other paper figures from behind. All seemed to be smoking, and their arms and legs curved in the breeze. A good high wind would pull them up and away and they would land perhaps among the tops of the trees.

Shadrack took the plunge. Four steps and he was on the grass heading for the gate. He kept his head down to avoid seeing the paper people swerving and bending here and there, and he lost his way. When he looked up, he was standing by a low red building separated from the main building by a covered walkway. From somewhere came a sweetish smell which reminded him of something painful. He looked around for the gate and saw that he had gone directly away from it in his complicated journey over the grass. Just to the left of the low building was a graveled driveway that appeared to lead outside the grounds. He trotted quickly to it and left, at last, a haven of more than a year, only eight days of which he fully recollected.

Once on the road, he headed west. The long stay in the hospital had left him weak—too weak to walk steadily on the gravel shoulders of the road. He shuffled, grew dizzy, stopped for breath, started again, stumbling and sweating but refusing to wipe his temples, still afraid to look at his hands. Passengers in dark, square cars shuttered their eyes at what they took to be a drunken man.

The sun was already directly over his head when he came to a town. A few blocks of shaded streets and he was already at its heart—a pretty, quietly regulated downtown.

Exhausted, his feet clotted with pain, he sat down at the curbside to take off his shoes. He closed his eyes to avoid seeing his hands and fumbled with the laces of the heavy high-topped shoes. The nurse had tied them into a double knot, the way one does for children, and Shadrack, long unaccustomed to the manipulation of intricate things, could not get them loose. Uncoordinated, his fingernails tore away at the knots. He fought a rising hysteria that was not merely anxiety to free his aching feet; his very life depended on the release of the knots. Suddenly without raising his eyelids, he began to cry. Twenty-two years old, weak, hot, frightened, not daring to acknowledge the fact that he didn't even know who or what he was ... with no past, no language, no tribe, no source, no address book, no comb, no pencil, no clock, no pocket handkerchief, no rug, no bed, no can opener, no faded postcard, no soap, no key, no tobacco pouch, no soiled underwear and nothing nothing nothing to do ... he was sure of one thing only: the unchecked monstrosity of his hands. He cried soundlessly at the curbside of a small Midwestern town wondering where the window was, and the river, and the soft voices just outside the door ...

Through his tears he saw the fingers joining the laces, tentatively at first, then rapidly. The four fingers of each hand fused into the fabric, knotted themselves and zig-zagged in and out of the tiny eyeholes.

By the time the police drove up, Shadrack was suffering from a blinding headache, which was not abated by the comfort he felt when the policemen pulled his hands away from what he thought was a permanent entanglement with his shoelaces. They took him to jail, booked him for vagrancy and intoxication, and locked him in a cell. Lying on a cot, Shadrack could only stare helplessly at the wall, so paralyzing was the pain in his head. He lay in this agony for a long while and then realized he was staring at the painted-over letters of a command to fuck himself. He studied the phrase as the pain in his head subsided.

Like moonlight stealing under a window shade an idea insinuated itself: his earlier desire to see his own face. He looked for a mirror; there was none. Finally, keeping his hands carefully behind his back he made his way to the toilet bowl and peeped in. The water was unevenly lit by the sun so he could make nothing out. Returning to his cot he took the blanket and covered his head, rendering the water dark enough to see his reflection. There in the toilet water he saw a grave black face. A black so definite, so unequivocal, it astonished him. He had been harboring a skittish apprehension that he was not real—that he didn't exist at all. But when the blackness greeted him with its indisputable presence, he wanted nothing more. In his joy he took the risk of letting one edge of the blanket drop and glanced at his hands. They were still. Courteously still.

Shadrack rose and returned to the cot, where he fell into the first sleep of his new life. A sleep deeper than the hospital drugs; deeper than the pits of plums, steadier than the condor's wing; more tranquil than the curve of eggs.

The sheriff looked through the bars at the young man with the matted hair. He had read through his prisoner's papers and hailed a farmer. When Shadrack awoke, the sheriff handed him back his papers and escorted him to the back of a wagon. Shadrack got in and in less than three hours he was back in Medallion, for he had been only twenty-two miles from his window, his river, and his soft voices just outside the door.

In the back of the wagon, supported by sacks of squash and hills of pumpkins, Shadrack began a struggle that was to last for twelve days, a struggle to order and focus experience. It had to do with making a place for fear as a way of controlling it. He knew the smell of death and was terrified of it, for he could not anticipate it. It was not death or dying that frightened him, but the unexpectedness of both. In sorting it all out, he hit on the notion that if one day a year were devoted to it, everybody could get it out of the way and the rest of the year would be safe and free. In this manner he instituted National Suicide Day.

On the third day of the new year, he walked through the Bottom down Carpenter's Road with a cowbell and a hangman's rope calling the people together. Telling them that this was their only chance to kill themselves or each other.

At first the people in the town were frightened; they knew Shadrack was crazy but that did not mean that he didn't have any sense or, even more important, that he had no power. His eyes were so wild, his hair so long and matted, his voice was so full of authority and thunder that he caused panic on the first, or Charter, National Suicide Day in 1920. The next one, in 1921, was less frightening but still worrisome. The people had seen him a year now in between. He lived in a shack on the riverbank that had once belonged to his grandfather long time dead. On Tuesday and Friday he sold the fish he had caught that morning, the rest of the week he was drunk, loud, obscene, funny and outrageous. But he never touched anybody, never fought, never caressed. Once the people understood the boundaries and nature of his madness, they could fit him, so to speak, into the scheme of things.

Then, on subsequent National Suicide Days, the grown people looked out from behind curtains as he rang his bell; a few stragglers increased their speed, and little children screamed and ran. The tetter heads[3] tried goading him (although he was only four or five years older than they) but not for long, for his curses were stingingly personal.

As time went along, the people took less notice of these January thirds, or rather they thought they did, thought they had no attitudes or feelings one way or another about Shadrack's annual solitary parade. In fact they had simply stopped remarking on the holiday because they had absorbed it into their thoughts, into their language, into their lives.

---

3. Heads with itchy sores.

Someone said to a friend, "You sure was a long time delivering that baby. How long was you in labor?"

And the friend answered, " 'Bout three days. The pains started on Suicide Day and kept up till the following Sunday. Was borned on Sunday. All my boys is Sunday boys."

Some lover said to his bride-to-be, "Let's do it after New Years, 'stead of before. I get paid New Year's Eve."

And his sweetheart answered, "OK, but make sure it ain't on Suicide Day. I ain't 'bout to be listening to no cowbells whilst the weddin's going on."

Somebody's grandmother said her hens always started a laying of double yolks right after Suicide Day.

Then Reverend Deal took it up, saying the same folks who had sense enough to avoid Shadrack's call were the ones who insisted on drinking themselves to death or womanizing themselves to death. "May's well go on with Shad and save the Lamb the trouble of redemption."

Easily, quietly, Suicide Day became a part of the fabric of life up in the Bottom of Medallion, Ohio.

1920

It had to be as far away from the Sundown House as possible. And her grandmother's middle-aged nephew who lived in a Northern town called Medallion was the one chance she had to make sure it would be. The red shutters had haunted both Helene Sabat and her grandmother for sixteen years. Helene was born behind those shutters, daughter of a Creole whore who worked there. The grandmother took Helene away from the soft lights and flowered carpets of the Sundown House and raised her under the dolesome eyes of a multicolored Virgin Mary, counseling her to be constantly on guard for any sign of her mother's wild blood.

So when Wiley Wright came to visit his Great Aunt Cecile in New Orleans, his enchantment with the pretty Helene became a marriage proposal—under the pressure of both women. He was a seaman (or rather a lakeman, for he was a ship's cook on one of the Great Lakes lines), in port only three days out of every sixteen.

He took his bride to his home in Medallion and put her in a lovely house with a brick porch and real lace curtains at the window. His long absences were quite bearable for Helene Wright, especially when, after some nine years of marriage, her daughter was born.

Her daughter was more comfort and purpose than she had ever hoped to find in this life. She rose grandly to the occasion of motherhood—grateful, deep down in her heart, that the child had not inherited the great beauty that was hers: that her skin had dusk in it, that her lashes were substantial but not undignified in their length, that she had taken the broad flat nose of Wiley (although Helene expected to improve it somewhat) and his generous lips.

Under Helene's hand the girl became obedient and polite. Any enthusiasms that little Nel showed were calmed by the mother until she drove her daughter's imagination underground.

Helene Wright was an impressive woman, at least in Medallion she was. Heavy hair in a bun, dark eyes arched in a perpetual query about other people's manners. A woman who won all social battles with presence and a conviction of the legitimacy of her authority. Since there was no Catholic church in Medallion then, she joined the most conservative black church. And held sway. It was Helene who never turned her head in church when latecomers arrived; Helene who established the practice of seasonal altar flowers; Helene who introduced the giving of banquets of welcome to returning Negro veterans. She lost only one battle—the pronunciation of her name. The people in the Bottom refused to say Helene. They called her Helen Wright and left it at that.

All in all her life was a satisfactory one. She loved her house and enjoyed manipulating her daughter and her husband. She would sigh sometimes just before falling asleep, thinking that she had indeed come far enough away from the Sundown House.

So it was with extremely mixed emotions that she read a letter from Mr. Henri Martin describing the illness of her grandmother, and suggesting she come down right away. She didn't want to go, but could not bring herself to ignore the silent plea of the woman who had rescued her.

It was November. November, 1920.[4] Even in Medallion there was a victorious swagger in the legs of white men and a dull-eyed excitement in the eyes of colored veterans.

Helene thought about the trip South with heavy misgiving but decided that she had the best protection: her manner and her bearing, to which she would add a beautiful dress. She bought some deep-brown wool and three-fourths of a yard of matching velvet. Out of this she made herself a heavy but elegant dress with velvet collar and pockets.

Nel watched her mother cutting the pattern from newspapers and moving her eyes rapidly from a magazine model to her own hands. She watched her turn up the kerosene lamp at sunset to sew far into the night.

The day they were ready, Helene cooked a smoked ham, left a note for her lake-bound husband, in case he docked early, and walked head high and arms stiff with luggage ahead of her daughter to the train depot.

It was a longer walk than she remembered, and they saw the train steaming up just as they turned the corner. They ran along the track looking for the coach pointed out to them by the colored porter. Even at that they made a mistake. Helene and her daughter entered a coach peopled by some twenty white men and women. Rather than go back and down the three wooden steps again, Helene decided to spare herself some embarrassment and walk on through to the colored car. She carried two pieces of luggage and a string purse; her daughter carried a covered basket of food.

As they opened the door marked COLORED ONLY, they saw a white conductor coming toward them. It was a chilly day but a light skim of sweat glistened on the woman's face as she and the little girl struggled to hold the door open, hang on to their luggage and enter all at once. The conductor let his eyes travel over the pale yellow woman and then stuck his little finger into his ear, jiggling it free of wax. "What you think you doin', gal?"

Helene looked up at him.

So soon. So soon. She hadn't even begun the trip back. Back to her grandmother's house in the city where the red shutters glowed, and already she had been called "gal." All the old vulnerabilities, all the old

---

4. Second anniversary of the armistice ending World War I.

fears of being somehow flawed gathered in her stomach and made her hands tremble. She had heard only that one word; it dangled above her wide-brimmed hat, which had slipped, in her exertion, from its carefully leveled placement and was now tilted in a bit of a jaunt over her eye.

Thinking he wanted her tickets, she quickly dropped both the cowhide suitcase and the straw one in order to search for them in her purse. An eagerness to please and an apology for living met in her voice. "I have them. Right here somewhere, sir . . ."

The conductor looked at the bit of wax his fingernail had retrieved. "What was you doin' back in there? What was you doin' in that coach yonder?"

Helene licked her lips. "Oh . . . I . . ." Her glance moved beyond the white man's face to the passengers seated behind him. Four or five black faces were watching, two belonging to soldiers still in their shit-colored uniforms and peaked caps. She saw their closed faces, their locked eyes, and turned for compassion to the gray eyes of the conductor.

"We made a mistake, sir. You see, there wasn't no sign. We just got in the wrong car, that's all. Sir."

"We don't 'low no mistakes on this train. Now git your butt on in there."

He stood there staring at her until she realized that he wanted her to move aside. Pulling Nel by the arm, she pressed herself and her daughter into the foot space in front of a wooden seat. Then, for no earthly reason, at least no reason that anybody could understand, certainly no reason that Nel understood then or later, she smiled. Like a street pup that wags its tail at the very doorjamb of the butcher shop he has been kicked away from only moments before, Helene smiled. Smiled dazzlingly and coquettishly at the salmon-colored face of the conductor.

Nel looked away from the flash of pretty teeth to the other passengers. The two black soldiers, who had been watching the scene with what appeared to be indifference, now looked stricken. Behind Nel was the bright and blazing light of her mother's smile; before her the midnight eyes of the soldiers. She saw the muscles of their faces tighten, a movement under the skin from blood to marble. No change in the expression of the eyes, but a hard wetness that veiled them as they looked at the stretch of her mother's foolish smile.

As the door slammed on the conductor's exit, Helene walked down the aisle to a seat. She looked about for a second to see whether any of the men would help her put the suitcases in the overhead rack. Not a man moved. Helene sat down, fussily, her back toward the men. Nel sat opposite, facing both her mother and the soldiers, neither of whom she could look at. She felt both pleased and ashamed to sense that these men, unlike her father, who worshiped his graceful, beautiful wife, were bubbling with a hatred for her mother that had not been there in the beginning but had been born with the dazzling smile. In the silence that preceded the train's heave, she looked deeply at the folds of her mother's dress. There in the fall of the heavy brown wool she held her eyes. She could not risk letting them travel upward for fear of seeing that the hooks and eyes in the placket of the dress had come undone and exposed the custard-colored skin underneath. She stared at the hem, wanting to believe in its weight but knowing that custard was all that it hid. If this tall, proud woman, this woman who was very particular about her friends, who slipped into church with unequaled elegance, who could quell a roustabout with a look, if *she* were really custard, then there was a chance that Nel was too.

It was on that train, shuffling toward Cincinnati, that she resolved to be on guard—always. She wanted to make certain that no man ever looked at her that way. That no midnight eyes or marbled flesh would ever accost her and turn her into jelly.

For two days they rode; two days of watching sleet turn to rain, turn to purple sunsets, and one night knotted on the wooden seats (their heads on folded coats), trying not to hear the snoring soldiers. When they changed trains in Birmingham for the last leg of the trip, they discovered what luxury they had been in through Kentucky and Tennessee, where the rest stops had all had colored toilets. After Birmingham there were none. Helene's face was drawn with the need to relieve herself, and so intense was her distress she finally brought herself to speak about her problem to a black woman with four children who had got on in Tuscaloosa.

"Is there somewhere we can go to use the restroom?"

The woman looked up at her and seemed not to understand. "Ma'am?" Her eyes fastened on the thick velvet collar, the fair skin, the high-tone voice.

"The restroom," Helene repeated. Then, in a whisper, "The toilet."

The woman pointed out the window and said, "Yes, ma'am. Yonder."

Helene looked out of the window halfway expecting to see a comfort station in the distance; instead she saw gray-green trees leaning over tangled grass. "Where?"

"Yonder," the woman said. "Meridian. We be pullin' in direc'lin."

Then she smiled sympathetically and asked, "Kin you make it?"

Helene nodded and went back to her seat trying to think of other things—for the surest way to have an accident would be to remember her full bladder.

At Meridian the women got out with their children. While Helene looked about the tiny stationhouse for a door that said COLORED WOMEN, the other woman stalked off to a field of high grass on the far side of the track. Some white men were leaning on the railing in front of the stationhouse. It was not only their tongues curling around toothpicks that kept Helene from asking information of them. She looked around for the other woman and, seeing just the top of her head rag in the grass, slowly realized where "yonder" was. All of them, the fat woman and her four children, three boys and a girl, Helene and her daughter, squatted there in the four o'clock Meridian sun. They did it again in Ellisville, again in Hattiesburg, and by the time they reached Slidell, not too far from Lake Pontchartrain, Helene could not only fold leaves as well as the fat woman, she never felt a stir as she passed the muddy eyes of the men who stood like wrecked Dorics[5] under the station roofs of those towns.

The lift in spirit that such an accomplishment produced in her quickly disappeared when the train finally pulled into New Orleans.

Cecile Sabat's house leaned between two others just like it on Elysian Fields. A Frenchified shotgun house,[6] it sported a magnificent garden in the back and a tiny wrought-iron fence in the front. On the door hung a black crepe wreath with purple ribbon. They were too late. Helene reached up to touch the ribbon, hesitated, and knocked. A man in a collarless shirt opened the door. Helene identified herself and he said he was Henri Martin and that he was there for the settin'-up.[7] They stepped into the house. The Virgin Mary clasped her hands in front of her neck three times in the front room and once in the bedroom where Cecile's body lay. The old woman had died without seeing or blessing her granddaughter.

No one other than Mr. Martin seemed to be in the house, but a sweet odor as of gardenias told them that someone else had been. Blotting her lashes with a white handkerchief, Helene walked through the kitchen to the back bedroom where she had slept for sixteen years. Nel trotted along behind, enchanted with the smell, the candles and the strangeness. When Helene bent to loosen the ribbons of Nel's hat, a woman in a yellow dress came out of the garden and onto the back porch that opened into the bedroom. The two women looked at each other. There was no recognition in the eyes of either. Then Helene said, "This is your . . . grandmother, Nel." Nel looked at her mother and then quickly back at the door they had just come out of.

"No. That was your great-grandmother. This is your grandmother. My . . . mother."

Before the child could think, her words were hanging in the gardenia air. "But she looks so young."

The woman in the canary-yellow dress laughed and said she was forty-eight, "an old forty-eight."

Then it was she who carried the gardenia smell. This tiny woman with the softness and glare of a canary. In that somber house that held four Virgin Marys, where death sighed in every corner and candles sputtered, the gardenia smell and canary-yellow dress emphasized the funeral atmosphere surrounding them.

The woman smiled, glanced in the mirror and said, throwing her voice toward Helene, "That your only one?"

"Yes," said Helene.

"Pretty. A lot like you."

"Yes. Well. She's ten now."

"Ten? Vrai?[8] Small for her age, no?"

Helene shrugged and looked at her daughter's questioning eyes. The woman in the yellow dress leaned forward. "Come. Come, chère."

Helene interrupted. "We have to get cleaned up. We been three days on the train with no chance to wash or . . . "

"Comment t'appelle?'

"She doesn't talk Creole."

"Then you ask her."

"She wants to know your name, honey."

With her head pressed into her mother's heavy brown dress, Nel told her and then asked, "What's yours?"

"Mine's Rochelle. Well. I must be going on." She moved closer to the mirror and stood there sweeping hair up from her neck back into its halo-like roll, and wetting with spit the ringlets that fell over her ears. "I been here, you know, most of the day. She pass on yesterday. The funeral tomorrow. Henri takin' care." She struck a match, blew it out and darkened her eyebrows with the burnt head. All the while Helene and Nel watched her. The one in a rage at the folded leaves she had endured, the wooden benches she had slept on, all to miss seeing her grandmother and seeing instead that painted canary who never said a word of greeting or affection or . . .

Rochelle continued. "I don't know what happen to de house. Long time paid for. You be thinkin' on it? Oui?"[9] Her newly darkened eyebrows queried Helene.

"Oui." Helene's voice was chilly. "I be thinkin' on it."

"Oh, well. Not for me to say . . . "

Suddenly she swept around and hugged Nel—a quick embrace tighter and harder than one would have imagined her thin soft arms capable of.

" 'Voir! 'Voir!" and she was gone.

In the kitchen, being soaped head to toe by her mother, Nel ventured an observation. "She smelled so nice. And her skin was so soft."

Helene rinsed the cloth. "Much handled things are always soft."

"What does 'vwah' mean?"

"I don't know," her mother said. "I don't talk Creole." She gazed at her daughter's wet buttocks. "And neither do you."

When they got back to Medallion and into the quiet house they saw the note exactly where they had left it and the ham dried out in the icebox.

"Lord, I've never been so glad to see this place. But look at the dust. Get the rags, Nel. Oh, never mind. Let's breathe awhile first. Lord, I never thought I'd get back here safe and sound. Whoo. Well it's over. Good and over. Praise His name. Look at that. I told that old fool not to deliver any milk and there's the can curdled to beat all. What gets into people? I told him not to. Well, I got other things to worry 'bout. Got to get a fire started. I left it ready so I wouldn't have to do nothin' but light it. Lord, it's cold. Don't just sit there, honey. You could be pulling your nose . . . "

Nel sat on the red-velvet sofa listening to her mother but remembering the smell and the tight, tight hug of the woman in yellow who rubbed burned matches over her eyes.

Late that night after the fire was made, the cold supper eaten, the surface dust removed, Nel lay in bed thinking of her trip. She remembered clearly the urine running down and into her stockings until she learned how to squat properly; the disgust on the face of the dead woman and the sound of the funeral drums. It had been an exhilarating trip but a fearful one. She had been frightened of the soldiers' eyes on the train, the black wreath on the door, the custard pudding she believed lurked under her mother's heavy dress, the feel of unknown streets and unknown people. But she had gone on a real trip, and now she was different. She got out of bed and lit the lamp to look in the mirror. There was her face, plain brown eyes, three braids and the nose her mother hated. She looked for a long time and suddenly a shiver ran through her.

"I'm me," she whispered. "Me."

Nel didn't know quite what she meant, but on the other hand she knew exactly what she meant.

---

9. *Will you?* (literally, *Yes?*) Below: '*Voir* (and "*vwah*"), short for *Au revoir—see you again.*

"I'm me. I'm not their daughter. I'm not Nel. I'm me. Me."

Each time she said the word *me* there was a gathering in her like power, like joy, like fear. Back in bed with her discovery, she stared out the window at the dark leaves of the horse chestnut.

"Me," she murmured. And then, sinking deeper into the quilts, "I want . . . I want to be . . . wonderful. Oh, Jesus, make me wonderful."

The many experiences of her trip crowded in on her. She slept. It was the last as well as the first time she was ever to leave Medallion.

For days afterward she imagined other trips she would take, alone though, to faraway places. Contemplating them was delicious. Leaving Medallion would be her goal. But that was before she met Sula, the girl she had seen for five years at Garfield Primary but never played with, never knew, because her mother said that Sula's mother was sooty. The trip, perhaps, or her new found me-ness, gave her the strength to cultivate a friend in spite of her mother.

When Sula first visited the Wright house, Helene's curdled scorn turned to butter. Her daughter's friend seemed to have none of the mother's slackness. Nel, who regarded the oppressive neatness of her home with dread, felt comfortable in it with Sula, who loved it and would sit on the red-velvet sofa for ten to twenty minutes at a time—still as dawn. As for Nel, she preferred Sula's woolly house, where a pot of something was always cooking on the stove; where the mother, Hannah, never scolded or gave directions; where all sorts of people dropped in; where newspapers were stacked in the hallway, and dirty dishes left for hours at a time in the sink, and where a one-legged grandmother named Eva handed you goobers from deep inside her pockets or read you a dream.

1921

Sula Peace lived in a house of many rooms that had been built over a period of five years to the specifications of its owner, who kept on adding things: more stairways—there were three sets to the second floor—more rooms, doors and stoops. There were rooms that had three doors, others that opened out on the porch only and were inaccessible from any other part of the house; others that you could get to only by going through somebody's bedroom. The creator and sovereign of this enormous house with the four sickle-pear trees in the front yard and the single elm in the back yard was Eva Peace, who sat in a wagon on the third floor directing the lives of her children, friends, strays, and a constant stream of boarders. Fewer than nine people in the town remembered when Eva had two legs, and her oldest child, Hannah, was not one of them. Unless Eva herself introduced the subject, no one ever spoke of her disability; they pretended to ignore it, unless, in some mood of fancy, she began some fearful story about it—generally to entertain children. How the leg got up by itself one day and walked on off. How she hobbled after it but it ran too fast. Or how she had a corn on her toe and it just grew and grew and grew until her whole foot was a corn and then it traveled on up her leg and wouldn't stop growing until she put a red rag at the top but by that time it was already at her knee.

Somebody said Eva stuck it under a train and made them pay off. Another said she sold it to a hospital for $10,000—at which Mr. Reed opened his eyes and asked, "Nigger gal legs goin' for $10,000 a *piece?*" as though he could understand $10,000 a *pair*—but for *one?*

Whatever the fate of her lost leg, the remaining one was magnificent. It was stockinged and shod at all times and in all weather. Once in a while she got a felt slipper for Christmas or her birthday, but they soon disappeared, for Eva always wore a black lace-up shoe that came well above her ankle. Nor did she wear overlong dresses to disguise the empty place on her left side. Her dresses were mid-calf so that her one glamorous leg was always in view as well as the long fall of space below her left thigh. One of her men friends had fashioned a kind of wheelchair for her: a rocking-chair top fitted into a large child's wagon. In this contraption she wheeled around the room, from bedside to dresser to the balcony that opened out the north side of her room or to the window that looked out on the back yard. The wagon was so low that children who spoke to her standing up were eye level with her, and adults, standing or sitting, had to look down at her. But they didn't know it. They all had the impression that they were looking up at her, up into the open distances of her eyes, up into the soft black of her nostrils and up at the crest of her chin.

Eva had married a man named BoyBoy and had three children: Hannah, the eldest, and Eva, whom she named after herself but called Pearl, and a son named Ralph, whom she called Plum.

After five years of a sad and disgruntled marriage BoyBoy took off. During the time they were together he was very much preoccupied with other women and not home much. He did whatever he could that he liked, and he liked womanizing best, drinking second, and abusing Eva third. When he left in November, Eva had $1.65, five eggs, three beets and no idea of what or how to feel. The children needed her; she needed money, and needed to get on with her life. But the demands of feeding her three children were so acute she had to postpone her anger for two years until she had both the time and the energy for it. She was confused and desperately hungry. There were very few black families in those low hills then. The Suggs, who lived two hundred yards down the road, brought her a warm bowl of peas, as soon as they found out, and a plate of cold bread. She thanked them and asked if they had a little milk for the older ones. They said no, but Mrs. Jackson, they knew, had a cow still giving. Eva took a bucket over and Mrs. Jackson told her to come back and fill it up in the morning, because the evening milking had already been done. In this way, things went on until near December. People were very willing to help, but Eva felt she would soon run her welcome out; winters were hard and her neighbors were not that much better off. She would lie in bed with the baby boy, the two girls wrapped in quilts on the floor, thinking. The oldest child, Hannah, was five and too young to take care of the baby alone, and any housework Eva could find would keep her away from them from five thirty or earlier in the morning until dark—way past eight. The white people in the valley weren't rich enough then to want maids; they were small farmers and tradesmen and wanted hard-labor help if anything. She thought also of returning to some of her people in Virginia, but to come home dragging three young ones would have to be a step one rung before death for Eva. She would have to scrounge around and beg through the winter, until her baby was at least nine months old, then she could plant and maybe hire herself out to valley farms to weed or sow or feed stock until something steadier came along at harvest time. She thought she had probably been a fool to let

BoyBoy haul her away from her people, but it had seemed so right at the time. He worked for a white carpenter and toolsmith who insisted on BoyBoy's accompanying him when he went West and set up in a squinchy little town called Medallion. BoyBoy brought his new wife and built them a one-room cabin sixty feet back from the road that wound up out of the valley, on up into the hills and was named for the man he worked for. They lived there a year before they had an outhouse. Sometime before the middle of December, the baby, Plum, stopped having bowel movements. Eva massaged his stomach and gave him warm water. Something must be wrong with my milk, she thought. Mrs. Suggs gave her castor oil, but even that didn't work. He cried and fought so they couldn't get much down his throat anyway. He seemed in great pain and his shrieks were pitched high in outrage and suffering. At one point, maddened by his own crying, he gagged, choked and looked as though he was strangling to death. Eva rushed to him and kicked over the earthen slop jar, washing a small area of the floor with the child's urine. She managed to soothe him, but when he took up the cry again late that night, she resolved to end his misery once and for all. She wrapped him in blankets, ran her finger around the crevices and sides of the lard can and stumbled to the outhouse with him. Deep in its darkness and freezing stench she squatted down, turned the baby over on her knees, exposed his buttocks and shoved the last bit of food she had in the world (besides three beets) up his ass. Softening the insertion with the dab of lard, she probed with her middle finger to loosen his bowels. Her fingernail snagged what felt like a pebble; she pulled it out and others followed. Plum stopped crying as the black hard stools ricocheted onto the frozen ground. And now that it was over, Eva squatted there wondering why she had come all the way out there to free his stools, and what was she doing down on her haunches with her beloved baby boy warmed by her body in the almost total darkness, her shins and teeth freezing, her nostrils assailed. She shook her head as though to juggle her brains around, then said aloud, "Uh uh. Nooo." Thereupon she returned to the house and her bed. As the grateful Plum slept, the silence allowed her to think.

Two days later she left all of her children with Mrs. Suggs, saying she would be back the next day.

Eighteen months later she swept down from a wagon with two crutches, a new black pocketbook, and one leg. First she reclaimed her children, next she gave the surprised Mrs. Suggs a ten-dollar bill, later she started building a house on Carpenter's Road, sixty feet from BoyBoy's one-room cabin, which she rented out.

When Plum was three years old, BoyBoy came back to town and paid her a visit. When Eva got the word that he was on his way, she made some lemonade. She had no idea what she would do or feel during that encounter. Would she cry, cut his throat, beg him to make love to her? She couldn't imagine. So she just waited to see. She stirred lemonade in a green pitcher and waited.

BoyBoy danced up the steps and knocked on the door.

"Come on in," she hollered.

He opened the door and stood smiling, a picture of prosperity and good will. His shoes were a shiny orange, and he had on a citified straw hat, a light-blue suit, and a cat's-head stickpin in his tie. Eva smiled and told him to sit himself down. He smiled too.

"How you been, girl?"

"Pretty fair. What you know good?" When she heard those words come out of her own mouth she knew that their conversation would start off polite. Although it remained to be seen whether she would still run the ice pick through the cat's-head pin.

"Have some lemonade."

"Don't mind if I do." He swept his hat off with a satisfied gesture. His nails were long and shiny. "Sho is hot, and I been runnin' around all day."

Eva looked out of the screen door and saw a woman in a pea-green dress leaning on the smallest pear tree. Glancing back at him, she was reminded of Plum's face when he managed to get the meat out of a walnut all by himself. Eva smiled again, and poured the lemonade.

Their conversation was easy: she catching him up on all the gossip, he asking about this one and that one, and like everybody else avoiding any reference to her leg. It was like talking to somebody's cousin who just stopped by to say howdy before getting on back to wherever he came from. BoyBoy didn't ask to see the children, and Eva didn't bring them into the conversation.

After a while he rose to go. Talking about his appointments and exuding an odor of new money and idleness, he danced down the steps and strutted toward the pea-green dress. Eva watched. She looked at the back of his neck and the set of his shoulders. Underneath all of that shine she saw defeat in the stalk of his neck and the curious tight way he held his shoulders. But still she was not sure what she felt. Then he leaned forward and whispered into the ear of the woman in the green dress. She was still for a moment and then threw back her head and laughed. A high-pitched big-city laugh that reminded Eva of Chicago. It hit her like a sledge hammer, and it was then that she knew what to feel. A liquid trail of hate flooded her chest.

Knowing that she would hate him long and well filled her with pleasant anticipation, like when you know you are going to fall in love with someone and you wait for the happy signs. Hating BoyBoy, she could get on with it, and have the safety, the thrill, the consistency of that hatred as long as she wanted or needed it to define and strengthen her or protect her from routine vulnerabilities. (Once when Hannah accused her of hating colored people, Eva said she only hated one, Hannah's father BoyBoy, and it was hating him that kept her alive and happy.)

Happy or not, after BoyBoy's visit she began her retreat to her bedroom, leaving the bottom of the house more and more to those who lived there: cousins who were passing through, stray folks, and the many, many newly married couples she let rooms to with housekeeping privileges, and after 1910 she didn't willingly set foot on the stairs but once and that was to light a fire, the smoke of which was in her hair for years.

Among the tenants in that big old house were the children Eva took in. Operating on a private scheme of preference and prejudice, she sent off for children she had seen from the balcony of her bedroom or whose circumstances she had heard about from the gossipy old men who came to play checkers or read the *Courier,* or write her number.[1] In 1921, when her granddaughter Sula was eleven, Eva had three such children. They

---

1. (Illegal) lottery number.

came with woolen caps and names given to them by their mothers, or grandmothers, or somebody's best friend. Eva snatched the caps off their heads and ignored their names. She looked at the first child closely, his wrists, the shape of his head and the temperament that showed in his eyes and said, "Well. Look at Dewey. My my mymymy." When later that same year she sent for a child who kept falling down off the porch across the street, she said the same thing. Somebody said, "But, Miss Eva, you calls the other one Dewey."

"So? This here's another one."

When the third one was brought and Eva said "Dewey" again, everybody thought she had simply run out of names or that her faculties had finally softened.

"How is anybody going to tell them apart?" Hannah asked her.

"What you need to tell them apart for? They's all deweys."

When Hannah asked the question it didn't sound very bright, because each dewey was markedly different from the other two. Dewey one was a deeply black boy with a beautiful head and the golden eyes of chronic jaundice. Dewey two was light-skinned with freckles everywhere and a head of tight red hair. Dewey three was half Mexican with chocolate skin and black bangs. Besides, they were one and two years apart in age. It was Eva saying things like, "Send one of them deweys out to get me some Garret, if they don't have Garret, get Buttercup,"[2] or, "Tell them deweys to cut out that noise," or, "Come here, you dewey you," and, "Send me a dewey," that gave Hannah's question its weight.

Slowly each boy came out of whatever cocoon he was in at the time his mother or somebody gave him away, and accepted Eva's view, becoming in fact as well as in name a dewey—joining with the other two to become a trinity with a plural name . . . inseparable, loving nothing and no one but themselves. When the handle from the icebox fell off, all the deweys got whipped, and in dry-eyed silence watched their own feet as they turned their behinds high up into the air for the stroke. When the golden-eyed dewey was ready for school he would not go without the others. He was seven, freckled dewey was five, and Mexican dewey was only four. Eva solved the problem by having them all sent off together. Mr. Buckland Reed said, "But one of them's only four."

"How you know? They all come here the same year," Eva said.

"But that one there was one year old when he came, and that was three years ago."

"You don't know how old he was when he come here and neither do the teacher. Send 'em."

The teacher was startled but not unbelieving, for she had long ago given up trying to fathom the ways of the colored people in town. So when Mrs. Reed said that their names were Dewey King, that they were cousins, and all were six years old, the teacher gave only a tiny sigh and wrote them in the record book for the first grade. She too thought she would have no problem distinguishing among them, because they looked nothing alike, but like everyone else before her, she gradually found that she could not tell one from the other. The deweys would not allow it. They got all mixed up in her head, and finally she could not literally believe her eyes. They spoke with one voice, thought with one mind, and maintained an annoying privacy. Stoutheated, surly, and wholly unpre-

2. Brands of snuff.

dictable, the deweys remained a mystery not only during all of their lives in Medallion but after as well.

The deweys came in 1921, but the year before Eva had given a small room off the kitchen to Tar Baby, a beautiful, slight, quiet man who never spoke above a whisper. Most people said he was half white, but Eva said he was all white. That she knew blood when she saw it, and he didn't have none. When he first came to Medallion, the people called him Pretty Johnnie, but Eva looked at his milky skin and cornsilk hair and out of a mixture of fun and meanness called him Tar Baby. He was a mountain boy who stayed to himself, bothering no one, intent solely on drinking himself to death. At first he worked in a poultry market, and after wringing the necks of chickens all day, he came home and drank until he slept. Later he began to miss days at work and frequently did not have his rent money. When he lost his job altogether, he would go out in the morning, scrounge around for money doing odd jobs, bumming or whatever, and come home to drink. Because he was no bother, ate little, required nothing, and was a lover of cheap wine, no one found him a nuisance. Besides, he frequently went to Wednesday-night prayer meetings and sang with the sweetest hill voice imaginable "In the Sweet By-and-By."[3] He sent the deweys out for his liquor and spent most of his time in a heap on the floor or sitting in a chair staring at the wall.

Hannah worried about him a little, but only a very little. For it soon became clear that he simply wanted a place to die privately but not quite alone. No one thought of suggesting to him that he pull himself together or see a doctor or anything. Even the women at prayer meeting who cried when he sang "In the Sweet By-and-By" never tried to get him to participate in the church activities. They just listened to him sing, wept and thought very graphically of their own imminent deaths. The people either accepted his own evaluation of his life, or were indifferent to it. There was, however, a measure of contempt in their indifference, for they had little patience with people who took themselves that seriously. Seriously enough to try to die. And it was natural that he, after all, became the first one to join Shadrack—Tar Baby and the deweys—on National Suicide Day.

Under Eva's distant eye, and prey to her idiosyncrasies, her own children grew up stealthily: Pearl married at fourteen and moved to Flint, Michigan, from where she posted frail letters to her mother with two dollars folded into the writing paper. Sad little nonsense letters about minor troubles, her husband's job and who the children favored. Hannah married a laughing man named Rekus who died when their daughter Sula was about three years old, at which time Hannah moved back into her mother's big house prepared to take care of it and her mother forever.

With the exception of BoyBoy, those Peace women loved all men. It was manlove that Eva bequeathed to her daughters. Probably, people said, because there were no men in the house, no men to run it. But actually that was not true. The Peace women simply loved maleness, for its own sake. Eva, old as she was, and with one leg, had a regular flock of gentleman callers, and although she did not participate in the act of love, there

was a good deal of teasing and pecking and laughter. The men wanted to
see her lovely calf, that neat shoe, and watch the focusing that sometimes
swept down out of the distances in her eyes. They wanted to see the joy
in her face as they settled down to play checkers, knowing that even
when she beat them, as she almost always did, somehow, in her presence,
it was they who had won something. They would read the newspaper
aloud to her and make observations on its content, and Eva would listen
feeling no obligation to agree and, in fact, would take them to task about
their interpretation of events. But she argued with them with such an
absence of bile, such a concentration of manlove, that they felt their convictions solidified by her disagreement.

With other people's affairs Eva was equally prejudiced about men. She
fussed interminably with the brides of the newly wed couples for not
getting their men's supper ready on time; about how to launder shirts,
press them, etc. "Yo' man be here direc'lin. Ain't it 'bout time you got
busy?"

"Aw, Miss Eva. It'll be ready. We just having spaghetti."

"Again?" Eva's eyebrows fluted up and the newlywed pressed her lips
together in shame.

Hannah simply refused to live without the attentions of a man, and
after Rekus' death had a steady sequence of lovers, mostly the husbands
of her friends and neighbors. Her flirting was sweet, low and guileless.
Without ever a pat of the hair, a rush to change clothes or a quick appli-
cation of paint, with no gesture whatsoever, she rippled with sex. In her
same old print wraparound, barefoot in the summer, in the winter her
feet in a man's leather slippers with the backs flattened under her heels,
she made men aware of her behind, her slim ankles, the dew-smooth skin
and the incredible length of neck. Then the smile-eyes, the turn of the
head—all so welcoming, light and playful. Her voice trailed, dipped and
bowed; she gave a chord to the simplest words. Nobody, but nobody,
could say "hey sugar" like Hannah. When he heard it, the man tipped his
hat down a little over his eyes, hoisted his trousers and thought about the
hollow place at the base of her neck. And all this without the slightest
confusion about work and responsibilities. While Eva tested and argued
with her men, leaving them feeling as though they had been in combat
with a worthy, if amiable, foe, Hannah rubbed no edges, made no demands, made the man feel as though he were complete and wonderful
just as he was—he didn't need fixing—and so he relaxed and swooned in
the Hannah-light that shone on him simply because he was. If the man
entered and Hannah was carrying a coal scuttle up from the basement,
she handled it in such a way that it became a gesture of love. He made
no move to help her with it simply because he wanted to see how her
thighs looked when she bent to put it down, knowing that she wanted
him to see them too.

But since in that crowded house there were no places for private and
spontaneous lovemaking, Hannah would take the man down into the cellar in the summer where it was cool back behind the coal bin and the
newspapers, or in the winter they would step into the pantry and stand
up against the shelves she had filled with canned goods, or lie on the flour
sack just under the rows of tiny green peppers. When those places were
not available, she would slip into the seldom-used parlor, or even up to
her bedroom. She liked the last place least, not because Sula slept in the

room with her but because her love mate's tendency was always to fall asleep afterward and Hannah was fastidious about whom she slept with. She would fuck practically anything, but sleeping with someone implied for her a measure of trust and a definite commitment. So she ended up a daylight lover, and it was only once actually that Sula came home from school and found her mother in the bed, curled spoon in the arms of a man.

Seeing her step so easily into the pantry and emerge looking precisely as she did when she entered, only happier, taught Sula that sex was pleasant and frequent, but otherwise unremarkable. Outside the house, where children giggled about underwear, the message was different. So she watched her mother's face and the face of the men when they opened the pantry door and made up her own mind.

Hannah exasperated the women in the town—the "good" women, who said, "One thing I can't stand is a nasty woman"; the whores, who were hard put to find trade among black men anyway and who resented Hannah's generosity; the middling women, who had both husbands and affairs, because Hannah seemed too unlike them, having no passion attached to her relationships and being wholly incapable of jealousy. Hannah's friendships with women were, of course, seldom and short-lived, and the newly married couples whom her mother took in soon learned what a hazard she was. She could break up a marriage before it had even become one—she would make love to the new groom and wash his wife's dishes all in an afternoon. What she wanted, after Rekus died, and what she succeeded in having more often than not, was some touching every day.

The men, surprisingly, never gossiped about her. She was unquestionably a kind and generous woman and that, coupled with her extraordinary beauty and funky elegance of manner, made them defend her and protect her from any vitriol that newcomers or their wives might spill.

Eva's last child, Plum, to whom she hoped to bequeath everything, floated in a constant swaddle of love and affection, until 1917 when he went to war. He returned to the States in 1919 but did not get back to Medallion until 1920. He wrote letters from New York, Washington, D.C., and Chicago full of promises of homecomings, but there was obviously something wrong. Finally some two or three days after Christmas, he arrived with just the shadow of his old dip-down walk. His hair had been neither cut nor combed in months, his clothes were pointless and he had no socks. But he did have a black bag, a paper sack, and a sweet, sweet smile. Everybody welcomed him and gave him a warm room next to Tar Baby's and waited for him to tell them whatever it was he wanted them to know. They waited in vain for his telling but not long for the knowing. His habits were much like Tar Baby's but there were no bottles, and Plum was sometimes cheerful and animated. Hannah watched and Eva waited. Then he began to steal from them, take trips to Cincinnati and sleep for days in his room with the record player going. He got even thinner, since he ate only snatches of things at beginnings or endings of meals. It was Hannah who found the bent spoon black from steady cooking.

So late one night in 1921, Eva got up from her bed and put on her clothes. Hoisting herself up on her crutches, she was amazed to find that she could still manage them, although the pain in her armpits was severe. She practiced a few steps around the room, and then opened the door. Slowly, she manipulated herself down the long flights of stairs, two crutches under her left arm, the right hand grasping the banister. The sound of her foot booming in comparison to the delicate pat of the crutch tip. On each landing she stopped for breath. Annoyed at her physical condition, she closed her eyes and removed the crutches from under her arms to relieve the unaccustomed pressure. At the foot of the stairs she redistributed her weight between the crutches and swooped on through the front room, to the dining room, to the kitchen, swinging and swooping like a giant heron, so graceful sailing about in its own habitat but awkward and comical when it folded its wings and tried to walk. With a swing and a swoop she arrived at Plum's door and pushed it open with the tip of one crutch. He was lying in bed barely visible in the light coming from a single bulb. Eva swung over to the bed and propped her crutches at its foot. She sat down and gathered Plum into her arms. He woke, but only slightly.

"Hey, man. Hey. You holdin' me Mamma?" His voice was drowsy and amused. He chuckled as though he had heard some private joke. Eva held him closer and began to rock. Back and forth she rocked him, her eyes wandering around his room. There in the corner was a half-eaten store-bought cherry pie. Balled-up candy wrappers and empty pop bottles peeped from under the dresser. On the floor by her foot was a glass of strawberry crush and a *Liberty* magazine. Rocking, rocking, listening to Plum's occasional chuckles, Eva let her memory spin, loop and fall. Plum in the tub that time as she leaned over him. He reached up and dripped water into her bosom and laughed. She was angry, but not too, and laughed with him.

"Mamma, you so purty. You so purty, Mamma."

Eva lifted her tongue to the edge of her lip to stop the tears from running into her mouth. Rocking, rocking. Later she laid him down and looked at him a long time. Suddenly she was thirsty and reached for the glass of strawberry crush. She put it to her lips and discovered it was blood-tainted water and threw it to the floor. Plum woke up and said, "Hey, Mamma, whyn't you go on back to bed? I'm all right. Didn't I tell you? I'm all right. Go on, now."

"I'm going, Plum," she said. She shifted her weight and pulled her crutches toward her. Swinging and swooping, she left his room. She dragged herself to the kitchen and made grating noises.

Plum on the rim of a warm light sleep was still chuckling. Mamma. She sure was somethin'. He felt twilight. Now there seemed to be some kind of wet light traveling over his legs and stomach with a deeply attractive smell. It wound itself—this wet light—all about him, splashing and running into his skin. He opened his eyes and saw what he imagined was the great wing of an eagle pouring a wet lightness over him. Some kind of baptism, some kind of blessing, he thought. Everything is going to be all right, it said. Knowing that it was so he closed his eyes and sank back into the bright hole of sleep.

Eva stepped back from the bed and let the crutches rest under her arms. She rolled a bit of newspaper into a tight stick about six inches long, lit it and threw it onto the bed where the kerosene-soaked Plum lay in snug delight. Quickly, as the *whoosh* of flames engulfed him, she shut the door and made her slow and painful journey back to the top of the house.

Just as she got to the third landing she could hear Hannah and some child's voice. She swung along, not even listening to the voices of alarm and the cries of the deweys. By the time she got to her bed someone was bounding up the stairs after her. Hannah opened the door. "Plum! Plum! He's burning, Mamma! We can't even open the door! Mamma!"

Eva looked into Hannah's eyes. "Is? My baby? Burning?" The two women did not speak, for the eyes of each were enough for the other. Then Hannah closed hers and ran toward the voices of neighbors calling for water.

1922

It was too cool for ice cream. A hill wind was blowing dust and empty Camels wrappers about their ankles. It pushed their dresses into the creases of their behinds, then lifted the hems to peek at their cotton underwear. They were on their way to Edna Finch's Mellow House, an ice-cream parlor catering to nice folks—where even children would feel comfortable, you know, even though it was right next to Reba's Grill and just one block down from the Time and a Half Pool Hall. It sat in the curve of Carpenter's Road, which, in four blocks, made up all the sporting life available in the Bottom. Old men and young ones draped themselves in front of the Elmira Theater, Irene's Palace of Cosmetology, the pool hall, the grill and the other sagging business enterprises that lined the street. On sills, on stoops, on crates and broken chairs they sat tasting their teeth and waiting for something to distract them. Every passerby, every motorcar, every alteration in stance caught their attention and was commented on. Particularly they watched women. When a woman approached, the older men tipped their hats; the younger ones opened and closed their thighs. But all of them, whatever their age, watched her retreating view with interest.

Nel and Sula walked through this valley of eyes chilled by the wind and heated by the embarrassment of appraising stares. The old men looked at their stalklike legs, dwelled on the cords in the backs of their knees and remembered old dance steps they had not done in twenty years. In their lust, which age had turned to kindness, they moved their lips as though to stir up the taste of young sweat on tight skin.

Pig meat. The words were in all their minds. And one of them, one of the young ones, said it aloud. Softly but definitively and there was no mistaking the compliment. His name was Ajax, a twenty-one-year-old pool haunt of sinister beauty. Graceful and economical in every movement, he held a place of envy with men of all ages for his magnificently foul mouth. In fact he seldom cursed, and the epithets he chose were dull, even harmless. His reputation was derived from the way he handled the words. When he said "hell" he hit the *h* with his lungs and the impact was greater than the achievement of the most imaginative foul mouth in the town. He could say "shit" with a nastiness impossible to imitate. So, when he said "pig meat" as Nel and Sula passed, they guarded their eyes lest someone see their delight.

It was not really Edna Finch's ice cream that made them brave the stretch of those panther eyes. Years later their own eyes would glaze as they cupped their chins in remembrance of the inchworm smiles, the squatting haunches, the track-rail legs straddling broken chairs. The cream-colored trousers marking with a mere seam the place where the mystery curled. Those smooth vanilla crotches invited them; those lemon-yellow gabardines beckoned to them.

They moved toward the ice-cream parlor like tightrope walkers, as thrilled by the possibility of a slip as by the maintenance of tension and balance. The least sideways glance, the merest toe stub, could pitch them into those creamy haunches spread wide with welcome. Somewhere beneath all of that daintiness, chambered in all that neatness, lay the thing that clotted their dreams.

Which was only fitting, for it was in dreams that the two girls had first met. Long before Edna Finch's Mellow House opened, even before they marched through the chocolate halls of Garfield Primary School out onto the playground and stood facing each other through the ropes of the one vacant swing ("Go on." "No. You go."), they had already made each other's acquaintance in the delirium of their noon dreams. They were solitary little girls whose loneliness was so profound it intoxicated them and sent them stumbling into Technicolored visions that always included a presence, a someone, who, quite like the dreamer, shared the delight of the dream. When Nel, an only child, sat on the steps of her back porch surrounded by the high silence of her mother's incredibly orderly house, feeling the neatness pointing at her back, she studied the poplars and fell easily into a picture of herself lying on a flowered bed, tangled in her own hair, waiting for some fiery prince. He approached but never quite arrived. But always, watching the dream along with her, were some smiling sympathetic eyes. Someone as interested as she herself in the flow of her imagined hair, the thickness of the mattress of flowers, the voile sleeves that closed below her elbows in gold-threaded cuffs.

Similarly, Sula, also an only child, but wedged into a household of throbbing disorder constantly awry with things, people, voices and the slamming of doors, spent hours in the attic behind a roll of linoleum galloping through her own mind on a gray-and-white horse tasting sugar and smelling roses in full view of a someone who shared both the taste and the speed.

So when they met, first in those chocolate halls and next through the ropes of the swing, they felt the ease and comfort of old friends. Because each had discovered years before that they were neither white nor male, and that all freedom and triumph was forbidden to them, they had set about creating something else to be. Their meeting was fortunate, for it let them use each other to grow on. Daughters of distant mothers and incomprehensible fathers (Sula's because he was dead; Nel's because he wasn't), they found in each other's eyes the intimacy they were looking for.

Nel Wright and Sula Peace were both twelve in 1922, wishbone thin and easy-assed. Nel was the color of wet sandpaper—just dark enough to escape the blows of the pitch-black truebloods and the contempt of old women who worried about such things as bad blood mixtures and knew that the origins of a mule and a mulatto were one and the same. Had she been any lighter-skinned she would have needed either her mother's protection on the way to school or a streak of mean to defend herself. Sula was a heavy brown with large quiet eyes, one of which featured a birthmark that spread from the middle of the lid toward the eyebrow, shaped something like a stemmed rose. It gave her otherwise plain face a broken excitement and blue-blade threat like the keloid scar of the razored man who sometimes played checkers with her grandmother. The birthmark was to grow darker as the years passed, but now it was the same shade as her gold-flecked eyes, which, to the end, were as steady and clean as rain.

Their friendship was as intense as it was sudden. They found relief in each other's personality. Although both were unshaped, formless things, Nel seemed stronger and more consistent than Sula, who could hardly be counted on to sustain any emotion for more than three minutes. Yet there was one time when that was not true, when she held on to a mood for weeks, but even that was in defense of Nel.

Four white boys in their early teens, sons of some newly arrived Irish people, occasionally entertained themselves in the afternoon by harassing black schoolchildren. With shoes that pinched and woolen knickers that made red rings on their calves, they had come to this valley with their parents believing as they did that it was a promised land—green and shimmering with welcome. What they found was a strange accent, a pervasive fear of their religion and firm resistance to their attempts to find work. With one exception the older residents of Medallion scorned them. The one exception was the black community. Although some of the Negroes had been in Medallion before the Civil War (the town didn't even have a name then), if they had any hatred for these newcomers it didn't matter because it didn't show. As a matter fact, baiting them was the one activity that the white Protestant residents concurred in. In part their place in this world was secured only when they echoed the old residents' attitude toward blacks.

These particular boys caught Nel once, and pushed her from hand to hand until they grew tired of the frightened helpless face. Because of that incident, Nel's route home from school became elaborate. She, and then Sula, managed to duck them for weeks until a chilly day in November when Sula said, "Let's us go on home the shortest way."

Nel blinked, but acquiesced. They walked up the street until they got to the bend of Carpenter's Road where the boys lounged on a disused well. Spotting their prey, the boys sauntered forward as though there were nothing in the world on their minds but the gray sky. Hardly able to control their grins, they stood like a gate blocking the path. When the girls were three feet in front of the boys, Sula reached into her coat pocket and pulled out Eva's paring knife. The boys stopped short, exchanged looks and dropped all pretense of innocence. This was going to be better than they thought. They were going to try and fight back, and with a knife. Maybe they could get an arm around one of their waists, or tear . . .

Sula squatted down in the dirt road and put everything down on the ground: her lunchpail, her reader, her mittens, her slate. Holding the knife in her right hand, she pulled the slate toward her and pressed her left forefinger down hard on its edge. Her aim was determined but inaccurate. She slashed off only the tip of her finger. The four boys stared open-mouthed at the wound and the scrap of flesh, like a button mushroom, curling in the cherry blood that ran into the corners of the slate.

Sula raised her eyes to them. Her voice was quiet. "If I can do that to myself, what you suppose I'll do to you?"

The shifting dirt was the only way Nel knew that they were moving away; she was looking at Sula's face, which seemed miles and miles away.

But toughness was not their quality—adventuresomeness was—and a mean determination to explore everything that interested them, from one-eyed chickens high-stepping in their penned yards to Mr. Buckland Reed's gold teeth, from the sound of sheets flapping in the wind to the labels on Tar Baby's wine bottles. And they had no priorities. They could be distracted from watching a fight with mean razors by the glorious smell of hot tar being poured by roadmen two hundred yards away.

In the safe harbor of each other's company they could afford to abandon the ways of other people and concentrate on their own perceptions of things. When Mrs. Wright reminded Nel to pull her nose, she would do it enthusiastically but without the least hope in the world.

"While you sittin' there, honey, go 'head and pull your nose."

"It hurts, Mamma."

"Don't you want a nice nose when you grow up?"

After she met Sula, Nel slid the clothespin under the blanket as soon as she got in the bed. And although there was still the hateful hot comb to suffer through each Saturday evening, its consequences—smooth hair—no longer interested her.

Joined in mutual admiration they watched each day as though it were a movie arranged for their amusement. The new theme they were now discovering was men. So they met regularly, without even planning it, to walk down the road to Edna Finch's Mellow House, even though it was too cool for ice cream.

Then summer came. A summer limp with the weight of blossomed things. Heavy sunflowers weeping over fences; iris curling and browning at the edges far away from their purple hearts; ears of corn letting their auburn hair wind down to their stalks. And the boys. The beautiful, beautiful boys who dotted the landscape like jewels, split the air with their shouts in the field, and thickened the river with their shining wet backs. Even their footsteps left a smell of smoke behind.

It was in that summer, the summer of their twelfth year, the summer of the beautiful black boys, that they became skittish, frightened and bold—all at the same time.

In that mercury mood in July, Sula and Nel wandered about the Bottom barefoot looking for mischief. They decided to go down by the river where the boys sometimes swam. Nel waited on the porch of 7 Carpenter's Road while Sula ran into the house to go to the toilet. On the way up the stairs, she passed the kitchen where Hannah sat with two friends, Patsy and Valentine. The two women were fanning themselves and watching Hannah put down some dough, all talking casually about one thing and another, and had gotten around, when Sula passed by, to the problems of child rearing.

"They a pain."

"Yeh. Wish I'd listened to mamma. She told me not to have 'em too soon."

"Any time at all is too soon for me."

"Oh, I don't know. My Rudy minds his daddy. He just wild with me. Be glad when he growed and gone."

Hannah smiled and said, "Shut your mouth. You love the ground he pee on."

"Sure I do. But he still a pain. Can't help loving your own child. No matter what they do."

"Well, Hester grown now and I can't say love is exactly what I feel."

"Sure you do. You love her, like I love Sula. I just don't like her. That's the difference."

"Guess so. Likin' them is another thing."

"Sure. They different people, you know . . . "

She only heard Hannah's words, and the pronouncement sent her flying up the stairs. In bewilderment, she stood at the window fingering the curtain edge, aware of a sting in her eye. Nel's call floated up and into the window, pulling her away from dark thoughts back into the bright, hot daylight.

They ran most of the way.

Heading toward the wide part of the river where trees grouped themselves in families darkening the earth below. They passed some boys swimming and clowning in the water, shrouding their words in laughter.

They ran in the sunlight, creating their own breeze, which pressed their dresses into their damp skin. Reaching a kind of square of four leaf-locked trees which promised cooling, they flung themselves into the four-cornered shade to taste their lip sweat and contemplate the wildness that had come upon them so suddenly. They lay in the grass, their foreheads almost touching, their bodies stretched away from each other at a 180-degree angle. Sula's head rested on her arm, an undone braid coiled around her wrist. Nel leaned on her elbows and worried long blades of grass with her fingers. Underneath their dresses flesh tightened and shivered in the high coolness, their small breasts just now beginning to create some pleasant discomfort when they were lying on their stomachs.

Sula lifted her head and joined Nel in the grass play. In concert, without ever meeting each other's eyes, they stroked the blades up and down, up and down. Nel found a thick twig and, with her thumbnail, pulled away its bark until it was stripped to a smooth, creamy innocence. Sula looked about and found one too. When both twigs were undressed Nel moved easily to the next stage and began tearing up rooted grass to make a bare spot of earth. When a generous clearing was made, Sula traced intricate patterns in it with her twig. At first Nel was content to do the same. But soon she grew impatient and poked her twig rhythmically and intensely into the earth, making a small neat hole that grew deeper and wider with the least manipulation of her twig. Sula copied her, and soon each had a hole the size of a cup. Nel began a more strenuous digging and, rising to her knee, was careful to scoop out the dirt as she made her hole deeper. Together they worked until the two holes were one and the same. When the depression was the size of a small dishpan, Nel's twig broke. With a gesture of disgust she threw the pieces into the hole they had made. Sula threw hers in too. Nel saw a bottle cap and tossed it in as well. Each then looked around for more debris to throw into the hole: paper, bits of glass, butts of cigarettes, until all of the small defiling things they could find were collected there. Carefully they replaced the soil and covered the entire grave with uprooted grass.

Neither one had spoken a word.

They stood up, stretched, then gazed out over the swift dull water as an unspeakable restlessness and agitation held them. At the same instant each girl heard footsteps in the grass. A little boy in too big knickers was coming up from the lower bank of the river. He stopped when he saw them and picked his nose.

"Your mamma tole you to stop eatin' snot, Chicken," Nel hollered at him through cupped hands.

"Shut up," he said, still picking.

"Come up here and say that."

"Leave him 'lone, Nel. Come here, Chicken. Lemme show you something."

"Naw."

"You scared we gone take your bugger away?"

"Leave him 'lone, I said. Come on, Chicken. Look. I'll help you climb a tree."

Chicken looked at the tree Sula was pointing to—a big double beech with low branches and lots of bends for sitting.

He moved slowly toward her.

"Come on, Chicken, I'll help you up."

Still picking his nose, his eyes wide, he came to where they were standing. Sula took him by the hand and coaxed him along. When they reached the base of the beech, she lifted him to the first branch, saying, "Go on. Go on. I got you." She followed the boy, steadying him, when he needed it, with her hand and her reassuring voice. When they were as high as they could go, Sula pointed to the far side of the river.

"See? Bet you never saw that far before, did you?"

"Uh uh."

"Now look down there." They both leaned a little and peered through the leaves at Nel standing below, squinting up at them. From their height she looked small and fore-shortened.

Chicken Little laughed.

"Y'all better come on down before you break your neck," Nel hollered.

"I ain't never coming down," the boy hollered back.

"Yeah. We better. Come on, Chicken."

"Naw. Lemme go."

"Yeah, Chicken. Come on, now."

Sula pulled his leg gently.

"Lemme go."

"OK, I'm leavin' you." She started on.

"Wait!" he screamed.

Sula stopped and together they slowly worked their way down.

Chicken was still elated. "I was way up there, wasn't I? Wasn't I? I'm a tell my brovver."

Sula and Nel began to mimic him: "I'm a tell my brovver; I'm a tell my brovver."

Sula picked him up by his hands and swung him outward then around and around. His knickers ballooned and his shrieks of frightened joy startled the birds and the fat grasshoppers. When he slipped from her hands and sailed away out over the water they could still hear his bubbly laughter.

The water darkened and closed quickly over the place where Chicken Little sank. The pressure of his hard and tight little fingers was still in Sula's palms as she stood looking at the closed place in the water. They expected him to come back up, laughing. Both girls stared at the water. Nel spoke first. "Somebody saw." A figure appeared briefly on the opposite shore.

The only house over there was Shadrack's. Sula glanced at Nel. Terror widened her nostrils. Had he seen?

The water was so peaceful now. There was nothing but the baking sun and something newly missing. Sula cupped her face for an instant, then turned and ran up to the little plank bridge that crossed the river to Shadrack's house. There was no path. It was as though neither Shadrack nor anyone else ever came this way.

Her running was swift and determined, but when she was close to the three little steps that led to his porch, fear crawled into her stomach and only the something newly missing back there in the river made it possible for her to walk up the three steps and knock at the door.

No one answered. She started back, but thought again of the peace of the river. Shadrack would be inside, just behind the door ready to pounce on her. Still she could not go back. Ever so gently she pushed the door with the tips of her fingers and heard only the hinges weep. More. And then she was inside. Alone. The neatness, the order startled her, but more surprising was the restfulness. Everything was so tiny, so common, so unthreatening. Perhaps this was not the house of the Shad. The terrible Shad who walked about with his penis out, who peed in front of ladies and girl-children, the only black who could curse white people and get away with it, who drank in the road from the mouth of the bottle, who shouted and shook in the streets. This cottage? This sweet old cottage? With its made-up bed? With its rag rug and wooden table? Sula stood in the middle of the little room and in her wonder forgot what she had come for until a sound at the door made her jump. He was there in the doorway looking at her. She had not heard his coming and now he was looking at her.

More in embarrassment than terror she averted her glance. When she called up enough courage to look back at him, she saw his hand resting upon the door frame. His fingers, barely touching the wood, were arranged in a graceful arc. Relieved and encouraged (no one with hands like that, no one with fingers that curved around wood so tenderly could kill her), she walked past him out of the door, feeling his gaze turning, turning with her.

At the edge of the porch, gathering the wisps of courage that were fast leaving her, she turned once more to look at him, to ask him ... had he ...?

He was smiling, a great smile, heavy with lust and time to come. He nodded his head as though answering a question, and said, in a pleasant conversational tone, a tone of cooled butter, "Always."

Sula fled down the steps, and shot through the greenness and the baking sun back to Nel and the dark closed place in the water. There she collapsed in tears.

Nel quieted her. "Sh, sh. Don't, don't. You didn't mean it. It ain't your fault. Sh. Sh. Come on, le's go, Sula. Come on, now. Was he there? Did he see? Where's the belt to your dress?"

Sula shook her head while she searched her waist for the belt. Finally she stood up and allowed Nel to lead her away. "He said, 'Always. Always.'"

"What?"

Sula covered her mouth as they walked down the hill. Always. He had answered a question she had not asked, and its promise licked at her feet.

A bargeman, poling away from the shore, found Chicken late that afternoon stuck in some rocks and weeds, his knickers ballooning about his legs. He would have left him there but noticed that it was a child, not an old black man, as it first appeared, and he prodded the body loose, netted it and hauled it aboard. He shook his head in disgust at the kind of parents who would drown their own children. When, he wondered, will those people ever be anything but animals, fit for nothing but substitutes for mules, only mules didn't kill each other the way niggers did. He dumped Chicken Little into a burlap sack and tossed him next to some egg crates and boxes of wool cloth. Later, sitting down to smoke on an empty lard tin, still bemused by God's curse and the terrible burden his own kind had of elevating Ham's sons,[4] he suddenly became alarmed by the thought that the corpse in this heat would have a terrible odor, which might get into the fabric of his woolen cloth. He dragged the sack away and hooked it over the side, so that the Chicken's body was half in and half out of the water.

Wiping the sweat from his neck, he reported his find to the sheriff at Porter's Landing, who said they didn't have no niggers in their country, but that some lived in those hills 'cross the river, up above Medallion. The bargeman said he couldn't go all the way back there, it was every bit of two miles. The sheriff said whyn't he throw it on back into the water. The bargeman said he never shoulda taken it out in the first place. Finally they got the man who ran the ferry twice a day to agree to take it over in the morning.

That was why Chicken Little was missing for three days and didn't get to the embalmer's until the fourth day, by which time he was unrecognizable to almost everybody who once knew him, and even his mother wasn't deep down sure, except that it just had to be him since nobody could find him. When she saw his clothes lying on the table in the basement of the mortuary, her mouth snapped shut, and when she saw his body her mouth flew wide open again and it was seven hours before she was able to close it and make the first sound.

So the coffin was closed.

The Junior Choir, dressed in white, sang "Nearer My God to Thee" and "Precious Memories,"[5] their eyes fastened on the songbooks they did not need, for this was the first time their voices had presided at a real-life event.

Nel and Sula did not touch hands or look at each other during the funeral. There was a space, a separateness, between them. Nel's legs had turned to granite and she expected the sheriff or Reverend Deal's pointing finger at any moment. Although she knew she had "done nothing,"

---

4. Because Ham, the ancestor of the African tribes, saw his father Noah naked, the patriarch curses Ham's son Canaan: "a servant of servants shall he be unto his brethren" (Genesis 9:22–25).

5. Hymn by J. B. F. Wright, which speaks of mem-

ories as "unseen angels"; the 1841 hymn by Sarah Flower Adams (1805–1848) consoles the sufferer ("... So by my woes to be/ Nearer, my God, to thee").

she felt convicted and hanged right there in the pew—two rows down
from her parents in the children's section.

Sula simply cried. Soundlessly and with no heaving and gasping for
breath, she let the tears roll into her mouth and slide down her chin to
dot the front of her dress.

As Reverend Deal moved into his sermon, the hands of the women unfolded like pairs of raven's wings and flew high above their hats in the air.
They did not hear all of what he said; they heard the one word, or
phrase, or inflection that was for them the connection between the event
and themselves. For some it was the term "Sweet Jesus." And they saw
the Lamb's eye and the truly innocent victim: themselves. They acknowledged the innocent child hiding in the corner of their hearts, holding a
sugar-and-butter sandwich. That one. The one who lodged deep in their
fat, thin, old, young skin, and was the one the world had hurt. Or they
thought of their son newly killed and remembered his legs in short pants
and wondered where the bullet went in. Or they remembered how dirty
the room looked when their father left home and wondered if that is the
way the slim, young Jew felt, he who for them was both son and lover
and in whose downy face they could see the sugar-and-butter sandwiches
and feel the oldest and most devastating pain there is: not the pain of
childhood, but the remembrance of it.

Then they left their pews. For with some emotions one has to stand.
They spoke, for they were full and needed to say. They swayed, for the
rivulets of grief or of ecstasy must be rocked. And when they thought of
all that life and death locked into that little closed coffin they danced and
screamed, not to protest God's will but to acknowledge it and confirm
once more their conviction that the only way to avoid the Hand of God is
to get in it.

In the colored part of the cemetery, they sank Chicken Little in between his grandfather and an aunt. Butterflies flew in and out of the
bunches of field flowers now loosened from the top of the bier and lying
in a small heap at the edge of the grave. The heat had gone, but there
was still no breeze to lift the hair of the willows.

Nel and Sula stood some distance away from the grave, the space that
had sat between them in the pews had dissolved. They held hands and
knew that only the coffin would lie in the earth; the bubbly laughter and
the press of fingers in the palm would stay aboveground forever. At first,
as they stood there, their hands were clenched together. They relaxed
slowly until during the walk back home their fingers were laced in as
gentle a clasp as that of any two young girlfriends trotting up the road on
a summer day wondering what happened to butterflies in the winter.

1923

The second strange thing was Hannah's coming into her mother's room
with an empty bowl and a peck of Kentucky Wonders[6] and saying,
"Mamma, did you ever love us?" She sang the words like a small child
saying a piece at Easter, then knelt to spread a newspaper on the floor
and set the basket on it; the bowl she tucked in the space between her
legs. Eva, who was just sitting there fanning herself with the cardboard

---

6. A kind of green bean.

fan from Mr. Hodges' funeral parlor, listened to the silence that followed
Hannah's words, then said, "Scat!" to the deweys who were playing chain
gang near the window. With the shoelaces of each of them tied to the
laces of the others, they stumbled and tumbled out of Eva's room.

"Now," Eva looked up across from her wagon at her daughter. "Give
me that again. Flat out to fit my head."

"I mean, did you? You know. When we was little."

Eva's hand moved snail-like down her thigh toward her stump, but
stopped short of it to realign a pleat. "No. I don't reckon I did. Not the
way you thinkin'."

"Oh, well. I was just wonderin'." Hannah appeared to be through with
the subject.

"An evil wonderin' if I ever heard one." Eva was not through.

"I didn't mean nothing by it, Mamma."

"What you mean you didn't *mean* nothing by it? How you gone not
mean something by it?"

Hannah pinched the tips off the Kentucky Wonders and snapped their
long pods. What with the sound of the cracking and snapping and her
swift-fingered movements, she seemed to be playing a complicated instrument. Eva watched her a moment and then said, "You gone can them?"

"No. They for tonight."

"Thought you was gone can some."

"Uncle Paul ain't brought me none yet. A peck ain't enough to can. He
say he got two bushels for me."

"Triflin'."

"Oh, he all right."

"Sho he all right. Everybody all right. 'Cept Mamma. Mamma the only
one ain't all right. Cause she didn't *love* us."

"Awww, Mamma."

"Awww, Mamma? Awww, Mamma? You settin' here with your
healthy-ass self and ax me did I love you? Them big old eyes in your head
would a been two holes full of maggots if I hadn't."

"I didn't mean that, Mamma. I know you fed us and all. I was talkin'
'bout something else. Like. Like. Playin' with us. Did you ever, you know,
play with us?"

"Play? Wasn't nobody playin' in 1895. Just 'cause you got it good now
you think it was always this good? 1895 was a killer, girl. Things was bad.
Niggers was dying like flies. Stepping tall, ain't you? Uncle Paul gone
bring me *two* bushels. Yeh. And they's a melon downstairs, ain't they?
And I bake every Saturday, and Shad brings fish on Friday, and they's a
pork barrel full of meal, and we float eggs in a crock of vinegar . . ."

"Mamma, what you talkin' 'bout?"

"I'm talkin' 'bout 18 and 95 when I set in that house five days with you
and Pearl and Plum and three beets, you snake-eyed ungrateful hussy.
What would I look like leapin' 'round that little old room playin' with
youngins with three beets to my name?"

"I know 'bout them beets, Mamma. You told us that a million times."

"Yeah? Well? Don't that count? Ain't that love? You want me to tinkle
you under the jaw and forget 'bout them sores in your mouth? Pearl was
shittin' worms and I was supposed to play rang-around-the-rosie?"

"But Mamma, they had to be some time when you wasn't thinkin'
'bout . . ."

"No time. They wasn't no time. Not none. Soon as I got one day done here come a night. With you all coughin' and me watchin' so TB wouldn't take you off and if you was sleepin' quiet I thought, O Lord, they dead and put my hand over your mouth to feel if the breath was comin' what you talkin' 'bout did I love you girl I stayed alive for you can't you get that through your thick head or what is that between your ears, heifer?"

Hannah had enough beans now. With some tomatoes and hot bread, she thought, that would be enough for everybody, especially since the deweys didn't eat vegetables no how and Eva never made them and Tar Baby was living off air and music these days. She picked up the basket and stood with it and the bowl of beans over her mother. Eva's face was still asking her last question. Hannah looked into her mother's eyes.

"But what about Plum? What'd you kill Plum for, Mamma?"

It was a Wednesday in August and the ice wagon was coming and coming. You could hear bits of the driver's song. Now Mrs. Jackson would be tipping down her porch steps. "Jes·a piece. You got a lil ole piece layin' 'round in there you could spare?" And as he had since the time of the pigeons, the iceman would hand her a lump of ice saying, "Watch it now, Mrs. Jackson. That straw'll tickle your pretty neck to death."

Eva listened to the wagon coming and thought about what it must be like in the icehouse. She leaned back a little and closed her eyes trying to see the insides of the icehouse. It was a dark, lovely picture in this heat, until it reminded her of that winter night in the outhouse holding her baby in the dark, her fingers searching for his asshole and the last bit of lard scooped from the sides of the can, held deliberately on the tip of her middle finger, the last bit of lard to keep from hurting him when she slid her finger in and all because she had broken the slop jar and the rags had frozen. The last food staple in the house she had rammed up her baby's behind to keep from hurting him too much when she opened up his bowels to pull the stools out. He had been screaming fit to kill, but when she found his hole at last and stuck her finger up in it, the shock was so great he was suddenly quiet. Even now on the hottest day anyone in Medallion could remember—a day so hot flies slept and cats were splaying their fur like quills, a day so hot pregnant wives leaned up against trees and cried, and women remembering some three-month-old hurt put ground glass in their lovers' food and the men looked at the food and wondered if there was glass in it and ate it anyway because it was too hot to resist eating it—even on this hottest of days in the hot spell, Eva shivered from the biting cold and stench of that outhouse.

Hannah was waiting. Watching her mother's eyelids. When Eva spoke at last it was with two voices. Like two people were talking at the same time, saying the same thing, one a fraction of a second behind the other.

"He give me such a time. Such a time. Look like he didn't even want to be born. But he come on out. Boys is hard to bear. You wouldn't know that but they is. It was such a carryin' on to get him born and to keep him alive. Just to keep his little heart beating and his little old lungs cleared and look like when he came back from that war he wanted to git back in. After all that carryin' on, just gettin' him out and keepin' him alive, he wanted to crawl back in my womb and well . . . I ain't got the room no more even if he could do it. There wasn't space for him in my womb. And he was crawlin' back. Being helpless and thinking baby thoughts and dreaming baby dreams and messing up his pants again and smiling all the time. I had room enough in my heart, but not in my womb, not no more. I birthed him once. I couldn't do it again. He was growed, a big old thing. Godhavemercy, I couldn't birth him twice. I'd be laying here at night and he be downstairs in that room, but when I closed my eyes I'd see him . . . six feet tall smilin' and crawlin' up the stairs quietlike so I wouldn't hear and opening the door soft so I wouldn't hear and he'd be creepin' to the bed trying to spread my legs trying to get back up in my womb. He was a man, girl, a big old growed-up man. I didn't have that much room. I kept on dreaming it. Dreaming it and I knowed it was true. One night it wouldn't be no dream. It'd be true and I would have done it, would have let him if I'd've had the room but a big man can't be a baby all wrapped up inside his mamma no more; he suffocate. I done everything I could to make him leave me and go on and live and be a man but he wouldn't and I had to keep him out so I just thought of a way he could die like a man not all scrunched up inside my womb, but like a man."

Eva couldn't see Hannah clearly for the tears, but she looked up at her anyway and said, by way of apology or explanation or perhaps just by way of neatness, "But I held him close first. Real close. Sweet Plum. My baby boy."

Long after Hannah turned and walked out of the room, Eva continued to call his name while her fingers lined up the pleats in her dress.

Hannah went off to the kitchen, her old man's slippers plopping down the stairs and over the hardwood floors. She turned the spigot on, letting water break up the tight knots of Kentucky Wonders and float them to the top of the bowl. She swirled them about with her fingers, poured the water off and repeated the process. Each time the green tubes rose to the surface she felt elated and collected whole handfuls at a time to drop in twos and threes back into the water.

Through the window over the sink she could see the deweys still playing chain gang; their ankles bound one to the other, they tumbled, struggled back to their feet and tried to walk single file. Hens strutted by with one suspicious eye on the deweys, another on the brick fireplace where sheets and mason jars were boiled. Only the deweys could play in this heat. Hannah put the Kentucky Wonders over the fire and, struck by a sudden sleepiness, she went off to lie down in the front room. It was even hotter there, for the windows were shut to keep out the sunlight. Hannah straightened the shawl that draped the couch and lay down. She dreamed of a wedding in a red bridal gown until Sula came in and woke her.

But before the second strange thing, there had been the wind, which was the first. The very night before the day Hannah had asked Eva if she had ever loved them, the wind tore over the hills rattling roofs and loosening doors. Everything shook, and although the people were frightened they thought it meant rain and welcomed it. Windows fell out and trees lost arms. People waited up half the night for the first crack of lightning. Some had even uncovered barrels to catch the rain water, which they loved to drink and cook in. They waited in vain, for no lightning no thunder no rain came. The wind just swept through, took what dampness there was out of the air, messed up the yards, and went on. The hills of the Bottom, as always, protected the valley part of town where the white people lived, and the next morning all the people were grateful because there was a dryer heat. So they set about their work early, for it was canning time, and who knew but what the wind would come back this time with a cooling rain. The men who worked in the valley got up at four thirty in the morning and looked at the sky where the sun was already rising like a hot white bitch. They beat the brims of their hats against their legs before putting them on and trudged down the road like old promises nobody wanted kept.

On Thursday, when Hannah brought Eva her fried tomatoes and soft scrambled eggs with the white left out for good luck, she mentioned her dream of the wedding in the red dress. Neither one bothered to look it up for they both knew the number was 522.[7] Eva said she'd play it when Mr. Buckland Reed came by. Later she would remember it as the third strange thing. She had thought it odd even then, but the red in the dream confused her. But she wasn't certain that it was third or not because Sula was acting up, fretting the deweys and meddling the newly married couple. Because she was thirteen, everybody supposed her nature was coming down, but it was hard to put up with her sulking and irritation. The birthmark over her eye was getting darker and looked more and more like a stem and rose. She was dropping things and eating food that belonged to the newly married couple and started in to worrying everybody that the deweys needed a bath and she was going to give it to them. The deweys, who went wild at the thought of water, were crying and thundering all over the house like colts.

"We ain't got to, do we? Do we got to do what she says? It ain't Saturday." They even woke up Tar Baby, who came out of his room to look at them and then left the house in search of music.

Hannah ignored them and kept on bringing mason jars out of the cellar and washing them. Eva banged on the floor with her stick but nobody came. By noon it was quiet. The deweys had escaped, Sula was either in her room or gone off somewhere. The newly married couple, energized by their morning lovemaking, had gone to look for a day's work happily certain that they would find none.

The air all over the Bottom got heavy with peeled fruit and boiling vegetables. Fresh corn, tomatoes, string beans, melon rinds. The women, the children and the old men who had no jobs were putting up for a winter they understood so well. Peaches were stuffed into jars and black cherries (later, when it got cooler, they would put up jellies and preserves). The greedy canned as many as forty-two a day even though some of them, like Mrs. Jackson, who ate ice, had jars from 1920.

Before she trundled her wagon over to the dresser to get her comb, Eva looked out the window and saw Hannah bending to light the yard fire. And that was the fifth (or fourth, if you didn't count Sula's craziness) strange thing. She couldn't find her comb. Nobody moved stuff in Eva's room except to clean and then they put everything right back. But Eva couldn't find it anywhere. One hand pulling her braids loose, the other searching the dresser drawers, she had just begun to get irritated when she felt it in her blouse drawer. Then she trundled back to the window to catch a breeze, if one took a mind to come by, while she combed her hair. She rolled up to the window and it was then she saw Hannah burning. The flames from the yard fire were licking the blue cotton dress,

7. The reference is apparently to a dream book in which Hannah's dream is #522 and well known; Eva plans to buy #522 in the daily "numbers" lottery.

making her dance. Eva knew there was time for nothing in this world other than the time it took to get there and cover her daughter's body with her own. She lifted her heavy frame up on her good leg, and with fists and arms smashed the windowpane. Using her stump as a support on the window sill, her good leg as a lever, she threw herself out of the window. Cut and bleeding she clawed the air trying to aim her body toward the flaming, dancing figure. She missed and came crashing down some twelve feet from Hannah's smoke. Stunned but still conscious, Eva dragged herself toward her firstborn, but Hannah, her senses lost, went flying out of the yard gesturing and bobbing like a sprung jack-in-the-box.

Mr. and Mrs. Suggs, who had set up their canning apparatus in their front yard, saw her running, dancing toward them. They whispered, "Jesus, Jesus," and together hoisted up their tub of water in which tight red tomatoes floated and threw it on the smoke-and-flame-bound woman. The water did put out the flames, but it also made steam, which seared to sealing all that was left of the beautiful Hannah Peace. She lay there on the wooden sidewalk planks, twitching lightly among the smashed tomatoes, her face a mask of agony so intense that for years the people who gathered 'round would shake their heads at the recollection of it.

Somebody covered her legs with a shirt. A woman unwrapped her head rag and placed it on Hannah's shoulder. Somebody else ran to Dick's Fresh Food and Sundries to call the ambulance. The rest stood there as helpless as sunflowers leaning on a fence. The deweys came and stepped in the tomatoes, their eyes raked with wonder. Two cats sidled through the legs of the crowd, sniffing the burned flesh. The vomiting of a young girl finally broke the profound silence and caused the women to talk to each other and to God. In the midst of calling Jesus they heard the hollow clang of the ambulance bell struggling up the hill, but not the "Help me, ya'll" that the dying woman whispered. Then somebody remembered to go and see about Eva. They found her on her stomach by the forsythia bushes calling Hannah's name and dragging her body through the sweet peas and clover that grew under the forsythia by the side of the house. Mother and daughter were placed on stretchers and carried to the ambulance. Eva was wide awake. The blood from her face cuts filled her eyes so she could not see, could only smell the familiar odor of cooked flesh.

Hannah died on the way to the hospital. Or so they said. In any case, she had already begun to bubble and blister so badly that the coffin had to be kept closed at the funeral and the women who washed the body and dressed it for death wept for her burned hair and wrinkled breasts as though they themselves had been her lovers.

When Eva got to the hospital they put her stretcher on the floor, so preoccupied with the hot and bubbling flesh of the other (some of them had never seen so extreme a burn case before) they forgot Eva, who would have bled to death except Old Willy Fields, the orderly, saw blood staining his just-mopped floors and went to find out where it was coming from. Recognizing Eva at once he shouted to a nurse, who came to see if the bloody one-legged black woman was alive or dead. From then on Willy boasted that he had saved Eva's life—an indisputable fact which she herself admitted and for which she cursed him every day for thirty-seven years thereafter and would have cursed him for the rest of her life except by then she was already ninety years old and forgot things.

Lying in the colored ward of the hospital, which was a screened corner of a larger ward, Eva mused over the perfection of the judgment against her. She remembered the wedding dream and recalled that weddings always meant death. And the red gown, well that was the fire, as she should have known. She remembered something else too, and try as she might to deny it, she knew that as she lay on the ground trying to drag herself through the sweet peas and clover to get to Hannah, she had seen Sula standing on the back porch just looking. When Eva, who was never one to hide the faults of her children, mentioned what she thought she'd seen to a few friends, they said it was natural. Sula was probably struck dumb, as anybody would be who saw her own mamma burn up. Eva said yes, but inside she disagreed and remained convinced that Sula had watched Hannah burn not because she was paralyzed, but because she was interested.

1927

Old people were dancing with little children. Young boys with their sisters, and the church women who frowned on any bodily expression of joy (except when the hand of God commanded it) tapped their feet. Somebody (the groom's father, everybody said) had poured a whole pint jar of cane liquor into the punch, so even the men who did not sneak out the back door to have a shot, as well as the women who let nothing stronger than Black Draught enter their blood, were tipsy. A small boy stood at the Victrola turning its handle and smiling at the sound of Bert Williams' "Save a Little Dram for Me."[8]

Even Helene Wright had mellowed with the cane, waving away apologies for drinks spilled on her rug and paying no attention whatever to the chocolate cake lying on the arm of her red-velvet sofa. The tea roses above her left breast had slipped from the brooch that fastened them and were hanging heads down. When her husband called her attention to the children wrapping themselves into her curtains, she merely smiled and said, "Oh, let them be." She was not only a little drunk, she was weary and had been for weeks. Her only child's wedding—the culmination of all she had been, thought or done in this world—had dragged from her energy and stamina even she did not know she possessed. Her house had to be thoroughly cleaned, chickens had to be plucked, cakes and pies made, and for weeks she, her friends and her daughter had been sewing. Now it was all happening and it took only a little cane juice to snap the chords of fatigue and damn the white curtains that she had pinned on the stretcher only the morning before. Once this day was over she would have a lifetime to rattle around in that house and repair the damage.

A real wedding, in a church, with a real reception afterward, was rare among the people of the Bottom. Expensive for one thing, and most newlyweds just went to the courthouse if they were not particular, or had the preacher come in and say a few words if they were. The rest just "took up" with one another. No invitations were sent. There was no need for formality. Folks just came, bringing a gift if they had one, none if they didn't. Except for those who worked in valley houses, most of them had never been to a big wedding; they simply assumed it was rather like a

8. Egbert Austin Williams (1874–1922), a great vaudeville and Broadway comedian, wrote as well as performed novelty songs. Black Draught: a vegetable laxative.

funeral except afterward you didn't have to walk all the way out to Beechnut Cemetery.

This wedding offered a special attraction, for the bridegroom was a handsome, well-liked man—the tenor of Mount Zion's Men's Quartet, who had an enviable reputation among the girls and a comfortable one among men. His name was Jude Greene, and with the pick of some eight or ten girls who came regularly to services to hear him sing, he had chosen Nel Wright.

He wasn't really aiming to get married. He was twenty then, and although his job as a waiter at the Hotel Medallion was a blessing to his parents and their seven other children, it wasn't nearly enough to support a wife. He had brought the subject up first on the day the word got out that the town was building a new road, tarmac, that would wind through Medallion on down to the river, where a great new bridge was to be built to connect Medallion to Porter's Landing, the town on the other side. The war over, a fake prosperity was still around. In a state of euphoria, with a hunger for more and more, the council of founders cast its eye toward a future that would certainly include trade from cross-river towns. Towns that needed more than a house raft to get to the merchants of Medallion. Work had already begun on the New River Road (the city had always meant to name it something else, something wonderful, but ten years later when the bridge idea was dropped for a tunnel it was still called the New River Road).

Along with a few other young black men, Jude had gone down to the shack where they were hiring. Three old colored men had already been hired, but not for the road work, just to do the picking up, food bringing and other small errands. These old men were close to feeble, not good for much else, and everybody was pleased they were taken on; still it was a shame to see those white men laughing with their grandfathers but shying away from the young black men who could tear that road up. The men like Jude who could do real work. Jude himself longed more than anybody else to be taken. Not just for the good money, more for the work itself. He wanted to swing the pick or kneel down with the string or shovel the gravel. His arms ached for something heavier than trays, for something dirtier than peelings; his feet wanted the heavy work shoes, not the thin-soled black shoes that the hotel required. More than anything he wanted the camaraderie of the road men: the lunch buckets, the hollering, the body movement that in the end produced something real, something he could point to. "I built that road," he could say. How much better sundown would be than the end of a day in the restaurant, where a good day's work was marked by the number of dirty plates and the weight of the garbage bin. "I built that road." People would walk over his sweat for years. Perhaps a sledge hammer would come crashing down on his foot, and when people asked him how come he limped, he could say, "Got that building the New Road."

It was while he was full of such dreams, his body already feeling the rough work clothes, his hands already curved to the pick handle, that he spoke to Nel about getting married. She seemed receptive but hardly anxious. It was after he stood in lines for six days running and saw the gang boss pick out thin-armed white boys from the Virginia hills and the bull-necked Greeks and Italians and heard over and over, "Nothing else today. Come back tomorrow," that he got the message. So it was rage, rage and a determination to take on a man's role anyhow that made him press Nel about settling down. He needed some of his appetites filled, some posture of adulthood recognized, but mostly he wanted someone to care about his hurt, to care very deeply. Deep enough to hold him, deep enough to rock him, deep enough to ask, "How you feel? You all right? Want some coffee?" And if he were to be a man, that someone could no longer be his mother. He chose the girl who had always been kind, who had never seemed hell-bent to marry, who made the whole venture seem like his idea, his conquest.

The more he thought about marriage, the more attractive it became. Whatever his fortune, whatever the cut of his garment, there would always be the hem—the tuck and fold that hid his raveling edges; a someone sweet, industrious and loyal to shore him up. And in return he would shelter her, love her, grow old with her. Without that someone he was a waiter hanging around a kitchen like a woman. With her he was head of a household pinned to an unsatisfactory job out of necessity. The two of them together would make one Jude.

His fears lest his burst dream of road building discourage her were never realized. Nel's indifference to his hints about marriage disappeared altogether when she discovered his pain. Jude could see himself taking shape in her eyes. She actually wanted to help, to soothe, and was it true what Ajax said in the Time and a Half Pool Hall? That "all they want, man, is they own misery. Ax em to die for you and they yours for life."

Whether he was accurate in general, Ajax was right about Nel. Except for an occasional leadership role with Sula, she had no aggression. Her parents had succeeded in rubbing down to a dull glow any sparkle or splutter she had. Only with Sula did that quality have free reign, but their friendship was so close, they themselves had difficulty distinguishing one's thoughts from the other's. During all of her girlhood the only respite Nel had had from her stern and undemonstrative parents was Sula. When Jude began to hover around, she was flattered—all the girls liked him— and Sula made the enjoyment of his attentions keener simply because she seemed always to want Nel to shine. They never quarreled, those two, the way some girlfriends did over boys, or competed against each other for them. In those days a compliment to one was a compliment to the other, and cruelty to one was a challenge to the other.

Nel's response to Jude's shame and anger selected her away from Sula. And greater than her friendship was this new feeling of being needed by someone who saw her singly. She didn't even know she had a neck until Jude remarked on it, or that her smile was anything but the spreading of her lips until he saw it as a small miracle.

Sula was no less excited about the wedding. She thought it was the perfect thing to do following their graduation from general school. She wanted to be the bridesmaid. No others. And she encouraged Mrs. Wright to go all out, even to borrowing Eva's punch bowl. In fact, she handled most of the details very efficiently, capitalizing on the fact that most people were anxious to please her since she had lost her mamma only a few years back and they still remembered the agony in Hannah's face and the blood on Eva's.

So they danced up in the Bottom on the second Saturday in June, danced at the wedding where everybody realized for the first time that except for their magnificent teeth, the deweys would never grow. They had been forty-eight inches tall for years now, and while their size was unusual it was not unheard of. The realization was based on the fact that they remained boys in mind. Mischievous, cunning, private and completely unhousebroken, their games and interests had not changed since Hannah had them all put into the first grade together.

Nel and Jude, who had been the stars all during the wedding, were forgotten finally as the reception melted into a dance, a feed, a gossip session, a playground and a love nest. For the first time that day they relaxed and looked at each other, and liked what they saw. They began to dance, pressed in among the others, and each one turned his thoughts to the night that was coming on fast. They had taken a housekeeping room with one of Jude's aunts (over the protest of Mrs. Wright, who had rooms to spare, but Nel didn't want to make love to her husband in her mother's house) and were getting restless to go there.

As if reading her thoughts, Jude leaned down and whispered, "Me too." Nel smiled and rested her cheek on his shoulder. The veil she wore was too heavy to allow her to feel the core of the kiss he pressed on her head. When she raised her eyes to him for one more look of reassurance, she saw through the open door a slim figure in blue, gliding, with just a hint of a strut, down the path toward the road. One hand was pressed to the head to hold down the large hat against the warm June breeze. Even from the rear Nel could tell that it was Sula and that she was smiling; that something deep down in that litheness was amused. It would be ten years before they saw each other again, and their meeting would be thick with birds.

Part Two

1937

Accompanied by a plague of robins, Sula came back to Medallion. The little yam-breasted shuddering birds were everywhere, exciting very small children away from their usual welcome into a vicious stoning. Nobody knew why or from where they had come. What they did know was that you couldn't go anywhere without stepping in their pearly shit, and it was hard to hang up clothes, pull weeds or just sit on the front porch when robins were flying and dying all around you.

Although most of the people remembered the time when the sky was black for two hours with clouds and clouds of pigeons, and although they were accustomed to excesses in nature—too much heat, too much cold, too little rain, rain to flooding—they still dreaded the way a relatively trivial phenomenon could become sovereign in their lives and bend their minds to its will.

In spite of their fear, they reacted to an oppressive oddity, or what they called evil days, with an acceptance that bordered on welcome. Such evil must be avoided, they felt, and precautions must naturally be taken to protect themselves from it. But they let it run its course, fulfill itself, and never invented ways either to alter it, to annihilate it or to prevent its happening again. So also were they with people.

What was taken by outsiders to be slackness, slovenliness or even generosity was in fact a full recognition of the legitimacy of forces other than good ones. They did not believe doctors could heal—for them, none ever had done so. They did not believe death was accidental—life might be, but death was deliberate. They did not believe Nature was ever askew—only inconvenient. Plague and drought were as "natural" as springtime. If milk could curdle, God knows robins could fall. The purpose of evil was to survive it and they determined (without ever knowing they had made up their minds to do it) to survive floods, white people, tuberculosis, famine and ignorance. They knew anger well but not despair, and they didn't stone sinners for the same reason they didn't commit suicide—it was beneath them.

Sula stepped off the Cincinnati Flyer into the robin shit and began the long climb up into the Bottom. She was dressed in a manner that was as close to a movie star as anyone would ever see. A black crepe dress splashed with pink and yellow zinnias, foxtails, a black felt hat with the veil of net lowered over one eye. In her right hand was a black purse with a beaded clasp and in her left a red leather traveling case, so small, so charming—no one had seen anything like it ever before, including the mayor's wife and the music teacher, both of whom had been to Rome.

Walking up the hill toward Carpenter's Road, the heels and sides of her pumps edged with drying bird shit, she attracted the glances of old men sitting on stone benches in front of the courthouse, housewives throwing buckets of water on their sidewalks, and high school students on their way home for lunch. By the time she reached the Bottom, the news of her return had brought the black people out on their porches or to their windows. There were scattered hellos and nods but mostly stares. A little boy ran up to her saying, "Carry yo' bag, ma'am?" Before Sula could answer his mother had called him, "You, John. Get back in here."

At Eva's house there were four dead robins on the walk. Sula stopped and with her toe pushed them into the bordering grass.

Eva looked at Sula pretty much the same way she had looked at Boy-Boy that time when he returned after he'd left her without a dime or a prospect of one. She was sitting in her wagon, her back to the window she had jumped out of (now all boarded up) setting fire to the hair she had combed out of her head. When Sula opened the door she raised her eyes and said, "I might have knowed them birds meant something. Where's your coat?"

Sula threw herself on Eva's bed. "The rest of my stuff will be on later."

"I should hope so. Them little old furry tails ain't going to do you no more good than they did the fox that was wearing them."

"Don't you say hello to nobody when you ain't seen them for ten years?"

"If folks let somebody know where they is and when they coming, then other folks can get ready for them. If they don't—if they just pop in all sudden like—then they got to take whatever mood they find."

"How you been doing, Big Mamma?"

"Gettin' by. Sweet of you to ask. You was quick enough when you wanted something. When you needed a little change or . . ."

"Don't talk to me about how much you gave me, Big Mamma, and how much I owe you or none of that."

"Oh? I ain't supposed to mention it?"

"OK. Mention it." Sula shrugged and turned over on her stomach, her buttocks toward Eva.

"You ain't been in this house ten seconds and already you starting something."

"Takes two, Big Mamma."

"Well, don't let your mouth start nothing that your ass can't stand. When you gone to get married? You need to have some babies. It'll settle you."

"I don't want to make somebody else. I want to make myself."

"Selfish. Ain't no woman got no business floatin' around without no man."

"You did."

"Not by choice."

"Mamma did."

"Not by choice, I said. It ain't right for you to want to stay off by yourself. You need . . . I'm a tell you what you need."

Sula sat up. "I need you to shut your mouth."

"Don't nobody talk to me like that. Don't nobody . . ."

"This body does. Just 'cause you was bad enough to cut off your own leg you think you got a right to kick everybody with the stump."

"Who said I cut off my leg?"

"Well, you stuck it under a train to collect insurance."

"Hold on, you lyin' heifer!"

"I aim to."

"Bible say honor thy father and thy mother that thy days may be long upon the land thy God giveth thee."[9]

"Mamma must have skipped that part. Her days wasn't too long."

"Pus mouth! God's going to strike you!"

"Which God? The one watched you burn Plum?"

"Don't talk to me about no burning. You watched your own mamma. You crazy roach! You the one should have been burnt!"

"But I ain't. Got that? I ain't. Any more fires in this house, I'm lighting them!"

"Hellfire don't need lighting and it's already burning in you . . ."

"Whatever's burning in me is mine!"

"Amen!"

"And I'll split this town in two and everything in it before I'll let you put it out!"

"Pride goeth before a fall."

"What the hell do I care about falling?"

"Amazing Grace."[1]

"You sold your life for twenty-three dollars a month."

"You throwed yours away."

"It's mine to throw."

"One day you gone need it."

"But not you. I ain't never going to need you. And you know what?

9. Exodus 20:12.
1. Hymn (1779) by John Newton (1725–1807)— "Amazing grace! how sweet the sound/ That saved a wretch like me!/ I once was lost, but now am found,/ Was blind, but now I see." Above: a paraphrase of Proverbs 16:18—"Pride goeth before destruction, and an haughty spirit before a fall."

Maybe one night when you dozing in that wagon flicking flies and swallowing spit, maybe I'll just tip on up here with some kerosene and—who knows—you may make the brightest flame of them all."

So Eva locked her door from then on. But it did no good. In April two men came with a stretcher and she didn't even have time to comb her hair before they strapped her to a piece of canvas.

When Mr. Buckland Reed came by to pick up the number, his mouth sagged at the sight of Eva being carried out and Sula holding some papers against the wall, at the bottom of which, just above the word "guardian," she very carefully wrote Miss Sula Mae Peace.

⊚ ⊚ ⊚

Nel alone noticed the peculiar quality of the May that followed the leaving of the birds. It had a sheen, a glimmering as of green, rain-soaked Saturday nights (lit by the excitement of newly installed street lights); of lemon-yellow afternoons bright with iced drinks and splashes of daffodils. It showed in the damp faces of her children and the river-smoothness of their voices. Even her own body was not immune to the magic. She would sit on the floor to sew as she had done as a girl, fold her legs up under her or do a little dance that fitted some tune in her head. There were easy sun-washed days and purple dusks in which Tar Baby sang "Abide With Me" at prayer meetings, his lashes darkened by tears, his silhouette limp with regret against the whitewashed walls of Greater Saint Matthew's. Nel listened and was moved to smile. To smile at the sheer loveliness that pressed in from the windows and touched his grief, making it a pleasure to behold.

Although it was she alone who saw this magic, she did not wonder at it. She knew it was all due to Sula's return to the Bottom. It was like getting the use of an eye back, having a cataract removed. Her old friend had come home. Sula. Who made her laugh, who made her see old things with new eyes, in whose presence she felt clever, gentle and a little raunchy. Sula, whose past she had lived through and with whom the present was a constant sharing of perceptions. Talking to Sula had always been a conversation with herself. Was there anyone else before whom she could never be foolish? In whose view inadequacy was mere idiosyncrasy, a character trait rather than a deficiency? Anyone who left behind that aura of fun and complicity? Sula never competed; she simply helped others define themselves. Other people seemed to turn their volume on and up when Sula was in the room. More than any other thing, humor returned. She could listen to the crunch of sugar underfoot that the children had spilled without reaching for the switch; and she forgot the tear in the living-room window shade. Even Nel's love for Jude, which over the years had spun a steady gray web around her heart, became a bright and easy affection, a playfulness that was reflected in their lovemaking.

Sula would come by of an afternoon, walking along with her fluid stride, wearing a plain yellow dress the same way her mother, Hannah, had worn those too-big house dresses—with a distance, an absence of a relationship to clothes which emphasized everything the fabric covered. When she scratched the screen door, as in the old days, and stepped inside, the dishes piled in the sink looked as though they belonged there; the dust on the lamps sparkled; the hair brush lying on the "good" sofa in the living room did not have to be apologetically retrieved, and Nel's grimy intractable children looked like three wild things happily insouciant in the May shine.

"Hey, girl." The rose mark over Sula's eye gave her glance a suggestion of startled pleasure. It was darker than Nel remembered.

"Hey yourself. Come on in here."

"How you doin'?" Sula moved a pile of ironed diapers from a chair and sat down.

"Oh, I ain't strangled nobody yet so I guess I'm all right."

"Well, if you change your mind call me."

"Somebody need killin'?"

"Half this town need it."

"And the other half?"

"A drawn-out disease."

"Oh, come on. Is Medallion that bad?"

"Didn't nobody tell you?"

"You been gone too long, Sula."

"Not too long, but maybe too far."

"What's that supposed to mean?" Nel dipped her fingers into the bowl of water and sprinkled a diaper.

"Oh, I don't know."

"Want some cool tea?"

"Mmmm. Lots of ice, I'm burnin' up."

"Iceman don't come yet, but it's good and cold."

"That's fine."

"Hope I didn't speak too soon. Kids run in and out of here so much." Nel bent to open the icebox.

"You puttin' it on, Nel. Jude must be wore out."

"*Jude* must be wore out? You don't care nothin' 'bout my back, do you?"

"Is that where it's at, in your back?"

"Hah! Jude thinks it's everywhere."

"He's right, it is everywhere. Just be glad he found it, wherever it is. Remember John L.?"

"When Shirley said he got her down by the well and tried to stick it in her hip?" Nel giggled at the remembrance of that teen-time tale. "She should have been grateful. Have you seen her since you been back?"

"Mmm. Like a ox."

"That was one dumb nigger, John L."

"Maybe. Maybe he was just sanitary."

"Sanitary?"

"Well. Think about it. Suppose Shirley was all splayed out in front of you? Wouldn't you go for the hipbone instead?"

Nel lowered her head onto crossed arms while tears of laughter dripped into the warm diapers. Laughter that weakened her knees and pressed her bladder into action. Her rapid soprano and Sula's dark sleepy chuckle made a duet that frightened the cat and made the children run in from the back yard, puzzled at first by the wild free sounds, then delighted to see their mother stumbling merrily toward the bathroom, holding on to her stomach, fairly singing through the laughter: "Aw. Aw. Lord. Sula. Stop." And the other one, the one with the scary black thing over her eye, laughing softly and egging their mother on: "Neatness counts. You know what cleanliness is next to . . ."

"Hush." Nel's plea was clipped off by the slam of the bathroom door.

"What y'all laughing at?"

"Old time-y stuff. Long gone, old time-y stuff."

"Tell us."

"Tell *you?*" The black mark leaped.

"Uh huh. Tell us."

"What tickles us wouldn't tickle you."

"Uh huh, it would."

"Well, we was talking about some people we used to know when we was little."

"Was my mamma little?"

"Of course."

"What happened?"

"Well, some old boy we knew name John L. and a girl name . . ."

Damp-faced, Nel stepped back into the kitchen. She felt new, soft and new. It had been the longest time since she had had a rib-scraping laugh. She had forgotten how deep and down it could be. So different from the miscellaneous giggles and smiles she had learned to be content with these past few years.

"Oh Lord, Sula. You haven't changed none." She wiped her eyes. "What was all that about, anyway? All that scramblin' we did trying to do it and not do it at the same time?"

"Beats me. Such a simple thing."

"But we sure made a lot out of it, and the boys were dumber than we were."

"Couldn't nobody be dumber than I was."

"Stop lying. All of 'em liked you best."

"Yeah? Where are they?"

"They still here. You the one went off."

"Didn't I, though?"

"Tell me about it. The big city."

"Big is all it is. A big Medallion."

"No. I mean the life. The nightclubs, and parties . . ."

"I was in college, Nellie. No nightclubs on campus."

"Campus? That what they call it? Well. You wasn't in no college for—what—ten years now? And you didn't write to nobody. How come you never wrote?"

"You never did either."

"Where was I going to write to? All I knew was that you was in Nashville. I asked Miss Peace about you once or twice."

"What did *she* say?"

"I couldn't make much sense out of her. You know she been gettin' stranger and stranger after she come out the hospital. How is she anyway?"

"Same, I guess. Not so hot."

"No? Laura, I know, was doing her cooking and things. Is she still?"

"No. I put her out."

"Put her out? What for?"

"She made me nervous."

"But she was doing it for nothing, Sula."

"That's what you think. She was stealing right and left."

"Since when did you get froggy[2] about folks' stealing?"

Sula smiled. "OK. I lied. You wanted a reason."

"Well, give me the real one."

"I don't know the real one. She just didn't belong in that house. Digging around in the cupboards, picking up pots and ice picks..."

"You sure have changed. That house was always full of people digging in cupboards and carrying on."

"That's the reason, then."

"Sula. Come on, now."

"You've changed, too. I didn't used to have to explain everything to you."

Nel blushed. "Who's feeding the deweys and Tar Baby? You?"

"Sure me. Anyway Tar Baby don't eat and the deweys still crazy."

"I heard one of 'em's mamma came to take him back but didn't know which was hern."

"Don't nobody know."

"And Eva? You doing the work for her too?"

"Well, since you haven't heard it, let me tell you. Eva's real sick. I had her put where she could be watched and taken care of."

"Where would that be?"

"Out by Beechnut."

"You mean that home the white church run? Sula! That ain't no place for Eva. All them women is dirt poor with no people at all. Mrs. Wilkens and them. They got dropsy and can't hold their water—crazy as loons. Eva's odd, but she got sense. I don't think that's right, Sula."

"I'm scared of her, Nellie. That's why..."

"Scared? Of Eva?"

"You don't know her. Did you know she burnt Plum?"

"Oh, I heard that years ago. But nobody put no stock in it."

"They should have. It's true. I saw it. And when I got back here she was planning to do it to me too."

"Eva? I can't hardly believe that. She almost died trying to get to your mother."

Sula leaned forward, her elbows on the table. "You ever known me to lie to you?"

"No. But you could be mistaken. Why would Eva..."

"All I know is I'm scared. And there's no place else for me to go. We all that's left, Eva and me. I guess I should have stayed gone. I didn't know what else to do. Maybe I should have talked to you about it first. You always had better sense than me. Whenever I was scared before, you knew just what to do."

The closed place in the water spread before them. Nel put the iron on the stove. The situation was clear to her now. Sula, like always, was incapable of making any but the most trivial decisions. When it came to matters of grave importance, she behaved emotionally and irresponsibly and left it to others to straighten out. And when fear struck her, she did unbelievable things. Like that time with her finger. Whatever those hunkies[3]

2. Nervous, jumpy as a frog.   3. Whites.

did, it wouldn't have been as bad as what she did to herself. But Sula was so scared she had mutilated herself, to protect herself.

"What should I do, Nellie? Take her back and sleep with my door locked again?"

"No. I guess it's too late anyway. But let's work out a plan for taking care of her. So she won't be messed over."

"Anything you say."

"What about money? She got any?"

Sula shrugged. "The checks come still. It's not much, like it used to be. Should I have them made over to me?"

"Can you? Do it, then. We can arrange for her to have special comforts. That place is a mess, you know. A doctor don't never set foot in there. I ain't figured out yet how they stay alive in there as long as they do."

"Why don't I have the checks made over to you, Nellie? You better at this than I am."

"Oh no. People will say I'm scheming. You the one to do it. Was there insurance from Hannah?"

"Yes. Plum too. He had all that army insurance."

"Any of it left?"

"Well I went to college on some. Eva banked the rest. I'll look into it, though."

". . . and explain it all to the bank people."

"Will you go down with me?"

"Sure. It's going to be all right."

"I'm glad I talked to you 'bout this. It's been bothering me."

"Well, tongues will wag, but so long as we know the truth, it don't matter."

Just at that moment the children ran in announcing the entrance of their father. Jude opened the back door and walked into the kitchen. He was still a very good-looking man, and the only difference Sula could see was the thin pencil mustache under his nose, and a part in his hair.

"Hey, Jude. What you know good?"

"White man running it—nothing good."

Sula laughed while Nel, high-tuned to his moods, ignored her husband's smile saying, "Bad day, honey?"

"Same old stuff," he replied and told them a brief tale of some personal insult done him by a customer and his boss—a whiney tale that peaked somewhere between anger and a lapping desire for comfort. He ended it with the observation that a Negro man had a hard row to hoe in this world. He expected his story to dovetail into milkwarm commiseration, but before Nel could excrete it, Sula said she didn't know about that—it looked like a pretty good life to her.

"Say what?" Jude's temper flared just a bit as he looked at this friend of his wife's, this slight woman, not exactly plain, but not fine either, with a copperhead over her eye. As far as he could tell, she looked like a woman roaming the country trying to find some man to burden down with a lot of lip and a lot of mouths.

Sula was smiling. "I mean, I don't know what the fuss is about. I mean, everything in the world loves you. White men love you. They spend so much time worrying about your penis they forget their own. The only thing they want to do is cut off a nigger's privates. And if that ain't love and respect I don't know what is. And white women? They chase you all to every corner of the earth, feel for you under every bed. I knew a white woman wouldn't leave the house after 6 o'clock for fear one of you would snatch her. Now ain't that love? They think rape soon's they see you, and if they don't get the rape they looking for, they scream it anyway just so the search won't be in vain. Colored women worry themselves into bad health just trying to hang on to your cuffs. Even little children—white and black, boys and girls—spend all their childhood eating their hearts out 'cause they think you don't love them. And if that ain't enough, you love yourselves. Nothing in this world loves a black man more than another black man. You hear of solitary white men, but niggers? Can't stay away from one another a whole day. So. It looks to me like you the envy of the world."

Jude and Nel were laughing, he saying, "Well, if that's the only way they got to show it—cut off my balls and throw me in jail—I'd just as soon they left me alone." But thinking that Sula had an odd way of looking at things and that her wide smile took some of the sting from that rattlesnake over her eye. A funny woman, he thought, not that bad-looking. But he could see why she wasn't married; she stirred a man's mind maybe, but not his body.

◉ ◉ ◉

He left his tie. The one with the scriggly yellow lines running lopsided across the dark-blue field. It hung over the top of the closet door pointing steadily downward while it waited with every confidence for Jude to return.

Could he be gone if his tie is still here? He will remember it and come back and then she would ... uh. Then she could ... tell him. Sit down quietly and tell him. "But Jude," she would say, "you *knew* me. All those days and years, Jude, you *knew* me. My ways and my hands and how my stomach folded and how we tried to get Mickey to nurse and how about that time when the landlord said ... but you said ... and I cried, Jude. You knew me and had listened to the things I said in the night, and heard me in the bathroom and laughed at my raggedy girdle and I laughed too because I knew you too, Jude. So how could you leave me when you knew me?"

But they had been down on all fours naked, not touching except their lips right down there on the floor where the tie is pointing to, on all fours like (uh huh, go on, say it) like dogs. Nibbling at each other, not even touching, not even looking at each other, just their lips, and when I opened the door they didn't even look for a minute and I thought the reason they are not looking up is because they are not doing that. So it's all right. I am just standing here. They are not doing that. I am just standing here and seeing it, but they are not really doing it. But then they did look up. Or you did. You did, Jude. And if only you had not looked at me the way the soldiers did on the train, the way you look at the children when they come in while you are listening to Gabriel Heatter[4] and break

4. Longtime popular radio news commentator who always had "good news tonight."

your train of thought—not focusing exactly but giving them an instant, a piece of time, to remember what they are doing, what they are interrupting, and to go on back to wherever they were and let you listen to Gabriel Heatter. And I did not know how to move my feet or fix my eyes or what. I just stood there seeing it and smiling, because maybe there was some explanation, something important that I did not know about that would have made it all right. I waited for Sula to look up at me any minute and say one of those lovely college words like *aesthetic* or *rapport*, which I never understood but which I loved because they sounded so comfortable and firm. And finally you just got up and started putting on your clothes and your privates were hanging down, so soft, and you buckled your pants belt but forgot to button the fly and she was sitting on the bed not even bothering to put on her clothes because actually she didn't need to because somehow she didn't look naked to me, only you did. Her chin was in her hand and she sat like a visitor from out of town waiting for the hosts to get some quarreling done and over with so the card game could continue and me wanting her to leave so I could tell you privately that you had forgotten to button your fly because I didn't want to say it in front of her, Jude. And even when you began to talk, I couldn't hear because I was worried about you not knowing that your fly was open and scared too because your eyes looked like the soldiers' that time on the train when my mother turned to custard.

Remember how big that bedroom was? Jude? How when we moved here we said, Well, at least we got us a real big bedroom, but it was small then, Jude, and so shambly, and maybe it was that way all along but it would have been better if I had gotten the dust out from under the bed because I was ashamed of it in that small room. And then you walked past me saying, "I'll be back for my things." And you did but you left your tie.

The clock was ticking. Nel looked at it and realized that it was two thirty, only forty-five minutes before the children would be home and she hadn't even felt anything right or sensible and now there was no time or wouldn't be until nighttime when they were asleep and she could get into bed and maybe she could do it then. Think. But who could think in that bed where *they* had been and where they *also* had been and where only she was now?

She looked around for a place to be. A small place. The closet? No. Too dark. The bathroom. It was both small and bright, and she wanted to be in a very small, very bright place. Small enough to contain her grief. Bright enough to throw into relief the dark things that cluttered her. Once inside, she sank to the tile floor next to the toilet. On her knees, her hand on the cold rim of the bathtub, she waited for something to happen . . . inside. There was stirring, a movement of mud and dead leaves. She thought of the women at Chicken Little's funeral. The women who shrieked over the bier and at the lip of the open grave. What she had regarded since as unbecoming behavior seemed fitting her now; they were screaming at the neck of God, his giant nape, the vast back-of-the-head that he had turned on them in death. But it seemed to her now that it was not a fist-shaking grief they were keening but rather a simple obligation to say something, do something, feel something about the dead. They could not let that heart-smashing event pass unrecorded, unidentified. It was poisonous, unnatural to let the dead go with a mere whimpering, a

slight murmur, a rose bouquet of good taste. Good taste was out of place
in the company of death, death itself was the essence of bad taste. And
there must be much rage and saliva in its presence. The body must move
and throw itself about, the eyes must roll, the hands should have no
peace, and the throat should release all the yearning, despair and outrage
that accompany the stupidity of loss.

"The real hell of Hell is that it is forever." Sula said that. She said
doing anything forever and ever was hell. Nel didn't understand it then,
but now in the bathroom, trying to feel, she thought, "If I could be sure
that I could stay here in this small white room with the dirty tile and
water gurgling in the pipes and my head on the cool rim of this bathtub
and never have to go out the door, I would be happy. If I could be certain
that I never had to get up and flush the toilet, go in the kitchen, watch
my children grow up and die, see my food chewed on my plate . . . Sula
was wrong. Hell ain't things lasting forever. Hell is change." Not only did
men leave and children grow up and die, but even the misery didn't last.
One day she wouldn't even have that. This very grief that had twisted her
into a curve on the floor and flayed her would be gone. She would lose
that too.

"Why, even in hate here I am thinking of what Sula said."

Hunched down in the small bright room Nel waited. Waited for the
oldest cry. A scream not for others, not in sympathy for a burnt child, or
a dead father, but a deeply personal cry for one's own pain. A loud, stri-
dent: "Why me?" She waited. The mud shifted, the leaves stirred, the
smell of overripe green things enveloped her and announced the beginnings of her very own howl.

But it did not come.

The odor evaporated; the leaves were still, the mud settled. And finally
there was nothing, just a flake of something dry and nasty in her throat.
She stood up frightened. There was something just to the right of her, in
the air, just out of view. She could not see it, but she knew exactly what
it looked like. A gray ball hovering just there. Just there. To the right.
Quiet, gray, dirty. A ball of muddy strings, but without weight, fluffy but
terrible in its malevolence. She knew she could not look, so she closed her
eyes and crept past it out of the bathroom, shutting the door behind her.
Sweating with fear, she stepped to the kitchen door and onto the back
porch. The lilac bushes preened at the railing, but there were no lilacs
yet. Wasn't it time? Surely it was time. She looked over the fence to Mrs.
Rayford's yard. Hers were not in bloom either. Was it too late? She fastened on this question with enthusiasm, all the time aware of something
she was not thinking. It was the only way she could get her mind off the
flake in her throat.

She spent a whole summer with the gray ball, the little ball of fur and
string and hair always floating in the light near her but which she did not
see because she never looked. But that was the terrible part, the effort it
took not to look. But it was there anyhow, just to the right of her head
and maybe further down by her shoulder, so when the childern went to a
monster movie at the Elmira Theater and came home and said, "Mamma,
can you sleep with us tonight?" she said all right and got into bed with
the two boys, who loved it, but the girl did not. For a long time she could
not stop getting in the bed with her children and told herself each time
that they might dream a dream about dragons and would need her to

comfort them. It was so nice to think about their scary dreams and not about a ball of fur. She even hoped their dreams would rub off on her and give her the wonderful relief of a nightmare so she could stop going around scared to turn her head this way or that lest she see it. That was the scary part—seeing it. It was not coming at her; it never did that, or tried to pounce on her. It just floated there for the seeing, if she wanted to, and O my God for the touching if she wanted to. But she didn't want to see it, ever, for if she saw it, who could tell but what she might actually touch it, or want to, and then what would happen if she actually reached out her hand and touched it? Die probably, but no, worse than that. Dying was OK because it was sleep and there wasn't no gray ball in death, was there? Was there? She would have to ask somebody about that, somebody she could confide in and who knew a lot of things, like Sula, for Sula would know or if she didn't she would say something funny that would make it all right. Ooo no, not Sula. Here she was in the midst of it, hating it, scared of it, and again she thought of Sula as though they were still friends and talked things over. That was too much. To lose Jude and not have Sula to talk to about it because it was Sula that he had left her for.

Now her thighs were really empty. And it was then that what those women said about never looking at another man made some sense to her, for the real point, the heart of what they said, was the word *looked*. Not to promise never to make love to another man, not to refuse to marry another man, but to promise and know that she could never afford to look again, to see and accept the way in which their heads cut the air or see moons and tree limbs framed by their necks and shoulders . . . never to look, for now she could not risk looking—and anyway, so what? For now her thighs were truly empty and dead too, and it was Sula who had taken the life from them and Jude who smashed her heart and the both of them who left her with no thighs and no heart just her brain raveling away.

And what am I supposed to do with these old thighs now, just walk up and down these rooms? What good are they, Jesus? They will never give me the peace I need to get from sunup to sundown, what good are they, are you trying to tell me that I am going to have to go all the way through these days all the way, O my god, to that box with four handles with never nobody settling down between my legs even if I sew up those old pillow cases and rinse down the porch and feed my children and beat the rugs and haul the coal up out of the bin even then nobody, O Jesus, I could be a mule or plow the furrows with my hands if need be or hold these rickety walls up with my back if need be if I knew that somewhere in this world in the pocket of some night I could open my legs to some cowboy lean hips but you are trying to tell me no and O my sweet Jesus what kind of cross is that?

1939

When the word got out about Eva being put in Sunnydale, the people in the Bottom shook their heads and said Sula was a roach. Later, when they saw how she took Jude, then ditched him for others, and heard how he bought a bus ticket to Detroit (where he bought but never mailed birthday cards to his sons), they forgot all about Hannah's easy ways (or their own) and said she was a bitch. Everybody remembered the plague of robins that announced her return, and the tale about her watching Hannah burn was stirred up again.

But it was the men who gave her the final label, who fingerprinted her for all time. They were the ones who said she was guilty of the unforgivable thing—the thing for which there was no understanding, no excuse, no compassion. The route from which there was no way back, the dirt that could not ever be washed away. They said that Sula slept with white men. It may not have been true, but it certainly could have been. She was obviously capable of it. In any case, all minds were closed to her when that word was passed around. It made the old women draw their lips together; made small children look away from her in shame; made young men fantasize elaborate torture for her—just to get the saliva back in their mouths when they saw her.

Every one of them imagined the scene, each according to his own predilections—Sula underneath some white man—and it filled them with choking disgust. There was nothing lower she could do, nothing filthier. The fact that their own skin color was proof that it had happened in their own families was no deterrent to their bile. Nor was the willingness of black men to lie in the beds of white women a consideration that might lead them toward tolerance. They insisted that all unions between white men and black women be rape; for a black woman to be willing was literally unthinkable. In that way, they regarded integration with precisely the same venom that white people did.

So they laid broomsticks across their doors at night and sprinkled salt on porch steps.[5] But aside from one or two unsuccessful efforts to collect the dust from her footsteps, they did nothing to harm her. As always the black people looked at evil stony-eyed and let it run.

Sula acknowledged none of their attempts at counter-conjure or their gossip and seemed to need the services of nobody. So they watched her far more closely than they watched any other roach or bitch in the town, and their alertness was gratified. Things began to happen.

First off, Teapot knocked on her door to see if she had any bottles. He was the five-year-old son of an indifferent mother, all of whose interests sat around the door of the Time and a Half Pool Hall. Her name was Betty but she was called Teapot's Mamma because being his mamma was precisely her major failure. When Sula said no, the boy turned around and fell down the steps. He couldn't get up right away and Sula went to help him. His mother, just then tripping home, saw Sula bending over her son's pained face. She flew into a fit of concerned, if drunken, motherhood, and dragged Teapot home. She told everybody that Sula had pushed him, and talked so strongly about it she was forced to abide by the advice of her friends and take him to the county hospital. The two dollars she hated to release turned out to be well spent, for Teapot did have a fracture, although the doctor said poor diet had contributed substantially to the daintiness of his bones. Teapot's Mamma got a lot of attention anyway and immersed herself in a role she had shown no inclination for: motherhood. The very idea of a grown woman hurting her boy kept her teeth on edge. She became the most devoted mother: sober, clean and industrious. No more nickels for Teapot to go to Dick's for a breakfast of Mr. Goodbars[6] and soda pop: no more long hours of him alone or wandering the roads while she was otherwise engaged. Her

5. To keep evil away.   6. Candy bars.

change was a distinct improvement, although little Teapot did miss those quiet times at Dick's.

Other things happened. Mr. Finley sat on his porch sucking chicken bones, as he had done for thirteen years, looked up, saw Sula, choked on a bone and died on the spot. That incident, and Teapot's Mamma, cleared up for everybody the meaning of the birthmark over her eye; it was not a stemmed rose, or a snake, it was Hannah's ashes marking her from the very beginning.

She came to their church suppers without underwear, bought their steaming platters of food and merely picked at it—relishing nothing, exclaiming over no one's ribs or cobbler. They believed that she was laughing at their God.

And the fury she created in the women of the town was incredible—for she would lay their husbands once and then no more. Hannah had been a nuisance, but she was complimenting the women, in a way, by wanting their husbands. Sula was trying them out and discarding them without any excuse the men could swallow. So the women, to justify their own judgment, cherished their men more, soothed the pride and vanity Sula had bruised.

Among the weighty evidence piling up was the fact that Sula did not look her age. She was near thirty and, unlike them, had lost no teeth, suffered no bruises, developed no ring of fat at the waist or pocket at the back of her neck. It was rumored that she had had no childhood diseases, was never known to have chicken pox, croup or even a runny nose. She had played rough as a child—where were the scars? Except for a funny-shaped finger and that evil birthmark, she was free of any normal signs of vulnerability. Some of the men, who as boys had dated her, remembered that on picnics neither gnats nor mosquitoes would settle on her. Patsy, Hannah's one-time friend, agreed and said not only that, but she had witnessed the fact that when Sula drank beer she never belched.

The most damning evidence, however, came from Dessie, who was a big Daughter Elk[7] and knew things. At one of the social meetings she revealed something to her friends.

"Yeh, well I noticed something long time ago. Ain't said nothing 'bout it 'cause I wasn't sure what it meant. Well . . . I did mention it to Ivy but not nobody else. I disremember how long ago. 'Bout a month or two I guess 'cause I hadn't put down my new linoleum yet. Did you see it, Cora? It's that kind we saw in the catalogue."

"Naw."

"Get on with it, Dessie."

"Well, Cora was with me when we looked in the catalogue . . ."

"We all know 'bout your linoleum. What we don't know is . . ."

"OK. Let me tell it, will you? Just before the linoleum come I was out front and seed Shadrack carryin' on as usual . . . up by the well . . . walkin' 'round it salutin' and carryin' on. You know how he does . . . hollerin' commands and . . ."

"Will you get on with it?"

"Who's tellin' this? Me or you?"

"You."

"Well, let me tell it then. Like I say, he was just cuttin' up as usual

7. Member of a black social organization.

when Miss Sula Mae walks by on the other side of the road. And quick as that"—she snapped her fingers—"he stopped and cut on over 'cross the road, steppin' over to her like a tall turkey in short corn. And guess what? He tips his hat."

"Shadrack don't wear no hat."

"I know that but he tipped it anyway. You know what I mean. He acted like he had a hat and reached up for it and tipped it at her. Now you know Shadrack ain't civil to nobody!"

"Sure ain't."

"Even when you buyin' his fish he's cussin'. If you ain't got the right change he cussin' you. If you act like a fish ain't too fresh he snatch it out of your hand like he doin' you the favor."

"Well, everybody know he a reprobate."

"Yeh, so how come he tip his hat to Sula? How come he don't cuss her?"

"Two devils."

"Exactly!"

"What'd she do when he tipped it? Smile and give him a curtsey?"

"No, and that was the other thing. It was the first time I see her look anything but hateful. Like she smellin' you with her eyes and don't like your soap. When he tipped his hat she put her hand on her throat for a minute and *cut* out. Went runnin' on up the road to home. And him still standin' there tippin' away. And—this the point I was comin' to—when I went back in the house a big sty come on my eye. And I ain't never had no sty before. Never!"

"That's 'cause you saw it."

"Exactly."

"Devil all right."

"No two ways about it," Dessie said, and she popped the rubber band off the deck of cards to settle them down for a nice long game of bid whist.

Their conviction of Sula's evil changed them in accountable yet mysterious ways. Once the source of their personal misfortune was identified, they had leave to protect and love one another. They began to cherish their husbands and wives, protect their children, repair their homes and in general band together against the devil in their midst. In their world, aberrations were as much a part of nature as grace. It was not for them to expel or annihilate it. They would no more run Sula out of town than they would kill the robins that brought her back, for in their secret awareness of Him, He was not the God of three faces they sang about. They knew quite well that He had four, and that the fourth explained Sula. They had lived with various forms of evil all their days, and it wasn't that they believed God would take care of them. It was rather that they knew God had a brother and that brother hadn't spared God's son, so why should he spare them?

There was no creature so ungodly as to make them destroy it. They could easily if provoked to anger, but not by design, which explained why they could not "mob kill" anyone. To do so was not only unnatural, it was undignified. The presence of evil was something to be first recognized, then dealt with, survived, outwitted, triumphed over.

Their evidence against Sula was contrived, but their conclusions about her were not. Sula was distinctly different. Eva's arrogance and Hannah's self-indulgence merged in her and, with a twist that was all her own imagination, she lived out her days exploring her own thoughts and emotions, giving them full reign, feeling no obligation to please anybody unless their pleasure pleased her. As willing to feel pain as to give pain, to feel pleasure as to give pleasure, hers was an experimental life—ever since her mother's remarks sent her flying up those stairs, ever since her one major feeling of responsibility had been exorcised on the bank of a river with a closed place in the middle. The first experience taught her there was no other that you could count on; the second that there was no self to count on either. She had no center, no speck around which to grow. In the midst of a pleasant conversation with someone she might say, "Why do you chew with your mouth open?" not because the answer interested her but because she wanted to see the person's face change rapidly. She was completely free of ambition, with no affection for money, property or things, no greed, no desire to command attention or compliments—no ego. For that reason she felt no compulsion to verify herself—be consistent with herself.

She had clung to Nel as the closest thing to both an other and a self, only to discover that she and Nel were not one and the same thing. She had no thought at all of causing Nel pain when she bedded down with Jude. They had always shared the affection of other people: compared how a boy kissed, what line he used with one and then the other. Marriage, apparently, had changed all that, but having had no intimate knowledge of marriage, having lived in a house with women who thought all men available, and selected from among them with a care only for their tastes, she was ill prepared for the possessiveness of the one person she felt close to. She knew well enough what other women said and felt, or said they felt. But she and Nel had always seen through them. They both knew that those women were not jealous of other women; that they were only afraid of losing their jobs. Afraid their husbands would discover that no uniqueness lay between their legs.

Nel was the one person who had wanted nothing from her, who had accepted all aspects of her. Now she wanted everything, and all because of *that*. Nel was the first person who had been real to her, whose name she knew, who had seen as she had the slant of life that made it possible to stretch it to its limits. Now Nel was one of *them*. One of the spiders whose only thought was the next rung of the web, who dangled in dark dry places suspended by their own spittle, more terrified of the free fall than the snake's breath below. Their eyes so intent on the wayward stranger who trips into their net, they were blind to the cobalt on their own backs, the moonshine fighting to pierce their corners. If they were touched by the snake's breath, however fatal, they were merely victims and knew how to behave in that role (just as Nel knew how to behave as the wronged wife). But the free fall, oh no, that required—demanded—invention: a thing to do with the wings, a way of holding the legs and most of all a full surrender to the downward flight if they wished to taste their tongues or stay alive. But alive was what they, and now Nel, did not want to be. Too dangerous. Now Nel belonged to the town and all of its ways. She had given herself over to them, and the flick of their tongues would drive her back into her little dry corner where she would cling to her spittle high above the breath of the snake and the fall.

It had surprised her a little and saddened her a good deal when Nel behaved the way the others would have. Nel was one of the reasons she had drifted back to Medallion, that and the boredom she found in Nashville, Detroit, New Orleans, New York, Philadelphia, Macon and San Diego. All those cities held the same people, working the same mouths, sweating the same sweat. The men who took her to one or another of those places had merged into one large personality: the same language of love, the same entertainments of love, the same cooling of love. Whenever she introduced her private thoughts into their rubbings or goings, they hooded their eyes. They taught her nothing but love tricks, shared nothing but worry, gave nothing but money. She had been looking all along for a friend, and it took her a while to discover that a lover was not a comrade and could never be—for a woman. And that no one would ever be that version of herself which she sought to reach out to and touch with an ungloved hand. There was only her own mood and whim, and if that was all there was, she decided to turn the naked hand toward it, discover it and let others become as intimate with their own selves as she was.

In a way, her strangeness, her naïveté, her craving for the other half of her equation was the consequence of an idle imagination. Had she paints, or clay, or knew the discipline of the dance, or strings; had she anything to engage her tremendous curiosity and her gift for metaphor, she might have exchanged the restlessness and preoccupation with whim for an activity that provided her with all she yearned for. And like any artist with no art form, she became dangerous.

She had lied only once in her life—to Nel about the reason for putting Eva out, and she could lie to her only because she cared about her. When she had come back home, social conversation was impossible for her because she could not lie. She could not say to those old acquaintances, "Hey, girl, you looking good," when she saw how the years had dusted their bronze with ash, the eyes that had once opened wide to the moon bent into grimy sickles of concern. The narrower their lives, the wider their hips. Those with husbands had folded themselves into starched coffins, their sides bursting with other people's skinned dreams and bony regrets. Those without men were like sour-tipped needles featuring one constant empty eye. Those with men had had the sweetness sucked from their breath by ovens and steam kettles. Their children were like distant but exposed wounds whose aches were no less intimate because separate from their flesh. They had looked at the world and back at their children, back at the world and back again at their children, and Sula knew that one clear young eye was all that kept the knife away from the throat's curve.

She was pariah, then, and knew it. Knew that they despised her and believed that they framed their hatred as disgust for the easy way she lay with men. Which was true. She went to bed with men as frequently as she could. It was the only place where she could find what she was looking for: misery and the ability to feel deep sorrow. She had not always been aware that it was sadness that she yearned for. Lovemaking seemed to her, at first, the creation of a special kind of joy. She thought she liked the sootiness of sex and its comedy; she laughed a great deal during the raucous beginnings, and rejected those lovers who regarded sex as healthy or beautiful. Sexual aesthetics bored her. Although she did not regard sex as ugly (ugliness was boring also), she liked to think of it as wicked. But as her experiences multiplied she realized that not only was it not wicked, it was not necessary for her to conjure up the idea of wickedness in order to participate fully. During the lovemaking she found and needed to find the cutting edge. When she left off cooperating with her body and began to assert herself in the act, particles of strength gathered in her like steel shavings drawn to a spacious magnetic center, forming a tight cluster that nothing, it seemed, could break. And there was utmost irony and outrage in lying under someone, in a position of surrender, feeling her own abiding strength and limitless power. But the cluster did break, fall apart, and in her panic to hold it together she leaped from the edge into soundlessness and went down howling, howling in a stinging awareness of the endings of things: an eye of sorrow in the midst of all that hurricane rage of joy. There, in the center of that silence was not eternity but the death of time and a loneliness so profound the word itself had no meaning. For loneliness assumed the absence of other people, and the solitude she found in that desperate terrain had never admitted the possibility of other people. She wept then. Tears for the deaths of the littlest things: the castaway shoes of children; broken stems of marsh grass battered and drowned by the sea; prom photographs of dead women she never knew; wedding rings in pawnshop windows; the tidy bodies of Cornish hens in a nest of rice.

When her partner disengaged himself, she looked up at him in wonder trying to recall his name; and he looked down at her, smiling with tender understanding of the state of tearful gratitude to which he believed he had brought her. She waiting impatiently for him to turn away and settle into a wet skim of satisfaction and light disgust, leaving her to the postcoital privateness in which she met herself, welcomed herself, and joined herself in matchless harmony.

At twenty-nine she knew it would be no other way for her, but she had not counted on the footsteps on the porch, and the beautiful black face that stared at her through the blue-glass window. Ajax.

Looking for all the world as he had seventeen years ago when he had called her pig meat. He was twenty-one then, she twelve. A universe of time between them. Now she was twenty-nine, he thirty-eight, and the lemon-yellow haunches seemed not so far away after all.

She opened the heavy door and saw him standing on the other side of the screen door with two quarts of milk tucked into his arms like marble statues. He smiled and said, "I been lookin' all over for you."

"Why?" she asked.

"To give you these," and he nodded toward one of the quarts of milk. "I don't like milk," she said.

"But you like bottles don't you?" He held one up. "Ain't that pretty?"

And indeed it was. Hanging from his fingers, framed by a slick blue sky, it looked precious and clean and permanent. She had the distinct impression that he had done something dangerous to get them.

Sula ran her fingernails over the screen thoughtfully for a second and then, laughing, she opened the screen door.

Ajax came in and headed straight for the kitchen. Sula followed slowly. By the time she got to the door he had undone the complicated wire cap and was letting the cold milk run into his mouth.

Sula watched him—or rather the rhythm in his throat—with growing interest. When he had had enough, he poured the rest into the sink, rinsed the bottle out and presented it to her. She took the bottle with one hand and his wrist with the other and pulled him into the pantry. There was no need to go there, for not a soul was in the house, but the gesture came to Hannah's daughter naturally. There in the pantry, empty now of flour sacks, void of row upon row of canned goods, free forever of strings of tiny green peppers, holding the wet milk bottle tight in her arm she stood wide-legged against the wall and pulled from his track-lean hips all the pleasure her thighs could hold.

He came regularly then, bearing gifts: clusters of black berries still on their branches, four meal-fried porgies wrapped in a salmon-colored sheet of the Pittsburgh *Courier*, a handful of jacks, two boxes of lime Jell-Well, a hunk of ice-wagon ice, a can of Old Dutch Cleanser with the bonneted woman chasing dirt with her stick; a page of Tillie the Toiler comics, and more gleaming white bottles of milk.

Contrary to what anybody would have suspected from just seeing him lounging around the pool hall, or shooting at Mr. Finley for beating his own dog, or calling filthy compliments to passing women, Ajax was very nice to women. His women, of course, knew it, and it provoked them into murderous battles over him in the streets, brawling thick-thighed women with knives disturbed many a Friday night with their bloodletting and attracted whooping crowds. On such occasions Ajax stood, along with the crowd, and viewed the fighters with the same golden-eyed indifference with which he watched old men playing checkers. Other than his mother, who sat in her shack with six younger sons working roots,[8] he had never met an interesting woman in his life.

His kindness to them in general was not due to a ritual of seduction (he had no need for it) but rather to the habit he acquired in dealing with his mother, who inspired thoughtfulness and generosity in all her sons.

She was an evil conjure woman, blessed with seven adoring children whose joy it was to bring her the plants, hair, underclothing, fingernail parings, white hens, blood, camphor, pictures, kerosene and footstep dust that she needed, as well as to order Van Van, High John the Conqueror, Little John to Chew, Devil's Shoe String, Chinese Wash, Mustard Seed and the Nine Herbs[9] from Cincinnati. She knew about the weather, omens, the living, the dead, dreams and all illnesses and made a modest living with her skills. Had she any teeth or ever straightened her back, she would have been the most gorgeous thing alive, worthy of her sons' worship for her beauty alone, if not for the absolute freedom she allowed them (known in some quarters as neglect) and the weight of her hoary knowledge.

This woman Ajax loved, and after her—airplanes. There was nothing in between. And when he was not sitting enchanted listening to his mother's words, he thought of airplanes, and pilots, and the deep sky that held them both. People thought that those long trips he took to large cities in the state were for some sophisticated good times they could not imagine but only envy; actually he was leaning against the barbed wire of airports, or nosing around hangars just to hear the talk of the men who were fortunate enough to be in the trade. The rest of the time, the time he was not watching his mother's magic or thinking of airplanes, he spent in the

---

8. Making folk medicine.
9. Powders, charms, and so forth sold for luck, strength, health.

idle pursuits of bachelors without work in small towns. He had heard all the stories about Sula, and they aroused his curiosity. Her elusiveness and indifference to established habits of behavior reminded him of his mother, who was as stubborn in her pursuits of the occult as the women of Greater Saint Matthew's were in the search for redeeming grace. So when his curiosity was high enough he picked two bottles of milk off the porch of some white family and went to see her, suspecting that this was perhaps the only other woman he knew whose life was her own, who could deal with life efficiently, and who was not interested in nailing him.

Sula, too, was curious. She knew nothing about him except the word he had called out to her years ago and the feeling he had excited in her then. She had grown quite accustomed to the clichés of other people's lives as well as her own increasing dissatisfaction with Medallion. If she could have thought of a place to go, she probably would have left, but that was before Ajax looked at her through the blue glass and held the milk aloft like a trophy.

But it was not the presents that made her wrap him up in her thighs. They were charming, of course (especially the jar of butterflies he let loose in the bedroom), but her real pleasure was the fact that he talked to her. They had genuine conversations. He did not speak down to her or at her, nor content himself with puerile questions about her life or monologues of his own activities. Thinking she was possibly brilliant, like his mother, he seemed to expect brilliance from her, and she delivered. And in all of it, he listened more than he spoke. His clear comfort at being in her presence, his lazy willingness to tell her all about fixes and the powers of plants, his refusal to baby or protect her, his assumption that she was both tough and wise—all of that coupled with a wide generosity of spirit only occasionally erupting into vengeance sustained Sula's interest and enthusiasm.

His idea of bliss (on earth as opposed to bliss in the sky) was a long bath in piping-hot water—his head on the cool white rim, his eyes closed in reverie.

"Soaking in hot water give you a bad back." Sula stood in the doorway looking at his knees glistening just at the surface of the soap-gray water.

"Soaking in Sula give me a bad back."

"Worth it?"

"Don't know yet. Go 'way."

"Airplanes?"

"Airplanes."

"Lindbergh know about you?"

"Go 'way."

She went and waited for him in Eva's high bed, her head turned to the boarded-up window. She was smiling, thinking how like Jude's was his craving to do the white man's work, when two deweys came in with their beautiful teeth and said, "We sick."

Sula turned her head slowly and murmured, "Get well."

"We need some medicine."

"Look in the bathroom."

"Ajax in there."

"Then wait."

"We sick now."

Sula leaned over the bed, picked up a shoe and threw it at them. "Cocksucker!" they screamed, and she leaped out of the bed naked as a yard dog. She caught the redheaded dewey by his shirt and held him by the heels over the banister until he wet his pants. The other dewey was joined by the third, and they delved into their pockets for stones, which they threw at her. Sula, ducking and tottering with laughter, carried the wet dewey to the bedroom and when the other two followed her, deprived of all weapons except their teeth, Sula had dropped the first dewey on the bed and was fishing in her purse. She gave each of them a dollar bill which they snatched and then scooted off down the stairs to Dick's to buy the catarrh remedy they loved to drink.

Ajax came sopping wet into the room and lay down on the bed to let the air dry him. They were both still for a long time until he reached out and touched her arm.

He liked for her to mount him so he could see her towering above him and call soft obscenities up into her face. As she rocked there, swayed there, like a Georgia pine on its knees, high above the slipping, falling smile, high above the golden eyes and the velvet helmet of hair, rocking, swaying, she focused her thoughts to bar the creeping disorder that was flooding her hips. She looked down, down from what seemed an awful height at the head of the man whose lemon-yellow gabardines had been the first sexual excitement she'd known. Letting her thoughts dwell on his face in order to confine, for just a while longer, the drift of her flesh toward the high silence of orgasm.

If I take a chamois and rub real hard on the bone, right on the ledge of your cheek bone, some of the black will disappear. It will flake away into the chamois and underneath there will be gold leaf. I can see it shining through the black. I know it is there . . .

How high she was over his wand-lean body, how slippery was his sliding sliding smile.

And if I take a nail file or even Eva's old paring knife—that will do—and scrape away at the gold, it will fall away and there will be alabaster. The alabaster is what gives your face its planes, its curves. That is why your mouth smiling does not reach your eyes. Alabaster is giving it a gravity that resists a total smile.

The height and the swaying dizzied her, so she bent down and let her breasts graze his chest.

Then I can take a chisel and small tap hammer and tap away at the alabaster. It will crack then like ice under the pick, and through the breaks I will see the loam, fertile, free of pebbles and twigs. For it is the loam that is giving you that smell.

She slipped her hands under his armpits, for it seemed as though she would not be able to dam the spread of weakness she felt under her skin without holding on to something.

I will put my hand deep into your soil, lift it, sift it with my fingers, feel its warm surface and dewy chill below.

She put her head under his chin with no hope in the world of keeping anything at all at bay.

I will water your soil, keep it rich and moist. But how much? How much water to keep the loam moist? And how much loam will I need to keep my water still? And when do the two make mud?

He swallowed her mouth just as her thighs had swallowed his genitals, and the house was very, very quiet.

◉ ◉ ◉

Sula began to discover what possession was. Not love, perhaps, but possession or at least the desire for it. She was astounded by so new and alien a feeling. First there was the morning of the night before when she actually wondered if Ajax would come by that day. Then there was an afternoon when she stood before the mirror finger-tracing the laugh lines around her mouth and trying to decide whether she was good-looking or not. She ended this deep perusal by tying a green ribbon in her hair. The green silk made a rippling whisper as she slid it into her hair—a whisper that could easily have been Hannah's chuckle, a soft slow nasal hiss she used to emit when something amused her. Like women sitting for two hours under the marcelling irons only to wonder two days later how soon they would need another appointment. The ribbon-tying was followed by other activity, and when Ajax came that evening, bringing her a reed whistle he had carved that morning, not only was the green ribbon still in her hair, but the bathroom was gleaming, the bed was made, and the table was set for two.

He gave her the reed whistle, unlaced his shoes and sat in the rocking chair in the kitchen.

Sula walked toward him and kissed his mouth. He ran his fingers along the nape of her neck.

"I bet you ain't even missed Tar Baby, have you?" he asked.

"Missed? No. Where is he?"

Ajax smiled at her delicious indifference. "Jail."

"Since when?"

"Last Saturday."

"Picked up for drunk?"

"Little bit more than that," he answered and went ahead to tell her about his own involvement in another of Tar Baby's misfortunes.

On Saturday afternoon Tar Baby had stumbled drunk into traffic on the New River Road. A woman driver swerved to avoid him and hit another car. When the police came, they recognized the woman as the mayor's niece and arrested Tar Baby. Later, after the word got out, Ajax and two other men went to the station to see about him. At first they wouldn't let them in. But they relented after Ajax and the other two just stood around for one hour and a half and repeated their request at regular intervals. When they finally got permission to go in and looked in at him in the cell, he was twisted up in a corner badly beaten and dressed in nothing but extremely soiled underwear. Ajax and the other men asked the officer why Tar Baby couldn't have back his clothes. "It ain't right," they said, "to let a grown man lay around in his own shit."

The policeman, obviously in agreement with Eva, who had always maintained that Tar Baby was white, said that if the prisoner didn't like to live in shit, he should come down out of those hills, and live like a decent white man.

More words were exchanged, hot words and dark, and the whole thing ended with the arraignment of the three black men, and an appointment to appear in civil court Thursday next.

Ajax didn't seem too bothered by any of it. More annoyed and inconvenienced than anything else. He had had several messes with the police, mostly in gambling raids, and regarded them as the natural hazards of Negro life.

But Sula, the green ribbon shining in her hair, was flooded with an awareness of the impact of the outside world on Ajax. She stood up and arranged herself on the arm of the rocking chair. Putting her fingers deep into the velvet of his hair, she murmured, "Come on. Lean on me."

Ajax blinked. Then he looked swiftly into her face. In her words, in her voice, was a sound he knew well. For the first time he saw the green ribbon. He looked around and saw the gleaming kitchen and the table set for two and detected the scent of the nest. Every hackle on his body rose, and he knew that very soon she would, like all of her sisters before her, put to him the death-knell question "Where you been?" His eyes dimmed with a mild and momentary regret.

He stood and mounted the stairs with her and entered the spotless bathroom where the dust had been swept from underneath the claw-foot tub. He was trying to remember the date of the air show in Dayton. As he came into the bedroom, he saw Sula lying on fresh white sheets, wrapped in the deadly odor of freshly applied cologne.

He dragged her under him and made love to her with the steadiness and the intensity of a man about to leave for Dayton.

Every now and then she looked around for tangible evidence of his having ever been there. Where were the butterflies? the blueberries? the whistling reed? She could find nothing, for he had left nothing but his stunning absence. An absence so decorative, so ornate, it was difficult for her to understand how she had ever endured, without falling dead or being consumed, his magnificent presence.

The mirror by the door was not a mirror by the door, it was an altar where he stood for only a moment to put on his cap before going out. The red rocking chair was a rocking of his own hips as he sat in the kitchen. Still, there was nothing of his—his own—that she could find. It was as if she were afraid she had hallucinated him and needed proof to the contrary. His absence was everywhere, stinging everything, giving the furnishings primary colors, sharp outlines to the corners of rooms and gold light to the dust collecting on table tops. When he was there he pulled everything toward himself. Not only her eyes and all her senses but also inanimate things seemed to exist because of him, backdrops to his presence. Now that he had gone, these things, so long subdued by his presence, were glamorized in his wake.

Then one day, burrowing in a dresser drawer, she found what she had been looking for: proof that he had been there, his driver's license. It contained just what she needed for verification—his vital statistics: Born 1901, height 5'11", weight 152 lbs., eyes brown, hair black, color black. Oh yes, skin black. Very black. So black that only a steady careful rubbing with steel wool would remove it, and as it was removed there was the glint of gold leaf and under the gold leaf the cold alabaster and deep, deep down under the cold alabaster more black only this time the black of warm loam.

But what was this? Albert Jacks? His name was Albert Jacks? A. Jacks. She had thought it was Ajax. All those years. Even from the time she walked by the pool hall and looked away from him sitting astride a wooden chair, looked away to keep from seeing the wide space of intolerable orderliness between his legs; the openness that held no sign, no sign at all, of the animal that lurked in his trousers; looked away from the insolent nostrils and the smile that kept slipping and falling, falling, falling so she wanted to reach out with her hand to catch it before it fell to the pavement and was sullied by the cigarette butts and bottle caps and spittle at his feet and the feet of other men who sat or stood around outside the pool hall, calling, singing out to her and Nel and grown women too with lyrics like *pig meat* and *brown sugar* and *jailbait* and *O Lord, what have I done to deserve the wrath*, and *Take me, Jesus, I have seen the promised land*, and *Do, Lord, remember me* in voices mellowed by hopeless passion into gentleness. Even then, when she and Nel were trying hard not to dream of him and not to think of him when they touched the softness in their underwear or undid their braids as soon as they left home to let the hair bump and wave around their ears, or wrapped the cotton binding around their chests so the nipples would not break through their blouses and give him cause to smile his slipping, falling smile, which brought the blood rushing to their skin. And even later, when for the first time in her life she had lain in bed with a man and said his name involuntarily or said it truly meaning *him*, the name she was screaming and saying was not his at all.

Sula stood with a worn slip of paper in her fingers and said aloud to no one, "I didn't even know his name. And if I didn't know his name, then there is nothing I did know and I have known nothing ever at all since the one thing I wanted was to know his name so how could he help but leave me since he was making love to a woman who didn't even know his name.

"When I was a little girl the heads of my paper dolls came off, and it was a long time before I discovered that my own head would not fall off if I bent my neck. I used to walk around holding it very stiff because I thought a strong wind or a heavy push would snap my neck. Nel was the one who told me the truth. But she was wrong. I did not hold my head stiff enough when I met him and so I lost it just like the dolls.

"It's just as well he left. Soon I would have torn the flesh from his face just to see if I was right about the gold and nobody would have understood that kind of curiosity. They would have believed that I wanted to hurt him just like the little boy who fell down the steps and broke his leg and the people think I pushed him just because I looked at it."

Holding the driver's license she crawled into bed and fell into a sleep full of dreams of cobalt blue.

When she awoke, there was a melody in her head she could not identify or recall ever hearing before. "Perhaps I made it up," she thought. Then it came to her—the name of the song and all its lyrics just as she had heard it many times before. She sat on the edge of the bed thinking, "There aren't any more new songs and I have sung all the ones there are. I have sung them all. I have sung all the songs there are." She lay down again on the bed and sang a little wandering tune made up of the words *I have sung all the songs all the songs I have sung all the songs there are* until, touched by her own lullaby, she grew drowsy, and in the hollow of near-sleep she tasted the acridness of gold, left the chill of alabaster and smelled the dark, sweet stench of loam.

1940

"I heard you was sick. Anything I can do for you?"

She had practiced not just the words but the tone, the pitch of her voice. It should be calm, matter-of-fact, but strong in sympathy—for the illness though, not for the patient.

The sound of her voice as she heard it in her head betrayed no curiosity, no pride, just the inflection of any good woman come to see about a sick person who, incidentally, had such visits from nobody else.

For the first time in three years she would be looking at the stemmed rose that hung over the eye of her enemy. Moreover, she would be doing it with the taste of Jude's exit in her mouth, with the resentment and shame that even yet pressed for release in her stomach. She would be facing the black rose that Jude had kissed and looking at the nostrils of the woman who had twisted her love for her own children into something so thick and monstrous she was afraid to show it lest it break loose and smother them with its heavy paw. A cumbersome bear-love that, given any rein, would suck their breath away in its crying need for honey.

Because Jude's leaving was so complete, the full responsibility of the household was Nel's. There were no more fifty dollars in brown envelopes to count on, so she took to cleaning rather than fret away the tiny seaman's pension her parents lived on. And just this past year she got a better job working as a chambermaid in the same hotel Jude had worked in. The tips were only fair, but the hours were good—she was home when the children got out of school.

At thirty her hot brown eyes had turned to agate, and her skin had taken on the sheen of maple struck down, split and sanded at the height of its green. Virtue, bleak and drawn, was her only mooring. It brought her to Number 7 Carpenter's Road and the door with the blue glass; it helped her to resist scratching the screen as in days gone by; it hid from her the true motives for her charity, and, finally, it gave her voice the timbre she wanted it to have: free of delight or a lip-smacking "I told you so" with which the news of Sula's illness had been received up in the Bottom—free of the least hint of retribution.

Now she stood in Eva's old bedroom, looking down at that dark rose, aware of the knife-thin arms sliding back and forth over the quilt and the boarded-up window Eva had jumped out of.

Sula looked up and without a second's pause followed Nel's example of leaving out the greeting when she spoke.

"As a matter of fact, there is. I got a prescription. Nathan usually goes for me but he . . . school don't let out till three. Could you run it over to the drugstore?"

"Where is it?" Nel was glad to have a concrete errand. Conversation would be difficult. (Trust Sula to pick up a relationship exactly where it lay.)

"Look in my bag. No. Over there."

Nel walked to the dresser and opened the purse with the beaded clasp. She saw only a watch and the folded prescription down inside. No wallet, no change purse. She turned to Sula: "Where's your . . . "

But Sula was looking at the boarded-up window. Something in her eye right there in the corner stopped Nel from completing her question. That and the slight flare of the nostrils—a shadow of a snarl. Nel took the piece of paper and picked up her own purse, saying, "OK. I'll be right back."

As soon as the door was shut, Sula breathed through her mouth. While Nel was in the room the pain had increased. Now that this new pain killer, the one she had been holding in reserve, was on the way her misery was manageable. She let a piece of her mind lay on Nel. It was funny, sending Nel off to that drugstore right away like that, after she had not seen her to speak to for years. The drugstore was where Edna Finch's Mellow House used to be years back when they were girls. Where they used to go, the two of them, hand in hand, for the 18-cent ice-cream sundaes, past the Time and a Half Pool Hall, where the sprawling men said "pig meat," and they sat in that cool room with the marble-top tables and ate the first ice-cream sundaes of their lives. Now Nel was going back there alone and Sula was waiting for the medicine the doctor said not to take until the pain got really bad. And she supposed "really bad" was now. Although you could never tell. She wondered for an instant what Nellie wanted; why she had come. Did she want to gloat? Make up? Following this line of thought required more concentration than she could muster. Pain was greedy; it demanded all of her attention. But it was good that this new medicine, the reserve, would be brought to her by her old friend. Nel, she remembered, always thrived on a crisis. The closed place in the water; Hannah's funeral. Nel was the best. When Sula imitated her, or tried to, those long years ago, it always ended up in some action noteworthy not for its coolness but mostly for its being bizarre. The one time she tried to protect Nel, she had cut off her own finger tip and earned not Nel's gratitude but her disgust. From then on she had let her emotions dictate her behavior.

She could hear Nel's footsteps long before she opened the door and put the medicine on the table near the bed.

As Sula poured the liquid into a sticky spoon, Nel began the sickroom conversation.

"You look fine, Sula."

"You lying, Nellie. I look bad." She gulped the medicine.

"No. I haven't seen you for a long time, but you look ... "

"You don't have to do that, Nellie. It's going to be all right."

"What ails you? Have they said?"

Sula licked the corners of her lips. "You want to talk about that?"

Nel smiled, slightly, at the bluntness she had forgotten. "No. No, I don't, but you sure you should be staying up here alone?"

"Nathan comes by. The deweys sometimes, and Tar Baby ... "

"That ain't help, Sula. You need to be with somebody grown. Somebody who can ... "

"I'd rather be here, Nellie."

"You know you don't have to be proud with me."

"Proud?" Sula's laughter broke through the phlegm. "What you talking about? I like my own dirt, Nellie. I'm not proud. You sure have forgotten me."

"Maybe. Maybe not. But you a woman and you alone."

"And you? Ain't you alone?"

"I'm not sick. I work."

"Yes. Of course you do. Work's good for you, Nellie. It don't do nothing for me."

"You never *had* to."

"I never would."

"There's something to say for it, Sula. 'Specially if you don't want people to have to do for you."

"Neither one, Nellie. Neither one."

"You can't have it all, Sula." Nel was getting exasperated with her arrogance, with her lying at death's door still smart-talking.

"Why? I can do it all, why can't I have it all?"

"You *can't* do it all. You a woman and a colored woman at that. You can't act like a man. You can't be walking around all independent-like, doing whatever you like, taking what you want, leaving what you don't."

"You repeating yourself."

"How repeating myself?"

"You say I'm a woman and colored. Ain't that the same as being a man?"

"I don't think so and you wouldn't either if you had children."

"Then I really would act like what you call a man. Every man I ever knew left his children."

"Some were taken."

"Wrong, Nellie. The word is 'left.' "

"You still going to know everything, ain't you?"

"I don't know everything, I just do everything."

"Well, you don't do what I do."

"You think I don't know what your life is like just because I ain't living it? I know what every colored woman in this country is doing."

"What's that?"

"Dying. Just like me. But the difference is they dying like a stump. Me, I'm going down like one of those redwoods. I sure did live in this world."

"Really? What have you got to show for it?"

"Show? To who? Girl, I got my mind. And what goes on in it. Which is to say, I got me."

"Lonely, ain't it?"

"Yes. But my lonely is *mine*. Now your lonely is somebody else's. Made by somebody else and handed to you. Ain't that something? A secondhand lonely."

Nel sat back on the little wooden chair. Anger skipped but she realized that Sula was probably just showing off. No telling what shape she was really in, but there was no point in saying anything other than what was the truth. "I always understood how you could take a man. Now I understand why you can't keep none."

"Is that what I'm supposed to do? Spend my life keeping a man?"

"They worth keeping, Sula."

"They ain't worth more than me. And besides, I never loved no man because he was worth it. Worth didn't have nothing to do with it."

"What did?"

"My mind did. That's all."

"Well I guess that's it. You own the world and the rest of us is renting. You ride the pony and we shovel the shit. I didn't come up here for this kind of talk, Sula . . . "

"No?"

"No. I come to see about you. But now that you opened it up, I may as well close it." Nel's fingers closed around the brass rail of the bed. Now she would ask her. "How come you did it, Sula?"

There was a silence but Nel felt no obligation to fill it.

Sula stirred a little under the covers. She looked bored as she sucked her teeth. "Well, there was this space in front of me, behind me, in my head. Some space. And Jude filled it up. That's all. He just filled up the space."

"You mean you didn't even love him?" The feel of the brass was in Nel's mouth. "It wasn't even loving him?"

Sula looked toward the boarded-up window again. Her eyes fluttered as if she were about to fall off into sleep.

"But . . . " Nel held her stomach in. "But what about me? What about me? Why didn't you think about me? Didn't I count? I never hurt you. What did you take him for if you didn't love him and why didn't you think about me?" And then, "I was good to you, Sula, why don't that matter?"

Sula turned her head away from the boarded window. Her voice was quiet and the stemmed rose over her eye was very dark. "It matters, Nel, but only to you. Not to anybody else. Being good to somebody is just like being mean to somebody. Risky. You don't get nothing for it."

Nel took her hands from the brass railing. She was annoyed with herself. Finally when she had gotten the nerve to ask the question, the right question, it made no difference. Sula couldn't give her a sensible answer because she didn't know. Would be, in fact, the last to know. Talking to her about right and wrong was like talking to the deweys. She picked at the fringe on Sula's bedspread and said softly, "We were friends."

"Oh, yes. Good friends," Sula said.

"And you didn't love me enough to leave him alone. To let him love me. You had to take him away."

"What you mean take him away? I didn't kill him, I just fucked him. If we were such good friends, how come you couldn't get over it?"

"You laying there in that bed without a dime or a friend to your name having done all the dirt you did in this town and you still expect folks to love you?"

Sula raised herself up on her elbows. Her face glistened with the dew of fever. She opened her mouth as though to say something, then fell back on the pillows and sighed. "Oh, they'll love me all right. It will take time, but they'll love me." The sound of her voice was as soft and distant as the look in her eyes. "After all the old women have lain with the teen-agers; when all the young girls have slept with their old drunken uncles; after all the black men fuck all the white ones; when all the white women kiss all the black ones; when the guards have raped all the jailbirds and after all the whores make love to their grannies; after all the faggots get their mothers' trim;[1] when Lindbergh sleeps with Bessie Smith and Norma Shearer makes it with Stepin Fetchit;[2] after all the dogs have fucked all the cats and every weathervane on every barn flies off the roof to mount the hogs . . . then there'll be a little love left over for me. And I know just what it will feel like."

She closed her eyes then and thought of the wind pressing her dress

1. Ornaments and clothing; *faggots*—derogatory term for male homosexuals.
2. Charles Lindbergh (1902–1974) became an All-American hero when, in 1927, he was the first man to fly solo and nonstop across the Atlantic; Bessie Smith (1895–1937), a black, was perhaps the greatest of all blues singers; Norma Shearer (b. 1900), an elegant film star of the thirties, was called by her studio (MGM) "The First Lady of the Films," while Lincoln Theodore Monroe Andrew Perry (b. 1902), known as Stepin Fetchit, played stereotyped lazy, readily frightened black roles in films from the late 1920s to the early 1950s.

between her legs as she ran up the bank of the river to four leaf-locked trees and the digging of holes in the earth.

Embarrassed, irritable and a little bit ashamed, Nel rose to go. "Goodbye, Sula. I don't reckon I'll be back."

She opened the door and heard Sula's low whisper. "Hey, girl." Nel paused and turned her head but not enough to see her.

"How you know?" Sula asked.

"Know what?" Nel still wouldn't look at her.

"About who was good. How you know it was you?"

"What you mean?"

"I mean maybe it wasn't you. Maybe it was me."

Nel took two steps out the door and closed it behind her. She walked down the hall and down the four flights of steps. The house billowed around her light then dark, full of presences without sounds. The deweys, Tar Baby, the newly married couples, Mr. Buckland Reed, Patsy, Valentine, and the beautiful Hannah Peace. Where were they? Eva out at the old folks' home, the deweys living anywhere, Tar Baby steeped in wine, and Sula upstairs in Eva's bed with a boarded-up window and an empty pocketbook on the dresser.

• • •

When Nel closed the door, Sula reached for more medicine. Then she turned the pillow over to its cool side and thought about her old friend. "So she will walk on down that road, her back so straight in that old green coat, the strap of her handbag pushed back all the way to the elbow, thinking how much I have cost her and never remember the days when we were two throats and one eye and we had no price."

Pictures drifted through her head as lightly as dandelion spores: the blue eagle that swallowed the E of the Sherman's Mellowe wine[3] that Tar Baby drank; the pink underlid of Hannah's eye as she probed for a fleck of coal dust or a lash. She thought of looking out of the windows of all those trains and buses, looking at the feet and backs of all those people. Nothing was ever different. They were all the same. All of the words and all of the smiles, every tear and every gag just something to do.

"That's the same sun I looked at when I was twelve, the same pear trees. If I live a hundred years my urine will flow the same way, my armpits and breath will smell the same. My hair will grow from the same holes. I didn't mean anything. I never meant anything. I stood there watching her burn and was thrilled. I wanted her to keep on jerking like that, to keep on dancing."

Then she had the dream again. The Clabber Girl Baking Powder lady was smiling and beckoning to her, one hand under her apron. When Sula came near she disintegrated into white dust, which Sula was hurriedly trying to stuff into the pockets of her blue-flannel housecoat. The disintegration was awful to see, but worse was the feel of the powder—its starchy slipperiness as she tried to collect it by handfuls. The more she scooped, the more it billowed. At last it covered her, filled her eyes, her nose, her throat, and she woke gagging and overwhelmed with the smell of smoke.

---

3. Cheap brand of wine.

Pain took hold. First a fluttering as of doves in her stomach, then a kind of burning, followed by a spread of thin wires to other parts of her body. Once the wires of liquid pain were in place, they jelled and began to throb. She tried concentrating on the throbs, identifying them as waves, hammer strokes, razor edges or small explosions. Soon even the variety of the pain bored her and there was nothing to do, for it was joined by fatigue so great she could not make a fist or fight the taste of oil at the back of her tongue.

Several times she tried to cry out, but the fatigue barely let her open her lips, let alone take the deep breath necessary to scream. So she lay there wondering how soon she would gather enough strength to lift her arm and push the rough quilt away from her chin and whether she should turn her cheek to the cooler side of the pillow now or wait till her face was thoroughly soaked and the move would be more refreshing. But she was reluctant to move her face for another reason. If she turned her head, she would not be able to see the boarded-up window Eva jumped out of. And looking at those four wooden planks with the steel rod slanting across them was the only peace she had. The sealed window soothed her with its sturdy termination, its unassailable finality. It was as though for the first time she was completely alone—where she had always wanted to be—free of the possibility of distraction. It would be here, only here, held by this blind window high above the elm tree, that she might draw her legs up to her chest, close her eyes, put her thumb in her mouth and float over and down the tunnels, just missing the dark walls, down, down until she met a rain scent and would know the water was near, and she would curl into its heavy softness and it would envelop her, carry her, and wash her tired flesh always. Always. Who said that? She tried hard to think. Who was it that had promised her a sleep of water always? The effort to recall was too great; it loosened a knot in her chest that turned her thoughts again to the pain.

While in this state of weary anticipation, she noticed that she was not breathing, that her heart had stopped completely. A crease of fear touched her breast, for any second there was sure to be a violent explosion in her brain, a gasping for breath. Then she realized, or rather she sensed, that there was not going to be any pain. She was not breathing because she didn't have to. Her body did not need oxygen. She was dead.

Sula felt her face smiling. "Well, I'll be damned," she thought, "it didn't even hurt. Wait'll I tell Nel."

1941

The death of Sula Peace was the best news folks up in the Bottom had had since the promise of work at the tunnel. Of the few who were not afraid to witness the burial of a witch and who had gone to the cemetery, some had come just to verify her being put away but stayed to sing "Shall We Gather at the River"[4] for politeness' sake, quite unaware of the bleak promise of their song. Others came to see that nothing went awry, that the shallow-minded and small-hearted kept their meanness at bay, and that the entire event be characterized by that abiding gentleness of spirit to which they themselves had arrived by the simple determination not to

4. Popular hymn (1864) written by Robert Lowry (1826–1899) amid an epidemic; the river ("where angel feet have trod") is the river of death.

let anything—anything at all: not failed crops, not rednecks, lost jobs, sick children, rotten potatoes, broken pipes, bug-ridden flour, third-class coal, educated social workers, thieving insurance men, garlic-ridden hunkies, corrupt Catholics, racist Protestants, cowardly Jews, slaveholding Moslems, jack-leg⁵ nigger preachers, squeamish Chinamen, cholera, dropsy or the Black Plague, let alone a strange woman—keep them from their God.

In any case, both the raw-spirited and the gentle who came—not to the white funeral parlor but to the colored part of the Beechnut Cemetery— felt that either *because* Sula was dead or just *after* she was dead a brighter day was dawning. There were signs. The rumor that the tunnel spanning the river would use Negro workers became an announcement. Planned, abandoned and replanned for years, this project had finally begun in 1937. For three years there were rumors that blacks would work it, and hope was high in spite of the fact that the River Road leading to the tunnel had encouraged similar hopes in 1927 but had ended up being built entirely by white labor—hillbillies and immigrants taking even the lowest jobs. But the tunnel itself was another matter. The craft work—no, they would not get that. But it was a major job, and the government seemed to favor opening up employment to black workers. It meant black men would not have to sweep Medallion to eat, or leave the town altogether for the steel mills in Akron and along Lake Erie.

The second sign was the construction begun on an old people's home. True, it was more renovation than construction, but the blacks were free, or so it was said, to occupy it. Some said that the very transfer of Eva from the ramshackle house that passed for a colored women's nursing home to the bright new one was a clear sign of the mystery of God's ways, His mighty thumb having been seen at Sula's throat.

So it was with a strong sense of hope that the people in the Bottom watched October close.

Then Medallion turned silver. It seemed sudden, but actually there had been days and days of no snow—just frost—when, late one afternoon, a rain fell and froze. Way down Carpenter's Road, where the concrete sidewalks started, children hurried to the sliding places before shopkeepers and old women sprinkled stove ashes, like ancient onyx, onto the new-minted silver. They hugged trees simply to hold for a moment all that life and largeness stilled in glass, and gazed at the sun pressed against the gray sky like a worn doubloon, wondering all the while if the world were coming to an end. Grass stood blade by blade, shocked into separateness by an ice that held for days.

Late-harvesting things were ruined, of course, and fowl died of both chill and rage. Cider turned to ice and split the jugs, forcing the men to drink their cane liquor too soon. It was better down in the valley, since, as always, the hills protected it, but up in the Bottom black folks suffered heavily in their thin houses and thinner clothes. The ice-cold wind bled what little heat they had through windowpanes and ill-fitting doors. For days on end they were virtually housebound, venturing out only to coalbins or right next door for the trading of vital foodstuffs. Never to the stores. No deliveries were being made anyway, and when they were, the items were saved for better-paying white customers. Women could not

5. Unordained.

make it down the icy slopes and therefore missed days of wages they sorely needed.

The consequence of all that ice was a wretched Thanksgiving of tiny tough birds, heavy pork cakes, and pithy sweet potatoes. By the time the ice began to melt and the first barge was seen shuddering through the ice skim on the river, everybody under fifteen had croup, or scarlet fever, and those over had chilblains, rheumatism, pleurisy, earaches and a world of other ailments.

Still it was not those illnesses or even the ice that marked the beginning of the trouble, that self-fulfilled prophecy that Shadrack carried on his tongue. As soon as the silvering began, long before the cider cracked the jugs, there was something wrong. A falling away, a dislocation was taking place. Hard on the heels of the general relief that Sula's death brought a restless irritability took hold. Teapot, for example, went into the kitchen and asked his mother for some sugar-butter-bread. She got up to fix it and found that she had no butter, only oleomargarine. Too tired to mix the saffron-colored powder into the hard cake of oleo,[6] she simply smeared the white stuff on the bread and sprinkled the sugar over it. Teapot tasted the difference and refused to eat it. This keenest of insults that a mother can feel, the rejection by a child of her food, bent her into fury and she beat him as she had not done since Sula knocked him down the steps. She was not alone. Other mothers who had defended their children from Sula's malevolence (or who had defended their positions as mothers from Sula's scorn for the role) now had nothing to rub up against. The tension was gone and so was the reason for the effort they had made. Without her mockery, affection for others sank into flaccid disrepair. Daughters who had complained bitterly about the responsibilities of taking care of their aged mothers-in-law had altered when Sula locked Eva away, and they began cleaning those old women's spittoons without a murmur. Now that Sula was dead and done with, they returned to a steeping resentment of the burdens of old people. Wives uncoddled their husbands; there seemed no further need to reinforce their vanity. And even those Negroes who had moved down from Canada to Medallion, who remarked every chance they got that they had never been slaves, felt a loosening of the reactionary compassion for Southern-born blacks Sula had inspired in them. They returned to their original claims of superiority.

The normal meanness that the winter brought was compounded by the small-spiritedness that hunger and scarlet fever produced. Even a definite and witnessed interview of four colored men (and the promise of more in the spring) at the tunnel site could not break the cold vise of that lean and bitter year's end.

Christmas came one morning and haggled everybody's nerves like a dull ax—too shabby to cut clean but too heavy to ignore. The children lay wall-eyed on creaking beds or pallets near the stove, sucking peppermint and oranges in between coughs while their mothers stomped the floors in rage at the cakes that did not rise because the stove fire had been so stingy; at the curled bodies of men who chose to sleep the day away rather than face the silence made by the absence of Lionel trains, drums, crybaby dolls and rocking horses. Teen-agers sneaked into the Elmira

6. In many states until quite recently oleomargarine could be sold only uncolored, a dead-white; small capsules or bits of powder were often included in the package to be squeezed or mixed in for coloring.

Theater in the afternoon and let Tex Ritter[7] free them from the recollection of their father's shoes, yawning in impotence under the bed. Some of them had a bottle of wine, which they drank at the feet of the glittering Mr. Ritter, making such a ruckus the manager had to put them out. The white people who came with Christmas bags of rock candy and old clothes were hard put to get a Yes'm, thank you, out of those sullen mouths.

Just as the ice lingered in October, so did the phlegm of December—which explained the enormous relief brought on by the first three days of 1941. It was as though the season had exhausted itself, for on January first the temperature shot up to sixty-one degrees and slushed the whiteness overnight. On January second drab patches of grass could be seen in the fields. On January third the sun came out—and so did Shadrack with his rope, his bell and his childish dirge.

He had spent the night before watching a tiny moon. The people, the voices that kept him company, were with him less and less. Now there were long periods when he heard nothing except the wind in the trees and the plop of buckeyes on the earth. In the winter, when the fish were too hard to get to, he did picking-up jobs for small businessmen (nobody would have him in or even near their homes), and thereby continued to have enough money for liquor. Yet the drunk times were becoming deeper but more seldom. It was as though he no longer needed to drink to forget whatever it was he could not remember. Now he could not remember that he had ever forgotten anything. Perhaps that was why for the first time after that cold day in France he was beginning to miss the presence of other people. Shadrack had improved enough to feel lonely. If he was lonely before, he didn't know it because the noise he kept up, the roaring, the busyness, protected him from knowing it. Now the compulsion to activity, to filling up the time when he was not happily fishing on the riverbank, had dwindled. He sometimes fell asleep before he got drunk; sometimes spent whole days looking at the river and the sky; and more and more he relinquished the military habits of cleanliness in his shack. Once a bird flew into his door—one of the robins during the time there was a plague of them. It stayed, looking for an exit, for the better part of an hour. When the bird found the window and flew away, Shadrack was grieved and actually waited and watched for its return. During those days of waiting, he did not make his bed, or sweep, or shake out the little rag-braid rug, and almost forgot to slash with his fish knife the passing day on his calendar. When he did return to housekeeping, it was not with the precision he had always insisted upon. The messier his house got, the lonelier he felt, and it was harder and harder to conjure up sergeants, and orderlies, and invading armies; harder and harder to hear the gunfire and keep the platoon marching in time. More frequently now he looked at and fondled the one piece of evidence that he once had a visitor in his house: a child's purple-and-white belt. The one the little girl left behind when she came to see him. Shadrack remembered the scene clearly. He had stepped into the door and there was a tear-stained face turning, turning toward him; eyes hurt and wondering; mouth parted in an effort to ask a question. She had wanted something—from him. Not

7. "America's Most Beloved Cowboy" (1905–1974), film star of the 1940s elected both to the Cowboy and   Country Music Halls of Fame.

fish, not work, but something only he could give. She had a tadpole over her eye (that was how he knew she was a friend—she had the mark of the fish he loved), and one of her braids had come undone. But when he looked at her face he had seen also the skull beneath, and thinking she saw it too—knew it was there and was afraid—he tried to think of something to say to comfort her, something to stop the hurt from spilling out of her eyes. So he had said "always," so she would not have to be afraid of the change—the falling away of skin, the drip and slide of blood, and the exposure of bone underneath. He had said "always" to convince her, assure her, of permanency.

It worked, for when he said it her face lit up and the hurt did leave. She ran then, carrying his knowledge, but her belt fell off and he kept it as a memento. It hung on a nail near his bed—unfrayed, unsullied after all those years, with only the permanent bend in the fabric made by its long life on a nail. It was pleasant living with that sign of a visitor, his only one. And after a while he was able to connect the belt with the face, the tadpole-over-the-eye-face that he sometimes saw up in the Bottom. His visitor, his company, his guest, his social life, his woman, his daughter, his friend—they all hung there on a nail near his bed.

Now he stared at the tiny moon floating high over the ice-choked river. His loneliness had dropped down somewhere around his ankles. Some other feeling possessed him. A feeling that touched his eyes and made him blink. He had seen her again months? weeks? ago. Raking leaves for Mr. Hodges, he had gone into the cellar for two bushel baskets to put them in. In the hallway he passed an open door leading to a small room. She lay on a table there. It was surely the same one. The same little-girl face, same tadpole over the eye. So he had been wrong. Terribly wrong. No "always" at all. Another dying away of someone whose face he knew.

It was then he began to suspect that all those years of rope hauling and bell ringing were never going to do any good. He might as well sit forever on his riverbank and stare out of the window at the moon.

By his day-slashed calendar he knew that tomorrow was the day. And for the first time he did not want to go. He wanted to stay with the purple-and-white belt. Not go. Not go.

Still, when the day broke in an incredible splash of sun, he gathered his things. In the early part of the afternoon, drenched in sunlight and certain that this would be the last time he would invite them to end their lives neatly and sweetly, he walked over the rickety bridge and on into the Bottom. But it was not heartfelt this time, not loving this time, for he no longer cared whether he helped them or not. His rope was improperly tied; his bell had a tinny unimpassioned sound. His visitor was dead and would come no more.

Years later people would quarrel about who had been the first to go. Most folks said it was the deweys, but one or two knew better, knew that Dessie and Ivy had been first. Said that Dessie had opened her door first and stood there shielding her eyes from the sun while watching Shadrack coming down the road. She laughed.

Maybe the sun; maybe the clots of green showing in the hills promising so much; maybe the contrast between Shadrack's doomy, gloomy bell glinting in all that sweet sunshine. Maybe just a brief moment, for once, of not feeling fear, of looking at death in the sunshine and being unafraid. She laughed.

Upstairs, Ivy heard her and looked to see what caused the thick music that rocked her neighbor's breasts. Then Ivy laughed too. Like the scarlet fever that had touched everybody and worn them down to gristle, their laughter infected Carpenter's Road. Soon children were jumping about giggling and men came to the porches to chuckle. By the time Shadrack reached the first house, he was facing a line of delighted faces.

Never before had they laughed. Always they had shut their doors, pulled down the shades and called their children out of the road. It frightened him, this glee, but he stuck to his habit—singing his song, ringing his bell and holding fast to his rope. The deweys with their magnificent teeth ran out from Number 7 and danced a little jig around the befuddled Shadrack, then cut into a wild aping of his walk, his song and his bell-ringing. By now women were holding their stomachs, and the men were slapping their knees. It was Mrs. Jackson, who ate ice, who tripped down off her porch and marched—actually marched—along behind him. The scene was so comic the people walked into the road to make sure they saw it all. In that way the parade started.

Everybody, Dessie, Tar Baby, Patsy, Mr. Buckland Reed, Teapot's Mamma, Valentine, the deweys, Mrs. Jackson, Irene, the proprietor of the Palace of Cosmetology, Reba, the Herrod brothers and flocks of teen-agers got into the mood and, laughing, dancing, calling to one another, formed a pied piper's band behind Shadrack. As the initial group of about twenty people passed more houses, they called to the people standing in doors and leaning out of windows to join them; to help them open further this slit in the veil, this respite from anxiety, from dignity, from gravity, from the weight of that very adult pain that had undergirded them all those years before. Called to them to come out and play in the sunshine—as though the sunshine would last, as though there really was hope. The same hope that kept them picking beans for other farmers; kept them from finally leaving as they talked of doing; kept them knee-deep in other people's dirt; kept them excited about other people's wars; kept them solicitous of white people's children; kept them convinced that some magic "government" was going to lift them up, out and away from that dirt, those beans, those wars.

Some, of course, like Helene Wright, would not go. She watched the ruckus with characteristic scorn. Others, who understood the Spirit's touch which made them dance, who understood whole families bending their backs in a field while singing as from one throat, who understood the ecstasy of river baptisms under suns just like this one, did not understand this curious disorder, this headless display and so refused also to go.

Nevertheless, the sun splashed on a larger and larger crowd that strutted, skipped, marched, and shuffled down the road. When they got down to where the sidewalk started, some of them stopped and decided to turn back, too embarrassed to enter the white part of town whooping like banshees. But except for three or four, the fainthearted were put to shame by the more aggressive and abandoned, and the parade danced down Main Street past Woolworth's and the old poultry house, turned right and moved on down the New River Road.

At the mouth of the tunnel excavation, in a fever pitch of excitement and joy, they saw the timber, the bricks, the steel ribs and the tacky wire gate that glittered under ice struck to diamond in the sun. It dazzled them, at first, and they were suddenly quiet. Their hooded eyes swept over the place where their hope had lain since 1927. There was the promise: leaf-dead. The teeth unrepaired, the coal credit cut off, the chest pains unattended, the school shoes unbought, the rush-stuffed mattresses, the broken toilets, the leaning porches, the slurred remarks and the staggering childish malevolence of their employers. All there in blazing sunlit ice rapidly becoming water.

Like antelopes they leaped over the little gate—a wire barricade that was never intended to bar anything but dogs, rabbits and stray children—and led by the tough, the enraged and the young they picked up the lengths of timber and thin steel ribs and smashed the bricks they would never fire in yawning kilns, split the sacks of limestone they had not mixed or even been allowed to haul; tore the wire mesh, tipped over wheelbarrows and rolled forepoles[8] down the bank, where they sailed far out on the icebound river.

Old and young, women and children, lame and hearty, they killed, as best they could, the tunnel they were forbidden to build.

They didn't mean to go in, to actually go down into the lip of the tunnel, but in their need to kill it all, all of it, to wipe from the face of the earth the work of the thin-armed Virginia boys, the bull-necked Greeks and the knife-faced men who waved the leaf-dead promise, they went too deep, too far . . .

A lot of them died there. The earth, now warm, shifted; the first forepole slipped; loose rock fell from the face of the tunnel and caused a shield to give way. They found themselves in a chamber of water, deprived of the sun that had brought them there. With the first crack and whoosh of water, the clamber to get out was so fierce that others who were trying to help were pulled to their deaths. Pressed up against steel ribs and timber blocks young boys strangled when the oxygen left them to join the water. Outside, others watched in terror as ice split and earth shook beneath their feet. Mrs. Jackson, weighing less than 100 pounds, slid down the bank and met with an open mouth the ice she had craved all her life. Tar Baby, Dessie, Ivy, Valentine, the Herrod boys, some of Ajax's younger brothers and the deweys (at least it was supposed; their bodies were never found)—all died there. Mr. Buckland Reed escaped, so did Patsy and her two boys, as well as some fifteen or twenty who had not gotten close enough to fall, or whose timidity would not let them enter an unfinished tunnel.

And all the while Shadrack stood there. Having forgotten his song and his rope, he just stood there high up on the bank ringing, ringing his bell.

1965

Things were so much better in 1965. Or so it seemed. You could go downtown and see colored people working in the dime store behind the counters, even handling money with cash-register keys around their necks. And a colored man taught mathematics at the junior high school.

8. Where there is danger of a cave-in during excavation, a pole or plank is sometimes thrust into the ground ahead of the digging and used as support.

The young people had a look about them that everybody said was new but which reminded Nel of the deweys, whom nobody had ever found. Maybe, she thought, they had gone off and seeded the land and growed up in these young people in the dime store with the cash-register keys around their necks.

They were so different, these young people. So different from the way she remembered them forty years ago.

Jesus, there were some beautiful boys in 1921! Look like the whole world was bursting at the seams with them. Thirteen, fourteen, fifteen years old. Jesus, they were fine. L. P., Paul Freeman and his brother Jake, Mrs. Scott's twins—and Ajax had a whole flock of younger brothers. They hung out of attic windows, rode on car fenders, delivered the coal, moved into Medallion and moved out, visited cousins, plowed, hoisted, lounged on the church steps, careened on the school playground. The sun heated them and the moon slid down their backs. God, the world was *full* of beautiful boys in 1921.

Nothing like these kids. Everything had changed. Even the whores were better then: tough, fat, laughing women with burns on their cheeks and wit married to their meanness: or widows couched in small houses in the woods with eight children to feed and no man. These modern-day whores were pale and dull before those women. These little clothes-crazy things were always embarrassed. Nasty but shamed. They didn't know what shameless was. They should have known those silvery widows in the woods who would get up from the dinner table and walk into the trees with a customer with as much embarrassment as a calving mare.

Lord, how time flies. She hardly recognized anybody in the town any more. Now there was another old people's home. Look like this town just kept on building homes for old people. Every time they built a road they built a old folks' home. You'd think folks was living longer, but the fact of it was, they was just being put out faster.

Nel hadn't seen the insides of this most recent one yet, but it was her turn in Circle Number 5 to visit some of the old women there. The pastor visited them regularly, but the circle thought private visits were nice too. There were just nine colored women out there, the same nine that had been in the other one. But a lot of white ones. White people didn't fret about putting their old ones away. It took a lot for black people to let them go, and even if somebody was old and alone, others did the dropping by, the floor washing, the cooking. Only when they got crazy and unmanageable were they let go. Unless it was somebody like Sula, who put Eva away out of meanness. It was true that Eva was foolish in the head, but not so bad as to need locking up.

Nel was more than a little curious to see her. She had been really active in church only a year or less, and that was because the children were grown now and took up less time and less space in her mind. For over twenty-five years since Jude walked out she had pinned herself into a tiny life. She spent a little time trying to marry again, but nobody wanted to take her on with three children, and she simply couldn't manage the business of keeping boyfriends. During the war she had had a rather long relationship with a sergeant stationed at the camp twenty miles down river from Medallion, but then he got called away and everything was reduced to a few letters—then nothing. Then there was a bartender at the hotel. But now she was fifty-five and hard put to remember what all that had been about.

It didn't take long, after Jude left, for her to see what the future would be. She had looked at her children and knew in her heart that that would be all. That they were all she would ever know of love. But it was a love that, like a pan of syrup kept too long on the stove, had cooked out, leaving only its odor and a hard, sweet sludge, impossible to scrape off. For the mouths of her children quickly forgot the taste of her nipples, and years ago they had begun to look past her face into the nearest stretch of sky.

In the meantime the Bottom had collapsed. Everybody who had made money during the war moved as close as they could to the valley, and the white people were buying down river, cross river, stretching Medallion like two strings on the banks. Nobody colored lived much up in the Bottom any more. White people were building towers for television stations up there and there was a rumor about a golf course or something. Anyway, hill land was more valuable now, and those black people who had moved down right after the war and in the fifties couldn't afford to come back even if they wanted to. Except for the few blacks still huddled by the river bend, and some undemolished houses on Carpenter's Road, only rich white folks were building homes in the hills. Just like that, they had changed their minds and instead of keeping the valley floor to themselves, now they wanted a hilltop house with a river view and a ring of elms. The black people, for all their new look, seemed awfully anxious to get to the valley, or leave town, and abandon the hills to whoever was interested. It was sad, because the Bottom had been a real place. These young ones kept talking about the community, but they left the hills to the poor, the old, the stubborn—and the rich white folks. Maybe it hadn't been a community, but it had been a place. Now there weren't any places left, just separate houses with separate televisions and separate telephones and less and less dropping by.

These were the same thoughts she always had when she walked down into the town. One of the last true pedestrians, Nel walked the shoulder road while cars slipped by. Laughed at by her children, she still walked wherever she wanted to go, allowing herself to accept rides only when the weather required it.

Now she went straight through the town and turned left at its farthest end, along a tree-lined walk that turned into a country road farther on and passed the cemetery, Beechnut Park.

When she got to Sunnydale, the home for the aged, it was already four o'clock and turning chill. She would be glad to sit down with those old birds and rest her feet.

A red-haired lady at the desk gave her a pass card and pointed to a door that opened onto a corridor of smaller doors. It looked like what she imagined a college dormitory to be. The lobby was luxurious—modern—but the rooms she peeped into were sterile green cages. There was too much light everywhere; it needed some shadows. The third door, down the hall, had a little name tag over it that read EVA PEACE. Nel twisted the knob and rapped a little on the door at the same time, then listened a moment before she opened it.

At first she couldn't believe it. She seemed so small, sitting at that table in a black-vinyl chair. All the heaviness had gone and the height. Her once beautiful leg had no stocking and the foot was in a slipper. Nel wanted to cry—not for Eva's milk-dull eyes or her floppy lips, but for the once proud foot accustomed for over a half century to a fine well-laced shoe, now stuffed gracelessly into a pink terrycloth slipper.

"Good evening, Miss Peace. I'm Nel Greene come to pay a call on you. You remember me, don't you?"

Eva was ironing and dreaming of stairwells. She had neither iron nor clothes but did not stop her fastidious lining up of pleats or pressing out of wrinkles even when she acknowledged Nel's greeting.

"Howdy. Sit down."

"Thank you." Nel sat on the edge of the little bed.

"You've got a pretty room, a real pretty room, Miss Peace."

"You eat something funny today?"

"Ma'am?"

"Some chop suey? Think back."

"No, ma'am."

"No? Well, you gone be sick later on."

"But I didn't have no chop suey."

"You think I come all the way over here for you to tell me that? I can't make visits too often. You should have some respect for old people."

"But Miss Peace, I'm visiting *you*. This is *your* room." Nel smiled.

"What you say your name was?"

"Nel Greene."

"Wiley Wright's girl?"

"Uh huh. You do remember. That makes me feel good, Miss Peace. You remember me and my father."

"Tell me how you killed that little boy."

"What? What little boy?"

"The one you threw in the water. I got oranges. How did you get him to go in the water?"

"I didn't throw no little boy in the river. That was Sula."

"You. Sula. What's the difference? You was there. You watched, didn't you? Me, I never would've watched."

"You're confused, Miss Peace. I'm Nel. Sula's dead."

"It's awful cold in the water. Fire is warm. How did you get him in?" Eva wet her forefinger and tested the iron's heat.

"Who told you all these lies? Miss Peace? Who told you? Why are you telling lies on me?"

"I got oranges. I don't drink they old orange juice. They puts something in it."

"Why are you trying to make out like I did it?"

Eva stopped ironing and looked at Nel. For the first time her eyes looked sane.

"You think I'm guilty?" Nel was whispering.

Eva whispered back, "Who would know that better than you?"

"I want to know who you been talking to." Nel forced herself to speak normally.

"Plum. Sweet Plum. He tells me things." Eva laughed a light, tinkly giggle—girlish.

"I'll be going now, Miss Peace." Nel stood.

"You ain't answered me yet."

"I don't know what you're talking about."

"Just alike. Both of you. Never was no difference between you. Want some oranges? It's better for you than chop suey. Sula? I got oranges." Nel walked hurriedly down the hall, Eva calling after her, "Sula?" Nel couldn't see the other women today. That woman had upset her. She handed her pass back to the lady, avoiding her look of surprise. Outside she fastened her coat against the rising wind. The top button was missing so she covered her throat with her hand. A bright space opened in her head and memory seeped into it.

Standing on the riverbank in a purple-and-white dress, Sula swinging Chicken Little around and around. His laughter before the hand-slip and the water closing quickly over the place. What had she felt then, watching Sula going around and around and then the little boy swinging out over the water? Sula had cried and cried when she came back from Shadrack's house. But Nel had remained calm.

"Shouldn't we tell?"

"Did he see?"

"I don't know. No."

"Let's go. We can't bring him back."

What did old Eva mean by *you watched?* How could she help seeing it? She was right there. But Eva didn't say *see,* she said *watched.* "I did not watch it. I just saw it." But it was there anyway, as it had always been, the old feeling and the old question. The good feeling she had had when Chicken's hand slipped. She hadn't wondered about that in years. "Why didn't I feel bad when it happened? How come it felt so good to see him fall?"

All these years she had been secretly proud of her calm, controlled behavior when Sula was uncontrollable, her compassion for Sula's frightened and shamed eyes. Now it seemed that what she had thought was maturity, serenity and compassion was only the tranquillity that follows a joyful stimulation. Just as the water closed peacefully over the turbulence of Chicken Little's body, so had contentment washed over her enjoyment.

She was walking too fast. Not watching where she placed her feet, she got into the weeds by the side of the road. Running almost, she approached Beechnut Park. Just over there was the colored part of the cemetery. She went in. Sula was buried there along with Plum, Hannah and now Pearl. With the same disregard for name changes by marriage that the black people of Medallion always showed, each flat slab had one word carved on it. Together they read like a chant: PEACE 1895–1921, PEACE 1890–1923, PEACE 1910–1940, PEACE 1892–1959.

They were not dead people. They were words. Not even words. Wishes, longings.

All these years she had been harboring good feelings about Eva; sharing, she believed, her loneliness and unloved state as no one else could or did. She, after all, was the only one who really understood why Eva refused to attend Sula's funeral. The others thought they knew; thought the grandmother's reasons were the same as their own—that to pay respect to someone who had caused them so much pain was beneath them. Nel, who did go, believed Eva's refusal was not due to pride or vengeance but to a plain unwillingness to see the swallowing of her own flesh into the dirt, a determination not to let the eyes see what the heart could not hold.

Now, however, after the way Eva had just treated her, accused her, she

wondered if the townspeople hadn't been right the first time. Eva *was*
mean. Sula had even said so. There was no good reason for her to speak
so. Feeble-minded or not. Old. Whatever. Eva knew what she was doing.
Always had. She had stayed away from Sula's funeral and accused Nel of
drowning Chicken Little for spite. The same spite that galloped all over
the Bottom. That made every gesture an offense, every off-center smile a
threat, so that even the bubbles of relief that broke in the chest of practically everybody when Sula died did not soften their spite and allow them
to go to Mr. Hodges' funeral parlor or send flowers from the church or
bake a yellow cake.

She thought about Nathan opening the bedroom door the day she had
visited her, and finding the body. He said he knew she was dead right
away not because her eyes were open but because her mouth was. It
looked to him like a giant yawn that she never got to finish. He had run
across the street to Teapot's Mamma, who, when she heard the news, said
"Ho!" like the conductor on the train when it was about to take off except louder, and then did a little dance. None of the women left their
quilt patches in disarray to run to the house. Nobody left the clothes
halfway through the wringer to run to the house. Even the men just said
"uhn," when they heard. The day passed and no one came. The night
slipped into another day and the body was still lying in Eva's bed gazing
at the ceiling trying to complete a yawn. It was very strange, this stub-
bornness about Sula. For even when China, the most rambunctious whore
in the town, died (whose black son and white son said, when they heard
she was dying, "She ain't dead yet?"), even then everybody stopped what
they were doing and turned out in numbers to put the fallen sister away.

It was Nel who finally called the hospital, then the mortuary, then the
police, who were the ones to come. So the white people took over. They
came in a police van and carried the body down the steps past the four
pear trees and into the van for all the world as with Hannah. When the
police asked questions nobody gave them any information. It took them
hours to find out the dead woman's first name. The call was for a Miss
Peace at 7 Carpenter's Road. So they left with that: a body, a name and
an address. The white people had to wash her, dress her, prepare her and
finally lower her. It was all done elegantly, for it was discovered that she
had a substantial death policy. Nel went to the funeral parlor, but was so
shocked by the closed coffin she stayed only a few minutes.

The following day Nel walked to the burying and found herself the
only black person there, steeling her mind to the roses and pulleys. It was
only when she turned to leave that she saw the cluster of black folk at the
lip of the cemetery. Not coming in, not dressed for mourning, but there
waiting. Not until the white folks left—the gravediggers, Mr. and Mrs.
Hodges, and their young son who assisted them—did those black people
from up in the Bottom enter with hooded hearts and filled eyes to sing
"Shall We Gather at the River" over the curved earth that cut them off
from the most magnificent hatred they had ever known. Their question
clotted the October air, Shall We Gather at the River? The beautiful, the
beautiful river? Perhaps Sula answered them even then, for it began to
rain, and the women ran in tiny leaps through the grass for fear their
straightened hair would beat them home.

Sadly, heavily, Nel left the colored part of the cemetery. Further along the road Shadrack passed her by. A little shaggier, a little older, still energetically mad, he looked at the woman hurrying along the road with the sunset in her face. He stopped. Trying to remember where he had seen her before. The effort of recollection was too much for him and he moved on. He had to haul some trash out at Sunnydale and it would be good and dark before he got home. He hadn't sold fish in a long time now. The river had killed them all. No more silver-gray flashes, no more flat, wide, unhurried look. No more slowing down of gills. No more tremor on the line.

Shadrack and Nel moved in opposite directions, each thinking separate thoughts about the past. The distance between them increased as they both remembered gone things.

Suddenly Nel stopped. Her eye twitched and burned a little.

"Sula?" she whispered, gazing at the tops of trees. "Sula?"

Leaves stirred; mud shifted; there was the smell of overripe green things. A soft ball of fur broke and scattered like dandelion spores in the breeze.

"All that time, all that time, I thought I was missing Jude." And the loss pressed down on her chest and came up into her throat. "We was girls together," she cried as though explaining something. "O Lord, Sula," she cried, "girl, girl, girlgirlgirl."

It was a fine cry—loud and long—but it had no bottom and it had no top, just circles and circles of sorrow.

1973

AFTERWORD

Sula is, first of all, a novel about being black and female in America in the early and middle years of the twentieth century. When Sula Peace and Nel Wright are twelve years old they meet each other in school, and immediately "they felt the ease and comfort of old friends. Because each had discovered years before that they were neither white nor male, and that all freedom and triumph was forbidden to them, they set about creating something else to be." Eighteen years later, when Nel visits the ill Sula, she tells her she cannot both be independent and not work; she can't have it all.

> "Why? I can do it all, why can't I have it all?"
> "You *can't* do it all. You a woman and a colored woman at that. You can't act like a man. You can't be walking around all independent-like, doing whatever you like, taking what you want, leaving what you don't."

Both women want to be themselves. As a girl, even before meeting Sula, Nel says to herself. " 'I'm me. I'm not their daughter, I'm not Nel. I'm me. Me.' " When, at twenty-seven, Sula returns to her hometown after an absence of ten years, her grandmother tells her she needs to settle down and have babies, but Sula responds, " 'I don't want to make somebody else. I want to make myself.' "

Nel chooses the conventional path: she marries and has children, lives in her hometown, is a member of the church. Sula goes off to college and wanders over the country before she returns, dressed like a movie star but without a husband or "visible means of support." She lives as she can, never letting anyone tell her what to do, never making demands—"Sula never competed; she simply helped others define themselves." She accepted people as they were, made Nel, at least, feel good about herself, and made her laugh, a deep "rib-scraping laugh." For her, however, anything forever is hell (just as for Nel change is hell); she scorns others for having safety nets, fearing the "free fall," which to her means fearing life: "she lived out her days exploring her own thoughts and emotions, giving them full reign, feeling no obligation to please anybody unless their pleasure pleased her." She takes men as she wants them, doubly offending the community wives by sleeping with their husbands just once, and then rejecting them as if she had found them wanting. Without loving him, she even seduces the husband of her only friend, Nel, whose whole life is built around her domesticity. Sula does not really seem to understand that Nel will be bothered by her husband's adultery, that it will virtually ruin her life; after all, Sula says, "I didn't kill him." When Nel asks her how she could do such a thing when Nel had been so good to her, Sula replies, " 'Being good to somebody is just like being mean to somebody. Risky. You don't get nothing for it.' "

Yet despite their differences the two women are bonded. None of Sula's men will talk to her (until Ajax comes into her life), and she craves that other half of self. With Nel she talks and laughs, or, as on one summer day when they are twelve, walks and plays an unpremeditated game, digging a hole, together, communicating, acting in concert, without speaking. Nel has been the only real "other" person to her. When death comes to Sula but comes without pain, despite their estrangement, she thinks, " 'Wait'll I tell Nel.' " And twenty-five years after Sula's death, the "soft ball of fur" that has been on the periphery of Nel's vision since her husband left her breaks.

"All that time, all that time, I thought I was missing Jude." And the loss pressed down on her chest and came up into her throat. "We were girls together," she said as though explaining something. "O Lord, Sula," she cried, "girl, girl, girl-girlgirl."

It was a fine cry—loud and long—but it had no bottom and it had no top, just circles and circles of sorrow.

And that is how this moving, tough, tender, and powerful novel ends.

It's certainly a novel about growing up female, and growing up black, and about bonding. But let's look a moment at that bonding. Domesticity, security, virtue are the cornerstones of Nel's rational life. In moments of crisis, she is cool, while Sula, governed by emotions, is ineffectual. Sula, who cuts the tip of her finger off to demonstrate her courage to a group of boys who are hassling them; who watches her mother burn to death "with interest," and who callously puts her grandmother into a home; who sleeps around and seduces Nel's husband; who seems a sociopath, with no sense of right or wrong—Sula says, in her last conversation with Nel:

"About who was good. How you know it was you?"
"What you mean?"
"I mean maybe it wasn't you. Maybe it was me."

Those are the last words of Sula *Peace* to Nel *Wright.*

Twenty-five years later Nel visits Sula's ancient grandmother in the home. The old lady accuses Nel of having thrown a little boy, Chicken Little, into the river more than forty years earlier.

"I didn't throw no little boy in the river. That was Sula."
"You. Sula. What's the difference? . . ."

She repeats herself, and in her senility confuses Nel with Sula. Nel questions herself and finds that she had not just *seen* but *watched* Chicken Little arc into the water and disappear, as Sula had watched her mother burn.

All these years she had been secretly proud of her calm, controlled behavior when Sula was uncontrollable, her compassion for Sula's frightened and shamed eyes. Now it seemed that what she had thought was maturity, serenity and compassion was only the tranquillity that follows a joyful stimulation.

Who is the virtuous one? Is the head or the heart the seat of virtue?

Do we see Sula the sociopath (the Devil, as the black community believed her to be) as good? Is she admirable? Is she right in the way she chose to live? Why, then, does she get her come-uppance? Why, when she finally finds a man for whom she wants to build a nest, does he—her male equivalent—leave her, just as Jude Greene left Nel? If we make her representative of a way of life—uncommitted, free, amoral—is the outcome of her life representative too? Why does she, like the unconventional Daisy and Amy, die young, and apparently as a result of her independent mode of life? She tells Nel she knows she's dying, but she's "going down like one of those redwoods" while all the other black women, who are also dying, are going down like stumps. And if her independent life is a lonely one, she says, Nel is lonely too, but Nel is lonely by another's choosing and Sula by her own. We know Sula has not really chosen to have Ajax go away; Nel believes Sula's bravado is just showing off. Is it?

If the wages of sin are death, the wages of virtue as Nel practices it are loveless survival; all she has of love is her children—a love described in one of those brilliant homey images that sparkle through the novel like bright thread—"a love that, like a pan of syrup kept too long on the stove, had cooked out, leaving only its odor and a hard, sweet sludge, impossible to scrape off." Which (if either) is virtuous? Which (if either) chooses the proper path? Eventually, these seem almost meaningless questions. Falling free and going down like a redwood may be mere romantic bravado covering a somewhat lonely and sordid life and death; going down like a stump is all too painfully real. Growing up black and female, there is no freedom and triumph, no "right" way. Sula and Nel, Peace and Wright, are alternative paths to similar goals. The two women are in effect doubles, in which we are not sure which is Jekyll and which Hyde, in each of whom good and evil can neither be separated nor even defined.

We may be able to outline the way the novel educates us in Sula's character and evaluates her career by controlling our expectations and pattern-making. Four times in *Sula* our reading is punctuated by three dots stopping us (on three of the four occasions each dot being enclosed in a small circle). The first three punctuation marks, those with the circles, mark time breaks. Just before the first, Sula callously has her grandmother put, against her will, into a home. Though Eva, Sula's grandmother, is tough, Sula is tougher. Eva's toughness has usually been exercised to help her children live (or die). Sula's toughness here is to help herself. The mark is followed by her friend Nel's feeling a special magic in that May time and attributing it to the good effect, the magic of Sula's recent return home. Before the marks we pause and put together what seems to be the completed life story of Eva (it is not the last we hear of her, but it looks that way); we think about Sula: Is she as cruel as she seems, or as wonderful as Nel thinks her?

On the second occasion, Jude, Nel's husband, is sizing up Sula too: "A funny woman, he thought, not that bad-looking. But he could see why she wasn't married; she stirred a man's mind maybe, but not his body." What goes on in *your* mind as you pause there? You think back about what you know of Jude's marriage, Nel's friendship with Sula, Sula's way with men, her mother's way with men, and you think, "Oh, no, Sula wouldn't do that, not to her best friend. . . . Would she?" You remember what she did to her own grandmother, and you think, "Okay, man, your body isn't stirred, but I know Sula better than you do, and you're in for it." And more, much more. Whether these are exactly the thoughts and feelings you have, the author's stop sign is designed to and is likely to make you stop, think back, perhaps to the three dots and Eva, evaluate the situation and its implications, and frame some sort of expectation of what is to come next.

The timing of the next appearance of the encircled dots could not be more different: Sula and her man, her free and independent male counterpart Ajax, have just made love, "and the house was very, very quiet." Then we see the three dots. By now we know they signal a change and we remember that they have been associated with an act of self-indulgence or amorality on Sula's part. We think back, we make a pattern, we anticipate. What? Some of us will probably expect Sula to tire of Ajax, cast him off as she has others, or—since in her love she has thought of getting beneath his skin, beneath the black to the gold, and with "a nail file or even Eva's old paring knife," getting beneath the gold to the alabaster, and with hammer and chisel, beneath the alabaster to the loam—we may expect her to commit some act of violence on her lover, to cut, burn, murder him. After all, she is the woman who, as a girl, cut off the tip of her own finger, and who watched with interest as her mother burned to death.

We're wrong. Beyond the dots the paragraph begins, "Sula began to discover what possession was." She starts to make a nest, and a few hundred words later, just before the next break (though without dots), Ajax makes "love to her with the steadiness and intensity of a man about to leave for Dayton." This time it is Sula who is abandoned. These divisions may help us, then, answer some of the questions we have asked about the evaluation of Sula's behavior or way of life.

Though Nel and Sula may be representative, they are also highly individualized, and though each seeks to be herself, the novel embeds each in a history and community. The novel is one-sixth over before they meet and almost a third over before they assume center stage. Nel may deny being her parents' daughter, she may delight in the female household of the Peace family and its warm slovenliness, but she is Helene Wright's daughter in her respectability, rejecting as her mother did the gaudy hell of her grandmother's life in a New Orleans whorehouse or its equivalent. Her respectability is her independence; she lives so that she will never have to smile that obsequious, flirtatious smile her mother gives the brutal white trainman to appease him, will never bring the look to the eyes of black men her mother's behavior did to the eyes of the black soldiers on the train. But she does bring that look to the eyes of her husband when she interrupts his sex-play with Sula.

A great deal more time in the novel is spent on the Peace family than on the Wrights, and Sula's grandmother Eva and mother Hannah are two of the triumphs of the novel. Eva is tough, some would say mean. She endures, but not like Faulkner's stolid Dilsey in The Sound and the Fury. She manages to have her own leg cut off by a train for the pension money to support her father-abandoned children. One of those children, her "boy," whose life she had saved as an infant by using the last of her food as a suppository to relieve his life-threatening constipation, she "executes" when he returns home after World War I a helpless drug addict. When Sula cuts off the tip of her finger to protect herself, we are reminded of Eva. Hannah Peace is an easy-going sexy woman who takes lovers casually and warmly, making men feel good about themselves. Sula is not so gentle and not at all submissive like her mother, but some of her casual attitudes toward sex, her seductiveness, and her carelessness she has learned from her mother. Though Sula is different, is herself, "Eva's arrogance and Hannah's self-indulgence merged in her. . . ."

The portrait of Sula without Eva and Hannah would not only deprive us of two memorable and fully realized characterizations, but even if its abstraction would make it seem more representative, it would lack the vibrancy, resonance, and reality that it now has and that makes the novel significant, in the full sense of that word. "The novel," D. H. Lawrence says, "is the highest example of subtle interrelatedness that man has discovered. Everything is true in its own time, place, and circumstance, and untrue outside of its own place, time, circumstance." Sula shows that interrelatedness and particularity.

Like Old Mortality, it uses dates for chapter titles. It begins, after a brief prelude, in 1919, not with Sula, Nel, or anyone from either family, but with a "shell-shock" victim of World War I, Shadrack, and a thumbnail sketch of the incident in 1917 that deranged him, a scene in hospital, his release, and his founding of National Suicide Day, a day he thought would get the fear of unexpected death out of the way for the rest of the year. A fair amount of time early in the novel is spent on Shadrack and we may expect him to play a greater role in the novel than he in fact does. He does, indeed, thread his way through the rest of the novel without being entirely necessary for any of the major action. Sula goes to his hermit's cabin on the river when Chicken Little is drowned to see if he has seen anything; they speak at cross-purposes but with an eerie sense of significance; Sula accidentally leaves her belt, and she, his one visitor, he singles out in the town for unique attention.

The townspeople, years later, think his respect a sign that Sula, like the mad Shadrack, is a devil. Indeed, these two do seem to have a special relationship as outsiders inside the community. When Sula dies, Shadrack loses his enthusiasm for Suicide Day, and he is now greeted with laughter rather than fear. At the very end of the novel, it is Nel's passing Shadrack, "each thinking separate thoughts about the past," that triggers Nel's whispering "Sula?" and her final recognition that it is her friend and not her husband she has been missing all these years. So Shadrack, while not being a double or a symbol, is an important pigment in the portrait of Sula, and to get just the right tone, we must see him too in significant particularity.

Sula, her family, her friend Nel and her family, her lover Ajax, the people in the community, the times are in subtle interrelatedness, so it makes no sense to ask whether the novel is about Sula, the community, being black in the Midwest from 1919 to 1965, being black and female, because the answer to all these questions is yes. There is, however, little historical background in the usual sense. There is the World War I scene, but no specific mention of the Depression, though more than half the novel occurs between 1937 and 1941—the black community of Medallion was always, in its fashion, depressed. World War II, so far as I can remember, is represented only by the casual mention that Nel had a boyfriend who was a sergeant stationed nearby and by its later effect on the town's growth. The only "political" event is the unpremeditated attack on the tunnel construction site where no blacks have been hired for honorable labor, ending with a cave-in and the deaths of a good many blacks. The undated prefatory chapter describes the disappearance of the black neighborhood in the hills above Medallion known as the Bottom and gives a bit of its history.

The final chapter, "1965," begins,

> Things were so much better in 1965. Or so it seemed. You could go downtown and see colored people working in the dime store behind the counters, even handling money with cash-register keys around their necks. And a colored man taught mathematics at the junior high school.

To Nel's fifty-five-year-old eyes, however, things were not better than they were forty years earlier. The beautiful boys of 1921 were no more, "Nothing like these kids." Even the whores in the old days were better, truly shameless, getting "up from the dinner table and walk[ing] into the trees with a customer with as much embarrassment as a calving mare." The "good old days" of Medallion in 1921 were no more truly good or better than any nostalgic memory of the good old days, but Nel's nostalgia is true to her, and even the reader, who has seen the calendar turning and the times changing throughout the novel, shares it to a degree.

There is a deep sense of time and of time passing conveyed in this short novel. Perhaps one of the ways in which it is achieved is in the rhythmic repetition or recollection of early events throughout the later portions of the novel. Nor is this merely a device for rendering time—repeatedly the recollection not only mimics the reader's recapitulation of the past as he moves through the novel, but also shows the conditioning power of the past on the lives of the characters. Nel's final "We was girls together" is only a summary of the effect of experience, lived life, the past on the present. Sula's swinging the boy Chicken Little by the hands, letting go, only to see him disappear under the waters of the river, is recalled time and again through the novel.

Earlier that day, Sula, passing the room in which her mother was talking to neighbors, all of them complaining about their children, hears her mother say she loves Sula but does not like her. Seventeen years later, the events of that day in 1922 serve to explain what the community feels is Sula's "evil."

Their evidence against Sula was contrived, but their conclusions about her were not. Sula was distinctly different. . . . hers was an experimental life—ever since her mother's remarks sent her flying up those stairs, ever since her one major feeling of responsibility had been exorcised on the bank of a river with a closed place in the middle. The first experience taught her there was no other that you could count on; the second that there was no self to count on either. She had no center, no speck around which to grow.

National Suicide Day and Shadrack, the look of the soldiers on the train headed for New Orleans, the burning of Hannah Peace, Sula cutting off her fingertip, the death of Chicken Little stitch the novel together with a rhythm as subtle and supple as the prose, creating a sense of depth in the characters and in their lived experience, a sense of causal and emotional connection in the events in their lives, forcing the reader to remember what he or she has read and so linking his or her own past to that of the characters, lending to *Sula* that depth, scope, and emotional as well as intellectual complexity that realizes the potentiality of the novel as a form and marks the short novel off from the short story.

ALICE MUNRO

The Beggar Maid

"If I am a regional writer," says Ontario-born Alice Munro (b. 1931), "the region I'm writing about has many things in common with the American South." Her Jubilee is rural and Calvinist, rooted in the land, the family, the past, and the Bible. Her first two volumes of short stories, *Dance of the Happy Shades* (1968) and *Something I've Been Meaning to Tell You* (1974), as well as her first "novel," *Lives of Girls and Women*, (1971) which reads like three interlocking short stories (or short novels), are set in Ontario, are profoundly regional and culturally specific, but with a psychological sophistication and a feminist orientation that would seem to belie their "provinciality." Munro says she is "very, very excited by what you might call the surface of life," and she captures that surface with brilliant, precise, and lucid beauty. But that surface, seeming—most of the time—so ordinary, is always ready to surprise, to leap into what seems almost another dimension, the extraordinary, the grotesque, even the fantastic.

Munro's two most recent collections of stories, *The Beggar Maid* (as it is known in the United States; the collection was first published in 1978 as *Who Do You Think You Are*) and *The Moons of Jupiter* (1983), are still in some measure provincial and small town, but they also involve life in the cities of western and eastern Canada and the urban world and folk.

She might say of all her works, it seems, what she says of *Lives of Girls and Women*: "This novel is autobiographical in form but not in fact." The stories and novels are so convincing, so detailed and fully realized, that it is difficult not to think of them as literally biographical, virtual transcriptions. What they give to the reader is what Henry James calls "the illusion of life," but Alice Munro does not really write in the tradition of Henry James but in that of George Eliot, D. H. Lawrence, and Doris Lessing. Not a bad league to be batting in.

The Beggar Maid

Patrick Blatchford was in love with Rose. This had become a fixed, even *Determined* furious, idea with him. For her, a continual surprise. He wanted to marry *to get her* her. He waited for her after classes, moved in and walked beside her, so that anybody she was talking to would have to reckon with his presence. He would not talk, when these friends or classmates of hers were around, but he would try to catch her eye, so that he could indicate by a cold incredulous look what he thought of their conversation. Rose was flattered, but *possessive* nervous. A girl named Nancy Falls, a friend of hers, mispronounced Metternich[1] in front of him. He said to her later, "How can you be friends with people like that?" *Mean?*

Nancy and Rose had gone and sold their blood together, at Victoria Hospital. They each got fifteen dollars. They spent most of the money on evening shoes, tarty silver sandals. Then because they were sure the bloodletting had caused them to lose weight they had hot fudge sundaes at Boomers. Why was Rose unable to defend Nancy to Patrick? *Intelligent*

Patrick was twenty-four years old, a graduate student, planning to be a history professor. He was tall, thin, fair, and good-looking, though he had a long pale-red birthmark, dribbling like a tear down his temple and his cheek. He apologized for it, but said it was fading, as he got older. When he was forty, it would have faded away. It was not the birthmark that canceled out his good looks, Rose thought. (Something did cancel them out, or at least diminish them, for her; she had to keep reminding herself they were there.) There was something edgy, jumpy, disconcerting, about him. His voice would break under stress—with her, it seemed he was always under stress—he knocked dishes and cups off tables, spilled drinks and bowls of peanuts, like a comedian. He was not a comedian; nothing could be further from his intentions. He came from British Columbia. His family was rich.

He arrived early to pick Rose up, when they were going to the movies. He wouldn't knock, he knew he was early. He sat on the step outside Dr. Henshawe's door. This was in the winter, it was dark out, but there was a little coach lamp beside the door. *Pitying him*

"Oh, Rose! Come and look!" called Dr. Henshawe, in her soft, amused voice, and they looked down together from the dark window of the study. "The poor young man," said Dr. Henshawe tenderly. Dr. Henshawe was in her seventies. She was a former English professor, fastidious and lively. She had a lame leg, but a still youthfully, charmingly tilted head, with white braids wound around it.

She called Patrick poor because he was in love, and perhaps also because he was a male, doomed to push and blunder. Even from up here he looked stubborn and pitiable, determined and dependent, sitting out there in the cold.

"Guarding the door," Dr. Henshawe said. "Oh, Rose!"

Another time she said disturbingly, "Oh, dear, I'm afraid he is after the wrong girl."

Rose didn't like her saying that. She didn't like her laughing at Patrick.

---

1. Klemens Wenzel Nepomuk Lothar von Metternich (1773–1859), Austrian statesman; there are many ways to mispronounce his name.

She didn't like Patrick sitting out on the steps that way, either. He was asking to be laughed at. He was the most vulnerable person Rose had ever known, he made himself so, didn't know anything about protecting himself. But he was also full of cruel judgments, he was full of conceit.

You are a scholar, Rose," Dr. Henshawe would say. "This will interest you." Then she would read aloud something from the paper, or, more likely, something from *Canadian Forum* or the *Atlantic Monthly*. Dr. Henshawe had at one time headed the city's school board, she was a founding member of Canada's socialist party. She still sat on committees, wrote letters to the paper, reviewed books. Her father and mother had been medical missionaries; she had been born in China. Her house was small and perfect. Polished floors, glowing rugs, Chinese vases, bowls and landscapes, black carved screens. Much that Rose could not appreciate, at the time. She could not really distinguish between the little jade animals on Dr. Henshawe's mantelpiece and the ornaments displayed in the jewelry store window, in Hanratty, though she could now distinguish between either of these and the things Flo bought from the five-and-ten.

She could not really decide how much she liked being at Dr. Henshawe's. At times she felt discouraged, sitting in the dining room with a linen napkin on her knee, eating from fine white plates on blue placemats. For one thing, there was never enough to eat, and she had taken to buying doughnuts and chocolate bars and hiding them in her room. The canary swung on its perch in the dining room window and Dr. Henshawe directed conversation. She talked about politics, about writers. She mentioned Frank Scott and Dorothy Livesay.[2] She said Rose must read them. Rose must read this, she must read that. Rose became sullenly determined not to. She was reading Thomas Mann. She was reading Tolstoy.

Before she came to Dr. Henshawe's, Rose had never heard of the working class. She took the designation home.

"This would have to be the last part of town where they put the sewers," Flo said.

"Of course," Rose said coolly. "This is the working-class part of town."

"*Working* class?" said Flo. "Not if the ones around here can help it."

Dr. Henshawe's house had done one thing. It had destroyed the naturalness, the taken-for-granted background, of home. To go back there was to go quite literally into a crude light. Flo had put fluorescent lights in the store and the kitchen. There was also, in a corner of the kitchen, a floor lamp Flo had won at Bingo; its shade was permanently wrapped in wide strips of cellophane. What Dr. Henshawe's house and Flo's house did best, in Rose's opinion, was discredit each other. In Dr. Henshawe's charming rooms there was always for Rose the raw knowledge of home, an indigestible lump, and at home, now, her sense of order and modulation elsewhere exposed such embarrassing sad poverty, in people who never thought themselves poor. Poverty was not just wretchedness, as Dr. Henshawe seemed to think, it was not just deprivation. It meant having those ugly tube lights and being proud of them. It meant continual talk of money and malicious talk about new things people had bought and whether they were paid for. It meant pride and jealousy flaring over something like the new

2. Canadian poets (b. 1899 and 1909 respectively) both of whom are concerned with social issues, though Scott is an experimental poet influenced by T. S.

Eliot, and Livesay writes personal and passionate as well as public poems.

pair of plastic curtains, imitating lace, that Flo had bought for the front window. That as well as hanging your cloths on nails behind the door and being able to hear every sound from the bathroom. It meant decorating your walls with a number of admonitions, pious and cheerful and mildly bawdy.

THE LORD IS MY SHEPHERD
BELIEVE IN THE LORD JESUS CHRIST AND THOU SHALL BE SAVED

Why did Flo have those, when she wasn't even religious? They were what people had, common as calendars.

THIS IS MY KITCHEN AND I WILL DO AS I DARNED PLEASE
MORE THAN TWO PERSONS TO A BED IS DANGEROUS AND UNLAWFUL

Billy Pope had brought that one. What would Patrick have to say about them? What would someone who was offended by a mispronunciation of Metternich think of Billy Pope's stories?

Billy Pope worked in Tyde's Butcher Shop. What he talked about most frequently now was the D.P.,[3] the Belgian, who had come to work there, and got on Billy Pope's nerves with his impudent singing of French songs and his naive notions of getting on in this country, buying a butcher shop of his own.

"Don't you think you can come over here and get yourself ideas," Billy Pope said to the D.P. "It's *youse* workin for *us*, and don't think that'll change into *us* workin for *youse*." That shut him up, Billy Pope said.

Patrick would say from time to time that since her home was only fifty miles away he ought to come up and meet Rose's family.

"There's only my stepmother."

"It's too bad I couldn't have met your father."

Rashly, she had presented her father to Patrick as a reader of history, an amateur scholar. That was not exactly a lie, but it did not give a truthful picture of the circumstances.

"Is your stepmother your guardian?"

Rose had to say she did not know.

"Well, your father must have appointed a guardian for you in his will. Who administers his estate?"

His *estate*. Rose thought an estate was land, such as people owned in England.

Patrick thought it was rather charming of her to think that.

"No, his money and stocks and so on. What he left."

"I don't think he left any."

"Don't be silly," Patrick said.

And sometimes Dr. Henshawe would say, "Well, you are a scholar, you are not interested in that." Usually she was speaking of some event at the college; a pep rally, a football game, a dance. And usually she was right; Rose was not interested. But she was not eager to admit it. She did not seek or relish that definition of herself.

On the stairway wall hung graduation photographs of all the other girls, scholarship girls, who had lived with Dr. Henshawe. Most of them had got to be teachers, then mothers. One was a dietician, two were librarians, one

---

3. "Displaced Person," or refugee from the Nazis.

was a professor of English, like Dr. Henshawe herself. Rose did not care for the look of them, for their soft-focused meekly smiling gratitude, their large teeth and maidenly rolls of hair. They seemed to be urging on her some deadly secular piety. There were no actresses among them, no brassy magazine journalists; none of them had latched on to the sort of life Rose wanted for herself. She wanted to perform in public. She thought she wanted to be an actress but she never tried to act, was afraid to go near the college drama productions. She knew she couldn't sing or dance. She would really have liked to play the harp, but she had no ear for music. She wanted to be known and envied, slim and clever. She told Dr. Henshawe that if she had been a man she would have wanted to be a foreign correspondent.

"Then you must be one," cried Dr. Henshawe alarmingly. "The future will be wide open, for women. You must concentrate on languages. You must take courses in political science. And economics. Perhaps you could get a job on the paper for the summer. I have friends there."

Rose was frightened at the idea of working on a paper, and she hated the introductory economics course; she was looking for a way of dropping it. It was dangerous to mention things to Dr. Henshawe.

She had got to live with Dr. Henshawe by accident. Another girl had been picked to move in but she got sick; she had T.B., and went instead to a sanitarium. Dr. Henshawe came up to the college office on the second day of registration to get the names of some other scholarship freshmen.

Rose had been in the office just a little while before, asking where the meeting of the scholarship students was to be held. She had lost her notice. The Bursar was giving a talk to the new scholarship students, telling them of ways to earn money and live cheaply and explaining the high standards of performance to be expected of them here, if they wanted their payments to keep coming.

Rose found out the number of the room, and started up the stairs to the first floor. A girl came up beside her and said, "Are you on your way to three-oh-twelve, too?"

They walked together, telling each other the details of their scholarships. Rose did not yet have a place to live, she was staying at the Y. She did not really have enough money to be here at all. She had a scholarship for her tuition and the county prize to buy her books and a bursary of three hundred dollars to live on; that was all.

"You'll have to get a job," the other girl said. She had a larger bursary, because she was in Science (that's where the money is, the money's all in Science, she said seriously), but she was hoping to get a job in the cafeteria. She had a room in somebody's basement. How much does your room cost? How much does a hot plate cost? Rose asked her, her head swimming with anxious calculations.

This girl wore her hair in a roll. She wore a crepe blouse, yellowed and shining from washing and ironing. Her breasts were large and sagging. She probably wore a dirty-pink hooked-up-the-side brassiere. She had a scaly patch on one cheek.

"This must be it," she said.

There was a little window in the door. They could look through at the other scholarship winners already assembled and waiting. It seemed to Rose that she saw four or five girls of the same stooped and matronly type as the girl who was beside her, and several bright-eyed, self-satisfied babyish-looking boys. It seemed to be the rule that girl scholarship winners looked about forty and boys about twelve. It was not possible, of course, that they all looked like this. It was not possible that in one glance through the windows of the door Rose could detect traces of eczema, stained underarms, dandruff, moldy deposits on the teeth and crusty flakes in the corners of the eyes. That was only what she thought. But there was a pall over them, she was not mistaken, there was a true terrible pall of eagerness and docility. How else could they have supplied so many right answers, so many pleasing answers, how else distinguished themselves and got themselves here? And Rose had done the same.

"I have to go to the john," she said.

She could see herself, working in the cafeteria. Her figure, broad enough already, broadened out still more by the green cotton uniform, her face red and her hair stringy from the heat. Dishing up stew and fried chicken for those of inferior intelligence and handsomer means. Blocked off by the steam tables, the uniform, by decent hard work that nobody need be ashamed of, by publicly proclaimed braininess and poverty. Boys could get away with that, barely. For girls it was fatal. Poverty in girls is not attractive unless combined with sweet sluttishness, stupidity. Braininess is not attractive unless combined with some signs of elegance; *class*. Was this true, and was she foolish enough to care? It was; she was.

She went back to the first floor where the halls were crowded with ordinary students who were not on scholarships, who would not be expected to get A's and be grateful and live cheap. Enviable and innocent, they milled around the registration tables in their new purple and white blazers, their purple Frosh beanies, yelling reminders to each other, confused information, nonsensical insults. She walked among them feeling bitterly superior and despondent. The skirt of her green corduroy suit kept falling back between her legs as she walked. The material was limp; she should have spent more and bought the heavier weight. She thought now that the jacket was not properly cut either, though it had looked all right at home. The whole outfit had been made by a dressmaker in Hanratty, a friend of Flo's, whose main concern had been that there should be no revelations of the figure. When Rose asked if the skirt couldn't be made tighter this woman had said, "You wouldn't want your b.t.m. to show, now would you?" and Rose hadn't wanted to say she didn't care.

Another thing the dressmaker said was, "I thought now you was through school you'd be getting a job and help out at home."

A woman walking down the hall stopped Rose.

"Aren't you one of the scholarship girls?"

It was the Registrar's secretary. Rose thought she was going to be reprimanded, for not being at the meeting, and she was going to say she felt sick. She prepared her face for this lie. But the secretary said, "Come with me, now. I've got somebody I want you to meet."

Dr. Henshawe was making a charming nuisance of herself in the office. She liked poor girls, bright girls, but they had to be fairly good-looking girls.

"I think this could be your lucky day," the secretary said, leading Rose. "If you could put a pleasanter expression on your face."

Rose hated being told that, but she smiled obediently.

Within the hour she was taken home with Dr. Henshawe, installed in the house with the Chinese screens and vases, and told she was a scholar.

She got a job working in the Library of the college, instead of in the cafeteria. Dr. Henshawe was a friend of the Head Librarian. She worked on Saturday afternoons. She worked in the stacks, putting books away. On Saturday afternoons in the fall the Library was nearly empty, because of the football games. The narrow windows were open to the leafy campus, the football field, the dry fall country. The distant songs and shouts came drifting in. The college buildings were not old at all, but they were built to look old. They were built of stone. The Arts building had a tower, and the Library had casement windows, which might have been designed for shooting arrows through. The buildings and the books in the Library were what pleased Rose most about the place. The life that usually filled it, and that was now drained away, concentrated around the football field, letting loose those noises, seemed to her inappropriate and distracting. The cheers and songs were idiotic, if you listened to the words. What did they want to build such dignified buildings for, if they were going to sing songs like that?

She knew enough not to reveal these opinions. If anybody said to her, "It's awful you have to work Saturdays and can't get to any of the games," she would fervently agree.

Once a man grabbed her bare leg, between her sock and her skirt. It happened in the Agriculture section, down at the bottom of the stacks. Only the faculty, graduate students and employees had access to the stacks, though someone could have hoisted himself through a ground-floor window, if he was skinny. She had seen a man crouched down looking at the books on a low shelf, further along. As she reached up to push a book into place he passed behind her. He bent and grabbed her leg, all in one smooth startling motion, and then was gone. She could feel for quite a while where his fingers had dug in. It didn't seem to her a sexual touch, it was more like a joke, though not at all a friendly one. She heard him run away, or felt him running; the metal shelves were vibrating. Then they stopped. There was no sound of him. She walked around looking between the stacks, looking into the carrels. Suppose she did see him, or bumped into him around a corner, what did she intend to do? She did not know. It was simply necessary to look for him, as in some tense childish game. She looked down at the sturdy pinkish calf of her leg. Amazing, that out of the blue somebody had wanted to blotch and punish it.

There were usually a few graduate students working in the carrels, even on Saturday afternoons. More rarely, a professor. Every carrel she looked into was empty, until she came to one in the corner. She poked her head in freely, by this time not expecting anybody. Then she had to say she was sorry.

There was a young man with a book on his lap, books on the floor, papers all around him. Rose asked him if he had seen anybody run past. He said no.

She told him what had happened. She didn't tell him because she was frightened or disgusted, as he seemed afterward to think, but just because she had to tell somebody; it was so odd. She was not prepared at all for his response. His long neck and face turned red, the flush entirely absorbing a birthmark down the side of his cheek. He was thin and fair. He stood up without any thought for the book in his lap or the papers in front of him. The book thumped on the floor. A great sheaf of papers, pushed across the desk, upset his ink bottle.

"How vile," he said.

"Grab the ink," Rose said. He leaned to catch the bottle and knocked it on the floor. Fortunately the top was on, and it did not break.

"Did he hurt you?"

"No, not really."

"Come on upstairs. We'll report it."

"Oh, no."

"He can't get away with that. It shouldn't be allowed."

"There isn't anybody to report to," Rose said with relief. "The Librarian goes off at noon on Saturdays."

"It's disgusting," he said in a high-pitched, excitable voice. Rose was sorry now that she had told him anything, and said she had to get back to work.

"Are you really all right?"

"Oh yes."

"I'll be right here. Just call me if he comes back."

That was Patrick. If she had been trying to make him fall in love with her, there was no better way she could have chosen. He had many chivalric notions, which he pretended to mock, by saying certain words and phrases as if in quotation marks. *The fair sex*, he would say, and *damsel in distress*. Coming to his carrel with that story, Rose had turned herself into a damsel in distress. The pretended irony would not fool anybody; it was clear that he did wish to operate in a world of knights and ladies; outrages; devotions.

She continued to see him in the Library, every Saturday, and often she met him walking across the campus or in the cafeteria. He made a point of greeting her with courtesy and concern, saying, "How are you," in a way that suggested she might have suffered a further attack, or might still be recovering from the first one. He always flushed deeply when he saw her, and she thought that this was because the memory of what she had told him so embarrassed him. Later she found out it was because he was in love.

He discovered her name, and where she lived. He phoned her at Dr. Henshawe's house and asked her to go to the movies. At first when he said, "This is Patrick Blatchford speaking," Rose could not think who it was, but after a moment she recognized the high, rather aggrieved and tremulous voice. She said she would go. This was partly because Dr. Henshawe was always saying she was glad Rose did not waste her time running around with boys.

Rather soon after she started to go out with him, she said to Patrick, "Wouldn't it be funny if it was you grabbed my leg that day in the Library?"

He did not think it would be funny. He was horrified that she would think such a thing.

She said she was only joking. She said she meant that it would be a good twist in a story, maybe a Maugham story, or a Hitchcock movie. They had just been to see a Hitchcock movie.

"You know, if Hitchcock made a movie out of something like that, you could be a wild insatiable leg-grabber with one half of your personality, and the other half could be a timid scholar."

He didn't like that either.

"Is that how I seem to you, a timid scholar?" It seemed to her he deepened his voice, introduced a few growling notes, drew in his chin, as if for a joke. But he seldom joked with her; he didn't think joking was suitable when you were in love.

"I didn't say you were a timid scholar or a leg-grabber. It was just an idea."

After a while he said, "I suppose I don't seem very manly."

She was startled and irritated by such an exposure. He took such chances; had nothing ever taught him not to take such chances? But maybe he didn't, after all. He knew she would have to say something reassuring. Though she was longing not to, she longed to say judiciously, "Well, no. You don't." But that would not actually be true. He did seem masculine to her. Because he took those chances. Only a man could be so careless and demanding.

"We come from two different worlds," she said to him, on another occasion. She felt like a character in a play, saying that. "My people are poor people. You would think the place I lived in was a dump."

Now she was the one who was being dishonest, pretending to throw herself on his mercy, for of course she did not expect him to say, oh, well, if you come from poor people and live in a dump, then I will have to withdraw my offer.

"But I'm glad," said Patrick. "I'm glad you're poor. You're so lovely. You're like the Beggar Maid."

"Who?"

"King Cophetua and the Beggar Maid.[4] You know. The painting. Don't you know that painting?"

Patrick had a trick—no, it was not a trick, Patrick had no tricks—Patrick had a way of expressing surprise, fairly scornful surprise, when people did not know something he knew, and similar scorn, similar surprise, whenever they had bothered to know something he did not. His arrogance and humility were both oddly exaggerated. The arrogance, Rose decided in time, must come from being rich, though Patrick was never arrogant about that in itself. His sisters, when she met them, turned out to be the same way, disgusted with anybody who did not know about horses or sailing, and just as disgusted by anybody knowing about music, say, or politics. Patrick and they could do little together but radiate disgust. But wasn't Billy Pope as bad, wasn't Flo as bad, when it came to arrogance? Maybe. There was a difference, though, and the difference was that Billy Pope and Flo were not protected. Things could get at them: D.P.'s; people speaking French on the radio; changes. Patrick and his sisters behaved as if things could never get at them. Their voices, when they quarreled at the table, were astonishingly childish; their demands for food they liked, their petulance at seeing anything on the table they didn't like, were those of children. They had never had to defer and polish themselves and win favor in the world, they never would have to, and that was because they were rich.

Rose had no idea at the beginning, how rich Patrick was. Nobody believed that. Everybody believed she had been calculating and clever, and she was so far from clever, in that way, that she really did not mind if they believed it. It turned out that other girls had been trying, and had not struck, as she had, the necessary note. Older girls, sorority girls, who had never noticed her before, began to look at her with puzzlement and respect. Even Dr. Henshawe, when she saw that things were more serious than she had sup-

4. Painting in the Pre-Raphaelite style by Edward Burne-Jones (1833–1898), whose somewhat stylized figures Rose describes a little later in the novel.

posed, and settled Rose down to have a talk about it, assumed that she would have an eye on the money.

"It is no small triumph to attract the attentions of the heir to a mercantile empire," said Dr. Henshawe, being ironic and serious at the same time. "I don't despise wealth," she said. "Sometimes I wish I had some of it." (Did she really suppose she had not?) "I am sure you will learn how to put it to good uses. But what about your ambitions, Rose? What about your studies and your degree? Are you going to forget all that so soon?"

Mercantile Empire was a rather grand way of putting it. Patrick's family owned a chain of department stores in British Columbia. All Patrick had said to Rose was that his father owned some stores. When she said *two different worlds* to him she was thinking that he probably lived in some substantial house like the houses in Dr. Henshawe's neighborhood. She was thinking of the most prosperous merchants in Hanratty. She could not realize what a coup she had made because it would have been a coup for her if the butcher's son had fallen for her, or the jeweler's; people would say she had done well.

She had a look at that painting. She looked it up in an art book in the Library. She studied the Beggar Maid, meek and voluptuous, with her shy white feet. The milky surrender of her, the helplessness and gratitude. Was that how Patrick saw Rose? Was that how she could be? She would need that king, sharp and swarthy as he looked, even in his trance of passion, clever and barbaric. He could make a puddle of her, with his fierce desire. There would be no apologizing with him, none of that flinching, that lack of faith, that seemed to be revealed in all transactions with Patrick.

She could not turn Patrick down. She could not do it. It was not the amount of money but the amount of love he offered that she could not ignore; she believed that she felt sorry for him, that she had to help him out. It was as if he had come up to her in a crowd carrying a large, simple, dazzling object—a huge egg, maybe, of solid silver, something of doubtful use and punishing weight—and was offering it to her, in fact thrusting it at her, begging her to take some of the weight of it off him. If she thrust it back how could he bear it? But that explanation left something out. It left out her own appetite, which was not for wealth but for worship. The size, the weight, the shine, or what he said was love (and she did not doubt him) had to impress her, even though she had never asked for it. It did not seem likely such an offering would come her way again. Patrick himself, though worshipful, did in some oblique way acknowledge her luck.

She had always thought this would happen, that somebody would look at her and love her totally and helplessly. At the same time she had thought that nobody would, nobody would want her at all, and up until now, nobody had. What made you wanted was nothing you did, it was something you had, and how could you ever tell whether you had it? She would look at herself in the glass and think: *wife, sweetheart.* Those mild lovely words. How could they apply to her? It was a miracle; it was a mistake. It was what she had dreamed of; it was not what she wanted.

She grew very tired, irritable, sleepless. She tried to think admiringly of Patrick. His lean, fair-skinned face was really very handsome. He must know a number of things. He graded papers, presided at examinations, he was finishing his thesis. There was a smell of pipe tobacco and rough wool about him, that she liked. He was twenty-four. No other girl she knew, who had a boyfriend, had one as old as that.

Then without warning she thought of him saying, "I suppose I don't seem very manly." She thought of him saying, "Do you love me? Do you really love me?" He would look at her in a scared and threatening way. Then when she said yes he said how lucky he was, how lucky they were, he mentioned friends of his and their girls, comparing their love affairs unfavorably to his and Rose's. Rose would shiver with irritation and misery. She was sick of herself as much as him, she was sick of the picture they made at this moment, walking across a snowy downtown park, her bare hand snuggled in Patrick's, in his pocket. Some outrageous and cruel things were being shouted, inside her. She had to do something, to keep them from getting out. She started tickling and teasing him.

Outside Dr. Henshawe's back door, in the snow, she kissed him, tried to make him open his mouth, she did scandalous things to him. When he kissed her his lips were soft; his tongue was shy; he collapsed over rather than held her, she could not find any force in him.

"You're lovely. You have lovely skin. Such fair eyebrows. You're so delicate."

She was pleased to hear that, anybody would be. But she said warningly, "I'm not so delicate, really. I'm quite large."

"You don't know how I love you. There's a book I have called *The White Goddess*.[5] Every time I look at the title it reminds me of you."

She wriggled away from him. She bent down and got a handful of snow from the drift by the steps and clapped it on his head.

"My White God."

He shook the snow out. She scooped up some more and threw it at him. He didn't laugh, he was surprised and alarmed. She brushed the snow off his eyebrows and licked it off his ears. She was laughing, though she felt desperate rather than merry. She didn't know what made her do this.

"Dr. *Hen*-shawe," Patrick hissed at her. The tender poetic voice he used for rhapsodizing about her could entirely disappear, could change to remonstrance, exasperation, with no steps at all between.

"Dr. Henshawe will hear you!"

"Dr. Henshawe says you are an honorable young man," Rose said dreamily. "I think she's in love with you." It was true; Dr. Henshawe had said that. And it was true that he was. He couldn't bear the way Rose was talking. She blew at the snow in his hair. "Why don't you go in and deflower her? I'm sure she's a virgin. That's her window. Why don't you?" She rubbed his hair, then slipped her hand inside his overcoat and rubbed the front of his pants. "You're hard!" she said triumphantly. "Oh, Patrick! You've got a hard-on for Dr. Henshawe!" She had never said anything like this before, never come near behaving like this.

"Shut up!" said Patrick, tormented. But she couldn't. She raised her head and in a loud whisper pretended to call toward an upstairs window, "Dr. Henshawe! Come and see what Patrick's got for you!" Her bullying hand went for his fly.

To stop her, to keep her quiet, Patrick had to struggle with her. He got a hand over her mouth, with the other hand beat her away from his zipper. The big loose sleeves of his overcoat beat at her like floppy wings. As soon as he started to fight she was relieved—that was what she wanted from him,

5. A 1947 anthropological and mythological study by the poet and novelist Robert Graves, which argues that poetry originated from the ritual worship of the goddess of fertility and the moon.

some sort of action. But she had to keep resisting, until he really proved himself stronger. She was afraid he might not be able to.

But he was. He forced her down, down, to her knees, face down in the snow. He pulled her arms back and rubbed her face in the snow. Then he let her go, and almost spoiled it.

"Are you all right? Are you? I'm sorry. Rose?"

She staggered up and shoved her snowy face into his. He backed off.

"Kiss me! Kiss the snow! I love you!"

"Do you?" he said plaintively, and brushed the snow from a corner of her mouth and kissed her, with understandable bewilderment. "*Do* you?"

Then the light came on, flooding them and the trampled snow, and Dr. Henshawe was calling over their heads.

"Rose! Rose!"

She called in a patient, encouraging voice, as if Rose was lost in a fog nearby, and needed directing home.

Do you love him, Rose?" said Dr. Henshawe. "No, think about it. Do you?" Her voice was full of doubt and seriousness. Rose took a deep breath and answered as if filled with calm emotion, "Yes, I do."

"Well, then."

In the middle of the night Rose woke up and ate chocolate bars. She craved sweets. Often in class or in the middle of a movie she started thinking about fudge cupcakes, brownies, some kind of cake Dr. Henshawe bought at the European Bakery; it was filled with dollops of rich bitter chocolate that ran out on the plate. Whenever she tried to think about herself and Patrick, whenever she made up her mind to decide what she really felt, these cravings intervened.

She was putting on weight, and had developed a nest of pimples between her eyebrows.

Her bedroom was cold, being over the garage, with windows on three sides. Otherwise it was pleasant. Over the bed hung framed photographs of Greek skies and ruins, taken by Dr. Henshawe herself on her Mediterranean trip.

She was writing an essay on Yeats's plays. In one of the plays[6] a young bride is lured away by the fairies from her sensible unbearable marriage. "Come away, O human child . . ." Rose read, and her eyes filled up with tears for herself, as if she was that shy elusive virgin, too fine for the bewildered peasants who have entrapped her. In actual fact she was the peasant, shocking high-minded Patrick, but he did not look for escape.

She took down one of those Greek photographs and defaced the wallpaper, writing the start of a poem which had come to her while she ate chocolate bars in bed and the wind from Gibbons Park banged at the garage walls.

> Heedless in my dark womb
> I bear a madman's child . . .

She never wrote any more of it, and wondered sometimes if she had meant headless. She never tried to rub it out, either.

6. *The Land of Heart's Desire* (1894), by William Butler Yeats (1865–1939).

Patrick shared an apartment with two other graduate students. He lived plainly, did not own a car or belong to a fraternity. His clothes had an ordinary academic shabbiness. His friends were the sons of teachers and ministers. He said his father had all but disowned him, for becoming an intellectual. He said he would never go into business.

They came back to the apartment in the early afternoon when they knew both the other students would be out. The apartment was cold. They undressed quickly and got into Patrick's bed. Now was the time. They clung together, shivering and giggling. Rose was doing the giggling. She felt a need to be continually playful. She was terrified that they would not manage it, that there was a great humiliation in store, a great exposure of their poor deceits and stratagems. But the deceits and stratagems were only hers. Patrick was never a fraud; he managed, in spite of gigantic embarrassment, apologies; he passed through some amazed pantings and flounderings, to peace. Rose was no help, presenting instead of an honest passivity much twisting and fluttering eagerness, unpracticed counterfeit of passion. She was pleased when it was accomplished; she did not have to counterfeit that. They had done what others did, they had done what lovers did. She thought of celebration. What occurred to her was something delicious to eat, a sundae at Boomers, apple pie with hot cinnamon sauce. She was not at all prepared for Patrick's idea, which was to stay where they were and try again.

When pleasure presented itself, the fifth or sixth time they were together, she was thrown out of gear entirely, her passionate carrying-on was silenced.

Patrick said, "What's the matter?"

"Nothing!" Rose said, turning herself radiant and attentive once more. But she kept forgetting, the new developments interfered, and she had finally to give in to that struggle, more or less ignoring Patrick. When she could take note of him again she overwhelmed him with gratitude; she was really grateful now, and she wanted to be forgiven, though she could not say so, for all her pretended gratitude, her patronizing, her doubts.

Why should she doubt so much, she thought, lying comfortably in the bed while Patrick went to make some instant coffee. Might it not be possible, to feel as she pretended? If this sexual surprise was possible, wasn't anything? Patrick was not much help; his chivalry and self-abasement, next door to his scoldings, did discourage her. But wasn't the real fault hers? Her conviction that anyone who could fall in love with her must be hopelessly lacking, must finally be revealed as a fool? So she took note of anything that was foolish about Patrick, even though she thought she was looking for things that were masterful, admirable. At this moment, in his bed, in his room, surrounded by his books and clothes, his shoe brushes and typewriter, some tacked-up cartoons—she sat up in bed to look at them, and they really were quite funny, he must allow things to be funny when she was not here—she could see him as a likable, intelligent, even humorous person; no hero; no fool. Perhaps they could be ordinary. If only, when he came back in, he would not start thanking and fondling and worshiping her. She didn't like worship, really; it was only the idea of it she liked. On the other hand, she didn't like it when he started to correct and criticize her. There was much he planned to change.

Patrick loved her. What did he love? Not her accent, which he was trying hard to alter, though she was often mutinous and unreasonable, declaring in the face of all evidence that she did not have a country accent, everybody talked the way she did. Not her jittery sexual boldness (his relief at her virginity matched hers at his competence). She could make him flinch at a vulgar word, a drawling tone. All the time, moving and speaking, she was destroying herself for him, yet he looked right through her, through all the distractions she was creating, and loved some obedient image that she herself could not see. And his hopes were high. Her accent could be eliminated, her friends could be discredited and removed, her vulgarity could be discouraged.

What about all the rest of her? Energy, laziness, vanity, discontent, ambition? She concealed all that. He had no idea. For all her doubts about him, she never wanted him to fall out of love with her.

They made two trips.

They went to British Columbia, on the train, during the Easter holidays. His parents sent Patrick money for his ticket. He paid for Rose, using up what he had in the bank and borrowing from one of his roommates. He told her not to reveal to his parents that she had not paid for her own ticket. She saw that he meant to conceal that she was poor. He knew nothing about women's clothes, or he would not have thought that possible. Though she had done the best she could. She had borrowed Dr. Henshawe's raincoat for the coastal weather. It was a bit long, but otherwise all right, due to Dr. Henshawe's classically youthful tastes. She had sold more blood and bought a fuzzy angora sweater, peach-colored, which was extremely messy and looked like a small-town girl's idea of dressing up. She always realized things like that as soon as a purchase was made, not before.

Patrick's parents lived on Vancouver Island, near Sidney. About half an acre of clipped green lawn—green in the middle of winter; March seemed like the middle of winter to Rose—sloped down to a stone wall and a narrow pebbly beach and salt water. The house was half stone, half stucco-and-timber. It was built in the Tudor style, and others. The windows of the living room, the dining room, the den, all faced the sea, and because of the strong winds that sometimes blew onshore, they were made of thick glass, plate glass Rose supposed, like the windows of the automobile showroom in Hanratty. The seaward wall of the dining room was all windows, curving out in a gentle bay; you looked through the thick curved glass as through the bottom of a bottle. The sideboard too had a curving, gleaming belly, and seemed as big as a boat. Size was noticeable everywhere and particularly thickness. Thickness of towels and rugs and handles of knives and forks, and silences. There was a terrible amount of luxury and unease. After a day or so there Rose became so discouraged that her wrists and ankles felt weak. Picking up her knife and fork was a chore; cutting and chewing the perfect roast beef was almost beyond her; she got short of breath climbing the stairs. She had never known before how some places could choke you off, choke off your very life. She had not known this in spite of a number of very unfriendly places she had been in.

The first morning, Patrick's mother took her for a walk on the grounds, pointing out the greenhouse, the cottage where "the couple" lived: a charming, ivied, shuttered cottage, bigger than Dr. Henshawe's house. The couple, the servants, were more gentle-spoken, more discreet and dignified, than anyone Rose could think of in Hanratty, and indeed they were superior in these ways to Patrick's family.

Patrick's mother showed her the rose garden, the kitchen garden. There were many low stone walls.

"Patrick built them," said his mother. She explained anything with an indifference that bordered on distaste. "He built all these walls."

Rose's voice came out full of false assurance, eager and inappropriately enthusiastic. "He must be a true Scot," she said. Patrick was a Scot, in spite of his name. The Blatchfords had come from Glasgow. "Weren't the best stonemasons always Scotsmen?" (She had learned quite recently not to say "Scotch.") "Maybe he had stonemason ancestors."

She cringed afterward, thinking of these efforts, the pretense of ease and gaiety, as cheap and imitative as her clothes. "No," said Patrick's mother. "No. I don't think they were stonemasons." Something like fog went out from her: affront, disapproval, dismay. Rose thought that perhaps she had been offended by the suggestion that her husband's family might have worked with their hands. When she got to know her better—or had observed her longer; it was impossible to get to know her—she understood that Patrick's mother disliked anything fanciful, speculative, abstract, in conversation. She would also, of course, dislike Rose's chatty tone. Any interest beyond the factual consideration of the matter at hand—food, weather, invitations, furniture, servants—seemed to her sloppy, illbred, and dangerous. It was all right to say, "This is a warm day," but not, "This day reminds me of when we used to—" She hated people being *reminded*.

She was the only child of one of the early lumber barons of Vancouver Island. She had been born in a vanished northern settlement. But whenever Patrick tried to get her to talk about the past, whenever he asked her for the simplest sort of information—what steamers went up the coast, what year was the settlement abandoned, what was the route of the first logging railway—she would say irritably, "I don't know. How would I know about that?" This irritation was the strongest note that ever got into her words.

Neither did Patrick's father care for this concern about the past. Many things, most things, about Patrick, seemed to strike him as bad signs. "What do you want to know all that for?" he shouted down the table. He was a short square-shouldered man, red-faced, astonishingly belligerent. Patrick looked like his mother, who was tall, fair, and elegant in the most muted way possible, as if her clothes, her makeup, her style, were chosen with an ideal neutrality in mind.

"Because I am interested in history," said Patrick in an angry, pompous, but nervously breaking voice.

"Because-I-am-interested-in-history," said his sister Marion in an immediate parody, break and all. "History!"

The sisters Joan and Marion were younger than Patrick, older than Rose. Unlike Patrick they showed no nervousness, no cracks in self-satisfaction. At an earlier meal they had questioned Rose.

"Do you ride?"

"No."

"Do you sail?"

"No."

"Play tennis? Play golf? Play badminton?"

No. No. No.

"Perhaps she is an intellectual genius, like Patrick," the father said. And Patrick, to Rose's horror and embarrassment, began to shout at the table in general an account of her scholarships and prizes. What did he hope for? Was he so witless as to think such bragging would subdue them, would bring out anything but further scorn? Against Patrick, against his shouting boasts, his contempt for sports and television, his so-called intellectual interests, the family seemed united. But this alliance was only temporary. The father's dislike of his daughters was minor only in comparison with his dislike of Patrick. He railed at them too, when he could spare a moment; he jeered at the amount of time they spent at their games, complained about the cost of their equipment, their boats, their horses. And they wrangled with each other, on obscure questions of scores and borrowings and damages. All complained to the mother about the food, which was plentiful and delicious. The mother spoke as little as possible to anyone and to tell the truth Rose did not blame her. She had never imagined so much true malevolence collected in one place. Billy Pope was a bigot and a grumbler, Flo was capricious, unjust, and gossipy, her father, when he was alive, had been capable of cold judgments and unremitting disapproval; but compared to Patrick's family, all Rose's own people seemed jovial and content.

"Are they always like this?" she said to Patrick. "Is it me? They don't like me."

"They don't like you because I chose you," said Patrick with some satisfaction.

They lay on the stony beach after dark, in their raincoats, hugged and kissed and uncomfortably, unsuccessfully, attempted more. Rose got seaweed stains on Dr. Henshawe's coat. Patrick said, "You see why I need you? I need you so much!"

She took him to Hanratty. It was just as bad as she had thought it would be. Flo had gone to great trouble, and cooked a meal of scalloped potatoes, turnips, big country sausages which were a special present from Billy Pope, from the butcher shop. Patrick detested coarse-textured food, and made no pretense of eating it. The table was spread with a plastic cloth, they ate under the tube of fluorescent light. The centerpiece was new and especially for the occasion. A plastic swan, lime green in color, with slits in the wings, in which were stuck folded, colored paper napkins. Billy Pope, reminded to take one, grunted, refused. Otherwise he was on dismally good behavior. Word had reached him, word had reached both of them, of Rose's triumph. It had come from their superiors in Hanratty; otherwise they could not have believed it. Customers in the butcher shop—formidable ladies, the dentist's wife, the veterinarian's wife—had said to Billy Pope that they heard Rose had picked herself up a millionaire. Rose knew Billy Pope would go back to work tomorrow with stories of the millionaire, or millionaire's son, and that all these stories would focus on his—Billy Pope's—forthright and unintimidated behavior in the situation.

"We just set him down and give him some sausages, don't make no difference to us what he comes from!"

She knew Flo would have her comments too, that Patrick's nervousness would not escape her, that she would be able to mimic his voice and his flapping hands that had knocked over the ketchup bottle. But at present they both sat hunched over the table in miserable eclipse. Rose tried to start some conversation, talking brightly, unnaturally, rather as if she was an interviewer trying to draw out a couple of simple local people. She felt ashamed on more levels than she could count. She was ashamed of the food and the swan and the plastic tablecloth; ashamed for Patrick, the gloomy snob, who made a startled grimace when Flo passed him the toothpick-holder; ashamed for Flo with her timidity and hypocrisy and pretensions; most of all ashamed for herself. She didn't even have any way that she could talk, and sound natural. With Patrick there, she couldn't slip back into an accent closer to Flo's, Billy Pope's and Hanratty's. That accent jarred on her ears now, anyway. It seemed to involve not just a different pronunciation but a whole different approach to talking. Talking was shouting; the words were separated and emphasized so that people could bombard each other with them. And the things people said were like lines from the most hackneyed rural comedy. *Wal if a feller took a notion to,* they said. They really said that. Seeing them through Patrick's eyes, hearing them through his ears, Rose too had to be amazed.

She was trying to get them to talk about local history, some things she thought Patrick might be interested in. Presently Flo did begin to talk, she could only be held in so long, whatever her misgivings. The conversation took another line from anything Rose had intended.

"The line I lived on when I was just young," Flo said, "it was the worst place ever created for suiciding."

"A line is a concession road. In the township," Rose said to Patrick. She had doubts about what was coming, and rightly so, for then Patrick got to hear about a man who cut his own throat, *his own throat,* from ear to ear, a man who shot himself the first time and didn't do enough damage, so he loaded up and fired again and managed it, another man who hanged himself using a chain, the kind of chain you hook on a tractor with, so it was a wonder his head was not torn off.

Tore off, Flo said.

She went on to a woman who, though not a suicide, had been dead in her house a week before she was found, and that was in the summer. She asked Patrick to imagine it. All this happened, said Flo, within five miles of where she herself was born. She was presenting credentials, not trying to horrify Patrick, at least not more than was acceptable, in a social way; she did not mean to disconcert him. How could he understand that?

"You were right," said Patrick, as they left Hanratty on the bus. "It is a dump. You must be glad to get away."

Rose felt immediately that he should not have said that.

"Of course that's not your real mother," Patrick said. "Your real parents can't have been like that." Rose did not like his saying that either, though it was what she believed, herself. She saw that he was trying to provide for her a more genteel background, perhaps something like the homes of his poor friends: a few books about, a tea tray, and mended linen, worn good taste; proud, tired, educated people. What a coward he was, she thought angrily, but she knew that she herself was the coward, not knowing any way to be comfortable with her own people or the kitchen or any of it. Years later she would learn how to use it, she would be able to amuse or intimidate right-thinking people at dinner parties with glimpses of her early home. At the moment she felt confusion, misery.

Nevertheless her loyalty was starting. Now that she was sure of getting away, a layer of loyalty and protectiveness was hardening around every memory she had, around the store and the town, the flat, somewhat scrubby, unremarkable countryside. She would oppose this secretly to Patrick's views of mountains and ocean, his stone and timbered mansion. Her allegiances were far more proud and stubborn than his.

But it turned out he was not leaving anything behind.

Patrick gave her a diamond ring and announced that he was giving up being a historian for her sake. He was going into his father's business. She said she thought he hated his father's business. He said that he could not afford to take such an attitude now that he would have a wife to support. It seemed that Patrick's desire to marry, even to marry Rose, had been taken by his father as a sign of sanity. Great streaks of bounty were mixed in with all the ill will in that family. His father at once offered a job in one of the stores, offered to buy them a house. Patrick was as incapable of turning down this offer as Rose was of turning down Patrick's, and his reasons were as little mercenary as hers.

"Will we have a house like your parents?" Rose said. She really thought it might be necessary to start off in that style.

"Well, maybe not at first. Not quite so—"

"I don't want a house like that! I don't want to live like that!"

"We'll live however you like. We'll have whatever kind of house you like."

Provided it's not a dump, she though nastily.

Girls she hardly knew stopped and asked to see her ring, admired it, wished her happiness. When she went back to Hanratty for a weekend, alone this time, thank God, she met the dentist's wife on the main street.

"Oh, Rose, isn't it wonderful! When are you coming back again? We're going to give a tea for you, the ladies in town all want to give a tea for you!"

This woman had never spoken to Rose, never given any sign before of knowing who she was. Paths were opening now, barriers were softening. And Rose—oh, this was the worst, this was the shame of it—Rose, instead of cutting the dentist's wife, was blushing and skittishly flashing her diamond and saying yes, that would be a lovely idea. When people said how happy she must be she did think herself happy. It was as simple as that. She dimpled and sparkled and turned herself into a fiancée with no trouble at all. Where will you live, people said and she said, Oh, in British Columbia! That added more magic to the tale. Is it really beautiful there, they said, is it never winter?

"Oh, yes,!" cried Rose. "Oh, no!"

She woke up early, got up and dressed and let herself out of the side door of Dr. Henshawe's garage. It was too early for the buses to be running. She walked through the city to Patrick's apartment. She walked across the park. Around the South African War[7] Memorial a pair of greyhounds were leaping and playing, an old woman standing by, holding their leashes. The sun was just up, shining on their pale hides. The grass was wet. Daffodils and narcissus in bloom.

Patrick came to the door, tousled, frowning sleepily, in his gray and maroon striped pajamas.

"Rose! What's the matter?"

She couldn't say anything. He pulled her into the apartment. She put

7. The Boer War, 1899–1902, in which Great Britain fought against the predominantly Dutch colo- nists of the Transvaal and Orange Free State.

her arms around him and hid her face against his chest and in a stagey voice
said, "Please Patrick. Please let me not marry you."

"Are you sick? What's the matter?"

"Please let me not marry you," she said again, with even less conviction.

"You're crazy."

She didn't blame him for thinking so. Her voice sounded so unnatural,
wheedling, silly. As soon as he opened the door and she faced the fact of
him, his sleepy eyes, his pajamas, she saw that what she had come to do
was enormous, impossible. She would have to explain everything to him,
and of course she could not do it. She could not make him see her necessity.
She could not find any tone of voice, any expression of the face, that would
serve her.

"Are you upset?" said Patrick. "What's happened?"

"Nothing."

"How did you get here anyway?"

"Walked."

She had been fighting back a need to go to the bathroom. It seemed that
if she went to the bathroom she would destroy some of the strength of her
case. But she had to. She freed herself. She said, "Wait a minute, I'm going
to the john."

When she came out Patrick had the electric kettle going, was measuring
out instant coffee. He looked decent and bewildered.

"I'm not really awake," he said. "Now. Sit down. First of all, are you
premenstrual?"

"No." But she realized with dismay that she was, and that he might be
able to figure it out, because they had been worried last month.

"Well, if you're not premenstrual, and nothing's happened to upset you,
then what is all this about?"

"I don't want to get married," she said, backing away from the cruelty of
I don't want to marry you.

"When did you come to this decision?"

"Long ago. This morning."

They were talking in whispers. Rose looked at the clock. It was a little
after seven.

"When do the others get up?"

"About eight."

"Is there milk for the coffee?" She went to the refrigerator.

"Quiet with the door," said Patrick, too late.

"I'm sorry," she said, in her strange silly voice.

"We went for a walk last night and everything was fine. You come this
morning and tell me you don't want to get married. *Why* don't you want to
get married?"

"I just don't. I don't want to be married."

"What else do you want to do?"

"I don't know."

Patrick kept staring at her sternly, drinking his coffee. He who used to
plead with her *do you love me, do you really*, did not bring the subject up
now.

"Well I know."

"What?"

"I know who's been talking to you."

"Nobody has been talking to me."

"Oh, no. Well, I bet. Dr. Henshawe has."

"No."

"Some people don't have a very high opinion of her. They think she has an influence on girls. She doesn't like the girls who live with her to have boyfriends. Does she? You even told me that. She doesn't like them to be normal."

"That's not it."

"What did she say to you, Rose?"

"She didn't say anything." Rose began to cry.

"Are you sure?"

"Oh, Patrick, listen, please, I can't marry you, please, I don't know why, I can't, please, I'm sorry, believe me, I can't," Rose babbled at him, weeping, and Patrick saying, "Ssh! You'll wake them up!" lifted or dragged her out of the kitchen chair and took her to his room, where she sat on the bed. He shut the door. She held her arms across her stomach, and rocked back and forth.

"What is it, Rose? What's the matter? Are you sick!"

"It's just so hard to tell you!"

"Tell me what?"

"What I just did tell you!"

"I mean have you found out you have T.B. or something?"

"No!"

"Is there something in your family you haven't told me about? Insanity?" said Patrick encouragingly.

"No!" Rose rocked and wept.

"So what is it?"

"I don't love you!" she said. "I don't love you. I don't love you." She fell on the bed and put her head in the pillow. "I'm so sorry. I'm so sorry. I can't help it."

After a moment or two Patrick said, "Well. If you don't love me you don't love me. I'm not forcing you to." His voice sounded strained and spiteful, against the reasonableness of what he was saying. "I just wonder," he said, "if you know what you do want. I don't think you do. I don't think you have any idea what you want. You're just in a state."

"I don't have to know what I want to know what I don't want!" Rose said, turning over. This released her. "I never loved you."

"Ssh. You'll wake them. We have to stop."

"I never loved you. I never wanted to. It was a mistake."

"All right. All right. You made your point."

"Why am I supposed to love you? Why do you act as if there was something wrong with me if I didn't? You despise me. You despise my family and my background and you think you are doing me a *great favor*—"

"I fell in love with you," Patrick said. "I don't despise you. Oh, Rose, I worship you."

"You're a sissy," Rose said. "You're a prude." She jumped off the bed with great pleasure as she said this. She felt full of energy. More was coming. Terrible things were coming.

"You don't even know how to make love right. I always wanted to get out of this from the very first. I felt sorry for you. You won't look where you're going, you're always knocking things over, just because you can't be bothered, you can't be bothered noticing anything, you're wrapped up in yourself, and you're always bragging, it's so stupid, you don't even know how to brag right, if you really want to impress people you'll never do it, the way you do it all they do is laugh at you!"

Patrick sat on the bed and looked up at her, his face open to whatever she would say. She wanted to beat and beat him, to say worse and worse, uglier and crueller, things. She took a breath, drew in air, to stop the things she felt rising in her from getting out.

"I don't want to see you, ever!" she said viciously. But at the door she turned and said in a normal and regretful voice, "Good-bye."

Patrick wrote her a note: "I don't understand what happened the other day and I want to talk to you about it. But I think we should wait for two weeks and not see or talk to each other and find out how we feel at the end of that time."

Rose had forgotten all about giving him back his ring. When she came out of his apartment building that morning she was still wearing it. She couldn't go back, and it seemed too valuable to send through the mail. She continued to wear it, mostly because she did not want to have to tell Dr. Henshawe what had happened. She was relieved to get Patrick's note. She thought that she could give him back the ring then.

She thought about what Patrick had said about Dr. Henshawe. No doubt there was some truth in that, else why should she be so reluctant to tell Dr. Henshawe she had broken her engagement, so unwilling to face her sensible approval, her restrained, relieved congratulations?

She told Dr. Henshawe that she was not seeing Patrick while she studied for her exams. Rose could see that even that pleased her.

She told no one that her situation had changed. It was not just Dr. Henshawe she didn't want knowing. She didn't like giving up being envied; the experience was so new to her.

She tried to think what to do next. She could not stay on at Dr. Henshawe's. It seemed clear that if she escaped from Patrick, she must escape from Dr. Henshawe too. And she did not want to stay on at the college, with people knowing about her broken engagement, with the girls who now congratulated her saying they had known all along it was a fluke, her getting Patrick. She would have to get a job.

The Head Librarian had offered her a job for the summer but that was perhaps at Dr. Henshawe's suggestion. Once she moved out, the offer might not hold. She knew that instead of studying for her exams she ought to be downtown, applying for work as a filing clerk at the insurance offices, applying at Bell Telephone, at the department stores. The idea frightened her. She kept on studying. That was the one thing she really knew how to do. She was a scholarship student after all.

On Saturday afternoon, when she was working at the Library, she saw Patrick. She did not see him by accident. She went down to the bottom floor, trying not to make a noise on the spiraling metal staircase. There was a place in the stacks where she could stand, almost in darkness, and see into his carrel. She did that. She couldn't see his face. She saw his long pink neck and the old plaid shirt he wore on Saturdays. His long neck. His bony shoulders. She was no longer irritated by him, no longer frightened by him; she was free. She could look at him as she would look at anybody. She could appreciate him. He had behaved well. He had not tried to rouse her pity, he had not bullied her, he had not molested her with pitiful telephone calls and letters. He had not come and sat on Dr. Henshawe's doorstep. He was an honorable person, and he would never know how she acknowledged that, how she was grateful for it. The things she had said to him made her ashamed now. And they were not even true. Not all of them. He did know how to make love. She was so moved, made so gentle and wistful, by the sight of him, that she wanted to give him something, some surprising bounty, she wished to undo his unhappiness. Then she had a compelling picture of herself. She was running softly into Patrick's carrel, she was throwing her arms around him from behind, she was giving everything back to him. Would he take it from her, would he still want it? She saw them laughing and crying, explaining, forgiving. *I love you. I do love you, it's all right, I was terrible, I didn't mean it, I was just crazy, I love you, it's all right.* This was a violent temptation for her; it was barely resistable. She had an impulse to hurl herself. Whether it was off a cliff or into a warm bed of welcoming grass and flowers, she really could not tell.

It was not resistable, after all. She did it.

When Rose afterward reviewed and talked about this moment in her life—for she went through a period, like most people nowadays, of talking freely about her most private decisions, to friends and lovers and party acquaintances whom she might never see again, while they did the same—she said that comradely compassion had overcome her, she was not proof against the sight of a bare bent neck. Then she went further into it, and said greed, greed. She said she had run to him and clung to him and overcome his suspicions and kissed and cried and reinstated herself simply because she did not know how to do without his love and his promise to look after her; she was frightened of the world and she had not been able to think up any other plan for herself. When she was seeing life in economic terms, or was with people who did, she said that only middle-class people had choices anyway, that if she had had the price of a train ticket to Toronto her life would have been different.

Nonsense, she might say later, never mind that, it was really vanity, it was vanity pure and simple, to resurrect him, to bring him back his happiness. To see if she could do that. She could not resist such a test of power. She explained then that she had paid for it. She said that she and Patrick had been married ten years, and that during that time the scenes of the first breakup and reconciliation had been periodically repeated, with her saying again all the things she had said the first time, and the things she had held back, and many other things which occurred to her. She hopes she did not tell people (but thinks she did) that she used to beat her head against the bedpost, that she smashed a gravy boat through a dining-room window; that she was so frightened, so sickened by what she had done that she lay in bed, shivering, and begged and begged for his forgiveness. Which he granted. Sometimes she flew at him; sometimes he beat her. The next morning they would get up early and make a special breakfast, they would sit eating bacon and eggs and drinking filtered coffee, worn out, bewildered, treating each other with shamefaced kindness.

What do you think triggers the reaction? they would say.

Do you think we ought to take a holiday? A holiday together? Holidays alone?

A waste, a sham, those efforts, as it turned out. But they worked for the moment. Calmed down, they would say that most people probably went through the same things like this, in a marriage, and indeed they seemed to know mostly people who did. They could not separate until enough damage had been done, until nearly mortal damage had been done, to keep them apart. And until Rose could get a job and make her own money, so perhaps there was a very ordinary reason after all.

What she never said to anybody, never confided, was that she sometimes thought it had not been pity or greed or cowardice or vanity but something quite different, like a vision of happiness. In view of everything else she had told she could hardly tell that. It seems very odd; she can't justify it. She doesn't mean that they had perfectly ordinary, bearable times in their marriage, long busy stretches of wallpapering and vacationing and meals and shopping and worrying about a child's illness, but that sometimes, without reason or warning, happiness, the possibility of happiness, would surprise them. Then it was as if they were in different though identical-seeming skins, as if there existed a radiantly kind and innocent Rose and Patrick, hardly ever visible, in the shadow of their usual selves. Perhaps it was that Patrick she saw when she was free of him, invisible to him, looking into his carrel. Perhaps it was. She should have left him there.

She knew that was how she had seen him; she knows it, because it happened again. She was in Toronto Airport, in the middle of the night. This was about nine years after she and Patrick were divorced. She had become fairly well-known by this time, her face was familiar to many people in this country. She did a television program on which she interviewed politicians, actors, writers, *personalities*, and many ordinary people who were angry about something the government or the police or a union had done to them. Sometimes she talked to people who had seen strange sights. UFO's, or sea monsters, or who had unusual accomplishments or collections, or kept up some obsolete custom.

She was alone. No one was meeting her. She had just come in on a delayed flight from Yellowknife. She was tired and bedraggled. She saw Patrick standing with his back to her, at a coffee bar. He wore a raincoat. He was heavier than he had been, but she knew him at once. And she had the same feeling that this was a person she was bound to, that by a certain magical, yet possible trick, they could find and trust each other, and that to begin this all she had to do was go up and touch him on the shoulder, surprise him with his happiness.

She did not do this, of course, but she did stop. She was standing still when he turned around, heading for one of the little plastic tables and curved seats grouped in front of the coffee bar. All his skinniness and academic shabbiness, his look of prim authoritarianism, was gone. He had smoothed out, filled out, into such a modish and agreeable, responsible, slightly complacent-looking man. His birthmark had faded. She thought how haggard and dreary she must look, in her rumpled trenchcoat, her long, graying hair fallen forward around her face, old mascara smudged under her eyes.

He made a face at her. It was a truly hateful, savagely warning, face; infantile, self-indulgent, yet calculated; it was a timed explosion of disgust and loathing. It was hard to believe. But she saw it.

Sometimes when Rose was talking to someone in front of the television cameras she would sense the desire in them to make a face. She would sense it in all sorts of people, in skillful politicians and witty liberal bishops and honored humanitarians, in housewives who had witnessed natural disasters and in workmen who had performed heroic rescues or been cheated out of disability pensions. They were longing to sabotage themselves, to make a face or say a dirty word. Was this the face they all wanted to make? To show somebody, to show everybody? They wouldn't do it, though; they wouldn't get the chance. Special circumstances were required. A lurid unreal place, the middle of the night, a staggering unhinging weariness, the sudden, hallucinatory appearance of your true enemy. She hurried away then, down the long varicolored corridor, shaking. She had seen Patrick; Patrick had seen her; he had made that face. But she was not really able to understand how she could be an enemy. How could anybody hate Rose so much, at the very moment when she was ready to come forward with her good will, her smiling confession of exhaustion, her air of diffident faith in civilized overtures?

Oh, Patrick could. Patrick could.

1977

AFTERWORD

This is a love story—of sorts. Or is it an unlove story? It certainly begins like a love story—"Patrick Blatchford was in love with Rose." But Patrick is not the beggar maid and it is not Patrick in whom we are primarily interested or from whose perspective we see the story.

We go where Rose goes, and it's her perceptions and feelings we share—up to a point, for she is not very communicative about just what she is feeling. From the beginning we are not even sure exactly how she feels about Patrick, so we cannot be sure whether it's to be a love- or unlove story. It's not that she's blind. We learn from the first very brief section that begins "Patrick Blatchford was in love with Rose" that she thinks him "edgy, jumpy, disconcerting"; "stubborn and pitiable, determined and dependent"; "the most vulnerable person Rose had ever known," but also "full of cruel judgments . . . and conceit." We know that for her his good looks are somehow "canceled out," and that she is continually suprised by his loving her and wanting to marry her. This is not exactly the kind of description you would expect from a young lady smitten by love, but there is just enough working for him— he is vulnerable, pitiable, dependent; he has good looks (canceled or not)—to make it just possible that she may love him. We don't know for sure because she does not just come right out and say exactly how she feels about him. Perhaps she does not know herself.

This clear-eyed confusion persists to the very end of the novel. At first it contributes to the narrative suspense: will she or won't she (love him, marry him)? Then it contributes to what might be called "character-" or "interpretive-" suspense: will she or won't she (come to understand herself, know definitively what she really thinks or feels)? Rose is very perceptive and seems even-handed in her presentation of the evidence of her senses, but perhaps that even-handedness is evidence of her own uncertainty, her own unwillingness or inability to commit herself to a decision, a judgment, or an action. On the other hand, we perhaps should not be too quick to judge, even if she is too slow to do so; she may be more clear-eyed and more honest than we are used to in fiction, in our own lives, in ourselves. Or, she just may be smarter than we are. But perhaps I'm misjudging you, and you find Rose not weird or indecisive, but typical of a young person (woman?) in the confusion of a mobile, ever-changing, valueless (or multivalued) society.

Although we may get impatient with her, we do not, I believe, dislike Rose for her indecisiveness or her rather harsh judgment of others. For she is at least as hard on herself as she is on Patrick. She tells us honestly about her chocolate fits, her enjoying worship in the abstract—but not in actuality, her enjoying the envy of others, even if she does not think much of those others who envy her or of their values. She herself reveals that she feels superior intellectually and even morally to her family and to others in her hometown. She even feels superior to the other scholarship students— better-looking, more wellrounded. And of course she presents her own confusion of feelings, thoughts, and action.

She sees clearly but cannot choose, select, or commit herself. She does not seem to know what she thinks, or even what she truly feels. To the end, she does not know why, once she had the courage to tell Patrick that she did not love him, never loved him, would not marry him, she took it all back and went ahead and married him anyway. Years later, after their ten-year marriage had ended in divorce, when she told the story to friends or acquaintances, she still did not know for sure why she relented. Sometimes she said that she had just been afraid of the world; sometimes that she had pitied him and his loneliness; sometimes that it had been because he was rich and she was greedy, and sometimes that she had gone back to him out of vanity, just to show that she could throw him away and get him back. Finally, what she concludes is that the reason she came back to him had been because of something "like a vision of happiness." Their marriage was stormy, she tells us, full of fights (even beatings), reconciliations, and of peaceful periods that went on for a long time but were more like truces than real peace. Then, at odd times there was happiness, or at least "the possibility of happiness," that would come "without reason or warning":

> Then it was as if they were in different though identical-seeming skins, as if there existed a radiantly kind and innocent Rose and Patrick, hardly ever visible, in the shadow of their usual selves. Perhaps that was the Patrick she saw when she was free of him, invisible to him, looking into his carrel. Perhaps it was.

Characteristically, there is still the "perhaps," and she concludes, "She should have left him there." So even what seems to be at last the final and definitive explanation is itself negated.

The scene in which she does not "leave him there" is one of the most interesting and enigmatic bits of narration in the novel. It is never literally presented but is projected in Rose's mind: she imagines, somewhat romantically, but in great detail, almost as if it were happening, what the scene would be like were she to go back to him:

> Then she had a compelling picture of herself. She was running softly into Patrick's carrel, she was throwing her arms around him from behind, she was giving everything back to him. Would he take it from her, would he still want it? She saw them laughing and crying, explaining, forgiving. *I love you. I do love you, it's all right, I was terrible, I didn't mean it, I was just crazy, I love you, it's all right.* This was a violent temptation for her; it was barely resistable. She had an impulse to hurl herself. Whether it was off a cliff or into a warm bed of welcoming grass and flowers, she really could not tell.
> It was not resistable, after all. She did it.

We are used to people—or at least to fictional people, characters—who know what they feel and know what they mean when they talk of love, and know they will not marry of their own volition unless they feel "true love" and a sense of commitment. So Rose's uncertainty is likely to leave us feeling uncomfortable, perhaps wondering whether there are not people like that, and we look around—or inside. How certain *are* we, indeed, about what it is we really believe, really feel, even about love? (Wasn't there once a time when we thought we loved him / her? How could we have been so wrong?) Do we know no one who has made a serious decision, even, perhaps, about marriage, with as little conviction as Rose? Is Rose less unique than we want to believe, perhaps even as typical of modern young women—or men—as the heroines—or heroes—of true romance? Perhaps we ought not to take out all our feelings of discomfort on poor Rose.

This is not to suggest that Rose be exonerated from all blame for her unintentionally destructive shilly-shallying, but that at least we try to understand her. After all, poor thing, she, like you and me, is not perfect. Even to the end she does not understand herself, or, to put it another way, does not understand how she looks to others. When, nine years after the divorce, she bumps into Patrick, he makes "a truly hateful, savagely warning, face; [an] infantile self-indulgent, yet calculated" face at her. She sees that face, its meaning and its emotions—and its weakness—very clearly indeed. Still she is puzzled: "How could anybody hate Rose so much . . . ?" she asks herself. Her answer is not in terms of her self of her behavior: "Oh, Patrick could. Patrick could."

What are we to make of this, then? Is it, as Rose seems to mean it to be, an indictment of Patrick? Is he the spiteful little wimp who could hate, even hate the essentially good, if somewhat weak; kindly, if somewhat indecisive; well-meaning, if sometimes unintentionally hurtful, Rose? Or is this the final indictment of Rose's failure to understand herself and of the destructiveness of her failure not just to see but to think and feel clearly and to act decisively?

Perhaps we need to look at Rose and Patrick more particularly and specifically: they are not Everywoman and Everyman, or even Every-young-modern-woman and -man. Whatever else they are, they are intellectuals. He is a graduate student of history, and Rose first meets him and finally agrees to marry him in his library carrel. She is a scholarship girl from the provinces, works in the library, lives in the home of a retired woman English professor. Neither Patrick nor Rose seems particularly interested in "campus life"—in football games or fraternity parties, or the like. In the first paragraph of the novel, Patrick asks Rose how she can be friends with a girl who mispronounces "Metternich." Though the story is not heavily allusive, Patrick refers to Robert Graves's The White Goddess and Rose to Yeats's plays, and Rose, a college freshman, is reading Thomas Mann and Tolstoy.

It is often claimed that intellectuals are inevitably indecisive, that seeing too many possibilities makes it all but impossible to make definite and lasting choices or to act decisively. What we see of Rose's intellect is chiefly her clear and complex vision and her perhaps too complex mind, a mind that see too many motives and too many possibilities, interpretations, explanations, so that it lacks simplicity, single-minded-ness, decisiveness, effectiveness, "common sense." Patrick does not seem so indecisive, but then, despite his hours in the library, he does not seem so genuinely intellectual, but just well educated and sophisticated; he does, after all, rather blithely give up his chosen career to go into his father's business. Rose is also different from the other scholarship students, it seems. Patrick and Rose seem more "practical" and ambitious, more like yuppies or overachievers than convinced intellectuals:

> It seemed to be the rule that girl scholarship winners looked about forty and boys about twelve. . . . [T]here was a pall over them, . . . a true terrible pall of eagerness and docility. How else would they have supplied so many right answers, so many pleasing answers, how else distinguished themselves and got themselves here? And Rose had done the same.

But, we know from the inside, Rose is different, more reluctant, if she sometimes succumbs in the end, to "supply the right answer." It is her very difference, or perceived difference, that makes us sympathize with her.

There is also her role as the underdog, for, though Patrick is rich, she is just a poor girl from the provinces and an orphan at that. Rose's poverty is alluded to in the title of the novel, which is itself, as a footnote tells you, an allusion to King Cophetua and the Beggar Maid. The king is left out of the title of the novel for it is the beggar maid Rose on whom our attention is focused. As Rose points out, Patrick is hardly a swarthy, forceful, barbarian like King Cophetua. His wealth does make him a modern king, however; Dr. Henshawe calls him—apparently in all seriousness—"the heir to a mercantile empire." He also appears to belong to some past, courtly era: Rose recognizes, for example, that part of the reason he fell in love with her was that she was a "damsel in distress" when first they met, and that "it was clear he did wish to operate in a world of knights and ladies; outrages; devotions."

Though not a beggar—unless sitting for a scholarship examination is thought of as a form of begging—Rose is poor enough, and she realizes that Patrick sees her as "the Beggar Maid, meek and voluptuous, with her shy white feet. The milky surrender of her, the helplessness and gratitude." She realizes, too, that Patrick does not truly comprehend what it means to be actually poor. When he asks who administers her deceased father's "estate," that is, he explains, "his money and stocks and so on," and Rose says, "I don't think he left any [estate]," Patrick says in disbelief, "Don't be silly."

Rose knows what it is to be poor, never more so than after she has lived in Dr. Henshawe's home; poverty, she understands,

> was not just deprivation. It meant having those ugly tube lights and being proud of them. It meant continual talk of money and malicious talk about new things people had bought and whether they were paid for. It meant pride and jealously flaring over something like the new pair of plastic curtains, imitating lace, that Flo had bought for the front window. That as well as hanging your clothes on nails behind the door and being able to hear every sound from the bathroom.

She gets an even more graphic picture of the difference between the rich and the poor when she visits Patrick's home and meets his family. It was not just the half-acre of manicured lawn, the greenhouse and the servants, the rose garden, that separated them from her, but the fact that they "had never had to defer and polish themselves and win favor in the world, they would never have to, and that was because they were rich."

The struggle between Patrick and Rose, then, is not just a struggle between them as individuals. They come, as Rose says, from different worlds, and, as she does not say, they almost seem to be representative of different worlds, or different classes—or at least of intellectuals who are beginning to or who wish to transcend their class origins. Patrick, of course, returns to the bosom of his family when he returns to the family business. Rose, unhappily, cannot go home again: she has been educated out of her class. She had recognized the intellectual limitations and the restricted lives and vision of Hanratty and of her family before she had ever left home and could not wait to get away. After her experience in the larger world, when she brings Patrick home to meet her family and tries to see them through his eyes, as it were, she recognizes even more its tackiness and crudity, but,

> Now that she was sure of getting away, a layer of loyalty and protectiveness was hardening around every memory she had, around the store and the town, the flat, somewhat scrubby, unremarkable countryside. . . . Her allegiances were far more proud and stubborn than his.

Rose's shaky sense of identity, then, her vacillations, may be due as much to her not having a well-defined social identity or "place" as it is to intellectual complexities or character. It is even possible that her class origins, and Patrick's return to his class origins, contribute to his thinking of her as an "enemy," and her escape from her origins makes her unaware of the class conflict behind—or reinforcing—his apparent hatred of her.

Goodbye, Columbus is also about a love affair that ends unhappily and one that involves crossing class lines. The first-person narrator of the Roth novel and the title character and center of consciousness of the Munro novel are both the lower-class members of the couple; in both, the richer member of the couple has a boorish father who made the family fortune and a somewhat more refined mother whose family's status is a bit older. Both—perhaps more than coincidentally—have scenes that take place in libraries. And there are many more resemblances of greater or lesser moment. Indeed, if you assume that *Goodbye, Columbus*, published in 1959, ends in the present of the narration, the late 1950s, and that the "love story" portion of *The Beggar Maid*,—first published in 1977—takes place almost twenty years before the final scene (the marriage lasted ten years and they have been divorced for nine), and that that final scene takes place more or less in the "present" of the late 1970s, then the two love stories are almost contemporaneous.

But the narration, the writing of the novels, is not. Though there are many differences, no doubt, in the Canadian and "American" experiences and literary traditions, and many differences in talent and temperament (not to mention gender) between Roth and Munro, it may nonetheless be fruitful to think of these novels as 1950s and 1970s versions of similar stories of love and class supposedly set in the same era. Though the Roth novel cannot be said to have ended any more "happily" or definitively than the Munro novel, its narrator-protagonist seems to have learned something and seems to be heading for a better life with a deeper understanding of himself and society. Not so Rose, apparently. She is successful enough, it is true, having her own talk show on television, but her life does not seem very full nor is her understanding of herself or of how she looks to others very clear (remember the Roth narrator seeing himself reflected in the library window—Rose never seems to see herself from the outside). Brenda may not be any nobler than Patrick, but Neil seems at least ethically nobler than Rose. Was there a certain amount of confidence in the future in the 1950s that had been lost by the 1970s? Was the earlier hope based in part on having defeated Hitler so recently, Victory for the good guys? Does Vietnam, even in Canada, have anything to do with the uncertainties of *The Beggar Maid*? Whatever the cause—personal, national, philosophical—the tones of these stories do seem, somehow, to share the tones of their times of composition.